FOR MY GREAT FOLLY
AND
THE MONEYMAN

TWO COMPLETE NOVELS

For My Great Folly

AND

The Moneyman

TWO FAMOUS NOVELS BY

Thomas B. Costain

GARDEN CITY, NEW YORK

Doubleday & Company, Inc.

FOR MY GREAT FOLLY
Copyright, 1942, By Thomas B. Costain
All rights reserved

THE MONEYMAN
Copyright, 1947, By Thomas B. Costain
All rights reserved

For My Great Folly

To My Wife

PREFACE

THERE was a John Ward, of course. His story, as I have told it, follows the historical facts closely enough. He organized the Free Rovers in the Mediterranean and won a series of victories which loosened Spain's tight grip on the seas, returning then to find that his welcome home took the form of a hostile salvo from the guns of the *Rainbow*. Barred from England, which he loved with deep patriotic fervor, the real John Ward sailed back to Tunis, where he set himself up in high state, in a fine marble palace and with a harem. Here Captain John Smith visited him, possibly the last white man to see the bold sea-rover alive. Little is known about the man himself, and so the picture of him presented in these pages is completely imaginary.

There was an Ann Turner also, a pretty woman who invented yellow neck ruffs and did a thriving business with the ladies of the court of James I, ending up on the gallows as a result of her participation in the notorious Overbury case. The real Ann was undoubtedly much more guilty than I have made her out here, but some question arose at the time as to her share in the poisoning. She won a great deal of sympathy, and so she could not have been all bad. Archie Armstrong was the court jester, and it is a matter of record that he bullied and berated the king. His candor did not sit as well with the successor to the throne, the "Baby Charles" who became Charles I and lost his head by adhering to the stubborn policies his father had set. Archie, stout fellow, lost his post and returned to private life, marrying a rich widow and living comfortably ever after. The rest of the active characters are as fictitious as the train of events in which I have involved them.

My most serious purpose has been to present a full picture of the life of those crucial times, and I want to say that here I have adhered absolutely to the facts. There were Upright Men in England then, and curtals and foins and nips and patricos; shareholders bought the privilege of loquacity by rolling coins to the center of the board; the fine clothes were worn on wire frames and men trussed up their hose with "points"; sailors died in the Basket at sea, and Derrick was kept busy at home—Derrick, the hangman who gave his name to tools for the elevation of heavy bodies; people stuffed their noses with wormwood to escape the Plague and dosed themselves with "hickery-pickery" and snail-water; "cant" was on every tongue, and so the talk of the day had a bawdy edge to it, which is my excuse for some of the phrases which will be encountered in what follows. I have done my best to make the picture complete and authentic, having read or consulted considerably more than three hundred books.

T.B.C.

BOOK ONE

1

THE BONFIRE WE BUILT on Shrubsole High was blazing furiously a good half-hour before John Ward arrived. Everyone was there, even Sheriff Cropper, who seemed at a loss as to what he should do under such circumstances. His eyes darted about suspiciously above a nose so curiously flattened at the point that I had often wondered if a sea mew figured somewhere in his ancestry.

The town drunkard sniffed with disappointment and demanded: "Where's the roasted ox and the fountain flowing with wine? Must we drink the great man's health in Adam's-ale? A fine nip-cheese lot, ye are!"

Sir Bartlemy Ladland created a momentary diversion by riding past and waving to us. He must have been in a great hurry, for he did not stop. I noticed that his saddle and stirrups were still swathed in black cloth, and that the tail of his horse was tied with a sable bow. It was over a year since his brother had died in Ireland, but he was very punctilious about such matters.

I was the first to see a horseman at the turn of the road from Wayland Spinney. He had a blue plume in his hat and long golden hair, so I knew it must be John Ward. I shouted in a voice hoarse with excitement: "He's coming! There he is! There he is!"

Someone near me chimed in: "Yes, that's Ward. I can make out his owling beak from here."

The cheer which went up could have been heard well out in the estuary. We had good reason to cheer. John Ward was a hero not only in our town, where he had been born and raised, but in all England. As a boy of seven he had seen the orange sails of the Spanish Armada from the side of a tiny English sloop, and he had been all over the world since. Now he was the most successful of the captains who braved the King's displeasure by harrying the Dons on the high seas. The thrill of earlier days had been recaptured when the word came that he had taken two great ships, the *Madalina* and the *Little John*, their holds stuffed with treasure. Ever since that day, the ballad makers had been comparing our bold John with Francis Drake of glorious memory.

He cantered up on a big gray horse, managing it very well for a

sailor. His faithful friend, Joralemon Snode, followed on a scrubby
roan. We were still cheering, and every hat was waving in the air.
What a remarkable-looking man he was! I knew he still had three
inches the better of me, though I was considerably over the average in
height. His fine head was carried on a massive pair of shoulders. His
long legs bulged in his flame-colored hose, a matter for envy to spare-
shanked fellows like me. A fur-tipped cloak of pease-porridge tawney
was thrown about him, but it did not conceal the richness of his doublet
with its many gold buttons (fifty-two, he told me afterward). The
plume in his hat was almost as long as his hair, and his shoes were of
lemon Cordovan leather. I always felt as though my mouth were hanging open when I looked at John Ward.

He twirled an arm above his head and shouted to us: "Here we are,
fellow citizens! Back home again after giving the mangy beard of the
Spanish king another good singeing."

There was a struggle for the honor of holding his horse. He got
down and walked to the bonfire. His eye picked me out, and he
laughed and called: "Holy Olaf, is that Roger Blease? I see you're
trying to grow up to my size, my brave nooker." He came over and
shook hands with me. "Roger, I had to look twice to be sure it was
you."

The butcher brushed past me with his red ham of a hand extended.
"Give us yer famble, Ward."

"It's great to be back," cried John in his booming voice, starting to
shake hands all around.

Someone demanded, "A speech, Cap'n Ward, a speech!" The rest
took it up. "Tell us what ye think of the gorbellied King, John," and
"Tell us how ye beat the Jew-roasters, Cap'n Rufflecoat."

John Ward's blue eyes blazed around the tightly packed circle. "I'm
a man of action, not words. But if it's gan-music you want . . ."

The word of his homecoming had reached us that morning. The
Court-to-Dover mail does not ride through our town, and so there was
much excitement in the punch-cutting shop when the horn of the
return carrier sounded its brazen note outside. "It's a letter, and it's for
you, master!" shouted Tod Tarsty, carrying it in with an eager hand.
He was sure it was a matter of life and death, for above the address the
words had been written: *Haste, Post, Haste!* and across the bottom
was another urgent admonition with plenty of exclamation marks: *Ride
for thy life! For thy life!! For thy life!!!*

"Tod," said Temperance Handy, taking the letter and smiling, "you
act as though you had never seen one before, you ignorant young sprat."

"And no more have I, master," answered the apprentice.

"Don't you know that everyone who sends a letter through the mail
tries to speed its delivery this way? They know the King's men have a
liking for taverns. Well, I'm afraid it's nothing more than word from

my brother Toby in Dover that our Uncle Griggs has died at last and left me the magnificent sum of five pounds out of his thousands."

The outer sheet, smudged with ink from his thumb, fell to the floor as he read. I saw him shake his head as he flipped the page. "Uncle Griggs *is* dead and he's left me nothing at all. It's just like the old curmudgeon, but—well, it's a disappointment, boys. I meant to use my share in getting out that new Gothic face. Something strong and fine and simple, with none of those gaudy, tricked-up figures of saints the French call capitals. Now we'll have to wait."

My tutor (the curious relationship between us will be explained in due course) had two prime grievances which cankered in his mind and led to frequent outbursts. One was that the art of making type should be called punch-cutting. To his way of thinking, anything that had to do with the making of books was the noblest of occupations, on a level with painting and sculpture and far above the scribbling of sonnets to a lady's eyebrow. The other was the preference which our printers still had for French type. "Behold!" he would say when a new book came into his hands. "How can such lettering be read? This French stuff prints as black as the Old Rogue himself. If this sort of thing keeps up, I swear that every scholar in the world will be blind by 1650 at the latest!" He had a special dislike for the work of the great Geofroy Tory, who claimed he could not design a new letter unless he worked on a large sheet ruled off into as many as two thousand squares to allow him a proper sense of balance and proportion.

As I watched him skim the rest of his letter, I saw his expression change suddenly. "Lads, there's real news after all!" he exclaimed. "The *Royal Bess* put in at Dover last night. John Ward came ashore, and he sends word by Toby that he'll be home by four o'clock today!"

My feet came down from the block on which I had been resting them and struck the floor with a thump. The Spanish grammar fell from my hand.

"John Ward back!" I cried. "We must build a bonfire to welcome him, sir."

"That we must, in spite of King James and his treaties," said my tutor. He despised the new king because of the peace he had made with Spain, as everyone did, for that matter. "Well, Tod, you were right after all. Wash your face and get yourself uptown to spread the news."

When Temperance Handy ordered his remaining pair of apprentices back to their work, I realized that I had reached an important decision. I got up from my chair in the corner where for so many years I had explored the mysteries of science and the world of strange tongues under his kindly tutelage.

"I'm through with studies," I said.

His bushy eyebrows, which gave him something of the look of an aged fisting-hound, went up in surprise. "Well, Roger," he said mildly,

"I'm of the opinion that you've gone as far as you can under my poor direction. You might still go to college, and I've said so to your mother many times. But why this sudden decision? Can it have anything to do with the word about John Ward?"

I made sure there were no other ears within hearing distance. "That's it, sir," I said. "I'm going to sign on with him. It's not sudden, though. I've had my mind made up for a long time."

"Was it to become a sailor, then, that you've got yourself grounded in the classics? What will your mother and your aunt think about it?"

I knew only too well what they would think. "I've always intended to be a sailor," I said. "Father helped lick the Armada, and he always said I should become a captain like him. I'm a Blease, and every Blease has been a sailor as far back as anyone can remember. It's time I stood up for myself."

"Mark Blease was a fine sailor, and you're his son. But you're a Pirie too. The Piries have never been sailors." He took one of my hands and studied it with a shake of his head. "The human hand is the surest index of character. Yours is too soft for splicing ropes. I can't picture you climbing the shrouds, my boy. I'm afraid you're better suited for scholarship than a life at sea."

"I'm not a Pirie." I could feel the stubbornness come over me which I always experienced when Aunt Gadilda preached about the grandeur of their side of the family.

"Well, you have your own life to live. But I'm sure, Roger, you should talk to them before doing anything rash."

Now I must explain something about myself and how I came to be taking my studies in a punch-cutting shop. My mother was the youngest child of Sir Ludar Pirie of Great Lunnington, and there had been a mighty to-do when she ran away and married Mark Blease, a fishing captain. Since my father's death there had been little money in the house, but both Mother and Aunt Gadilda had been determined to have me educated like a gentleman. They could not afford a regular tutor, but neither would they countenance the idea of sending me to the town school. Aunt Gadilda had thought of a compromise plan.

Everyone regarded Temperance Handy as the smartest man in town. His wealthy Uncle Griggs, a mercer in Dover, had wanted to make a minister of him and had paid his way through Cambridge. He had come out a Brownist, however, and so more of a candidate for the stake than for the stole. His uncle had washed his hands of him and had never forgiven him for choosing then the lowly occupation of a type maker. Handy had always been a rebel, a believer in all the wrong things. He was against the social order and had been known, in his rasher moments, to praise John Ball and the peasant leaders of central Europe. He was a scoffer also, laughing at all the pet beliefs of sober people, which was much harder for them to accept. There was no such thing as magic, he declared; and nothing stirred him to wrath more easily than the common fear of witchcraft. In this he was flying in the face of the Word, which warned men of evils the human eye could not see. Everyone knew that many old women, and some young ones as well, made compacts with the devil; that he visited them in the guise of a huge brown dog with a gold collar; and that, when they went out alone at night, milk pails detached themselves from their hooks on the wall and went clattering after them, a sure proof of satanic powers.

"We'll pay Temperance Handy to teach him," Aunt Gadilda had decided. "The man may be queer and a dissenter, but he *is* a scholar, and he can coach our Roger as well as any popish doctor at college."

He had been glad enough to earn the three pounds a year they offered him, even agreeing more or less publicly not to air his unorthodox views in his role of teacher. I had spent the greater part of my time since in a corner of his shop that he allotted to me. I liked him from the start, and he, for his part, had proved himself a good instructor. It had not been easy for me. I had to be up each morning at four for services at home, with Mother yawning and quite as unhappy as I was over such early rising and Aunt Gadilda eyeing us both with bitter reproof as she read from the Book. Breakfast never varied, a dish of wheaten flummery without cream, summer and winter alike. It was a long walk to the shop, and sometimes I would eke out my meager fare by robbing apple and pear trees on the way. The hardest part of all was finding the Handy household, including the apprentices, breakfasting on roast ham and new bread when I arrived. Dame Handy was famous for her hams, which she prepared by a special recipe of her own, curing them in a mixture of stale beer, saltpeter, and rum, and rubbing black pepper into the bones. She never failed to offer me a slice, and I as regularly refused. The delicious odor of it nearly drove me crazy with longing, but I could not bear to let them know how poorly we fared at home. I would be at work on my books by five o'clock, and it was seldom I returned home before the shadows of the medlar trees were long on the stone fences of the town.

The results had justified all these efforts, I suppose. At any rate, I had acquired a good classical education and could write and speak French tolerably well. I was now working on Spanish, Aunt Gadilda having become convinced that a knowledge of that abominable language was necessary since King James was so determined on close relations with the Dons. One thing I had missed: there had been little time to steal down to the docks and talk to the sailors there, who were always willing to be friendly with a son of Mark Blease. On rare occasions I had gone out with them and had found the lift of the deck under my feet more exciting than the best story from the classics and the bite of a raw wind on my cheeks more to my liking than any sport. At least I had said to myself that I did; it generally happened that I became seasick.

But now I was through with books and studies. I was determined to sail with our great captain of Free Rovers.

"Men of England," said John Ward, waving a hand on which gleamed a ring with an enormous diamond, "I'm proud to be welcomed home so warmly. I could not be sure that our windy old porridge-pot at Theobalds"—he was referring to the King!—"allowed men to express their approval of what I am doing. But now I see that I was wrong. Englishmen will not be dictated to by a craven ruler who gives in to our mortal foes."

I had never heard the general contempt for the King stated as openly and daringly as this. He seemed to have no fear at all. He called James a "quaking puffin" and a "pusillanimous pander" who was so anxious to keep the peace with Spain that he shut his eyes to the undeclared war the Spaniards (he called them the Faggoters) were waging on our merchant ships everywhere. The King had sent my Lord Howard all the way to Madrid to make this disgraceful peace, with a train of forty gentlemen dressed in black velvet and riding black horses with gold trappings.

"He wasted ten thousand pounds to impress the Spaniards!" shouted Ward. "If he had spent that money on the upkeep of the Navy, the Dons would have sent forty gentlemen to London to ask peace. Instead we must now suffer under the one-sided treaty these gentlemen in black velvet brought back."

I could see the face of Sheriff Cropper growing redder as the speech went on, and I wondered if he was getting ready to take some action. He did nothing, however; and Captain Ward concluded with the statement that he was sailing back to the Inner Sea as soon as he could get his *Royal Bess* outfitted for a long cruise and that he would then "impress the Dons in the only way they understand, by the weight of my shot."

Everyone crowded around him at the finish to clap him on the back and tell him what a great man he was, and to ask envious questions about the loot from the captured ships. There were women in the crowd, and at this point a bold piece named Doll Saunders brushed her way up close to him and insisted that she was going to have a kiss. John was only too glad to oblige. He swung her up in his arms until her heels were two feet off the ground and gave her a resounding buss.

"There you are, Fubbs," he said. "There's only one thing I would rather do than fight a Spaniard, and that's kiss a pretty English girl. Are there any more?"

There were plenty more. Every woman there, married or single, wanted to be treated the same way. The men cheered them on as they lined up in a giggling row. John went down the file, sometimes adding for good measure a sound smack on the blind-cheeks.

I wanted to get a word with him, but I realized there would be no chance here. I edged up close to Joralemon Snode, who was standing unnoticed beside his resplendent captain. Joralemon was a deeply religious fellow who had wanted to be a parson (I almost wrote it "heavenbeck," being more accustomed to that word) but had gone to sea because he worshiped John and always followed his lead. I noticed that he was thinner and more sickly-looking than ever.

"Jore," I whispered, "I want to ship with you this time. When can I get a word with John?"

His startled eyes came round to mine. "You too, Roger? Every boy in town has the same idea. Half a dozen have spoken to me already." He shook his head doubtfully. "Better think it over. It's a rough life. I'm not sure you could stand it."

"My father stood it. And you seem to have survived a long spell of it."

"I don't count. John has made me a combination parson and clerk. I don't stand watch, and I've never been aloft." His voice sank to an earnest whisper. "I mean it, Roger. Let rougher men fight this war out. It's going to be a bloody business. It's not for the like of you."

"I want to go, no matter what it's like."

"You'll live to regret it if you do. But I'll tell John what you've said. He'll be at the Cygnet's Head after eight o'clock tonight. You could get a word with him there." He shook his head again. "Seven men from town didn't come back with us this trip."

I was not happy over the doubts being expressed of my fitness for the sea, and so I was in no mood for further remonstrances when Temperance Handy came up behind me and insisted on adding to what he had already said on the subject.

"Listen to me, Roger. After that speech—and, mind you, I agreed with him—I'm more set against your going than before." His eyes, peering into mine, showed how deeply concerned he was. He dropped a hand on my shoulder. "It isn't just the dangers you'll face at sea. I'm beginning to realize where all this is leading. Ward is right, but he's a firebrand; he goes much too far. You'll be involved in worse things than fighting Spaniards, my boy. In piracy and"—his voice sank lower —"in treason even. I don't want to see you hanged at Wapping Stairs. And that's what it's likely to come to, mark my words."

"I'll have to chance that," I said, although I had given no thought before to such possibilities. "If he's right, and you say he is, then I should be prepared for any risks. England needs John Ward, and John Ward needs all the men he can get."

"He can get them without any difficulty—men trained to the sea. They're the kind he needs, not young sprats like you. No matter how willing you are, it would be folly to go. A great folly."

I answered that I was going if John would have me, and that I would thank him to let the matter drop. "What's more," I added, with some heat, "I hope you won't go to Mother about it. I don't want any more lectures."

He looked at me reproachfully. "You ought to know me better than that. I won't go behind your back."

Nothing more was said, and he drifted off toward home, turning up the collar of his jerkin, for it was growing chilly.

The last hand having been shaken and the last girl kissed, John disappeared with a group of his old friends. The crowd began to dissolve, and I decided it was time to go home also.

The air had a nip of autumn in it, and the sky over the treetops was still as blue as the cloaks all women were wearing nowadays in imitation of Queen Anne. Above the distant line of Wayland Spinney I could see the handsome towers of Appleby Court, and it was natural for my thoughts to turn on Katie Ladland, who lived there; and equally I could not think of Katie without indulging in speculation on the subject of perfection in general. How lucky it was, I said to myself, that I had been born in this great age when life had come to such a complete and final flowering. The last important secret had been wrung from Mother Earth when Columbus proved the world to be round. The incomparable verse of Spenser and Donne and Sir Philip Sydney would never be bettered, nor the plays of our great dramatists. No man could be braver than John Ward or wiser than Coke. All men, in fact, were more learned as well as taller and stronger than ever before. The very peak of perfection had been reached in habit and manner and dress. We were building handsomer homes and more enduring churches, and the ships we sent out to sea were tall and fast and ineffably lovely with their bright sails and carved hulls. Yes, it was a great age, as close to the millennium as man would ever get; and I was happy that now I was going out into the world to play my part in it.

2

MY SPIRITS DIPPED as I turned to go home. Perhaps everyone was right in saying that I was not cut to the pattern of a sailor. John Ward might agree with them and refuse to have me. I was worried also because I had taken my station so close to the bonfire that a flying spark had burned a hole in my gray galligaskins. As I came in sight of our tall oak-beamed house, I was thinking dismally: What will Aunt Gadilda say to this?

Deciding that I had better put a bold face on it, I threw back my shoulders and stamped into the square room at the front of the house. I tossed my cap on the refectory table, which was already spread for supper, and said in confident tones: "John Ward's back, Mother. The whole town turned out to see him. We built a grand bonfire, and Sir Bartlemy Ladland rode by and waved to us. I got so close to the fire that I ruined these old gallyslops."

Before Mother could answer, Aunt Gadilda sniffed and said sharply: "You and your John Ward! I declare, young man, you should take shame to yourself. Your poor mother slaves and saves to provide for you, and you burn great holes in your fine warm clothes. Let me see just what you've done, you good-for-nothing rogue."

Mother interposed in a tone of almost timid remonstrance: "Now, Gaddy, don't be hard on the lad. I think the damage can be easily mended."

"It's not so much the harm to the breeches, Meggy," grumbled my aunt, as she shrugged closer into her shabby old shawl. "Must he always be running after this low rascal of a John Ward? It's in no way meet that the own grandson of Sir Ludar Pirie of Great Lunnington should hold such friendship for the son of an owling fisher captain. What will come of our plans for him if he demeans himself in this way?"

"My father and John's sailed together," I reminded her. "Was Father a smuggler too, then?"

They were huddled in front of the smallest fire that could be kept alive and still advertise itself to the outside world by a wisp of smoke at the top of the chimney. Mother was tiny and pretty, with deep gray eyes and hair that was still black and crisply curling. She always looked trim and neat, and yet she wore her starched ruffs as long as Aunt Gadilda did hers. My poor aunt, who was two years older, never looked anything but wilted and untidy. She also was small, but she was gaunt and rawboned where my mother was dainty.

The three of us sat down to supper without further words. I was hungry, and I looked at what had been provided with a deep sense of dissatisfaction. Here we were, the first family of the town if one left out of consideration Sir Bartlemy Ladland, whose great manor house lay a half-league north of the limits; and yet I was ready to wager that none other would be supping on such meager fare. I had hoped there would be herb pie, my favorite dish, in which the piquant flavor of chervil or sage was blended with the sweet of almond paste. There was a long dish of scalloped oysters, a loaf of raveled bread, and three small mugs of ale. The oysters were done in the French manner, with many herbs and a dash of brandy, and they were served on a fine silver dish; but this did nothing to disguise the fact that they were the commonest and cheapest of food in a town where the Free Dredgermen of the Hundred and Manor maintained the largest oyster beds in England. They were served so often at the behest of Aunt Gadilda that my stomach was ready to turn over at the very sight of them. I knew also before tasting it that the ale in my fine silver tankard was new and thin.

I dipped an unwilling spoon into the mess on my plate and remarked in grumbling tones: "We must be very poor, Mother. Why don't we ever have beef or mutton? Must we always starve ourselves on fish and oysters? Every home where I go has wheaten bread, and sometimes even manchet."

Aunt Gadilda spoke up, clipping her phrases in a curious manner as though she considered words a luxury and therefore to be indulged in sparingly. "Must we go all over that again, Roger?" she demanded. "If we waste our money now, how will we be able to fit you out when the time comes for you to take your proper place in the world? You must have a post at court, dear boy. For that you'll need a horse and a servant of your own, and the very finest of clothes. Isn't it worth a little scrimping now if it means you'll wear silks and satins for the rest of your life and sit at the King's table?"

I felt the secret inside me ready to explode into words at this, and I almost gave myself away. It was the sight of Aunt Gadilda herself, pecking with no appetite at a slice of the bread, which restrained me from speaking. Our Spartan regimen was, after all, hardest on her. She hated oysters and would never eat them. Any kind of fish, in fact, had a malignant effect on her, causing her face to swell and turn a yellowish shade like a ripe May apple; and so the economies she ordained left her with little to live upon but bread. I felt like saying that it was unjust to starve herself and Mother in order to lay by funds for my future, especially as I did not intend to go to court. But we had been all through that argument many times. My often-asserted desire to be a sea captain like my bold and bluff father, dead these ten years, affected Aunt Gadilda even more adversely than the taste of fish. Any mention of the sea or of seamen would send her stomping out of the room, her pinched face reflecting the scorn she had always felt for the poor match that the youngest daughter of Sir Ludar Pirie had made. Father had commanded the one ship our town fitted out for the Crown under the charter of the Cinque Ports. He had been a fine seaman, a duly elected jurat, and he had sat in the Guestling. I was jealous of his memory, for he had been a brave and forthright man and had enjoyed the respect of everyone, with the exception of the members of my mother's family.

Knowing that nothing I could say would do any good, I bit the words back and proceeded to eat my oysters with as good a will as I could summon.

Mother, who was making the best supper of the three of us, asked about Sir Bartlemy Ladland. Had he seen me when he rode through Shrubsole High? Had he said anything to me? Had he been wearing his plum-colored cloak with the collar of miniver?

"Of course he didn't see me," I answered with some impatience. This took my thoughts back to John Ward, and I began to give them an enthusiastic description of him. "You should have seen him, Mother. He paid twelve pounds for his doublet alone. Jore Snode told me. His hat was Spanish and cost sixty shillings without the plume. His hose didn't wrinkle at the knees the way mine do. I wish——"

Mother laughed. "Your friend John Ward has a handsome leg," she commented. "I've often noticed it. You are on the lean side, my poor Roger, and so you must always expect that your hose will wrinkle. You don't take after your father in that respect. Nor me either, for that matter."

Aunt Gadilda sniffed and said in hostile tones, "Really, Meggy, must you say such coarse things?"

"The old queen noticed men's legs and talked about them a great deal," protested Mother in self-defense. "They say Sir Walter Raleigh won favor with her first because he had such a well-turned shank. And King James likes trim men around him."

Aunt Gadilda looked daggers at her for this last remark, and my mother blushed and said hurriedly: "The Piries are thin-shanked on the male side. Do you remember, Gaddy, that even when Father became so very heavy near the end, his legs were still skinny? I think he should have worn pads. Well, Roger is that much of a Pirie, at any rate."

My thinness was a sore point with me, so I hastened to change the subject. "Sir Bartlemy still has black stirrups, but he was wearing the cloak with the miniver collar. He didn't stop."

"I was hoping he said something to you about our going to Appleby Court for Christmas," said Mother. "I'm counting on it, and I'm sure Katie would like us to be with them again this year."

I began to blush. It was no secret in the family that I was in love with Katie Ladland, but I felt foolish and presumptuous when any open reference was made to it. Aunt Gadilda, who had developed a recent dislike for Lady Ladland, sniffed and said she would prefer to spend the day right here at home. Mother replied sharply that she was taking a selfish attitude, and a dispute ensued which continued even when Albert Pett came in to remove the dish of oysters for his own supper with Fanny Trimble in the buttery.

We had to keep servants, of course. They were a necessary part of the struggle to maintain an outward semblance of genteel superiority. Albert Pett came into the room through a dark little serving pantry, in which he kept a handsome red suit of clothes. He was under orders to change into these company habiliments before answering the front door, but he would get back into his russet tunic and baggy smalls the instant the company left, or catch it from Aunt Gadilda. She never let a day pass without examining the red livery for traces of moths or wear. It had been in use now for seven years and still looked as good as new.

"I zee bonfire, M'ims," remarked Albert with a pleased smile. "That John Ward, now, he's a one to give they Dons a fair trouncing. Ay, M'ims, whole town is proud o' John Ward."

"What is the man saying?" demanded Aunt Gadilda in an aggrieved voice. She was never able to make out what he said, or pretended not to, because she objected to his habit of addressing us familiarly.

"He's speaking of the bonfire this afternoon," explained Mother.

"I see the flames from yard, M'ims," declared Albert. Fire was an exciting thing to him, perhaps because he enjoyed so little of it in our cold house. "A bunny fire, M'ims, forty feet high. Pother o' wood burned to make such a fire."

Fanny Trimble put her head through the door to contribute a piece of news on the subject. She was a plump wench who kept Albert on a taut rein by refusing to marry him, although she was not adverse to an occasional scuffle in the buttery from which she would emerge with a red face and cap in disarray. "Plenty townsmen going wi' Captain Ward when he sails again," she said. "My brother Sim, and Harry Engle, and both they Bledsoe's. They hopes to come back wi' pockets full o' Spanish gold."

Aunt Gadilda sat up stiff in her chair and said in an angry voice, "Meggy, *must* we spoil our servants in this way?"

"I'm sure, Gaddy, I am very much interested in what Fanny was saying about the men of the town sailing with Captain Ward," declared Mother. She nodded at the pair, however, and they took the hint by disappearing through the door promptly. "It will be a good thing for Sim Trimble, I'm sure. He's never been worth his salt on land, certainly, and so let us hope that he *does* come back with his pockets full of gold."

"You know full well, Meggy, that His Majesty has forbidden his subjects to fight the Spanish," declared Aunt Gadilda. She was speaking ostensibly to my mother, but I could see that her eye was fixed on me, and I knew that the lesson in what she said was intended for my benefit. "Those that disobey him are pirates and subject to punishment. I hope that none of the men of the town are weak enough to go with this wicked Captain Ward. They'll suffer for it if they do."

Mother and Aunt Gadilda went back to their eternal needlework; and I, with great inner reluctance, took up a Spanish book. It was a loosely bound volume in tough brown leather with a wood print in the front of Philip II of Spain, that bloody-minded monarch whose name was linked in every English mind with the Armada. I hated the book, and King Philip as well, but I had to make some effort to please them on what might be my last night at home.

I tried to appear studious as I stretched my legs out in front of the meager fire and glared at the scorbutic countenance of the hated king. My thoughts were not with Spanish syntax, however. They were concerned with the decision I had reached this day and the effect it would have on the lives of all of us.

"Roger!" exclaimed Aunt Gadilda. "You're sitting on the cushion. It will be threadbare if you *will* be so careless."

I put the velvet cover carefully to one side. It was the first time I had ever offended in this respect. "Sorry, Aunt," I said. "I didn't think about it."

She nodded in forgiveness, believing that my absorption in study had been responsible for the lapse. In reality, however, I was thinking back over the years to that sad day when the word had reached us of the sinking of my father's ship with all on board. It was a cold fall day, with a wind lashing the upper branches of the oak trees about the windows, and it had seemed to me that the end of the world had come. I had loved my tall father with his fine ruddy cheeks and his blustering ways and had been looking forward to the day when I would go to sea too, as all the Bleases had done. Never afterward could I hear branches brushing against our plastered walls without my thoughts reverting back to that time which had brought such a change in my life, with a longing to hear again the deep tones of my father's voice as he said, "Ay, Roger, ye're a pindling little lubber, but I'll make a sailor of ye yet."

Aunt Gadilda had posted down from Great Lunnington the very next day and had taken charge of the household. I remembered her saying to Mother: "There will be no more nonsense now, Meggy. You'll have to live here, for both Geoffrey and Ralph have moved their families to Great Lunnington, and there's no room left. But I'm going to stay with you and see to it that Roger is raised right. He's a Pirie now, not a Blease. There's to be no more talk of his going to sea. Nothing must satisfy us but a place at court for this fine little man of ours. It's going to be hard. Father can't help us, but we will save every penny. You and I will manage it somehow, Meggy."

They had managed it somehow. Money had been laid away, in spite of the fact that outwardly we maintained some of the traditions of Great Lunnington. The people of the town had been taught to regard us as gentry and to pay us the respect due to the name of Pirie. And yet I knew that more had been laid out on the livery for Albert Pett than either of them spent on clothes for themselves. Aunt Gadilda had proved herself an adept at all the sorry expedients incidental to the carrying out of their plan, and Mother also had come to learn.

I remembered in particular one afternoon when Lady Ladland was to pay us a call. I was very young at the time, and my excitement was almost unbearable when our dining-room table blossomed out with fresh fruit, with decanters of fine muscadine wine and ossy caprie, and, more important than all, a platter of marchpane, silvered on top with sugar and rich with almonds. It had needed all of Aunt Gadilda's vigilance to keep me from looting that fabulous display before our guest arrived. I stalked around it like a cat around a jug of cream, and I was too occupied in rosy anticipations to be interested at all in the fact that Lady Ladland brought her daughter Katie with her.

"Now, Roger, you must sit down and talk to little Mistress Catherine," said Mother. "She has come all the way from Appleby Court to visit you."

It was the first time I had seen Katie, and I thought her nice enough, and pretty enough; but I was too fearful that her presence would weigh against my chances in the distribution of the marchpane to be glad that she had come. Her eyes were large and as round as an Old Harry sovereign, and she seemed to find me worth staring at. She told me about her pet dog, who was called Walter, after Sir Walter Raleigh, I supposed, and I found this interesting because I had no dog of my own and wanted one more than anything in the world. She explained that she had not been allowed to bring Walter, which I thought a pity but entirely in line with the kind of injustice which children had to endure.

Between intervals of talk I maneuvered about the gorgeously laden table but was never able to help myself without discovering the bony hand of Aunt Gadilda clamped tightly on my wrist. Katie was helped liberally and, I thought, proved quite greedy in the matter of the marchpane. My share was two figs and a small cake which had lost most of its frosting.

After Lady Ladland had left, with the reluctant Katie in tow, I smacked my lips over the residue of that magnificent feast, thinking how well we would do at supper. But it was far from Aunt Gadilda's idea to let a greedy small boy benefit to that extent. Rich food could be used only to further social aims, and so the rector's wife and her three healthy children were invited over at once.

There had always been money enough for a necessary book, but never a penny for the things I craved. The only dog we ever had was Bessy, a spiteful little fisting-hound which one of my uncles sent to Mother. She had loved the miserable beast, but that had given her no understanding of my longing for a real dog, a mastiff or a gazehound to romp with when I went out to the sand dunes or wandered in the thick groves of sorb and asp which fringed the town.

What I disliked most of all about it was that everything had to be done with an eye to appearances for the furthering of my all-important future. Our home was imposing from the front. Visitors were shown in through screens of richly carved oak, and there were tapestries and paintings from Great Lunnington on our walls. Back of this, however, and particularly in the bedrooms above, the house was as bare as a windswept moor. We had glass from Venice on the sideboard, a few fine pieces, but we used cheap specular stone to replace any panes which broke in our upper windows. Fanny Trimble rustled in a silk skirt when she waited on guests, but the coverlets on our beds were of the coarsest dagswain or even hopharlot. I hated this shabby kind of life, but I had endured it because I knew how unselfish was the love back of everything they did.

And now it was to end. The scheming and slaving of ten long years would soon be over, for I had made up my mind. I was going to take things into my own hands. I felt guilty over the decision I had reached, and yet the thought of what it was going to mean set my blood to racing. I dared not raise my eyes from the book for fear they would read my plan in them.

The tall clock in the corner struck nine. Mother smiled and yawned. "I'm tired and I'm cold. I think I shall go to bed, Gaddy. It's been a hard day, and you should come too. Will you continue your studies, Roger?"

"Yes, Mother," I answered. I was barely conscious of what she had said, for my mind now was with John Ward and that amazingly bold cruise of his through the forbidden Mediterranean—forbidden to English ships by order of another Philip, son of the well-hated king who had launched the Armada against England. I was dreaming of hot blue seas around Sicily, of the Lion of St. Mark's where the flat-capped Doges waged undeclared war against Anglo-Saxon mariners, of the fabulous port of Tunis, the home of the corsairs. My mind was filled with visions of palm-fringed islands and of Spanish galleons coming up over the horizon like castles awash.

Mother's hand fondled my hair as she passed me. I thought Aunt Gadilda was going to do the same, but she thought better of it and resolutely folded her arms under her shabby shawl. She was looking ill and, I thought, a little wistful.

"Roger," she said, "you've grown up. You're a man now."

I protested at this. I was sure that I would continue to grow. In fact, I was going to be very unhappy if I failed to pick up the three inches that John Ward had over me.

"You're as tall as your grandfather," declared Aunt Gadilda, as though it were wrong to wish for more than that. "I saw little of your own father, but I think you've outgrown him a full inch. You're taller than any of your cousins at Great Lunnington."

That went without saying. My cousins, who lorded it over me because I belonged to a poor branch of the family, were a lumpish lot, and I had always entertained an inner conviction of superiority as far as they were concerned.

She gave vent to a deep sigh. "I'm afraid, Roger, we can't expect much from any of the boys at home. We're depending on you to set the Piries back where they belong. You are our one hope."

One light only was burning in the wrought-iron candelabrum. She moved it nearer to me. "I hope you're not straining your eyes," she said anxiously. "You know, Roger, we would be only too happy if we could make things easier for you. It makes me sad to see you reading with one candle. But—well, it won't be long now."

I nodded absent-mindedly. She came nearer and put a frail hand on my shoulder. "You know that everything we do is for your own good, don't you?"

"Yes, Aunt," I said.

This did not seem to satisfy her. Perhaps she had some inkling of the things which had been running through my mind. There was a catch in her voice as she repeated the question. "Roger, you do know that? You must never think we live like this because we are mean or miserly. Money means nothing to your mother or to me. We've done everything for you, Rogerkins. For your future. So that you too can be a great man, as your grandfather was. You must never believe anything else."

She walked slowly toward the stairs, favoring her bad foot a little more than usual. I knew that she would go to bed in the dark, as Mother had done. A sense of guilt took possession of me, and for several minutes I was sure that my plan would have to be abandoned after all. They had devoted their lives to building a secure future for me, and I must not disappoint them now. But by slow degrees my resolution hardened again. After all, it was my own life. They had never consulted me about their plans. I had stood as much as I could of this cramped, petticoat-ridden existence. I had the blood of Mark Blease in my veins. I knew that I was not intended for the kind of life that a great city like London offered. I had no stomach for the future they had planned, no willingness to scramble for favor at the court of a cowardly and unpopular king.

I was not a pindling little lubber any longer; and, as my father was not here to do it, I was going to make a sailor of myself. I was going to sea with John Ward.

3

WHEN I PUSHED THROUGH the door of the Cygnet's Head, it seemed that every man in town was there, the solid citizens as well as the tickle-pitchers and the swill-bellies. The return of John Ward had stirred things up, and feeling was running high over the Spanish question. From somewhere in the rear a voice was declaiming the words of a song which had swept the country:

> He cites as thieves and pirates we,
> Who fight to keep the sea lanes free.
> No English ship will turn and flee!
> *The harbor bar is cleared!*

He, Philip of Spain, had been claiming, ever since the peace had been signed by our chicken-hearted Jamie, that no English ships had the right to venture into the Midland Sea or to trade with the Levant. Around the bonfire that afternoon there had been talk of what had happened to an honest merchantman, the *Trial*, overhauled by a Spanish ship-of-war near the island of Rhodes. The crew had been lodged in prison for two months, and they had been bastinadoed and drawn upon beams, until only four of them had been left alive. These poor fellows had then signed the confessions shoved under their noses and had been hanged at once for piracy; and the Spanish ambassador had taken the papers to Whitehall where King James had wagged his over-sized head and acknowledged that the seizure of the ship was right and just. As I stood in the doorway, looking about me for a sight of John Ward, I heard a sailor reciting more details of this grim affair.

"First they took the purser and strung him up by the arms," he was saying. "I knew him well these ten years, a decent little fellow from down Bristol way, with a wife and three tow-headed kinchers of his own. They tied cannon balls to both of his feet and then turned a ram loose on deck. It butted him back and forth until his wrists were cut to ribbons and he screamed so loud that even some of the cursed Dons begged the captain to cut him down. They didn't let him off until both arms were broken and his muscles were hanging in shreds. And he still shook his head and swore himself an honest sailor and no pirate."

Another voice chimed in bitterly: "Why must we have a Scotch loon for a king? It was an ill day for England when the old virgin drank her last glass of canary."

This was heady talk, and it confirmed me in my resolution. If King James refused to uphold our rights on the seas, then all Englishmen must follow the lead of John Ward and take the fight on themselves.

John was nowhere to be seen, but Andrew Widdigate, the landlord, caught sight of me and motioned me to follow him. He led the way back to the kitchens where his wife and two maids were scurrying like mad to cook for their many guests. A goose and a haunch of beef were browning on spits, and Dame Widdigate was filling baked florentines with rich jam. The sight and smell of this wonderful food made me ravenously hungry.

"He's gone," whispered the landlord. "The harman-beck was here. John said you were to shake a stamper after him."

I knew enough of tavern talk to make out of this that the constable had been in looking for John, and that the latter had left word I was to follow him. The cant of London was creeping more and more into everyday use. Temperance Handy lectured me continuously about it, saying that the purity of our well-nigh perfect tongue was being threatened. It did little good, I am afraid, for I was rather proud of my ability to "cut whids" with the best of them.

"Where did he go?" I asked.

The landlord looked cautiously at his wife and then winked. "He's glazing a jill-flirt," he said. "Can't leave the little dells alone, that John.

Go to the apothecary shop of Aaron Blazeby on the High. Back door."

I said to myself: So Ann Turner's back. I hope she didn't bring her husband with her, or John may get into trouble.

He laid a slice of the goose on bread and handed it to me. "Tib o' the buttery, roasted to a turn. Nothing to beat it. Powder into that before you go."

I fell to with a great appetite, although by custom I was inclined to refuse. Did they guess how closely we ran things at home? Before I could give it more than a thought, the food had vanished. Widdigate then took me through a long and musty passage which led to the stables. Here he laid a cautioning hand on my shoulder.

"There's something afoot," he said. "The harman-beck's been in twice. Tell John to watch out. And tell him he's to see Sir Bartlemy Ladland tonight. Without fail. Now off with ye, lad."

I passed our house on the way and was relieved to see that no lights were showing; my absence, then, had not been discovered. I was mystified over one part of my errand. Why was John to see Sir Bartlemy Ladland? Was he counting on Sir Bartlemy's help in getting out of his difficulties? The rest was not hard to understand at all. The apothecary's niece had always been favored with John's attentions when he was home. To be honest about it, there had been a time when I went out of my way to pass the shop on the chance of seeing her about. She was very pretty, with golden hair and deeply shadowed violet eyes and a neat ankle. I nearly always caught a glimpse of her through the murky shop windows, and she never failed to smile. I had felt a little sorry for her. She was certainly well enough mannered, but for some reason the other girls in town would have nothing to do with her. They had been delighted when she married and moved to London.

The establishment was in darkness when I arrived. I went to the back door and gave a discreet knock. Apparently I was expected, for I heard a stealthy step inside at once. A low voice asked, "Who is it?"

"A friend of John Ward's," I answered. "I was told to call for him here."

"Yes," said the voice. I heard a bolt being drawn. The door swung back. "Come in, Roger."

It was Ann Turner. She closed the door and then held up the candle so we could see each other better. She was dressed in black and was prettier than ever. In the uncertain light her eyes looked enormous.

"I didn't know you were back," I said.

"I arrived today. I'm a widow. Did you know? It's going to be a very short visit. I'm returning to London as soon as possible."

"I didn't know. I'm very sorry to hear it."

She got out another candle and lighted it from the one she was holding. Now I could see better, and I realized that there was something curiously different about the way she was dressed. She had discarded the farthingale which held women's skirts out stiffly at the sides—that was it. As a result her trailing black gown fell gracefully and easily about her, even revealing something of the slender line of her hips. There was a pleasant swish and rustle every time she moved. I wondered why women did not always dress this way.

"You needn't be too sorry," she said. "My marriage wasn't much of a success. My husband was a doctor, but I soon found out that he worked for the Upright Man."

The Upright Man! That was a predicament for a young bride. Before I could make any comment, she went on: "I hope you won't think I'm hardhearted, Roger, but it was a great relief when I was free again. He was an old man and he drank heavily. He didn't treat me very well. I married him to get out of this dreadful place. I guess you knew that."

I had suspected it to be the case, for she had had a lonely time of it. I wanted to ask if her husband's connection with the powerful head of London's criminals had involved her in any difficulties; but, remembering that I had an urgent message for John Ward, I asked where he was.

"He's upstairs." She hurried to explain the reason. "He was hurt on the way here. But don't look so startled; it wasn't very serious and my uncle is attending to it now. John says he must leave as soon as it's dressed."

"The sheriff seems determined to get his hands on him."

A step was heard approaching the shop. We stood close together, not daring to make a move. My companion clasped my arm tightly with her free hand, and I could hear her breath coming in excited gasps. I was afraid the light of the candles might show but found on a glance around that the curtains had been drawn tightly across the windows.

The steps seemed to pause but then moved on. We both sighed with relief. Ann even managed to laugh.

"I thought they were coming for him. What would have happened to us, Roger? Would they have taken us all? Living the way we did in London made me afraid of every knock on the door."

"I must give him my message at once," I said. "Every minute counts now."

She was still holding my arm. "You're looking well, Roger. I think you've grown a lot since I left town."

"I'm an even six foot."

"My! And you're only eighteen."

"I'm more than that," I protested. "I'm nearly nineteen."

We moved into the front room, which Aaron Blazeby used as his workshop. There was a large mortar on an acid-stained table and beside it a dudgeon knife with a jagged edge. The walls were lined with bottle-filled shelves, and a skull grinned down at us from the darkness above.

At one side was a flight of stairs without a handrail. Ann said, as I began to climb: "Be careful. They're very narrow and steep. They should be, for they lead to a lady's bedroom."

I knew she was watching me, but I kept my eyes down. I did not know what kind of an answer I should make to that.

A door was open at the head of the stairs, and I saw John standing by the side of a bed. He was wearing his flame-colored hose, which covered him as far as his muscular hips, but otherwise he was naked. The apothecary stood beside him, applying something to his shoulder.

"Well, my kinchin coe, you got here," said John with a friendly grin. "I had an argument with one of the sheriff's men on the way, and he had a nervous manner of handling his petronel. The ball took a little skin off my shoulder."

"Something more than skin," grunted Aaron Blazeby, paying no attention to me but going on with his work. He had cauterized the wound and was now clamping a bandage on it. The apothecary was a little man, not especially clean, and with a twist in his neck which caused him to carry his head sideways.

The room was Ann's, as she had warned me. I saw an article of feminine apparel on the floor and the wire understructure of her farthingale in one corner.

"You'll have a stiff shoulder, Cap'n Ward," warned Blazeby.

"I'm not concerned about that. I'm afraid the harman-beck will have more than a stiff shoulder. I dropped him on his head over the nearest wall. Well, Master Apothecary, I won't need you for anything else. Roger will help me dress."

When Blazeby had made his way down the steep steps, John picked up his shirt from the bed, wincing perceptibly. "I judge from the look of you," he said, "that you have news for me."

I gave him the message from Widdigate and then added: "I want to go with you this time, John, if you'll have me."

He grunted with pain as he struggled to raise the shirt above his head. "Jore said something about it. So you want to be a pirate, do you? That's what we're going to be in the eyes of the King's law from now on."

"I don't care what we're called. I want to be in it."

"That's the spirit! If you feel that way, I can use you; and many more like you. I'll make a good sailor and a fighting man out of you, Roger. We're going to go on breeding seamen in England in spite of old King Quodlibet. What do the family say about it?"

"I haven't told them yet."

"They won't like it. Your mother will blame me for it."

He stood without moving for a full minute. He was holding his shirt above his head with his good arm. It was of the finest silk and richly embroidered with gold thread. I was sure our house was run for a full year on what he had paid for it. His hair, which was the color of gold, fell below his shoulders. He might not be considered a handsome man by some, for his nose had the curve of a hawk's and his jaw was too square; but he was a truly magnificent physical specimen. I wondered at the whiteness of his skin. Most deep-sea sailors were tanned to the shade of mahogany.

"So, I'm to see Sir Bartlemy Ladland," he said at last. "This means our brave Jamie has refused to wink at my little exploits. I suspected as much when the constable creased my skin for me. I'm not surprised. He swore before I sailed that he would hang me if I took a fall out of his good friends the Dons. Well, we'll have to move fast. I have no desire at all to swing on the chats. Nor do I want to keep the Great Man company in the Tower."

He was referring, I knew, to Sir Walter Raleigh, who was still in the Tower under a sentence of death pronounced some years before. The last of the great captains of Queen Elizabeth's time had outgrown his earlier unpopularity and was now recognized for what he was, the most versatile and remarkable man of his age. All England was angry at the way he was being treated, particularly as no one believed the trumped-up charge of treason on which he had been convicted. It was well known that King James was plucking him piecemeal of all his possessions for the benefit of his favorites.

John had tucked his gorgeous shirt under the top of his hose and was buckling a belt of soft leather around his waist. It had at least a score of eyelet holes in its lower edge, corresponding with an equal number in the reinforced silk of the hose top. He proceeded to bind them together with leather thongs, called points. It was a complicated business, and I watched with considerable interest. My own leggings were held up by no more than four points, tied to the bottom of my tunic, which accounted partly for the slackness which invariably showed at my knees. When John had finished with the last of them, he was so tightly trussed up that the silk of his hose fitted him like his own skin.

"What has Sir Bartlemy to do with this?" I asked.

John had drawn on his brown trunk breeches, which were slashed with velvet of the same color as the hose. This necessitated more tying of points to the upper edge of the belt. His fingers moved with impatient haste.

"Has it ever occurred to you, Roger," he asked, "that it takes money to equip a ship-of-war? Behind every freebooter there's always a man of position and wealth, or a group of them. They supply the money for the expedition and then sit comfortably at home and enjoy a very large share of the profits without taking any of the risks. I'm backed by such a group. Sir Bartlemy is one of them; in fact, he's the main one. There is in addition a young man, very close to His Majesty, who was supposed to secure immunity for me. The others are wealthy men in the City, aldermen and the like. I deal mostly with Sir Bartlemy. He negotiated my letters of marquee from the Low Countries when Old Rumbleguts refused. Keep a close tongue about this, my lad, for Sir Bartlemy would be in serious trouble if his part in it were known." He had clamped a frame of wire around his neck and was attaching his starched ruff to it. The ruff was an enormous affair, a full two feet wide. "Snap the wire at the back, Roger. And tie the ruff so that none of the wire shows. I always need help in getting into these things. That's it. Now about Sir Bartlemy. I'm sure he has some urgent word for us, so we must get over there at once."

"We?" I was almost too surprised to speak. Surprises, in fact, had been piling up on me the last few minutes, the greatest being the amazing information about our powerful neighbor. Sir Bartlemy Ladland was a quiet and studious man who was supposed to have no ambitions other than a desire for occasional conquests in a gentler game than politics. I found it hard to believe that he was concerned in as stern a business as that on which John had sailed.

"You, of course," said John. "You're going with me tonight. That is, if you meant it about joining me."

"I meant it!" I exclaimed fervently. "But it hadn't occurred to me we would be leaving so soon."

"It's tonight or not at all," said my friend. "There will be no time for farewells, I'm afraid. I must go to Appleby Court and make my arrangements, and then we'll lose no time in getting away. I'm taking no chances on what that mammering old bastard of a king will decide to do. The *Royal Bess* is lying off the coast, ready to sail at a moment's notice. She was the *Madalina*, you know. I mounted thirty-two guns in her when I changed the name, and she's now the sweetest and fastest craft that ever sailed the Midland Sea."

He had slipped into his sleeveless doublet and had turned his back so that I could button him up. I performed this task with great care, having regard to the costliness of the material as well as the tender condition of his wounded shoulder. "No, Roger, there will be no time to see your mother or that old dragon of an aunt. Sir Bartlemy will supply us with horses, and we may make up our minds now to a long ride tonight."

"I'll write them," I said. I had no thought of backing out, but I was realizing that this would make the blow harder for them. I was conscious at first of a deep sense of guilt. Then I let my thoughts jump ahead to the end of this adventure and immediately felt much better about it. I would come back with so much Spanish gold that the need for saving and scrimping would be over for all time. I would bring them silks and satins and fine jewels, and I would marry Katie Ladland, which they both hoped for above everything.

John was now putting on his enormous puffed sleeves, which had to be attached to the doublet with many more points. He winced once while I attended to this for him but otherwise seemed to be taking no discomfort from his injury. He began to strut about the room in all his finery, the most magnificent figure of a man I had ever seen or ever hoped to see. I felt small and insignificant beside him.

"I promised to take some lads from the town, but there won't be time to collect them now," he ruminated. "It's a pity, for I could use them all. I hoped to have none but Englishmen in the crew this trip. Well, I can pick up a few stout Dutchmen if need be. They're good enough."

"Don't you think we should hurry?" I asked. "The sheriff may come any minute."

"Let him try it," replied John easily. "Do you suppose the bully boys of this town would stand by and see trouble come to John Ward? I hardly think so." He picked the garment off the floor and held it up with a sly wink. "The little baggage! She left it there on purpose. Our pretty Ann wears fine main buntlings. Satin, no less, and will you take notice of the fineness of the lace! I have nothing better myself. What do you say, Roger, shall we take this along and let it flutter from our masthead?"

I thought at first he was serious about it and was going to protest. It was bad enough, to my way of thinking, that we could not sail under the flag of England. Then I noticed there was a twinkle in his eye.

"I see you don't approve," he said. "Well, you're right. If she were French, now, or even a dark-eyed señorita! But we couldn't treat an English girl that way. Not even our little Ann. By the way, Roger, you knew, of course, that she was not entirely adverse to a little niggling in the old days? You were a sly young dog and knew all about it, I'm sure. She's a widow now, and I thought— Well, I confess that I came here tonight with far pleasanter anticipations than to have her dirty old uncle dress a wounded shoulder for me."

He stamped down the stairs, and I followed at his heels, not too happy over the confidences he had reposed in me. I had suspected it, of course, for there had been plenty of talk in town about them; but I was fond of Ann and would rather not have heard this confirmation of it. John was in high spirits again and began to sing a verse of the song I had heard earlier at the Cygnet's Head:

> We'll set our course and take our fee,
> From haughty Don and High Grandee.
> Philip, we'll sail in spite of thee,
> *And singe thy royal beard!*

Ann met us in the workroom below. Her uncle had retired to the back room, and I could hear him puttering about and talking to himself.

"It must be good-by now, my sweet and lovely Ann," said John in a gay tone. "I hoped to stay awhile in town and see a great deal of my little Mistress Goldenlocks. But Old Jamie won't have it that way. So I'm off. Give me a buss, sweetheart."

He put his good arm around her and squeezed her tight. Ann seemed to take it coolly enough, for she kept an interested eye on me over his shoulder the while. When she found that the width of his ruff made it impossible for him to kiss her, she puckered up her lips and looked at me as though to say: Perhaps *you* would have better luck.

"Take a heart-felt word of advice from me, Roger," said John. "When you have love-making in mind, never get yourself all dressed up like this. I have had no chance to ask you about your plans, Ann. Do you intend to stay here? It would be dull for you, I'm thinking."

"I'm going to London," she answered, trying to free her face from the close proximity of his ruff. "I'm going to open a little shop. Widows have to live, you know."

"A shop? What are you going to sell?"

"Clothes for ladies of the court. Fine ruffs and caps. And other things."

"Especially the other things," declared John. "The ladies of the court will be sure to think that they would look as well as you do in—the other things. I'm sure you'll have a great success. But when I come back, that will be a different matter, Fubbs. There'll be no keeping of shops then."

Ann's face puckered up into a smile, but she continued to look at me around the huge puff of his sleeve. "Roger will come and see me in London, I hope," she said.

"No, Roger won't come and see you in London," declared John. "Roger is sailing with me."

She stepped back from him. "You didn't tell me that," she said, looking in my direction.

"I wasn't sure he would take me."

"This is your doing, John Ward!" said Ann. "You've talked him into it!"

"I've had nothing to do with it. It's his own idea. And I can't see that it's any concern of yours, Mistress Ann."

"No, it's no concern of mine and thank you, John Ward, for reminding me." Her face wore a look of real distress. "Roger, do you want to go? I don't think it's a—a very good idea."

John said impatiently, "I'm going to make a seaman of our Roger. He shall play Grenville to my Drake. Keep your fingers out of men's affairs, Fubbs."

She looked at him intently. "I'm not interested in *your* affairs. I'm beginning to think I don't like you any more. But I've always liked Roger."

4

WE LEFT TOWN by a back road which led through the closely set firs of Wayland Spinney. There was a steep hill here, and when John and I had puffed our way to the top we could see that the Great Hall at Appleby Court was lighted up.

"Sir Bartlemy must have guests tonight," I said.

John frowned. "Sir Bartlemy is a cautious soul, and he won't be happy if anyone should see us there. Even if we had the King's approval, he wouldn't want it known that he has dealings with a gory-handed pirate."

"He sent for you," I reminded him.

We plodded on in silence for a few minutes. "Roger," said my friend suddenly, "I've been thinking. This may be all wrong. I have no right to take you away from home. You've no idea what's ahead of you. It's the hardest kind of a life. What Ann said back there set me thinking. It's a filthy business, and the fighting is of the bloodiest kind. And what's at the end of it? Death, perhaps, in a Spanish prison—a very unpleasant death, I promise you. Or at the end of a rope. The glory of it is all in the beholding. Roger, you must be sensible about it. Turn around and go home. I won't think any the worse of you if you do."

"But what will I think of myself?" I demanded. My mind was running on the glory that Englishmen had won in the days of great Queen Bess. I was thinking of Drake sailing around the world, of Sir Richard Grenville and the *Revenge*, of the dread Armada turning tail and running to its destruction with English hornets stinging it to death. My father had fought against the Armada, and so had John's, and John himself. These men must have felt some of the glory they had earned. England needed men who were capable of the same kind of gallantry now, and men of commoner clay to work and fight back of the leaders.

I wanted to tell him what I was thinking, but all I could manage to say was, "No, I am going."

"There will be times when you'll regret it bitterly," said John. "Some days your flesh will crawl with the heat, and the sea will look like green fire, and the ship will stink like a charnel house. You'll live on the roughest food, and your hands will be cut to ribbons on the shrouds, and you'll never know what it is to have a full and decent sleep. You'll see things done every day which will sicken you to your very soul. I'm being honest with you, Roger. This is no life for a man with a single grain of fineness in him."

"I always thought Drake and Frobisher and Cavendish were fine men," I declared.

"No," replied John, "they were great men. There's a big difference."

"It's my duty to go. I've thought it all over, and I can see no other way. I want to go. The Bleases have always been sailors, and I am a Blease."

John had nothing further to say for a full minute. Then he nodded. "Have it your own way, Roger. Probably you're right about it, but I wanted to be sure you went in with your eyes wide open. I'm glad you're coming with me."

The drawbridge over the moat at Appleby Court had not been raised for so long that the rusted chains had been cut. As we crossed the bridge I looked up at the gatehouse tower, and it seemed at such close range to stretch all the way to heaven. I was suddenly conscious of my mended jacket with its plain camelet sleeves and unmatched buttons of pewter and my ill-fitting kersey hose. Beside my gorgeous companion I would look like a plucked country crow, and so I had no stomach for facing Katie Ladland. She had no idea of the way I felt about her, of course; but I did not want to appear at such disadvantage in her eyes.

Hugh Parler, the porter, led the way in and escorted us up a winding stone staircase. This brought us to an apartment with a log snapping cheerfully in a stone fireplace. I recognized it as the first of the guest chambers which took up the full front wing of the house. I smiled as I read the couplet cut into the stone over the mantel.

The sloven and the careless guest, the roynish nothing nice,
To lodge in chamber comely decked, are seldom suffered twice.

The point was well taken. It was a handsomely furnished room, and the habits of guests were often marked by a lack of care, to say the least. There was a long draw-table, several cushioned chairs, and even a Turkey carpet covering the stone floor. I went to a window which looked out over the quadrangle and saw that the Great Hall was crowded with guests. A tall oriel window gave me a full view of the interior, and I could see them bowing and dipping and swaying to the music. They were dancing a coranto, a slow and dignified measure.

"Who shall I say?" asked Parler, looking dubiously at us.

John answered him. "No names, if you please," he said. "Just say to your master, 'Little John and the Middle Course.' Can you remember that?"

When the porter had gone, John joined me at the window and said with a broad grin: "Sir Bartlemy entertains in high state. I ought to be leading a measure down there myself, because I've paid for a large share of all this. I brought back plenty of gold in the hold of the *Royal Bess*. I'm going to make a great heiress of little Katie Ladland before I'm through." Then he looked at me and his smile broadened. "Haven't I heard it rumored that one Roger Blease is very much enamored of the daughter of Appleby Court? No cause to blush, my boy. I'm sure it's an honest attachment, and the Piries can match quarterings with the Ladlands any day. An excellent plan all around. It would keep the loot in the family, in a way of speaking."

I was thinking that Katie would not be dancing, not being old enough to mingle with the guests. She would be in the East Gallery and peeping over the tapestried rail at the company. None of the ladies with their jeweled coifs and wide farthingales, who posed and bowed and swung in the slow turnings of the coranto, would be half as pretty as my Katie, with her sweet gray eyes and hair as black as the outside sky. My Katie? What presumption! I knew that I was an imbecile to harbor such a dream.

John had taken to pacing up and down the room with his incredibly long strides. "Sir Bartlemy wants me to try the Americas," he said, in a ruminating tone. "They're all for it, in fact, the fine young gentleman at court and the worthy merchants in the City. I don't agree with them. Granted there is more chance for gold off Barbados or Jamaica. But that isn't what I'm risking my life for, and the lives of all my crew. I aim to show the Dons that the flag of England has as much right in the Midland Sea as the red and yellow bars. I shall attack and sink any ship carrying the crest of Castile as long as they continue to seize English merchantmen. If we pick up cargoes in doing so, it will be so much gain. But, Roger, we don't sail for gain! That point must be made very clear to our gallant gentlemen."

Katie's father came into the room at this point, and it was clear that he was both troubled and annoyed at seeing me there. He was as richly attired as John, and I realized more fully than I ever had before that he bore a close resemblance to pictures of old King Harry. He sat down at the end of the table and tucked his thumbs aggressively in the slashings of his doublet.

"I expected you alone, Captain Ward," he said in his rich bass voice. "Why is Roger with you? I'm at a loss to understand this."

"Roger is sailing with me," declared John, seating himself at the other end of the table. His manner said plainer than words: That is how it is and I don't give a snap of the finger what you may think or say about it.

A look of genuine concern showed itself on Sir Bartlemy's broad and whiskered visage. "Indeed, Captain Ward! I'm not sure I can agree to that. Roger is young, and his mother has other plans for him. This is— Really, this is an annoying situation. It puts me in a most difficult position." He folded one silk-clad knee over the other and turned in my direction. "Roger, have you told your mother of this? I can't believe she has given her consent."

"I haven't spoken to her yet," I answered reluctantly. "It was this afternoon that I made up my mind. I intended to tell her tomorrow, but now it seems I must leave with John tonight, or not at all. I'm going to write her, sir. She will understand." I began to argue my case with all the earnestness at my command. "I am of sailor stock, as you know, sir. My father went to sea when he was ten years old. It's high time I made a start."

He continued to regard me with a worried frown. "I don't like this," he muttered. "Really, I don't like it at all. I have a great respect and affection for Mistress Blease. What would she think if she knew I had been a party to sending you off to sea?"

"She'll never know, sir," I declared eagerly. "Certainly she'll never hear of it through me. How else could it reach her?"

Sir Bartlemy ran vexed fingers through his straggling beard. "I know you well enough to be sure you will keep a still tongue, Roger," he said at last. "Otherwise I would have no course open but to send you home. There is this to be said for you, my boy: your father wanted you to be a sailor. He said so many times. The decision, as I see it, then, is in your own hands."

He turned back to John. "Ward, we have matters of importance to discuss. Things have taken—well, quite a difficult turn. I'm deeply concerned. We must consider our course with the utmost care. It may not be wise for me to run too contrary to the royal will. I don't mind saying that I am disturbed, seriously disturbed." He got to his feet and patted out a wrinkle at his knee. "There's a small room off my library where we will be safe from intrusion. In fact, I'll make sure of it by locking the door. Then some food will be served here. For you and Roger." He looked at me again and smiled with a little more cordiality. "Catherine will want to say good-by. The little baggage was told to go to bed, but I'll swear it was her head I saw from a corner of the East Gallery not ten minutes ago."

They left the room together, and in a very few minutes Firk Besson came in, carrying a tray above his head. He began to lay plates and dishes of food on the table, grumbling openly at the additional labor which our coming had imposed on him.

"There," he said, slapping down the spoons and knives and whisking a slice of cold mutton into his own mouth. "Meat and a veal pie and the best bread in the house. And suckets. The best food you've had in many a long day, Master Blease. You'll make your knife move lively with *this* food I've brought you." He frowned at me. "No making yourself sick over it, mind you."

I waited until he had gone and then, I am afraid, my knife did move lively. There was a pitcher of red wine on the table. I had filled my cup and was lifting it to my lips when the door opened again. I heard a rustle of skirts and looked up.

It was Katie. She smiled and came a few steps into the room. Then she stopped as though not entirely sure of the propriety of paying me a visit.

I scrambled to my feet, almost spilling my wine. She had just turned fifteen but was looking very much grown up. Her hair was done in a new way, dressed high on her head with loops of seed pearls and allowing the tips of her ears to show. I had never seen her ears before. Her eyes were bright with excitement, and she was managing her wide skirts with an air which said plainly: I am no longer Katie, if you please; I am Catherine Ladland, and what do you think of me? I longed to tell her exactly what I thought of her but did not dare.

"Roger," she said in a whisper. "Father sent word I was to go to bed but also that you were here. I think he expected I would come. What does it mean? Are you going away?"

"Yes," I answered proudly. "I'm going with John Ward. To fight the Spaniards."

She gave me a frightened look and came a little farther into the room. "Roger, what do you mean? You're going to sea? I can't believe it. You—why, you're going to London soon. I have been thinking— Roger, you look different tonight. You look so *very* much older."

"We both look different tonight," I said, getting up my courage to tell her what was in my mind. "I could hardly be sure at first it was you. I thought it must be one of the ladies from downstairs, you looked so grown up and—and lovely. You took my breath away." I paused and then added hopefully. "Katie, I never intended to live in London. I had to pretend because of Mother and Aunt Gadilda, but I've always meant to be a sailor. When John came home today, I made up my mind once and for all. I'm going with him."

She was standing beside me now and looking up with troubled eyes. "I believe I would want to go too, if I were a man," she whispered. "But I'm frightened. Roger, you might be killed—or taken prisoner. I don't dare think what that would mean."

"You do like me, then?"

Katie had always been honest about things, and she did not hesitate to answer now. "Of course I like you. I always have. You know that, Roger. I like you well enough not to want anything to happen to you."

We sat down on opposite sides of the table. I drank a little of the wine and began to talk about John Ward's plans. He was going to Tunis first and was going to organize all the Free Rovers into one fleet. Then he was going to drive the Dons off the seas. It was going to be like old times, like Drake sailing into Cadiz and burning the whole Spanish fleet under the king's nose. Leaning both elbows on the table, Katie cupped her chin in her hands and regarded me with serious eyes.

"But I don't understand," she said finally. "Isn't this country at peace with Spain now?"

"Nominally," I answered. "The two kings have signed a peace. But it's one-sided, Katie. The Spaniards are not observing it. They seize every English ship they find and then say they were pirates. They intend to gobble the trade of the whole world. They couldn't beat us, and so now they aim to get what they want by trickery. King James won't see what they are up to, and so men like John must fight the English cause on their own."

The frown between her eyes deepened. "Everything you say makes me more frightened," she said. "It will be very dangerous. I don't want you to go, Roger. Your mother's plan *must* be the best. You might become a great man in London. I—I may go to court soon myself. Father thinks Queen Anne will make me a maid of honor when I'm a little older. Perhaps in another year."

We talked it over for a long time. I indulged in bold predictions as to what it was going to mean to fight under John Ward. Glory and wealth and the esteem of all men—all men except King Jamie, of course. Perhaps even the King would change his mind when he found what we would do to the Dons. Katie continued to shake her head. I could see she had never heard of the *Trial*, and it was quite clear that she knew nothing whatever of her father's partnership with John Ward. When I told her that John was in the house and closeted that very minute with Sir Bartlemy, she opened her eyes wide.

"What business has he with Father?" she asked.

"He's seeking advice, no doubt, as to what he should do. All men of the town look up to your father."

"I want to see him!" she said eagerly. "Is he as handsome as everyone says? I hear he's the tallest man in England."

"I don't know about that, although I've never seen a taller. But I do know he's the bravest man in England." I leaned across the table and looked earnestly into her eyes in my anxiety to make her understand. "Katie, if you feel that way about him, how do you suppose I feel? I would die of shame if I didn't join him now that the chance has come."

She nodded slowly. "I suppose so," she said. Getting to her feet, she looked down at her skirt to make sure it had not become rumpled. "You haven't said a word about my dress, Roger. Do you like me in it? You're going away, and I won't see you for years. I'll be a lady of the court when you get tired of fighting and decide to come back. I'll have suitors, I hope. Perhaps I'll even be married. Have you thought of that?"

"Katie!" I exclaimed. I wanted to implore her to wait for me, to promise that she would not marry, no matter how many suitors she had. But I could not manage to say it.

She may have known what I was trying to tell her, but if she did she made no effort to help me. "We must be reconciled, then, to not seeing each other for a long time," she said in a lighter tone. "Does that worry you at all? Still, there's nothing more to be said." Then she smiled and gave me one of her hands. "Would you care to watch the dancing? It's quite exciting."

Finally we came to the cavernous corner kitchen where fires blazed on open hearths and supper was being prepared for the guests. The Great Hall lay just beyond. We went through the buttery and climbed a short flight of narrow wooden steps to a balcony from which we could look down on the dancers. We sat on the floor and peeped through holes in the tapestry which covered the railing.

I had dined in the Great Hall on the preceding Christmas. There had been a huge Yule log burning, and the place had seemed bright and full of cheer. It looked much larger now. The roof was so high above us that the pennons hanging up there in the darkness made a faint and ghostly rustling in the drafts. Such sounds could be heard at odd intervals only, however, for the musicians were playing with might and main. The citterns were twanging and the bysardens wheezing and the drums thumping. The guests were dancing a galliard, and I found it hard not to laugh when it came to the lavolta, which is a sudden spring in the air; for the farthingales of the women were not well suited to such acrobats. They looked like marionettes when the strings are operated by amateur puppet-masters. I had heard much of the beauty of court costumes, but I must say that I was disappointed, for the V-shaped bodices worn by the women made them look unnaturally long-waisted. The men cut better figures, I thought. Katie saw nothing of this. Her interest in everything was almost breathless.

"Isn't it beautiful?" she said. "I can hardly wait to go to court. The Queen is a very fine dancer and loves masques. I love them too. There is Lady Govern now. I wonder what color her hair really is? Perhaps it's gray. I don't think I want to live to be that old."

"You needn't worry about that," I said. "You will always be lovely, Katie."

She squirmed around to look at me more closely. "Why, Roger, you *are* growing up," she said. "You've made me a courtly speech. Did you really mean it?"

I was finding it intoxicating to sit so near her in the darkness. My courage began to come back.

"Katie, will you wait for me?" I asked.

She looked at me intently and then shook her head. "I will make no promises," she answered. "You're going away and you'll be gone two years. Perhaps longer. I'll be at court, and there will be many men there. I might fall in love with one of them. It would be very easy for me to give you a promise now, but later I might forget it. I wouldn't want things to happen that way. When a promise is given, it must be kept. And so I think it would not be right for me to say yes to you now."

I watched the strutting gallants on the dance floor, thinking that sooner or later Katie would fall in love with some stripling of the court.

She interrupted my train of thought by whispering, "I think we had better leave now."

I got to my feet and helped her to rise. My face must have shown what I was thinking, for she squeezed my hand and said: "You needn't be so tragic about it. I haven't said I *would* fall in love with another man. I may never meet one I'll like better than—than my memory of you."

It was so late by this time that she decided we would be unlikely to meet anyone if we crossed the quadrangle. Perhaps she was not feeling equal to another venture through the Long Gallery. At any rate, we went out through the buttery door and proceeded cautiously in the dark through the inner gardens. It was very dark, and I stepped on a tennis ball, falling flat on my back and seeing immediately all the stars that the night clouds hid. It was most humiliating, for I had been dramatizing my disappointment by stalking in dignified gloom. Katie began to laugh. At first this made me angrier still, but then I saw the humor of it and was able to laugh also. "Poor Roger," said Katie.

John was seated at the supper table when we reached the chamber in the gatehouse. He shoved his wine cup to one side when his eyes lighted on Katie and rose slowly to his great height. He stared at her for a moment and then turned to me.

"Roger," he said accusingly, "you're a lying, quibbling, conniving, understating dog. You only said she was beautiful." Then he turned back to Katie. "You are Mistress Catherine Ladland, of whom I have heard not nearly enough. I am John Ward, a poor sea captain of no official standing, and from this moment thenceforth your most faithful servant and abject admirer."

Have you ever stood by and watched something that you have treasured within yourself crumble away before your eyes? Perhaps old King Harry had felt as I did now when they broke the news to him that his second Catherine had been unfaithful with a young blade of the court. Katie was looking at John Ward with a light in her eyes that I had never seen there before. But how could it have been otherwise? John was so big and compelling, with his hawklike nose, his bold mouth, and his blazing blue eyes. He was born to command the loyalty of men and the love of women. He had always had the one from me, and now Katie perhaps was in a fair way to yield him the other.

I had never been in a theater, but the thought went through my head that plays must be something like this: the three of us standing there with this situation between us and none of us saying a word.

It was John who broke the silence. "You've heard bad reports of me, I'm sure. That I'm enticing your friend Roger off to sea where I'll make him into a pirate like myself."

"No," answered Katie, never taking her eyes off his face. "I've heard only the best reports of you, Captain Ward."

"I'm glad of that," declared my friend. "I would be very unhappy if you thought badly of me, Mistress Catherine. I've heard you may soon be going to court, and I'm wondering if you'll change your mind about me then. It's the rule there to agree with everything King Jamie says."

"I won't change my mind," said Katie. "Not even if I go to court."

"What do you think of our bold Roger's electing to throw in his lot with me?"

She gave me a quick look, and then her eyes turned back to him, like iron to a magnet. "I'm not sure," she answered. "At first I was against it. But now I—I think I'm able to understand it better."

"Well spoken," declared John. He leaned over and clapped me on the shoulder. "If the three of us had lived two hundred years ago, you would be begging the right to wear her colors, my bold Roger. And I—" He looked at Katie and added slowly, "I perhaps would be disposed to contest that great privilege with you."

Katie blushed deeply and said, "I must go now. It's very late."

But John was not through. He had a receptive audience, and he was going to make the most of it. "I'm wondering about the future," he said. "Your destiny, Mistress Catherine, is easy to read. In part, at least. You'll be a court beauty, and plenty of men will be in love with you. It will be difficult for you to remember two humble sailors fighting for a cause which went into eclipse when the Great Queen died. And yet I have a sense of conviction that you *will* remember. As for Roger, he has a head on his shoulders, and I think he may become the Ulysses of freebooters. Or a councillor high in royal circles if he ever elects to return to a life ashore. In that event, it seems to me certain that no one will be able to contest with him the right to wear those colors we were speaking of. As for me, I'm not a modest man, and so I make bold to assert that I shall give this country what she needs most at the moment: someone to fill as well as he may the shoes of the great Drake. The common men of England will think well of me even though the King stretches my neck at Wapping Stairs. My destiny is the easiest to read, for there's no doubt as to the course I must follow. No more doubt than there is to another matter: the devotion I'll always feel for Mistress Catherine Ladland."

Much as I admired John, I felt some impatience at the length of this speech. He was showing off for Katie's benefit. It was clear, however, that he had her full attention. She was too bemused to make any comment; and, to my relief, Besson broke up the tableau by putting in an appearance.

"It's very late," she said then. "I'm sure father thinks I retired long ago."

She looked at me briefly, then much longer at John, or so I thought. She gave us a curtsy and left the room. While in the room she had seemed quite mature and grown up, but it was little Katie Ladland I watched going down the steep stone staircase of the gatehouse, even though she wore a fine blue gown and had loops of pearls in her hair. I found myself wishing she had not changed.

"Have you supped, Roger?" asked John.

Firk Besson looked at the table and snorted. "It's well for him if he has," he said. He didn't seem to know who John was, but it would have made no difference.

Firk was right. A sparrow would have made out badly on what was left. The mutton was gone, and the veal pie was a hollow shambles of crust. The suckets, highly sugared fruit confections, had vanished. John was a hearty eater.

When the serving man had loaded his tray and departed, John went back to his chair and stretched himself out at full length. "There's been a change of plan," he said. "We're to stay here until tomorrow night. In the strictest seclusion, of course. Sir Bartlemy is developing nerves. He hasn't the heart for a gentleman adventurer, and he's hoping to get things patched up with the royal gander. Tomorrow night we set out to make two important calls. One in London. The other—" He paused and winked at me to increase my suspense. "Where do you suppose we're to make our other call? At Theobalds."

"Theobalds!" I exclaimed. "The King's palace?"

"Yes, my bold Roger. We go to the King's palace. But not to see the King. Nothing as rash as that. I've no thought to let him get his greasy paws on me. We're going to talk instead to the young man I told you of before." He looked at me as though doubtful of the wisdom of further explanation. "Perhaps you're too young to know about this king of ours. He has—peculiarities. He likes men about him, young men. The one we go to see has rosy cheeks and curly hair and legs like a dancing master's. They say he can twist King Jamie around his finger. Sir Bartlemy is hoping he can persuade his master to look with a more lenient eye on my activities. I shall propose that a large share of future profits find lodgment in the empty royal purse."

I had heard plenty of talk about the King which I had never fully understood. I covered up my ignorance by asking who we were to see in London. My companion went into a second explanation with more relish.

"A man of a different stripe," he said. "You remember Chirp Bird, of course. A miserable fellow, Chirp. He was born a foin and would have become no better than a clapperdudgeon if luck hadn't come his way." I agreed entirely about Chirp Bird, who had been a thief at school and had always run whining at our heels. "Well, Chirp is in London and has become quite a swaggerer. But it's not Chirp we're to see, although we're sure to run into him. It's the man just above him. The boss of the cohorts of crime. The Upright Man of Alsatia."

"Things have been changing in the criminal world," John went on. "The Rogue-stalled are well organized today. There's an Upright Man in every town, and they're as powerful in their way as our old lummocks at Whitehall. Yes, there are kings of crime. Every nip who cuts a purse must turn part of it in. The looting of apple-squires goes into a common fund. The morts who walk the streets belong to the system as well as the owners of the ordinaries where gentlemen try their luck at the gaming tables. Well, we must see the boss crook of Alsatia because he and he alone can turn what we rieve from the Dons into good English mint."

He could see that I was puzzled, so he proceeded to explain his last point more clearly. "There's a business side to freebooting, Roger. When we take a Spanish ship, it is loaded to the gunnels with fine goods. Tapestries, gold plate, furniture, silks and satins and leather goods, sometimes even precious stones. What are we to do with them? Sir Bartlemy and his friends can't open a shop in Cheapside to dispose of them or hawk them around the country like Irish toyles. The Upright Man takes all that off our hands. He can sell the stuff, at good prices too, although he won't turn back to us as much as half of what he gets. Still, it's the only way. I must talk to this rank fellow in Alsatia and strike a bargain with him."

I was feeling thoroughly disillusioned. It had never entered my head that there could be anything like this to sea adventuring. I had pictured it as clean and open fighting to prove our rights and to rescue the poor devils who pulled oars in Spanish galleys, not as a furtive business which made us partners with criminals. John sensed what was running through my mind and patted my knee encouragingly.

"Easy now, youngster," he said. "Drake had to do the same thing, and Cavendish, and even the Great Man in the Tower. The old queen used to drive a hard bargain for her share; and a big share it was. Would you have us throw the stuff overboard? Well, then, there you have it. You must face one bitter truth, Roger: the rosy dreams of youth are soon lost when you turn your hand to man's work. It's not only at sea, my fine sprat. Have you any idea what you would have faced if you had decided to go to court instead? Making friends with panders and pimps with noble tags to their names. You would have to wink at all manner of evil trades. A court post is trafficking in scandal and lies. Get this into your head: all life is piracy of one kind or another."

I was doing my best to digest this unpalatable statement and so made no answer. John changed the subject by remarking in an elaborately casual tone: "Your Katie is a pretty child. Perhaps you would be wiser after all to stay home and marry her."

I hesitated. "I'm very much afraid that Katie isn't for me," I said. "Why not?"

"You've said yourself that her father is a rich man. Look at this place, and you have the answer. Would Sir Bartlemy consider me as a son-in-law? I won't come into any property worth mentioning."

"Money isn't everything. If Sir Francis Drake had been unmarried when he won his greatest fame, he could have had anyone in England. No heiress was too high-placed for a man like that. Great deeds level rank."

"Another Drake might have a chance. Were you thinking of me when you suggested that?"

He looked at me soberly. "To be perfectly honest, Roger," he said, "I wasn't."

5

SIR BARTLEMY was so determined to keep the fact of John Ward's presence in the house a secret that he escorted us himself to the library where we were to spend the night. It was in a corner of the left wing and had been the chapel in earlier days, when men thought much of religion and very little of learning. Our host looked up at the light flooding in through the stained-glass windows—it was a strange green glow, and I had started to wonder as soon as we entered how we would manage to sleep in such an eerie atmosphere— and said in apologetic tones: "This is the best I can do for you. The place is as full of guests as a granary with rats; and some of them not much more welcome, if I may speak my mind. In any event, it's highly unwise for any of them to know you're here. There are comfortable couches, and I left orders for blankets to be brought."

When he had gone I picked up our solitary candle and made a tour of inspection, cupping a hand around the flame to protect it from the drafts. The place was as cold as a tomb and about as cheerless under these circumstances. Partial partitions of dark oak had been built out from the walls on each side, having the appearance of high pews. They were banked with books, and on that account I looked about me with an awe that the ecclesiastical past of the place could never have induced. I could see nothing but the backs of fine tomes bound in red, blue, and brown leather—thousands of them, musty with age and containing no doubt the accumulated wisdom of the centuries. For the first time I felt a faint touch of regret that I had elected to go to sea. A man could spend a lifetime both pleasantly and profitably in such company as this.

John complained that his shoulder was stiff and that it was causing him some pain. I helped him to undress, even undoing his endless points. Then I wrapped him in blankets on a deep couch in one of the embrasures which I selected because it seemed to have the least smell of damp leather about it. He fell asleep immediately and snored with the complete surrender of perfect physical condition.

I wakened early, feeling cold and cramped. With my first flash of reason, I wondered if I had made the mistake of spending the night in St.

Martin's, our rather fine tenth-century church. John sat up and rubbed
his eyes, remarking cheerfully that he felt much better. The light
through the windows was bright and reassuring now, having something
of the yellow of the sun about it.

I had slept in my clothes, having made sure that John got the better
of the blanket division. He shook his head when he noticed my rumpled condition. "You're an untidy gilpie," he said. "Holy Olaf, you
must never venture out in such a rig on a Fifth of November, or they'll
burn you for an effigy of Guido Fawkes."

He grumbled while I helped him to dress because he had to wear
the same clothes. I was to learn during the long time I was with him
that he was the greatest of dandies. "I wish she could see me in my
new green and yellow," he muttered, wincing a little as I adjusted the
sleeve on his bad shoulder.

"She?"

"Your Katie. I've taken quite a fancy to her. She's a gay little spark,
isn't she? I swear I've never seen the equal of her eyes."

This recalled to me what had happened when they met the previous
evening, and my spirits took a drop. "I doubt if we'll see her at all
today," I managed to say. "So it wouldn't do you any good if you had
your other clothes."

"Probably not. Old Timid-and-Touchy will see to it that his one
sweet chick isn't exposed any more to piratical influences." His voice
showed a trace of irritation. "You speak as though I had two suits only.
I'll have you know, my gentry-cove, that I've got fourteen."

Old Timid-and-Touchy came in to visit us shortly after, entering
through a low door which communicated with his bedroom. He was
muffled up in a brown shamoy robe which trailed on the floor but did
not conceal the fact that he was in bare feet. On the top of his head
was a ridiculously small nightcap of brown cloth, tied under his chin
with a leather strap. He was in a mood of great amiability and greeted
us with the hope that we had slept well.

His good spirits did not surprise me. It was known to everyone in
town that Sir Bartlemy invariably wakened with a blandness which
tapered off during the day and left him acid and unhappy in the hours
of evening. It had been the reverse with his late-lamented brother, who
rose in the deepest melancholy and did not enjoy any lift in mood
until candlelight time, when he became so excessively jovial that he
was ready to sell his birthright for much less than a mess of potage;
he had, in fact, done that very thing and had died in Ireland in a condition of extreme poverty.

"There will be some breakfast for you soon, my good lads," said
our host, stretching himself out on the couch which John had vacated.
I noticed that the soles of his feet were black. "I think it advisable to
keep the servants in the dark about all this, and so my Katie will fetch
it for you."

"You're being very kind, Sir Bartlemy," said John, winking at me over his huge shoulder.

"No, no, not at all. I'm only sorry that I couldn't put you in my best bedrooms. After all, you're fighting for a good cause, and that would be my warrant." He drew the shamoy collar tightly around his neck, for the cold was enough to strike into the very marrow of your bones. "I won't have an opportunity to talk to you much today, and so I must take advantage of the present. Answer a question, if you please, Ward. What is your opinion of Macherie?"

"Macherie?" John was stamping about to keep himself warm. "Sir Nevil Macherie? I think less than nothing of him."

Sir Bartlemy looked startled at this. "Come, come. He's one of you. A Free Rover. He's been cruising in the south for over a year, and I hear he's done rather well."

John picked up his gold chain, which had fallen to the floor, rubbing with an impatient finger the emerald which dangled from it before draping it around his neck. "Sir Nevil Macherie," he declared, "is a long-snouted coward who knows nothing of navigation. You asked my opinion, and there you have it."

It was proof of the matutinal amiability of our host that he was able to laugh, even though there was a slightly embarrassed ring to it. "I had hoped to hear the opposite from you. Sir Nevil's a neighbor, in a sense. He has a place about ten miles south of here, as you probably know. Some gentlemen hereabouts assisted in fitting him out. His honesty, of course, is above suspicion."

"I hope you were not induced to join in raising funds for him, Sir Bartlemy. His backers will get no good of it, I promise you."

"Of course not. Ah—one venture of the kind is proving enough for me, I assure you."

"Profitable enough, at any rate," declared John.

There was an uncomfortable pause. Our host, whose face had become somewhat red, said with a suggestion of a titter: "If what you say is true, I've been completely wrong about the man. I even thought once —it was a fleeting idea, of course—that he might be a suitable husband for my daughter."

John's laugh boomed out at that. "I'm sure you never gave it any serious thought. Mistress Catherine is entitled to someone much better than this slab-flanked fellow." He looked at me slyly. "What do you say, Roger?"

I was sure Sir Bartlemy had introduced the topic for a purpose. "I think," I said, "that Katie should have the best man to be found in all England."

"I am going to see that she gets him." I did not expect him to say anything more, but he proceeded to discuss his daughter's future with great seriousness, mentioning the sons of various great noblemen as possible candidates. They rolled glibly off his tongue: the heir of the

Earl of Totness, the second son of "Charlie" (who turned out to be one of the Howards, the oldest family in England), and the nephew of the wealthy Lord Blessington. No subject could have been more distressing for my ears, and I thought John found no more enjoyment in it. He seemed as glad as I was when Katie herself appeared with a tray of food.

"We've been discussing your future, Doll," said her father, watching me out of the corner of one eye. "Both Roger and Captain Ward agree you must marry the finest and richest man in the country. I thought you would be glad to know of their good opinion."

Katie, who was wearing a dress which matched the gray of her eyes, seemed to like this no more than we did. "I'm sure it's very kind of them, Father, but if you don't mind I'll choose my own husband. I would prefer not to be discussed in this way."

Her father got to his feet. "I thought they would both be interested, my dear. We'll leave them to their breakfasts now, Doll. I must request, gentlemen, that you confine yourselves to this room until I let you know that it's safe to appear. Some of our guests are not departing until late in the afternoon. The books are at your disposal." He glanced down at the tray. "I see you've brought brandy. It may serve to keep the young men warm. A fire, I regret to say, is out of the question. I can't risk sending a servant in to lay it."

Katie seemed reluctant to go, but her father took her by the elbow and urged her through the door.

John was furious. He shook his fist at the closed door. "Was there ever a poorer creature than that?" he demanded. "I'm getting completely out of patience with him. He's afraid of his own shadow, and he hems and haws like a noddie saying grace before meat." He calmed down a little and gave me a wink. "But he's got a sharp eye in his head. He had noticed something, and so he went to great pains to serve notice on us, and on her as well. No trespassing!"

Katie had hardly looked at me while she was in the room. This was not to be wondered at after what John had said about my appearance. But she had watched him closely. I said to myself that it didn't matter now; we would both be away for years, and when we returned she would be married to the second son of Charlie or to someone equally suitable. My daydreams had come to an end.

After breakfast I began an inspection of the books, discovering that those in the embrasure where we had slept were all comparatively new. Of recent years there had been a general interest in what was called self-improvement, and many books had been printed on the subject. They were all here. I skimmed over the titles, surprised that there were so many: several issues of the *Horne-Book*, *The Mother's Blessing*, *Richard Whittington and His Great Rise*, *The Mirror of Worldly Fame*, *Directions for a Man to Choose His Mate*, *How to Become Rich*, *Panaceas for Health*. None of them appealed to me in my then state of mind, but I found something in another niche, a history of the Hundred Years' War. I was soon deep in its pages, with a blanket around my shoulders.

John found himself in less fortunate case. He had no liking for books, and so he paced up and down the room, stopping in front of me at intervals to complain of my absorption. "You'll never learn from print how to round Cape Passer in the teeth of a heavy blow," he said. "Do you find there how to trim a mains'l or to set your course when there's not a star in sight?"

As I paid no attention, he tried to catch me with talk of more urgent matters. "Roger," he said, "no matter how greedy Sir Bartlemy is for profits, I'll never stop a ship with English goods in the hold. He must get that through his cunning head." Another time he said: "Your Katie looks very well in gray. I've made love to plenty of women in my time. French girls and Spanish señoritas, and women of the desert with eyes like sloes. But there's nothing to compare with the sweetness of an English girl. There are times when I regret that I've been such a rough swad."

Tiring of the history, I found a moldy old book with dull gold lettering on the cover which I was able to decipher as *Sir Jehan Mandeville, His Travels*. I opened it, and then for a long time the mutterings of my companion fell on deaf ears. The chronicle of Prester John, that I found there, held me in complete thrall.

I don't know how long I read, but many hours must have been consumed in that way. I looked up finally and saw by the angle of the light through the windows that we had reached midafternoon. There was an emptiness in my stomach which confirmed this. Then I heard voices at the other end of the room and a sudden silvery explosion of feminine laughter. I tucked the book under my arm and proceeded in that direction.

Katie was seated on the top of a four-step library ladder, her skirts tucked in tightly around her ankles, her eyes fixed on John Ward as he did justice to the dinner she had brought. She looked up at me with a contrite and, I thought, somewhat guilty air.

"Oh, dear, I hope your dinner isn't spoiled," she said.

John grinned at me over the rim of his ale tankard and said that he had called me. Katie nodded confirmation. "So did I."

"How long have you been here?" I asked.

She started to say, "Not long—" and then stopped herself. "Half an hour, I'm afraid. I feel very guilty, Roger. I should have gone for you. Now your dinner is cold."

"I hope you've had an interesting talk. But it was my fault. I was reading and didn't hear you call."

"It's a very bad habit," said John. "I've warned you against it. Some day it will cost you more than the loss of a dinner."

Katie looked at the tray with an anxious eye. John had made serious inroads. I seated myself beside him and found myself facing the remains of what had probably been a very fine dinner. The book slipped from under my arm, but I did not pick it up; and, now that I come to think of it, I have never finished the story of Prester John.

"Captain Ward has been telling me stories of the sea," said Katie. It was clear that she had enjoyed them. There was an almost breathless catch in her voice, and her eyes were shining. Her hair was done the old way again, and I decided that I liked it much better. "He makes it all sound fascinating, and I can understand now why you want to go, Roger."

"It's the only life for a man," declared John. "But there won't be any time for reading, Master Roger. When you hear the cook call, you'll have to shake a lively stamper if you don't want to go hungry."

I did my best with the scraps of meat while John told her about sea superstitions. He was a good talker and made everything sound either very funny or very grim. Katie drank it in, giving me nothing more than scraps of attention. I said very little. I was thinking that another one should be added to the list of common superstitions: *never* let the girl you love meet a handsome and fascinating friend.

When I had finished, and it did not take long, Katie said regretfully that she must go; that her father had told her not to stay long. She stepped down easily from the ladder, giving no more than a glimpse of ankle in a froth of lace.

She held out a hand to me and said in a tone that had become completely serious: "I'm proud of you, Roger. It's a brave thing you're doing, and I'm sure you'll become very famous. I'll think of you always."

"Thanks, Katie." There were many things I wanted to say; but this, I knew, was not the time to say them. I was acutely aware of the poor figure I cut, an "untidy gilpie" beside my tall captain in his handsome velvet. I contented myself with adding, "I'll think of you too. All the time."

She gave her hand to John then, and he squeezed it in both of his. "I'll take good care of the young man," he said. "And I shall expect my reward for it when I return. We'll come back like conquering heroes, with bay leaves in our hair and our pockets full of rolling Spanish ribbin. Spare a little place in your thoughts for me."

"I shall," she said.

When she had vanished, with a swish of silk skirts and a very serious last backward glance, there was silence for a moment. "Well," said John, "our Katie is a most lovely and amusing lady. It's amazing how fast she grew up. She was a mere bantling with her hair in braids when I went away, and I'm sure she gave no promise at all of *this*."

"Our" Katie! Soon, I thought, he will advance the relationship another step and make it "my" Katie.

It was dark when Sir Bartlemy paid us another visit. He came in briskly, wearing the kind of short cloak which King Harry had made popular but which was seldom seen nowadays. The shoulders and sleeves were so extravagantly padded that a good six inches was added to the width of the wearer on each side. There was a portrait of the old king on the wall, and our host posed himself in front of it, his feet splayed wide apart and his thumbs tucked in the folds of his peg-topped breeches. It was clear he was very proud of the close resemblance.

"I'm afraid we're going to quarrel, Captain Ward," he said. The amiability of the morning had vanished, and there was a deep line of vexation between his eyes. "I've just learned of the very unwise things you said in your speech yesterday. You talked like a fool, Ward." His voice trembled. "I must insist that in future you exercise more care. You must keep that unruly tongue of yours under control, or we'll all be in trouble."

"What I say is my own concern, Sir Bartlemy Ladland," declared John. "And I may add that I allow no man the right to insist on anything where I am concerned."

"But what you said amounted almost to treason. The King's Council might construe it as such."

"If that is treason, things have come to a pretty pass in England. I don't care what construction the King's Council puts on my words. They all accept pensions from Spain, which seems to me much more treasonable than the honest criticisms I made."

This seemed to increase the irritability of our host. "If you want to put your own head in the noose, it's your right. But I must say this to you: if we're to continue on our—our present basis, you owe it to me to put a curb on that tongue of yours."

John said impatiently: "I'll find someone to buy out your share, Sir Bartlemy. I'm as tired of our present basis as you seem to be."

"No, no, there's no call to go to extremes. We'll get on, Ward, we'll get on well enough in spite of everything. I've no wish to withdraw. A little more caution is all I ask. Well, you can be on your way now. You'll find horses tethered in Wayland Spinney, and food in the saddle bags. Don't ride through London." His voice took on a note of excessive anxiety. "Use the utmost discretion, Ward. Stop first at the Bandy Tar. It's a mile or so from Theobalds. Here's a note for Sir Everard Clement. Send it over by messenger, and don't show a nose outside the inn until you get his answer. It's a dangerous errand you are on."

John said in angry tones: "Be easy in your mind. I'll take every precaution." He added in a whisper to me, "The peery old fool is taking good care that we have no chance to see our Katie before we leave."

6

OUR OBJECTIVE was the small town of Cheshunt; and, to avoid notice as much as possible, we set ourselves a roundabout course, riding through Southwark and the scattered suburbs to the west of London before cutting north into Hertfordshire. I had done very little riding, and so I was a mass of aches and pains by the time we reached the Bandy Tar.

It proved to be a small inn, filled with a smell of sour beer. Although it was barely six in the morning when we arrived, there were a number of people in the bar.

I had observed that there were women in the party, who had eyed us boldly, but I was too weary to take an interest in anything but the two beds in the low-raftered room to which we were escorted. It had been my intention to write a letter to Mother, but I tumbled into one of the beds without a moment's delay. It was six in the evening when I wakened up.

I realized at once that it was the sound of voices which had roused me from my deep sleep. John was sitting in a chair by the one window in the room, with his massive arms folded on his chest. I saw that he was seriously disturbed, for he was frowning unhappily at a most proper-appearing gentleman seated opposite him. I looked at the stranger with considerable interest, for it was clear that he was a great dandy. His golden hair was hanging in long curls over his broad white ruff. There was a tippet of green sarsnet around his shoulders and canions of the same color attached to his padded breeches. His cork-soled pantoffles were of bright yellow leather and of such a neat size that I wondered how he had managed to get his feet into them. His looks suggested that he was of an easy and even a languid disposition, but his voice by contrast was sharp and peremptory.

"I regret that I'm in no position to help you, Captain Ward," he was saying. "In fact, I'm disposed to regret even that I've had a hand in this at all. The royal temper is most uncertain. I might as well be frank with you and acknowledge that His Sowship looks at me these days with an unseeing stare in his eyes. He has no regard for anyone but a long loon from Scotland, a certain Robert Carr. 'Ud's blood, I find it galling to mention the fellow in civil conversation! Master Robert Carr comes from a flea-bitten place with the heathenish name of Ferniehurst, and he got himself trampled on in a tournament to attract the attention of His King's Grace. I'm completely out of favor. Master Carr is so set to oust me that all he would need would be a whisper about our little dealings, and I would be unrigged."

I sat up in bed. The effort involved was so great that I groaned aloud, and the two men at the window turned their heads in my direction. The stranger's eyes were blue and as large as a woman's, but a hard and calculating gleam showed in them when he realized that I had been listening.

"I trust, Captain Ward, that your young friend will know enough to keep a still tongue," he said uneasily.

"I'll answer for Roger Blease," said John. "You may rely on it, Sir Everard, that no word of this will get out through him."

Sir Everard Clement frowned and ran an impatient finger between his neck and the tight folds of his starched ruff. I wondered if it was the heat from the fire in the chimney or the agitated state of his mind which was responsible for his discomfort.

"If Master Carr continues to advance in the kingly favor, I may have to go to sea myself," went on our visitor in a tone of deep aggrievement. "I'm a poor man, or I should never have thrown in with you, Ward. And now His Sowship is turning all my prerogatives over to Master Carr. I shall starve, egad, if it keeps up. If our business overseas had not turned out so well, I wouldn't have a James shilling in my purse." He meditated darkly for a moment and then continued: "The country has come to a pretty pass when a lean Scot, with an empty head and a belly stuffed with collops, can lead the King around by the ear."

"That's not the worst thing we face," declared John. "It's hard to believe that our command of the seas could be lost in a few years without a blow being struck. And all because of a cowardly quirk in one twisted mind!"

"To be perfectly frank with you, there are compensations in my present situation," said Sir Everard with frowning concentration. "Now that I'm out of favor, I no longer have to occupy one of the three beds around the royal couch at night. One at each side and one at the end." His handsome lips twisted in a sardonic smile. "He's much given to fears, our doughty James. You must have heard that his clothes are padded because of his fear of assassins, and that the cellars are searched every night for more gunpowder. But even that doesn't allay the royal trepidations. 'Ud's teeth, he must also be securely hedged in by loyal supporters before he can go to sleep." He sniffed with disgust. "It's not pleasant. His Majesty has an aversion to bathing, and he sleeps with all the windows clamped down tight. The air in the royal chamber becomes positively foul before morning!"

I had managed by this time to get my feet to the floor. Every move I made in pulling on my hose sent waves of agony through my stiffened muscles. I was wondering what I could do about the crop of blisters I had raised, but at the same time was not neglecting to keep an eye on the pair at the window. I was surprised to note that John had fallen into a thoughtful note. He did not even smile at the ex-favorite's description of the kingly sleeping quarters.

"Clement," he said with sudden earnestness, "I'm wondering if you appreciate the gravity of the situation. This goes much deeper than a mere determination on the part of a few sailors to disregard royal orders. I'm placing myself in the shadow of the gallows because I know that the future of this country depends on what her seamen do today. This is a small island, and the destiny of its people lies on the sea." He had placed his hands on his knees and was leaning forward, his eyes gleaming with ardor. "Spain has the world by the throat because of a lucky accident. An Italian found the Americas for them and so tossed untold wealth into their laps. It's unfortunate for the Dons that the Atlantic lies between them and the new El Dorado. They're compelled to maintain a great navy and to police the lanes of the Middle Course. If they did it well, they would hold all Europe in thrall. But they aren't sailors, they have no real liking for the sea, and so they do it badly. But we English are sailors. It's in our blood. We can sail around them like dogs around a bear at a baiting. When it comes to fighting, we beat them every time. They still frighten disobedient children with the name of El Draque."

He got to his feet and began to pace about the room. "We have broken their stranglehold on trade before and we can do it again. We still have the greatest opportunity ever offered to Englishmen. But mark this, Sir Everard: we must not give them a breathing spell. They have cozened James into making a peace they don't keep themselves. If we leave them alone now, they'll win a hold on the seas that we'll be unable to break later. They are recruiting sailors from other races. If we give up today, we surrender our chance to become a great nation. England will never again be anything but a small island, and the whole world will be harnessed to the might of Spain!"

I had never heard John make a long speech before. The earnestness back of what he said was a revelation to me. It made an impression on our resplendent visitor also, for I saw that Sir Everard had become thoughtful and attentive. He nodded gravely when John finished.

"God's-trewth, I believe you're right, Ward," he said. "I had never looked at it that way before. You talk like the Cornishman."

"I've never enjoyed the privilege of an acquaintance with Sir Walter Raleigh," answered John, "but I'm sure he must think about this as I do. If we had Raleigh to lead us now, things would be different, king or no king." He stopped short and felt his shoulder as though suddenly aware of the wound he had sustained before leaving home. "Is there no spirit left in England that we allow our eagle to be caged on a charge as flimsy as the gauze of a dancing girl's veil? Has the law lost its teeth?"

Clement held up a restraining hand. "Such words come close to treason, Ward. I still enjoy some small share of the King's favor, and

I am frank to say I don't want to lose it. He won't see reason in the case of Raleigh. Prince Henry has tried to move him a score of times without any success. Our Jamie is obstinate, and he hates the Great Man. I'm afraid Raleigh will not enjoy freedom again as long as James is king." He paused to help himself to snuff from an elaborately jeweled ivory case. "In spite of everything, I have a certain sympathy for the poor old fellow. He is a timorous man, born to rule over a tough race in a particularly violent period. He has a craze for peace because he thinks his personal safety depends on it. He's a coward, I grant you, but—you can't expect a puffin to act like an eagle, my dear Ward."

"The young prince will make a good king when his time comes," observed John. "God grant it won't be too late!"

There was a loud knock on the door. John and the courtier looked at each other with uneasy eyes. I could see that Sir Everard was disturbed, but he motioned John to stand back out of the light and went himself to answer the summons.

A truly amazing figure stalked into the room. At first I could not be entirely sure that the newcomer was human. He was so thick and squat of build that he reminded me of the curious creatures who thronged the pages of Mandeville. His eyes puzzled me most. There was a wild gleam in them as he stood in the doorway, rocking back and forth on his heels and staring at each of us in turn. They made me think of the eyes of an animal. In spite of this there was something a little ludicrous about him. He was like a wolf with a sense of humor.

"I heerd ye were here wi' company," he said to Sir Everard, "and I made bold to join ye."

I was surprised to see that Sir Everard was no longer worried. He even laughed.

"It's Archie," he said.

I had heard of Archie Armstrong, the court jester, of course. King James had brought him down from Scotland, and I knew that the English nobility, bitterly resentful of the influx of Scotsmen, had been especially critical of this importation. Archie was the exact opposite of their conception of a court fool, they being accustomed to sly fellows who skipped and pranced and sang bawdy songs. Archie was a man of deep opinions which he never hesitated to vent, no matter whose toes might be trampled on. King James might be the only one at court to laugh at the pawky sayings of his outspoken jester, but the impression was gaining ground in the country that under his plain woolen jerkin Archie was quite a bit of a man.

"Ay, it's Airchie," he said, with a dripping Lowland accent. "Airchie, the keeper o' the royal conscience. A frail an' chancey theeng, the royal conscience. I tell it to His Mujesty's ain face that the keengdom wud be better aff wur Airchie the keeng an' James the jester. Do ye doot that Airchie cud play the keeng?"

A change came over him so suddenly that I could hardly believe my eyes. He drew in his mouth until his protruding tongue seemed too large for it. His eyes became shifty and uneasy. The bones in his thick body seemed to have turned to water, for he sagged and swayed on wobbling legs. A reedy, whining voice, so unlike his own that at first I suspected someone else was in the room, issued from his pursed-up lips. "I wull hae ye ken I am Keeng o' England, and I maun hae ma ain way. I am vury, vury oopset that ma soobjects doot the weesdom o' the fine peace I hae made. Ony mon breaking the Keeng's peace shall feel the heft o' the Keeng's hond. John Waird shall hangit i' chains frae a bludy pirut. I swear it."

It must have been a good imitation of His Majesty, for Sir Everard Clement doubled up with laughter. Though he had made a wry face at the allusion to hanging, John also was laughing. I joined with them as I pulled on my patched shoes.

"Archie," declared the courtier, when his mirth had subsided, "I have a surprise for you, mon. Look well at this great hulking sailor. He's a friend of mine, although on that point I count on you to keep a still tongue. His name happens to be John Ward."

John was startled, but he need not have feared the consequences of this frank introduction. The muscles of the jester settled back into their customary mold. His eyes began to shine as before, except that now they were filled with surprise and admiration.

"Is it, noo?" he exclaimed. "I micht hae kenned it wur John Waird. John, I am prood ta mak the acqueentance o' sae bonny a fichter. Dinna fash yersel, lad. Airchie can keep a secret. Mon, mon, I theenk weel a'ye!"

"And so you have told His Majesty a hundred times," affirmed Clement. "Archie, this bold fellow has come to me in the hope that I had some influence to wield in his behalf. I've told him that a certain Master Carr has the royal ear at the moment, and that it would be safer for him to get back on his ship and put the full length of the Channel between himself and the King's justice. What do you say?"

Archie nodded his head in assent. He agreed it would be the canny thing for John to get back on the high seas until the royal displeasure had abated. Then he sat himself down on his broad haunches and plied my friend with questions about his adventures at sea. Fixing his wide, staring eyes on the face of the freebooter, he begged to hear everything about the capture of the *Madalina* and the *Little John*, smacking his lips gustily over the details of the fighting. "Ay, mon, ay," he kept repeating. "So ye trouncit they popish diels!"

Supper was brought up, to my great satisfaction, for I was so ravenously hungry I could have gorged myself on Poor-John-and-a-Mullet. The four of us rubbed elbows as we plied our knives at a small table. Archie acknowledged that he had already supped but managed nevertheless to keep pace with us, doing full justice to the cold roast beef and old nappy ale. He never took his eyes off John and muttered at intervals, "Weel, weel, the turrible John Waird, is ut?"

He was truly an amazing fellow. He monopolized the conversation, blasting the members of the royal household and the highest officials of the land with shrewd and unsparing invective. He ridiculed the foreign policy of the King and spoke with bitter scorn of his theological pretensions. James, he declared, was a gnat-straining nonentity, a quibbling quodlibet, a caudge-pawed dunce, a pig in a pickadell. There was so much gusto to his talk that after no more than a half-hour of it I felt mentally exhausted.

He immediately obliged with imitations when new games were introduced into the conversation. His broad-featured face became by turns belligerent, crafty, mordant, sly, malevolent, lascivious. His accent could be laid aside completely when necessity arose, and several times he fell into the soft and cultivated manner of speech which was associated with the great universities. It was astonishing to me that he could even achieve a suggestion of half-tipsy but haughty languor when giving us his version of Queen Anne, flirting imaginary skirts with a preening desire to give glimpses of a fine ankle.

Once he laid down his knife to remark that it was a pity John was "no a sonsy laddie wi' his lugs still damp beneath his biggin."

"Why?" demanded John, frowning as though he did not relish the suggestion.

Archie explained that then he might attract the notice of King James, who liked tall young men. Had he not showered titles and wealth on a baker's dozen already? And now he was a "fair loon" over the long-legged Carr, even setting himself to educate the callow recruit from Ferniehurst. Laughing loudly in anticipation of our applause, he added in plain English: "He has dressed him up in satin and is teaching him dog Latin. He'll fill his mind with civil lore, and make him, eke, a councillor. He'll strap the Garter on his knees, and let him share the royal fleas. So mark my words, this empty loon will rule o'er all of England soon." He rattled this off with unfaltering glibness, never finding it necessary to pause for the word he needed. After a long elaboration of the same theme, he concluded in all seriousness, "His Sowship will bring ill to the land with his daughty favorites."

It was dark before he finally ran down and remembered that he was long overdue at Theobalds to entertain the King. Even then he was loath to leave so appreciative an audience. He thumped both John and me on the back and announced that he had a plan. How would we like to enjoy a glimpse of the King "wallowing in his frowsty pigsty of a court?" It could be arranged with complete safety if we so desired it. Was not he, Archie Armstrong, the very Machiavelli of Merry Andrews? Leave everything to him. A word in the ear of Timothy a Pycons, who stood guard at the gatehouse and was a gossip of Archie's, would see us in with no questions asked. There was a window in the jester's own quarters which looked down over the Presence Chamber. Here we could sit and watch the high jinks, and no one would be the wiser.

Although I was nervous of the possible consequences, I found that the idea appealed to me very much. It might be my only chance to see the King, now that I had chosen a life at sea. It was clear that John was keen for it also. Sir Everard Clement was against the plan; but, when he realized how taken we were with it, he shrugged his shoulders and gave in. He even allowed that he would accompany us to supply the element of sanity to the proceedings which undoubtedly would be needed before the evening was over.

We set out on foot. A cloak had been supplied me at Appleby Court, and I wrapped myself up snugly in this. It was a monstrous thing of coarse brown cloth with a hood capacious enough for a full-wigged head, and make me look like a servingman. John and his rival in sartorial splendor, Sir Everard, had velvet cloaks with miniver collars, spangled in gold thread and lined inside with tufted satin. Archie wore no wrap of any kind and did not seem to feel any lack.

There is no part of the country more lovely than the strip of Hertfordshire through which the gentle New River meanders on its way to join the Thames. Elizabeth's Lord Burghley had appreciated this when he chose it for his handsome country seat at Theobalds. James had visited there on his way from Holyrood to London and had fallen in love with the long, gracious mansion at first sight. Nothing would content him but that it should become his own; and so Robert Cecil, son of Burghley by a second marriage and now the chief adviser of the King, had been forced to make a trade by which he was given Hatfield House instead. Sir Everard talked of this as we walked over from Cheshunt, and Archie contributed some biting comments on Cecil, who was believed to be in the pay of Spain.

A brisk stretching of legs over pleasant country lanes, easy-sodded to the foot and arched with trees in which swifts rustled, brought us in short order to the red brick wall encircling the royal park. My heart began to beat a little faster when I saw the turrets of Theobalds looming up over the wall in buttressed tracery against the starry autumn sky. James might be all that rumor said; he might even be as gross as depicted by the unbridled tongue of the loquacious jester; but he was still King of England, and this was his favorite home, a shining mark to chain the fancy of a country boy.

Archie told us with a touch of awe that it took ten miles of brick wall to enclose the park, and that the upkeep of the palace cost enough to feed all of "auld Reekie," meaning the Scottish city of Edinburgh. He whispered in the ear of Timothy a Pycons and convinced that morose individual we were not objects of suspicion. The guard nodded and waved us in with his lantern. The jester then turned us sharply off the tiled walk leading to the main entrance and led the way across grass sward to an unlighted door in the right wing. I was so consumed with curiosity that I had fallen behind the others and did not hear what passed between our guide and the armed attendant at the door. Apparently the explanation given was satisfactory, for we were admitted without questioning.

We climbed a dark stairway single file and came out on a long corridor. Except for the thickness of the carpet, which completely muffled the sound of our footsteps, it was not as richly appointed as the galleries at Appleby Court. There was an undeniably musty odor about it which I found hard to reconcile with an abode of royalty. Archie turned sharply into a side hall and led the way up another narrow stair. Then we traversed a number of connected and rather mean apartments, at the end of which was a whitewashed room with two windows. One was small and high up near the ceiling, the other was lower and, although heavily curtained, emitted a narrow slit of light from the room beyond.

This was the jester's home, for he whisked a tartan jacket and cap from the one chair and motioned John to sit down. Sir Everard and I were bidden to make ourselves comfortable on an unmade bed in one corner, but the courtier shook his head and announced that he thought it wise on his part to put in an appearance below. He disappeared almost immediately with a suggestion of alacrity.

"I am late mysel'," said Archie. He produced a flask of wine from a cupboard, looked at it anxiously and even affectionately, and laid it with open reluctance on the table. His air conveyed the thought that we were to apply ourselves to it if our thirsts should develop beyond the point of restraint, but that he hoped such a dire pass would not be reached. He then demonstrated that we could see everything that happened below by raising no more of the curtain than an inch at each side.

"Dinna show yoursel'," he urged. He added that he would return as soon as his part in the proceedings was over, and that he thought it wise to lock the door in the meantime. We had best remember that he had succeeded in getting us through as his cousins Dugald and Sandy from Auld Reekie. Estimating the length of the single candle with a canny eye, he volunteered the conviction that we would see better if the room were in darkness and, receiving no denial from us, snuffed out the tiny flame with an almost savage thumb. A moment later, John and I were alone in the room.

John rose from the chair. "I have placed my neck in jeopardy on the word of a fool whose tongue clacks gossip at both ends," he said. "Well, we might as well find if what we came to see is worth the risk."

My angle of vision proved as satisfactory as Archie had predicted. I could see most of the Presence Chamber, which was long and stately and two stories in height. At one end was a raised dais with high-backed chairs on which were seated the King and Queen. My eyes focused instantly on the royal pair, and I drank in every detail of their appearance.

King James was fashioned so closely on the lines of the jester's imitation that I believe I could have recognized him even if he had not occupied the dais. His eyes had the same sly look, and his mouth was so drawn in that hollows showed in both cheeks. He was, I thought, rather meanly attired, except that he wore a massive gold chain around his neck and that diamonds glittered on his fingers. Queen Anne, who had a reputation for dowdiness, was handsomely dressed in spite of it, with a farthingale so wide that the skirts flared enormously on both sides and even obtruded themselves on the shins of her royal spouse. She had been a pretty woman, I thought, for her hair was light and wavy and her eyes were pleasant. She seemed very much interested in the masque which was being performed on the floor of the Chamber, but the King's attention to it was openly intermittent. He lolled in his seat and scratched his chest with an absent-minded air.

It was a dull masque, done by the ladies and gentlemen of the court. They had not been too well coached; some of them boggled and stammered over their lines, and none of them displayed any gift for elocution. I recognized all the stock characters: Error, Rumor, Curiosity, Credulity, Malice, Cupid.

The King yawned and looked as though he longed for the end of it. For the first time I felt sympathy for the much-criticized monarch and fancied that I could detect evidences of a dry humor in his rather melancholy visage. The masque finally reached its conclusion, and the Queen rose immediately and bowed to the King. Apparently she asked his permission to withdraw, for His Majesty bowed and there was much rustling all over the Chamber as the ladies of the court prepared to follow their queen into retirement for the night.

I was conscious of a deep sense of disappointment. Where were Prince Hal and the Princess Elizabeth? The hopes of the nation were centered in the manly young first-born, while the pretty young princess was the darling of all England, her popularity being enhanced by the fact that so little liking could be felt for the monarch himself. She was said to be lovely and high-spirited and very much like her unfortunate grandmother, Mary Queen of Scots. I had looked forward to seeing the royal children even more than the King and Queen, and I whispered a question about them in John's ear.

"They have their own homes, and it's very seldom they put in an appearance *here*," answered my friend, with an emphasis on the last word which conveyed his contempt for the court and the people in it.

I turned back to watch the proceedings below us. The Queen had already withdrawn. A tall young man with blond locks and ruddy cheeks had been motioned to a seat on the steps of the dais close by the King, and I was in time to observe that he did not take up his post until after a colloquy with a very young and very lovely lady in blue with straps of ermine on her bodice. I had already noticed her and had voted her the most attractive one there. Her eyes sparkled vivaciously, and she had chattered without pause in the ear of a vulpine-nosed nobleman with drooping black mustache and beard and a somber air. This veteran courtier had wagged his head and displayed his teeth in tittering appreciation of her sallies. He stood waiting for her now as she exchanged a final word with the handsome youth.

John had been watching this display also. He said to me in bitter tones: "Mark that lecherous old buzzard. Lord Harry Howard himself, Earl of Northampton, by grace of treachery and such consummate lying that Ananias himself has lost his pre-eminence. Lord Harry is Warden of the Cinque Ports as well as Privy Seal. A price-chiseling draper would make a worthier Warden than this bootlicking hypocrite and pander. My stomach turns at the sight of him. The girl is his niece. They married her to the young Earl of Essex and then packed the bridegroom off to the Continent to give the pair a chance to grow old enough for the privileges of matrimony. She's a lovely chit. How do you think she compares with our Katie?"

I had been thinking grudgingly that she was quite as beautiful, although lacking the sweet winsomeness and inner grace of the daughter of Appleby Court; but I now asserted stoutly that there was no comparison at all.

"No," agreed John. "She can't hold a candle to our divinity. But I'll hazard a guess that the lively eyes of this hoyden will create plenty of havoc when she's a little older." The world was to learn later how accurate he was in this surmise. But John's attention had now shifted to the gilded youth with the blond locks. "I'm of the opinion that yon long loon is the Master Carr we've been hearing so much about."

I had already reached this conclusion myself; for, with the ladies gone, King James had begun to run his hand affectionately through the long locks of the handsome Scot. The whole air of the gathering had changed. The King's indifference had vanished. He beamed over the edge of a tall gold winecup and called out impatiently for the merry-making to begin. The courtiers, talking exuberantly and without any restraint, arranged themselves along both sides of the Chamber, leaving the center space empty. It was apparent that most of them were already in an advanced stage of intoxication.

The fun began with a loud roar of welcome for two stout young men who appeared at each end of the Chamber. One of them was accompanied by Archie and the other by a squat individual who, as we learned later, was Tom Derry, the Queen's jester. Both masters of the motley were equipped with market baskets on their arms, and they carried broomsticks which, it was clear, were to be employed as lances. Archie had made himself up to resemble a knight, with a cock's feather in his cap and breastplates of painted cardboard. He posed and strutted about the place, bowing with exaggerated gallantry to imaginary ladies in the balcony. Then he mounted on the back of one of the strapping youths, and Tom Derry followed his example at the other end. I could see that the King's sides were already quaking with mirth.

"Ma siller's on Airchie!" he cried, leaning back and crossing one

clumsy leg over the other. "Ten pund he unseats the Derry wi'oot ony
trooble at a'."

"No one will take that bet," said John. "I hear His Majesty never
pays when he loses. Roger, there's more to this buffoonery than meets
the eye. I'm told that Archie has a great contempt for this other fellow,
who returns it in kind. They've been egged on to fight it out. The
Queen should have stayed to see fair play, I'm thinking."

What followed was so funny that both John and I laughed as heartily
as the foolish old monarch. The two youths charged as fast as they
could, with such heavy burdens on their backs, meeting in the middle
of the room. Archie had all the better of the encounter. He aimed his
broomstick with such deadly accuracy at the basket of the less agile
Tom Derry that he sent the rival jester and his mount sprawling on the
floor. Dismounting, he stalked over to his fallen opponent and planted
a foot on his face, while declaiming in the high falsetto tones that court
heralds employed: "Sir Archibald Armstrong, champion of His Most
Christian Majesty, proclaims himself the victor and asserts his right
under the rules of knightly combat to dispose of the trappings of his
adversary to his own advantage. To wit, one pair of well-worn gallyslops and one moth-eaten jerkin, which will be gladly exchanged for a
pot of ale. He further charges the defeated Sir Thomas Derry to betake
himself back where he belongs and never show his ugly face again,
nor match his weak wits in competition with his betters."

"Weel spoken, Airchie!" exclaimed the King. "I kenned wha' the
ootcome wad be but nane o' ye wad cover ma ten pund. Ye are a puir-
spirited lot."

He had risen to his feet to watch the fun and was laughing so hard
that his weak underpinning gave way. He tottered down the steps of
the dais and then collapsed in a heap of cushions from which his well-
padded posterior protruded so conspicuously that, even from where we
sat, it was possible to see that a large patch had been inserted in the
green silk of his breeches. The whole gathering went into roars of
merriment over the mishap. Archie immediately took his broomstick in
hand and charged across the room, aiming the point at the royal back-
sides.

"Even Tom Derry couldna miss that target," he exclaimed.

But the King had already managed to squirm around into a sitting
position. It was clear that he had not enjoyed his mishap and that he
resented the laughter at his expense. There were tears of mortification
in his weak eyes.

"Bad boys, bad boys!" he quavered. "Making sport o' your puir auld
dad and gossip. This is maist unseemly. Maist unseemly. I willna forget
it, dinna fear."

John turned away from the window and looked at me with disgust
written all over his face. "And that," he muttered, "is the King of England. I hope you were properly edified, Roger."

Proceedings below settled down after that. Tom Derry disappeared, perhaps to doff the forfeited gallyslops and jerkin. Archie continued to strut about and prate of his skill. The King regarded him with a wrathful eye.

"Ye're a fause loon, Airchie," he said. "I am of a mind to hae yer wagging tongue sewed up."

"Dinna ca' in the royal tailor then," countered the jester. "I wouldna want as puir a job done on ma tongue as he did on the royal breeks."

The King smiled feebly. "Airchie, Airchie," he childed. "I shouldna pay oot guid siller to a graceless loon wha flouts me tae ma vera face."

"It was no yer face I was a' set to flout," responded Archie.

"Some day ye wull gae too far," promised the monarch, "and then back ye'll gang to the feelthy byre ye cam frae, wi'oot ears as weel as tongue."

"I've seen and heard enough," declared John, returning to his chair. He proceeded to light the candle and even cast a speculative eye on the wine flask. "I don't enjoy sitting in the dark, so we'll burn an inch or two of tallow, even if it breaks the heart of our canny host. His wine we'll respect, however, but only because I judge it to be of the cheapest quality. Well, Roger, are you convinced you were wise in deciding against a career at court?"

"There was no doubt in my mind at any time."

John fell into a reflective mood. "It hurts my pride to think of England with such a king," he said. "I believe it's true that sailors have a greater love for the homeland than those who stay ashore. They see foreign lands and judge them all poor in comparison, no matter how many tall tales they tell after they return. I'm happy when I feel the quarter-deck under my feet and the sea running high, but even then it's likely that I'm thinking of England and the joy I'll feel when I see her again. I grant you there are wondrous things to be seen. Off Tunis there's magic in the blue of the sky and the dazzling white of the shore, yet I never come in sight of Gouletta but I think with regret of the chalk cliffs of Dover or the gentle rise of soft green hills behind the harbors of Devon. There's nothing lovelier in the whole world than Wayland Spinney. The love of England grows in you when you sail the seas, Roger. But it's going to be hard for me to forget the spectacle we've watched tonight."

He went on in the same vein, expanding his belief in the greatness of our destiny. I listened avidly, but once, when he paused, I went back to the window and saw that a late supper was being served. The courtiers were eating and drinking with gusto, and the King was feeding himself soup with a spoon two feet long. This unusual utensil was necessary on account of the width of his ruff, but I saw that His Majesty was not too expert in the handling of it. A trickle of soup was running down a pleat in the ruff and dripping on the table.

Archie joined us, his eyes fired with his triumphs below. He said nothing about our use of his candle, but I noticed that he darted an appraising glance at the wine flask and seemed relieved to find there had been no lowering of the contents.

"Did ye see me spill Tam Derry?" he demanded. "The saft loon willna show his face here again in a hurry. Did ye hear them laugh when I nearly splintered ma lance on the royal prat?" He slapped his thigh and exploded into a loud roar of self-approval. Then he checked himself and said in serious tones, "It's best ye bing a waste noo. Servents will soon be aboot like cackling-cheats, laying fires and putting warming-pans in beds. It's high time ye wur aff."

I needed no second invitation myself, as I was becoming fearful for John's safety. We left the palace by the same route, but Archie then diverted our course to the rear, leading the way through a series of formal gardens. I had heard much about the beauty of the grounds at Theobalds and regretted that the sky had become overcast, making it impossible for me to see much. We passed through what I judged was the Dove House Court and walked by the Falconry and the Camel House before reaching a side gate in the brick wall. When we had passed to the road outside, Archie instructed us in whispers to take the first left turn, which would lead us back to the inn.

"The next brush ye hae wi' the Spanish diels, gie them a stiff blow frae Airchie," was his parting admonition.

To our surprise, we found Sir Everard Clement at the fork of the road with a groom and two fresh horses. He seemed almost desperately anxious to be rid of us.

"I think you would be wise to avoid Cheshunt," he declared. "There's no telling what might happen if you showed your face in public again, Ward. Your score has been settled at the inn, and I have taken the precaution of providing fresh horses for you. I make no secret of the fact that I'll feel much better when I have seen the last of you." He lowered his voice to a cautious whisper. "Did you see dainty Master Carr? And were you amused by your glimpse of the King's gentlemen at their evening diversions?"

"Yes, to the first question," answered John, swinging a leg over his mount. "It will be no news to you that I wasn't overly impressed with the young man. As to your last question, I can only say that I shall be glad to feel the deck of the *Royal Bess* under my feet again."

I climbed painfully into the saddle, wondering how I would manage to survive the ride ahead of us.

"I trust you'll reach your ship safely," said Clement. He began to scratch his ribs with almost vicious energy. "Why is the King so fond of this place? It's full of fleas!"

7

JOHN, WHO RODE like a sailor, did not seem to be enjoying himself. He was as relieved as I was when we reached the outskirts of the city.

"London," he said, "is a city for men. I've seen Paris and Rome and Venice, and I've even been as far inland as Vienna. They are all soft and dangerous, like women of the streets. London is the only town fit to welcome back a man from the sea. It's a quarrelsome, hearty, speak-your-mind place. It feeds you solid beef and ale, and you need not question the honesty of the gold it gives you. The others are like old witches with sharp claws, or hunchbacked panders; but here in London your thief is a stout fellow who will have your purse or slit your weasand for you. You know just what to expect. When it comes to big towns, I'll take London every time, and the Old Ruffian cly the rest of them!"

It was midnight when our horses felt paving stones under their feet, for we heard the nightwatch declaiming:

> *"Twelve o'clock, look well to your lock.*
> *Your fire and light, and so good night."*

We struck south toward the river, crossing Fleet Street and proceeding with great caution down Blackfriar's. I knew we were now in the section of London known as Alsatia, where criminals of all kinds found harborage and the roots of the nether world were sunk deep. The streets seemed unusually crooked here, and there was a sinister suggestion about the tall dark houses from which no sounds issued. Several times the doors of taverns swung open to disgorge revellers, and I caught hasty glimpses of dimly lighted interiors and of ill-clad men who gathered in close groups as though plotting mischief. Once the flank of my horse butted against a lone pedestrian who scuttled to the side and then blistered us with the foulest flow of profanity I had ever heard. I began to wonder if John had been entirely justified in his hearty praise of London town.

A mariner's sense of direction can desert him when he falls into a maze of twisting lanes and dark mews, and finally John had to stop at a tavern to ask directions. The landlord's close-spaced eyes narrowed into suspicious slits.

"So it's Robin Humpery ye're seeking," he said. "What have ye been up to, my fine buck? Have ye broken the head of an alderman or run foul of the watch? Robin's your man, in either case, but you'll have to pay him handsomely before he dups the jigger of Alsatia for ye."

"I want to play him stooleball for a tansey," declared John, looking his questioner steadily in the eye. "Is that enough for you to know before you answer a civil question?"

"Listen to me," said the landlord. "You're now in Alsatia, where the law runs the same for the poorest abram-man as for a flaming gentry cove. Until I know your business, I'm of no mind to tell you where Robin is to be found."

John spun a gold coin in the air. It rolled under a table. The landlord winked and said: "Two blocks south and one to the right. A small house with a double window over the front door. Ye can't miss it, for the scrippets will be there to look ye over. If ye've let daylight into your man, ye'll pay plenty for a stalling ken."

No one made a move until the door closed behind us. Then we heard scuffling and a sound of bitter wrangling, ending in a loud wail of pain.

"What was it he said to you?" I asked.

"A stalling ken is a hide-out from the law," explained John. "Alsatia is recognized as a sanctuary, and no one is likely to come here at this hour of the night unless the King's men are after him. A scrippet is a watcher. I have a feeling that eyes have been on us from the moment we set foot in this stinking morass of crime."

We followed the landlord's direction and came to the house he had indicated. It stood in an unpaved square, backing at an angle against a taller building of brick. It was mean and inconspicuous and gave no outward signs of life. The square itself looked deserted, and so I was surprised to find, when we reached the door, that two men had materialized beside us.

"Who are ye and what do ye seek here?" asked one of them in a husky whisper.

He was a shapeless hulk of a man who nevertheless moved without any apparent effort. His companion, who was small and thin, was ostentatiously clicking a long bagonet in its scabbard.

"My business is within and will be explained on the other side of that door," said John.

The big fellow leaned so close to us that I got an unpleasant whiff of damp clothes and unwashed flesh. He studied us as well as he could in the darkness.

"Ye're not hoskers," he muttered. "Ye're not stalled to the Rogue."

"No," said John, "we are not night workers and we have never taken your oath. Nor are we law-breakers looking for sanctuary. But mark this, my malodorous friend, *I have milled the sea.*"

The smaller man pushed his companion to one side. "That's the kind of talk we know," he said. "Get inside, Core, and tell the curtal."

A few moments later we were motioned inside, and the doors closed behind us with a disturbing metallic rattle. We were in complete darkness.

"They take extraordinary precautions," muttered John. "There are inside doors of solid metal. I think they may be of steel. At any rate, they closed automatically behind us."

My eyes were getting accustomed to the dark, and I could see we were standing in a small anteroom and that another door faced us at the top of a short flight of stairs. I climbed the steps and tapped lightly with my knuckles. The inside door was of metal construction also. A wicket opened to our right, flooding the place with light. An arm shoved a lantern through and hung it on a bracket. The arm was then withdrawn and the wicket closed. Almost at once there was a click in the inner door, and a slot opened in the top panel, letting more light in.

"The dogs take no chances," whispered John in my ear. "They're looking us over up there. It's harder to see their plaguy leader than King Jamie himself."

Finally the inner door opened with a rattle of metal hinges. A familiar voice said, "Cly me, if it isn't John and Roger," and a tall fellow with skinny calves bowed to us elaborately in the strong light from the room beyond. I recognized my former playmate, Chirp Bird.

It was quite a different Chirp Bird, however, from the cringing hanger-on we had cuffed around so contemptuously on the commons off Shrubsole High. He now wore a white ruff and breeches with flashy codpieces, and there was a sword buckled to his belt. It was clear that he had come to fancy himself, for the dull blue eyes in his yellow freckled face watched us eagerly as though he wanted to ask: How does all this magnificence impress you?

"Keep names out of this, Chirp," said John. "I think you must know the business that brings us."

"I know the business that brings you," repeated Chirp importantly. "I've been expecting you. But I wasn't expecting Roger. This is a surprise, I must say. What is our little gentry-cove doing here?"

"I'm sailing with John," I said, with pride in the announcement.

"Well, so you're sailing with John! What does proud Mistress Blease think of that and the good Aunt Gadilda?"

"What they think is no concern of yours, Chirp," said John impatiently. "Since you know what brings us here, see to it that we're taken to Robin Humpery at once. We have no time to waste in gossip."

"Now I must ask *you* to keep names out of this," declared Chirp. "We've as good reasons as you for not wanting them bandied around in the hearing of everyone."

We were standing in a hallway which opened on a large room filled with men and women who were too busy over their cards and dice to pay us any attention. There was a hectic note to the play, and I could hear them scoring and counting with covetous emphasis—"tib and

towser" from one, "tiddy and the ace" from another. Money passed
from hand to hand with bitter grudging. The men were an ugly and
pock-marked lot, and the women had been recruited from the trulls
and callots of London. One only of the crew took any interest in us.
He was a furtive wraith of a man, with a long purple-veined nose and
a frightened eye. He was pacing up and down the hall, keeping his
head alertly cocked on one side as though it were necessary even here
to watch over his shoulder. I could sense a consuming fear in every
line of him.

This unhappy individual plucked at Chirp's elbow and asked in an
almost breathless whisper: "Will he see me now? God's furies, man,
time presses!"

Chirp shook him off with impatience and, I thought, some fear as
well. "Bide yer time, Culleton," he said. "He'll see ye soon enough, for
your comfort. Don't touch me! You have blood on your hands!"

The suppliant shuffled away, and Chirp's thin mouth twisted into a
grimace of distaste. "He knifed a wench in Southwark, and now he
wants us to see him through. We'll do it, on one condition. His
pockets must be well lined!" He looked at John and winked. "All who
do business with the Upright Man must have pockets that clink. How
are yours, Sir Captain?"

"Again that is no concern of yours," declared John. "I'm in as great
a hurry as that evil-faced dog yonder, although for a different reason.
Take me to your Rich-arrayed Robin now. That's all I ask of you,
Chirp Bird."

Chirp was determined to impress us with his importance. "You can
talk to me as well as Rich-arrayed Robin," he said sulkily. "I'm the
curtal of Alsatia, if you want to know. Your business can be settled
between us."

John's patience was wearing thin. He sank his fingers in the velvet
folds of my former playfellow's doublet and gave him a shake. "I
didn't come here to waste my time with an oyster dredger, dressed up
to pass as a man. Take me in to your master, and no more words about
it!"

Chirp slipped out of his grasp and brushed his finery into place with
furious fingers. "Did you hear me say I'm the curtal of Alsatia?" he
demanded. "The word is out for ye, John Ward. Speak gently or you'll
find yourself in the queer-ken. Ye're not on your own quarterdeck
now, to strut and give orders. We rule this roost."

"Robin Humpery knows I'm to see him," declared John, controlling
himself with an effort. "You've done your strutting, Chirp. Now take
us in."

Chirp glanced back over his shoulder to see if this byplay had been
observed. The gamblers were intent over their games, and the fear-
ridden Culleton had gone back to his nervous pacing. Convinced that
he had lost no face, the curtal of Alsatia led the way down the hall

to a metal door at the far end. He rapped three times, and it swung back to admit us into a room with a high ceiling and a stone fireplace in which a log was blazing.

I judged we were now in the tall building against which the smaller house had backed. There was a suggestion of faded magnificence about the place. The wainscoting was elaborately carved, and the walls were covered with tapestries. Clearly, it had once been the home of someone of importance.

There were three men in the room. Two of them were playing backgammon on an antique board with red ochre squares on black leather. The third was writing in a corner. All three looked furtively at Chirp and then settled back to their occupations.

"There's something you must bear in mind, John," said Chirp, motioning us to sit down. "The man you're going to see has no gift for patience. An ill-timed word, and you might find yourself with half a blade sticking into the least convenient part of your handsome body, my friend. I pass that advice on for old time's sake."

"Thanks for the word," said John cheerfully. "But you need have no worries about me. I'll get along fine with Rich-arrayed Robin. Let's get to business. It will mean some hours to talk to go over everything in detail."

"Roger can stay here," ordered Chirp. He had never had any liking for me, and I could see that our visit had not resulted in any diminution of his ill-will.

He took John back through a door which opened on a small apartment. As far as I could see it was empty, but there was a table with ink and paper and a flagon of wine. The door swung shut, and I sat down and watched the backgammon players. It was a game I had often played with Mother. I had developed some skill at it, and I could see that neither of them knew anything about the finer points. They grumbled and swore and seemed more interested in me than in the clumsy moves they were making. The man in the corner, who had a suggestion of holy orders about him, although I couldn't tell why, went on with his scribbling.

Chirp came back in a very few minutes. I could see that he was discomfited because he had not been bidden to stay and take his part in the talk between his superior and John Ward. His pale eyes darted at each of the three men in turn and then settled on me.

"Will ye have a drink, Roger?" he asked. "Or would a dish of flummery with Adam's-ale be more to your taste?"

Flummery was a porridge and Adam's-ale was the cant word for water, but I refused to let the question nettle me. I replied that I desired nothing. Chirp then seated himself and crossed one lank knee over the other with an air that was meant to prove his acquaintance with the manners of fine gentlemen.

"Did you understand what it meant when I said I was curtal here?"

he demanded. "I'm next to the Upright Man. He leaves most matters in my hands. Isn't that so, Clem?" One of the backgammon players nodded with surly assent. "I control the sacking-law. The woman traffic, Roger. When pretty Ann Turner opens her shop, she will come to me for protection. I see that interests you, Roger. You always did make sheep's-eyes at our willing Ann, didn't you? She had such a fine waggle in her backside, eh, Roger? She had no use for me then, but things will be different now. She is going to run a shop here in London, I hear, and sell pleated chemises and silk petticoats to the ladies of the court. That's all very proper and fine, but she's likely to sell love potions and charms and philters too. That will bring her under our control. No one can dabble in the black-law without the consent of the Upright Man. When our pretty Ann finds that out, she will come here to pay the bill. And she'll have to make a deal with me. I'm looking forward to that."

My fingers were itching to get at his skinny neck, but I controlled myself and said nothing.

"Did ye ever climb through her window, Roger?" he asked, with an eager smirk. "John did, many's the time. I used to watch, and I wondered what good it would do me if I climbed in after him and offered to blow the show. But I never did. I bided my time. And now things are coming my way, I won't have to climb through her window. She'll have to walk in through my door."

He took a goldpiece from the pocket of his scarlet breeches and tossed it in the air.

"Shall we match, Roger? But I was forgetting. You're not likely to have gold, are you? You're poor. You belong to the gentry. The outer fringe of the gentry. But you're poor, nevertheless."

"I'm poor," I said shortly. "Leave it at that."

Chirp stretched out his spindling shanks. "I have gold to spend every day of the week," he exulted. "Plenty of gold. And how I spend it! On the very best of everything. And on women, Roger. I supped tonight with two handsome little sparrows. We had mutton with gallandine sauce and all the best muscadel wine we could drink. Do you ever have wine, or do you still drink such poor stuff as hippocras?"

"I still drink poor stuff," I answered.

"I thought so." He patted the velvet of his doublet with a gloating hand. "Twenty shillings the yard, Roger. The best to be had in all London. Quite handsome, don't you think? What did your jacket cost?"

"It cost nothing. It was made from old clothes of my father's."

Chirp began to laugh. He laughed until there were tears in his watery eyes. It fed his pride to lord it over me in this way, but I did not care. I could see the cheap soul of him under his flashy clothes, and it did not matter a whit to me if he stuffed himself every day on mutton with gallandine sauce and cased his bony frame in the best velvet in all London. Chirp Bird would never be anything to me but the cadging son of a thieving oysterman.

"So you're going to be a pirate," he went on.

"No!" I declared, my pride on fire at last. "I'm going to fight the Spaniards. John is carrying on the work where Sir Francis Drake and Sir Richard Grenville and Sir Walter Raleigh left off. I'm going to help, as all true Englishmen should."

Chirp's long nose quivered at its sharp end. "That's all bambury-chat and swish-swash!" he cried. "Your great John Ward is making a deal now with Rich-arrayed Robin Humpery to clear the stuff you lift from Spanish ships. You're one of us, Roger. The grandson of Sir Ludar Pirie has come down to my level. No, not to my level. You'll be a cabin-boy on a stinking pirate ship. And I—I am the curtal of Alsatia!"

There was enough truth in what he said to make me cringe inside. I had been carrying a deep feeling of hurt ever since John had talked so frankly to me at Appleby Court. Sailing under the colors of John Ward was not going to be all that I had hoped for and dreamed about. He would finance himself out of the cargoes he captured, and that meant an association with the Upright Man and his spaniels like Chirp Bird.

I could think of no suitable answer, and so it was fortunate that John put his head through the door at this moment. I could see that a plump individual was seated at the desk and that two burly fellows were standing back of him. The Upright Man kept himself well guarded, it seemed.

"We're in for a full night of talk," said John. "Better go to bed, Roger. Chirp is to see that you're comfortably settled. And, Chirp, your master is not too well pleased at the ease with which we cracked our way in here tonight. He says you're to put a flea in the ears of those two scrippets in the street. No one is to be allowed in tonight, not even if it were King Jamie himself."

Chirp's face went white with anger. He did not like to be given orders, it was clear, nor did he relish John's tone. He clamped his slack lips tight, however, and said nothing. He motioned me to follow him.

We went up a stairway, with carved oak bannister and an ancient lantern on the newel post, to a noble bedroom with a huge four-poster bed. The curtains at the window were old and fine and almost served to conceal the fact that there were metal shutters under them.

"The best bed you have ever slept in," said Chirp, with a return to his former mood of sly malice. "A proper libbege for the grandson of Sir Ludar Pirie. But don't let yourself dream, Roger. You might fancy yourself in prison or swinging on the gallows they keep for pirates at Wapping Stairs."

He walked back to the door but then paused for a final gibe. "How did you leave Katie Ladland?" he asked. "Was she blooming like a rose? Did you ever climb in her window, Roger?"

This was too much. I sprang across the room and drove my fist into his grinning face. His head cracked so sharply against the edge of the door that a dazed look came into his eyes. He tried to reach his sword, but I clamped his wrist tight with one hand while I threatened to repeat the medicine with the other.

"Keep your foul tongue from her!" I warned. "You may be the curtal of Alsatia, Chirp, but to me you're nothing but a cheap coward and a crook. Call up your crew from downstairs, and I'll repeat every word I've said. I wouldn't be afraid of you if you had every cutthroat in London at your back."

I let him go then. He left without a word. I remembered that he had always been a physical coward. His sudden rise to power in the world of crime had done nothing to change that.

I tried to open the metal shutters but found they were too tightly cramped. Then I drew back the curtains of the imposing bed. It was spread with the finest linen and pillow-beres of satin, but I knew from the damp smell that it had lacked airing for a long time. I touched the pillow lightly, and my fist went right through the linen cover.

I dropped the curtain and went to sleep in a corner of the room, with my cloak wrapped around me.

8

THE BARRED SHUTTERS of my room kept out the sun, and I would have overslept next morning if a fight in the street below had not wakened me. Two passers-by had fallen foul of each other and had progressed from bandying words to an exchange of blows, a proceeding which seemed to delight the whole neighborhood. I could hear enthusiastic shouts of "crack 'is nab, Squire," and "rip his weazand, the gawping old huffsnuff!" and such like, a chorus made up at least in half of feminine voices.

The rooms below were deserted of all but the guards, who pinned suspicious eyes on me from every hall and doorway, and Chirp Bird, who was eating breakfast in a black mood. He looked at me and scowled. There was a red mark on one side of his jaw, which, I suspected, was the result of contact with my fist the night before.

"John's gone," he said shortly. "He brangled with the Upright Man all night and then started back at daylight to see the—the fine gentleman who supplies the mint. He left word for you to go to an inn and wait until he comes back."

I was well pleased at this news, for it meant I would have at least one day free in London. For as long as I could remember I had been looking forward to the time when I would see the wonders of the great city. Now the chance had come.

"How's the weather?" I asked. The windows were still shuttered, and the atmosphere of the room suggested that all of Hobson's horses had been stabled there.

"A fine day," answered Chirp. His hand strayed gingerly to his bruised chin and then dropped, as though he did not want to acknowledge that he carried a souvenir of our encounter. He looked at me with elaborate scorn. "I'll see you to an inn. You would be lost if I turned you loose." He made quite a ceremony of wiping his hands and face and then shambled to his feet. "Come along. I'll see you safe."

I had no desire to see London for the first time in the company of a cadet of Alsatia, and so I told him. Chirp swept my objection aside magnanimously.

"Do ye think I want to be seen with you?" he demanded. "All you need is a cloth cap and a belly-cheat to pass for a draper's apprentice. But I promised John Ward to see you safe, and I'll do it."

So I did not argue the point any further and followed him outside. The air was cool and bracing, and between the housetops I caught glimpses of a speckless blue sky. It was a lovely day, but when I looked about me I realized that the boon of fine weather did nothing to ameliorate the ugliness of the slums. The houses hung so closely together that I was afraid at first glance they might fall. They were dark and forbidding and in both respects no different from the people who lived in them. No one seemed to work. Men stood about in whispering groups on the streets, and frowsy women leaned from doorways and windows to shrill abuse at one another. Sooty faces looked up at us from cellars, and leering faces popped out of every opening in the walls.

There were taverns everywhere, but even so the public thirst seemed to require the service of bowse boys, who were running back and forth with piping soprano cries: "Ole nappy ile! Bowse, my marsters, bowse!"

A chimney sweep, already so drunk that I was sure he would come to grief if any employment were offered him, was sounding his trade cry in a mournful singsong:

> "Sweep, chimney sweep, Mistress!
> Hey, dery sweep.
> From the bottom to the top,
> Sweep, chimney sweep!
> Then shall no soot fall in your porridge pot,
> With a hoop-dery, dery, dery, sweep!"

I could not help thinking that to clean the chimneys of these filthy slums would be a superfluous operation, but when I said this to my companion he treated me to another scornful glance.

"Do ye suppose sweeping is their real trade?" he demanded. "There's no better way to spy a ken. That fellow takes his orders from us, and he isn't as drunk as he seems. Every lilywhite in London is stalled to his Upright Man. It's the same with most of the food vendors and the potboys in the inns."

"Is there more than one Upright Man?" I asked in surprise.

"Three in London," replied Chirp. "We've divided the town into districts, but it doesn't work very well, I can tell you. The Wapping lot and the gentlemen from across the river poach on us all the time. And do we cut in on them! Some day they'll all come in under one head. All that's needed is a strong hand to guild the town." It was clear from his tone that he did not consider Rich-arrayed Robin Humpery the man for the task. Perhaps it was in his mind that the one to rule as the overlord of Rome-ville (the cant name for London) was none other than Chirp Bird himself.

We cut through a tangle of slime-encrusted alleys and came out at Whitefriar's Stairs, and here caught my first glimpse of the Thames by daylight. The grand old river was running strong with quite a showing of whitecaps. It was dotted with barges and looked so clean and brisk and gay in the strong sunshine that I began to feel better at once.

We turned eastward to the City and for half an hour were never completely out of sight of the river. This was a different London, a busy and cheerful town of solid streets with fine shops and substantial homes. St. Paul's enthralled me, and I stopped a dozen times on Cheapside to stare in the open booths of the goldsmiths and drapers. I enjoyed everything so much that I was not concerned when apprentices laughed at my country garb and bawled "apple-squire!" at me. Chirp kept a few paces in the rear as though unwilling to be seen in the company of a goggling visitor from rural parts.

We came finally to a tavern with a faded sign. I was delighted to recognize it as the Draw the Pudding, a rather famous inn of which I had heard often.

"You're to stay under cover until ye get word from John," he admonished. He regarded me with an unfriendly scowl. "Better stay close, bumpkin. And keep your fives in your gallyslops. If you use 'em here, some cuffin will sink a blade in your ribs. They won't be as easy on you as I've been."

He had meant to leave at once, but the tavern was buzzing with excitement, and he decided to see what it was all about. His sharp eyes darted about the crowded common room. "There's going to be trouble," he said.

The common room was three stories high, with an oak-studded

balcony around it on two sides and a cavernous fireplace. The balcony railings were hung with souvenirs which caught my eye instantly, as it was clear they came from foreign parts. There were curious heathen masks and the shrunken heads of cannibals, Mayan cloaks of intricate color design, ostrich plumes from the headpieces of caciques, and the long tobacco pipes of American Indians. I recognized most of them, for I had heard long descriptions of such things from sailors at home. The floor was crowded with tables which in turn were crowded with customers, drinking, dicing, and quarreling.

As we stood there, a tall fellow got suddenly to his feet and began a heated oration. He was a seaman, for he had a chain of shark's teeth about his bronzed neck, and the dialect of Devonshire dripped from his tongue. All other talk in the room ceased.

"The King's come back to Greenwich today," he declaimed. "He'll be able to see his fine ships rotting at their moorings and with barnacles on their bottoms, the ships which ought to be out protecting our merchantmen. Tell me this: what good is a king who refuses to fight for his subjects? Our pious old fraud of a king says we must let the thrice-cursed Dons drive us off the seas. He swears he'll hang bold John Ward. Are we going to sit by and let him sell us into slavery?"

There was a clamor of approval from all parts of the room. The Spanish question was not the only bone his subjects had to pick with royal James, however. His return to the city had stirred up other grievances in the minds of the townsmen. A sober-appearing merchant stood up and protested against the imposts which were being levied. "No sovereign may tax the people without the consent of the Commons," he declared. "It was that way before the Normans came over. Have we brought a king from Scotland to set our liberties at naught?" The King's choice of ministers was another point which came in for open discussion, and it was made abundantly clear that the Cecils and the Howards found little favor with the hard-headed men of the capital. "They're all in the pay of Don Sarmiento," called out one man, Don Sarmiento being the London nickname for Gondomar, the much-hated Spanish ambassador. A suggestion came from somewhere that His Majesty should make Archie Armstrong his Secretary of State and be done with it, a sally which brought a general laugh. "Good for Archie!" called a loud voice. "He's a wise 'un which makes him different from the other fools."

I stood in the doorway and drank in everything that was being said, amazed at the boldness of the talk and finding that it did a great deal to bolster my own resolution. This was what right-minded Englishmen were saying.

My eyes rested on a table in a corner when I saw that Chirp was watching it intently. One man sat there alone, a massive individual with small darting eyes in a squashed-pudding face. He had arrayed himself in the manner of a court gallant and resembled a sucking pig which had been decorated with hollyberries and apples for Christmas consumption. It was clear that he was of some importance, for none had dared to occupy the other chairs at his table. I observed, moreover, that furtive-looking fellows were seated near by who watched every move made in that part of the room. I concluded they were acting as bodyguards.

"Chirp," I whispered, "that bloated meal sack who thinks himself the Emperor of India, who is he?"

My companion looked at me as though I had been guilty of sacrilege. "That's Barnaby Cloud," he answered cautiously. "The Upright Man of Wapping. He's a tough cove, and one of these days we shall have to fight it out with him. Keep an eye on him, Roger. He's going to put in his say."

Chirp was right. The Upright Man of Wapping got to his feet, and almost immediately a silence fell on the room. Every eye was turned in his direction. I was surprised to find, when he spoke, that the voice issuing from that gross mass of flesh was cultivated and clear.

"Good men of London," he began, "the time has come to let the councillors of His Majesty know that we find serious fault with the policies they are following. Impositions have been placed on merchants and other men of business—"

"Who have nothing left to pay taxes with when you get through with them, Barnaby," called a voice from the back of the room. A loud laugh followed.

"I protest," said the Wapping leader in an aggrieved tone. "I am a man of business myself. I provide protection from evil-doers for the merchants of London."

A chorus of indignant denial arose from all parts of the room. "And you also protect Simon Forman, the magician, and poisoners, and doxies, and cutpurses, and pickpockets!"—"Barnaby Cloud, the prince of prancer-priggers!"—"A fine state of affairs when the king of the crooks raises his voice against the King of England!"

"The royal poltroon—" went on the Upright Man, raising his voice over the hubbub.

The first speaker got to his feet again. It was clear that he had no stomach for support in this quarter. "These are grievances for honest men," he thundered. "Since when have thieves and doxie-masters set themselves up as makers of public opinion? What, my lively lads from Devonshire, are ye going to sit on your haunches or are ye going to flay the impudence out of this evil-faced city dog?"

"I told ye there would be trouble," said Chirp. I saw that he had gone pale and remembered again that he had always been a physical coward, ready to run like a jack rabbit when fists began to fly.

The appeal of the seaman met with an instant response. Brawny sailors converged on the Upright Man from every corner of the room. His bodyguards placed themselves around him, tugging at their dirks with nervous hands. I looked for Chirp, to observe the effect of this on him. He was nowhere to be seen.

The fracas was a short one. The rush of seamen split the criminal squad wide open. Barnaby Cloud and his henchmen went down under the wreckage of the table. Daggers flashed. After several moments of frantic tussling on the floor, the Upright Man was yanked to his feet again, pinioned in the grasp of two lusty sea dogs. He was rushed from the room and propelled into the street while his lieutenants were disarmed and mauled unmercifully. I would have enjoyed a hand in the affair myself, for I had seen enough since coming to London to know it was high time these lordly masters of crime were taught a lesson.

When it was all over and some kind of order had been restored, I sought out the landlord and asked for a room. He had a harried look in his eyes and was sweating profusely, and at first he paid no attention to my demand. I finally got it through his addled head that I was a customer with the price of a room in my pocket. This being clear, he turned me over to a fat servingwoman, who led me up two flights of stairs to a large bedroom with windows looking out over the roofs of the city.

"Ye're a country boy," she said in friendly tones. "If ye could just see now down three squares and then two to the right and a sharp jog to the left, ye would put eyes on the very spot where the King sits with his parlyment. Yes, m'lad, and wouldn't ye like to see the Marshalsea and the Clink, and the place where they hang them and cut out their innards, and burn them afore their very faces? There's a lots of rare sights to see in Lunnon. Would ye be anxious for a little fun, now?"

I assured her I was not anxious for a little fun and that all I required was paper and a pen. She brought these, and I settled down to my delayed task of writing to Mother and Aunt Gadilda.

I found it hard to tell them what I had done and what I proposed to do about my future. My gentle mother, I felt sure, would understand me well enough, and perhaps even have a little sympathy for the course I had elected to follow; but it would be different with Aunt Gaddy. She was so set in her ideas, so sure that the plan for which she had slaved and scrimped and starved was the only proper one. It was going to break her heart. Her poor pinched face would go white with misunderstanding and grief when she read what I was putting down. I owed it to her to break the news as kindly as I could. But the right words would not come.

I chewed the quill desperately and struggled for ways to make my message less unfeeling, but only the shabbiest of phrases got themselves down on the paper in front of me. My fingers were well inked by the time I was through, and I was well aware that the two who loved me best in the world would find no reason for comfort in what I had written. Still, it could not be helped. There was man's work to be done these bitter days, and nothing could be more right than that a son of Mark Blease should take his place beside stout John Ward. I finished the letter, sealed it, and took it down to the post. Then, with my mind torn between regret over the thing I had been compelled to do and high anticipation of what the rest of the day held for me, I sallied out to see London on my own.

I dined heavily on slices of hot roast beef and a steamed roll pudding in a near-by bakeshop. As I emptied my platter, I watched through a steamy window the barbershop opposite where the proprietor was using a hot iron to curl the long hair of a gentleman of fashion. In front of the place was a tall pole, painted red and white, and a long coil of twine on which were strung the teeth which had been extracted from customers. There were many hundreds of them, and I suppose they proved that tooth-pulling was a fine art with the worthy barber.

The pangs of hunger fully satisfied, I inquired the way to Parliament Place and wended my way there first of all. I spent some time in Westminster Abbey, thinking with proper awe of the noble dust that lay under its imposing monuments. I looked at the outside of the old chapel where the Commons sat and at the royal palace where the king no longer lived, but which contained the House of Lords. All the time, however, I was conscious of an urge to follow the other sightseers who gave no more than a passing glance at these institutions and then hurried down a narrow lane leading toward Queen's Bridge. I gave in to my curiosity and joined the procession, finding myself in due course in front of a stone house.

I knew without asking anyone that this was Vinegar House. It was mean and unpretentious, built against a wing of the Lords, and it seemed to me not only well named but well suited to the dark purpose of the gloomy men who had used it. In this cold and bitter tenement the most famous conspiracy of history had been hatched, the Gunpowder Plot. It was now some years old, but it was still England's most grateful topic of conversation. It seemed as though people would never stop talking about it, and I was not surprised that the feet of visitors turned to this spot first of all.

I found myself in a crowd of considerable size. For the most part, the people gazed at the awesome house with gaping jaws and said nothing. Such comments as were made showed how ignorant they were of the real facts.

"It were so full o' poother ye could see the barrels from the bedroom winders," declared one man in a shivery voice. I knew this was wrong. None of the powder had been stored in Vinegar House. The plotters had found they could not cut through the walls of the palace and had boldly carted the barrels away and stored them in the coal cellars of the palace.

Hawkers were plying the usual wares among the credulous onlookers:

pieces of the rope with which Guy Fawkes had been hanged, odd scraps of things which had been found in the cellars, even twists of paper containing (or so they said) quantities of the actual powder itself. Shillings were changing hands briskly, and guides were organizing parties to go up to Butcher Row and see the house where Guy Fawkes had lived. "He were four inches longer when they took 'im off the rack," announced one of them cheerfully. "Come now, only a twelver to see and hear *everything*. Things to make your flesh creep, good people; even the beads they took offen 'im when they cut out 'is bowels. Something to talk about the rest o' yer nateral lives."

The house was empty and had a haunted look about it, as though all the hates and fears which had resulted in the Gunpowder Plot had remained after the plotters themselves had gone to their deaths, to lie stagnant here; a more dangerous brew than all the gunpowder in the world. I found myself reciting under my breath the words of an inscription which had been cut on a panel after the event, from copy prepared by the King himself:

> *"Jacobus Magnus, Magnae Britanniae, Rex, pietate, justitia, prudentia, doctrina, fortitudine, elementia, ceterisq—"*

It sounded highly ironical to me. "James the Great, King of Great Britain, illustrious for piety, justice, learning, hardihood, clemency and other regal virtues—" Had Guy Fawkes actually been four inches longer when they removed his tortured frame from the Tower rack?

I decided not to invest one of my few shillings in the satisfaction of curiosity, although I confess it was hard to resist doing so, and struck off eastward on foot. I did not stop until I came to the foot of the wharf which surrounds the Tower of London on the water side. I was hoping to walk out on the wharf and see the Traitor's Gate and, if I were lucky enough, catch a glimpse of Sir Walter Raleigh walking on the terrace of the Bloody Tower. To my intense disappointment, however, I found that barriers had been set up so that no one could get any farther than the street. I pressed tightly against the bars and craned my neck over them, hoping that I might still be rewarded by a fugitive glance of the noble prisoner, but a guard came along and poked the blunt end of his pike in the direction of my stomach, causing me to retreat to a safer distance.

It was no consolation when a dark-skinned fellow pressed against my shoulder and whispered that for a shilling he would sell me the recipe of Sir Walter Raleigh's Great Cordial, about which the whole world was talking, believing it to be a cure for every human ailment. At first I was sure he must be one of the natives of Guiana, who had been brought to England by Raleigh and who were supposed to be living in lodgings near the Tower in order to be close to their white god, but then I detected a smack of Alsatia in his voice. I concluded that the darkness of his skin might very well be due to an application of walnut stain. I decided against this investment also.

Then I crossed London Bridge, stopping to count the heads of the so-called traitors which decorated the pikes over the central span. Thirty-two! Many of them had been up there so long that they retained no human suggestion at all, but I marveled that the people of London, milling back and forth across the bridge, paid no more heed to this ghastly display than to the flocks of gulls which perched on the tops of the houses.

Descending the ramp on the far side, I passed the inns of Tooley Street and gave a few curious glances to the stewhouses and the Cardinal's Hats which infested the neighborhood. I paused in front of the Globe Theatre and read a notice to the effect that "Volpone, a recent Play by B. Jonson" would be presented there the following day. I visited a bear-baiting pit and found the stench rising from it intolerable. Nevertheless, houses had been built close around it, and I had heard that the residents did very well by renting out their upper windows.

Retracing my steps over London Bridge, I looked up and counted thirty-three heads on the pikes. Had I been in error before or had another trophy been added to this exhibition of royal clemency while I was sightseeing on the other side of the river? There was one head I did not recall seeing on my way over, that of a young man with long golden locks which tossed in the lively breeze. I shuddered as I thought that, if James had his way, still another might soon be added to the lot, that of my friend John Ward. *Jacobus Magnus, Rex, pietate, clemential*

Of the many things which London had always meant to me, the most important of all remained to be seen. I paced with weary footsteps back to the heart of the city until I reached the busy spot where Bread and Blowbladder streets came together near West Cheap. Here stood a tall inn with nothing to make it stand out from the hundreds of other inns of the great city. Certainly there was nothing about it from the outside to excite the feelings of passers-by, and yet I found my heart thumping as I looked up at its plain façade. This was the Mermaid Tavern, the very heart and soul of England!

I made no move to go inside. At best I would see groups of well-dressed men at supper; and none of them, perhaps, would bear the great names with which the Mermaid was associated in my mind. It was much more satisfying to stand outside and tell myself that an illustrious company was within: Will Shakespeare and Ben Jonson; Fletcher with his towering brow and Chapman with his merry round beard; Dekker and Drayton; and Will Sly the actor; and even some of the brave spirits who had sailed the seas with Raleigh and had first come here as members of his Bread Street Club. I told myself that the conversation within would be serene and sparkling and elevated. There would be no gossip of gunpowder plots, no talk of court intrigues, no idle speculation about the latest royal favorite. They would be concerned only with great truths, universal truths, with the world of letters, which was so much finer than the real world, with what the future would bring, and of England's part in that future.

Yes, here was the real heart of England. No one, I thought to myself, could look at the Mermaid Tavern, where so many great projects had been born, and go away content with the royal dictum that Englishmen must forswear their heritage on the high seas. London had disappointed me up to this point. The filth of the slums had been worse than I had expected, the Tower had seemed much smaller than I had conceived it to be and not especially awe-inspiring, the wonder of London Bridge had been spoiled by the rotting row of heads which looked with sightless eyes up the broad river. But the Mermaid Tavern made up for all this. No city could harbor so magnificent a shrine without being truly great. I turned, with spirits which had soared again to the heights, and decided that I had seen enough.

It had grown dark by this time, and I was not sure I knew the way back to my inn. I was pondering what I had better do when a beggar sidled by, intoning his dismal chorus of "alms, good people, alms!" As he passed, he gave me an upward squint from downcast eyes and said in a sharp whisper, "If ye're Roger Blease, go on to the next left turn. I'll speak to ye there."

I was too startled to make any immediate response; and the beggar, hobbling painfully on his weak legs, was well beyond me before I recovered my self-possession. I paused irresolutely; and then, in response to an impatient glance that he threw back at me over his shoulder, I began to walk slowly toward the designated corner. He was already there when I arrived.

"Turn to the left," he admonished me. "Walk slowly. Gawp around and whistle if ye can. Free and easy, mind ye."

I did as he bade me, turning down one of the darkest and narrowest lanes in all London. I was not at all free in my mind about following such instructions, and yet the man knew me by name and very clearly had some message for my ears. There did not seem to be anyone about, and yet I was sure I could hear rustling in the darkness on each side. I began to feel decidedly nervous about all this and was on the point of turning and retracing my steps when a whisper came out of the gloom.

"Nah, then, my gentry-cove. Do ye want to be picked up by the King's men? Keep on walking."

I resumed my course. It was ridiculous to suppose that I could be in any danger from the King's men, and yet I had been traveling with John Ward and had spent a night at the headquarters of the Upright Man of Alsatia. Did such circumstances make me a law-breaker? I was trying to figure this out when there was a sound of sudden footsteps behind me. My arms were clasped from the rear with such vicious strength that I felt as though a steel trap had closed on me. At the same second a hand grasped me by the mouth and yanked my head backward. A gag was slipped into my mouth so effectively that I was not able to utter a sound.

"Come on, Master Blease," said the voice I had heard before. "Do as ye're bid and ye'll keep a whole skin."

9

I WAKENED NEXT MORNING in a soft bed with light filtering dimly through rich curtains. My jaw was sore; and, as I rubbed it with a careful thumb, I began to cast back over the events of the night.

I remembered being half carried and half propelled for a distance of several hundred yards. At intervals my abductors had halted; and at these times I had sensed, from the tensity with which they gripped me, that they were under a strain. Once I had heard many footsteps passing us and a creaking sound which I thought might be made by the swinging of lanterns in the hands of the city watch. Finally we had entered a house; and, after stumbling up a long flight of stairs, I had been thrust into this room. The gag had been removed, and I had been told in a fierce whisper to keep my jaw closed if I valued my life. I must have gone to sleep almost immediately after.

I sat up in bed and realized at once that I had been sleeping in the bedroom of a lady of quality. It was enormous, and neither at Appleby Court nor at Theobalds had I seen anything to compare with its appointments. When I dropped my stiffened legs over the side, my feet sank into soft carpet. There was a lingering trace of perfume in the air. I walked to one of the windows and pulled back the curtain a cautious inch. A blind wall of ivy-covered brick faced me.

I did not dare touch a thing. The room was done graciously in the softest tones. There was a dressing table with a tall mirror framed in gold and a great variety of bottles and other toilet articles, the uses of which I could no more than guess at. I recognized a red leather box with an embossed likeness of the old queen as a sweet coffer, a container of perfume. A pomander on a gold chain lay carelessly beside it, and I got the impression that the lady who occupied the room had departed in a hurry.

A door beside the dressing table was half-open, and I peered through into a small marble-tiled room. It contained nothing but a stone bathtub, shaped like a tulip with drooping petals, its four dragon-clawed feet bolted to the floor. I closed the door with an intensified conviction of intrusion.

Silence gripped the place. I could be sure of one thing only: my abduction had been ordered from Alsatia. The beggar in front of the Mermaid Tavern had addressed me by name, and it was only through Chirp Bird that he could have known it. I had been spirited away for some reason which had to do with John Ward's business in London, and in due course I would learn what it was all about. In the meantime I would have to make the best of it.

The only other door opening into the room was tightly closed. It was a full hour later that I heard steps coming cautiously toward it and the turning of a key in the lock. It swung open, and a thickset fellow in a gray jerkin looked in. He had watery eyes in a face which resembled that of an ill-tempered badger.

"Breakfast," he announced in a grudging tone.

He came slowly into the room and set down a bowl of food and a whiskin filled with ale, saying in a hoarse voice: "No use cagging at me. Curtal's coming. Save yer gab for him."

The bowl contained some slices of cold meat and a sizable hunk of excellent bread. I had disposed of everything by the time Chirp Bird put in an appearance. He came into the room and sniffed. His greedy eyes took in the richness of the furnishings with a kind of reluctant envy.

"If my advice had been taken, you wouldn't be here," he said, after a moment.

"Why am I here? I don't understand this at all."

"Of course you don't, you totty-headed country lob," said Chirp venomously. "If I had my way, you would be feeding the fishes this very minute, Master Roger Blease! It's a mistake to let you live, and we're all going to suffer for it." The hostility in his eyes deepened. "A pretty mess, this is. They'll lag us all."

"You might tell me what it's about," I suggested, with a feeling of growing apprehension.

He seated himself in front of the dressing table and drew his thin knees together. "John Ward was seen at Cheshunt," he said, with a trace of a quaver in his voice. "That's what it's about."

"They haven't caught him?" I asked, with sudden alarm.

"Gog's Nownes, no!" cried Chirp. "If they had, you wouldn't be here. Listen, Roger, John Ward was recognized. The word got to the King, and the peery old gander was sure it was another plot on his life. He's been squeaking like a pig-widgeon ever since they tried to plant that gunpowder under him. He got the jumbles, and nothing would do but the court must be moved. They've moved back to Greenwich Palace already. A double row of guards has been set around the walls, and a dozen armed men were in the royal chamber last night. Do ye see what it's all about now?"

I was beginning to see, and I was sharing Chirp's fears. I did not need to be told what would happen if either John or I were caught.

"By four o'clock yesterday every inn in London had been searched for John Ward and *a thin, dark boy dressed in gray!*" said Chirp. "We heard about it and tried to find you. But you, you nick-ninny, had gone out to see the sights! Didn't I tell ye to lie low?" The thought of the consequences if I had been caught was so upsetting still that he wiped perspiration from his brow with a shaking hand. "If we hadn't lagged you when we had, they'd be stretching you now on the Duke of Exeter's Daughter where they racked Guy Fawkes, and you'd be bleating out everything you know and a lot you don't know. And you ask me what it's all about!"

"But there was no plot!" I exclaimed. "John went to Theobalds to see—"

"No names!" cried Chirp with a white face. "Not even here. That's what they would get out of you. Names! Everyone you had seen and spoken to. This king has men around him who make it their business to tell him his life is in constant danger. If they laid hands on you, my fine kinchin coe, they wouldn't let you off the rack until you had sworn that Raleigh and every man in the anti-Spain party was back of you." His face was a greenish white with the fear that gripped him. "Think of me. I was seen all over London with you! I can feel the dirty fingers of the topping-cove on my neck right now!"

He was in a pitiable state of fright; and, if the truth must be told, I was little better myself. I was seeing crowds of goggling natives, and hawkers selling them bits of the rope with which Roger Blease had been hanged at Tyburn.

The door opened again to admit my first visitor. The man jerked a thumb over his shoulder and said: "There's another one of them. What's to be done?"

Chirp was as puzzled by this piece of information as I was. "What do you mean?" he demanded. "Another who? Speak up!"

"Another one of them," repeated the man. "Outside. Clem the Cuckold just brought him in."

"Is he a sailor?" asked Chirp.

The man shook his head. "I think he's a lob. Says his name is Snode."

If our situation had been less critical, I would have enjoyed the look of consternation which showed on Chirp's face at this news.

"Snode!" he cried. "Jore Snode here? That brattle-mouthed fool in London?" It was too much. He looked at me as though I were to blame for this addition to his problems. "Where did Clem find him?"

Joralemon Snode was to have met us in London and gone on with us to the *Royal Bess*. All yesterday I had been expecting to hear of his arrival at the Draw the Pudding, and I had been worrying about him while Chirp had been explaining the dangers of our situation.

"Clem saw him as he set foot on Lunnon Bridge," explained the man. "He cut with him, thinking he might have a glag or two in his pocket. When he let out he were looking for a Roger Blease, Clem brought him here. By water, straight to the stairs."

Chirp said grimly: "Bring him up, then. Bring him up. I want a few words with Joralemon Snode." He looked at me and glowered. "Well, Roger, we'll be thinking we're back on Shrubsole High if this keeps up. Jore Snode in London!" Suddenly he began to laugh. "All we need is Ann Turner and Katie Ladland to keep us company while we wait for them to come and take us. It would help a little. You needn't look at me like that. I can have your throat slit from ear to ear any time I give the word!"

Joralemon Snode appeared in the door and peered at us uncertainly. I looked at him more closely than the first day and saw that he had a thin and shriveled appearance.

Chirp took him by the arm and jerked him into the room.

Snode looked at both of us and said: "Chirp! And Roger! This *is* a surprise."

Chirp began to ply him with questions in an almost breathless haste. "Did you come alone? Did you speak to anyone before Clem got his hands on you? Did you mention Roger's name to anyone else?"

"No. I spoke to no one else."

"Are ye sure? You said nothing to man, woman, or child? Did you pass the time of day or throw a word to a beggar? Are ye ready to swear it?"

"It will not be necessary to take the name of the Lord in vain," said Jore stiffly. "I spoke to no one save that evil-tongued son of Belial who brought me here."

"How did you get to London?"

"I walked every foot of it."

Chirp's face took on a tortured look. "And spread the word of what was bringing you all the way from Shrubsole High to London Bridge! I know you, Jore, so you needn't deny it. Did you name John Ward? Or Roger Blease? I must have the truth. How often did you tell?"

"Never once," answered Jore, drawing himself up with offended dignity. "John warned me about it, and I spoke to no one."

"Don't try to lie out of it!" exclaimed Chirp. "You've been clacking about sailing with John Ward and what a great man you are. I know that loose tongue of yours, Jore. Didn't you tell Clem the Cuckold you were seeking Roger Blease?"

Joralemon nodded slowly. "Ay, that much is so. I did speak to him the once. But London was so large, and I didn't know where to begin looking. I asked him the way to the Draw the Pudding, and then he asked who I expected to see there. The name slipped out."

I was as anxious as Chirp and not yet sure that Jore had told us everything. "This is most important," I said to him. "Did your tongue slip any other time? Think hard, Jore. Our lives may depend on it."

He raised his hand. "On my hope of salvation, I spoke to no one else. And it seems I was right to do so then, for it has brought me here to you, Roger."

This satisfied me, and I could see that Chirp was relieved also. He began to ask more questions, however.

"What orders did John give you?"

"John's orders were given to *me*."

I interposed then, to avoid an explosion, and told Jore how necessary it was for us to know everything. He finally accepted my word for it and explained that he had left the night before on orders from John. He was to go to London and look for me at the inn. The two of us were then to get out of the city and make our way to the *Royal Bess*, where John himself would join us as soon as possible.

"Where is the *Royal Bess*?" demanded Chirp.

Snode shut his mouth tight. The whereabouts of the ship was a secret and nothing would induce him to tell it, not even threats to cut his throat if he refused to give in. Chirp raved and swore but got no satisfaction. Finally he gave up the effort.

"That brain-sick ox of a Ward should have known better than to send anyone to London!" he declared. "What would have happened if Clem hadn't seen Jore when he did? Every inn is being watched. Ward should have known the danger. That's how close he's come to giving the thing away. Our great hero hasn't the brains of a bantling!"

He began to pace about the room, his legs bent at the knees and his face puckered with uneasy thoughts. Finally he stopped in front of me. "Is it necessary to warn you not to shove your nose out of here? Either of you?"

"No," I said. "You may depend on us now, Chirp. We want nothing better than to stay right here."

"Then I'll leave you," he said. He added with a bitter scowl: "I hope you realize it's almost as dangerous for me to show myself as you. But, worse luck, it's got to be risked."

As soon as it seemed safe to indulge in confidences, I told Joralemon the whole story. He looked a little frightened for the first time.

"God is watching over us, Roger," he affirmed after a moment. "It was no accident that led me to speak with that evil man who brought me here. He suffereth not the sparrow to fall, and He stayeth the hand of the ungodly. He will guide us to safety in His own good way."

"I trust you're right," I said fervently. I dropped my voice to a whisper, although it was highly unlikely that we were being spied upon. Whatever guards had been set would avoid this part of the house. "We can't stay here, Jore. Chirp is itching for an excuse to put us out of the way. Dead, we would no longer be a menace to him and the rest of his crew. As I see it, our only chance is to get out of here as soon as it's dark and take our chances on reaching the ship."

Snode nodded in agreement. He had taken to breathing lightly also and seemed more afraid of the air of the place than of the dangers which lurked outside. He found it difficult to give me any information when I asked him about the location of our hiding place.

"It's on the river," he said. "An old house but quite handsome. There are deep grounds and a high wall around them. They brought me in through a rear door, and I saw very little."

It was cold in the house, but no one did anything about it. For my part, I was not disposed to hunt for wood to make a fire and, as for poor Joralemon, he had allowed himself to sink into a mood of speechless apprehension, in spite of the consolation he sought from the leaves of his Bible. He had produced it from his doublet and was turning the pages in search of reassuring passages. More food was brought at noon, but neither of us was able to muster any appetite.

At four o'clock or thereabouts Chirp paid us another visit. He looked more frightened than before and reported that the city was being turned upside down. The King's councillors had whipped up the royal fears to a fine frenzy, and even Sir Walter Raleigh had been questioned in the Tower.

"They've been all over Alsatia," he said. "A few likely lads for Paddington Fair were picked up." By this he meant execution day. "That fellow Culleton, for one. He'll have you to thank for it when the rope tightens around his neck."

"Have they found out who we saw at Theobalds?" I asked. All day I had been worried for the safety of Sir Everard Clement and Archie Armstrong. The jester, in particular, had been continually in my thoughts.

Chirp shook his head. The royal council was so set on proving our visit part of a deep-laid conspiracy that they had overlooked the obvious lines of investigation, and had been winding up in a series of dead ends. I felt enormously relieved at this.

But there was nothing to raise my spirits in the attitude of our frightened ex-townsman. Chirp's nerves were close to the breaking point, and I could read in the looks he gave me that he would know no relief as long as Jore and I were alive. His eyes were saying: Dead men tell no tales. We would not see the light of day again if we remained within his reach. I knew how dangerous it would be to sally out, but certain death waited for us here.

Chirp left, and a dead silence settled down over the empty house. Darkness fell outside. It proved quite easy to get away after all. When the time seemed ripe, I motioned to my companion, and we stole out of the room with what turned out to be an unnecessary excess of caution. The door had been left unlocked, so certain were our guards that nothing could persuade us to venture forth. We avoided the front of the mansion and made our way cautiously to a steep flight of steps in the rear.

We heard no sounds other than what we made ourselves, and there was no one about when we reached the grounds. There was no one stationed at the stone gate opening on the wharf. We heard nothing but the vigorous swish of water against the stone base of the wall as we detached the lock from the heavy inside chain.

The river was as black as the overcast sky, but pinpoints of light showed on passing boats. "A proper night for us, Master Roger," said Jore. He stepped to the end of the pier and called in a voice which quavered in spite of his effort to make it bold, "Eastward Ho!"

There was an immediate answer from the river of, "Right y' are, Guv'nor. Eastward Ho, it is."

I saw a light close to shore dip as the wherry which carried it came sharply about. I watched and listened anxiously, but no sounds came from the grounds of the deserted mansion. The wherry came in, and we sprang aboard. It was not until the boatman had sent his craft out into the current again with a stiff thrust of an oar against the side of the mooring that I heard sounds of running feet in the gardens.

"Let them come now," I whispered to Snode. "We're out of danger as far as honest Chirp Bird is concerned."

"Ay," said Jore, with a sigh of relief. "This air is good, Roger."

I was drawing in great draughts of the salt-laden breeze myself, happy to be free of the dank atmosphere of the house. I could have shouted with sheer relief when the bargeman brought the wherry from under the lee of the sheltering stone walls. Then he heeled her about and she caught the breeze. Her sails bellied, and I could feel the pull of the current as we swung off down the river.

10

I SHALL NEVER FORGET my first sight of the *Royal Bess*, anchored well off the coast and shining against the blue of early morning like a ship of magic from a sailor's Land of Cockayne. Her masts were almost bare, but even without a spread of canvas she was a blaze of color. The hull was green with bands of white to outline the carvings, and there were paintings on the taffrails. No Spanish shipmaster would have selected the Tudor colors, so I knew the choice was John's, a gesture of defiance to a Stuart king who was tearing down what his predecessors had raised.

We had put in at Southend and had traveled overland to Felixstowe. Most of the time we had had to depend on shanks-his-mare; and, as we had come along hell-bent, my bones were aching with a degree of fatigue I had never known before. Still, when Joralemon Snode pointed over the top of a knoll standing between us and the sea, and I per-

ceived masts tightly wrapped with tawny sails, I scrambled to the top
of the obstructing land with no consciousness of effort.

"She's a beauty!" I called down to Jore. John had given me some details, and so I had known she was a four-master; but I had not been
prepared for such a display of carrying power. The foremast was stepped
far forward, and the bowsprit was steeved at an unusual angle. I drank
in the details, realizing in how many respects this leviathan differed
from the greatest of the Elizabethan ships-of-war. Both fore and main
masts were square-rigged, and the mizzen carried a lateen sail. "She'll
show her heels to anything on the high seas!" I boasted to my weary
companion.

"Ay," answered Jore, with no enthusiasm. "I've been told she's fast,
but I know nothing of nautical matters. Could she hold her own with
the mighty ships which set out from Tyre in the days when Solomon
was building his temple? I think not, Roger. Let not pride get the better of you."

It was six o'clock in the morning when we climbed over the rail of
the ship, but howls of drunken merriment reached our ears from below
decks. The tall man in discolored kersey smalls who greeted us was
finding it hard to maintain an air of tipsy dignity. He had an enormous
spread of shoulders, and his eyes, which darted at us from under narrowed lids, were sharp and cruel. In spite of his condition, there was a
suggestion of authority about him. Could this, I wondered, be Hale
Harry Gard, John's much-vaunted first mate?

"Well, if it isn't Joralemon Snode!" said this individual, planting
himself so squarely in front of us that we could not advance a step.
"My holy Jore, you're a day late, and I'm of a mind to lay the salt-cel
over your shoulders. Where have ye been, my sanctimonious Snode,
rollicking in vaulting-schools or playing knave-noddy with city sharps?
Joralemon Snode, Joralemon Snode, there's a bawdy look about ye, and
I know ye've been up to no good." He turned his narrow slits of eyes
on me with an almost feral appraisal. "Who's this, in God's good
name? Another joskin for me to lick into shape? Can ye handle yerself on the shrouds, boy? Look at him, doing a cuddy-jig and the ship
hove to! How will ye keep yer legs in a blow, you shag-bag of bones!"

"You're drunk," declared Jore, standing up to him like a man. "Is
this the way you go on when Captain Ward's ashore? This is Roger
Blease, a friend of the Captain's who's shipping with us. He's gentry,
what's more, and he'll want no more talk from you."

The mate's angry eyes shifted back to me. "So, this is Roger Blease,
and he's a friend of John Ward's! And he's gentry, is he? What am I
supposed to do, kiss his blind-cheeks? I'll kiss his skinny ribs with the
bimster!" He gave a drunken stagger and had to grasp the rail for support. He began to laugh in a high-pitched cackle. "My holy Jore, I have
a story for your ears. Have ye heard about the sailor who wanted to

marry the landlady of a tidy little inn down Islington way? But it seems—"

"I'll have none of your filthy stories, Harry Gard!" said Jore sternly. "Stand aside, so we can find our quarters below."

He laid a hand on my shoulder and led the way down the waist of the ship. I saw almost with awe that there were jeers to hoist the yards (I had never seen them used, but they were the latest thing in ship-building) and that the sails were as shiny new as James shillings. The decks were clean, and every inch of wood was freshly painted. Poor John, I thought; he had seen to it that his ship was spick and span for the grand reception he had hoped to receive. He had come home like a bridegroom but would set sail again like a thief in the night!

"I'll speak to the Captain about that fellow," said Jore in my ear. "He's a good enough sailor, but the devil is in his heart. Do you hear the voices of women? It's hard to believe that even Gard would allow them on board here."

There could be no doubt on that score, however, for the shrill note of feminine laughter could be distinguished in the din. I had been conscious of it from the moment we set foot on deck.

"It's always this way when we lay over in port," said Jore sadly. "I've fought with the Captain about it, but he's blind to the evil. He says it's necessary for the men to have their go. But I had hoped we would be free of it here. They are English women down there, Roger."

I was much more interested in the splendid appointments of the ship. Ahead of us the superstructure loomed up like the high towers of Appleby Court. The *Royal Bess* was of Spanish build, and it had always been the way of the Dons to sail the seas in state. I had seen ships like this from the docks at home sailing majestically up the Thames but had never set foot on one before. I held my breath in wonder.

"Come," said Jore. "I'll show you your quarters. Then we must see to getting you rigged out properly. You would freeze to death in that thin jerkin."

I followed him below. The Spanish idea was to provide stately quarters for the officers and such passengers as might be carried, and to herd the men in filthy congestion on the orlop-deck where the air was foul and the floors damp from the bilge. In renovating the *Royal Bess*, John had done what he could to correct this fault. What had once been the chapel, a magnificent chamber occupying a large part of the two top decks, fitted with mahogany and roofed like a cathedral with high-arching timbers, was now an ordnance room. The crew were using it for a different purpose, however, as we learned when Jore swung open its carved and copper-studded door. A blast of sound assailed our ears. The men were there in full force, squatted on powder kegs or sprawling on the floor. Jore slammed the door shut so fast that I caught no more than a glimpse of naked fattish figures seated on the knees of the sailors or flitting with tipsy efforts at grace among those on the floor.

My companion's face was set in grim lines. "God forgive me for saying it," he declared, "but I would rather see that fine chamber used for popish mummery than turned into a drinking ken for sailors and harlots. Roger, my boy, I hope you'll be wise enough to leave women alone. I say it with grief, but John must not be your model in such matters. It's his one flaw, and I pray the good Lord every night to forgive him for it."

My cabin was on the top-deck, with a porthole and a netting already slung. I could stand in the center and touch all four walls with my outstretched fingers; but there was a chair strapped to the floor, a chest for clothes under the hammock, and even a silver-backed mirror on one wall, a souvenir no doubt of the days when the ship had been the *Madalina* and had sailed proudly under the flag of Castile.

"I'm next to you," explained Jore. "John's cabin is beyond mine. It's large and handsome, but I'll leave it to him to invite you there. We're friends ashore, but here he's the captain, and he never lets you forget it. You must always address him as Captain Ward." He slipped his hand into his doublet and produced a testament in limp leather. "Will you take this, my boy? I brought it for you when I heard you were joining us. You'll find it a great comfort, times without number. Roger, I must warn you that things will happen on this ship which cause the angels in Heaven to hide their heads in shame. I'm not blaming John, mind you. It's not his fault. It's the way of the sea."

John did not arrive that day, nor the next. The men had been refused shore leave, and they became more unmanageable all the time. They began to grumble openly. The drinking increased, and boats plied back and forth from shore, bringing supplies of all kinds and, of course, more women. The chief mate, who seemed to me the drunkest of them all, looked on the antics of the crew with a tolerant eye, although sometimes he would yank his bimster (a rope's end waxed to a steellike hardness) from his belt with a savage gesture and lay it across the shoulders of a sailor for no apparent reason at all. Once he lashed a poor silly fellow into insensibility for stumbling as he passed. A pail of salt water was thrown over the victim, and he was left to recuperate as best he could in the scuppers. No one paid any attention to him.

I am sure the mate would have been less tolerant if he had not found more satisfying targets for persecution in Joralemon and me. He would back Jore into a corner and compel him to listen to obscene narratives, fixing him the while with a belligerent and zestful eye. He sang foul songs at the top of his lungs or gave imitations of a parson whenever Jore hove in sight. For my part, I had to listen to dire predictions as to what would happen to me when we got under way; and, as a foretaste, he set me to all manner of impossible tasks from which I emerged with bleeding hands and broken fingernails, my tormentor laughing uproariously as he watched me. He seemed to realize instinctively that I was sensitive about my thinness and called me nothing but Spindle-shanks.

"When he's sober there's no better sailor afloat," Jore said to me several times. That was no extenuation in my eyes, for I was beginning to hate the man and to feel the first faint regret for the comfortable life I had left.

I was sick with worry over John's failure to appear. Had he been caught? All through that second day I had visions of him in the Tower with sly interrogators picking his brains and the King writing another Latin tablet. It was only a matter of time, I was sure, before boats filled with soldiers would be putting off to take possession of the *Royal Bess*. The identity of the ship must be well known to people ashore, and the only reason that some action had not already been taken was that news traveled slowly. Word of the hue and cry for John Ward and his unidentified companion had not yet reached the coast towns. I made up my mind to jump overboard before I would let myself be taken.

Jore and I were discussing the situation in my cabin on the second evening. We were certain by this time that John was in prison. We were so depressed that our talk was fitful and filled with long pauses. It did not help any to hear the drunken roaring of the crew, proof that the revelry had reached a still wilder level. They were in a fighting mood, and sounds of bitter altercation frequently drowned out the tipsy screaming of the Madame Vans.

"I must see if I can do anything to stop it," said Jore finally, getting to his feet. "Throats will be cut if this keeps up."

"If you go down there, your own throat will be the first to be cut."

Suddenly all sound ceased. It was uncanny how quickly and completely the rioting subsided. We could hear feet scurrying in the passageways, and once or twice a sharp command from Hale Harry Gard. I knew at once what it meant.

"They're coming for us," I said. I clasped in my hand the testament that Jore had given me. "This is the end. I'm not going to be taken alive, Jore."

He shook his head. I was surprised to see that the tense look on his face had been replaced by a smile of confidence. "John's coming," he declared. "Let's go up on deck. You will see I am right, Roger."

I was sure he was wrong, but I followed him to the waist. The whole ship was alive with activity. I saw the mate striding up and down and could sense a new note in his hoarse voice as he barked commands right and left. The women were being bundled unceremoniously down the ladders, where an inadequate number of small boats were waiting for them. Many of them were still naked and were carrying their clothes in bundles over their shoulders, squealing curses the while. Gard's handy bimster was leaving its mark on their flabby backs.

I began to take heart. Perhaps Jore was right after all. The preparations did not suggest an impending visit from officers of the law.

"Get to your stations, you sham-abrams!" roared the mate, when the last of the women had gone over the rail. "I'll have ye all in the garters if the Captain finds anything amiss!"

My relief was so great I could have shouted. So John was coming after all! I leaned over the rail and saw a boat breasting the waves. It carried a lantern on the prow which heaved and dipped with the motion of the water. Jore stood beside me and chattered excitedly in my ear.

"He gave them the slip," he exulted. "Trust the Captain for that. The sheriff has never been born to lay a hand on the shoulder of John Ward. I think I can see him, Roger. You'll find things different now. No more drinking or wenching. They'll be up in the shrouds and ready to set the tops'ls when the Captain gives the word. Look at Hale Harry! I believe he has sobered up already."

The boat reached the side, and I saw John Ward coming up the ladder. He was giving orders before a first heel had been cast over the rail.

"Gard!" he cried. "Break out the anchor! Are the tops'ls set? Let fall your mains'ls and on with the bonnet and drabbles."

He saw Jore and me and ran over to us. His heavy hand fell on my shoulder.

"Thank God, you made it, Roger!" he said. "I was afraid they had lagged you. Now I can get away with a free mind. I've a lot of news for you, but it will have to wait. There isn't a second to lose. Well, Joralemon, my doughty old soul-driver. I wouldn't have given a win for your chances either, and here you are with your peak braided and ready to go. No Paddington Fair for you this time, my old hell-raking Jore!"

He climbed to the poop-deck, three steps to the stride, bellowing orders at the top of his lungs. I did not dare follow him, but stood and watched in an immense upsurge of happiness. Jore was sniffling with relief.

"Gard, there's going to be weather," called John. "We've got to chance it. Get us away, man, get us away! Tallow the parrels! See that the ordinaries are lashed. Strike your top masts to the cap. Make them jump to it, Gard."

We got under way in what I was sure was record time. Joralemon called to me to go below, but nothing could have dragged me away from the rail. I was violently seasick already.

BOOK TWO

11

"Look!" exclaimed Joralemon Snode, pointing to the east where the sun was lighting up the blue waters of the Inner Sea. "So must the Ark of the Covenant have looked to the children of Israel when the Lord sent it back to them. There is a promise of help from on high in that mighty light. The Lord will be with us today."

"The Spaniards will be seeing the same sunrise," I pointed out, although nothing would have been more comforting than an assurance that He would be fighting on our side.

I had never before failed to respond to the glory of a sunrise over the Mediterranean, but this morning I had no eyes for it. A full hour earlier I had been roused by Gard's booming command, "Clear for action!" I had stumbled through the gun-deck, where sweating squads were loading and opening the gun-ports, to take my station in the waist. Now the deck of the *Royal Bess* was black with squatting men, the stillness of the morning disturbed by the low mutter of talk and the thump of pike butts on the planking. As soon as John Ward gave the order, we would issue out from behind the tall hills of the island where we now lay, and a Spanish ship-of-war from Barcelona would have an unpleasant surprise. If the Dons stood up to us, as we expected them to, I would have my baptism of fire. A nervous tapping against my side was proof that one vital organ at least was still functioning. Otherwise I felt as though a clumsy surgeon had removed everything from inside the basket formed by my ribs.

Joralemon moved along, his eyes fixed on the rising sun, seeing no doubt the dread mien of Jehovah in the wisps of vapor which drifted on the horizon. I stayed where I was, one of a glum group of four in the scuppers. My mind could not detach itself from what lay ahead. I wondered how it would feel if the end of a pike were driven through my ribs. Would I die at once, or would there be a long period of agony? How would it feel to run my own weapon between the ribs of a Spaniard? I really believe this second conjecture gave me the most concern. What kind of sound would it make? Would his eyes lay a curse on me before he died?

The other three were members of my watch, but I did not know the real names of any of them. They came out of the same pod, and sometimes I found it hard to tell them apart. There were, however, slight deviations of type between them, and on these differences nicknames had been tagged. One was called Maltworm because his absorption in the delights of drunkenness excelled that of his fellows in some small degree. The second carried the sobriquet of Dandyprat, due to his being somewhat less untidy in dress and habit. Clim the Cod's-head was the third. There was an especially naïve quality to his ignorance which made him stand out from the rest, dull clods though they were.

In all the dreaming I had done of the day when I would fight for the glory of Old England, it had never occurred to me that I would do so finally in the company of three such men as Maltworm, Dandyprat and Clim the Cod's-head.

"Clim," demanded Maltworm, breaking a long silence, "would ye rather fight a Spanisher or a Portugall?"

Clim thought this over with ponderous absorption. "A Portugall," he decided finally.

"Clim would rather fight a Portugall," announced Maltworm. He began to laugh. Why this should be funny I did not know, but apparently there was a humorous side to Clim's preference. The word passed down the deck, and everyone began to laugh. Clim joined in himself, proud of his accomplishment in stirring amusement among his mates. "Ay, a Portugall," he repeated.

The cook came along, carrying a bucket of brandy from which he ladled out drinks in a tin cup. The bite of the liquor on the well-gogged tongue of Maltworm stirred him to fresh loquacity.

"Shanks," he said to me, "mayhap ye're a-going to die today. Would ye rather have a pike head turned full around inside yer guts or a musket ball in yer belly?"

I had proof instantly that the sensation of emptiness inside me was a false one. My stomach turned completely over.

"If I'm going to die," I said, "I would rather die by a musket ball. In the head."

This remark had some strange capacity also to rouse the risibilities of my mates. "Shanks wants to 'ave 'is nab shot off," declared Maltworm, laughing uproariously. Everyone joined in. I could hear my words being repeated all along the deck, to the accompaniment of loud guffaws and much slapping of muscular thighs.

"There's a gentry-cove for ye!" commented Dandyprat. "'E doesn't want to be all messed up. 'E wants to die easy and clean."

I was not surprised at the level of the talk. John had abandoned me completely to the not at all tender mercies of Hale Harry Gard, and I had been assigned to a watch which included my three present companions. For four months I had been listening to this kind of thing and wondering if in time I would come to be like the rest of them. Everything about the life had been hard; but this, I think, had been the hardest.

I had lived and worked as the others did, but with the one privilege of having a berth to myself. The meals were coarse and monotonous, salt pork and sea biscuit being the backbone of every meal. The stench of the galley from which this food was brought to us in iron kettles never left my nostrils. The crew were a rough lot, suspicious, vindictive, foul-mouthed, but peculiarly childlike in certain respects. They talked of nothing but fighting, drinking, and the sex habits of native women. There was no fire of patriotic spirit in them, no deep feeling for self-sacrifice in a glorious cause. When I spoke of England's destiny on the seas, they looked at me with dull eyes and jeered obscenely. They had all joined up for a chance to pocket Spanish gold.

In spite of the doubts John had expressed that night when we walked to Appleby Court, he had done nothing to smooth my path. He believed, no doubt, that Gard's methods would harden me quickly to the ways of the sea. But, as I sat on the deck this morning and waited for what lay ahead of us, I knew that the method had failed. Each day had found me withdrawing inside myself more and more. The mate had exceeded whatever orders he had received. When I was not on duty with the watch, he had kept me busy with menial tasks. I had washed dishes in the stinking galley and had scrubbed decks until my back was ready to break in two. I had even been set to cleaning out the croppin-ken, a malodorous corner of the orlop-deck with crude sketches on the walls and proofs everywhere of the carelessness of sailors. I had said to myself on this occasion: You may not like it, Roger Blease, but never forget that this is the one and only path to glory. They've all been through it—John himself and, in their day, Drake and Cavendish and perhaps even Christopher Columbus. Why should your stomach rebel at doing what these great men had to do? But, unfortunately, my stomach did rebel. Try as I might, I could not overcome my squeamishness.

John's words of warning had been amply borne out. If I had been asked how I liked it at sea, I would have declared as stoutly as I could manage that it was the only life for a man. But down in my heart there was a different answer. I knew now that I was not cut to the measure of a sailor. Perhaps it was the soft Pirie strain in me which made me shrink from the work I had to do under the gimlet eyes of the mate and from the contacts with my messmates. My hands were calloused and covered with jagged cuts. My shoulders were black and blue from the impact of the bimster. The purely physical effects were not the worst, however. I could take the hardships, although there were times when, through sheer weariness, I could have wept. It was what these four months had done inside me which had convinced me of the truth.

There had been two sources of consolation for me: the company and friendly guidance of Joralemon and an intense interest in gunnery. I had a knack for mechanical things, and I had spent every spare moment on the gun-deck, studying the great iron monsters and learning what I could about the handling of them. The Master was always glad to have me there, for I helped him in many ways. I soon learned to set a true dispart on the muzzle-rings, and I could figure the degrees of randon in my head while he was chalking them out painfully on the side of a gun carriage.

My spirits had gone up the night before when the word had passed around that a Spanish ship-of-war was due our way. At last I should see some action. On the two previous occasions when the *Royal Bess* had come within sight of Castilian sails I had been in hospital, but I had shared in the general disappointment of the crew when the Dons had shown clean heels.

There was sudden commotion. Gard came down the ladder from the poop deck. "We're off!" said Maltworm. "The mate's got his orders from Captain Rufflecoat."

Gard began to bawl at us, and the crew scrambled to their stations. We were putting out to sea. The feeling at the pit of my stomach tightened. I thought of what Maltworm had said: "Maybe ye're a-going to die today." Suddenly I was sure of it. A musket ball would find its mark, and I would not be there to see the Spaniard strike his colors.

The mate had changed in some unaccountable way. I had never seen him completely sober before, but now I would have sworn he had not touched a drop. His eyes had lighted up, and there was a clear and exultant note in his voice. Had the prospect of battle done this to him?

"The great day at last, Shanks," he said, dropping a heavy hand on my shoulder. He actually smiled. "I'm expecting to see ye show yer mettle today. The Captain said to send ye up to him."

I could have shouted with relief. John had sent for me at last. He had not spoken to me for a month at least, and I had been more than half afraid that I was condemned for all time to the company of Maltworm, Dandyprat, and Clim the Cod's-head. Perhaps the days of my apprenticeship were over.

John was in the steering room, making some calculations on the traverse board. He had arrayed himself in smoke-colored velvet with touches of pink in the folds of his sleeves and breeches. Only the fact that he was wearing breastplates and a steel helmet gave any hint of the business in hand. He looked up and nodded.

"You're looking fit, Roger," he said. "How much weight have you put on?"

"Half a stone, Captain Ward," I answered.

"I would have guessed more. There isn't a single wrinkle in your hose. I've done that much for you, at any rate." He laid down the dividers and smiled at me. "Has it been hard, Roger?"

"Hard enough."

"The worst is over now, I think. Gard tells me you can climb the shrouds like a yonker, and that you know a sprits'l from a clew-garnet. All that's left is to make a fighting man of you, and I judge that won't be difficult. How do you feel about this little venture we're trying today?"

I managed to smile. "I'll be right enough if I can control my stomach."

John laughed. "Don't let that worry you. I spewed all over the deck when we caught the first glimpse of the sails of the Armada. It's the usual thing, Roger. You'll get over it fast enough when we come to grips with the sallow-faced devils. I have just one word of advice for you if it comes to hand-to-hand fighting today. They're shifty, the Dons. When you square up to your man, watch his eyes. He'll always look where he's going to thrust. Remember that, and you'll have better than an even chance of coming through with a whole skin."

"Will they fight us this time?"

"Yes. They won't dog it today." His eyes began to glow with an almost fanatical light. "We're going to match strength with one of their largest ships, the *Santa Caterina*. Does that name mean anything to you? It should. The *Santa Caterina* it was that captured the *Trial*. She's setting out for the Cape Verde Islands, according to the reports I received. And mark this, Roger: Don Pedro Alonzo Maria de Vente is still in command, the gallant gentleman who strung our poor fellows up by the wrists, and put them to the rack, and then hanged what was left of them at the yardarm. We have a score to settle with Don Pedro. I'm not going to be content until I've seen his well-shod heels dancing on thin air."

I began to share his eagerness. It was the tragedy of the *Trial* which had convinced me I should go to sea with John Ward. My stomach seemed to have settled down.

"Are they carrying any gold?" I asked.

John shook his head. "Not likely. The Spaniards never take gold to the West. They bring it back from there. It's revenge we're looking for this time, not booty. Satisfaction in the name of all England for a great wrong done to us."

He picked up his instruments again and continued with his work. "Roger," he said, after a moment, "I don't want anything to happen to you today. Mistress Blease would never forgive me. And there is Katie to think of as well."

"I want to take my chances with the rest of you."

"You'll get your share of the fighting, of course. But I meant what I said, Roger. I promised Katie to look after you."

This put me on my mettle. I did not like to think that Katie had confided my safety to his care. I could look after myself. "It was kind of her to think of me," I said stiffly. "I don't believe it would matter much to her now."

John glanced up from his work. "You can never tell about women," he said. "Katie is young. Just turned sixteen, isn't she?"

"Her birthday was ten days ago."

"I was a romantic figure in her eyes," said John. "Time may make quite a difference. When you go back to England and they build bonfires for you, who can tell what may happen? You'll be handsomely togged out, and you'll have an ostrich plume in your hat, and everyone will think you a great hero. Perhaps Katie may decide then that she preferred you all the time. She must have her chance to decide, you know. And then there's the possibility that I may never be able to return to England." His eyes went back to the traverse board. "We must stick together today, Roger. If I get in trouble, you'll help me out. I'll do the same for you. What do you say?"

"I joined for the chance to fight with you, John!" I said fervently.

He overlooked my lapse. "That's the talk I like. Between us we'll strike a few shrewd blows for England. We'll even the score for those poor fellows on the *Trial*."

He walked out to the quarter-deck, and I followed, full of pride and with eagerness for what lay ahead. My stomach felt better. The *Royal Bess* had maneuvered out from under the shelter of the island and had taken a northern course. A brisk datoo, blowing in from the Straits, had filled our sails. John shaded his eyes and scanned the horizon.

"There she is!" he exclaimed, pointing straight ahead. "The *Santa Caterina!* Just as I figured. Don Pedro is coming on with a full head of sail. Coming like a bridegroom in his finest attire and with a heart full of arrogance and pride."

All trace of fear had left me. I strained my eyes at the spread of orange sails in the distance. I thought of the *Trial* and could hardly wait for the fighting to begin. It was a bracing day, and the air was like wine. I drank it in with gusty eagerness.

"We have him!" exulted John. "He's hooked like a Yarmouth capon. This is the first of March, and Don Pedro is offering us a fine Taffy Day prize."

He was staring at our prospective foe, his feet spread wide apart, his blue eyes dancing with excitement. Every minute seemed to diminish the distance between the two ships. Don Pedro had no fear of us, for he had clapped on more canvas. I could now make out the red and yellow standard flapping proudly at his peak. The *Santa Caterina* looked enormous, standing high out of the water and with the most majestic spread of sail I had ever seen. Her decks and rigging were alive with men.

"What do you think of our chances, my kinchin coe?" asked John, turning to me with a grin.

"These tall ships are all crank-sided," I declared, drawing on the nautical lore I had been picking up in the fo'c's'le. "We can sail all around her. If we can get in close enough, she'll fire right over us."

"Right!" cried John. "When you look at the *Royal Bess* by herself, she stands up like the Tower of Babel; but against this top-heavy specimen of Spanish pride she seems trim and low. They never learn anything, the Dons. They seem to think the art of shipbuilding is to get as near as they can to the cruel God they worship. We'll teach them a few things today. We'll rip her guts with lead and get no worse in return than a few holes in our tops'ls. And there may be a few yellow boys rolling around in her coffers after all. You may find your pockets heavy with Spanish ribbin before the day's out."

The Spaniard came on, a perfect picture of confidence. We were ready for him. Our gun crews were at their posts, and the yonkers aloft had their muskets loaded and set. The boarding party lined the sides, swishing their cutlasses or beating an eager tattoo with the butts of their pikes. Hale Harry Gard seemed to be in a dozen places at once, bellowing orders, bulldozing, cautioning. I began to feel an unwilling admiration for him.

The Dons fired first, and jets of water spouted up a full hundred yards ahead of us. John snorted in disgust at such waste and shouted an order to the mate. I had expected we would race in to close quarters, but instead we clewed up and waited.

"If they want to spend themselves shooting at an impossible target, I am ready to give them a chance," said John.

The guns of the enemy continued to roar. They were doing us no harm, but it takes both fortitude and patience to play target, and I could see our men were growing impatient. The voices of the yonkers demanded that we "give it back to the bloody Faggoters." We were now at closer range, and a single shot crashed into the side of our pilot-house, filling the air with splinters. The cutlass which John had given me suddenly became too heavy to hold. My arm felt limp. The feeling of nausea returned. Now that the supreme test was ahead, I doubted if I would be able to meet it. Could I muster up the strength and the heart to follow John up the side of that towering wall of wood, and face the slash and cut of steel which would greet us at the top? I was far from sure of myself. I realized how little I wanted to die.

What followed will always remain in my mind as a mad and utterly fantastic dream. The *Santa Caterina* had swung in close, cutting off the wind. Our guns roared for the first time, tearing holes in the proud hull. We were so near that I could hear the screams of the wounded on the gun-deck of the enemy. The Spanish guns were useless now, but they continued to vomit shot which tore through our rigging.

"Don Pedro will dance a lively lavolta at the yardarm!" exulted John. "My foot must be the first to touch his deck. Follow right along, Roger. Jump when I give the word."

I looked up and shuddered. The Spanish guns seemed right above us, sticking out like the heads of angry black serpents, spitting venom. My ears throbbed with the pressure of the sound. I realized that the real danger now came from the small-arm men in the enemy rigging who were raining lead on us. One of our tops'l-men crashed down from above, striking full on the rail of the poop-deck and straightening out like a bow before plunging into the water. His blood splattered over me.

"Truss up your bullions!" cried John in a high and unnatural voice.

"We're going over! There'll be a hemp-widow in Spain this night, or I'll be a dead man myself!"

The grappling irons had shackled the two great swaying hulls together. The waist of the Spaniard was six feet above the rail of our own poop-deck. I saw John grasp a carved projection and swing himself up. His feet dangled for a moment above my head, and then he was over.

I knew that I must follow him, but not a muscle could I move. It was as though a paralysis had gripped me. The agonizing thought took possession of my mind: I'm a coward. I haven't the courage to face death. Now the terrible truth is out. I had always turned giddy when facing any kind of a climb, and I knew that what I feared most was the danger of falling. I looked up, and it seemed as though the canvas of the two ships had merged, forming a solid sheet of orange shot through with the flash of musket fire like forks of lightning. The ships jarred apart and then came together again with a grinding crash. Without any knowledge of how it had happened, I found myself clinging to a raised beam, my feet dangling in space. My cutlass was in my teeth. My fingers gripped the wood desperately, and I knew that if they failed me I would be crushed between the hulls or fall into the churning waves below.

The stimulus of mortal fear caused me to heave my body up. I caught the rail with one hand and hung on desperately. The end would come soon, for I had no power to climb further and I knew that I could not cling here much longer. The strain on my arms was almost unbearable.

I felt the ship sway and feared the motion would dislodge me from my desperate position. Instinctively I heaved myself forward again. The motion of the vessel aided my effort to climb. I found myself astride the rail.

I could see John ahead of me, cutting and slashing with his long sword, a ring of Spaniards pressing in on him. As my feet touched the slippery deck, I had a momentary flash of the inevitable end. I saw myself lying in the scuppers, and in agonized imagination I could feel the rip of steel in my throat.

A face loomed up in front of me, a yellow face with wildly distended eyes. I lunged with my blade, and the face disappeared. Others took its place. I lunged and cut and thrust, without any conscious thought of direction or control. What had John said about their eyes? I could not remember. There were eyes all about me, mad, furious, frightening eyes. There was nothing to be done about them but to strike when they came close enough. My arm became weak with the effort, and I was sure after each stroke that I would be unable to go on. But I knew that I had to go on fighting if I wanted to live, if I wanted to keep those hostile eyes away from me. I was gasping like a gaffed fish, sick with the effort; but my arm continued its nerveless work.

Suddenly the pressure about me eased. The ring of eyes fell back. I was conscious that I no longer stood alone, that other blades had joined mine. I slumped back against the railing and clung there weakly, gasping for breath. My cutlass point touched the deck.

Our men were all over the place now. I could hear them cursing bitterly as they drove against the line of defenders. One man was chanting, "Death to the dogs of the Inquisition!" Another man was singing the words of "Bold Francis Drake." They moved ahead steadily. I began to feel better. Strength came into my arm, and I raised my cutlass again. A fighting rage took possession of me. I shouted the first line of the Drake song and rushed in to help.

The solid front of the enemy had broken by this time, and the nature of the fighting had changed. Individual duels had become the order, and I could see that we were getting the better of it. The rain of bullets from above had ceased, for the Spanish marksmen could no longer distinguish friend from foe.

I saw the towering figure of our captain a few paces ahead of me and knew a feeling of relief that he had come through so far. He was engaging a thickset Spanish officer. When a second antagonist came at him from one side, I ran in to lend what aid I could. John glanced over his shoulder when the second man turned to meet me.

"Thanks, Roger," he called.

My man seemed to have little heart left for the struggle. He gave ground before my wild thrusts and finally dropped his sword, raising his arms in token of surrender. It did him no good, however, for a pike lunged over my shoulder, catching him squarely between the eyes. His face seemed to split open like a ripe apple and when the point was withdrawn he crumpled up. He fell forward, his head squashing against my knee. I glanced back and saw that the blow had been struck by Clim the Cod's-head. Clim was blubbering in a furious fighting rage. "They got Dandyprat!" he muttered. "A splinter in his belly. They'll pay for it, Shanks. A dozen of them to pay for Dandyprat!"

A gap had opened in front of me, and I saw the black muzzle of a portable gun pointed in my direction. A Spanish soldier was behind it with a lighted fuze, while another was shoving it forward on a long iron pintle. In a moment the gun would vomit lead through our ranks.

I closed my eyes, expecting the next moment to be my last. Then I heard a shout and opened my eyes to see the pike in Clim's hands cut down the gunner. The ship gave a heave, and the gun slid across the deck, crushing the body of the fallen Spaniard against the bulwarks. Clim had saved my life, but I had no chance to thank him then. His berserk rage had already carried him farther along the deck, his pike flailing in lethal sweeps.

I learned later that this first phase of the struggle, which decided the day, was a short one. It had lasted a very few minutes, although it stayed in my mind as an almost endless fury of stroke and counterstroke. I saw now that the Spanish soldiers were giving in with what

appeared to be suspicious haste. They wanted no more of it. All over
the place they were dropping their arms and pleading for mercy.

The second phase, which consisted of putting down sporadic resistance, took considerably longer. It was waged below deck, for the most
part, where small squads were hunted down and disarmed. Hale Harry
Gard was in charge of this operation, while John took on himself the
task of clearing the Spaniards from the rigging.

My share of the fighting was over. John gave me an approving pat
on the back and told me to stay with him. The order came just in time.
Now that the excitement had subsided, my stomach was beginning to
assert itself again at the sight of dead bodies wherever we went. Blood
was running in the scuppers like filth in a London sewer. I followed
our captain from bow to stern, keeping my eyes averted as much as
possible but seeing nevertheless many strange and disturbing things. I
saw a tall Spanish officer, whose sword had been broken, scorn the
summons to surrender and defend himself bravely with a belaying pin,
only to go down as I passed from a ferocious stroke of Clim's pike.
Clim, it seemed, had not yet wiped off the score and was fighting on
in a blind rage. I saw the bodies of a dozen or more of our men which
had been hastily collected in one heap with an English flag spread
over them. I saw a score of brown-skinned slaves break loose from
below and come gibbering at us for mercy. They were as thin as scarecrows and covered with sores. A water cask at the foot of the mainmast
had been punctured by many bullets and was spouting thin streams of
water like the fountain on Shrubsole High on the Queen's birthday. I
saw a priest with one side of his head broken by a musket ball administering the sacrament to dying men. Finally, I saw a family of kittens
in a basket outside the cook's galley. They had slept peacefully through
it all.

The Spanish captain had surrendered his sword early and was being
held on the poop-deck. John waited until Gard reported that all resistance below was over and then went up. A curious tableau greeted
us there. Don Pedro Alonzo Maria de Vente was seated in an X chair
with his feet on a velvet cushion. This seemed a strange affectation for
a captain who had struck his colors and whose ship was running with
the blood of his men. He was most handsomely attired in plum-colored satin. A group of his officers stood back of his chair and watched
us with haughty but uneasy eyes. Behind the officers were several women,
one a young and beautiful girl. I judged the girl to be of gentle birth,
for she also was seated and she had a plump servingwoman at her
elbow. She was the only one in the group whose eyes reflected defiance
without a trace of fear.

In spite of my upset condition, I found myself watching this girl
with active curiosity. She was small and slim, with a proud arch to
her nose and the longest of lashes to shade her dark eyes. Little as I
liked the Spanish race, I had to concede that she was the loveliest

woman I had ever seen. Her servant was young and in a swarthy way attractive also.

The vanquished commander rose and bowed when John appeared on the deck. To do so he had first to detach a small monkey which had been perched on his shoulder. The little animal felt the tension, for it whimpered and curled its tail around the arm of the chair.

"You are Don Pedro Alonzo Maria de Vente," said John, acknowledging the bow with a curt nod. I was glad now that Aunt Gadilda had insisted on my Spanish studies, for I was able to follow what was said. John had picked up his knowledge of the tongue in the course of his continuous sea campaigning. He spoke it with an accent all his own.

"I am," answered the Grandee. "I have the honor of serving as admiral in the navy of His Serene Majesty. And you are John Ward."

"Captain Ward, if you please. Sir Admiral, it has come to my ears that you captured an English merchantman some months back. It was named the *Trial*."

I detected a shade of anxiety on the swarthy face of the Spaniard as he bowed in affirmation.

John's voice boomed out in stern accusation. "The *Trial* was engaged in honest trade, and she was manned by a crew of sixteen. Where are those men, Don Pedro?"

The admiral wet his lips nervously. "The vessel in question had been preying on Spanish shipping, a fact established by the depositions of several members of her crew. They were dealt with as befitted their crime."

"You lie, Don Pedro!" cried John. "Those depositions were wrung from my unfortunate countrymen by torture, and the few survivors were then hanged in defiance of all the laws of God and man. I should balance this grievous wrong by hanging sixteen of the subjects of His Serene Majesty. But would it be fair to punish your men, who acted in obedience to orders? I've no desire to mete out Spanish justice. The guilt rests on your shoulders, Don Pedro Alonzo Maria de Vente, and I've decided that you alone shall pay the penalty for this crime."

I had always heard that the noblemen of Spain were as brave as they were cruel. Don Pedro apparently was cast in a less heroic mold. He became a sickly white at John's words.

"Captain Ward," he stuttered, "I acted in accordance with my instructions. I am a prisoner of war, and I demand honorable treatment as befits my rank."

"You're a murderer with the blood of innocent men on your hands!" declared John. "It's my intention to treat you as such. A few minutes will be allowed you to make your peace with your God."

The group about the Admiral stirred. Don Pedro's lieutenants were brave men but, lacking arms, there was nothing they could do in his defense. The girl sprang to her feet and advanced several yards in our direction.

"You will not dare lay a hand on an admiral of Spain!" she cried. "Even an English pirate would not be guilty of such a crime!"

John seemed to be aware of her for the first time. He looked at her intently. Her eyes had become larger and darker with the intensity of her emotion. A black lace shawl, which she had worn on her hair, had slipped to her shoulders.

"Madame," said John, bowing to her gravely, "I'm not at all happy in this duty which has devolved on me. I'm a sailor, not a hangman. And I am being most lenient, I think. One life for sixteen? Surely that is fair enough." He looked scornfully at Don Pedro, who seemed on the point of collapse. "A poor life at that, Madame. The men who were butchered by his orders were stanch and honest sailors with wives and children at home. He showed no pity for them."

"I have been taught to hate the English," declared the girl. "Now that I have seen you, I understand why. In spite of your fine clothes, Sir Pirate, you are nothing but a blaspheming heretic and a butcher."

"I'm sorry you think so badly of me. Particularly as the only course open to me will increase your antipathy."

"Would it do any good if I begged you for my uncle's life?"

"Madame, my duty is clear."

The servingwoman, her black eyes as full of blazing defiance as those of her mistress, ran up to him and shook her fists in his face, pouring out a torrent of abuse. John gave a few feet and smiled tolerantly.

"Well," he said, "I'm gaining a high opinion of the spirit of the women of Spain. It might be better for His Serene Majesty if he were to entrust his fine ships to them. Still, I can't allow justice to be delayed any longer." He turned to the cringing Don Pedro. "Sir Admiral, I shall be as gentle with you as I can. In your last moments your feet will rest on a softer cushion than that dainty piece of velvet. Perhaps they will dance as lively a measure as the ignoble feet of those poor fellows on the *Trial*."

"You cannot hang me!" cried Don Pedro. "I am of noble birth. I demand a hearing!"

John laughed at this and turned to Harry Gard. I saw for the first time that the mate had brought a ram on deck and was holding it on a tight rein. The animal was huge, and Gard was having his troubles with it.

"He demands a hearing," said John. "Very well, he shall have it. The same kind of hearing he gave the poor purser of the *Trial*. The evidence you got from my countrymen, Don Pedro, was forced evidence. It was extracted from them when they could no longer endure the agonies of a Spanish hearing. The position now is somewhat different, I'm glad to say. I aim to extract the truth from you, not lies. Since you have demanded it, we will now string you up by the wrists and permit this mute assistant of your judicial proceedings to refresh your memory by the points of his horns. Tie cannon balls to his ankles first, Gard. We must follow his practice on all points. I think, Don Pedro, you'll not delay long in acknowledging that the evidence you wrung from those poor sailors was false and that you had no other proofs on which to hang them. Then I shall have every right to hang you in turn. I am very glad you raised the point. It will be more regular this way."

"No, no!" cried the Admiral. "For the love of God, not that! You must give me time to explain. My officers will bear me out."

"He's changed his mind," said John. "Never mind the weights, Gard. He doesn't want a hearing, after all. Not the kind of hearing he thought fit for others. He doesn't seem to think well of Spanish justice."

"Sir," said the girl, wringing her hands, "grant him a chance to explain. He will convince you, I am sure. I fear the harsh things I said have hardened your resolution. If that is true, I beg you to forget them. I humbly crave your pardon."

"I'm influenced only by the known facts of his crime," declared John, in solemn tones. "Truss him up, Gard. We have no more time to waste."

I kept my eyes on the deck for the next fifteen minutes, not daring to watch the proceedings. I heard the scuffling of feet as Gard and several members of the crew pinioned the wildly protesting nobleman, the bitter protestations of the other prisoners, the screams of the women. I noticed that the purple cap of the monkey had fallen off, and I tried desperately to rivet my attention on the frightened animal. However, I knew when the victim had been propelled to the yardarm by the silence which fell suddenly. The wind had freshened, I decided, for the deck began to heave. I felt much sicker now than I had before scaling the hull of the *Santa Caterina*.

A priest was saying a prayer in Latin. I heard the Spanish officers whispering among themselves. I could see out of one corner of my eye that John was standing rigidly to attention.

I looked up once and regretted it instantly. I caught a glimpse of Don Pedro's squat figure twisting and turning at the end of the rope. His movements, as John had predicted, were grotesquely similar to the sudden hops of the lavolta. I felt a sense of shame that I could think of such a thing while a man was dying.

I am sure there can be nothing harder to watch than a hanging, for it is so apparent that the victim is dying painfully. A reedy whistling was the only sound to be heard, and I knew it came from the throat of the strangling grandee. My own throat felt so constricted that I clutched it with one hand. Someone collapsed on the deck, and my first thought was that it must be the Spanish girl. Out of the tail of my eye, however, I saw that the prostrate figure was that of her servingwoman. Her many colored petticoats were spread out in all directions. The sensation of nausea in my stomach became so acute that I gulped deeply in an effort to keep my windpipe full of fresh air. Someone near me was sobbing.

It seemed an interminable time before I heard John say in a relieved voice, "Well, it seems to be over. Cut him down, Gard."

I looked up then and could see nothing but the eyes of the Spanish girl. They were filled with the deepest horror, but there was still no trace of fear in them. John began to speak.

"I want to express again my great regret that this ugly duty fell to my lot. The man who has just died was guilty of a great wrong and richly deserved his fate. What I have done is the answer of Englishmen to the policy of the King of Spain, who has declared that death waits any of our sailors who fall into his hands. The murder of a whole crew has been avenged. Now, Gard, get the men to their posts. A hard day's work is ahead of us."

The voice of the mate exploded in a series of orders. There was a rush of feet. It seemed to me that Gard had reverted already to the tyrant of the main deck, and I would not have been surprised to feel the cut of his ready bimster when I failed to jump at his bidding. I paid no attention, however. I had one thought only, an overwhelming desire to be back in my quiet home off Shrubsole High, training myself for a gentler manner of life than this.

12

I HAD BEEN SURE that relaxation would follow victory, but I soon discovered my mistake. For the rest of the day every man left alive labored incessantly. Part of the crew, under Mate Gard, returned aboard the *Royal Bess*. Brandy was passed around to the rest of us, and then we were divided into two squads, one to work on repairs to the ship, the other to dispose of the bodies and scrub the decks free of blood. I was assigned to the second.

I was still feeling too sick to do more than wield a careless mop, and I paid little attention to the rumors which spread among my companions. The stories they passed back and forth were made out of whole cloth for the most part.

"I hear the Don's pockets was stuffed full of diamonts," declared Maltworm, pausing from his work to straighten his back. "What good will they be at the bottom of the sea? I could make good use of some of them myself."

"There's plenty to be had from the rest of them," contributed another man. "The Cap'n should have the lot of them searched."

Maltworm snickered. "Shanks," he asked, "how would ye like to search that Spanish gel?"

Someone volunteered the information that the girl was a niece of the hanged man and a very great lady. That interested me, and I raised the question as to what Captain Ward would do with her. My question met with a chorus of guffaws. "What will he do with 'er?" said Maltworm. "That's a good one, that is. Was ye thinking he might pass 'er around after he's through with 'er? Not our Captain Rufflecoat!"

The report that aroused the most discussion had to do with the finding of some instruments of torture in the hold. My companions went after this one in full hue and cry and before long had convinced themselves that the ship was filled with thumbscrews and racks to be set up in England. From that they drew the belief that a new Armada was being organized and that the King of Spain had sworn to stretch English bones until every man, woman, and child was six feet tall.

Clim joined us while they were still engaged in these speculations, and I took advantage of the chance to thank him for saving my life. It took him a full minute to recall what had happened. Then he grinned and said: "It were nothing, Shanks. I couldn't lose two friends on one day, now could I?"

The big, slow-thinking fellow regarded me as a friend! I looked at him with new interest and realized for the first time that there was a steady light in his eyes which made me think of a faithful dog. The resemblance went further, for he had the lumbering frame of a mastiff, and his heavy jaw was not unlike the muzzle of that sturdy animal. I found myself liking him very much.

The talk had veered to the possibility of finding gold on board. Maltworm was sure there was plenty of it.

"I know what I'll do with my share of the yellow boys," he declared. "I'll set me up in a tidy little pub outside Rome-ville on the Turkish side of the river. I'm going to drink up the best of the stock myself. What will ye do with yours, Clim?"

Clim was still too concerned over the death of Dandyprat to think in terms of booty. He did not answer for a moment.

"I can't get the sight of him out of my head," he said finally. "He were such a jolly one, and there I see him with his belly tore wide open. I rather have Dandyprat alive than all the gold in Chiny."

The talk came back to the women on the ship, and then Clim brightened up. He had definite ideas on the woman question. He liked them big and fat and "not too peery." In fact, he already had his eye on one of the captives. Under questioning, he divulged that it was the buxom maidservant.

Around noon orders reached me to report at once in the captain's cabin, and I straightened up with a sigh of relief. My companions were sure this meant that the discussion of rewards was to begin.

"Put in a word for me, Shanks," said Clim. "None o' these little monkeys for me. I want a long-meg."

"I want my share of the yellow boys," decided Maltworm. "And a bottle of the best wine. You can have the women, Clim."

I gave a gasp of astonishment when I set foot in the main cabin. It was almost as grand as the great hall at Appleby Court. It was a long, high-ceilinged apartment with magnificently carved wainscoting and majestic beams, lighted by three bronze lamps and innumerable candle sconces along the walls. I had little time to take in details, but I saw on the far wall a clock with a face of solid gold to represent the sun. A sideboard glittered with gold plate. I recognized a somber painting as a portrait of Philip of Spain. Even the bell pulls were made of cloth of gold and embroidered with what I believed were real pearls. In the center of the room was a table heaped up with letters and documents.

John was seated at the far end, and to my great surprise I saw that the Spanish girl was with him. Her women hovered near them, keeping a look of black hostility on our tall captain. The girl was speaking when I entered, and it was clear from the tone of her voice that she was subjecting him to a bitter indictment. John was watching her closely, and there was a hint of a smile around the lines of his mouth. He got up at once and joined me at the door.

"Roger, I think you read Spanish well enough," he said in a whisper. "I've some work for you. These papers are to be looked over."

I nodded, finding myself disinclined to raise my voice in this cathedrallike room. I was watching the girl, who had turned her head away from us. Her hair was black with the faintest hint of red, and she had made no effort to dress it high on her head in the prevailing mode. It hung low about her ears in the most charming disorder.

"Every scrap of paper on board has been collected," went on John, nodding in the direction of the table. "There will be plenty of information in the lot, and I want it sifted through. There isn't much time for it. Three other ships-of-war are within striking distance, and I may have to scuttle the *Caterina* and run for it. Get right at it, my fine scholar, and see what gold you can cull from all this dross."

I followed him into the room, looking about me with growing wonder.

"Dona Cristina," said John, in a tone which seemed to me to carry a hint of amusement, "you think so badly of all Englishmen that I hesitate to introduce one of them to you. However, this is Roger Blease, who belongs to one of the best families of Kent—the least barbarous part of our island—and who's a scholar as well as a gentleman. This interruption to our pleasant conversation is necessary because Mr. Blease is to examine these papers."

The girl turned her head in my direction but made no other response to the introduction. Her eyes were cold and hard.

"You have letters of mine there," she said. "They are personal and of no possible value to you. Is it in your power to understand that I would rather not have them read and passed around?"

"Even an Englishman can appreciate your desire," answered John, with a wink for my benefit. "They shall be kept from the scrutiny of our rude and unlettered eyes. When you find Dona Cristina's letters, Roger, lay them aside in a separate pile. They're to be returned to her unread."

"You treat me as though I were a child!" protested the girl. "I find this condescension as hard to bear as the proofs you have given us of your barbarity."

"On the contrary, I'm only too well aware that you're a beautiful woman. I have at the moment no thought save a most sincere desire to do everything in my power for your comfort and your ease of mind." He seated himself and smiled encouragingly. "And now, Dona Cristina, if you care to proceed with the recital of all my iniquities, I'm prepared to listen."

"I have nothing further to say," she asserted haughtily. "I came to make a plea on behalf of my fellow prisoners. They know you are sailing to Tunis, and they fear you will turn them over to the Turks. That I beseech you not to do."

"I have no such intention."

The conversation between them went on for a long time. Seated at the far end of the table and busy at my task, I made no effort to follow what was being said. Her tones ran the scale from stormy protest to a restrained form of feminine pleading. John's responses never seemed to vary and conveyed a hint of mockery. Once, as I skimmed through a sheaf of orders for naval supplies with a casual eye, I heard him remark: "I can't believe you despise me as much as you say. I've been fighting for many years, and in that time I've learned one lesson. Individuals can maintain normal relationships even when their countries are at war. You're Spanish, Dona Cristina, and so represent a race which has done my country and my people great harm. I've been raised to hate Spain and everything she represents, and yet the only feeling I have for you is one of the greatest admiration. In fact, I find the light in your eyes quite devastating. If we had met under different circumstances, I would be eager to prove my devotion."

What would Katie Ladland think of that speech? I said to myself.

It was apparent from the first that in the mass of material there would be much of value to us. There were orders from the Escurial which proved the hostile intentions of Spain and the unalterable determination of Philip to bar the English and Dutch from the seas. I found extracts from the reports of Gondomar, Spanish ambassador to England, in which the peace between the two countries was treated lightly as a means to an end, and from which Spain was to reap all the benefit. There were specific references to the pensions paid by Philip to the ministers of James. These I laid carefully aside. I found also that Madrid was following closely the affairs of the English trading concerns, the companies formed to operate in Muscovy, Virginia, and the Levant and the newly formed East India Company in particular. There was full information on the size and number of their ships, one memorandum giving details of the new leviathan of the sea, the *Trade's Increase*, which had recently been launched by the East India Company, with King James officiating. I found references to the prisoner in the Tower and the possibility of hardening the heart of James so that he would send Raleigh to the block.

I became so absorbed in my work that I did not hear when the others left the room. Becoming aware finally that all talk had ceased, I looked up and saw that I had the room to myself. I indulged for a moment in speculation about John and the Spanish girl. She likes him, I said to myself. In spite of everything, she was as much taken with him as my poor Katie was.

Piles of valuable documents kept accumulating while the floor around me became white with discarded notes and letters. I located Dona Cristina's personal mail and laid it aside. I found many official references to her as well. Her name was Cristina Isabella de Vente. Her mother being dead and her father continuously abroad in the colonial service, she had been educated in a convent at Seville. She had reached the decision a few months before that duty prompted her to join her father at Trinidad. This had created much discussion in court circles and been the cause of an interminable number of royal orders. The King had been opposed at first, having had it in his mind to select a husband for her from among the grandees of his court. Only the insistence of the girl herself had won a grudging consent from Philip. I located a memorandum on the jewelry she was taking with her and whistled aloud at the value of it.

The afternoon wore away, and I worked on alone, finding constant matters for speculation in the mass of documents; and increasingly glad in my mind that a knowledge of the language had been forced on me. By four o'clock it was dark in the cabin, and I found it necessary to detach a candle from its sconce and place it on the table. The candle was shaped like the Mexican serpent god, and I examined it closely. I decided it belonged in this setting, for it seemed to me cruel, strange, and sinister, all of which qualities belonged certainly to the conquerors of America. But my interest in the tallow god vanished when I chose from the dwindling pile a yellowish sheet covered with the scrawling penmanship of the defunct Don Pedro, and my eye chanced to focus on the word *Trial*. It turned out to be a copy of the report the Admiral had made on the capture of that ship and the disposition of the crew. My excitement mounted as I read it, for Don Pedro had told the story with complete candor. His guilt was abundantly established.

With this discovery in hand, I hurried out in search of John. The

sound of axes and hammers came from all directions. I saw that some
of the prisoners had been pressed into service. Our head carpenter, a
gaunt North Country man known as Shaves, was directing the work.

"Where is Captain Ward?"

Shaves opened an almost toothless mouth in a broad grin. "He wur
cagging wi' Spanish gel," he said, "but noo he be below wi' nim-
gimmer."

I entered the cockpit with hesitation, realizing from the appalling
sight which greeted me that my stomach would be put to a severe
test. There were still at least a score of men waiting their turns, all of
them stripped naked and rolling in agony on hard benches. I saw
bodies which had been torn by cannon shot or lacerated by flying
splinters; faces which had been reduced to bloody masks by the slash
of cutlass or the impact of pike; the bleeding stumps of legs and arms.
All this seemed more horrible than the mutilated corpses I had helped
to throw overboard, for inside these mangled husks the spark of life
still stirred. The stench of the place was unbelievable.

The screams and groans of the unfortunate men mingled with the almost frenzied orders of the two harried chirurgeons. John was there
in the middle of things, stripped to the waist, his muscular arms covered with blood and his face gleaming with perspiration. To my surprise, I saw that Joralemon Snode was also assisting. He was wearing
nothing but a loincloth, and was doing all the menial and revolting
tasks for which the others had no time. He had not gone over with
the boarding party, not being a fighting man, but he was showing his
mettle now in a role which called for a higher degree of courage. He
stopped beside me for a moment to say: "We should all have a dozen
hands here, Roger. Most of these poor fellows will die before we can
get around to them. We can't attend to their bodies, let alone their
souls. May the Lord forgive us all!"

The Spanish chirurgeon, looking like a gorilla in his seminudity, was
preparing to amputate the leg of a fellow countryman. Joralemon ran
at his nod to the far end of the gallery, where he plied the bellows
on a small fire. Flames sprang up, giving the place an even closer
resemblance to pictures of Purgatory. He then plunged the cauterizing
irons into the blaze. The Spaniard studied the blade of a long dudgeon
knife with a doubtful frown, and I heard him mutter to himself, "The
edge is gone. It is well that this fellow is only a thief."

The victim was small, but it took all of John's strength to hold him
when the chirurgeon went to work. He had been given a stiff drink
of brandy, but he screamed like a gutted stallion when the knife cut
into his thigh, and he writhed so viciously that John called for help.
I seized one of his arms and bore down with all my weight. I could
not see what the chirurgeon was doing, but apparently his doubts about
the instrument proved groundless. It seemed no more than a few seconds before he reached for his saw and began to cut the bone. There

is nothing terrifying about the rasping bite of a saw until you know that it is ripping its way through a human frame; then the sound becomes the most horrible that the mind can conceive. Drops of sweat from the chirurgeon's brow fell on my arm, and I heard him say, "Thank God, his bones are small."

I knew when he applied the white-hot iron to the stump by the smell of searing flesh. Fortunately the victim fainted at this stage, for my arms were no longer capable of anything. I ran to an open porthole. In a moment John joined me there.

"This is much worse than fighting!" he gasped. It was a relief to my pride to see that he had been affected as much as I had. After a moment he said in a thin voice: "It's good there are few of our fellows here. We got off light today."

Joralemon went right on with his work. He was wrapping bandages about the stump, his skinny arms moving with skill and dispatch. John looked at him and shook his head in puzzled admiration. "He's a better man than either of us, Roger," he said.

As soon as I was able to catch my breath, I told him what I had found. His eyes lighted up, and he motioned me to follow him outside. He frowned as he placed a foot on the rope ladder leading from the cockpit to the deck and said to me: "The poor devils were carried down *that!* I've never given the matter a thought, but now I see it's high time something was done about this. There should be proper hospitals on all ships. I must see to it, Roger."

He read the admiral's report as soon as we reached the deck, and I could see that it afforded him great satisfaction. He smacked me on the shoulder with his blood-reddened hand.

"This takes a load off my mind," he declared. "I had to hang that fellow. But now the whole world will get the facts, and no one will be able to blame me. Even—" He broke off for a moment and then smiled broadly. "What will old King Rumbleguts say to this? He has already pronounced the Spaniards within their rights in seizing the *Trial.* Now the addled old swillbelly will have to eat his words. Come along, Roger, I must break this news to our high-stomached prisoners who have been looking down their long noses at me as though I were a common topping-cove."

My mind was still so filled with the agonized, "*Madre! Madre mia!*" of the suffering thief that I paid no attention to the fact that my captain had not waited to remove any of the traces of the charnel house. I followed him to a sumptuous cabin where we found all our prisoners sitting in a grim-lipped circle. They were attired in their best and were trying hard to maintain an air of haughty superiority. I could see that fear sat on the shoulders of most of them nevertheless.

John stalked in, looking like a butcher with his disheveled hair and blood-streaked torso. He paused for a moment and then held up the report, smacking it emphatically with his other hand.

"Here we have it, my fine ladies and gentlemen," he declared. "The proofs of the late Don Pedro's perfidy. It's here in black and white, set down in his own hand. I owe you no explanation or apology, but I've so much regard for my own reputation that I shall report what your commander has written." He read the note aloud and then handed it back to me. "I now dare any of you to say that the fate which overtook Don Pedro this morning was not a just one."

"I say so," declared Dona Cristina calmly. "That ship was sailing in forbidden waters."

"Forbidden?" repeated John, without looking in her direction. "Forbidden by whom? Since when has Spain owned the Inner Seas?"

The rest of the company sat in tense gravity, fearing no doubt that the uncovering of this proof would lead to further reprisals. One of the women fell into a fit of hysterical weeping, and I saw Dona Cristina lean over to whisper reassuringly in her ear. John sensed what was in their minds and proceeded to allay their fears.

"The episode is closed," he said. "One life only has been taken for the many who died on the *Trial*. The rest of you are in no danger." He paused and frowned. "It's an easy thing for a beautiful woman to speak her mind boldly. All women, beautiful or not, are safe in the hands of Englishmen." He seemed to be conscious for the first time of his condition. "I apologize to the ladies for my appearance. Perhaps they will forgive me when I say that I've been doing what I could to assist in saving the lives of the wounded Spaniards of low degree who fill the cockpit below us."

No one ventured any comment, so he went on to explain the situation which had developed. "It may prove necessary to sink the *Santa Caterina*," he said. "There is still a chance that I'll be able to make a southern port. In any event, your safety will be seen to and, as far as possible, your comfort. You'll be held as prisoners for exchange or ransom. If the fear of the galleys has been in the minds of any of you, you have my word that you may banish it at once. No Christian, no matter how richly he may deserve it, will ever go to pull an oar on heathen benches because of John Ward. All I ask is that you obey orders and do nothing to add to the difficulties under which my crew and I are laboring."

All through this scene I had been aware that Dona Cristina's eyes had never wandered from him. John had not looked in her direction, and he did not do so even when he added a final word which concerned her particularly.

"It is not my intention to hold the niece of your late commander. What has happened has been especially painful for her, and I should like to make what amends are in my power. If at all possible, she will be landed where other ships for the West will call. One formality now remains. You haven't yet been subjected to search, and it is my duty to see that this is attended to at once. Again this order does not apply to

Dona Cristina. She is at liberty to leave if she desires, but the rest of you must remain here."

I wondered if he had any idea of the value of the jewelry she was carrying, but of course I said nothing. I intended to keep my knowledge on the subject to myself.

"I prefer to remain," said Dona Cristina.

Their eyes met for the first time, and I could not help thinking what a contrast they presented, the Spanish girl with her grave and lovely eyes, and the enormous Englishman, naked to the waist, with his golden hair straggling over the grimy muscles of his great shoulders.

"That shall be as you wish, Señorita," he said.

A new note pervaded the decks when we arrived there, a cheerfulness due to the arrival of the supper kettles. I became aware for the first time that I had not had a morsel of food all day. The odor of stewed lamb made me hungry. We sat down immediately, John taking a seat on the planking with us. We supped enormously on the lamb and some loaves of crusty Spanish bread which had been found in the galley. Quantities of fresh fruit then appeared and a single cask of wine. The order had gone out that there was to be no heavy drinking until the end of our labors was in sight and the first glimpse had been had of an African port on the horizon. We were to take no manner of chances.

I saw John in a new light during this meal. The disciplinarian had vanished. He joked with the men while he dipped his huge hands in the kettle for lamb bones and munched great segments of the fine fresh bread. He praised every one of us in turn for the parts we had played in the fight. Surely, I thought, he must have eyes in the back of his head as well as a capacity for seeing through wood and metal to have observed all the individual instances of stanch conduct to which he now alluded. The men were thrown into a happy state of pride by the lavishness of his praise. Even Clim the Cod's-head threw out his chest and grinned all over his rather foolish face when the Captain spoke of the swathe he had cut with his avenging pike. I could judge of the sentiments of the rest of them by the gratification I felt when he mentioned the help I had given him.

And yet through it all I had a curious sense of unreality. I, Roger Blease, had no place in this company of rough-living, hard-fighting men. Even though I had managed somehow to play a part with reasonable credit, I did not belong. I would never belong. I was realizing this more surely all the time.

John's mood changed to one of sly anticipation. He smiled around the squatting circle and said: "Well, my bingo-boys, I now have a morsel of good news for your greedy ears. There is gold on board, after all, and, I think, a rather pretty supply of gauds. You've been on short rations, and there hasn't been one stroke of good luck to make up to you for the work you've done and for the reasty foods you've packed into your hungry bellies. Now I can make you all a promise. When we get back to Rome-ville, there will be yellow boys in your pockets. Enough to get you the best of everything. You'll be weighed down with mint, and there will be trinkets for all your women. There has been no time yet to cast a reckoning but—well, I'm making a guess that we shall all do rather well."

The men cheered him lustily as he got to his feet. He winked at me and said in my ear: "And now, Roger, I'm going to struggle with those damned points again and buckle a very fine ruff around my neck. There are some differences of opinion between me and a certain haughty lady which must be talked over at once. I'll see you later. Do you think you can finish the papers before you turn in?"

I nodded in assent as I got to my feet, painfully conscious of the stiffness of my muscles and of a sense of complete fatigue which weighed me down. I walked slowly to the captain's cabin and settled myself to my task. John had vanished with suspicious alacrity.

I did not expect to find anything much of value in what was left, and I'm afraid that my work was performed in a perfunctory way. Weary from the day's excitement, and filled with food and wine, I drowsed over the dull and often illegible documents, blinking my eyes to keep them open. Several times I found myself with my drooping head in dangerous proximity to the lighted end of the candle.

It was by the greatest of luck, therefore, that I stumbled on an important discovery. Hours had passed, I believe, for silence had settled over the ship and the documents in front of me had dwindled to a mere handful. I found myself with a creased note in my hand which was no different from scores of similar ones which had already joined the pile on the floor. I glanced with tired eyes at the opening sentence without grasping what it meant. Then a sixth sense came to my assistance and warned me that here was something which required my attention. I read it again, and a tingle of excitement ran through my veins. I found myself wide awake instantly.

SIR ADMIRAL:
This is to inform you that within a very short time it is our belief a truce will be concluded with the government of the Low Countries. You will receive advance information and in the meantime you are to govern your activities—

My eyes raced across the closely written page. This was certain to prove a serious matter for John Ward, for me, for every English sailor now on the high seas. My heart was thumping as I deciphered the stilted phraseology of the instructions.

In brief, Don Pedro was ordered to assist in a drive against the English rovers in the Mediterranean as soon as the truce had been signed. He was, therefore, to change his plans and not continue to America with the *Santa Caterina*, which had apparently been the original plan. Instead, he was to drop his passengers at the Cape Verde Islands, where another vessel would pick them up, and to put back at once to Cadiz. It was the intention of the Spanish Government to use the entire strength of the Navy in a sweeping operation from Gibraltar to the Levant, a dragnet in which every English ship would be caught inevitably, thus putting a stop to free roving for all time. It was anticipated that the truce would be concluded within six weeks of the date on which the letter had been dispatched. I glanced at the date: February 18.

There would be another month, then, before the might of Spain would be unleashed for our destruction. This was reassuring, for I knew it would allow time for a warning to be broadcast and for all Englishmen to get safely away. I sensed another difficulty which would face us once hostilities ceased between the Low Countries and Spain. We were sailing under Dutch letters of marque, and these would be canceled. We would be left with no flag to fly. We would become pirates in the eyes of the world.

I went out on deck in search of John. It was a beautiful night, with a moon close to the full and a sharp breeze blowing from the west. We were sailing under as heavy a head of canvas as was possible in view of the damage the ship had suffered, and I could see that our course was set for the southeast. For Tunis, I concluded, where safe anchorage would be found. The *Royal Bess* was a good half-mile in advance of us, with lanterns in her rigging to guide us in following her. I paused to watch, thinking of the difficult days which stretched ahead for all such craft. In spite of my growing disinclination to life at sea, I was proud of the *Royal Bess*, proud that I had played a part in the most spectacular of her victories. It would be a sad blow if she were recaptured and sailed once more under the flag of Spain.

The lookout men were at their posts, but the decks otherwise were deserted. I concluded that John would be in the pilot-house if he had not already turned in, and I made my way there. He was standing near the wheel, staring straight ahead at the lights of the *Royal Bess* with an air of complete concentration. I told him my news.

To my surprise, he did not seem seriously concerned. He had been expecting this for some time, he said. The refusal of King James to assist the Low Countries had made it inevitable. The Dutch apparently had decided to make as good terms as they could.

"What will you do?" I asked.

"What will I do?" He looked at me with eyes that glowed fiercely. "I will not give up the fight! Did Sir Richard Grenville quit when he found himself pitted against the full might of Spain? I've sworn to keep at this as long as I have a sound hull under me and a single gun to man." He began to pace up and down the narrow space, his long arms swinging in pace with his thoughts. "It's very lucky, Roger, that you found this letter. Now we know what time we have and can prepare.

I must get word at once to all Englishmen in the Inner Sea. In one sense I'm glad it is happening this way, for now they can no longer hold out against the course I've been advising. We must combine! We must operate as a single fleet and from the same base. When the Dons come out to catch us, they'll get an unpleasant surprise. They'll find themselves pitted against a fleet of the greatest fighting ships ever gathered together. I think it will be rather amusing, my brave Roger!" He stopped in front of me, and I was surprised to see how excited and happy he had become at the prospect. "Perhaps the admiral of that surprise fleet will be none other than your old friend and townsman, John Ward himself!"

I had been confident that his reaction to the news would be the opposite of this, that he would have set himself to plans for a quick exit from these dangerous waters, but I began to catch fire from his enthusiasm. This was the great chance for which I had enlisted under his colors, the opportunity to fight the enemy of our country, not as a single ship skulking in hidden roadsteads, dodging in and out for stray prizes, but as a mighty fleet with the power to strike smashing blows for the freedom of the seas. Every other consideration left my mind. I forgot the hardships of my daily lot, my shrinking from the cruelty and greed of my companions. I found myself meeting his enthusiasm with equal zeal, as eager as he for the struggle which loomed ahead.

We talked it over at full length, going over every detail of the campaign. It was getting on into the small hours when John sat down with an air of sudden weariness.

"Time to turn in, Roger," he said. "The ache in my bones has reached my head at last. What a day this has been!"

I got painfully to my feet. Tired as I was, I had one more question to ask.

"How did you succeed with Dona Cristina? Did the—the differences resolve themselves?"

John managed a rather poor attempt at a smile. "I didn't succeed at all," he confessed. "The lady is very proud, and she has a sharp tongue in her head. She found all the loose joints in my moral armor. If we had more time, it would be a great satisfaction to me to set her right."

13

FOR TWO DAYS the westerly wind blew strongly, carrying us beyond all danger of pursuit. Then it died down, and the two ships lay motionless on a glassy sea under the blistering sun. The heat was so great that there were times when I found it difficult to breathe. The men sulked and had to be driven to work. John paced the decks like a caged animal, knowing that every inactive hour was bringing closer the day when Spain and the Netherlands would come to terms. His temper grew short. I was kept so continuously busy with clerical work and in seeing that all the valuables on board were baled up that I had no time to share in other worries.

In spite of my activities, however, I was constantly conscious of the atmosphere of hate and strain which gripped the ship. On the second day a Spanish prisoner broke loose from detention and seriously injured one of our men. An hour later he was swinging from the yardarm while the rest of the prisoners watched in glowering silence. Every few hours, it seemed, one of the poor devils in the hospital would be sewn up in canvas and thrown overboard. Don Pedro's pet monkey, which had taken to the rigging and had refused to come down for food, was kicked into the sea by the irritable foot of one of our men. Floggings were administered constantly. I began to feel as though life had changed into a long and hideous nightmare.

Then Clim the Cod's-head got himself into trouble. He had found his long-meg, a Spanish servingwoman with a face as forbidding as a thundercloud. He was proud of his conquest, and when a Dutchman who had signed on with us at Marseilles vied with him for her favor, he evened the score by sinking his knife between his rival's ribs. There were some infractions of discipline that John would wink at, but I knew this could not be condoned.

The crew were lined up in the waist, and Clim was brought forward for sentence, his arms trussed behind him. He looked puzzled at the sudden change in status from hero to prisoner, and his dull eyes were filled with savage resentment. I was so concerned over what might happen to him that I could not watch the proceedings. I let my eyes wander to the towering superstructure of the ship back of me and was surprised to see Dona Cristina standing in one of the upper galleries. John had sought her company continually during the days which had elapsed but, so far as I could tell, with indifferent success. Once, however, I had stumbled on them in the same gallery where she now stood. It had been late in the evening, and for the first time her maid had not been with her. They were conversing in low tones, and it had seemed to me that her attitude had been less resentful.

Several other prisoners were standing at the railing, but I noticed they kept their distance from her. Did they resent her intimacy with the English captain? If so, she did not seem to be concerned about it. She was holding her head high, and her eyes were fixed intently on the tall figure of John Ward.

"Clement Duvver," declared John, "you have been guilty of a murderous assault on one of your fellows. The offense calls for the most severe punishment. I know that quarrels can't be avoided, but I expect the men of my crew to settle them with their fists in the English way."

He went on to describe the fault of the unfortunate Clim in scathing terms. I found myself wondering about the name Duvver, which I had not heard before, and speculating as to whether it could be a corruption of De Vere. There was a suggestion in the straight nose and broad skull of the sailor of good blood gone to seed generations back. I knew that the best Norman names often turned up in curiously Anglicized form. Clim, who had been born and raised in Wapping, and whose mind at best was a flame which flickered fitfully, might perhaps be able to trace his descent back to one of the proudest of those great families which had broken Saxon England to the yoke of feudalism. The possibility made me feel still more sorry for him.

"It's lucky the man is not going to die," concluded John. "I'm going to consider also the bold part you took in the capture of this ship. Your punishment, therefore, will be light. Your share in the pool will be cut in half, and you will be kept in the garters for two days. That will give you plenty of time to think, and I hope you'll decide to keep a hold on your temper in future. The next time you're guilty of an infraction of the rules, I shall be much less lenient."

Clim was led away, and I went back to my work, relieved that the punishment had not been more severe. I decided that later in the day I would pay Clim a visit and try to talk him into a better frame of mind.

About midafternoon broken clouds gathered on the horizon, and a puff of wind stirred our dead sails. In an hour our hull was rising and falling gently with a promise that sent the watch scrambling up the shrouds while John shouted orders to them in a brisk and cheerful voice. I went out on deck to watch and was gratified to see that our luck was in again. We were under way.

John took my arm and led me back to the pilot-house. He put a finger on the map that was spread out on the table. "Observe, Roger," he said happily. "This is Tunis, where the Dey gives us harborage and his blessing in fighting the Dons. Here is Sicily. Did you ever blow up a pig's bladder and tie it in the middle? Well, that's the Mediterranean for you. It's divided off into two parts, and this narrow bit of water between Tunis and Sicily is all that joins them. If we can control this stretch, we cut Spain off from the East and the trade of the Levant." He laughed with an exultant catch in his voice. "This is my plan, Roger. I'm going to assemble all the English and Dutch privateers in the port of Tunis, like spiders with a web reaching over to Sicily. Once that is managed, no ship with the Spanish flag at its peak will dare to sail between the two points. Give me twenty ships, and the trick is done."

"They will send their whole fleet against us," I warned.

"Let them. I would not mind a riffle with all the admirals of Spain. But even if they're too strong to meet in the open, we can always drop back to our bases. And wait. They can't keep the royal fleet out there permanently." He chuckled. "I've a notion to proclaim the Inner Seas closed to Spanish shipping. That would get Philip's dander up. But, of course, I must get my fleet together first. I promise you it won't be hard. When these hard-headed English captains hear what's in the wind, they'll come tailing into Tunis with every inch of canvas on. They know the side of the stream where the jack barrel run. They'll throw in with me—Harris from Bristol, and those two tough Cornishmen, Halsey and Longcastle; and Giffard and Glanville and Jennings and the rest of them. They're stout fighters, Roger, and they did the cuddy-jig in their cradles. I must get word to all of them."

"Sir Bartlemy mentioned a man named Macherie," I reminded him.

He frowned. "Sir Nevil Macherie, our one aristocrat," he said. "Yes, I suppose I must invite him to join us, much as I dislike the fellow. And then there's Basil Sleath, the wild Irishman. I'll need him more than Sir Bartlemy's fine friend. Did it occur to you that Sir Bartlemy was one of Macherie's backers? He seemed concerned over my hint that there would be no profits."

"I doubt it," I answered.

"Well, we haven't any time to lose. I've lost three days as it is."

"I've finished the inventory," I said, drawing a paper from my doublet. "Their purser helped me when I gave him your promise of an early release. There are thirty-two tapestries, four of them large and quite old. The purser says they're worth three thousand pounds."

"They'll sell easily enough in London. Rich-arrayed Robin will attend to that. But I'm sure our greedy gentleman from Alsatia will see to it that we get no better than seven or eight hundred for our share."

I nodded. "Then here are a score of fine paintings. Another thousand pounds for the lot. Four clocks and eight crucifixes of solid gold, seven mirrors with gold frames, eighty candle sconces of silver, a solid-gold dinner service of ninety pieces, sixteen swords with jeweled hilts. Eight thousand worth, in the opinion of the purser. The bullion you already have under lock and key. There are enough uncut gems to fill a temperade basin, and the jewels we collected from the passengers are easily worth two thousand. There are four hundred books and eight illuminated missals heavy with gold leaf. There are eight thousand yards of the richest materials and a chest of ostrich plumes. Twenty-one thousand pounds is a safe estimate of the value of everything, apart from the gold."

John did not seem particularly interested. "Pleasant news for our fine gentlemen at home," he said. "It can be put ashore at Marseilles with our agent there. Some of it may be disposed of in France, but the bulk of it will go to Rome-ville. If you feel disposed to take pride in the fact, we English have the best fencing kens in the world. The old queen saw to that. No one ever got a sice the better of her." He grinned at me. "We'll keep the bullion ourselves. The men prefer to take their shares out in Old-Mr.-Gory. You'll be having a heavy purse of your own, Roger, if the matter interests you."

I handed him the paper and was preparing to leave when he laid a detaining hand on my shoulder. I could see that he had something important to say and that he did not know just how to go about it.

"I've never told you what happened when I was detained at Appleby Court," he declared, clearing his throat. "Sir Bartlemy was in a panic over the trouble at London, and he didn't think it safe for me to venture out until the hue and cry died down. He kept me cooped up in a snug little cell in the gatehouse, but I saw the members of his family on two or three occasions." He paused unhappily. "I give you my word, Roger, it was not my fault; but I fell in love with Katie so completely that I'll never get over it. There has never been her equal. I don't have to tell *you* that, I know. One evening I stole out for a breath of fresh air in Wayland Spinney and she—she joined me there. I'm telling you this because I want to be honest with you. You've a right to know everything. We talked for a few minutes; on my word of honor it was not more than a quarter of an hour. She promised me she would wait until the *Royal Bess* came back. I asked her about you, and she said things that would have made your ears burn with pride had you heard them. But, Roger, the truth of the matter is, she's in love with me."

I had been expecting this, but to hear it put into words left me with the feeling that my whole world was toppling. The stark realities of life at sea had been stripping me of my illusions one by one; and now I found that Katie's regard for me had been as unstable as everything else. For a moment I felt sick at heart, but this was followed by anger. John had known that I loved Katie and that she had reciprocated in some degree at least. He should not have allowed any romantic notions touching her to become lodged in his mind. If he had not permitted her to see that he had been so much taken with her on that first meeting in the gatehouse chamber, she would soon have recovered from the impression he had made on her.

Almost immediately, however, this feeling of anger passed. I realized that John had not been able to help himself. He had fallen in love with her, and that was all there was to it. Nor could Katie be blamed. He was a national hero, a romantic figure, who had suddenly appeared in her life and swept her off her feet. Her girlish preference for me had not been strong enough to stand against the attraction of John Ward. What had happened was inevitable.

"Does Sir Bartlemy know?" I asked.

"God forbid!" exclaimed John. "He has other plans for Katie, as he made clear. And that, Roger, is the only thing that gives me any peace of mind in this matter. You have no place in his plans either. He wants a fine match for his little Katie. A penniless cadet of Great Lunnington wouldn't do."

I nodded in agreement. Even when I had allowed myself to indulge in daydreams, I had always known somewhere in the back of my mind that the ambitious plans of Katie's father would stand in the way.

"I was careful not to make any trouble for her," explained John. "There was a fall of snow the evening she met me in Wayland Spinney, and I was afraid our footprints would show. I carried her back, taking care to plant a foot in every track she had made." He indulged in a reminiscent smile. "That was what brought matters to a head, I'm afraid. I give you my word, I had intended to keep my feeling for her a secret. But—well, I leave it to you, Roger. She was all bundled up in an ermine wrap, and her eyes were sparkling, and she looked like a little snow fairy, if there is such a thing. My good resolutions melted away. I told her then that I loved her, that a lifetime at sea would not be long enough to banish the image of her from my heart. On my honor, Roger, I couldn't help it."

"I'm glad," I said, "that you took such pains to protect her. But don't you think you ought to continue in the same course?"

He looked at me with a puzzled frown, not perceiving at first what I meant. Then he nodded and began to laugh.

"You refer to the Señorita? My stanch old sobersides, there's nothing to that. The lady had conceived a very bad opinion of me. I couldn't bear to have her continue in so grievous an error, and so I've set out to show her she's wrong. I owe it to my country to teach her that Englishmen are not all crude and bloody-handed barbarians. That, Roger, is the only reason for the pains I've taken to cultivate her better acquaintance. I give you my solemn word on it."

"That she's lovely has played no part in it, of course," I said. "I feel sure of one thing: if Katie knew of Dona Cristina, she would prefer to have her continue in her erroneous opinion of Englishmen rather than have her educated to the truth in this way."

John opened the leather pouch at his belt and drew out a pipe and a handful of tobacco. The pipe was the handsomest thing of the kind I had ever seen, with a long curved stem and a diamond-studded bowl. He began to fill it, eyeing me the while with a look that was compounded of amusement and annoyance.

"So, I'm to have two guides to my conscience now!" he commented. "It's not enough to have Snode preaching at me all the time. You must begin as well." He pressed down the tobacco with an impatient thumb. "Get this into your head once and for all: Everything changes when you lose sight of shore. The pretty little set of pink morals that the parsons set up for our guidance are nothing but bambury-chat to sailors, my boy. Why do you suppose I let the brims on my ship whenever we touch port? Men must have their mutton-in-long-sleeves. Don't be too hard on me, Roger. I can run after a dozen women, even a fine lady like the lovely Dona Cristina, and still remain true in my heart to the one girl I love at home."

I did not believe this, and said so. John brushed aside my arguments with increasing impatience.

"You'll find out for yourself," he declared. "Wait until you've been at sea for the better part of a year. The first thick-beamed callot you set eyes on will look to you like Venus rising from the foam. You don't think so now, but you'll find I know what I am talking about."

He sprawled himself out in a chair and puffed vigorously at his pipe. As a concession to the heat he had discarded his ruff and was wearing a wide lace collar which lay flat on his shoulders and left his neck free. His doublet was of thin green silk, covered with designs in gold thread of ships under full sail. I was certain, however, that underneath he was as tightly trussed up as ever, for the green hose he was wearing fitted his legs like the bark of a tree. I had been amazed at the way he blossomed out each day in a fresh set. His supply of hosiery seemed inexhaustible.

"I warned you of this," he said. "Leave my morals to the tender care of Joralemon Snode and we'll remain good friends. Don't try to make Nature over, Roger."

I had been hearing this all my life. The sailors I had talked with on the water front at home had said the same thing in even grosser terms. I had caught similar phrases in the talk of the captains that father had brought home. The boys I had run with at school had been equally sure of masculine privileges. I was still not convinced. I was sure that the words "honor" and "chivalry" meant something. King Arthur's knights, who had spent their lives seeking adventure, had remained true to plighted troths. Was the wind at sea corrupting, instead of clean and strong, so that a sailor could not keep his ideals untarnished?

John got to his feet and mopped his face with a handkerchief of fine linen. He was too thorough an Englishman to enjoy such intense heat.

"In a few days," he remarked, "we should round Cape Blanc and see the white roofs of Gouletta ahead of us. These infidels have built their hovels on stones that knew the tread of Hannibal's feet. A classical scholar like you will find that interesting, I suppose. I dislike the whole country intensely myself. I think I would lose my mind if I had to see much of it. Give me the chalk cliffs of Kent or the low green hills back of a Cornish port."

"Or Wayland Spinney when the snow is on the ground," I suggested.

He looked at me closely, as though trying to judge how much bitterness lay back of my remark.

"I'm all English in my preferences," he said. "I like cold brisk winds and the green of the country after rain. I like solid food and heady drinks. I prefer gray eyes to black."

"The Señorita's eyes are the blackest I've ever seen."

"Then don't let yourself look too deeply into them," he advised lightly. "You might find it easy to lose yourself in eyes like that."

Early in the evening I paid my visit to Clim in the ship's prison. It was so dark on the orlop-deck that I had to hold a torch close to the bars before I could make him out. He was sitting in a corner with his head in his hands and so sunk in spirits that he was making no effort to shift his feet when the motion of the boat flooded his side of the deck with bilge water. The stench of the place was almost unbearable.

"Clim!" I called.

He looked up. I could see now that he was chained by both arms to the wall. He was sitting on a low bench covered lightly with damp straw.

"It's Roger Blease," I said.

A flicker of interest showed on his swollen face. "Shanks," he said in a hoarse whisper, "get me out o' here. Tell Cap'n I done nothing wrong. He were on'y a Hogen-mogen. A Hogen-mogen, Shanks." Clim, I realized, had his full share of the racial pride which counts no law valid where foreigners are concerned. It had been a great blow to his pride to have a Dutchman, a "Hogen-mogen," take his woman away from him; and now he could not understand why he was being punished for what he had done.

"You shouldn't have used a knife on him, Clim," I said.

"But, Shanks, he were on'y a Hogen-mogen." That quite apparently was the only point his mind was capable of retaining.

I held the torch up and inspected the place. There were several other prisoners, chained to the wall at intervals of six feet, all of them broken specimens of mankind with wildly staring eyes. One began to jabber at me in frenzied tones.

"I oughtn't be here wi' Spanishers and Portugalls," protested Clim. "I killed a dozen Spanishers. A dozen, Shanks. You see me do it yourself. I oughtn't be here."

It was clear that the praise he had received since the capture of the *Santa Caterina* had gone to his head. In his dim and slow-moving mind he had been dramatizing himself as a hero. It seemed to me likely that he would not have been so offended otherwise over the loss of the woman.

All the prisoners now were clamoring at me, and the din suddenly seemed to drive Clim berserk. He poured out a stream of oaths and tried frantically to free himself from his chains.

"Take it easy, man," I shouted, finding it difficult to make myself heard. "I'm going to speak to Captain Ward. He won't do anything for you if you carry on like this."

"I won't be treated like a Hogen-mogen or a Portugall! You tell that to Cap'n, Shanks. You tell him that."

Finding that John had already turned in, I went to his cabin and knocked on the door. There was no sound from within for several moments and then John called, "Who's there?"

"It's Roger Blease, Captain Ward."

"Oh." A moment later he opened the door a few inches and peered out at me. The cabin was in darkness.

I explained the situation I had found below and urged him with all the earnestness I could summon to release Clim from serving out his sentence.

"That fellow has been getting above himself," grumbled John. "Still, he's a good man, and he fought like a demon the other day. It's a mistake, I'm afraid; but I'll give in to you this time, Roger. Get him out. I suppose that chicken heart of yours would keep you from sleeping tonight if you couldn't get him free at once. I'll have a talk with this Clim the Cod's-head tomorrow and put some proper ideas of discipline into his head."

The door closed with suspicious haste. I stood outside for a moment or two, trying to convince myself that there had not been a faint trace of perfume on the air. Then I went below to see that Clim was released.

14

WE OVERHAULED the *Royal Bess* in the lee of the island of Zimbra, and John issued orders for a number of us to transfer back to her with him. I was included in the order. Most of the wounded had died, and there was nothing more to be done for the survivors, so Mickle, our chirurgeon, and Joralemon Snode were also named.

I was glad of the change. I had been sleeping on a hard couch in the main cabin. The meals had been irregular and the work unremitting. And yet I had some regrets. A feeling of mystery pervaded the stately upper decks of the great ship. My daily quests into the contents of cabinets and chests had been spiced with anticipation of curious discoveries.

I needed to make no preparations for the transfer. All I had brought on board was a cutlass and a palpitating heart, and all I would take back were a few trinkets and old papers which I had found in the secret drawers of the high cabinets of cypress and tulip wood.

Maltworm was returning with us, and very glad of it. Clim was being left behind, however, with the squad to man the *Santa Caterina*. I think that the decision to leave him was a deliberate one on John's part. Clim, after all, was entitled to some punishment.

He took it hard. The order had made it clear that the prize crew would be on continuous duty. They would be allowed no chance to go ashore, no opportunity to traffic with the mysterious women of Tunis about whom they had been speculating so avidly. Clim seemed particularly disturbed over the fact that Mickle, the chirurgeon, was transferring with us. He had respect for none but fighting men.

"He be nought but a nim-gimmer," he growled when I tried to comfort him. "Let him stay wi' the poor fellows below decks and not go ashore. Tell Cap'n to let me change wi' him, Shanks."

I saw that the gold in his purse was what made his selection for duty on the prize ship so irksome, and I was assuring him that he would have plenty of opportunities later to spend it when my attention was attracted by a curious tableau on deck. John was standing in the waist, giving some last-minute orders, when Dona Cristina's maid approached him with her arms full of bundles. She said something to him in a whisper. John's face took on immediately a shade of the deepest chagrin. He said something in reply which caused the buxom maid to shake her head in emphatic dissent. I was trying to figure out what it was all about when Dona Cristina herself appeared.

I understood the situation then and, in spite of a certain feeling of sympathy for my friend, I found it hard not to laugh at the difficulty in which he had involved himself. The Spanish girl had a white lace wrap around her head and a crucifix clasped in her hand. She glided over to him with such grace that she seemed to move without physical effort. Her flaring white skirt neither rippled nor swayed. Even at a distance I could see that her face was serious and intent.

I heard John say in a tone of remonstrance: "Dear lady, this is rank folly. It is impossible. I—I cannot allow it!"

They talked for several minutes in low tones, the helpless chagrin on my captain's face growing deeper all the time. Then he motioned me to come over.

"Roger," he said, in English, with a gesture which indicated he had reached the end of his verbal rope, "our lovely prisoner has made up her mind to go with us. I've already planned it so that she will be taken to Cadiz where she can go aboard the first ship for Trinidad. She refuses to consider it. You're a better talker than I am. Take the minx in hand and see if you can batter some common sense into her."

The girl indulged in a brief and unhappy smile. "I speak some English," she said. "I do not understand the word minx, but it is clear you are very angry with me. It will do you no good, Don John. I go ashore with you. Nothing can change my mind."

John reverted to Spanish with a somewhat sheepish air. He was not very fluent in that tongue, and he chose his words with some difficulty. "My sweet child," he said, "I'm alarmed over what this would mean." He turned to me, his face a study in earnest bafflement. "Roger, think of some reasons to make her change her mind. We must protect her, you know. Tunis is a vile and corrupt hole, the center of all the wickedness in the world. She couldn't live there."

Dona Cristina shook her head. "I know all that. I have no illusions. But I must go with you. There is no other way."

Sensing what John had wanted me to explain to her, I said: "Captain Ward has plans which will keep him at sea continuously. It is impossible to tell you why, Señorita. There would be no one in Tunis to protect you. You might fall into heathen hands."

"I'm an excellent sailor," she asserted. "You are his friend, and so I appeal to you. Make him see my position please, Don Roger. I cannot go to America now. My father would disown me. Little as I may find it to my liking, I have no alternative but to go with you. I am prepared for whatever it may mean. Stay in Tunis or sail with you, it is all the same."

John's face was a study. He had arrayed himself in a festive suit of bright yellow satin with slashings of blue, and I could not help feeling some amusement over the contrast between the gaiety of his clothes and the unhappiness mirrored on his face. He turned a mute look of appeal in my direction.

"We're English and you are Spanish," I urged. "Have you thought how difficult it would be for you with the enemies of your race?"

"I am not expecting happiness," she answered. "Nor peace of mind."

There was a moment's silence, and then she said in low and intense tones: "In spite of everything, I cannot stay here. Look back of us. There you will see my reason. They are all watching us, I am sure. They haven't spoken to me for many days. The women draw their skirts aside when I pass them, and I can read scorn in the eyes of the men. They *know*. Time does not soften hatred with my people, John. It grows deeper all the time. Now do you understand?"

It did not require more than one glance at the faces of our prisoners, who lined the railing of one of the upper decks, to realize she was right. They were so still they looked like images; a grim and forbidding group with tight-lipped mouths and black smoldering eyes. There was something unnatural about their silence, but I could feel more hatred in their passive attitude than if they had spat it out with torrents of abuse.

John lifted his hat from his head with such a sweep that its enormous blue ostrich plume touched the deck. "I shall be very happy to take you with me," he said.

We left immediately. John went first, followed by the girl, who managed to negotiate the swaying ladder with ease and still keep her skirts tightly wrapped about her. I glanced up as I began the descent and was surprised to see that the group of prisoners had not yet moved. Then a single voice was raised, sounding almost like a sob from the intensity of feeling which prompted it, *"English dogs!"* This broke the spell. Immediately they were all gesticulating and shouting at the top of their voices, a flood of curses which enveloped us as we made our way down the ladder. Some of the invective was directed at us, but most of it at the girl, for I heard constant repetition of a term which convinced me I had not been mistaken that night at the door of John's cabin.

John grinned at me as we took our seats in the boat. "They couldn't hold it in any longer," he said.

He sat in the rear with Dona Cristina, and without looking back I knew that he was holding her hand. Joralemon Snode sat with me, and his long, pinched features expressed a degree of disapproval which almost equaled that of the prisoners we had left behind.

"He must be mad!" he whispered to me. "Is he going to marry her? Great harm will come of this, Roger, mark my words. She's put a spell on him with her wicked black eyes!"

"If anyone has been guilty of placing spells, it's John," I answered shortly.

The next morning I was up at dawn, happy to feel the planking of the *Royal Bess* under my feet again. John was pacing the poop-deck with a preoccupied air. He had donned his helmet and breastplates, and his sword clanked against his calves at each step.

"Roger," he said, "I feel unhappy and even a little unclean when it's necessary to make use of this heathen port. He's a sly fellow, the Dey. He tells me he's my friend, but there's always a calculating look in his eyes. He's driving a hard bargain with me. I may operate out of Tunis and make war on the Spaniards, but I must show his Tunizeens how to handle square sails and tall ships like these. I must teach the dogs how to fight against Christian fleets. It goes bitterly against the grain, but what else can I do? All civilized ports are closed to me. I can't go home. And, after all, we can't cruise forever. Do you feel how badly we're rolling? We must lay up long enough to get our hull well scraped—cleaned and ready, Roger, for the fight ahead of us. That's all that counts."

"I've heard that Tunis is full of renegados," I commented. "If you refused, the Dey could get some of them to teach his sailors."

"That's true," said John. "And it eases my conscience a little. It goes further than that, of course. This little scorpion of a Dey has cut a great many throats in his time, and he believes he's buying security by having English sailors about him. Perhaps ambition is eating at his mean soul. He wants Tunis to be the most important port on the African coast. One way and another, he needs us badly; and so we must play our game with him. We need him just as badly."

He stopped his pacing and pointed straight ahead to where a single white column showed above the green of the shore line. "Gouletta," he said. "Keep your eyes open today, Roger. There's going to be much to see. The hill of Sidi-bou-Said has looked down on the making of history. Old Khair-ed-Din, the greatest of the Barbarossa, crossed these waters many times. He used Tunis, as we're doing, in his war against the Spaniards. His men needed no other flag when he stood on the prow with his red beard waving in the breeze. There wasn't an ounce of honesty in his whole body nor a drop of compassion in his veins; but, God of Battles, the scoundrel was a fighter! He could teach us all something."

"Even Drake?" I asked.

He looked at me impatiently. "Barbarossa scoured the seas for twenty-five years, but there was not one second in all that time when he was worthy to stand on the same quarter-deck with Sir Francis Drake. You should know by this time, Roger, that our great English captain was so far above all other men that he couldn't be judged by the same standards. He would have crumpled up the fleets of Barbarossa like so many toy boats on Hampstead Pond and then nailed that old Turk's beard to his mast as a gesture of contempt."

Dona Cristina joined us as we watched the white roofs of Gouletta rising slowly above the hot blue of the sea. John drew her arm through his and led her to the rail. I heard him explaining that this was the port only, that the city of Tunis lay some miles back on a lake into which only the smallest of boats could ply. I could not help thinking what a handsome pair they made.

A Moorish galley was gliding in to anchorage just ahead of us. The sweep of its oar-banks was regular and easy. Colors floated from the masts. The shouting crew had manned the rigging, and a gun at the prow was firing a triumphant salvo. John called me over.

"Do you know what that means?" he asked. "The dogs have sunk a Christian ship! I get a sick feeling at the pit of my stomach every time I see this. Listen to the din the blackamoors are making! It's partly for our benefit. They hate us, and it's all the Dey can do to give us protection in port. Can you imagine how this sounds to the poor cringing devils of prisoners down in the hold? That's where they'll have them, chained together, men and women alike. The women will be sold into harems. Some of the men will go to the galleys; the rest will be put up at auction in the Souk-el-Barka."

"Do you suppose it was an English ship?"

"If they're English, I can make a deal with the Dey," answered John. "It would be expensive. I would probably have to turn over our haul from the *Santa Caterina*. A sore blow to our lords and gentlemen at home, but I would make the deal without a moment's hesitation." He turned and looked at the girl. "The grandfather of your present king cleaned this nest out once most thoroughly. It's high time someone did it again. I would like to undertake that little task myself. With six ships like the *Royal Bess* I could pound Gouletta to pieces in a few hours. It would be a pleasure. But, to speak of more immediate concerns, you can't go ashore like this. Your maid must find native clothes for you. A veil is most necessary. I couldn't answer for your safety without one."

Excitement had gripped the port. The water front was packed with screaming mobs. "It always happens this way," said John. "When one of their galleys captures a Christian ship, they get a religious fever.

Listen to the drums! The dogs pound away at them with as much relish as though they were the soles of Christian feet."

The ship was warped in skillfully to the foot of a steep stretch of green-stained stone steps. A group awaited us at the top, made up of officials of some sort, and I was surprised to see a tall Englishman in sober gray among them. He called out a greeting to us in the cultivated tones of Oxford. "Welcome, Captain Ward! I've been waiting two weeks for you."

"Mundy Hill!" boomed John. "You old gray fox, I'm delighted to see you." Over his shoulder he explained. "Sir Sigismund Hill. What a stroke of luck! He carries the shrewdest head in all Christendom on that long neck of his. His advice will be most helpful."

I had heard much talk of Sir Sigismund Hill, one of the founders of the Levant Company. He had never commanded a ship, but for many years had been the eyes and ears of that courageous band of English merchants who had set themselves the task of opening up trade with the East. He had spent years in Turkey and Persia and had even gone overland as far as India. He could speak half a dozen Eastern languages, and I had heard that he talked of some fantastic scheme to connect the Mediterranean with the Red Sea by means of a canal and so make a quick route to the magic Orient. He was often called the English Ulysses. I was surprised to see that this famous rover was mild and almost bookish in appearance, with a thin frame and a twinkling gray eye.

A turbaned official stood at Hill's elbow, a gaunt individual who glared down at us with open hostility. The group was surrounded by a guard with drawn swords.

Dona Cristina had retired to her cabin to don a more suitable costume, and while we waited for her John looked the crowded water front over with an anxious eye. A blast of music from a native band now reached our ears. It was strangely like the unearthly shriek of an instrument used by the Scots, called, I believe, the bagpipe.

"The reitas," explained John. "They'll play away at them until they fall down in a frenzy. I don't like the look of things at all."

I had been surprised to see that many of the natives were wearing green turbans. When I asked about them, John shook his head soberly. "That's what worries me most," he said. "A green turban can be worn only by the Shorfa. They're a special lot, descendants of Mohammed, no less. Whenever they appear it means trouble. Listen to them! I know a little of their vile tongue. Enough to tell that they're screaming for the death of all *koffers*. That's us. Whenever you hear that chant of *Hagi Baba! Hagi Baba!* look to yourself."

The two Spanish women rejoined us in native costume. Dona Cristina's eyes looked enormous over the top of her veil. John motioned to me to take care of them and then made his way down the rope ladder, followed by half a dozen of the men.

"Are these infidels all mad, Don Roger?" whispered the girl. "They have froth on their lips. I have confidence in your captain, but still I do not feel very comfortable about this."

"No more do I," I replied. I was able to reassure her on one point, however. "There's a lot of sham about it. They get that froth from the mouths of camels. They're not as mad as they seem."

The maid liked the looks of the jeering, milling mob even less than her mistress. She clung to the railing and refused to budge until one of the sailors urged her down with a sharp prod from his pike. I followed her, extending a hand to Dona Cristina. I could tell from the intensity with which she grasped my fingers that her fears had not been allayed. I wondered if she had begun to regret her decision.

I looked upward when my feet touched the bottom step and saw John shake hands cordially with Sir Sigismund Hill. Then he turned to greet the turbaned official. The latter shuffled forward and extended his left hand. To my amazement, I saw John strike the proffered hand aside with an angry gesture. Then I remembered that he had told me it was an insult for a Tunizeen to offer the left hand in greeting.

The din subsided instantly. The calm before the storm, I said to myself, being sure that John's brusqueness would bring the natives down on us. Dona Cristina sensed that something was wrong, and her dark eyes asked me a silent question.

"Be ready to get back up that ladder as fast as you can," I warned. "There's going to be trouble."

She began to climb the steps instead. I reached for her arm to hold her back, but she shook my hand off. I hurried after her, doubly surprised to find that the maid had also begun the climb.

The crowd above us remained strangely silent. Then I heard the native officer say in whining Spanish, "Sidi, I crave your forgiveness." He cringed and bowed profusely. His attitude had an effect on the mob, for they continued to hold back. When the din was renewed, the belligerent note was missing.

John had taken the only course under the circumstances. I realized that the native temper would have risen if he had failed to cap the insult with an even greater one. Now the danger was over for the time being.

John presented me to Sir Sigismund with a complimentary reference to the part I had played in the capture of the *Santa Caterina*. The great traveler smiled warmly and said he had known my father. When Dona Cristina was presented, he lifted his shaggy gray brows. "You haven't chosen the best day to come ashore, Señorita," he said. "Gouletta is generally as calm as the streets of Seville in the heat of noon. Today the spell of the Prophet is on them. But have no fear. The Dey thinks too well of Captain Ward for anything to happen to him or to any member of his train."

He turned back to John. "I crossed France and took ship from Marseilles three weeks ago," he explained. "I made the journey to bring you news. Important news, John. Something that will give you a great deal of pleasure, I think. And I have a packet of letters."

"You have me at a loss, then," said John. "I can conceive of no form of news from England which would give me pleasure now. I've news for you, Mundy, and I am sure that mine will give you no pleasure at all. The Dutchmen are giving in. A truce for twelve years will be concluded with Spain in a few weeks. Have you heard any word of it?"

Hill looked grave. "No word of this had reached London when I left," he said. "Nor did I hear any rumors of it in France. This is indeed the blackest of news, John, although I must say I have been expecting it for a long time. The Low Countries couldn't be counted upon to fight alone forever. Have you decided on any course?"

"I have," declared John. "We'll have to carry on the fight ourselves. My plans are all made. I think we had better get on to Tunis at once, for I must get the ear of the Dey as soon as possible. Fortunately that sly little heathen has as much reason to fear the truce as we have. The news and the letters you bring will have to wait, Mundy. Where are your quarters?"

"In Tunis. A partly dismantled palace has been put at my disposal. I eat and sleep in a hammock which I've swung high enough to keep me free of the rats and lizards. Such as it is, you and your men may share it with me." He glanced at the two women and then added: "There's room for everyone, in fact. We can go by boat through the canal, although it's the slowest way."

"Let's start at once," said John.

15

I ESCORTED DONA CRISTINA about Sir Sigismund's domain while we waited for John to return from his audience with the Dey. Her eyes, taking in the crumbling walls and the gardens choked with weeds, were not happy.

It had, however, been a great palace once. It stood high above the white-roofed expanse of Tunis, and its walls were of marble. It was clear that it had been in Christian hands at some time, for one of the rooms on the ground floor had been used as a chapel, and from the tangle in the outer court protruded the mutilated heads of sculptured saints. I would have liked to investigate this, but my companion was too tired to show any interest. The trip through the city had been a nerve-racking business for her. Hundreds of natives had followed us, keeping up their shrill chorus of "Hagi Baba!" and pressing in as close

as they dared. I had ridden in the rear, and one green-turbaned scarecrow had clung to the tail of my horse, pelting me with offal from the
streets which he scooped up with his free hand. We could still hear
them milling about outside, and at intervals rocks came hurtling over
the walls. It was not surprising that her nerves were slightly jangled.

"Don Roger," she said, when the noise outside the walls reached an
especially high note, "I do not think I like this."

Sir Sigismund Hill joined us at this point. "There's nothing to fear,"
he said. "I don't mean that those howling dervishes out there wouldn't
enjoy tearing us limb from limb. They're in one of their religious fevers
today. But they'll take it out in noise. As long as Captain Ward is useful
to the Dey, we're as safe here as on West Cheape."

"We passed a slave market on our way," I said. "I saw white men
chained to pillars. It wasn't a reassuring thing to see. I don't like this
either."

"Don't judge hastily. In its normal moods, Tunis is a city of enchantment. I've been here many times, and I'm always glad to come back. It
has life and color and mystery. You can find anything you seek here.
Even peace. Time means nothing. I think I am reasonably hard of
head, and yet I tell you that on hot still nights I've fancied I could see
the ghosts of Hannibal's men marching out to Zama." He paused and
smiled. "I'm going to make a confession. I prefer Tunis to most Christian
cities. Even to London."

"London!" There was the deepest contempt in Dona Cristina's voice.
"I hear it is a dismal city. Cold and foggy and very dirty. They treated
our Queen Catherine badly in London. I think you are comparing one
form of barbarism with another. Have you seen any of the cities of
Spain?"

"Yes, dear lady, I've seen them all. They make me think of beasts of
the jungle sleeping in high grass through the heat of midday. They
seem peaceful and lovely; but you know that they might at any moment
be roused to blood-lust." He smiled apologetically. "I'm speaking my
mind frankly, Señorita. As for London, it is clear you don't know it's
the richest city in the world. Even the merchants of mighty Rome-
ville live in homes as fine as the palaces of your noblemen in Seville. I
mention the fact with pride, although you'll think perhaps I'm giving
further proof of the barbarity of the place."

"I do indeed," she said.

"It's a great city, Señorita. I know nothing more inspiring than to
sail up the Thames and watch the life of London unfolding and multiplying on each bank. But I'm never happy there. I confess it. To me
London is the personification of human energy and the determination
of man to make over God's good earth to suit himself." He paused and
shook his head. "Strange talk, this, from me. I've spent my life in finding ways to increase the number of ships on the Thames."

We had climbed a narrow stone stairway, slippery from the moisture which dripped through leaks in the roof, and now stood on a long gallery overlooking the main hall of the palace. It had been imposing once, but now there were wide cracks in the colored tiling of the walls, and the inlaid marble floor was warped and split.

"The knights of Charles V of Spain dined here once," said Sir Sigismund, reflectively. "And the place has been shunned like a pesthouse ever since. Even the beggars of the city refuse to seek shelter inside these polluted walls. Please don't think I say this as a reflection on your people, Señorita. The heathen hate us all equally. And, as it happens, I'm half Spanish myself."

He was so completely English in appearance, with his mild gray eyes and thin, high-bridged nose, that I was as much taken aback at this statement as our companion.

"My mother was Spanish," he explained. "I don't remember her, but I believe she was quite a beauty. I think she must have looked somewhat like you, Señorita. My father, who was an astronomer of some small repute, went to Portugal with George Buchanan when that great Scotsman was invited to lecture at the University of Coimbra. There my father met the daughter of an obscure Spanish poet and married her."

The Señorita had forgotten her fears and was listening to him with absorbed interest. I watched her with more interest than I had for Sigismund's explanation, noting the stamp of pride in her fine features and the sensitive curve of her lips.

"I was born the very day that the officers of the Inquisition came for my father and other foreign lecturers. He was kept in prison for a year. My mother carried me in her arms when she met him at the prison gates with the welcome news that he was free to leave the country. The pardon came too late. He was reduced to skin and bone, and a rat had gnawed away one ear while he lay unconscious in prison."

"He was a heretic—" began the Señorita.

"There is a choice of terms," said Hill. "My father had imbibed his religious beliefs under a truly great man. His name, Señorita, was John Knox, though I doubt if it can mean anything to you. He didn't survive the voyage home, and my mother died a few months after we landed. I was brought up by an uncle, a wool merchant in London. He taught me to believe that the devil had put his mark on every Spaniard. When quite a young man I spent several months on a walking tour of your country, and I realized then how wrong he had been. I wasn't able to locate any of my mother's people, but I made many friends. Some of them continue friends to this day."

He regaled us with anecdotes of his travels in Spain as we completed our inspection of the place. In the chapel we found a crucifix of solid gold attached to the wall. Sir Sigismund regarded it with thoughtful eyes.

"My mother was treated coldly in England because she was a Catholic," he said. "Years later a young cousin of mine, a girl and quite lovely, was burned at the stake by Queen Mary's orders because she was a Protestant. And now observe this crucifix, the symbol of the Christian faith. It's hated so intensely by the Mohammedans that it has been left untouched all these years. It would have made a rich man out of any beggar who carried it away. I vow, my young friends, that this would be a peaceful world, and a pleasanter one to live in, if men could only learn to take their religion with less intensity."

I called attention to the fact that the servingwoman had been following us at a respectful distance from the moment we began our inspection.

"Poor Luisa!" said the Señorita. "She is afraid to be left alone. At home she would run and hide herself at the sight of a brown face. You may judge of her loyalty when she insisted on coming with me."

Sounds of conflict reached us from the street. I could make out English voices above the treble clamor of the natives. "John has arrived with a squad," I said. "They'll soon get the streets cleared."

It took a very few minutes, and then John entered through the front gate. He was grinning happily. "That will teach the beggars a lesson," he said. He swept a low bow to the Spanish girl. "If the Señorita will excuse us for a few minutes, I have important news for you, gentlemen."

He led the way to a corner of the weed-infested courtyard where we seated ourselves on the rim of what had once been a marble fountain. A bronze fawn stood in the center and afforded us a little shade from the heat of the sun.

"The Dey is a badly frightened little man," said John. "He has agreed to everything."

Hill nodded. "I expected as much. The Dons have a heavy score to settle with him. He needs your help badly."

"He went limp with apprehension when I told him about the truce. I didn't need to explain what I planned to do. He began by begging me to organize all the Free Rovers into a fleet to operate from this port. If we agree to engage any Spanish squadron which rounds Cape Blanc, he will give us certain supplies free of charge and forego his percentage of the spoils. His fears got the better of his bargaining instinct. He sat there biting his nails and making concessions so fast that I found it hard to keep up with him. If I had held off, I believe the little heathen would have offered me the half of his kingdom and the run of his harem."

"He's a great promiser," commented Hill, "but he'll bear watching. When he thinks he has no more need for you, he'll throw you to the dogs, Ward. And now, perhaps, you'll condescend to hear the news I bring you. I think you'll find it a great surprise."

John laughed. "I'm all ears. Does good King Jamie offer me the half of *his* kingdom?"

"Not exactly. But you've made a shrewd guess. His Majesty has changed his mind. He wants you back."

I could hardly believe my ears, although I realized from the serious expression on the lean face of the great traveler that he was speaking the truth. I felt like jumping up and shouting for joy. This meant we would return to England at once, with the profits of a successful cruise in our pockets and the plaudits of the whole nation in our ears. I glanced at John to see how he was taking it and was surprised to see that he was frowning.

"I can accept a joke in good grace, Mundy," he said. "But you're letting your fancy stray too far. What, in God's name, are you trying to tell me?"

The girl had retired to a shaded corner of the courtyard. Here she had seated herself on a stone bench and was watching us with an intensity which under the circumstances I found pathetic. It was clear she knew her own fate was bound up in what we were discussing. I wondered what John would do with her now, for it was certain he could not take her back to England with us. Poor lady! This great news, which had set my blood racing with exultation, would be nothing short of tragic for her.

Luisa was standing behind her mistress and had placed a reassuring hand on her shoulder. Apparently the maid also had sensed that a crisis was at hand.

"It's official, John," said Hill. "I had my instructions in the matter direct from my Lord of Nottingham. He requested me to tell you how great is his own pleasure in the decision. I'm sure His Lordship has important plans for you."

John got slowly to his feet. Taking his plumed hat from his head, he tossed it solemnly in the air.

"I'm so happy I can hardly speak," he said. I was not surprised to see that his eyes were filled with tears. "I've never desired anything better than to fight for my country under the flag of my King. I promise you that His Majesty will find me a loyal servant." His voice suddenly boomed out with a rush of enthusiasm. "Tremble, Philip of Spain! Your filthy beard is ripe for singeing! The might of England is to be unleashed at last. And, glory to God, John Ward is to have his share in it!"

I was puzzled by the expression on Hill's face. Was he withholding something? Were there strings to the offer from London which he had not yet mentioned? My spirits took a sharp decline.

John began to pace about, his hands sunk deep in the pockets of his yellow breeches. We all watched him, Hill with a growing air of apprehension, the Spanish girl with an agitation that outstripped my own. I was sure now that matters were not as perfect as they had seemed.

"I'm convinced, Mundy," boomed John, "that His Majesty knows the negotiations between Spain and the Low Countries are ending in this truce. He has a wise head on his shoulders, after all. He may endeavor to block it by throwing in actively with the Dutch. Or it may be that he realizes England will soon face a fight single-handed against Spain. Thank God, he's facing the issue at last."

Hill shook his head in dissent. "You're leaping far ahead of the royal purpose," he said. "His Majesty is not thinking in terms of war with Spain. On the contrary, he's as strongly persuaded to peace as ever."

John stopped his excited pacing. "He doesn't intend to fight? I don't understand this. What does he propose to do with me, then?"

Hill smiled bleakly. "There's plenty of work for you. Have you any idea how much real piracy there is about our own shores? Lundy Island is still a menace to shipping in the Severn. It's high time something was done to clean out that foul nest. Things are bad in the northern reaches of the Irish Sea. Grace O'Malley and Fineen of the Ships are dead, but there are a dozen or more taking their places. That's the task His Majesty has for you, John."

"I see. Hire a pirate to catch other pirates. So that's the King's plan! I might have known."

John sat down again. I knew what his answer was going to be, and somewhere down deep within myself I found a spark of agreement. But it was not strong enough to take the edge off my disappointment.

The rosy dreams in which I had been indulging disappeared. We would not be returning to England after all. I felt so bad that I did not dare raise my eyes. Instead I kept them fixed on a green lizard which was creeping around the base of the fountain. It was the largest and gaudiest specimen I had ever seen.

"I can't make any sense out of this at all," went on John. I could tell from his voice how sick he was feeling. "Gondomar must be clamoring for my head. Has the King found new courage to resist Spanish demands?"

"You would find it easier to understand if you knew what happened after you sailed," explained Hill. "All London started to laugh when the word got out that the King had suspected you of a plot against his royal person. The country took it up. The laughter became so general and so boisterous that echoes of it finally reached the royal ears. He had enough common sense to see he had made a fool of himself, particularly when a paquin of Archie Armstrong's got about. It began like this:

> "King Jamie peered beneath his bed,
> But John Ward wasna there. . . ."

"I could supply the rest of the lines myself," said John glumly.

"His Majesty realized at last that the people of the country were for you and against him in this matter. He made up his mind, grudgingly I am sure, to grant you a pardon and get you back in his service before more harm was done to his kingly popularity. I'm assuming that he has another purpose. Relations with Spain will remain unsatisfactory as long as you continue to give them cause for complaint. His Majesty sees that, the sooner you are called off, the easier it will be for him to get the peace he desires. And there you have the whole story."

"Not quite all. His Majesty didn't know then that I would add to my long list of crimes by hanging Don Pedro Alonzo Maria de Vente. Wait until he hears about that!" He began to laugh bitterly. "This, then, is the situation: I will be taken back to do the King's dirty work and spend my life chasing the owling brotherhood of the Irish Sea. In the meantime Spain will conclude her truce with the Dutch and will be free to concentrate her fleets in the Mediterranean and on the lanes to the Americas. There will be no one to organize any resistance to them, and English shipping will be driven from the seas."

Hill made no comment, and after a moment John asked him what the effect would be on the Levant Company. "We're in a dilemma," was the answer. "Our ships may be put into coastal service or sold to the East India Company. The route around Africa will remain open."

"Don't be too sure of that!" declared John. "Once we're driven out of here, the Spaniards will be in a position to close off the Middle Course. Be honest with me, Mundy. Are you happy over this situation?"

Hill hesitated and then said gruffly, "No." They sat in silence for several moments before he added: "I'm not happy about it. I refrained from expressing myself one way or the other because I didn't want to influence your decision. It would be to your own best interest to take the offer, my boy. If you don't—" He left the sentence unfinished.

John crossed his knees and stared straight ahead with the deepest gloom. I glanced in the direction of the Señorita, and she raised her hand in a gesture which I construed as an invitation to join her. I walked over, and she drew her skirts aside to make room for me on the bench.

"What is it all about?" she whispered. "I have been watching your faces and have seen that you are all very unhappy."

"Captain Ward has been offered a pardon and reinstatement in the Royal Navy."

Her face clouded over, and at first she made no comment. "But that is what he wants, is it not?" she asked finally.

"Yes. But there are conditions attached which he doesn't like."

There was another pause. "He will accept?" she ventured.

I shook my head. "I don't think so. If he doesn't, it will probably mean that we will never see England again. Certainly not for many years."

"Would he not be wise, then, to accept the conditions?"

All my doubts suddenly dissolved. "No, Señorita. He would be untrue to everything he believes if he returned to England now. I'm sure he has already made up his mind to refuse. And that's what you want, isn't it?"

She gave me a steady glance from under her long black eyelashes. "Yes, it is what I want," she said. "But I am sorry for you, Don Roger.

John has told me a great deal about you, and sometimes I have watched you when you did not know it. You do not like this life. You are very young, and it does not seem right that you should be an exile all your life."

This put me on the defensive. "It may not last forever. The King's son will change things when he comes to the throne. He's a brave prince and sees the need for fighting Spanish pretensions as much as most Englishmen do."

She sighed. "You all hate my country. I think you do not like me either."

I had been keeping my eyes on John and Sir Sigismund, but this was a challenge which forced me to turn and face her. Her face was a perfect oval of delicate ivory against the soft fold of her lace rebatoe. The dress into which she had changed was white except for a few touches of black in the embroidery of her sleeves and on the barred petticoat which showed under her divided skirt. I could not help contrasting her slim grace with the artificial effect of the farthingale, to which English women still clung. She was wearing no jewelry, with the exception of a large emerald set in a ring of curiously carved gold.

"You're wrong about that," I said. "I like you very much."

She began to speak in low and hurried tones. "We have interests in common, Don Roger. You must know that I would not be here if I had not been so foolish as to fall in love with your tall captain. One day we had a very bitter quarrel, and he told me then about the girl in England and about you. See, Don Roger, we will make a bargain between us. You will go home and marry this girl. And I, I will see that John does not care." She went on in a tense whisper, "I could not bear it if a memory stood between us. The memory will fade quicker if you marry her. Do you think me immodest to say this? I cannot afford to be modest now."

"Roger!" called John.

"Remember," she whispered, as I got to my feet. "We are partners. We must stand together."

"We're partners," I said. "But I'm afraid things won't happen the way we want them. I've no chance at all. Katie's in love with John."

John looked at me curiously when I rejoined them. "You're learning fast, my kinchin coe," he said. "What were you and the Señorita talking about with your heads so close together?"

"You, for the most part."

He laughed and clapped me on the shoulder. "I'm not so sure of that. You've a guilty look about you. But come now, we've a decision to make." He seemed to have regained his spirits, which to me was an indication that the decision had already been made in his mind. "Mundy, what is your final thought?"

"There's one point I haven't mentioned yet," said Hill. "With the offer from His Majesty goes a promise of knighthood within as brief a space of time as may seem necessary to the maintenance of the royal dignity. Sir John Ward—it has a round ring to it. Perhaps that is the argument you need to decide the matter for you."

John drew his sword from its scabbard. The hilt was made of gold and elaborately chased. He held the blade out in front of him.

"I'm proud of this sword," he said. "The steel was forged by a smith of Damascus several centuries ago. I won the hilt in fair combat with a subject of His Most Catholic Majesty of Spain. I'm not ashamed of any use to which it has been put since it has belonged to me. I prefer to keep my record as clean as this fine blade." He thrust it back. His voice rose. "You may inform the Earl of Nottingham that I refuse the King's offer! I would rather be plain John Ward, a pirate if you like and a man without country or flag, fighting by myself to keep the sea lanes open, than Sir John Ward, tame piglet in His Sowship's sty. That is my decision."

"John," said Hill, "you're a great fool. But as an Englishman I am proud of such folly."

They shook hands on it. John turned his head in my direction. "What about you, Roger? I think you would be well advised to return with Sir Sigismund. Anyone who stays with me will find himself forever under the royal ban. I don't want to have that happen to you."

"I'm going to stay," I answered. "I signed up for the duration of the cruise. Would you have me back out now when there is rough water ahead?"

"Bravely spoken," said John. "I knew you would want to stay. And now, Mundy, what have you provided for our dinner? All this talk has made me hungry."

When Sir Sigismund left to see what could be done about refreshments, John took me by the arm and said in a low tone, "I suppose you're wondering what my plans are for the fair captive?"

I assured him that I was very much interested, and that I was sure the Señorita herself would like to learn what was in his mind as soon as possible.

"I've thought of an excellent plan." He spoke with assurance, but I was certain that he was suffering from inward misgivings. "There's an Englishman living with his wife in Sicily, Sir Ninian Phippins from up Ipswich way. His health was so bad that he was given up for dead, and he then conceived the completely mad scheme of leaving England and living on this island. Ten years ago it was, and by some curious chance he's still alive. Lady Phippins is a motherly soul, and they have no chick of their own. I hear they are lonely, and they have a large stone house with a garden looking out over the sea. Well, I shall send the Señorita to them. I'll give her as much as I can, and she can make her home with them; and in time, no doubt, she'll marry some fine young fellow. Don't you think it is a perfect solution?"

"No," I answered. "It's far from a perfect solution."

"In God's name, why not?" His manner showed irritation, and yet I knew he had expected no other answer.

"She'll tell you herself when you propose this plan to her. Why not do it at once? The poor lady is consumed with anxiety."

I left the courtyard, observing out of a corner of my eye that he had made a bad start. Tapping the servingwoman familiarly, he said, "Run along, Fubbs, I've something to say to your mistress."

The Señorita frowned. "Disrespect for the maid is disrespect for the mistress. Perhaps you do not know that in England."

I went into the inner court, and from there could hear their voices distinctly enough to know that John's plan was not receiving a favorable hearing. The talk went on for the better part of an hour, at the end of which time Sir Sigismund announced that food was ready for us. The discussion stopped, and I saw Dona Cristina walk into the house, her head held high and a trace of color in her cheeks. John followed with a slightly chap-fallen air and, as I fell into step with him, he said, "The lady has a temper."

16

THE MEAL WAS SERVED in the high-ceilinged chamber which we had observed from the gallery earlier in the afternoon. Some pretense at furnishings had been managed in the meantime. A long table had been set up on the uneven floor, and half a dozen oddly assorted chairs had been placed about it. In one corner was a tabouret with a set of tall ivory chessmen.

"Do either of you play?" asked Hill. "I always carry these men with me. I'm reasonably expert. No one in England has ever beaten me, and once I achieved a draw with the great Ruy Lopez de Segura in Spain. But that means little, for I've been beaten by many players in the East. There is one dried-up little mummy of a man in Damascus, a rug merchant, who can give me the queen—he calls it the *farzi*—and defeat me with the greatest ease."

I owned to a slight acquaintance with the game, and it was arranged that we would play after dinner. He would give me a rook to begin with; or did I think I might need both?

The Señorita joined us, and Sir Sigismund took the head of the table, placing her on his right while I sat on her other side. She looked across the table at John with stormy eyes but said nothing.

A single dish was placed before us, a huge platter heaped high with food. "Couscousou, the great dish of the East," explained Sir Sigismund.

"I'm afraid we must help ourselves with our hands. It's the custom."
The Señorita and I looked at each other with considerable doubt, but
our two companions began to eat with appetite, assuring us it was
capital food. Accordingly I dipped a hand into the platter and was rewarded with a tender piece of mutton. It was so good that I threw my
scruples to the wind and proceeded to make a hearty meal. Dona Cristina could not be persuaded to participate, however.

"The base of this dish," said Hill, tossing a bone over his shoulder,
"is a wheaten substance called seminola. They put into it everything
they can find—meat, eggs, vegetables, butter, spices. Then it's steamed
slowly for hours. You're making a great mistake, Señorita. It's the best
food in the world."

"I can't go that far," protested John. "This is excellent in its way, but
give me the food at home. Roast beef and marrow puddings, collops
and hotch-potch; goose at Christmas and pancotto and fruit suckets.
There's nothing better."

Sir Sigismund protested vigorously. Had John any acquaintance with
the curried foods of India, for instance? He considered French cookery
overestimated but, even at that, much superior to anything found in
England. A ragout, now, a turbot in wine sauce, or a mess of lam-
preys—these were royal dishes. They argued with some heat, tossing
the names of favorite foods back and forth: Jack-of-Dover, quaking
puddings, goodicakes, syllabub, temperade, hartshorn jellies. My silent
neighbor looked at me once and smiled to show how dull she found
the topic.

The platter was removed, and water bowls with linen towels were
placed in front of us. I used mine with alacrity, being sure that I had
achieved as greasy an appearance as the two disputants. Then a tall
dish of fruit was brought in. There were strawberries, the largest grapes
I had ever seen, some early peaches, and pomegranates. As a Bible
student I was much interested in the latter and bit into one eagerly.
John laughed when he saw how disappointing I found it.

"If the Children of Israel had known the taste of an English apple,"
he declared, "their prophets would have devoted less time to singing
the praises of this bitter fruit. A Cornish codlin or a red biffin, for my
taste. Still, we must manage somehow to like these desert fruits. We're
going to have a long acquaintance with them, I'm afraid. All of us."
He nodded at the Señorita, who had looked up in surprise. "A very
long acquaintance. You in particular, Roger. I've decided you're the man
to act as our agent in port."

My pride took immediate alarm. "That's landsmen's work!" I protested.

"Don't judge too soon. You've acquitted yourself like a veritable
David, but you've also shown a turn for the details of management.
That's a quality I lack most completely." Seeing that I was going to
protest, he went into an explanation. "You have no idea of the im-

portance of this work I want to shift onto your shoulders. If we get all the Free Rovers with us, you'll be busier than any captain in the fleet."

"I've served in that capacity in my time," said Hill. "It's hard work, I assure you."

"There's always a shortage of water in Africa, but you will have to be ready on the shortest notice to fill the casks of any number of ships I may bring in. I'm hoping to have as many as thirty. You must keep us supplied with food and powder and medicines. And canvas and silk and rope. The petty tally alone is enough to keep a man busy."

Hill nodded. "Many a night did I sweat over my books. I've stood between captain and owner and taken abuse from both. Thirty captains to suit? You'll need a cool head on your shoulders."

The girl whispered to me, "It will be better for you ashore."

The magnitude of the work had begun to frighten me. When I said this, John declared emphatically: "You can do it, Roger. I've been watching you, and I'm sure of it. I'm also sure," he added with a smile, "that you'll find it much more to your liking than playing joskin under Hale Harry Gard."

It did not take me long to make up my mind. The scope of the work was terrifying, but I knew I was better fitted for it than for life aboard ship. I felt easier about the prospect when John explained that I would have the assistance of a wily old Turk named Abadad, who knew the household of the Dey inside out and could be relied on to match official guile with a degree of cunning at least as great.

"Abadad," said John, "has been with me since my first visit to Tunis. He's as ugly as the Prince of Sin, and he'd cut his grandfather's throat if I ordered it. He steals less than any Christian agent I've ever known. He works twenty hours a day and devotes half of his leisure time to prayers. I'm fond of the old rascal."

"Where will I live?" I asked.

"At Gouletta. We have an old stone building which Queen Dido must have built, for it's at least a thousand years old. You'll have a room to yourself, and the walls are so thick that you'll be reasonably cool. You'll live on the fat of the land while the rest of us are starving at sea on wormy biscuit and rancid salt meat. And, of course, you'll be entitled to the share of a mate. That's something to consider."

I nodded my final acceptance, and the talk turned to details of supply. Naturally we fell back into English, for it was impossible to speak of such matters as the drawing and hand-hackling of hemp in foreign terms. Sir Sigismund was particularly concerned about the manufacture of cloth for sails, which had been started in England for the first time some ten or twelve years before.

"They're not sailors, the French, and the mildernex we bought from them to rig out our ships could not be trusted," he declared. "There is a shoddiness to the French which comes out in what they do. Now that we're making our own, we have sail cloth to stand the bitter threshing of an Arctic gale. Unfortunately, Roger, you'll have to take what you can get here."

I saw that John was keeping an uneasy eye on the Señorita as the talk flowed monotonously along. He seemed ill at ease and fidgeted in his chair. It was a flimsy thing and creaked alarmingly under his weight. He consumed an immense quantity of fruit, throwing the rinds through a fissure in the marble floor. Knowing little of English, Dona Cristina sat with bowed head, turning and re-turning the emerald ring on her finger.

"That's a fine stone," John said finally, addressing her directly for the first time.

"My father sent it to me from America," she answered, without raising her head. "It is an Inca ring and is supposed to have the power to bring fulfillment of wishes to anyone who wears it. I believed in it at first, but now I am afraid I am losing faith."

Sir Sigismund leaned over the table to study it. "It's of great value," he said. "I'm very much interested in what you say about its power because I've seen many magic stones in the East. I've heard of Yogis bringing fine crops to arid soil by touching the first furrow turned with a piece of jasper. Generally the stones of the East are used for harmful purposes. I saw a large toadstone on the dirty finger of a Persian magician, and it was said he could cast a spell on anyone who crossed him by rubbing it with his thumb."

"Did you see any proofs?" I asked.

"Many strange things happened. I must confess that I took great care not to arouse the man's enmity, I see there's an inscription on the band, Señorita. Do you know what it says?"

She shook her head. "No one has been able to read it. Not even the natives of the country where it came from. It is a very old ring."

"I've never seen a lovelier one," said Hill. "I'm disposed to believe the story. The cool deep green of the emerald has a suggestion of beneficence as well as mystery about it. Ask nothing but good of it, Señorita, and I'm sure it will fulfill your wishes. It's meant to bring love and happiness."

John cleared his throat. "Perhaps you've lost faith too soon," he said.

The girl raised her eyes and looked at him steadily. I sensed that a crisis in their relationship had been reached and wondered what John would say next. He turned toward Sir Sigismund. "I've arranged with the Dey to take over this place when you leave, Mundy. He gives it to me outright as part of the bargain."

"What do you plan to do with it?"

"I'm going to restore it to its former glory. The Dey promises me all the workmen I'll need. I'm going to raise the wall to twenty feet and broaden it so watchmen can stand on it. The chapel will be restored.

Water will be piped in from the city reservoir. The fountains will run again, and I'm going to install baths. I'll station half a dozen men of the crew here to act as a guard." He paused. "I'm hoping, Señorita, that you'll accept it as your home. You'll be able to live here as comfortably as you did in Castile. There will be security for you, and peace. I hope some happiness also."

She sat for a moment without answering. Then she rose and said, "You are very kind," and left the room. John gazed after her with a hurt and puzzled look.

"I thought she would be pleased," he said.

"You great dolt," said Sir Sigismund. "She's so happy about it, she couldn't trust herself to say anything more." He winked at me. "And now, Sir Agent, we may get to our game of chess."

I joined him at the tabouret, and we matched for the first move. I lost. John got to his feet with careful nonchalance and strolled from the room.

Sir Sigismund swept both his rooks from the board and advanced his king's pawn. "I think the ring has power after all," he said, with a broad smile. "The lady has won. We won't see either of them now for a time. That's just as well, for now we'll have an uninterrupted game. She's quite beautiful, don't you think?"

"Yes, very beautiful."

"What a contrast to our apple-cheeked girls at home." He pounced triumphantly on a knight which I had advanced carelessly. "The last time I was in Spain was just before war was declared. They were assembling the Armada, and they were very sure of victory. Governors were being appointed for all our cities. Philip was going over the lists himself, and he was having medals struck to reward his captains. Feeling was running high, and I had to get out of the country fast. There was a song I heard being sung everywhere. It dealt with the faults of Englishmen and was so amusing that I went to the trouble of translating it. One verse had to do with love.

> "A Spanish maid in love might fall,
> Mayhap with reasty Portugall,
> With an Irish kern, a Paris clown,
> A Moorish thief with skin of brown,
> A scurvy knave of roynish clan;
> *But never! No, never, an Englishman!*"

He advanced a bishop and said, "Check!" I was in a difficult position, and while I studied what to do he went on: "I'm afraid our lovely Señorita had never heard that particular verse. It would have been better for her if she had. When things go wrong between them—as they will, of course—she will either put a knife between his ribs or go quietly away and die of a broken heart. In my judgment, the poor lady will take the second course. Well, there's nothing to be done about it. She's fallen in love, and with an Englishman. By the way, Captain Ward will be in port a great deal from now on. Don't be surprised if he decides you are too crowded at Gouletta to accommodate him."

17

A BREEZE BLEW IN from the sea during the evening, giving us a welcome respite from the drugging heat of the day. John and I adjourned to an upper balcony to take advantage of it, and there went into a discussion of supplies. After a short nap, Sir Sigismund joined us with a packet of letters in his hand. Three of them were for me, the rest for John.

I did not open mine for several minutes. Looking at the familiar handwriting on two of them and at the slanting girlish scrawl of the third, I had become desperately homesick. I did not need to read them to get the feel of happier things: the bustle and chatter of Shrubsole High; the pleasant calm of an evening in front of the fire at home with Mother smiling at me over her embroidery and Aunt Gadilda grimly absorbed in some more practical task; the sway of light breezes in the sorb groves; and the unmusical voices of brisk dredgermen at the wharves. I found myself longing to be back in that easy and secure life. The sounds of heathen gabble, reaching us faintly from the rooftops in the town below, intensified my desire for the sweet tedium of home.

John, whose interest in our talk of powdered pork and ammunition had been limited by the fact that, from where we sat, we could see the slim figure of the Spanish girl pacing slowly up and down in the outer courtyard, was already deep in his mail. I was undutiful enough to read Katie's note ahead of the others. It was the first I had ever received from her, and my eyes skimmed eagerly over the closely written pages.

DERE ROGGER; [Katie was never much of a scholar]

Father has sede Sir Sigismund Hill will carry latters for me and so I am writing you and Captane Warde [she had set down 'John' first and then crossed it out] to tell you how happie I am you are soone to return home. Father does not agrie and says Captane Warde is needed wear he is. I am sure he wud be angrie with me for feeling diffrunt—

It was a chatty note, filled with details which I absorbed eagerly. She was in a jubilant mood because she was to become maid of honor in the household of Queen Anne in the fall and had written down ecstatic descriptions of the dresses she was going to take with her to London. There was a whole page about tippets of sarsenet, pickadells, rebatoes, purles, fulles and frislets, buskpoints and whalebone wheels. She had seen my mother in town one day, and they had talked about me for a long time. Her old dog Walter had died, and she did not think she would get another because it was said the Queen did not like dogs and would not want one at court. Did I remember a forward minx named Ann Turner? Of course I did; all the men of the town had been interested in the girl. She had opened a frippery shop in London, and all the ladies of the court were going to it. So she, Katie, would probably go too, if only out of curiosity. She wondered what presents I would be bringing her.

I was much feared [she concluded] when there was so grate a trubble in London and Captane Warde was hideing with us. We thought you had been taken to the Tower and so I was most happie when Father heard that the Royal Bess had sailed. You are much in my thoughts, Rogger, and I will not fele easy until you and Captane Warde have returned safely. I have missed you grately.

I read it over several times, picturing her in my mind in each episode she described. I told myself it was exactly the kind of letter she would have written me if she had never set eyes on John Ward, and that I had no reason for disappointment. Nevertheless I found myself watching him and wondering if his letter from Katie was longer than mine, and if it had been couched in more intimate terms.

He was a long time in reading it. Then he fell into a brown study, his eyes fixed on the sky to the north. Finally he said to Hill: "I want you to know, Mundy, that it's not ambition which keeps me here. I've no desire to add to my reputation. I would be the happiest man alive if I could sail home this very night."

I knew then that what he had told me was true. Katie had made her choice.

I turned to the rest of my mail with a sinking heart. There was much news of the town in the letters from Mother and Aunt Gadilda. They both indulged in a few mild expressions of reproach, but it was easy to see they were secretly proud of what I had done. Each referred to the rumor that we were returning soon and were very happy about it, although Aunt Gadilda added a phrase which puzzled me. "Your mother," she wrote, "does not explain how she heard this welcome news, fearing my disapproval, and rightly."

I was so much at a loss over this that I read what she had said to John. "Sir Bartlemy, no doubt," he said, with a grin. "He's a great gossip and quite a bit of a beau as well. It was said all over town he had a soft spot for your pretty mother. No doubt he stopped in to tell her the news, and your righteous aunt didn't approve."

I knew at once that he was right. Thinking back, I recalled many occasions when the owner of Appleby Court had called at our house on one pretext or another. It had never occurred to me then to connect his calls with the fact that afterward Aunt Gadilda was always in what Mother called her mood. One afternoon I had been in my bedroom and, hearing voices below, had opened my door with the intention of going down. Aunt Gadilda was standing at the head of the stairs, her head bent forward to catch what was being said in the drawing room. This had seemed strange, and I had changed my mind and returned to my room. Later I saw Sir Bartlemy ride away, looking very gallant in his velvet cloak and plumed hat.

John saw at once that I was bothered over what he had said, for he added hastily: "Come now, I meant no offense. Sir Bartlemy is a giddy old fool, and he never misses a chance to talk to a pretty woman."

I let the matter drop without any comment, and John went back to his mail, throwing an occasional word over his shoulder about the contents of the letters. There was one from the Upright Man of Alsatia to confirm arrangements for the shipment of goods by the overland route from Marseilles. He read it aloud, chuckling over its stilted phrases. There was a brief note from Richard Hakluyt, raising the point of publication of any manuscript which John might have in preparation. This interested me so much that I forgot my dismal speculations over the probable contents of the letter he had received from Katie. I had read most of the *Divers Voyages* which Hakluyt had published, getting the loan of them from Appleby Court; and the stirring tales they contained had done more than anything else to keep me resolute in my intention to become a sailor. John let the sheet flutter over the railing. He had never heard of Richard Hakluyt.

The most interesting letter of all was a brief scrawl from Archie Armstrong which John read aloud:

The mental acrobatics of our great noddie of a King have amazed everyone. He has turned a neat cat in a pan and now has nothing but the fondest things to say about you, my good Sir Pirate. But a word to the wise. Our doughty monarch changes his mind more often than he does his shirt. Given his own gait, he would rather see you swinging at Wapping Stairs than strutting it on the poop-deck of a royal ship-of-war. Think it over well, John Ward.

"Archie is right," said John. "I put no trust in pious Master James and his half-promises. I would as soon find myself in the power of this web-spinner at the Bardo. The Dey, at least, knows how best his own interests can be served."

Hill nodded in agreement. "The King's mind," he said, "is a quick one, but it is a small one. A dangerous combination."

The sun went down, and darkness fell over the city almost immediately. I could never get accustomed to this curious trick of Nature. Twilight at home was gradual and pleasant; I always felt we were in a different world when night came down like a black curtain. Silence fell over the city. My two companions got to their feet, Hill with a deep yawn, John with a rueful reminder of letters he must write as a result of his talk with the Dey.

I descended a stone stair and made my way through a passage to the inner court. A dozen lanterns had been brought ashore and had already been hung in different parts of the palace. One was suspended on the wall of the court, but the light it cast was so small that I did not see the Señorita until she came forward from the corner where she had been sitting alone.

"I thought you would never be through talking," she said. "It must have been a matter of great importance to keep you all so long."

I nodded. "John has letters to write now. He's summoning all the Free Rovers to Tunis."

Her face showed mixed emotions at this piece of news—fear mostly, but a trace of pride as well. "It will do him no good," she declared. "How can he hope to face the navy of Spain? He and his Free Rovers will be swept off the sea. What will happen to all of us then, Don Roger?"

"It will not be as easy as you think," I answered. "Have you forgotten the fate of your Armada?"

She had a black shawl over her shoulders although the breeze had died down again. I noticed that her eyes were a little red.

"We must not quarrel," she said. "I have been in trouble with Luisa. She is sure I should go home and enter a convent. She is very religious and thinks only of saving my soul. More than I do myself, I am afraid. Just now she made a discovery which shocked her very much. She has prostrated herself in prayer, and I cannot get her to speak to me. She found that part of this building had been used as a harem. The thought of remaining in such un-Christian surroundings is too much for her."

Our tour of the afternoon had not included the quarters of the women, and my interest was aroused at once. "Where is it?" I asked.

She motioned toward a small door in the wall farthest from us. "In there," she whispered. She looked up at me and smiled doubtfully. "I—I am almost ashamed to say it, Don Roger, but I am very curious to see what it is like. Would it be too unseemly for us to go in?"

I detached the lantern from the wall and led the way to the door. It was of copper, and there was a huge key still in the lock. The hinges screeched a protest when I threw it open. My companion caught her breath as she followed me in.

I held the lantern high above my head. We were standing in a long room with a green marble floor and a sunken bath in the center. The walls were high, and there were latticed windows at least ten feet above the level of the floor. "This must have been the common room," I said in a whisper. "Their lord and master saw to it they were kept closely. No outside eye ever saw them here."

"Poor creatures!" said Dona Cristina. After a brief pause, she added: "Still, they had something precious here. They had peace."

"Peace? A dozen women living together in quarters like this! Anything but peace, I would say."

We found, on climbing a flight of steps to a corridor back of the common room, that at least twenty doors opened off it. I held the lantern in front of one of them and we looked inside. The room was just large enough for a bed and a few small articles of furniture. There was a window high up on the wall with colored glass.

My companion had been speaking in English, choosing her words slowly and with some difficulty. Now she reverted to her own tongue. "It's just like a prison. No, Don Roger, the poor women couldn't know peace in such surroundings. Luisa was right. There's something very wicked about this. I shall ask to have this wing closed up."

She spoke such perfect Spanish that my book learning enabled me to follow her with little difficulty. From that time on she never spoke anything else with me.

At the end of each corridor were narrow embrasures with tall windows which had served to give the inmate a view of the outside world. Vines grew thickly over the glass now. At the end of the long row of small rooms was a dark cell with a barred iron door. Holding the candle through the bars, I saw there were iron bracelets sunk into the masonry.

"What is it?"

"A punishment room, I think. Oriental husbands see to it that wives who disobey them are brought to their senses quickly."

She indulged in a shudder. "I think we had better go back now. What a cruel and senseless life! I'll never be able to get this picture out of my mind."

I pointed out the handsome decorations on the walls. The tiles were hexagonal in shape and carried yellow inscriptions on a dark-blue background. The cornices were loaded with gilding which had stood the ravages of time and neglect remarkably well. My companion was not impressed. When I called attention to a dark stairway leading underground, and made the suggestion that it led to the quarters of the eunuchs, she shuddered again.

"We'll leave that part unvisited, if you please. I'm sure we would find bastinado boards and whipping posts. I've seen enough."

When we descended again to the common room, we found John standing in the doorway. He was holding a lantern above his head and scowling doubtfully.

"Well," he said, his voice echoing through the bare room. "This is where you are. I've been looking everywhere and more than half suspecting an elopement." He made the suggestion lightly, but I could see he was not pleased.

"We've been looking over the harem," I said.

"What do you think of it?"

"It's wicked, and unfair and unclean!" said the girl. "I'm sorry I came."

John laughed. "I'm not so sure the idea is entirely wrong. Why should the women be unhappy? They live an easy life with no cares or responsibilities."

"Can any woman be happy who shares a husband with twenty others?"

"Perhaps not. But my sympathies are with the husbands."

She answered scornfully. "I was sure they would be. You boasted to me that you had a roving eye—"

"I didn't boast about it. I stated it in a properly penitent mood."

"You would be completely happy here, I'm sure. Your eye could rove along that row of doors—"

"Come now, we'll be quarreling in a minute. Roger has had more than his fair share of your company. I claim the rest."

I realized that I was tired, and so decided I would go to bed. I said good night to my companions and went in search of the room where the nettings from the ship had been hung. It proved to be close and airless, and I found it impossible to sleep there. After a time it occurred to me that it would be more comfortable on the roof. Unhooking the netting, I gathered it up in my arms and started out.

I reached the roof after a quarter-hour of stumbling along dark corridors and up stairs which ended in blank walls. It was hot even here, but the beauty of the sky was enough to compensate for any physical discomfort. The stars were out, and my first impression was that I could pluck any of them by extending an arm.

There was no possibility of swinging my netting from the stone parapet, so I rolled it up to serve as a pillow and stretched myself out on the stone roof. Sleep continued to evade me, for voices rose with surprising clearness from the garden below. I tried not to listen when I realized that it was John and the Señorita, but only by covering my ears could I have avoided hearing something of the conversation. She was calling him "Beau Brimstone," which surprised me because it was the least-used of the many nicknames the crew had coined for their captain. Once she began to sing in a pleasant throaty voice, and I recognized the air and words of the song to which Sir Sigismund had referred that afternoon. She had known it after all. John laughed at the finish and asked, "And is that the way you feel about Englishmen?" If she made any answer it was in too low a voice to reach as far as the rooftop.

Their voices went on and on, and finally I began to get drowsy. I heard John say, "You wouldn't be content, then, with one share in twenty?" I caught the answer this time: "I would not be content with nineteen shares." I became fully awake again when John said, "You need have no worries on that score, my sweet. It will not be difficult for you to command my entire devotion."

He was carrying Katie's letter in his pocket. I did not know which I felt sorrier for, Katie or Dona Cristina.

18

A MONTH LATER the roadstead was filled with English sails, and the Free Rovers assembled in the stone house at Gouletta to discuss John Ward's plan. They were a nondescript lot, some of them handsome enough and with traces of good breeding, others as rough as the trade they followed. I kept an eye on Sir Nevil Macherie, remembering the idea that Katie's father had once entertained. He was tall and sleek and very dandified in his manners.

Macherie was strongly in favor of the plan until he found that John would be selected as commander. He then began to hedge, to find objections and to question every suggestion with a supercilious air. It was clear that he regarded himself as of superior clay to the rest of them. He would sit by himself, cool and immaculate in spite of the stifling heat, and look around him with the utmost insolence. I took so great a dislike to him that I sometimes chimed in on the other side during the debates.

John disliked him fully as much as I did. Once he whispered in my ear: "This superior young gentleman needs a lesson. I wish I could afford to give him it."

Sir Nevil acquired a small following, but in the end he was outvoted. The impending truce between Spain and the Low Countries made it necessary for the Free Rovers to do something in self-defense, and John's plan was the only feasible one. They had to come to it finally. It was settled after two acrimonious days that they would join forces and take their orders from John Ward. Macherie was named second in command, perhaps because of the blue blood in his veins, perhaps to win his assent to the plan.

It was agreed also that I was to take charge ashore. This was done in spite of vigorous protests from Sir Nevil. He contended that I was "a raw gilpie, and an insolent one to boot." He wanted the Irishman Sleath to have the post but received practically no support on that. It had been decided that the cargoes of captured ships would be stored in port until an even division could be made, and the other captains were too well aware of Sleath's propensities to trust him with the fruits of their combined operations.

I had been watching Macherie closely during these stormy meetings. He was sparely built, with lathlike shanks and a habit of carrying his head well forward when he walked. This, combined with the fact that his skin was unusually white, made me think he resembled a high churchman of earlier days. There was nothing in his record to confirm this suggestion, however.

John stopped him, after the final meeting, to say that he had seen Sir Bartlemy Ladland recently and that he, Sir Bartlemy, had expressed the hope that they would meet. Macherie seemed to find the matter of small interest.

"Ah, yes," he said, rubbing his long nose. "Sir Bartlemy Ladland. Yes."

John turned away abruptly, but Sir Nevil reached an arm to detain him.

"Ward! What do you think of this venture? Do you see success in it for us?"

"Of course." John's manner was short. "We'll make it so hot for the Spaniards that they'll elect to leave our shipping alone."

"You *do* beat the drum of patriotism loudly, Ward. Fid's florins! I was thinking of something quite different. I was thinking of gold, man, gold for you and me and the rest of them. I need all I can get. My patrimony"—he paused to flick a speck of dust from the padded sleeve of his black doublet—"is somewhat depleted."

This was an understatement. I did not know what the Macherie estate had been earlier, but I had seen where Sir Nevil now lived: a few acres on a wooded scaur, without water or pasture land, the house an unpretentious block of green stone named Hodleyhaw, although the people of the neighborhood insisted on calling it Old Rattle-slates.

"I must get the family land back," went on Macherie. "You can't keep up a name in England without land. You probably don't follow me in that, Ward. You've never had land."

"No." John twisted his neck around to wink at me. "Like all the rest of the old and illustrious family of Ward, I've had to put my roots down in the deck of a ship."

Later he said to me, "The fellow is a perfect woolly-crown." I did not agree with that. In spite of his foppish ways, Macherie impressed me as dangerous.

I had been fighting against a sense of impending trouble for days. It had started when I realized that the three captains now taking their turn at a layover in port were, by some mischance, the only open adherents of Sir Nevil Macherie in our group of thirty. My apprehensions had grown as I watched the trio with their heads together in long serious talks. Something was afoot; and, whatever it might be, it boded our enterprise no good.

The table I used for a desk was piled high with papers, but I was in no mood for work. I had moved it so far forward that I sat almost in the open, and beneath me the ships at anchorage were massed so closely together that they made me think of an immense floral border in full bloom, even though I was close enough to see tarry patches and badly mended rents in the sails of blue, green, and orange. Over this barricade of color I could gaze clear across the bay. The surface of the water was almost glasslike, but gray clouds were banking over the horizon with a promise of coolness later.

I doubt if any tavern in Wapping had ever harbored a more villainous-looking lot than the assorted group which filled the room back of me. A file of natives squatted along the wall, waiting their turns with the utmost patience. I knew that any one of them would slit a throat for a handful of copper aspers. Their business was the transport of slaves through the inferno of sand country which lay to the south. I had refused to deal with them a dozen times, but they still came back with insectlike persistence, buzzing in my ear the latest quotations on healthy white men and comely white women. They filled the room with a heavy musky odor.

Two of the captains sat at a table in the corner. They were a little tipsy and were playing a bitter game of snogo. I could hear Black Jack Blunt from up Newcastle way expostulating with Basil Sleath as he slapped down his greasy cards: "The devil take yer luck! I won't have a single king's picture left." Sleath, who was dark and Irish, was saying nothing as he raked in his winnings, although once or twice he winked in my direction. Out of a corner of my eye I saw Captain Pooley join them and rest his great weight on the rickety table. His knee-high boots had been slit down the front to accommodate his enormous calves; and, although it was but ten in the morning, he was so drunk he could hardly stand. Bristol Bill Pooley was closer to Sir Nevil Macherie than either of the others.

I was thinking how the bold scheme hatched in the brain of John Ward had brought golden rewards. English sails had swept the narrow stretch of water between Tunis and Sicily, and as a result Spain's trade with the Levant had been completely disrupted. Prizes had been brought back with such regularity that up in the Bardo the Dey was beginning to regret his bargain and to demand his full percentage. I had been to see him twice about the matter, and now settlement of the dispute waited on John's next visit. In the meantime our warehouses bulged with spoils, and I had found it necessary to rent two state bagnios for the care of our prisoners.

The broad back of Captain Pooley interposed itself between me and the tiny breeze blowing in from the bay, and immediately I felt perspiration beading out on my head and neck. He moved aside, and I felt relief. His one good eye, sunk deep in layers of tallowy fat, turned in my direction.

"When is Ward coming in?" he demanded in a reedy voice. "Slit my windpipe, if I like the looks of things here. We have more gold than the Pope of Rome, and that old malkin sits up there on his hill like a cat watching a lot of fat mice. One of these days he'll turn his sally men loose on us. Wouldn't you like to get away while there's still time, Master Blease?"

"Not so loud," I cautioned. "Where could we go, Captain Pooley, if we pulled out from here?"

"The world is large." He spread out his enormous arms. "There's the Far East, and there's the south part of Africa, which some say is the real Land of Cockayne at last, and there's the Americas. We might even go home. Macherie says it would be safe—for some of us. He has influence."

The man was so drunk that I thought it possible to squeeze some information out of him. I decided on a bold course. "If we depended on Sir Nevil Macherie," I said, "there would be nothing left for the Dey to covet. He hasn't brought in a single prize. And now it seems he wants to run away with his share of this gold he's done nothing to earn. How many prizes have you brought in, Captain Pooley?"

He rose to the bait. His solitary eye gleamed sullenly. "You speak boldly for a mere rum-bob," he growled.

"Where would you expect Captain Ward to be? He has taken on himself the hardest task of all. He has the western patrol, to watch for the coming of the Spanish fleet."

"Ay," said Pooley. "And who's watching for the Flat-caps."

"The Venetians?"

"Ay, the Venetians. They're planning to take us in the rear. Does Captain Ward know that?"

"Does Sir Nevil Macherie know it?"

Pooley laid a heavy hand on my shoulder. "Not yet. While our great men are at sea, it's left to plain William Pooley to get at the truth. The word was brought direct to me, and what do you think of that, my fine young cock?"

It was working. Drink had broken down his caution, and he was in a boastful mood, which gave me the chance I had been looking for. I glanced over my shoulder and saw that the card players were still absorbed in their game. In another corner, Abadad was arguing monotonously with a port officer on the ever-pressing problem of water, each of them stripped down to soiled drawers and caftan. It was reassuring to find him there, for I knew I was going to need him. An ugly white slash across his coffee-colored cheek gave him a villainous appearance, but I had grown to accept John's estimate of him during the six stifling weeks we had worked together.

"We have no quarrel with Venice," I said. "I think you've been listening to bambury tales, Captain Pooley. And that surprises me, because I've always believed you to have a shrewd head on your shoulders."

"I've been listening to no bambury tales. It's the truth I'm telling you. You'll believe me when you find yourself pulling an oar in a Venetian galley."

I got to my feet and motioned him to follow me out on the stone balcony. He shambled after me, nodding his head in tipsy triumph.

"Captain Pooley," I said in a whisper, "I'm convinced you've heard something of importance. You're too wise to be taken in by idle rumors, but what I can't understand is how you get this important information here in port."

"Well, my rum-bob, so you believe me now, do you? One of the Dey's galleys came in a few nights ago and tied up board-and-board with my pinnance, the *Cornish Lass*. They had an English prisoner, a tough little Tynsider named Gormish. He cut through his chains with a file and climbed the side of the *Cornish Lass* during the night. He brought me the word."

"And how would a prisoner on a Tunizeen galley know anything about the plans of the Doges? Do you expect me to believe that?"

This put him on the defensive, and he proceeded to tell me the story in full detail. The sailor had been a prisoner in Venice as a result of a stabbing scrape over a Livornese girl. All the prisoners had been offered their freedom if they would enlist for a campaign which was being planned by Spain, with the assistance of the Venetian government, to clean up privateering in the Mediterranean. He had agreed to sign but had managed to make his escape when the recruits were marched in a body from the prison. He had seen that the harbor was full of Spanish and Venetian ships-of-war and had heard the talk in the tavern of what was afoot. Warehouses were bulging with stores, and he had seen with his own eyes the loading of hundreds of barrels of powder and shot. He crossed Italy on foot and had the good fortune to get away from Genoa on a small French trading vessel. There his luck had ceased, but the boat was picked up by the Tunizeens and he had found himself chained to a heathen bench.

"It's a lucky thing he managed to get away," concluded Pooley, with a wag of his oversized head. "I for one have no wish to rot in a Spanish nask or swing in a nubbing party under the Lion of St. Mark's."

"Has the fleet put out from Venice yet?"

"Gormish thinks so. The taverns were buzzing with a neat plan they intend to work on us. They'll send *La Solderina*, their largest carrack, on ahead. As a decoy." I nodded, having heard John speak admiringly of *La Solderina* as the finest ship in the Levant trade. "They expect us to pounce on her. While we're busy with the decoy, their fighting ships will come up on us from two directions."

"We can take care of that. The Flat-caps have never stood up to us yet."

"Ay," affirmed the captain. "We can blow them off the seas like foam from a whiskin. But, remember, part of the fleet will be Spanish. And they're playing with tatts this time. If they catch us in force, they'll run for it, drawing us after them. When that happens, the full Spanish fleet will come in behind us. First, they'll attack here and burn every ship they find. Then they'll follow us up, and we'll be caught between them with no port to make and no base of supplies."

"How can you be sure this man Gormish is telling the truth?"

Pooley waxed indignant at the suggestion that he could be taken in by falsehoods. "What good would come to him of lying to me? He knows well enough that he would die in the Basket if he tried it. No, Master Blease, the fellow is telling the truth. You can be sure of it."

"It's a neat plan," I said. "But now that we know what's in their minds, we can catch them easily. We can play with loaded dice ourselves. All we have to do is get word to Captain Ward, and he'll bait a trap of his own."

The information for which I had been fishing came out then. "Ay, all we have to do is get word to Captain Ward, and he will play Peter Lug with them. But where is the mighty, the sagacious, the all-seeing Captain Ward? Cruising boldly in open water and thumbing his nose in all directions! We must lose precious time catching up with him while the net closes on us!"

"I have the course the *Royal Bess* is following. One of you could reach him in two days."

Pooley's great bulk began to shake with mirth. "We've no intention of finding Captain Ward, my young vaulting squire. I may tell you we've lost confidence in your great Captain Rufflecoat. By dawn tomorrow we'll be on our way. We'll pick up Sir Nevil and such others as may care to join us, and we'll sail for new seas where the picking will be easier, with no need to stomach more of the whiddled nonsense your great man is always preaching."

My mind seemed incapable of clear thinking; and yet, with John away, there was no one else to cope with the situation. What should I do? It was beyond my power to change the minds of these tough-willed seamen. They would save their own skins and leave the rest of our fleet to be crushed between the converging battle squadrons.

The problem was mine, and somehow I must find a way of solving it. In an effort to gain time, I walked to the railing and looked down over the crowded wharves. Pooley's pinnace was directly below, one of the smallest ships of the fleet, with dirty white sails and a brown hull from which the paint was peeling. Two sailors with raised morglays were keeping a free space on the landing for a crew of loaders. Pooley had not been indulging in idle talk, then. He was getting ready to sail.

As I watched the busy scene below, I found it easier to put two and two together. It was clear they would not cat their anchors and get

away without an effort to raid our well-filled warehouses. If Pooley
had been honest in saying they would sail at dawn, the attempt would
be made during the hours of the night. Well, they would not succeed
in that. The Dey was keeping a close eye on the warehouses and could
be depended on to nip their plan in the bud. My problem boiled down
to finding some way of getting word to John without the help of the
Dey. He must not know that we were in grave danger, for I was sure
his first thought would be to profit from our difficulties by seizing
everything. I thanked my lucky stars that I had caught Bristol Bill
Pooley in a drunken moment.

I had picked up a little of the native tongue. In as casual a tone as I
could command, I spoke over my shoulder to Abadad. His face did
not change expression, and he went on talking with the port official,
scratching his fleas indolently with one hand. The official looked surprised at some remark he made and replied in a sharp tone. In an
instant they were at it, hammer and tongs, bandying insults like a
pair of camel drivers. The altercation exploded so suddenly that Captain Blunt looked up from the game with a vigorous, "Stubble it, ye
lousy sons of Satan!" I walked back to my table, and Pooley followed.
I judged from the expression on his face that he was beginning to
regret his looseness of tongue.

Abadad got to his feet and reached down a snowy linen robe from
a peg on the wall. He draped it over his shoulders with one expert
contortion, and smiled at me with a suggestion of resignation.

"Sidi," he said, in halting English, "may Allah make of him an
infidel dog. He sees fit to refuse my most humble requests. Now I go
to speak with those who will compel him to a better frame of mind."

With a curt nod to the unhappy port officer, who seemed completely
taken aback by the sudden shift of the wind, and a servile bow to the
captains, Abadad backed out of the room. I felt an immense surge of
relief. So far, so good, I said to myself. I spoke sharply to the row of
slave-dealers, ordering them to leave at once. They shuffled reluctantly
to their feet and departed, followed by the crestfallen official.

"And now, Captain Pooley," I said, resuming my seat, "we can talk
this matter over at our leisure."

The card players looked up with sudden uneasiness. Blunt dropped
his hand and glared at Pooley.

"What matter?" he demanded. "What have you been telling him,
Pooley?"

I began to shuffle some of the papers in front of me. For a moment
nothing was said. Then I faced around, holding a letter toward them.
"Here is a report from London which I am sure all of you will find
very interesting. It tells of the interview Gondomar had with King
James immediately after the truce had been signed between Spain and
the Low Countries. It seems the good Don Sarmiento was quite sharp
with the King and laid down the law in no uncertain tones. England,

he said, must watch her step. The King made him plenty of promises, among them an assurance that all English Free Rovers would be hanged as pirates as fast as he could lay his hands on them. The situation at home is worth a thought, gentlemen. It doesn't seem the best time to think of returning. Even with the influence back of you that Sir Nevil claims to have."

"Who said anything about returning to England?" Blunt got to his feet and advanced close to where I sat.

"Where do you plan to go, then, if not to England? I understood Captain Pooley to say you were planning to leave at once. Tonight, in fact. Things are getting too hot for you here, apparently."

"Have you no brains in that empty costard, Pooley?" roared Blunt, turning on his companion.

Basil Sleath looked at me with his pale gray eyes. I knew him to be the most dangerous of the trio, a quiet Irishman who had learned his trade under a great master, Sir Fineen O'Driscoll, the now almost legendary Fineen of the Ships.

"Under the circumstances," said Sleath, "it seems fortunate the room has been cleared. But most unfortunate, I'm thinking, for Master Blease himself."

Pooley's enormous hand fell on my shoulder, forcing me down hard into my chair. He was breathing heavily.

"There's only one way to repair your error, Pooley," went on the Irishman, in a tone little above a whisper. "There's a court back of here filled with rubbish. It will be easy to hide the body there."

I was not seriously disturbed at the threat and made no effort to free myself from Pooley's iron grip. I even managed a smile.

"What do you suppose I said to Abadad just now?" I asked.

Silence fell on the room. Pooley dropped his hand from my shoulder and looked at his companions in slack-jawed contrition. Basil Sleath moved his chair nearer to me without letting his eyes stray from my face.

"And *what* did ye say to the dirty heathen, my brave Roger?" he asked.

I answered in easy tones, "He has had plenty of time to set a guard about the building. No doubt he's seeing now to the other precautions I suggested."

"And what might they be?"

"They might include a message to the Dey, requesting that no ships be allowed to leave harbor until further notice. They might also have to do with the placing of native guards on all our warehouses. I'm sure you would have thought of these things if you had been in my place, Captain Sleath."

The Irishman turned his unblinking gaze on Bristol Bill Pooley. "Do ye hear that? The boy knew what to do with the high cards ye shoved into his hands. What do ye suggest now?"

"Slit his throat for him!" declared Pooley. "And take a chance on getting away before the Dey can act."

Sleath shook his head. "And sail with our holds as empty as our pockets? Na, na, Pooley. I have a weakness for the yellow boys. We must think of something better."

I waited for them to make the next move. As a matter of fact, my instructions to Abadad had been confined to the placing of guards about the building, as I saw the danger of letting the Dey know that dissensions had risen among us. I was still clinging to the hope that a way would be found to send one of the three ships with warning of the enemy plans. The trio withdrew to a corner and began to argue with bitter intensity. Sleath said little, but I was sure he would dictate whatever decision they reached. They made no move to stop me when I walked out on the balcony again. Glancing down into the street, I saw that Abadad had already followed out my orders. Tunizeen soldiers were grouped about the door, and Abadad himself was there, talking to an officer in a red turban. Sleath joined me at the railing in a few moments, and I drew his attention to the guards and also to the presence of a dozen war galleys in the basin.

"You have less than five hundred men between the three of you," I said. "Captain Ward figured we would need no more than that to protect our interests ashore. But—it's not nearly enough to carry out what you have in mind, Captain Sleath."

"Four hundred and eighty of us against a cityful of heathen? I don't dislike the odds."

"But you need the advantage of surprise. Now that has been lost, and you would be well advised to give it up. If I care to give the signal, I can have you all lodged in the Bardo." In an earnest effort to win him over, I went on: "I would rather arrange things some other way, Captain Sleath. We're here on sufferance as it is. It will be dangerous if the people find we're divided among ourselves. There would be no holding them if the Dey had to step in."

"We could cut our way out of here with the greatest ease. But then we would have to leave those hard-earned yellow boys for the heathen. I'm concerned about that and nothing else, Master Blease."

He spat reflectively over the rail. "It's indeed a devil of a mess, and I see no profit in it at all. The Spaniards and the Venetians have made up their minds to be rid of us once and for all. They'll do for us this time."

"They'll run us down one by one if we split up again as Macherie suggests," I argued. "But they can't beat us if we stick together."

Sleath pointed along the teeming water front. "We have enough wealth stored down there to make us all easy for life. But Ward and the rest of them will never make this port again. They'll be caught in the trap. Those of us here can break through. That much is clear enough; but can we get our hands on the loot first? I tell you again, boy, I'm interested in nothing else."

"There's only one way it can be done," I argued. "We must beat the Spanish and come back here in force to claim it. Even then we'll have to divide with the Dey. Did you seriously believe that he would have let the three of you loot the warehouses tonight and show him your heels? I tell you, Captain Sleath, it's only as victors that we can hope to collect what we have down there."

The voices of Pooley and Blunt reached us from inside in angry disagreement. Sleath paid no attention. He was regarding me with a thoughtful frown.

"It's a shrewd head ye have on yer shoulders," he said finally. "I'm half convinced ye're right. I don't like the great John Ward, and I wouldn't raise my good Irish blade to help him beat the Dons. Still and all, my share is worth protecting." His pale eyes studied me closely. "Perhaps there'll be a way of getting at this. A way to make it worth my while if I throw in with ye."

I waited for him to continue. After taking a glance at the quarreling pair in the room behind us, he winked slyly and said: "It's in full charge of things ye've been. All the fine jewels we've taken off the Dons, and the gauds and the little bits of stones; ye have them stored away, I take it, and could put yer hands on a parcel of them if ye had a mind to it. What would ye say, Master Blease, to a little agreement like, just between the two of us?"

I still maintained silence. "Just supposing I give these two noddies the slip and took ye out with me. Supposing that I took ye straight to John Ward. When ye set foot on the ladder of the *Royal Bess*, perhaps ye might slip into my hand a bag containing a little something for myself alone. As fair return for services rendered, eh, Master Blease?"

"I have everything of the kind hidden safely away," I answered. "Against the time when a fair and open division can be made. What makes you think I would steal from the common pot to pay you?"

Sleath chuckled. "Because it's the only way open to ye. Make it worth my while or sit here and do nothing while the Dons gobble up yer friends. Ye're a smart lad and can cover it up."

He had me. I had known it as soon as he broached the matter. It was the only way out, and I was sure that John would approve if I fell in with the scheme.

"Take me to the *Royal Bess*," I said. "It's a bargain, Captain Sleath. The minute I set foot on the ladder, I'll place in your hand a leather bag containing twenty uncut diamonds."

"And not a word said about it? Ye swear to that?" His eyes had lighted up with excitement. "Twenty, ye say? Are they of good size? It's no deal if they're not white."

"They'll make a rich man of you. And make both of us thieves at the same time. I don't suppose that will weigh heavily on your conscience."

"I'll lose no sleep over it." He seized my arm with a vicious pressure. "How can I be sure of ye? How can I tell ye won't show me a clean pair of heels up the ladder and give me nothing but a laugh for my pains?"

"How can I be sure you won't lift the stones as soon as I go aboard with you? I'll be taking a longer chance than you, Captain Sleath."

He shook his head. "Ye'll be safe with me, and well ye know it. I want my full share as well. Ye have me there."

"We'll have to trust each other."

He seated himself on the railing and thought it over. I could see it went against the grain to repose trust in anyone on a deal of such importance. Finally he got back to his feet and said with a deep sigh: "There's no other way. I must take your word for it, little though I'm liking it. And remember this, nipperkin: a whisper to anyone afterward, and I'll run my sword through that belly of yours as quickly as I'd gut a herring."

"No one will ever hear of it," I said. "I can juggle the lists so that the loss won't show. I'm robbing the rest, but I see no other way of saving their lives. No honest way."

"Honesty is a word much used by fools," declared Sleath.

He fell into a deep study. After several moments he announced that we would sail with the turn of the tide in the evening. In the meantime it would be necessary to pull the wool over the eyes of the two fuddle-cups inside. He would tell them that a deal would have to be made with the Dey, and he would see to it that they became thoroughly drunk.

19

I WENT TO SEE Cristina in the new white and blue palace, and told her what happened that morning. I did so with some hesitation. She was Spanish; and, in spite of her love for John, her sympathies would be with the red and yellow fleet. She listened silently and did not interrupt until I came to the matter of my deal with Captain Sleath. I did not go into details, but she must have sensed that a bribe figured in his change of heart, for she shook her head furiously. "We know how to deal with such men in Spain," she said.

She remained silent for some time after I finished. "I am afraid I shall never see any of you again," she said finally.

I hastened to assure her that the prospects were not as black as that.

"We can win," I said, "if John can manage it so that we fight them separately. His plan, I think, will be to throw back the ships from Venice first and then turn to meet the Spaniards. Together they would crush us easily enough, just as the Armada would have beaten us in the Sleeve if we hadn't been able to break it up. If there's a way, John will find it."

We said nothing more for several moments. There was an ivory-topped tabouret between us and a tray with coffee in small gold cups. She took a cup and began to sip it. I had never tasted coffee, but the odor was most appetizing.

"John's ship will be in the middle of it," she said.

"You mustn't worry about him. Destiny has put a mark on John Ward. He can't die yet; not in a busking foray. He'll come back, never fear." I reached over and touched her hand, which lay tightly clenched at her side. "He'll come back, and then we'll have a wedding. With a beautiful bride, and music to make it complete."

She replaced the cup on the yellowed table top. Her hand was none too steady. "No, Roger. There won't be a wedding. No priest would marry us, and to me any other ceremony would not be binding. No more binding than the—the tie between us now." She paused. "John has no thoughts of marriage. You see, I have no illusions about my situation at all."

I took another sip of the coffee and found it slightly less distasteful. What she had said about her relationship with John had set me thinking. He had stayed at the palace during the visits he had paid ashore in the three months since the meeting of the Free Rovers. He had a good excuse at first, the need to supervise the renovations; but when the last whisk of mortar had been removed, he just continued on without making any explanation. I had many occasions to be with them and had tried to keep my eyes shut to what was going on. Their relationship was not as one-sided as I had feared it might be. There was passionate tenderness on her part, but something not too far short of that on his. Their tastes were similar enough to make companionship a pleasure. They were fond of music, and many times I heard John's deep baritone trolling sea songs to the twanging of her bandore. They shared a lively humor; in fact, their laughter helped to carry them over the quarrels which were inevitable. They bickered frequently and violently but always about the small things, mostly his lack of care in matters of deportment and the vulgar edge to his tongue. The real issues between them were never mentioned. They seemed to be keeping them in abeyance, as though afraid to let the uncertainties of the future dim the pleasure they were finding in the present.

She asked suddenly, "Is she very beautiful?"

"Katie Ladland?"

"Yes."

"It's hard to tell you about her. She has a sweetness I can't describe. I think she's beautiful."

"Does John think so too?"

"Yes, I suppose he does. But I've heard him say you're the most lovely woman he has ever seen."

"Thank you. I'm sure John is a competent judge of beauty in women, so I should be proud of his praise." She changed the subject abruptly. "He ought to be very glad of what you've done today."

"It was lucky I found out in time. We'll have a chance now."

"Can you depend on this Captain Sleath? I don't trust him; he has evil eyes."

"I think he'll go through with his bargain. I don't trust him any more than you do, but he has everything to gain by it."

She said with sudden vehemence: "I'm hoping you win this battle. It's a terrible thing for me to want! I'm Spanish. I love my country. I'm proud of everything she stands for. And yet I can wish to see her beaten so that no harm may come to John Ward, her worst enemy!"

"I'll tell John you said that. It might help him."

She shook her head. "No. I shouldn't have said it. It is bad enough for me to think that way. Please don't tell him. I'm afraid I have humbled myself in his eyes too much as it is."

Sleath came out on the balcony behind us. His pale eyes took in the beauty of my companion with a hungry look.

"Time to be off, my brave Roger," he said. "It's sorry I am to be taking you away from such fine company."

I stood up. Cristina took my hand in both of hers and pressed it hard. "You must come back," she whispered. "You and John. My prayers will follow you."

Sleath and I made our way to the street through a side gate so that our departure would not be observed. The sun struck against the white walls of the palace with greater intensity than ever. I found it hard to breathe. I loosened my collar with a damp finger and reflected dismally on the long tramp ahead of us through the steaming alleys of the city.

"A dozen picked men have gone on ahead," said Sleath. "I must have a talk with Pooley and Blunt and spin a yarn for their benefit." He looked at me and winked. "A dainty chick. What a light in her eyes, what a delicate curve to her little breasts! I was thinking back there I might prefer to take her from Ward than the diamonds."

"It's an easier matter to steal the diamonds, Captain Sleath," I said.

20

WE WENT OUT on a leeward tide. Sleath drove his skeleton crew into feverish activity as soon as his foot touched the deck of the *Grace O'Malley*. I watched the skyline recede, and then, with a sigh of relief, turned into the pilot-house.

The redheaded steersman winked at me and remarked that it was a pleasant evening. Would it be nice to take a girl down the Beaux Walk and into Stephen's Green? Or didn't I think so? I winked back to express agreement and turned to study the sand in the roning glasses. I knew the hour already, but time had become a matter of such supreme importance that I could think of nothing else. I was desperately afraid that we would be too late. There was no way of telling when the hostile fleets had sailed nor how long the Tunizeen galley had taken to make port. If it had dawdled up the coast in quest of stray prizes, the scattered Free Rovers might already be caught in the pincers. I tried to put this thought out of my mind, but it persisted. I could see the *Royal Bess* surrounded by Spanish ships-of-war, raked by their broadsides, her hull battered, her rigging cut to shreds, fighting on to the inevitable end as the *Revenge* had done.

I knew the *Grace O'Malley* was scudding along at a good rate, but I wanted to go out on the quarter-deck and demand of Sleath that he tack on every square inch of canvas that the ship could carry.

He saved me from this error by coming into the pilot-house. "Hola, bar!" he shouted. "Keep full and by!" The steersman threw his weight against the whipstaff, and I could hear a rattle of chains below. The captain looked at me and scowled. "If it's speed ye're wanting, ye'll be getting more than yer stomach can stand. And do ye happen to know that looby-clown of yours is on board?"

Clim on the *Grace O'Malley*? I did not believe it at first.

"Someone told him what was afoot, and here he is," declared Sleath impatiently. He led the way to the gun-deck; and there, sure enough, was Clim. His arms were bound with rope and he was grinning foolishly.

"He's drunk," said the captain. "He's your man, so I leave him to ye. My advice would be to have some sense lashed into him. Luke here will oblige."

When he had gone, I said to the tall sailor on guard: "Cut him loose, Luke. We'll give him a chance to sleep it off first."

I decided to spend the night on deck. The odors which assailed my nostrils from every hatch had warned me of what I might expect below. Some of the beer casks had burst, saturating the ballast and giving a sour edge to the atmosphere. But that was not all of it. The *Grace O'Malley* was a slattern ship. When a captain is slack, conditions below become indescribable in hot weather.

I stretched my netting in a corner of the quarter-deck and fell into a heavy sleep almost immediately. It must have been several hours later when a tug at the hammock forced me into wakefulness. The stars were out in full, and the moon was well overhead. The wind had fallen off.

"Shanks," said a cautious voice which I recognized as Clim's. "I had to come, Shanks. When there's fighting, I'm the man for it. I'm no cheap-jack landsman."

I sat up and dropped my feet to the deck. Then I rubbed my eyes and looked about me. Clim was crouched down under the rail where the lookout could not see him. From his voice I judged him to be sober.

"I had to come," he repeated. "You see that, don't ye, Shanks?"

"I don't see it. You were stationed ashore by Captain Ward's orders. He considered it necessary to have men as guards at the palace. You were one of them, and here you've run away. What's he going to say about that?"

Clim was still filled with a sense of his importance. "He'll say 'good man' when he sees me. He's going to need me. There's fighting ahead."

"He's more likely to stick you in the bilboes or have you keel-raked. And I won't be able to do anything for you this time. I got you out of the garters, but the Captain won't listen to me again." My impatience grew as I considered what his leave-taking might mean. "Who told you there was fighting in prospect? You didn't get it from me."

"I heard it from one of Sleath's men. I made up my mind as soon as I heard it. I want my share of the dibs, Shanks."

"You heard it from one of Sleath's men? Did everyone know about it?"

He nodded his head. "I expect so. Blunt's men and Pooley's were angry when they found out. They didn't relish being left ashore."

"Blunt and Pooley are both dead drunk. Suppose their men take it into their heads to follow us?"

His voice took on a sulky note. "All the better if they do. When there's fighting, we need every pike."

"And who would be left to protect our interests ashore? Would you like to lose your share of what we have in those warehouses?"

That shook his confidence a little. "I didn't think of that."

"No, I'm sure you didn't. Why didn't you come and tell me what was being whispered around instead of sneaking off by yourself? What will happen to Dona Cristina if trouble starts ashore and none of us there to protect her? You didn't think of that either."

His tone had become thoroughly humble. "No, Shanks."

"Captain Ward left you with her because he thought he could depend on you. Do you see what you've done now?"

"Yes, Shanks, I do."

I got to my feet and scanned the horizon. A small point of light showed on the horizon back of us. I pointed this out to Clim.

"A ship's lantern," he said.

"It's either the *Cornish Lass* or the *Albicore*. They're following us. We'll find, Clim, that every man sober enough to climb a ladder is on board. Sleath's men as well. It may go hard with those left behind. And Dona Cristina."

He slumped down in his corner and said in a penitent voice: " 'Fore God, I wouldn't want harm coming to the lady. She was kind to me, Shanks. I wanted to tell ye, but I knew ye would keep me ashore if I did."

I began to feel sorry for him and dropped a hand on his shoulder. "Well, the wind's coming from the wrong quarter, but we may weather it still. There's this to be said: John is going to need every ship. Perhaps we'll be able to get back before things go wrong ashore. If only we had Dona Cristina with us! That is what worries me most."

By dawn it was certain that my surmise was correct. There were two ships plowing along in our wake. Standing on the quarter-deck with Captain Sleath, I recognized them as the *Cornish Lass* and the *Albicore*.

Sleath was in a savage mood. He paced up and down the tiny deck, pausing at each turn to gaze with bleak face at the oncoming pinnaces. Finally he stopped in front of me to say that both Blunt and Pooley deserved "a touch of cold steel in their innards." Drunk they might have been, he went on, but they should have been able to control their men. He was ready to wager an Old Harry against a win that both of them were snoring in their bunks and not yet aware that everything was "up in the boughs." It had not occurred to me that the two captains would be with the ships, but when I put my doubt into words he brushed it aside impatiently.

"Do ye think the mates would put off without them?" he demanded. "That would be mutiny, and they want none of that dish. Na, Master Blease, ye can be sure the two swill-bellies were carried aboard before a single robin was loosed."

I saw the sense of that at once. "Do you suppose," I asked, "that either of the mates had sense enough to leave a force ashore?"

He gave me a curiously intent look before answering. "A great deal depends on that point, my fine gentry-cove. I was coming to that very point myself. You see, I gave Hughie Haight his orders to stay ashore for the purpose. Do ye know Hughie? He's my first mate, a black Irishman from up Antrim way. I assigned a hundred of my men to stay with him. Enough to hold the warehouses until we can finish up and get back. But how can I be sure he stuck to his post when the rest of them decided to come along?" He squinted over the rail at the unwelcome sails behind us and shook his head. "I must find out what Hughie did, Master Blease."

I realized from the tone of his voice that my life was hanging in the balance. If the mate had stayed at his post, Sleath would still carry out our plan, counting on a victorious return to port. But if Haight had followed with the other ships, he would reckon our stores of plunder lost and act accordingly. That would mean death for me and Clim, who blundered his head into the same noose. Sleath would take the diamonds and then get rid of us before changing his course due westward in the hope of slipping through the Spanish dragnet. I was so sure of this that I trembled when he turned his fish-gray eyes in my direction.

"I'll haul to and let them come up," he said. "I must know about Hughie Haight."

That settled it. I could read death in the look he gave me. I wanted to run in search of Clim, so great was my desire for the sight and support of a friend, the only one within a hundred miles. But in spite of this feeling of panic, I was able to realize the danger of any delay now.

"We'll lose several hours if we wait for them, Captain Sleath," I said. "Every minute counts. We may be too late as it is."

"That's important only if Hughie is following my orders. I'm going to wait." He smiled, but I was not able to gain any comfort from that. It was a cold smile and did not disturb in any degree the calculating expression in his eyes. "I'm thinking, my young friend, you had better be turning over those baubles now."

"That was not the agreement," I protested, although I knew there was no profit in contesting the point. "You were not to be paid until I put a foot on the ladder of the *Royal Bess.*"

"That's true." He treated me to another smile, colder and less comforting if possible than the first. "But it doesn't seem likely now that you will live long enough to set a foot on that ladder. I'm not taking any chances." When I still made no move, he suddenly blazed at me: "D'ye hear me? Hand them over! If I'm to be mumped out of my full share, I'll have the diamonds at least."

"But supposing you find the mate has stayed ashore—"

He reached out and pinioned my arms. "In that case we go through with our bargain. With this little difference—I'll have the stones a few hours earlier than we agreed."

He released one arm, and I fumbled inside my doublet. I had donned my new finery, and the belt under my coat was full of points. A bag was attached to the belt, and my fingers fumbled so long with the knot that Sleath shook me with exasperation. Then, with a sudden change of mind, he freed my arm.

"It's best no one sees us," he said. "Come into the cabin."

Inside he emptied the contents of the bag on a small table attached to the wall. His hands trembled with eagerness, and he had to count the stones twice.

"Many of them are small," he grumbled. He picked up one and shoved it accusingly under my nose. "What would a fencing-cove give me for that? Little enough, perhaps no more than a single Job. Ye're cheating me, Master Blease, and I swear I'll take it out of your hide."

"You have a fortune in your hand, Captain Sleath."

He lifted one of the larger stones and nodded unwillingly. "This one is handsome enough. It might keep the black ox off my feet for a spell. A few are not bad, my yarrumsop, not bad at all." He looked up at me and winked. "I'll be doing better than the rest of them, and that's something."

"If we delay now," I said, "most of them will have death as their only share."

"That's no concern of mine." He looked me over closely and winked again. "It's a fine caster ye're wearing. Do ye think it might fit me?"

My control was beginning to slip. "It's cut to a full man's size, and so might be a little ample for you, Captain Sleath. But no one else will want it, for it is full of the stench of your ship already."

He scooped up the stones and poured them into a leather bag at his belt. The round shape that the bag assumed seemed to please him, for he patted it affectionately. Then he looked at me, and his face darkened. "So ye think poorly of my ship. She's a trig little lady, and I happen to be fond of her. If what ye say is true, then I have need of a swabber. The idea would not appeal to ye, belike? I thought not. Still, I must give it some consideration, Master Blease. There might be some satisfaction in keeping ye here under my thumb. More perhaps than in throwing ye overboard as I have had it in mind to do."

We hove to and drifted aimlessly for a matter of two hours while the other ships came up. Clim had been ordered aloft to repair ratlines. In his purple doublet and yellow-striped hose he looked like an enormous insect perched at the top of the shrouds. I was left to my own devices, and my first thought was to write letters. There were messages I wanted to send before I died, if it should come to that. I wanted to tell Katie how much I loved her and all the things I had never dared say to her face. I wanted to tell Mother and Aunt Gadilda how sorry I was for the grief I had caused them. Also, I wanted to let John know the things Cristina had told me, in the hope that it might bring them to a better understanding.

I knew that nothing I wrote stood any chance of being delivered. There would have been some comfort, however, in spending those slow hours in the company of the people I loved. As it happened, there was not a single sheet of paper on board, which surprised me for, the skipper showed some traces of education. I made one discovery in my search for writing materials which I knew would be useful, a Spanish bagonet. Its leather sheath was covered with mold, but the blade was in good condition. I slipped the dagger inside my doublet.

The vessel was in shocking condition. The sails were dirty and patched. The bull ropes had never been properly tarred, and the types were old and frayed. It was clear enough that Sleath's yonkers took their lives in their hands every time they went aloft. The upper structure of the ship had been without paint for a long time, and some of the wood was rotten. Even the captain's cabin stank like a butcher's jetty on the Thames.

The *Cornish Lass* was the first to come up, and I saw Sleath climb the ladder to the quarter-deck as the two vessels drew close together. Clim had worked his way down by this time, and I called to him to join me in the waist. His face was streaked with perspiration, for he had been working in the full glare of the sun. His doublet was torn and smeared with tar.

I told him of Sleath's purpose. His face showed no sign of fear as he listened. Stout Clim! He patted me reassuringly on the shoulder and with his other hand tugged at the dagger in his belt.

"We'll give 'em a tussle," he said confidently. "Are ye armed, Shanks?"

I showed him the Spanish knife, and he nodded briskly. "We'll make for the lookout," he said. "They'll have to come up there for us, and we'll show them a thing or two." He seemed almost happy at the prospect. "The dirty teagues! I hope that Sleath is the first to show a head. I've a score to settle with him."

I heard Sleath bellowing across the water from his post on the quarter-deck and a voice answering from the *Cornish Lass*. It sounded to me like the deep rumble of Captain Pooley. I strained my ears to hear what was being said but could not make out a single word. Well, we would know soon enough. If Haight had joined them, it would mean a quick climb and death eventually for both of us high up in the air. I shuddered, sure in my mind that the worst had happened. I could feel my heart beating wildly with the strain. I tried to drag the dagger from inside my doublet in readiness, but my hands seemed numb. I was not sure I would be capable of a mad scramble up the swaying shrouds and told Clim he had better start while there was time.

Clim shook his head and chuckled. "Here we are, Shanks, the both of us all dressed up like Essex when he bussed the old virgin. And nothing but a bloody fight on our hands. It's just as well. I allus wanted to go out in the best, like a strutting gentry-cove." He gripped my shoulder. "Here he comes, Shanks. Get set for it!"

Sleath was climbing down to the main deck. He turned and began to walk toward us.

"Easy," said Clim. "You go first. I'll stay back and break his ugly head for him."

I was watching the captain, trying to read our fate in his expression. He was smiling, but I took no comfort from that.

"Well, Master Blease," he said, "Not planning any mischief between ye, I trust? Not that it would matter, things being as they are. Hughie Haight has a wise head on his shoulder. He stuck to his orders and stayed behind. Ye owe the black Irishman something, I'm thinking. He saved yer life."

My lungs seemed to explode in the intensity of my relief. Clim, however, did not seem to be convinced. He said in a whisper: "He may be lying."

"I don't think so," I whispered back. "He means it."

Sleath turned away from us. He cupped his hands over his mouth and shouted: "Step into it, men! Set the tops'ls. Let fall the mains'l. Lively does it, my lads! We have two hours to make up."

The men scrambled up the shrouds. Sleath then turned to me and said in even tones: "It's God's truth, Master Blease, although I'm not blaming ye for holding back. Hughie Haight is looking after our interests ashore." He motioned me to step closer, and I obeyed without hesitation. "We'll go on with our bargain. I have the pay, and I'll take ye to Ward as I promised. All Ward is to know is that we got wind of things and came out to have our share of the fighting." He sunk his voice to a whisper. "Any hint from ye to the contrary, and it will go hard with ye. I'm a man of my word, Master Blease. If ye don't want the Ten Commandments carved on yer back, keep a still tongue in yer head."

21

JOHN WARD'S LUCK, always good, was holding. He had summoned his captains for a conference off Cape Passer, and when we arrived with our news they were all there.

I was back on the *Royal Bess* and the "bloody colors" were suspended from the main shrouds. We could see skiffs and shallops coming from every direction in answer to the summons. The sea was dotted with sails in all quarters, and I found it an inspiring sight. Many of the ships were famous for exploits about which all England had talked with pride: the *Fair Rosamonde*, which had captured three Spaniards single-handed off San Lucar; the *Alcibiades*, which had been as far east as China; the *Prester John*, which had come closer than any other ship to finding the Northeast Passage. My confidence in the outcome rose as I watched this mighty fleet. It would take more than the Latins to beat us.

I stood in the waist with Joralemon Snode and watched the captains come over the side. John was there to greet them with a jovial word for each. "You're ratsbane to the Flat-caps, Harris. I'm glad you're here because they seem disposed to pick a quarrel with us."—"Now I can be easy in my mind, Dick Longcastle."—"Halsey, wait until I tell you the news. You've been looking for a fight, and now you'll have a real one."

But pious Joralemon saw it in a different light. He told me in whispers about each arrival. They were without exception roaring bullies, with no respect for God or man, and all of them ripe for hell-fire.

Joralemon was in what John called his "weeping Jeremiah" mood. I knew the reason for it. When I arrived the night before and went to John's cabin, I had found him stretched out in a chair with a girl reclining on the arm. He had looked a little crestfallen and had explained hurriedly that she was a German girl who had been taken off an Italian ship. She was to be sent home as soon as an opportunity arose. The girl, who was redheaded and ample-bosomed, had pinched his ear as she rose from her position. John had grinned and said, "She's very grateful to us for rescuing her." I could not look at her without thinking of the one visit I had paid to the Souk-el-Barka, the slave market of Tunis. There I had seen naked women for the first time, chained to black pillars for the inspection of buyers. I could not look at this grateful German girl without picturing her in my mind rid of her trailing blue dress and wide ruff. No other woman had ever had this effect on me, and I had felt so guilty about it that I kept my eyes away from her during the whole of my talk with John.

Joralemon had told me about her later, scoffing at her claims to gentility and berating John because of the weakness he had shown for the "foreign Jezebel."

I pricked up my ears when Macherie came over the side to be welcomed by John with a friendly, "Hail, Sir Nevil." His manner had its usual edge of condescension, and I found it a great temptation to blurt out what I knew about him. He said, "Well, Ward, what's all this about?" and John answered, "The devils are loose, Macherie, and we have a fight on our hands."

Sir Nevil strolled over to talk to his three henchmen, who were standing in a group by the rail. When the last of the captains arrived, John led the way to the main cabin, and the rest trailed after him. I took advantage of the chance to pay a visit to Clim, who was sitting out his sentence of six hours in the bilboes. I could see that his wrists were already pinched and red in the sharp iron stocks.

"Take it easy, Clim," I said. "Just an hour more."

The pain must have been great, but he was accepting his punishment cheerfully. "I don't mind," he said. "It's what I deserved. I disobeyed my orders and left the lady when I shouldn't of. I'm getting off light enough."

I helped him to a drink of water, which was against the rules. Joralemon had followed me, and as we walked off together he said: "It's a good thing Gard didn't see you, Roger. He would have planted you beside Clim for a spell of it yourself." His mind was still running on the German girl, for after a pause he asked darkly: "Will there be another establishment set up on shore? Another scarlet whore of Babylon for honest sailors to guard? How can he expect the Lord to prosper him?"

He left me, muttering mournfully to himself. I wandered aimlessly about the deck, speculating as to what course of action would be settled upon in the council of war. The girl came out on the quarter-deck. The wind blew her skirts tightly around her, but she did not seem disturbed about it. She smiled down at me.

The meeting broke up in an hour's time. John came out on deck with an arm over the shoulder of Sir Nevil, saying in a confident voice: "That will do it for the Dons, Macherie. You have a great opportunity."

Sir Nevil answered with dry confidence, "I think I shall be equal to it, Ward."

I was not to know what had been decided until several hours later. In the meantime the assembled captains drank a noisy toast and departed for their ships. The supper kettles were brought on deck. Two of the men got into an argument. The rest took sides, and for a quarter of an hour the air was thick with ugly profanity. Released from the iron grip of the bilboes, Clim made a hearty meal, although it was difficult for him to lift his arms.

Early in the evening I was summoned to the coach, as the men called the captain's cabin. I found John with a map spread out in front of him, a candle at one elbow and a flagon of white wine at the other. The German girl, whose name I had learned was Aurora, was curled up in a chair beside him. He was in an exuberant mood.

"We have them in the hollow of our hands!" he predicted. "Thanks to your promptness in getting the news to me, I'm in a position to lay a neat trap for them. I've just had a talk with Gormish, and he has given me a lot of valuable information about the strength of the fleet coming from the east." He paused and, sensing that I was disturbed by the presence of the girl, added: "Don't worry about her, my old Sobersides. She doesn't know a word of English, so we can talk freely."

"That wasn't what I was worried about. I was thinking of Katie."

His face lost its happy expression. "'Od's bones, Roger, I call you in to praise you, and all you're concerned about is a trifling matter like this! How many times must I tell you not to attach any importance to these little passing fancies of mine?"

"Is Cristina a passing fancy? I've become very much attached to her and don't want to see her hurt."

"You needn't preach at me, Roger." His face had taken on a sulky look. "You can leave that to Parson Snode. He never gives me any peace. It would be good for both of you if you would get yourselves native women. It might make you more human. As for this willing bit of fluff, I'm pretty well convinced she comes right out of a vaulting school. Macherie took a fancy to her today, so perhaps I'll ease myself of your disapproval by transferring her to his ship. Will that satisfy you, in God's name?"

The girl said something in a soft, slurring voice. John listened with a frown, apparently finding it hard to follow her. He answered in a few halting words, the only one familiar to me being the usual "Fubbs." Then he grinned at me and winked. "She says she knows we're talking about her and wants to know what we're saying. I said you had taken a fancy to her and were threatening to steal her from me. You'll have to watch yourself now. She's a forward minx."

He straightened up in his chair with an air that dismissed the matter and laid a finger on the map in front of him. "Now let's get to work. First, I want to thank you for the way you handled things. You've done nobly. I suspect you haven't told me everything because I know what precious scoundrels you had to deal with. But that story can wait. I want to explain what was decided today. The Spaniards think they'll catch me with a divided fleet. It's clearly in their minds that the appearance of the ships from the east will draw away a good part of ours, and that we can be disposed of piecemeal. Well, I am going to leave all but six here so they will find us in strength when they come sweeping in. That will prove a most unpleasant surprise for the Dons. In the meantime, the six will keep the Venetians in play."

"Six against a whole fleet!"

He indulged in a confident laugh. "And why not? The *Revenge* stood out for a whole day against the might of Spain. Surely with six ships I can hold them for as long as may be necessary. I'm taking that part of the operation on my own shoulders."

"And who will command against the Spaniards?"

"Sir Nevil Macherie."

"Macherie!" I launched into a heated protest. "You can't trust him. He was planning to run away and leave you in the lurch. Sleath, Blunt, and Pooley were in it with him. They were going to steal everything we had in port. I found out about it in time." I had promised Sleath not to talk, but I considered myself absolved when the fate of the fleet was at stake.

John nodded soberly. "I can believe it. Do you suppose I would adopt such a course if any other were possible? I have nothing but contempt for Macherie and would as soon lose the sight of both eyes as give him the chance for all the glory of a big victory. But personal feelings can't be considered at a time like this. Macherie has been second in command, and if I had tried to pass him over there would have been bad blood at once. I couldn't risk that. In any event, I'm assuming the main responsibility because everything will depend on my ability to hold them in the east while the main fleet engages the Dons."

"But suppose he gets himself beaten?"

John rose to his feet and led me over to a porthole, from which we could see the lanterns at the mastheads of the waiting ships. He dropped his voice to a cautious whisper. "I can play a deep game as well as our wily Sir Nevil. I've a private understanding with the wisest heads among the captains—Harris and Jennings and Longcastle. Macherie has agreed to consult them on all decisions. If things don't go to their liking, they'll step in and relieve him of the command. He won't be allowed much rope.

"Halsey and Glanville have agreed to go with me. Two of the stoutest fighters England has ever seen." He paused and winked. "Who do you suppose I've selected to make up the balance? Your three friends, Sleath, Blunt, and Pooley."

"Can you trust them?"

"When it comes to a scrap, they're as good as any. Sleath particularly I rank high. Their own skins will be at stake, so I'm not concerned on that score. The advantage I see is that Macherie won't have them to back him up if there's any trouble. In fact, I think I've managed it so that their hands are securely tied." He pointed to one of the nearest of the ships. "That's the *Grace O'Malley*. As you know, Sleath is badly undermanned, and I've promised to find him some men to make up his full complement. His master gunner got left behind in Tunis by mistake. You've been very much interested in gunnery, Roger, and I'd like you to fill in for him."

There was nothing I wanted to do less than renew my acquaintance with Captain Sleath or set foot again on the greasy deck of the *Grace O'Malley*. In addition, I was not at all confident of my ability to handle a gun crew. It was clear, however, that John was counting on me and that personal inclinations could not be considered. I nodded reluctantly.

"That's my stout Roger! There's no one else available, or I wouldn't have asked it of you. There's this to be said for Sleath: you couldn't serve under a better man when the decks are stripped for action. I'm sending your friend Clim with you. Don't let him get into any more trouble. He has two black marks on his record now, and the penalties are rigorous for third offenders. Keep an eye on the fellow. He's too good a man to swing at the yardarm."

Joralemon was sitting in the waist when I went out, mending a rent in his trunk hose by the light of a lantern. He continued to ply his needle but invited me with a nod to sit down with him.

"I'm being transferred to the *Grace O'Malley*. Did you know?"

He shook his head with a doubtful frown. "You know more of petty tallies and cockets than you do of gunnery," he said. "I wish you were staying on the *Bess*."

"I've wondered why you stay on. You're less of a seaman than I am, Jore. Is it because you've always followed John?"

"That's it." He studied his handiwork with a critical eye. "We lived in the same end of town, as you probably remember. John was always a god in my eyes. I looked up to him and took his word for everything. I was not very strong as a boy, and he fought my battles for me."

"I remember the day he tore the coat off Chirp Bird because he laughed at you."

"You must have been a little fellow then. Yes, John and I were always very close. I don't know why he tolerated me, for no two boys were ever less alike. Perhaps it was because of my father. John would spend hours in the hut at the foot of our yard where the old man worked, listening to his stories." There was a touch of pride in his voice. "John's father had never been much out of sight of land, but mine saw the ramparts of Nombre de Dios and the brown waters of the Platta before he settled down to sail-making ashore. I'm afraid he often drew a long bow when he had us to listen to him. He would tell stories to make your blood run cold. About the dread kraken, and renora monsters which sucked ships down from below. He swore by St. Erasmus, not being of the true faith then, that he had seen the ghosts of dead Spaniards haunting the tops of the shrouds in southern waters, and that lights played about them like the fires of hell. John would sit there and take it all in. Everything the old man said made him keener than ever for the sea. It had the opposite effect on me. But when John went it never occurred to me to do anything but follow him." He sighed profoundly.

"We've had twelve years of it. Twelve years of misery for me. I always meant to study Latin and become a minister of God, but instead I've been a self-appointed parson to crews of bloodthirsty rovers. It's been so different from everything I had counted on, and hoped for, that sometimes I think it must be a dream and that I'll waken to hear the church bells ringing on Shrubsole High." He had fallen into a reflective strain, and I let him go along without any interruptions. "Our first important cruise was in Arctic waters. The Muscovy Company sent a ship to find the Northeast Passage, and we signed on. John was a full mate by the time we put back. There was trouble on board because the captain was slack. It came to mutiny, and two of the men were hanged finally. I'll never forget that voyage!

"You won't be surprised," he went on, "when I tell you there was a tall Norwegian girl on the dock to see us leave. She looked so sad that I took John to task for the first time. A handsome lass, much like John's mother. Do you recall Mistress Ward?"

"Dimly. I remember her as a tall woman with yellow hair and the kindest eyes. I was quite young when she died."

"A fine woman. She was much too good for Enoch Ward. John took after her in looks, and he got all his best qualities from her as well. Certainly he got his worst from his father. I was outside the Bull and Stump when the husband of that redheaded woman stuck a knife between Enoch Ward's ribs. A little, swaggering fellow, he was, with an eye for the wenches all the time. It's hard to believe our great yellow

John could be get of his. But Mistress Ward was always like a mother to me. My own was dead, you know. I would go home with John after my father had filled us with his tales and she would always have something good for us. Humble pie or collops perhaps. Food to put muscle on your bones." He paused and looked at me as though begging understanding. "You mustn't take me seriously, Roger, when I speak harshly about John. I've two things only against him: his lack of interest in the Word and his ways with women. I've said much harder things to his face than behind his back. I always try to remember that he couldn't be a great captain if he were any different. His virtues and faults are all of one piece. You must believe that also, Roger."

With the thought of Katie and Cristina in my mind, I found it hard to condone his ways with women, and I said so.

"It's not all his fault," Joralemon protested earnestly. "They run after him. All the time. Look at this woman." He jerked his head back in the direction of the cabin. "When she came aboard, with her wicked ways and wanton eyes, I knew at once what would happen. She took one look at John and—well, you've seen for yourself."

"I have his word he's going to send her away."

"But after she goes there will be many more. I've seen them come and go all these years."

"I hoped he would feel differently about the Señorita. She's good as well as beautiful, and she loves him. Her whole life has been wrecked because of this."

"She is popish!" It was the one unforgivable sin in his eyes. "It was the likes of her that burned our martyrs by the thousands! I can't look at her without smelling the faggots. If I had to choose between them, I would rather he took this brazen light-o'-love. She's of the true faith, at any rate."

"Do you think it possible for him to love one woman in spite of everything? He says he loves Katie Ladland, and yet it seems to make no difference. It's become a sore point with me because—well, I love Katie myself."

"I know." He leaned over and patted my knee. "Yes, I believe it's possible. John might love one woman all his life and still not alter his ways."

"But what will it mean to Katie?"

"She's young. She saw John a few times only. She goes to court soon, you say? I think she may soon forget him; and you as well, if you stay away too long. No, I'm not sure she's in need of much sympathy, nor you, for that matter. I think in the long run it will be John we should feel sorry for."

He got to his feet and walked to the rail. I joined him there, and we studied the ring of motionless ships about us. We could see little but the light of their lanterns.

"A beautiful night." He sighed again. "The dawn will be even love-
lier, but it will see us on our way. Off on an errand of death, Roger.
Have you that testament I gave you? Never let it be far from you.
You'll need the comfort you can find only between its covers."

22

"IT'S NONE TOO PLEASED ye are to be back on the
Grace O'Malley," said Captain Sleath, squinting at me out of one
corner of his narrow eyes. "Ye'll be wise to remember ye're under my
orders. One wrong move, and it's over the side with ye to feed the
sea-apes."

We had been watching a full week for the enemy fleet, our little
squadron of six spread thinly across the water south of Cape Passer.
The captain had ridden me with spurs the whole time, and I had come
to hate him intensely. I was not alone in this. The members of my gun
crew would mutter, whenever he passed. They were a fine lot of
fellows, answering to such names as Jamesey Dowcra, Felim McSwyne,
and Con O'Relye. I liked them all and had come to rely strictly on
one of them, a black lath from Belfast who called himself Henry Oge
O'Neal, son of Brian, son of Manus. This was almost like a ritual
with him, and he rattled it off with the greatest pride at every opportunity. He knew more about guns than anyone else and had names
for each of our black-snouted monsters. One was Ree Shamus, after
King James, a cranky specimen which gave us a lot of trouble. Another
was the Great Boar of Thomond; a third, Old-Bear-a-Bob, which means
"friend in need." He talked to them during gunnery practice as though
they were alive. "Na, na, Ree Shamus," he would mutter, "ye're a full
ten bandles off yer mark." Or, "If ye've a mind to it, *ma bouchal*, ye
can split his binding-strakes for him." It was Henry Oge who ran the
gun crew, and I considered myself lucky to have him.

"I'll have ye know, my gentry-cove, that at home I'm called Basil of
the Tops," went on Sleath. We were standing at the head of the after-
ladder, and he had placed himself sideways in order to watch the skyline full ahead. "My mother, bless her, was a Bourke of Tirawly, the
Lower Bourkes, and so I've no taste for the high nose ye give me,
Master Blease. In fact, I like ye not at all."

I made no answer, for my eyes had fixed on what seemed to me a
faint streak of light on the horizon. When I became sure of it, I told
the captain, and he studied it for a long time under a cupped hand.

"I'm thinking it's *La Solderina*," he said finally. His manner changed as completely as Harry Gard's had on the morning we set out to engage the *Santa Caterina*. He grinned with sheer delight, and one of his feet tapped out the first steps of a dance. "Ye call us dirty teagues behind our backs, and now ye'll see how the dirty teagues can fight. Tell me this: would the great John Ward have ventured out with no more than six of us if one of the six hadn't been Irish? I think not."

"He told me you were a fine fighting man, Captain Sleath."

"Did he now?" His pale eyes showed how pleased he was at this praise from John Ward. "For once he's right. I'll say this for him: he's fair at it himself." Suddenly he burst into action and began to bawl orders at the top of his voice. The watch came tumbling out, and almost instantly the shrouds were full of straining figures. "Furl the mainy'rd! Out with the waistcloths and top-armings, ye abbey-lubbers!"

For frenzied activity there's nothing to compare with a ship in the process of stripping for action. As I slid down the after-ladder, forgetting that only officers were allowed to use it, I could see the cooper lashing fast the halfbutts and hogsheads while his helpers soaked blankets and sheets in the water and then spread them about the deck where they would be handy if fire broke out in any part. The red cloth of the top-armings was already stretched over the cubbridge-heads and would soon encircle our whole upper works, thus creating a screen through which the enemy would not be able to see our deck, and very little but the tops of our rigging. I knew the carpenter and his men would be down in the hold, clearing everything away from the sides so that any damage could be quickly reached and repaired.

I found the gun-deck filled with men. They had stripped the tomkins and fids from the guns and were now rubbing tallow into the trunnions under the busy eye of Henry Oge. It was dark, and glancing up I saw that the scuttles, which serve the double purpose of letting air in and smoke out, had not yet been opened. I shouted to Jamesey Dowcra to remove the canvas covers. Several of the others I set to work on the black clay powder pots and the stink-balls which later would be tossed on enemy decks. The air became filled with the smell of saltpeter and asafetida.

In half an hour we were ready, and I went up on deck to report the fact to the captain. He was pacing the quarter-deck, stripped to the waist and with his head bound in a red handkerchief instead of the tarry blue caubeen he usually wore. He was muttering angrily, and the reason for his ill-temper was not hard to find. The ship we had sighted had grown from a half-inch of white sail into a full-rigger under a heavy head of canvas, and was almost certainly the long-expected *La Solderina*; but off to our right the *Royal Bess* was a good mile or more nearer the prey than we were. Sleath came to the rail and scowled down at me.

"Captain Rufflecoat is ahead of us!" he called. "He'll have her kid-neyed before we can get close enough to have a hand in it. He has all the luck, and I am of a mind to haul to and let him have the whole bloody mess to himself."

He did not mean it, for almost with the same breath he was issuing orders to clap on more sail. This did us small good, for the *Royal Bess* had behind her what little wind there was. *La Solderina* had come about in the meantime and was preparing to run for it. Even to my inexperienced eye, it was clear she handled clumsily. I wondered if her slowness was part of the plan to lure us into the trap.

I missed the first act in the play because the captain suddenly ordered me back to my post. Nothing could be seen from the portholes on the gun-deck, so I sat about with the men and speculated as to what was happening. None of them had any fear as to the outcome. They shared their captain's opinion that all the Latin ships in the world were no match for the Irish-manned *Grace O'Malley*. Henry Oge O'Neal straddled Old-Bear-a-Bob and boasted that he would blow the colors off the flagship with a single shot.

We changed our course several times, which made it clear that Captain Sleath was trying frantically to be in at the death. I knew that he had failed in this when Clim peered down through one of the scuttles with a broad grin on his face.

"She's took, Shanks," he called. "It wur a sight for English eyes. Cap'n Ward had the wind of 'er, and so he tacked about and give them a taste of iron from his bow pieces. Then he lay alongside, louse-and-louse, and give 'em a broadside what took all the fight out of the Flat-caps. Twenty minutes it took, Shanks, and not a second more. Down came the colors. They could hardly wait to be through with it."

I looked at the faces about me and saw no trace of jubilation over the news. Henry Oge scowled up at the triumphant Clim and swore that the *Grace O'Malley* would have done it in half the time, and he damned to Captain Ward and his whole crew for a lot of caudge-pawed loiterers. There was a loud chorus of assent at this. I was afraid Clim would let himself down through the scuttle to settle the point with them, so I interposed hastily with a question as to what had happened to the carrack. Clim answered that a prize crew had already been installed, and that *La Solderina* was running due west. The rest of the enemy fleet was closing in from north and south, and by noon the battle would be on.

We spent two stifling hours waiting for the action to begin. The little air which reached us through the narrow scuttles did nothing to alleviate the heat of midday. The men grumbled and drank deeply of the green-scummed water in a corner cask. Finally Henry Oge motioned me to join him at one of the portholes. The view it allowed us was due north, and I caught my breath with surprise and involuntary admiration. What had been before a bare expanse of hazy blue water was now alive with ships—great four-masters with gaudy-colored sails and long rows of black muzzles sticking out from their sides. I realized how the Great

Armada must have looked, sailing majestically up the Sleeve to conquer England. It was a terrifying spectacle, and yet at the same time beautiful.

Henry Oge said in envious tones: "Will ye look at those guns! If we had them, we could blow the whole bloody lot of them out of the water. The Flat-caps don't know how to use them. They're a peery lot, and they'll start popping at us when they're still a quarter-mile off. What are the orders, Master Shanks?"

"We're not to fire until the word is given us. I'm inclined to think we won't loose a round until we're right under them. We can't afford to waste a single ball."

He nodded his head approvingly. The men were too excited to return to their posts. In sheer exuberance of spirits they began to play a new game called leap-frog. They played it with gusto, shouting, "Shule!" while waiting their turns and trying to kick the under man as they vaulted over him.

I let this go on for a few minutes and then whistled them to their places. "When we fire, it will be at point-blank range," I said. "No need to think about elevations. All we have to do is give it back to them faster than they can give it to us."

The roar of guns soon reached us from all sides. The enemy was firing at long range, as O'Neal had predicted. I shook with excitement, longing for the moment when we could pay them back in the same coin. I watched from the nearest porthole and could see that a towering carrack was coming up to engage us. Jets of smoke spouted from her bow as she maneuvered about to get at closer range. She seemed twice as large as the *Grace O'Malley*.

When a broadside from the enemy struck us full on, I knew that the two ships had drawn into line. They had fired high, but a sound of splintering wood reached us from the deck and the screams of wounded men. I could feel the eyes of every man in the line fixed on me, waiting for the word. I ran directly under the first scuttle and looked up, one arm raised to relay the order when it reached me. Nothing happened. Had I mistaken my orders? Or had Captain Sleath forgotten to send them? Then I saw a blood-stained hand in the opening, and my arm dropped.

A roar filled the low galley, greater than any thunderclap I had ever heard. I thought my ears would burst. Through the thick smoke which filled the air I could barely see the recoil of the gun carriages and the torsos of the men as they raced with the reloading. I returned to my porthole and saw that our fire had torn great jagged rents in the enemy hull. I wanted to shout the good news, but the acrid fumes had filled my throat and I was capable of nothing more than an exultant croak. What amazed me more than the havoc we had caused was the closeness with which the scarlet and brown hull of the enemy had drifted. It filled my whole range of vision. I was on the point of signaling for another round when the two ships came together with a grinding crash. Waving both arms to the gunners to withhold their fire, I stumbled through the smoke to Henry Oge.

"They're boarding us!" I shouted.

He shook his head. "Na, na," he said. "They won't be boarding us. They have no stomach for fighting it out at close range. We're boarding them. None of us must leave here until we get our orders."

We had come through without a single injury to any member of the squad. Such luck could not last. Out of the corner of one eye, I saw that the canvas over the farthest scuttle had caught fire. A piece of the burning material fell through the opening, below which was an open budge-barrel of powder. I was too far away to do anything about it, but my frantic shout of warning brought Henry Oge into action. He leaped over a gun which stood in his way and threw himself headlong in the direction of the keg. He was too late to prevent an explosion, but his body fell across the top and muffled it. Even at that, the shock of it threw me off my feet and I tumbled against a gun barrel. The air was full of smoke again and I could see nothing. From the cries of pain around me, I knew that some of the men had been hurt.

When the air cleared, we found there was nothing left of poor Henry Oge. He had been blown to pieces. The deck, the rough ceiling, and all the nearest guns were splattered with his blood. My head was aching, and I was too dazed to do anything but stumble blindly to my feet.

Then I saw something which caused a feeling of horror to creep up my spine. A strange black ball was lodged on the carriage of Old-Bear-a-Bob, a good twenty feet from the spot where the explosion had occurred. I had never seen anything like it before. Then, with growing agitation, I noticed that one side of it was not as black as the other, and that it bore a faint resemblance in shape to a human head. Old-Bear-a-Bob had been the favorite gun of Henry Oge O'Neal, son of Brian, son of Manus, so there seemed something fitting in the spot that chance had found as a resting place for all that was left of him.

I could not restrain my tears and, not wanting the others to see me, crept into a corner behind one of the guns. The ache in my head had become a violent, throbbing pain, and I leaned my forehead against the black barrel. All around I heard excited talk of what was happening above us and speculation on the possibility of spoils. Nothing was said about the dead gunner until one voice observed, "It's little use poor Henry Oge will be having for his share." Another added, "He's a wife and childer at home."

I went on deck just as the enemy struck his colors. It had taken no longer than the capture of *La Solderina*, but my head was aching unbearably, and I was unable to feel any sense of triumph when our men came back over the side with Captain Sleath at their head.

Clim was right on the captain's heels. The men who walked beside the big fellow were thumping him on the back approvingly, so it was clear he had distinguished himself again. His doublet had been cut to shreds, nothing being left of it but a few slashes of velvet over his chest and the remains of a puffed sleeve on one arm. He waved at me and grinned in triumph.

"Cut the grappling irons!" cried Sleath. "There's no time to lose. She'll blow up in a few minutes."

The shrouds were full instantly. I asked the man nearest me what had been done with the prisoners. He answered impatiently that they had been driven below and the hatches battened down. I stared at him, refusing to believe what I had heard.

"Do you mean," I asked, after a moment, "that they'll be blown up with the ship?"

"Of course. What else can we do with them?"

I glanced around me, expecting to find in some of the others a reflection of the horror I was feeling. No one seemed to be concerned in the slightest degree. I tried to figure out how many prisoners there would be. Several hundred, without a doubt. The pain in my head became worse. Was it possible that these men, with whom I had lived and fought on the best of terms, and most of whom I had come to like and respect, could acquiesce in the killing of hundreds of helpless human beings?

"This is murder!" I shouted desperately. "Captain Sleath, there's still time to get them off in the boats."

No one paid any attention. The stretch of water between the two ships began to widen, but I could still hear the voice of Sleath urging the men on to greater exertions. When we were well under way, he came over to where I was standing and looked at me with a kindling eye.

"Did I tell ye right?" he demanded. "What would John Ward have done this day without Basil Sleath and his fighting Irish?"

"It was magnificent," I said. "But, Captain, you can't mean to let those poor devils die? If you'll order a boat lowered, I'll go back and open the hatches for them. They must have a chance to get away."

The smile he turned on me had a puzzled note in it. "And get blown to hell with the rest of them? I thought ye had more sense." He suddenly became very angry. "Ye're more of a looby fool than I thought. What would they've done to us if the tables had been turned? Set us down to meat and drink and asked kindly about our health? They would have strung us up as fast as they could slip the nooses around our necks."

"But they can't be left to die like rats in a trap!"

He laughed. "Would your Captain Ward do any different? I think not." He paused and looked at me with professional interest. "That's a handsome slash in the head ye got for yerself."

It had not occurred to me that I had been wounded. Ever since the explosion on the gun-deck, I had been conscious of dampness on my cheeks, but had thought it due to the intense heat. Now I passed a hand over my face and found on inspection it was covered with blood.

"More of them will be down on us," said Sleath. "Get that little cut attended to and then back to yer post, ye soft-hearted fool."

Clim tore the shirt off the back of a dead man on the deck to wipe the end of his pike, and then came over to where I stood. He examined my head with a worried look. "A splinter," he said. "It's cut in pretty deep, Shanks. I'll bind it for ye."

Nothing else being available, he ripped the velvet off his arm and used it as a bandage. His fingers were clumsy, and it took some time. I watched the enemy ship through a rent in the top-armings and saw when it blew up. Even at that, I started so violently that the knot came loose. I looked at Sleath and saw him cross himself.

"Peace to them," he said, adding almost immediately: "A poor lot they were. They had us three to one. We deserve more than glory for what we've done, but I'm afraid it's nothing more we'll be getting."

Clim whispered in my ear: "Let him go on thinking that. I've something to tell you later, Shanks."

The red felt of the top-armings closed us in like the dome of a cathedral, and I found it necessary to go to the rail in order to see anything of the battle. It was raging on all sides. Three ships were in flames, two of the enemy and one of ours. It was Pooley's *Cornish Lass*, and I could see that the little pinnace was in bad shape. All of our ships, however, were too closely engaged to give any help.

A hurried count brought one reassuring fact to light: the enemy fleet did not number more than a score. They were tall and powerful ships with great batteries of guns; but, with the odds not much worse than three to one, we might have a chance after all. A number of them were already in such plight that they had dropped out of the battle line. The *Royal Bess* was engaged with their flagship, and I felt a surge of pride when I saw what a heavy time the Venetian was having. Her mainmast was down, and a fire had broken out on her deck. There was something about the way she handled which made me sure she had little stomach left for fighting. As I watched, the *Bess* came about and rocked the towering flagship with a blast from her port pieces.

That duel will soon be over, I said to myself.

Feeling the eye of Sleath on me, I went below to my post. The men were all there, some of them wearing bandages. The better part of an hour passed, and then I saw that the tack we were on would bring us under the guns of a high-pooped monster with a band playing martial airs on her deck. They were already firing at us, and I could see jets of water spouting up at a sufficient distance from us to prove the poorness of their marksmanship. They continued to riddle the seas without doing us any manner of harm at all, but their guns went silent when we slung in beside them. The reason, I concluded, was that the barrels had become too heated for use. It was hard to believe they could have been guilty of such a miscalculation; but there it was. My order to fire was delivered with an exultant shout.

There was not enough draft to carry the smoke up through the scuttles, and so for ten minutes we worked in a haze which our burning eyes could not pierce. Only by the sounds could I tell when the carriages had been driven back into position after each recoil. The figures of the crew, seen through the fumes, seemed gigantic. They moved with frenzied haste, and it would not have been hard to believe I had been translated to the Lower Regions where spirits skipped over the flames.

We fired half a dozen rounds. Then a hand tugged at my shoulder, and the voice of Jamesey Dowcra reported that we would have to stop until the guns cooled. I glanced through the porthole and saw that it did not matter. No further medicine was necessary to complete the cure. The enemy was veering off, her hull as full of holes as a fish-leek, her band silent, and smoke issuing from every port. She had had more than enough, and her one thought clearly was to get as far away as possible from the sting of our little Irish hornet.

I went up on deck, and Sleath called down to me from the rail of the quarter-deck, "Not bad, Master Blease, not bad at all."

I had arrived in time to witness the end of the unfortunate *Cornish Lass*. The blazing hulk, lacking power to strike back, had been caught between two of the enemy. They proceeded to pour volley after volley into her with almost fiendish glee, as though paying back in this coinage for the punishment they had received from the rest of us. There was no trace of life on the doomed ship, but I winced every time a shell struck her. Finally they opened a hole in her well below the water line, and she then settled fast. She went down by the stern. One moment we saw her standing straight up in the air as though held by some force other than human; the next she was gone. It looked as though one of old Jore Snode's renora monsters had gripped her by the keel and dragged her down beneath the waves.

"Every last mother's son of them gone," said a sailor beside me, in a lugubrious voice. "That's how we'll all end up. And very soon, I'm thinking. They're all around us. It's nothing but a bull-baiting from now on."

I was not convinced that our position was as desperate as that. They had closed around us, but on signals from the *Royal Bess* we had pulled in together and were in a position to fight on almost equal terms. The enemy seemed to have little desire left for the task of breaking up our compact squadron. They tacked about and fired at us from a safe range. The guns on all our ships were silent. We could afford to wait and conserve our supplies.

The afternoon was wearing away, and I felt I could now take the time to have my wound properly dressed. Forgetting that there was no chirurgeon on board the *Grace O'Malley*, I made my way to the cockpit. The wounded had been carried there, and some of the worst cases had been given what little attention their mates were capable of supplying. The stumps of legs and arms had been rudely bandaged, but little else had been done for the unfortunate fellows who rolled on the decks and screamed with their pain. The planking was slippery with blood, and I fell on my back, rolling with the pitch of the ship to the far end and encountering two dead bodies on the way.

The hopelessness of the situation made things seem worse than the horrors I had encountered on the *Santa Caterina*. Nothing could be done for the sufferers. They must lie here until they died or until the battle ended and help could be secured from the other ships. I struggled to my feet, cursing Basil Sleath for his carelessness and penury.

When I told him of the conditions below, he did not seem very much concerned. "We all take chances," he said. "They staked their lives against a share of the loot. They've lost. The rest of us so far have won." He crossed himself. "What can we do for them?"

"They must have brandy. You haven't seen fit to provide a chirurgeon and a proper medicine chest for the poor devils, but at least you can make it easier for them."

"Ye can't cure them with brandy. We're short of it; but break out some bottles if ye must." He glowered at me. "It's glad I'll be when I've seen the last of ye, Master Blease."

I think the wounded men gained some relief from the drinks which I served with a lavish hand. I knew, however, that few of them would survive if help did not reach us soon; and that seemed impossible.

Night fell, and the five battered survivors drew closer together. The enemy maintained a patrol around us, but at such a distance that their lanterns seemed no larger than fireflies against the blackness of the sky. Dawn might bring them a renewal of fighting spirit, but in the meantime we could rest satisfied with the results of the day's struggle.

Too weary to find any other resting place, I sank down in the scuppers and propped my pain-racked head against the rail. I was not alone, for men were sleeping all over the deck, with musket and pikes beside them, their vigorous snores sounding louder in my ears than the "All's well!" which came at intervals from the lookout. Clim found me there, picking his way cautiously among the sleepers with a candle in his hand. He snuffed it out with a satisfied chuckle and sank down on the deck.

"Is it hurting ye much?" he asked in a whisper. "When ye get a splinter in the nab, it's like the devil was driving nails in ye with a red-hot hammer. I've had 'em many's the time. But in a few day's ye're as good as new. It was lucky ye didn't get it in the belly like poor Dandyprat. There's no cure for *that*." He dropped his voice so low that I found it hard to hear what he was saying. "Shanks, there was gold on the ship we took. They had it hidden on the orlop-deck, and a couple of us found it. On the orlop-deck, Shanks. Do ye see what that means?"

I shook my head with weary lack of interest. Clim, who seemed on the point of bursting with excitement, went on to explain. "One of the lads with me was Danny Boy O'Donnell, and he says anything found on the orlop-deck belongs to the men. It's in the Lotman Code, Shanks. Danny Boy O'Donnell says we divide it up, and no one else can lay a finger on a single win of it. Cap'n Sleath will spit blood when he hears, but it'll do him no good. It was in small bars, and we brought them over in our trunk hose."

My mind was wandering, and I found it impossible to follow what he was saying. It was as though I had moved away from my body and was floating above where we sat. I could look down at the pair of us there in the scuppers, and I could catch scraps of his talk. "We'll be rich, Shanks"—and "Danny Boy O'Donnell says—" Then my mind went far afield. I was back on Shrubsole High, watching the huge bonfire built for John's homecoming and hearing him say, "No law beyond the Line!" Everything became very confused after that. I thought we were in the inn near Theobalds, and a gigantic figure with a face like Archie Armstrong's was laughing loudly and quoting bits of verse that made no manner of sense. I saw Chirp Bird sprawling in a cushioned chair, with his skinny legs cased in crimson silk, saying, "I'm the Upright Man of all London." I knew there was something wrong about that, for Chirp was only the curtal of Alsatia.

Finally I seemed to be in Wayland Spinney. There had been a light fall of snow, and the rabbits came out and frisked around as though I were not there, and then Katie came running to meet me. She was wearing an ermine coat, and there was a glad light in her eyes. Now I was sure that everything was wrong. It was John that Katie had met in Wayland Spinney, and the glad look had been for him and not for me. Still, it was wonderful to see her, and I hoped she would stay a long time, even though I was pretty certain it was not real. I was on the point of saying, "You're a gay little spark, Katie," but checked myself when I realized that John had used those same words. She went away almost at once, and I became aware again of Clim's voice: "The Cap'n can do nothing about it, Shanks. Danny Boy O'Donnell knows the Code from beginning to end, and he says we'll fight for our rights."

The rim of the sun was over the horizon when I wakened. I was so stiff that I had to reach up to the rail with both arms in order to get on my feet. I nearly fell in turning to look out over the water.

Not an enemy ship was in sight.

23

I WAS GLAD to get away from the celebration which followed on the *Grace O'Malley*. Instead of breaking out a cask of brandy,
which was the customary thing after a victory, Captain Sleath compromised by having kettles of hot-pot prepared, a mixture of ale and
brandy boiled together. There was more ale than brandy in the con-
coction, but even so it possessed a diabolical potency. In no time at all
most of the crew had a touch of the jumbles. They seemed determined
to submit the less drunken members to physical indignities and so,
when the captain announced the wounded were to be taken to the
Royal Bess for treatment, I was quickly over the side.

The sea was choppy and the trip in a cranky skiff did not prove
pleasant. We were not crowded, for half of the poor fellows I had seen
in the cockpit had died during the night. Most of the survivors were
delirious. One of them kept singing over and over the first lines of an
old Irish battle song in a voice as reedy as a bird call. Another was
determined to jump overboard; and, as the few sound men with us were
busy with the oars, it fell to my lot to restrain him. He was a great
hairy fellow whose jaw had been broken by a musket ball, and it was
like wrestling with a demented bear. The pain in my own head had not
abated, and every move I was compelled to make sent waves of nausea
over me. The singer changed to a gentler song as we swung in beside
the *Royal Bess*:

> "I'll trade my plate, I'll give my bowl,
> I'll sell my everlasting soul—"

Joralemon Snode was waiting for me at the top of the ladder with a
warm smile. He was stripped to the waist and smeared with blood, so I
knew he had spent the night with the wounded. When he saw the
condition of the men we had brought, he shook his head.

"We'll do what we can for them, with the Lord's help," he said.
"But, Roger boy, we're at our wit's end as it is. We were in the thick
of it from the beginning, and our best fellows went down like the sons
of Israel before the slingshots of Midian." He ran over the list of those
who had been killed, and it sounded like a roll-call in the Cinque
Ports. I listened with a sinking heart, for I had been fond of most of
them. "Nearly everyone has some hurt. John got a musket ball in the

neck, but it did no more than crease the skin of the great lucky zany. It's been a costly victory."

"But a great one."

I tried to sound jubilant but did not succeed entirely, I am afraid. This was not altogether due to the condition of my head. Ever since I had wakened up, a sense of impending disaster had been filling my mind. I was sure that Clim was headed for trouble. All my efforts to talk sense into him had been without result. During the drinking he had stood with one arm over the scrawny shoulders of a redheaded fellow with the look of a fox about him—Danny Boy O'Donnell, no doubt. They were in a state of tipsy self-congratulation, chuckling and winking at each other. Clim's guileless face had been more than ever like that of a big schoolboy playing truant. The pair were very sure of themselves and laughed uproariously when I tried to warn them.

"First, I'll have a look at that head of yours," said Joralemon. He pulled off the velvet bandage, clucking anxiously at the condition of it. "Might as well have used a swabber's rag. The head of the splinter's in there still. You'll think the thumbscrews are on you when I go after it. Come below and I'll get to work on you."

It took a few minutes only, but he had been right about the pain. When a clean bandage had been bound over the wound, I was only too glad to gulp down a noggin of brandy and stretch myself out on a wooden bench. I lost consciousness immediately. Whether I swooned or fell asleep, I don't know; but it was hours later when I wakened.

Mickle, the chirurgeon, and Joralemon were still hard at work. The latter came over to me as soon as I sat up.

"Take things easy and you'll be all right," he said. "I wish I could say as much for the rest of them." His face lighted with righteous anger. "The fires of everlasting hell are not punishment enough for a captain who doesn't look after his men! I was glad when I heard there was trouble on the *Grace O'Malley*."

Trouble on the *Grace O'Malley*! I felt sick at this confirmation of my fears. What had Clim and his new friend been up to? I remembered what John had said about the penalties for third and fourth offenders. If Clim had been concerned in the trouble, it would be his third offense.

"First, they signaled for help," went on Joralemon. "We came about and boats were being manned when they strung up another message. They were sending a boat to us." He shook his head soberly. "There's a skiff-full of them now on the way over. I don't like the looks of it."

"Jore," I said, "the penalty for mutiny is death, isn't it?"

He nodded. "I've seen plenty hanged for less than that. I didn't mean it when I said I was glad. I'm sick at the thought of what may be ahead of us."

I heard the word "mutiny" as soon as I placed a foot on deck. The watch were standing about in whispering groups, and I knew they were speculating as to what had happened on Sleath's ship. Mutiny is an ugly word when you hear it spoken at sea. It means the breaking down of authority, the coming of violence and bestiality and sudden death. A grim and terrifying word. The watch were talking in low tones as though they shared my dread of it.

Sleath himself was the first over the side. He was followed by several members of the crew, all of them fully armed. There was a short delay, and then I saw Clim come up the ladder. He was chained to Danny Boy O'Donnell and another man whose name I knew was Flynn.

There had been an attempted mutiny and it had failed—that much was certain. Clim looked sullen and defiant, but his two companions were chalky with fear. I heard one of the newcomers say to a member of the watch: "A bloody mess, it was. They did for Mat Byrnes." I knew then it would go hard with Clim. Mat Byrnes was second mate of the *Grace O'Malley*; and the killing of an officer is gallows-business.

I was edging over to get a word with Clim when John came out of the pilot-house. He walked slowly to the rail. I wanted to go to him and say, "Have the courage to be merciful." With that in mind I had reached the foot of the ladder when Joralemon came up behind and held me back.

"You'll only make matters worse," he whispered. "He wouldn't relish interference now."

John looked down at the crowded deck. "Good day, Captain Sleath," he said. "It would seem you have been having some trouble."

Sleath found the greeting not entirely to his liking. "It's not help I'm needing in the handling of my own men. I can attend to my affairs, and it's swinging they would be from the yardarm this very minute if I had the settling of it. But the worst offender is one of yours, and so we must handle it between us. That's why I'm here."

I heard tense breathing over my shoulder and turned to find a solid row of the men behind me. Many others had climbed into the shrouds and were staring down with sober faces. Jackes, the cook, was standing outside his galley, and his face had the same pasty look to it as the dough in a pan he was gripping under his arm. Hale Harry Gard appeared from somewhere and took his place at John's side.

"What's happened?" asked John.

"Mutiny," answered Sleath. "Theft, first. And then resistance to orders. Four men were killed."

John climbed slowly down the ladder, followed by the mate. The two captains faced each other on the deck with no effort on the part of either to conceal their dislike.

"Mutiny?" said John. "Give me the details, if you please, Captain Sleath."

The Irishman answered in an aggrieved tone, "My word on that should be enough. But since you ask, Captain Ward, I'll tell you. It came to my ears this morning that some of my men had found a considerable store of bullion on the ship we captured yesterday. They were keeping it for themselves." His voice began to rise. "When I summoned them before me and demanded that they hand the gold over, they told me to my face, these filthy gallows-birds, that it belonged to them. They proposed to divide it up there and then." He looked at the three men in chains and spat furiously.

"And you refused."

"I refused. What do I care for their code? I told them I had a code of my own, and I would have the lot of them keel-raked for their insolence." He paused and then went on in more moderate tones, "It was on your suggestion, Captain Ward, that we agreed to lump all our takings and have an even division at the end. Everything has been turned in since that time."

"Had you explained it to your crew?"

"That I had. It went sorely against the grain to talk to the canats at all, but I explained it again. It made no difference. They defied me and stood by their code."

"How many men were concerned?"

"A score of them finally. But most of them were misled by the lying tongue of O'Donnell. I am holding none but the three leaders responsible. Two of them are mine, O'Donnell and Flynn. The third is yours, Clement Duvver."

John looked at the prisoners for the first time. "You again," he said to Clim. "I swear you've caused me more trouble than any dozen of the crew."

A voice called from behind me, "And he's the best man ye've got, Captain Ward!" This drew a loud chorus of assent.

"We didn't think to make trouble, Cap'n Ward," said Clim. "But we knew our rights. Danny Boy O'Donnell said it was ours, and he ought to know. He was with O'Driscoll. He said what was found on the orlop-deck always went to the men."

The prisoner Flynn broke in with sudden fury: "And a fine division it's been! What's found in the cabins goes to the officers. The jewels and the fine clothing and the gold clocks and the feather beds. What did us ever find on the lower decks? Old clothes and bilge water!"

It was apparent from the torrent of sound which broke loose at this point that all the men were thoroughly in accord with this view of things. A voice from the rear shouted: "It's the same in everything, mates. They drive us off the land to starve in the cities. We get tired of begging and dodging the harman-becks and we go to sea. What do we get then? Wormy food and the bimster on our backs, and what little's left over after our betters are through!" I recognized this as coming from Jackes, the cook, who was always preaching about men's rights and how to get them by revolution.

Danny Boy O'Donnell, forgetting his fears in the face of such open support, stuck his red head out from behind his two tall companions and said in a high-pitched voice: "The only time we ever find something rich, what happens? Black looks and threats from the captain and orders to hand it over. Is that fair play, Cap'n Ward?"

"Enough of this!" thundered John. He looked around him at the angry faces of the crew. "I want every one of you to give me an honest answer before we go any further. Did you understand that the old code had been set aside and that the men on all ships were to share equally at the finish?"

The cook was the first to respond, elbowing his way to the front rank with his pan of dough still under his arm. "We knew it, but we were given no word in the making of the agreement. And we didn't like it. It's always Hobson's choice for common men. First the owners gets half of everything. Then the cap'n takes ten shares and the mates two, and some of us gets one share but most a half. And it's all drunk up and wenched before we get home."

"I want an answer from all of you."

There was an unwilling murmur of "aye" from the men in the circle behind me. John turned to Clim. "Did you understand it?"

Clim had a puzzled look in his eyes. "I heard what you told us, Cap'n Ward, like the rest," he said. "But I didn't think much about it. I knew you would look out for us, and that's all I needed. But Danny Boy said the gold was ours anyway."

"It's becoming clear that your man O'Donnell was responsible for this trouble," declared John. "Unfortunately it may not prove enough excuse for the rest of them. Will you oblige me, Captain Sleath, by telling now what happened when the men refused to hand over the gold?"

"I ordered the three leaders put in the bracelets. Mat Byrnes, my second mate, put a hand on the shoulder of your fellow and was pitched into the scuppers for his pains. Twenty of them lined up against my authority. It was open mutiny, Captain Ward, and you'll be needing no further proofs. Before we got the better of them, we had a harder fight for it than the Flat-caps give us yesterday. Four men were killed, two on each side. Mat Byrnes had his skull cracked."

"Who killed the mate?"

Clim spoke up. "I killed him, Cap'n Ward. I didn't mean to, but he came at me with a pike, and it was him or me. I'm sorry it happened that way. I liked the mate."

My mind had been casting about frantically to find grounds on which leniency could be claimed, but I knew how damaging this admission was. I could see that John dreaded the making of a decision, and I tried to catch his eye. He carefully avoided looking in my direction.

"You're right, Captain Sleath," he said slowly. "It was mutiny, and we must deal with the offenders in the manner prescribed. The fact that at least one of the men concerned has a splendid record in action cannot, I'm sorry to say, be taken into consideration."

The three of them would be hanged. I had known it would come to this, but with the pronouncement made I was swept away with a furious determination to prevent it. I looked around me and could see the same feelings reflected in every face—pity and anger and baffled desire to do something. I called out in a strained voice that no one could have recognized as mine: "His record must be considered, Captain Ward. I demand it on behalf of the crew!"

A roar of approval followed my words. It was what they had been waiting for, apparently. Vehement voices joined in my protest from all quarters. "We don't want Clim to die!"—"He don't deserve it!" —"Good for you, Shanks!" Approving hands clapped me vigorously on the back.

John shook his head gravely. "I feel this as keenly as the rest of you," he said. "Clim is a good man, a fine fighter. But no other course is open to me. If the trouble had occurred here, it would have been in my power to consider your feeling for the prisoner. I don't mean," he added hastily, "that I would have spared the offender, unless there had been the very best of reasons for doing so. Discipline must be maintained at any cost. In this case, the trouble occurred on Captain Sleath's ship, and I can't extend leniency without his consent."

"And that ye'll never get," declared Sleath. "I propose to hang both O'Donnell and Flynn as soon as I get them back aboard the *Grace O'Malley*. I expect ye to give this fellow what he's entitled to."

His eye was fixed on me, and I wondered if he was striking at me through Clim. His nod of sly triumph was as much for my benefit as for John when the latter said, "If that's your final word, there's nothing else for me to do."

The mood of the men was growing sharply belligerent, but this had no effect on Sleath. He looked at John and said: "It's not my final word. There was more than mutiny to it. They stole the gold first. That makes two offenses, Captain Ward. That's to be taken into consideration."

Gard, standing beside John, nodded in agreement. "He's right about that," he said.

"What difference can it make?" John was growing impatient. "The penalty for mutiny is death."

"Aye," said Sleath. "But it makes a difference in the manner of death prescribed."

A cold chill of apprehension took possession of me. What did he mean by that? Was he striving to fix something more painful for poor Clim than death at the yardarm? The men seemed to understand what he meant, for their mutters of protest grew in volume. Jackes, at my elbow, was cursing furiously.

"How many offenses does this make for your man?" persisted Sleath, his eye still singling me out.

Gard took it on himself to answer. "Four."

"Four?" Sleath's tone was openly triumphant now. "There you have it, Ward. Death in the Basket!"

Death in the Basket? I recalled that Captain Pooley had made mention of it that morning in Gouletta. I did not know what it meant, but I was sure it would prove something unspeakably cruel, the epitome of all the horrors of the code under which seamen lived. I glanced at the cook and saw that his face had gone a tallowy white. It was apparent that this possibility had not occurred to John, for he looked almost as dismayed as the rest of us. I did not dare look at Clim.

"It's a clear case," said Sleath. "Well, we'll now return to the *Grace O'Malley*, as I prefer to hang these mutinous dogs from my own yardarm."

From the start I had known there was something I could say as a last resort, but I had held back, being well aware of the consequences. Even now I hesitated. If I told what I knew, the vengeance of Sleath would find me out sooner or later. I prayed for courage, and something inside me responded. I heard myself say: "It's not a clear case. So far we've heard nothing but Captain Sleath's version of what happened."

He turned a furious eye on me. "And are ye doubting it, Master Blease?"

I could not back out now. "Yes," I said.

His hand closed on the hilt of the short demihag in his belt, and he made a move in my direction. John stepped between us and motioned him back.

"You've done it now, Roger. As you've expressed a doubt of the captain's veracity, there's nothing for it but to hear what you have to say. You'll accept the consequences, whatever they may be."

"I'm prepared to accept them."

Complete silence had settled over the ship. The men were watching me with set faces. Sleath drew the dagger from its horn sheath and began to edge closer.

"No man can give me the lie," he said.

"We'll hear this thing through first," declared John, laying a hand on his arm. "Out with it, Roger. What do you know?"

"I know nothing about what occurred today. But I know a great deal about Captain Sleath." I was well aware that I might pay with my life for what I was going to say, but it was too late to turn back. Fear had left me. "He ordered these men put in irons. That was what started all the trouble. Was he right in doing so? No! They were refusing to live up to an agreement they had no hand in making. An agreement, moreover, that he had already broken himself."

All along I had felt Joralemon tugging at my elbow in a frantic effort to keep me quiet. To my amazement, I now heard him chime in with shrill agreement. "That makes a difference, Captain Ward! We want to hear both sides!"

"You've made a bold charge," said John. "But I can't see that it has much bearing on the case."

"It has a bearing," I declared. "Can you condemn men to death on the word of a thief?"

Pandemonium broke loose then. The men began to cheer wildly. The head of Danny Boy O'Donnell popped out again like that of a turtle, new hope showing in his beady eyes.

"We're with ye, Shanks!" cried the cook. "Tell them what ye know."

"Yes, we're with you," echoed Joralemon, jumping with excitement.

The crew moved in front of me by way of protection from any move that Sleath might make. I found myself so hemmed in that I could see neither of the captains.

"You'll have a chance to justify what you've said." I heard John's voice. "As soon as we've settled this case, you'll come to my cabin. I want Captain Sleath there at the same time. We'll hear what you have to say."

"Very well!" I shouted. "I can make good my charge, never fear. See that he isn't allowed out of sight with that bag at his belt. The proof of what I have to say is in it."

The noise redoubled in volume at that. I caught a glimpse of Sleath's face, purple with fury, as he fought to break through the file in front of me. Two of the men were holding him by the arms. Then, to my complete surprise, I saw the head of Clim appear behind them.

Later I was given the story in full by those in a position to see what happened. Clim had been standing at one side, his wrists clamped in the chain which bound him to his two fellow prisoners. As he was much taller than either of them, he had been bending over to ease the strain on their arms. When Sleath sprang in my direction, he straightened up suddenly and dragged them across the deck after him. Sensing danger, Sleath broke loose from the men who were holding him and turned face about.

I was able to see what followed. The chained arms of the infuriated Clim were raised in the air. "I'll do for him myself, Shanks!" he cried. He brought the chain down on top of the captain's head. There was a sharp cracking sound, and Sleath disappeared from view. I did not need to be told that he was dead when I saw his body stretched out on the deck a moment later. Both legs were crumpled up under him, and his broken head was twisted to one side.

"Every man to his post!" shouted John. They scurried to obey without a word. The body of the murdered captain lay there in full view for the better part of a minute. Then John walked over and took the leather bag from his belt.

"What will I find?"

"Diamonds," I said, finding difficulty with my voice. "There should be twenty of them."

He motioned Gard to join him, and they examined the contents together. "Twenty there are," he said. I could see that he was relieved. "You knew what you were talking about, it seems. I'll hear your story later. Gard, signal the captains to come aboard. They must all have a voice in this. Select witnesses to give them the story of what happened both here and on the *Grace O'Malley*." He hesitated and then added in solemn tones: "As for Clim, we have no way out now. Have the carpenter build the Basket."

Clim was relieved of his chains and allowed to sit in the scuppers while the carpenter went to work. Tears were streaming down his cheeks, but I knew this was due to the fighting rage with which he had finished off Basil Sleath and not because he was sorry for himself. He wiped them off with his sleeve and called a good-by to O'Donnell and Flynn when they were helped over the side to the waiting skiff. I sat down beside him while he drank a glass of wine and finished a bone of powdered beef which the cook had brought him. He had a good appetite.

"I'll speak to the Captain," I managed to get out in spite of the lump in my throat. "I'll get around him somehow. You're too good a man to lose, Clim."

He shook his head. "It's the end for me. There's nothing can be done now. Not after I killed him. I'm not sorry about that, Shanks. I'm glad."

I was finding it hard to hold back my own tears. "You did it to save me, Clim. Twice you've done it. And they're going to make you pay for it."

The carpenter was building a wooden cage in full view of us. It was about four feet square with a solid base. He wielded his ax with a reluctant arm as though conscious of the bitter eyes which watched him from every quarter. Once he looked directly at us and shook his head. "Don't hold this against me," he said. "I'm only following orders."

"It's all right, Shaves," said Clim. "Make a snug little home for me. And be sure it's strong. I don't want to drown."

John had disappeared into his cabin, but Gard stood by and watched the carpenter complete his work. Joralemon joined us and began to talk to Clim of the eternal life into which he was soon to enter.

"The Lord will forgive you all your sins if you go to Him with a penitent heart," he said, turning the leaves of his Bible with unsteady fingers.

Genuine tears came into the unfortunate man's eyes at this. "I been a pretty bad lot," he said. "I don't see what use the Lord can have for me. Make the prayers strong, Parson Snode. I'm going to need them."

He brightened up almost immediately and finished his drink. "Shanks, will ye find my hat with the pink feathers? It's all that's left of my fine clothes. I want to wear it."

I found the hat in the fo'c's'le, where it had been left when we transferred to the other ship. Clim indulged in a rueful inspection when I brought it to him. One of the plumes was missing. "Someone stole the biggest feather," he said. "I won't look right."

The cage was finished, and Gard tied a twenty-foot rope to one of the top bars. "Ready, Clim," he said.

A look of fear showed in the victim's eyes for the first time. He glanced about him as though calculating his chances of resistance. Then he pulled himself together and got to his feet. He straightened his hat and laid a hand on my arm. "Tell the lady I'm sorry I ran away," he said. "She was good to me. You too, Shanks."

I followed them at a distance to the stern. I saw Clim take his place in the cage and the carpenter nail down the last of the bars. A bottle of wine and a loaf of bread were handed in to the prisoner. Then Gard tested the edge of a knife he had carried in his belt and handed it to Clim. The Basket was lowered from the spanker-boom. I looked about me and did not see a member of the crew.

I stopped Gard on his way back and asked him the purpose of the knife. For the first time in my knowledge of him, the mate answered in an almost kindly tone.

"Ye're feeling pretty bad about this, Shanks. It's no use, for it can't be helped now. The knife? He'll use it to cut the rope. When he's had as much of it down there as he can stand."

24

BLUNT HAD BEEN too drunk to answer the summons, so I told my story to a group of three composed of John and the two remaining captains, Halsey and Glanville. There was a moment's silence at the finish. I knew that I had told the story badly, my mind being too full of what had happened for lucid narration. Then Halsey, who had the darkest and most expressive eyes I had ever seen in an English face, asked what course I would have followed if the dead captain had not forced me to let the cat out of the bag.

"I was going to tell Captain Ward and leave the matter in his hands," I replied.

Glanville said, between puffs on a long-stemmed ivory pipe: "If it had not been so contrived that we got the word in time, most of us would have been picked up by the enemy. I am strongly of the opinion that our young friend did the only thing possible and that he acted with admirable decision. We owe him a heavy debt of gratitude."

Halsey chimed in with a hearty, "I agree to that," and John smiled at me across the table and said, "Roger, you may consider that we approve what you did."

Glanville then rubbed his long nose with a puzzled air and asked: "What are we going to do about Blunt? I've always considered him a hulvering fellow."

It was decided that Blunt would be forced to withdraw from the Free Rovers after the return to Tunis. Glanville asked, "And Macherie? There's something rancid about him also." John pointed out that Sir Nevil's participation in the scheme had not been proved, and that we would have to look into the matter first. Halsey did not seem entirely convinced of the wisdom of this, saying that we would soon find ourselves with an Upright Man of the Inner Seas if we didn't watch the rascal closely.

I rose to withdraw. John looked at his fellow captains for their concurrence, and then remarked that the question of doing something handsome for me would be discussed later. This was the opportunity I had been waiting for, and I walked back to the table eagerly.

"There's only one thing I want. You know what it is, Captain Ward. A pardon for Clim."

Dissent registered on all three faces instantly. John shook his head. "And that is the one thing we can't grant," he said. "It shouldn't be necessary to tell you the reasons."

"You give me credit for saving our ships from capture, so perhaps you'll agree that I saved also a great many lives. I'm asking only one in return."

John frowned. "You saw how the men acted out there today. There's never more than the thinnest margin between obedience and mutiny. If we gave in to you, there would be no holding them. Discipline would dissolve into thin air. Where would we be then?"

"Can you compel obedience by injustice?"

"Injustice?" Halsey took up the argument. "Your man killed a captain on the open deck!"

"But the captain had been at fault in his treatment of the men."

"The evidence does not prove it," declared Halsey.

"You know that Sleath's word couldn't be depended on. He goaded them into open resistance."

"That has no bearing on the case. He represented authority."

Glanville's sympathetic attitude had made me hope for support from him, but he now said, in a not too happy tone: "Discipline is as necessary as a sound hull. I've sent many men to the yardarm in my time and slept badly of nights because of it. It's an evil thing, but it stands in the way of things that would be still more evil. You've heard,

I'm sure, that Sir Francis Drake had to hang his best friend on the voyage around the world?"

I had heard the story many times, and it had seemed to me the one blot on the reputation of our great sea hero. Before I could voice this opinion, John broke in: "I feel badly about this, Roger. I would spare the poor fellow if I dared. *But it can't be done!* Do you want us to succeed? We face every handicap as it is, and we need that fine edge of discipline if we're to have a chance at all." He looked at me earnestly as though trying to compel my understanding. "I've seen leniency tried. It was on my first long voyage, in the northern seas. A man should have been hanged, but the captain let his heart get the better of him. Five men died finally because of it, three of them innocent members of the crew, in a full day of fighting. The trouble-maker was hanged *then*."

"Captain Ward is right," said Glanville. "The code of the sea may not seem important to one as young as you, but we have to live by it. And die by it sometimes."

"Roger," said John earnestly, "consider that there have been five offenses in a row, ending with mutiny and the murder of a captain! I might as well turn the command over to that loud-mouthed cook if I let your man go now."

I argued the case bitterly but futilely. They had closed their minds. Clim would have to die a lingering death, swinging behind the ship in a frail wooden cage, without food or water under the blistering rays of the sun. He would die in torment, but the crew would have the lesson of obedience driven home to them in a way they were never supposed to forget. I bowed and left.

A member of the watch stopped me when I set foot on the main deck. He was a simple-looking country fellow with lank hair and frightened eyes.

"Any luck?" he asked.

"None."

The sailor fell into step beside me. "Will they leave him there until he starves to death?" he asked in a horrified whisper.

"Yes. Unless he goes mad with the heat first."

His lower jaw was trembling, and he found it hard to speak. "My brother and I signed up together. He was killed yesterday." He gulped back his tears. "He went overboard when they shot away our sprits'l. I saw him in the water, hanging onto the spar. We were fighting one of the Flat-caps, and it was a full hour before we left the spot. I wanted to go after him, to do something! But the mate kept me at my post. I saw the look in his eyes when we sailed away and left him there to drown. My stout little Will!" The tears were streaming down his face now. "I can't stand this bloody, beastly life, Shanks, I can't stand it!"

I answered in a whisper, "Neither can I!"

I walked the deck for hours, taking care to avoid the stern. The stars came out and a breeze sprang up. We began to make good head-way. I thought of the cage swaying at the end of the rope, knowing the added discomfort this would bring the unhappy occupant. A dozen times I made up my mind to go back to the cabin and repeat my de-mand, but each time I drew back. It would do no good.

Joralemon joined me finally. For a time we walked along in silence. Then I pointed to the stars above us. "It's a beautiful night. How can there be so much cruelty under a sky like that?"

My companion answered quietly: "There are thousands of men dying tonight. In fine beds as well as in filthy spital-houses and in the cockpits of ships. Some are dying in great pain. Some are dying be-cause of the wickedness of other men. It goes on all the time, Roger. Perhaps you and I will go to our Maker in His good time with more suffering than Clim will know in the next few days. There has always been pain and shame in the world as well as beauty and peace."

I knew that what he said was true, but it did nothing to ease my mind. Could I stand by and see a friend die under my very eyes? I must do something, anything, not walk the deck like a coward. There must be some way out of this. Something I had not been able to think of. The things the three captains had said kept revolving in my mind. There must have been an answer I could have given to convince them.

"You haven't eaten anything all day," said Joralemon. "Come below now and we'll see what the cook can do for us. Then you'll be able to sleep."

Jackes dipped down into a barrel and hauled out a slab of salt pork. "It's well powdered," he said, cutting a slice and handing it to me on a biscuit. "Cap'n didn't eat any supper either. Can't be feeling good." His thick lips, under a small waxed moustache, quivered with the ques-tions he hesitated to ask while Joralemon was there. I took a mouthful but found I couldn't swallow.

"I can't eat," I said.

The cook proceeded to dispose of the food himself. Between mouth-fuls he said: "He's been very quiet. Not a sound out of him. He's a game one, Clim is."

"Yes. He's game."

"You were talking with the Captain?" Jackes kept looking back and forth from one of us to the other.

"I talked with Captain Ward. Nothing can be done."

He ejected a mouthful of the food with furious energy, as though he were casting out privilege and all its manifestations. On the boards be-hind him was a figure chalked with crude originality, a caricature of a gentleman with a pleated ruff and tall feathers in his hat. Seizing a piece of chalk, the cook inscribed a noose around the neck and then sketched in a gallows.

"Some day it will be like that," he said, grinning furiously. "You're a scholar, Shanks. Did ye ever read of a man named John Ball? They hanged him and cut out his innards before he was dead. Because he was a great man and had a message for the world. There was another man named Jack Cade. They hanged him too."

I could not sleep at all. I tossed in my netting for several hours, then dressed and went out on deck. The breeze had died down. I walked to the stern. I went with stealthy steps as one might in approaching a haunted chamber, and it took all the power of will I possessed to look over the side. The Basket was swaying gently on the end of the rope.

"Clim!" I called.

There was no answer. I called again but received no response. Apparently he was sleeping. Feeling slightly relieved, I returned to my cabin and stretched out in the netting, hoping that sleep would come to me also. It was a vain hope.

I was out at dawn. The watch was being changed, and each man up from the fo'c's'le wore a sullen look. The air was filled with the threat of a hot day.

I paid another visit to the stern. Clim was awake, for I could see the pink plumes move. The loaf of bread and the bottle of wine were gone. The knife had been stuck in one of the wooden bars above his head.

"Clim, are you all right?"

He changed his position so suddenly that the cage tilted, and he slid down against the bars on the lower side. He stuck out a hand and waved at me.

"I'm fine, Shanks. A snug little place to have all to myself. But I'm hungry. I'm fair starved."

I nodded to him by way of promise. Gard was not in sight, so I ran to the galley and begged Jackes to let me have some food. He was only too glad to tie up some meat in a red handkerchief. To this he attached a length of fish-line.

"Keep casting until it lands on the top," he said.

I tucked it under one arm, hoping that the folds of my sleeve would conceal it. By the worst of luck, however, I ran into the mate as soon as I set a foot outside. He give me one look and then wrenched the parcel away from me with an impatient oath.

"You looby fool!" he exclaimed. "Didn't ye hear the orders? No one goes near him. Do ye think it a kindness to keep him alive down there? The sooner he uses the knife, the better it'll be for him. Try this little trick again, and you'll earn a spell in the bilboes for yerself."

With one angry motion of his arm, he hurled the food far out over the side, fish-line and all. The eyes of the cook, watching us from inside the galley, were blazing; and I half expected to see him hurl the dudgeon knife in his hand. If he had any such intention, he thought better of it.

It grew so hot by midday that the pitch boiled out between the seams in the deck. It must be unbearable in the Basket! The bars would provide no shade from the blazing rays of the sun. I tried to tear my mind away to other subjects but found it impossible. How long did it take for a man's tongue to become black and swollen when he lacked water? What could Clim do if the sun heated up the wood on which he sat as much as it did the deck?

Toward the end of the afternoon, one of the men said out of a corner of his mouth as he passed me, "He's calling for ye." I scrambled to my feet and started back, trying to find a path where the deck was in shade. I had discarded my shoes and in my disturbed state of mind could not remember where I had left them; with the result that my feet found the warmth of the exposed planking unbearable. As I drew near, I heard a voice which I did not recognize calling at regular intervals like the ticking of a clock, "Shanks! Shanks! Shanks!"

Mate Gard loomed up in my path and demanded to know where in the name of Almighty God I thought I was going. I said impatiently, "Can't you hear?" and tried to brush by him. He took me roughly by the arm.

"Won't you ever learn? Don't you know what orders mean? Listen, no one is allowed to speak to him, and that means gentry-coves as well as common seamen! It's water he wants anyway. Supposing I was soft enough to let you get him some, how would ye get it down to him? Now then, get some sense into your head."

"I'm going to speak to him, orders or no orders."

When I tried to dodge by him, he reached out with sudden fury and seized me by both shoulders. I was unable to move a muscle. He held me for several moments and then gave a shove which sent me sprawling on my back. "Ye're nothing but a joskin to me, Master Blease, and I'll treat ye as such," he said.

I got slowly to my feet. My trunk hose had been ripped in the fall, completing the ruin of my once wonderful clothes. My blue velvet doublet was blackened with powder burns, and my black silk hose were full of holes and bagging at the knees in the old familiar way. I had been allowed a few hours only to strut in magnificence, and I might never be able to afford anything so fine again. Well, it did not matter.

I borrowed a needle from the cook, but my fingers refused the task. Joralemon came along and took over the work of repair, sewing up the rent with a skillful hand. "You'll be seeing the tailor again when we get back to port," he suggested.

I shook my head. Rags and tatters were good enough for those who lived this unclean and Godless life. I would never try to deck myself out like a gentleman again.

"You preach to us of God!" I said bitterly. "How can you expect anyone to believe in Him when He lets this go on?"

"You must not blame God for the ways of men."

"You'll lose your chance with the crew, Parson Snode, if you do nothing about this. Why don't you go to John? He might listen to you."

"I have. I was with him an hour ago. He—he says there's nothing to be done."

"The men must be taught a lesson: that's what he said, I suppose. Well, it's having the opposite effect. Have you noticed how quiet and grim they all are?"

He shook his head. "But they jump to the word of command on the second, Roger. I—I'm afraid that John is right. I've been through similar things. The killing of a captain can be punished in no other way."

I turned and stared at him. "Are *you* in favor of this kind of a lesson, then?"

He did not reply for a moment. Then in a quiet voice he said: "When Christ was on the cross, Roger, there was a little group which watched, knowing that he was the Saviour. They suffered as much in spirit as He did in the body. 'They stood afar off, beholding these things.' They did nothing, because there was nothing they could do." He laid a hand on my shoulder. "I'm not drawing a parallel between that sublime scene and this sordid case of human justice. I'm trying to show you there are things which must be endured. You must do as those humble followers of Jesus did. You must stand afar off."

"You needn't preach to me of Christian meekness," I said. "I've been playing the coward as it is. First I let John and the other captains talk me down instead of standing up to them and fighting it out. Then I let the mate keep me from going to Clim when he called."

Joralemon finished his task and broke the thread with an expert finger. "Did this little accident happen in a scuffle with the mate? You got off light."

"Clim will think I've deserted him."

"You've done everything possible. Nothing you could have said would have made any impression on the captains. And what else could you have done with the mate? He could break your back with one twist of his wrist."

"I should have had the courage to stand up to him, at any rate. Instead I came skulking back here with the crew laughing at me because my trunk hose had been torn."

"They are not laughing at you, Roger. You've made a friend of every man in the fo'c's'le, if that is any consolation."

It was no consolation at all. I could think of nothing but Clim, suffering out there in the blazing heat. After several moments' silence, I asked, "Is it going to be very hard for him?"

My companion sighed. "It's not an easy death. I'm afraid the Leveche is due. He'll have a bad time of it then."

The supper kettles were brought up, but my stomach still refused food. The cook whispered that he had a pudding for me, but I thanked him and shook my head.

The hot wind that Joralemon had predicted began to blow over the water from Africa. It became unbearably hot, and the men slept on deck. Joralemon took his place beside me and fell asleep almost immediately. I envied him the oblivion he was enjoying. My own eyes refused to close, and all through the night I believed I could hear Clim's voice calling me, "Shanks! Shanks!" Just at dawn I dozed off, but it was worse than the wakefulness, for I dreamed of Clim stretched on the rack with John turning the crank. John was wearing a red jerkin and a mask, and he kept saying, "There's nothing I can do; discipline must be maintained."

A thought occurred to me suddenly. If we got back in time to help in the engagement with the Spanish fleet, it would mean a reprieve for Clim. We would not go into action with one of our best men swinging in the Basket behind us. John would order him taken out and, of course, he would not be sent back after that. Here was the chance I had been trying to find.

I sprang to my feet and ran to the rail. The sky ahead of us was still dark. I gazed hopefully in every direction. There was no trace of a ship's lantern to be seen.

I tried to reckon distances. We had been sailing due west for two days and two nights, and the winds had been favorable. Surely we would make contact with the rest of our fleet very soon. I murmured a double prayer: that the Spaniards would be coming up on schedule, that Clim would have the strength to hold out until then.

The wind from the south was freighted with the choking breath of the desert. An order from John set me to the task of copying documents in the comparative coolness of the ordnance room. Although I suspected he had sent the order in the hope it would keep my mind occupied, I tried my best to concentrate. My mind was incapable of it. After an hour, I looked at the paper in front of me and discovered I had been setting down letters at random. I gave it up then.

I went out on deck and the sudden impact of the heat made me catch my breath. God, what must it be like in the Basket! Could any human being stand it? I walked with determination to the stern. Gard was not in sight, but it would not have made any difference if he had been there. I had made up my mind that nothing would stop me this time. I leaned over the rail and looked down.

Clim was sitting without moving, his head a bare inch from the edge of the knife. He had lost his hat, and his head and neck were mottled and fiery red.

"Clim!" I called. "They wouldn't let me come before."

He answered without moving. "Is that you, Shanks? I feared ye had given me up."

"No, no! I'll never stop trying to get you out. Listen to me, Clim: if I can't persuade the captain, I'm going to talk the crew into action. He'll have to do something if we go to him in a body."

There was a moment's silence and then, speaking with great difficulty, he said: "No, Shanks. That's how mutiny starts. We mustn't have any more of that. See what come to me of going against orders. They'll put ye down here with me if ye try it."

I found it equally difficult to speak. "When you saved my life, you said you couldn't let me die because I was a friend. You're a friend of mine, Clim, and I can't let you die."

"There's nothing now ye can do." His voice was so low and husky I could hardly make out what he was saying. "I don't want you to go through anything like this. But can ye get me water? That's all I want. Water, in God's name!"

I became aware that Gard was standing at my elbow. I faced around and saw that he was favoring me with an intent smile. He made no move to interfere, however.

"I'll see what can be done," I called. "Don't give up hope, Clim. I'm going to the Captain."

When I turned away, the mate fell into step beside me. I saw that he was fingering the bimster in his belt. "So ye went against my orders, Master Blease," he said. "And now ye're going to the Captain, are ye? Well, my fine young gentleman, ye're not going to the Captain. He's feeling this nigh as much as you are, and I'll not have ye making it any harder for him. I'm giving you an order. No going to the Captain, understand? If you do, I'll tie ye up to a grating and beat some of the flesh off your ribs!"

Joralemon heard what had happened, and after that I could not shake him off. When I started to climb the ladder to the quarter-deck, he seized one of my arms and hung on with all his strength.

"He means it! You'll have to take the consequences if you go against orders again. You mustn't play the fool, Roger."

When I insisted on tramping the hot decks, he pattered after me, entreating me to be sensible and stay in the shade.

"Is Clim in the shade?" I demanded. "I can't sit in comfort when I think what he's going through."

"It will do him no good if the both of us get a touch of the sun," argued Joralemon.

I asked every man we met how far he thought we had gone, and how soon we would be off Marsa Ali, where the rest of the fleet was stationed. All they could do was guess, and even their guesses were wide apart. Clim became slightly delirious during the latter half of the afternoon. He sang patches of sea songs until his swollen throat gave out. After that he gabbled continuously in a throaty voice which suggested Bedlam. The sound of it carried all over the deck, and I saw it was having an effect on the men. A few who were Catholics crossed themselves. When I could bear it no longer, I went below to my cabin. The heat was stifling there, and the wound in my head began to bother me again. Joralemon looked in at me once but withdrew hastily when I screeched at him to leave me alone.

Night closed in. Unable to bear the confinement of the cabin any longer, I went out on deck. The Leveche was blowing steadily, and on the port side it was like standing in the door of a baker's oven. I joined a group of the men sitting to starboard and was given an almost affectionate welcome. They disagreed widely when I asked how far we had gone during the day. They were sure of one thing, however: the only sails sighted since we headed westward were those of our four sister ships.

Was the luck of wind and tide running against us? Would Clim lose this last thin chance?

I was amazed to find that my companions were in a mood bordering on cheerfulness. Perhaps this was due to the fact that the voice from the Basket could no longer be heard. They fell into a boastful train of talk, each man dilating on the part he had played in the great victory. When any mention was made of John, they spoke in terms of pride, calling him in turn Captain Rufflecoat, Beau Brimstone, and Gaffer Johnny. For the moment all resentment had been laid aside.

"That *Solderina* were a rich prize," said one man, smacking his lips. "Ye'll be having that snug little tavern on London River after all, Maltworm."

I had not known until then that the third member of the unlucky trio was in the group. He had said nothing, which was natural if he shared my feelings in any degree. When he spoke up now, however, his voice seemed to reflect the same curious forgetfulness.

"Aye," he said. "I've been thinking about it. I'm going to call it the Free Rover. How do ye like that for a name, mates?"

"Why not call it the Basket?" I demanded. "It's the only way you'll have of remembering poor Clim. He won't be dropping in for a mug of ale or to talk over old times."

In the silence that fell we found that the suffering prisoner had begun to babble again. It was clear that his strength was failing him. Although it was too dark to read anything in the faces around me, I sensed that their mood had changed. I seized the opportunity thus offered.

"We could save him yet," I said. "The Captain likes this no better than the rest of us. If we went to him in a body, he might give in to us."

I could see that some of the heads were shaking dubiously. "We'll all end up in the bracelets if we try it," said one man. "Gard won't like it. He'll take it out on all of us."

"Suppose he does take it out on us," I argued. "Are you content to sit here and let a friend die without raising a hand to help him? Are we all cowards? I'm going, if I have to go alone."

I talked with furious haste. Wouldn't we need Clim when we faced the whole Spanish fleet? Wasn't he the best fighting man we had when it came to going over the side? What would we tell his friends when we went back home? They began to come around. Finally, Maltworm swung over to my view.

"No harm in trying, mates," he said. "Clim's one of us, ain't he? We've a right to speak to the Cap'n."

"That's man's talk!" Jackes the cook had joined us. He was carrying something in his hand which resembled a butcher's knife. "We've rights, ain't we? We're men, ain't we? Let's do as Shanks says. The Cap'n will have to listen to the fo'c's'le."

There was a sound of scuffling as the men got to their feet. They were full of fight now. "We'll all go," shouted one man. "Shanks and the cook will do the talking for us."

A square figure loomed up suddenly in the dark, and I heard Gard say: "So Shanks and the cook are to do the talking for ye! I'll do all the talking right now—with my fists. See if ye like what they have to say."

He was facing me as he spoke. I saw his arm draw back. I could not get out of the way of the blow because the men behind me were pressing against my shoulders. I raised my arm to ward it off.

I came to in my own cabin. I knew where I was because the first object my eye lighted on was a Spanish sword I had selected from the loot of the *Santa Caterina*. It was hanging from a peg on the wall facing me.

I felt so weak I couldn't raise my head. Everything began to whirl about me, and I saw a score of Spanish swords with tasseled hilts. I heard Joralemon say, "He's coming to," and then the voice of the surgeon, Mickle, "I'm very glad of that."

"Were you getting worried?" asked Joralemon.

"I was. When we picked him up off the deck, I was sure his neck was broken. I think I would rather be hit by an iron pintle than Gard's fist."

"I'm all right," I said. It surprised me that speech could involve such physical effort. The throbbing in my head was as hard to bear as in the first hours after I received my wound. I managed to add, "What's happened?"

"Well," said Joralemon, "you've had a narrow escape, for one thing. Gard turned on the cook after knocking you down. He broke his nose for him. He's feeling bad, the cook is."

"Have any ships been sighted?"

"Never a one. Why?"

"We've got to reach the others," I said. "Tonight. It might be too late tomorrow. What time is it?"

"Near midnight. It's been over two hours since you went down, Roger. I was beginning to fear you were done for."

The chirurgeon gave me something to drink. It must have been

potent, for I felt a little better at once. They left me then, and I must
have fallen asleep soon after. Daylight was showing through the porthole when they returned. I tried unsuccessfully to sit up. Still, I knew
that I was better, for the sword was stationary in its usual place on
the wall. My head was throbbing.

"The Leveche is still blowing," said Joralemon. Mickle felt my jaw
with a gentle hand. I noticed that both their faces had a taut appearance as though they had been scorched. How must Clim look by this
time?

"The bone's not broken. You have an exceptionally strong jaw, young
man."

"Have we sighted the fleet?"

"No."

"How far are we off Marsa Ali?"

"No one can be sure. There's no sign of land yet."

My hopes went down. We should be in sight of the end of Sicily,
which had been set as the rendezvous. Had our ships sailed farther
west in search of the enemy? If that had happened, the last hope of
saving Clim would be gone. In a faint voice I asked, "How is he?"

Joralemon did not answer for a moment. "Clim was in his right
mind for a few minutes after dawn," he said then. "I spoke to him.
I hope the Lord will forgive me, but I—I urged him to cut the rope.
It isn't right for him to go on suffering this way. But he said no, he
wouldn't kill himself. He even managed to smile."

I was incapable of comment for several moments. Then I managed
to ask, "Can it last very much longer?"

The chirurgeon answered: "The heat will be worse today, I'm afraid.
I've been through this several times, and they've never lasted out the
third day in weather like this. But you can't tell about Clim. He's
such a fine physical specimen."

I turned my aching head in Joralemon's direction. "Is anything going to be done?"

"Nothing more. The men are in a submissive mood since last night.
Captain Ward hasn't appeared yet. I reported what had happened to
him last night and told him how we all felt. His dinner was on a
table beside him. He hadn't touched it. He had been drinking and he
roared at me to get out."

They left me then. I must have been out of my mind for a while,
what with the heat and the lack of food and sleep. At any rate, I
believed that I was in the Basket myself. It was much more vivid than
any dream I had ever had. I was sitting with my knees drawn up
close and my head bent over them, for in no other position could I accommodate myself to the cramped space. The cage was so flimsy that
I had the sensation of hanging over a tall cliff with the terror of
illimitable space under me. Every time we swayed with the wind, I
held my breath. At the same time the sun was beating down on me

with searing intensity. The boards were hot to the touch, and I could feel my flesh shrink from the heat striking at me through the bars. I tried to draw myself in still closer to escape it. My throat felt as though live coals had been sprayed through my lips.

When I dared a glance beneath me, the sea had the appearance of a mass of molten flame. Was it the sea? Or was I suspended over the lake of everlasting fire?

I would come back to full consciousness at intervals but then almost immediately would relapse into my illusion. Once I saw Hubert, the Captain's swabber, come in with a flagon of wine under one arm and heard him say, "The Captain's compliments, sir."

I managed to get up on my elbow. "Has the fleet been sighted yet?"

"No, sir. Will I pour a glass for you?"

"Take it back to the Captain with my compliments."

He looked at me with reproach and said, "It's muscadine." I drifted back to my nightmare and did not see him leave.

It was a long time after this when Joralemon returned. He was looking grave.

"What time is it?" I asked.

"It's getting dark."

I tried to sit up. "Have I been here all day? I should be out. What has happened, Jore?"

"You've been here two days. We've been in to see you half a dozen times. You've been in a high fever."

"We must have come up with the fleet. Have they met the Spanish?"

"No signs of them yet. John is getting worried." He paused and then said in solemn tones, "Roger, Clim is dead."

I could feel my hands trembling. There is nothing more terrible than the irrevocability of death. Clim had gone. I had let him die. For two days I had allowed myself to lie here while nothing was done to save him. And now it was too late.

"He didn't use the knife. I was sure he would come to it in the end. But I didn't know how stanch his spirit was." He laid a hand on my arm as though to give me what comfort he could. "Ten minutes ago I noticed he had fallen over on the floor, and I had one of the men climb down the rope. He reported it was all over. I'm going to hold a funeral service now."

"I must go."

He frowned doubtfully. "Are you strong enough?"

By way of answer, I threw one leg over the side. I felt so dizzy that I needed his help in getting to a standing position. My knees displayed an uncomfortable tendency to buckle under me. The swabber had left the flagon after all, and Joralemon poured me a full glass. Muscadine is a rich and heady wine, and I could feel some of my strength coming back as I swallowed it. When I attempted a step, however, I found it hard to locate the floor. "A strong potion to take on an empty stomach," said Joralemon, clamping an arm through mine.

He was carrying a Bible in his hand. The members of the crew not on duty fell in behind us as we walked down the deck. Instinctively we adopted a slow pace, and the men behind kept step. Tramp. Tramp. Tramp. There was something of the finality of doom about it.

When we took up our positions near the ensign staff, Joralemon said, "Ready, Jones," and I was surprised to see that it was Maltworm who responded. With a knife between his teeth, he climbed out on the boom until he was directly over the rope on which the Basket was suspended. I remembered then that the real name of this tough-fibered seaman was Edwin Jones.

I did not turn, but I could tell that the deck back of us was filled with men. Joralemon opened his Bible and began to read. His voice, becoming full and resonant as he intoned the service, seemed to fill the space about me. When he came to the words, "We therefore commit his body to the deep," he raised his hand, and I saw Maltworm's knife flash in the evening sun. A moment later there was a thud as the Basket struck the surface of the water. The tragedy of Clim the Cod's-head had come to an end.

When I turned to go back, I saw that John had been standing back of the last file of men. His hat was in his hand, and he was looking grave and unhappy. He faced about at once and descended to the waist.

Back of me I heard Maltworm saying, "He were the only one ever put in the Basket what didn't cut the rope." There was deep pride in his voice. Clim had died bravely, and his comrades would take a great deal of satisfaction out of it.

Suddenly I found myself struggling with a desire to laugh. "Edwin Jones!" I said, stifling the hysterical impulse with the greatest effort. "Edwin Jones is a name for a haberdasher of nouns. Not for a man like Maltworm!"

Joralemon drew an arm through mine. "Easy, Roger," he whispered. "Don't let yourself get out of hand."

He led me over to the rail to let the rest of them pass. I looked straight ahead into the west, and suddenly my heart seemed to stop. I counted seven sails on the horizon.

25

JORALEMON INSISTED I should be in bed, but I brushed the suggestion aside when I heard John say to Gard, as they watched the main section of our fleet on the skyline: "No more order than a stinking pout fleet! I tell you, they haven't done well. There's a hangdog suggestion in the set of their sails."

There was still enough light to see the low thumb of land where Marsa Ali lay. I examined it carefully in the hope of finding the remains of the walls and fortifications which Charles V of Spain had destroyed seventy years before. The harbor had been a pirate nest then, and the doughty king had hoped to stamp out the trade by robbing the corsairs of their base. All pirates had brown skins in those days. It had remained for a watery-eyed king of our own to put that label on Englishmen who refused to let Spain rule them off the seas. However, we were too far off to see anything, and I turned my attention to matters which concerned us more immediately.

The talk which reached my ears from the groups seated around the supper kettles indicated that the men were in a dissatisfied mood. They were discussing the old code, and I heard envious references to the value of what they would have divided under it, the loot found on the lower decks of our prizes. It was clear that the death of Clim had set them thinking. Joralemon heard the talk also. He looked at me and shook his head soberly. "John values the good will of his men above everything," he said. "This will make him very unhappy. Will he blame you, Roger, for the way they're talking?"

"He's brought it on himself," I asserted.

The cook, with little but his eyes showing through bandages, had squatted on the deck and was holding forth on the rights of common men. "They hang us at the yardarm and starve us to death in the Basket," he declared in a loud voice. "But have patience, mates. Some day it will be the spawn of the spital-houses who wear ermine on their jackets and the gentle-born who jumped from the gallows-tree."

John heard something of what was being said, for he crossed the upper deck and looked down into the waist. Jackes saw him but went right on. "Clim is dead. Who will get his share?" he demanded. "Will it be divided up among us? Not a sice of it will we see. It will go to the owners. They're glad to see us run foul of the code. It means gold in their purses when Shaves builds the Basket."

"That's a lie, Jackes!" declared the Captain, in a voice which could have been heard at the top of the shrouds. "Clim's share will be divided among his mates. That is in the agreement, and well you know it. Keep that tongue of yours under control, you scullery cank!" He turned and walked back toward the pilot-house, but not until he had looked in my direction as though to say, "You've stirred all this up."

I did not care how he felt about it. My bitterness over the death of Clim blinded me to all other considerations.

In spite of my condition, I remained on deck long enough to watch the arrival of Sir Nevil and the captains of the main fleet. Night had settled down, and the bobbing of lanterns on the bows of their skiffs reminded me of the will-o'-the-wisp on Haverstraw Marsh at home. It was easy to read dissatisfaction in their faces as they came over the side, but Macherie himself was as arrogant as ever. He slapped John on the back with a patronizing hand.

"Well, Captain Rufflecoat!" he said. "Or is it John Lacklatin your men call you? It's apparent you have seen some action. I count only five ships. Where is the sixth?"

"At the bottom of the sea. Four of the enemy are with it, I'm proud to say. We sent them about their business with plenty of good English lead in their bellies. La Solderina is safely in Tunis by this time. The richest prize I've ever taken, Sir Nevil. And now what report have you to make? Haven't the Jew-roasters put in an appearance yet?"

"Oh, yes. They came up in accordance with their plan. I think they cared little for the reception we had prepared for them. At any rate, they put about at once and showed us their heels."

"You are much too modest, Sir Nevil. I am sure they didn't get away as easily as that. You warmed their heels for them, of course."

Captain Harris from Bristol took it on himself to reply. "They gave us the slip. Don't ask me how it happened, Ward."

"They got clean away? I can't believe it."

The Bristol man exploded with pent-up indignation. "Not a shot was fired on either side. A pretty farce it was! We should have cut off a round half-dozen of the stragglers, but instead we scurried around like a flock of cackling-cheats!"

Macherie's hand went to his sword, and John interposed hastily with the suggestion that all discussion be postponed until the full council assembled. The baronet agreed in sulky tones; and, when the last of the captains had arrived, they went in a body to the ordnance room. By this time I was barely able to stay on my feet, and I did not demur when Joralemon insisted that I go below. He helped me to my cabin, and I crawled into my netting without removing any clothing. When he returned an hour later to report on what had occurred, I was nearly asleep, but I pulled my drifting faculties together sufficiently to hear the news. Macherie's handling of the fleet had been bitterly criticized by every captain. Joralemon had picked up one story, which was later confirmed, that Sir Nevil had been more interested in the German wench than in the control of operations, and that he had not put in an appearance for a good half-hour after the Spanish fleet was sighted. "He's been put most thoroughly in his place," said Joralemon gleefully. "They refuse to serve under him any longer. He's sailing back to Tunis with us, and then he's going to take himself off. Blunt's going with him. Good riddance to the pair of them!"

"Are we heading for port?"

"At once. The Spaniards have broken up. Half are on their way back to Barcelona, the rest for Malaga. The danger is over."

John's plan had worked, then! He had won on every point. The plans of the enemy had been foiled, and all the credit for this belonged to him. He had scored a complete victory over a force more than three times the size of his own, while Macherie's efforts had ended in a sorry fiasco. The dissension in our ranks was at an end. I forgot everything else in my feeling of satisfaction over this result, and I drifted off to sleep in a glow of elation.

I slept until noon of the following day and then went on deck with an appetite which overrode every other feeling. The Leveche had blown itself out, and we had a favorable wind for the return to port. The cook plied me lavishly with food and news.

"There'll be a split after the division," he said. "Some of the mighty captains think we've given the Dons such a beating they'll leave us alone now. A few of them have a desire to try their luck on the lanes to America."

"Let them go, then," I said. "We won't be needing them now. They couldn't all pick up a living in these waters."

"Some are for going home." He looked at me closely. "How are you feeling about all this cheering and hullabaloo?"

"I could be thoroughly happy," I answered, "if Clim were here to share it."

"I see." He spat disgustedly. "You let all this talk of victory blind you to injustice. Well, you're gentry, after all."

I found that most of the men were still in a sulky mood. John must have sensed this, for he never stepped off the upper deck. I did not have a word with him until we caught the first glimpse of land. He sent for me then.

"Roger," he said, "we haven't been seeing eye to eye, have we? You've shown courage through the last few days, and I admire you for it. But this sort of thing is very bad for discipline. The men seem to be accepting your belief that I should have spared Clim. No other course than what I took was open to me; but we'll say no more about that. I called you here to point out that I love most of these poor fellows and don't want to be forced to harsh measures again. It comes down to this: we must forget this Clim incident."

"That will be hard."

"I know it. Perhaps it will be harder for me to forget than for you.

I see you don't believe that. But—his voice reached my ears as well as yours. It's over and done with now, and I'm still sure I acted for the best." He looked at me intently. "We don't want any more trouble. I've no wish to see my yards turned into gallows-trees."

A lump had come into my throat. "I didn't think you cared about what happened."

"It was the hardest thing I've ever had to do. It was hard because I could have ended it with a word. It's sometimes the hardest of all things to have authority."

"You told me something like this might happen that night when we walked to Appleby Court. I see now I shouldn't have come."

"I'm glad you did," he said quickly. "Put that out of your head. If it hadn't been for you, where would we be now?"

"I knew you had reason on your side, but—there was no malice in poor Clim. He killed Sleath to protect me."

"You may find this hard to believe." He smiled and dropped a hand on my shoulder. "The truth of the matter is, Roger, I would gladly have changed places with you during the last few days."

We had been talking in a corner of the pilot-house. John looked out and then called a sharp order to the man at the wheel. "Gouletta ahead. We'll know soon now what the Dey has been up to in our absence. The fighting you've seen so far, Roger, may be child's play compared to what faces us here." He smiled again. "No more hard feelings? Good! That's a great load off my mind."

The first clue to what had happened ashore was apparent when we stepped out on the quarter-deck. *La Solderina* was anchored in the roadstead ahead of us and our flag floated from her masthead. "If he hasn't laid a hand on that handsome prize," said John, "it is likely he has lived up to his bargain all around. I can't understand it. He has a covetous soul, and it must irk him to think of all those warehouses of ours. Of course, he doesn't know yet how we have fared. He'll have something up his sleeve."

It had been arranged the night before that three of the ships would put into the docks while the rest anchored in the roadstead. Most of the captains were going ashore, however, and several of them were now with us. They were as puzzled as John over the peaceful appearance of the port. Every pair of eyes was filled with the same query as we drew closer in, and the white and red frieze of the water front began to break up into recognizable details.

"There are two flags above one of our warehouses," said John, gazing intently ahead. "It looks as though we're in luck. One is English, the other Dutch. I think we'll find Haight and his men have had no trouble at all. It surprises me, but there it is."

The first man up the ladder when we docked was a little fellow with a dark face and the talking eyes that are found most often among the Irish and the gypsies—moon men, I had heard Sleath call the latter, and a good name for them it is.

"It's glad I am to see ye, Cap'n Ward," said Haight. "Never an eye have I closed for weeks, and when I have it's been to dream of the dirty heathen climbing over the walls to get at us."

"You've had no trouble, then?"

"None but what I'm telling ye. It's all safe and sound, Sir. Not a length of rope or a bolt of cloth missing."

When he was told of the death of Sleath, he crossed himself and said, "Peace to his soul," adding immediately, "It's captain I'll be then."

"Yes. And a good captain, I'm sure."

"I'll try to be that. I'm telling ye they're a fine crew, Irish to a man, and honest as the day is long; now that Danny Boy is gone, I'm meaning."

Outwardly our offices looked the same. A few slave traders squatted along the walls, and there were other natives waiting who stank of villainy but whose purpose in being there was not clear. Abadad greeted me with a profound obeisance, his ugly features reassembling themselves into a smile which lighted up his face. Plucking at my sleeve, he led me out on the balcony.

"Sidi," he whispered, "they have been through everything. The place has been searched several times by order of the Alcayde."

I looked at him with dismay, knowing the endless work I would be put to if all my records had been lost. Abadad bobbed his head reassuringly. "I had taken it on my unworthy shoulders, Sidi, to remove all papers of value to the house in Tunis. They are safe. I have letters here."

Letters from home! Nothing was ever so welcome. It was a miracle that any reached us at all, for they had to pass through many hands, progressing slowly along one of the three overland routes with a chancey trip across the Inner Sea as the final stage. Most were lost on the way.

There was one letter only for me. It was in Aunt Gadilda's hand, and I knew before I broke the seal that the news it contained was not good. I read it through in a daze and then let the sheets fall to the ground.

Mother was dying. Aunt Gadilda had tried to break it to me gently, but the truth was clear to me almost from the first line. Mother had been unwell for several months, and the town doctor had finally become convinced that she could not recover. He was still in the dark as to the nature of the sickness but was disposed to think it some form of malignant fever. She had a continual pain in her head and at times was delirious. Bleedings and clysters brought her ease for a short while, but it was seldom that she could take any nourishment. It was, wrote my aunt, in every way similar to the trouble which had carried my

grandmother off at Great Lunnington in that terrible year when two
of the maidservants had died and the gardener's boy as well.

The stilted sentences in the cramped hand gave me a picture of
my poor mother, lying so patiently in the big bed in the front chamber,
a bare room with no carpet and the cheapest kind of curtains, her
face flushed with the fever, her eyes, usually so smiling, dimmed with
the pain. I had always thought her the prettiest of women, so dainty
and trim in spite of the cheapness of the materials in which she
dressed. A poor kind of a life she had lived, and now it was coming
to an end; if, indeed, it had not already ended.

I picked up the sheets and went through them again, weighing every
phrase, trying to find in each sentence some gleam of hope, some
comfort, however small. She was most patient, wrote Aunt Gadilda,
and resigned to her fate. At first she had kept a good face about it and
had said she was going to get well in spite of the doctor and his
Latin words; nothing could prevent her from staying to see her sailor
son come home with his face bronzed with the winds, and full of
honor and glory. She had insisted each day that she was better and
would be up and about tomorrow. But, alas, each day found her weaker,
until finally even she had been convinced that there was no hope. She
had one desire only now, to see me before she died.

There was a final paragraph which puzzled me, even though I conned
it carefully many times. Aunt Gadilda had always been one to read
great meanings into things. No casual word of greeting, no chance
expression was ever as simple as that to her. She would search everything said or written for hidden meanings or implications. On that
account I was inclined at first to put little stock in what she had
written, believing that she was at her old tricks. This mystifying paragraph read:

You must not take any blame on yourself, dear boy, for your poor
mother's condition. She has worried much about you but there has been
both pride and satisfaction for her in the thought of what you are doing.
Her illness is due entirely to another trouble which has been visited on
us but which I must not explain here. We will tell you about it when
you return home, Roger, your mother and I, if she is still alive to greet
you, which I am forced to doubt. Come as soon as you can, dear Roger,
and may God grant that she will be here to give you her blessing. She
asks me to tell you that you are never out of her thoughts and how
proud she has been of her fine big son.

Another trouble? What could it be? I thought of all the possibilities,
my mind as leaden as my heart. It could not have to do with money.
They had a small income to live on as well as the savings of years.
Could they have been subjected to some form of persecution because
I was serving with John Ward? This was an infinitely remote possibility
because everyone in our town was openly proud of John and of all the
men who had sailed with him. English law does not pass on punishment

directly to the kin of offenders. I decided it could have nothing to do with that. Finally, I remembered what Aunt Gadilda has said in her previous letter about Sir Bartlemy Ladland. Was he connected in any way with this new trouble, this tragic circumstance which was costing my pretty young mother her life?

I got to my feet and paced about the room, conscious of the rows of dark eyes which fixed themselves on every move I made. I struggled to bring my mind into some kind of order, to think and plan sanely. Mother was dying, and here I was, a thousand miles away and with no earthly means of getting to her in time. There was nothing I could do about it. The same maddening sense of irrevocability which I had felt at the death of Clim took possession of me.

If only I could start back without a moment's delay! There would have been some relief in physical motion, even if it were confined to fruitless tramping under the hot African sun. I could have felt that each step brought me that much nearer home.

John had been talking in the next room with several of the captains, going over the points to be threshed out with the Dey. He put his head through the door with a question. When I did not answer, not being conscious that it had been addressed to me, he looked at me closely and then came into the room.

"What's wrong?" he asked. "You look as doleful as a galley slave with salt-water boils."

He sobered when he heard the news. "I'm damnably sorry to learn of this. I can hardly credit it. Your mother is so young. Isn't it possible your aunt is exaggerating the danger? Women have a way of doing that, you know."

I shook my head. It was only too true, I said. Everyone had given up hope, even my mother. That was what convinced me, for she had always looked on the bright side.

"Then you must start for home at once," he said briskly. "We will be sending several of the ships to Marseilles as soon as we can get them loaded. You can go along and then strike across France. A month or six weeks will do it."

I pointed to the date on the letter. It was already two months old. "She's gone by this time. I'm sure of it, John. I think I knew it before I opened the letter."

"No sense in looking on the black side." He laid a hand on my shoulder and pressed it hard. "I was at sea when my mother died. We were off Norway when the letter reached me that she was ill. Mother had been buried a year when I got back. You can imagine how I felt. I thought I was to blame in some way. But there was nothing I could have done, just as there's nothing you can do." He paused. "Abadad tells me things are in excellent shape. Go over the figures with him again today so that you can get away when the ships sail."

"You had no thought of returning when the word reached you about your mother?"

"There was no way of getting back."

"If there had been, would you have gone?"

He gave some thought to that. "I had signed on for the whole cruise. No, I suppose not."

"And I've signed on for this one. I'm not a deserter, John."

He looked at me steadily and then returned to the other room without saying anything more. I went out on the balcony and sat there for the better part of an hour, looking north across the water and thinking of home. My fear grew into a certainty as I sat there. Mother was dead. She could not have survived two months in the condition Aunt Gadilda had described. There was no reason for me to go home, much as I longed to do so.

John came back into the room with a serious look on his face. He was carrying an open letter.

"Roger," he exclaimed, "you must get back to England after all as fast as you can. There's work for you there. This king of ours, this boggling looby of a king, is proving himself more knave than fool. He has set all England by the ears. I find it hard to believe, and yet here is the proof of it. This is from Mundy Hill, although that's a secret we must keep between us. The King's Council would say it smacked of treason."

He began to stride up and down, declaiming loudly. "He has invented a new phrase, this mitching mooncalf. 'The divine right of kings!' Think what that means, Roger. He believes his selection to rule comes from God and not from the people of England! He's answerable to no one but God, and he's already made it clear that he thinks the Almighty inclines an ear downward to learn what James of England thinks about the problems of the Universe. Never until this slobbering coward came down from the land of mists have we had a king who professed to rule by any right save the will of the people. The things he has been doing make my blood boil. I tell you, Englishmen will become no better than slaves if King James has his way."

I had no idea what work he had in mind for me, but I was ready to undertake any mission—anything to get back to England, to the land of soft rains and green woods, where I could see my mother's grave, where in time I might again enjoy a normal life in which bloodshed and cruelty had no part.

"He's determined to rule in his own sweet way," went on John. "He's making laws and imposing taxes as he sees fit."

"Surely the Parliament will see to that," I said.

John snorted. "He disregards Parliament. He's making laws by proclamation and raising money by impositions more sweeping and unfair than anything the Tudors dreamed of. He's creating new courts of law. He declares that men must worship God in the manner he decrees.

He's refused to permit the erection of new buildings in London because he fears the growing power of the city."

I began to share his excitement. "No king can do that."

"This king can. He has. He has more guile, more stubbornness, in that oversized head of his than any tyrant the world has ever seen." He sat down at the table and spread the closely written sheets in front of him. "He found England one of the three great powers of the world. In seven years he has brought us down to the third rank. He has lost us the fear and respect of the world. I thought no king could do worse than that. But what he is setting out to do at home is far more dangerous."

We had the room to ourselves, for I had dismissed the natives when he came in. "What do you want me to do?" I asked.

"All right-minded men are seeing the danger. A strong opposition has developed already. According to this letter, they're getting together to discuss means of checking the royal program. We're in a position to help them by supplying proofs of the weakness of his naval policy and the veniality of his ministers. I want you to take these proofs back to England."

This was a mission I would gladly undertake. I forgot the personal reasons for returning which had filled my mind up to this point. I nodded my willingness.

"There is Don Pedro's report on the case of the *Trial* and the other papers you found on the *Santa Caterina* which prove Spain's determination to bar us from world trade by every foul means. They will show also that pensions are paid by Spain to the ministers the King keeps about him. These proofs are to be placed in the hands of men who will know how best to use them. They are too important to be entrusted to any messenger."

"I'm ready to go," I declared.

"It's a dangerous errand." He looked at me with sudden gravity. "If the King's ministers get wind of what you are about, they'll stop at nothing. If they get their hands on you with these papers in your possession, they'll hang you. Think it over well, Roger. You will be in graver danger in England than here with me."

"I'll go," I repeated.

"Very well," said John. "I'll tell you the names of the men you are to see. You must commit them to memory; it would be dangerous to put such a list down on paper. I'll see that the ships sail before nightfall tomorrow. Every day counts now."

He got to his feet. "I must go to see the Dey and learn what is in his mind. You had better take Abadad to Tunis and get to work with him on the records. I'll join you there in a few hours." He looked at me in a half-shamefaced way and added: "I hope your passion for truth is less active than usual today. I would esteem it a favor if you made no mention of those few hours the German flounce spent with me."

Those few hours! According to Joralemon, she had been on the *Royal Bess* ten days before her transfer to Macherie's ship was arranged. I grinned and promised.

Abadad and I took a boat across the lake and then traversed the city on foot. I looked about me with more interest than I had ever felt before. Tunis has many open squares, all of them ringed tightly with tiny booths. I looked longingly at the six-foot store of my little grasshopper of a tailor in the square where the "cucumbers" plied their patient needles. I saw the dark hole in the wall where the father of Clim's widow squatted amid his bales of cloth. We passed the Souk-el-Barka, and I saw that there were many women on sale. All of them, fortunately, were black, stout wenches from the interior of Africa with fuzzy hair and wide hips. One little fellow, with a caved-in chest and flushed cheeks, struggled at his chains when we passed and cried in a desperate voice, "White fellas, please save Italia man!"

When we reached the palace under the city walls, I had to chase a beggar away from the entrance, a shrunken beanpole with skin the color of a decayed tooth. One of the guards came running along the top of the twenty-foot masonry, shouting eagerly, "What news? What news?"

"The best," I answered, making my way into the garden. It had suffered from the summer heat but was still a vision of beauty and peace to eyes surfeited with the glaring blue of sea and sky. "We gave them a sound beating. Our whole fleet is lying out there in the roadstead."

A figure in black came racing through the iron grating of the inner court. It was Cristina, and she was in such a state of agitation that at first she could not speak.

"He's safe," I said.

She sank down on the rim of the fountain and let her arms fall limply by her sides. She was breathing quickly. It was several moments before she could achieve a smile.

"When I saw you standing there," she said finally, "I didn't believe you were real at first. I had been thinking the very blackest of thoughts, and I was sure you were all dead." She was still a little breathless. "John is really safe? You're sure? When is he returning?"

"He's here now. As soon as he's through with the Dey, he's coming to see you."

She sighed with intense relief. Linking an arm in mine, she led the way back to the cool greenness of the inner court. We found a seat in the shade of a small palm tree.

"I'm still afraid it's too good to be true. I've thought of nothing else. You look like the Angel Gabriel to me, Roger, even if you are more ragged than ever."

I spread out my arms. "My fine new clothes! One day's fighting did it all. I wonder if you'll ever see me in respectable attire?"

"You've been in my mind a great deal."

"I'm glad I had a small share of your thoughts."

She favored me with an affectionate smile. "It could be called small only because the other is so very large. And now you must tell me everything."

She seemed relieved to hear that the main Spanish fleet had not been engaged. When I told her of Clim's death, omitting any mention of the manner of it, her eyes filled with tears. "My poor Clim! I had become so fond of him. Will John be ashore much now?"

"I'm sure he'll be a full month in port this time. The ships will all need refitting."

I told her then what my letter had contained, and she gave me a compassionate look. "It must be hard to face the loss of someone you love," she said. "I never saw my mother. I was so young when Father sailed to America that I can't be sure what he looked like. He's never been back. I seem to remember he had a long yellow beard and very dark eyes." After a moment she asked, "Is she very much like you, your mother?"

"They say I resemble her a little. Not very much, though. She's quite young. Much too young for this to happen."

Abadad put his head through the grating at this point, his arms crammed with documents.

"Work? So soon? You ought to have at least one free day to celebrate your safe return. I suppose it will be the same with John when he gets here."

Abadad and I began at once on the task of setting our records straight. We labored over them for many hours. I heard John's voice in the outer court, but he did not join us, having matters of greater importance to engage him. More time passed, and the sun fell so low that the walls around us were completely in shadow. The air became a little cooler, and John put his head through the grating, winking at me to get rid of Abadad.

"We've had a time of it with that old cross-biter in the Bardo," he said when Abadad had pattered away with the finished work. "His eyes went completely blank when he heard we had beaten them. He was profuse enough in his praise, but I knew he was regretting the bargain he struck with us at the start. He soon came around to demanding his full share of the spoils."

"He made it clear to me that he would."

"He mentioned you. He said you were shrewd for so young a man. Well, we refused to consider any change from the original terms, and the little heathen got almost hysterical. He talked about the reluctance of his people to harbor *koffers* in the city. I could feel trouble in the air when we left. I don't know what he'll try, but he has something in mind. We'll soon find out what it is."

"Wouldn't it be wiser to give in?"

"Most of our captains are too close-fisted for that. They say that with all of them in port we can snap our fingers at him. If it were my decision alone, I would be inclined to let the little spider have what he wants. It would save us trouble in the end." He frowned and ran his fingers impatiently through his golden beard. "I wish I knew what he's planning."

He dined alone with Cristina, as I thought it tactful to leave them to themselves. A dish of couscousou was sent out to me in the garden, rich with meats and savory with spices, a small pyramid as mysterious as the great peaks of Egypt, for each venture into it yielded something quite new and unexpected. With it was a flagon of Spanish wine, a warm amber sparkling as though the sunlight which had ripened the grapes had been caught in the presses and distilled into the liquid, where it flashed like golden fins in a stream. I drank quite a little of the wine, for both at home and aboard ship I had been accustomed to the heavy red kinds, sweetly musty in taste. My spirits improved in consequence. After dinner Abadad returned and we worked for several hours longer.

It was verging on midnight when we scanned the last of the petty tallies. I stretched and suggested that it was time for us to be going. The old man smiled, a trick which he seemed to manage with a twist of his down-curving nose, and said, "Sidi, we must hurry before the last of the city gates are closed."

I did not want to leave without saying good-by to Cristina, but I was sure she was asleep by this time. I walked slowly to the gates, wondering if I should have her wakened. She solved the problem by running out after me.

"Roger!" Her tone was both hurt and indignant. "Were you going to leave without seeing me?"

"I didn't want to. But I was afraid you had gone to bed long ago."

"You didn't tell me you were returning home," she said accusingly.

"I thought John should do that."

"I cried when he told me. Things will be so different without you. I've always wanted you to go home, but I feel very sad about it now that it's happening. Why must it be so soon? Can't you have even one day's rest?"

"The ship sails tomorrow. I must go then or wait indefinitely."

"Of course. There's a chance you may still see your mother." She unfolded a silk handkerchief she had been holding tightly and placed what it contained in my hand. "Keep it, please," she whispered. "It may bring you good fortune. In love, and perhaps in other things as well."

It was the emerald ring. The diamonds which encircled the large green stone sparkled as it rested in my hand.

"I can't take this," I said. "You must never part with it."

"But it's not mine. No one ever owns it. When it has accomplished for you what you want most, you must pass it on."

There were no paths and she found it necessary to hold her skirts up as she walked beside me. I saw that she had slipped bare feet into white satin slippers.

"I'm very happy tonight, Roger. That's why you must have the ring. It can't go to John because he's concerned in what it has brought me. Remember that its power will be lost if it isn't passed on after your wishes are granted."

I looked at the fortune I held in my hand. "I can't find words to thank you for this."

We had reached the gate. "I'll never see you again," she said. "You've been so kind to me, Roger. I'm not sure what I could have done without you. I'll be very lonely when John leaves again. But I've nothing else to worry about now. John and I—"

When she did not go on, I said, "I'm very glad to know that."

"Poor Roger! You've been having such a bad time! John told me everything that happened. And about Clim's death. I'm sure you're happy to be going."

"Yes, I'm happy about it. I have just one regret—I don't like to think of you here. It will never be safe."

"Oh, we've made wonderful plans. As soon as we can, we're going to Italy. Or perhaps to France."

"Then I'll certainly see you again."

"Perhaps. Let's hope so, Roger."

The moon had climbed high, and the noise of the city had dwindled to the faint cries of the watchmen at the gates. Abadad was anxious to make a start, as I could see.

"I mustn't keep you any longer." She held out both her hands. "Good-by, Roger. I'll always think of you."

"Good-by, Cristina. I hope everything will come out well for you."

The gate swung to behind us, and the watchman on the wall called a cheery "Good night, mates." I followed Abadad through the narrow alleys of the city. The only sound we heard was that of our own footsteps. The light of the moon, touching the white tops of the buildings like the fire I had seen on our mastheads at night, had a disquieting effect. I found it hard to believe it was the same moon which looked down so benignly on the green hedges and peaceful fields of England. It had set the level head of Sir Sigismund Hill to seeing the soldiers of Hannibal on the march. I thought of the turbulent history of the city: Dido, mounting the funeral pyre at Byrsa; Regulus returning while copper-hued mobs screamed for his blood; Scipio grinding out the life of Carthage under his iron heel; Barbarossa dragging white captives after him in chains. History of a kind to set the imagination flaming had been made here; and now John Ward and the Free Rovers were adding a new chapter. I did not feel entirely happy that my part in that chapter was drawing to a close. It was impossible to escape the feeling that I was running away.

26

I WAS WAKENED AT DAWN by the sound of voices along the water front. Standing on my toes to look out of the high latticed window, I saw that scores of our men were beginning work on the loading of the ships.

It was a wonderful morning. No artist would have dared to lay on canvas the streaks of flaming red which radiated from the east. Certainly day was never ushered in at home with such flamboyance. There were some things about life here, I told myself, that I would miss.

John was in the next room, and I could hear him cursing over his points. I looked in the door as he engulfed his arms in a honey-colored doublet. This did not mean that he had spent the night here, however. He never wore the same clothes two days in succession if he could help it.

"Good morning," he said. "Would you be kind enough to fasten this thing for me?"

My adventure with him had begun when I helped him to dress that evening in the apothecary's house at home, and so it was fitting that it should end the same way. I proceeded with my task while John used a pair of scissors to trim his beard. It took him quite a time, for he was most meticulous about it, studying himself in a mirror from every angle as he snipped.

"There'll be trouble today," he said. "I don't like the look of things, Roger. It was still dark when I rode through the city, but the squares were already full of people. They screamed 'Arfi!' at me, and several times I thought they were going to pull me off my horse."

"Perhaps it's a holy day."

"There's more to it than that." He shook his head. "I begin to suspect the Dey has given orders for a demonstration. He may want to convince us that it's difficult for him to keep the people in hand. An argument to make us break the agreement in his favor. If that's the reason for this, it may not prove too troublesome; provided, of course, the beggars don't get out of hand."

The noise in the streets below was growing all the time. I went to a window and looked out.

"There are plenty of green turbans down there," I reported.

"They'll be out in full force. Well, we'll see what develops. I have another audience with the Dey this afternoon."

John made a careful selection among the half-dozen hats he had brought ashore. Then he turned to me with a serious face.

"A final word with you, young fellow. There's something I want you to din into the ears of every man you meet on your mission. This is going to be a different world from now on, a smaller world. Our islands are tiny; and if we want to be a great people we must see to it that the seas are made free. Make them realize that, Roger! Everything depends on it. The English flag must be found in every port in the world."

He began to pace up and down the room. "No Spanish king, with underslung jaw and greedy claws, can gobble up this great world on the nod of a Pope of Rome! What right have these skulking sons of shore-huggers to put a ban on the bold rovers of the north? It was Norsemen who found America. I heard them talking of it when I was in Norway. It was centuries before this mewling Italian went pattiecaking over the easy waters of the Middle Course. As for the world's being round, Roger Bacon knew that long ago. Not Bacon? Well, it must have been some other Englishman."

He dragged a map out from a corner and spread it on the floor. He crouched on his knees and pointed out places in unexplored parts with an eager finger. "We must have colonies here," he said. "And here. And here. All long the coast of America. Raleigh had the right idea. We must have trading stations in Africa and factories in the Indies. We must bring spices from the East, ivory from Africa, gold from the Americas. These Jew-roasters can't corner the wealth of this world. It is England's duty to see that they don't. The Dutch are too busy with their religious troubles to lend a hand, and none of the others count in this. We must do it ourselves. That's what all Englishmen must be made to see."

The increasing tumult below drew us both to the window. The work of loading was being hampered by the screeching natives in the streets. We could hear the sound of the *reitas* over the shouts of the mob.

"It begins to look like the real thing," said John. He turned around suddenly with a look of deep concern. "Cristina! 'Fore God, Roger, I must get her out of there! If this keeps up, it will be dangerous for her in the city." He paused for a moment to consider the best course. "I'm going to take a dozen men with me and we'll ride out by the Taenia Road and from there around the lake. Will you ask Halsey to take things in hand here while I'm away? We should land more men and place a cordon around the water front. They must be told not to fire unless the situation becomes desperate. We must avoid bloodshed if at all possible."

Halsey came in at that moment, stretching himself to get the sleep out of his bones and complaining about the noise. He became wide awake in a moment when John explained what was afoot.

"I'll take things in hand here," he said briskly. "Get on your way, Ward. Nothing must happen to your lady."

John vanished before anything more could be said. Halsey took charge with decision, and in no time at all the rioters had been shoved back from the paved road which skirted the water front into the narrow alleys leading from it. We could still hear the shrill cries of *"Arfi!"* and *"Hagi, Baba!"* but no move was being made to rush our lines and so I concluded that the worst was over. I retired to my room and proceeded to study the list John had given me of the men on whom I would call when I reached England. There were at least fifty of them, and I decided that I could best commit them to memory by the rhyming method Temperance Handy had taught me. It became easier immediately, and soon I was chanting to myself:

> Mark Beston, Hugh Weston, and eke my Lord Harley,
> Squire Robson, Squire Dobson, Sir Ninian Varley.

When I was sure that I could jingle off the whole list without referring to the notes, I destroyed the paper, as John had advised. It had taken me a couple of hours. From my window I could see that the work of loading was going ahead briskly. I estimated that they would be through with it on time, which meant that we would weigh anchor before the end of the afternoon. I proceeded to pack my few belongings.

I had not been seriously concerned about the situation in the city, but as hour after hour passed without any sign of John I began to worry in real earnest. His audience with the Dey would consume considerable time, but even allowing for that it was clear that something had happened to delay him. I thought of many possibilities, all of them disturbing. Had he been too late? Had they been trapped in the city by the fanatical mobs? Was the Dey holding him at the Bardo as a hostage to compel acceptance of his terms?

The time for our departure drew close, and still no sign of John and his party. I joined Captain Longcastle, who was to be in charge of the ships for Marseilles, and found him in an impatient mood.

"We'll sail on the hour, Ward or no Ward," he said.

"I can't leave until he returns," I answered. "Something has gone wrong, or he would be here by this time."

"Do as you wish about that. I must be well out into the Gulf by nightfall."

I was certain now that something had gone seriously wrong, and in a fever of apprehension I paced up and down the roughly cobbled road in front of the slip where Longcastle's ship lay. The captain squinted at the sun and said, "I give you fifteen minutes more, Blease."

Before the quarter-hour was up John and his men arrived. I saw him dismount from his mustard-colored horse and walk slowly over to where we were standing. He did not raise his head.

"I was too late," he said.

Too late! Had Cristina—I could not finish the sentence even in my mind.

"I should have turned back at once when I found how things were this morning in the city," John went on bitterly. "I should have realized what would happen. How could I have been so blind!"

"But Cristina! What about her?"

"She was carried off." He was finding speech difficult. "The other women were taken with her. The men—I knew what had happened as soon as we reached the foot of the street. The gates had been broken in. All of the guards had been killed. Their skins were nailed to the outside of the wall." He paused. "They had been flayed alive!"

"If Clim had stayed—" I began.

"He would have died with the rest of them. That may be some consolation for you, Roger. Do you want to hear the rest of it? It isn't pleasant telling."

"What has been done about it?" demanded Longcastle.

"Done?" cried John. "I've been for two hours with the Dey. I practically took him by the throat and demanded he get her back or see his palace pulled down around him! I told him six thousand of the best fighting men that ever sailed the seas would exact a price for their butchered fellows. He has been sending men out in frantic haste, I promise you. The women will be found and returned. He's agreed to hang the leaders."

"We'll back you up, Ward," said Halsey, who had joined us in time to hear the story.

"I'm sure of that. This doesn't concern me alone. The safety of every man in the fleet depends on what we do about this now. I'm sure of one thing: the demonstration started on orders from the Dey. He tried to force our hand, and the devils got out of control. He must be made to pay!"

"I'm ready to sail; but if you need us, Ward, we'll stay and see it through," said Longcastle.

John shook his head. "There will be enough of us left to bring him to his senses. It's important for you to leave at once. By sending off the stuff, we let him see we mean what we say. I want a word with you, Roger, before you leave."

We walked to one side. "You can go with an easy mind. Cristina will be found, or I'll raze this place as thoroughly as the Romans did!"

"Last night she insisted on giving me her ring," I whispered. "Do you suppose she had some idea this might happen?"

He brushed the suggestion aside. "I put no stock in such things. I would drop the ring in forty fathoms of water if I were you."

He stood for several moments in deep thought. "This may be a long farewell, my kinchin coe. I wouldn't wager a single sice now against a purse full of Old Harrys on my chance of getting back. I may never ruffle a cloak down Shrubsole High again. Of course the royal swill-belly may drink himself to death, but that's a remote possibility."

"I'll do the work you've set me with a real will."

"Do nothing until you see Mundy Hill. You mustn't get yourself in trouble over this." He held out a hand. "When you think of me, think of the day we went together over the side of the *Santa Caterina*. Try to forget the flinty-hearted captain who sent Clim to the Basket. As for Katie, go in and win. You have my best wishes, Roger. Well, I shall spoon my sails and run before the wind. God in Heaven alone knows where it will take me."

"Time to be off," called Longcastle.

BOOK THREE

27

SIR NEVIL MACHERIE accompanied us to Marseilles and, to my surprise, came ashore there. He was followed by the girl Aurora and two sailors to carry his handsome sea chests. His ship was to risk a dash later through the Straits of Gibraltar, but he had decided to make an overland trip to Calais, business in Paris being the reason he gave. Apparently he had not known I was going to England, for he began to ply me with questions.

"You go on some mission, I take it."

"I'm returning for personal reasons. It's my hope to rejoin the *Royal Bess* later."

"Personal reasons?"

"My mother is dying."

"A convenient excuse, Master Blease. I still believe you're going on some errand for your rascal of a Captain Rufflecoat."

I knew he was not trying to pick a quarrel with me. He considered it his right to say anything he desired. He was much younger, I now saw, than I had believed; and rather handsome in spite of his blackness and his vulpine nose.

"There's no reason for me to explain my movements to you," I said.

"I could force the truth from you." His fingers were tapping impatiently on the lid of the shell-backed agenda he carried at his belt. It gave out a hollow sound, and so I knew it was a sham. In all probability he used it, being such a great dandy, to carry white cypress powder for his face. I had heard that he always kept with him a gold toothpick and a pair of ivory head-rubbers. In the fleet he had been given credit for a wardrobe exceeded in point of size and costliness only by that of John Ward. He seemed to run to black, however, while John's fancy was for every color in the rainbow.

"You're lying, of course," he added in a languid voice.

I retorted angrily: "I don't permit you, or anyone, to question my word!"

Macherie began to laugh. "So! Our young fire-eater assumes the privileges of a gentleman." His hand fell carelessly on the hilt of his sword. "I could spit you with one pass, my bold cockerel. But I don't propose to be accused of murder, so I'll let your bad manners pass without correction." He had the reputation of being one of the best swordsmen in England and considered it his right, apparently, to treat such matters lightly. "On the whole, I hope you're telling the truth. If you do go back, you'll have something to tell your blackguard captain and the other ruffians associated with him."

"Whose number is now less by one."

"Keep a guard on that tongue of yours. I'm no more disposed to bandy words with you than to cross swords; but there's a limit to my patience. This is what I want Ward to know." His manner of saying John's name was an insult in itself. "I've been done a great injustice by that pack of rogues and cutthroats, and I'm making it my purpose in life to see that all of them pay for it. That's my chief reason for returning to England. I expect to see every one of them hanged in chains as they richly deserve. I shall have a hand in bringing them to that most fitting end."

"Why didn't you tell Captain Ward of your purpose before you left?"

"Ward," he said easily, "is beneath notice. I've never considered it fitting to quarrel with him."

"Or was it the same lack of courage you showed when the Spanish fleet came up?"

He laughed again but on a different note. "I think it highly likely, Master Blease, that you'll be the first of the lot to hang."

He was dressed for travel when he emerged next morning from the water front inn where he had put up with his party for the night. His finery had been replaced by a shamoy doublet of flowered design and trunk hose of the same material. Five horses, one a stout-backed palfrey and one a pack horse, were standing in the tavern yard. The girl followed on his heels, elaborately swathed in trailing blue, and was with some difficulty hoisted into her saddle. They cantered off without a word, although Aurora fluttered a surreptitious hand in my direction. She jounced ungracefully and fell at once into the rear.

It took four days to complete arrangements with our Marseilles agent, a talkative fellow with no appreciation at all of the value of time. I chafed at the delay, but it served one purpose in allowing me an opportunity to acquire some suitable clothes. When I set out alone on the fifth day, there was a fine outfit packed away in my saddle bags, and I was wearing a rather handsome brown cloak and a tall beaver hat with plume and gold buckle. The hat alone had cost me five sovereigns.

Saladin was the name of my horse, a completely misleading one, for he was an easy-going gray. His steadiness of gait, however, made him a treasure for a novice like me. I allowed him his head for the first two days, with the result that my saddle burns had ceased to bother me by that time. From then on I made good time, so good, in fact that I was surprised to reach Paris without overtaking Sir Nevil and his companions.

My mind was so full of my many troubles that I had little thought for the beauty of the country. There was scarcely a moment that I did not think of Cristina and wonder if she had been rescued or of my mother's condition. I was aware that the land through which I rode was gentle and sunny, that the air of Provence had a languorous softness which was like heaven after the fierce heat of Africa; but this seemed of little moment when a spark of hope inside me was urging that no second should be lost in getting home. I could not fail to notice, however, that the people were prosperous and happy and most voluble in praise of their great king. Henry IV was a god in their eyes; they loved his bluffness, his human qualities, his earthly tastes, even his way with women. How different it was in England!

I acquired a great liking for French food. At first I hesitated over omelettes sprinkled with brandy and strange fishes smothered in bilious-looking yellow sauces. Once tried, I found everything surprisingly good. The white wines they brought in cool stone bottles were infinitely satisfying after a day in the saddle. King Henry had once said his chief aim was to see a fowl in the Sunday pot of every peasant; I was sure, from what I observed, that no one ever lacked a pair.

Paris nevertheless was disappointing. It was an effeminate city, as John had said, and not at all like robust Rome-ville. The men were cox-combs, foppish in dress and simpering in manner. Voices were brittle, conversation volcanic, tempers short. I stayed just long enough to read *Le Mercure Français* over a wonderful dinner and to buy for ten *testons* (a matter of three shillings) a thumbed copy of Bayard's *Histoire* with plenty of woodcuts. This acquisition compensated me for every lack I found in the great city.

I arrived in Calais early one afternoon. In spite of my many anxieties, I felt exhilarated at being so near the end of my long journey. It was one of those magnificent days when the late summer sun carries the first hint of autumn sharpness. A smudge on the horizon was England, faintly to be seen over the whitecapped waters of the Straits. My spirits continued to rise as I cantered through St. Pierre and crossed the canal to the old town. Calais was not a cheering spectacle for an Englishman, but it was easy to forget our loss of this last strip of continental soil. By nightfall my feet would be planted on good English earth!

I put up at an inn which seemed old enough to have been there when King Ned first planted the English standard over Calais. While the landlord prepared a capon for my dinner, I sallied out with the intention of seeing something of the town, but I got no farther than the yard where a dusty carriage was being sloshed with water by a slow-moving groom. It occurred to me that any travelers arriving in such haste must be headed across the Sleeve, and I dropped a *teston* in the man's hand.

"English," he grumbled, in answer to a question. "One gentleman, one lady. Gentleman, very grand. Lady— Ah, M'sieur should see lady!"

This description made me sure that I had at last overtaken Sir Nevil, and I turned back with an instinctive feeling that the papers in my battered old capcase should not be left unguarded. The landlord con-firmed my suspicions. The gentleman, he told me, was in a great hurry,

so great that he was using his rooms only to change clothes and have
a bath before catching the boat for Dover. Conceive, M'sieur, a bath
and the gentleman about to go on the water anyway! Two maids had
been kept busy carrying up pails of hot water; were Englishmen like
fish, that they must cover themselves with water to take a bath? Convinced that it was Macherie, I gave orders to have my dinner served
upstairs and walked to the stairs.

A resplendent vision was on the way down, pointed pink shoes showing under rustling blue skirts at every step. It was the German girl,
with a frothy rebatoe around her neck, and above it a warm smile of
welcome for an old friend. Quite apparently she had been picking up
a slight acquaintance with the language of her most recent lovers, for
she remarked in slurring accents on the excellence of the weather.

"Are you continuing on to England?" I asked.

This proved an unfortunate query. She immediately assumed an air
of deep distress and engulfed me in a torrent of fervid German. I tried
to get away, but her eyes beseeched me to stay. Using an occasional English word and lapsing oftener into French, which she spoke badly, she
made it clear that she was very much in need of help. Without knowing
quite how it came about, I found myself ensconced with her in a
window embrasure. I had given no orders, but the landlord appeared
at my elbow with a bottle of very fine and expensive wine which he
proceeded to serve.

My companion talked incessantly, rolling her round blue eyes in a
way that most men would have found seductive. My only desire was
to get away as soon as I could, but at the same time I could not help
feeling sorry for her. The few stray sheaves of meaning that I was able
to glean from the harvest of her words made it clear that what I had
expected was true. Macherie was planning to leave her here, with his
best wishes and a purse that she considered to be nothing short of
niggardly. She was far away from her native land and did not know
what to do. Strange countries frightened her—I swallowed that one
with a grain of salt—and she spoke so little of the French! Would I
intercede with Sir Nevil in her behalf? I said that Sir Nevil and I were
hardly on speaking terms. She laid a plump white hand on my arm
and begged me to do what I could. Would I help her to reach England?
Her eyes were promising rewards, but I argued strongly against the
idea of crossing the water, pointing out that in England she would be
farther away from home than ever. That did not prove to be a real
objection after all. She had heard that all Englishmen were kind to
ladies in distress and, with one mean exception, generous. She was sure
she would be happier in London than in any part of France. She asserted
vehemently that she did not like Frenchmen.

I squirmed in my seat for a good ten minutes before I had the
inspiration to lay several fat gold pieces between the dimpled elbows she
had rested on the table. She smiled and scooped them up without

pretense of reluctance, making no further effort to detain me. "See?" she remarked, squeezing my arm. "The Englishmen *are* generous."

I hurried to my room. There was nothing to indicate that it had been visited in my absence. My cloak and hat were on the bed where I had tossed them, my capcase on the floor beside it. I sighed with relief. As a final reassurance, I opened the capcase; and found, to my intense dismay, that the worst had happened. The documents were gone!

Macherie had visited the room while the girl engaged my attention below and had stolen them. This was the only possible explanation. I was filled with panic, for among the papers was a letter to Sir Bartlemy Ladland which almost certainly would contain some references to his connection with John Ward. I loosened the dagger in my belt, pondering my chances if it came to a struggle. Small enough, I decided, particularly if the landlord were in league with them, as seemed likely.

Hearing the grind of wheels on the stones of the courtyard, I rushed to the window in time to see a swirl of blue skirts in the door of the carriage and the driver curling his whip over the heads of the horses. It was an antiquated type of coach with leather side blinds which had been rolled down, making it impossible to see inside.

I went down the steps three at a time, nearly upsetting the landlord, who stood at the foot.

"I've been robbed!" I shouted.

"Robbed?" I heard him say as I made for the door. "But impossible, M'sieur!"

"Bring my horse around!" I ordered.

The groom, who was watching with slack-jawed interest, made no move to obey. I gave him an impatient shove, but it was clear that he could not get Saladin ready in time. I raced out into the street and started on foot after the rapidly disappearing coach. I ran at the top of my speed, shouting to them to stop and interjecting indignant cries of "Thieves! Robbers!" Curious heads bobbed out of windows as I passed and men came pouring out of taverns to see what all the excitement was about, some of them running along after me.

It was no use. The driver of the carriage whipped up his horses and plunged into a maze of narrow streets, and I was left hopelessly behind in short order.

I returned to the inn, almost ready to weep over my failure and my realization of what this would mean. I found my horse saddled and ready at last, and the landlord standing beside it with an apologetic air and his bill. I took him by the throat and shook him until his teeth rattled and his precious bill fell out of his hand.

"How much did he pay you to keep me below?" I demanded.

He swallowed painfully and protested his innocence. He was devastated, he declared, but what could he have done? The gentleman was well-mannered and prosperous; how could he be expected to know he was a thief?

I sprang into the saddle. "I'm off now to lodge a complaint. I'll see you lodged in jail for this as you deserve."

"The gentleman was English," said the innkeeper, rolling a crafty eye. "M'sieur also is English. How could I decide between you?"

"Where is he going?"

"As God is my judge, I don't know."

"You may take what I owe you out of what you got from him," I said.

He made no response, which, in a French innkeeper, was a confession of guilt. I let my whip flick across his shoulders as I rode out of the yard.

As I turned Saladin's head in the direction of the water front, I wondered why Macherie had gone to such pains to search my belongings. He had acted on suspicion only, for he had no way of knowing what I carried. He would realize the value of his find as soon as he examined the papers. I was sure he was looking them over already, his eyes slanting greedily down his long nose as the carriage bumped over the rough paving of the streets. It would be clear to him that he held a bargaining weapon of great value, a certain lever for the King's pardon and favor.

I knew he would drive to another port and delay his departure until he was sure I had gone. I might ride up and down the coast in the hope of finding him, but it would be waste of time. Even if I did locate him, what steps could I take to recover the papers? I had no way of proving they belonged to me. There was only one course open: to sail at once for Dover. It would be dangerous to attempt an entry after the documents had reached official hands in England. The only real hope I had was that Macherie might be foolish enough to sail from Calais as he had first intended.

Needless to state, he did not do this. At the appointed hour, the French captain climbed over the side and bawled an order to cast off. With a heavy heart I considered how serious the consequences of my carelessness might prove. I would have given anything to undo the events of the last few hours.

"In London I'll find a way to even the score," I said to myself.

28

DURING THE YEAR I had been away, my home town had remained in my mind as the one bright landmark in a grim world. I had thought of it always as a place of pleasant thatched houses in a setting of gentle green, its garden walls lined with the inquiring faces of marsh mallows, the sun (not the fierce sun of the South, but a thing of friendly warmth) slanting down Shrubsole High to the square at the end where our old gray church reared its spire like a symbol of peace and security against the sky. I had hoped that there would be a welcome for me, perhaps even a bonfire. I had expected congratulations and much hearty slapping on the back and drinking of toasts.

Never was homecoming more depressing than mine. In the first place, I arrived in a despondent frame of mind. I knew that I had been a failure as a sailor, in spite of the part I had managed to play in John's success. I had been placed in a shore post (what would my bluff father have said to that?) and I had been responsible for creating a mutinous spirit among the men. To cap everything, I had been careless enough to lose the papers which John had entrusted to me, and so had laid the train for troubles the magnitude of which I could not yet foretell. I felt so completely out of conceit with myself that I was glad the danger of my position made it necessary for me to arrive at night. I could not have met my old friends with a bold face.

It was quite late when I rode up Strawberry Hill, from which ordinarily one could see the whole town; and it was so damp and gray with fog that I shivered, partly from cold but more from disappointment. I was glad a fire had been built in the brazier standing on high iron legs above the square. The light from it showed clearly enough through the mist to guide me home. To my great relief I met no one on the way.

The row of quicken trees in front of our house looked ghostly instead of warm and welcoming. I tied my horse to one of them and looked up at the front gable where I hoped to find a light still burning in Mother's bedroom. The whole house was dark and still.

I rapped gently on the front door; then, receiving no response, with more vigor. Several moments passed before I heard a cautious step on the stair within. More moments passed and then Aunt Gadilda's voice asked, "Who's there?"

"It's Roger," I said in a low tone. Apparently my voice did not carry, for there was no response. I had to repeat, in a bolder tone: "It's Roger, Aunt, I'm back."

I heard excited hands drawing the bars, and then the door swung back from the pressure of my hand. A voice, so wrought up with emotion that I did not recognize it, said in the blackness ahead of me: "Roger! Is it really you? Oh, Roger, you've come home at last!"

I closed the door. "Have you no candles? I thought I could find my way all over this house in the dark, but a year seems to make a lot of difference. I've gained twenty pounds, Aunt Gaddy. Wait till you see the things I've brought you!" I had little idea what I was saying. I knew I was leaving unasked the one question that filled my mind because I dreaded the answer. Then I heard her trying to light a candle, and I did not hesitate any longer. If Mother were dead, I wanted to hear of it in the dark. "Aunt, what has happened? Is—is Mother—"

There was a long silence, and then the candle flared. Aunt Gadilda was holding it in front of her face, a meager inch of tallow which she cupped in one hand. I was amazed at her appearance. She seemed to have shrunk, to have turned into an old woman, with bent back and trembling arms. Her eyes, looking out of hollowed sockets, told of long suffering.

"Roger," she said in a whisper, "your poor mother is dead. We buried her eight weeks ago come Wednesday."

All I could say was, "Then I couldn't possibly have returned in time."

Aunt Gadilda led the way into the drawing room, holding the candle above her head. The house was in deepest mourning, as I had expected, knowing how zealously she clung to all forms and rules. The floors were spread with black felt, and there were funereal hangings on all the ceilings. There were even black bows on the sideboard and the sturdy old bink (which had come to us from Great Lunnington when my grandfather died and was said to date back to the time of Richard II), from the open shelves of which all the silver and pewter pieces had been removed. I suspected she had borrowed these trappings of death from Great Lunnington, for no household in town could boast the like.

She held the candle in front of my face and studied me closely.

"Oh, Roger," she said, in a pitiful whisper. "If Meggy had only lived to see you like this!"

I placed a chair for her and insisted that she sit down. Then I found a pair of full-length candles and lighted them in spite of her involuntary gasp of protest, placing one on the table and one on the bink.

"Where are Fanny and Albert?" I demanded.

"I had to part with them." She smiled defensively. "How foolish it would have been to keep them, two husky servants to wait on one old woman!"

"So you're saving their wages, are you? Two pounds a year apiece!"

"And their food," she protested. "How that Albert could eat! And the quantities of ale!"

"Is there any food in the house?"

"Very little, I'm afraid. Are you hungry, dear boy? I'll see what I can get you right away."

"Never mind about that now." As a matter of fact, I had eaten nothing since morning, having taken the back roads from Dover to escape notice. I studied her lined face. "You've been starving yourself. If I hadn't come back, there would have been another funeral in this house soon. What are you saving for now? Has it become habit?"

"You must know, sonny, that Meggy's income was for her life only. We had the same from Father's will, thirty pounds a year. That isn't much."

"You had saved plenty." I unstrapped a belt under my doublet and opened the catch. A stream of gold pieces cascaded on to the top of the table. Her eyes fixed themselves on the yellow pyramid with fascinated intentness.

"Roger! The window! Someone will see."

"The windows are all shuttered. What would it matter anyway? I'm going to take you away from this miserable house. We'll live in London. On the fat of the land, Aunt Gaddy. Things are going to be different from now on. No more starving and freezing. If Mother had only lived to share in it!"

She began to cry. "Poor Meggy! She wanted so badly to live until you came back. We talked so often of how you would look."

To keep myself from crying also, I asked: "Have you any brandy in the house? I think we both need a stimulant."

"Aren't you feeling well?" I could see the look come back into her face with which she always met my ailments, an eagerness to apply her homemade simples and remedies. To escape any suggestion now of flowers of sulphur or *hickery-pickery*, or her most extreme cure, snail-water. I said that all I wanted was a swallow of brandy to warm me after my ride. She took one of the candles and went back into the blackness of the household offices. While I waited, I looked about the room, noticing that one window had been broken and that the glass had been replaced by a sheet of linen steeped in oil. I thought to myself that Mother had perhaps been willing enough to leave the kind of life they lived here—starving, scrimping, saving, for an ungrateful son who ran away to sea.

When I had swallowed a small glass of the brandy, and had seen to it that she did the same, I faced her with the question I had been wanting to ask since I entered the house.

"What was this mysterious trouble?"

She dropped her eyes. "Trouble? Mystery? I'm sure I don't understand what you mean, Rogerkins."

"Then what did you mean in your letter? You said Mother's illness was due to something you couldn't explain in writing."

She kept her eyes averted. "I think perhaps I shouldn't say anything more about it."

"Aunt Gaddy, I must know!" I said. "I'm not a boy any longer. What was it? I've been racking my brain ever since without finding any rhyme or reason in what you hinted. I can't wait another minute. I must know what it was."

She gave in reluctantly. "It was Lady Ladland. She—she thought her husband came here too often. She was jealous of poor Meggy. One day she followed him here. They were sitting where you and I are now; talking quietly, about you, I think. She came in and charged them with dreadful things. In a loud voice. It was a warm spring day and all the windows were open. The whole neighborhood heard what she said." She shook her head with sudden asperity. "She never was a lady, Fanny Plumptre! Her father made his money as a victualler to the Navy, and everyone said the poor sailors starved on the wormy food he supplied.

She was handsome enough, but I'm sure Sir Bartlemy married her for her money. He bought Appleby Court with it."

"What happened then?" I had been prepared for something like this but, now that it was out, I felt very hollow and miserable inside. I might never be able to see Katie again.

"She went out to her carriage, still talking in that high, ill-bred voice of hers. I've never seen anyone in such a temper. Sir Bartlemy said something to Meggy and then rode after her. He never came back, of course. Lady Ladland took Catherine to London with her and opened their town house. Appleby Court has been closed ever since." She was folding and unfolding her hands nervously. "The whole town heard about it. There was a great deal of talk because—well, it seems Sir Bartlemy has a bad reputation. Your poor mother never set foot outside the house after that. She was too shamed to face anyone. I could see her pining away before my very eyes. When this sickness took hold of her, she had no strength at all to resist it."

I began to stride about the room, my mind full of a ventless rage. My mother's death, then, could be laid at the door of the Ladlands, husband and wife; but I could think of no way to make them pay. The memory of Katie faded out of my mind, driven away by my bitter resentment over what had occurred. My sweet, unselfish mother! It was unbearable that such a thing could have happened to her; and on top of the disappointment I had caused her. I stopped beside my ink-stained old scriptine and saw that my pen was still in the place where I had left it. The Spanish book lay beside it.

"Don't let's talk about it any more," I said. "I don't know what to think or what to do. There ought to be some punishment for a woman who would act like that; who could think that way about Mother." I picked up the Spanish book and then let it drop with a listless hand. To bridge the uncomfortable silence, I said: "Some day I'll tell you how fortunate it was for me that I could speak some Spanish. You did me a good turn in that, Aunt Gaddy."

After a long and unhappy interval, during which neither of us spoke, I returned to my chair. "We'll have to try to forget the past," I said. "I won't be able to take you to London right away, Aunt. I must make sure that I'm not wanted for piracy first. Don't look startled; I have plenty of friends, and I won't be in any danger in any event. I'll get the situation straightened out soon. I'm afraid I must leave tonight, but in a very short time I'll write you with instructions. You'll have to be careful, Aunt, and follow them to the letter. It will be necessary, I'm afraid, for you to leave town quietly. I don't want anyone to know when you go or where you're going. In the meantime I want you to be comfortable here." I scooped up a handful of the coins and poured them into her lap. "Get the servants back. One of them, at any rate. Keep the house stocked with food! I want you to have some flesh on your bones when I see you next. Keep fires going. You must be warm and comfortable." I paused. "Some day, Aunt Gadilda, I want to hear everything, but I don't think I can talk about it now."

I began to pack the gold back into my belt. My fingers must have been cold, for I fumbled at the task. Aunt Gadilda watched me with anxious eyes.

"Are you thinking this has made a difference with Katie?" she asked.

I put away the last of the coins and clasped the belt about my waist. "I don't believe she would let it change her feelings," I answered. "Not that it would make any difference. Can you conceive of Sir Bartlemy accepting me as a son-in-law?"

Aunt Gadilda became indignant at once. "And why not? You have better blood in your veins than Katie Ladland! Never forget you're a grandson of Sir Ludar Pirie. The Piries have been one of the best families of Kent since long before the Wars of the Roses. Your grandfather was knighted by old King Harry himself. Can the Ladlands show anything like that? I think not! Fanny Plumptre, indeed!"

"Well, I guess it doesn't matter much now." I sat down to figure out what I should do. I was tired and the thought of a night's sleep in my comfortable old bed upstairs appealed to me strongly. Could I take the risk? I decided that it would be unwise, however, as we had no stabling for the horse. I got to my feet again and took one of the candles. "I may never set foot in this house again," I said. "I think I'll take a look around. Could you get me a bite of supper? I should be away in another hour."

Nothing was changed upstairs except that there were black pillowberes and drooping bows of black silk on the testers of the beds. Aunt Gadilda was thorough in such matters!

I looked with a feeling of deep regret at the small room where I had spent so many happy hours. For a keepsake, I slipped under my doublet a tiny galleon carved out of black wood which an old sailor had given me when I was a small boy. I knew it was an odd choice, considering what a poor sailor I had turned out to be. After a few minutes in Mother's room, looking at the familiar furnishings with a sense of compassion and shame, I went below to find that a supper of bread and stringy ram-mutton had been set out.

"You're indeed a man now," said Aunt Gadilda, watching me as I struggled with the meager fare. "You'll find someone to your taste, never fear. Someone prettier than Katie Ladland."

"No one in the world is prettier than Katie. And I don't want to find anyone else."

She shook her head solemnly. "Then you're sure to have trouble and sorrow, Roger. I wish you could put her out of your mind."

An hour later, I rode away. The fog was lifting a little, but forks of flame were still shooting up from the brazier on the square. I turned my reluctant Saladin, who showed what he thought of night-riding by refusing to stir out of a slow trot, off the main road. We came finally to the soft gravel path through Wayland Spinney. I swept all other thoughts from my mind by speculating as to the exact spot where Katie had met John Ward, looking "like a little snow fairy." My spirits did not improve as a result. Katie might keep other trysts in Wayland Spinney, but if she did they would not be with me.

The towers and chimneys of Appleby Court rose dark and majestic over the thinning fog. It was not yet midnight, but there was no sign of a light in the huge pile; apparently Lady Ladland was still nursing her spleen in London. I skirted the moat until I came to the rear, where there was a cluster of outbuildings like a small village. It was clear enough now to make out most of them, the mill-house, the squillery, the scalding-house, the malting and brewhouse, the saw-pit, the root-chamber. No lights showed here either.

A squat figure, coming out of the mist on the other side of the moat, halted at sight of me.

"Off with ye!" called a rough voice. "No hoskers here! I've a loaded gun with me."

I recognized the voice. "Firk Besson!" I called. "I want a word with you. I'm Roger Blease."

Besson walked forward until he faced me across the water. "So, our bold pirate's back, is he? It wur said as how you and John Ward wur coming home. But that wur a good two months back. If ye'd come then, ye wud 'a seen yer poor mother afore she died."

"I didn't know in time. I was a long way off when I heard; nearly a thousand miles, Firk. I came as soon as I could."

"And little good ye'll get of it now. They'll be after ye, Master Blease. I think ye'll be wise to turn around and go back where ye came from."

"Is the Court empty?"

"It won't be tomorrow. They're coming back. But not Mistress Katie, if that's what ye want to know. *She's* not coming. She's a great lady at coort now. Maid to the Queen, no less. What do ye think o' that, Master Blease?"

"I'm glad to hear it, Firk. She always wanted to go to court."

"And a great little beauty she's become, if that's of interest to ye. It needn't be; ye'll never be seeing Mistress Katie again, Master Blease."

John's instructions had been to see Sir Bartlemy as soon as possible so I decided to stay and get a word with him the following day. A coin changed hands, with the result that Besson took my horse in hand while I crossed the moat at the rear bridge. I spent the night on a cot in the Squillery, unable to sleep because of all that I had heard, my nose full of the curious scents of drying herbs.

29

MY TALK WITH SIR BARTLEMY proved as difficult as I had feared. It was late afternoon when he came out to the Squillery to see me, ostentatiously consulting the watch he wore around his neck. It was an unusually small one, no larger, in fact, than a saucer and presumably most expensive on that account. He made it clear he was not glad to see me, fidgeting about and keeping an eye on the door as though fearful someone would break in on us. He brightened up, however, when I told him of the great victory and of the spoils to be shared.

"John Ward is a great fellow," he said. "A great fellow, indeed."

The note of approval dropped instantly when I told him of Macherie's theft. He went as white as chalk when I explained that one of the letters had been addressed to him.

"This may be the finish of me," he said, staring around with a panicky eye. "His Majesty is set against the Free Rovers and all who have dealings with them. If that letter falls into his hands, it may cost me everything I possess. I might even lose my head."

He refused to listen to any explanations. "I must see Macherie as soon as he arrives," he went on, shaking his head despondently. "Perhaps I can make a bargain with him. Why did I ever listen to that smooth-tongued scoundrel of a Ward? It was an ill day for me when I decided to take a part in his ventures!"

I thought it wise not to point out that he had profited enormously thereby, although I was tempted to do so. He paced up and down the narrow space of the Squillery, brushing his head against the bundles of herbs hanging from the ceiling and muttering to himself in agitated undertones.

"What was said in the letter?" he demanded finally.

"I don't know. It was sealed, of course."

"It gave everything away I'm sure. Ward is a rash and heedless person. As for you, Roger, I can't find words to tell you what I think of such criminal lack of care. I knew something evil would come of it when Ward said you were to sail with him. The best thing you can do is to leave now and never let me see your face again."

He was too sunk in his fears to say anything of my mother's death—though I considered it likely that he would not have mentioned it in any event. I left immediately and spent the rest of the day and the night following in a dirty inn on the river.

I went to London by water the next day and got off at Wapping

Stairs. Saladin had been left in the care of Firk Besson, where his identity would be lost among the scores of horses in the Ladland stables. Observing with an uneasy eye the dirty, lumber-strewn court where so many seamen had gazed their last on the sun, I hoped that I would be able to lose myself as successfully here in London.

The streets were humming with talk of a recent murder. Pausing on the skirts of one gabbling group, I learned to my great surprise that the victim had been none other than our unwelcome confederate, the Upright Man of Alsatia. There was considerable mystery about the affair, it appeared; and the avid gossips in the street were retelling the details with almost drooling delight.

"He wur cut up like a griskin," I heard one man say in exultant tones. "Twenty holes in his bleeding hide, and the body propped up in a tall chair with a paper crown on his nab. He wur getting a notch above himself, wur Master Humpery, and some 'un saw to it he wur brought down proper."

"He'll make hisself the dimber-damber in hell," declared another. "Even the Old Rogue won't be able to hold *him* down. He's always top man."

"Better there than here," said a third.

I made some discreet inquiries and learned that the body had been found the previous day, exactly as described, in a house on the edge of Alsatia. It seemed to be accepted that there would be no investigation. Anyone of the thousands who had suffered at the hands of Robin Humpery might have been responsible, and after all it was a case of good riddance as far as the city authorities were concerned. He had been on my list, and I felt a sense of relief that now I would not have to see him. Then it occurred to me that another Upright Man would take his place immediately.

"Who will be the new one?" I asked.

Everyone seemed to know the answer to that—Chirp Bird. One man volunteered the information that he had seen Chirp on West Cheape late the previous evening. "He wur dressed to the nines and there wur a dozen ugly customers with him. He's a right bad 'un, Chirp Bird."

I said to myself: I know who planned the murder.

I found my way with some difficulty, the streets of mighty Rome-ville being as many and as crooked as a maze, to a tall house which stood just off the Poultry. It was a pretentious place with colored glass in its casement windows and a mounting-post of marble in front of the door. I went through a high-arched door and into a waiting room, where I asked for Sir Sigismund Hill. A clerk waved me to a seat along the wall, already partly occupied by two men of curiously different stamp.

I watched them while I waited. One I knew to be a sea captain, for his skin was as brown as a Tunizeen's and there was about him an air of bluff authority. The other was city-bred, a pursy fellow in murrey jacket and hose, who kept uneasy fingers laced over his swelling paunch. They whispered continually, and I got the impression that they were sharing some reason for chagrin.

All I had told the clerk was that I was from the south. He returned shortly and motioned me to follow him. We proceeded into a handsome apartment with a high oriel window looking out on an inner court. Sir Sigismund came from behind his long desk to welcome me, holding an opened letter in his hand.

"I've been expecting you, my boy," he said, "for exactly ten minutes. I've just finished reading the letter which announced your coming. What grand news! What a magnificent victory! I could hardly believe my eyes."

I was rather taken aback that any letter could have reached London before me, but I made no comment, as Sir Sigismund was too full of the news it had contained to think of anything else. His eyes were shining. "We've been sorely in need of something like this!" he exclaimed. "Six against twenty! It's like old times again. You must tell me all about it."

He listened eagerly to the details I supplied. "Marvelous!" he cried at the finish. "As fine a thing in its way as the defeat of the Armada. The Inner Sea wide open again—that's news for our shipping companies! John Ward, John Ward, you've done more for us than you promised!" He thumped me on the back with enthusiasm. "I must spread the news at once. The Privy Council meets this morning to discuss naval matters. It will sit ill on their stomachs when all London begins to roar over our victory."

"I don't understand how you received the word," I said, when his excitement had subsided sufficiently.

"Ward sent me the letter on the ship that took you to Marseilles, my boy," he explained. "It came right through while you waited over to attend to your affairs there. Even at that you almost caught up with it."

I was still unsatisfied. "But who brought it?"

He let his voice fall into a confidential pitch. "Did you ever hear of the Stranger's Post?" he asked. "It was set up by foreign merchants here to attend to their mail and keep them informed quickly of affairs on the Continent. About thirty years ago it was abolished. It has always been my belief that the real reason was the old queen's men didn't like letters delivered which they couldn't read first. Everything which went into the mails then passed under the eyes of Walsingham, as you probably know. The merchants didn't relish having their privilege withdrawn, and they've succeeded in keeping the service in operation without the government's knowing it. Couriers ride for them regularly from Brussels and the south, and the letters are smuggled across the Channel in ways that I prefer not to disclose. I've been making use of this clandestine post for many years. You must, of course, consider this as confidential."

I proceeded then to give him the rest of my news. He shook his head gravely when I told him of the abduction of Cristina.

"John must have taken it hard," he said. "The lady will hardly be returned in the best of condition. I know the Tunizeens too well to expect anything else. I wonder if the Dey wanted her for himself? He has a great liking for white women. He had the effrontery once to ask me what I could do for him in that way."

"The city was being turned upside down when I left," I said.

He shook his head. "Let's hope for the best. I won't rest easy about it until we've had further word."

"I came home," I said then, "because of the letter you wrote to John."

He smiled broadly. "Ah, yes. You might as well know the truth about that right away. John felt you had done your share, that you should come home while there was still a chance for you. He tells me he tried to persuade you, and that you refused. He decided then to—well, to beguile you into coming."

I looked at him blankly. "I don't understand, sir."

"He invented a reason for getting you back. That's what it amounts to."

"You mean there was no need for me to come? That there's nothing for me to do, now that I'm here?"

"I'll find plenty for you to do, never fear. There's important work for you, my boy. But it was not John's intention to have you make a tour of the country on an errand that would be very close to treason. He spoke of that because he was sure you would still refuse to come unless you were convinced the danger here would be the equal of what you were leaving. Don't look so disturbed about it. I assure you he was thinking of your best interests."

I was completely dumfounded. I could not be sure that the reason he was giving for John's action was the true one. Had I been sent back because of the dissension I had caused in the crew? I had a very sick feeling that this was closer to the truth.

"Then there's no discontent in the country over the King's policy? Was it all made up for my benefit?"

"There's plenty of discontent," declared Sir Sigismund. "Everything he said was true enough. I had given him a faithful picture of how things were at home here. But, of course, he had no intention of sending you out to risk your neck on any such errand. And, if he had, I would soon have put a stop to it myself."

"It's clear, then," I said, "that he wanted to be rid of me."

He looked up sharply. "Why do you think that?"

I found the explanation hard. "Things happened that you don't know about, Sir Sigismund. I very nearly caused a mutiny. John forgave me but—I'm sure he thought it best for me to return."

"I know everything about it. The whole story is in this letter. That, and many other things. You don't seem to realize how much affection he has for you. He had no other reason than his desire to save you from the fate he sees for himself."

"I know I was a great disappointment to him."

"Roger, if you knew what he said about you in his letter, you would rid yourself quickly of that idea. He gives you credit for saving the fleet and for showing great courage under the most difficult circumstances. He praises you to the skies."

I was still in somewhat of a fog. "Then I must disregard the instructions he gave me?"

"Just that. It was certainly not his idea to have you sent to prison on a charge of treason. That's what would happen to you if you went around the country preaching discontent."

"But if the country feels the way you say it does, why shouldn't I do it?"

My companion smiled grimly. "Have you ever seen a man executed for high treason? It's not a pleasant spectacle, I assure you. First, he's hanged, but not long enough to kill him. He's cut down before he loses consciousness, and then the executioners proceed to carve him with knives heated to a white edge. The process has been planned to give the victim the most terrible suffering. He is castrated, then his bowels are cut out and burned before his eyes—if he's still alive, as many of the poor wretches are—and finally he's cut into quarters, and the pieces are sent to various cities to be hung up as an object lesson. No, it's not a pretty thing to watch, and I leave it to you what kind of a death it is to die.

"I think, Roger," he went on, "you had better dismiss from your mind the notion of offering yourself as a candidate for that kind of a ceremony."

In spite of what he had described, I managed to say: "I've no desire to die that way, or any way. But can we permit fear of the consequences to keep us from doing our duty?"

"There are times when we should not. But what is your duty under the circumstances? I can't see that you would help the cause by placing your head in the noose. You can be more valuable to us alive. We can make good use," he added, "of the papers you brought over with you. They can, with perfect safety as far as we're concerned, be placed in the hands of certain public men who'll know what use to make of them."

The humiliating truth had to come out now. "They were stolen from me," I said.

A look of consternation spread over his face. "Stolen! In God's name, how did that happen?"

I told the story, not sparing myself at all in doing so. He sat for a few moments deep in thought after I had finished. "It's fortunate in a way that Macherie is the thief. I know him well enough to be sure that he'll follow whatever course he believes will bring him the most profit."

"Is it likely," I suggested, "that he has already arrived and that the meeting of the Privy Council was called to discuss the matter?"

"That's exactly what I've been wondering myself." He sat up with an air of decision. "Well, this makes it doubly clear that you must do nothing rash. Orders will be out for your arrest as soon as our worthy ministers have had an opportunity to examine the documents he turns over to them. That won't mean all, by any means. I'm sure Macherie will keep some of them for his own purposes."

"Do you think he'll keep the letter to Sir Bartlemy Ladland?"

"Yes. He's not likely to turn that over. Not at first, at any rate. He may find a use for that, and any other letters of the same kind." After further reflection, he added: "They'll have to move cautiously. They would hardly dare to charge you with piracy while the whole country is ringing with the news of Ward's great victory. His Majesty is getting too sensitive to public disesteem to be guilty of anything as grossly stupid as that. I'm inclined to think they'll wait for a few days. Then, if they can get their hands on you, they'll charge you with some less serious offense. Your case will be disposed of very quietly; but very effectively, I assure you. The public might never hear a whisper about it. Well, we must see that they don't get their hands on you."

"I must leave London at once, then."

"On the contrary, you must stay here. You can go into hiding more easily in London than anywhere. This city is like a morass; you can sink into it and never leave a trace. You mustn't venture out until I can make arrangements for you. If need arises quickly, there's always a safe sanctuary ready for you." He nodded in the direction of the tall stone fireplace. "There's a room back of that, the secret of which rests exclusively with me. I haven't looked in there for many years, and my memory is that it's limited in point of bodily comfort. Still, it would serve nicely."

He added after a moment: "There's no need for any great haste. The King's ministers move slowly and ponderously to a decision. We certainly have many hours of complete security, perhaps even a day or two. In the meantime, you are a young friend of mine from the country. The name, shall we say, Richard Strange?"

The clerk put his head into the room to report that the Beadle had returned and that none of the shareholders had fulfilled their extra assessments. Hill seemed more annoyed at this piece of news than he had been over the complications in which I had involved him.

"I declare, my name should be Job," he said. "These merchants and greedy gentlemen subscribe for shares in a venture at sea. They think only of the profits they hope to make and never of the responsibilities. When we find a need for additional funds, they refuse to pay their share. I think we shall have to send some of them to jail as an example."

"Surely they can't be imprisoned for that!"

"And why not? Can you think of a more serious offense than jeopard-

izing the success of a great business venture? It must not be allowed.
I could go to the Privy Council and get orders for their bodies or chattels
to make good our claim. I could indeed." He shook his head in
exasperation. "But that's only one of the things with which we have to
contend. Did you notice those two sly individuals outside? One is a
captain in our service, the other a rather large shareholder. I've caught
them in a very old trick. The captain accepted money from our honest
partner and delivered a part of the cargo to him instead of to the
company. A precious pair of thieves!"

"They seemed uneasy."

"And well they might. I have all the evidence I need. I'm letting
them cool their heels out there before bringing them in. I think it will
come to dismissal for the captain and a very heavy fine for the shareholder; although they deserve prison, the rascals. Let me show you
something else."

He led the way to a small dark room opening off a corridor in the
rear. Scores of uniforms made of the stiffest and coarsest of cloth were
hanging on the walls.

"Observe," he said, taking one down from its peg. "No pockets. We
have to dress our workmen in these when we unload a ship. If we
trusted them, they would come to work with secret pockets under their
jerkins and fill them with the most costly spices. I had these clothes
made after catching one fellow with a fortune hidden on him—four
pounds of pepper, a quart of ginger, and even some galangal. They used
to wear shoes with hollow heels and fill them with cloves. I sometimes
wonder if there are any honest people in the world."

Further down the hall was a large room from which a rumble of
noise had reached us as soon as we left the office. Sir Sigismund said it
would be safe for me to go as far as the door; everyone inside would be
too busy to notice me. I saw that elaborate efforts had been made to
give it a suggestion of the East. The walls were of imitation marble,
and the arched doorways had fretted frames. Two dark-faced attendants,
their foreheads triangled in snowy turbans, stood at the entrance. The
effort went no further, however. At one end of the room an English
clerk was standing behind a table, his face blond-bearded and beefy,
his voice nasal with the twang of the docks. He was wielding a wooden
mallet with an impatience which had no effect at all on the large group
of men seated in front of him.

They were all Londoners, quite obviously. They were handsomely
dressed without exception, but in colors much more sober than the
gentlemen of the court. Each man had the crest of his guild embroidered
on his sleeves. I noticed another point of difference: the fashion among
the gentry ran to a lathlike thinness, but these busy merchants were
heavy in build, with comfortable stomachs and bulging thighs. There
was a keen quality about them; their eyes were cool and hard, the line of
their mouths shrewd. The noise they were making was the only note

out of character; they were all shouting and gesticulating in a frenzy of competitive excitement.

Back of the table were piles of fine fabrics: velvets, velours, and brocades of great weight and value; and silks so fine and rare that the hot gold sunlight of the Orient seemed to have been spun into them. The air was laden with unfamiliar scents, tantalizing and exotic.

"It's an important roup today," explained Sir Sigismund, who seemed to have become infected with some of the excitement. "We're selling off a great variety of goods. The spices are up now. I question if there's a spice to be found anywhere which we haven't got. Things you may never have heard of, my boy—spikenard, peppermint, cubeb, nutmeg, galangal. That red-grained stuff is the galangal. It's too hot and acrid for me, but it brings a beautiful price. This will be worth watching for a few minutes. Stand close behind one of these fellows, and no one will notice you."

I could see that the noise was not all due to the excitement of the roup. Turbaned attendants were handing around wine and ale, and there was a well-laden table of food at one side. Here was a noble roast of prime beef, sliced down to the pink-and-brown stage; a great pile of mutton slices, richly rimmed with fat; a tall Dorset cheese, blue-veined and old; a meat pie crammed with richness under its arch of buttery yellow coffin crust; a mountain of sugar-iced marchpane and huge bowls of fruit. The merchants kept going back and forth between their chairs and this table, and munching enormously while they followed the progress of the sale.

Sir Sigismund left me to investigate the figures on a slip at the front table. He shook his head and frowned. The clerk promptly announced in an awed tone: "Gentlemen, Sir Sigismund Hill is not satisfied with the prices we're getting today. I'm not surprised. Gentlemen, we must do better. We really must do better."

Coming back to the doorway, Hill whispered: "As a matter of fact, the prices are not bad. Still, we must brisk things up. Give them the chance, and they'll sit here all day and chaffer. We're going to try a candle roup now. Watch this closely; it can be quite exciting."

A plump fellow who had been sitting in a corner got up now. I had already identified him as the Beadle; he carried a tall staff and wore an expression of official severity as though ready at a moment's notice to take charge of delinquents. He carried in a candle on a board, a mere coating of tallow with a short wick. The candle was lighted and then shoved well forward on the table.

The commodity now offered was a quintal of one of the rarest spices. Perhaps I should explain that a quintal is an Oriental measure, a little in excess of one hundred pounds. As the light flickered, the voices of the bidders began to acquire a new stridency. The price mounted rapidly. Sir Sigismund said to me with a chuckle: "The bidding stops when the light goes out, and the last offer heard is accepted. They can never be sure how long it will run."

As the last of the tallow burned away, the price mounted rapidly. Seven! Seven and a half! Eight! Eight and a quarter! The Beadle raised his staff. Eight and a half!

The light was gone.

The Beadle pointed his staff at the lucky bidder. "Eight and a half," he intoned. "Sold to Guy Casterby for eight and a half; Guy Casterby will kindly come to the table and pay his deposit."

My companion whispered in my ear: "Eight and a half shillings a pound. A good price, better than we'd have had after a half-hour of leisurely bidding. It's like a game this way; they get excited and forget their caution. Still, the stuff is rare."

The rest of the day I spent in seclusion in a small room under the leads, which had been given me for temporary sanctuary. I had for company my copy of *Bayard* and for sustenance a rib of cold beef, a loaf of wheaten bread, and a stone bottle of ale. It was dark outside when Sir Sigismund joined me. He was smiling triumphantly.

"London has gone stark roaring mad over the word of the victory," he announced. "They're toasting John Ward in every tavern in town, and in every fine house as well. Cheapside is so crowded you can't get from one end to the other. The word I get from court is that our King has gone into a fit of sulks. Archie is drunk and in disgrace."

I opened the window and looked down. Crowds were milling in the street below, and I could see torches waving above the heads of the people.

"They'll be burning effigies tonight," said my host. "The King of Spain. Guy Fawkes, of course. Perhaps some of the King's Privy Council."

"Not the King himself?"

"They're not likely to go that far. But talk runs high against the old zany. They're clamoring for war with Spain."

"I wish John were here to see this."

Sir Sigismund seated himself in a chair with an air of weariness. "It's been a full day. We held a council at five, and I swear I've never seen our worthy shareholders in a more gabby mood. Even Percentage Tuttle laid his shilling on the board five times on one question alone. That's a rule we have: no member may speak oftener than twice on any matter without paying a shilling fine. Usually it puts a damper on their loquacity. There were more than a dozen of them paid their two-and-six for interrupting other speakers. The coins rattled on the wood like dice. And would you believe that the point in question was whether our ships should expend gunpowder in answering salutes at sea? The decision was for the frugal course; no guns to be fired but the members of the crews to have instructions to cheer."

"Who gets the fines?"

"They're turned into a fund to provide Bibles for our ships and stations." He turned his attention to more serious matters. "I've made all arrangements for you, Roger. You're to have the top floor in the house of a respectable widow. Her husband was in hides; and now that he's dead, she ekes things out by letting rooms on occasion. Remember, your name is Richard Strange, and you're a student. What you're studying for is a matter I leave to you—the law, the church, whatever seems best. A load of books is being sent in for you. Immerse yourself in them and never go out except at night; and as little as possible then. The hue and cry will be on soon. Dame Witchie is discreet enough, and I vouch for her honesty. But she's a woman and has a lively curiosity. You'll move in tonight."

I tried to express my gratitude, but he waved that aside. "I've a selfish interest in your safety, Roger," he said. "Every merchant in England has, for that matter." He nodded his head gravely. "Have you any idea of the importance of the Eastern trade today? It comes to this: London does six times as much trade as all the rest of the country put together, and a very large part of it is with the Eastern countries. It's become so vital that I used to go each year to the Barbary Coast and pay tribute to protect our ships from the Corsairs. Two thousand pounds a year! It cut into the profits, I tell you. That's over with, now that John Ward and the rest of them are keeping the control of the seas. Did you know we pay something to the Free Rovers? Much less, of course, but a goodly sum. That will give you an idea of where the interests of the merchants of England lie."

This explained many things about which I had wondered. I had never understood his reason for being in Tunis and the freedom allowed him there.

"I'm going to say something now that you may not agree with, because it's so contrary to the general belief," he went on. "Get this into your head, Roger: Those men you saw downstairs today are more necessary to England than all the courtiers and the soldiers and the fine gentry. Trade is what counts in the long run. People must be kept employed, they must eat and clothe themselves, and it takes your merchant for that. Kings make wars, but there's always some necessity of trade behind it. We pull the strings, and we provide the money for wars. Your merchant is looked down on; his wife isn't allowed to dress in silk; he's given the worst of it in any legal disputes with a noble. But he runs the country in all things that deal with money; and some day his importance will be recognized."

After a moment he added: "There, I've done enough preaching for one night. Here's what you're to do: Two porters are going to Denmark House. We make it a rule to send Her Majesty a few presents each time a ship comes in—some of the best spices, perhaps a bolt of fine silk, sometimes even a piece of jade. I've instructed them to take a special route tonight. Follow them as far as the Boar's Head, and you'll be within a few squares of the house. It's on Gracechurch Street, not far from Old Swan Stairs. You can't miss it; a doctor had it once, and his lantern is still suspended from the second story, though its color has been changed from red to blue. Dame Witchie will be waiting for you."

I followed the porters at a safe distance. They dawdled along, stopping at every square where effigies were being burned and making one protracted stay at a mean little inn. It was called the Great Can, but I was sure it was intended for "Khan," as the sign outside depicted a potentate of swarthy hue on an anemic elephant. The streets were still thronged, and I took a keen pleasure in the merrymaking spirit which gripped the city, feeling that I had had a share in bringing it about. I realized, however, that the temper of the people was beginning to change. A day of drinking had engendered an uglier mood. Before the night was over, Catholic glass would be splintered all over London, and blood would be spilled. This did not apply to all who were celebrating the victory. Once the door of a humble home opened as I passed, and I caught the notes of a hymn sung by many voices. I recognized the fine roll of "We Light This Day a Candle" and knew that the singers were Puritans, or even Brownists, and that they also were offering humble thanks for what had happened.

I did not stop at the Boar's Head, as Sir Sigismund had directed, but continued to dog the footsteps of the porters at a discreet distance. I had decided to follow them as far as Denmark House and treat myself to a glimpse of the palace where Katie lived. I was sure it was the closest I would come to seeing her for a very long time.

30

DENMARK HOUSE made me think of Paris, for it had a completely foreign look about it. Its tall circular chimneys stuck up in the air like slender fingers, and there were fanciful touches to the brick façade which were not English in any sense.

Two guards, the very picture of dismal vacancy, stood at each side of the gatehouse entrance; but it was not difficult to get in. All manner of people were passing in and out, and I decided that I might as well have a look at the interior of the place now that I had come this far. Nothing was said to me as I stepped with assumed briskness through the squared portal. I found myself in a crowded anteroom. Most of the visitors, I suspected, had no more right to be there than I had; some of them, in fact, had dropped in to use the privy room. In one corner an elderly fellow with a pack on his back was making some repairs on a sleeve of dingy shagg; two eager bargainers were looking over samples of velvet of the very finest kind, worth, I judged, at least three pounds a yard; a group of servants in the palace livery surrounded a chirurgeon who was extracting a tooth from one of them.

No one paid any attention to me, and I walked to the rear of the gatehouse where I could see the main block of buildings on the other side of the quadrangle. Katie was somewhere in this imposing pile, probably in attendance on Her Majesty and trying to look very grown up and proper; or perhaps she had already been dismissed for the night and had gone to her own room. I picked out one small light which winked at me from the top story and pretended to myself that it was hers. She was sitting at her work table and was writing a letter (but not to me); her hair was piled high on her head in that new way she liked so much, and her sweet brow was puckered with the effort involved in composition (I have explained that Katie was no scholar). I could see how stiffly she held the quill, and that the tip of her tongue had been caught between her lips, and that her eyes were happy with thoughts of the lucky one to whom the note was addressed. Or perhaps she was ready for bed, one arm free from her night-rail and reaching to snuff out the candle. I decided it was still too early for this last picture, especially as the light I had picked as hers continued to burn steadily.

I saw a gentleman, with an ill-tempered pucker to his features, take charge of the goods the porters had brought. He was someone of importance, for he was wearing the George; but he was of careless habit, and the symbol of his rank dangled over a stained doublet of black velvet. A lady with powdered hair, looking almost doll-like in her exaggerated farthingale, spoke to him about the presents, and they whispered together for several moments. I got the impression that they were sharing some anxiety, but I was not aware that they had become interested in me until the gentleman plucked at my sleeve with officious fingers.

"Young man, did you come about these presents for Her Majesty?" he asked.

"No, my lord." I judged he was of the peerage from his possession of the George.

"You came in with the porters," he grumbled. "And I can tell you're a sailor. Come now, you're just back from the East."

"I'm just back from sea, my lord."

The lady, who had come up behind him, said: "It's worth trying, Gerald. Her Majesty is finding things very dull this evening."

This seemed to increase his irritability. "It's always the way! Keeping a pack of women amused who haven't a thought in their heads beyond—" He broke off and studied me with angry intentness. Finally he made up his mind and addressed me again in tones of brisk authority. "I don't know why you deny your connection with the Company. What would you be doing here otherwise? I shall take you to Her Majesty, young man. It may cheer her up to hear some stories of adventure in the East."

I realized then how foolish I had been in coming here. "My lord," I protested, "I must crave your indulgence. I'm a plain sailor. I—"

"You're of gentle blood." He waved my objections aside. "I'll risk it. Come with me, young man."

"But, sir—"

"You don't understand. It's a command."

I should not have stood on ceremony. I should have left there and then; but something inside me was urging that I see this through. What the impulse was, I have never been able to figure out. I hoped to see Katie, of course; but, great as the pleasure might be from that, it was hardly in proportion to the risk I was taking. Whatever the reason, it kept me on his heels until I found myself at one end of a long and lofty apartment. There was a hush about it which warned me that I stood in the presence of royalty. I saw that a bevy of women were clustered about a high-backed chair in which the Queen was sitting. There was no backing out now. I followed my guide down the long stretch of floor, our heels making an unseemly din on the marble. I was dimly aware that we passed a long series of tapestries which told some story from the Bible.

"May it please Your Majesty," I heard my guide say, bowing so low that the George swung out a full foot in front of his chest, "this is a young sailor from Eastern waters. I thought Your Majesty might find some interest in the stories he has to tell. His name—speak up, sir, what is your name?"

"Roger Blease, Your Majesty," I said, gulping with nervousness.

The Queen's chair had been placed at an angle so she could enjoy the heat from a log flaming on the immense hearth. Now that I saw her at close range, I realized she was much handsomer than reports gave her credit for being. Her features were good, her hair, once flaxen, was still attractive, her eyes a warm and lively brown. She smiled at me encouragingly and said with the slightest suggestion of foreign accent:

"An excellent idea, my lord. It has been a tedious evening. Are you with the Gentlemen of the Levant, young sir?"

"No, Your Majesty."

I had not dared look at the group of ladies, but now I gave a hurried glance about me. I saw Katie at once. She was sitting cross-legged on a cushion beside the Queen's chair, which made me sure that she was in high favor. She was lovelier even than I had expected. I glanced away at once and let my eyes rove quickly over the rest of the attendants. Some of them were young and many were pretty; all were richly attired, with wide ruffs and flowers in their hair; but none of them, I said to myself, was capable of holding a candle to the newest and youngest member of the circle. From that moment I was always conscious of

Katie's eyes fixed on me with an expression both of amazement and alarm. She had given no sign of recognition.

"But you came in on the latest ship from the East, no doubt?"

"No, Your Majesty. I've just arrived from the south. But I've sailed in Oriental waters."

The officer frowned at me and said in sulky tones: "He told me, Your Majesty, that he was from the East. He said it, most positively."

The Queen smiled at me again and said: "It doesn't matter, my lord. No doubt the young man has some stories to tell which will relieve our tedium."

There was an awkward pause. Then something happened inside me which I can no more explain than the impulse which had brought me into this difficult situation. My mind cleared, and I was no longer conscious of either nervousness or fear. I knew that a rare opportunity had been thrown my way by chance. Everything I said here would be reported and talked about; in time it would reach all parts of the country.

"If I might have Your Majesty's indulgence," I said, "I would like to depart from the usual custom. There's a story I could tell of a very brave man. But he wasn't a captain or a man of gentle blood. He was a common sailor."

The Queen drew her wide skirts tightly about her ankles with a gesture which I learned later was characteristic of her. It permitted the tips of her shoes to show above the needlepoint footstool. "Proceed, then," she said. "It will be a novelty. We've never heard stories of common sailors."

"He was called Clim the Cod's-head," I said. It proved an easy story to tell. I began with the day we captured the *Santa Caterina*, being careful not to give myself away by the use of names. I told it without sparing a single detail of Clim's share in the struggle. Everyone was listening, I could see. I stole another glance at Katie; she was sitting up straight now and watching me with wide-open eyes. Her Majesty followed the recital with as much attention as her ladies were giving, taking an occasional sip from a goblet of wine with a jeweled edge. Out of the corner of one eye, I saw that a curious activity was being carried on by a manservant in front of the blazing fire. Five bottles of wine were kept there in a row, and at regular intervals one was removed and a new one placed at the other end of the file. When the Queen made a gesture toward her goblet, one of the ladies would empty it and then see that it was filled from the first bottle. This puzzled me until I realized that it was done to make sure the wine she sipped was heated always of the right degree for her taste.

I went on with the saga of my unfortunate friend, telling of his involvement in Danny Boy O'Donnell's tragic error, and of his lingering death in the Basket. When I reached the point where the rope was cut and the cage fell into the sea, I was aware that most of the ladies, including Her Majesty, had tears in their eyes.

"Poor fellow!" said the Queen. "We were hoping to the very end of your story that something would happen to save him. He was a brave man, your—what was the name you gave him?"

"Clim the Cod's-head, Your Majesty."

She smiled and blew her nose on a pearl-edged handkerchief. "Clim the Cod's-head," she repeated, as though not quite sure of the meaning. "He should have been called Clim the Stout-heart. But now, perhaps, you have other stories to tell us. Something a shade more cheerful. We have had enough of tragedy for one evening."

"Yes, Your Majesty, I might tell you of a sea battle in which I played a very modest part but which was won by the greatest bravery." She nodded permission, and I began to describe our great victory off Cape Passer. Again I held back no detail, no matter how grim, telling of the battle as I had seen it myself, first from my porthole on the gun-deck and later from under the red swathe of the top-armings. I related everything: the death of poor Henry Oge and my finding of his powder-blackened head; the blowing up of the ship captured by Sleath with all on board; the horror of the conditions I found below; the masterly maneuver by which our ships were drawn into close formation; and, finally, of the glorious sunrise when we roused to find no enemy sail on the horizon. Although telling it from my own standpoint, I kept John Ward, unnamed, in the front of the picture at all times. I think I succeeded in making them see him as he was that day, a great leader and a gallant gentleman. I was sure that I had done so when the Queen said: "You are too modest, both on your own account and for these brave men you fought beside. You give us no names. Who was this daring young man who commanded your ships?"

"His name, Your Majesty, was John Ward."

A spark passed through the company. The Queen straightened up in her chair with such suddenness that the footstool toppled over. It was serving the double purpose of foot-warmer, and the pan under the needlepoint rolled out of its frame, spilling the water on the floor. There was a rush of servants to repair the damage and bring another rest for the royal feet. By the time this was done, the shock of my announcement had spent its force.

"Well," said Her Majesty, "you have given us a surprise. Are you telling us, young sir, that you belong to that lawless band who disregard their King's commands?"

"I've served a year with John Ward, Your Majesty."

"It's hard to believe." She turned to an elderly lady who sat on her right. "Susan, does this young man look like a pirate to you?"

"I'm no judge of such matters, Your Majesty. It's true he lacks the villainous aspect one usually expects in pirates."

Another voice chimed in with an opinion. "I can't imagine a pirate without a beard, Your Majesty." The Queen paid assiduous attention to her goblet while a discussion developed among the ladies. They talked me over as freely as though I were an inanimate object, but they were all kind enough to express the belief that I was too young and innocent in appearance to have been involved, except indirectly, in any proceedings which might be defined as piratical. Katie took no part in the debate.

"Ladies, you are probably right," said Her Majesty, when they were through. "But we remember clearly what happened once when we were a small girl at our father's court in Denmark. A band of pirates had been caught. They had been operating in the Baltic and had caused many complaints from the cities of the Hanseatic League. We saw them being led away after their trial, and one was a very young man with a gentle face and golden hair which fell over his shoulders. We went to the King and begged him to save the life of the young man. The King refused. He was a kindhearted man, but the band had been a thorn in his flesh for several years, and he said no exceptions could be made. We wept bitterly for hours about it. But"—her eye lighted on the series of tapestries; I saw now that they told the story of Esther and that the final one showed the execution—"they were all hanged, including the handsome young man, as high as the gallows of Haman!"

"Your Majesty," I asked, "may I say a word in my own defense?" She nodded a somewhat unsteady head. "By all means. We remember too well what occurred that time to want— Proceed, young sir."

"Your Majesty, the winds and the seas have always been the heritage of the men of the north—the English, the Norse, the Danes. Now that we know the world is round—and Norsemen found the proof of that long before Columbus—we can be sure there are new continents and strange seas still to be explored. Must we let our ships rot in port because a Spanish king has drawn lines across the globe and decreed that no vessels but his own may venture into these new oceans? Are we to sit by while he monopolizes the trade of both East and West? Is it piracy to contest the right to sail the seas with the Spanish?"

A voice issued from somewhere in the group in frightened and perhaps involuntary agreement, "No, no!" I paused. The results of such outspoken criticism of the royal policy might be serious, but I had set my feet in the furrow and might as well continue to the end.

"John Ward is warring on Spanish shipping because they war on ours. He keeps them so busy that now our merchantmen are coming through from the East again without interference. He is carrying on the work that Drake and Cavendish and Frobisher began. He's not a pirate, Your Majesty; he's a patriot; and his one aim is to make the land His Majesty rules over the greatest in the world."

The Queen leaned forward and studied me with such intentness that I expected to hear her order me taken in charge. Instead she laughed. "You're very bold, young sir. That's to be expected, perhaps, and we don't say we dislike it. It's unfortunate His King's Grace was not here to listen to your story."

"Your Majesty, I think it's fortunate for me he isn't here."

She laughed again. "Perhaps you're right. The King has little liking for such troublesome subjects as your John Ward. We confess to some curiosity about the man. Is he as handsome as they say?"

"What has been said about him is no exaggeration."

"We hear he has mistresses in every port."

"I'm sure that can't be true, Your Majesty. I know he's a most chivalrous gentleman."

"Then what of yourself? You must have seen many beautiful ladies on your travels. The women of the East are fascinating, are they not?"

"I didn't find them so."

"But you are in love, surely. All young men are in love."

"Yes, Your Majesty. I'm in love with an English girl."

I kept my eyes fixed on the row of tapestries, not daring to look in Katie's direction. The Queen smiled at me approvingly.

"Was it to see this English girl that you returned?"

"That was one reason, Your Majesty."

"But how does it happen that you're here tonight?"

"I throw myself on Your Majesty's indulgence. It was curiosity. I wanted to see the home of the Queen of England. My lord saw me and became convinced I had some concern with presents which had been delivered for Your Majesty."

She smiled indulgently. "We have no quarrel with your curiosity, Sir Pirate. Many hundreds come here every day for the same reason." She held a jeweled hand to her mouth to stifle a yawn, and I felt the court officer tug at my arm. I bowed and began to back away.

"Accept our thanks for a most diverting evening," said the Queen, rising with a careful arm on each side of her chair. She was still smiling, and I felt that, no matter what might happen to me, I could count on her support. "We were finding things very dull this evening. There was even some talk of filling in time by playing a child's game that was a great favorite when we were young. It's called 'Rise, Pig, and Go,' and it would have been a poor substitute for the stirring stories you've told us."

"I'm happy to have been useful, Your Majesty."

"You were very bold to come here with such stories. We hope His King's Grace will be disposed to regard you with as much indulgence as we do. You have our permission to retire." She laughed unsteadily. "Rise, Pirate, and go."

31

IN THE ANTEROOM the court officer, who had been striding angrily ahead of me, turned about and said in vicious tones: "Bold indeed! Your presumption will get us all in trouble; perhaps even Her Majesty. Gog's Nownes, what did you mean by it? If I'd known you were one of Ward's men, I would have turned you over to the watch!"

I could tell that he wanted to do that now and was holding back because he was not safe in taking any action after the cordial reception I had received from the Queen. He muttered: "I hope it won't be necessary to face you at a questioning before the Council. It will probably come to that. What a tight spot you've placed me in!"

He had no intention of being seen further in my company, so I crossed the dark quadrangle alone. This was most fortunate, for a voice said out of the darkness behind me, "If you please, sir, I have a message for you."

I stopped. A servingmaid approached and dropped a hurried curtsy.

"From Mistress Ladland, sir. She wants a word with you. Will you follow me, sir?"

She led me back to the wing overlooking the river. We entered a dark doorway at the extreme east end, and I found myself in a mean room with no fire and a tall screen cutting off one corner. It was used by the palace watchmen, I judged; a horn lantern was hanging on one end of the screen, and a pair of high boots, caked with mud, had been carelessly deposited under the table.

The servingmaid left, after lighting another candle, and in a few minutes Katie came breathlessly in. We stood and looked at each other for several moments without saying a word.

She had grown in the past year, in height as well as in beauty. I have made no serious effort to describe her before, fearing that in any such attempt I would run to superlatives; but now it must be done. I will give the necessary details first: Her brow was broad and white under her dark hair, so broad that it gave her face the shape of a heart; her eyes were wide-spaced and a deep gray; her nose was straight and of a pleasing lack of length (pleasing to me, as I don't like long noses, my own quite as little as Macherie's); her mouth was a perfect index always to the mood of the moment. Much more important than these particulars was the continual aliveness of her—the fact that her eyes never failed to sparkle, that her voice had a lilt, that she seemed always a little excited and delighted with life. Animation of this kind is so rare that it lifts up those who possess it; and it turned her sweetness and charm of feature into real beauty. There is something cold and detached about beauty of figure, and I hasten to report that Katie did not have it. In this particular she remained no more than pretty; pretty in every line, in every movement; the prettiness of youthful roundness, of dimpled elbow, of slender ankle. It was always a delight to watch her.

If I have not succeeded in giving as accurate a picture as a painter could achieve with his brushes, I am sure I have made it clear why all my share of coolness and detachment deserted me the instant I saw her.

"Roger," she said, "I was so proud of you! But I was frightened. You must go in a very few minutes."

"More than a few, surely."

"But you're in great danger. You shouldn't have come here. The Queen enjoyed the stories you told, and I'm sure she likes you. But the word you were here will get around so fast! I tremble to think what might happen! One of the ladies told me the King was very angry when he heard about the battle. He drank too much and had to be put to bed."

"Is he here?"

"No, of course not. He and the Queen keep separate courts. Didn't you know? They see each other seldom. I'm glad of it because the King's household isn't a very nice one. If you should want to send me a message at any time, you can have it delivered at the east wicket. Address it on the outside to Elsie Windiyard, my maid. I can trust her. I heard Her Majesty whisper to one of the ladies, Roger, that she thought you handsome. I think so too. You're so tall now; almost as tall as Captain Ward. You won't stay in London, of course."

"Yes, I must for a time. It's the safest place I can find. I'm going into hiding."

"Why did you come, Roger? I couldn't believe my eyes when I looked up and saw you." She noticed the small scar on my forehead. "Were you wounded? You didn't tell us about that."

"It wasn't much. A splinter. But it hurt enough at the time. John's neck was creased by a bullet, but it was slight too. We were lucky, both of us. Eight of the men from town were killed."

There was a moment's silence. "Captain Ward is well, then?"

"Yes. We talked about you a great deal. We got your letters at Tunis."

"But you never wrote me." Her tone was reproachful. "I got no letters at all. I was very hurt about it."

"Then they must have been lost. I wrote you three letters."

We were standing close together, and she was looking straight up into my eyes. "Roger," she asked, "did you mean me?"

"When I said I was in love with an English girl? Of course I meant you. But I shouldn't have said it; I was taking an unfair advantage."

She looked puzzled. "An unfair advantage? I don't understand."

"John isn't here. I wouldn't have said it, but I knew you realized how—how I feel about you."

She sighed. "I shouldn't have asked. Things are different now."

I made no comment on that, knowing only too well what she meant. "You are different, Katie," I said. "You're much lovelier even than when I went away. I shouldn't say things like that either. It's unfair to John."

"It isn't unfair to pay me compliments. Lots of men do that, if you want to know."

"I was sure you would have plenty of admiration. Do you remember telling me that you would have suitors when you came to court?"

She looked up again and smiled. "I haven't been—well, unnoticed exactly. Men do pay me compliments. I have one suitor." She hastened to add, as though compelled to be honest about it: "He isn't a very exciting suitor. He's a year younger than I am, and he doesn't talk about anything but horses. He seems to think horses are the most interesting things in the world. Sometimes he talks about dogs. He sent me poetry once. It didn't seem to me that it was very good poetry. He got someone to write it for him. I found out."

"Are you happy here?"

She nodded in almost ecstatic agreement. "Oh, it's wonderful! I've never been so happy. Her Majesty seems to like me. Sometimes she sends for me and talks for the longest time. She tells me about the days when she was a girl at her father's court in Denmark, and sometimes about the awful life they had in Scotland. Witches were always trying to put spells on the King. Or at least he thought so; he's terribly afraid of witches. When her children were born they were taken away from her and given to the wives of noblemen to raise. She never saw them for months at a time. She and the King quarreled about it. They hardly spoke for a year."

"Then you're fond of Her Majesty?"

"I love her, Roger. Didn't you like her?"

I agreed enthusiastically on that point. "She was very kind to me just now. She must have been lovely once."

"Beautiful! No one should believe the silly stories they tell about her. She likes wine but she never gets—what is that funny new word?"

"Typsy?"

"That's what I meant. She never gets typsy, although people say she does. You've no idea how graceful she is and how well she can dance. There's no one so wonderful as she is."

"I'm glad you're happy. I'm afraid I should go now. If you ever want to get in touch with me, you can send a note in care of Sir Sigismund Hill. But be careful about it. It mustn't get out that he's helping me. Be very sure of the messenger you use." I paused. There was one matter that should be mentioned between us, but I hesitated to open it up. "Did you know my mother died?"

She had not known; that was clear, for she looked at me with instant and horrified compassion. "Mother writes me sometimes, but she never mentioned it. They haven't been at Appleby Court, so perhaps they didn't hear. Oh, Roger, I'm sorry! Your mother was so young. It's hard to believe. When did it happen?"

"Eight weeks ago."

"And that was why you returned?"

"It was another of the reasons." After a moment's hesitation, I went on. "You know what happened before, of course?"

She nodded unhappily. "I was so sorry about it! Roger, I don't think Mother behaved very well. I didn't speak to her for days afterward. I wanted her to go back and talk to your mother; but she wouldn't. That's what I meant when I said—" She left the sentence unfinished.

"That things were different?"

"Yes. Mother's very hard. I'm afraid she hasn't changed; that she still believes what she said."

"Things are different in many ways. There's John too."

We had no chance to say anything more. Footsteps were heard coming down a stair behind the room. Katie looked frightened and motioned me urgently to leave. I whispered to her as she left the room on tiptoe: "I brought something for you, but it will have to wait."

The maid was outside and led the way to the eastern postern. The watchman looked us over and grinned evilly. "It's late for cosseting, my girl. How would ye like it, now, if I stuck to orders and refused to let him out?"

I slipped a coin in his hand as he swung back the iron-studded door. "She's a lively 'un, my fine buck," he whispered.

The street was clear, but I lost no time in getting away from the neighborhood. I dodged into dark corners whenever I heard sounds which suggested the approach of the watch. I had plenty to think about, but my mind never veered from the subject of Katie. I found myself dwelling lingeringly on the way she had looked up at me with her fine gray eyes, on the white roundness of her neck, on the sudden coming and going of the dimple (she had one only) in her right cheek. Although I had talked to her calmly enough, it had taken every ounce of resolution I possessed to keep from seizing her in my arms and telling her that nothing mattered in life but the hope that some day my devotion might be returned.

This was completely wrong and futile as well; I knew that well enough. Katie was in love with John. Even had things been different in that respect, the situation would still have been hopeless. Her parents would never consider me as a suitor for her hand. I was the cadet of a once-wealthy family, and I had no prospects. On top of everything there was the rift which had led to my mother's death and to Lady Ladland's unbending hostility.

I knew all this, but logical thought has no chance to survive in the

face of youthful optimism. Something would happen to change everything; her parents would relent finally, she would come to prefer me
after all; it was unthinkable that things could end in any other way.
By the time I reached the house with the blue lantern near Old
Swan Stairs, I was no longer aware of the blackness of the streets.
The white light of my hopes had cast a rosy glow even over the slums
of London.

32

I HAD A WINDOW in the front of the house from which
I could look over the river. The prospect was pleasant enough, but the
rooms themselves were dingy, being immediately under the roof, and
so small that I could go from one end to the other in ten strides. As
Sir Sigismund had promised, there was a fine supply of books. As I
glanced at the titles I realized that my term of confinement would
have its compensations. There were several volumes of Hakluyt that
I had never seen before, and I decided to begin on these. Now that
I was safely back from sea, and not likely to leave dry land again, I had
a consuming desire to read of other voyages.

My landlady seemed glad to have someone in the house, for she visited me twice during the morning on slender pretexts. Later she
brought up my dinner herself, although there were two servants in the
house, a middle-aged maid and a poor clod who answered to the name
of Stevecorn and whose activities were confined to the cellar and the
high-fenced plot of ground at the rear. He was afflicted with the falling-
sickness, I learned later, and Dame Witchie did not like him on the
streets. It was a meal fit for a king, and she urged me to do my very
best, at the same time jabbing with a parsimonious poker at the few
bits of green wood in the fireplace. She was a study in contradictions,
and I never did get to understand the workings of her mind.

Late in the afternoon she came up the stairs again with a singularly
light step for one so generously endowed with flesh. She laid a parcel
on my table. "From Sir Sigismund Hill," she said. He was an important
figure in her eyes, quite clearly, and she was deeply curious about the
parcel. A note had come with it which said nothing more than: "A payre
of cards you may like to use. H."

"Playing cards," I said, watching to see what her reaction would be.

"Cards!" She drew in her lips primly. "I'm surprised at Sir Sigismund. I am indeed! Cards are the devil's tools, Master Strange. What
would the Reverend Humility Brown think if he knew I allowed play-

ing cards to be brought into my house!" Her ample bosom heaved with indignation, but her breath was proof that she had found occasion during the day for frequent visits to her brandy stock. I wondered how the Reverend Humility Brown viewed such generous indulgence in strong liquor.

When she had gone I broke the seal of the parcel. The cards were of French make and very fine; not at all like our limp homemade kind. They were stiff and glossy, Beniere's no less, with boldly printed figures in gay colors. I noted that the king of clubs, the only one of the four monarchs allowed a crown, was made in the likeness of the King of France; while the four vulgar and shifty-looking knaves were labeled with names of Kings of England.

There was a note immediately under the king of clubs, without a signature.

The hounds are out in full cry. If the fox is sensible, he will stay close to his lair. The Master of the Hunt is in a determined mood and swears to be in at the kill. N.M. is back and is said to be in high favor.

P.S. There is much talk around of a very foolhardy thing that happened last night. Have you taken leave of your senses completely?

I was disturbed by the reference to Macherie. If he became powerful at court, it would mean trouble for all of us. I remembered his vow to even the score with his fellow Free Rovers. I had put the weapons he needed for the purpose into his hands by my carelessness at Calais.

I was reminded continually during the next few days that it might devolve on me to take steps against him. My side window looked on the courtyard of a down-at-heels inn which had once catered to a better trade than the low city custom with which it had now to be content. No carriages stopped at its door; the mounting-post in front was used only by urchins playing leap-frog; and the mews at the rear had been converted to other use than the stabling of horses. It was easy to decide what that use was, for men in fine clothes went in and out at all hours of the day, and I could hear the clanging and rasping of steel and breathless cries of: "On Guard."—"Ha, octave!"—"A neat riposte!"—"Faugh, flanconnade!"

If I ever dared to confront Sir Nevil Macherie with charges of ill-faith and theft, I must be prepared to enforce my complaint at the point of steel. Knowing nothing of swordsmanship, I decided that here was an unexpected opportunity to acquire some skill in the handling of the weapon with which gentlemen arbitrated their differences. If it had not been for the urgent note of warning from Sir Sigismund, I would have visited the converted stables at once. As it was, I waited until the third night. The place had not had any visitors for a matter of two hours, and only a dim light showed through the circular window above the entrance. I made my way downstairs cautiously, not wanting to arouse the curiosity of Dame Witchie. Her voice reached me, however, as I gained the front door.

"You're going out, Master Strange? There's a nip in the air at night now. Are you warmly dressed?"

She came down the hall, holding a candle above her head and carrying a handsome cloak over her other arm. She had brought it for me to wear, I concluded; but some inner sense of caution held her back from offering me its use. Instead she cautioned me to make my walk a brief one and to keep myself warm by moving briskly. I promised to obey both injunctions.

When I put my head into the fencing school, I thought at first it was deserted. It was lighted by a single lantern hanging on the wall, and my feet resounded as hollowly on the paved floor as though I had entered a church. My eyes becoming accustomed to the dim light, I saw a man sitting behind a table at the far end, with his head hunched down over a bowl of food. He appeared enormous, and he was eating with a great appetite.

"What do you want?" he demanded truculently.

I walked over to the table. "I've urgent need for some degree of skill with the sword," I said.

His appearance was not reassuring. Under a thatch of tousled hair, he had a set of rough-hewn features, contorted for my benefit into a heavy scowl. He said scornfully: "I'm the best swordsman in the world, but what could I hope to make out of the likes of you?"

"My money will be good, at any rate."

He got to his feet grumblingly, and I was amazed at the size of him. He was well over six feet, and his stomach was as round as a washtub. He must have weighed well over twenty stone. Seizing my arm, he flexed it roughly.

"Well, not bad," he conceded. "You're tall enough, though I've got three inches on you. About nineteen and a half? I thought so. As a matter of fact, I never make a mistake in the age, height, and weight of any man. Gentry, too. Why haven't you done something in this line before?"

"I've been at sea. It's a different kind of fighting there."

"I knew it from the tan of your cheeks. Can you handle a pike?"

I admitted to some acquaintance with the use of a pike. He scowled and said he could take on three of me at that game. Once he had beaten a whole watch with nothing but a blunt morglay in his hands. The recollection seemed to put him into a better mood, for he asked me in an almost friendly tone why my need for instruction was so urgent.

"I expect to fight a duel."

He snorted. A fine fist I would make of a duel! My antagonist would carve me to a cow's thumb. He did not fancy having any pupil of his in a brangle where he would get daylight through him at the first pass. Suddenly he threw back his massive head and called in a high-pitched voice: "Dirk! Dirk, you lazy bastard, where are you?"

A skinny fellow with surprisingly long legs and arms came in from the rear. He had been indulging in a nap, for he blinked at the light and rubbed his lids with the back of one hand.

"Can we do anything with this one?" demanded the big man.

"We've had worse looking 'uns, Dom Bass," answered the newcomer, looking me over as though I were a horse up for sale. "He's got length to him. His legs has spring. I don't care much for the set of his shoulders. He's been a scholard."

"He's a rum-bob at this."

"We all has to start once, Dom Bass."

"Take him in hand, then." The big man waved an arm carelessly and returned to his meal. Dirk proceeded to set up a target. Then he drew a line on the floor seven feet in front of it and handed me a sword with a blunted point.

Under his instructions I stood on the line and practiced lunging at the center of the target. Dom Bass watched me over the rim of his bowl with a scornfully critical eye. My right foot had to touch the floor at the same time that the point touched the target; a fraction of a second off either way, and he would roar as though suffering actual pain. I was supposed also to strike the exact center and with no more force than the whisk of a fairy's wing. If I failed either way, his reaction was immediate and bitter.

"You caudge-pawed monkey!" he would shout. "You've no feel for it. Get it through your head that skill with the sword is all a matter of physical precision. Everything must work together—your legs, your arm, your back, your eye—and your brain if you have one. You'll never do; you've got about as much skill and touch as a suffolk-punch."

I did not enjoy being compared to a draught horse, but after each outburst Dirk would whisper: "Let it go, sir, he's the best fencing master in all Lunnon, and it's worth the abuse to have him." So I swallowed my pride and went on with the first lesson. The weapon I was using was heavy, and in a short time I began to feel the strain of the continual lunge and recover, lunge and recover. My arm felt like lead, my breath came in gasps. My mentor watched me with an unfeeling eye while he discoursed over his food on the art of fencing.

"They say the French and the Italians are the best swordsmen," he grumbled. "Let me tell you, I come from a country which has produced better men than any spindly Frenchman or the smartest Roman that ever lived. Portugal!" I was surprised, for he spoke with no trace of an accent. "You thought I was English, did you? That shows what twenty years in your miserable fogs can do to a man's throat! I've never seen such poor hands with a blade as your damned Englishmen. Attack, attack, slash and cut, blood and thunder! No finesse, no sense of balance or time. You stay with me, my fine rum-bob, and I'll make you the best fencer among Englishmen; I'll promise you that much. You'll learn to stand on guard, to play the other man like a lunging pout, to watch your chance. Not that I don't believe in attack at the right time. When I go into action, I blow them all in front of me."

I came in twice a day after that. Early each morning, before any of the other patrons put in an appearance, I would exercise on a wooden horse with sharp ears which caught me neatly if I failed to achieve enough height in my vaults. Dirk would see to it that I went over it at least a hundred times. The routine varied, however. The first time I was supposed to arrest all motion on landing, remaining poised on the tips of my toes. The next time I would spring to the right, the third to the left. He kept making the horse higher until finally it took all my strength and agility to get over it. Each morning also he set me to running around the room, twenty, thirty, then forty times; and he would bend over to watch me, shouting, "Faugh!" if I as much as touched a heel to the ground. This was "to put spring into me" and improve my wind. At regular intervals he would make me stand against the wall, touching the stone with every part of my body. "Head, shoulders, buttocks, thigh, shank, and heels," he would intone. "That'll teach ye to stand straight."

Dom Bass, whose name I found was Sebastian de Vagez, never appeared in the mornings. He liked to sleep late. I never did find out when poor Dirk was supposed to sleep; he was always hard at it until they closed at night and it seemed that he was still going when I arrived in the mornings. He did everything—sweeping out the place, cooking the meals, fetching and carrying, and jumping like a jack-in-the-box whenever Dom Bass shouted from his easy chair, "Dirk, you lazy bastard!"

In the evenings I practiced at the target. Nothing else was given me for a full week, but Dirk kept moving the shield back an inch or two until finally it took a full spread to reach my mark. If I failed to recover in perfect order even then, the huge Portugall would roar at me with his favorite metaphor, that I had no more control over my miserable body than a waddling walking mort.

I was happy when they allowed me to attempt some of the preliminary steps to engagement at arms. I was taught the position of the guard, the advance, the retreat, the lunge. I began to think that I had some aptitude after all, for I was quicker on the recovery than Dirk. This became more apparent when we went on to parries, counterparries, single ripostes, and the more elementary feints.

I smiled happily once when I had managed a rather neat invitation in tierce, which is an inside thrust delivered after a parry in quarte. Unfortunately Dom Bass observed my satisfaction. He got to his feet.

"I'll take a hand in this myself," he said, selecting his own pet weapon from the rack on the wall.

I was delighted. At last I was to engage a swordsman of recognized merit. I was so content with the progress I had been making that I felt reasonably sure of giving a good account of myself.

My satisfaction lasted no longer than a moment. Dom Bass attacked at once, and it was as though I stood in the teeth of a great blast from the north, a blistering, raging storm which nearly swept me off my feet, a head of flashing steel on every roaring gust. I had no more chance of defending myself against this breathtaking onslaught than King Canute had to stem the incoming tide. I stood with my sword in front of me like the rankest of beginners, which I was, knowing that he could have penetrated my guard with each stroke. Finally I felt a tug on my wrist and my sword left my hand. It described a slow circle in the air and landed on the floor an ignominious ten feet away.

Dom Bass gave vent to a high-pitched cackle and handed his blade to Dirk to be replaced in the rack. He sank back into his chair and called to Dirk to fetch a light for his pipe.

"That'll teach you not to be so damned sure of yourself," he said. After a few puffs on his pipe, he added: "You were getting too smug. Why, I could take on three like you with my left arm and both eyes shut!"

My days were spent in reading. The weather had turned warm again, and I found it very irksome to stay indoors. Whenever I tired of my books, I would ensconce myself in the front window and watch the busy life of the city below. Once I saw a dismal procession pass our door, an apprentice boy tied on the back of a bony horse, his face to the tail. Armed men marched both front and rear to keep the crowds back. Dame Witchie told me later that he had been caught throwing paving stones through the windows of the Spanish Embassy on the night of the victory celebration, and that he was to be publicly whipped at Charing Cross. What a fine king we had, who would order a subject whipped to placate an arrogant, scheming Spaniard!

Dame Witchie came pattering up the stairs one day, holding her skirts high enough to show that her ankles had remained slim in spite of the heaviness of the rest of her. I had observed on other occasions that she took pride in the fact, but nothing was further from her thoughts now. I could see that she was thoroughly frightened.

The Death had broken out! The return of warm weather had started the trouble again in the slums, and a score of cases had been reported. Her chin twitched as she dilated on the danger. On no account must one of us put a foot outside. If it became necessary to let any fresh air in, we must first stuff our ears with rue and our nostrils with wormwood. Fortunately there was plenty of rosemary in the house; there wasn't anything surer than rosemary, and she would see that I had a full bowl of it to keep under my nose and beside my pillow at night. I had heard too many stories of what happened when the Plague clutched London with its deadly fingers, and the death carts began to rumble through the streets at night, to balk at any precautions. I assured her that I would go nowhere but to the academy next door, and that I would use the rue and wormwood as she prescribed.

I was very much surprised, therefore, when Sir Sigismund Hill paid us a visit that evening. His nostrils were free of wormwood, and he pooh-poohed the protestations of the widow over his rashness. It was nothing, he said. There was always the Death around, and always would be. It could not be helped, and it was as much a part of London as the Tower and Bow Bells. My landlady became a little easier in her mind then and even responded with a faintly coquettish smile when he pinched her cheek in dismissal.

"As a matter of fact, Roger," he said, when we were alone, "this is all most fortunate. It's too late in the season for the Plague to get under way, but the King has gone already to Theobalds, and the whole court is following pell-mell. His Majesty has no stomach for the Death. In truth, he's a great coward, as everyone knows. He can't bear the sight of a bare blade, and he nearly put out the eye of a courtier the other day when he was knighting Millard Lucas. Well, his officers will be too concerned with keeping free of the disease to pay any attention to locating a certain Roger Blease. You'll be perfectly safe as long as this lasts."

He had brought me a letter which had been delivered to him that morning by "a trim little slut with a nice brown eye"—I recognized Elsie Windiyard at once—and he was sure I would find it an antidote to the weariness of spirit I must be feeling after so long a confinement. I was eager to open it at once, but decided to wait until after his departure. I tucked the note into my doublet with as casual an air as I could manage.

"Macherie has not gone with the court. He's staying behind to attend to personal concerns which promise to improve his financial position considerably. Manasseh Griggs came to see me this morning and told me something in strict confidence which made my blood run cold." He paused. "Griggs is the wealthiest man in the Mistery of Feltmakers, and a solid, sober fellow. He helped back Macherie, advancing a large sum to fit out his ship. As your personal safety is concerned in the matter, Roger, I'm going to tell you the story; but you must give me your solemn promise that it won't be repeated."

I nodded, and he went on: "Macherie told Griggs that the King was desperately in need of funds—everyone knows that, of course—and that he, Macherie, was going to suggest that the royal treasury be filled by the simple expedient of levying fines on all who have invested with the Free Rovers."

I could hardly believe my ears. Could any man be guilty of such a breach of faith? Sir Sigismund waited to let the full ignominy of the plan strike home before proceeding: "Every nobleman in England, more or less, and a great many London merchants, have had a finger in the pie. It's a shrewd scheme. Macherie came out with it boldly, according to Griggs; no sly beating about the bush, but a straight statement of his villainous purpose. He let Griggs see the danger in which he stood."

"You mean that he threatened to inform on his own backer?"

"He made it quite clear that such was his intention. He was aware that Griggs hopes to be elected Lord Mayor of London and to become Sir Manasseh. Our worthy feltmaker could accept the terms he offered or see his chance for these high honors vanish. Well, the risk was too great; Griggs gave in, which means that he promised to wipe the transaction off the books. Macherie now owns most of the ship, and no claim will be made for a share of the very handsome profits. The man is absolutely without honor!"

"Will he stop at that?"

Sir Sigismund shook his head in gloomy denial. "You can judge for yourself. This morning he paid a visit to Sir Bartlemy Ladland. I'm having him followed, and the report I received was that he stayed a matter of two hours. It was given out later that Sir Bartlemy was ill and had taken to his bed."

"You think, then, that he'll go the rounds?"

"It looks like it. Sir Bartlemy won't be the only other victim. Macherie has his chance to make himself a wealthy man, and he'll take advantage of it without a doubt."

My sense of guilt over the episode at Calais had been growing with each word said, but my companion did not agree when I pointed out that my lack of care was responsible for the situation. "The papers he stole have been useful to him in getting his own pardon, but that's all. You can be sure of this: all the time he was with the Free Rovers, the rogue kept his long ears open. I'll warrant he found out the names of every man who had invested with his fellow captains. He had this in mind from the first. I'm quite sure of that."

"What can be done?"

"Nothing at all at this stage." He regarded me with a serious frown. "I hope you realize that this makes it all the more necessary for you to keep under cover. If they get their hands on you, they'll squeeze out of you everything you know. Perhaps more than you know; the Iron Maiden is a persuasive questioner. No more visits to Denmark House, if you please. It was a bold stroke, I grant you. No one talked of anything else for days." The severity of his expression relaxed. "You did us a lot of good that time, Roger. But it won't bear repeating. There's too much at stake now."

He got to his feet and slipped his cloak over his shoulders. "There have been no letters from Ward," he said. "I wish we had some word. Not a day passes that I don't think about our poor Cristina."

Not an hour passed that I did not think of her and hope that she had been rescued. I begged him to let me know instantly when he received any reports from the south. He promised, and on his way to the door he paused to warn me against the coddling of Dame Witchie.

"She's a fine woman, and it wasn't so long ago that she was considered the best-looking burgher's wife in London. But she gets very jumbly, and she'll salt you down in mithraditum and grease you with wormwood if you give her the chance."

Katie's letter was long and chatty and so fearfully and wonderfully original in point of spelling that it took me a long time to master its contents.

There had been, she informed me, a great disagreement between His Majesty and the Queen over my visit. The King had come to Denmark House, looking most stern and forbidding, and had rated his spouse roundly. Queen Anne had shown her usual spirit and had refused to accept his chiding. She had said that, if His King's Grace thought she would refuse to hear a stout tale of adventure told by a "pursable yung pirut," he misunderstood her character completely. The argument had been a long and stormy one, and all the ladies of the court had enjoyed it.

Still, the King was very angry, and I had better stay in hiding wherever I was, much as she would like to see me again. She would not have taken the risk of writing me except that she knew I ought to be warned of my great danger.

She then proceeded to deal with more personal matters. I had been better dressed than she had ever seen me. Brown was my color, and I ought to wear it always. I must have found a good tailor, for all the ladies had remarked on how well my hose had fitted. What present had I brought her? She knew she would have to wait, but she was consumed with curiosity about it. One of the other maids of honor was down with the measles, but no one was wasting any sympathy on her. She, Katie, had been to Ann Turner's shop on Oldcastle Street. The Mistress of the Sweet Coffers had gone with her. They had both worn dark-blue bongraces and velvet masks of a lighter blue, and they had found the shop fascinating. The brazen baggage was very pretty, and it was no wonder all the men of the court went there to buy presents for their wives—and other ladies. She had bought some fine silk and a string of beads that Mistress Ann said had come from the Americas. Did I know that love philters could be bought which would cause any man to fall into the deepest state of love?

Dere Rogger [the letter concluded], you half seldome ben out of my minde sith I hearde you speke up so welle and so boldlie. Her Majestie lerned that we come frum the same towne and she sed I must be the

Inglish girle you loved but I sed Noe. She did not belief me and she smiles nowinglie everie time she sees me. It is pleasunt to share a secrut with the Queene of Ingland.

33

EARLY THE NEXT MORNING I received a note from Sir Sigismund which raised my spirits considerably. Macherie had not gone with the court to Theobalds, having been stricken with some malady; not the Death, unfortunately, but something sufficiently serious to keep him on his back for a time. The unpleasant circumstances we had been discussing would, therefore, progress no further until the amiable knight was on his feet again.

I was delighted with the news and decided to take advantage of it in spite of Sir Sigismund's warning. I was determined to see Chirp Bird, it having occurred to me that the new Upright Man was involved in this as much as we were. He might be in a position to put pressure on Macherie. At any rate, he should know what was happening; and I had thought of a way of seeing him without incurring the danger of a visit to Alsatia.

I asked Dame Witchie for directions to Oldcastle Street. It was evident at once that she disapproved of my interest in that neighborhood. "It's but two squares away, more's the pity," she said. "I'm surprised at you for asking, Master Strange; and disappointed, I must say. It's not a proper street at all. It has shops for the sale of gauds and even worse things, charms and spells and blackest witchcraft. There are even places where ladies, so called—" She checked herself hastily and concluded by saying that it was a wicked place and that no young gentleman could be seen there and retain his self-respect.

To placate her, I said that I had no purpose beyond a visit to the fencing school, and that I would take every precaution. I found the place deserted and Dom Bass in a disgruntled mood in consequence. "The timid bantlings!" he said. "The peery-gutted mammets! A lousy beggar dies of the Spanish-pox and everyone says it must be the Death. So all my fine gentlemen run to the country!"

When I said that I was glad of it because he could now give me all of his time, he scowled and asked if I could make it worth his while. He demanded a *portague* each fortnight, and I agreed, although it was a heavy fee, nearly four pounds in English money. With that settled, and the equivalent of the first *portague* jingling in his pocket, he condescended to give me a lesson himself. I must have handled myself reasonably well, for he grumbled very little and even declared at the end that I was coming along; that I might become expert enough in time, for an Englishman.

It was late in the afternoon when I set out to find my way to Oldcastle Street. I encountered very few people. The fear of the Plague had become general, apparently; for those I met were scurrying along with furtive haste and all of them gave me a wide berth. For a penny in hand, a ragged urchin escorted me to the street and identified the house for me. It was quite tiny and wedged in between two of much greater height.

It was Ann Turner herself who answered my rap. Her eyes opened wide when she recognized me, and she took me by the wrist and almost dragged me across the threshold without opening the door any wider.

"Roger!" she said. "You shouldn't be out on the streets in daylight. Did anyone see you?"

"No one recognized me, at any rate."

We were standing in a narrow hall. She took my arm and squeezed it tightly. "I'm glad to see you, even if you have become a dangerous character. But I don't want them to catch you. If you ever do me the honor of another visit, you must make it at night."

We entered a large room which managed to be cheerful and bright in spite of the small share of daylight permitted by its one window. This was due to the bright yellow of its walls and ceiling and the white tile of the fireplace. It was filled with articles of clothing, many of an embarrassingly intimate nature, hanging on frames or displayed under sheets of glass. Ann waved her hand lightly about the room.

"I'm doing quite well," she said. "So well that I'm proud to have you see."

I was amazed at the costliness of everything displayed there. I saw handsome ruffs with loops of pearls on the edges; superb cloaks of plush ("Fifty pounds for that one, my Roger," she said, when my eye lighted on one very fine specimen); ruffled buntlings; gloves embroidered in gold thread; dainty shoes with the tops turned back to show the fineness of the satin linings. It was clear her customers were people of wealth.

"All the ladies of the court come to me." She had kept hold of my arm, and now she twined her fingers in mine. "Fanny Howard runs in and out all the time. She's the Countess of Essex, you know; though I doubt if my Lord of Essex is sure of it yet. Oh, I'm quite the rage. It's Mistress Ann this and Mistress Ann that. Some of the gentlemen visit me too, and I always ask them higher prices." She tilted her head back to look up at me. "Katie Ladland has been here. She's prettier than ever, I thought; but I don't need to tell *you* that. She talked of you and John Ward, but I didn't say I knew either of you."

"I saw Katie one night at court."

"I heard all about it. You were very brave to do it, Roger. I was proud of you." She came right back to her own concerns. "Would you like to know how I managed to get such a fine trade? I wrote to Fanny Howard and said I wanted to show her some things I had for sale. When I went to see her I was wearing a yellow ruff. You see, I've found a starch which makes linen yellow, and I don't mind saying it's *very* effective. She noticed it at once, and I explained how it was done. Nothing would suit her but she must know the recipe, and I agreed to show her laundress. When the laundress came, the mistress was with her, as I had expected she would be. She fell in love with my shop, oh-ing, and ah-ing about everything I had. I gave her some things, so of course she came back. Soon all the ladies were coming too. It was lucky for me, wasn't it?"

"It was very clever of you, I think."

"Well, I did plan everything. Now I must show you the rest. You seem a little embarrassed at all these intimate little things. My other stocks won't bother you, I promise."

The apartment to which we repaired was quite different from the bright front room. It had no windows and was lighted by a cluster of candles in one corner. The walls were covered with heavy hangings of black velvet, and the only articles of furniture were a small table and two chairs. The table had a sable drape which swept the floor. When my eyes became accustomed to the gloom, I noticed that this cover as well as the wall hangings were marked with curious insignia. The place smacked of magic. Temperance Handy had always scoffed at such things, but I am free to confess that I did not feel entirely comfortable.

"You look quite impressed." She indulged in a giggle. "It's good, isn't it? But it's all for effect. I bring only my very special patrons here, and it never fails to put them in the right mood. I went to see a very famous magician named Simon Forman. Have you heard of him? I copied some of his things. That parchment on the wall is a very powerful charm; or so he said. And look at that black scarf with all the white crosses. It means something quite sinister. All my patrons are impressed when they look at it. I have phials and philters and curious little bottles full of liquids in strange colors. Do you need anything of the kind, good sir? A charm to create the proper degree of passion in the heart of—shall we say, Katie Ladland?"

"No thanks," I answered hastily.

"Are you so sure of yourself, then? As a matter of fact, Roger, you're quite right. My charms wouldn't advance your cause, if you wanted it advanced. I sell my ladies and gentlemen nothing more potent than scented water with a little *hickery-pickery* to give it a taste. But don't ever tell. I don't want my trade spoiled."

She left the room and returned with two goblets filled with an amber-colored wine. "This at any rate is real, and I can recommend it as likely to have more effect on the senses than my silly charms," she said, seating herself in one chair and motioning me to the other. I had been getting nothing but good small beer at Dame Witchie's, and so I found the wine most agreeable. Ann sipped hers and smiled at me over the top of the goblet. She had a curious way of smiling, crinkling up her brows as though prepared to frown instead; but the effect was pleasing.

"I've often thought it would be pleasant to share a glass of wine with Roger Blease," she said. "Perhaps other things too. Now, don't be alarmed. I'm actually very well behaved. I'm most prim and proper with my grand ladies and gentlemen. But now that you *have* paid me a visit, I want to make the most of it."

"Perhaps I shouldn't have come. It might get you in trouble if it became known I'd been here."

She put down her goblet. "I'm not afraid of that. I'm glad to have you at any price; and I'm going to feel badly if you don't come again. I can't tell you how proud I am of you—and of John too. The night we heard of the victory, I wanted to go out on the streets with a torch and shout myself hoarse." She filled my glass, giving me a pat on the arm as she handed it back. "Because I've been married, I'm sure you think I'm much older than you are. It's just under a year, really. You must grow a beard now, Roger. I've a very handsome gold comb out there that I've been hoping to sell to some rich dandy. I'll give it to you when you have a nice little black beard curling just under your chin."

Her hands were always busy, gesturing lightly, fluttering over her goblet, or patting me on the hand. "Roger," she said, "this is a great occasion for me. I always wanted to know nice people at home, but they never cared to know me. You represented everything I wanted then. Did you know I used to run to the window to watch you go down the street? Well, I did." She sighed. "I didn't have a very good time, and I'm afraid I was very foolish. I'm trying to make my life over now, and that's the reason for all this. I'm going to make as much money as I can here so that I can live afterward as I've always wanted to. Not in London, of course, nor at home either. I'll go some place where I'm not known and where I can pretend I'm a lady. Perhaps they won't find me out."

"I always liked you, Ann."

"I thought you did." She sighed again. "Others did too, and they weren't as backward as you. Do you know how important that beast of a Chirp Bird has become?"

"I hear he's the new ruler of Alsatia. King Nicholas the First. He'll end up on the gallows."

She shuddered. "He comes here all the time. I have to make payments to him. If I sold nothing but silks to the ladies and fucus for their faces, I wouldn't have to deal with him. But having this"—she waved her hand to indicate the macabre trappings of the room—"puts me in a class with the soothsayers and magicians, and I have to pay for protection. It's called 'paying the pill.' I hate everything about it—but mostly I hate Chirp Bird. He makes it clear he wants payment in a different coinage—a kind that real ladies wouldn't mention." She made a wry face. "He will never collect from me that way. I would die first. I can't tell you how much I fear and hate him. Some day, I'm sure, he's going to do me a great injury."

"I've heard about paying the pill," I said. "There's another term that goes with it that you must know, 'fencing-cove.' Well, Chirp is our fencing-cove, and I have dealings with him because of that. I should have seen him before this, but I haven't dared show my face on the streets. It's too dangerous for me to go to Alsatia. I would be in his power there, and he wouldn't hesitate to turn me over. He could get a good price for me; his own immunity, perhaps."

She showed real concern at once. "You must never trust him, Roger. Why couldn't you meet him here? It would be the safest way."

I had hoped she would suggest this. "Are you sure you wouldn't mind? I don't want to involve you in my troubles."

"How could we arrange it?"

"I'm living a few squares away. Could you send me word when he arrives?"

"Of course." She got up and removed my empty goblet, her sleeve brushing across my cheek. She was using a most unusual perfume; not penetrating and sweet, but subtle and provocative and suggestive of the East. "Does it occur to you, however, that there's another way? You could come here often enough to be sure of seeing him when he pays his next visit. No, I'm a designing woman, Roger, so I know you would prefer it the other way. Don't think you must dissemble. I can read what you've been thinking. But I'm not as bad as I make myself out to be. I want people to believe I know Father Forman's secrets. Spells and charms and incantations, even poisons. I can talk mysteriously about white arsenics and powder of diamonds and all other kinds of mystic drafts. It's good for my trade. But, Roger, I don't know a thing about it, not a thing. I don't believe in it at all, and that's the solemn truth." She drew her brows together again in that characteristic half-frown, half-smile. "I want you to tell the truth now. Will you come back only because you want to meet Chirp Bird?"

"Of course not."

"I know how you feel about Katie Ladland; or how you did. But I don't care; I'll take what I can get. You must have a great deal of time on your hands. Spare me a little of it. It would be perfectly safe to come here after dark."

As we walked toward the front rooms, arms linked tightly (Ann saw to that), she drew aside the hangings near the door and revealed a row of shelves covered with curious objects. I could not identify any of them, although it was clear they belonged to the practice of white magic in which my companion was dabbling. She picked up something with her free hand and held it up for my inspection. It was an ivory cube, inscribed in a strange script.

"The dread name!" she said in a deep whisper. Then she laughed. "It's all very silly, Roger. Father Forman is a clever old man, but he has no more power to do good or evil than my stupid maid Betsy."

I had heard strange stories of Simon Forman, and I was not at all sure she was right. Certainly Merlin and Michael Scott, and perhaps Roger Bacon, had possessed mysterious powers. I had read about the greatest magician of them all, Simon Magus, and the amazing things he had done at Samaria in the days of Christ.

"I'll send Betsy to you when the great man of Alsatia arrives next. It won't be long, my most honorable young friend."

"My name now is Richard Strange," I reminded her.

"Richard Strange. It suits you rather well. If you continue to give all your devotion to one lady, one you can't see, moreover, you're indeed well named. Constancy of that kind is a strange thing nowadays. Well, good-by, Richard Strange. I may work some magic on you before you come again." Her brows drew together without any suggestion of a smile. "When I think of Chirp Bird, I wish there was such a thing as black magic. I would practice some of it on him!"

34

MY SUMMONS CAME LATE in the afternoon of the second day. Dame Witchie handed a note to me, her face acid with disapproval, reproof in the rustle of her green and black kirtle. "A girl brought it," she said. "A forward, smirking minx. I'm wondering what kind of company you've been getting into, Master Strange."

"I've got to go out," I said, after reading the note hurriedly. Her mouth drew into such a stubborn line that I hastened to add: "It's a very important matter in which Sir Sigismund Hill is concerned. I'll return as soon as possible."

Ann Turner greeted me again at the door of the Oldcastle Street house. She was dressed in braided black with artificial yellow flowers at the point of her wide collar. She smiled at me, but I noticed that her cheeks had an unusually high color, and that her hand trembled as she touched mine.

"He's here, the beast!" she whispered. Then she said in normal tones: "This is indeed a surprise. Come in. There's an old friend of yours here."

Chirp was straddling the one chair in the bright showroom, looking like a large and ugly spider in the petals of a yellow rose. He was wearing his hat, a much taller beaver than mine, with a jeweled buckle and a cascade of rich plumes on one side. He scowled when he saw me.

"Well, the returned hero!" he exclaimed. His face had broadened since I had last seen him, and even his skimpy legs had a suggestion of bloat about them. "'Od's bowels, where have you been? I've had my whole sacklaw ging on the look for you."

"Is it necessary to explain that I've been in hiding? This is a lucky chance, Chirp. I've wanted to see you."

"You knew where to find me." He threw out his chest as he said it.

"Indeed yes!" exclaimed Ann. "Everyone should know where to find Chirp Bird. The great Chirp Bird!"

"The Upright Man of Alsatia," I added.

"Of London!" His eyes devoured mine with a savage triumph. "Have you heard what happened to Barnaby Cloud?"

The name did not mean anything to me at first. Then I remembered Barnaby Cloud as the unpleasant individual who had been manhandled at the Draw the Pudding. He was the Upright Man of Wapping, and therefore the rival of Alsatia.

Chirp grinned at us slyly. "He can't be found. Two nights ago he had his late bite as usual. A conger eel in oil and a slice of cold beef on the side. He went out for some air, a scrippet on each side of him. They didn't come back. None of them." He snapped his fingers. "They vanished, just like that. Odd, wasn't it?"

"Very odd," I said.

There was a pause. "With Barnaby gone, I'll soon make myself the Upright Man of all London," declared Chirp. He crossed one leg over the other and regarded Ann with a gloating look. "I'll have this city in my fambles then. I'll have as much power as the King himself. What do ye think of that, Ann?"

We had been standing in front of him, as he was occupying the only chair in the room. Ann looked at me sideways as though to ask: Must we put up with him? Then she said: "What do I think about it? I think it's quite remarkable how important all of us have become. John and Roger and Chirp and Ann; and all from the one small town."

"And Joralemon Snode," I said. "We mustn't forget Jore."

"Nor Katie Ladland," said Chirp. "Maid of Honor to the Queen. That's something. We mustn't forget Katie." He spoke with a snicker, but there was no hint of amusement in his eyes. They were watchful and unfriendly. I noticed that he had ear muffs attached to his hat and a handkerchief knotted above his ruff; he had used them apparently to keep out the plaguy air of the streets.

"Katie's out of your reach now, my proud cock robin," he said. "Are you turning to Ann for consolation? Well, I'm giving you warning: I'll not have you cloy Ann away from me." He drew an enormous pipe from the leather pouch at his belt and filled it with tobacco, spilling careless shreds of it on the yellow carpet. "A light!" he demanded.

Ann glared. Nevertheless she walked slowly across the room to the small white fireplace in one corner. There was no fire in it, but the ashes were piled high at one side. I followed her and knelt down to brush the ash away.

"The filthy beast!" she whispered.

The juniper fire was glowing under the ashes. I lighted a spill from the smoldering wood and then packed the ashes back again; with proper care, a fire could be kept alive thus for weeks. Ann took the blazing spill from me and carried it to the Upright Man. He started the tobacco burning, puffing clouds of smoke from his mouth and his splayed nostrils with gusty enjoyment. It was apparent from the odor that he had soaked the stuff in sacklees, a custom that all good smokers condemned. The charred spill dropped to the floor.

"Please!" exclaimed Ann tartly. "You'll ruin the carpet."

"What of it? I'll buy you a dozen carpets. You know how generous I'd like to be where you're concerned, my sweet Ann."

She flashed him an angry look and left the room. Chirp squared around in his chair at once. His manner changed; the half-smirk he had worn while Ann was with us vanished completely.

"Now then, where have you been?" he demanded. "Why haven't you come to see me? I'm beginning to wonder. Have you been coming here a lot? Trying your fine gentleman wiles on Ann?"

"Where I've been is no concern of yours," I retorted. "We've plenty of matters to settle between us, so let's take advantage of this chance and go into them now. We've no time to waste."

"Big talk for a green country cank," he said. His pale, lashless eyes studied me with open dislike. "Waste no more time, eh? I'm getting surer *you* haven't been wasting any time. If I find I'm right—well, we'll settle that between us later. Now you'll tell me one thing: where's your stalling ken?"

"That's the one thing I won't tell you. I don't trust you, Chirp. You'd think nothing of turning me over if it suited your purpose."

He grinned savagely. "That's what you think, is it? Perhaps you're right, my flash gentry-cove. Some day I may have the pleasure of looking in at you through the visitor's door at the Clink. I'd like to see you strapped up in Little Ease."

"What makes you think you'd be on the right side of the bars in that case?"

He indulged in another mirthless grin but made no rejoinder. Without further altercation we settled down to the various matters of business between us, which had to do for the most part with the disposal of the plunder from the *Santa Caterina*. A great deal of it had reached England: the finer tapestries, the paintings, the armor, the jewelry, even the gold crucifixes, for which there was a profitable clandestine demand. Very little money had been received from Alsatia from the sale.

"Do you expect looby miracles from me?" he demanded. "The King's dipped his hand into every well-filled kick in the country. I'll sell your shag-bag loot when things get better."

"You've already sold everything," I said. "We happen to know all about it. Why hasn't our full percentage been paid over?"

"So, you think I've been cloying from you." He took his pipe out of his mouth and thrust his head forward at a belligerent angle. "What if I say you're right? What is there you can do, my gentle cock robin?"

"You've no idea how much valuable stuff was taken in after the capture of the *Santa Caterina*," I said. "We took a great fortune off *La Solderina* alone. The best of it is being held at Marseilles. It will be disposed of there if it becomes evident that we can't trust our agents in this country. You must make up your mind quickly. If you don't make a full accounting for the first lot, you'll have no chance at the greatest store of stuff ever thrown on the market. Think it over, Chirp. It doesn't matter to us one way or the other."

Indecision was written all over his greedy face. He had to decide between returning what was due us on the first lot and losing a future profit on all the rest. It was a difficult choice for him to reach, and I could see he was suffering from the effort to make up his mind. Finally he said in a grumbling voice, "I'll think it over." I knew then that he would give in, but that he did not want me to have the satisfaction of hearing him say so.

I changed the subject at once. His face went the color of dissolving tallow when I spoke of the danger we might all be in if Macherie told everything he knew. "That's why I haven't been to see you," I said. "I was afraid you might use me to buy your own immunity."

"My immunity!" He wet his lips with a nervous tongue. "What do you mean by that? What have I got to do with it?"

"That ought to be plain enough. The gentlemen and the rich merchants would get off with fines, but there would be need for a sharper example. Some of the little fellows would be hanged. The agents and the go-betweens probably; certainly the fencing-coves."

Suspicion struggled with fear in his eyes. "Why are you telling me this?" he demanded.

"It's only fair to warn you of the danger, but I've a selfish purpose as well. I know that I'd get short shrift myself, and I want to make sure that you realize the full risk there would be in turning me over to them. They might make you promises, Chirp, but they would hang you in the end. If they needed an excuse, they could look into the murders of Robin Humpery and Barnaby Cloud. There's only one thing for you to do: lie low for the time being; say nothing and do nothing to attract attention to yourself. If I hang, there will be a rope ready for you also."

He was beginning to shiver. "It's cold here," he muttered. Then he bawled out in sudden anger: "A fire, in God's name! This place is like a tomb."

The maid answered his demand, carrying in an armful of wood. She used the juniper fire to light it and then threw in a little nard. A pleasant odor filled the room.

Ann returned and looked at us curiously. "What's the matter, Chirp?" she asked. "Have you and Roger been quarreling?"

I took it on myself to answer. "We've been getting along famously. In fact, I think we've come to a complete understanding on several important points. Chirp is leaving now."

He got to his feet in an almost humble mood and proceeded to knot the handkerchief over his mouth. He hardly looked at her as he went out the door.

"Well! What did you do to our great man?"

"I frightened him with a picture of what might happen to him under certain circumstances. I'm inclined to think he'll leave me alone now."

"I've never seen him like this before. He even looked pale."

She insisted that I take the one chair and then perched herself on the arm. "I'm glad he's gone," she said. "He makes me feel creepy. He must have been terribly frightened to go away and leave you here."

"He has a purpose in that. By going first, he can have a watch set on me. There will be one of his men outside when I leave with orders to trail me home. Chirp's in a chastened mood, but he'll feel safer if he knows where he can put his hands on me."

She looked down at me anxiously. "Won't that put you in great danger?"

"No. I'll manage to give his man the slip."

This did not reassure her. "Supposing you don't?"

"I'll have to chance that."

"Roger," she said, "I won't let you go. The man may have orders to kill you. I know Chirp Bird. It's too dangerous to leave now."

"He'll have his orders to hang around until I do. There will be less danger in leaving now than if I wait until it's dark."

"Then you mustn't leave at all. I'll keep you here until you can go safely. I don't care how long it takes." Her hand had been resting lightly on my shoulder. It tightened perceptibly.

I hurried to point out the inadvisability of a long stay. "Chirp is jealous enough as it is. Do you want to stir him up further? No, it won't do. I'm not going to endanger you, Ann. There's no telling what he might do to you."

"I don't care."

"But I do. I didn't come here to cause you trouble like this. Think what it might do to your reputation."

"I don't care what happens to my reputation." She laughed. "I don't care at all. I'm willing to have it smashed into a million pieces. And what do you think of that, Roger Blease?"

"I think it would ruin your trade. You have to be very careful."

"It might help my trade. But, either way, I'm not concerned about it. Let people talk as much as they like."

I was beginning to flounder. "Come, Ann. It's nice of you to be concerned about me this way. But we've got to be sensible. I'm not afraid of this fellow outside. I'm sure I can give him the slip."

"Must we be sensible?"

"Yes. The sooner I get away, the safer I'll be, now that Chirp knows I'm here."

"But, Roger, I'm *sure* Chirp has given orders to have you killed. You threatened him, didn't you? The streets are so narrow here. You'll be stabbed in the back before you get a square away. I know it; and I won't let you take the risk."

"But, Ann, I can't stay here indefinitely." I tried to speak in a lighter tone. "Do you want a permanent lodger? Your house is very small, too small to hide away anyone as big as I am. Think of the inconvenience of it for you."

She said softly: "It would be no inconvenience at all to keep you here. None at all, my Roger. It's true that my house is small but"— she began to run her cheek up and down against the edge of my ruff —"but my bed isn't."

I must have shown how startled I was, for after a moment she laughed again. "This is the very first time anyone has said that to you."

"No, not exactly."

"I'm sure it is. And you didn't like it, did you?"

I did not know what to say. I would have been less than human if I had not realized how tempting she was. She was so close that I could feel the softness of her shoulder and arm. The strange perfume she used was having an exciting effect on me. While I was struggling for words, she gave my shoulder a pat and slipped down from the arm of the chair.

"Don't look so worried, my dear," she said lightly. "I didn't mean it, of course. I like to make you blush. It's so rare to find a man today who can. Your face went positively scarlet, Roger. You poor innocent!"

The situation was solved by the sound of a carriage stopping in the street and a loud rapping at the door. Ann went to the window and peered through a corner of the curtain. She turned back and frowned.

"It's Fanny Howard," she said. "I thought she had gone with the court. It must be something important to bring her back. I'll have to see her at once. It's a great nuisance, but the lovely Fanny is my chief sponsor." She ran back and laid an urgent hand on my arm. Her face was flushed. "And now you'll go and you won't come back. I know you, Roger. I may never see you again."

"I'll go. I intended to from the first. But I'll see you again after all these troubles blow over."

"No." She shook her head. "You won't come back. Not when you've thought it over. You're a regular Puritan at heart."

We faced each other silently for a moment. "What a silly sense of humor I have," she said. "I must cure myself of it. Good-by, Roger."

The back door of the house opened on an alleyway. It was getting quite dark already. I glanced carefully in both directions before venturing out; no one was in sight. I had reached the street into which it led and was congratulating myself on having eluded the watcher when I noticed a tall man emerge from the doorway of a corner house. He sauntered along in the direction I was taking.

I quickened my pace, keeping a watchful eye over my shoulder. He fell back a little. Perhaps his presence was a coincidence after all. I turned down another street, going in the opposite direction from Dame Witchie's house. I walked with considerable briskness and did not look back for several minutes. When I ventured another glance, the tall man was still in sight. He was striking as vigorous a stride as my own.

I knew now it was not a coincidence. There were few people out, and I confess that I did not like the look of things. Ann might be right about Chirp's intentions. It was not a pleasant speculation, and my hand sought the dagger at my belt. I was glad of the lessons I had been taking in self-defense.

When the streets I chose were empty, the man fell back, but he shortened the distance between us when there were people to pass. He was taking no chance on losing sight of me. I wondered what I could do to elude him. I did not dare enter any of the taverns we passed. Once in a particularly narrow thoroughfare I heard a voice from above intone the customary word of warning, "Ware, below!" and deliberately hurried my steps so that my pursuer had to increase his gait also. I was delighted to see that he arrived just in time to receive the full benefit of the pail of slops emptied from above. He shook himself with an oath and came on.

A wind had sprung up. It whistled through the streets, carrying the first leaves of autumn with it. I don't know where they came from— there were no trees in sight; but they whirled by me like swifts on a warm summer night, twisting and swooping and vanishing over the tops of houses and in the darkness of lanes and enclosures. The sound added to my sense of fear. It was the right kind of night for violence.

My first chance to give him the slip came when I saw that people had gathered at an intersection to watch a street show. A torch flared on the top of a pole which had been set up beside a low platform. A saltimbanco was going through his tricks and giving a poor performance. I wedged into the crowd and watched him flutter an English flag in front of him, causing it to change suddenly into the red and yellow bars of Spain. The spectators did not respond to this as they should, and the juggler's work became more limp and discouraged as a result. He produced a rabbit from his hat, the commonest trick of all, then kept three knives in the air, finally adding a tin maser bowl for good measure.

I realized that the chance to escape had been thrown my way. The torch would have to be extinguished first, so I let myself sag against the back of the onlooker standing directly in front of me, emitting a groan at the same time. I could feel him cringe away from me while his voice gave vent to a startled cry, "The Death!" The cry was taken up instantaneously. People began to rush about blindly, crashing into each other and shouting in panic. I had calculated the distance carefully, and with one bound I reached the side of the stage. I tore up the pole and doused out the light on the ground. The confusion became worse, and a splintering sound told me that the platform had been upset. I took sanctuary in the porch of a house well in the rear where there was plenty of shadow in which to hide.

In a few minutes the turmoil had subsided completely, and the street had emptied. I looked out cautiously. Becoming sure that my man had gone on with the rest, I was preparing to make my way back along the route by which I had come when a disturbing sound reached me. It came, I decided, from the juggler, who was sitting among the ruins of his platform and his few poor bits of magic property.

He was crying, I found; a slow, hopeless show of grief over his misfortune; his head sunk between his shoulders and his body heaving with each sob. I knew that I should be on my way, but I also knew myself as the instrument of his bad luck. I stopped beside him.

"How much is your loss?" I asked.

He did not bother to look up. "I'm done for," he muttered. "I may as well go and throw myself in the river. I'll starve if I don't."

"Come, now. It can't be as bad as that."

He said with sudden passion: "I've taken in five sice in two days! Can I get together another outfit with that? It's all I've got. And Ralph Roister-Doister was killed."

"Who?"

"My rabbit. The best little fellow I've ever had. I was training him. He could sit up on his haunches and beg, and wiggle his ears when I told him to. He'd have been a draw for me in time, a real win-pincher." He gulped miserably. "They trampled on him, my poor little Ralph. His back was broken."

I handed him a sovereign. He took it mechanically and then, with a gasp of surprise, squinted down at it to make sure his sense of touch had not played him a trick. He exclaimed with rapture: "An Old Harry! St. Simon and the Turk, a real Old Harry!"

"Will it make up your loss?"

He licked one hand and slapped it down smartly on the palm of the other where the coin was cupped. "I'm set up again!" he cried. "Young gentleman, do you know how long it would take me to save a whole pound from the earnings of a miserable trade like mine? A lifetime, sir; and I mightn't get to do it then. Some days I don't take in more than I've done today, a few sice. I carry my traps on my back, and half the time when I reach a new town the harman-becks make me move on. Save? It can't be done! I never expected to see the day when I'd have an Old Harry in my hand, and know it was all clear and my own."

"Don't drink it up, then."

"God, sir, I won't buy as much as a mug of hum-cap. I'll get myself new props, that's what I'll do with it. I'll learn the bagonet trick and the 'vanishing hodman.' Perhaps even the 'seven cackling cheats.' I may get off the high-pad, after all." He paused, and some of the enthusiasm oozed out of his voice. "If only they hadn't killed Ralph Roister-Doister!"

"Good luck," I said, starting on my way.

35

THE RIGOROUS TRAINING which I had been through under the scornful eye and blistering tongue of Dom Bass was having its effect. I had never felt better in my life. There was a new spring to my step, and my arms were hard and strong. My doublet pinched me over the shoulders, and I no longer had to adjust the points to make my hose fit me snugly. I was growing a beard, a thin stubble of black under my chin. It was a feeble start, I am afraid, although Dame Witchie praised it every morning when she brought up my breakfast. Manhood and a beard were synonymous terms with her.

The morning after my encounter with Chirp Bird, I was honored by a special lesson from Dom Bass himself. He stripped himself to the waist, exposing a mountainous and hairy stomach; and the attack he unleashed was as furious as on the first occasion when we crossed steel. I found to my delight that I could defend myself now against his devastating onslaught. Remembering the advice which he had barked at me so often from his comfortable chair on the side, I kept my sword well forward, refusing to be trapped into side parries or lunges and avoiding contact with his devious blade as much as possible.

"Not bad, not bad," he said once, puffing a little from his exertions. "Keep your point down, Mooncalf! It must be lower than your hand.

Always advance on a steady guard. Work straight ahead. Glide along my blade, but keep your own free. Give me one little opening, and I'll poach you. One careless second, and I'll gut you like a wriggling pout! And watch my eye, you stupid cank, watch my eye!"

He began to show me a variation of the flanconnade, a favorite stroke of his own. It consisted of seizing forcibly the feeble of your opponent's blade, then dropping the point under his wrist and thrusting home suddenly and savagely with the movement of the octave. For the first time I was able to execute it, and I even succeeded in making him skip backward with the agility which so amazed me in a man of his gargantuan bulk.

"Dom Bass," I said, disengaging and stepping a pace to the rear, "will you teach me that favorite trick of yours?"

I referred to his ability to disarm me any time he cared to. The request seemed to stagger him. He looked at me blankly for a moment and then indulged in one of his short angry laughs.

"No one in the world knows that one but me," he said. "I worked it out myself. I've never told anyone how to do it, not even Dirk. Why, Master Cock Robin, should I tell you how it's done?"

"I told you at the start," I answered, "that some day I might have to fight a duel. I think it will be soon now. The man I'm going to fight is older and stronger than I am, and I hear he's a remarkably good swordsman."

"The way to stay alive," declared Dom Bass, "is not to fight anyone better than yourself. All I can give you is advice; and that's it."

"But I have to fight him. And it's terribly important for me to win, Dom Bass. He was with John Ward, but now he's gone over to the other side. Don Gondomar should pay him a pension because he's proving himself the most active help to Spanish policy."

I introduced this reference to Spain deliberately because the Portuguese hate that country even more than the English do. He pondered the point, frowning at me dubiously.

"What do you know about John Ward?" he demanded.

"That," I said, "is my secret."

He began to laugh. "And I never guessed it. You mealy-mouthed young sprat, I believe you're this elusive boy pirate they've been looking for. Well, Roger Blease, if that's who you are, I'll have to consider your request after all. This puts a different face on it." His laugh rose to a high-pitched cackle. "You've given them the slip nicely. But who would take you for a pirate, you bread-and-butter bantling?"

"You're right. I'm Roger Blease."

"And you're a gentleman," he said. "That ought to mean your word is worth something. Will you swear to keep it to yourself? To use it only when you need it; to save your own life or to give this Spanish agent the finishing stroke?" He glowered at me. "Can I depend on you? I would cut your miserable throat from ear to ear if you ever let anyone else know how it's done!"

I assured him earnestly that he could depend on my discretion. He raised one hand in a gesture of reluctant consent and ordered me sharply to set myself on guard. For a brisk half-hour we went through the motions. I had to catch him off balance; that was the first essential and, with so adroit a master of the game, it was no simple task. The opportunity created, it was a matter of a quick stroke to drive his blade downward, then an equally fast reversal of the wrist, a twist with all the strength of the arm and—there it was! I had to try it fifty times before I did everything exactly right and has the intense satisfaction of seeing a flash above my head as his sword spiraled upward.

"Remember this," he said, recovering his blade in a bad humor, for it went against the grain with him to be caught, even though it was by a master stroke he had himself invented. "His arm must stiffen before it's safe to try it. Wait for it. The stiffness will show if he gets the least bit off balance. I can make the chance myself; you'll have to wait for it."

I returned to my room in a jubilant frame of mind. I felt as safe as though a master magician had put the secret of life and death in my keeping. If the chance came to fight Macherie, I should be equal to it. I was sure that I had enough skill to stand up to him and keep him in play until the golden moment showed itself. Stevecorn was standing in the back hall, and I rumpled up his hair as I passed. I called a cheerful good morning to Dame Witchie, who was peering down over the balustrade. She thought I had been drinking, for I could feel her sharp black eyes on my back, vibrant with suspicion, as I climbed the top flight of stairs.

Late in the afternoon, as I drowsed over my books, I heard male voices in the lower hall. Dame Witchie's excitement was evident in the treble note of her responses, so I knew it must be Sir Sigismund Hill. I was greatly surprised, however, to find that he had brought Archie Armstrong with him.

The jester wore a glum look, but he thumped me on the back and said: "Weel, if it isna' the leetle pirutical rum-bob himsel'. The weel-o'-the-wisp that Jamie's men ha' been poorsuing wi' sich seengular lack o' success! The puckfeesting blawer wa' filled the fair ears o' oor ain Queen wi' tales o' bludy fichting! It wur shrewdly done, Maister Pirut."

Sir Sigismund winked at me cautiously. "I suppose you're surprised at having guests, Roger. You need have no fear. Archie is the soul of discretion; and, as it happens, he finds himself at the moment in the same position as a great many other men who allowed themselves to take more than a casual interest in the Free Rovers."

"Ay," muttered the jester. "I'm in a sair pickle."

"In other words," said Sir Sigismund, "he risked a little siller with the other backers of John Ward."

"Verra leetle!" protested Archie in agonized tones. "Verra leetle. Nae mair than a tooken o' ma faith in the long loon."

"And now the King has found out about it. Some ill-wisher filled the royal ears with the story."

"It wur Maicherie. The lee'ing, treacherous dog!"

"I suspect it was. Well, the upshot is that Archie at the moment is under a cloud. His Majesty has banished him from court and has ordered his pension stopped. I hope he'll be able to escape the attentions of Derrick."

This reference to the London hangman had no effect on Archie. He even managed a rather dismal imitation of a grin. "Ye maun hae yer leetle joke, Sir Seegismund," he said. "I'm no afeered o' Derrick. But I'd be in a fair dither if ye told me o' threats to ma purse."

"What did the King say when he banished you into outer darkness?"

Archie grinned again. "Ye've struck it parfectly. It wur lak Jee-hovah thrawing Satan oot frae Paradeese. King Tiddy wur in rare foorm. But, mark ma woords, he'll no be happy wi 'oot Airchie. He canna get along wi 'oot me."

"There's this to be said for His Majesty," pointed out Sir Sigismund. "He heard the news of your rash venture at the wrong time. You had been bearing down hard on him, Archie. Your tongue has a sharp edge; and I'm told you have been pointing out his faults in no friendly way. He heard of your association with John Ward at a moment when his pride had been touched on the raw. But perhaps you would like to hear some details of the fighting. It might take your mind off your troubles."

Archie assented to this and proceeded to shower me with questions. In the role of backer, he was particularly interested in the rewards of our victory. Had there been much siller in the hold of *La Solderina*? Had we found plenty of rich, yellow, clanking Spanish ribbin? Were there fine paintings and rich jewels? I told him that we had done very well indeed in this respect, and that those who had thrown in with John Ward would reap an abundant harvest. His spirits became better immediately. He listened to me avidly, sitting in a low chair which projected his square knees to a level with his chin, his eyes gleaming with interest.

"If Archie will excuse us now, I've something to tell you," said Sir Sigismund. He motioned me to follow him to the window. Archie said he would pick a little at a morsel of food while we talked, and I waved him cordially to the table where the remains of my dinner still stood. There was a round of mutton, a rich suet pudding speckled with raisins-of-the-sun, and a half-full tankard of ale. His eyes lighted up, and when I saw him attack the mutton, I wondered how Dame Witchie would regard such lusty picking.

"I've had a letter from Ward," said Sir Sigismund in a grave tone. "His news is good in one respect. The Dons have made no hostile move. They haven't interfered with any English merchant ships, and John is sure they've learned a lesson. The Free Rovers are breaking up. Some of the captains have elected to try other fields, and some will risk a return to England. I don't like that part of it. They won't get the reception they hope for. It's the worst kind of folly because the King isn't in a forgiving mood."

Archie's sharp ears had caught what was said. He lowered the ale tankard long enough to remark: "They'll hangit in chains, the puir loons. Naething less will do frae Jamie. Is Waird coming back?"

Sir Sigismund shook his head. "He's remaining in Tunis. A number of them will stay with him. Enough of them, he thinks, to keep the Dons in their present chastened mood."

"He musna put hissel' in Jamie's poo'er," said Archie, wiping his lips with a doubled-up fist. "Gude Keeng Jamie! What a roaring, de'il-may-care auld sea-dog he is!"

"The rest of the news is not good," declared Hill. He seemed reluctant to go on. "Roger, the Señorita is dead. Ward said little about it; I'm sure he felt it too deeply to indulge in any details. They traced her to a town on the edge of the desert, but the rescue came too late. Ward didn't see her alive." He swallowed noisily. "I know how you must feel. She was a splendid little person; I had quite a soft spot in my heart for her myself. Well, it was in God's hands. Perhaps the poor child was spared much disappointment and suffering."

I could not say a word. I had been prepared for bad news, but it had never occurred to me that this could have happened. She had been so sure of the future, so confident of happiness. My hand touched the squared surface of the emerald ring which I carried in a pouch under my doublet. I had almost forgotten I had it. I wondered now if her parting with it had been the cause of her death. She had been carried off the day after she gave it to me. A picture of her as she had looked that last night came into my mind: her lovely face, lighted by the tenderness in her eyes, the eloquence of her expression as she spoke of the future, the soft mist of her dark hair. She was dead, and all that beauty and fineness of spirit lost!

Sir Sigismund added: "Ward wrote that he had sent you a letter also. But only the one came through."

"John must have suffered," was all I could manage to say.

"Yes. I'm afraid your friend Ward will have many occasions for feeling badly from now on." He shook his head gravely. "His affairs won't prosper. I don't like the look of things at all."

Archie was now eating his way through the pudding. As we had finished our talk, he began to speak of affairs at court, referring to the sharp things he had said to the King, with the purpose no doubt of justifying himself in our eyes for his forthrightness. I found it hard to follow, not only because of the thick coating of his Lowland accent, but also on account of the nicknames with which he larded each sentence. My mind was so full of the tragic news I had heard that it took me a long time to get these names straightened out. His Majesty was King Tiddy; Master Carr, now Lord Rochester, was my Lord Gleek. I knew these were card-playing terms, but I could not understand their exact application. When he referred to the very lovely and voluptuous Countess of Essex as Madame Tup-tup, the reason was much easier to find. He spoke of these three so continuously that the names began to run through my head like a monotonous refrain: *Tup-tup, Tiddy and Gleek, Tup-tup, Tiddy and Gleek.* For a long time, that was all I made out of it.

My Lord Gleek, he explained finally, was feeling called upon to rule. Soon he would be Master of the Horse, and Secretary, and Treasurer. All offices in the kingdom would have to be rolled into one to create a post fit for the supreme talents of my Lord Gleek; and the long-legged loon had no more aptness for it than a two-year-old bairn. He had said this to King Tiddy, not once but many times. As for little Madame Tup-tup, always making sheep's-eyes at my Lord Gleek, and with a fine young husband of her own, what would she think if she knew that Towser (a new one, referring, I concluded, to Sir Thomas Overbury, Carr's special crony and confidant) had written all those passionate notes which she received from Gleek and which made her little heart go pitty-pat? She must always be the white ewe, this lively Madame Tup-tup, but he was sure—and he had said it to the King—that a Cardinal's Hat on Turnbull Street was the proper sphere for *her* talents.

Just the other day he had said he asked King Tiddy what he proposed to do if the Dons sent another Armada against him. He had no ships ready, and he had outlawed all his best captains. Would he fight them with texts? Or would he send out my Lord Gleek with a fleet of bumboats to drive them back? He had told the King there was biblical sanction for turning the other cheek; but the trouble with his doughty Tiddy was that he made the proffer by bending, not turning.

His Majesty couldn't get enough of this ungodly game of cards called Maw. Time and again he had told him such worldliness in a ruler would be frowned on by the Great King in Heaven. Would we believe that he was too indolent to hold up the cards for himself? Archie must hold them for him; and whisper the right plays in his ear; and then throw the proper card on the table. But who collected the winnings? Not Archie; they were swept up and handed to my Lord Gleek. But he, Archie, had managed to get his revenge. There had been one occasion when the stakes on the table were heavy, and both King Tiddy and my Lord Gleek were smacking their lips because the winning cards were in the King's hand. The cards were of French make; and he, Archie, had called attention to the fact that the knave was marked the King of England. They were wrong, these French cardmakers, he had remarked, for truly the King of England was less knave than fool. King Tiddy had thrown down his hand in a rage and so had failed to win the stakes. There had been quite a scene as a result.

"And he's surprised the King is angry with him," said Sir Sigismund. "However, I think it will blow over in time. For some curious reason, His Majesty will take more from this gentle critic in motley than from any other living soul, not excepting my Lord Rochester."

"Is there any news of Macherie?" I asked.

"He's showing his hand at last. He's been in to see me; in fact, I think he's making the rounds. He's very suave about it; but he makes himself abundantly clear. It's Dane-geld he has in mind. If they will do something for him, something in the nature of gold in hand or the deeds to a few tidy manor houses, he'll keep a discreet tongue in his head. Otherwise, he seems to think it will be impossible for him to retain his secrets any longer."

Archie had finished everything by this time and was disposed to go. He paused on his way to the door, however, to remark that paying Dane-geld was a very bad thing. Your money never came back in any form, but the Danes always did, clamoring for more. King Tiddy, who was as timid as a bowdled hen, tried to run the kingdom by paying Dane-geld; and he had become as a result little better than a vassal of Spain.

"There's to be a meeting of gentlemen in the North in a fortnight or so," said Sir Sigismund, rising to join his companion. "We may want you to go, Roger. It will depend on whether it seems safe for you to leave the city."

They left then, and I spent a long and cheerless evening pondering the tragic news they had brought.

36

I HAD OBSERVED that Dame Witchie never left the house, and that both of the servants followed her example; but I did not know until much later that they were acting on instructions from Sir Sigismund. He had told them that I was the stepson of a Catholic peer who wanted to be rid of me and was determined to send me to Spain; and that I, having no stomach for exile, was hiding from him. My supposed stepfather was very powerful, in spite of his faith, and the only chance I had was to keep out of his clutches. The story had had the desired effect, all three being deeply religious and anxious on that account to help me. This was fortunate; for, as it developed later, the authorities were sure I was still in the city and a thorough search was being made. If any of the neighbors had learned there was a new lodger in the house, it would have been searched promptly.

I gave up all outside visiting myself when I heard from Dirk that a deputation from Alsatia had appeared at the fencing academy. This made me sure that Chirp Bird was having a search made of the neighborhood, and that it was doubly necessary for me to remain in strict seclusion.

On the morning of the third day I had unexpected visitors. I could tell from Dame Witchie's face that something out of the ordinary had happened when she came to announce them.

"There are ladies to see you, Master Strange," she said. "One of them's a lady, and I think the other's her maid. I'm sure they're from the court."

It must be Katie. I wondered what had happened. Sir Sigismund would not have risked telling her where I was if the matter had not been urgent. In spite of my uncertainty, I went into the small back room where my bed was set up and found the present I had brought back for her.

I was so pleased with it that I had been looking forward eagerly to the time when I could place it in her hands. It was an ivory fan. When my eye had first lighted on it in a Marseilles shop, I had known at once that it was the perfect thing, and I had decided to get it in place of the leather purse I had brought from Tunis. The fan was tipped with ostrich plumes and elaborately inlaid with opals, a beautiful stone very little known in England. It was the finest thing I had ever seen. I showed it to my landlady. Her eyes opened wide. "Master Strange!" she exclaimed. "It's fit for a queen! I declare, I've never seen anything so wonderful."

Her enthusiasm delighted me. "Look at this," I said. I spread the fan open, revealing a tiny mirror set in the handle. This was a clever device; the holder could inspect her face without anyone knowing or watch over her shoulder during a dance. The French merchant had made much of both points.

"I declare," said my landlady. "I really don't see how they can make such things. Is some lucky lady to get it, Master Strange?"

I could hardly wait now to see Katie's face when I placed the fan in her hands. I slipped it eagerly under my doublet and followed Dame Witchie to the ground floor. She stopped in the door and said in flurried tones, "Master Strange, my lady."

Katie was wearing a complexion mask. She removed it and said to her companion, "Run along, Elsie. The good woman will show you where." When the maid had disappeared in the wake of Dame Witchie's voluminous skirts, she said to me, "So, I've found you at last!"

"I can't tell you how happy I am to see you."

"You're a regular man of mystery, Roger. Why haven't you written me? I've waited and waited."

"I didn't write because I was afraid it might get into the wrong hands." She was so lovely in her blue tammil wrap and white ruff that I found it hard to keep my thoughts in order. "I didn't want to get you into any trouble."

"I've been worried about you. And I've had so much to tell you."

"I'm surprised Sir Sigismund let you come."

"Oh, I didn't go to him. I found out where you were all by myself." She looked up at me and smiled. "Well, I suppose I might as well confess. I was at Mistress Ann Turner's, and she told me."

"But, Katie," I said. "How does it happen you're in the city? Isn't the court at Theobalds still?"

"Yes." Her mood sobered. "Father wrote me that he wanted to see me. He seemed very much concerned about something, so I asked Her Majesty for leave to come. She didn't want me to. She was afraid I might get the Plague."

"It's pretty well over now. There were only a few cases this time."

"She was very much disturbed about it. Roger, she's so good to me. I'm beginning to love her very much."

She motioned me to follow her to the front of the room and then said in lowered tones: "There's something going on that I don't understand. Is Father in any kind of trouble?"

"Of course not. Sir Sigismund told me he hadn't been feeling well. That's all there is to it, I'm sure."

"No. It's not that. It's something much more serious. I'm sure it has something to do with Captain Ward."

"You mustn't worry, Katie. I'm certain there's nothing wrong."

"Roger." There was a hint of impatience in her voice. "You must tell me what you know. I *won't* be put off. There was something in Father's note—Roger, the King knows that many gentlemen have been helping the Rovers. The court talks of nothing else. Captain Ward was at our place twice before he sailed. How could that happen if Father hadn't been concerned with him?"

"If there's anything to tell, your father will have to tell you himself."

"Then it's true."

"I haven't said so. Even if it were true, there would be no cause for worry. So many prominent men are concerned that the King wouldn't dare do anything about it."

She was very close to tears. "You don't know the King, or you wouldn't say that. He swears he's going to stop all this trafficking in piracy. He even sent Archie away."

"I know. Archie was here one evening. Katie, the whole country is against the King. The Queen differs with him, and Prince Henry and the Princess Elizabeth. You ought to hear the talk in the city."

"Nothing can make the King change his mind. Roger, I *know*. I'm afraid to think what might happen if Father's involved." She dabbed at her eyes with a small handkerchief. "Sir Nevil Macherie has been back at court the last few days. I'm sure he knows something about it.

He tries to talk to me and follows me about. Roger, I'm afraid of him. I don't know why."

"Macherie will be taken care of when the time comes," I declared.

"It's all very well to say that. But I'm sure he knows about Father and Captain Ward. If he hasn't told the King already, he intends to."

"Macherie is a liar and a thief!" I declared. "I'm going to call him to account myself."

This added to her fears at once. "It's dangerous to even say such things. They say at court he's fought a great many duels. What chance would you have against him?"

"Do you think I'm too young? I'm nearly twenty, you know. Please don't think I'm boasting when I tell you I'm not afraid of Macherie at all. I've been taking lessons from the best fencer in the world. You ought to see him, Katie. He's an enormous fellow. It's like standing up to Hercules when you cross swords with him. He's been teaching me everything he knows. I'll be able to take care of Macherie when the time comes."

"Haven't we enough trouble as it is?" She was weeping now. "He would kill you. I know he would. He's a cruel man; I can see it in his eyes. I don't want you killed, Roger. Please, you must promise to give up this foolish idea. I won't go until you do."

"I can't promise that. You see, I'm responsible for his being in a position to make trouble. Your father will probably tell you why. If there's any way to make amends, I must take it."

She turned away to repair the effect of her tears. She looked so small and helpless that I experienced a still more bitter sense of regret over my carelessness that day at Calais, and I made a mental vow that no risk would be too great to take.

"Then there's nothing more to be said now." She turned back and smiled. "Perhaps we're taking too gloomy a view of things."

"I'm sure we are."

"It may have nothing to do with this at all. Father may have something entirely different to tell me. Perhaps"—she smiled again—"he's going to say that he's arranging a marriage for me. He and Mother have been talking about it, you know."

There was a pause at that. "I'm afraid I prefer it the other way," I said finally.

She had regained her usual animation. "I'm of marriageable age. Do you want me to be left on the shelf? And perhaps you'll condescend to tell me what you've been doing all this time. Besides paying visits to Mistress Ann Turner."

"I've been right here. Reading all manner of books and catching up on some studies I had neglected. I'm working hard at Spanish again, and I'm even trying my hand at Arabic."

"And do you expect me to believe that, sir? It was a different report I had from Mistress Ann."

"I've seen her twice only. I went there for a special reason. I wanted to see Chirp Bird. Do you remember him? He came from home, you know."

Her brows drew into a frown of concentration. "Wasn't he the bad boy of the town?"

"Yes. And he hasn't changed. He's the Upright Man of Alsatia now."

"Is he *that* Chirp Bird!" Katie showed her astonishment at the news. "I hadn't any idea. There's been a lot of talk about him at court. Everyone says the King should do something about him."

"We had some business to talk over. I heard he was paying regular visits to her, so I arranged to meet him there."

She nodded her head and smiled. "I knew it all the time. At least, I knew you went there to meet someone. She didn't tell me who it was. Is your friend Chirp Bird in love with her?"

"I wouldn't besmirch such a beautiful word by applying it to the feelings of Chirp Bird."

"Roger." She hesitated as though uncertain how to express what she had in mind. "It's wonderful having a post at court. I like the Queen and it's a great honor and privilege to serve her. But—there are things about it I don't like. I'm sure many of the men are no better than your Chirp Bird. I hear the most dreadful stories of things that go on."

"I'm sure all of them are true. I hear stories too. From Archie Armstrong."

"Oh, Archie." She smiled. "He's very funny, isn't he? I like him. He annoys the King by holding his nose when he comes into the royal reception room. His Majesty says that some day he will order the hangman to cut his nose off. I'm afraid I must go now. The carriage is waiting for us at Mistress Turner's shop. It's been so nice seeing you again. You promised me to be very careful, didn't you, Roger?"

"No," I answered. "I made no promises. But I do promise now that I'll be as discreet as possible. Will you make me one in return? That you won't worry?"

"I'll try not to." She sighed. "I seem to be all mixed up in my mind. I can't be sure of things any more. Everything has changed. I can't even feel sure about my father."

"You're sure of one thing. That you love John Ward."

She gave me a quick and searching look. "Do I? Did he tell you? Or are you just guessing? Why are you so sure I love anyone? I'll have you remember, Roger Blease, that I belong to Her Majesty's household. I meet all the best men in the country. Some of them may fall in love with me; you said once yourself that they would. I'm going to wait for a man who is very handsome and rich and who has a title—a great title, mind you—and who loves me very much. I'm going to be sensible, you see." She gave another sigh. "I'm not sure I mean that; and yet I'm not at all certain that I don't. I tell you, I'm all mixed up inside. As for you, sir, I advise you to stop your visits to Mistress Turner. She's very attractive. Much too attractive, I think. Let your friend the Upright Man have a clear field."

"That's a promise I *can* make." I fumbled under my doublet. "May I give you the present I brought back?"

"Yes, please! I've been so curious about it. What do pirates bring back to their—to friends at home? A charm from the East, perhaps?"

I produced the fan. She held out a hand for it and said: "Roger, it's beautiful. How sweet of you to bring me such a lovely gift."

Her voice had the right note of enthusiasm, but I was not deceived. I was watching her eyes; and I realized, with a sinking of the heart, that she did not like it. I was so disappointed that I could say nothing. What was wrong with it? Was it gaudy? I looked at the inlaid edges of the thing, and somehow it did not look nearly as fine as I had thought it. It *was* gaudy; I could see that now, and I wondered why I had fallen into such a display of poor taste. To cover up my embarrassment, I demonstrated the working of the mirror.

That pleased her, for she laughed with a spontaneous note which could not be misread. She opened and reopened the fan and studied her face in the glass. "That's very clever," she said. "How their eyes will open when I carry it at court! I'm sure no one has a fan with a mirror like that." She began to wave it languidly in imitation of the airs of a lady of fashion. Sensing perhaps that I was disappointed, she hurried into more praise of it. "It's beautiful, Roger."

I loved her more than ever for the effort she was making to appear happy over it. I wanted to take her in my arms and tell her how sorry I was that I had been taken in by a tawdry article because a high price had been set on it, that I would try hard to acquire better taste. All I could manage to say was that, if she didn't really like it, I would give her instead a leather purse I had picked up in Tunis. It was very old and quite handsome in its way.

"Give up my lovely fan for an old purse! I wouldn't think of it. But I suppose now you'll give the purse to some other girl. To Ann Turner, perhaps?"

I shook my head. "I'll save it for you. I'll give it to you as a wedding present. When you marry that rich man with the big title."

"Then I may have to wait a long time for it. There's no telling how long it will be before he appears. Perhaps never, Roger, and I'll have to go on the shelf. Well, I really must run on. Will you summon my maid for me?"

When I returned to the room, she placed an urgent hand on my arm and looked up at me with eyes full of almost tragic alarm. "There's real trouble ahead for all of us," she whispered. "I *know*. I didn't tell you at first because it seemed that you had enough to worry about as it was. A meeting was held at Theobalds yesterday. All the King's councillors were there, and they had long faces. I heard they were discussing naval matters and piracy. And, Roger, one of the captains has been caught! He landed at Bristol, and the Warden put him in prison and seized the ship."

"Did you hear his name?"

She shook her head. "I heard it, but I can't remember it now. He's to be brought to London for trial. They say the King is determined to have him hanged. And any others he can get his hands on. You must be very careful, my dear."

37

I DID NOT LEAVE my room for three days. It was a trying ordeal, for I knew that things were happening outside which concerned me vitally, and also everyone in whom I had an interest. No word came from Katie. Had she found, then, that the summons from Sir Bartlemy had no bearing on the situation in which we were all involved? This was too much to hope for, and yet the lack of any message gave me some ground for relief. I wondered which one of the Rover captains had been taken. Harris was a Bristol man, but he was a shrewd fellow and not likely to be caught in a trap so easily. I hoped it was not Harris; he was able and brave, and the time was coming when the country would need men of his stamp.

The time passed slowly. I dared not show myself openly, but when my eyes grew weary of reading I would sit well back in the front window and stare out over the roofs of London. Beneath me the old doctor's lantern swung and creaked on its rusty bar. A small iron shield covered the joint, and under its peeling blue paint I could see it was stamped with the Caduceus, the serpent-twined wand of Mercury; I wondered if this meant that medical aid moved on winged feet, and laughed at its inaptness. Across the street the houses were much lower, and I was able to see above them as far as the river.

It was not an inspiring view. London is speckled with slums, and the district immediately south of us was one of the very poorest regions of all. The houses were small and dirty, of crazy design for the most part, with latticed upper stories leaning out over the streets and closing off the sky. They made me think of drunken men with dropsical stomachs teetering in unsteady files. The roofs broke away from convention in fantastic angles which had no sense or reason; and under them, I knew, unhappy people lived in filthy squalor.

There was one church in view, its austere spire standing up high over the brawling roofs, as completely and coldly detached from this display of architectural horror as the faith it served was from the dreary

problems of common people. I caught glimpses of chains at the inter-
sections which could be drawn across the streets in case of emergency,
to confine the teeming denizens of dinginess to their own particular
share of this inferno of darkness and disease. The streets themselves
were unbelievably narrow, but not too narrow to make place for pillories
and harmans at the corners: punishment would be futile if not carried
out in full view of everyone.

The people rose at four o'clock in the morning. At this hour, with
much clack of canting tongues and clatter of pails, the men poured out
to their work, their faces sullen under cloth caps, their bodies huddled
into greasy jerkins. There seemed no limit to the capacity of the
tatterdemalion houses, for the workers kept emptying out like ants from
a hill. The district boiled and fought and raged with coarse invective all
day, but silence closed down quickly at night; perhaps because early
bedding was a necessity; more likely, I thought, it was a deep-placed
memory of curfew which drove them indoors as soon as the tiny shafts of
light, percolating through the converging roofs, turned dark and the
piping winds beat about the eaves with threat of cold and rain.

Many hours I spent watching the sick life of the slums; and I was no
longer sure that the world had attained the flavor of perfection. Something would have to be done to give relief to these children of gloom
before we achieved an earthly millennium.

Things had been moving while I watched and fumed in idleness. On
the morning of the third day a note was handed in to me from Ann
Turner. I knew who the sender was before I broke the seal, for the
paper carried a trace of her curious perfume. It was a brief note.

MY DERE ROGER [she was not much of a scholar either]:
I have had a customere todaye and am likelie to sell menny artickles
for an earlie wiving. I must not give the name of the faire bride but I
thoughte you shoulde knowe what is in the winde.

ANN

I realized at once what had happened. Sir Bartlemy and Lady Ladland
had lost no time in finding a husband for Katie—a wealthy one, no
doubt; an alliance which would relieve the strain of any financial losses
rising out of Sir Bartlemy's rash ventures with John Ward. Perhaps the
King had a hand in it; for Katie, being a member of the Queen's household, was subject to royal direction in the matter of a husband. I was
sure that some deal had been made which would free her father of all
complications and, perhaps, enrich the kingly purse. The fears aroused
by this communication from the frippery shop were confirmed that
afternoon when my landlady informed me that "the same pretty lady
was in the parlor and desired a word with me." Dame Witchie was all
smiles.

Katie had removed her complexion mask when I joined her in the parlor. She smiled and said: "Well, Richard Strange, here I am again. Isn't it shameful of me to pursue you in this way? I'm a forward minx, am I not?"

She was looking grave in spite of the lightness of her greeting. I studied her face carefully. Her eyes were tired and listless, her cheeks pale. It was the first time I had seen her with no trace whatever of her usual animation.

"What has happened?" I asked.

She did not answer but walked to the front of the room where an embroidery frame had been set up. Dame Witchie had been working on it and had left in too great a hurry to put away the ball of fine silk. Her striped cat, Winkle, had taken charge of it and had succeeded in getting the silk prettily tangled around the legs of the frame. I seized Winkle while Katie set to work to untangle the thread. My hand touched hers in the operation, and I was not surprised to find it cold and limp.

Katie studied the pattern my landlady was developing in the taut square of white linen and nodded her head with apathetic approval. "We all do Black Work at court," she said. "I suppose this is going to be a portrait of Queen Elizabeth. It's quite good, isn't it? But why Elizabeth? Why not our present queen?"

"People still think a great deal of the Old Queen," I said. "Haven't you seen the Memoriam that Francis Bacon has written? I hear King James didn't like it." I might have added that it was significant how little impression the new royal family had made on the feelings of the country. Prince Henry and the young Princess Elizabeth were popular with the people, but a glum silence was all that the King drew on his rare appearances on London streets.

"It's not fair!" There was a hint of real heat in her voice. "You've no idea how fine my mistress is! If people only knew, they would soon forget about the Old Queen. Instead they listen to silly stories. She does *not* drink too much. She is *not* in love with my Lord Pembroke."

"Both stories are generally believed."

"They're not true! They're not!" Her voice had risen to a note almost of passion. I was amazed to find that her eyes were filled with tears.

She returned to her chair. "I'm being very silly. I'm upset today. Please forgive me."

"Katie, what's the trouble?"

"There's really no trouble at all. I just— Well, I'm in a mood, as Mother says." She dabbed her eyes with a pearl-edged handkerchief. "It's just as well I didn't bring my fan, Roger. I don't want to see how dreadful I look. Your fan made a very fine impression. When she heard I had received a present from you, Mother wasn't going to let me keep it. But she fell completely in love with the fan and changed her mind. I think she would like to have it herself."

"Let her have it then. I have something else for you. I think I told you about it. I'm sure you'll like it better."

"But you said you were keeping it for—another purpose."

"Yes. As a wedding gift. I'm afraid it will be useful soon."

There was a long silence. "How did you know?" she asked finally.

"I was sure something had happened. Something tragic. Nothing could be more tragic than that. So it's true?"

She nodded. "Yes. It's very sudden, isn't it? I had no idea of it when I saw you. And that was—just three days ago."

"Who are you going to marry?"

She looked away before she answered. "I'm almost afraid to tell you, Roger, after the way I spoke the other day. I even said I didn't like him. It's Sir Nevil Macherie."

Macherie! I could hardly credit it. Since receiving the note from Ann, I had been indulging in glum speculations; but this incredible selection had never occurred to me. My face must have shown how I felt, for she hurried into explanations.

"You've every reason to be surprised, I know. But—I've changed my mind about him. He's really very handsome and amusing, and he's being most kind and thoughtful in every way. Everyone thinks it a most suitable match. Father and Mother are pleased. Her Majesty doesn't know about it yet, but the King has given his consent. You see, Sir Nevil has properties near ours."

"A hundred acres of sand and stone," I said bitterly. "And a tumble-down stone house."

"He's in high favor at court," she went on. "Father says he's to be made a peer."

"A reward for his treachery." I was trying to keep my feelings in check, to spare her as much as possible, for her part in it was clear enough; but I could not control my tongue entirely. "I'm sure your father is pleased. Why shouldn't he be? He arranged it. That is the only possible explanation for this—this terrible thing you're telling me."

Somehow we were standing, facing each other. Her face, looking up into mine, was completely drained of expression.

"You must try to understand, Roger."

"Oh, I understand. You're marrying him, Katie, as the price of his silence. That's clear enough. You're being forced into it. Don't deny it. I know it's the truth."

"I won't let you say such things. If it were true, it would be Father's work. You have no right to say such things about him. Do you understand that, Roger Blease?"

My mind was incapable of further thought. Katie married to Nevil Macherie! It was preposterous, unbelievable; it was wrong, unthinkable, obscene; but it was going to happen. Macherie had demanded a different kind of price from Sir Bartlemy; not gold or land, as he had from the others. And Sir Bartlemy, to save himself from the consequences of exposure, was willing to sacrifice her. Katie, always loyal, would go through with it.

There was nothing to be done about it; nothing, at least, short of convincing the country that the King's foreign policy was wrong and by force of concerted opinion compel a change. Relieved of the danger of prosecution, Sir Bartlemy would soon send Macherie about his business. I said to myself grimly that I would begin at once on the work I should have been doing, that I would no longer skulk in London to save my own skin. But would there be time?

I realized that I must spare her feelings. She was entitled to every consideration on my part; certainly I had no right to reproach her.

"Please forget what I said. I—I was overwrought. Any step you are ready to take must be right, Katie. But let's be entirely honest with each other."

She continued to look up at me with sober eyes.

"Yes. I think it would be better."

"I want to know one thing. Are you sure, Katie, that this is the only way? Can't some other solution be found?"

She shook her head. "It's the only way, Roger. I'm quite sure. I've thought and thought about it—and there's nothing else to be done." She walked to the front of the room and stood for several moments at the window. Then she turned suddenly, and I saw that there were tears in her eyes. She said, with a catch in her voice, "Oh, Roger!"

"Katie, you can't do it! Surely your father—"

She dried her eyes slowly. "I'm to keep my post. His Majesty has promised that. He knows the Queen likes me; but I don't think he would let me stay if he knew why. He would probably send me packing if he ever found out. It's because of the Gowrie Plot."

"The Gowrie Plot!"

She nodded. "Yes. You remember about it, don't you? It was when they were in Scotland. The Queen was very lonely, and she became fond of one of her maids of honor, Beatrice Gowrie. The Gowrie family was involved in a conspiracy against the King—or the King thought they were—and her two brothers were killed. Beatrice was sent away. The Queen never got over it. She's never had anyone she's been able to like since. That is, until I came. She likes me because she says I look like Beatrice Gowrie. She speaks of it all the time."

"Beatrice Gowrie must have been very lovely."

"It's nice of you to think so." She smiled faintly. "The wedding will be at Appleby Court, but I'm to return to court at once. I'm very much afraid that Mother won't be content with anything but a large wedding. She's making arrangements already." She added with sudden vehemence: "I can't be honest about it! Don't let's try. Let's pretend that—everything is as it should be. That's what I intended to do when I came. You might even wish me happiness. It's customary, you know."

"I can't do that. I'm not very good at pretending."

"You might try."

"I'm the cause of all this. Can you imagine how I feel about it? If I hadn't—"

"There's no use talking about it, Roger, I'm to be Lady Macherie, and you—what will happen to you? I'm more worried about you than I am about myself. I hear what's being said at court."

Dame Witchie interrupted us at this point by bustling in with a tray in her hands. It contained a long-necked amber bottle and two small glasses. She smiled at Katie with excessive cordiality.

"You must taste my dew-of-the-sun, my lady," she said. "I make it myself. It will be good for you on a raw day like this. Try it; do, my lady."

"Thank you," said Katie. When the landlady had left, she looked at me with a wan smile. "I suppose we must drink it."

"I suppose so."

"It's very silly of us. One might think we were celebrating. We haven't anything to celebrate, have we? We're both in a terrible plight, and there's nothing we can do. Not a toast, please. I don't think I could stand that." She sipped the warm liqueur. "Are you thinking terrible things about me?"

"You know what I think about you. I'm drinking a toast, Katie; a silent one."

We replaced our glasses on the tray, and Katie tied the neck of her wrap with an unsteady hand.

"The wedding may be very soon," she said.

After dark I made my way to Sir Sigismund's tall house near the Poultry. By the greatest of luck he answered my knock himself. "The servants are out," he said, hurrying me in and closing the door.

He was careful to snuff out all but one candle before we seated ourselves at the big desk. Then he proceeded to fill his pipe, lighting it from juniper fire, which he kept well packed with ash in a metal box. He was studying me with a shrewd eye.

"What is it?" he demanded. "I can see by your manner that the whole universe has gone awry."

"Katie Ladland is to marry Macherie."

His eyebrows raised in surprise. "Indeed! I thought perhaps the King had been blown up in another Gunpowder Plot or the moon had neglected to come out. I had no idea of the real gravity of your news."

I told him the circumstances back of the coming wedding, although I was sure he had guessed already.

"There's nothing you can do about it, my boy." He paused and then added: "Sir Bartlemy is a sorry specimen, but I didn't think him capable of this. The little lady has more courage than her father."

For a few moments nothing more was said. Then I nodded in the direction of my capcase, which I had deposited just inside the door.

"I'm not going to play the coward any longer. I must start on the work

John set me. He expected me to do it anyway; I'm sure of that, and I'm going ahead with it. At once; tonight, in fact. I think I would go crazy if I stayed cooped up in that room another hour."

"Perhaps you're right. Some good is bound to come of it. Ward had a shrewd idea; the country should be wakened to the danger of our present policy. But you'll have to be extremely cautious. Have you thought of the consequences?"

I answered bitterly: "I've thought about them too much. I've hesitated and hung back because of thinking of them. I've been a rank coward. Now I'm going to make up for it."

"It's a courageous thing to do. As you feel so strongly about it, I'll withdraw my objections. We must figure things out carefully first." He fell into reflection, puffing on his fat-bowled pipe. "You must go first to some of the safer men. I'll go over the list with you now. They'll pass you along, and perhaps save you from falling in with those who lack real resolution; the Sir Bartlemys, of whom unfortunately there are many."

We discussed names and routes for an hour or more. Then Sir Sigismund went to a cupboard beside the fireplace and drew out a bottle of wine.

"Madeira," he said, smacking his lips. "The very best of all wines, though few people in this country know much about it yet. Some day they'll want nothing else, mark my words. The Portuguese make it in a peculiar way, keeping the grapes under high temperature for a long time. It gives body and flavor to it." He savored his glass with relish. "Well, my boy, success to your venture. And the best of luck in it yourself."

He began to speak of other matters. "We had another Council tonight and, my, how the shillings rattled! Our shareholders want the basis of investment changed. You see, they now put their money into a single voyage. If the ship comes back, they make as much as one hundred per cent profit; if it goes down, they lose everything. Now they're suggesting that they should invest in the company and take a share of all ventures. They figure they would have a sure profit that way, though smaller, of course. There's something in it; but it's a radical idea. One can't be sure where such innovations might lead. Frankly, I'm afraid of it. I know the Privy Council will forbid it; they have no stomach for radical change."

He was talking, I could see, to take my mind off more serious matters. After a third glass of the warm wine, he got to his feet and said: "You must be off before dawn. I'll have a good horse for you and a warm cloak. You're going to need both. In the meantime, you must have some sleep. A clear head will be needed for what you're setting out to do."

38

IT WAS LATE OCTOBER when I began my journey and late March when it ended. Fear sat on my shoulder every minute of the time; and every man I spied on the road was a King's officer until he passed. I changed horses three times, for it proved a bitter winter and very hard on the poor beasts. Snow fell continuously, and the roads were frequently so icy that we struck sparks at every stride. The winds, sweeping down from the north, made me intensely grateful for the fur-lined castor Sir Sigismund had given me. I did most of my riding by night, as it was not safe to show myself in public inns.

I think I must have been in every county in the kingdom in the course of those bleak months, going from one great house to another, with letters from my last host to commend me to the next. It was a hole-in-corner business and almost as hazardous for them as for me. None of them seemed to take that part of it seriously.

I attended the meeting of which Sir Sigismund had spoken, and it may be described as typical of many others. The reports I had received on my host were so favorable that I was rather taken aback by my first glimpse of his house. It did not appear large, and there was something almost furtive about its location. I came upon it suddenly, a huddle of gray chimneys at the mouth of a valley. A storm was blowing, and I rode through heavy drifts to a glumly silent entrance. The snow, sometimes falling sullenly and sometimes swirling on the wind, had lodged in the eaves and gable ends, making me think of enchanted houses I had read about as a boy. It sifted down on my face as I lifted the huge iron knocker. I would not have been surprised if a witch or a magician had answered my summons.

This impression vanished as soon as I set foot inside. It was warm and cheerful and much larger than it had looked from the outside; quite impressive, in fact, with high ceilings and sculptured stone stairways on each side of the entrance hall. The master welcomed me warmly. His wife was there to second him, a pretty woman much younger than her lord, with a kind smile and a white hand for me to kiss. We went at once to the Great Hall through brown-paneled passages decorated with an amazing number of inscriptions in Latin; the work, I judged, of a long line of scholarly owners, for many of them were in the oldest of script. The company had assembled in the Great Hall, half a dozen gentlemen with their backs to the fire and an expression of watchfulness on their faces. They were friendly enough, although there were no introductions and no naming of names. The rules which govern seating before the fire were abandoned, and I was ensconced at once in a chair quite close to the blazing logs, a foot-warmer and a glass of hot brandy provided for my immediate comfort.

"Well, Sir Pirate," said my host, in a booming voice. "I must say you carry no outward signs of your sinful trade."

The others laughed; and one of them, who had all the earmarks of a parson, remarked that fighting the Spaniards was doing the work of our Heavenly Master.

They were a sober lot as compared with the fine gentlemen of London. None of them sported the gay colors, the doublets of pease-porridge tawney, or the popinjay blues which were so popular at court. Most of them wore gray or brown, with collars lying flat on their shoulders, and there was not a single stitch of gold thread among the lot of them. They might lack the subtlety and sparkle of court gallants, but there was something very reassuring in the fine gravity of their eyes and in the serious note of their conversation. I had heard that the Puritan influence was beginning to show itself among the smaller gentry, and here was the proof of it.

The first scraps of talk made it clear that they were religious men and bitterly opposed to the copes and wafer-cakes of the new English Church. They were even more concerned over the way things were going in the political world. They returned continuously to the imposts the King was applying and his refusal to listen to Parliament. Most of them, I judged, sat in the House, if it could be called sitting when His Majesty summoned it so seldom and dissolved it on the first sign of opposition.

It was clear they understood the necessity for the work John Ward and his captains had been doing. I knew that all of them had taken some hand in the fitting out of the ships, and on that account I dwelt chiefly on the documents which we had located on the *Santa Caterina*: the proofs of Madrid's determination to drive us off the seas, the cold-blooded treatment of captured crews, and the payment of pensions to ministers of the Crown. They listened quietly enough until I came to the matter of the pensions, and then an indignant rumble arose. Dishonesty was more than a political sin in their eyes; it was an offense against God and not to be borne in silence.

"Where are the proofs of all this?" asked my host.

I am sure I looked as crestfallen as I felt when I explained that they had been stolen from me and turned over to the King's ministers.

"And the name of the thief?"

"It was an English gentleman, one of the Free Rovers, I'm ashamed to say. Sir Nevil Macherie. He's in high favor at court as a result."

Someone laughed. "I know Macherie. And I have no hesitation in believing this. He's quite capable of it."

On a nod from my host, I launched into a circumstantial story of everything that had occurred, beginning with the assembling of the fleet.

I could see a gleam in every eye when I came to the fight with the Latin ships. Our host slapped his thigh and laughed loudly. "You've told this story at least once before. To the Queen."

"Yes, sir. I told exactly the same story to her Majesty at Denmark House."

"You may not know it, my boy," said one of them, "but you were speaking to more than the Queen that night. You were speaking to the whole of England. Everyone has heard it since. I don't mind saying it was the boldness you displayed on that occasion which persuaded me to come here today." He paused and let his eye flit from one to another. "Well, gentlemen, I for one am disposed to believe every word of it, proofs or no proofs."

The talk became general after that. I waited my chance and threw in a word about John's belief that a great empire could be built if once the grip of Spain were loosened on the trade routes. This set them to much eager speculation about the Americas. They did not seem to understand the East. There was something unreal, and almost ungodly, about India and China in the eyes of these quiet gentlemen. But the continent to the west was different; there, they agreed, was land fallow for Anglo-Saxon hands.

While we talked, I became aware that we had an uninvited visitor. I could see a pair of eyes and a flounce of scarlet skirt around the edge of the screens at the far end of the Hall. At first I thought it was a child. She became bolder, however, and ventured a little way into the open, and I realized she was in her middle teens; a daughter of the house, for she had all of her mother's comeliness and the same lively eyes. She watched us with interest, but apparently she knew that she had no right to be there; she scurried back when her father, suddenly becoming aware of her, waved her impatiently to leave. I saw, however, that she lingered long enough to scratch something with her finger on a pane in the oriel window at the side.

The glass was thickly frosted, and what she had written was still legible when I found an opportunity to stroll in that direction. She had added one more inscription to the many; but she had not employed the stately Latin of the rest.

Who's afrade of a pirut?

"The baggage!" said her father, over my shoulder. "She heard you had sailed with Captain Ward, and so nothing would do but she must have a look at you. I think she expected someone more on the bearded and ruffianly order. I trust you're not offended."

She was not seen again. I thought to myself: Suppose John Ward had been in my place?

The debate lasted for several hours, and then dinner was served. So far I had not glimpsed a single servant, and I was not surprised when our host led the way to a small room where we found a table laden with an assortment of dishes. We helped ourselves; it was noble fare, a chine of beef, a roast of mutton, a large fish curled head to tail and covered with a rich sauce, a brace of ducks, and plenty of kickshaws on the order of pastries and marchpane. There was no fruit and no vegetables, as such things become almost nonexistent in England when winter sets in. I was hungry and did full justice to everything.

When the dishes had been emptied, we returned to the Great Hall and found on a low stool in front of the fire the largest bowl I had ever seen, filled with a hot punch. Our host saw that all glasses were filled and then raised his own in front of him with a solemn air.

"The King!" he intoned.

"The King!" echoed the rest of the company with a fervor that I found hard to understand after the tone of the conversation. The expression on each face was one of complete loyalty to the head of the state, and it was only after a long silence that one voice added: "May it never be necessary for us to honor that toast with less than our whole hearts."

One episode of the visit remains to be told. After an hour's relaxation in front of the fire, by which time the bottom of the bowl was in clear view, the owner turned to me with a serious expression.

"No one knows of our meeting today. The servants have been kept from this part of the house, and I'm sure that none of them could name you. It's only because of your youth that I point out the danger of a careless word or an unthinking reference to what has been said or done."

"My own life depends on my discretion," I pointed out.

"They had an easier way of imposing silence once." Our host walked to the side of the fireplace and fumbled along the paneling. There was a grating sound, and I saw that a portion of the floor had dropped in an alcove to the right of the screens. Going over, I found myself looking down into a shaft twenty feet or more deep, at the bottom of which water swirled. The water came from the moat, I concluded, for snow and broken ice churned about on the surface. It was an *oubliette*; I had never seen one before and it was not pleasant to look at, nor was it pleasant to think of the enemies of the house who had made their exits here in bygone days.

"It hasn't been used for a century at least," said the owner with a chuckle. "I keep the spring oiled, however. You can never tell. My Lord Rochester might pay us a visit; or the honorable gentleman who stole those papers from our young friend."

I spent Christmas Day in a very small town on the edge of the fen country. It was a dismal place with nothing to give it distinction but the fact that a year before one of its citizens had been burned alive. He had been too outspoken in his refusal to conform to the King's ideas of how his subjects should worship God. I do not know the extent of his heresy; perhaps he did not acknowledge the Godhead of Christ, or he may have voiced the common comparison between the sacrament and a jack-in-the-box. Whatever it was, he had been placed in a tarred barrel on the town square and a fire had been lighted around it; the barrel and the unfortunate man and his nonconformity all vanishing together in short order.

Christmas is always a merry day in England, even in glum towns such as this. The purpose of my visit was to speak with some of the leading dissenters, all of them humble folk without spare beds, and so I had been put to the necessity, and the danger, of staying at an inn. From my high window, I saw the holiday procession start early in the morning with the elected Lord of Misrule in the lead. He was not a very impressive-looking master of revels, but he wore a scarlet cloak of camlet thrum, held up by a chorus of mummers, chanting:

> "Wassail, wassail,
> In snow, frost and hail."

He had a good-natured face, and he managed to cut a few amusing capers before the procession wove out of sight. Later he would lead the way back to the inn and there would be a feast, with the boar's head carried in to the table in full state; and the worthy gaffers of the town would do some substantial holiday drinking.

I thought of the Christmas we had spent at Appleby Court, when the Yule log had been twenty feet long and the boar's head had been brought in by four huntsmen with green scarves and drawn faucions; and I had stepped a measure with Katie in the dancing which followed, and she had allowed me to squeeze her hand. Had the marriage already taken place? It seemed certain that it had, for she had said it was to occur soon. That was a dismal thought with which to begin a Christmas celebration, but it stayed with me throughout the day. Would the world ever be right again, with my mother dead, John Ward in exile, and Katie married to Sir Nevil Macherie?

I took dinner at the home of a humble Puritan family on the outskirts of the town. The solemnity of the occasion was deepened by the fact that the martyr of the previous year had been a brother of the head of the household. There was, however, a quiet air of thankfulness in the little circle which I found more agreeable than the usual extremes of Yuletide gayety. They had a roast of braun, served with hot mustard, and a fine pudding with holly on top, and the children had received small gifts which they carried about with them all day in a high state of pride. I felt sorry for the children because I knew they would not be allowed to play any of the games which make up Christmas night: shoe-the-mare, hot-cockles, or hodman-blind. But they did not seem to mind the omission, and were quite happy with their Yule cakes (but without the customary imprint of the figure of Jesus, which the Puritans considered sacrilegious) and their thin rations of sugared candy.

The talk was all of leaving England and finding a new home in Leyden where a colony of English dissenters had already been established. There they were worshiping God in their own way under a great preacher named Robinson, who could "ding the pulpit to blads" as soundly as John Knox himself. There were pamphlets in the house which had been printed in the Low Countries for distribution in England. King James had banned all printed matter of the kind, but they showed me copies without any trace of fear, even though they knew a barrel of blazing pitch might be their reward. For the first time I heard talk of America as a possible sanctuary for those who took their religion in the spirit of Calvin and abhorred a bishop's rochet as the mark of the beast.

They were men of peace, but they exulted in what the Free Rovers had done, believing that we had struck hammer blows against the power of the papacy. They drank no toasts to royal James. They had none of the class loyalty of gentlemen to a weak head of the state, and I felt a reluctant admiration for them on that account. They were forthright men, and there was only one thing they asked of life. I said to myself that, if the overweening pretensions of the King were to be haltered, it would be these humble citizens who would fasten the checkreins; and many years later I knew that I had been right in that.

Five months were consumed in my travels, and I expected that each day would be my last of liberty. I knew that the King was aware of what I was doing, and that he was urging his officers on to lay me by the heels. It was proof of the deep feeling pervading the country that anyone was ready to receive me under these circumstances. We took every precaution, naturally. I was passed from house to house, traveling by night and taking back roads wherever possible. I skirted all towns of any size and did not show myself in inns or taverns.

Everything I heard in that time convinced me the country was bitterly opposed to the policies of the King. All men felt baffled at the incongruity of a monarch chosen by the people of the country, laying claim to divine sanction and assuming powers that verged on the despotic; and they felt a great sickness of the soul because our once-great country had fallen in less than ten years of his rule to the rank of a third-rate power.

39

I CAME TO THE END of my travels in a mood of deep dejection. Had I accomplished anything besides putting my head in jeopardy? I doubted if I had. Every time that I fell into talk about the policy of the King, I would hear the incisive voice of the master of Gorhambury saying, "We must consider the irks of our present situation as the price we are paying for our great chance." If he were right, and I did not doubt it, we could not hope to accomplish any improvement in the conduct of national affairs. All that we could look forward to was a great convulsion which would shake England at some time in the future, and from which we would hope to emerge with a new freedom.

I was to make my last call next day. My man, Sir Ninian Varley, had guests at his home; and so it was impossible for me to spend the night with him. I decided it would be safer to select an inn where the poorest class of travelers put up, but I was not prepared for the dinginess of the room to which I was escorted by a bulging landlady in a frowsy coif. It had the smell of a flinch-gut about it, and I made up my mind to sit the night through on a bench downstairs. Late in the evening, however, my resolution weakened. The company consisted of a half-dozen townsmen who persisted in bawling the chorus of "Labandola Shott" until the discord drove me out into the peril of the town.

I paced the muddy streets and dark alleys, my thoughts busy with a letter I had received that morning from Sir Sigismund Hill. It had been handed to me by a ruddy-faced squire with whom I had spent the night, after having passed through numerous careful hands, and it was the first communication of any kind that had reached me. It was completely unsatisfactory in one respect, for it contained not one lone bit of information about the Ladland family; but it had outlined a plan for my future.

"We must appoint a new agent at Damascus," he had written, "and I have talked so much of the merits of one Richard Strange that my partners are disposed to leave the matter entirely in my hands." Three years' residence would be entailed, at the end of which time it might be safe for me to return, "it being reasonable that the odor of piracy will by then have deserted the royal nostrils." As he had reported me in France at the moment, I would join the ship at Brest or Marseilles, and I could take my Aunt Gadilda with me. She had been ailing (how kind of him to have found this out), and the warm sun of the East would be the very thing for her. A comfortable house on a palm-shaded hillside went with the post.

The prospect appealed to me very much. I could not remain in hiding forever, and John did not want me back, out of regard for my well-being. The East, then, was the place for me. I could live there in security, and the work should not be beyond my capacity; my experience in Tunis would stand me in good stead there. There was one drawback: a whole continent would lie between me and Katie. The prospect of never being able to see her robbed me of any real content with the plan.

There had been disturbing news in the letter as well. More of the Free Rovers had returned and had been taken in charge. Sir Sigismund feared that the King's purpose was to see them "hangit in chains," as Archie had predicted. The letter had been written more than a fortnight before it reached my hands, and I wondered with a sinking heart what had happened in the meantime to our stout captains.

A warm sun had shone during the day, melting the last of the snow and bringing the townspeople out from their winter-chinked homes to welcome the arrival of spring. They were still about, hobnobbing at the corners or in the doors of taverns. I remembered Temperance Handy's saying once that the weakest feature of English life was that the social activities of the common people centered in the streets; but that, unfortunately, if any attempt were made to drive them indoors, they would only go to the taverns. After what I had seen of their homes from my window at Dame Witchie's, I felt that they could not be blamed for seeking diversion and comfort elsewhere.

Suddenly, to my intense surprise and alarm, I heard my assumed name pronounced in a high-pitched voice. My first impulse was to turn and run, but a wise second thought held me back; by doing so, I would attract attention to myself, and that was the one thing I could not afford to do. I looked about me. All the people in the immediate neighborhood had been drawn into a tight group farther down the block, and I decided the cry had come from there. While I hesitated, not knowing what to do, the call was repeated. There was something unreal about it, a ghostly cachinnation which sent a shiver of fear down my spine. "*Richard Strange! Richard Strange!*"

I was now sure that it issued from somewhere within the crowd, and that I would have to find out what it meant. I could not leave with the mystery of that summons unsolved.

It was a Motion that had drawn the people together. By the light of an elevated torch the puppet-master was giving an elaborate performance of the most recent and most popular of all marionette shows, *Luke Hutton, the Rhyming Highwayman; or, Hemp Passeth Green Holly*. The bystanders were enjoying it very much and cheering loudly when the bouncing and declamatory figure of the footpad held up the fine gentleman; and shouting, "Buss 'er, Luke!" in his scenes with the heroine, a strapping spital-house trull. They were enjoying it so much they accepted an innovation of the puppet-master as a new piece of comedy. Hutton would accuse the woman of being unfaithful to him and demand the name of the other man, whereupon she would answer in that high voice which had so nearly scared me out of my wits, "Richard Strange!" The audience guffawed every time it happened. I understood now that it was a summons to me to remain, and I stayed on the edge of the crowd.

It was a sociable gathering. Bowse-boys threaded their way through the pack, doing a brisk business with their trays of ale mugs. A pastry vendor was selling tiny pork pies at a rag (a farthing) apiece, and the crunching of jaws almost drowned out some of the lines. No one paid any attention to me, for the drama of the Motion was reaching a high

pitch of intensity. The Rhyming Highwayman had been captured and
was trussed up in Little Ease, waiting for the inevitable ride to the
chats. He was intoning the words of his famous lament:

> "My name is Hutton, yea, Luke of bad life;
>   Oh, woe is me, woe is me, for my great folly;
>   Who on the highway did rob man and wife;
>   Take warning, young wantons, hemp passeth green holly!"

The puppet-master issued from behind the boxlike stage at the end
of the piece, accepted the applause of the good-natured audience with
a slightly derisive bow, and proceeded to pass through them with his
extended hat. He seemed to do rather well, much better than the poor
saltimbanco had done; the cap, with its greasy cock-feather, was soon
weighted down with rags, and even the more desirable wins. I waited
until the people had melted away and the master was busy packing up
the figures, and then went back of the theater.

"Well, my man," I said.

He was a surly fellow. "Well, yourself," he grumbled, going on with
his task.

I spun a coin in his direction and said in a whisper, "Richard Strange."

He looked up then and grinned. "Ye're to come along of me." He
finished the packing, collapsing the walls of the theater into so small a
space that the whole thing could be slung over his shoulder. Putting out
the torch, he struck briskly toward the center of the town, not giving
a glance to see whether I followed or not. I did so with great misgivings.

He stopped in front of a house standing on a side street in complete
darkness and said gruffly: "A double part for Brose Totten tonight.
Pimp as well as Motion-master. Well, it pays good, I must say. She
wur a likely looking baggage. Give me another of the same, my gentry-
cove, and I'll drink to yer success with her."

My cautious knock was answered at once, and I found myself admitted into a dark hall. A familiar voice said: "Roger! At last! Praise
God, I've found you!"

It was Ann Turner. Even if I had not recognized her voice, I could
not have mistaken the perfume which pervaded the air. She found my
arm and pressed it with passionate relief. "You were in great danger,
Roger. But now let's hope it's over. We had better go back before I
light a candle. No sense in taking chances, my dear."

The candle lighted up a long room which served many purposes,
being parlor, dining room, kitchen, and pantry all in one. There were
hams and bunches of aromatic herbs hanging from the rafters at one
end, and at the other there was a refectory table set out with the
cheapest kind of knives and plates on a scarlet rush cover. I looked at

Ann and saw that her eyes were a trifle red, as though she had been crying.

"Don't dare look at me," she said. "I'm a sight."

"Were the King's men on my trail?"

She achieved one of her nicest brow-knitting smiles. "Yes," she answered, almost breathlessly. "You were to see a Sir Ninian Varley tomorrow, weren't you?" I nodded. "He gave you away. They'll be at his place to take you. What a narrow escape, Roger! I didn't hear of it until this morning, and I came right down. The driver of the coach must have thought I was starting alone on an elopement, for I called 'faster!' every time he let his horses slow down. He wished me happiness when we got here. Fortunately I have an uncle in this town. This is his house. I packed the family off on a visit and took possession. That part of it was easy enough. But I've been almost frantic ever since, trying to locate you."

"How did you find out about this?"

"Fanny Howard told me. *She* heard about it from Lord Rochester. She visited the shop early and as usual gave me all the gossip. She was selecting some—I won't tell you what, Roger, you're so modest—and I'm afraid I hurried her rudely. I could hardly wait to get her out of the place."

"Thank God for your Fanny Howard."

"I didn't know what to do when I got here, except to send a man around to all the inns in search of a Richard Strange. There was no Richard Strange to be found."

"I use a different name in each place I visit. And I never go to inns unless it's absolutely necessary. As it happened, I did go to one tonight, but I gave my name as Ludar Blayne."

She was still overwrought from the anxiety she had suffered. "I couldn't think of anything else to do about it," she said. "I almost cried my eyes out. Then I thought of using a Motion to get your name cried on the streets. It was smart, wasn't it? How lucky you heard!"

"Lucky, indeed!" I said fervently. I wondered how I could ever repay these brave efforts on my behalf. She was dressed in black, which became her immensely, and her ruff was white; a sensible precaution, for I knew that her use of yellow had become very well known and might have identified her. "You *were* clever, Ann. But you were taking a desperate chance. The officers may be in town tonight; I think it's almost certain they are. Supposing they had wondered what all this calling of Richard Strange was about? They might have followed the man here."

"What if they had?" She was studying me closely by the small light of the one candle. "Just as long as they didn't find *you!* As far as I'm concerned, it would have been easy enough to explain; I'd have fobbed them off with hints of a tryst. They would have believed it. They might have thought that this mysterious Richard Strange was a lucky man; what do you think, Roger?"

"They couldn't very well help it."

"You've grown a beard! I love it." She came over and took both of my ears in her hands and rocked my head from side to side. "You rascal, you're positively handsome. Does it curl up that way naturally? It's the latest thing, you know. The men at court use irons to make their beards curl in exactly that way. I sell plenty of them. Some men even use curlers in bed."

"It must be natural with me. I haven't time for curlers, and I don't often have a bed to sleep in. I leave that sort of thing to Sir Nevil Macherie."

She backed away, still shaking her head admiringly. "Have you supped? I'm so glad you haven't; we can have supper together. That will be nice, won't it?"

I was struck with a disturbing thought. "Do you think we're safe? They might pick up the master and make him bring them here."

She said triumphantly: "I thought of that! I paid him to leave town at once. He's on his way to London now. My, Roger Blease, you've been costing me a lot of money!" She stopped and looked at me with sudden gravity. "I've bad news for you. Perhaps I should tell you now."

"I'm getting used to bad news. Yes, I'd rather hear it at once."

"Mistress Ladland was being married today. It was to be a very elaborate wedding. Many of the court were going down for it. Fanny Howard told me all about it. She wasn't going herself; she doesn't seem to care much for Mistress Ladland."

I should have been prepared, but this confirmation of my worst fears made me feel as though the end of the world had come. There should have been tremors of the earth and chasms yawning around us. Nothing now was left, nothing worth-while to be fought for, nothing left to fill the mind any longer with hope. I could not say a word. Ann looked at me with sympathy and proceeded to elaborate on her information.

"It isn't strange that Fanny doesn't like Mistress Katie. I'm sure she dislikes every woman at court. I knew a lot about the marriage myself because I supplied some of the clothes. The finest laced day cornets and coifs, half a dozen dresses, and a stomacher on which I sewed her mother's pearls. It's going to be a lovely wedding, Roger; you'll be glad of *that*, for her sake, I'm sure. I hear the presents are wonderful. The Queen gave her a ruby ring." She paused and smiled. "You must think I'm weak-minded, talking this way. I'm doing it to help you get over the shock, my dear. I know how badly you're feeling."

"I've been expecting it, Ann. I was sure, in fact, that it took place long ago. I've had no news of things."

"It's hard when you can't have the one you want." She began to set some dishes on the table. "I haven't been too happy myself lately. I've had to do things I don't like."

Remembering that strange room back of her shop, I took alarm at once. "What kind of things?"

"For Fanny Howard. That innocent-looking little beauty; you wouldn't think she would say *boo* to a goose. But she's a—a determined *fiend!* I mean it, a fiend. She doesn't want her husband, and she does want my Lord Rochester. She demands charms to chill love in the one and stimulate it in the other. I've taken her to Father Forman. But, Roger, his silly charms won't do anything."

"Why are you so sure of that?" I was not at all sure myself.

She shook her head decidedly. "It's all nonsense. She won't get her lover that way. Nor get rid of her husband either. What then? I'm afraid she'll stop at nothing. First—poison!"

Poison! Just one whisper of that sort of thing around, and my companion would find herself in prison with the threat of the rope or the stake hanging over her. King James was desperately afraid of witches —"cummers," he called them. "Ann," I said, "have nothing more to do with the woman! Give it all up, in God's name!"

"I know. I must stop. But it isn't as easy as you think. Fanny Howard's my best customer. She brought the whole court to my door, and I mustn't offend her. I know what she's capable of if she's crossed in anything."

"We both seem to have plenty of troubles, Ann."

"Yes. Let's mingle our tears together, shall we?" Her animation left her. "Sometimes I hate her. She frightens me. And then there's Sir Thomas Overbury. You must have heard about *him*. The great friend of Lord Rochester. Watching, watching, all the time. He doesn't like Fanny; he doesn't want his friend to become involved. He wants to run the King and the country through Lord Rochester, and Fanny is getting in his way. He knows everything that's going on. I'm afraid of him too. There may be trouble for all of us before we're through."

She finished laying out the supper, and we took our places at the table. I tried to eat but found that my appetite had deserted me. I laid down my knife and saw that she had done likewise.

"I'm not hungry after all." She smiled at me across the table. "Well, let's have some wine. Perhaps it will make us both feel better."

We each had a glass of very good wine, and it accomplished its purpose in part. After a second glass I felt very much better. I looked at my companion and saw that her spirits had improved also.

"Let's forget our troubles," she said. "You know there are always compensations in life, my Roger. I may find myself involved in a court scandal; but I *am* accomplishing what I set out to do. I'm making a great deal of money, and before very long I may be able to move away from London. I'll find some respectable young man to marry. He'll have to be tall and dark—I've decided that much—and I think

I'd like him to have a beard that curls naturally. Of course, I mustn't expect everything! And then I'll settle down to a quiet life. Do you think it will be hard for me to do that?"

"Not as far as finding the husband is concerned. That will be very easy for you. They'll fight over you, Ann. Tall and short, dark and fair alike."

"Thank you, Roger. You think I'm pretty, then? But not as pretty as Katie Ladland." She added immediately: "There, I've gone and reminded you, and just when we were beginning to forget all about it. It was stupid of me, wasn't it? Especially when I knew you wouldn't give the answer I wanted. Well, another glass may help you to forget again."

It helped considerably. We settled down to talk about the old days at home, about John Ward and Chirp Bird and the rest. Her eyes began to sparkle, and I realized that, with one exception, she was prettier than anyone I knew. I told her so. She was wearing a new kind of bodice which had the ruff only in the back and opened in a low V. I noticed that her throat was slender and white, and I began to like the curious perfume she used.

Once she reached out suddenly and took hold of my right hand. "I must see," she said. "I've been afraid to ask for fear of what I might find. The wine has given me courage, I guess." She spread my fingers open and examined the palm. Her eyes lighted up almost immediately. "It's not here! You're safe, Roger. They won't catch you. Oh, what a relief!"

"What isn't there?"

"The sign. The fatal sign, my dear. Everyone who is going to die on the scaffold has it. It's always in a certain place, and it can't be mistaken for anything else. Father Forman told me. He said it was infallible, and for once I believed him. I can't tell you how relieved I am."

I was very much relieved myself, for I believed, as everyone did, in palmistry; even Temperance Handy had once said that the Bible warned us of the signposts of destiny on our hands. She curled my fingers back slowly.

"Roger."

"Yes, Ann."

"I'm sensible enough not to expect the impossible. I know what can be and what can't be. But life always has its compensations. I said that before, didn't I? Some day all your difficulties will clear up, and you'll settle down to the life of a gentleman. You'll marry someone of your own class. I hope you'll have every happiness when you do. What will happen to me is much less certain. But—there's a mean-time, my dear. For both of us."

I nodded in agreement. All my own expectations had been shattered; but, as she said, there was a meantime.

"Come over and sit beside me."

I carried my glass around the table and drew a chair up beside hers. She twined her arm through mine.

"I frightened you that day at my shop. Poor Roger! I've never seen such a startled look on any face. Well, I may be going to frighten you again. Prepare for a shock, young fellow!" She pressed my arm against her. "You're going to stay quite a while with me this time. What do you think of that? All tonight and all tomorrow. Are you properly startled? I can't see your face." It was clear that she could not, for her head was against my shoulder; and, in any event, the one candle provided little light.

"It wouldn't be safe to venture out tonight," I said. "I won't dare go for my horse at the inn. It's too bad; he was a steady fellow and I liked him."

"You and your horse! I'm not concerned about your horse at all. Did you hear what I said?"

"Yes, I heard. I agree that I can't leave tonight. But it's a different matter about tomorrow. Why should I continue to make you share my danger?"

"It's the only safe way. You must travel back to London with me. I've arranged everything. A coach is coming at daybreak. You'll go with me as my servant." She squeezed my arm again and laughed. "You'll make a very handsome servant. I even have a livery for you, a rich maroon with silver trimmings. I can hardly wait to see how you look in it. You ought to see the ruff; I'm sure you'll need my help with it. You'll have to be very dignified to play the part; very stern and stiff. And I have a warm beaver hat for you which can be drawn down over the ears. If it's cold you can wear a muffler around your face, so you'll be most completely disguised."

I shook my head. "There's a limit to the risks I'll let you take. It won't do, Ann. I'll leave before you do. Before daylight. I must strike out on my own."

"And travel on foot? What chance would you have that way? No, my dear, my plan is the only possible one."

"You've been too good to me as it is. I don't know how I'll ever repay you."

"I've been too good to you?" She laughed softly. "You have no idea how good I'd like to be. No, my most chivalrous Roger, you won't add to my perils by traveling with me. It will be still dark when we start, and we'll strike south to avoid the main roads. It will take us all day, and then it will be dark again when we reach London. It will be cold again tomorrow, I'm sure, and I won't have the heart to keep a servant out in the cold, much as I would like to travel with a fine big footman on the box. No riding outside for you, my Roger. Are you blushing again? I can't see in this light. Now, it's all settled."

40

I RODE ON THE BOX during the greater part of the next day after all, for the weather proved too mild to provide any excuse for a servant to share the carriage with his mistress. I pulled the beaver hat down over my brows and looked straight ahead when we passed people on the road. Fortunately my fine maroon livery stamped me undeniably, and no one paid me any attention at all. The driver was surly, and we talked very little.

Late in the afternoon it began to rain, and Ann rapped sharply on the panel back of us. It was clearly a summons to me to get under cover. When I seated myself opposite her, she leaned forward and smiled delightedly. "Roger, Roger, Roger! My, what a fine-looking servant you make. So tall and straight and dignified. Can't I persuade you to stay in my service?" Her smile became arch. "You would be very useful around the house."

"I wouldn't pass muster long. I'm afraid the driver has his suspicions about me as it is. My way of speaking doesn't strike him as just right. I dragged in a few cant words to throw him off, but he knows I'm new to this kind of thing."

"Silly! Of course he does. He thinks this is an elopement and that you're wearing livery as a disguise. I was careful to plant that idea in his mind before we started."

"You seem to think of everything."

She sobered at that. "Yes. I try to think of everything. And that prevents me from harboring foolish fancies, even when I want to believe them possible. About us, for instance. It would be wonderful to believe we might go on like this. But I know it can't be. I can even see that we must separate as soon as we reach London. You'll be safer in the streets there than riding in a carriage with Mistress Ann Turner. Chirp will know I left town, and he's certain to have men watching for me."

The coach crawled through the back roads of Surrey, splashing through the mud. The rain lashed down, getting through the side hangings and dampening the seats. We talked about the future. Ann dropped her coquettish airs and discussed plans with complete seriousness.

"You must get to the Continent at the earliest possible moment," she urged. "Why not go to France? You speak French, and I hear the King is very wise; he could find some use for you. He must need men with experience at sea."

"Hale Harry Gard would enjoy a laugh if he heard you say that. As far as the sea is concerned, I'm still a green joskin. But it's already arranged, Ann, that I'm to leave for the East. I'll be gone three years."

"Three years!" There was so much real dismay in her voice that I began to feel still more guilty about what had happened. "Then it's likely, Roger, that I'll never see you again. Three years seem like all eternity. Before you come back, I'll be away from London; if all goes according to plan, that is. You may not be able to find me." She looked at me with somber eyes. "What's still more awful about it, you won't want to find me."

I tried to speak in a light tone. "Are you imagining that I'll return with a wife? I can promise you *that* won't happen. I don't care for women with brown skins."

"It's not that. You'll forget me in three years. I'm afraid you'll want to forget me." She raised the side curtain to inspect the weather but dropped it at once. It was still raining hard, and her sleeve had become wet. Her eyes were wet also, but I was sure it was not from the rain. "Perhaps it's the best way. I think you'll remember me pleasantly if we part now. I want you to remember me that way."

She became practical then and plied me with questions. Did I have enough money for my needs? Did I have a safe sanctuary in London for the time I must stay there? It must be safer than Dame Witchie's; she was sure Chirp Bird had uncovered that address by this time. Had all the details of my leaving been arranged? She had enough influence in high quarters to be of help to me if anything were needed.

"You must leave London as soon as possible," she said finally. "Tonight if possible. Promise me you won't stay a moment longer than is necessary! It's terribly important, Roger. I *know*. Have you heard that several of your captains have been caught and brought to London?"

It was news to me that they had been taken to the city. The King, then, was taking justice into his own hands and not trusting to the magistrates in the ports where they had landed. This augured badly for their chances. I asked her if she knew the names of any of the prisoners.

"I heard them, but they meant nothing to me and I can't recall them now. The gibbets have been set up at Wapping Stairs already. Roger, there will be one for you if you're not careful! Oh, I know you haven't the sign on your hand; but I don't put complete faith in that."

"I've a safe place to go." I felt so sick over the news about the captains that it was difficult to speak. "You mustn't worry about me, Ann. They won't catch me in London. And I'm sure my friends will get me safely away. All arrangements have been made."

We were in the outskirts of the city by this time, for the wheels of the carriage were grinding on wet paving stones. She motioned me to sit beside her and then laid her head against my shoulder.

"We must say good-by in a few minutes," she whispered. "A long good-by, my dear. You can't keep a woman like me in your life. I've no illusions, you see. Certainly I've none about the future. I let myself dream about the things I want to do, but—I'm afraid they won't work out as I want them to. I haven't told you everything. Some day I may be in as much danger as you are now. Don't ask me about it; I don't want to talk now. Well, we've had these twenty-four hours. That's something, isn't it? I don't want to say anything more. Let's just sit like this until you have to leave."

I left the carriage as soon as we had crossed the river. Ann leaned out of the door and waved her hand. She looked white and tired, but she managed to smile. "I'm afraid you'll catch cold," she said.

The rain had mounted until now it was a regular March gale. It swirled down between the houses and nearly swept me off my feet at the street corners. I was soon soaked to the skin. I was glad of the storm, however, for the few people who had to brave it took no interest in a bedraggled pedestrian in a once-handsome maroon livery. I gained Sir Sigismund's house without mishap.

I wondered if he would still feel disposed to take me in; I would be doubly troublesome now to one in his position. His first words reassured me.

"I had almost given you up. You've been treating the hounds to a real run, but I'm thinking they are close on your heels now. Did anyone see you come in?"

"No," I answered, still a little out of breath. "The storm has driven everyone indoors. I was afraid you might not want to see me."

He smiled. "I can think of safer guests to have in one's house. But don't give that a thought. I'm in this now as deep as I can get. It's as necessary to me to get you out of the country as it is for you to go."

We went to the small room where the unloading uniforms were kept; and, on a suggestion from him, I stripped off my wet clothing and donned one of the pocketless suits. My host smiled dryly and said it made me look like a prisoner, but he was sure there was nothing prophetic about it. The room was without windows and on that account the safest place to talk. We sat down on stools, and I proceeded to tell him briefly what had happened since I started on my travels.

"I'll say this for you," he commented at the finish: "you've been energetic. I had no idea you would get to so many of them. And you've succeeded in keeping His Majesty in a tantrum. Archie has advised me of what's going on at court."

"Then he's been restored to favor?"

"Oh, yes. He was right about it. The King can't get along without him. He's managed to get his stipend restored, which shows how His Majesty feels about him. To be honest, I never expected to see you again. Archie told me they have been trying to spread a net for you the last six weeks. You've been lucky."

"I've been lucky in my friends."

"We must see to it that your luck holds." He fumbled with his amber pibeam but, because of the impossibility of lighting it where we were, tucked it back again under his belt. "Some of the others haven't done as well as you. Have you heard about it?"

I nodded unhappily. "I heard that several captains have been caught."

"They're being held here. For some reason, they've been scattered among all the jails. Harris is in the Marshallsea."

"Harris! I hoped he wasn't one of them. He's the best of the lot, a gentleman and a stout fighter. Can't anything be done? Surely the people of England won't stand by and see a man like Harris hanged!"

Sir Sigismund made a despairing gesture. "What can they do? Harris is from Bristol, and his friends there have offered the King eight hundred pounds to buy him free. That's a big sum to raise in small amounts. James needs the money badly, but refuses it nevertheless. He has been fairly drooling for vengeance, and now he has his chance. They'll swing, all of them."

"Who else?"

"Halsey. He's being held at the Fleet."

Halsey! I think I had liked him best of all, in spite of his refusal to help poor Clim. And now he was to die himself, a felon's death, as a reward for his brave work at sea!

"Longcastle is in the Clink. I've a great regard for Longcastle. There's a fine and gentle strain in him. He'll go with the rest. His Cornish friends are moving heaven and earth to save him, but they'll get nothing but trouble for their pains."

I got to my feet and began to pace about the room. I was finding it hard to breathe. It was almost as bad as during those terrible days when Clim was dying in the Basket. Three gallant men were to hang because of the passionate resentment of an unkingly ruler! Was England, the green and happy home for which I had longed so passionately, no better after all than heathen lands where all men were slaves?

"There are nineteen of them," said Sir Sigismund. "The rest of them are humbler victims, mates and a few common sailors. Every one of the nineteen fought in the battle off Cape Passer."

"When is it to happen?"

He hesitated. "No date has been set. The gibbets are up. Some of the gentlemen of the court paid a visit to Wapping Stairs yesterday to inspect them. Will you believe it that there were ladies in the party? I think the King is waiting in the hope of making it an even twenty." His expression suddenly took fire. "Don't let that frighten you, Roger. We'll see to it that he never has that satisfaction! You can stay here in perfect safety. I swear they'll never find you in that dark room of mine."

"Two close acquaintances of yours," he went on after a moment, "have been very helpful to His Majesty in this—this epic of injustice. The Upright Man ran down all of the common sailors who had taken refuge in the city. He did it for a price. There had been a restive feeling about the boldness of his operations, and something might have been done about it. Now he can rest easy; the law will continue to wink at what goes on."

"Don't they know," I demanded, "that Chirp Bird is in it as much as any of the prisoners? That he's been fencing for the Free Rovers?"

"Everyone knows it, of course. I suppose there's been a deal made. Your friend Chirp will turn all the profits over to the big men at court. You ought to hear what Archie has to say on *that* point! But you needn't think that Bird's immunity will last long. He's useful to them now, but some day soon the King's ministers will realize how dangerous he is. He'll be brought to book, never fear. I went to see him when I first got wind of all this and advised him to have no hand in it. But it was too late. Eight of the arrests had already been made as a result of information he had given."

"You took a great risk in going to him."

"None whatever." The cool face of Ulysses of the Trades broke into a smile. "I know too much about our Upright Man. All I had to do was to mention a certain circumstance in connection with the death of Barnaby Cloud which had come to my ears in a curious way. The Upright Man became anything but upright; he fairly groveled at my feet. But it was too late for him to draw back."

"I'll never forget that visit," he went on. "Master Bird has moved from Alsatia. He wants to be a gentleman, and he's taken quite a large place fronting on the river. Right in the middle of the finest homes in London. There was an uproar about it, but nothing could be done; he had the deed in his pocket before anyone knew what was happening." He shook his head and smiled with sardonic satisfaction. "You should see the place now! The King, you know, has a collection of wild animals at Theobalds; and so nothing would do but Master Bird must have the same. There are iron pens in his front garden, and he keeps a toothless lion and a mangy old camel in them. The creatures are so poorly kept that the stench annoys his noble neighbors."

In spite of my upset state of mind, I managed to laugh at the thought of Chirp Bird living in a London palace with lords and ladies on each side of him. He had always been full of big ideas; and now he was living up to them.

"The inside of the place is beyond description. He's picked out for himself all the gaudiest stuff you sent from the South. The top of his dining table is made of stained glass! His favorite chair—incredible as this may sound, I swear it's the truth—is on a dais, and he wears a purple suit whenever he sits in it. He has the largest bed in England, with crowns carved on the headboard. He says twenty men could sleep in it with their heads together in the center and their bodies stretched out fanwise. Yes, we have a second king now, the Monarch of Mummery, the Sovereign of the Spital-spawn!"

"You spoke of two men who had assisted the King," I reminded him.

"Macherie, of course, is the other. I understand most of the arrests started from information he gave. It's certain, at any rate, that he told where Halsey and Longcastle were to be found. I'm convinced he came back with the idea of avenging himself. They played right into his hands by returning."

"You know that he's married to Katie Ladland?"

He nodded. "I heard the marriage was taking place. Poor child! Macherie set a high price on his silence; but not too high, apparently, for our stanch Sir Bartlemy."

I think he saw that I was tired, for he got to his feet and said he would see me to my quarters. It would be uncomfortable, he warned, but I must be prepared to put up with it. The house might be searched at any time.

It developed that there was another entrance to the secret room which he considered safer to use. We climbed to the bedroom under the roof which I had used on my first visit. My host opened the closet and pressed down heavily on the floor with his feet. A trap door opened slowly and with much creaking, and I looked down into a black shaft not more than three feet square. I confess that the thought of descending into this narrow aperture gave me an empty feeling at the pit of the stomach.

"It's the only safe way," said Sir Sigismund, noting my reluctance. "The lower entrance hasn't been used in a generation, and it wouldn't be wise to disturb it now. You see, there's a ladder sunk into the bricks. Go down carefully; a mistake would mean a long fall! I'll visit you in the morning."

It seemed to me that I would never reach the bottom. The rungs of the ladder protruded an inch only from the brick surface, and so I had to exercise the greatest care. I doubt if I could have managed it if the shaft had not been so narrow that I could brace my back against the other side and so relieve my arms of much of the strain. My sword kept getting in the way. I heard rats scuttling about between floors, and once a bat struck against my face with a blood-chilling squeak. I decided that the bricking was part of the chimney and there was an open hole somewhere in the shaft, for I heard other bats both above and below me.

I kept going down until I thought my arms would give out. I counted the steps: thirty, forty, fifty, sixty. I would never make it! My legs were shaking with the strain, but I did not dare to stop, even if relief could have been secured that way. When I came to the seventieth step, my foot, to my intense relief, touched solid bottom.

I had no candle. Feeling cautiously about me I discovered that my new home was a hole not more than twelve feet by six and so low that I could touch the top with my hands. A couch, covered with blankets damp to the touch and moldy with age, filled nearly half of the space. It was so cold that my teeth chattered; a reaction not entirely due, perhaps, to the atmospheric conditions. I heard rodent claws scratching on the floor.

All manner of terrifying thoughts filled my mind. What would happen to me if Sir Sigismund took sick, if he were arrested, if an accident overtook him? No one else knew of the existence of this foul and noisome hole. Here I would be, in a dark pit at the bottom of a narrow fifty-foot shaft. No one would hear my cries for help. Could I raise the trap at the top by myself? For that matter, could I ever manage to climb up it to the top? If none of these things came about, how could he manage to get food to me? What if the house caught fire?

Underneath these speculations was a curious kind of fear I had never experienced before. I felt as though the building had closed in on me, that I could not move my arms, that very soon I would not be able to breathe. The sensation was so horrible that I had to press my face against the brick wall of the chimney to prevent myself from screaming. What did it mean. Was I going mad?

Finally I managed to rid myself of this hallucination, and I dropped on the couch, shaking with exhaustion. I tried to force my mind into normal channels but found it impossible to get away from one fact: here I would have to stay as long as I remained in London, alone, with nothing to occupy myself, days, weeks even. I was sure I was doomed to starve, if nothing worse happened to me.

I shivered with the cold, which struck into the very marrow of my bones, and tried to get some degree of warmth by clasping my arms about my chest. Nothing could have induced me to wrap myself in the soggy bed coverings. How could I tell what ghastly living things were under them?

This went on for a long time, an hour at least, I was sure; and then I found, to my surprise, that a certain warmth had begun to manifest itself. I reached out a hand and discovered that the wall in front of me was warm. I knew then that a fire had been lighted in the fireplace, and that the heat was coming through. This was the only comforting thing about my situation; I would not suffer continuously from the cold.

I overcame my repugnance sufficiently to throw the coverings off the bed, and then stretched out on the wooden slats. Here I stayed for endless hours, twisting continually to transfer the strain to new muscles, my peace of mind not helped at all by the sound of rats parading and convening and fighting beneath me.

I did not sleep, but once I fell into a sort of coma which came to an end when I sat up suddenly, trying to decide if my eyes were deceiving me or if a gray shape hovered in the blackness above me. Was it a ghost? Men undoubtedly had died in this foul hole; did their spirits still haunt it? I sat in terror, my heart seeming not to beat, for I don't know how long; I am sure it was many minutes before I was able to convince myself that it was nothing more than an optical illusion.

I knew it was morning when I heard a scuffling noise in the shaft above. It must be Sir Sigismund coming down; but the thought of company, comforting though it was, had one terrifying aspect. I was not sure he would be able to make it; and if he were to fall, what chance would I have of getting out?

He succeeded in reaching the bottom, but I could hear him puffing and gasping long before his feet touched the floor.

"Are you all right?" he asked, in an exhausted whisper.

"Yes."

I heard him strike a flint against the wall, and then a tiny light showed in the intense darkness of the place. He lighted a candle and set it in a niche in the wall. He had strapped a bundle on his back, but before getting rid of it, he looked about the narrow cell and shook his head.

"No one has been here in years," he said, clucking apologetically. "I had no idea it was as bad as this! Whew! It smells like the animal pens of our Upright Man. The ventilator in the shaft must be closed. I *am* sorry. But I didn't expect you, Roger, and there was no chance to do anything about it."

"I would be a lot worse off in prison, sir."

He had brought several dozen candles which he placed in another niche where they would be out of reach of the rats. "Better keep one going all the time," he advised. "There's too much danger in striking lights down here. If a fire started, the flames would shoot right up the shaft, and you would never be able to get out in time. I brought long enough candles to last many days."

He had brought also a bundle of food, a bottle of wine, and a heavy blanket. I discovered that I was ravenously hungry and bit at once into a loaf of bread.

"At any rate," he said, "they'll never find you here. That's some consolation for you. No one else knows of the existence of this princely apartment." He sat down on the end of the couch, making a wry face at the odor rising from it. "Well, Roger, I have news for you."

"Bad news?"

"On the contrary. The best possible. The wedding didn't take place after all."

I found it hard not to shout at this unexpected information. Katie was not married! What could have occurred to prevent it? I was not capable of clear thinking, but I was sure that, whatever the reason, it meant she would never marry Macherie.

"I can't believe it! Are you sure, sir? It was to take place two days ago."

He smiled at my eagerness. "I thought that would do you some good. Perhaps this miserable kennel won't seem so bad now. Yes, I'm quite sure. The guests who went down to Appleby Court were received with the word that the bride had changed her mind. No reason was given, but the story everyone believes is that your stanch little lady refused to marry Macherie when she found he had informed on his friends."

He was right; I no longer found the discomforts of my cell unsupportable. The cold walls and the darkness overhead seemed to have vanished; I felt as though a dazzling light filled the place.

"What about her father?"

"Sir Bartlemy," said my host, "seems to have been completely in accord with her. There was a limit, apparently, to what he could demand from the girl. I hear he behaved with firmness and dignity. There are all manner of rumors in the city about it. It's said the King was furious, and I can believe that he was. Sir Bartlemy is now certain to face unpleasant consequences. At the least reckoning, he will be stripped of everything he possesses."

"Then it's come out that he was backing John Ward?"

He nodded. "Yes, the whole story is out now. Macherie created a scene and threatened Sir Bartlemy openly."

My regret over the plight in which Katie's father now found himself was tempered by another thought. Katie would no longer be an heiress, certain on that account to be forced into a good marriage. She was no longer, wonderful thought, out of my reach. If I could escape from my present difficulties and stay away from England long enough for everything to blow over, it was not inconceivable that I might in time secure a pardon; in which event I might have a chance after all to win her. I made a silent vow that I would devote my life to regaining for her something of what she had lost.

With this happy and exciting chain of thought went one reflection which left me with a deep sense of regret and shame. If I could only blot out the last two days from my life!

"Some friends are supping with me tonight," went on Sir Sigismund. "Archie will be with us, and I'm sure he'll have the whole story for me."

"Where are they now?"

"The Ladlands? At Appleby Court, I'm sure. Sir Bartlemy will be wise enough to stay as far away from the King as he can manage. Not that it will do him much good now." He smiled. "The only overt action the King has taken so far has been a sharp demand that the present sent by Her Majesty be returned."

"None of this would have happened if I had been more careful that day at Calais," I said, beginning to realize how serious the situation had become for Katie's father.

"You mustn't think that. Macherie had plenty to go on before he stole those papers." He got wearily to his feet. "It's going to be a hard pull to get up there again. I hope I can manage it. One thing's certain: I won't try it again. I'm afraid you'll have to do whatever climbing's necessary from now on."

We arranged that I would make the trip each night at eleven o'clock when the servants would be in bed and sound asleep, and he left his watch with me so that I could keep track of the time. Once a day he would lower food and other supplies to me on a rope. This settled, he began the ascent with obvious misgivings. It took him a long time to reach the top; but, to my intense relief, he finally accomplished it.

The day passed more easily than I would have thought possible; entirely due, of course, to the turn of events which had switched my thoughts into pleasanter channels. I dipped into a book he had brought for me but found reading hard in the small light available. I remained most of the day on the couch with my new blanket wrapped around me. Even then the cold was hard to stand.

I made all manner of plans. I would save every penny during the three years in the East. Aunt Gadilda would help me in that, for no nip-cheese could excel her in making one shilling do the work of half a dozen. Some chance to distinguish myself would present itself, and my reward would be a pardon from the King. My fancy mounted to dizzy heights. I would become rich and famous: I would win a title, a great title, not a mere knighthood or baronetcy; I would be one of the foremost builders of the empire which John Ward talked so much about; I would buy Appleby Court, if it passed out of Sir Bartlemy's hands; and, of course, I would marry Katie. The time passed quickly with such rosy speculations trooping through my mind.

At eleven o'clock to the minute I began the ascent. I had taken off my shoes, and the climb proved not as difficult as I had feared. I tapped cautiously on the trap door and felt a great relief when I saw it open above me. I blinked hard when the light struck my eyes.

The room was warm and cheerful, with a splendid fire crackling in the fireplace. Sir Sigismund had a plate of hot food ready for me and a glass of brandy, and very little was said while I consumed both. Then he motioned me to a mirror on the wall, under which were a basin of hot water and a towel. My face, I discovered, was as black as a chimney sweep's.

"With a hoop-dery, dery, sweep," I said cheerfully, as I proceeded to give myself a thorough scrubbing.

"The house was searched today," announced Sir Sigismund when I had completed my ablutions. "I've been under suspicion for some time, of course. Luckily they can prove nothing. I haven't a shilling

in any other venture than our own. They seemed to have hopes of
finding you, and they made a very thorough job of it. Did you hear
them thumping around the fireplace? It was just as well we left the
panel undisturbed. The officer in charge said he was sure you were
using this as your 'stalling ken' and that he would be back."

"Then I must continue to use the shaft. Or do you think it would
be safer to get away?"

"Where would you go? No, the hunt is on in real earnest now.
They're sure you are in London, and they're very much puzzled over
how you managed to get to the city. They picked up your scent hot
thirty miles away." I hoped they would never find the answer to that!
"The only thing to do is to stay right where you are."

The sense of that was so apparent that I nodded. "Did Archie have
any news?"

"Some odds and ends of gossip. It seems the King and Queen have
been brangling over you. Her Majesty is reported to have said that
she didn't want to see 'her nice young pirate' in any kind of trouble.
You seem to have made a very favorable impression on her that night.
But her advocacy only makes the King more set against you. They
don't agree either on what is to be done to Sir Bartlemy. The Queen
favors leniency, having such a soft spot in her heart for Mistress Katie."

"Then nothing has been decided?"

"Nothing yet. I'm afraid the King's greed will prevail in the end.
He needs money too badly to let an erring subject escape without
a thorough unrigging. It's certain Appleby Court will be confiscated.
Archie says the court gossips have begun to chew on one juicy morsel
of rumor: that Sir Bartlemy backed Macherie also."

This was hard to believe in the face of the course Macherie was
taking; but, remembering what Sir Bartlemy had told us, I was sure it
was true. I explained the circumstances to my host, and he shook his
head with a puzzled frown.

"The dishonesty of the man passes all understanding," he said.
"Well, this should give that acute conscience of yours a rest. If Macherie was backed by Sir Bartlemy, he knew all about the Ward matter
as well. That stands to reason."

"What about the prisoners?"

"The whole country's in an uproar. The King's under heavy pressure to pardon them. There's a chance now that he'll yield, but I'm
not counting on it. They say he still falls into a rage when one of
the captains is mentioned. Of course, my Lord Rochester and the
Howards are bolstering him in his desire to stand firm. They stay
in favor by backing every royal whim."

He proceeded to tell me that plans had been completed for my
own departure. The ship on which Richard Strange was to sail was
leaving in two weeks. I would depart from London at night and sail
down the river in a flory to a point near the city of Reading. There

I would be met by a trusted servant of Sir Sigismund's, who would escort me to the home of a retired sea captain near Plymouth; and from there I would sail across the Sleeve on a fishing smack. The ship would put in at Brest for me, and my Aunt Gadilda would be aboard.

I returned to my dark cell in a mood far different from the exalted one which had carried me through the day. I could think of nothing but the gibbets erected at Wapping Stairs. Nineteen gallant seamen would die there within a few days if a miracle did not happen to save them. My own prospect for a safe departure lost its savor in the face of that grim picture.

I managed to exist through two more days of confinement. On the evening of the second, I found my host in a depressed mood. He said nothing at all by way of greeting.

"What is it?" I asked.

He shook his head soberly. "The warrants have been signed. They die tomorrow morning unless something happens tonight to change the King's mind. I'm sure there's little chance of that."

I had no appetite for the food he had provided for me. "Then there's no hope?"

"Frankly, I see none. The court's at Greenwich, and I went there this evening in the hope of an audience. It was refused. Curtly. The city is seething, and there's a lot of wild talk about a rescue. Nothing will come of it. Gondomar was with the King this evening, and you can guess what *that* means. Nothing will satisfy Spain but the death of these men." He paused as though reluctant to go on. "There's worse to it than that. I saw Archie, and he whispered a disturbing bit of news in my ear. John Ward is on his way back."

This amazing news left me completely tongue-tied. If John returned, he could expect no better fate than the nineteen unfortunate men who would die in the morning. I could not believe he would be guilty of such folly. He knew the vindictive streak in the King too well to put himself in the royal power.

"I can't credit it," I said finally. "John is too wise for that."

"All I know is what Archie told me. He said orders have been given for a hasty refitting of the *Rainbow*. The old flagship has been rotting in port for the last ten years. As Archie puts it, 'Why should she be scraped and painted and provided wi' new laces and stays lak an auld strumpe' if some extraordinary need hasn't risen for her services?' He's quite sure a warm reception is being prepared for John Ward."

"If it's true," I said, "we must find some way of warning him."

"And how would we set about it?"

I knew how it could be done, but I did not go into that, being sure that he would raise objections.

"The bad news comes all at once," he said. "Appleby Court has been confiscated by royal order and a fine imposed as well which will strip Sir Bartlemy of many of his other possessions. His town house will have to go, certainly. I understand he'll have enough left to live comfortably on one of his farms. The disposition of the estate is what amazes me most." He shook his head slowly as though unwilling to speak of such things. "Appleby Court passes into the hands of Sir Nevil Macherie! Yes, to the most treacherous dog this country has produced in my lifetime. A deal has been made, of course. I suspect that Macherie will divide with Rochester in the matter. Some substantial sum may find its way into the royal treasury, which is completely bare at the moment. It's a pretty business all around! Well, my boy, there it is. Macherie lost the heiress, but he made sure of the estate."

At various stages of my adventures I had been forced to act with some boldness. When I had risen to the need, it had always been with inward misgivings and with no stomach at all for the course forced on me by circumstances. I was not cut to heroic measure by any means, as must be apparent by this time. But now I was conscious of an anger so deep that no considerations of caution entered my mind at all. Macherie must be made to pay! I had been preparing myself for the time when he could be called to account, and now that time had come. I wanted nothing on earth so much as a chance to try conclusions with him. I knew that I would have no peace of mind until I had done so.

"Sir Sigismund," I said, "this makes a change of plan necessary. I must go to Appleby Court first."

He dissented strongly. "Why, in God's name? You're in enough danger as it is. Don't you suppose they've set a watch for you at home? You'll walk straight into a trap."

"I've no intention of going near my own home. Nor to the Court directly. I've a matter to settle with Macherie, and I'm sure that I'll find him there now."

"There's no sense to it. No sense at all."

"There may be no sense to it, but I've got to go. Even if it means losing the chance of getting out of the country."

He studied me intently. "I'm afraid you mean it. Well, it's your own decision. I can't stop you if you want to drop the noose around your own neck. But let me say this much: Mistress Ladland doesn't need any such rash proof of your devotion."

"I hope she doesn't. But this is a matter between Macherie and me. Sir Sigismund, I'll find my own way to Plymouth after—I'm through with Macherie. Can the rest of the arrangements stand?"

He pondered the matter. "I suppose so. But it adds to the chanciness of it. Is there anything else you need?"

"Yes." My voice raised above the cautious level we had always used. "Suitable clothes. A horse. At once! Tonight!"

41

APPLEBY COURT lies west of the town, and I sighted it at daybreak. I reined in my horse and studied its tall chimneys, from which no smoke was issuing, with a feeling of complete bafflement. Nineteen brave men who had fought for England's rights at sea were dying in London this morning. John Ward had been proscribed and would meet the same death if the King's law ever reached him. Sir Walter Raleigh, the last of the titans of the old queen, was a prisoner in the Tower and would die when the King nerved himself to take the step. But a traitor and a coward was receiving this lordly domain as a reward for betraying his comrades. Things had reached a strange pass since James came to the throne!

I tethered my horse in a thick copse in Wayland Spinney and then took my station near the edge of the wood, where I could watch the road from town. I could make out from where I stood the square bulk of Temperance Handy's shop, and I found my thoughts turning longingly to the peaceful times I had spent under his tutelage. The future had been full of rosy dreams then. I had been sure that bravery and self-sacrifice led to a fair reward, that right always triumphed in the end. It had taken little more than a year to destroy all these beliefs and illusions.

I saw someone emerge reluctantly and carry a bucket to the well at the foot of the garden. It would be one of the apprentices; I thought I recognized Tod Tarsty, and I knew how he would be groaning and muttering over the necessity of rising so early. He had one prospect which I lacked —a substantial breakfast would be preparing to which he would soon sit down. One of Dame Handy's hams would be warming in front of the fire, from which thick slices would be cut for each apprentice. There would be hot and crusty bread and foaming mugs of ale. In spite of my troubled state of mind, I was ravenously hungry.

At nine o'clock I spied a small party of horsemen riding out from town. When they came closer I saw that the man in front had a long nose and a black beard curling under his chin. I had been right in my calculations, then; Macherie had not waited in the city for the executions but had ridden out at once to claim his prize. I wondered if any thoughts of the tragedy being enacted in London disturbed his satisfaction.

Some people of the town were following behind Macherie and his party. I could not make out who they were, and I could only guess at their reasons for coming out so early; curiosity, I decided, was the most likely motive. I was glad to see them; I needed an audience for the challenge I proposed to deliver.

I untethered my horse and rode out to meet Macherie. His eyes narrowed when he saw me.

"Well!" he said, reining in. "Ward's jackal! I didn't expect to meet you today. You were wanted badly for a little ceremony which took place in London this morning." He smiled. "It seems I can be of assistance to His Majesty in arranging a repeat performance."

I rode up alongside. There were three men with him. One was an official of some kind, a court bailiff perhaps; the other two were servants. None of the trio showed any inclination to come any closer.

"This isn't chance," I said. "I came here this morning to meet you. I was sure you wouldn't stay in the city while your old comrades were paying the price of your treachery." I saw that some of the townsmen were now within hearing. I recognized many of them and felt sure that I could count on support. "I came to tell you that you're a traitor, a liar, and a thief! You stole papers from me and then used them to make trouble for many honorable gentlemen. The confiscation of Sir Bartlemy's property is one result of your thievery."

He had dropped one hand to the hilt of his sword, but otherwise he made no move. I went on: "Nineteen men have been hanged because of your treacherous tongue. All nineteen served in the same cause as you, and served much more bravely than you did, Sir Judas Macherie. Will you fight me now, or must I add the word coward to the others?"

He went into action then. Seizing my bridle reins, he shouted: "Hugh! Frank! Take this gallows-bird in charge! One on each side of him. He's wanted in London, and I'll see you get your share of the reward."

"Will you, now!" said a voice in the crowd. The horse of one of the servants began to balk, and I saw Brose Bettenham take it by the bridle and lead it to the side of the road. Another townsman named Welch, who had been employed a great deal on the Ladland estate and so had reason to resent the change, edged close to the other servant and seemed prepared to interfere if the man made a move. I heard someone say, "Judas is the right name for him, the lying dog!" Boys who had trailed along in the wake of the procession took it up and began to shout, "Judas! Judas!" This, together with the nervous pawing of the horses, created quite a din.

"I warn you all!" cried Macherie in a rage. "This fellow is a criminal. You'll put your own heads in the noose if you help him get away."

"Are nineteen not enough for you?" demanded the voice which had spoken first. I saw now that it was Widdigate of the Cygnet's Head.

We were sitting our horses thigh to thigh. Macherie's face was white with anger, and I could see small purple spots on his long nose. I removed one glove and slapped it across his cheek, demanding, "Now will you fight me?"

This move was so unexpected that all noise ceased at once. Macherie glared at me with incredulity turning quickly to white fury. We both dismounted.

"You've brought it on yourself!" he declared. "Apparently you prefer to die by the sword of a gentleman rather than at the end of a rope. There's nothing for me to do but oblige you."

He tugged at his weapon, bringing it out from the scabbard with such furious energy that those nearest him had to skip lively to avoid the blade. "Move back, all of you!" he ordered, glaring at the growing circle of townsmen. I wondered where they were all coming from. "I call to your attention that this has been forced on me. The hangman would have attended to this lying cub in due course, and it's by no wish of mine that I take over the task. He has insulted me publicly, and there's only one answer to that. Stand back!"

"You're right, there's only one answer to that," I said, drawing my sword. "I came here for the sole purpose of forcing you to fight. I've declared you openly a thief, a liar, a traitor, and a coward. The responsibility is mine."

"I'm going to kill you!" He looked around the circle of faces and frowned. "There's not a gentleman here. What can we do about seconds?"

"I'm willing to dispense with all formality."

A more cautious mood was taking hold with him. "It's true you're of man's size," he said, looking me up and down. "But I'm not anxious to lay myself open to criticism. What do you know about swordsmanship? I can spit you like a collared braun."

I felt a tug at my arm and looked around into the worried face of Mine Host Widdigate. "You'll not have a chance," he whispered. "Better make a run for it while there's time."

I shook him off and turned to Macherie. "At your service," I said.

We moved to a flat space on Fritchett's Meadow on the other side of the road. One of the townsmen used a dagger to trace two lines on the ground ten yards apart. By the code we must fight it out inside the lines and under no circumstances step beyond them.

Macherie proceeded to make himself ready by removing first the watch from around his neck and handing it to one of his servants; it was an oval-shaped Nuremberg Egg and as large as a platter. Then he stripped off his rich blue doublet without caring that under it he was wearing tight-laced whalebone stays. These went next, revealing a lawn shirt elaborately embroidered in colored satin. Finally he removed his shoes and took his station in the center.

Being unsure of the condition of my shirt, I contented myself with removing my shoes.

"On guard!" said my opponent.

I knew as soon as our blades touched that this was going to be different from any other encounter in which I had figured. After his first attack, a lightning thrust which I turned aside with no more than a fraction of an inch to spare, he went steadily to work, an amused smile on his dark features. He had learned his trade in a better school than any of the gentlemen I had practiced with in the course of my travels that winter. It was not "slash and cut, blood and thunder" with him. He did not rush it; his thrusts were straight and deadly, his timing perfect; although sometimes he would deliver an attack with a savage energy which made me think of Dom Bass. I was kept strictly on the defensive and, with a tightening feeling at the heart, I realized that I would be lucky if I came out of this with my life.

I fought as warily as I knew how, keeping the point of my blade a shade lower than my hand and engaging his steel as lightly as possible. I shifted ground frequently, for I saw that his one weakness was his footwork. His legs were spare and a trifle clumsy; each shift threw him a little off balance and so gained me time.

There was no sun, and therefore no advantage in position. I stood with my back to Appleby Court and facing the town. I could see more people streaming down the road, some on horseback, some on foot. Clearly the word of what was afoot had been carried back. Carriages had stopped on the road. I realized that Sheriff Cropper could not fail to hear as well and that my chances of getting away would be slim even if I managed to emerge unscathed.

The only comfort I had was Macherie's obvious discomfiture over the steadiness of my defense. He had not expected to find me so well prepared. Once he stepped back and said, "Well, Sir Jackal, you seem to know something of it after all." The smile had not left his face, however, and it was clear he entertained no doubts of the final outcome. He began to exercise a still greater degree of guile, shifting his tactics with such suddenness that I never knew what to expect next. At each pause he would toss remarks at me calculated to keep me uneasy in mind. "Would you have danced as lively at Wapping Stairs as you do here?" or "Pray your Maker for mercy now; my blade will be through your ribs in a moment."

My arms began to grow weary with the strain. I blamed myself bitterly for not having practiced more regularly. Was he feeling the strain also? I doubted it, for his smile was confident as ever, and his blade wove around mine with unabated vigor. I continued to shift ground, hoping to tire him in that way. My only chance, I knew, was to catch him with the master stroke Dom Bass had taught me. As the minutes passed, it became increasingly unlikely that I could take him in that trap. His touch was always feather-light, and he avoided my approaches to it with ease.

Once I caught a glimpse of Temperance Handy's face back of the front rank of watchers. He had come in a great hurry, for he wore no hat and he was panting. I saw that he was as white as chalk, and that his lips began to move, perhaps with prayers for my benefit. I thought desperately that I was going to need them!

My chance came so unexpectedly that I was never able afterward to understand how I managed to take advantage of it. I think Macherie had decided to finish me off; perhaps he was feeling the strain as much as I was. At any rate, he shifted to the right and lunged with more fierceness than he had yet displayed. I parried, and the weary muscles of my arm conveyed the welcome message that he had put too much effort into his stroke. At last his grip had stiffened! I drove his blade downward in the manner I had been taught, reversed my wrist, and gave his steel a twist. O blessed and omnipotent Dom Bass! It worked perfectly! Macherie gave a grunt of surprise, and I saw the first glint of fear in his eyes. His sword was twisting slowly in the air above me.

I had been vaguely aware of comments from the watchers before this, mutters of, "Hold him, Roger, hold him." Now the air was full of deafening noise. A shout went up from the packed circle. Hats were thrown in the air; some of them indulged in gestures and dance steps of delight. "Go in and finish him!" shrieked the townsmen, knowing that the code now compelled him to defend himself against me with his dagger. His face showing desperation and fear, Macherie backed over the line until the solid bank of spectators made further retreat impossible.

I dropped the point of my sword. "My opponent," I said, "has supplied proof of one of my charges. He has shown himself a coward."

The crowd shouted their agreement, forcing him forward until he stood inside the line again. He had drawn his bagonet, and his face had the look of a cornered animal.

It was my privilege to go in and finish him. I knew that I should act quickly; my own life depended on it. I took a step in his direction and then stopped. Could I run a helpless man through in cold blood? My arm refused the task. If our positions had been reversed, he would have shown me no mercy. I knew that well enough. But I stepped back.

"Pick up your sword," I said. Something inside me clamored that I was acting like a fool, that I would lose my own life because of this. I wanted to kill him and end it; but my arm still refused the butcher's task.

Macherie gave me the look of a man who has won a reprieve on the gallows. At first it was one of incredulity, then of intense relief. He ran for his sword. The crowd howled their disapproval, and I thought for a moment they would break the circle and prevent a renewal of the conflict. I caught another glimpse of Temperance Handy's face. He was smiling in anxious agreement. I was glad then. I remembered something more that Dom Bass had taught me, a variation of the disarming stroke. If I could catch my antagonist off guard again, I would do things differently.

We were facing each other again, Macherie's face wreathed with malignant purpose. I was facing the other way, and I saw that another carriage had stopped where the road curved off toward Appleby Court. A feminine figure was standing on the steps. It looked like Katie, but I could not be sure.

"You've indulged yourself in a very fine gesture," said Macherie, advancing to the attack. "I suppose I should thank you. But in matters which concern my own safety I'm always willing to take advantage of such weakness. You won't have another chance. On guard, Sir Jackal! This time I intend to finish you quickly."

I could hear murmurs from the spectators as our blades crossed. He meant what he had said; there was the deadliest of menace now in the feel of his questing, darting sword. I kept myself completely on the defensive, hoping that another chance would come. I had no illusions, however; my squeamishness had probably cost me my life.

His attack had more subtlety of design than before, his own fear back of it. I fended him off with the greatest difficulty. Sweat poured down my face, almost blinding me. I was barely conscious of the excitement of the watchers, who were imploring me to disarm him again. My only thought was to wait, wait, for the chance which might come a second time. I never let my gaze wander for as much as a second from his confidently smiling eyes.

I decided after an eternity of this that I must resort to a subterfuge. The muscles of my arms were giving warning that I could not maintain my defense much longer. I must do what I could to end it, and do it at once. An idea flashed through my head. I knew from the comments of the crowd that Cropper had arrived; and so, taking care to keep a watch on my opponent from the corner of one eye, I pretended to be disturbed over his presence and looked back in his direction. Macherie saw his chance and lunged. It was a vicious, all-out thrust, delivered with a forward step. As his blade slashed along mine, my arm conveyed the same message: he was off balance, and he had stiffened his grip to drive the steel home. I was able to parry in time and to force his blade down. This time I did not reverse my wrist; instead I followed the lethal instructions of my great Dom Bass and thrust forward with an inward twist of the shaft. The steel encountered solid resistance.

Desperately I drove it home.

My opponent's face wore a bewildered look which turned in the merest trace of time to one of intense agony. Then it lost all expression, as though a hand had smoothed out the lines. He dropped forward with unnatural slowness. His sword, which had stuck in the ground, impeded his descent; and it seemed as though his body would never reach the earth.

For the first time the spectators were completely silent, stunned by the suddenness of it. Nothing was said as the men nearest the body rushed in to examine it. Knowing how deeply my sword had penetrated, I was not surprised when Widdigate said, "It's all up with him, Roger."

Someone shouted, "He's gone to Pegtantrums!" There was no cheering, which surprised me in view of the clamor they had created at every other stage. Perhaps the presence of Cropper had something to do with it. I sensed a new feeling of apprehension around me. I caught a momentary glimpse of my old tutor's face in the swerving wall of tense watchers;

tears were streaming down it. Immediately I was caught up in such a whirl of movement that I had no chance to think of anything. I saw Cropper's predatory face forcing its way through the press, but only for a moment. A mounted man swung his horse directly across the sheriff's path. He applied his spurs, and the poor animal reared and whinnied with pain, forcing Cropper and his aides to drop back. Before I knew how it happened, I had been dragged up into my own saddle and found myself riding off the field with mounted companions on each side of me. The spectators gave full vent to their feelings at last, and a wild chorus of cheers sounded on the heels of our galloping horses.

My two companions were young men. I had never seen either of them before, but they were regarding me with a friendliness which I found most reassuring.

"A beautiful stroke!" one of them threw at me over his shoulder.

I gasped in reply, "The greatest fencer in the world taught me that one."

We thundered down the road and then turned off to the right. I had forgotten everything but the great need to get away, and I would have ridden past the coach there without a glance if the lady on the steps had not waved at me as I went by. I looked back then. It was Katie! Her face was white and tense, but her eyes told me how happy she was that I had come through safely. I drew in sharply on my bridle and would have stopped if one of my companions had not kicked my mount on the flank to set him back into full stride. "Danger!" he cried. All I could do was to wave back. She would understand, of course.

Apparently, however, no serious effort was made at pursuit. We rode due south for several miles and then came to a fork in the road with an arrow marked west and under it the name Newnham. We pulled up, and one of my new friends said in an apologetic tone: "I must turn back here. My good lady's having her yearly visit from the midwife, and nothing short of a duel or a witch-burning would have brought me out. It's going to be a boy this time. Will you go on with him a piece, Fitz?"

The other, who seemed very little older than myself, said: "That I will. Get back to your Sophie, Jack. I'll see him safely on his way. It's certain to be a boy. One in four, surely."

"I'd advise turning off before you come into Newnham and striking down Godersham way. No sense in being seen any more than you can help. Good luck to you, Blease. You struck a shrewd blow for the right cause today. Going to name him Luke."

I rode with my remaining companion for several more miles, encountering a lone farmer's wagon on the way and nothing else. My mind was blank of all emotion in spite of the fact that I had just killed a man. Perhaps it was the fatigue which was now manifesting itself in the aching muscles of my back and arms. Perhaps also the fact that I had dreamed so long of fighting Macherie, and had hated him so violently, made his death seem right and just. At any rate, I was conscious of no sense of regret. My mind was filled instead with the picture of Katie as she stood on the steps of the carriage and waved me good-by. Would I ever see her again? In my jaded condition of mind and body, I was ready to believe that this brief glimpse of her would be my last.

My new friend had the reddest hair I had ever seen and the friendliest eyes. When we reached an intersection in the middle of a thick blanket of woods, he reined up and pointed to the right. "Now I must leave, I'm afraid. Keep riding west, and you'll be well beyond London by dark. What are your plans?"

"To get out of the country as soon as I can. I want to keep my head on my shoulders. I'm going to the East."

"The East? Do you mean China? And India?" He was very much excited at once. "I want to go to those countries more than anything else on earth. But my mother and sisters depend on me. We've three farms, and there's work to keep me busy all the time." He looked at me enviously. "What I'd give to be in your shoes! All England will hear about what you did today, and approve. A first payment for those poor fellows hanged in London. It's a beastly shame the way things are going in this country; and I don't care who hears me say it. Some day we'll meet again. I hope so; and I hope it'll be somewhere in the East."

He insisted on changing mounts when he realized that I had ridden down from London the night before. "Take good care of old Jeremy," he said. "He's a stout fellow and my favorite. If you'll leave him with an uncle of mine, Sir Anthony Basing, near Tunbridge Wells, he'll give you another in exchange and put you up for the night as well. He's a capital fellow, but a bit garrulous in his cups. Give the old boy some cock-and-bull story; anything but the truth."

"Thanks," I said. It was amazing to me how willing people were to help, knowing as they did that my life was forfeit to the government. "I don't know why you do all this for me, but I must say it's wonderfully kind of you."

"You saved my life." He laughed loudly at the puzzled look on my face. "Sooner or later I'd have found it impossible to stand that beast of a Macherie as a neighbor, and I'd have challenged him myself. After what I saw today, I know I wouldn't have stood a dotterel's chance against him. So, by doing it first, you unquestionably saved my life."

"Where will the Ladland family live?"

"At one of their farms, I think. Burchall's East Farm, a fine bit of land." I knew the place, a hundred acres or so with a stone house ringed on three sides by a small stream. It was a long step down from Appleby Court, but they would be comfortable enough there. I hoped the Queen's influence would ease matters for them in time.

My new friend mounted my weary nag and said cheerfully: "Spare me a thought, Blease, when you get to China. I'll be at home with the horses and the cows and the chickens. I haven't even got a sweetheart. Do'ye suppose Katie Ladland would look at me?"

42

CAPTAIN AMOS STARKLE, to whom I carried a note
from Sir Sigismund Hill, lived far out from Plymouth on the Penlee
Road. I knew he had commanded ships in the Eastern trade, and that
later he had lived for many years in Persia, becoming rather handsomely
opulent in the process, and so I expected to find in his household the
rigid discipline which seems to govern the lives of all retired captains. To
my surprise I discovered that he lived in an atmosphere of indolence and
bodily comfort; a reflection, I realized later, of his luxurious life in the
Orient.

The Hoe, where Francis Drake bowled while the sails of the Armada
hove in sight, was visible across the Sound when I arrived, so it seemed
fitting that Captain Starkle should be enjoying a game back of his house
with a friend. Still, I was surprised; for, although the season was well advanced and the almond and cornelian trees were already in bloom, the
grass was tender and the ground soft. They were hard at it in spite of
this, shouting, "The bias isn't working, man!" and, "There's a Mary for
ye, straight to the Block!" He came out at once to greet me, carrying a
muddy bowl in one hand; a thickset man rolling sailorwise on the balls of
his feet, his eyes like lighted garnets and his hair so completely gone that
his long beak of a nose made him resemble a parrot.

"Hill wrote me to expect ye," he said, in a high-pitched voice, "but
ye're a day or two ahead of time. Ye're younger than he led me to believe.
Well, now, I see ye're surprised to find us at the game so soon. We're
bowlers here, sir; we can hardly wait for the frost to get out of the
ground." He looked back over his shoulder at his opponent. "Be off
home, Syl. Game's over."

The house was broad and low, and covered with a yellow Italian material called stucco which had been introduced into England a very short
time before. I did not care much for it, I must confess; it looked too
unsubstantial and gibe-crakey for a rugged English landscape. There were
surprises in every room; lovely rugs from the East on the floors and hangings on all the walls in the gayest color combinations I had ever seen;
cool tiled partitions in place of the usual dark oak screens, and ivory
tables; and, most unusual of all, a pair of salaaming servants in snow-
white turbans and trousers as broad as a lady's farthingale. The room to
which I was escorted had a bathtub made of tile instead of wood and
high enough to bring the water right up to the armpits. I was into it as
soon as I could untie my points, not having had an opportunity to wash

properly for many days. The water was hot, and there was an oval of soap which smelled of rose-water and lavender. There was even a fine linen cloth for the teeth and a special soap to aid in scrubbing them clean.

Over a supper of curry, which he explained was an Eastern dish of meat smothered with crushed herbs, and which was very tasty, although I thought the first mouthful would take the roof off my mouth, my host talked incessantly. His favorite habit was the quoting of verse, by preference in English, although he could roll out Latin as well. Everything said reminded him of something from Spenser or Donne or "that new fellow, William Shaxbird," and he would then recite flawlessly and at great length, fixing me the while with his avid eyes. It was not until we were at our wine that he began to ply me with questions.

"Why has the *Rainbow* been fitted out for action?" he asked, twisting his head in the direction of Plymouth. "She lies over there, and I hear no shore leave's being allowed."

"It was rumored in London," I answered cautiously, "that Captain Ward was returning and that His Majesty planned a reception for him."

"Ay, I heard the same. But what manner of reception? Will the captain of the *Rainbow* read the great Ward an address of welcome, or will he use a round of langrel-shot instead?"

"I don't think they plan to have masques and fireworks," I answered. "Has the news reached you that nineteen of the Free Rovers were hanged in London a few days ago?"

"Ay, and the whole town's gone into mourning over it. We hear the ballad makers of Paul's Walk have turned out songs on the hangings that will send some of them to the chats if the King can find who wrote them. Can it be that ye know John Ward?"

"I was raised in the same town with him."

"And sailed with him, belike?"

Sir Sigismund had said that I could trust him completely. "Yes, I sailed with Captain Ward. I was in the battle off Cape Passer. I consider him a great man, and I'm proud to say that I've been making myself troublesome to the King. He would have made it twenty if he had got his hands on me."

"I judged ye right, then, although our old Ulysses didn't tell me much about ye."

"Now that you know that much, I might as well give you my whole record. I killed Macherie in a duel on the morning of the hangings."

He whistled. "Ye killed Macherie! I didn't know about that. It's extraordinary, quite extraordinary! Ye must be a rare hand with the blade, my young cock."

"You're harboring a dangerous guest, Captain Starkle. If you say so, I'll leave at once, and no hard feelings. I don't want to see you in any trouble."

He clapped his hands, and one of the servants came into the room, bowing so low that he seemed to double up like a spring knife. I wondered if my host would give orders for my capcase to be delivered to me at once. Instead he ordered more wine. When the blackamoor was gone, he laid a reassuring hand on my knee. "Don't ye like the ways of the East, Master Pirate, that ye talk of leaving so soon? Ye made a friend of every salt in England when ye let daylight into that lying bully-huff. I tell ye I have no love for the King, and the more trouble ye make for him, the better I'll like ye. No, no, we'll get along fine together."

I sighted the *Royal Bess* on the morning of the third day. I believed it was Ward as soon as my magic cylinder picked up her sails on the horizon, and it did not take long to be sure. I felt an intense relief; for now I could save John from the fate waiting for him ashore and still get to Brest in time.

We fought our way out through a powerful sea-gate. The *Royal Bess* paid no attention to my first hail, and so my skipper had to lay the sloop alongside the hull of the plunging monster while I repeated it. Finally I heard the voice of Mate Gard bawling orders from the quarter-deck. The great ship heaved and lay to.

Gard had recognized me, for I heard him say, "It's Blease, or I'm a culping sea-ape!" A line was thrown me, and I managed to climb up the side, getting myself thoroughly soaked to the waist; a final proof that I would never make a sailor. The rail was crowded, and I heard jubilant shouts as I pulled myself over. "Shanks! Good for you, Shanks!"

I was given a hearty welcome. They had been feasting their eyes since dawn on the hilly coastline of England, and I suppose my arrival seemed to them a confirmation that things were right ashore. At any rate, they slapped me on the back as though I were bringing them the news they wanted and indulged in all manner of delighted capers. One man danced a hornpipe. I looked about me and was struck with the fact that many of the faces were new.

They felt no better than I did. The shadow of the rope, which had hung over me from the moment I landed, had vanished at last. I had escaped; I was free; the chance to begin a new life in the East stretched ahead. I was so happy I would have joined in the hornpipe if I had known the steps. For the moment everything else was forgotten.

Maltworm, his face tanned to the color almost of charred wood, was one of the first to shake hands. "Shanks, we're proud of ye," he boomed. "We heard about ye. Pouring bambury-chat into the ears o' the Queen!"

The cook, looking out from the galley, called to me: "Greetings to ye! Will ye take us all to the palace to see the old lady?"

"She isn't old," I said. "She's young and pretty."

"All the better! Nownes, to see a pretty face again!"

"Ye'll make the rounds in Rome-ville with us, Shanks," said Maltworm. "If only Clim and Dandyprat could go with us too! We'll have a girl on each arm, and we'll drink all the ale in England, and the gorbellied old King will wave at us from his window."

"And our pockets full of ribbin!" shouted someone else.

One of the men in the shrouds took that up and started to sing the ribbin song: "Ribbin, ribbin, rolling Spanish ribbin!"

The whole crew joined in, shouting the words and slapping their breeches pockets in anticipation of the easy times ahead:

> "Ribbin, ribbin, rolling Spanish ribbin!
> Angel, noble, yellow boy,
> Darby, rhino, dust o' Troy.
>
> Ribbin, ribbin, ruddy Spanish ribbin!
> Setting busk and making law,
> Waxing in a nip-cheese claw.
>
> Ribbin, ribbin, richest Spanish ribbin!
> When the sailors go ashore,
> Hear the callots call for more
> Ribbin, ribbin—"

It was one of those continuous things, and they would have sung it through if John Ward had not appeared on deck. He came down the ladder on the run and shook hands with me.

"Roger, boy! I'm delighted to see you!" The white plumes in his hat trembled with the eager pumping of his arm. With a sinking of the heart, I realized he had dressed himself up like a bridegroom in anticipation of a triumphal visit ashore. His doublet was of white velvet, and his trunk hose slashed and embroidered in gold, tapering down to below the knee. He even wore low shoes with white Tudor roses. I wondered dismally how I could break the news.

"Why, you swaggering lob, you've grown a beard!" exclaimed John. "I hoped you would get wind of our coming. How are things ashore?"

I hesitated. "I'm afraid, Captain Ward, you won't find things as you expected. The fact is, you musn't risk it."

The smile on his face died. "No?" he said. "Just what do you mean, Roger?"

"I came out to warn you."

I was conscious that complete silence had fallen over the ship. The seamen were edging up as close as they dared, to hear what was being said. Their faces had become sullen.

"Nineteen men were hanged at Wapping Stairs a week ago," I went on. "I'd have been with them if they had caught me."

John reached forward and gripped me by the shoulders. His eyes seemed to have shrunk to pinpoints.

"Nineteen! Were they Free Rovers? Did they belong to the ships that came home ahead of us?"

I nodded unhappily. "Four of the captains. Halsey—"

"Halsey!" cried John. "Halsey hanged! This passes belief. Halsey was one of the finest fighting men this country ever bred." He paused and breathed deeply. "Who else? In God's name, who else?"

"Harris, Longcastle, and Jennings."

John's arms dropped to his sides. He walked to the rail and stood there in silence for several minutes. When he turned back, his face was stern and set.

"Did Macherie have a hand in it?" he demanded.

"Yes. But there's nothing left to be done about him. I killed him in a duel the morning of the executions."

He looked at me incredulously. "You killed Macherie in a duel? I would like to believe it, but—"

The men were stirring again. The news of the hangings had struck them dumb, but it was apparent they were getting some consolation out of the killing of Macherie.

"A fencing master had taught me a special trick," I explained. "I was able to use it before he wore me down. We fought on one of the meadows near Appleby Court."

John took me by the arm and led me back to the quarter-deck ladder. "Roger," he said, "it's clear now they had set a trap for me. Two months ago I received word that the old offer held; I could return home and take a post with the Navy. It didn't come from my Lord of Nottingham, but —well, I'll name no names here. It seemed official enough, and I was sure I could trust my man. Several of the captains had received promises of pardon and had already sailed for home. I decided I could take it this time. The Dons had left the Inner Sea wide open since we whipped them. English ships were putting through without interference. We'd done what we set out to do."

"Macherie was back of it, I'm sure."

"His hand didn't show, but I think you're right. I was foolish enough to believe there had been a change of heart. I'm a weak-headed dolt; and you've saved me again. Well, I don't need a soothsayer to read the future for me now!"

He walked back and faced the crew. "Men," he said, "this is bad news for all of us. We've been chasing a wild goose. We can't land; it would be the rope for all of us if we did. There's nothing to it but to put back to where we came from. Heathen ports are the only ones open to us still. Any man inclined to risk it has my permission to leave and go ashore. But I advise against it."

No one spoke. The faces of the men were glum with the final dashing of all their hopes.

"The *Rainbow* is in Plymouth Harbor," I said. "She's been fitted out for action. She's fully manned, Captain Ward. The word ashore is that she's been ordered to capture the *Royal Bess*."

He threw back his head and laughed. "The *Rainbow* is a stout old lady, but we've nothing to fear from any ship manned by King's officers. We could blow the abbey-lubbers out of the water!" He paused. "But I see what you meant. We'll have to get away. We can't fight an English ship."

"We need fresh supplies, Cap'n Ward," put in Gard. "Two more down with the scurvy today. That makes six. They'll all have it if we put back with nothing but powdered pork and sea biscuit."

"I don't intend to run like a fox at the first sound of the horn. We'll put in at some port west of here and pick up what we can. Bring her about, Gard. We've no time to spare."

He took me back to his cabin and there heard the whole story. At first he listened with complete apathy, his eyes full of the disappointment he had suffered. When I began to relate the details of Macherie's course, however, his interest became bitterly active.

"I hated the man from the first time I saw him," he said. "Well, you wiped that score off neatly. You'll have to show me that trick, Roger; there must be a touch of black magic about it, for I've seen Macherie in action, and he was a dimber hand with the blade."

"I'm under promise not to describe it. Dom Bass made me take an oath before he taught me."

After a moment he sighed deeply and said: "I wish it had been a little further on into spring. There's so little green out! I've been looking forward to seeing apple blossoms and cowslips. Things won't be at their best for a month or more."

"We may never see England again."

He sat up at that and said with an attempt at briskness, "Well, no use repining, my stout Roger. We're being turned away, but it could be worse; by this time Macherie has been driven from the gates of heaven and is on his way south to a warmer clime than Tunis. I wouldn't trade places with him. As a matter of fact, I'm free of all strings now. I'll carve out some kind of life for myself; and, by all the angels above, I'll have a good time doing it. I'm free now, I tell you."

"Things may right themselves in time, John. The Queen is for us, and young Prince Henry. There's a powerful party against the King, as I found when I made my rounds."

"Yes. But he's the king, and what the rest of them think and want doesn't matter." He managed a smile. "Your audience with the Queen was a bold stroke, Roger. But I didn't expect you to risk your neck that way. I was sure Mundy Hill would put a check-rein on you."

"I take no credit. I didn't do anything until my conscience drove me to it."

"Well, you did it. You laid the train; let's pray something will set it off!" His hands slipped listlessly to his knees, and all the animation left him. I could see he was thinking again about the bleak future stretching ahead of him. There was a suggestion of moisture in his eyes when he said in hopeless tones: "I'm no longer an Englishman. I'm a man without a flag or country. Must I keep going now like the Wandering Jew? God, Roger, was ever mortal in such a plight before?"

He had told me that Joralemon was down with the scurvy, so I slipped away to pay a visit to the hospital. It was on the orlop-deck, a dark corner with one porthole and a latticed opening through the inner partition to give some circulation of air. The atmosphere was foul beyond description. Joralemon essayed a smile when he saw me, but it was a feeble effort.

"What's being done for you?" I demanded, for the place reeked of neglect. "I'm afraid John is falling into lax ways."

He rose at once to the defense of his hero. "Nothing more can be done. We'll be right again as soon as we can have a bite of fresh food and some milk to drink. It's always amazing how quickly a man can get over this trouble. This is my third spell of it, and right now my teeth are so loose I could pull them all out like raisins from a cake. But I'll be right in a day or two."

I examined the medicine cabinet which stood in one corner. It was almost completely bare. There was a bottle of *hickery-pickery* and another containing a colorless powder, and that was all. The handles of two knives were visible above the chirurgeon's table, and on top of it there was a large mazer-bowl in which some nauseous ingredients had been mixed. The bowl had been handsome once, but the silver was tarnished yellow now, and I had difficulty in reading the inscription on the rim, "Forget not thy beginning, Think of thine End"; a cheerful sentiment for a sick room!

"We'll have fresh food in a few hours," I said, returning and seating myself on a joint-stool beside his hammock. "How have things been going, Jore?"

He whispered cautiously so that none of the other patients could hear: "Badly, Roger. So many of our English crew have been killed that we've had to take on anyone we could get. A lot of Dutchmen and Italians and a few French. They're a wicked lot! Terrible things happen on board now. Beastly things; I can't put a name to them. I can't do a thing with these new men. They jeer at me all the time. Gard tries to beat it out of them; but that's no good either. The *Royal Bess* is a hell, a sink of the foulest iniquity. Well, it will be over soon. Didn't I hear that the coast has been sighted? It will be wonderful to be home in England!"

I hesitated about telling him the truth and then decided he would be sure to get the news immediately anyway. "The ship can't go in, Jore. The King is hanging the Rovers as fast as he can lay his hands on them. John is going to lay in fresh stores and then sail back to Tunis."

His face went even whiter than it had been before. His eyes closed. "Then it's better if I die," he muttered. "Lord, if it be Thy will, take me from this scene of wickedness!"

43

WE DROPPED DOWN THE COAST and anchored off the mouth of a small river where the thatched roofs of a village showed through the trees. A boat was sent ashore and returned in a few hours, well laden with everything obtainable in the line of food—tall crocks of milk, some bags of vegetables which had managed to survive the winter in root-cellars, quarters of beef, and whole carcasses of hogs, and, most enticing of all to the starved nostrils of the sailors, dozens of loaves of bread, hot from the ovens. The men seized the loaves tossed to them by Gard and tore them apart with their fingers, then devoured them with ravenous smacking of lips.

They had no more than a few minutes to eat, for the sails of the *Rainbow* had been sighted. The old flagship was coming up with the obvious purpose of cutting us off. John Ward held all officers of the Royal Navy in the utmost contempt, but he was anxious to avoid a clash, knowing that lives inevitably would be lost; so he signaled Gard to up anchors and away as soon as the boat had been raised.

I stood beside him on the quarter-deck, and I could see that the *Rainbow* was being handled well enough. At any rate she came up fast, and it was apparent that we could not get away without a brush. Realizing this, John frowned and cursed King James under his breath.

Some years later a song was written about what happened that day.* It became a great favorite, and I heard it sung wherever sailors congregated. It was a poor bit of doggerel, as far from the truth as could be imagined, and full of bombastic messages exchanged between the King and John Ward. John was said to have offered "full thirty ton of gold" for a pardon. There was a brisk fight, according to the ballad writer, with the piratical craft getting all the better of it, for "they were brass on the outside but Ward was steel within."

It did not happen that way at all. It is true that the new guns in the bow of the *Rainbow* spat at us angrily when we proved that we had the heels of them. The shots were pitifully wild, causing spouts of water to kick up a hundred yards in front of us. John shook his head sorrowfully when he saw how bad their marksmanship was.

"They're no better now than the Jew-roasters," he said. "Can you believe that's all we have left of the stout navy which pounded the Armada

---

* "John Ward and the *Rainbow*" (1620).

to pieces? Still, bad as it is, this must be stopped. I can't risk an injury to the *Bess*."

I followed him below to the gun-deck, where Master Gunner Gracey had his men lined for immediate action.

"One shot only, Gracey. We'll give him a scare, but I don't want any of the poor fellows hurt. Do you suppose now that you could damage his rigging for him?"

It was a stiff order. While Gracey and I argued about the degrees of randon, John himself got to work and had one of the guns trained on the flagship. He sighted it himself, carelessly it seemed to me, and without doing any figuring at all. "That should be about right," he said.

Miracles will happen for men like John Ward. To my amazement, and the delight of the whole gunnery crew, the shot struck the mainmast of the *Rainbow* squarely, sheering it off as neatly as a cocoanut at a fair. The billowing head of white sail collapsed at once. I can think of no simile to describe it except that the same effect might have been gained if a giant hand were to reach up and drag from the sky a bank of fleecy clouds.

John rubbed his hands and grinned at me. "What's all this talk about degrees of randon and setting a true dispart?" he demanded.

That was all there was to the epic fight between John Ward and the *Rainbow*. The flagship was soon nothing more than a stationary speck on a darkening ocean. It was cock-shut time, and the swabber put his head out of the coach to say that the Captain's dinner was ready. The Captain paid no attention. He had walked to the rail and was watching the receding shoreline. I went over and stood beside him.

"It's so green!" he said, after a few moments of silence. "When I try to find a reason for the way I feel, it comes back to that. France and Spain get a baked and parched look when the summer wears on, but England is always green. Green and fresh and peaceful. You know, Roger, my mother had a little of the poet in her, and she used to say that the streams and brooks all murmured, 'Slowly I flow, sadly I go.' They wanted to linger as long as they could before leaving England and joining the sea. I think she was right."

"This time I've had no chance to listen to brooks," I said, "but I'm sorry to see that shore fading away."

"I can't believe yet," he said, "that I'll never again walk the streets of our grand, noisy, fighting Rome-ville. I love it! You know that song, 'The grave I choose at last to fill must lie where I may hear them still, Bow Bells, rapt, in Rome-ville.' It keeps running through my head."

He gave a short laugh. "Why should I keep repeating those words? The grave I'll fill will be under desert sands; and, if there's any sound of bells to be heard, they'll belong to stinking camel trains!"

We were interrupted by a loud cry of pain. I had already noticed that one of the crew was a Moor, a huge fellow with coarse features under a dirty turban. He had passed behind us on shuffling feet and about twenty paces on had encountered a knife dropped from the shrouds. It struck him squarely in the shoulder, and he fell to the deck, calling loudly on Allah and the One Prophet.

"God in Heaven," cried John, "what's come over this ship! Gard, Gard, find out who did it! Find the murdering dog and bring him here! I'll put a stop to this business of dropping knives if I have to hang half the crew!"

The mate, who was already bending over the wounded Moor, straightened up. "I'll find who did it, Cap'n. But think that matter of hanging over carefully before stringing any of them up. I'm shorthanded, Cap'n Ward; I haven't two full watches as it is. And remember this: none of them wanted us to take on the heathen dog. Just think it over, Cap'n."

"All right, all right," said John, throwing up his arms. "Have it your way, Gard. I must wink at murder so long as the ship keeps under way!" He stopped and then went on in his normal tones. "Gard, there must be some punishment for this. Find who did it and have him keel-raked. See that he gets a good one. I want him scraped down one side and up the other; and when he comes to the surface I want to see that he's close to drowned and has half the skin raked off his filthy hide."

"Keel-raked it is, Cap'n," said Gard. "If ye say so. But I'm against it. They're close to mutiny now, Cap'n Ward. They don't take kindly to this business of being shut out of England. They're not praising Cap'n Rufflecoat down in the fo'c's'le tonight, and I might as well tell ye the truth."

"See that he's roped and thrown over at once," said John sharply. "I want the whole crew on hand when it's done. We must get back to proper discipline, Gard. This malingering's got to stop. I won't have a crew of mine fed out of pap-boats! They'll step lively from now on. I want the ship scraped and painted, from top to bottom. Work's what they need, the dirty abbey-lubbers!" His eyes roved about the ship, frowning at the evidences of laxness which he saw. His face became red with rage when he detected the head of a seaman over the forward rail. "Get him off that seat! Are they too dainty to go below any more?"

I could not help laughing at that. Many times I had seen Captain Ward himself on the side seat, and I had been caught there often and been well drenched when the sea was running high. John looked at me sternly for a moment, but then broke down and began to grin himself.

"Let that go, Gard," he said. "But don't misunderstand me about the main issue. Have evening prayers as usual at Compline. See that every man's on hand. Then truss your man up while they're there. He'll need prayers afterward, I trust."

Before going in to dinner, he visited the pilot-house and exploded into new rage when he saw that the sand in the roning glass had been allowed to run out. He scowled at the man on the wheel. "I'll have another talk with Gard. Holy Olaf, we're falling into slack ways!"

We had dinner together in his cabin. The cook had celebrated the securing of new supplies by providing a roast of beef. John helped me liberally and then cut off a full rib for himself. It had been done as a matter of habit, however, for he picked at the meat in an abstracted mood. He said nothing. I tried to talk about various matters, but he did not seem to hear. Sometimes I thought that I detected a glint of tears in his eyes.

"The roast beef of Old England," he muttered once. "Will I ever taste it again?"

He drank steadily, and in time this had its effect. His mood lifted. He sunk his knife in the red meat, and his elbows began to work with their accustomed heartiness. He finished the beef and then proceeded to devour half a dozen thick slabs of new cheese. He wound up the meal by cracking walnuts with the hilt of his fine sword.

The sea was rough. The lantern, suspended from the ceiling by a chain of Castilian brass, swayed so much with the pitching of the ship that we were in semidarkness half of the time.

John fell into an oratorical mood. "I've given the trade of the world back to my country," he said. "I've handed the Levant on a platter to our merchants, with dressings of olives and cloves of garlic. And this is my reward! I'll die under an African sun with heathen gabble in my ears. Or perhaps the Dons will get me finally, and I'll appear before my Maker with a red welt around my neck. Well, my brave Roger, I propose now to make the best of it. If I must cast in my lot with the heathen, I'll take what ease and pleasure I may out of heathen ways. Have you any quarrel with that, my strait-laced friend?" After a moment he added: "Did you know that most of the people ashore refused to take money for the supplies we picked up today? It's a fact; and it shows that their hearts are stanchly in the right place. *They* think well of John Ward. That will be something for me to remember under the stinking hot walls of Tunis!"

The creak of the swaying lantern was the only sound heard for several minutes. John had lighted his pipe but it refused to draw.

"I suppose you want to hear about Cristina," he said finally. "I don't like to talk about it yet and, after all, there's so dismally little to tell. I went to the place where they had taken her, but she was dead before I arrived. I saw her, poor child. That was some consolation, for I could be sure they hadn't made up the story of her death to throw me off. She— she was very thin. She left a letter for me. It was a brave note, and I'll always treasure it." He puffed furiously at his unwilling pipe. "My son died with her. If you don't mind, that's all I want to say about it."

We came to the subject of Katie shortly after. "Well, we've both lost her now," he said. "She'll be married when you come back from the East; if they ever let you, that is." As though I did not know it! I thought about it continually. "The state of the family purse will make it doubly necessary for her to take a rich husband. Did she tell you I wrote her?"

I shook my head.

"She wouldn't, of course. What I said was that she ought to marry you.

Oh, it was no magnanimous gesture, like a hero in a play at the Globe. I had no chance myself, and I wanted you to have her in preference to anyone else. That was all, so don't be thanking me. It might have worked out that way if you had walked on eggs like a sensible man. The King would have pardoned you. I think Mundy Hill could have seen to that."

I shook my head again. "I doubt it. Pardons were to be had, but at a stiff price. A stiffer price than I wanted to pay."

"I'm not so sure. The old gander might have done handsomely by you. But no, you looby fool, you had to preen yourself before the Queen and then spread sedition up and down the land." He smiled at me. "It was well done, Roger. I'm proud of you. But you probably lost our Katie by it."

When I said nothing, being deep in recollection of her as I had last seen her on the edge of Fritchett's Meadow, he went on: "She's the only one I've ever had any real love for. Not even my poor Cristina. You may not want to believe it, Roger, after seeing the way I live; but I remember every word she said on the few occasions that I saw her. I can recall every expression on her face and every little move she made. Well, there it is. She'll marry some sober landowner and will raise a flock of proper little ladies and gentlemen; and we'll both rot under tropic suns."

"John," I said, "you've done what you set out to do. Why not drop it now? Come on with me to Damascus. There are independent traders in the East, and they do well for themselves. The King might pardon both of us in time."

He shook his head. "And what about my men? There are still fifty or more of them who signed on with me at home. I couldn't take them with me. What then? Leave them to fend for themselves? The poor devils would all wind up in Spanish nasks. No, I must see it through. I got them into this, and I must do the best I can for them."

He continued to fill his wine cup, and his spirits rose as the wine went down. Finally he insisted on a demonstration of the stroke that had won for me against Macherie.

"I'm not asking to know how it's done," he said. "I'm just curious to see if it can be played on me. I'm a dimber-damber with the blade myself, you know."

Anyone who had ever seen him in action could believe that. When we boarded the decks of the *Santa Caterina*, his sword had cut a swathe about him like the mighty brand of Roland at Roncesvalles. He had been the equal of six ordinary men, a slashing, raging human torrent; the greatest fighter, I am sure, in the world. I had no faith whatever in my ability to disarm him.

As soon as our blades crossed, however, I realized that, in spite of his prowess in combat, he was not in the technical sense a good fencer. He had most of the faults that Dom Bass had ascribed to Englishmen: a tendency to attack with ill-considered fury, a looseness of stroking which left him open to the ripostes of an opponent, and little sense of economy in the strength of his thrusts. Because of the fitful light, we fought warily, but I knew from the start that I could disarm him at any moment I saw fit. Out of regard for his pride, I delayed the culminating twist.

"I guess you find me different from Macherie," he declared, beaming over the flash of his busy blade. "When does it come, this magic trick? My sword's still in my hand, oh, my doughty Roger. I begin to think you were drawing a long bow; or perhaps I'm too good to be caught by the trick of a mere fencing master."

I knew then that I must let him off. His pride was too closely engaged, and he needed whatever satisfaction he could win after what he had been through this day. Finally I stepped back and lowered my point.

"You must know it after all," I said. "I can't catch you, John. You would have run Macherie through in short order if the privilege of meeting him had been yours instead of mine."

He smiled at me with great satisfaction. The outcome of our little brush had restored his spirits.

"I thought so," he exulted, sheathing his sword with a bang of triumph. "Well, it's getting late. You'll be seeing old Kochab over the left shoulder soon. Better turn in, my kinchin coe." He dropped a huge hand on my shoulder and began to propel me toward the door. "Look in on Jore, will you? My poor old heaven-beck needs cheering up. Perhaps you could work your trick on *him*."

There was a rap on the other door of the cabin which led to a smaller one adjoining it. His face, already red from the exertion, became even more ruddy. He shrugged his shoulders and gave a somewhat shamefaced grin.

"I didn't want you to know," he said. "Well, it doesn't matter now. You know well enough already that I've always had a roving eye. She's French and as lively as a young wildcat. I saw her when we touched a small Sicilian port, and she swore she needed a protector. I declare, Roger, that if things had gone right I would have shipped her home to France so quietly that no one would ever have known."

Who was I to judge him?

As I stepped out the door, I heard him call, "Come in, Fubbs."

44

I WAS THREE DAYS in Brest, waiting for the ship to put in, and I was glad of the delay, for it afforded me a chance to get some suitable clothes. The paunchy little French cucumber to whom I went insisted on the use of light silks when he found I was to live in the East, where velvets and kersey cloths would be uncomfortable. That was most sensible, as I discovered later, but he took his own head about other matters, with the result that I was never very happy with my new wardrobe. He made everything the French way in spite of my earnest instructions to the contrary. The trunk hose were shorter than we were accustomed to in England—so short, in fact, that they made me feel like a pumpkin on top of long props. The doublets had all manner of little Gallic surprises, such as yellow ruffles around the armpits and lace on the sleeves which drooped down over my hands. In time, of course, I became accustomed to the gibe-crakey look of everything, but I never did get used to the lack of points to hold my doublet and breeches together. The tailor had spliced them in the new French way, with curved pins welded together in pairs. He called them "sure-pinnes" and was voluble in declaring that I would soon get to prefer them. I never did, however; they never gave me the fine sense of security that only points can supply.

It was late in the afternoon of the third day when the *Empress* arrived. I went out to her at once, uncomfortably aware of my new clothes. The captain, a North Englishman from his accent, welcomed me as I climbed over the side and said that the ladies were waiting for me in their cabins.

Ladies? I expected Aunt Gadilda, of course, but I could not understand his use of the plural. It seemed highly improbable that prudent Aunt Gadilda had brought a maid with her.

The explanation proved the greatest and most wonderful surprise of my life. The captain led the way to a door facing his own cabin, knocked, and then quickly faded away. A voice said, "Come in." When I obeyed the summons, I found myself face to face with Katie.

"Here I am, Roger," she said. She was trying to make her tone sound casual, but there was a breathless catch in her voice. "Don't you think you had better close the door?"

I obeyed mechanically. The surprise was so great that I could not find a word to say. I just stood there, looking at her, wondering if it would turn out to be a dream. She had been on deck, apparently, for she was still wearing a bongrace, and the wind had put a glow in her cheeks. As I watched her, I saw a change in her manner. She seemed suddenly to become unsure, even a little frightened.

"Roger! I don't believe you're glad to see me!"

"Glad to see you! Katie, I—I don't know what to say. It's too good to be true!"

"Then you *did* mean it?"

"Mean what?"

"If you don't know, I can't tell you."

"If it had anything to do with my feeling for you, I meant it."

"That's a little better. But—must I go on? You're being very stupid, Roger. Do you remember when you appeared before the Queen and you told her you were in love with an English girl? And right afterward you said you meant me?"

"I'll never forget it as long as I live. Yes, I meant what I said that night. I wish I could tell you how much I meant it." I took both her hands in mine and pressed them tight. I still could not be sure that her presence meant what I wanted it to mean.

"That's very much better. It's almost what I wanted you to say." She closed her eyes. "Well, then, I think you had better kiss me. It's quite proper for you to kiss me. The captain is going to marry us right away."

I did not kiss her at once. I held her in my arms lightly, trying to convince myself that everything had turned out right after all. She was not going to marry a wealthy landowner in order to mend the Ladland fortunes. She was going to marry me. She was going to marry me right away and live with me at my post in the East. She was here, in my arms, and the world had suddenly become a wonderful place again.

I kissed her once only. The first kiss is a milestone in life, the most important of all, something to remain clearly in the mind for all time, and so not to be confused with other kisses. She seemed to understand and to want it that way too.

"I was afraid you were in love with John," I said, when speech became possible again.

She looked up at me intently. "I know you thought that. I'm beginning to understand you pretty thoroughly, my Roger, and so I think we had better settle this once and for all. I don't want any doubts or reservations between us. There *was* a time when I thought I was in love with him. But it was such a long time ago."

"All of a year."

"But I was very young then."

"It's still no more than a year."

She protested indignantly. "A year makes the greatest difference. I've lived at court since. I've learned a great deal. It seems so long ago that I can hardly remember how I felt about it. Roger, you've got to believe me. I only *thought* I was in love with John. I suppose I was swept off my feet. I was impressed by the great things he was doing. How am I going to convince you of that?"

The fact that she was here with me proved it. I did not need anything else to convince me; but I said nothing because I wanted her to go on. She stood for several moments in the circle of my arms, and I saw that her eyes were closed. Suddenly they popped wide open. "I can't see him any more!" she cried. "I've been trying to but I can't! I know he had long golden hair and a large nose and blue eyes. I can remember each feature separately, but when I try to put them together I don't see anyone at all. Roger, I can't be sure now what he looks like." She began to laugh. "Does that convince you? Are you going to believe me and never have any other thoughts about it as long as you live?"

I did not answer with words, but I think she found my response en-

tirely satisfactory. After a long interval, I asked her when she had made
up her mind about me.

"Must you know now?" she demanded. "I don't think I'll tell you yet.
We're going to be together a long time—have you any idea how long
it's going to be? Years and years, forever and ever, and it can't be too
long for me—and if I don't tell you everything now, perhaps I'll be able
to keep you really interested in me. There will always be something for
you to find out. A wife has to think about such things, you know. I've
been at court, and so I know a great deal about husbands. No, you'll
have to be content with what I've told you already. It ought to be enough,
my lord." After another long interval, she said: "I'm going to tell you
after all. I want to. It was when you came to court. I fell in love with
you as soon as you walked into the room. Roger, it—it almost frightened
me! It was so different from the way I had thought about John Ward.
You looked so handsome and brave, and you talked right up to the
Queen. I was so proud of you I wanted to cry."

"Do you really mean it?"

"Is it weak of me to tell you such things? I'm doing all the talking,
all the confessing. But I've been weak about everything, writing you
notes and running in to see you on any little pretext. Didn't you see
that I was pursuing you?"

"You don't expect me to believe that."

"You're much too humble. That's all right as far as being my husband
is concerned. But you've been humble about things, and *that* has
got to stop. Do you understand?"

"I'm sure I'll never be humble after what has happened to me today.
I'm fairly bursting with pride. I feel as though I could go out now and
conquer the whole world."

"That's what I want. I want you to bring me the world. Not that
I would know what to do with it, but because I'm going to need some
such proof of your devotion."

"You'll never need proofs of that, darling. I fell in love with you the
first time I saw you. No, the second time."

"And why not the first time, pray?"

I took her in my arms and held her close, laughing with the sense
of happiness which filled me. "Because, my sweet and beautiful and
adorable one, the first time you were just a little bit greedy about the
marchpane. You took all the cakes I had picked out for myself."

"Did I really?" She joined in my laughter. "I always was greedy about
marchpane. I still am. Are you going to see that I always have plenty?
And are you going to be sensible enough now to claim your share?"

"You're all the marchpane I'll ever want now. Sweet and tempting
and beautifully iced. And good enough to eat. Would you be afraid if
you knew how much in danger you are of being devoured right now?"

"That's very much better. I'm beginning to think you're really glad I
came. I was so frightened when you walked in and looked at me so

queerly. You looked cold and *stony*. I didn't know what to think."

"There's one thing more I *must* know. How was it arranged, this great miracle which has happened to me?"

"Must I make another confession? I arranged it myself. I was ill after the duel—are you surprised at that?—and it was decided I must be taken back to London to see a doctor. But when I got there, I went at once to that nice old man at the shipping offices. I told him I was de-termined to follow you, and that he might as well help me because I knew he had been looking after you. He said he thought it could be managed and that he was entirely in favor of having me go, but that I would have to obey his instructions closely. He sent me to Dover in a coach, and I went aboard there. I went under the name of Mistress Deborah Willis —it was his choice, not mine—and I was supposed to come from New-castle. I wore a bonnet which came down over my face, and I was going to France to visit relatives. Do English people ever have relatives in France? It seemed an improbable story, but we couldn't think of a better one."

"Had word of the duel reached London?" I asked.

Her eyes began to sparkle. "I should say it had! Everyone was talking of it. You were the hero of London. They were even selling a ballad about you on the streets, *The English David and Sir Goliath*. If I hadn't thought of it before, I would certainly have followed you after all the things I heard there. You were fully as popular with the people as John Ward."

"What did the King think about it?"

"I didn't hear because, of course, I didn't dare go near the court. I'm sure he was more furious than ever. Sir Sigismund Hill told me that Archie Armstrong said to His Majesty it was a good thing his name wasn't King Saul, or the new David would be sure to get his throne. The King didn't like *that* very much." Her expression changed suddenly to one of contrition. "I'm being very selfish, Roger. You must go in and see your aunt now."

"Where is she?"

"In the next cabin. I'm afraid I must make still another confession. I wasn't glad at all when I heard she was coming with us. She's always been such a grim old thing. It shows how determined I was to have you that I didn't change my mind. I came, and now I'm sure I'm going to like her. I think she's going to like me, though I don't think she cared for the idea at first either. You see, we have an interest in common, and that was a very great help. I'm really glad we're going to have her with us."

I had two more surprises when I visited the next cabin. The first was Aunt Gadilda herself. She was well, quite amazingly well, in fact. The sea had done something for her in the few days since they sailed. She looked rested, better fed, almost happy. Many times later I thought how ironic it was that things should work out this way. Aunt Gadilda, who had thought so scornfully of Mother's marriage to a sailor and who had hated the sea because she knew I had an urge to follow it, was in reality a natural sailor, never seasick for a moment, never so content as when she could sit on deck and watch the great waves following in the wake of the ship; while I, who longed to be a sailor, who wanted to carry on the tradition of my father's family, had no more aptitude for it than a dancing master.

The other surprise was the state of the cabin. It was small enough to begin with, but she had crammed it full to overflowing with an amazing variety of things. She had even brought my scriptine and the old corner bink, neither of which had she been able to think of leaving behind. I heard later that they had been taken aboard by block and tackle, to the intense annoyance of the mate, who objected anyway to having women passengers. There was a portrait of Grandfather Pirie and miniatures of Mother and herself as girls. There was a gold mazer-bowl from Great Lunnington and a dozen pewter tankards with the crest of York (we never knew how they came into the family, but I suspected they were loot from the Wars of the Roses). All my books were piled up in a corner and all my old clothing; which, of course, I had completely outgrown. She had apparently lacked the heart to leave anything behind. How she managed to live in the space that was left remained a mystery to the end of the voyage.

"I never expected to see you alive," she said, hugging me tightly with her thin old arms. "Sonny, sonny, I'm so happy! The Lord has had you in his keeping and has brought you safely through."

"I have a great deal to be thankful for," I answered. "Much more than I ever expected."

She knew what I meant by that, and nodded her head with the least suggestion of hesitation. "I never thought to like a daughter of Fanny Plumptre," she whispered. "But I do, Roger, I do indeed. She's a sweet child, and I'm so glad you're to marry her. I think she'll make you a fine wife, Roger."

"Richard, Aunt Gadilda. You must get used to calling me by my new name. I'm to be Richard Strange for the next three years. Perhaps for much longer. There's no telling."

"I'll do my best. But I'm afraid I'll make many a slip."

"I'm glad to see you looking so well. You seem to be the real sailor of the family."

She made no reply to that. Taking me by the arm, she drew my head down close to hers and whispered: "If anything should happen to me, sonny, remember it's in the secret drawer of the bink. I packed it in with sawdust. It's all there."

"What's all there?"

"The gold, Roger. All that we own between us. No one will ever be able to find it. There's—there's much more than you might think. Your poor mother and I were saving to set you up well in life." She drew back her head with a look of pride. "We're doing better for you than Fanny Plumptre will ever be able to do for her daughter."

"I don't want Lady Ladland to do anything for Katie. I'll be quite capable of looking after my wife, I think."

"Of course you will. She's going to be a lucky girl."

I shook my head. "I'm the lucky one. I can hardly believe it's true yet."

I had further evidence of my luck when I returned to my cabin, *our* cabin, I should say. Katie, her cheeks flushed with pleasure, had brought out her whole wedding wardrobe for me to admire. The place blazed with color. There was so much to be seen that the only place left for me to sit on was the floor. I squatted there while my bride-to-be held up each article for my comment and approval. I struggled to appear suitably impressed, but all I could see was Katie herself.

I realized, however, that it was an astonishing outfit. There were at least a dozen dresses, flounced and gored and embroidered, of the softest and finest materials, silk and satin and velvet, all of them rich with gold braid and jeweled buckles and loops of pearls. They had pleats and tassets and ruffs, bodices of old lace, cuffs like spun gold. I lost count of the caps and coifs, lacey affairs all of them, worked through with pearls and sparkling with buckles and buttons of gold and silver. There seemed a never-ending succession of more intimate garments: petticoats (I almost wrote "main buntlings") of silk and stammil, as foamy as the surf off a sandy shore; silk stockings, a dozen or more, and worth (so Katie told me pridefully) five pounds the pair; slippers and boots and shoes, with rose buckles and gold-leaf tracery, some of them the richest polonian with furred tops. I was astounded at the number of pearls, in strings or loops or set singly in rosettes of colored lace. My head buzzed with the names which tripped from her tongue: falles and buskes and puffs, rebatoes and pickadells and palisadoes, pendulets and fillets. Never, I decided, had there been such a harvest for the costumers in the whole long history of marriage-making.

Katie came and sat beside me on the floor when the last delicate morsel of frippery lace had been displayed and put away. She rested her head against my shoulder. "I'm not bringing you a dowry, Roger," she said. "I'm a very poor bride. But I don't believe it can ever be said that I came to you naked."

"I'm still dizzy with it all. I'm sure Queen Anne Boleyn and Gabrielle D'Estree and the Queen of Sheba are turning in their graves this very minute. But is it sensible for the bride of a poor man to have such royal clothes?"

"Now you're talking like Mother. She was against my bringing the whole wardrobe. I think she was of the opinion that it would be wise to sell as much of it as we could. But Father put his foot down. He insisted that I should have everything they had bought for—well, the *other* wedding. You can hardly believe how changed he is. He's so sweet and understanding now. It's true he wanted me to marry Sir Nevil at first, but he was afraid then that a charge of treason was to be brought against him. When we found out what Sir Nevil had done about the other captains, he was ready to support me when I said I could never marry him. He was different at once; he didn't seem to care what happened to him. He even put on a cheerful face when the word came that he was losing Appleby Court."

"I'm surprised you dared tell them you were coming away with me. Did your parents object?"

"Father was glad. He had been singing your praises ever since the duel. It was his idea that I should go to you with everything, my dear. To do anything else would be an insult, he said. Mother—well, Mother is different. I can't seem to remember any time in all my life when Mother and I have agreed about anything. Father and I had our way; and so here I am without a shilling to my name and a wardrobe fit for a queen. Does that seem silly to you?"

"I can't begin to say how proud I am that your father thought enough of me to do this. He didn't think well of me at all before."

"Do you know," she said thoughtfully, "I believe he's happier now than he's ever been before. He talks of improving his land, and he reads all the time about cattle and sheep and crops. He has an idea he can grow the things Sir Walter Raleigh brought from America."

"Maize and potatoes?"

"Yes, and even tobacco. He says he intends to be a rich man again. Mother will never be happy until they have Appleby Court back. You see, it was bought with the fortune she brought him. She'll never let him forget it. Poor Father!"

She had cuddled into the shelter of my arms. After a short silence, she said:

"Roger."

"Yes, Katie."

"Wouldn't it have been awful if you hadn't meant it! What would you have done? Packed me off to John Ward like a bad load of flour or wheat or something of the kind?"

"I don't think I would have had the courage to fight Macherie if I hadn't been in love with you; and if I hadn't fought him, your father would never have let you come. So the speculation is a completely idle one. But one thing's certain: I would never let you go to Tunis. It's no place for a white woman."

There was another silence, and then she asked: "Was the Spanish girl in love with John?"

"Yes. So much in love with him that she gave up everything. How did you know about her?"

"He wrote me a letter, you know. He mentioned her, and I put two and two together. Did you know about the letter?"

"Not until a few days ago. He told me about it then. His purpose was to convince you that you should marry me. That's the way he has always been."

"As it happened," she said, "I didn't need convincing. He said he wasn't worthy of a good woman's love. What did he mean? Do you think he was in love with the Spanish girl?"

I shook my head. "You happen to be the only woman he has ever loved. I owe it to him to say that much, after all he's done for me. Especially when I think how much of a failure I was."

"Now you're being humble again. He said in the letter you had been wonderful; that you saved the fleet and that you fought like a lion."

"I made trouble for him. About Clim. Sir Francis Drake would have hanged me for it if he had been my captain. You see, Katie, I was a failure as a sailor. All my life I dreamed of going to sea; and then I discovered I wasn't meant to be a sailor. Finding out about the Spanish plans was luck."

"What about the things you've done since you returned?"

"It took me weeks to get up my courage to it. I've no illusions at all about the part I've played."

"Well, Sir David, I saw you fight the duel. That's all I ever need to know about you."

"*That* was different. I was fighting for you."

To change the subject, I produced the emerald ring and placed it in her hand. She gasped over the beauty of it.

"Roger, where did you get it? I've never seen anything so lovely. The Queen herself has nothing finer."

I explained about it. She listened intently, turning it over and over and admiring it from every angle.

"What wish did you make?"

"None. There was only one thing in life that I wanted, and it would have been unfair to wish for that—as long as John Ward was my rival."

"And your wish came true after all? Or am I assuming too much?"

When I had assured her on that point, and I took plenty of time in doing so, she said: "I think she gave it to you with this in mind. She must have been very fine, Roger. And now you must leave me and send your aunt in. I must get dressed. For your wedding. You haven't condescended to ask when it's to take place. Hasn't it occurred to you that the necessary words haven't been spoken over us yet to give you the right to sit with me alone in a ship's cabin?" She laid her cheek against mine. "I'll hurry, Roger. The captain will marry us here as soon as I'm ready. It has to be done that way because you must marry me with your real name. Captain Thomson knows who you are, but no one else does, of course. Run along now, darling."

It was a good half-hour before I was admitted again, but I understood when I saw her in her wedding gown. She looked radiantly beautiful. At the time I was incapable of observing details, and all I knew about the gown was that it was white and that there was for me a suggestion of the angelic about it. Later Katie explained it to me in earnestly enthusiastic detail, and so I am setting down for those who may be interested.

I shall begin with the collar, which was of lace and more than one hundred years old. It was cut low in front, but grew into a ruff in the back to provide a white frame for her head. It was edged with looped pearls and at each point a larger pearl dangled on silver thread. The bodice molded her slender breasts in close-fitting simplicity, and it was only on the most careful inspection that one could detect the embroidery in white satin which covered it, a design of hymeneal suggestion with hearts and cupids and angels playing raptly on harps. Contrary to the usual custom, it was laced in the back, and so continued severely plain to the slim waist, where it cascaded over the narrow farthingale in frothy tucks and rosettes. There were plain puffs of satin at the shoulders, and the sleeves consisted of white velvet ribbons attached only at top and bottom; so many of them that they allowed no more than an occasional glimpse of the silk base beneath, although they rippled with each movement of the arm. The cuffs were of the same ancient lace, falling so low over her hands that I could barely see the prayerbook she carried. The skirt was full and sweeping, opening in an inverted V in front to reveal an underskirt crossed with corded velvet; its lines gracious and gay and even voluptuous; a little demure also, never allowing so much as the toe of a satin slipper to show.

The wedding veil, fastened in front with a diamond brooch, was what I remembered best. It was drawn back from her brow, covering her lovely dark hair and descending around her shoulders like mist above a waterfall.

It is not to be wondered at, therefore, that the hearty voice of Captain Thomson, intoning the wedding service with puritanical unction, was no more to me than an indistinguishable rumble. I suppose I made the right responses, for the ceremony proceeded without delay or hitch. I heard Katie say, "I do" and that was all I needed to know about it. The miracle, for which I had been hoping all my life, had come to pass. Katie Ladland had become my wife.

"And now, *Richard Strange,*" said the captain, closing the book and putting special emphasis on the name, "I must give you a word of warning. It's for your good lady as well, and for Mistress Pirie. You must be continually on your guard. I want no slips of the tongue. I would not like to place a bridegroom in irons, but that is what I shall have to do if the name of Roger Blease is so much as whispered. My crew are very curious about you as it is."

We had a light supper and a single glass of wine. The captain toasted our healths in a speech larded with biblical quotation and then, seeming reluctant to go, launched into talk about Damascus.

"You're going to the oldest city in the world, my young friends," he said with pulpit emphasis. "Older than Jerusalem, older than the wicked cities which perished under the wrath of God. It is now a ranting, lying, thieving, heathenish city. But it has played its part in the building of God's glory on earth. You will see the Street called Straight and the road on which Paul walked when the great white light blinded him and he heard the mighty voice of Jehovah; and the place on the wall where he was lowered to safety from the persecution of his enemies. You will find much to study and ponder to the good of your immortal souls." He looked at me with solemn earnestness. "The old city is given over to trading now, and you will find little use for that sword at your belt. From all that I hear, you have an uncanny knack with it. Keep it in its scabbard, my young friend. Let your ways henceforth be the ways of godliness and peace. Not," he added, "that I find any fault with the use to which it has already been put."

He got to his feet and shook hands with all of us. "I must return to my duties. A blow is coming up across the bay, and you may find it a trifle uncomfortable tonight. Be easy in your minds; we are in the Lord's hands, and Isaiah Thomson is worthy of your confidence. Good night, my young friends. I am sure you have things to talk about more interesting than anything I have to say."

He was entirely right about that.

BOOK FOUR

45

IT WAS EXACTLY three years and a half later when we returned to England, on a warm day in September, when the medlars were loaded with fruit and the bullaces and hollyoaks were at their best, and the feeling of harvest was in the air. There were still three of us, but Aunt Gadilda did not make the third. After more than two years in our white-walled Eastern home, broken by an ecstatic journey to Jerusalem which included a progress around the Sea of Galilee and up the River Jordan, she had passed away peacefully; her greatest regret, I am sure, the necessity of leaving my fine little son, John. It still seemed absurd to me for Katie to be a mother; she had not changed a particle; but it was the pleasantest kind of absurdity. I had made the discovery that there is nothing in life to equal the sight of the girl you love sitting with your first-born in her lap, counting over his fat toes with the usual ritual: "Harry Whistle, Tommy Thistle, Harry Whible, Tommy Thible," and, coming to the small toe, "Little Oker Bell"; or jouncing him on her knee to the jolly air of the old nursery rhyme: "No one's at home but Jumping Joan, Father, Mother, and I."

It had not been easy to raise him, which was not strange when you consider how few babies manage to survive the perils of infancy. Katie had not been able to nurse him for the full two years, and, needless to state, we had not considered the hiring of a brown-skinned wet nurse. Goat's milk was out of the question; we could not be sure of its purity, in addition to which Aunt Gadilda had clung zealously to the belief that babies fed on it develop beards or, at the very best, dewlaps. It had been necessary, therefore, to raise him on gruels and soups and, a little later, on vegetables and morsels of meat. He had thrived on it, particularly after I insisted on his release from the confinement of the swaddling board. I had stood as long as I could seeing him bound up each night in rollers, stays, swathes, fillets, clouts and bands, until he could not move a leg, to be left there until the following night. Aunt Gadilda had been stubborn on the point—children had always been kept that way, so it must be right—but I had won Katie around; and after that my son was left as free as the native babies, to kick his heels and grow straight and strong.

We were returning with the King's pardon and a fair fortune to show for our years of exile. I had acted on the hints of Sir Sigismund and Captain Starkle, dealing in currency exchange and picking up fine rugs and bits of ivory on my own, which had later been sold at a neat and legitimate personal profit. We had received letters, of course, and so had kept ourselves informed on the main currents of the news at home. We had heard of the success of the Countess of Essex in getting her divorce—a shady business, it had seemed—and her subsequent marriage to Master Carr, now Earl of Somerset. We had heard whispers that the star of the favorite was beginning to wane, and that a certain gay and handsome young man named George Villiers was rather more in the royal eye these days. Also we had learned of the death of Prince Henry, a sad blow to the hopes of the whole nation; although Baby Charles, the second son, had now recovered from the lameness his nurses had afflicted him with and was turning into a fine young man with legs capable of doing their part in the masques Queen Anne loved to arrange. There had been compensation in the marriage of the Princess Elizabeth (a beautiful and high-spirited girl like her grandmother, Mary of Scots) to the Elector of the German Palatinate, a Protestant prince and therefore more suited than the Spanish husband King James had wanted for her. The King had persisted in his stubborn course, refusing to summon Parliament, except for brief and stormy interludes, and ruling by imposition and royal decree. He still prated of divine right in the face of the growing exasperation of the people. More and more of the Puritans were slipping over to Holland to live, and some of them were talking openly of going to America to find homes where men could worship God as they pleased.

It was late at night when we dropped anchor, and so we decided to postpone going ashore until the morning. Katie was tired and said she was going to take herself and Jack Thumbkin to bed at once, but I elected to sit up and talk with Percentage Tuttle, who had come aboard as usual; which proved how avid I was for talk.

Percentage Tuttle was a shrewd member of the Mistery of Feltmakers, who had decided years before that the way to make money in the shipping trade was to place small sums on all the vessels we sent out instead of large amounts on a few, thereby assuring himself, on the principle of averages, of a fair and sure return. He was not thought well of in the city, as he had adopted curious ways of doing business. Instead of keeping his apprentices at work in his own home, he had taken several tumbledown hovels in the worst of the slums and had turned them into a large and dismal shop where his men made hats and caps in amazing quantities. He preferred, he said, to sell inexpensive headpieces to thousands of common men instead of a few handsome bonnets to men of the court. Perhaps there was some sense in it, for Percentage Tuttle had become a wealthy man. He was unbelievably greedy, and it was his custom to visit our ships as soon as they warped into dock, as though unable to wait for word as to the value of the cargo.

He had been, as usual, the first man over the side, and for the past hour had been prying and rummaging in the hold. He came on deck now, his tight little mouth pursed up with the satisfaction of certain profits.

"A fine cargo, sir, a bounteous cargo, I may even say a satisfactory cargo, sir," he wheezed, rubbing his hands. "You have done well, sir. If there is talk of a small compensation for you, I shall throw my shillings on the board for the opportunity to speak in favor of it. Ah, such fine silks, such desirable cloths and leathers! Such delicious spices! Secured, I trust, at fine, low costs." He peered at me anxiously as though seeking confirmation on that important point. "I see you have been careful and zealous in your trust, young sir. There will be nice round profits, there will indeed!"

"Would you care for a glass of wine?" I asked.

There was nothing he wanted more. We settled down in the captain's cabin, the master having taken himself ashore for a full night in a Cardinal's Hat, and my companion supped up a first mouthful of wine. "Company stuff?" he asked suspiciously. His thirst increased when I assured him it was private stock which I had purchased for my own use. He was easily led then into talk of what had been happening in my absence.

Trade, he averred cautiously, had been fair, better than fair for those who had been canny enough. The new Council Chamber had been finished at the Guildhall; a shocking extravagance, which would feed nothing but the pride of purse-proud fools. The King, and here he shook his head spitefully, had been making more forced loans, which, of course, would never be repaid. He had been forced to make such a loan himself—but he could not go on with the details of an outrage which, clearly enough, had shocked him to the very core of his being. Yes, the Spaniards were leaving English ships alone, thanks to the work of my friend (a grin and a bob of the head went with that) John Ward. He did not know much about Ward's present activities, except that he was holding out alone.

"I heard it said the other day," said my companion with a chuckle, "that our ambassador in Venice, Sir Henry Wotton—who owes me a bill I won't collect until he returns home, if then—made a demand on the Doges and backed it up by saying England could loose a dozen Wards on them if they did not come to their senses. It brought the Flat-caps around, that did."

"But it was an exaggeration," I declared. "There's only one John Ward."

"More's the pity," said Percentage Tuttle. "He's the friend of honest merchants, he is indeed."

He went on to talk about the course of royal policy with a grumbling and uneasy candor. "Tongues can be slit for what I'm saying, but I'm a free Englishman and a man of some substance, and I've a right to speak my mind. Have you heard the latest? Men can't dress as they please any more. The King has issued an order that apprentices must not wear this and that. I tell you, it's the truth. No facing on their hats wider than three inches—and what profit is there in the making of such tawty things as that?—no lace at all, no fine material for their breeches, no Spanish shoes. Well, I've never held with men getting too far above their station in life, but soon he'll be telling all honest men how they're to dress. No feathers or gewgaws in hats, perhaps? What would that do to the trade of Joshua Tuttle? It's not to be borne. Soon he may be telling us what we may eat and drink and who we may take to wife!" He paused and then gave vent to a wheezing and unwilling laugh. "It took Archie to tell the King what men thought of all this. He told him to his face that he had better concern himself with the shortness of his courtiers' morals instead of the length of apprentices' cloaks."

"Archie is the boldest man in England."

"He is indeed. And the sad part of it is that he's not only a fool but a Scotsman as well."

It was growing late so he was able to give me no more than a hint of a great scandal which had been uncovered recently. "Somerset is in prison," he said, smacking his lips with relish. "He went too far, and even King James could not stand by such wickedness. I hope he pays for it with his neck. And his lady too."

"A conspiracy?"

"You might call it such. Well, I must be off, for it's incumbent on me to rise early. My lazy sprats would never do an honest stroke of work if I wasn't there to drive them to it. I'll be wishing you good night."

Katie brought our son out on deck early the next morning. They were dressed to go ashore, and both very much excited about it. My wife's cheeks were flushed and her eyes were sparkling.

"Oh, how good it is to be back!" she cried. "England is so lovely. You can fairly drink the air. I must see the Queen as soon as possible and thank her for what she did. And, Roger, we must see to it at once that Jack Thumbkin is christened, now that we can get it done. I'm going to ask Sir Sigismund to stand as his godfather."

I looked at Master John and realized that Katie was right in saying there should be special clothes for children instead of dressing them up like little men and women. The native nurse we had brought back with us had not paid proper attention to his points, and as a result his hose had the sag to them that I knew so well. He was wearing his Black Pudding cap, well padded to protect his head in case of a fall. It had a fine feather in it, but he looked like an odd little sobersides in spite of that.

"Yes," I agreed, "he must be christened right away. And I think we'll send that heathen woman back and get him a real English nurse."

"Well, we'll have to think about that," said my wife. She added in an almost breathless tone: "I can hardly wait to get an apple. A big red one. Will you buy me one at the first fruit stall?"

Despite the early hour the streets were full of people, and they seemed in a jolly and excited mood. The bowse-boys were doing a fine trade everywhere, and the taverns were overflowing. There were no carriages in sight, so we had to walk, with Master John perched upon my shoulder and cooing with delight at the noise and strange sights.

"I *love* London," exclaimed Katie. I believe she would have stopped to buy a pint of ale for herself if we had not been in such a hurry. "I think there must be a Fair today. Everyone is in such good spirits."

"It's either that," I answered, "or a hanging. They take both the same way."

"I'm afraid, my lord and master, that the East has soured you."

Sir Sigismund was delighted to see us and properly amazed at the size of our son. "My fine kinchin coe," he said. "We'll make a sailor of you in no time at all. But I'm very much afraid you're not going to look like your mother."

He sat us down to a real English breakfast of roast ham and apple sauce and a broiled fish. His face showed fresh surprise when Katie requested a dish of wheaten flummery for John. "Really?" he said. "He *is* growing up fast. Don't you think it might stir up something inside him?" The dispatch with which my son attended to the dish when it arrived kept him so interested that it was not until the meal was over that he began to ask questions.

"You must tell me about your life out there," he said then. "I know you enjoyed it from what you wrote me."

"It was lovely in some ways," answered Katie. "We had a white house on the side of a hill with a deep garden and a fountain, and servants to do everything. I slept every morning until six o'clock and loved it so much that I'm afraid I'll always be lazy now. Since my Jack Thumbkin couldn't be born in England, it was much the nicest place we could have found for him. It was so cool and shady, and I could watch the caravans winding by on their way to the city. I loved having flowers and fruits all the year around. Yes, it was nice; but I can't tell you, Sir Sigismund, how happy I was when the word came that Her Majesty had talked the King into a pardon for Roger. I've been counting the hours ever since."

"It took a lot of talking," said Hill with a smile. "The Queen never forgot her little Mistress Katie, and she gave the King no peace."

"She's wonderful!" exclaimed my wife. "I love her. I think I would be willing to die for her."

"I would have something to say about that," I interposed hastily.

"His Majesty gave in with very bad grace," went on our host. "And only because he needed a favor in return. Something about the wedding of the Princess, I think. Or perhaps it had to do with Master Carr; but I won't go into that possibility."

"I'm an old married woman now," Katie reminded him.

"Still," said Sir Sigismund with a smile. "Of course, I didn't let it be known where you were until the papers were signed. I was taking no chances on the flighty whims of His Sowship. I thought, Roger, when he found you had been working for us all the time, it would be necessary for someone to beg a pardon for me. He's very grumpy about it still." He looked at Katie with an air of deep sympathy. "I hoped you would get home in time. I knew your father had been ailing but, as it happened, he died less than a week after the pardon was signed."

Katie nodded silently. The fact that Sir Bartlemy had died while we were away was the one sad thing about our return. He had worked hard, and not too successfully, to make his land pay. I suspected that this lack of results had played a part in his sudden demise. Lady Ladland had gone to live with a married sister in the North. To change the subject, I asked for information about the trouble in which Carr had become involved.

"I don't like to spoil your first visit ashore with such a sordid tale," he said. "You knew about the divorce and the marriage later of Somerset—he's an earl now, you know—to the Howard woman? It seems that Overbury, his closest friend, was against the marriage. The woman knew it, and contrived to have Overbury put into the Tower for some trivial offense. Well, they were married then. It was a brilliant affair, and the bride looked very lovely, they say. Quite innocent and fresh and dewy-eyed. Everything went well for a time. Somerset was running the Privy Council without his friend's help. Of course, the Howards were behind him, and they were gobbling up all public offices and favors for themselves."

My son created a diversion at this moment. He had been set down from the table and had decided to show how well he could walk by himself. Our host, his lined face beaming with pleasure, promptly squatted on the floor and held out his arms.

"Come, my stout little kincher!" he exclaimed. "Come to your Uncle Mundy. I tell you, Roger, you've got a fine boy here. Look at the gait of him, will you? He rolls as though he were walking the deck of a ship. He's a born sailor."

"Then he doesn't take after his father!" I said.

Katie took her son up in her arms, saying with indignation: "He's not going to be a sailor! Not my precious little Handy-spandy-Jack-a-dandy. He's not going to sea; he's going to stay at home with his mother, and ride a horse, and be a fine little gentleman."

"I withdraw the suggestion," said our host, getting to his feet. "And I think you're right, my dear. There are better trades than that of the sea. But, whatever you do with my godson, don't plan on sending him to court."

"You were telling us about the Earl of Somerset," I reminded him.

"Yes. I'm always glad of interruptions when speaking of such matters." He lighted his pipe with slow care. "Well, it happened that in the Tower this unfortunate fellow Overbury was given something to eat that didn't agree with him. He died. Soon after the marriage it became known that he had been poisoned. A good friend of yours, Roger, had something to do with the working out of the case."

"A friend of mine?"

"The Upright Man. It seems he had been disappointed in his pursuit of a pretty woman named Turner"—with a sinking of the heart, I realized now where the story was leading—"and he took advantage of something he heard from her to delve into it. He uncovered some facts and put them into hands that were far from friendly to the Howard faction. A shrewd fellow, your Chirp Bird. But, as it happens, too shrewd for his own good. He should not have acted on his desire to make trouble for the Turner woman."

I could see that Katie was distressed also. "What has happened?" I asked.

"There was no difficulty in getting at the truth, once suspicions were aroused. Some confessions were secured, and the lot of them were clapped into prison, Somerset and his beautiful bride as well as their accomplices. The Upright Man was taken in charge as well." He paused and gave us a wry smile. "I had something to do with that. I saw to it that certain facts about the murder of his predecessor came to the ears of the Council. They got out of him everything he knew about the Somerset case and then held him for murder. I'm afraid he's been having a bad time of it."

"Has he been tried yet?"

"Our honest Chirp has been duly tried, convicted, and sentenced. In the meantime the whole country has gone stark mad over the case. The favorite has always been unpopular, and all that was needed to set the people by the ears was a story like this. There's a great clamor for the Somersets to be punished. Two of the men they hired have been hanged already. Did you notice how crowded the streets are this morning? That's because the woman hangs today."

Katie looked horror-stricken. "The Countess of Somerset!"

He shook his head. "Neither of the principals have been tried yet. It's the Turner woman who dies this morning."

I felt too sick to speak. Katie and I looked at each other, and I wondered if my face were as white as hers.

I had been expecting this from the first moment he mentioned Ann's name. I remembered how reluctant she had been to share in the activities of the determined Fanny Howard; that she had been strangely obsessed with fear of the future. Had she foreseen this? I recalled that, when studying my palm, she had said nothing about her own. Had she found the sign there already?

"This is dreadful!" cried Katie. "Can't something be done to save her?"

Hill shook his head. "I doubt if anything could have been done for her, but certainly it's too late now. Public opinion is too inflamed for mercy to be shown. Not that any of them deserve it on the evidence. It's a clear case."

"I'm sure she had no part in the poisoning," I said. "I know her, Sir Sigismund. I swear she isn't guilty."

"I'll go to Denmark House and speak to the Queen," declared Katie. "She might be willing to do something about it."

"The court's not in London." Our host shook his head. "You mustn't concern yourself about this, my dear. The woman is guilty enough. She took the Countess to Simon Forman, who first gave them the poison. She acknowledged that on the stand. Fortunately for him, Forman died before it was used. No, your Ann Turner was in it deep enough, and there isn't a thing that can be done for her. I believe there would be a revolution if any of them were let off. The King won't want to see Somerset die, and he'll try to appease the country first by hanging everyone else. That's the situation."

"I can't believe it," said Katie. She had begun to cry.

I got to my feet. "I must go and see her," I said. "She can't be left alone today. If I can't do anything else, I can do that."

Katie also got up. "I'll go with you."

"The idea does you both credit," declared Sir Sigismund, "but you mustn't try it. It will do the poor woman little good, and it might do you a lot of harm. After all, Roger, you're back in England under sufferance. It would be unwise to attract the King's attention again. I'm serious about this. It would be a great mistake."

"I must go," I said. "Which prison is she in?"

"She's being held in the house of the sheriff. I don't think you'll succeed in getting in. And that is the only reason I won't try to stop you."

I persuaded Katie that she should stay at home and then started out on my errand with a heavy heart.

46

THE STREETS WERE PACKED with people now, all hurrying in one direction. A woman was to be hanged by the neck until she was dead, a young and pretty woman and an innocent one, if they had only known. They were glad of it. I knew that they thought her a witch and a poisoner and that their desire for her death was part of the public resentment against the abuse of power in the hands of unworthy favorites, and yet I felt a bitter anger at their attitude.

I heard someone ask, "Will they hang her in her yellow ruff?"

"The ruff she wears today should be as black as her dirty soul!" cried an old woman who was hobbling along frantically in the fear that she would be too late for the spectacle.

If I had not felt the need for haste I would have stopped and shouted at them that Ann Turner was innocent, that she was the unhappy victim of circumstances. It would have done no good, of course; I might even have been mobbed for my pains. I took my resentment of them out in angry jostling as I hurried through the narrow and muddy thoroughfares.

The house of the sheriff, where Ann had been held since her trial, was an ugly structure of mortar and frame, with a high towerlike wing which rose more than a dozen feet above the main structure. This curious addition had one window only, a narrow cusped slit about halfway up; and its roof was so grotesquely slanted that it gave the house a crazy, tipsy air. I shuddered as I thought that the wing resembled a coffin.

I forced my way through the masses swarming in the neighborhood to a door opening on a side alley. I knocked, conscious of the fact that all eyes were on me. They thought, no doubt, that I had come on some official errand.

A red-faced fellow opened the door and demanded to know what, in the name of the Old Rogue and all his foul fiends, I thought I wanted here at a time like this.

"I want to see Mistress Turner," I said.

He laughed at that. "So you want to see Mistress Turner, do ye? Well, ye'll see her soon enough, but ye'll have to go to Tyburn to do it. And ye'd better hurry, my young gentry-cove, if ye expect to get within a half-mile of the spot."

I dropped a coin in his palm. "I must see her now. There may be some small service I can do her."

"Are ye a friend of hers?"

"Yes," I said, although I knew the danger of such an admission. "Here, I'll double that. Get me in to her, man."

He closed his fist hurriedly over the second coin and frowned uneasily. "I don't want no trouble. Orders is to let no one see her. What kind of thing might ye have in mind?"

"I don't know," I answered desperately. "She's all alone in there. We came from the same town and we grew up together. I'm sure she would like to see one friendly face before she dies."

"Is that all?" He slipped the money into a pocket of his galligaskins and motioned me to come in, slamming the door after me. We stood then in a narrow passage, smelling strongly of soapsuds, from which a few steps led up to an inner door.

"Now here's how it is, young fellow," he said. "Ye can't see the woman. That's plain. That's orders, and I don't break 'em, not if ye was a Lord of the Council hisself or the Beeshop o' Cantyberry. It ud be no use anyhow; she's gone into the jumbles, and Dame Cripps can hardly keep her up with brandy and smelling powder. But I can do one thing: I can fetch Derrick to see ye. Perhaps ye can do something for the poor lass that way. Another one of the same and I'll do that much for ye."

Derrick was the hangman. He had been so long the custodian of his terrible office that already men were calling after him any device for hoisting heavy objects. I certainly did not relish the idea of speaking with this grim functionary; but there was nothing else apparently that I could do for Ann; so I waited.

Master Derrick proved to be a morose individual with sparse red hair and a curious way of speaking in a slow and expressionless voice.

"What might it be that you want?" he asked. It sounded as though he were a new scholar reading lines from a grammar.

"I came to see if I could do anything for—for the prisoner. I'm not allowed to see her, so I thought there might be—well, ways of making it easier for her."

"There is something can be done for her," he said, after staring at me for several moments with his cold eye. "Yes, something can be done. Have you an idea of paying me?"

I dropped three sovereigns in his hand, the last of the gold I had brought out with me. He clinked the coins with the first sign of animation I had been able to detect on his face.

"It is this way," he said. "I know my trade, young man. If I get the knot exactly under the left ear and see that she stands in the proper position on the car, her neck will crack with the fall. It is easy enough to die that way and as quick as scat. But not nearly as easy, my master, if it does not happen just that way."

"In God's name, then, take every care!" I exclaimed. "There'll be as much again for you, if you do." Talking to him on such a grim matter made me feel as though I had been translated out of the realm of decent things into some bestial kind of world. "I'll have you watched. You won't get the gold if you make any slip."

"I will make no slip," he assured me in his horrible and monotonous voice. "I know my trade, my master. If anything should happen— but nothing will, nothing—I will have Gregory attend to her. Gregory is my assistant. He will hang onto her legs and his weight will do it. That will always do the trick just as well."

I realized that I would be ill if I talked to him any longer. I muttered, "You'll get the money, then," and rushed out. I think the crowd noticed my paleness and concluded it had something to do with the condition of the prisoner. At any rate they watched me with avid interest as I struggled through them.

"Are ye ill?" asked the keeper of the first tavern I could find. "Brandy!" I ordered.

He set the brandy in front of me. "It'll be a fine nubbing party," he said pleasantly. "A real sight, eh? It's not been my luck to get anywhere near the chats for many's the year. Paddington Fair days are always the very best for trade, so here I has to stay. I'd give a shilling or two to see this little yellow-haired vixen kicking on the end of a rope, that I would."

I had taken one swallow only. I let him have the rest of the brandy full in his grinning face. He was still gasping and spluttering curses when I went out the door.

I had made up my mind not to go to Tyburn; the thought of watching Ann die was more than I could bear. At the same time it seemed that I would be deserting her if I left now. I wandered from place to place along the route to the gallows. I saw that all the windows were filled, and the rooftops crowded with people. Finally I came to Snow Hill, and here I managed to wedge myself into the expectant throng. A wait of an hour or more followed. I tried not to hear the talk going on around me.

Two sober citizens were standing immediately in front. I knew they were vintners from the three *tuns argent* embroidered conspicuously on their sleeves. They were talking soberly enough of the business ahead and expressing the doubt that seemed to be in every mind: would the wicked countess and her perhaps equally guilty husband be brought to punishment as well as the minor actors in the crime? I detected in their tones a deep sense of dissatisfaction with the way justice was being administered.

At last someone shouted, "They're coming!" and the crowd pressed forward and fought feverishly for better positions. First came a carriage containing the sheriff, a corpulent individual carrying the staff of his office with an air of proper solemnity. It was seldom that the sheriff accompanied a prisoner to the place of execution, so his presence could be taken as evidence of the importance attached to this last act in the tragedy of Ann Turner. His coach was piled high with flowers, but this curious fact, I knew, had no relation to the matter in hand; it was merely an indication of his fear of the Plague, flowers being regarded as a preventative. Some guards followed on horseback and then came a creaking, jolting cart with more guards riding on each side. There were no flowers in this grim conveyance.

Ann was sitting on a bale of moldy straw, her back to the horses and her arms strapped behind her. In accordance with one of the many cruel customs which had grown up around English justice, the rope with which she was to be hanged was coiled around her neck and breast, one end of it dangling over the side of the cart. All along the line, jeering spectators were reaching out in vain efforts to pull at the rope.

Ann was pale and incredibly thin. She was staring up at the sky and she seemed, happily, to be completely oblivious to the wild shouting and the horseplay of the mob.

"The poor lamb!" I heard a woman say near me.

"Poor lamb, indeed!" cried another savagely. "Witch, poisoner, bawd, thief! That's what the judge said she was. She ought to be burned alive, that's what she should!"

Suddenly I felt that I could not let her be carried away without making an effort to save her. She had risked her life to rescue me from the fate which was now overtaking her; could I do any less? Shouting, "Ann! Ann!" I threw my weight against the solid mass of people in front of me. It was so closely packed that I did not progress more than a foot. The two respectable vintners turned around in mild expostulation. Common sense returned, and I drew back again. Ann had not heard me. Even if it had been possible for her to hear over the din in the street, she was too far sunk in the emotion which had gripped her to pay heed. I stayed where I was until the cart had jolted out of sight.

For an hour or more I wandered about the streets, recoiling from the holiday-making which went on around me but not feeling capable yet of returning to the house near the Poultry. Finally I stopped at a dilapidated tavern and bought myself a much-needed drink.

The place was crowded, and the talk was all of the execution. The customers were discussing every phase of it with a relish which seemed hardly human. My eyes turned to an old man sitting silently alone at a small table in a corner. Perhaps it was the fact that he had nothing to say which attracted my attention. He had a purple-veined nose and was dressed in shag-bag woollens, but I thought I could detect evidences of better days about him.

"They'll be tuning up the kits in hell this very minute to give her a proper reception," exulted a loud voice from the far end of the room.

The old man sat up in his chair suddenly. "Are you sure it isn't harps that are being tuned?" he asked.

Apparently he was known in the place, and respected. The gabble of talk ceased. The old man rubbed his eyes with a weary gesture and went on: "Although I have little use for my time these days, I don't spend it all here as you may think. I was interested once in the law; it's nothing to you why or when that interest came to an end; but sometimes still I return to—to the scene of former crimes, shall I say? It happened I was in court when this unfortunate woman was tried. I did not get the impression she was guilty. She had erred clearly enough, but the degree of her wrongdoing did not seem to warrant what has just occurred." He shoved his tankard away from him. "Well, they hanged the poor creature. I might feel a little less badly about it if I knew the answer to this: What of my Lord Somerset and his wife?"

Someone said, "Everyone's asking that one, Old Fuddle-cup."

"I'm afraid I can guess. They will be tried, and the ax will be carried with the sharp edge toward them when they leave the court. Yes, they will be found guilty. I'm sure of that. But will they die? I am afraid they will be held in prison for a time and then pardoned by the King."

"The people of England will have something to say about that!" shouted one of the listeners.

"The people of England will have nothing to say about it. There's a different law for gentlemen than for the Ann Turners." The old man got to his feet and walked to the door, pausing to say over his shoulder in a completely passionless voice, "This is a great country for hanging."

47

SIR SIGISMUND INSISTED that we must remain with him until permanent arrangements could be made. We took possession of the top floor, with the coffee-colored nurse and a personal maid Katie hired, a feeble-spirited girl with a perpetual sniffle. I was very busy, having reports to prepare on trading conditions in the East and consultations to endure with all the profit-hungry shareholders.

Two weeks after our arrival, Chirp Bird had his turn with Derrick. I heard that he died badly, screaming for mercy and clutching at the knees of the executioner. He was the last of the Upright Men, for his arrest had thrown the organization into complete confusion, and no effort was made to set up anyone in his place. The house on the river was confiscated by the Crown, and so a highly disgraceful episode in the life of the great city came to an end. I had no reason to feel sympathy for Chirp, but I made a point of being out of London the day he journeyed to Paddington Fair.

The next day a full meeting of the Council was held to consider my recommendations and, as it developed, to settle my future with the Company. It was a brisk session and, although most of my ideas were adopted finally, it was not without heated debate. Each shareholder had plenty to say, and as a result the shillings, and the less frequent contributions of two-and-six, rolled on the board continuously. Even Percentage Tuttle paid an occasional coin for the privilege of additional participation in the arguments.

I emerged at the conclusion with my head in the clouds. It had been decided that I was to remain in London as assistant to Sir Sigismund, and when the time came for him to retire I was to be in charge of the operations of the Company. I was to be allowed to buy a full share for five hundred pounds, and my salary was to be based on a percentage of the profits. On these terms I could not fail to become a wealthy man in the course of time.

I was completely happy. I loved the work, the planning and managing of voyages, the inspection of vessels back from the East laden with rich cargoes and aromatic with spices, the control of the roups and the striking of deals, even the laborious detail of the petty tallies. I was born for the shipping trade.

Katie was out when I reached our apartments after the meeting. I could hear my son and his nurse in the little room where he slept, and I said to myself: "Master John Ward Blease, I'm going to see to it that you come into something rather substantial. There will be a fine property for you, and perhaps even a title. You're a lucky kincher, my fine John. And now I must do some figuring on a home for you."

I got out a large sheet of paper and began to make a sketch. I planned the details with care and concentration.

Katie came in while I was still at work. She was wearing one of the wraps from her wedding outfit—there had been few opportunities to wear her fine clothes in the East—and I gloated over the certainty that now I could provide a suitable setting for my lovely wife. I noticed that she had an anxious air, but I was too full of my news to give it any thought.

"We must have a special dinner tonight," I said, trying to keep my spirits under restraint. "Herb pie, and nightingales' tongues, and the finest wines we can find. We have something to celebrate tonight."

"Have we?" she said, failing to catch my mood.

I launched into an account of the meeting. "It's exactly what I wanted, darling," I exulted. "I'll be a rich man some day, almost as rich as the husband you deserve. You won't have to leave England again. I'm already planning a house for us. But that's not all of it. Think of the opportunity

I'll have. We're going to build a great empire, just as John and Sir Sigismund have planned, and I'm going to have a hand in it."

"Yes, Roger," was the only comment she made.

I brought out my sketch. Burchall's East Farm had been left to her by her father's will, and I had taken the stone house standing on it and added wings. The additions brought the ends of the house close to the curve of the stream and gave the suggestion of a moat. Katie's eyes lighted up when she looked at it.

"Why, it's lovely!" she exclaimed. "I had no idea the place could be made so fine. It's positively imposing."

"Could you be happy in such a home?"

She made no answer for a moment. Then she said: "Put away the plans for a while, please. I've something important to tell you. The royal family have returned to London, and I saw the Queen this afternoon."

So that was what made her so preoccupied! I asked, "Was she glad to see you?"

"She seemed to be. She talked to me for more than an hour. She asked me lots of questions. About our life in the East, and about you, and the baby."

"You told her how grateful we are to her, I'm sure."

"Of course. She laughed about it and said His Majesty was still far from reconciled to the idea, but that you needn't worry. She and her Good Dog would look after us."

"Her Good Dog?" I was puzzled, needless to state. "What does that mean?"

"I'll explain later." She seemed unwilling to say anything further. After a short space, she asked me if I remembered the boy who had fallen in love with her when she was at court. I nodded. "He's married now. I met his wife, and she said she saw you years ago when you visited her father's place. She wrote something about you on a pane of glass, but she didn't think you saw it."

"Of course I saw it. She wrote, 'Who's Afraid of a Pirate?' and, as I recall it, her spelling was very bad."

"Then she was interested in you, and she had no right to tell me about it. I'm sure I won't like her."

"You won't have to like her, darling, because you may never see her again. We're not going to court, you know. In any case, I didn't get as much as a good look at her, and I couldn't tell her now from Dame Witchie. I got the impression she was rather lively, and that makes me sure she'll lead your tame ex-suitor a merry dance."

"Roger."

"Yes, darling."

"I met someone else. Her Majesty's Good Dog. Sir George Villiers. He came for an audience, and the Queen made me stay while she talked with him."

"A great honor, I'm sure. Is that why you're acting so strange?"

"He's very handsome and amusing. He's much nicer in every way than the Earl of Somerset."

"Then I hope he doesn't end up in prison too." I looked at her closely. "Katie, I'm afraid you like this new favorite."

She answered thoughtfully: "No, not exactly. But he has a way of making people feel cheerful and happy. You never heard so much laughing! The Queen likes him, Roger. They say she got him his start at court to get rid of the other one. Her Majesty told me he was to become Master of the Horse at once."

"Another rapid rise to eminence through sheer merit." I was feeling very superior because of my own advance, and on that account contemptuous of court affairs. "Still, if we must have these handsome boys at the head of the state, I'll take your word for it that Master Villiers is an improvement over Master Carr."

She seemed reluctant to go on. Instead she changed the subject by asking me about the secret passage. I had told her all about my incarceration, and it was natural that she should be curious about it. I decided there would be no harm in showing her the upper exit, particularly as I was to be head of the house some day. I walked to the alcove and pressed my foot on the concealed trap door. It swung open slowly.

Katie looked down into the dark hole and shuddered. "How far does it go?" she asked.

"To the ground floor. At the bottom there's a chamber just high enough for a man to stand up in. If the King changes his mind about us, you and I and Jack Thumbkin might have to live down there for a while."

I said it in a joking tone, but her eyes became distended with real terror. "Just to think about it makes me want to scream!" she exclaimed. "Close it, please. It frightens me." After a moment she managed to smile and say, "I suppose it wasn't brave of you to live down there alone for a whole week!"

"It wasn't courage sent me down that ladder. It was fear. I knew it was the only place in London where I would be safe."

"We needn't ever argue about your courage again because I watched you fighting that duel. I hated every man there because they were standing back and letting you risk your life. I was sure you were going to be killed." She smiled again. "If you had stopped when it was over, I was going to ask you to take me with you. I waved at you to make you stop, but you galloped right past. I wasn't even sure you had seen me."

I took both her hands in mine and pressed them tight. "I wanted to stop and swing you up in front of me. But it wouldn't have done, darling. I had to travel fast. And I couldn't involve you in my danger. The arrangements made later—"

"Which I made."

"Which you made, darling, worked out much better. No man ever had a more wonderful surprise, or felt half as happy as I did, when I walked into the cabin and found you there."

"I was almost mad before you came. I kept thinking, 'Suppose he doesn't love me after all?' and 'Suppose he doesn't want me here?' The ship was a day late, and I suffered agonies every minute. I almost decided to slip ashore before you could see me."

The memory of that day was still so fresh and green for both of us that we sat there and smiled happily at each other without saying anything more. I was thinking how well it had worked out now that my future was comfortably assured. I would build towers at both ends of the new house and throw the whole central part into a Great Hall. The present building provided enough height for the purpose. A new entrance would have to be planned to allow for screens and a stairway at the side. An oriel window could be placed in the rear, and there would be room on one wall for a gallery.

"Roger."

"Yes, darling."

"There's something I must tell you. I'm almost afraid to say it. I want so much to go on just as we are."

"You're being very mysterious. What is all this?"

"Roger, what would you rather have happen, apart, that is, from all the wonderful things that have happened to us? And will happen."

"That's easy to answer. I want to see John receive a pardon so he can come home too."

She nodded her head eagerly. "I was sure of it. That makes it easier for me to say what I have to now. The Queen has thought of a way. It would mean a great sacrifice on your part, my dear. A great sacrifice for all of us."

I had no idea what she meant. "Isn't it a case of Her Majesty's asking him until he gives in, as he did with me?"

"No, it isn't going to be as easy as that. She says the King is still set in his mind against John, and nothing she could say or do would ever have any effect. It will depend on Sir George Villiers."

"Villiers!" I was beginning to feel alarm. "What has he to do with it?"

"Everything, I'm afraid. The Queen says he's the only one who could ever make the King change his mind. He must be persuaded to do the asking; and you'll have to persuade him."

I began to laugh. "Katie, I have as much chance of getting your Sir George Villiers to do that as I have of reading Persian cuneiform. I don't know him, and it's most unlikely I ever shall."

Sounds from the other room distracted my wife's attention at this point. She rushed out and did not return for quite a long time. When she did, it was apparent that another worry had taken possession of her mind.

"Our son isn't well," she said. "I'm sure it's that roast mutton he had this morning. I knew it would be too strong for him."

"But, Katie," I protested, "he can't be fed on milk all the time. We don't want him growing up into a weakling."

She shook her head in voilent dissent. "He's not as strong as you think. After all, he isn't two years old yet. I'm sure he shouldn't have so much meat. Beef and mutton all the time! Well, fortunately it doesn't seem to be anything serious. I think he's got a touch of the thrush in his throat. I gave him some medicine and he's gone off to sleep, the little lamb."

I objected to the medicines given our son as strongly as Katie did to his diet. Powder of crab's-eyes and chalk! I said nothing on that score, however, as I could see she was upset enough as it was. "We were talking about Sir George Villiers," I reminded her.

"Oh, yes." She seemed reluctant to resume the discussion. "The Queen says you'll have to cultivate him, Roger. Nothing but that will ever bring him to the point of asking the King for the pardon."

"Darling, your Sir George Villiers is going to be Master of the Horse. Very soon, no doubt, he'll be an earl or even a duke. I'm going to be a humble and very busy shipping merchant. And so the idea of a close acquaintance between us is impossible, not to say completely absurd."

"Not—not as absurd as you think. Her Majesty can arrange it. In fact, darling, she *has* arranged it."

I began to feel serious alarm for the first time. What did she mean? What had the Queen arranged?

"The Queen sent for him on purpose while I was there. She took things right into her own hands, and nothing I could say would stop her. Darling, when he becomes Master of the Horse, you will be appointed one of his equerries. He agreed as soon as the Queen suggested it. It's a fine post, Roger, and you'll probably be knighted at the same time."

I still did not perceive the full extent of the tragedy which threatened me. "But, Katie, an equerry must be at court all the time. It's not an honorary position. I couldn't possibly take it and still do my work here."

"Roger," she said, with a catch in her voice, "you don't seem to understand. You would have to give up your work."

That possibility had not occurred to me seriously. I tried to make light of it. "You're joking," I said. "I couldn't consider it. This is too important."

"The Queen's idea is that when you're an equerry you'll see Sir George continually and become such good friends that he'll be willing to help you about John. He admires John very much. He told her so."

I began to think of objections with almost frantic haste. "Her Majesty is very kind to take such an interest in the matter, I'm sure. Please don't think I'm not appreciative. But how can we be certain anything would come of it? After all, Villiers is a new man at court. He may lose favor as Carr did."

"The Queen says that by the time you know Villiers well enough to persuade him to do this, he'll stand so high with His Majesty that he'll be able to get anything he wants. She has no doubts about it at all." She looked at me with understanding eyes. "I don't want it any more than you do, Roger. But I—I'm afraid it's the only way."

I got up and began to pace about the room. I was very much afraid the Queen was right. There might be a chance this way. If Villiers grew in favor, the time would come soon when the fatuous monarch would refuse him nothing. If Villiers admired John Ward sufficiently, it might be possible to win his interest in a pardon. But it would mean relinquishing my career, my chance for honorable advancement. It would mean living at court and giving up the idea of building a home. The pay of an equerry would do no more than keep us living on a respectable scale; most officers of the court were continuously in debt with no prospect of ever getting out. If a title went with it, the honor would be unearned and, as far as my feelings were concerned, a thoroughly empty one.

"Katie," I said, stopping in front of her, "do you realize what this would mean? For both of us? For our son?"

"Yes," she answered, "I think I do. I prefer the other kind of life. I don't want to go back to court."

"Is Her Majesty doing this to get you back?"

"Partly, I think. But she's really interested in John's case and would like to help him. I was going to add that I don't want to return unless you would be unhappy about it the other way. I know you, my dear. I'm afraid your conscience would hurt you if you didn't do what you could for John Ward."

I was sure of that too. John had done so much for me that I could never repay him.

"I thought at first," went on my wife, "that I wouldn't tell you about it at all. I could have persuaded the Queen not to do anything more."

I put my arm around her and pressed her close. "I'm glad you thought of that. But, of course, you couldn't have done it, not even to protect me from my sense of duty. Your conscience is too active for that."

I resumed my pacing. There was a stir in the other room, and Katie ran in to see what it was. By the time she returned, I had my thoughts more clearly organized.

"It would mean living the life of a courtier," I said. "Consorting with panders and standing every day in the anteroom of a man who himself would be courting the favor of the King. An idle, empty, filthy life. We would be involved in intrigues and, if we didn't watch out, in scandals. We would have to drag along wherever the King went and have a couple of small hot rooms assigned to us up under the leads. Men would make love to you, and I wouldn't be able to do anything about it. Not if they were placed high enough."

"But you would do something about it," she said with a smile.

"I suppose I would. And then all our sacrifice would go for nothing. We would have to act lies and make flattering speeches and wink at deceit and treachery. It would mean our fine little John would be raised in that kind of an atmosphere. And our other children; if we have more."

"I know, Roger. I thought of all that. I almost didn't tell you about it."

I began to laugh. "It's exactly what my mother and Aunt Gadilda wanted for me. A post at court. It meant magnificence and comfort and honor in their eyes. I went to sea to escape it, and now the great honor has caught up with me after all. There's something ironic about it, isn't there? I wonder if they'll be happy about it, if they know?"

"I don't think they would be any happier about it than I am. Is it too high a price to pay, Roger? After all, we have our own lives to live, haven't we?"

"I used to think we were living in the perfect age," I said. "Well, my eyes have been opened. There's nothing fine about it. It's an ugly, treacherous, cruel age. I realize more all the time that we're living in a world as filthy as a cow byre."

Katie spoke up sharply at that. "You're wrong, Roger. It *is* a lovely world. We have each other, and Jack Thumbkin. Isn't that enough?"

"Perhaps we ought to go to America. We would be far enough away from people then." I patted her cheek. "I'm going to accept the post. We would be unhappy, both of us, if I didn't. I suppose I intended to from the first. I owe John that much at least. Well, it may not take so very long after all. This new longshanks may accomplish our purpose sooner than we think, and then we can go back to the kind of life we want. I guess we've been looking too much on the dark side. Forgive me if I've made the decision too difficult for you."

I picked up the sketch and tore it into small pieces.

48

AS THINGS TURNED OUT, I did not have to go to court after all. Several days later a visitor came to Sir Sigismund's house, a bluff and untidy individual who stamped into the anteroom and demanded in a loud voice to see "a certain Roger Blease." I drew him into a corner and said that I was Roger Blease, that I was in a great hurry, and what did he want with me?

"I'm Captain John Smith," he said. "You've heard of me, I'm sure. I'm the greatest traveler in the world. I've been all over the East, and I've been in Virginia. I'm sorry I left the primeval forests of that great new land to come back to this stinking sinkhole of crime and fraud." He always talked like that, I found, a combination of erudition and sea-going bombast. "If you're Roger Blease, I have a message for you. From John Ward."

"Then," I said eagerly, "you're the most welcome visitor I could have. I take it you've seen him."

"Yes, I've seen him. A matter of two months ago. In Tunis."

"I want to hear everything. Let's find a quiet spot where we can talk at our leisure over a bottle of wine."

That suited Captain John Smith, and when we were comfortably ensconced in a near-by inn he launched into a long story.

"A remarkable man, John Ward, Terror of the Seas," he said. "He made me think of many things: a god with more than a touch of the whipjack as well; a Noah, forbidden to build his ark, sailing around Ararat on a raft; a hearty Jove, in velvets and laces, lording it in a noisy Cardinal's Hat—"

"But how is he faring? Is he well?"

Captain John Smith looked at me soberly. "To the best of my knowledge," he said, "John Ward is dead."

He told his story with so many long diversions and so much obscure metaphor that it will be better for me to restate it in my own words.

John Ward was on the wharves at Gouletta when a man with a white skin stepped off the plank of a slattern coaster from Tripoli. He forced his way through the screaming natives and was by the side of the newcomer in a matter of seconds, saying in an eager voice: "You're an Englishman. It's lucky I'm here, or they might tear you to pieces. I'm Captain Ward."

The man looked at the hostile mob. "I was in two minds about coming ashore," he said. "I hope you're right about the luck. At this particular moment it seems to me uncertain. I guessed you were Ward." It was not a difficult guess, for the one-time commander of Free Rovers was arrayed in all his old magnificence, and a huge diamond sparkled in his hat.

"We had better get out of here. I don't like the look of things," said Ward.

As they struggled toward the rear, the newcomer asked: "How did you pick me for English? My cloak is Venetian, my shoes are Spanish, and I stole this molting nab-cheat in Turkey."

"Holy Olaf, man, I could see roast beef and Jack-of-Dover sticking right out of your ears. What's your name?"

"Captain John Smith."

"I've heard of you. You're a traveler and you write books."

Smith grinned. "The greatest traveler in the world. I don't claim as much as that for my writing."

"You had better come along with me. It's fine to see an English face again. And you'll be safer. The whole yellow coast is rupping with hate for the whites. It happens often, but this time there seems to be a more fanatical edge to it than usual."

They sailed across the lake and then took horse through the scattered outskirts of the city, coming finally to the palace under the city walls. Smith asked many questions on the way.

"Are you privileged here?"

"Yes. I'm useful to the Dey. At the moment my immunity seems to have worn thin."

"Do you sail any more?"

"No. I'm a retired pirate." John smiled at his companion without any suggestion of mirth. "A great anomaly. Can a pirate retire without his sins' catching up with him? My retreat was forced on me, Smith. My original crew dwindled, and I had no stomach for training foreigners to take their places; although I tried it at first. I traded the *Royal Bess* to the Dey, who wanted it for his personal use."

"May I ask what you got in exchange?"

"Something much less tangible. The right to live in Tunis without embracing their beastly faith." He shook his head bitterly. "The poor old lady is carmined to the teeth now like an aging callot. I never show myself when she's in port. It goes against the grain to see her covered with heathen flags."

When they turned in at the palace gates, Smith looked about him with wonder. "Don't tell me this is yours, Ward."

"It's mine," answered John indifferently. "Some years ago a great tragedy happened here, and I swore then to use it no more. But many pleasant things had happened here too. So I made it my permanent home after all." He smiled at his companion. "Spanish gold paid for this place; rolling Spanish ribbin. I'm a rather rich man."

Smith was a shrewd fellow, and he kept an eye open when they reached the outer courtyard, where dusky servants took their horses. The place was imposing, but there were signs of carelessness everywhere. Smith saw under the rim of the fountain the heel of a yellow shoe, the frayed end of a sky-blue baldrick, and a broken wineglass. The grass was long. The scum of neglect was on the walls and, inside, the rooms had a faintly moldy smell. He looked closer at his host and saw that Ward himself was not in the best of condition. He had grown stout, his face was flaccid, and there were purple pouches under his eyes.

"What goes with all this?" asked the guest.

"A certain amount of power. The Dey consults me about many things. I have luxury and ease; more of both than the King of England. I decided years ago to make the best of things. If I had to live with the heathen, I would get all I could out of it. I even have a harem."

"I heard whispers of that," said Smith eagerly. He had seen something of harems in his day, but not enough to take the edge off his curiosity.

Joralemon Snode joined them then. Jore quite apparently had been keeping up his wardrobe with his own efforts. The gray homespun doublet he wore had been mended so often that on close inspection it appeared to be covered with hit-and-miss embroidery. His cheeks were hollow and his nose so thin that it had a razor sharpness. He looked, according to Smith, like an unhappy anchorite.

It was growing dark, and a meal was served at once. The three of them sat down together on the balcony over the inner court where I had often dined with Cristina. I wondered, while listening to the story, if her spirit had hovered over them. The air was so close and moist that the visitor found it difficult to breathe. Joralemon said a long grace, ending with: "And, O Lord, continue to let the rain fall gently in England so that the land will always be green and cool, and grateful to those happy enough to live there. And let the winds blow lightly and not as here with the sting of the hot desert, and let the crops be plentiful. And, more than anything, O Lord, put it into the mind of the King to rule England better so there will be peace and prosperity in the land. And let them sometimes give a passing thought to those less fortunate who live far away."

At the close he and John looked at each other silently for a long moment and then John said, "Amen!"

The food was strange but good. First there was a thick brown soup with flecks of white on top, into which John spilled grated ginger with a lavish hand. Smith, great traveler though he was, tried it with mental reservations, finding it, however, savory and satisfying.

"My cook is a villainous Spaniard who turned renegado," explained the host. "But the fellow can cook. He can cook anything but English dishes."

A whole baby lamb followed, roasted until the skin was crisp and brown while the inner meat remained tender and succulent. Then there was an immense Carthage hen. Both had a pungent taste which John identified for his guest as garlic used with the greatest care. Finally there was a rich pastry and clove-scented chocolate to drink with it. Throughout the meal there was plenty to drink, the finest wines that Smith had ever tasted.

The atmosphere seemed to be getting more oppressive all the time. Smith, drenched with perspiration, had very little appetite. Joralemon Snode, saying nothing, did little more than peck at the food. John Ward partook enormously of everything, emptying his wine glass with an amazing regularity. "He's eating himself to death," thought Smith, noting the unhealthy color of his skin and the thickness of his waist. He felt a little sad about it, for John Ward was still a great hero to all Englishmen.

The conversation was desultory. At first the host brushed aside any talk of affairs at home, protesting that he had lost interest in matters so far removed. Instead, he discussed the situation in the Mediterranean, explaining with some detail a plan he had evolved to maintain a peaceful balance of power among the Christian nations. His idea was to detach Venice from Spain and set up a coalition which would accomplish what the Free Rovers had fought to secure—the freedom of the Inner Sea to

all commerce. It was plausible enough, but Smith wondered if his heart
was as much in it as he pretended.

Finally John tossed the last scrap of pastry over the balcony railing
with a gesture of satiety and settled back in his chair, a highbacked affair
of gilded wood and stamped leather which he had taken off a Spanish
prize. It creaked alarmingly with each move of his massive frame. The
stars had come out, and the servants had hung ship's lanterns on the walls
of the court beneath them. How well I knew the effect thus created, the
light shining faintly among the branches of the bigarade trees! John
reached down for one of the yellow globes of fruit on a limb beneath him.

"It's bitter," he said. "As bitter as the land where it grows."

"Now he's being honest about his feelings," thought the guest.

John smiled in a shamefaced way. "I haven't been deceiving you,
Smith. You must know how hungry I am for news of home. Start talking,
man. Tell us about England."

So Smith talked. He spoke first of national affairs and the dissension
over the policy of the King. He told of the pardon granted to the Earl
of Somerset and his wicked wife, and how the pair of them were living
in unhappy seclusion in the country, hating each other but forbidden any
other company. The rise of Villiers and the greediness for power of the
new favorite came in for long discussion. Then he turned to gossip: the
quips of Archie, the quarrels between Bacon and Coke, what the King
had said about this and the Queen about that. He talked for an hour or
more, and when he seemed to flag John prodded him into more recollec-
tions with eager questions. Joralemon Snode said little. Finally the leader
of the Free Rovers asked the question which had been on the tip of his
tongue from the first.

"Does King James show any signs of a change of heart in matters
which concern me?"

Smith shook his head. "On the contrary," he said, "the old sourbelly
grows more set in his ideas all the time. Gondomar has him completely
under his thumb. One of these days he'll send Raleigh to the block to
please the Dons. He's hankering now to marry Baby Charles to the
Spanish Infanta. She's a milky-cheeked, red-headed wench, so Baby
Charles himself is in favor of it. No, I'm afraid there will never be a
stand made against Spain as long as he's alive."

"Well," declared John, "it doesn't matter as much now. I pared
Philip's pretentions to a cow's thumb. English ships are safe again. I
take it that England won't be in need of the services of men like me."

He asked one more question only. "Have you heard anything of a
Roger Blease? He's a friend of mine and sailed with me for a time. He
married a girl that I knew, the daughter of Sir Bartlemy Ladland."

Smith had never heard of Roger Blease and knew nothing about Sir
Bartlemy except that he had been in disgrace and had died soon after.

John said: "I'm going to ask a favor of you, Smith. When you get back
to England, find Roger Blease and give him and his lady a word of

greeting from old Captain Rufflecoat. Tell them—tell them the seas are free again, and so he's well enough content with the way things have fallen out. I'm very fond of both of them, Smith."

The latter made a request in turn. He would like to have a look at the harem if such were not too strictly taboo. John grunted and said he was no damned Mohammedan to keep his wives locked away, but that the visit would be a great disappointment; the place was small and the women for the most part a lot of chattering margery-praters. Smith was insistent. He considered the women of the East most attractive in their mysterious way. Did he indeed, said John; he himself thought their beauty very much overrated, even the much-praised Circassian girls. It was clear, he pointed out, that Nature had designed their hips to relieve the discomforts of travel on camel back.

"Still, I'm a collector of impressions," said Smith. "I may never have such a chance again."

John pondered for a moment. "There's something I haven't told you about our situation here. I'm saving it for your ears later. Because of it, I don't see why you shouldn't have a glimpse of my happy little household. Come, Captain Smith, I'll initiate you into the sacred rites of Eastern conjugality."

Jore had disappeared, and the pair of them made their way down to the inner court. The copper door in the wall was opened by a native servant whose oxlike eyes rolled sluggishly under a turban as large almost as those silly rainbreakers which had been seen for the first time in London a few years before, called umbrellas. Smith followed his host on tiptoe.

The scene that greeted them was quite different from what Cristina and I saw the night we inspected the women's wing. The pool was filled with water, and a dozen women were squatting about it on cushions, drinking chocolate from silver mugs. The front wall had been opened to give a view of the city over the top of the palace walls. Little could be seen at the moment, however, but the star-specked sky. Candle-dips in wall sconces threw a faint light over the long apartment. The air was thick with perfume.

The weather being so oppressive, the women had thrown off much of their clothing, and the sudden appearance of the lord of their small creation, with a male guest at his heels, brought about a frenzied ducking under cushions and much hurried donning of garments and veils. They chattered and giggled in excitement. One, too far away from her clothes, turned and ran into the shadows at the far end, treating the intruders to a view of large brown limbs and a broad rear elevation.

"Is that Faussie?" asked John, shaking with laughter.

There was a chorus of assent, and the master of the household remarked that it was clear some of them, Faussie particularly, had been indulging themselves too liberally when the couscousou was on the table.

Something would have to be done about it; he did not value his wives according to weight.

Smith's eyes had become accustomed to the dim light, and he looked about him with retentive care. Most of the women were native, and their eyes glowed above the hastily donned veils with a promise of great beauty. Some were European, and he noticed they seemed less upset by the incident than their heathen sisters. Feeling an almost imperceptible touch on his ankle, he looked down and was a little startled to find an enormous pair of blue eyes looking up at him, framed in an oval face of olive tint. The woman was young and lovely and, quite obviously, enjoying a sly interest in his presence. The little vixen! said the traveler to himself. I would like to steal this one.

Another, small and vivacious in appearance, said something which the visitor did not catch, although he knew she had spoken in French. John frowned.

"Our guest, Francine," he said, "is an Englishman and a famous traveler. He has been in America and fought with savages who would think nothing of tearing all the hair off your pretty head. I sometimes think some such treatment is what you need."

The French girl also was pretty. The great John Ward has an eye for women, thought Smith. He was finding everything quite up to expectations. The languorous air, the perfume of the women, inflamed his senses. To end one's days in this way, he thought, had its compensations after all.

John had stopped beside a plump little woman with bright dark eyes in a round face, who smiled up at him. He dropped a hand on her shoulder and said, "Well, Fubbs."

He did not say anything more as they made their rounds of the long room. The lattices in the row of small private rooms were all closed. Smith stared through one but could make nothing out. He was wondering how things were managed. Did the master visit his wives in these tiny bowers, or did he have them sent to his own quarters? He had heard of both methods in his travels farther east.

"Now you've seen it," said John, not too cordially, when they had returned through the creaking copper door. "Would you trade your freedom for this sort of thing?"

Smith did not care to go that far, but he expressed himself with enthusiasm about the beauty of the women. John made no answer. He was looking up at the patches of sky through the branches of the trees. "Even the stars are different here," he muttered. "Does it seem to you that they are unfriendly?"

"I've seen the stars all over the world," said Smith. "They always look the same to me except when it comes to a matter of navigation."

John seated himself on a bench and motioned to his guest to join him. Feeling under the seat with a careful hand, he uncovered a small glow of juniper fire and lighted a spill. Both men started their pipes going.

"The natives say I keep a devil under this bench," remarked John with a short chuckle. "They won't come within ten feet of it. If I had valuables to hide, this would be a perfect place for it."

"You live in great comfort, Ward," said Smith, when their pipes were burning well.

John puffed loudly. "Comfort, yes. Too much, I fear. It might be an effort for me to climb the side of an enemy ship now."

Smith thought to himself, It would kill him if he tried it.

"This isn't always the paradise it seems. Some years ago the heathen came screeching over these walls. They skinned four of my men and nailed their bleeding hides to the wall outside. They also killed someone I thought a great deal of. It will happen again, Smith."

"By the Great Kochab, why do you stay, then? Don't you set any value on your life?"

John did not answer immediately. "Not a great deal. Would you have me go back to England and be hanged like my comrades?"

"There's France, Italy, Germany. You could live in any of them."

"Isn't one place of exile as good as another? The life here is easy and comfortable—for as long as it may last. I sometimes wonder if I could get away. The Dey has an exaggerated idea of what I have. He would strip me clean if I tried it." He said after a pause, with one of the bitter laughs which punctuated all his talk: "So you think my wives beautiful. Take their veils away and scrub the paint off their faces, and you would be surprised to find that some of them are as homely as little monkeys. Native women aren't completely human, you know. They fight and scratch and spit until the servants have to whip them apart. Sometimes they go fey, and then they sit up through the night and howl like dogs at the full of the moon."

"But they aren't all native."

"I saw you studying the white ones. Did they pass muster with such a discerning judge? One, Francine, is French."

"I thought she was."

"She comes from Marseilles. She's lively. But she has a venomous tongue in her head. All the rest are afraid of her. Did you notice a young one with lovely eyes? But of course you did; you couldn't overlook Maria."

"She's Italian, isn't she?"

"Sicilian. She's quite beautiful. I send for her often." So that point is settled! thought Smith. "She looks almost saintly, but she doesn't like being kept here. She would give herself gladly to any man who managed to break in. The only one who has any real regard for me is the little Greek. If I were ill, I wouldn't be afraid to lay my head on her shoulder."

"I heard you lived in state, Ward. But I had no conception of all this."

John said, with sudden fervor, "Even if security went with this, I would trade it gladly for a small thatched house on a green lane in Kent."

Smith then asked about Joralemon. In what capacity did he act?

"My good old Jore! He's everything—butler, secretary, friend. Most of all, he's my conscience. Not that I heed him much. He gives me no peace about these women whose charms have made such an impression on you. You may find it hard to believe, but he refuses to go inside that door. Perhaps that answers a question you didn't care to ask. Jore is a real saint, caught by circumstances in a sinful corner from which he can't escape."

"I couldn't fail to notice," commented the visitor, "that there wasn't an English woman. It surprised me, I must confess."

Then, for a moment, he saw the real John Ward. The massive form drew up straight. John spoke in a voice pitched low with the intensity of his feeling.

"I would count myself lacking in every quality that makes a man," he declared, "if I brought a woman of my own race inside the walls of this sepulcher. I'm not proud of the way I'm living, Captain John Smith. The women are waifs; they've been better off here, I suppose, than they'd have been anywhere else. But I wouldn't ask a woman I could respect to share my dishonor."

There was a long silence after that. Finally John, with considerable effort, heaved his great bulk around on the bench and looked intently at his companion. "You must leave tomorrow, Smith," he said.

"Has my company wearied you so soon?"

"I can't tell you what a pleasure it's been to hear an English voice. Your talk has been as welcome as water to a man dying of thirst on the desert. But—as I told you before, I don't like the look of things. I'm at serious odds with the Dey. He threatens to withdraw his protection. It will come to that, my friend. There's a ship sailing for France in the morning. They don't know it yet; but tonight my European wives are being sent aboard. I still have enough influence to manage a thing like that. You must go too."

"Then you must come with us," exclaimed Smith. "Great God, you mustn't throw your life away!"

John Ward said quietly: "I've never run away from my fate. Perhaps I've unconsciously accepted some of the philosophy of the East; it seems to me that a quick death is a welcome one. I'm not well, Smith; I seem to lack resolution these days. And even if I wanted it, I doubt if I could get away."

Smith knew that further urging would be useless. He contented himself with asking, "What about your man, Snode?"

John's face lighted up with the first genuine smile of their encounter. "My brave old Jore!" he said. "He's a splendid fool, Smith. He refuses to leave me. I've tried to talk sense into him, but he won't have it. I'm afraid he'll be here to the end." He tamped out his pipe. "It won't be long now before the heathen come over the walls again."

The Moneyman

To Nelson Doubleday

INTRODUCTION

STORIES speak for themselves and so an author's preface is, in most cases, superfluous. When the setting is historical, however, there are certain explanations which become necessary. It must be made clear to the reader where history ends and the work of the romancer begins and also which of the characters are real and which fictitious. With this as my excuse, I wish to point out that the story of Jacques Coeur, the Moneyman (L'Argentier) of Charles the Seventh of France; as set down in the pages which follow, adheres to the record as closely as possible. Some liberties have been taken in the matter of time sequences and, because the chronicles of the day are both scanty and full of gaps, it has been necessary to draw on the imagination for some of the details with which the bare skeleton of known facts has been fleshed and clothed.

It is surprising how little has been written about some phases of the career of the great Moneyman. Monstrelet and his fellow scribes of the day went to great pains to set down the activities of unimportant knights and to tell of the daily lives of dull kings and stupid princes but they seem to have been lightly concerned with the spectacular career of Jacques Coeur. There would be little known about his trial were it not for the happy discoveries of C. Joseph Jacques, as given in his *Un Scandale judiciaire au moyen âge*. Even with the explanation M. Jacques supplies of the parts played by Robert de Poitevin and Ferrand de Cordule, it has been necessary to reconstruct the scene and to invent more tangible and believable evidence.

Those who approach the past with reverence for the traditions of chivalry will perhaps object to the part I have given that great paladin, Jacques de Lalain. He devoted himself exclusively to challenge encounters with other knights (like the barnstorming prizefighters of the present day) but he did not fight the Sire d'Arlay, for the very good reason that the Sire d'Arlay had no existence in fact. I conceived the duel as necessary to point up the absurdity and the unfairness of the chivalrous practices of the day. As Jacques de Lalain was the recognized champion and, as a close study of his career had convinced me he would have behaved in exactly this way in the given circumstances, I cast him in the role of the bully who refused to fight for France but was ready to fight on any other pretext.

I have made no mention of Jacques Coeur's family for the reason that they played no real part in the events which brought his career to its climax. His wife, a gentle and retiring lady, died when the trouble began, and his sons seem to have adopted passive roles. When I attempted to introduce them into the story they got so much in the way that I decided finally it would be better to do without them. If I have done them an injustice I plead in extenuation that I have followed the lead of historians who give his family the scantiest of mention.

I have striven to give a faithful picture of Agnes Sorel, that lovely and unfortunate lady, and of Charles the Well Served. Robert de Poitevin lived and played his courageous part as described in the drama of the trial, as did Jeanne de Vendôme and Guillaume Gouffier, the villains of the piece. As Valerie Maret and D'Arlay and the Comte and Comtesse de Burey are fictitious characters, it follows that the train of events in which they are depicted as playing parts has been invented to supply a note of lightness and romance in what might otherwise be a grim story.

THOMAS B. COSTAIN

BOOK ONE

1

THE ROYAL STANDARD of France waved above the towers of the Louvre. It was an unusual sight, for the King bore Paris no love and seldom came there. The citizens, as might be expected, were making a carnival of it and the streets were filled with banners and pennons, and there were peep shows and Mysteries, and trading booths at every corner. They were having a good time and a profitable one (being shrewd enough to charge well for supplying the needs of the court) and yet they were viewing the proceedings with tongue in cheeks. They knew, these burghers of the wise and worldly old town, that the gallants who rode or strutted through the streets, their noses high in the air and their cold eyes unconscious of the rabble, had lost to the English all the great battles of the Hundred Years' War and would lose more if allowed their own way; and so sometimes above the creaking of leather and the stomping of horses and the shrillness of the silver trumpets could be heard jeers and catcalls and the bitter invective in which the Parisian excels.

Jacques Coeur could see the standard from the window of the white-plastered room which he used, when in Paris, for the direction of his many activities. He had been at work since five in the morning. Visitors had passed in and out in a seemingly endless procession and he had talked with them all, briefly and decisively, dismissing each one with a peremptory wave of the hand when convinced the purpose of the call had been accomplished. He had read mountainous piles of letters and documents, he had scrutinized lists, and had issued so many orders that all over the busy establishment his people were in the throes of carrying them out. He had exhausted completely the patience of his servant Nicolas.

He got to his feet and went to the window where he gazed through a break in the clustered rooftops at the turreted splendor of the Louvre. "Charles the Well-Served," he said in a half-audible tone. "You are well named, I think, my amiable but irresolute liege lord! I wonder what names they will have for you when the history of these days is written? . . . I wonder what will be written about Jacques Coeur?"

Seen from the rear he could not have been mistaken for anything save what he was, a prosperous and middle-aged man. When he turned about it was a different story, for then his eyes captured the attention and made everything else about him seem trivial and misleading. They were extraor-

dinary eyes, large and gray and very much alive. They smiled, laughed,
lighted up, sparkled, burned, smoldered, suffered, exploded into vivid
dramatization of every mood. They never lacked animation for a moment.
His voice, which was of an eager timbre, had something of the same quality.
It could not be denied that he inclined to the theatrical in his gestures,
but the lift and play of his fine white hands did no more than keep pace
with his constant and quick change of expression.

A closer view made it clear that he dressed with rather particular care.
His tunic was laced tight with cords of silver thread and there were pearls
in the tufting of his sleeves. His hose fitted him well and his shoes were of
the finest leather; although, being intended for active use, they lacked the
extravagant upward curl at the toe.

"I think, Nicolas," he said to his servant, "we may assume that we
have given this place a thorough shaking, like medicine in a bottle. The
other half of our day begins. I shall now wait on the King. A cloak, my
ever-smiling Nicolas."

Nicolas, as a matter of fact, had rarely been known to smile. If his outward appearance could be accepted as an indication of what went on
inside him, he lived in state of bilious discontent. His eyes moved with
painful slowness in yellow sockets and the corners of his mouth drooped.
He was a Norman, with a head shaped like a pear and a jowl the color of a
ripe plum.

This gloomy apparition produced a heavy cloak which was richly lined
with miniver, and held it out for his master.

"Must you go to court today?" he asked. "You've done a full day's work
already, my lord. My head buzzes with all the orders I've had."

"I am expected, Nicolas. And when the King expects, the subject obeys;
particularly if he happens to be the Moneyman."

"Truly I have a fool for a master," muttered Nicolas. "He will work himself to death. And then I will have no master and I will starve."

Jacques Coeur looked at the bottle-bellied figure beside him and smiled
cheerfully. "You could live for a long time on what you've stored under
your belt," he said. Then he felt the weight of the proffered cloak and
frowned doubtfully. "Is it cold enough out to wear this?"

"Would I bring it to you, master, if I didn't think you needed it?"

"That is true," admitted the merchant. "I should know by this time
that in such matters your judgment is better than mine."

"In matters of your comfort and well-being I am always right," admitted
the servant. "And you, master, are always wrong."

"I wouldn't have said my record was quite as blank as that," demurred
Coeur. "You will allow, perhaps, that in concerns of a rather more general
nature I display somewhat better judgment. Well, Nicolas the Omnipotent, lead the way. We shall walk today."

They descended by a stone staircase and emerged on the street through
wide bronze gates. The air was brisk and Coeur realized at once that his
servant's selection of a cloak had been a wise one. He wrapped it more

closely about him and stepped out at such a swift gait that Nicolas had
to go at a jog trot to keep on his heels.

"Master, master!" protested the servant. "Won't the King's affairs wait
a few minutes longer? Do you want to wear yourself out? After all, you're
not a young man any more."

The merchant's good nature was not proof against this suggestion. "I
may not be young," he said, with a sharp glance back over his shoulder,
"but I'm still as strong as I was in my twenties. You needn't shake your
head, Nicolas. You are ten years behind me in age and yet compared with
me you're doddering into senility. I can still outwork, outthink, and outwalk any man I know."

"You can outclaim anyone, master," puffed the servant.

It was at once clear that the people of Paris did not include the King's
Moneyman in the veiled hostility they felt for the rest of the court. Coeur
and his servant were followed by a company of admiring men and boys
like the tail of a comet. Cordial greetings reached them from the doors of
taverns and the windows of houses, "It's the Moneyman!" "Brava, good
Jacques!" and "Jaquet the Fox is our friend." Coeur returned these salu-
tations with readiness and good humor. It was apparent that he enjoyed
the attention paid him and so Nicolas stepped closer to grumble at his
shoulder, "They would gape just as wide if it was the hangman passing,
master."

When they reached the stone-lined ditch which surrounded the Louvre,
Coeur stopped abruptly. "Nicolas," he demanded, "has any word been received yet from the Sire d'Arlay?"

"Wouldn't I have told you if it had?"

Coeur would have realized, had he ever stopped to consider the matter,
that his cross-grained attendant seldom or never gave him a direct answer.
More often than not Nicolas countered with a question of his own, as in
this instance. But the Moneyman was too concerned with the question itself to give any thought to the nature of the response.

"This day," he said to himself, "may go down in history. It's unfortunate
I've had no reports from Robin d'Arlay. I'm sure what he has learned
would have enabled me to put additional ribbing on the familiar carcass
of my arguments."

The armed guard at the entrance to the palace smiled and motioned
the Moneyman to enter. Jacques Coeur, his fur-lined cloak flapping about
his well-shaped legs, made his way briskly through crowded halls to the
foot of the Great Staircase. Here a chamberlain in green-and-white livery
gave him an obsequious, "A fine day, my lord Coeur."

"Where shall I find the King?"

The chamberlain motioned up the staircase with a splayed thumb. "The
ladies and gentlemen of the court are with the Queen, my lord Coeur.
The King is expected to join them any moment now."

The Moneyman paused. "Tell me, Guyot, in what mood shall I find
the King? Is there any hint of a twinkle in the royal eye today? Does my
dread lord walk easily and with something of an air of expectancy?"

"It is my opinion the King does not feel well today. He walks slowly. He was silent all morning, according to report. No one has seen him smile."

A clatter of conversation fell on Coeur's ears as he entered the Great Chamber. The court had already settled down to its new preoccupation of the moment, the playing of *cards* with painted slips of stiff cardboard. The ladies and gentlemen were so engrossed in what they were doing that not a single pair of eyes was raised at his entrance. "Painted monkeys!" he thought. "Wasting all their time with their foolish games and wagers." Then, as usual, he began to think in terms of trade. "I must get an artist to paint a new set of cards, and copy them on the best of paper. They must be very special and costly. I might as well make a profit out of this."

He was careful to pause by the silk alms bag attached to the wall and to drop in a gold coin. Ordinarily the eyes of Queen Marie fixed themselves on each newcomer to make sure that this unwritten rule of the court was observed. Today, however, she was too occupied with her game to notice, and, as a result, the sound his contribution made suggested it had found little company in the alms bag.

The Queen was seated at the head of the room and Coeur knew she was playing *Glic* because her opponents were two in number. One was a young woman with a vivacious manner and a pretty dark face under a heart-shaped hennin, the other an enormous man in disorderly gray. Many other games of Glic were being played at small tables scattered over the floor but a good part of the company seemed to prefer watching the royal contest, standing in a silent and respectful circle.

The Queen was so absorbed that the Moneyman realized it would be unwise to interrupt her to pay his respects. Her overlarge nose, which robbed her otherwise pleasant face of any claim to beauty, showed a tendency to twitch, a sure sign that she was in a disturbed mood. Her well-rounded bosom was laced low in a dark green robe with broad bands of ermine sweeping in generous curves to the tips of her shoulders. The folds of her sleeves were so long that they sometimes touched the floor and so gave her much trouble in the handling of her cards. He heard her say in a distressed voice, "I am having *such* bad fortune today." The large man answered in a rumbling undertone, "In the game of Glic, liege lady, good luck can be compelled by a proper playing of the cards one holds."

Coeur found his way to a bench by the wall under a new tapestry representing in lurid realism the Seven Virtues and the Seven Vices. It had an occupant already, a soldier with a sword buckled to his belt and a look of distaste for his surroundings on his thin, leathery face.

"Dunois," said Coeur in a whisper, watching the attractive brunette who played with the Queen, "does it seem to you that Mademoiselle de Maignelais is pressing rather hard in her effort to usurp her cousin's place?"

"She's a pert minx," said the old soldier. "The lovely Agnes progressed to the King's notice through the favor of the Queen but I doubt if the method can be followed a second time."

"We mustn't feel too secure about it. The Queen is reconciled to Agnes Sorel. But it may be she thinks Agnes has been her rival long enough."

Dunois shook his head. "You and I have every reason to know how fickle our royal master can be; but in this matter his constancy verges on the miraculous. There's something about the fair Agnes which holds him on the tightest leading string. Will he ever be content with the raven locks of this little cousin on the pillow which has known the golden loveliness of Agnes Sorel?"

Coeur had fallen into somber speculation. "Agnes isn't well," he said. "Have you noticed how pale she is? She confesses to a malady of the spirit as well as of the body. I'm concerned about it, Dunois, deeply concerned."

The old soldier looked at his companion with a certain slyness of expression. "That I believe," he said.

An interruption was caused at this point by the entrance of the King. The voice of the single attendant who had preceded him was lost in the buzz of animated talk and it was several moments before the fact of the royal presence was generally recognized. Then there was a hurried clatter of heels as the ladies and gentlemen rose and made their bows.

"He looks his usual melancholy self," muttered Dunois.

Charles the Seventh stood for a moment in the entrance to the Great Chamber. His bow to the company was a perfunctory one and clearly a matter of habit. He sighed abstractedly and bowed again before beginning his progress through the room.

There were times when he looked every inch a king but this was not one of them, for he had donned his favorite short jacket of green which exposed his legs. The royal legs were not good. They were short and skimpy and bowed, and there was no denying that an unexpected lumpiness around the knees compromised seriously the dignity a wise monarch should always strive to maintain.

When he reached the Queen's table, he bowed moodily. "I have no wish to interrupt your—your new afternoon diversion, Madame," he said.

"We play only to fill the time until you honor us with your presence, liege lord," declared Marie of France.

"It is very clear, Madame, that you find this matching of wits most diverting. Under the circumstances"—the King seemed to suffer from sudden uneasiness and was careful to avoid her eyes—"you will be content that my stay must be unusually brief today. Matters of state demand my attention immediately. I must ask you to allow me the attendance of"—his glance strayed about the room—"of Gouffier, Chabannes, Dunois, Coeur. Questions of the utmost urgency demand our attention in my own chambers."

The Queen found it hard to conceal her chagrin. Drawing a linen kerchief from the broad gold-mesh belt at her waist, she dabbed at the end of her long nose. To forestall any open remonstrance, the King rose to his feet.

"My most profound regrets, Madame," he said. "I trust you will spend a pleasant afternoon."

2

The four men named fell into line behind him, Jacques Coeur bringing up the rear. All maintained a proper decorum as they left the room although each of them knew he was playing his part in an open farce. Even their selection had been a matter of routine, for they had been called out in this order many times before. Without a word being said, they passed through the screens and on to the landing of the Great Staircase. Instead of ascending to the apartments of the King on the floor above, they turned of one accord and proceeded down a long passage which ended at another staircase.

An iron door clanged to behind them. They began to descend in single file, as the steps radiating out from the ornate newel were not wide enough to permit them to walk two abreast. It was a curiously designed staircase, with a separate ascending tier; and the soffits were so low and carefully placed that it was impossible on either tier to see anyone going the other way. Coeur had often thought of this arrangement as a perfect reflection of the prevailing state of mind at the court—sly, secretive, suspicious, constricting.

Guillaume Gouffier, who preceded Coeur in the line, turned his head and grinned back at the Moneyman. His nose was so long that the act of smiling made his mouth curl up closely around its vulpine tip.

"A most convenient stair for—for the purpose," he whispered.

Reaching the ground floor, they proceeded down a flag-tiles passage. A guard was standing at the end and, at the first glimpse of them, he scuttled out of sight. The door at which he had been stationed was of oak, ornamented elaborately with a spreading branch of the surelle tree. Here the King halted and bowed to his followers.

The door opened immediately. They caught a glimpse of a well-lighted room and a tall *prie-dieu* with crimson tapestried panels. The King vanished within and the door closed after him with a speed which suggested a surreptitious intent.

Before it closed, however, they heard a pleasant feminine voice say in a tone of mock despair: "My lord, my lord! That very short jacket again!"

"The fair Agnes," declared Gouffier, "has never admired the royal legs."

The state ministers turned in a body into a small room on the other side of the passage. It had, apparently, been prepared for them; there were four chairs, a table with a flagon of red wine and a triangular slab of green-veined cheese, fire on the hearth.

"How long," asked Dunois, as they seated themselves, "have we played our inglorious parts in such mummeries as this?"

"Too long," answered Gouffier. He stifled a yawn and glanced covertly at Jacques Coeur. "Could it be construed as faintly treasonable if one voiced the opinion that it grows tiresome?"

"No one has been deceived from the start," grumbled the old soldier.

"All France knows that the King pays afternoon visits to the Lady Agnes. Too many know of the way he tries to cover his movements, and they laugh at him for his pains."

"And at us no doubt." Gouffier gave another sly look at the Moneyman. "One of us should convince the King that no purpose is served by going through these discreet motions. I lack the finesse for it myself. You, perhaps, Jacques Coeur?"

"The deception," said Coeur shortly, "is not of the King's will. It's the Lady Agnes herself who insists that a veil be kept drawn. You're all aware that she's of a pious turn and refuses an open avowal of——"

"Of her adultery," said Gouffier, when the Moneyman hesitated to use the word. He had cut himself a slice of the cheese and was consuming it with voracious bites. "We would be well advised, the four of us, to learn this game of Glic. I fear, my lords, a distaste for your faces will grow in me if I have to suffer them much longer in idleness."

"I had a distaste for your face," said Dunois bluntly, "long before the curtain went up on this far-from-sacred play."

Gouffier turned and scowled at him over the cheese. "It's a prerogative of military greatness to speak one's mind openly," he said. "But you may not always find it wise, my doughty Bastard, to abuse the privilege."

The soldier glanced at him and then at Chabannes, who was sprawling morosely in his chair. "We are two against two," he said, "and it's becoming increasingly hard for us to sit down together in peace. The Moneyman and I desire an immediate resumption of the war. You are in favor of continuing the present policy of inactivity. It would be idle for us to attempt any further persuasion. Your minds, I regret to say, cannot be swayed into a more patriotic way of thinking. It would be easier for us to sit here and blink at each other in the silence of mutual dislike; but, sirs, we might as well recognize that the issue must soon be resolved and so speak with complete frankness."

"If it's frankness you want," cried Gouffier, "I'm ready to say that I consider you nothing but an animated sword hand, Bastard of Orléans! Your views should carry no weight as they are dictated by self-interest, a desire to display your leadership again in action. As for the Moneyman, I say again what I have spoken openly on many occasions. We have come to a sorry pass when common men are raised to posts of responsibility in the state. If I had my way, Jaquet the Fox would be shorn of all his honors and herded back to where he belongs, the fashioning of furs for the wives of town burghers."

Jacques Coeur gripped the arms of his chair. He wanted to spring at the throat of the smirking state minister but was restrained by force of habit. He had never had any illusions as to the esteem in which he was held at court. Although he had been ennobled by royal decree, the aristocracy had never accepted him as one of them, and never would. It had been necessary to accept their rebuffs as part of the price of his rapid elevation. Outwardly he had remained impervious to the hostility of the court but inside he still suffered as much from each new proof of contempt as he had at the beginning. Trying to be philosophic about it, he had said to himself that his tormentors were men of narrow mind and that what they said and did was of no real concern; but there was no longer any concealing from himself that this constant bludgeoning of his pride was having its effect. The floodgates had been dammed so long that it might prove impossible to let them swing open. He did not want to become completely stultified.

He remained silent for several moments and then addressed himself to Dunois. "As you know, I have never sought honors at court. I serve the King at his own suggestion and command. When I can no longer be of service to him, I shall be happy to devote myself entirely to the control of my own affairs. In the meantime I can't be a good servant if I quarrel with those about him, even though I hold them in contempt."

Dunois nodded somberly. "Moneyman, I think you allow us to see that you have a strong stomach."

"My stomach," said Coeur, "threatens to rebel."

Silence settled on the room. The two courtiers devoted themselves to the flagon of wine and tossed an occasional word between them. The eyes of Dunois became fixed on the window and it was clear his thoughts had wandered to a more congenial plane. Perhaps he was dreaming of the days when he and the Maid had routed the invaders before Orléans. Jacques Coeur got to his feet and paced up and down, his arms folded on his chest. The comment of the old soldier rankled in his mind. "Is that what all men think, that I will swallow any insult?" he asked himself again and again. "Would it be better if I fought them with their own weapons?"

"As for the issue between us," said Gouffier suddenly, "I find that I have much to say."

"Ha!" cried Dunois, emerging instantly from his reverie. "Out with it then!"

An hour passed in bitter argument. They went over and over the old familiar ground, the two courtiers advancing the specious reasons with which the peace party bolstered their desire for a continuation of the treaty with the English invaders. Coeur took no part in it, the turmoil inside himself making any participation in the debate impossible.

He was on the point of announcing that a press of duties would compel his departure without waiting for the royal sanction when the sound of a door opening and closing reached their ears from across the hall. A moment later the King appeared in the doorway.

"I see you are at each other's throats again, gentlemen," he said. "Must this dispute go on forever? I confess that I weary of the sound of it." After a moment, he added in contrite tones: "I have been delayed. Please believe that I feel a deep regret at keeping you here so long. I fear it's too late now for a full discussion of the matters I had intended to propound for your advice and so I suggest we postpone our talk until tomorrow. There's still time for a turn in the gardens before supper."

3

In his capacity of comptroller of the royal purse, Coeur had a small room in the tower overlooking the Rue Beauvais. It was an inconvenient location, being far removed from the rest of the household offices, and as a consequence the officials who attended him there brought sulky looks with them as well as their accounts. He spent two busy hours after leaving the King, checking over lists of supplies and issuing instructions to a long succession of chamberlains, valets, almoners, even cooks. It was trying work, for thee minor servants took their cue from the nobility and treated him with condescension under the thinnest veneer of respect.

It was dark by the time he was through, and the wall hangings were rippling with the night drafts which found their way through the mullioned windows. He realized that the court supper was now over. That he had missed it was of no importance, for he lacked the intense interest in food which most men seemed to share. Perhaps, he reflected, it was just as well he had lost the chance to partake of the rich viands served by the royal cook; on the occasion of his last talk with the court physician he had been advised to watch his weight.

Free of all interruptions at last, he set himself to the task of writing letters. His pen moved rapidly and incisively. He never hesitated for a word.

When they were finished and sealed with an embossed ♡ and the motto underneath *A Vaillants Coeurs Rien Impossible*,[1] he began to undress without bothering to summon Nicolas. "I've had enough of his grumbling for one day," he said to himself. His movements now were slow and unwilling. It might have been construed from this that he felt he was laying aside with his clothes the responsibilities and the stimulating activities which filled his days, and that he regretted the necessity.

He was about to step naked into bed when there was a knock at the door. Ensconcing himself between the sheets, he called, "Come in." The only unlocked door perhaps in the Louvre opened at his summons to admit a minor court official.

"Your attendance is required, my lord Coeur."

"Is it the King?"

The official hesitated and then said, "Yes, my lord Coeur."

The Moneyman sprang out of bed with alacrity. He seemed glad to dress again and thus to resume the duties and the importance of his waking hours. It took no more than three minutes to complete his toilet.

The route by which he was conducted supplied the Moneyman with the reason for the officer's hesitation. They were not going to the apartments of the King. They proceeded to the ground floor and went out into the courtyard where the night guards had already been placed and were stamping their feet to keep warm. Jacques Coeur knew from the sounds

[1] To valiant hearts nothing is impossible.

which reached his ears that the chains were being drawn across all the streets leading to the palace.

After reaching the far end of the court they proceeded along a covered passage. This ended in three doors grouped darkly together. Opening one with a key, the official led the way up a short flight of stairs to a square apartment where the gloom of the outside was left behind suddenly and completely. There were a score of lighted candles and a cheerful fire crackling on the hearth and bundles of bittersweet and evergreens in pots and vases; a pleasant room and most distinctly feminine. Jacques Coeur did not need the surelle device which appeared in all the decorations and in the embroideries to tell him where he was. "We walked three times as far as was necessary to get here," he thought. "The King will take an even more roundabout way. And when he arrives tongues will be clacking all over the palace and everyone will know where he is!"

His reflections were cut short by the arrival of the lady to whom the apartment belonged. She paused in the doorway with a nod and a smile for the visitor. Their eyes met and held; and, if anyone else had been in the room, it would have been apparent that a look of understanding had passed between them.

"Is it to be tonight, then, my dear Lady Agnes?" asked Coeur.

"Yes, my old friend, it's to be tonight."

It is impossible to convey in words the full effect of Agnes Sorel's great charm. Her loveliness was owing only in part to the gold of her hair, the vibrant blue of her eyes, the delicacy of her features. It was in equal degree a matter of spirit. Hers was a fine and high spirit, in which vivacity, sweetness, and resolution were combined. Jacques Coeur, who understood her better perhaps than anyone, found himself instantly under the spell of it, as he did on every occasion they met. At the same time he noted, with a catch of his breath, that there were deep violet shadows under her eyes and more than a hint of weariness in her manner and bearing. He asked himself, "Must Time be so unsparing that even the beauty of Agnes Sorel suffers from its passing?"

She was dressed rather simply in blue velvet with a veil of ivory lace about her shoulders. With the courage which only a conviction of beauty can give, she had disregarded the stern dictate of fashion by which women wore hennins on their heads at all hours of the day; instead she kept her hair uncovered and piled high on her head in a profusion of curls. A prayer book in a gold case was suspended by a thin chain from her wrist.

She walked slowly into the room and it became apparent at once that her gown did not depend for effect on its simplicity. There was artfulness in the cut of it, particularly in the way the waistline fell to a V in front. There was art also in the slit of the skirt at one side, extending almost to the knee and allowing glimpses of a froth of lace on the under kirtle; this, however, the sole concession to the craze of the moment for elaboration and embellishment.

"I arranged it so you would arrive first," she said. "There is a matter to be discussed before the King comes."

Coeur was still concerned about her appearance of ill-health. He frowned and said, "You are tired, I fear."

"Yes, a little tired." Then she nodded her head slowly as though unwilling to be anything but entirely honest. "It's more than that, my kind Jacques. I haven't felt at all well of late. I am beginning to fail—in health as well as in looks."

"But you have never looked more lovely, my Lady Agnes!"

"Must you play the courtier with me? I can be honest enough with myself to believe what my mirror tells me. There are hollows in my cheeks and these great shadows under my eyes. I found three gray hairs this morning, and I tore them out as fiercely as a pious churchman casting out a sinful thought!"

"You are still so beautiful that you could do me another great favor. A new silk has reached us from the East, a rich variety stiffened with other material which makes it rustle with every movement. If you would condescend to wear a gown made of it, there would immediately be a great demand for the stuff."

Agnes Sorel rose to the bait with a look of eager interest. "A skirt that rustles as you walk? That would be quite enticing and very, very feminine. I will be glad to use some of this new material. We have introduced many new things between us, haven't we? And I don't believe anyone has ever suspected."

"What Agnes Sorel wears today, every woman in France wants tomorrow," said Coeur.

She began to speak in a low and hurried tone. "Old friend, it pleases me to hear you say I'm still fair to look at. God grant I never see the day when I'm too old and faded to find favor with men or"—she smiled wanly —"to start a new fad in dress. I think I never shall, for I must tell you that—that matters are serious with me. I suffer continually from a weakness in the limbs. It's no longer easy to rise in the mornings and I have no desire to walk or ride or dance. I've always been active and so I'm sure that—that I haven't much longer to live."

She drew closer and her voice dropped to a whisper. "I'm going to tell you a secret, Jacques Coeur, because it leads to something you may have to do soon. It was through the influence of the Queen's mother that I won the favor of the King. Do you find that hard to believe? I'm sure you must. And yet it's true. Yolande, with all her great goodness of heart and her fine understanding, established a rival for her own daughter."

"I don't find it hard to believe," said Coeur. "I understood the Queen's mother well enough to know the reasons she had."

"The old lady was very wise," whispered Agnes Sorel. "She knew the weak side of the King, that he would always have a mistress. She preferred to select one who would cause Queen Marie the least distress and who would help to keep His King's Grace from listening to the wrong advice. She chose me."

"And what a wise selection it has proven to be!"

"Thank you. . . . It hasn't been easy and I'm happy you think I have justified the choice." After a pause she went on in the same hurried tone: "She counseled me at every step. She urged me to use my influence in the matter of the ministers he kept around him. You, Jacques Coeur, she preferred to all others. Did you know that? Ah, what fine things she said about you; she was so sure that all would be well with France if the King continued to listen to you. Yes, she was very wise. It was a great loss for France when that wonderful old lady died."

"It was a great thing for France when Agnes Sorel was born." The Moneyman nodded. "I knew Yolande was at your shoulder all the time. You have been an apt pupil, Agnes."

"I know what she would say if she were alive today. She would say, 'My child, you must face the truth. Time is taking its toll and you must be ready to step down.' Yes, she would say that, even though she knew it might hurt me very much. I thought it all over last night and made up my mind to speak to you, to tell you that we have work to do between us. We must be ready to have someone else to—to continue what I have done. It wasn't easy, Jacques Coeur, to reach that conclusion; I am proud, I like to stand first, I like to have power. But I made up my mind to it; and last night in my dreams Yolande came to me and smiled—such a wise, sweet smile—as though she knew and was pleased with me."

"No one can ever take your place!" exclaimed the Moneyman. "The King's devotion is as complete as ever. It will be time enough to think of such things when he shows signs of wavering—if he ever does."

She shook her head positively. "I'm the only one in a position to judge. I'm growing old. Jacques Coeur, Jacques Coeur, I am nearly forty!"

"Years do not count when they prove as kind as they have to you."

"*Your* devotion will never lessen, I am sure, and there is much consolation in that." She shook her head and pronounced two of the most bitter of all words, "My successor—yes, my successor must be carefully chosen. We must be as wise as Yolande would have been. I think the selection must rest with you. I might not have the grace to be sufficiently detached in my judgment. Yes, I must be wise enough to entrust this to you and to abide by what you may decide. My friend, I have only one piece of advice to give. You must be ready—when the inevitable need arises."

"That you have the courage to say this to me," declared Coeur, "is even more remarkable than the wisdom of Yolande."

"The Queen has always known, I think. It's even possible that the old lady told her. She liked me very much at first and she has always been as tolerant as possible under such circumstances. What a strange situation for the three of us to face, Yolande and the Queen and me! It seems to me that the Queen will prove sympathetic when the time comes." She leaned closer to him and he was acutely conscious of the slow lift of the lids which enabled him to look full into her unusual blue eyes. "Now that I've summoned the courage to say this, I feel a great sense of relief. It's as though a burden had been removed from my shoulders—and added to the heavy ones you carry yourself."

"A heavier burden than everything else combined, dearest lady. The most unwelcome one I've ever assumed."

She continued to look at him intently. "You have always liked me, I think, Jacques Coeur."

"Yes," he answered slowly, "I have always liked you."

4

Charles of France entered the room a moment later. His chin was sunk in the collar of a long fur robe as though he desired not to be recognized, and the quick glance he cast about the room was both apprehensive and sulky. He made it clear at once that he had not expected to find his Moneyman there. "*You?*" he said. "Now what is the reason for this?"

"I asked you to come, sire," began Agnes Sorel, looking at the monarch with an air of supplication, "because we desired a chance to waken your great generosity. Ah, if you will only give that generous instinct full rein! There is a gift I hope you will grant soon. Not for me, sire—for the people of France!"

Charles shifted uneasily. "I should have known it!" he exclaimed. "Another lecture, my Agnes? Out with it, then! What can I do for France beyond what I have done already?"

The lady looked at Jacques Coeur as though seeking his support. When she failed to find the right words to continue with her plea, the latter took it on himself to reply.

"I think, sire, I know the nature of the gift she asks. Permit me to point out that the English are still in Rouen."

The King frowned with sudden impatience. "Is another war the boon you crave?"

"Sire," said Agnes, "the people of France will know no rest, no happiness, as long as the invaders hold a square inch of our soil. There is war now, even though undeclared. Part of your people groan under foreign rule. The rest are at the mercy of the Free Companies. It's not war we seek, sire, it's peace, the peace that can be won for the unhappy people of France only by a final effort to drive the English out."

"The time is ripe," declared Coeur. "The English are torn by dissensions at home and their garrisons are small. This is the golden opportunity to end a century of fighting. I, a man of peace, do not need to point this out, for no one can see the turth more clearly than you, sire."

"Am I to have no peace, in God's Holy Name?" cried the King. "You are always girding at me, Jacques Coeur, you and Dunois and De Brézé. And now you, my Agnes, to whom I have always looked for consolation after the cares of the day. Twenty years of war I have had already. By St. Denis, is it not enough?"

"There can be no peace, sire, as long as the English stay at Rouen," said Coeur.

Agnes Sorel slipped forward from her stool and rested on her knees beside the royal chair.

"My liege lord," she whispered, "when I was a child it was foretold o me that I would live to be honored by the love of the greatest king and captain of his day. Make it come true, sire! Finish the work you have begun so well!"

Charles drew his hand away from hers. "It's easy to talk of war. I gran you the English garrisons are small. But what if they pour their armie across the Sleeve again? Would we suffer another Crécy, another Azin court?"

"Has my liege lord talked with Jean Bureau?" asked Coeur.

"The bombard fellow? Yes, I have listened to him. I have heard him spin his fables about the big guns he can mount against the walls of Nor mandy. That is still a dream, Moneyman, but the arrows of the English archers are a reality. They have cut the chivalry of France to pieces in al the great battles of the past. We still have nothing to match them."

"Sire," Coeur exclaimed, "the winning of the war will not depend on the chivalry of France. That must sound like the rankest of heresy but I have no hesitation in saying it. I know that it's true. The men whose father lost us Azincourt and whose grandfathers died so helplessly at Crécy have learned nothing from the disasters of the past. They still think and talk o war as it was fought a hundred years ago. If the issue lay with them, they would die just as surely and in the same kind of defeat. But, sire, the English have not learned anything new either. They still depend on the longbow, thinking it the supreme weapon. They have no cannon like the powerful bombards of Jean Bureau. An Englishman named Walter Fitz Rauf, whose ancestor of the same name went to Cathay two hundred years ago and brought back word of the cannon of the Far East, was in Rouen this summer. Rumors of what he had to say have reached our ears. He was begging the English leaders to turn their attention to the use of gun powder and not to depend any longer on archery. They laughed at him The English beat us in the first campaigns because they had a weapon we did not understand. Today things are reversed. We have a new weapon and the English are refusing to recognize its possibilities. We can beat them easily, sire, and almost bloodlessly."

The King listened to this impassioned plea with a frown of suspicion. "You speak so glibly, my good Moneyman," he said, "that I suspect you have rehearsed all this in advance."

Coeur smiled. "That is true, sire. The issue is of such importance that I gave careful thought to what I should say. I would be a poor advocate if I left it to the promptings of the moment."

Charles frowned again. "Talk, all talk," he muttered. "How can I be sure there is truth in all this cant about our great cannon? I can't risl a defeat."

"My great king and captain can't be defeated!" cried Agnes Sorel.

The King began to stalk about the room. The long cloak he was wear ing made him seem more kingly than he had appeared in the green jacket of the afternoon. His face reflected the gloomy doubts which filled his mind. After a turn or two, he paused before a crucifix on the wall and fell into silence.

Agnes Sorel watched him for several moments before she turned to Coeur. "Have we made any progress tonight?" she asked in a whisper. "Do you think he listened to us in a more receptive mood? I thought so, but it may have been my fancy."

Coeur also had been studying the bent back of their royal master. After a moment he gave an affirmative nod. "I think so," he replied. "I've learned to read the kingly moods and it seemed to me he was on the point of giving in. He's slow at making up his mind, as you know, but in a very few minutes you may find, my most gallant lady, that your efforts haven't been in vain."

Her eyes lost their tired look. She leaned forward and touched his arm. "If you are right," she whispered, "I'll be well content. Even if what I suspect about this weakness of mine should prove to be true."

The Moneyman nodded slowly and, perhaps, reluctantly. "If needs be, I have another inducement to offer him. There's a great risk I can take to tip the scales. I've been turning it over in my mind, realizing all it might mean. After what you have just said, my sweet Agnes, I would be a coward if I hesitated any longer."

Jacques Coeur had the best of reasons, nevertheless, for hesitation.

His was the type of mind which sees far beyond the range of vision of the ordinary man. Starting as a furrier in his native city of Bourges, he had sensed the chance to revolutionize the whole face of trade by a new type of shop, one in which goods of every description would be offered for sale. The next step in his program was even more radical, the duplication of his first department store in all the major cities of France. He now had twenty-four; two in Paris, two in Tours where the court was located most of the time, four in Lyons, six in Bourges, four in Montpellier, and single shops scattered all over the face of the country. They were not, as he phrased it himself, "small holes in a wall behind a single pair of shutters." They were towering houses, stuffed with every kind of article which entered into the lives of people. They had made him enormously wealthy.

Back of these extraordinary moves was a basic discovery which had come to him early and had dictated each step he had taken. Combination! He had seen that trade could be made the most powerful force in the civilized world if it were no longer confined to the individual efforts of small men. He had realized that there must be a multiplying of interests, of manufacture, of shipping and selling. One of his first steps had been to establish a fleet of his own ships to bring goods from the East. Now he was building factories all over France for the manufacture of cloth, shoes, hats, gloves, armor. He was buying mines.

It was not solely the desire for power and wealth which had urged him on. The thought was firmly lodged in his mind that this was how things should be. The world was full of natural riches which men had not found the means to use. Commerce must be bound together, taking in the whole world if necessary, so that goods could be brought from all the far corners of the earth and then sold at prices which all people could pay. He had said on many occasions, "I want the wife of the artisan to wear silks like the fine lady of the court and the poorest tinker to have spices in his wine."

He was the earliest and the greatest of merchant princes. He was a monarch, presiding with infinite skill and almost incredible foresight over an empire of trade.

The inducement he had in mind to make the King would put this great empire in jeopardy.

The King faced about and walked back across the room. He still wore a frown but there was less uncertainty about the glance he gave them.

"Granted that all you've said is true," he began, "there is still a great difficulty we haven't yet mentioned. One to which I fail to find any answer. Money, Jacques Coeur. I don't need to remind you of the empty state of the treasury. How could we pay the cost of another war?"

The Moneyman said to himself: "Now it is your turn, Jacques Coeur, to make a sacrifice for France. You must throw everything into the scales— your fortune, your future, the great enterprises you have created. You may lose everything you possess. You may see your dream of a different world dissolve back into the mists of the past. Is it worth it? Have you the courage to take this step?"

"Money," sighed the King. "Always that same dire problem."

Coeur said deliberately, "We will pay the cost of the war with the fruits of peace, sire."

"But armies cannot be paid with promises. My soldiers cannot be equipped and fed on the hopes of a prosperous future. Where can we raise the funds? At what figure do you estimate the cost of this war you demand of me?"

"Two hundred thousand *écus*, sire."

The King looked startled, as though the figure exceeded even his worst fears. "I might as well reach for the moon as try to raise that stupendous sum!" he exclaimed. "I can't put fresh taxes on my people. They are overburdened now. What rash scheme is in your mind? To raise the salt gabelle? More land tailles; a heavier tax on hearths? Would you bring me to the danger of another revolt?"

Coeur found that all his hesitation had left him. "Liege lord, I will undertake to raise the necessary funds myself."

King and merchant faced each other in a tense silence for several moments. The monarch's expression had changed. His eyes had lighted up for the first time since the debate began.

"But how?" he demanded finally. "In your capacity as a minister of the Crown?"

Coeur shook his head. "Not as your minister, sire. As Jacques Coeur, a private individual. I am a rich man and I have extensive credit against which I can borrow if necessary."

"If we win, I could repay you. If we lose——" The King paused and shook his head. "Do you realize what that would mean? Are you prepared to stake everything on this—this great gamble?"

There was no trace of hesitation, of uncertainty, or of fear, in the answer of the Moneyman. "Do you think I value my fortune, the future of my enterprises, except for the use they can be now? I know the risk and I give it not a single thought. *Sire, what I have is yours!*"

2

IT WAS DREARY COUNTRY through which Pregent Kennedy had been riding all day, and the company of a fat priest on a broad-backed roan had done little to alleviate the monotony. The churchman had attached himself to the Scot for greater safety. The *écorcheurs* had been raiding freely hereabouts and as a result travelers rode in continual peril. The Free Companies had not only burned villages and castles but had wantonly destroyed everything, even the signposts at crossroads.

In no part of France was it more apparent that the country had been at war for a hundred years. All normal life had ceased and it was a rare and startling thing to see a human face peering out from the walls of a ruined house or a cow straying disconsolately in a blackened field. Even the roads seemed to have taken on the fears of the few travelers who ventured out on them. They did not march straight ahead nor strut with confidence; instead they were like dim rakes in a bewitched forest, and seemed to slink, to hesitate at crossings, to gaze uncertainly ahead before making a turn on lagging legs. The sun had lost the power to shine with warmth and good cheer (or so it seemed), and the only birds seen above the fields and the woods flapped ominously on black wings. A continuous wind blew from somewhere high up in the hills. Men met with suspicion in this desolation and parted in haste; and anyone who lacked food in his saddlebags rode on an empty belly.

The two companions had reached a crossroad and the priest fell silent for the first time that day as his eyes lighted on a long train approaching from the north. A nobleman of high degree and great wealth was on the move. Many knights were in attendance, their armor clanking as they rode, and there were squires and men-at-arms and almoners and lackeys without number in the cavalcade. In the center was a carriage of the type ladies used in following the hunt, being open on one side. This afforded a full view of a middle-aged woman wearing a hennin of majestic white plumes under which her face looked ailing and severe. In the lead was a young lady on a gaily-bedecked palfrey; the daughter of the house, without a doubt, for a page rode on one side of her and a priest on the other, and there was arrogance even in the way she held a hawk on her wrist. She was a plump young beauty with a curling plume in her high hat, a habit of peacock-blue velvet, and ruffles of ivory lace at her neck and wrists. The glossy tip of a red leather shoe showed briefly beneath her skirt.

The priest began to speculate aloud as to who they were. Had good King René of Sicily been on a visit to his sister and brother-in-law of France? Was it the rich Comte de Foix or, perchance, the great Comte de St. Pol? Or, rather, was it Havart, the esquire-carver of the King, who because of his office always appeared in azure velvet?

Pregent Kennedy paid no attention. Flicking the ends of his tartan around his long and somewhat stringy neck, he gazed instead down the side road along which a curious equipage was approaching. He slipped a hand out of its steel gauntlet to give a twist to the ends of his graying mustache and allowed an amused grin to spread over his long and usually severe face. "Now what," he asked himself, "can this be?"

The carriage was of the type known as a *chare* but with eccentricities all its own. The seat was perched precariously high on shafts which swayed so much with each turn of the wheels that the driver seemed in constant danger. It was drawn by a pair of ambling mules, and the clear treble voice of the girl at the reins could be heard urging them on to greater efforts. "Come, Olivier. We'll never reach an inn at this rate. Annette, Annette! Less of sloth, I beg of you!" Her anxiety was natural, for it could now be seen that she was alone.

"Here," said the Scot, to his companion, "we have two young persons of the gentler persuasion who present certain points of contrast. I can see that you're all agog over the damoiselle in velvet. I concede that she has her points. But, good Father Imbert, permit me to voice a preference for the brave little pea-chick who is closer to Heaven up there on that absurd Ark of the Covenant than some of us can ever hope to get."

The forest lined the roads so tightly at this point that the girl guided her weary mules to the center of the crossing before she had any inkling of the approach of the lordly train. Most unfortunately one of the wheels became wedged in a deep rut. The conveyance stopped. Realizing now the gravity of her offense, the driver urged her team on frantically but failed to rouse the lethargic mules to the effort needed to extricate the imprisoned wheel. The young lady at the head of the cavalcade was compelled to rein in.

"What is this?" demanded the latter in a petulant voice. "What impudence in the creature to drive directly in front of us! Eduard, see that she moves on at once."

The page, to whom this order had been directed, saw no way of obeying it. "The wheel is stuck, my lady," he pointed out. "We'll have to wait until it can be dragged clear."

"Then get down and shove, lazy one!" cried the damoiselle in a sudden gust of anger. "Down, all of you! Get this unsightly thing out of our way!" Then her mood veered and she began to laugh. "What is it, in God's Good Name? Is it a new kind of scarecrow and is the girl a part of it?

Stir the creature up, Eduard. Perhaps she's out of a circus and has trained monkeys under that filthy blanket."

The page answered eagerly, "If that's what you want, mistress, just watch me!" He dismounted and began to belabor the nearest of the mules with the shaft of a pennon. The animal strained at its harness but still failed to get the chare into motion. The boy redoubled his efforts.

"Stop! You'll do him an injury!" cried the girl from the seat above.

The boy grinned. "I want to do this stubborn old mule an injury," he said.

One of the men-at-arms came up at this point with a pike in his hands. "Watch *me!*" he declared. He drove the pike into the haunch of the mule and the animal gave a loud scream of pain. It lunged forward frantically, carrying its mate with it and causing the wheels of the chare to grind and churn. The ramshackle vehicle shook violently and then began to move. The man-at-arms followed up his success by smacking the wounded hindquarters of the mule with the butt end of the pike. The frightened team broke into a run, dragging the carriage over a brash of stones at the side of the road. The seat rocked like the top of a tree in a windstorm and the girl had to hang on with both hands to avoid being pitched out.

Most of the members of the noble train had hurried forward to watch this comic spectacle. The men doubled up with amusement. The women jeered and laughed. Even the daughter of the house unbent and joined in the merriment, and the priest laughed so hard that he had to wipe his eyes on the end of his sleeve.

Kennedy turned his horse with the intention of overtaking the runaway team and bringing it to a halt. He was too late, however. There was a sharp turn in the road and the frightened mules rounded it at such speed that the chare was thrown against the bank. One wheel was torn off and went spinning and bouncing down the road like a child's hoop. The carriage collapsed with a sound of snapping shafts and splintering wood.

Kennedy saw a black cat, which had been curled up unnoticed on the seat beside its mistress, leap into the air and achieve a claw-hold on the trunk of a tree. The girl was less fortunate, being thrown from her high perch to the road. She rolled over twice before coming to a stop. The Scot dismounted and ran to her assistance.

She accepted the aid of his arm in getting to her feet. The hood of her cheap chammer cloak had fallen back, revealing a head of fair hair which shimmered in the late afternoon sun like harvest grain. Kennedy said to himself, "I would like to see her in the clothes of the other one."

Her cloak, which had been old and worn to begin with, had sustained some rents in the fall and she was covered with dust from head to foot. Her hands had been scraped and there was a small cut on her forehead. It was with great difficulty that she was restraining herself from breaking into tears, and he thought at first this was from the pain of her injuries. He realized when she spoke that it was because of anger.

"The beasts, the cruel beasts!" she exclaimed. She rubbed at the dirt on her face with one sleeve. Then, seeing that the damoiselle was still watching with an amused air, she burst out with, "I would like to scratch her eyes out!"

She wheeled about and began to walk back to the intersection of the two roads. Kennedy took hold of her sleeve to restrain her. "Take heed, my child," he said. "It will be unwise to say anything to them. They will think nothing of beating you as they did your mule or even riding you down. I won't be able to protect you against all of them, and yet nonetheless I am a shrewd and doughty fighter—one of the best in all France, I'll have you know."

She shook off his hand and continued to walk forward with a determined air. He gave up and contented himself with muttering a proverb, "He who chases folly, soon catches it."

The girl halted a few yards from the daughter of the house. As the Scot had remarked, they presented a striking contrast: the aristocrat in her velvet and gold, so disdainful and yet so lovely with her lustrous black hair and bright black eyes, the other in her brownish cloak with its lack of fit and its ugly bell-shaped sleeves and yet quite as lovely because of the gold of her hair and the intense blue of her eyes. For several moments they regarded each other in a silent and growing antagonism, each conscious and resentful of the beauty of the other.

"You couldn't have known what you were doing!" said the girl on the ground. "No one, not even you, could be so cruel and callous!"

"If you say another word or delay us any longer," said the other, "I shall have my servants tie you to a tree and whip you soundly as you deserve."

"My carriage is broken." The voice of the one in the ugly cloak became choked with emotion. She was silent for several moments while she strove to control her feelings. "Under what you called that filthy blanket is the body of my father. He died last night. I was seeking a place where he could be buried." She crossed herself passionately. "And now what am I to do?"

A sudden silence fell on the group. The squires and men-at-arms gaped at the bereaved girl in a discomfort which manifested itself in a sheepishness of mien and in embarrassed scraping of feet in the dust of the road. Even the daughter of the house seemed nonplused for a moment. Then she tossed her head impatiently and called an order to the almoner.

"Father Ambrose! Give her some money. Enough to pay for repairs and the burial of her father. And now all of you get to your places! We've lost more time already than we can afford."

The almoner produced a small gold coin and walked over to the slim figure in the chammer cloak. He placed it in her hand with a hurried, "*Benedicte*, daughter," and then resumed his place in the train. The girl stood without moving for several moments, looking at the coin on her palm. When she raised her head her cheeks were flushed and her eyes were flashing angrily.

"It's true that I'm entitled to compensation for the breaking of the chare," she said clearly, "But this has been given as charity. I will have you know"—she was staring up straight into the eyes of the daughter of the house—"that I can't accept anything at your hands. Here!" She tossed the coin in the direction of the servants. "Divide it among you. My hand would sicken and wither if I held it any longer!"

"It's clear you don't know your place!" cried the girl on horseback. "You presume too much. I lack patience for such impudence as this!" Her anger getting the better of her, she blazed into invectives. "Guttersnipe! Base-born creature! You shall be well whipped for this!"

"Patience isn't the only thing you lack! I'm not afraid to tell you to your face that you lack decency and fairness!"

"Enough of this! Eduard, Bertrand, Jules! Get this dirty waif out of my sight! If you spare your whips on her back, I'll not be sparing in my punishment of you."

Before the order could be obeyed, one of the knights at the rear of the cavalcade rode forward and said, "One moment, if you please, Lady Alys."

There was an alien suggestion about him; for, having the hint of a stoop in his shoulders, he seemed almost scholarly, a quality which all good knights fiercely scorned. His hair and eyes were dark and his features tended to length and even gauntness. He was dressed with great richness and taste: a fine feather in his hat, a fur-lined cloak, hose which fitted his legs with the skinlike exactitude which fashion demanded. This, however, was in the way of secondary impressions. The first glance given this cavalier was always for his sword which was exceptionally long and with a jeweled handle in the manner of the East—an aggressive, even a truculent sword in an age when men carried weapons for constant use, and consequently out of keeping with the appearance of this sober knight of thirty years or so.

"Lady Alys," he said, reining in beside her with a diffident air, "I confess to finding your instructions hasty and not well advised. Permit me to say that your father, if he were here, would regard himself as in the wrong in this matter. His sole concern would be to make amends."

"I've tried to make amends, Sire d'Arlay!" cried the girl. "My offer has been spurned, as you've seen. She has dared to answer me back and that's something I can't allow!"

"I find myself in an awkward position," said the knight, regarding the offended beauty with some hesitation. "I've ridden in your train for two days and so consider myself as a guest. In spite of that I must say that I can't permit you or your servants to molest this unfortunate child."

The girl turned in her saddle. "You joined us for the protection we could afford you, Sire d'Arlay! It's a poor return to interfere in matters which don't concern you at all! My mother is ill and I'm sure she will join with me in demanding that you spare us your company further." Her eyes flashed angrily in his direction. "It will be pleasanter riding without you. There will be no taint of trade on the air!"

"You refer, no doubt, to my connection with Jacques Coeur. Is it possible you don't know how your father acquired his new lands in Beaune?" Then the frown on his face gave place to a smile. When this happened the suggestion of melancholy, which the serious expression of his eyes gave his face, vanished completely. "I know you well enough, Lady Alys, to be certain you don't mean the things you say when you're in a temper. Nonetheless I propose to delay my departure long enough to make sure that you don't indulge it any further."

The intervention of the knight had caused the servants to remain in their places. They now waited uneasily to see what course their mistress would take. To their obvious relief, she decided not to force the issue. Turning her horse's head back into the north, she called out an order for the cavalcade to proceed.

After watching the long train pass, the Sire d'Arlay looked at his servant who had stationed himself with discretion behind his master. "Helion," he said, "we've changed sides, it seems. What do you think of this new company with whom we find ourselves?"

The servant sniffed contemptuously. "A mangy crew," he said.

D'Arlay smiled. "I sometimes think, Helion, that you're more conscious of my rank than I am myself. I detect in you a tendency to look down that long nose of yours at people."

"I'm the servant of Robinet de Burey, the Sire d'Arlay. Isn't that just reason for pride? I was at Montagne-Noire when you were born, master. I've been in your service ever since you fell heir to the domain of Arlay. Who serves you has no regard for the rabble."

"What's your opinion of this tall soldier? The one with all the colors of the rainbow at his neck?"

"A tug-mutton, that one."

"A Scot? I believe you're right. What think you of the churchman?"

"A hedge-priest. He carries a knife in his sleeve."

"And the girl?"

Helion's air became less confident. "As for the girl, master," he said, "I can't make up my mind about her at all."

"You and I are in the same case there, my Helion. I haven't been able to make up my mind about her either."

2

Pregent Kennedy and the girl were standing beside the wrecked chare. He gave reluctant consideration to the shape under the blanket which was stretched on the floor of the conveyance.

"Was it the truth you told them?" he asked.

"Yes, my lord. My father died last night. It was very sudden. He was in great pain and I could do nothing to bring him relief. I tried to find help but there wasn't anyone, it seemed, within miles of us. And so I—I had to sit beside him and watch him die."

"I can see, my lass, that you've been taking it hard." Then he added in a grumbling tone, "You must be well left if you can refuse gold in such a lavish manner."

"I have no more than will pay for a single night at an inn."

Kennedy surveyed her downheld face with an air that verged on horror.

"What madness is this? Is your mind buzzing with waxwings that you could do such a thing? It was sinful pride, my lass, that made you do it!"

"There are the mules to be sold. They will be of no further use now that the carriage is ruined." Her face took on an expression of the deepest grief. "It will distress me sorely to part with them. They've been such faithful friends!" She walked over to the one which had suffered at the hands of the man-at-arms and put an arm around his neck. "My poor fellow! My patient old Olivier! How sad to be born a mule and have a master who keeps you on the road every day. And now you're old and they've hurt you badly and yet I must sell you to some stranger!" She was on the point of tears. "I'll never forgive myself, my good Olivier!"

Kennedy had been giving the team a critical appraisal, examining their teeth and running his hands over their haunches. "They'll be ready for the crows in another year," he commented. "Still, you're in luck, minikin. Anything that travels on four legs is so much in demand that you may get a good price for these hobbling ghosts."

"Will there be enough to pay for a decent funeral and for masses to be said?" asked the girl anxiously. "I loved him but—but, my lord, he will need the masses, and many of them. He was a drinking man and there was little piety in him even when he was sober."

"Aye. There will be enough—if we can find any way of getting him the burial. There may even be a few pence over for you. I'm a rare hand at a bargain and you will be wise to trust the selling of the mules to me."

"If you'll be so very kind, it will be a great load off my mind. I'm a very poor hand at a bargain."

The Sire d'Arlay had dismounted in the meantime. He walked over to them, studying the Scot first and then turning his attention to the girl. He stopped abruptly and it was apparent that he had experienced a surprise. "I've seen her before," he said to himself. Then he realized it was not that. She resembled someone he knew. There was a sense of shock about his discovery of the resemblance because he was sure that in some way it would prove of great importance to him. And yet everything was vague in his mind and he had no idea at all of whom she reminded him.

"May I inquire your name, Mademoiselle?"

"It is Valerie Maret." There was no trace of the pride she had shown in her encounter with the other girl. She kept her eyes lowered. "It was kind of you, my lord, to interfere in my behalf."

D'Arlay said to himself, "Her voice is low and rather beautiful. Where could she have learned to speak in such a way?" Aloud he asked, "And where do you come from?"

"We had no home, my lord. My father, who is dead, was Damian Maret, an actor in Mysteries. We lived on the road."

Kennedy had raised the blanket for a look at the dead man. He dropped it back into place and said to the girl: "He has a noble head, my lass. I would have judged him an expounder of the Holy Word or even a philosopher rather than an actor in wicked and heathenish nonsense."

Valerie Maret lost her diffidence at once. "You are wrong!" she declared. "The Mysteries are not wicked. They do much good."

"I've seen many and I agree with you," said D'Arlay, addressing the girl.

"My father was a very fine actor, my lord," said the girl proudly. "But it was a great tragedy for him! His legs were short and crooked and so he had to play the villains or sometimes, even, comedy parts! The best they ever gave him was Judas, and sometimes he was Malice, and once Envy." A desire to justify the Mysteries, aroused in her by Kennedy's criticism, led her on to boasting of her father's ability. "Ah, you should have seen him as Judas! And as Simon Magus. He learned to do magic tricks and sleight-of-hand to play Simon, and everyone agreed he was the greatest Simon since Anton Fresche, who was a German and had been a magician himself once. Ah, my lords, he longed so much to play the Part—Christ in the Resurrection. But how could he with such bandy legs? I think it was because of this he drank so much."

D'Arlay was still musing over the contrast between her way of speaking and the station of life in which she had been born. "She chooses her words like a lady of birth," he said to himself, "and not like the daughter of a common strolling player. Can there be a real mystery here? One in which she's playing a part?"

He had been watching her with intense concentration. Everything about her added to the effect of familiarity she created—her eyes, her hair, every play of expression. And yet the answer still eluded him. He would think he had it and then the clue would be lost. It would slip away from his mind like a firefly through the clutching fingers of a child.

It was with growing surprise that he noted details of her appearance. She had a fine brow, wide and white and intelligent. Her nose was straight and without any of the coarseness of line found in the peasant type. At first he had set her down as pretty but now he realized she was the possessor of real beauty.

Seeking for an explanation, he began to ask questions. "Were you born in Anjou?"

She shook her head. "No, my lord. I was born in Berri. At least it has always been so believed."

He grasped at this hint of obscurity in her past. "Surely your parents were not in any doubt?"

Her diffidence had reasserted itself and she seemed distressed at the necessity of answering. "It—it's a long story, my lord, and one which wouldn't interest you."

He said to himself, "This isn't the time to press her on that point. I'll find out about it later." Aloud he asked another question. "You've traveled about the country a great deal?"

"All my life we've been on the road. I've seen all of France save—you will smile at this, my lord—all save Paris itself!" Her eyes suddenly began to glow. "I have seen where the Maid was born. I stood there for hours and almost I was persuaded that the Voices were beginning to speak to me! Once, when Father had no part, I had him take me where she led our armies. Someday, when our King wakens up from his long slumbers and drives the Godons[1] out of France, I shall go to Rouen and offer a prayer on the spot where she died!"

"I think," said D'Arlay thoughtfully, "that it may be possible to go to Rouen soon now." He hesitated, as though uncertain of the wisdom of giving an explanation for this belief. "I also have been in every part of France during the past six months. I went to test the feeling of the country about the question of war. I found this: The people want war, they want it so badly that the King will have to yield."

"I pray God you are right, my lord. And that another Maid will come to lead the armies of France!"

"That," said D'Arlay dryly, "may not be necessary."

A pause ensued and then D'Arlay turned to the Scot to ask, "What is your name?"

"I am Pregent Kennedy." Apparently the Scot was surprised that the name evoked no sign of recognition for he frowned and added, "It must be that I am less well known than I thought."

"Unjustly, perhaps, I am unaware of the claims you have to fame, Monsieur Pregent Kennedy."

"I know more of bombards than any man in the world. Will it mean anything to you if I say I commanded a battery of the guns against the heathen Turk? I'm on my way now to see Jacques Coeur. *He* will know all about me and will see to it that I'm given a command when we fight the English again."

"I've heard Jacques Coeur speak of you. Will you forgive my lack of memory, Sir Scot?"

"My father fought at Azincourt as so many of my brave countrymen did," went on Kennedy, with a bitterly assertive pride, "and he died there with a Sassenach arrow in his throat. I have fought your battles for thirty years myself, Sir Knight, and little reward I've had." He looked up at the sky and shook his head. "There's a mizzle coming on from the tinge of things. We'll spend a damp night, I am thinking. . . . My mother was French but I'll have you know I was born at Maybole in Ayrshire. May she rest in peace, my sweet lady mother dead these many years, but she did me an ill turn by naming me after her own father. It fits ill with the fine Scottish name I bear though I swear I have done enough to lend distinction to the combination. I," he added grandly, "am a Kennedy of Cassilis."

"I presume it's a distinction of some importance."

"Aye," said the Scot. "It's important in Scotland. And," with a scowl, "wherever *I* happen to be."

There was a pause and then D'Arlay asked, with an air of deliberation, "You have ridden with the Free Companies?"

[1] Godon was a term of contempt applied to the English invaders. It was first used by Jeanne d'Arc.

The Scot looked at him sharply. "It is true," he said, after a moment. "I'm a soldier and I must live. I had my own band for a time. And," with rising emphasis, "I was doing handsomely. I always see to it that in anything I do there's a profit for myself, even though no more than a souldie, as you might say. Can you quarrel with that, Sire d'Arlay?"

"I quarrel bitterly with the right of any man to prey on innocent and defenseless people. Since the truce was signed with the English, the Free Companies have bled France white."

"The Free Companies are made up largely of Frenchmen," said the Scot. "What excuse can you offer for that, Sire d'Arlay?"

"I offer no excuse. Unfortunately it's true. Perhaps one hundred years of fighting has turned us into savages." With an air which terminated the discussion, D'Arlay turned to the priest. "Where do you hail from?"

He looked closely at the churchman while waiting his reply, noting the multitude of purple lines which gave his face an odd resemblance to a map of the world. At close range it was possible to read in Father Imbert an amiability and trustworthiness not apparent on first inspection.

"I am from Provence," answered the priest. "I carry papers to Paris."

"And now," said the Scot, in an impatient tone, "if your curiosity concerning us has been satisfied, may I inquire as to the prospects for supper? The lass has nothing in the carriage save a stone jug of wine which I suspect is thin and sour, and a loaf of bread of questionable age. The priest and I fed well at noon in expectation of locating an inn before nightfall. As a result our saddlebags are empty."

"What have we left, Helion?" asked D'Arlay.

The servant answered grudgingly. "Enough for all, master. There is the better part of a roast capon and some scraps of other meat. And there is meal and bread."

"We shall do famously," declared the Scot, with an expression of relief.

The girl spoke up in a hesitant tone. "I am a very good cook, my lords. If we can have a fire made, it will take little time to prepare a warm meal —if my lord is ready to trust the food to me."

"With the best will in the world, Mademoiselle. Helion has had much experience in the building of fires since we took to the road and will have a good blaze for you when it's needed. The rest of us had best use the interval in pitching tents against the prospect of rain which you've already noted, my brave captain of Free Companions."

Valerie Maret said to herself when she saw the variety of supplies which Helion produced for her use, "How wonderful it must be to have things like these!" Then she added hastily, "Since I have boasted of my skill, I must do my very best." She studied the supplies and decided to make a dish called a mawmenny which was a popular one with all who could afford it. Accordingly she poured oil and wine into a pan and dropped in sparing quantities of herbs and porret and the thinnest possible slice of garlic. This she stirred over the fire until the ingredients became crisp and brown. She then poured in the meal, whipping it furiously with a spoon as she did so. The cooked flesh of the capon was added, and it was not until the last moment that she stirred in the sliced dates and dried mulberries which give a mawmenny its full perfection of flavoring.

At exactly the right moment the pan was removed from the coals and placed on the ground between the three men (Helion remaining in the background) who had seated themselves in an impatient semicircle. When she made no move to join them, D'Arlay looked up inquiringly at the young cook. "The food will have no flavor if we lack your presence, Mademoiselle," he said.

She shook her head quickly. "It wouldn't be right, my lord. Always my father ate first, and then my mother and I sat down. It's a custom on the road."

"A custom, then, which we must break tonight." D'Arlay moved to one side to make room for her. "Sit here with me. I shall see to it, moreover, that you are served first."

He was unable to fulfill his promise, however, for Pregent Kennedy had already dipped a spoon in the savory dish. The Scot nodded his head with approval as the first mouthful vanished down his throat. "A toothsome dish," he said, smacking his lips. "In Scotland we call this a Bouce Jane. We cook it plain without all these knickknacks and kicksey-winseys. The wholesome food of Scotland," he went on defensively, "is what makes the strong backs and arms of the Scots, and the strong heads. These same strong arms will drive the English into the Channel for you when the chance comes." Sensing that this boast had roused resentment in the others, he added: "What I mean is this: The knights of France won't win the war, if war there is."

D'Arlay commented with some unwillingness, "I agree with that."

"It will be the cannon, the bombards. And many Scots, being shrewd and farsighted, will be serving as bombardiers."

Nothing more was said for several minutes. The men were all hungry and were applying themselves to the food with the good will which is the cook's accolade. D'Arlay was aware, as he consumed his share, that the girl had not started to eat. "It's not strange that you abstain from food," he said to her. "But it won't be wise to give yourself entirely to your grief. Come! Dismiss these gloomy thoughts and dip a spoon into the dish before these ravening wolves have scraped it clean."

"I have no appetite, my lord." She obeyed him, however, and began to eat, slowly and sparingly.

There was still no rain although the threat of it remained. Not a star was to be seen. Bats circled about them and swooped through the area of light on swiftly weaving wings. A belated wheatear fluttered by and vanished, and then returned to hover about uncertainly, uttering its startled "Chat! Chat!" before finally taking itself back into the gloom. An owl hooted continuously from somewhere close at hand.

Watching the girl with the interest which he had felt from the instant he detected the resemblance, D'Arlay saw that she was progressing mentally through a cycle of moods. At first she held her head down and was obsessed quite clearly with her grief, for she sighed and lost all concern with food. She passed from this stage into one where her eyes showed signs of agitation and her fingers gathered together tightly. He was convinced that she was thinking of the clash with the Lady Alys and he said to himself, "There's nothing passive about her; she has her share of fighting spirit." Gradually she became less tense. She relaxed into a spirit of reflection, her hands lying limply in her lap, her eyes fixed on the darkness which had closed in about them.

"What thoughts are in your mind," he asked, "which take you so far away from us?"

She flushed. "I would be ashamed to tell you, my lord. It was—it was something most trivial. You would have a very poor opinion of me if you knew."

The rest of the company were still eating with avidity and paying no attention. The chomp of Helion's jaws could be heard from the spot he had selected for himself which was not close enough to the fire to constitute lack of respect but not far enough away to lose him all benefit of the warmth. D'Arlay leaned closer to her.

"Tell me," he urged.

She still hesitated. "Truly, my lord, it's a matter for great shame that I —I can think at a time like this about"—she looked up at him and her face took on a deep flush—"about the beauty of the velvet dress the lady was wearing!"

He smiled. "I rode for two days in her company and I can't tell you now what color it was. Was it a very pretty habit?"

"Oh, it passes description! It was of a color one seldom sees, I'm sure the most lovely blue in the world." Now that she had begun to talk, the words came tumbling out. "And did you notice the lace at her neck and wrists? But of course you didn't, since you were not in an observant mood. Never have I dreamed of such beauty! And the plume in her hat! I longed to feel the softness of it in my hands. Her shoes——" She stopped suddenly and with a hurried motion of her arm draped her skirt over her own shoes in fear that he might look at them. She was too late. He had already observed, with a feeling of compassion, that they were old and broken and most meanly clobbered. He had noticed also that her hose, the one article of apparel in which all women, old or young, high or low, took the most meticulous interest, were cheap and covered with patches.

"And do you think clothes so very important, then?" he asked.

She hesitated and sighed. "I think they are most important when you lack everything you would like to have. I've made my own clothes since my mother died, six years ago. But I've little gift with the needle, my lord, as you must have noticed."

"You need good clothes less than anyone I've ever seen. You're so attractive, in fact, that I've been wondering about you. You must have found admirers wherever you went—to the extent even that it became a danger."

"Tinkers and barbers and ale-drawers in taverns." She was speaking in a lighter tone. "Yes, I've had admirers but they've been of the lowest degree. No girl traveling about as we've done could escape that kind of attention."

"Has it been difficult for you?"

"No-o-o." Her manner had now shown a definite change. For the moment she had forgotten her grief and distress. She even indulged in a smile as she started on an explanation. "I had ways of avoiding it. When we had money and could stay at an inn—it wasn't often, my lord, and so it was always a great event—I would usually do something like this when we went in."

She straightened up and said, "Observe!" The corners of her mouth drew down and something strange happened to the shape of her eyebrows. It was hard to believe and yet there was no gainsaying that she had succeeded in giving herself an air of slyness and ill-nature. Then it vanished, and she laughed with satisfied pride. "You can believe now, my lord, that they would take one look at me and that would be all. But sometimes, when there were many men about, and it seemed wise to be more thorough, I would pull my hood down over my forehead and make myself look like this."

This time she managed to create a suggestion of broadness about her face. Her eyes had a hard glint in them. She had become common, a drab, a vixen, and yet at the same time something of a goose-cap as well; and so completely lacking in attraction that no man would have given her a second's attention.

"That one always accomplished its purpose," she said. Her face had changed back to its normal lines. "My father said I would have been a fine actor if I had been born a man. He even said I might in time be as good as he was; and that, my lord, is the highest praise an actor ever gives."

Pregent Kennedy flicked the ends of his tartan lightly across his lips and sat back from the dish. He glanced about the circle of faces, barely perceptible now in the dark of evening.

"We have a problem to discuss," he said. "What's to be done about the body?"

It had become apparent to all of them that Father Imbert possessed no more than a limited share of understanding. He looked up now and said: "There must be a burial. But where? And when?"

"Here," answered the Scot. "And now."

"Do you want to know how far we are from a church?" asked the priest. "I will answer as best I can: I don't know."

Kennedy turned to D'Arlay. "Are you familiar with these parts, my lord?"

D'Arlay answered with a negative shake of the head.

"And you, child?"

Valerie responded in a low voice from which she strove to keep any hint of the emotion she was feeling, "I know little of this part."

"Then," said the Scot, "the burial must be here. It's fortunate we have Father Imbert to conduct the service."

The girl was distressed. She looked at Kennedy, her eyes full of supplication, and then turned in the direction of D'Arlay. "Please, my lords! Surely there is something else to be done!"

Kennedy proceeded to explain that none of them had time to waste in reaching their destinations. She could see for herself that the chare could not be used again. What other way, then, was there? "After all," he added, "your father will have an easier resting place than soldiers who fall in battle."

There was a long and uncomfortable pause. "I understand the difficulties," said Valerie finally. "You've all been so kind that I don't want to cause more trouble. And yet I—I can't reconcile myself to this."

D'Arlay asked, "Is your reluctance because he would be buried without a coffin?"

The girl nodded her head. "Yes, my lord. He wouldn't have any rest." She was on the point of tears and it was apparent that she found it hard to continue. "He suffered for many years from an ache in his bones. Many times he said to me, 'Never bury me in damp ground.' He said that all he asked of a grave was that it be wide and dry. Sometimes he laughed when he said it but I knew that he meant it." She turned her head toward the sky. "It will rain before morning, my lords, and the ground will be soaked."

D'Arlay indulged in some speculations. "I have a little skill with tools," he said finally. "If you're prepared to let me use what's left of the chare I could make a coffin of the wood."

Valerie said to him eagerly, "If you will do that for him, I will say a prayer for you every day as long as I live!"

"It will take me a long time and I'll need all the help you can give me." D'Arlay rose to his feet and called to his servant: "Helion! My ax!"

3

For two hours D'Arlay and the girl struggled with the task. The others had shown some inclination at first to assist but had given it up early. They were now asleep, stretched out on the ground with their feet turned toward the fire. Valerie had worked hard, keeping the fire going as well as undertaking the demolition of the chare (a task which caused her infinite regret, having always taken a pride in the family possession of a vehicle), and carrying the wood to D'Arlay.

"I have less skill than I thought," said the latter. "This is taking me a much longer time than it should."

Her face acquired at once a look of remorse. "I am shamed to be the cause of so much trouble, my lord."

D'Arlay laughed. "To be honest, I'm enjoying myself in spite of all the difficulties. I may say with just pride that I'm accomplishing quite a feat here. If it had been my good fortune to be born a carpenter, I might have been a success. Instead, I'm a landowner and a knight, and a sorry failure at both."

"I'm sure you are not, my lord."

"The only thing to my credit is that I've acquired a certain skill with that." He nodded in the direction of his sword which he had deposited on the ground. The blade shone in the light from the coals. "And skill with the sword is little considered. A knight should have a mastery of the lance, the battle-ax, and the morning star,[2] but the sword is counted a womanish weapon. I predict that someday it will be considered the only fit weapon for a gentleman. . . . Also I had the good fortune to fall in with the great Jacques Coeur and to become a friend, and, in a sense, a partner of his. That I've prospered is due entirely to the partiality of the Moneyman." He wiped his brow and flexed the muscles of his arms gratefully. "It would be wise for both of us to have a rest now and a drop of wine. Carpentering is thirsty work."

"You must be very tired," said D'Arlay, as they sat beside the fire, their thirst satisfied. "All the menial part of the work has fallen to your share." He paused and then made an abrupt demand. "Let me see your hands."

She held them out for his inspection. They were small and well shaped, the fingers slender and tapering. Although the palms were calloused and the skin rough and chapped, it was clear they were not the hands of a peasant girl. "Nor," he said to himself as he examined them, "the hands of the daughter of a strolling player. There's a story here and I must get to the bottom of it."

"You've had a great deal of work to do," he said aloud.

"Since he took so ill I've had everything—caring for the mules and making fires and setting up the tent." She held her hands in front of her and studied them ruefully. "That isn't hard to see, is it? They are hard and ugly."

"So far from ugly that I'm beginning to wonder." He turned about on the ground to face her squarely. "You said there was some doubt as to where you were born. Do you care to explain what you meant?"

Valerie hesitated. "We never told anyone," she said finally. "But now they're both dead and it's my secret—to tell if I wish. I didn't know about it myself until I was ten years old and then my mother—Madame Maret— told me." She looked up at him and added impulsively: "I'm sorely tempted to tell you, my lord. You are so kind."

He waited for her to make up her mind.

"It's this, my lord. I wasn't their daughter. They found me."

D'Arlay was not surprised. The long war, complicated by the operations of the écorcheurs who harried the countryside during the recurrent truces, had resulted in countless cases of a similar nature. Every army movement, every raid for plunder, left smoking ruins and charred fields and the bodies of victims without number. Parents were killed and the children left, to find homes where they might or die of starvation. All records had been destroyed and it was generally an impossibility to trace the missing. It was said that in the areas over which the contending armies had fought back

[2] A mace. So called because it was oftenest used in surprise attacks at daybreak when it was handy to bash out the brains of sleeping opponents.

and forth for so many generations there were few children who could be certain of their parentage.

"I thought so," said D'Arlay. "And I'm quite sure your real parents were from a higher station in life than the—the couple who raised you. I'm still amazed at the way you speak, for it's impossible you can have had any education."

"I've already told you that Monsieur Maret was a great actor," said the girl, with a trace of pride. "He often said that the only thing he could do for me was to teach me to speak properly. He began as far back as I can remember. He would recite lines from the Mysteries and have me repeat them after him. Sometimes he would read from the *Imitatio Christi*.[3] I had some education, you see—in listening to him and asking questions."

"Did he teach you to read yourself?"

She shook her head regretfully. "No, my lord. When I grew old enough there always seemed to be too much to do. My mother, Madame Maret, was an invalid."

"I can understand now why you have such a fine voice. But the rest can be explained in one way only. You have beauty, Mademoiselle, and of a kind which proves you come of good stock. Will you tell me under what circumstances you were found?"

Now that she had broken the ice, the girl was willing, nay, eager, to talk.

"I wish I had more to tell. They, Monsieur and Madame Maret, found themselves in a village which had been raided and burned. Some of the houses were still blazing, and so they knew the écorcheurs couldn't be far off. They were going to drive on quickly—and then they heard the cry of a child. Madame Maret insisted they must do something. She went to look and found me in a basket just inside the entrance to the church. A woman had gone there for sanctuary, taking me with her. But it had been of no use. The robbers had killed her. They had even stripped the church of all its vestments. I must have been hungry, for I was crying loudly."

"And you believe the murdered woman was your mother?"

Valerie hesitated before answering. "Madame Maret did not think so. The sheet in which I was wrapped was not of dowlas but of the very finest linen."

"Was the woman a peasant?"

"It seemed so. Madame Maret said she was plainly dressed and that her hands were large and rough. She was young and of a heavy build."

"She was being paid as a wet nurse. Everything points to that."

"We always believed so. But now there's no way of finding out anything more. They, the Marets, went back to the village six months later to make inquiries. It was still deserted and so they learned nothing."

"And they didn't go back a second time?"

The girl shook her head. "No, my lord. It's my belief they didn't want

[3] A book published in parts over a period of years which was widely read because of its inspirational power. The handwritten copies were so eagerly sought that it was, in fact, the first best seller.

to find out anything after I began to grow up. They thought of me as their own child. Monsieur Maret was very angry when he found I had been told. I could hear them quarreling about it after they thought I had gone to sleep. She said to him that he had been willing enough once to get a reward for returning me but he said that was at first. He had changed his mind."

D'Arlay remained silent for several moments, turning over what he had heard. "Is that all you know?" he asked finally.

"Madame Maret didn't have time to notice anything more. The roof of the church was blazing and so she picked up the basket and left at once. She saw that the woman was swarthy and that blood was running from a wound on her face. I curled my hand around her thumb while she carried me to the chare. And that's all."

"You know the name of the village?"

When she told him the name, he shook his head to indicate that he had never heard of it. "The chance of learning anything more as late as this," he said, "seems very small. But I think you should make every effort to see if you can discover your real identity."

She responded in an eager voice: "I intend to when the chance comes. I dream about it all the time. I'm sure in my own mind that the poor woman who was killed was not my mother. Who could my real mother have been? Is she still alive? If so, does she have any suspicion that I'm living also? Would she claim me if she knew?"

"There's one way in which I might help you. You remind me of someone I know."

"Who is it, my lord?"

"I don't know. All evening I've been trying to remember but I haven't succeeded."

"And you think it might lead to finding out who I am?" She was looking up at him with the most intense and eager interest. "Could it be a relative? A sister? My mother, even?"

He gave his head a shake of warning. "It won't be wise to build any hopes or expectations on it. The closest resemblances can be accidental. There's a man in Paris who looks so much like me that we might be thought twins. I went to see him once—and once only. He was a dull and timorous fellow who sniffled all the time. I felt irked that such a weak-spirited clod should walk the earth in the same guise as I."

"But——" She was far from content to leave the matter there. "Is there nothing to be done? I have a conviction, my lord, that I would learn who I am if you *could* remember."

"It will come to me soon, I'm certain." He got to his feet with some difficulty. The energy he had expended in unaccustomed toil had stiffened the muscles of his back and arms. "All I can do for you now, Mademoiselle, is to finish arrangements for the burying of the only one who might have been of assistance in getting at the truth. Do you feel equal to further effort tonight?"

Valerie rose promptly. "Of course, my lord."

An hour later he drove in the last nail. He thought, "I must contrive to give some small note of grace to this crude and clumsy thing," and began to carve a Latin text on the lid. He had succeeded as far as *Nil nisi bonum* when he glanced at his companion who was standing close by him to watch. He read both absorption and gratitude on her face.

"What does it mean?" she asked.

"I'm a poor scholar, but if my memory and my spelling are not at fault, it will mean, when I am through, something to this effect, *Think only good of the dead.* Do you approve of my choice?"

"Oh yes, my lord! I'm sure he would be grateful too, and proud, if he could see it."

Spurred on by this praise, D'Arlay said, "I'll try to carve some roses, and perhaps an angel with spread wings, when I finish the text."

He didn't go right back to work, however. The flicker of light across her face again stirred his desire to solve the matter of the resemblance. He said, "Stand over here where I can see you better." Dropping the ax, he placed a hand on each of her shoulders and proceeded to study her face with complete absorption.

He now perceived things about her which had escaped him before. Her fairness was of the kind which comes from the effect of the sun. It was as though its rays had become imprisoned in her skin and hair; and so she had none of the fragile and flowerlike prettiness of gold and pink and white but displayed instead a molten quality, the vitality and radiance of the sun itself. He could not be sure of the color of her eyes. They were, he thought, blue, a very light blue. But it was apparent also that there was a tawny quality about them as well. He realized that the distinctive quality of her looks came from her eyes.

"A most unusual kind of loveliness," he thought. "It should be easy to remember who it reminds me of. And yet it still eludes me."

Then, without knowing why he had stopped or when, he was thinking no longer of that point. He had been completely carried away. He was conscious only of the curious charm of the face turned up to his. Her eyes (how could he have believed that another pair like them existed?) held him in such subjection, such thrall, that he had forgotten everything else.

"What has come over me?" he asked himself. "Have I fallen under a spell?"

He felt an almost uncontrollable impulse to draw her into his arms. He said to himself, "I'm afraid that I'm falling in love," and this thought helped him to resist the temptation. He dropped his hands from her shoulders and stepped back. It would not do for him to fall in love. There were the best of reasons why it would not do.

He said to Valerie, "I must finish the carving," but to himself he was saying, "As soon as we've buried this poor actor fellow in the morning, I must be on my way."

3

THE glove was up! It was suspended over the gates of the city as a sign that a fair was being held. For the time it remained there, ordinary affairs would be forgotten. In the daytime people would trade in the booths set up along the streets and in the evenings there would be feasting and drinking and dancing, and merrymaking in general.

Valerie experienced a nostalgic feeling as soon as she came in through the gates. Fairs had always been the high spots in her not-too-gay existence. They had meant parts for Damian Maret and money once more in the family purse and, perhaps, a new dress for her or a hat or, at the very least, some ribbons. When she saw that a stage was being erected on the main square, with a block and tackle for the Ascension and a curtain on rings, she said to herself, "If poor Father were alive he might be picked at last to play the Part and he would be stamping up and down this very minute rehearsing his lines or he would be shouting to me to know if I had unpacked his costumes and wigs." She sighed, however, when the realization came to her that Damian Maret more likely would be in one of the taverns, drinking in advance to the success he hoped to achieve.

The errand which brought her here was in no sense a festive one. After the burial service and the departure thereafter of the Sire d'Arlay (she had been sorry to see him go and had wondered why such haste was necessary), she had known that the time had come to strike out on her own. Pregent Kennedy, who had sold the mules for a good figure, had given her sound advice. There was only one course open to her, he had pointed out: she must get married, and to a middle-aged husband, one with plenty of gold in the chest he would use for the headboard of his bed, and the capacity, which only an elderly spouse would have, of appreciating her good looks. As the best chance of finding such a husband was to go where the most men were to be found, she must accompany him to Paris. If the right kind of husband did not put in an appearance, there was always the certainty that a place of some kind could be found for her in one of the many establishments conducted by Jacques Coeur. The Scot's purpose in going to Paris was to see Jaquet the Fox and, of course, a word from him would suffice.

Valerie didn't want to go to Paris. Damian Maret had been afraid of the city. Perhaps he had heard so much of the greatness of the actors that he had secretly lacked the courage for such competition; perhaps he dreaded the poverty which would be his lot there. At any rate, although he talked loudly and overmuch of invading Paris and setting it agog with the splendor of his talents, he had always found some reason at the last moment for not going. His fears had been communicated to Valerie. She thought of the city on the Seine as a great walled prison. She had heard more of the bodies swinging in chains at Montfaucon than of the beneficent shadow of Notre Dame. Furthermore, she had lived all her life on the edge of destitution and one thing she had learned was that rosy hopes and expectations such as the Scot was holding out could easily be blasted. She had thought of a plan of her own which would be surer and safer. Accordingly she had listened respectfully to Kennedy's arguments and then she had quietly packed up and disappeared.

She was carrying a bundle of clothes in one hand and a basket in the other as she made her way through the crowded town. She kept her eyes wide open and was the first to jump to one side and flatten herself against the wall when a party on horseback came galloping at top speed down the narrow cobbled street. A murmur of curses rose around her as the knights disappeared and she saw nothing but faces black with hate. This was not new to her. Those who travel the roads and know the people of the spittal-houses and the slums learn all about their hates and fears.

She saw a tall blond youth in a shining hauberk and with a bill on his shoulder come striding through the crowd, whistling with easy confidence. The people made way, knowing him to be English from the leopards on his scarf. They would not have been so ready to respect the truce had they known the air he was whistling was the campaign song of the days of the great English victories, "Sir Robert Knowles All France Controls." Valerie looked at him in fear and wonder and took pains to make sure that he had nothing in the way of a tail. Most of the people of France, who knew the invaders by reputation only, were sure that the term applied to them of *Longues-Coues* was a literal description.

She stopped beside a friendly looking citizen in the flat cap of a vintner to ask, "Can you tell me, Monsieur, where the Giglet fair is being held?"

The man motioned over his shoulder. "In the yard of the next inn back, minikin," he said. Then he noticed the bundle and basket. "If you're thinking of offering yourself, you'll have to hurry. It's nearly over. They tell me the *Petit Gaste* is still to be suited. Take a hint and don't sign with him."

The innyard was crowded still and there was much chattering and laughing going on. The blue flag had been hoisted on a low platform and the clerk sitting under it was striving to inject a lively note into the proceedings by a continuous monologue.

"The Giglet fair is open!" he intoned. "Want you good servants, Messires and ladies? We have a number here for your inspection and questioning. Look them over well, you who are here because of your needs and not for gaping-seed. The men are strong and the women are diligent and neat. Look at them, Messires, standing there in youthful innocence and confusion at being forced to parade themselves in public. Never have we offered a better lot than you see before you today. Come up and make your selections!"

"The same lot, year after year," complained a merchant. He glared up at the clerk. "They're misfits, and well you know it. You know how poor they are when the Petit Gaste can't find one to suit him. They're doddy-polls, these, or they're lazy, or dishonest."

The candidates were standing on benches along each side of the yard, the men on one and the girls on the other. If they were covered with confusion or filled with youthful innocence, there was nothing on the surface to indicate it. Rather, they seemed to be enjoying themselves on this, their one day to strut in public, and were exchanging badinage of a heavy-handed variety with the spectators. Each wore a placard with a number lettered on it.

The spectators clearly were of the opinion that the matter in hand was part of the entertainment of the fair. There was a continual offering of witticisms. "Jacques," shouted one, "you'll have the Petit Gaste as your master if you don't find another soon. He'll cure you of sitting around on your fat blind-cheeks." Another raised a laugh by suggesting: "Flip up your skirts, Margot, and let them see your fat calves; that will get you hired if anything will."

Valerie's confidence in her plan had received a severe shock by this time. She looked about her and wondered if she could go on with it. The prospective masters, walking up and down the line and inspecting the candidates with a callous air, seemed to her as poor a lot as the candidates themselves. She had to fight down a wild desire to turn and leave while there was time.

A young man whose garb proclaimed him a mercer at this point tossed a coin in the direction of the girl Margot. To catch it would be to accept engagement. Margot did not lose a moment in reaching up and plucking it from the air. After biting it, with an impudent flash of eye for his benefit, she raised her outer skirt and dropped the coin into the pocket of the scarlet kirtle she wore underneath. Then she followed the custom of the fair by removing her placard and handing it to the clerk.

The latter went into brisk action. "Good Master Bellay," he said, "you've hired yourself a servant. It's affirmed that she's in good health, has no trace of contagion about her, and that she's not with child. If it should happen that a child *is* born at any time within nine months, it will not be your responsibility. After that—he, he!—it will be a different matter. If you find it necessary to beat her, it must be with a stick no thicker than your thumb and it must be limited to ten strokes. You will provide her with one warm dress of woolen material, a sleeping shift, two pairs of hose, and a cap. She will have four ounces of soap for the six months. You will pay her one denier a day."

"Agreed," said the mercer.

In accordance with custom, the girl said, "I accept you as my master for six months, and I promise obedience, and I will do every task set me with willing spirit."

Valerie had succeeded in edging up close to the platform. She now plucked nervously at the sleeve of the official in charge and said, "I desire to offer myself as a servant, Master Clerk."

The clerk was busying himself with a paper and did not look up. "Very well," he said. "I've no time to question you now but it can be done later. Get yourself up on the bench and, if you want a good master, smile." Then he chanced to look at her and his mouth gaped open with surprise. "St. Christophe! It won't be necessary for you to smile, my girl. You may get too good a master if you do."

He handed her a placard with the number sixteen, uttering a feeble joke, "Your age, no doubt, my little one." Valerie pinned it on the front of her cloak. Then she mounted to an empty section of the bench.

The appearance of a new candidate so late in the fair created something of a stir. The would-be employers moved forward with one accord to look her over. Painfully aware of the avid eyes which roved over her from head to foot, she clenched her hands and her lips in an effort to hold her feelings in control. She looked fixedly at the top of the innyard gates where a flimsy girouette jerked about in the wind.

As soon as she entered she had noticed a man of unusual size who was prowling about and grunting and snuffling and muttering to himself. Now she became acutely conscious of him for he had shouldered his way to the front rank and was staring at her like a tomcat at a caged bird. His exertions had brought out large globules of perspiration on his round face, making him look like a wax statue which was starting to melt.

Someone safely in the rear shouted: "How do you like her, Red Fins?" (An allusion to the custom butchers had of painting the fins of stale fish to make them seem fresh.) "Are you suited now?"

The unpleasant apparition began to speak in a high-pitched voice, addressing the company at large. "You say the Petit Gaste is hard to suit. Well, I'm suited now. This little chick is mine. I'll have you all notice that I'm the first to put in a claim."

This evoked an instant chorus of protest. "Wait, she suits me!" cried one man. "I want her myself," from another. A stern-looking woman, with the mustache which marks the approach of the late forties, at the most favorable reckoning, said, "It will be for the girl to decide."

The large man shoved his competitors back with an outward sweep of both arms. He scowled about him ferociously. "Any one of you who moves an inch closer will feel the weight of my hand," he announced. He looked up at Valerie (his head was almost level with hers as it was) with mounting approval. "I spoke first. But everyone knows that I'm a decent man and a fair one. You will all have a chance, even though I could knock your heads together and cave in your ribs and tweeze off your ears with one twist of my fingers!" He brushed his damp forehead with a grimy forearm. "We'll draw for her, my good fellow townsmen. Could anything be fairer than that? Here, Alain-All-Alone, a broom!"

When the inn servant had obeyed the command by producing the remnants of a broom, the giant pulled out a dozen straws of different lengths. He glanced about him until his eyes lighted on a shrinking little individual at the edge of the crowd. "You, Godenotte, come here!"

"Not me, Gaste! Please, not me!"

"Come here!" roared the big man, in a sudden fury. "Didn't you hear me right? Come at once or I'll tear out your teeth and use them to curry my mules!"

The small man came forward so slowly that the butcher reached out impatiently and yanked him the rest of the way. "All I want you to do, Calf-Lolly, is hold the straws. Here! Double your puny fist over them so that only the ends show. Now we'll see who's to be the lucky man."

Godenotte did as he was bade. One of the claimants, with more boldness than the rest, came forward with outstretched fist. Little Gaste stared at him for a moment in amazement and then cuffed his hand aside roughly.

"What! You would take first draw when I am giving you this chance out of the goodness of my heart? I shall have first draw myself."

The giant gripped the wrist of Godenotte so tightly that the fingers curled up under the pressure, revealing the lengths of the straws. Gaste examined them carefully before making his selection.

"And, now, the rest of you."

Afraid to cross him, each one of the claimants went through the farce of drawing a straw. Then the lengths were compared and the Petit Gaste was declared the winner. He looked about him with increased bellicosity.

"Are you all satisfied?" he demanded. "Was it a fair draw?"

Those nearest him, and thus the most exposed to danger, nodded at once and said, "Yes, it was fair."

He had hoped, apparently, to meet with some dissent. He looked now at those who stood in the rear and picked on one of them, a young fellow with a weak chin. "You haven't opened your mouth, Olim," he exclaimed. Stalking over, he proceeded to shake the victim with a pistonlike movement of his muscular arms. "Are you content, Olim? Are you, Olim? Say that you are, hulverhead, or I'll wrench your giblets loose!" He gave the young man a final shake and then sent him sprawling with a shove.

"Olim is content," he said, grinning about him.

The butcher turned then to look at the girl he could now claim as a servant without any hint of opposition. A blank look came over his face. The section of bench she had occupied was empty.

Valerie, watching the proceedings with feelings which can readily be imagined, had realized that she would have no chance to find employment unless she were prepared to accept the Petit Gaste as her master and this, needless to state, was a prospect she could not face. Taking advantage of the fact that the attention of everyone was focused on the drawing, she had discarded her placard and climbed down from the bench. When the triumphant butcher turned to claim her, she was already on her way to the entrance of the courtyard.

The Petit Gaste caught a glimpse of her and started in pursuit. Valerie fell into a panic when she realized this. She began to run in blind haste, saying to herself, "It was madness to come here!" Wheeling suddenly to escape his outstretched paw, she ran into the side of the platform. It col-

lapsed with a loud crash and she caught a glimpse of the clerk's heels high
in the air as he went over with it. A sound of breaking crockery made it
evident that a jug of wine which had been on the platform had come to
grief.

2

As usual a court had been set up to settle any disputes which might
arise during the time the fair lasted. It was called Pied Poudre (in England, where they followed the same plan, the name was corrupted to Pie
Powder) and it was quite literally a court of Dusty Feet, being conducted
by merchants who had come from great distances. The judge was a trader
in silks from Marseilles, an elderly man with a shrewd and kindly face.

The judge smiled as he said to the group assembled in front of him,
"But it's clear, Messires, that it was an accident."

"A costly accident for me," whined the clerk of the Giglet fair who
appeared as the complainant.

"The girl was frightened," went on the old judge. "She did not want
to be claimed by the Petit Gaste, which is easy to understand. That she
overturned the platform was unfortunate, I grant you, but there was no
intent in it."

"I've suffered heavy losses," declared the clerk. "Item, a valuable jug,
broken. Item, a gallon of good wine, spilled. Item, a rent in my cloak,
suffered in the fall. Must I, the victim of the mishap, assume this three-
fold loss?"

The judge asked with a twinkle in his eye, "Have you considered claiming damages from the Petit Gaste?"

"No!" answered the complainant hastily.

"I didn't deem it likely. The Petit Gaste might display a slight tendency to violence under such circumstances. I hinted earlier to the one
officer this court possesses for the carrying out of its decisions that it might
be necessary to collect from that—that amiable citizen. I was informed
he would rather lose his post than make any such attempt. In any event,
the legal claim on the worthy, if somewhat hasty, butcher is a slight one."
He reached out for a paper the clerk was clutching in his hand. "You have
the amounts there? Let me have it."

"Thirty-four deniers," he announced after studying it. He glanced down
at Valerie who was standing in front of him with a forlorn look on her
face. "It seems, my child, that you have created a loss amounting to that
sum. Are you in a position to pay it?"

"No, my lord judge," she answered in a frightened tone of voice.

"Have you anything to offer by way of compensation? Can you pay a
part of it?"

"I have no more than two deniers, my lord judge."

The judge looked about him. "I am reluctant to send this child to
prison——" he began.

Valerie caught her breath. She was under no illusions as to what a term in prison would mean. She would be thrown into one large cell with other prisoners (in the smaller towns the sexes were not separated) and there she would stay until her time was up, subsisting on the foulest food and exposed to every kind of disease. She knew that when poor people went to prison they were seldom the same afterward. She looked up with frantic appeal into the gentle face of the old judge.

He was continuing: "—or to order that she work long enough to pay the amount of the damages, inasmuch as that would mean entering the service of that kindly citizen who supplies the needs of the community in the matter of flesh and fowl. May I suggest that all present, including myself, make a donation and that the amount thus raised be accepted by you, Monsieur Clerk, as payment in full?"

The silence which followed this suggestion was a conclusive answer. The judge sighed. "I had hoped to strike a spark of generosity in your hearts, Messires," he said. "Having failed in that, I am under the necessity of——"

A voice spoke up from the rear of the courtroom. "I'll pay for her."

Valerie turned eagerly. The voice had a familiar ring to it and she was infinitely relieved to find that it belonged to Pregent Kennedy. The Scot came forward slowly, casting her a side glance as he passed which said as plain as words, "Now do you see how foolish you have been and what I am compelled to pay for your folly?"

"I know this girl," he said to the court. "I'm prepared to make a money settlement rather than see her sent to prison. But first I must cast an eye over the items on the bill of damages."

"Naturally," said the judge, handing over the paper.

"It's clear," declared the Scot, flourishing the paper after a quick survey of what it contained, "that the claimant has been guided by the promptings of hopes and, even, cupidity, rather than a sense of honesty and justice in fixing his estimates. What! Can it be that the wine which was spilled was costly Cyprus or Tokay? Did it come from the slopes of Lebanon and did flakes of gold float in its clear amber? Was the jug itself a chalice fit for the lips of a princess or a holy saint that he sets this absurd value on it? Monsieur Judge, I am a good whittler and this statement of claims will be like a willow wand in my hands."

Valerie felt a sudden weakness in her knees and, with a nod to the judge to beseech his permission, she walked to a bench at the side of the room where she seated herself. She watched the proceedings from there with a sense of relief so great that the leathery face of the Scot became to her like that of a guardian angel filled with wisdom and benevolence. She heard him brushing aside the passionate protestations of the clerk with a coldness of logic which reduced the claim to shreds.

"Seventeen deniers!" announced the judge, after an agreement had finally been reached. "This worthy soldier of an allied nation has been generous enough to pay that amount and so I am happy to declare the incident closed. May I add that I hope the Giglet fair will conclude with the Petit Gaste still unsuited."

Pregent Kennedy was honest enough to disclaim any undue credit when he escorted Valerie to the street. "I've a liking for you, minikin," he said. "But I'm compelled to tell you that it might have taken more than that to involve me in such a disastrous transaction as this. I am never prodigal with my"—he was compelled to fall back on his native tongue for the right word—"with my *siller*. There are other reasons for this seeming madness on my part. The Sire d'Arlay, who has a share of the wealth the Moneyman has created, left a sum in my hands to be used in just such an emergency. Further, I confess, minikin, that I was not as fast asleep that night as I appeared and so I heard what you were telling him about the mystery of your birth." When Valerie looked startled, he went on in a reassuring tone: "Your secret is safe with me. Nay, I think you lucky that I know. Let me help you, my child, and I'll dig out the truth for you like a dog with a long-buried bone."

"I'll be most happy to have your aid," said Valerie.

The Scot nodded his head. "I'm an honest man and I want you to understand at the outset that I am not actuated solely by generous instincts. I'm not above taking advantage of this to add to the weight of my purse. There must always be a souldie for me in everything I do." He looked at his companion with a dry smile. "Do you think you can unravel the secret if you sell yourself into service with butchers and the like? Nay, child, you must be prepared for bolder courses than that. Come with me to Paris and we will make a start on things from there."

"I'm ready to go," answered Valerie humbly.

4

THERE was a small section cut off by a low oak screen from the rest of the white-plastered room. Here, on benches against the wall, visitors waited the convenience of Jacques Coeur. The screen was not high enough to prevent them from seeing the great merchant himself as he sat behind his desk, and so the period of waiting served a double purpose. The visitors achieved a proper appreciation of the demands on his time before they were summoned inside; and, when he so desired, he could look them over and give them a quick appraisal in advance.

"Who are out there today?" Coeur asked Nicolas, not raising his eyes from the papers in front of him.

"A dowsy lot," answered the servant. "Gerhart the fuller. He wants to wheedle you about the debt he owes you. I hope you heat his ears for him. A priest from the University; he'll be begging for something. A pilgrim who says he's just back from the Holy Land and has a splinter of the Cross to sell. A fakir, that one."

"Tell Gerhart to come back another day. I'll see the priest as soon as I can. Send the pilgrim away. Who else?"

"A soldier who calls himself Pregent Kennedy. He talks with a foreign twist. *Ecossais*, I think."

"Pregent Kennedy?" Coeur repeated the name thoughtfully. "I've heard of this Scot. He's been in the East, in Constantinople. He handled the bombards in a campaign against the Turks. I'll talk to him, Nicolas. Who else?"

"A girl."

"A girl? Well, go on. What does she want?"

Nicolas was smiling wisely. "I don't know what she wants, master."

"If she's here to beg, give her something from the alms bag and send her away."

"In that case you had better have the Lombardy banker up. He's waiting your convenience below."

"Why didn't you say so at first? Filling my ears with talk about this catch of small sprate when the big fish is waiting!"

Before departing to obey the order, Nicolas said in an aggrieved tone, "You know I always save the best for the last."

On the other side of the railing Valerie was watching the great man with fascinated interest. At the same time she was uncomfortably conscious of the close scrutiny of the other visitors and was careful to keep her feet hidden under the skirt of her cloak, not wanting anyone to see how dilapidated her shoes had become. She had placed a small wicker basket on the floor beside her.

Pregent Kennedy leaned toward her and whispered, "What is there about Jaquet the Fox which interests you so much?"

"His eyes," she answered in a low tone. "I'm sure he can see right through me. And yet they're so kind and understanding. I think he must be a wonderful man."

"Wonderful?" The Scot peered across the screen at the Moneyman with a dry smile on his long features. "Aye, he's wonderful—in his own way. Hard, acquisitive, sharp. His mind's as nimble as a ropedancer."

Nicolas entered, escorting a weazened old man in a plain gray gown which swept the floor as he walked. The arms of the newcomer were folded under his chin as though to provide a rest for his palsied head.

"A banker, I'll swear, from the looks of him," whispered the Scot. "Now watch how quickly that old frame of bones will be allowed to see the great Jacques Coeur."

"I've thought it over," said the banker, when he had seated himself across the table from the Moneyman. "Ten of the estates I must have, Jacques Coeur. The list is here. I have put Beaucaire at the head. Beaucaire I must have most certainly."

Coeur looked at the little man with a bitter frown. "I have thirty-two estates in which most of my profits have been sunk," he said. "And you, leech from Lombardy, are demanding ten of them as security for this miserable little loan you're making me. The lands you demand would repay the loan three times over. Are you forgetting I must make other loans and that all my creditors have to be satisfied?"

"You call this loan a small one?" quavered the old man. "It is so considerable I must scrape the bottom of my coffers to find the money. And, bear in mind, it's for the making of war. If the Engloys beat you again, and well they may, for they are a rude and fierce race, they will take every acre you own, Jacques Coeur! How, then, would poor Guiseppi of Lombardy get back his forty thousand écus? Would your Engloy masters pay him? Na, na! It would be a total loss. The return must be heavy, and the security good, to make this terrible risk worth while."

"The return," said Coeur, with a wry smile, "*is* heavy. Thirty per cent interest!"

The Italian, who looked as though he had been living in a steam bath and had been reduced thereby to the human limits of desiccation, piped up sharply: "I would demand of the King of France forty per centum for such a loan. You may know by the difference, Jacques Coeur, how well I think of you." He plucked at his beard with hands so thin they seemed all nails and veins. "As to Beaucaire, it's far enough south to be out of the reach of the Engloys. Yes, yes, I must have Beaucaire."

"If the people of Paris knew what you were demanding of me, they would stone you to death in the streets."

The veil which had obscured the rheumy orbs of the ancient banker suddenly cleared. Coeur found himself looking into the most predatory pair of eyes he had ever encountered. They were ageless eyes and as much out of place in that shrunken body as a beating heart in a scarecrow. "Have a care to yourself, Jacques Coeur," shrilled the moneylender. "They are more likely to stone *you*. The common people do not like rich men. When they hear that Jaquet the Fox is paying the whole cost of the war himself, they will want to know where he got the money for it. They will say that it came out of *their* pockets. They say now that he is so rich he has his horses shod with silver shoes. They gaze after him with envy in their hearts." He paused and nodded his head several times. "You are a generous man and a brave one, Jacques Coeur. You may win them their freedom—and be stoned as your sole reward!"

Coeur had never doubted that he stood well with the common people, never doubted that they looked with pride at what he, who had been one of them, had accomplished. "Old age is robbing him of his wits," he said to himself. "His avarice has addled him."

And yet there was a prophetic ring to the words which nettled him with a first stirring of fear. He got to his feet and began to pace about in an effort to regain his self-confidence.

"Guiseppi of Lombardy," he said finally. "I am not modest. I know myself for a man of infinite resource. If these loans I am now compelled

to make should recoil like one of Jean Bureau's bombards and bring ruin
to my enterprises, I have enough inventiveness here"—touching his forehead with his hand—"to build a new and better structure on the ruins.
I'm afraid of nothing. I'm not afraid of the English. I can snap my fingers
at all who yap at my heels.

"I've made up my mind about the terms I'm prepared to accept on
this loan," he went on. "Banker, I won't give you Beaucaire as security.
I won't give you all the others you have demanded. Five you shall have
and no more; and I myself shall have the selection of them. Those are
my terms. *Aut cape aut relinque.*"[1]

"I must have time," whined the Lombard. "I can't risk my moneys
without due thought. My good lord Coeur, I must give the matter the
deepest consideration."

"Take a week," said Coeur. "Go back to the Grand Pont and think it
over well. I'll see you here one week from today. Wars can't wait for
moneylenders."

"Wars," declared the old man, recovering some shreds of his arrogance,
"can't be fought without moneylenders."

"You're wrong, banker. This one can be fought without moneylenders.
But not without Jacques Coeur."

The banker shuffled from the room, muttering to himself, and Jacques
Coeur returned to the papers heaped on his desk. He went through them
with the utmost speed, recording his findings with a decisive "Yes" or
"No" on the margins and scrawling at the bottom of each his bold "De♥."

Nicolas returned. "Robert de Poitevin is here," he said. "Because he's
the King's physician, should he stamp in here as though he owned us
body and soul?"

The Moneyman's face had taken on a grave expression. "I'm afraid
he's the bearer of ill tidings. Well, bring him in, Nicolas."

A sound of scratching could be heard from the other side of the screen.
Coeur frowned and demanded, "What's that?"

"A cat, master. The girl has it in a basket."

"Is she still here? I thought I told you to send her away. I've considered
sending *you* away a thousand times, my gome. This time I may do it."

Nicolas was not disturbed. "You needn't buy any flutes[2] from me today, master. You need me and full well you know it."

Coeur raised his hands in a gesture of resignation. "In the name of all
the saints! Bring the physician in!"

2

Robert de Poitevin was a small man who looked the world squarely in
the eye and feared nothing. He was not afraid of contracting the diseases
and mischiefs he encountered every day and so had never adopted any of

---

[1] Take it or leave it.
[2] In Paris jargon of the day, pick a quarrel.

the devices his fellow physicians used. He did not wear a tunic steeped in chemicals nor did he fill his ears and nostrils with rue or carry a clove of garlic under his tongue. Instead he dressed in a plain gray habit, and the only sign by which he could be identified was a small caduceus embroidered on his collar.

He walked in briskly and seated himself beside the Moneyman's chair without indulging in any form of salutation. "Jacques Coeur," he said, pointing at him with a forefinger, "Anges Sorel is going to present the King with another child."

The Moneyman was both shocked and disturbed. "But, my good Robert, she's in very bad health! Can she hope to survive childbirth when she's already in such a weakened condition?"

The physician answered in gloomy tones: "I'm not pleased, you may be sure."

"Have you told the King?"

Robert de Poitevin nodded. "An hour ago. His King's Grace was disposed to regard the news with pride at first. When I made it clear to him that the unfortunate lady was in no condition to stand the ordeal, he became very angry with me, as I knew he would. Our liege lord doesn't like to face unpleasant facts. He told me that he wasn't satisfied with my unsupported opinion. . . . Well, I shall have to call them in, Olivier de Bousse from the University, that great blowhard, that maker of empty phrases, and the rest of them. We'll have the consultation he demands and they will sit around solemnly for hours, talking in Latin texts and making it abundantly clear that they know nothing at all. And then they will say to our liege lord that his servant, Robert de Poitevin, has been hasty in his opinion, that they in their joint wisdom do not agree with him entirely. They will say that the Lady Agnes is undoubtedly quite ill but that, on the other hand, she is still a young woman and God's ways are inscrutable and why should any mortal take it on himself to know what is in the heavenly mind. Sometimes, my lord Coeur, I am ashamed of my calling! We pretend to know so much and in reality we know so very little! Consider the matter of poisons——"

"Come, my good Robert! If you get launched on that subject, you'll talk for hours. Frankly, I can't allow you that much time today. My hours are filled—and the news you have brought me will weigh so heavily that I can't hope to accomplish much."

The two men stared at each other in an unhappy silence for several moments. Then Coeur said, "Tell me the truth, Master Robert. Is there any hope for her?"

The physician shook his head slowly and sadly. "Jacques Coeur," he said, "Agnes Sorel is going to die!"

Nicolas watched his master from the other side of the room with a worried frown. It was unusual for Jacques Coeur to remain impassive for such a long time; the news he had received from the physician had been disturbing, quite clearly. When he fell into a mood of absorption like this it was better to leave him alone, and so it was with reluctance that the servant crossed the floor again. He said, "Master, he's here."

The Moneyman roused himself with some difficulty. "Who is here?"

"Would I disturb you again for anything short of a summons from the King? Or because the Sire d'Arlay has returned at last?"

"Robin has arrived?" There was a note of relief in the voice of the Moneyman. "I am glad to hear it. Bring him up, Nicolas, bring him up!"

3

That there was a bond of mutual esteem between the two men was apparent when D'Arlay entered. Coeur met him halfway across the room with both arms outstretched. He wrapped them around the newcomer and gave him an affectionate hug.

"How, Robin!" he cried. "I'm delighted to see you. You're as brown, my gadling, as though you had returned from another journey to the East with Jean de Village."

"I have much to tell you," declared D'Arlay, settling himself down in the chair the physician had vacated.

For an hour they talked. They discussed the results of the tour D'Arlay had made, his meeting with Coeur factors in the course of his travels (Coeur knew them all so well that he could have quoted the profits of each for any given year), the news from the East which the last ships in at Montpellier had brought, the presents that D'Arlay had picked up, particularly for Isabeau (Coeur's scowl was evidence that he did not approve the bringing of presents for Isabeau), and the state of the country generally.

They had not exhausted their interest by any means when a trumpet sounded in the street. Coeur sprang eagerly to his feet.

"The convoy from the south has arrived," he said. "You must see this, Robin. There has been a procession through the town so the people could gape at the marvelous things we shall have for sale."

He motioned D'Arlay to follow him. Donning his customary *houve*, a curious type of headpiece which closely resembled in shape an oriental turban, Coeur led the way out to the open gallery which overlooked the inner courtyard on all four sides at a height of about fifteen feet. It was a narrow and picturesque passage with elaborately carved stone pillars. They took up their station beside one of these. The merchant, all eagerness now, leaned over the stone railing.

The trumpet sounded again, a high, shrill note. A company of heralds rode into the courtyard, three abreast. They were astride fine black steeds and wore tabards of crimson with the Coeur device of heart and shell in gold thread and the familiar motto in bold letters, *A Vaillants Coeurs Rien Impossible*. Men in eastern costume followed, leading camels by their nose cords. The camels, clearly, were for display only; they carried no burdens save maidens in white who sat high up on the red leather saddles, and they swayed and minced along and raised their muzzles in demanding bleats. Above their veils the eyes of the riders sparkled with a lively sense of the part they were playing.

"The East, the magic East!" said Coeur, turning around to nod and smile at his companion. "It's the home of mystery. You never know what to expect. And it's the same with the goods which reach me from there. They are always a treasure trove of surprise. Who knows but what we may find in one of the bundles a tiara which once graced the brow of the Queen of Sheba or a lamp from which a dread genie may be released."

A train of jugglers followed, tossing knives of polished steel in the air, and after them a body of musicians who struck up a curious refrain on instruments of the East.

"How this takes me back!" sighed Coeur. "That music gets in your blood. How clearly I remember my first visit to Damascus. They thought ill of Frenchmen then and every night we were herded to prison and locked up. They treated us like pariah dogs. But I soon changed all that. They found they could trust Jacques Coeur, that he was the one to trade with first, instead of the wily merchants from Venice and Genoa. Today, as you know, my ships have the freedom of eastern waters and my captains get the cream of the trade."

The van of the procession, which was devoted exclusively to entertainment, had now unwound itself and taken station at one end of the courtyard. The musicians continued to play as the pack mules ambled in, loaded with bundles in red, green, and white canvas.

"It's hard for me to wait until the unpacking begins," said Coeur, shifting his feet as though he also found it hard to stand still. He stopped suddenly, his eyes fixed on the spectators below who had been forced to crowd back against the walls. He reached out one hand and touched D'Arlay on the shoulder. "Robin, do you see that girl?"

"I see a score of girls. Which one do you mean?"

"The one near the foot of the east tourelle. See, she has on a long gray cloak and a hood. It's extraordinary, Robin, quite extraordinary!"

D'Arlay looked in the direction indicated. The crowd, made up for the most part of customers who had been in the shop when the procession arrived, was so thick that he could not identify the girl in question. Certainly he saw nothing to account for the excitement which had taken hold of his companion.

"She looks like——" Coeur broke off and slammed a fist down on the top of the stone railing. "She's gone! Come with me, Robin. I mustn't let her get away. I must find her at once."

D'Arlay followed at his heels, wondering what had come over him. Coeur was so excited that he began to run as soon as they turned in from the gallery. He raced down a short stretch of hall, beckoning D'Arlay to do the same, and then footed it pell-mell up a narrow flight of stairs. This brought them to a door with a cresset burning rather fitfully above it. "I hope we're in time!" he muttered, opening the latch with an eager hand.

They found themselves in an unlighted corridor, so narrow that they could touch the wall on each side and so low that they had to bend over as they walked. There were apertures in the walls at regular intervals through which shafts of light appeared. Coeur peered ahead of him and shouted, "Antoine!"

"Yes?" answered a voice from somewhere in the gloom ahead of them.

"Sound the *Coquille!* Quick! The Coquille!"

They heard hurried footsteps and an instant later a bell tolled out. It was so loud and urgent that D'Arlay had no doubt it could be heard in all parts of the vast establishment.

"Now all the doors will be closed and guarded," explained Coeur, with a note of satisfaction in his voice. "No one will be able to leave. I think, Robin, we are in time."

"What is all this about?" demanded D'Arlay impatiently. "Why is it so important not to let this girl get away?"

The Moneyman motioned down the corridor. "This is a way I've found to prevent the theft of goods exposed for sale. The corridor runs all around the building and overlooks the sections where the most valuable articles are shown. I keep four men here as long as the shop is open. They watch what goes on below through the slits in the wall. Nothing which happens escapes them. If a customer takes a fancy to something beyond the reach of his purse, or hers, my man sees and pulls one of the ropes. The bell sounds, the doors are closed and they are not opened again until the guilty one has been located. The matter is always resolved to the great discomfort of the thief."

"A most ingenious arrangement."

Coeur led the way back through the door and closed it after them. "There are two ropes for the use of each watcher," he said, with an air of conscious pride. "The second is to warn of fire. They are in all parts of the building as well, each attached to the one bell. The theft bell is called the Coquille and the other the Incendie. They have different sounds and so there is no mistaking the reason for the signal in each case. I planned this method myself."

"This girl, I judge, is a thief."

Coeur laughed. "No, Robin, the girl isn't a thief. Do you think me so concerned over the loss of some paltry gewgaw that I would go to all this trouble myself? It happens that the Coquille is serving me in a matter which may be of the utmost importance."

"Explain it, then, in God's good name!"

"I prefer to leave the explanation," said Coeur, leading the way back to his own apartment, "until you can see the girl at close hand. It may be I've been deceived. I shall wait to see what you think."

4

Valerie followed Nicolas into the presence of Coeur and his companion. She was frightened, not knowing the reason for the brusque way she had been singled out, and she kept her eyes lowered. The reed basket was clutched tightly in both hands. When the servant urged her forward, her sense of alarm grew. She plucked nervously at his sleeve.

"Monsieur," she whispered, "what have I done that's so very wrong?"

"You needn't be afraid, Mademoiselle. The master means you no harm."

He found it necessary, in spite of this reassurance, to take her by the elbow and compel her reluctant steps forward. They halted in front of the table.

"Is this the one, master?" asked Nicolas.

The Moneyman took a glance at the downcast face of the girl and nodded triumphantly. "Yes, my argus-eyed Nicolas, this is the one," he said.

He got to his feet. Placing himself in front of the girl, he studied her face with care. Then he ejaculated a hearty, "Remarkable!" and seizing both her hands, patted them together exuberantly. "I was not mistaken!" he cried. "It's even closer than I thought. Remarkable, indeed! My child, who are you?"

D'Arlay had been so astonished when Valerie entered the room that he had brushed a hand across his eyes to make sure he was not being deceived. When he had left after the solemn ceremony of burying Damian Maret, there had been no talk of her coming to Paris. He had heard no discussion, in fact, of her plans. In leaving he had entrusted a sum to the Scot which he knew would suffice to cover her needs until such time as she became settled in some new niche in life. He had not expected to see her again.

Standing before the Moneyman in her badly tattered cloak, looking frightened and thoroughly bewildered, she had much the same effect on him as she had when, in the light from the campfire, he had placed his hands on her shoulders and drawn her close to him. He had known then that he was perilously close to falling in love. Now, he realized, he was walking even closer to the edge; one blind step would carry him over. "Was it fated that she should come here? That I should see her again?" he asked himself. It had required an accident to bring them together. If Jacques Coeur's eye had not happened to pick her out, she would have vanished immediately and been swallowed up forever in the great city.

"Her name is Valerie Maret," he said, stepping forward.

The girl looked up quickly and a smile of great relief lighted up her face. "I don't know why I have been brought here, my lord," she said. "I've done no wrong. Perhaps you will tell them that I'm honest and make them let me go."

It was Jacques Coeur's turn to be astonished. His eyes darted back and forth from one to the other. "You know her?"

"Yes," answered D'Arlay. "An accident brought us together one evening not so long ago in a desolate part of the country. I don't know what purpose you have in summoning her here but I'm sure she can't have done anything wrong."

Jacques Coeur's face became grave. He put into words the thought which had flashed through D'Arlay's mind a few moments before. "I can see the hand of fate in this. Why else should she have come, and today of all days? There can be no doubt about it. Everything fits into a curious pattern, even the refusal of this fellow of mine to obey the orders I gave him. A divine hand guided her to this spot, I swear."

D'Arlay smiled at Valerie as though to say, "I don't know what he means any more than you do but you mustn't let it disturb you."

"My child, what have you in that basket?" asked the Moneyman.

"A cat, my lord."

"And that's the final proof!" cried Coeur. "By St. Martin of Tours, I know it was not mere accident which brought her to my attention. Even the cat did its best to waken me. How unreceptive I was! I was determined not to see her. . . . Most fortunately it had been willed otherwise."

"Perhaps," said D'Arlay, "you will now condescend to tell us what you mean."

"Look at her!" exclaimed Coeur. "Surely you can see what I see."

"I've been aware from the first that Mademoiselle Maret resembles someone I have seen but so far I haven't been able to tell who it is."

"Think, Robin!" Coeur planted himself in front of his friend and stared into his eyes as though striving in that way to set his mind in the right direction. "Think back. Back many years. Back to the first time we met, you and I. You will recall the occasion well."

A light flooded D'Arlay's mind. He threw back his head and laughed triumphantly. "Of course!" he cried. "I see it now. How could I have been so very dense?" Then his mood sobered. "It's hard to believe and yet the resemblance is quite unmistakable."

5

D'ARLAY'S THOUGHTS had gone back to the saddest day in his life.

He was seventeen years old and Isabeau was marrying his brother. He walked in the procession, dressed most handsomely in ceremonious white, even to his shoes, which curled to a point in front like whitecaps on a rolling tide. His heart was heavy as he paced up the aisle and he kept saying to himself with an almost frantic insistence: "This is all a terrible dream. It can't be true! She was to marry me, not Regnault. Something will happen to put a stop to this, because it's wrong and unthinkable that she should wed anyone but me!" He hoped that a specter from his brother's unsavory past would rise up somewhere in the dark recesses of the cathedral to call a halt. He more than half believed that the all-seeing and wise God would send down a thunderbolt to prevent such an unseemly plighting of vows.

But nothing of the kind happened. In an unhappy daze he heard the solemn words of the bishop, the rise and fall of the choir chants.

"If a stop is to be put to it," he thought, "I must do it myself!"

He was standing, with no knowledge of having risen to his feet. There was a rustle of sound about him, faces staring up at him, amused and unfriendly faces, elbows nudging, whispers of surprise. He opened his mouth to say that the ceremony must not go on but no sound issued forth. A parched sensation in his throat made it impossible for him to speak, despite the torrent of protest which filled him. After a moment he brushed a hand across his forehead and it came away damp with perspiration.

He crushed his way out to the aisle, realizing that he had made a sorry spectacle of himself and unable, as a result, to sustain the amused scrutiny of all those peering faces. He began to walk down the aisle, arms held stiffly at his sides, his eyes fixed straight ahead.

"I'm a fool!" he said to himself. "A stupid, blundering fool! Everyone is laughing at me. Isabeau will hear about it and then she will laugh at me too."

Sometime later he found himself in the cathedral entrance. The ceremony was over. The sun was high, the sky a joyous blue, the talk of the people who crowded the steps loud and animated. This was all wrong, he knew. How could they chatter and laugh as though nothing had happened? For that matter, how could the sun think it worth while to shine so brightly in the face of this catastrophe?

A hand fell on his shoulder and he looked up into a friendly face under a most curious kind of hat. He roused himself sufficiently from his state of dejection to realize that the stranger was a walking example of everything that was unconventional. The newcomer's eyes proclaimed his moods openly instead of peering stealthily from behind an evasive curtain. He had a manner free of the stilted niceties of the court, a laugh which had the courage to be a real laugh, a jauntiness in the matter of dress which also required courage in this day of rigid adherence to set fashions.

"Is it possible," asked the stranger, regarding him with frank curiosity, "that you are the young brother of the bridegroom? I've nothing to say against my good gossip Regnault, who amuses me in spite of everything; but truly, my boy, the difference between you is remarkable enough to make one doubt the relationship."

"I am Robinet de Burey."

"I'm told you are of a bookish turn," went on the stranger. "That is surprising, and admirable, in itself; for the minds of all aspirants to knightly honors of your age do not seem to me to rise much above an interest in birds' eggs." The keen eyes under the strange hat studied him closely. "You look pale, my boy. Are you not feeling well?"

"I'm quite well, Monsieur."

"My name," said the man, "is Jacques Coeur. You have heard of me, no doubt."

Everyone had heard of the King's fabulous Moneyman, the furrier of

Bourges who had risen to such wealth and power. Despite the lacerated state of his feelings, young D'Arlay looked at his companion with a certain amount of interest, liking him at once and sensing in him a genuine warmth and friendliness.

"I'm of an interfering turn," said the Moneyman, "and you may resent what I'm going to say to you, Robinet de Burey. It happens that I have acquaintances in Anjou who have told me about—well, about you and your brother and the fair lady who has just pledged her vows to him and thereby acquired what she wanted most, an ancient title. Come, you need not look at me as though I had committed sacrilege and wounded you mortally in so doing. I've been guilty of no more than putting into words what you know inside yourself to be the full truth, my boy. My desire to help you is my excuse for this frankness of speech." He threw an arm around D'Arlay's shoulders and began to lead him down the steps. "It seems like the blackest of tragedies at this moment. Life has become a dreary affair, the future as dark as the plume in the hat of the brave Bastard of Orléans. But time is a great thing, my boy. It can cure almost any ill in its slow but very sure way. I can look back to a tragedy in my own life which was not entirely unlike yours; and there is now even a certain sweetness in my memory of it."

Not knowing how to answer this unexpected and uninvited confidence, D'Arlay said nothing. After a moment the Moneyman went on. "There are no limits to my capacity for interference," he declared, with a broad smile. "We are complete strangers and yet I'm going to be bold enough to propose a cure. You must go away. You must allow yourself time to become accustomed to what has happened."

D'Arlay found himself in instant agreement. This was the solution! He must get away, far away, where he could see nothing of Isabeau and Regnault and the friends they had in common. He was sure he could no longer maintain the pretense of indifference which he had assumed the instant Isabeau told him of her decision. This, clearly, was the course he must follow: to go away and, if necessary, to stay away forever.

"I think you're right, Monsieur Coeur," he said.

"I'm a busybody—but I'm many other things," declared Jacques Coeur. "I am, for instance, a shipowner. Perhaps you know I have some ships engaged in the eastern trade. Tomorrow my stout Jean de Village leaves for the south and he will take out my finest vessel from Montpellier on the run to Alexandria. Would you care to go with him? Egypt is a land of wonder. The whisper of dead centuries reaches your ears the instant you sight the roadstead. And you will have a chance to go on to the Holy Land and even up to Damascus."

D'Arlay made up his mind on the instant. He had always wanted to go to sea; the East had worked on his imagination like a magnet. He would take this chance so generously and gratuitously offered him, and if he never saw Isabeau again, it would be all for the best.

"You are so kind I can find no words to thank you," he said to the Moneyman. "I accept your offer, Monsieur Coeur! I accept it gladly."

"I thought you would. I was so sure of it that I risked a rebuff in coming to you like this. You'll soon get over this present mood of yours, I give you my word on that. The keen winds of the Inner Sea will sweep all the cobwebs of regret from your mind, my boy. Well, come to see me tonight. I'll have Jean de Village there to greet you. He's a famously fine fellow, this Jean of mine, and you will become the best of friends in less time than it takes me to sell a bolt of camelot cloth to a buxom housewife."

They had reached the street. D'Arlay glanced at his companion and suddenly found himself determined to assert a new manliness of sentiment over what had happened.

"I hate my brother!" he said. "And as for his wife, I shall never see her again as long as I live."

The Moneyman halted beside a carriage in the street with four mettlesome white horses. A lady sat inside and, as they stopped, she leaned out and smiled at Jacques Coeur. She was so beautiful that D'Arlay looked at her with an almost incredulous wonder. This being his first visit to Tours, he had few acquaintances among the people of the court and he found himself considering who she could be. That point was resolved at once by the Moneyman.

"Lady Agnes," he said, moving closer to the carriage and bowing low, "I'm happy to see that you've recovered so soon from your indisposition. May I present a new friend of mine? This is Robinet de Burey, Sire d'Arlay. My boy, this is the Lady Agnes Sorel who is, I am sure you already agree, the most lovely lady in all the world."

So this was Agnes Sorel, the mistress of the King! D'Arlay had heard the stories about her which circulated over France and even reached the secluded corner of Anjou where he had lived all his life, stories of her great qualities of heart as well as of her unusual beauty. Reports of royal mistresses were generally edged with malice and dislike but Agnes Sorel was so kindly regarded that many people were disposed to put some stock in the suggestion that she was not actually the mistress of Charles of France, that their relationship had been kept on a platonic plane. Even those who were not prepared to believe this were still willing to concede that her influence over the monarch was a beneficent one.

The boy bowed to her, finding himself somewhat discomfited by the frankness of interest with which she was regarding him. The reports he had heard of her had not been exaggerated in the slightest degree. She had a beauty which excited as well as pleased the senses. His attention went first to her eyes, which were a light blue, a most unusual blue, and then to her mouth. It was so vividly red that it suggested passion and yet, on closer inspection, he could see that it was gentle and highly sensitive.

"I've heard of the Sire d'Arlay," said Agnes Sorel, in a pleasantly low-pitched voice.

"He has made up his mind to sail East on one of my ships," announced Jacques Coeur, giving his companion an encouraging thump on the back. "We are men of quick decision, this young friend of mine and I; we thought of the plan no more than a minute ago and it was settled between us quicker than you could lirp a finger. He leaves tomorrow with Jean de Village and will sail at once from Montpellier."

Agnes Sorel smiled and nodded her head. "What an excellent idea," she said. "I'm sure, Sire d'Arlay, you'll find your journey most stimulating. It will be"—she looked at him with so much sympathy and understanding that he knew she had heard his story also—"it will be a great adventure for you. And the very best thing—under the circumstances."

"He will come back loaded with wealth," declared Coeur. "With precious stones and wonderful fabrics and spices and perfumes. Perhaps he will bring back also—who can tell?—a beautiful eastern princess as his bride."

D'Arlay had never seen Agnes Sorel again and so it was not to be wondered at that the resemblance borne her by this little waif had eluded him for so long.

2

"And now you know," said Jacques Coeur.

"And now I know."

The Moneyman, whose eyes were sparkling with excitement, took her hand again and gave it a reassuring pat. "My child," he said, "you must forgive us. We are talking in riddles. You must be patient until—until tomorrow, perhaps."

"Yes, my lord." It was clear from her tone that she was more puzzled than ever.

"One of two things will happen," went on the Moneyman. "I may say to you that a certain dream in which I had indulged myself has dissolved and that I won't have any use for you after all. If it turns out that way, there will be a little present for you to compensate for the strange way in which we've used you. On the other hand, I may have something quite different to say to you. In the meantime . . ." Coeur frowned as he pondered the question of what was to be done with her immediately. Then he gave a satisfied nod. "My factor lives with his family at the top of this building. There will be a room for you there, and a bed, and plenty of food. Later, I hope, it will be necessary to make permanent arrangements." He called to his servant, "Nicolas, I'm entrusting Mademoiselle Maret to you."

Valerie, now thoroughly bewildered, turned her eyes in D'Arlay's direction. Reading the question in them, he said, "I'm almost as much in the dark as you are, but I assure you, Mademoiselle, that you need have no fears."

"This way, Mademoiselle," said Nicolas importantly.

When they were alone, Coeur began to address D'Arlay in excited tones. "What a remarkable thing! The Lady Agnes is the acknowledged Queen of Beauty, she's without a peer in this or any age. And yet here is a girl with no advantages, who comes of peasant stock, if one may judge from the clothes she wears——"

"Her father was a strolling player named Damian Maret."

Coeur nodded his head with satisfaction. "That explains her voice. It puzzled me, for it shows definite traces of culture. Well, here is the daughter of a cheap cullion who's sufficiently like the Fair Agnes to be a full blood sister—or a daughter. It's hard to believe but we've seen the evidence with our own eyes."

"I saw the Lady Agnes once only and so I'm not the best judge. But it does seem to me that the resemblance is quite astonishing."

Coeur sat down in his chair and swung one parti-colored knee over the other. He began to enumerate the points of resemblance. "They are identical in coloring," he said. "There's the same blue of eye and the same yellow of hair. The girl even has some of the same characteristics. She looks at you with a slow raising of the lids just as the Lady Agnes does. She has the same way of lifting a hand to gesture." He swung around in his chair to face his companion. "And now, my gossip Robin, what can you tell me about her? Under what circumstances did you meet this extraordinary child?"

D'Arlay did not answer at once. He had no way of knowing why Coeur was taking such an interest in Valerie. He felt himself on the defensive. He was still amazed also at the unexpected depth of the feeling he had experienced when he saw her escorted into the room. He had realized then, from the exultant jump his heart had given, that he had been wanting to see her again, that he had been regretting his unceremonious leave-taking.

Reluctantly he began to tell of his meeting with her. He intended to make the recital a brief one but Jacques Coeur would not permit that. The Moneyman asked innumerable questions and was not satisfied until he had extracted a detailed report of the occurrence.

"Do you believe these people were her real parents?" asked Coeur at the finish.

D'Arlay hesitated. "No," he said finally. He pondered the question of how much more he should tell, his fingers busy with the pleated drapery of the roundlet he had removed from his head on entering. Finally he decided to repeat the whole story.

Jacques Coeur's face lighted up as he listened, and at the finish he nodded his head with the most intense satisfaction. "Of course!" he cried. "There's the best of blood in her. She's no child of the people, this small one, no get of a strolling player. The mark of quality is stamped all over her!" He paused for several moments and then burst out with, "How very fortunate this is!"

"Fortunate? Why do you say that? I don't understand why you are taking so much interest in her, Jacques."

The mood of the Moneyman underwent a quick change. "There's something I must tell you," he declared. "The King's physician came to see me no more than an hour ago. He told me that Agnes Sorel has a short time only to live."

"I'm sorry to hear such news."

After a long silence Coeur began to speak in a low tone. "It will be a great tragedy. Usually I take the optimistic view of things. I always expect that matters will come out right. But in this I find myself fearing the worst. I'm sure the outcome will be a sad one for—for her friends. And for France, D'Arlay, for France above all else."

"I still don't understand you."

"This is a strange King we have. I don't need to tell you that. We both know he has certain fine qualities and I confess to a deep affection for him. But"—Coeur shook his head solemnly—"his unguided choice of advisers has always been bad. If Agnes is not there to speak the right words in the royal ear, things will go wrong."

"I've no illusions about my own position," he went on. "I've slept in the royal bed and, for the moment, the King seems to have every confidence in me. But, Robin, my tenure in reality hangs on a single thread—a frail one and of the finest gold. If it breaks——" He paused. "I have more enemies than you know. The court is packed with them, whispering, running to the King with every malicious bit of gossip they can pick up or invent. The King lacks constancy. He did not bestir himself to save the Maid. Would he do more for me?"

After another minute of silent thought the Moneyman began to speak in a brisker tone. "The King will mourn Agnes deeply but he will soon take another mistress. Her vixen of a cousin is angling already for the succession. If that happened——Robin, has it ever occurred to you that I should have a candidate to offer?"

D'Arlay was so startled that he made no effort to reply.

"Have you noticed that the preferences of most men run to certain types? More often than not a second wife is much like the first one. No man has ever been more deeply enamored of a woman than the King of Agnes Sorel. She has suited him completely." He paused for a moment. "The most likely candidate would be one who resembled Agnes closely. Now you will understand, my good Robin, why I took an interest in this girl as soon as I set eyes on her."

D'Arlay sprang to his feet. "This is unheard of!" he cried. "It's absurd! You can't be serious about it!"

"I'm completely serious about it. Before I make any move, of course, I must convince myself that the child has character and courage as well as the physical likeness."

If D'Arlay needed any further proof of how he felt about Valerie, he had it now. "I can't yet believe," he said, "that you are in earnest. It's an idea of the moment. You'll brush it aside after giving it more thought."

Coeur looked up in surprise at the feeling he had detected in D'Arlay's voice. "Is it possible that you take a personal interest in her?"

D'Arlay indulged in serious thought before answering. "I like her. Perhaps it was because of the circumstances under which I met her but certainly I feel protective toward her."

Coeur spread out his hands in a questioning gesture. "Why are you so emphatic about it?"

"Surely there are better ways of meeting the situation—if it ever arises. Is the favor of the King worth saving at such a price?"

Coeur laid a hand on the other's arm. "It's not favor for myself which concerns me. You are honorable and patriotic, Robin. Will you acknowledge me to be the same?"

"You've given convincing proofs of your patriotism. And I know you to be the most honorable of men."

An even greater gravity manifested itself on the faec of the Moneyman. "It's regrettable that sometimes you must do things as a minister of the state which you wouldn't do as a man. When a certain step, which may be harmful for individuals, is best for the state of the nation, there can be no holding back. I have to do many things, Robin, which gall me bitterly. I don't need to tell you that there can be no recovery or prosperity for France, no happiness for her people, until the invaders are driven out. The King must be held in line! It's not only necessary to finish the war but to provide our sick and bleeding country with strong leadership through the first years of peace. Can we allow personal feelings to sway us in this all-important matter?"

"That much I grant you——"

"Listen to me! When Agnes Sorel dies, the King will fall under the spell of Antoinette de Maignelais—unless his fancy is directed elsewhere. The succession so far is in her hands—her selfish, grasping, cruel hands. She's committed to the other party, to men who will use her influence with the King to get power and wealth for themselves." He remained silent for several moments and then burst out with, "That must not happen!"

D'Arlay did not answer. His mind was occupied with the reflections natural to one who, realizing himself in love, is faced with a danger to the object of his devotion. The Moneyman went on by asking him a question.

"You see dishonor in the course I propose?"

"I shrink from the thought of it, Jacques!"

"Have you been blaming Agnes Sorel all these years?"

D'Arlay shook his head with some reluctance. "I must acknowledge that I've always had the deepest respect for her."

"Then it's clear that you are not being consistent. I'm prepared to strive for the salvation of France by any means whatever rather than to stand aside in scrupulous delicacy and see my country suffer. In matters of state the result justifies the means. I firmly believe it was fate brought this girl here. Why otherwise should a seemingly perfect instrument be delivered into my hands at this moment?"

"But the girl herself——"

"The girl may not have the capacity or the will for the part. That is still to be determined. And, of course, there's always the probability that she'll refuse to try."

"When anyone has lived the kind of life she has," declared D'Arlay, after a moment of uneasy reflection, "they can't be blamed if they accept such a chance."

Coeur regarded him steadily for the moment. "The aristocrat in you prompted that," he said. Then he asked a question, "Could France have been united under Charles if there had been no Jeanne d'Arc?"

D'Arlay frowned in a puzzled way. "Certainly. It was Dunois who commanded the army and saved Orléans."

"And is that view generally held in court circles and among the nobility?"

"Yes. You know it is."

Coeur leaned forward and began to speak in a tone of the greatest earnestness. "It's different with the people of France. They hold the Maid in the deepest reverence. They speak her name in whispers. She is the saviour of the country, a heroine, a saint, the one figure in history above reproach or blame. Someday all of France will come to see her in that light. Even the nobility, unlikely though that may seem now. Someday, perhaps, the whole world."

"We seem to be talking at cross-purposes."

"I've been leading up to this: if the girl accepts the proposal I may make her, it will be because of the inspiration of the Maid, because she also wants to serve her country. She won't see it as a chance to improve her lot."

"I had no intent to speak ill of her. On the contrary, I—I have a fondness for her. But I still believe the idea an impossible one. How could you hope to fit her for the part? And, if you succeeded, would the King stoop so low?"

"The King's infatuation for the original is so great that I'm sure he would be happy with a copy. We mustn't overlook the possibility that she has good blood, derived perhaps from the Sorels. Failing that, I can provide a pedigree for her while she's being made over. A pleasant little fiction can be arranged to cover the point."

"Are you prepared to go to such lengths as that? Kings don't enjoy being duped."

"If the King found her to his liking, he would be eager himself to supply the lack of a fitting pedigree. But why balk at obstacles we may never meet? I promise you one thing: any scheme I commit myself to will be so carefully prepared that it will stand the most hostile scrutiny."

D'Arlay tossed both arms in the air with a gesture of resignation. "What more can I say? Will it avail anything to point out that changing her into a lady will be a task possible only to someone who knows the ways of the court? Can you find such a person? Do you dare let another into such a dangerous secret?"

"As to that, I have a plan in my mind already."

D'Arlay said nothing more. After a few moments of silence the Moneyman leaned over and placed a hand on his companion's shoulder. His manner and the tone of his voice when he spoke seemed to beg for understanding. "Do you think I'm happy about this? My good gossip Robin, you must know this Jacques Coeur well enough to realize that he has no more liking for the plan than you have. The need to find a substitute for the Lady Agnes—— Robin, it's like a sword thrust in my heart. I still nurse a slender hope that the physician's report will prove wrong. But until such time as we know for certain, we must prepare for the worst. We must be ready to play for a big stake, the biggest stake of all—the saving of France!"

A still longer silence ensued. D'Arlay could not say, "I love her and so you must give up this scheme." He could not say it for a number of reasons. Time might prove that his interest in her had been temporary; but even if it were certain that his devotion would never lessen, he still could not say it. Only matrimonial intentions would give him the right to interfere further, and marriage was out of the question.

Both men were relieved when Nicolas came in with candles. As he placed one on the table beside his master, he asked in a grumbling tone, "What am I to do about the Scot?"

Coeur looked across the low oak screen. The anteroom was empty. "He seems to have lost patience and gone."

"He has lost patience, master, but he hasn't gone. He wasn't able to find his way back here. I heard he was making a disturbance in the Spicerie but by the time I got there he had wandered on to the Horsegear. I found him at last in Mortars, Pestles, and Pots. He demands two things, master: to see you at once and to know what has happened to the girl."

"I'll talk to him now."

When the servant had left, D'Arlay said in an urgent tone, "I strongly advise that the Scot be kept in ignorance of this rash plan."

Coeur laughed easily. "I've no intention of telling him anything. Beyond my promise to obtain a command for him with the guns, he'll have to be content with a few friendly words and perhaps a small purse of gold."

This assurance did not entirely allay D'Arlay's fears. "Did you know he had his own band of Free Companions?"

"I'm not surprised."

D'Arlay frowned uneasily. "He seems to be acting as her guardian and I'm not sure you can satisfy him as easily as that. Much as I shrink from what you have in mind, I don't want to see any trouble come of it. It might be wise if I took him along with me. I have plenty of room and Helion has a leg of lamb on the fire and a roast train[1] big enough for three. I suggest this because it will be necessary to keep an eye on the fellow."

"An excellent idea. I'll talk to him for a few minutes and then turn

[1] A batter of flour and wine flavored with ginger and sugar and baked about the meats.

him over to you." The Moneyman looked up at a huge clock on the wall over his head. It was marked off into the twenty-four hours and the hand was hovering over the fifteenth. "I should have been at the Louvre long before this. A full day's work awaits me there."

6

D'ARLAY did not regard Paris with the eyes of his king. He loved the city. He loved it so much that he forgot the things weighing on his mind as he and the Scot made their way toward his house in the Rue Grenier sur L'Eau. He nodded his head at the tangle of spires against the skyline. "It's unfortunate," he said, "that there has never been a poet capable of interpreting the spirit of Paris."

"I'm not a poet but I can do that for you. And in a very few words. The spirit of Paris is made up of bombast and insolence. Not to mention thievery."

"That comes in poor grace from the mouth of an alien," said D'Arlay angrily.

"I have fought and bled for France and yet in this city dirty little ur-chins shout 'Tug-mutton!' after me. When I stop at an inn, I am under-fed and overcharged. Women take one look at the tartan around my neck and turn away."

"Paris," declared D'Arlay, in resentment of these criticisms, "is so fine a city that even the smell of its streets, which is most peculiarly rank and penetrating, is like incense in my nostrils. The spirit of Paris is made up of wisdom, sparkle, irreverence, abandon, fortitude, and rebellion."

Kennedy was not to be put down. "All kindliness has gizzened out of Paris like water from a cask in the sun."

They came shortly thereafter to a spot in the town where an inn, tower-ing high above its sign which bore the name *La Galimafrée*, faced on the dilapidated sheds of a market. The space between was filled with men staring up at a balcony on the front of the tavern, which, at the moment, was empty.

There was a great deal of loud talk going on. "It's said," one of the watchers was remarking as they drew abreast, "that he took his battle-ax and sliced the flesh from the ribs of Don Guzman as evenly as a butcher cutting chops." A dissenting voice said, "But he's a Burgundian." That brought a quick answer. "And can't we, as Frenchmen, be proud of a Burgundian?"

Drawing on the resources of his own tongue, Kennedy demanded to know what all this *curfuffle* was about.

"I think," answered D'Arlay, "it has to do with the great Jacques de Lalain."

There was a stir at this moment, occasioned by the opening of the door at the back of the balcony. A tall knight sauntered out and waved a careless hand to the crowd assembled below.

"There he is, the greatest champion in the world," said D'Arlay. "I met him once and it was like talking to a battle-ax equipped with a small brain and a huge pride. He spends all his time traveling about and seeking new opponents to kill or maim." He turned to his companion. "Jacques Coeur said a very true thing once, that all knights-errant are like cruel small boys who have never grown up."

Jacques de Lalain was a powerful young animal, both tall enough and broad enough to make the squire, who had followed him out on the balcony, seem small by comparison. He was dressed in white from head to foot, with enormous tufted sleeves and an ermine cloak tossed over one shoulder with an affectation of carelessness. A nose like the beak of a parrot arched out from between eyes of an opaque blue. His hair was dark and straight, falling full-bottomed to his shoulders.

He advanced to the railing and looked about him with a smile of amused pride. "Ha, scum of Paris!" he called. "You've come to see Jacques de Lalain. Well, look at me closely. You will never see me again. You will never see me in the lists, canaille of Paris. Your brave knights have prudently abstained from taking up the cartel of defiance I sent on in advance." He stared about him with mounting arrogance. "I am the greatest fighter in all Christendom! I can defeat any knight born of woman with any weapon invented by man! Take one last look at me, starved and sniveling worm bait, for I shall never come back."

D'Arlay swore bitterly under his breath when the great champion withdrew out of a sight. The crowd was already scattering, well pleased, apparently, at the insulting reference to the chivalry of France. He motioned the Scot to follow him and was vigorously plowing his way to the side of the street when he heard his name called from the door of the inn. He stopped and looked back.

"The Sire d'Arlay! The Sire d'Arlay!"

"Who wants me?"

The squire responsible for the summons came out through the crowd. "My master," he said, "is sitting down to supper and begs the honor of your company."

D'Arlay asked in a tone of surprise, "Did your master see me from up there?"

"An eagle," said the squire with an intolerable air of pride, "can spot its prey in the air at a distance of a thousand feet. Is there reason for surprise when Jacques de Lalain recognizes the Sire d'Arlay at a mere twenty yards?"

"Convey my respects to your master and say that the Sire d'Arlay regrets his inability to accept. I have a friend who accompanies me to my own house for supper."

"My master said the bidding included the Scot if needs be."

Kennedy grinned. "He can pick out a tartan at twenty yards also, it seems."

The two recipients of the invitation looked questioningly at each other. D'Arlay whispered, "It might be interesting to watch the ravening boar of Burgundy at his feeding."

"Aye," said the Scot. "I wouldn't be above making my boasts that I had broken bread into the gravy with Jacques de Lalain."

D'Arlay turned to the squire. "Our thanks, then, to your master and say we'll join him as soon as we have washed and set our clothing in order. Warn him that by comparison with his own grandeur of raiment his guests will seem like plucked crows."

The squire belched indifferently. "They always do, my lord."

2

Jacques de Lalain received them in a room back of the balcony in which a table had already been spread for supper. He had dismissed his followers with the exception of one servant and was sprawled out in a chair, his massive white-clad legs spread wide for comfort. He got slowly and reluctantly to his feet.

"Robinet de Burey, Sire d'Arlay," he said with a stiff bow. "I'm happy to see you again. And this is the Scot? His name does not matter. This is most fortunate, as now I needn't sup in solitude."

"It's fortunate indeed, my Lord de Lalain," said D'Arlay, bowing in turn. He scrutinized his host's face closely, saying to himself, "There is something noble about him and yet his is the cruelest face I've ever seen."

The supper which the servant proceeded to serve had been chosen with discrimination. There was a loined sole, the very best of all fish, served with a white sauce in which the appetizing tang of porret predominated. This was followed by an unlaced mallard, and then the main dish appeared, a roast kid with flutings of ribbon around the tail. At the finish there arrived a rich *hastelet* of figs, raisins, and dates, cooked together and served with a gilding of egg yolks. D'Arlay watched this procession of noble dishes with inward pride. "I would like to tell him," he thought, "that only in Paris, and certainly never in his native Burgundy, could a meal like this be served."

Their host monopolized the conversation, speaking in a voice which seemed surprisingly thin to issue from a frame of such huge proportions. He confined himself to his own exploits, the antagonists he had worsted in single combat, the plans he had for future jousts. Once only did he deviate from this saga of self-glorification. Pausing to look his guest over, he remarked on the lack of resemblance between D'Arlay and his elder brother who had been at the French court when De Lalain had last visited there.

"The Comte is a mally old gossip," he said. "He made me laugh at some of his jibes—an indulgence I seldom allow myself. His lovely Lady

Isabeau"—the opaque eyes turned back questingly to D'Arlay—"reminded me of a fair creature—Spanish, as it happens—whose favor I carried on my lance when I fought Don Guzman in Castile a few months agone. But before I beguile your ears with the details of that pleasant little affair, I must pay tribute to the fair Comtesse. I consider her far more lovely actually than my little Spanish spark. She approaches the years when the flower of beauty begins to crisp on the stem but . . . Well, Sire d'Arlay, I confess to a liking for the tang of maturity."

"My fair sister-in-law," said D'Arlay, speaking in a carefully casual tone, "is most charming."

"Your good opinion of her was made known to me. You are not married, Sire d'Arlay?"

"No. I have no wife."

"Nor I." The Burgundian indulged in one of his admittedly rare laughs. "But for a different reason, I think."

D'Arlay felt a wave of resentment rising in him. He said to himself, "There's insolence in every word he utters." His distaste grew as he observed the exaggerated manners of his host: the ceremonious elevation of the goblet to a level with his closed eyes whenever he took a sip of wine as though drinking a silent pledge; the fastidious manipulation of spoon and knife; the regal gesture for silence before he began to speak.

"As I said out there, there are no champions in France who dare meet me," proclaimed De Lalain, going back to the topic which interested him most. "Now I must go to Scotland, to England, perhaps even to Italy, to find opponents worthy of me."

"The knights of France," said D'Arlay, "disregarded your challenge on the order of the King."

Jacques de Lalain snorted. "A brave lot of toy knights to hide behind a royal proclamation."

D'Arlay found his dislike growing every moment. When he spoke, however, it was in a casual tone. "The King is striving to prevent dueling as he will need every loyal subject with him when he renews the war." He replaced his wine goblet and looked at his host. "Why not fight with the knights of France instead of against them? You are a Burgundian, of course, and your duke may not share in the campaign. But the English are hard and shrewd fighters and we'll need all the strength we can muster. If Jacques de Lalain rode under the lilies of France, it would stimulate our men to greater exertion."

With a delicate gesture the Burgundian crushed *pimpernel aromatisante* into his goblet and then motioned to the servingman to fill it with wine. He took a deep sip before answering.

"I've no intention of serving with the French Army," he said.

There was a moment of silence and then D'Arlay said, "I confess that this is a surprise to me."

"Your feeling in the matter is of no importance. But if you want the reason, I'll strive to make you understand."

"I," said D'Arlay, "shall strive to follow your reasoning."

The knight-errant drew his ermine cloak around both his shoulders. The fire on the hearth was dying down and a chill had settled on the room. He motioned the servant to leave.

"I disapprove of the use of cannon," said De Lalain. "It's said you plan to make much use of these fire-spitting tubes called bombards. It's a sorry thing that war will no longer be an honorable meeting between brave knights with Almighty God as the arbiter." He turned his pale and expressionless eyes on his guest. "I can't fight for a country which resorts to black magic."

"The bombards," said D'Arlay quietly, "will be our answer to the magic of the English longbow."

The Burgundian brushed this aside. "I may tell you that my sympathies are with France. The English have been overlong on this side of the Channel and the time is ripe to drive them back to their own barbarous island. But I swear to you," he cried with sudden vehemence, "I would rather see you lose every battle than win by any means save by the might of the chivalry of France!"

D'Arlay stirred impatiently in his chair. "We can't drive the English from Normandy by losing battles," he said.

"You are of noble blood, Sire d'Arlay, and it should not be necessary for me to explain what I mean. The result of a battle is not the important thing. All that counts is the way it is fought. I hold firmly to the belief, as all good knights should, that God awards the victory to the side which strives most bravely and in accordance with the Code of Chivalry."

D'Arlay was finding it increasingly hard to hold his feelings in check. "It's that kind of thinking," he said, "which has cost France a hundred years of defeat and suffering."

"I'm a bombardier of some note," declared Kennedy, speaking for the first time since the supper had started, "and I tell you now, Sir Knight, that the guns will clear a way to the Channel with the greatest ease."

Jacques de Lalain did not deign to look at the Scot. "You're not a knight and my invitation to join us did not include the privilege of taking part in our talk." He turned to D'Arlay with a shrug of his padded shoulders. "I've no intention of disputing with you the principles of honorable warfare." He frowned and twirled his goblet as though reluctant to proceed with what he had to say. "I had a purpose in asking you to sup with me tonight. Your brother told me you were associated in some obscure manner with this greedy merchant who has put a spell on your king. I've heard also that your Jacques Coeur is the one who is urging the use of bombards. I must ask you to do something for me, to go to the Fox with a message." He shoved his goblet aside with a movement which indicated distaste for this necessity. "I have a cousin, Alain de Kersai. He has taken the vows of knighthood and is a goodly enough lad, though not capable physically of winning much glory for himself. I had intended making a place for him in the company I'll take with me to Scotland or on such other travels as I may decide upon." He paused and regarded D'Arlay with a frown which carried a suggestion of incredulity. "You'll find what

I must now tell you hard to believe. Alain has refused! The little fool is set on serving with the bombards. I have talked to him, I have reasoned with him, I have even made threats. He remains obdurate. I'm asking you, therefore, to say to Jacques Coeur that he must not allow Alain to join. He must help me in saving the boy from this great disgrace."

"It's no disgrace," said D'Arlay. He was keeping his eyes fixed on the table in front of him. "If we win the war, it will be by the use of the cannon you affect to despise. Your cousin could find no better way to serve."

"I've tried to consider Alain's youth and not judge him too harshly. His place is with me. Serving cannon is fit only for common men, blacksmiths and such."

"I'm thinking of serving under Jean Bureau myself," said D'Arlay.

The Burgundian settled back in his chair with a laugh. "I see now I made a mistake in thinking you might act as my advocate. My first impression of you was unfavorable, Sire d'Arlay. I should have realized that one who associates with the Fox would have no spark of knightly honor in him. Well, I must go to Jacques Coeur. Or I may take my case to the King himself. I shall demand that the boy be sent home." The face of the Burgundian suddenly became white with passion. "I've an affection for Alain, but I tell you, Sire d'Arlay, I would rather see him dead, and by my own hand if need be, than consorting with common men and—and noblemen who forget the obligations of their class."

"You would get no satisfaction from the King."

"I am sure," declared the Burgundian, "that the King of France would think twice before refusing a reasonable request from me. I am Jacques de Lalain, the greatest champion in all Christendom. My wishes are not to be disregarded."

It was no longer possible for D'Arlay to contain himself. "You are Jacques de Lalain, the greatest champion in Christendom!" he cried. "True. But you are also a fool, a blind and stupid fool! It's the duty of all patriotic men to see that our country is no longer shackled by such folly as you are preaching!"

Jacques de Lalain shoved back his chair and rose slowly to his feet. He rested his powerful hands on the edge of the table and stared down at his companion with the eagerness of a tomcat when an unwary mouse ventures out within reach of his claws.

"Robinet de Burey, Sire d'Arlay!" he said. "You have insulted me, grossly and wantonly. You're no fit opponent for me but the words you have spoken can be answered in one way only. I demand satisfaction."

"Satisfaction shall be yours."

The Burgundian looked at him in a kind of wonder, as though he had expected some effort to seek an escape by qualification of what had been said. D'Arlay had risen in his turn. Now that his first wave of anger had passed, he realized he had placed his life in jeopardy. "What chance will you have against this butcher?" he said to himself. "He will cut you to pieces with the greatest ease."

"I can fight only with men whose family lines show nobility for at least four generations on each side," said the Burgundian, willing perhaps to find a flaw in the D'Arlay genealogy.

"The De Burey family goes back more generations than most noble knights can count," answered D'Arlay. "My mother, as you may know, was Amalie de Mailly. Can you match that?"

The two men stared at each other for several moments in silence. Then an engraged flush took possession of the Burgundian's face and he gripped the handle of his sword. His anger was so great, in fact, that his enormous sleeves gave the impression of being puffed out by it.

"I was willing to give you a chance to withdraw," he said, with a snort. "You've disregarded it and now the issue between us can only be settled on the field of honor."

"I suggest we take our seats again," said D'Arlay, suddenly conscious of the fact that his legs were trembling. "We can at least make our arrangements in comfort. Now, I propose that first of all we explore the provisions of the Code of Chivalry bearing on this situation."

"The provisions," declared De Lalain, seating himself and raising his wineglass to take a long draught, "are explicit and to the point."

"They're not as simple as you seem to believe. As it happens, I know the Code as well as you do. Permit me to point out that the intent of the Code is to provide as much equality as possible where opponents are of unequal prowess. You, the greatest knight in Christendom, will concede that an inequality exists between us. That consideration will enter into the choice of weapons."

"The offended party has the choice of weapons. I am the offended party."

"On the contrary, it was you who provoked the quarrel between us."

The Burgundian raised an impatient hand. "Spare me your arguments. I'm not a lawyer. I fight with good and honorable steel and not with crafty words. You insulted me to my face as this fellow will attest. The choice rests with me."

D'Arlay realized that his life depended on the resolving of this point. "The giving of offense," he said, "is not always a matter of words spoken. The real incitement to a quarrel may consist in an overt act, a hostile look, even in a state of mind. You, Jacques de Lalain, have given mortal offense to me. From the moment I entered this room you showed contempt in every word you spoke. There was a rancid pride in the very curl of your nostril. The views you expressed were an insult to every man of French birth."

"The fact remains you spoke the words."

"If we cannot agree, what course do you propose? To carry the issue to a Court of Honor?"

The Burgundian snorted again. "If necessary."

"Then," said D'Arlay, "let us consider some other words which have been spoken this evening. You openly scoffed at the bravery and prowess of the knights of France. What would be the ruling of a Court of Honor on these open taunts?"

The quickness with which the Burgundian turned to look at his table companion was proof that his complacency had received a jolt.

"I spoke in general terms."

"That makes it worse. You reflected on the courage of the whole knightly body. Give a thought to the consequences before you take the decision outside this room."

Jacques de Lalain squirmed in his chair like a sulky schoolboy thwarted in some pet desire. It was several moments before he broke the silence. "What weapon would you select?"

D'Arlay answered quickly, "My sword."

The Burgundian broke into a loud and confident laugh. "The sword?" he cried. "Don't you realize I am the best swordsman in all the world?"

"My own sword," amended D'Arlay. "You would fight with one of the same weight, length, and shape."

The exuberance of De Lalain's mood subsided slightly. He said sharply, "Let me see it, if you please."

D'Arlay detached the weapon from his belt and laid it on the table. His opponent got to his feet and picked it up, touching an exploring finger to the point before hefting it with expert intentness.

"It's a curious one," he said. "Where did you get it?"

"This type of sword comes from the East originally. This particular blade reached me from Spain."

"I've never seen one quite like it," grumbled De Lalain. "It has a womanish blade but the point is keen."

"It will be used without armor of any kind."

"Ha, there would be conditions! I might have expected it. I can see that a shrewd thrust, or perchance a lucky one, would drive the point clear through a man's body." He gave D'Arlay a suspicious glance. "There is method in your suggestion. This begins to smack of trickery and I care little for the smell of it."

"The advantage would still rest with you. You have asserted your supremacy in the use of all weapons."

"I've never before held a sword such as this in my hand."

The Burgundian gave a quick cut at the air to test the balance of the blade. Then he raised the hilt and squinted at the tiny inscription in Arabic. It undoubtedly would have added to his misgivings had he been able to decipher the words.

Inalienably bequeathed by Alassir-al-Asmeed. May hostile hand that touches this steel wither and rot at the wrist.

"It may be you have a special skill in the use of this tricky blade," he said, after a moment.

D'Arlay nodded. "I have skill with it," he said. "It's the only weapon I use."

"I won't be fluddered into the choice of it!" The Burgundian threw the sword back on the table. "I find I've no will to fight you like a mincing master of arms."

"Then," said D'Arlay, "we must leave the matter to a Court of Honor."

De Lalain scowled. "I give you this as my last word: Leave the selection to chance; toss a coin in the air and abide by the result."

It was D'Arlay's turn to hesitate. An urgent thought hammered in his mind, "If you lose, you will surely die!" He said aloud, "It's only with the sword that we could fight with any reasonable degree of equality."

The Burgundian refused to move from the stand he had taken. He repeated stubbornly, "Let it rest on the toss of a coin."

Kennedy, who had been turning back and forth from one to the other and breathing hard with excitement, plucked at D'Arlay's sleeve and whispered in his ear, "By St. Andrew, you'll sign your own death warrant if you give in to this butcher!"

D'Arlay whispered back, "He will proclaim me a coward if I dispute the point any longer. I was rash enough to get myself into this quarrel and now I must face the consequences."

There was a moment of silence and then D'Arlay said loudly: "In God's name, let it be as you demand! Toss the coin!"

De Lalain drew a piece of gold from his purse and held it up. "An English noble of Harry Fift'. A great king and an honorable fighter. I claim the side with the King's head, D'Arlay. You may have the other with the Cross and arches trefoil. Is it agreed?"

"Agreed."

"I'm not content with a mere toss of the coin," declared the greatest knight in Christendom. "There are fingers nimble enough to throw this noble clear to the ceiling and still control the way it will fall. You consort with tricky company, D'Arlay, so I insist on doing it the Burgundian way. I'll spin the coin in the air and you'll catch it in a flute glass of good red Burgundian wine. You hand it to me and I turn it upside down. Then we shall see what the god of chance has decided."

"Agreed."

D'Arlay rose to his feet, resting his weight against the table. His whole body was trembling. The Burgundian, his face shining with excitement, gave the coin a preliminary toss, catching it on his wrist. He looked at the exposed face. "The King!" he cried exultantly. "There's an augury to give you pause! Come, D'Arlay, the goblet. Is your hand steady enough to hold it without spilling the wine?"

He threw the noble high into the air. D'Arlay, clutching the goblet in both hands, caught the spinning yellow disk in the wine. It required an effort of will to keep his hands steady as he handed it over to his opponent. The Burgundian turned it upside down on the table and the spilled wine spread out over the cloth in a widening stain.

"Lift it, lift it, my doughty antagonist!" cried De Lalain, almost dancing in his eagerness. "Which will we find staring up at us, the King or the Cross? The King, I swear; and, if it is, you will die miserably under the blows of my battle-ax. Come, are you afraid to look?"

D'Arlay reached out a hand and raised the goblet. He did not venture a look at the yellow noble resting on the red stain and his first intimation of the result came from the silence of his opponent and an exultant laugh from Pregent Kennedy.

"The Cross!" said De Lalain, in an angry voice. "By the Moine Bourru, it's the Cross!"

D'Arlay looked then. An intense relief flooded over him. "Never have I seen a more gratifying pattern inscribed on minted gold!" he said to himself. "An arched molding and a Cross potent. God has decreed I am to have a fair chance."

"I claim a delay," said the Burgundian sulkily. "I must have time to find another plaything like this and to train myself in the use of it. You'll have that much longer to live, D'Arlay." He scowled. "You will hear from me when I'm ready."

"Agreed," said D'Arlay.

"And now," said D'Arlay, when he and his companion found themselves again in the street, "we shall seek the comfort and security of the Rue Grenier sur L'Eau. I confess to a weariness both of mind and body."

The Scot snorted indignantly. "There will be no rest for you for another hour at least." He laid a commanding hand on D'Arlay's shoulder. "I know an arms master here in Paris, one Gaspard Soullaine, who has the best hand with the sword I've ever seen in action. You will be in need of his services, my lord, if you're to get yourself into proper condition to meet this great bully and braggart."

"I'm sure," said D'Arlay stiffly, "that I could teach your arms master some things about the use of the sword."

"When Jacques de Lalain summons you to battle," said the Scot earnestly, "he will have acquired so much skill with this piece of lath that he will be as hard to resist as a blustering wind from the north. Come! Gaspard's place is a half hour's walk from here. We must see him tonight and engage his services."

7

VALERIE went to bed in a such a confused state of mind that the only impression she got of her bedroom was of its terrifying grandeur. She roused next morning when the first light of dawn came through the windows. Wide awake at once, she was gratefully conscious of the softness of the bed on which she lay. She gave a low exclamation of wonder over the coverlet which was embroidered in blue and gold with a most curious device: the heart and shell which, as she learned later, was the Coeur insigne. The bed was an enormous one with a canopy above, and immediately under the canopy a shelf for books, and attached to the shelf a bag filled with aromatic herbs. There was a candlestick on a table and it was at least two feet high and as big around as her wrist.

She lay perfectly still for several minutes, thinking of what had happened the day before and wondering what plans were hatching in the mind of the owner of this huge stone building. "What a strange man!" she said to herself. "His eyes seem to burn. I know he's kind in spite of all his sharpness and the way he hurries. How I wish I knew what he has in mind to do with me!" She was certain of one thing: that all this mystery had to do with the problem of her parentage. Jacques Coeur had known at first glance whom she resembled and had assisted the Sire d'Arlay to the same knowledge. What else could it mean?

"Today," she said aloud, sitting up in bed and nodding her head emphatically, "I shall learn who I am."

Her thoughts went from there to the Sire d'Arlay and became firmly anchored. This second encounter with him had confirmed the impressions she had carried away from the first. He was not handsome and he had none of the airs and affected manners she associated with highest gentility, but in spite of that she had no doubt at all that he was a great gentleman. He was showing himself just as kind as he had during that long evening when they labored together at the fashioning of the coffin and she had confided to him so much about herself. She thought, with a surge of pride, "He likes me!" It was gratifying and exciting to know that he liked her even though she had made no serious effort to define for herself how she felt about him.

Her thoughts came back to the beauty and wonder of this room. She studied the *prie-dieu* against one wall. It was tall and had panels of red needlepoint. There was a bench piled up luxuriantly with velvet cushions, a carved chest with massive bronze hinges, a crucifix with so much compassion depicted on the face that her own eyes filled with tears. She measured the width of the bed with an incredulous eye and decided that as many as five people could sleep in it. "How fine to have it all to oneself and be able to stretch right out!" She had always been cramped as to sleeping space, in the Maret tent and in malodorous rooms in taverns. In fact, there had been for her something mean and furtive about slumber, a need to dress and undress hurriedly and under a certain constant inspection.

She threw back the covers and set herself to test the width by rolling across the bed. She accomplished six revolutions safely but the seventh projected her over the side. She landed on the floor with a loud thump.

She was on the point of raising herself, rather ruefully, when her eyes fixed themselves on a pair of shoes beside a chair. They were unbelievably lovely. The leather was soft and of a shade of green which suggested spring and the first foliage on the trees. The tops were turned back to reveal an inside lining of soft white material. The greatest glory of these amazing shoes, however, was the presence of a bow of yellow velvet on the instep of each.

She lay still and looked at them, not fully trusting the evidence of her eyes. Something was wrong! She had put her clothes the night before on this particular chair and had deposited her own shoes beside it, thinking at the time how out of place they looked. What had happened?

Slowly she raised her eyes, finding further food for surprise at each stage of the elevation. The chair was covered with clothes, but not the old and somewhat bedraggled objects she had left there before getting into bed. All her own clothing was gone and in its stead was a complete new outfit!

She sprang to her feet. She was shivering now, as much from excitement as the fact that, according to custom, she had slept naked.

"They must be for me!" she cried, in an ecstatic tone. She lifted with reverent fingers the tunic which was silk and of the same soft green as the shoes. "How lovely! These things are fine enough for a lady to wear."

She hesitated over donning the clothes, but another glance about the room convinced her that it was a case of taking this new outfit or not dressing at all. There were no signs of the worn garments she had discarded the night before.

First she picked up a linen kirtle which was intended for use next to the skin. It was quite plain but so cool that she shivered with delight at the first touch of it. The tunic came next and it fitted her perfectly, with a high waist and a rather daringly low bodice and tight sleeves diapered with gold at the wrists. She found, somewhat to her surprise, that it emitted a rustling sound with every move she made, as though the gown itself had feelings and was expressing its gratification over the fitting use to which it was being put. Then came the hose, which were of such finely spun white wool that she was able to mold them closely and neatly to her legs. Last of all came the shoes, and she marveled at the comfort of them in spite of the snugness of the fit.

There was a hat as well, a breath-taking hat of yellow velvet with an edging of the green. She held it up on one finger and knew it to be perfect.

Her mind was racing excitedly. "Who can I be," she asked herself, "that he thinks me worthy of such costly things?"

The tall stone building was coming to life. Valerie could hear footsteps in the halls and voices raised sharply in admonition and instruction. She went out on the landing of the narrow inside stairway and stared down. There was evidence of considerable activity below and curiosity took possession of her. Here was a chance to see at close range the inside of this fabulous shop. She began to descend.

She was conscious at once of strange and beguiling odors, heavy, rich, mysterious. Spices from the East! She glimpsed through an open door a long room with metal bins extending along both sides and, as the odors were almost overpowering here, she concluded this was the spice store-room. Through other doors she caught glimpses of rare things—beautiful furniture and shining armor and, most interesting of all to her, the sheen of colored materials draped over tall frames. A clerk, with a sheet of paper in his hand, passed her on the stairs at a running gait. She heard him hesitate and then stop; and she knew that he had turned and was watching her, and wondering, no doubt, who she could be.

On each floor she encountered oldish men and women, all of them attired in gray with a red heart on one arm, who were plying brooms and otherwise setting the place in order for the day's trading. One of the women, a sharp-faced crone, stopped sweeping as she passed and stared at her with eyes sunk far back in her wrinkled mask of a face.

"I saw you last e'en when you came," whispered the woman. "You wore a ragged chammer cloak then, my girl."

Valerie tried to brush by but the crone gripped her by the elbow. "What a pretty little *garce* you are! I could tell you things to your profit if you were of a mind to listen to old Dame Trix." The woman glanced about her furtively and then made a gesture with one finger crooked above the rest. "Do you know the meaning of that? It's the sign of the Coquille. You know what *that* is!"

"No," said Valerie, who was becoming frightened. "I'm from the country and I know nothing of Paris."

"You've brought yourself to the right market, my small one. I've been able to set many girls from the country in the way of neat profits." The hoarse voice of the old woman dropped still lower. "Now don't try to tell me you've never heard of the King of the Coquillards."

"I know of one king only," faltered Valerie. She had heard a great deal, as had everyone, about this organization which extended all over France. It was particularly strong in Paris where, she knew, the head of the order lived in hidden splendor. At the moment, however. she had one thought in her head only: to get away from this evil old creature.

"Ha!" grunted the crone. "*This* king rules the best subjects in Paris. Bold rufflers, with gold in their *pilles* and ready to spend it all on pretty girls like you. Vendenguns and mercerots and king-davids, who know how to please the ladies as well as pick locks." She nodded her head on its palsied stalk of neck. "If you want a man like that, my lively sprig, you come to me. Ask for Dame Trix. That's all, just Dame Trix. And"—leering with sudden malice—"if you have any regard for your baby face, you'll keep a still mouth about what I've said."

Valerie pulled herself free of the clutching fingers and ran blindly down a dark passage. The desire to get away filled her mind so completely that when she came to a door at one end of the hall, she opened it without thinking. The room in which she found herself seemed familiar to her at once. It had whitewashed walls and many windows through which the light of the early morning sun was beginning to shine. A low oak screen closed off the section in which she stood and beyond it she saw a man hard at work before a table. He looked up at the sound of the closing door and she saw it was Jacques Coeur.

"Good morning, my child," he said, smiling. "I seem to have been successful in the selection of clothes for you. And how pleasant it is to find that you're an early riser! I didn't expect to see you as soon as this. But here you are and there isn't anyone about yet to disturb us. This will be the best time for us to have our talk."

2

The Moneyman had discarded his outer tunic for greater comfort and facility in working and had turned down the collar of his smock. This gave a full view of his neck, which was brown and muscular, an entirely adequate pedestal for his impressive head. His leggings were scarlet on one half and green on the other, as she could see now that he had risen. He had kicked off his shoes and they lay on the floor beside his chair. They looked surprisingly small for a man of his robust proportions. The gold tassels on their upturned green tips would have appeared foppish to anyone not accustomed to the supreme elegance of the day.

"Come!" said Coeur to the girl who was so abashed at the mistake which had brought her into his presence that she had not ventured beyond the door. "Come over here and sit down. I have a hundred questions to ask you."

When she took a chair beside his table, he subjected her to a close scrutiny. Then he nodded his head in approval. "If I had entertained any doubts before, they would now be swept away. You look so much like—— But that I must leave until later."

It had been no exaggeration when he said he had a hundred questions to ask. He drew out the story of her life, eliciting more information than D'Arlay had secured in his talks with her. He was like a lawyer with a witness on the stand before him. Leaning forward so that no expression of hers escaped him, he shot his questions at her so rapidly that she was in much the same position as a French soldier when arrows from the English archers rained about him; and, if the truth must be told, with some of the same need to be wary.

When he had satisfied himself about her history, he began on questions of a more general nature.

"If I gave you a royal d'or, what would you do with it?"

"A royal d'or!" It was clear she was startled by the mere mention of such a princely coin. "I've never even seen one, my lord."

"All the better. What would you do with so much wealth?"

Valerie gave serious thought to the point. "I would have it changed into the smallest coins, even *rouges liards*, my lord. I would make sure the reckoning was in *Parisis* and not *Tournois* so that I wouldn't be cheated. Then I would put the coins away in many places, never more than two in one place. I would never show more than one liard at a time and no one would suspect me of having so much."

Coeur nodded his head approvingly before going on to the next question. "Suppose you had a choice to make. Let us say, between a Bible, a gold chain, and a bolt of the best camelot cloth. Which would you take?"

"The bolt of camelot cloth, my lord," she said without hesitation.

"I didn't expect you to say that. Can you tell me what guided you in making your selection?"

The girl said to herself with a trace of inner alarm, "Have I given the wrong answer?" After further thought she began on her explanation. "I would treasure a Bible above everything. But, my lord, I can't read and never expect to be able to. Would it be right, then, for me to have a Bible? There are so very few of them and it would be sinful to waste one on me. It would do so much more good in the hands of people who could read it."

"That," said Coeur, nodding, "is sound reasoning. You would be wrong to choose the Bible."

"If I had a gold chain," she went on, "they would say I had stolen it and I would be put in prison. When people like us are put in prison, even if we're innocent, we're put to the torture. And after that, my lord, we are never again of much use."

"And what of the bolt of camelot cloth?"

"It could be traded for many bolts of plainer material and perhaps even a band of fur and some good beads. There could be a little money over into the bargain; but not enough to get me into any trouble. So you see, my lord, the cloth would be the practical choice."

"You've convinced me, Mademoiselle, that your choice was the right one."

His next question was projected with a suddenness that suggested he hoped to catch her off guard. "Tell me about Damian Maret. Was he a mirliton player? Did he carry the gay-horse on the stage?"

Valerie looked up indignantly. "He was a fine actor, my lord. A very fine actor. He was a musician also, of course; all actors must be able to play in case of need. But"—drawing away and raising her head proudly—"they always gave him fine parts."

"If he was a fine actor, why did you live so poorly? I'm told he didn't treat you well."

The girl found it hard to keep her indignation from showing in her voice. "He did as well for us as he could."

"Come, Mademoiselle, you're shielding him. You know full well that he was a lazy rascal. I am told also that he drank to excess. Did he beat you when he was in his cups?"

Valerie sprang to her feet. Angry tears filled her eyes. "You've been kind to me, my lord, but you've no right to speak of him in this way."

"Come, my child," said Coeur, in a placating voice. "You must not take amiss what I have said."

"If he drank," she explained, "it was because he had such bad fortune! Now that I know what you think of us, I am sure there is no need for us to talk further."

Coeur indulged in an approving laugh. It was clear that he was well pleased with the way she had responded. "Sit down, Mademoiselle. For all I know, Monsieur Maret was the greatest actor in the world and a man of rare and goodly disposition. I was testing your mettle." He nodded his head and beamed at her. "I'm glad to find you so loyal. It would have disappointed me very much had I found you meek and unready to speak up.

"Mademoiselle," he went on after a moment, "I have one more question to ask. It refers to something that happened twenty-five years ago."

Valerie's head came up with sharpened interest. "Twenty-five years ago? That was when the Maid——"

"Yes." Coeur's voice carried a reverent note. "The most important date in all the long history of France, Mademoiselle."

They looked at each other intently for several moments and then the Moneyman smiled. "You're getting a hint of my purpose, I think," he said. "Yes, my child, we now come to the point of this questioning which you have so patiently endured. You've wondered why I asked so many things which seemingly lacked all reason. It was because I had to be sure in my mind first that you had spirit and intelligence, and some common sense as well, before I went any further.

"My doubts have been resolved," he continued, nodding his head. "And now tell me what happened twenty-five years ago."

"It was then the Voices began to speak to the Maid."

"Yes, the Voices spoke in the ear of a peasant girl and told her what must be done to save France. Many in high positions in the state knew already what must be done but they lacked the power to make the King see the truth. God selected His instrument well. He chose a girl of the common people. But, unfortunately for France, Jeanne D'Arc did not live long enough to finish the work to which she was called." He paused to allow his words to have the desired effect. "Valerie, if you had lived then, and the choice had fallen on you, would you have obeyed the Voices?"

"I trust I would have had the courage to obey as the Maid did," she answered in a low voice.

"I'm sure you would. I'm sure you would have that same great faith if— if a second summons came now."

"I think, my lord, that every girl in France dreams of the chance to follow in the footsteps of the Maid."

"Would you be prepared to face the consequences, whatever they might be? Think well, Valerie Maret, before you answer. It may be that the time has come for another summons. Not a summons to ride into battle in shining armor. The miracle of Jeanne D'Arc can never be repeated. It would take a far different form, my child. There would be no glory in it, and perhaps not more than half-a-dozen people would ever know the truth. Shame and not glory might be the reward you would find." He paused before asking, "Do you want me to tell you anything more?"

The girl looked into his eyes without any hint of reservation in her own. "Yes, my lord."

"There is a long explanation I must make first. I must take you deeply into my confidence and I must have your solemn promise that nothing I tell you will ever be repeated."

"You have my promise."

He began to speak, lowering his voice instinctively as he explained the purpose which had entered his mind when he first saw her.

3

When the Moneyman completed his explanation with no more than one sentence to tell what was expected of her, "Someone must take the place of Agnes Sorel, someone with the good of France at heart, and you, Mademoiselle, are my choice," her reaction was instant and instinctive. She cried out: "No, no, my lord Coeur! You can't mean it!"

"But I do mean it."

Her face had become scarlet. "I—I'm not suited. How could I pass myself as a lady at court?"

"You could be taught. I don't think it would be very difficult to fit you for the role. You've good blood in your veins, unless all the signs are at fault. You're bright and quick. Yes, my small one, you would soon learn all the tricks and wiles of a great lady."

"But, my lord, don't you see that—that I shrink from the thought of such a life!"

"The Maid didn't shrink from the kind of life she knew was ahead of her."

"But that was different! It was glorious! She rode in white mail at the head of the armies of France. There was nothing shameful about it."

"She died a shameful death, a cruel death. She knew from the first what would come of it but she didn't draw back. But, my child, it's not my intent to urge this on you. You must think it over and decide for yourself. All I want to say is this: I have no doubts whatever that you could carry on the part Agnes Sorel has played."

Valerie turned her head away so that he could not see her face. She fixed her eyes on the nearest window through which sunlight was now pouring generously. "My lord Coeur, does it not seem strange to you that it's the Lady Agnes I resemble?"

"When we have time to investigate thoroughly we may find some blood relationship to account for it."

She kept her head lowered as though unwilling to meet his eyes while talking of such matters. "What," she asked, "would I have to do to fit myself for life at court?"

"You would need an education. It would be necessary to read and write and even cipher with figures. Just the beginnings of such things, fortunately. A lady is not supposed to read like a scholar or write like an *écrivain*; her gentility would be suspect if she did. I'm sure, my child, that everything else would come easily enough to you. Down inside yourself you are more of a lady now than many I know who were born to great estate."

"How long would it take?"

"Six months perhaps."

"And after that? I mean, if—if the plan should succeed?"

The Moneyman's eyes narrowed in calculation. "The war will be finished in less than a year. I'm ready to stake my official head that it will be short and decisive. We'll clear France of the enemy before another winter. . . . The rudder must not fall into weak hands for five years after peace comes. . . . Your age is sixteen at a guess. You could give us six years and still have all the best of your life before you."

Valerie said in a low tone, "Would there be enough years left to—to make my peace?"

Jacques Coeur's face sobered at once. Reaching out, he took possession of both her hands. "Do you believe that what I have asked you to do is a sin in the eyes of God?" he asked. "I've never taken my God out of a book nor fashioned Him in my mind from priestly words. He may be stern but He is just. He knows how much France needs peace and honest rule, how terribly her people will suffer if these are denied them any longer. Can it be sinful to help bring this about?" He pressed her hands reassuringly. "The God I know is a very wise God, understanding and human, and He would not weigh a small transgression against a great accomplishment!"

Nothing more was said for several moments. She was turning over in her mind the things he had told her, sitting meanwhile in a rigid position, hands clasped tightly in her lap, eyes on the floor.

He was distressed to see that there had been a distinct change in her appearance. Her cheeks had become pale and there was a trace of violet shadow under eyes. The resemblance had become more pronounced.

Finally she began to speak. "I must have time, my lord. I know that everything you've said must be true. And yet—and yet I can't be reconciled to what it would mean."

"You must take all the time you want."

"Must you know today?"

"No, my child. Not today. Nor tomorrow. Nor the day after that."

She sighed deeply. "Then I will think about it. I will try to conquer my feelings, but I must tell you that I don't think I shall succeed."

He reached out a hand and raised her face so that he could look into her eyes. "Take all the time you need," he repeated slowly. "You must come to your decision only after thinking it out with the greatest care—and with your heart as well as your mind. I want you to know this: if the answer is Yes, it must be reached willingly. You must be entirely sure of your readiness to make this sacrifice. Otherwise, I want your answer to be No."

She turned and walked to the door. Here she stopped and hesitated. Finally, with a suggestion of color once more in her cheeks, she came back to him.

"Does—does the Sire d'Arlay know of this?"

"I told him yesterday what I had in mind."

"Is it—is it permissible to ask what he thought of it?"

Coeur looked at her shrewdly, suspecting that this might prove a crucial point with her. He answered, however, with complete frankness, "He was against it, my child."

"May I ask why?"

"The Sire d'Arlay is a man of high ideals and great generosity. But he's not logical. When a ship is on the point of foundering, it becomes necessary to throw the cargo overboard, no matter how valuable it may be. D'Arlay knows that the ship of state is in danger of being wrecked but he would rather go down with all hands than part, for instance, with his belief that the honorable and proper thing should always be done. That is fine for him but what of the poor crew?" The Moneyman paused and smiled. "I'm fond of Robin and you mustn't think I speak of him in anger. There is this also, Mademoiselle, to account for his attitude. He likes you, and wants to spare you."

Valerie bowed. "Thank you, my lord. It was kind of you to explain."

4

On the third day, having received no word from Valerie, Jacques Coeur went to the factor's wife. She was a talkative woman, with a tendency to dramatize everything: by intonation, by gesture, by expression, most of all with a flow of detail she employed to flesh the bare framework of fact.

"This girl I don't understand," she admitted. "She's interested in nothing. I talk to her; she doesn't listen. I cook for her the best; she doesn't eat. I make for her rye bread, fresh from the oven, and all women know it's good to preserve the beauty. Lentil soup by my own mother's recipe. And sambocades! Ah, such richness of curds and whey, baked in a coffin of crust and flavored as it should be with elder flowers. But will she eat? No, my lord, she takes a few bites and then she says, 'I have no more appetite.' But that cat, it eats enough for her! It eats everything I give it and then it goes back to my kitchen and steals the fish heads, and then it goes downsairs and eats the food of Old Benedisto who tends the rear gate and who brings his meals wrapped up in cabbage leaves."

"What does she do with her time?" asked the Moneyman.

"That, my lord, is hard to answer. She sits and stares out of windows and, if you ask her questions—which I have done a hundred times—she doesn't answer. She goes to the oratory and prays. Once only she seems to come to life. She laughs and talks about Mysteries and about her mules and about the time when the rope and the hook which lifted an actor off the stage broke and dropped him on his fat Guillaume. It was this morning, my lord. She even takes my children down to the grass bailey and plays with them there. She teaches them a game called Tat-and-Spat. And she imitates for them."

"Imitates?"

"Yes, my lord. She makes herself like people she has seen about the shop. Eduard, the little old bachelor who sells in Eastern Silks and who has to put his thumb in his mouth when he reckons. And Dame Trix who is a sweeper and who drinks. And Philbert the High Stepper who cleans out the stables. But it was for a short time only, my lord. She has the cockroach again as soon as she gets back, and not another word does she say."

Father François was even more disturbed about her. "Monseigneur, she prays by the hour," he reported. "I've tried to be of help to her but she says there is nothing she can tell me. I said to her, 'Daughter, what great sin have you committed which cannot be told to a man of God?' Her answer was that it was about the future she prayed and not the past. I've questioned her at length, Monseigneur, but she gives me no slightest hint of what she has on her mind."

Coeur said to himself, "She's not the tattling kind to run to neighbors or the priest with everything. That is good."

Father François seemed to feel that he was proving neglectful. What more can I do, Monseigneur? Must I stand by and see this poor child struggle alone with her troubles?"

"This much I know about it, Father: there's nothing you can do to help her."

The Moneyman encountered Valerie that afternoon. It happened to be in the Armory and she was standing in one of the windows, gazing out in the mood of complete preoccupation which had so disturbed the factor's wife. The sun was pouring through, making her hair glisten warmly and striking on the well-polished surfaces of a suit of mail by which she was standing. Coeur said to himself, "If an artist put that on canvas, people would think it a picture of the Maid."

She turned at the sound of his steps. When she came forward to meet him, she had shaken off the mood of abstraction entirely. He knew at once that she had made up her mind and, also, what her decision had been.

"I shall do as you wish in the matter, my lord."

Coeur studied her face with a gravity which matched her own. "Are you quite sure? Have all the fears and reservations left you?"

She nodded slowly. "Yes, my lord."

"And you're entirely willing to make the sacrifice?"

She answered in a low tone. "I've come to see that it's not only my duty but my privilege. Yes, my lord, I am willing. Sometimes even I find that I'm glad. I'm so sure about it now that I wonder why I didn't see it clearly at first. How slow and stupid I have been! Taking three days to make up my mind!"

"I'm glad you took the time, Valerie. Now your mind is made up so firmly that it won't change with every twirl of the weather vane. This won't be easy for you, my child. There will be plenty of ups and downs; there will be days when everything will seem wrong. There will be times when you will weary of the hard work and the uncertainty and the—the danger. You understand, of course, that there will be danger?"

"Yes, my lord. But at no time have I been concerned about *that*." She wore a worried frown, nevertheless, when she asked, "When do I begin?"

"I've a plan which I hope to get settled this evening. If all goes well, your education will start tomorrow."

Valerie tried to face this fact cheerfully but he noticed that her chin trembled a little. "I fear, my lord," she whispered, "that I will be a *very* poor scholar."

The Moneyman continued to study her face with an absorption which kept him silent for some moments. "Today you remind me of the young Agnes so much that I am carried back," he said at last. "I can almost believe myself at the King's court on the day when she first came. Ah, she was so young, so lovely, so very grave! She won all our hearts—and some of them she kept. You look exactly as she did the first time I saw her. She was in a green gown; and I think that memory must have prompted me in selecting this dress for you, my child. Her cheeks lacked the tan of yours and her hair was done in a different way. But otherwise you are the young Agnes I remember so well. . . . I think, my child, that the resemblance goes deeper than looks. You seem to have the same spirit, the courage, the sweet good temper I've always loved in her!"

8

JACQUES COEUR took a pride in having systems for everything. In the room he used at the Louvre—all the other ministers had suites, with chapels, refectories, pantries, even cellars of their own and stables for their horses and armories and formal gardens—there was a long table with an equally long bench behind it. Each day when he arrived, he would find piles of letters and documents at intervals along the table. When he had gone through one pile, he moved along on the bench to the next; and facing him would be the official with whom he was to discuss the matters contained therein. When he reached the end of the bench, his duties as Moneyman were over for the time being.

On the day Valerie reached her decision, he completed his tasks at a relatively late hour. Walking to one of the windows, he looked down into a busy courtyard at the palace. Men, looking dwarfed at the distance, were coming and going in the jingling harness of war. With a sudden sense of satisfaction he said to himself, "That's one thing they'll never be able to take away from me, that I persuaded Charles to the need of finishing the struggle."

Nicolas came stumbling through the dusk of the room, saying in an aggrieved tone: "And why didn't you light the candles, master? Do you think yourself above such ordinary needs as light or do you fancy yourself a cat to see in the dark? The Sire d'Antenne is waiting outside. I would like to slam the door in his face!"

There was a hint of jocularity in Coeur's voice as he said, "Show the splendid fellow in, Nicolas."

The "splendid fellow" proved to be a foppishly dressed young man with a black patch over one eye. Any observer who caught the slyness and greed in the other would have been forgiven for thinking that the accident, if accident it had been, would have been much more of a boon had it resulted in closing both.

Coeur waited for Nicolas to withdraw and then addressed his visitor. "Come and sit beside me, my honest Georges, so that we can talk in low tones. In no other way can we discuss the kind of business which always brings you here, my perfect paragon of honesty."

The visitor, whose skin seemingly was thick enough to absorb any amount of verbal pricking or bludgeoning, seated himself at the table with no suggestion of umbrage. He said in an even tone, "What I have for you today is worth double the usual fee."

"I'll judge of that," declared Coeur sharply, "after I have heard what it is."

The young man with the black patch was watching the Moneyman closely with his one eye. "It's the most vital piece of information I've ever had for sale. I've some hesitation about telling it, as you will understand, my lord Coeur. There is danger in passing it on."

"Speak up!" said Coeur impatiently. "We both know that the skin of an informer is always in some danger. Isn't it rather that the odor this time is so strong that even your well-seasoned nostrils can feel a distaste?"

The Sire d'Antenne proceeded to tell his story. He had called to see his sister, who was married to Guillaume Gouffier and was in ill-health because of the imminence of her fourteenth child. By some error of calculation (he smiled as he gave this information, as though proud of what he had done) he had found himself not in his sister's quarters but in a small room which opened into a larger apartment where Gouffier conducted his affairs. He had become aware at once that his sister's husband had important visitors. There was a murmur of voices from the larger room, many of which he had no difficulty at all in identifying. With a skill in such matters which he regarded clearly as an accomplishment, he had succeeded in opening the door slightly and in spying out the land. There were seven men in the room. He had recognized all of them.

The talk going on inside had reached his ears in snatches only but he had heard enough to realize that the gathering was not a chance one, that it had been called by Gouffier for a specific purpose. He paused at this point and waited.

"And what was the purpose, my expert at keyholes, my agile gatherer of gossip?"

"To discuss ways and means of persuading the King to dispense with the services of his Moneyman."

Coeur smiled as though he took a certain sardonic satisfaction in the situation. "They will find they are too early. I've not yet paid the whole cost of the war."

"They're not looking at the immediate future, my lord Coeur. They won't make any kind of move until after Rouen has been taken. Then, my not-too-generous employer, watch yourself! The pack will be upon you!"

"My ill-wishers grow more daring, it seems. They're no longer content to snap at my heels like a pack of jackals. What form will the attack take, when it comes?"

There had been talk, explained the informer, of getting together evidence to lay before the King. The management of the mint at Bourges, which Coeur had controlled in the earliest days of the reign, had come in for much discussion (Coeur smiled at this, for Charles had lived at Bourges then and had been so poor that he had needed to clip the coinage in order to have meat on his table), and there had been some talk about the supplying of bombards to the Turks to assist them in their war against Christian states.

While the bearer of tales was telling what he had seen and heard, Jacques Coeur was piling up coins on the table in front of him in the form of a pyramid. He had seemed completely absorbed in this occupation but in reality he had missed nothing. He looked up the instant the story came to an end.

"And you'll tell me the names of the seven men?"

"If the fee is to be doubled."

"The fee will be doubled, my spotless paladin, my cavalier of clean conscience. See! It's ready for you here."

The man with the black patch named the conspirators, counting on his fingers as he did so.

At the end Coeur nodded his head with a return of his sardonic mood. "I could have named them myself, I think," he said. "They would all profit personally by my removal. It happens that six of the seven are in my debt at the moment." He raised both hands and then dropped them inertly on the table. "These brave and honorable knights should be grateful to me. I'm paying for a war in which they will have a chance to display their gallantry and win renown for themselves. Instead they plot my ruin."

The Sire d'Antenne counted the coins with great care. Then he nodded and rose to his feet. He seemed well pleased with himself.

"That patch on your eye is the sign of a war pledge no doubt," said Coeur.

"Yes, my lord Moneyman-for-the-time-being. I've sworn not to discard it until I've performed some noble deed in the fighting with the Engloys."

Coeur laughed mirthlessly. "I've heard of half-a-dozen other great knights who are wearing patches for the same reason. I could give you the names of three who have forsworn a certain pleasurable rite, in which their ladies would play a part, until the enemy has been driven from the country. How unfortunate it would be for them if the war dragged on for another twenty years! I know of one who has declared himself not to bathe until his doughty arm has brought him just acclaim. Not that the oath will make any particular difference in his habits." His voice rose. "I would like to propose a more useful and logical oath for the lot of you to swear. That you will obey the orders of your leader when it comes to the fighting. That you won't charge when you see fit yourselves—as you did at Azincourt and so lost the battle—but wait until the order is given. That you won't scorn to protect your archers, because the poor fellows are of low degree, nor allow the enemy to cut them to pieces while his own bowmen rain deadly arrows on the army of France! In other words, that you will behave like real soldiers and not like sulky and overbearing fools!"

"You seem to have little respect for chivalry, my lord Coeur."

"So little, Sire d'Antenne, that I—— But let that go for the moment. I'm a buyer of secrets and so only a degree better than you, a seller. I don't need to tell you, my model of rectitude, that all ministers of the King employ spies to know what is going on! You sell to all of them, I don't doubt. But under the circumstances I'm not in a position to suggest that another oath you might take would be not to sell information about your friends."

The wearer of the patch smiled without a trace of rancor. "I need the money," he said. He waved a hand jauntily as he was leaving the room. "I'll continue to serve you, Jaquet the Fox, as long as you have gold to pay me."

Coeur called out in a sudden burst of anger: "Nicolas, Nicolas! Get a window open in there! That splendid fellow has polluted the air!"

2

Jacques Coeur was late in reaching the Grand Salon. The long tables were already filled and at *dressoirs* along the walls the court carvers were basting the roast meats with orange juice and rose water and sprinkling them with salt and sugar and spices. At first glance it was impossible to see much more of the company than the towering headdresses of the ladies. Some of these rose as much as three feet above the heads of their wearers and no two were alike. There were some which resembled windmills with broad surfaces of shimmering satin, a few which sported horns as widespread as a stag's, others which were heart-shaped with armorial bearings picked out in precious stones, and many which were further complicated by bands of velvet looped around the head and falling to the floor. The general effect was much the same as that produced by a company of standard-bearers in a victory processional or a saint's day parade.

Coeur perceived at once that the company had taken advantage of the fact that the royal family were enjoying their meal in the privacy of the Queen's own salon by relaxing ceremonial to the extent of supping *à deux*. Each gentleman was sharing his plate and cup with a lady, and already a certain boisterous levity had developed. There was one vacant chair and into this the Moneyman slipped quietly.

"I begged the privilege of your company tonight, my lord Coeur," said the lady who was to share his plate. "For a long time I've desired a chance to talk with you."

She was a mature beauty of thirty or perhaps even a few years in excess of that turning point in the lives of the women of the day. Her warm brown eyes smiled at him from under a comparatively inconspicuous hennin of velvet.

Coeur was surprised that the much-sought-after Comtesse de Burey should have expressed a preference for his company, and his manner showed it. "I'm most deeply honored, Comtesse," he said, with a bow. "This is doubly fortunate, as I've desired a talk with you. We have an interest in common."

"Yes," she agreed. "You refer, of course, to my brother-in-law. I had a note from him last night but I haven't seen him yet since his return." Isabeau de Burey allowed the furred edge of her fan to brush her companion's shoulder with the slightest suggestion of coquetry. "I make no secret of the fact that I'm interested in everything he does. But you need not look so disturbed, my lord Coeur. I was in accord with the purpose which kept him away so long."

The Moneyman studied her face with a steady eye. "I'm indeed happy to know that, Comtesse," he said. "We still need every adherent, particularly one whose charm can be of service to us."

"I've been such a loyal supporter of your policy that some on the other side have treated me coldly," whispered the Comtesse. "Even my husband had been won over to our way of thinking. Not"—with a sudden hardening of her very lovely eyes—"that Regnault's support would ever be of much help to you. He has shown such a capacity for making enemies!"

Despite his deep interest in the topic, Coeur had already begun to dip his spoon into the soup before them. "The royal cook is doing us special honor tonight," he said. "This *soupe dorée* was the great Taillevent's most conspicuous triumph. I can never resist it."

The rich potage clearly was a dish that none of the company could resist. It was made of slices of brown toast fried in yolks of egg and white wine and then floated in rose water, sprinkled with saffron and sugar. The ladies and gentlemen alike were spooning it up voraciously.

The Comtesse shook her head sadly. "It's too rich for me. I am no longer young"—she paused as though willing to have him enter a denial—"and there is no longer any doubt that I can take on weight too readily. It's a great trial."

He was well aware, nevertheless, that her throat and shoulders, generously exposed in the mode of the moment, displayed a dazzling white roundness of contour. "It seems to me that you grow lovelier every day," he said.

A *squire de gobelet* poured wine into the cup they were to share. Coeur raised it with an appreciative hand and offered it to his companion. "Saint-Pourcain!" he said. "We are indeed being honored. The very best of all wines. Will you condescend to take the first drink?"

The Comtesse took a sip and then handed the cup back to him. "Robin has been most secretive on one score," she said, returning to the subject which interested her most. "He has never let me know the exact nature of the relationship between you. Is it such a very great secret, then? I confess to being an inquisitive person, my lord."

Coeur took a deep swallow of the wine. "I see no reason why it should be a secret at all. D'Arlay has never shown any reluctance to having it known that he has an interest in my enterprises. In fact, I've every reason to believe he is proud his fingers have dabbled in—in what the rest of our company here tonight would call 'vulgar trade.' What is it you want to know?"

"Well," she said, "how it began, for instance."

"I can understand why he has never told you that. I saw him for the first time on an occasion when his spirits were very low. Someone he thought a great deal of, Comtesse, was being married. I advised him to go away and even took the liberty of suggesting he sail on one of my ships. He acted on the suggestion and it did him much good. We have been friends ever since."

As he spoke Coeur was watching the profile of his companion. It was well worth studying: a good brow, a delicately arched nose with proudly chiseled nostrils, full eyelids, and lashes of unusual length. "No wonder Robin was so unhappy when she threw him aside," he said to himself. "She must have been irresistible then." Now she had a reputation for ambition and selfishness, but he was not entirely inclined to accept this estimate. Court beauties were always the targets for envy and malicious tittle-tattle. He went over in his mind the stories circulated about Isabeau de Burey: She had tried hard but without success to succeed Agnes Sorel in the affections of the King; she thought of little else but her looks and even went to such extremes as bathing in strawberry juice and drinking vinegar instead of wine to retain the milky whiteness of her skin; she paid visits to a learned doctor at the University who was said to dabble in magic and who was even rumored to be on the point of discovering the Philosopher's Stone; she cared for her husband's brother much more than she did for the Comte and made it clear to the latter that she had married him for his title alone. Coeur was sure of one item only in this indictment, the last named.

"Quite a few years ago," went on the Moneyman, "I found myself needing funds rather badly. I was adding to my fleet of ships and I had, perhaps, rushed into construction more boldly than was wise. I was so hard pressed that it was a great help when D'Arlay made me a loan. I've always considered that he did me a great service."

"I *did* know of the loan."

"It was bold of him as well as generous. His share of the estates, into which he had just come, was badly stretched in the process. In fact, he found it necessary to put a mortgage on his lands."

"I didn't know of the mortgage. Regnault would have been furiously opposed if *he* had heard of it."

"I am telling you this in confidence, Madame. The loan was well protected. I did better for him than a bottomry bond by which he would have had for security a certain ship and could lose everything if that ship went down; I gave him his security, in fact, on the goods in my shops and so he couldn't lose. The loan was repaid quickly enough but I felt that his trust had placed me under a never-ending obligation. Ever since I have considered him a silent partner and he shares in certain of the profits. He will always do so."

The Comtesse continued to watch him with a speculative eye. "It's within the bounds of possibility then that my sweet Robin may become a very rich man?"

Their plate had been filled with gobbeted trout. The Comtesse refrained from eating but Jacques Coeur began to ply an enthusiastic knife. "Will you forgive me if I indulge in a boast?" he asked between mouthfuls. "He's a rich man now as a result of this share in my enterprises. He should become very much richer as time goes on."

"I'm very happy to hear it," whispered the Comtesse.

"You see, Madame," went on the Moneyman, not averse to fanning the regrets she might be harboring over her matrimonial mistake, "my enterprises are different from anything the world has ever seen before. There is no limit to the growth I foresee. Actually I've made no more than a start. Your brother-in-law continues to help me in many ways. He will continue a partner, a silent one it is true, in the—the empire of trade I am building."

The trout had been succeeded by venison and furmenty, a combination invented two generations before by Taillevent, the famous royal cook of that day. The wheaten flour of the furmenty was boiled in milk with melted sugar and cardamom seeds and the result was a piquant accompaniment to the strong flavor of the meat. It was a favorite dish of Coeur's but the Comtesse did not touch it, contenting herself with a small mound of *marrois* which one of the helpers placed on her side of the plate. Into this well-spiced combination of hashed fish and cod's liver she dipped a sparing knife at intervals.

"I'm the richest man in the world today," declared the Moneyman proudly. His eyes were glowing with enthusiasm but he was taking good care to pitch his voice so low that he could not be heard by anyone else at the table. "What will I do with my wealth if it continues to grow? I don't know. In fact, I never give that a thought. I'm not doing this for the sake of money. I like power but I'm not thinking of that either. I lack words to tell you the vision that prompts me to go on and yet I can see the future clearly enough. The world will be a different place, a better place, when commerce becomes man's chief interest and"—he paused significantly—"when soldiers are considered of small account. Comtesse, that's what I am striving to bring about: to make the rules of the countinghouse of more moment than the Code of Chivalry, to provide a greater degree of comfort and happiness for all people. It's coming. Nothing can hold it back. I want to bring that welcome day closer."

"I find it hard to believe in the possibility of such a future," said the Comtesse. "But—you are a most ardent advocate, my lord Coeur."

The royal cook had provided a special Warner, the dish which served as an intimation that the course had been finished and another was to begin. It consisted of two figures, almost life size, representing a shepherd and shepherdess made of various kinds of edibles. There was an artist in the kitchen, a potential Phidias born to waste his talents among pots and pans and to work in lard and pastry instead of enduring stone. The figures were startlingly real. The faces had been faithfully contrived out of browned dough and they smirked at each other in bucolic fidelity. Each carried a small basket. When the lid of one was lifted, a pair of canaries began to sing inside. Doves flew out from the other, a half dozen or more. They flapped confidently about the room and even perched on the shoulders of the company in expectation of being fed.

Jacques Coeur joined in the applause by clapping his hands briefly. He then plunged back into conversation without any delay.

"You've known D'Arlay a long time, Comtesse?"

"Yes, Monsieur. All my life. The estates of our families adjoined in Anjou, although the De Burey lands were much more extensive than my father's holdings. We were much of an age, Robin and I. You perceive, my lord, that my honesty is great enough for even such a damaging admission as that. We played together as children and I saw him every day as we grew up. Robin was a kind and gentle boy and a very good companion. I was always fond of him."

"But you married his older brother."

"Yes, I married his brother."

There was a pause. "You are an ambitious woman, I think, Comtesse," said Coeur.

Isabeau de Burey nodded in agreement. "That is true. I see no reason for not acknowledging that I would like to have more influence at court. I have some beauty and I'm sure I have more intelligence than most of these"—she lowered her voice cautiously—"these very stupid people about us."

"It was to better your chances, then, that you married the Comte de Burey? You wanted the title?"

The brown eyes of the Comtesse narrowed slightly before she nodded a second time. "You have asked me a direct question and I feel disposed to give you a frank answer. Yes, my lord Coeur, I married Regnault for his title and the position it would give me at court. He has been a great disappointment to me and I feel no need to conceal the truth on his behalf."

"Did D'Arlay understand the reason for your preference?"

"Not entirely. He charged me with it at the time but I—I denied it. He was even more modest then and so he found it easy to believe I could prefer his brother." She dipped her hands in a ewer of hot water offered by one of the servitors and dried them carefully on the linen towel draped on the handle. "I don't know why I am telling you this. I'm making admissions, in fact, which will give you a very bad opinion of me."

Coeur took a final drink of wine and shoved the goblet aside as a signal it was not to be refilled. He turned to study his companion more closely. "It is in your mind perhaps that you could be of use to me?"

The Comtesse returned his gaze steadily. "It has seemed to me possible. You need friends at court."

"Yes, Comtesse, it's possible I may need friends in the unpredictable days ahead of us. A lady of your position, and with your charm, could be useful to me." He asked, after a moment, "Are you in need of funds?"

"Always," she sighed. "My selfish spouse has been very extravagant. Our debts are heavy—so heavy that we are forced to the most trying expedients to pay his creditors and still keep up appearances."

"Have you ever applied to D'Arlay for assistance?"

She hesitated before answering. "I've been so frank with you already that I might as well tell you everything. Even if it gives you a still worse opinion of me. Yes, my lord, I have sought his help when—when things become particularly difficult."

"And has he been willing to help?"

"Of course. My dear Robin is the most generous of men. He has never needed more than a word from me."

"In return for what you may be able to do for me, you might prefer to come to me when the necessity arises."

The Comtesse did not withdraw her eyes. "That possibility has occurred to me."

A born bargainer, Coeur liked nothing better than to have the lead come from the other party to a transaction. He said to himself with satisfaction, "This is a fortunate coincidence. I'm in a position now to make arrangements to suit myself."

"It happens, Comtesse, that you could be of direct aid to me now," he said aloud. "There's a rather delicate undertaking which I think could be put safely in your hands. It would be a profitable venture for you."

The lady had an instinct for bargaining also. She said nothing.

"Before I explain the nature of it," Coeur continued, "I must touch on a delicate point without any bearing on the undertaking itself. I must make a stipulation. You won't like what I'm going to say but I'm always forthright in my dealings and I believe in speaking openly and to the point."

The lady's eyebrows raised slightly and involuntarily but she answered in even tones, "I'm ready to listen to anything you have to say, my lord Coeur."

"I'm very fond of Robin," said Coeur, after a moment. "It's a matter of deep regret to me to realize that he's not happy. I don't mean that he is actively unhappy. He enjoys such work as I entrust to him. He has his books and he dabbles a little in philosophy and science. But here he is, a man of thirty or so and still unmarried. He should have half-a-dozen children around his house by this time. Books are a poor substitute for a family, Comtesse. I'm beginning to fear he will never marry now; and that is a bleak prospect for a man of his disposition. I'm quite disturbed about him."

"I've never stood in the way of his marrying," said Isabeau.

"Not directly, or openly, perhaps. But I wonder if he's likely to think of any other women as long as a certain bond remains unbroken? If that bond were snapped or permitted to fray, I think he would soon find someone to suit him. I'm certain of one thing, Comtesse: you, and you only, are in a position to break that bond."

A long silence developed, each waiting for the other to break it. Coeur won.

"Am I to understand this is your stipulation?" she asked.

Coeur nodded. "Make me a promise to do everything you can to break that bond, Comtesse, and I'll be so generous with you in the other matter that you will never know any financial embarrassment again."

For the first time a touch of color showed in her usually cool white cheeks. Watching her closely, Coeur realized that she was finding it difficult to control her resentment. He waited anxiously, not sure that her need for security would get the upper hand.

She asked finally, "Must I give you this—this extraordinary pledge before you tell me the nature of the undertaking?"

The Moneyman said to himself triumphantly, "She's going to agree." Through force of habit he waited before answering. "I may tell you this much, that it would involve taking a young girl under your tutelage and care for a period. Before saying anything more, I must ask you a question. I must be sure that certain information I have received is correct."

"As you wish."

Convinced in his mind now of the outcome, he asked, "You had an uncle named Gilles de Voudrai with estates in the southern part of Berri?"

"Yes. My uncle Gilles died about ten years ago."

"He had many children, I believe, most of them illegitimate."

The Comtesse permitted herself to smile. "A great many."

"What did he do to provide for those born out of wedlock?"

"Nothing that I know of. My uncle was not a rich man. He had squandered his resources and his estate was in a sad condition when he died."

"Have his heirs concerned themselves over the plight of his illegitimate issue?"

"Knowing my cousins as I do, I'm quite sure they've done nothing at all. Do you wish to imply that they've been negligent or unnatural in the matter?"

Coeur shook his head. "I'm not concerned with the ethics of the situation. I want to be sure of one thing. Have your cousins kept track of them?"

Isabeau indulged in an easy laugh. "If you had known my uncle Gilles, you wouldn't require an answer. There were too many of them, Monsieur. I'm not sure that even he knew how many he had. There is nothing unusual about that."

Supper was over. There was a loud scraping of chairs on the stone floor as the company rose to leave. Most of them paused by the door where servitors offered them the spiced *boute-hors* which brought each meal to a close. There was a loud clatter of talk.

"I'm satisfied now to tell you what I have in mind, Comtesse," said Coeur. "Do you feel disposed to give me more of your time when we reach the apartments of the Queen?"

Isabeau kept her eyes lowered. "I—I must think of what you have said first."

Coeur smiled at her. "By all means. Whatever the decision, permit me to say this has been a most pleasant and profitable supper. I've enjoyed your company very much."

9

A GALE took possession of Paris that night. It came from the northwest and roared down the river and over the rooftops. It was not the mischievous kind, snatching at hats and making clotheslines dance, but a baleful storm with fingers of ice and lungs of steel. It brawled fiercely about the spires of churches and forced its way through faults in the glazing to mutter in the aisles like the whisper of heresy. It swirled down the streets and caused tavern signs to swing like bells in a steeple.

By morning the river was rolling in yellow turbulence. Masses were being sung in empty churches and the shutters of most shops remained up. D'Arlay had intended to make several visits but a single glance from the window of his bedroom on one of the top floors of the house in the Rue Grenier sur L'Eau was sufficient to dissuade him from that purpose. He decided to stay indoors.

Leaving the window, he paused beside an unfinished object made of clay which occupied a small table against one of the walls. It consisted of a round cylinder about two feet in length protruding from a cradle of crossbars. It was not hard to recognize, for it was an excellent model of a bombard, the new kind of cannon which was to be used against the English. He and Pregent Kennedy had filled in time by making it but had not yet finished the equipment for breech-loading and firing. And now it would remain unfinished, for Pregent Kennedy had left.

He had returned the previous noon after a visit to the headquarters of Jacques Coeur and had proceeded immediately to pack his saddlebags with his meager belongings. As usual he had volunteered no information at all.

"You are going away?" D'Arlay asked, standing over him as he meticulously folded in his one change of underclothes.

"Aye. I am grateful to you for your kindness in letting me fill a humble bed in your handsome house but I'll have no further use for it. I leave at once."

"May I ask what brought about this sudden change of plan?"

The Scot straightened up and gave frowning consideration to the advisability of answering. "I go," he said finally, "at the behest of the Moneyman."

"Does your mission concern Valerie Maret?"

Another long pause. "Aye. I go to Berri to make inquiries about her. I'll be gone for several weeks at the least reckoning."

D'Arlay nodded his head approvingly. He was glad an effort was to be made to trace the girl's parentage, and convinced that no better agent could have been selected.

By further questioning he learned that Kennedy knew nothing more, except that Valerie still lived with the family of the factor and was not to be seen by visitors. He, Kennedy, had been denied the opportunity of talking with her before leaving.

When the Scot had tossed the saddlebags over his shoulder and departed, D'Arlay realized that he could no longer keep up his pretense of indifference by staying away. It had required the exercise of all his strength of will to keep from rushing to Coeur to protest still more urgently than he already had done and to the girl herself to prevent her from making such a serious mistake. Each day he had paced up and down, wondering what had happened between Coeur and Valerie, even his anxiety about the forthcoming duel relegated to the back of his mind.

Having decided against the idea of venturing out into the rain-swept streets himself, he was surprised when a step on the stairs announced a visitor. It was Gaspard, the arms master. He came in with water dripping from his clothes and trickling down his cheeks and nose.

"I didn't expect you in weather like this," said D'Arlay.

"A man must live," declared the arms master cheerfully. "If I didn't come here, my lord, I would have nothing to do today and the state of my purse makes idleness a luxury I can't afford."

D'Arlay took down his sword from a metal fastener on the wall. He gave it a preliminary cut with the feeling of satisfaction he always enjoyed when it was in his hand.

"I'm disposed to think, Gaspard," he said, "that you will come off second best today. Very much second best. I feel in the mood for swordplay. This good blade of mine fairly tugs at my hand."

The arms master contented himself with saying, "I will do my best," as he threw off his sodden cloak and rolled up the sleeves of his tunic. He was a stockily built fellow with muscles which rippled under the brown skin of his arm. His movements were deliberate, but when he took a step forward it was easily to be seen that his whole body was like a beautifully adjusted machine.

D'Arlay advanced, treading on his toes in eagerness to begin, his blade extended in front of him. "On guard!" he cried.

The swords touched and held for the customary moment. Then D'Arlay drew back and lunged vigorously. There was a grind of steel as the arms master parried the thrust. The bout was on; and an exultant power coursed through D'Arlay's arm as he went seriously to work.

This mood did not last, however. Facing him, as he countered his opponent's steel, was a stained-glass window representing Samson with jawbone in hand. D'Arlay had never been pleased with the subject. Now, as he advanced and retreated and lunged and parried, he was less pleased than ever. The uplifted arm of the strong man seemed to him to represent the might of Jacques de Lalain and he fancied he could see a slight resemblance to himself in the cringing Philistine on whom the jawbone was descending.

Isabeau had been responsible for nearly everything about this house in the Rue Grenier sur L'Eau. As soon as he had acquired it, she had descended on him with a builder and a glassmaker in tow and had taken over the direction of the improvements. It was a house of the type known as foreland, with masonry foundations and a succession of frame upper stories, each of which reached farther out into the street until the roof seemed in imminent danger of toppling over; a picturesque structure in its original guise, with N-shaped beams and thatch of red and yellow plaster and an infinity of quaint design in the woodwork both inside and out. There were moments now when he did not like his Paris home at all. Isabeau had succeeded in converting it into an imitation of the pretentious hotels of the great families; but, he thought, a not particularly successful one, despite the fact that the windows blazed with all the hues known to the glassmakers and the ceiling of the ground floor had been ripped out to give him an imposing and thoroughly uncomfortable Great Hall.

Despite the parallel he had read into the subject of the glass window, he was quite pleased with himself when the bout came to an end. Wiping his streaming brow on the maroon velvet of his sleeve, he said to his opponent, "You didn't touch me once, Gaspard."

The arms master grunted. "That's true, my lord. I didn't get by your guard once. You have great skill with the sword."

Removing the cork from the tip of his weapon, D'Arlay added with an air of satisfaction, "On the other hand, I got through your guard quite often."

"Four times, my lord."

"Well," demanded D'Arlay, dropping on a bench and spreading out his long legs with the feeling of comfort that follows any physical effort, "what do you think of my chance?"

Gaspard did not answer at once. He was rolling down the sleeve of his tunic. Then he reached for his leather jerkin and struggled into it. It was a full minute before he ventured an opinion. "You will have no chance at all, my lord."

D'Arlay was puzzled as well as disturbed. "But why?" he asked. "What more can you expect of me?"

The arms master shook his head gloomily. "I've seen Jacques de Lalain in the lists. There has never been anyone to equal him. His strength passes belief and he fights with the fury of a gored bull. In addition he has great skill with all weapons."

"With the sword it's skill only which counts. The answer to his greater strength is in the lightness of the foot. I can keep out of his reach until I see an opening for a thrust of my own."

The man did not seem convinced. "But your legs lose their nimbleness when encased in grevières and with iron shoes on the feet."

"We're to fight without armor of any kind."

Gaspard looked his surprise. "Has the Burgundian agreed to that? It will make a great difference. You'll have a chance to spit him before his greater strength can have any effect. But," with a return of his doubts, "it will be wise not to depend too much on that. You must fit yourself for a long bout and that will mean much hard work."

"I'm prepared to do whatever you think necessary."

The arms master nodded his head approvingly. "If you are serious, I can promise to make a different man of you. It will mean"—Gaspard gave a quick glance to convince himself that the drastic advice he must offer would be accepted in the right spirit—"the greatest discomfort for you. You must eat nothing but the foods I select. There must be exercises twice a day and a long run to improve your wind. Our bout today was a short one, my lord, and yet you are still panting and covered with perspiration. When you have followed my advice for a long enough time, you will come through a little dancing lesson such as this without a damp hair on your head. I must be honest with you, my lord. You are soft and short of wind and you have muscles like a chitterling."

"As I said before, Gaspard, I'm ready to place myself in your hands."

The arms master reached for his cloak and hat. "May I ask how old you are?"

"I've turned thirty."

"You look younger than that. It's a late age to begin on the heavy work I must give you. I can say this much for you, my lord, you haven't got yourself a monstrous weasand like most men of your years." After a critical survey he went on, "There's a little extra fat here and there on your bones which we must get rid of at once. Eat sparingly. Soups and meat only. No bread, no pastry, not more than one drink of wine at each meal."

"A miserable kind of life you are plotting for me, Gaspard."

"But a longer life," ventured the arms master, "than you are like to have if you don't do everything I say."

D'Arlay had been reduced to a thoroughly unhappy frame of mind. "I thought he would be well impressed," he said to himself. "Well, I must set myself humbly to doing everything he says. I must forget I have a brain and a heart and remember only that I have muscles to be developed. I must strive to make myself into the kind of honorable knight who thinks only of killing other knights."

2

He was still engaged in these gloomy speculations when another visitor arrived. It proved to be the last person in the world he could have expected on such a day, his brother. The Comte de Burey slouched in on flat feet, leaning forward as he walked and peering ahead of him with the anxious pucker of shortsightedness. He had become paunchy and bald and his long face had the sallowness of bad health; but in spite of all this he still exerted some small vestige of what had once been a debonair charm. Dropping his wet cloak from his shoulders and allowing it to fall behind him on the floor, he revealed the fact that he was attired in the extreme of fashion. A ruffled tunic fell almost to his knees, his thinning shanks were covered by parti-colored hose, and the sleeves of his tunic were like the trunks of full-grown trees. He stopped and looked about him, teetering uncertainly. It was clear that he was at least partially drunk.

"Ha!" he said, squinting at his brother. "What have you been trying to do, make yourself a rival of Marco Polo? You've been away for six months and I've been needing you desperately. I heard last night you had condescended to return—and here I am, in all this rain, with an ache in my bones as though I had been put on the rack. *That* is how badly I need to see you!" He walked farther into the room, laying his feet down with the greatest care and balancing himself with difficulty. "There are times when I suspect the gout has laid its foul hand on me."

"Your sins are catching up with you, Naulty," said D'Arlay. Then he smiled and extended his hand. "I'm glad to see you."

"Ha!" snorted the Comte. "It's Isabeau you'll be glad to see. How could you stay away from her so long? By'r Lady of Marmoutier, I must have an eye to my health now that you're back. If I should die, you would strip the shoes off my feet before they were stiff in your haste to get into them."

"A jest in very bad taste, Naulty. And I doubt very much if you'll leave as much as a pair of shoes, the way things are going with you."

"It's bad taste to let the whole world know you're in love with your brother's wife, my Robin. Oh, I concede it's partly my fault. You wanted her and I took her away from you. I might have expected, knowing what a determined, unchanging young dog you are, that you would go on mooning after her. But now I confess to a growing distaste for your undying devotion, as I suppose you call it." He dropped limply into a chair. "Can't you see that I shall perish if you don't produce a hot posset at once to revive me? And do you call this feeble pindle of flame a fire? Is it by mean economies such as this that you keep yourself so affluent, my closefisted brother?"

D'Arlay called to his servant. "Helion! Mulled wine at once. And then another log for the fire."

"The days of your devotion to Isabeau are over," asserted Regnault de Burey when a flagon of wine had been brought him and the fire had been stirred up to a hot blaze. "That's what I've come to discuss with you. You must marry at once. I may tell you without more ado that I've found the wife for you."

"Has it occurred to you that I might prefer to find my own wife?"

The Comte glared over the rim of his flagon. "Has it occurred to you that we might have all the family estates taken away from us if we don't find a way at once of paying off my debts?"

D'Arlay's mood sobered. "Is it as bad as that, Naulty?"

"Things couldn't be worse. They hang over me like a flock of vultures, these bloodsucking leeches from Lombardy. They give me no peace. I can no longer pay the interest on my debts and at the same time keep up any pretense of living like a gentleman. Do you want to see the lands of your ancestors in the hands of filthy moneylenders?"

"No!" said D'Arlay. "I'm as concerned about that as you are, Naulty. The debts must be paid in some way."

"Are you in a position to pay them?"

"I've benefited through my association with Jacques Coeur, but not to that extent. It would take a very rich man to repair the damage you've done to the family fortunes, brother."

"It comes down to this. You can't dandle around fancy free any longer, my fine Robin. You must take a wife with a large enough fortune to save the lands of De Burey from going out of the family." He supped at his wine before adding in a tone of voice faintly apologetic: "There is also the matter of a male heir to succeed and carry on the name. That will be your responsibility also. I'm not likely to supply the deficiency. Make no mistake, it's not *my* fault. I've cast a dozen laggen-girds[1] around the countryside."

D'Arlay seated himself beside his brother. After several moments of intense and unhappy thought he began to speak. "I've always known, Naulty, that it would come to this sooner or later, that I would have to marry with an eye to both these considerations. My duty has always been clear to me but I've put off marrying as I haven't seen anyone I felt I could endure living with. Now it seems I must face the problem. It's unfortunate from my standpoint that the crisis should come at the very moment when I suspect I've fallen in love—and with someone with no name and no prospects. In fact, I couldn't have made a worse choice, as you would emphatically agree if you knew anything about the lady in question."

The Comte was so taken aback by this piece of news that he stared fixedly at his brother, the whites of his eyes showing (or what would have been the whites if they had not become a bilious brown) and his mouth open to display a prominent front tooth. "What Isabeau will think of *this*," he said, "will add to my discomfort for longer than I care to contemplate. By'r Lady of Marmoutier, she will take it ill!" He crossed one leg over the other and groaned with the pain. "But we have no difficulty here at all. If the wench is as lacking in prospects as you say, no one will want to marry *her* and you can keep her for yourself after you're married."

"You are wrong. In the first place, she has no idea that I've fallen in love with her. When I marry someone else—and it seems that I must—I shall never see her again."

"You would be well rid of one as uncomfortably virtuous as that."

They sat in silence for several moments and then D'Arlay asked, "Who is the lady on whom you've fixed your eye?"

The Comte answered with cheerful readiness. "A perfect choice, a flaw-

[1] A reference to illegitimacy.

less diamond among women, or at least nearly flawless. Listen to her perfections. A widow, well under thirty, one child only—a girl, quite sickly and not likely to survive—fair to look upon, lively, and so much property in her own name, mostly in the way of estates in Angoulême, that our debts could be paid off and still there would be enough to muffle up the whole family of De Burey against the winds of adversity."

"Who is this paragon?"

Regnault watched his brother with a slightly furtive air as he pronounced the name. "Clothilde de Trepant, widow of the Sire de Trepant who was killed in a lance-running at Bordeaux some six months back. He was killed, in fact, just as you began your endless travels and I've been watching for you ever since." Satisfied that D'Arlay had never heard of the lady who might become his wife, the Comte proceeded to an explanation. "There is one small circumstance which will bear telling. A few months after the sire's death, her page, standing behind her chair with company in the room, was observed to reach down and give her a sly pinch. It was assumed from this that she had been allowing the boy certain privileges."

In a tone of voice which seemed to say, "If I must marry for wealth does anything matter?" D'Arlay asked, "What of her looks?"

"Ha!" cried his brother. "There we are on the firmest ground. She has hair which tends to red, eyes on the order of green, a pert nose, and a figure that is most pleasantly slender. I can promise you this: by day, she will amuse you with her wit; by night, she will battle it out with you in the briskest and sweetest of dalliance." Regnault de Burey nodded his head like a lawyer at his summing up. "I have looked over the field with a thoroughness bred of desperation. This one is the pick. She will be both wife and mistress, she will be like a beautifully embroidered purse which will never empty no matter how often you reach into it for gold. Of all who possess the necessary property, she has the most virtues and the fewest faults. My advice to you, brother, is this: take her at once."

"You will allow me, I trust, to—to look about me first?"

"There's no time to waste." The Comte went on in a grumbling tone. "Touching this matter, I put little trust in you. There was the case of the Lady Alys de Guiraut a few weeks ago. Oh, I've heard all about it. You were riding north with the household of the Comte. The daughter, a pretty chick, was inclined to like you—for reasons which I fail to understand. And what did you do? You took sides against her with some half-wild creature, some greasy hobgoblin; and now the Lady Alys can't think of you without wishing the wind would set in another direction." He began to enumerate the holdings of the Comte de Guiraut. "A tract of eight hundred acres within a dozen miles of Tours. Sixteen sweet vineyards in the very heart of the wine country. Three châteaux, one on the Loire. A house in Paris. A castle on the Garonne large enough to hold an army. And you, my wise brother, offended her on behalf of this verminous trollop with the head of a turnip——"

D'Arlay said shortly, "I promise to waste no time in reaching a decision."

The Comte got slowly to his feet. He was on the point of leaving but then changed his mind and turned back. "Have you been sending money to Isabeau?" he demanded.

"No. I've neither seen nor been in communication with her for six months."

"Then where does the gold come from which has been in my house for the last two days? The servants have been paid. Isabeau, pretty creature, has been buying materials for dresses. Can it have anything to do with Jaquet the Fox paying her visits?"

D'Arlay sprang to his feet. A preposterous notion had entered his head —one which became less preposterous, but still completely unwelcome on second consideration. "Are you telling me that Jacques Coeur has been seeing Isabeau?"

"Twice in the last few days. Whispering together like a pair of conspirators. When I ask her what it's all about, she just stares at me—that cold stare my wife reserves for me alone. And now this cousin is coming. Not a full cousin, mind you. Some little chit, a bastard no less of my wife's rampaging bull of an Uncle Gilles. Why is this child being brought into my household?"

D'Arlay understood the whole story now. He walked over to a corner where clothes were hanging on pegs and took down a heavy cloak. He was thinking: "He's going too far. I won't permit it!"

"When I asked Isabeau the reason, she said the child was in need of a home. Ha, no doubt! But Uncle Gilles has his get scattered all over Berri, and all of them are in need of homes. Why this sudden solicitude over one of them? You know as well as I do that this wife of——" He stopped, clearing his throat, and erupted noisily in the general direction of the fire. "I almost said this wife of *ours*. That will show you how I feel about the way you patter after her and jump at her beck. Well, this wife of *mine* is a beautiful woman, as you will agree, a woman of intelligence and charm. We both admire her very much. But we both know that her heart is not the kind to swell up suddenly to the bursting point over the plight of a distant connection, one she has never seen, moreover. Why is she so concerned over this ill-begotten brat?" Another phase of the matter, one which seemed to cause him the most acute annoyance, occurred to the Comte. "If my house is to be filled with sniveling children, why is none of the money given to me?"

"Because, no doubt, they realize that giving money to you would be as sensible as feeding gold pieces to the fish in the Seine."

The head of the family continued to grumble. "I might be brought to see reason if they would give me a share of the fruits of this—this backstairs conspiracy, this underhanded foisting of bastards on me."

D'Arlay started to walk in the direction of the stairs. He was so filled with resentment that he found it hard to speak. "Come! I'm going with you! We must see about this at once!"

10

COEUR, who could be cheerful in most circumstances, looked about him as they mounted their horses and said, "The storm will surely moderate before we get there."

"It will become worse!" declared Nicolas tartly. "The Grant Oberie is washed out. A drunken fuller was drowned this morning in a pool near Saint-Gervais."

"In spite of that we must be on our way."

They rode out with their horses' hoofs splashing loudly in the water which swept down the street. Valerie was beside the Moneyman while Nicolas, grumbling audibly, brought up the rear. It became evident at once that the servant's estimate had been the correct one. The rain was coming down with all the fury and volume of that downpour which covered the earth after forty days and forty nights. They kept their heads down and made no attempt to talk except once when the wind ceased to howl and Valerie took advantage of the chance to ask, "What is she like, my lord Coeur?"

The Moneyman ruminated for a moment. "The Comtesse is very lovely," he said. "She has intelligence and charm, and a very great deal of determination. How you will find her when she first gets up in the morning, or if you stumble on her when her hair is down, I can't say."

The Hôtel de Burey, which they reached in due course, towered high above the street. The carved inscription and the family arms on the arched masonry shield over the postern gate were proof of the antiquity of the building as well as of the importance of the family, but nothing could offset the impression of dilapidation the house created. The copper gutters under the roof were full of holes and the water dripped from them in dreary persistence. The pointed sentinel towers, bulging out on each corner, had been so long in disrepair that they seemed ready to tumble down. The iron balconies were rusted. The only sign of habitation was a smudge of smoke from one chimney which the wind pounced upon and forced downward in wisps about the eaves and windows.

But to Valerie it was most grand and impressive. "It must be a very great family, my lord," she said, in a far from happy tone.

Coeur helped her down from her horse. "An old family," he whispered. "But because of the Comte's fondness for dicing and women, and his father before him whose fancy ran to lawsuits, they are as poor today as a beggar's cloak. My friend D'Arlay, though the youngest brother, is in better case than the Comte."

The Comtesse met them at the head of the stairs. "My lord Coeur!" she cried. "I had given up all hope that you would come on such a day."

She might have given up hope but that had not prevented her from being well prepared for the unexpected. Her flowing kirtle was of a diamond-shaped pattern of brown and yellow and was overwhelmingly becoming. Her sleeves, puffed generously at shoulder and elbow, were laced with straps of gold thread. Contrary to custom she wore nothing on her head. There was design in this, undoubtedly, for her hair had a crisp natural wave. Her fine wide brow showed no trace of the passage of the years; her eyes were as warmly responsive as a girl's; her generously exposed neck and shoulders were white and enticing. Following nervously in the rear of her escort, Valerie looked at the Comtesse and thought, "She must be the loveliest woman in the world, lovelier even than Agnes Sorel." Frightened though she was, the girl noticed that the kerchief of this beautiful lady was tucked under her waist and wondered if this was the custom at court. She saw also that there were no rings on the fingers of the Comtesse but that she wore one on a chain about her neck. "She thinks her hands look better without them," thought Valerie, "but she wears that one on a chain as proof of her regard for the person who gave it to her."

"You are drenched," said the Comtesse to Coeur, solicitously. She turned and looked at Valerie. "And this is the girl?"

"Yes, this is Mademoiselle Maret."

The Comtesse nodded. "You are welcome, my child."

The girl dropped a rather forlorn curtsy. She was feeling more awe with her surroundings each moment and in addition was acutely conscious of the condition to which the storm had reduced her. Rivulets of water were trickling down her cheeks and her hair was hanging in damp wisps.

The Comtesse looked her over critically and indulged in a puzzled shake of the head. "Well," she said, "there must be a reason for all this. Have I been told everything? The resemblance eludes me, my lord Coeur."

"Under better conditions it's unmistakable."

"Then I shall have to wait."

Valerie thought, "They talk about me as though I were not here. Is that one of the habits I must learn?" She was beginning to have doubts. "I think she's hard in spite of her beauty. She isn't going to like me at all."

The Comtesse continued to study her new charge. "Collect your wits, my child," she said. "You're supposed to be a cousin of mine, and the servants will wonder if you face them with so little assurance."

"Yes, my lady," quavered Valerie.

"You must accustom yourself to calling me 'cousin.' And your name from now on is Valerie de Voudrai. You must be very careful. A single slip might undo everything."

"Yes, Cousin."

"That is better." The Comtesse then called, "Guillaumette!" in a peremptory tone.

A middle-aged servant appeared promptly in the doorway, bowing and saying, "Yes, my lady?"

"This is my cousin, Mademoiselle de Voudrai, of whom I have spoken. As you see, Guillaumette, she's wet through. Show her to her rooms at once and see that she has everything she needs." Smiling at Valerie for the benefit of the maid, the Comtesse added in an affectionate tone: "I'm so happy you have come at last, my child. You must have a hot bath at once or you will be ill. I shall drop in for a talk a little later, dear Valerie."

"Come, Mademoiselle," said the maid. Under the deference of her voice there was a suggestion of the polite scorn felt by the servants of the great for lowly family relations.

Coeur had not failed to observe the evidence of panic in Valerie's manner. He walked over and said in a whisper: "You'll soon get accustomed to everything, even though it's strange to you now. You mustn't be frightened."

"I *am* frightened," she whispered back. He could not be sure whether the dampness of her cheeks was due entirely to the storm. "The Comtesse doesn't like me. I can tell by the way she looks at me."

"You're imagining it. She will soon be very fond of you."

"My dear Valerie," said Isabeau, with the slightest trace of impatience, "you will get a cold if you stay in those wet clothes any longer. Go with Guillaumette."

When they were alone, the Comtesse raised her fine dark eyebrows and smiled at her visitor. "Well!" she exclaimed. "All I can say to you is that I'll do my best."

"That is all I ask." Coeur smiled back at her. "During the few days we have been in partnership, I have conceived a great respect for my— my fellow conspirator. I'm sure this task is well within your powers." He bowed. "I must leave now. I'll return soon, tomorrow perhaps, to talk matters over with you further."

2

Coeur had been gone a few minutes only when the master of the house returned. The Comte was puffing by the time he reached the top of the stairs and, when he appeared in the doorway, he was so bedraggled in appearance that Isabeau could not help laughing. Then she noticed that his brother accompanied him and she cried out gaily, "Robin!" She ran to meet D'Arlay, saying, "How glad I am to see you! But I should be severe with you instead, for truly you've been most rude. Why have you been so tardy in coming to see us?"

"I'm happy now that I'm here," said D'Arlay. "As to my tardiness, which I humbly admit, there have been countless things to keep me at work."

She placed her hands on his shoulders and stretched up on tiptoe to give him a sisterly kiss on the cheek. Then, suddenly, her fingers tightened.

In a whisper so low that her husband could not hear, she said, "Robin, my dear Robin!"

D'Arlay stepped back rather hurriedly and turned to his brother. "You've made no secret, Naulty, of your feeling that my visits here are in the nature of intrusions. In spite of that, I must ask the privilege of a few minutes alone with Isabeau."

"Very well," said the Comte. "I'm depending on you to get to the bottom of this mystery. And"—wagging an admonitory finger—"you will be firm and let my sweet spouse know what we've decided between us."

Isabeau frowned when her husband had withdrawn. "Mystery? Be firm with me! What, pray, is all this?"

"By mystery he refers to the arrangement you've entered into with Jacques Coeur. It's no mystery to me." D'Arlay frowned. "I'm disappointed, Isabeau, that you've been weak enough to let yourself be persuaded into playing a part in it. It's not only the danger, which is serious enough in itself. Your reputation would be tarnished if this became public. As Regnault doesn't know about it, I'm taking it on myself to insist that you give the thing up."

The Comtesse placed a hand on his arm and by exerting a faint but unmistakable pressure directed him into a chair beside the hearth. She sat for a moment on an arm of it and allowed her head to rest against his shoulder. Then she got quickly to her feet.

"*That*," she said, in a whisper, "to let you know that I still love you as much as ever. I wanted you to know before—before we get very angry with each other. Which may happen in a few minutes." She lifted an arm with a graceful gesture to pat her bronze curls back into order above one ear. "If you had existed as we have for years in this dreadful, hateful poverty, you wouldn't be so quick, my dear Robin, to insist that I refuse the benefit of—of this regular supply of golden eggs which has been offered me."

"You mean, then, that Jacques Coeur has tempted you beyond the point where you can resist?"

There was still a trace of disbelief in the way she nodded her head. "He's being so generous that sometimes I believe I am living in a dream, a beautiful golden dream. Robin, Robin, you can have no conception of the difference it has made already! Some of the most pressing debts can be met. There is gold in the house. Gold, Robin, gold! The servants have received their wages. The candles in this room are made of wax. Real wax! Can you imagine such extravagance?" She smiled then and lifted her skirt a few inches, giving him a glimpse of a slender ankle. "Satin hose, and embroidered with gold thread! Robin, you must try to understand. I am free in my mind for the first time in years. Would you take this blessed relief away from me?"

D'Arlay studied her in silence for several moments. "It's not necessary for you to accept these fees from Jacques Coeur," he said finally. "Regnault and I have been discussing the future and we've decided there is only one solution to the tangle in which he has involved himself. I must find a rich wife for myself. He, in fact, has already found one."

Isabeau dropped her eyes so that he could not see the expression in them. "He has talked to me about this for years. It never entered his head that he might ease our troubles by economy on his part. No, he was determined to wait until you could be persuaded to a wealthy marriage. Now that *you* tell me this, I know it must be so, that you are going to marry— and that I'm going to be very unhappy about it." She looked up then. One of the candles only had been lighted and the room was dark in consequence. "You have been so faithful, my Robin. For so many, many years! We mustn't calculate how many; I am sure I shouldn't risk having the passage of time charted too closely. . . . I think you should know, Robin, that it was to save you from this that I agreed to what the Moneyman asked."

He may not have believed this. At any rate, he brushed it aside quickly. "No matter how generous he may prove with you, it wouldn't suffice to clear up the debts. And"—after a moment's pause—"there's the matter of an heir."

Isabeau had not won back his allegiance after her marriage, and held it all the years since, without the exercise of infinite tact and the employment of her full charm. She understood him thoroughly. One thing she realized about him was that to dispute a point was the surest way to confirm him in his determination but that he would yield quickly before any hint of ridicule.

She permitted a silence to fall after his reference to the need for an heir to the title and lands of De Burey. This, she knew in any case, was the point to which there was no answer. An heir must be forthcoming and it was now manifest that she would never present one to the present holder of the title. She permitted the silence to continue until she saw the first suggestion of uneasiness in his face. Then she hurried into the breach with a question.

"Who is she, this woman Naulty brings forward as his choice?"

"Someone I don't know. She's a widow and her name is Clothilde de Trepant."

Isabeau cried in a strained voice, "Oh no! Oh no!" After this first, and effective, reaction to the suggestion, she paused before going any further. "I might have expected it!" she said then, shaking her head hopelessly. "Naulty has no sense in such matters, none at all. This woman"—she pronounced the two words with a verbal reflection of the distaste a good housewife would display on finding a soiled undergarment folded away with the best linen—"might do as a mistress for your brother but never as a wife for you. Give the idea no further thought, Robin. I promise to convince him that he's wrong." Then, with calculation, she began to laugh. "*What* an idea! Really, my husband is an absurd creature! I'm sure we must disregard him from now on and settle these matters between ourselves."

Isabeau walked over to one of the windows. The rain was turning to hail and lashing against the glass with the uneven spatter of a drumming boy. Drawing the curtain back, she looked out into the storm. "You mustn't think of venturing out tonight. We have no other guests and so we shall sup *en famille*. I'm afraid we won't be very cheerful company. Our difficulties will weigh on our spirits. And, of course, the presence of this hedge brat will be a very great nuisance."

D'Arlay joined her at the window, where he looked out with an air of deep depression at the blur of roofs and chimney pots. She studied him openly, realizing, as she always did, that the quality of fineness about his features was more desirable than mere good looks and that there was both strength and sweetness in the habitual gravity of his expression. "I won't give him up! I won't give him up!" she said to herself. She had promised Jacques Coeur that she would, but without any serious intention of living up to her bargain. She had been on the point of making a reference to this absurd condition but she now felt an inner warning in time. It would be like her brother-in-law to decide, if he knew of it, that he shared with her the responsibility of carrying out her promise.

She turned and placed a hand on his arm. "I'm a selfish woman, Robin," she whispered. "Such a selfish creature, indeed! You have good reason to know that, haven't you? I married someone else and yet never since have I been able to bear the thought of losing you." She shook her head slowly back and forth. Then she smiled with a resigned gravity. "And now we face the situation which has been hanging over us for so long. You must at least grant me this: enough time to see if I can't turn my alliance with the Moneyman into a source of sufficient revenue to remove the— the grim urgency about it."

D'Arlay's response to this was so abrupt and bitter that she realized at once she must withdraw quickly and find a stronger position. "I came today to tell you," he said, "that under no circumstances must you go on with this. If you go against my wishes and the dictates of your own good sense and finer feelings, then you must accept——" He did not finish but she knew he had meant to say that she would never see him again.

She answered in a hurt voice, as though he had prevented her from making her meaning clear by breaking in prematurely. "My dear Robin! Will you allow me to go on? I was going to say that the arrangement with Jacques Coeur is a small matter, after all, one that can be broken at a moment's notice if needs be. But your agreement with Regnault that the time has come for you to marry is quite different. Your whole future life, your happiness, depends on *this*. I wanted to say that you mustn't move as quickly as your attitude threatened. You must be *very* sure. Feeling about you as I do, I can't sit quietly by and see you rushed into an absurd marriage with one of these lusty creatures your brother thinks will make suitable wives. My selfishness now has become a determination to see that you suffer as little unhappiness as possible." She leaned forward and looked up at him with her brows raised in a suggestion that, after all, they were perhaps being unnecessarily concerned. "And finally, my severe

Robin, I wanted to say that no matter what you must do and no matter how much I may be called upon to endure, you can at least"—a smile crinkled up the corners of her eyes—"forget it all for one evening and stay for supper, can't you?"

3

When the Comtesse entered the bedroom, Valerie was bundled up from ears to toes in a woolen houppelande, the most practical article of feminine attire. Her hair had been thoroughly dried and then combed and brushed until its usual golden glow had returned. The discreet use of strawberry foam had put a trace of color in her cheeks. The Comtesse looked at her in silence for a moment and then ordered Guillaumette to withdraw.

"I begin to understand," she said. "You are rather lovely, child. I can see the resemblance now. When you are properly dressed, it will probably be most striking."

"Thank you, my lady."

"Cousin. You must get into the habit of calling me that."

The Comtesse seated herself in a chair close to Valerie and studied her closely in silence. It was a bare room—the interior of the house reflected, as well as the exterior, the poverty which had hung over the family so long—with only two chairs, a chest against one wall, a small and somewhat decrepit *prie-dieu*, and a bed in one corner. It was a single bed, with plain coverings and the merest imitation of a canopy.

"And now it begins," said the Comtesse. "It's not going to be easy for you, child, nor for me either. Do you understand that you must be prepared to do whatever I say and to work very hard?"

"I shall at least be a willing pupil, my lady—my cousin."

"What a lady must know," continued Isabeau, "could probably be told in a few words. It comes easily and naturally when you are born a lady and grow up as one. But for you to acquire it now will not be easy. You must start by realizing that everything you have done and thought and believed is wrong."

"Yes, Cousin. That much I know."

"And it won't be enough to make a lady of you. If a certain pair of eyes are to be attracted, you must have some of the grace and sprightliness of the Lady Agnes. The sprightliness, at least, will be a real difficulty."

"Please don't judge me by today, Cousin," said Valerie. "I am a—a little abashed."

"Naturally, child. I didn't mean to be critical. I am trying to make you see that the change in you must be as complete as the improvements we will make in your wardrobe." Isabeau continued to study her charge with a discerning eye. "I must contrive to let you see the Lady Agnes. You must watch her closely and note every movement. She has certain mannerisms all her own, a little studied, perhaps, but undeniably effective. The happiest result would be if you could catch a suggestion of them but not enough to look deliberate. And now you must be dressed. You will sup with us tonight."

She summoned Guillaumette back to the room and issued detailed instructions in the matter of the clothes Valerie was to wear. "There will be no time for an aromatic bath," she added. "Use my best perfume, Guillaumette. And a touch, just a touch, of melilot on her face. Her hair suits me as it is."

Guillaumette was back in a very short time with a billowing armful of clothes. She proceeded then to remove the houppelande and the kirtle that Valerie wore under it. Accustomed to dressing in her own cramped corner behind a curtain in the Maret tent, the girl looked distressed at being thus publicly disrobed, particularly when the removal of the kirtle revealed that she wore a third garment under it, a pair of woolen leggings which fitted her snugly from waist to knees. The maid looked surprised at this discovery and turned to her mistress in a mute demand for instructions.

"What is that peculiar thing you are wearing?" asked the Comtesse.

"A winter garment, Cousin," faltered the girl. "Is it—is it not customary?"

"I have never seen one before," laughed Isabeau. "What a very ugly thing it is."

"But it's very warm."

"Comfort is the last thing a lady must consider. Do you think we enjoy wearing these high headdresses? I get a headache whenever I use a heavy hennin. It's quite as bad with sleeves. The very latest are long enough to touch the floor. They are a great nuisance and a great absurdity; but as they are the mode, they must be worn."

"Mademoiselle has perhaps never heard of the *toute-autour?*" ventured the maid. "It keeps one warm without the need for garments such as these."

Mademoiselle had never heard of the toute-autour but the promise of such a substitute brought her no comfort when Guillaumette proceeded to remove the leggings. She blushed when robbed of this last cloak to her modesty. There was no reason, however, for her to feel any shame. The Comtesse studied her nakedness and said to herself: "The little slut has a lovely figure as well. What pretty thighs!"

Fortunately for the girl's peace of mind, the maid quickly dropped a *robe-lingue* over her shoulders. It was long enough to reach below her ankles and was made of warm woolen material except for the sleeves and a band about two feet deep at the hem. These were of the finest linen, daintily embroidered in forget-me-not blue. A surcote of a darker shade of blue was then draped over the chemise. Valerie's nervousness left her at once and was replaced by an excited interest, for this was much the handsomest dress she had ever seen. It had a train at least a yard long, and open pointed sleeves with edges embroidered in gold. The skirt had V-shaped slashes on each side, crisscrossed with gold bands. The reason for the linen attachments to the chemise was now apparent. They showed through the slashes and under the sleeves with each movement of the arms.

Valerie looked at herself in a mirror that the maid held up in front of her and for one amazed second could not believe that the fine lady reflected there was herself. A touch of natural color appeared in her cheeks, growing to a rosy flush. She gave a short and excited laugh.

"I—I look quite different, I think."

She had a moment's worry over the low cut of the surcote, which revealed all of her neck and much more than a suggestion of the youthful line of her breasts, but she dismissed it at once, thinking, "I'm to be a lady and so it doesn't matter."

"And now, Mademoiselle, you will see what a toute-autour is," said Guillaumette, producing a long velvet band. This she passed through loops on the robe-lingue a foot above the ankles. The ends were then drawn together tightly and tied in a bow.

"It holds your chemise close to you, Mademoiselle, and so keeps you from getting cold," she explained, taking advantage of the fact that her mistress was looking elsewhere to give the girl's hand an encouraging pat. "There are loops also on the inside of the surcote. When the weather is windy, the toute-autour can be drawn through them as well. That holds all the skirts together snugly."

"It serves a double purpose," pointed out the Comtesse. "You can't take a long step. You had better practice, child, or you will stumble when you go down with me to supper."

Valerie found some difficulty in accustoming herself to the close confinement of the velvet band but, after pacing the length of the room several times, she was able to adjust her steps to it. The test was still in progress when a loud rap sounded on the door. Guillaumette answered it and they saw the long and solemn face of the Comte de Burey staring into the room over her shoulder.

"How dare you intrude yourself on us, Monsieur!" demanded his wife in a tone of the deepest annoyance.

The Comte pushed his way into the room, giving the maid a surreptitious pinch on the hip as he passed her. He was still feeling the effect of his libations, for he carried himself stiffly and essayed each step with all the care of a ropedancer. When he reached the center he stopped and bowed.

"I heard that the little cousin had arrived, Madame," he said. "It seemed to me fitting to wait on you at once and extend her my welcome."

"As you wish," said Isabeau carelessly. "This is Valerie, Monsieur. She will sup with us. If you had cared to contain yourself a few minutes longer, we would have joined you below."

The Comte found it necessary to take several steps nearer to see the new arrival closely. As soon as his nearsighted eyes had succeeded in taking her in, he reached enthusiastically for her hand and planted a kiss on it.

"Madame, my congratulations," he said. "Your cousin is charming. Having full recollection of your uncle Gilles, who bore a close resemblance to a heron or some member of the bird family, I am surprised and pleased. I am doubly happy to welcome her to our—our contented family circle. My respects, Cousin Valerie."

"Thank you, my lord," said Valerie.

"You resemble your mother, no doubt," added the Comte, peering at her closely. "Could I have seen her? There is a certain familiarity about your face, child, which makes me think I must have known her at some time."

Noting the animated beam in her spouse's eye, the Comtesse said impatiently: "If you'll favor us by withdrawing, Monsieur, Guillaumette will complete Valerie's toilet. The shoes remain to be put on."

"I have no intention of withdrawing," declared the Comte. "After all, she's my cousin, if only by marriage. Proceed with your pleasant task, Guillaumette. Ah, a neat foot, most commendably small. You will pardon me for saying, Cousin, that I was laboring under a misapprehension. I thought the girls of Berri ran to heavy hoofs like their horses."

"Your arm, Monsieur," said Isabeau, rising. "We are ready to accompany you to supper."

Even with the support he was able to get by leaning on his wife, the Comte found it hard to negotiate the stairs. He paused after each step, his breathing audible and labored.

"Madame," he whispered between wheezes, "are you prepared yet to tell me what this is all about?"

"I'm prepared to tell you nothing," answered Isabeau shortly.

"I squeezed a little out of that close-mouthed brother of mine. He's staying, no doubt? I need not ask. I note, Madame, that you are dressed with most particular care."

"Robin is staying, of course."

"Now, Madame, about this girl. You know the proverb, 'She shames her mother who does not resemble her father'? Your little Valerie does not resemble in any way that old bloated gander of an Uncle Gilles. If he sired this dainty little dabchick, I've lost all sense of blood lines."

"Have more care," demanded Isabeau. "The girl will hear you."

"Some conspiracy is afoot here, Madame. I must have a personal share in the prosperity which has visited our house so unexpectedly. Now that I've seen the cousin, my ideas as to the size of my share are going up. Going up, Madame, up, up, up!"

4

If there had been any doubts as to his feelings in D'Arlay's own mind, if he had felt that he still hovered on the brink of complete devotion, his first glimpse of Valerie descending the stairs in her new guise dismissed all such mental miswending by sending him headlong over the edge. He went down, down, down, his head in a whirl, his senses swimming in a new delight with her. It was with difficulty that he regained control of himself when he heard Isabeau say in an indifferent voice, "This is my cousin Valerie," adding immediately, "We'll go right in, as supper is ready."

The Comte dropped inertly into the master's chair on the dais, with his wife on his right and Valerie on his left. D'Arlay sat in a muse on the other side of the Comtesse.

The master of the household seemed to have a liking for proverbs. He said in a wheezy voice, " 'A short mass and a long dinner.' I trust, Madame, that the unwonted prosperity of the De Bureys will be reflected in the supper you have provided for us."

Valerie looked about her with astonishment, never having seen such a large and grand apartment before. The fact that it was also bare and shabby made no impression on her. The table below the dais was large enough to accommodate several score although not more than a dozen servants were seated there. The hall was so long, in fact, that she could not make out the subjects of the tapestries hanging on the walls at the far end. The candles lighting the dais were elevated in massive silver candelabra of such height that they spluttered in the drafts far above her head. Two pages in azure livery were engaged in serving the meal, though they found plenty of time to idle about the *dressoirs* and to whisper cautiously. The dishes on which the food arrived were of silver, embossed with the De Burey tree. A sense of excitement began to stir in her. "I had no idea," she said to herself, "that life could be as grand as this."

"Well, little cousin," said the Comte, leaning toward her and giving her arm a cautious nip, "you're a quiet kitten although I seem to read the promise of a lively spirit whenever you raise your eyes long enough to allow me a glimpse of them. It's clear you owe nothing to Gilles save the bare fact of paternity. You will bear me out that he always loved the sound of his own voice." His tone had been rising. "There are many douse stories I could tell about him——"

"I am sure, Monsieur, that our cousin has no desire to hear such memories of her father as have been retained in *your* mind," said Isabeau. She regarded her husband with a look of steady animosity. "As you've already imbibed rather generously, my Regnault, I've given orders that only one wine is to be served tonight."

The Comte was too deep in his cups to offer any defense. He blinked shortsightedly and fumbled at the front of his parti-colored tunic, producing with some effort an *oculus berellinus*, a pair of round crystal discs bound together by a bar of silver. These he fitted on the inflamed bridge of his nose and then proceeded to stare intently at his wife.

Valerie had heard there were magic instruments which people in derision were beginning to call "spectacles" but which were reputed to restore seeing power to weak eyes. Her own eyes grew round as she looked at him.

"Am I no longer master in my own house?" muttered the Comte. "Madame, you go too far."

Conversation lapsed after that. The Comte munched resentfully and cautiously, as though his teeth were giving him trouble. Isabeau and

D'Arlay talked together in low tones. Valerie was too busily engaged in noting all that was done to have anything to say. Her curiosity banished appetite also.

She was realizing how much she had to learn. Beside her plate she found a knife and a strange instrument with two straight prongs. Her first thought was that the latter might be used in conveying food to the mouth, but a tentative effort in that direction was a failure. The prongs refused to take a proper grip on the food and she hastily desisted, deciding that she must do nothing until she had seen how the others went about it. She noted then that they were using their forks (she was to learn the name later) to hold the meat while cutting it into slices for eating. The slices were lifted to the mouth on the circular ends of the knives which were indented to keep the food from slipping off. Spoons, circular in shape and quite large, were used for the pastries. When it came to fish, however, her companions threw nicety to the winds and went vigorously to work with their fingers. Valerie noticed the fastidious way in which her hostess dabbled her fingers at intervals in a ewer of water and was very careful to do the same.

To observe all this closely she found it necessary to lean forward slightly and this brought D'Arlay within her range of vision. She was pleased to see that, although his conversation with the Comtesse ran along without a break, he looked continuously in her direction. The Comtesse became aware of the fixed way in which he was regarding her charge. She glanced at Valerie with a hint of a frown and then, turning back to D'Arlay, said something which caused him to lower his eyes. He did not keep them averted, but it was only at intervals afterward that he allowed them to stray to the other end of the table.

The one glance that the Comtesse had directed at Valerie had been sharp, direct, and suspicious. It convinced the girl on one point. "She's not going to like me." This thought lodged itself so firmly in her mind that she began to indulge in rather dismal reflections on the kind of existence she might expect while she remained a member of the De Burey household.

To escape from these uneasy speculations she resolutely turned her thoughts to Jacques Coeur. How different he was from these people of noble birth! He had been so kind, so quick to understand her, so willing to accept her as an equal. In the short span of time since she had first seen him she had become convinced that he was the greatest man in the world. She was ready to follow his guidance in everything, being certain that whatever he said and did would be right. "Even," she said to herself, "if he tells me I must never disobey this cold Lady Isabeau."

To the great discontent of the Comte, supper consisted of a few dishes only. He partook of them all with a snuffling absorption and his fingers toyed impatiently with his empty wine cup. At intervals he addressed himself in aggrieved undertones to his wife. "Madame, you remain your frugal self in spite of everything," and, "A reasty supper, Madame, with which to welcome the pretty little cousin." His annoyance reached a still higher point over the fact that the fire on the hearth at one side of the long room, above which the azure band and the three silver stars of De Burey were almost regally blazoned, was not throwing out enough heat to make tenancy of the dais comfortable.

"I'm of a mind, Madame," he announced, pushing aside his plate on which he had heaped up a *blanc dessore* of minced pheasant mixed with milk of almonds, "to exile myself to the comforts of country life. There I will be warm at least."

The Comtesse roused herself to a sense of her own discomfort. She clapped her hands and called to the pages, "Alain, Froy, have them bring in more logs." Then she turned to the Comte. "An excellent idea," she said. "I'll put no obstacles in the way of your departure, Monsieur."

Regnault de Burey considered the point for several moments, then he adjusted his spectacles and squinted through them at Valerie. "On second thoughts, no," he said. "I have a conviction, Madame, that life here, in spite of the pestilential cold of this gloomy prison, will prove much more interesting."

11

LIFE for Valerie fell into a pattern the next day which was repeated more or less closely each day thereafter.

The bedroom was dark when Guillaumette awakened her. "Five o'clock, Mademoiselle, by God's good grace," said the maid. She was carrying a taper. Her face, shining moistly above a shapeless red garment, looked no more than half awake in the uncertain light. Valerie's mind was filled with uneasy speculation. She had no idea of what lay ahead of her but was sure that this would prove the most difficult day of her life. It was reluctance to begin the ordeal and not a desire for more sleep which caused her to shrink back under the bedcovers.

"Come, it's time to rise," said Guillaumette, giving the girl's bare shoulder a shake. "You'll want to go to the *Chambre Basse?*"

Valerie guessed at the nature of the suggestion and said, "Yes, Guillaumette."

The maid wrapped her in a warm robe and put woolen slippers on her feet. "It is a distance," she said.

It was indeed a distance. They descended a flight of stairs which were still as dark as in the middle of night, traversed a gloomy hall where the cold of the stone floor could be felt through the slippers, found their way down another staircase even darker than the first, passed a series of open doors through which servants could be seen preparing food, and finally arrived at a door with curtains draped on each side.

The maid drew the curtains together after them. "That's to warn any-one who comes," she explained, "that the room's in use."

The bareness of the great house had left Valerie unprepared for the luxurious nature of the Chambre Basse. The floor was carpeted and warm to the feet. A charcoal-filled brazier, standing beside the Bishop's Throne, was emitting a comfortable glow of warmth. The Throne itself, which seemed to the girl to stand up rather absurdly high, had arms padded with velvet and panels of needlepoint on both back and sides. The pavilion above it, to be let down when extra warmth was required or to pamper the modesty of the user, was of rich camelot cloth. There was a table containing a variety of bottles of perfume, rose water, and spirits of lavender.

After leaving here, they traversed halls in a different direction and came in time to a smaller room where another chair with a pavilion above it awaited the girl's occupancy. It was shaped somewhat like a jack-in-the-pulpit and turned out to be a bath in which she had to sit with her knees in close proximity to her chin. It was a pleasant experience, however, for Guillaumette poured into the warm water a succession of scented liquids, powder of eucalyptus, elder blossoms, mint, thyme, and dried lime blossoms, filling the whole room with their intoxicating odors.

Breakfast followed in Valerie's own room, consisting of a plate of lam-preys, a chop, a single slice of rye bread ("Madame insists on it because it does not make one fat," explained Guillaumette), and a glass of a fiery substance called *eau de vin*[1] instead of wine. All the ladies of the court had taken to drinking it, explained the maid, because the King's physician had recently given it out to be the most healthful of all drinks.

Guillaumette shook her head over the meal. "It is clear," she said, "that things have taken a turn for the better with us. Not that there was any improvement in *my* breakfast. It must be desired that Mademoiselle become most rosy and plump."

One swallow of the eau de vin caused Valerie to choke and refuse more of it, healthful or not. She shook her head at the chop but proceeded to make a good breakfast on the lampreys. Guillaumette watched her for a moment and then, having reached the conclusion that her charge was to be trusted, began to make talk.

"Is Mademoiselle going to like it here?"

Valerie answered, "Yes." Then, as though her question had a bearing on the one the maid has asked, "Is Madame the Comtesse as good as she is beautiful?"

Guillaumette answered with a wry smile. "Good? It's a word to be given many meanings. She's a good mistress, even though she has a sharp tongue and a swift hand for a box on the ears. She has a temper, the mistress. Watch out when the color of her eye changes to red! And she's a close one! She questions the *squire de gobelet* every day, and how she watches the food supplies in the kitchen! If a rat nibbles a corner of cheese, the

[1] Brandy, the making of which had just commenced.

mistress knows about it. She sees everything. I promise you she never misses a thing that Monsieur the Comte does."

"Even when he gives someone a pinch?"

"Mademoiselle also has a quick eye," said the maid. "Mademoiselle will find that Monsieur is a great one for pinching bottoms."

Valerie continued her meal in silence for several minutes. Then the maid said, "Madame should be in a better mood now that the Comte's brother has returned."

"Why should that make a difference, Guillaumette?"

The servant threw back her head and gave forth with a loud cackle. "What difference does it make? Mademoiselle! Madame the Comtesse has been in love with the Sire d'Arlay for years and years and years! Everyone knows it, even Monsieur the Comte."

After a moment Valerie asked, "And does he love the Comtesse?"

"Naturally. There was a time, when they were both younger, when he loved her to distraction. Ah, it was very sad!"

Valerie sat back from the table. She felt both uneasy and dispirited. The Sire d'Arlay had seemed to her the kindest of friends, one to whom she could always turn for help and support. That he was in love with the Comtesse should make no change in his relationship with her but she was realizing that it did. She felt that something had been lost which had been of the greatest importance to her.

Guillaumette began to tell everything she knew about the matter with much shaking of her head and winking to lend extra point to the narrative. D'Arlay had been in the East after the marriage but immediately on his return he had begun to visit his brother's house regularly. At first he always occupied a chair at the far end of the dais and from there he had watched the beautiful chatelaine with worshipful eyes. Gradually she had promoted him along the board until finally, one night, he was granted the supreme happiness of sitting beside her. From that time on he sat nowhere else and the talk between them had been of the kind which excluded all others, being conducted with heads bowed close together and in the lowest of tones.

That had been, the maid explained, when the Sire d'Arlay was young and so much in love that he had not been able to hide his feelings. As he grew older, he had become more guarded and had paid fewer calls. Nevertheless, there had been much talk on the outside and particularly at court. Some courtier had written a couplet about it to the effect that when he Comte had a sore throat it was *mal de rougegorge* (a play on the word for robin) and all the beautiful ladies and great noblemen had gone about quoting it and even singing it to a popular air. The Comte had been very angry that time and had raised a scene when he came home.

"But," said the maid, giving her head an emphatic nod, "it's my opinion, Mademoiselle, that now the rose has begun to wither on the vine. If it were not that Madame the Comtesse is such a one to hold on! . . . And now, of course, he must marry a rich wife and *that* will be the end of it."

"He must marry?" Valerie found it hard to keep from showing the dismay she felt at this further development.

Guillaumette raised her shoulders. "Certainly, Mademoiselle. He must marry to save the estates. The master has debts"—she made a circle of her arms to indicate that the debts were of mountainous proportions—"and they can never be paid unless the Sire d'Arlay brings a fortune into the family. We have all known this for years. It is clear, is it not?"

"Yes, it is clear," said Valerie unhappily. "Is it also known who he is to marry?"

The maid laughed again. "It hasn't gone that far. But when it does, Madame the Comtesse will try again to put porret in the syrup—to spoil the dish, you understand. This much I know. The Sire d'Arlay is now most unhappy about everything. I think he would like to run away to the far ends of the earth."

Valerie had other questions to ask but the chance for further conversation was ended at this point by the arrival of Madame Barquet. Guillaumette retired at once into the background to await such orders as might be given her.

Madame Barquet was reputed to know all the beauty secrets of the East, whence all such secrets came, and her services were much in demand among the great ladies of Paris; and even, it was whispered, among the wives of wealthy merchants who defied the sumptuary laws by insisting on dressing as well as the aristocracy. She came sweeping into the room with dry clothes, a sign that the storm had stopped at last, but bringing in on the end of her long train enough mud to prove that the effects of it were still to be encountered on the streets. She was an elderly woman with a succession of chins and a body like a tun of wine. Valerie looked at her with dismay and thought, "What can she know about beauty when she is so ugly and dirty herself?"

Madame Barquet had many curious habits which manifested themselves quickly enough but the most curious of all was apparent at once. She addressed many of her remarks to herself.

"Madame Barquet," she said, surveying the girl with a calculating eye, "you will have your hands full with this one. You will indeed, Madame Barquet." She bobbed her head so emphatically that the hennin she was wearing flailed about like a windmill in a storm. "Mademoiselle is from the country?"

"Yes, Madame," answered Valerie, feeling even more humble than ever.

"That is good. Mademoiselle knows nothing. She won't dispute with Madame Barquet who knows everything. Saints and sinners! When before, Madame Barquet, have you seen such fingernails! Is it possible the girl has been grooming horses?"

A long dissertation followed on the care of fingers and toes. Valerie, who had never thought of them as anything but adjuncts to her daily labors, was amazed when the woman proceeded to clip the nails almost to the quick. Her surprise mounted when they were dipped into a mixture she had always believed to be a deadly poison and then vigorously polished. The final step was the real surprise of all—the application of a stain which left them a warm and lustrous pink.

"Always," said Madame Barquet, when the operation had been completed, "I leave the nails until the last. But Mademoiselle's were in such a state that something had to be done about them at once."

She stood up then and considered the girl's figure with a speculative eye. Pleased, apparently, with what she saw, she proceeded to confirm her impression by running her hands over the bosom, arms, and hips. Her touch was quick and expert.

"The daily rubbing will be light," she said. "There is a little of the surplus weight of youth to be lost—it's always in the worst possible places, Mademoiselle—but mostly the rubbing will be needed to make you graceful. Ah, Madame Barquet, these middle-aged mountains of flesh who come to you to regain the bloom they have lost through stuffing their stomachs and bringing brats into the world every ten months or so, how much they would pay for such firm breasts, such a sweet roundness of limb!" After a moment's consideration she announced: "There will be no need to wear wrappings around the hips. The lightest of bands around the breasts will do."

A minute inspection of the face followed. "Saints and sinners!" she cried, in a reproachful tone. "A freckle on the point of the nose! Has she been so careless, so foolish, so unmindful of her advantages, as to expose herself to the hateful effects of the sun? Avoid the sun, Mademoiselle, it is the enemy of feminine beauty! The moon—ah, that is different. Every evening, if possible, you must expose yourself for at least an hour to the beneficent rays of the moon. It will make you lily white; and it's white flesh which makes desire grow in the eyes of men." Addressing herself to the maid: "Now for this treacherous freckle. Oatmeal paste and lemon juice must be applied to the nose every night before going to bed."

Madame Barquet, her labors for the time being completed, deposited her bulging form in a chair. "Guillaumette, the wine!" she said. While waiting for the order to be obeyed, she opened her mouth and proceeded to rub her almost toothless gums with a brown spice. At the same time she kept a sharp eye on her new charge.

"You've been told, Madame Barquet," she muttered, "that you are to see nothing and to say nothing. If the pay is steady enough, you will say nothing. But what you see would make a dainty little morsel to tell your ladies. Your ladies expect you to fill their silly ears with gossip while you pummel and rub and salve their fat bodies." She continued to mutter. "Is it really the fair Lady Isabeau she is cousin to? Now *that* is something to think about, Madame Barquet."

She departed after swallowing her wine. It was then the turn of the physician. He was small and sharp of eye and very restless and chipper of movement. "Like a squirrel," Valerie thought. The physician lacked the courage of Robert de Poitevin, for he had trussed himself up in one of the chemical-soaked tunics and his breath was lethal with garlic.

He found nothing wrong with Valerie. In fact, as a physician, he seemed to resent that she was so safely removed from the need of his ministrations. "It goes against all the laws of nature for one to be so healthy," he complained, in his chirping voice. Then he nodded his head in the maid's direction. "Calomel once a month. It will purge the poisons which are concealed somewhere inside her. See that she never drinks cow's milk. Half a cup of mare's milk a day if she craves it, but no more; it's dangerous stuff to take into the human stomach. We must guard against every kind of chance. Above everything see that her bed has red hangings. She'll never catch the smallpox if you do."

After the little man had departed, Guillaumette said, "The good father from the University is here to give you a first lesson in reading and writing."

Valerie felt a cold chill take possession of her. "They say," she whispered in an awed tone, "that one must have a very clever mind to learn letters. I am tempted to run away."

As it happened, the ordeal did not begin that morning after all. Before the priest from the University put in an appearance, a summons was received for Valerie to go at once to the apartments of the Comtesse.

2

The bare aspect of the old house was not reflected in the rooms dedicated to the comfort of the chatelaine. The main chamber of the Comtesse was fully and warmly furnished. There was a *secrétaire* under a canopy of brown velvet, a long table which obviously was many centuries old, a beautifully carved crucifix on one wall. The window hangings were of fine linen and most cheerfully blue. The Comtesse was sitting at one end of the table with a vanilla stick burning beside her.

It was clear that she had not been up long. Her hair, which showed reddish tints through the brown, was bound in braids on the back of her head, and the tip of a yellow bed slipper protruded under the hem of her skirt. She had a goblet of eau de vin in front of her.

"Good morning, Cousin," said Valerie.

"Good morning. I've just had a note from Monsieur Coeur, asking us to pay him a visit this afternoon at his largest shop in the city. He'll have an assortment of things to show us which may be useful for your wardrobe. We'll leave here at three o'clock and I suggest that you be ready before the hour."

"Yes, Cousin, of course." Valerie spoke eagerly. "It's a wonderful shop. I saw enough of it to know that it contains the most beautiful things."

Some of the severity went out of the voice of the Comtesse. "I'm looking forward to the visit. My own wardrobe needs replenishing. . . . I want to tell you, child, that you behaved yourself well at supper last night. You made no mistakes and you—you looked quite presentable."

"Thank you, Cousin. I watched you and I didn't do anything until I had seen you do it first."

"But," said Isabeau, with sudden sharpness, "you show a tendency to copy me in ways that I don't relish. After supper I went to your room to bid you good night and from the door I saw you walking in front of your mirror in what I suspect was an imitation of my manners and walk. I went away without letting you know I had been there. I want you to understand that I was deeply offended."

Valerie's cheeks flushed guiltily. "I'm sorry, Cousin. It's a habit I have and I see now that it's a very bad one. Need I say that it won't happen again?"

"I trust not." Isabeau hesitated before going on. She was deeply annoyed, it was clear. "I'm not in a position to judge of the excellence or otherwise of your aping of me. But this I must say: you're mistaken in thinking I swing my hips when I walk. The way you exaggerated the motions was—was vulgar in the extreme. I was very angry and very hurt."

"I'm sure it was a stupid attempt on my part, Cousin."

The Comtesse gave a cold nod of forgiveness. "We'll say no more about it then. I suggest that you return now to your lessons and that you be ready promptly this afternoon."

Valerie was thoroughly ashamed of herself for making such a mistake on her first day. As she left the room, however, she was thinking that the Comtesse did not look so lovely in the mornings and that she was undoubtedly older than she, Valerie, had at first supposed. "And," she added to herself, "she *does* swing her hips a little when she walks."

3

The shop of Jacques Coeur stood in a cluster of buildings back of the Louvre and within sight of the Hôtel d'Alençon and the Petit-Bourbon. It had been the city house of some great personage in its earlier periods. Planned both for show and security, its walls towered up in gloomy grandeur above the street to end in a confusion of stone turrets and flying buttresses.

The two ladies arrived promptly at half-past four and were escorted to a large apartment where a busy official asked them the nature of their needs. The mention of the name of De Burey had a magical effect. He drew himself up and said in an important voice: "Yes, my lady. You are expected. You are respectfully requested to visit the floor above."

They stepped out into a confusion as great as the daily hubbub of the streets. Torches blazed at all corners of the court, for the walls shut it in so closely that a blanket, seemingly, could have covered the square of sky visible above. Customers were passing to and fro. Porters with bundles on their backs were everywhere.

The walls were lined with open galleries, one above the other. Valerie began to count them but lost track in the upper reaches where the stone tracery of the railings merged into confusion. There were outside stairs at each end, one marked *Up* and one *Down*, and the clatter of heels on their stone steps added to the din. Their guide led the way to the upward-bound stair and from there to the white-plastered bureau of the master of this humming beehive.

Jacques Coeur greeted them in a jubilant mood. "In three more days," he told them, "this main bazaar of mine will be gnawed as clean as a rind in a cupboard. Did you know the building is to be used for war purposes? Some of the goods are being moved to other shops but the largest part of the stock is being purchased by the good people of Paris. Did you meet any of my heralds on the streets, crying the bargains to be found here?" His eyes were snapping with enthusiasm. "You must forgive me, Comtesse. I'm a merchant first and last, and at times like these I tread on light toes. I'm as excited and happy as a captain who has won a great victory. But you needn't fear that the cupboard is empty. I've seen to it that some of the very best things are left for you."

Valerie had arrived in a depressed mood to which a number of things had contributed: the information she had been given about D'Arlay, the reprimand from the Comtesse and, back of everything, the uncertainty and fear she felt whenever her mind cast on into the future.

Her spirits lifted, however, when the Moneyman led the way to an adjoining room which was well lighted by a score of candles. She paused on the threshold with a gasp of astonishment and pleasure. The place was filled with fabrics in all the rich colors of the East. There were frames along the walls hung with lengths of the rarest silks and the very choicest of satins while in the center a vermeil table was heaped with velvets and shimmering brocades. Smaller tables had assortments of camisoles and *baignoires* and chemises of Flemish linen, embroidered surcotes, flowered jupons, and lacy gorgets for the neck. One was given over entirely to purses and the gipsers which ladies wore at their waists, to hold the small coins their husbands trusted them with, and leather cases for prayer books. Another displayed hoods of velvet and hennins of all kinds.

Coeur said proudly, "The Queen of Sheba never had the likes of this to choose from."

He reached into one of the wall frames and held up a bolt of silk for their inspection. Both ladies exclaimed with involuntary delight and reached out simultaneously to feel its tempting texture. It was a cream color like the subdued glow of the setting sun. "From Cathay," he said reverently. "It's the finest silk to be found in the world today. They call this shade by a word that means kiss me. A good name for it. Not only does it hold the kiss of the sun but it promises that the wearer will create that desire in every male beholder."

The Comtesse took an end of the silk and held it against her cheek and hair. "I must have it," she said. "It's better suited to me. I shall have the bodice cut so tight that it won't matter where the line of the neck comes. It will drop low over the hips, still very snug, and then flare out into a fifteen-fluted skirt. The sleeves will widen at the shoulders and taper tightly to the tips of the fingers, and must be tufted, I think, with dull gold buttons."

Coeur was completely the merchant now. He studied her with an expert eye and agreed that this particular shade was better suited to her. He then turned to Valerie and considered the color of her hair before reaching down a bolt of velvet. "And this for Mademoiselle," he said.

It was blue with a hint of peacock green, a perfect shade for corn-colored hair. "It is called Angel's-Eye," he said. He draped a fold over her shoulder. "The East keeps the secret of this shade. We have fine blue dyes here in France but nothing to equal this. For trimming, I think it needs gold ornaments of the kind we call *orfrays* in the trade. Fortuantely there's a wide assortment of them still."

He brought out many more materials, each one seeming, if possible, more desirable than the earlier ones. A table had been cleared for the purpose and it was soon piled high with them. There were lengths of rich camocas (which was sometimes called Beyond-the-Sea), camelot cloth, cendal and satanin for linings, Alexandrine velvet, Turkey cloth dyed a deep red, satins in shades of pansy, canary, rye flower, summer gray, and amorous desire. The two visitors paid most attention to one called Lively Ghost, which derived its name from a tendency to change color. Sometimes it was gray, sometimes blue, occasionally it deceived the eye with suggestions of green, and at all times it seemed to shimmer and flash like a hint of distant lightning in a rain-washed sky.

If any piece of material did not seem suitable for Valerie, it was irresistible to Isabeau, and so not one of the beautiful specimens was allowed to be set aside. "You must have this," the merchant would say. The mound of accepted stuffs grew to a pyramid like a miniature Tower of Babel. "Surely," thought Valerie, her eyes glowing with excitement, "this would do for the trousseau of a princess!"

The Comtesse showed a trace of worry. "How are we to explain such fine things? Everyone knows how thin our purse is, and Valerie is to pass as a dependent relative."

"It can be said that she's a special pet of Jacques Coeur's." He gave the girl's cheek an affectionate pinch. "She *is* that already."

He began then to bring out accessories which caused Valerie's head to swim with delight. There were gold-mesh cornettes and bourselets for the head in lieu of the extravagant hennins; kerchiefs so finely wrought as to be almost transparent; gorgets of a shade called *ynde* which was a vivid blue; stiffened panels of embroidered Turkish velvet to be worn over the chemise; stockings of turquoise and gray-pearl and flamelet of sulphur.

The excitement mounted when he came to the question of shoes. Both ladies, it seemed, had an especial interest in this important adjunct of feminine apparel. Valerie was transported when he produced a pair *à la poulaine* which were of green Cordovan leather and curled up at the toe with a gold tassel. They were so small and delicately contrived that they looked like early spring buds. She continued to exclaim as he removed the ones she was wearing and put them on instead. They fitted perfectly.

"Never have I seen anything more lovely!" she said ecstatically.

She was equally pleased, however, with a second pair which he brought out. They were known as *fauves botes* and made of very softest leather, with coral velvet lining and spirals of gold thread in place of buttons in which seed pearls nestled like drops of dew.

"These," he explained, "can be used for a special purpose. When you wear them with the sides turned down like this, it means you have made a pledge. A love pledge, Mademoiselle."

He had left something for the last, considering it, quite clearly, to be the prize item of all. There was a trace of excitement in his fingers as he spread before them a bolt of cherry-colored cloth. "There is a story about this," he said. "It comes from a monastery in the southern part of China. The priests have magic powers and many secrets, the making of this cloth being one of them." He smoothed the surface with a careful touch. "It is much like camelot but finer and infinitely more durable. They spin it from the hair of newborn kids. It is as soft to the touch as silk and yet it will wear like a suit of Milan mail. They say it has a magic power to change its shade just enough to suit anyone who wears it; provided, however, that the wearer has a heart without envy or malice. It will lend our little Mademoiselle a vivid quality. She will look in this like an autumn wood sprite or a princess from the high mountains where it was made." He turned to the Comtesse and beamed happily. "When our Galatea is clothed in this, she will be fairer than Helen and Cleopatra and Balkis combined!"

They were breathless when the time came to go. "Have you calculated the cost?" asked Isabeau, in a weak voice.

"The cost? It doesn't matter. That is my responsibility, dear lady. If we beat the English, we will all walk in paths of glory, and such small matters will be forgotten. If we lose? In that event, the victors will have less to pick from my bones."

12

TUDDUAL THE HERALD wiped his hands on the front of his emblazoned tabard and winked across the table at Guillaumette. "By Gis! They're a glum lot tonight," he said.

Guillaumette looked up at the three silent figures on the dais. There had been little conversation since the meal began. "Madame's not happy. When Madame has the cockroach, the others are unhappy too. It's very simple."

The herald demanded, "And why does Madame have the cockroach?"

"You're a stupid mome if you lack the answer to that, my Tuddual," said the maid, with a scornful sniff. "The Sire d'Arlay has not been here for"—she paused to make an accurate count—"for a month and three days. Is it not enough to put an edge to her temper? She has been boxing ears right and left. It's very hard for those who cannot keep themselves at a safe distance."

The herald gawped up at the figure of his mistress, sitting very straight and staring ahead of her. "What keeps the sire away?" he asked.

"It may be that he's ill. It may be that some other lady is filling his eye. It may be the Comte has told him to stay away. Who am I to know? Truly, Tuddual, I wonder sometimes that you have enough wit to sound your horn." The maid indulged in a reminiscent giggle. "You should see the getling's imitation of you!"

"Mademoiselle?"

"Who else could I mean? Mademoiselle, of course. She's a rare one to mimic. She takes you off to a white—you and your look of an ox and your silly questions. I tell her she takes you off better than any of the others."

The herald's slow gaze turned toward Valerie. All he could see of her was her head and shoulders, for the table on the dais was several feet higher than the one at which the retainers were eating. He could tell, however, that she was more handsomely attired than usual. Her headdress was of the finest velvet and of a rich blue shade to match her ermine-trimmed tunic. She was lifting slices of preserved ginger to her mouth with a fastidious motion of her fingers which would have passed scrutiny at the court itself.

"Mademoiselle imitates *me?*" The idea seemed to please him. His eyes, which resembled partly poached eggs both in shape and color, seemed almost to achieve animation. "I would like to see it, Guillaumette. When can I see her imitate me, Guillaumette?"

"She's a clever one!" said the maid pridefully. "Ah, what a mimic! You should hear her when she does Master Alain whose voice is beginning to crack. It's enough to make you split your sides. And she does old Gracien, with his nose which always runs and his bumbling and his lameness in the one leg. But she's best when she does you, my Tuddual."

"Does she do the mistress? Or Monsieur the Comte?"

Guillaumette snapped at him. "You great mome! Most certainly she does not."

The Comte de Burey was not comfortable. He shifted uneasily in his chair and grunted. One of his feet had swelled and was causing him much pain.

He crunched an *échande* in his mouth and mumbled a question to his wife, "Have you quarreled with that brother of mine?"

Isabeau raised her brown eyes in an admirable simulation of surprise. "Have I quarreled with Robin? Of course not. What put that idea in your head?"

"My amiable spouse," said the Comte, dropping his voice, "it's the only conclusion open to me. I've missed his earnest face. The only thing that would keep him away would be a disagreement with you. So—unless this damnable pain in all my muscles has destroyed my reasoning powers, there has been a rift."

The Comte began to munch another of the small pastries, making a wry face when he discovered there was a fig in it. His bodily discomfort was so great that he was getting little satisfaction from wearing new clothes. He had on a parti-colored velvet jacket, brown on the right half and yellow on the left, which was as new as a chicken just out of the shell. Ordinarily the luxurious feel of the fresh finery would have put him in a preening mood.

Valerie was watching them as closely as she dared. She knew that the prolonged absence of the Sire d'Arlay had been the cause of the many spells of nervous anger in which the Comtesse had been indulging. So far the servants had been the victims of her upset state of mind but Valerie had been expecting that the winds of displeasure would begin to blow in her direction. She leaned forward sufficiently to see her mentor, saying to herself, "She looks so cool and white and unruffled and yet underneath, I'm sure, she's burning with vexation." Isabeau, certainly, had never looked more charming. She was wearing a gown fashioned from one of Coeur's materials, a warm brown silk with bands and trimmings of gold. Only the possessor of real beauty of shoulder and breast could wear a bodice so tightly fitted.

"I was at court this morning," said the Comte, breaking the silence again. "I bring news which you will like as little as I do."

Isabeau looked up quickly. "Indeed?"

"The King walked in the gardens this morning with—— Who do you suppose shared the royal saunter, my heart?"

"Antoinette de Maignelais, of course."

"Yes, it was the De Maignelais vixen. She minced along beside him and looked up into his face and trilled with delight at every word that fell from his lips." The Comte gave an apprehensive glance at Valerie and then dropped his voice to a whisper. "Are you not likely to be too late?"

Isabeau looked up quickly. "What do you mean?"

"There's no need to explain. We understand each other, my sweet one. When I saw her garcing along beside him, I felt quite disturbed and sure the—*the new entry*—would be too late in the field."

Isabeau answered coolly, "I think not, Monsieur."

"Why are you so confident? I tell you the lusty little creature was taking full advantage of her opportunity this morning."

"She's trying too hard—and too soon."

The Comte shook his head with a lack of conviction. "I'm not at all sure you're right."

"Agnes Sorel is not dead." Isabeau spoke in such a low tone that only her husband could hear. "She knows of her cousin's behavior and at the proper time she will take steps. Someday she will appear at the King's side again. She will be pale and wan; but make no mistake, she will still be lovely, as lovely as ever, if in a different way. The King will fall under her spell again. It has never failed, Monsieur. The vulgar little Antoinette will be forgotten immediately."

The Comte chafed the bridge of his nose and squinted down into the composed face of his wife. "I'm told the Lady Agnes is too ill to make an appearance."

"She won't be too ill to show her power for the benefit of the over-anxious cousin. She'll never be too ill to wind Charles of France around her finger."

The Comte hesitated. His manner indicated that he was deeply concerned over the news which he now had to tell. Leaning toward his wife, he asked, "Has it come to your ears that Jacques de Lalain is back in Paris?"

Isabeau shook her head. "I've never taken any interest in the exploits of that great ox."

"It's clear then," said her husband, "that my brother has not told you that there is a duel pending between them."

The shock Isabeau felt at hearing this was so great that she did not notice something which her eyes would have been quick to detect under any other circumstances, that Valerie was as distressed as she was.

"It can't be true! Robin wouldn't have been so foolhardy——" The coolness of the Comtesse had deserted her. Her cheeks had taken on a flush. "Regnault, do you mean it?"

"Unfortunately, it's true. It seems they met the first night of Robin's return, and quarreled. The story I had today was that the Burgundian insisted on enough time to acquaint himself with the use of the new type of sword. They're to fight, it seems, with the sword. There's a slight satisfaction there. Robin has skill with the weapon." The Comte shifted uneasily in his chair. "I asked you about him a moment ago because I was hoping the stubborn fellow had confided something to you which would serve to allay my fears."

"Have you forgotten," asked Isabeau, with a desperate suggestion of hopefulness in her voice, "that the King has issued an edict against dueling?"

"That won't prevent them from meeting. All Paris has gone mad over the prospect of seeing the Burgundian in action, particularly in view of the unusual conditions. It has gone too far for the will of the King to stop it." The Comte remained sunk in uneasy speculation for several moments. Then he blinked solemnly and turned to look at his wife. "This is what I hear. The duel will be fought somewhere outside the city. The place won't be given out but the word will be circulated quietly at the last moment to a limited number. That will throw the officers of the Crown off the scent —or such is the hope. In any event, I doubt if the King will try to stop it. It would be a most unpopular move and our liege lord is tender toward the feelings of his subjects."

Isabeau was looking down at her plate. After several moments of silence she asked in a strained voice, "Will he have any chance?"

"Little enough. The Burgundian is the greatest fighter in the annals of chivalry."

"This duel mustn't be fought!" Her voice rose with a suggestion of hysteria. "I shall go to the King and demand that his edict be enforced!"

Her husband responded gloomily, "It would do no good, my heart." He shook his head slowly. "Everyone wants the fight to go on. Even if our liege lord strove to prevent it, some way would be found to set his authority at naught."

"Where is Robin?" demanded Isabeau. She was showing signs of panic. "Why can't he be placed under arrest in advance? That has often been done to prevent duels. Why can't Jacques de Lalain be ordered to leave Paris now? Has the King no power at all?"

"Neither Robin nor Jacques de Lalain can be found." The Comte sighed hopelessly and fumbled with his aids to vision. "It's clear they've gone into hiding to prevent any such steps being taken. They won't be seen until they appear in the lists tomorrow at whatever place is decided on."

"Why has Robin kept this to himself? Was he afraid he might be put under arrest?"

The Comte nodded his head. "That was his reason quite clearly. Even the Moneyman knew nothing of it until today. He was at court and heard it the same time I did. I talked to him afterward and he seemed stunned by the news. It was his intention to urge action on the King but he had little hope of succeeding."

Isabeau burst out suddenly. "Has he gone mad? Is he determined to throw his life away? Regnault, there must be something we can do!"

"Have you ever heard, my spouse, of the Code of Chivalry? There's nothing we can do."

Well down below the salt Guillaumette said to those around her: "Why are they so silent up there? I'm sure they haven't said a word for at least ten minutes."

13

AS JACQUES COEUR GALLOPED across the Petit-Pont, causing the wooden planking to rock and creak, he was conscious that never before had he seen the ill-fated old bridge (it was continually falling or being washed out in the floods) so crowded. A continuous stream of horsemen were crossing with as much tendency to haste as he was showing himself. Foot travelers were striding ahead and spitting their resentment like gibbed cats when forced to step aside for the more fortunate wayfarers who rode. An occasional carriage rumbled along in the single-minded procession.

The Moneyman was in no doubt as to the meaning of this activity. "The secret, which was to be so closely held," he said over his shoulder to Nicolas, "is known, quite apparently, to all Paris."

"Did you expect anything else, master?"

They pulled in to a more circumspect pace on leaving the bridge. As they rode through the dark arch of the Petit-Châtelet, Coeur looked up at the windowless walls of that grim old prison. "It would be in the power of our liege lord to throw everyone who attends this duel into jail," he said to Nicolas. "Yet all Paris is going—laughing and joking and looking for chances to gamble on the outcome. There's less respect for law here, I believe, than anywhere else on earth."

Emerging into the light, they pulled up in front of a house with a single window set in its beamed and plastered front like the one eye of Cyclops, and Coeur whistled a bar from "The Old Man of the Mountain." In a very few minutes D'Arlay came out, pulling the brim of his roundlet well down over his eyes to escape recognition. He swung a leg over a horse hitched at the mounting post and rode off with them. Coeur's critical appraisal of him netted the conviction that he was cool and composed in spite of what lay ahead of him.

"You've had your pains for nothing," said Coeur. "You could have remained comfortably at home and the law wouldn't have raised a hand to interfere with you. Last night I laid the papers for your arrest before the King and begged him to sign them. He shook his head and said you were a bad subject—everyone is a bad subject who doesn't please him at the moment—but that he would take no steps. I offered to tell him the place selected for the encounter and he smiled and asked if I thought him less informed than the poorest citizen of Paris. I suggested that, as a state of war will soon exist, Jacques de Lalain be treated as an alien and sent immediately on his way back to Burgundy. It did no good. Our liege lord seems perfectly content to have his law broken."

D'Arlay indulged in a wry smile. "It's possible, Jacques, he would like to be rid of such a bad subject."

"If he were rid of everyone to whom he has applied that term," declared the Moneyman, "he would be left with a thinly populated country to rule."

D'Arlay did not seem aware of the reason for the hurrying crowds. "What is happening?" he asked. "Is it another Exodus? Have English armies been reported up the river?"

"Doesn't it occur to you that these crowds are on their way to see you fight the Burgundian?"

D'Arlay gave his friend an incredulous stare. "But it was given out we were to meet on the other bank, in the fields a mile beyond the Grange-Bâtelière. It was expected that anyone curious enough to want to attend would be thrown off the scent and go there instead."

"You are to fight," said Coeur testily, "in a secluded dip of land to the right of the Chartreuse Monastery and every idle mother's son in Paris is on his way there. The original twoscore who were to share the secret has grown to a mere twenty thousand. Well, what can you expect? This is Paris."

"I've made a new will," said D'Arlay, taking advantage of the fact that the pressure of the crowds had forced them so close that he could speak in a low tone. "With the exception of one bequest, everything is to be applied to paying off the debts. I've taken the liberty again of naming you as executor."

"Do you wish to tell me anything about the one bequest?"

"No, not now, Jacques. It's to someone for whom I have a—a great affection."

Coeur said in a grave tone, "God grant there will be no need to apply its provisions."

Despite the ever-present evidence of the milling crowds, they found it hard to credit what they saw when they reached the place selected for the encounter. It was a flat stretch of land with a slope at one side which became wooded after a rise of perhaps twenty feet. An enclosure had been marked out, using the slope as one side, and pavilions had been erected at each end. The enclosure was two hundred yards long and a third of that in width but already the space around it was tightly packed with people, except the slope, which was being reserved for spectators of noble birth. The waiting crowds were at least fifty feet deep, and still farther back they were using the stumps of trees, overturned carts, and any convenient rise of ground to obtain a view of the enclosure. Entertainers were plying their trades: magicians, jugglers, ropedancers, and mountebanks of all kinds. One enterprising butcher had dug a long ditch and built a fire in it, over which the carcasses of three oxen were turning on spits; he would reap a rich harvest later, when the duel was over and the spectators could give a thought to bodily appetites. Paris, in short, was turning the occasion into a holiday.

They reined in their horses on a hillock overlooking the scene. D'Arlay's eyes rested for several moments on the pavilion at the far end of the enclosure. It was of spectacular size, purple and rust in color, and with the flag of Burgundy flapping insolently on a tall shaft in front. Signs of activity about it indicated that Jacques de Lalain and his party had already arrived. D'Arlay's own pavilion was a much smaller one, of plain gray with the azure band and silver stars of De Burey on the shield suspended at the entrance. It was so small, in fact, that he could barely see it over the heads of the mob. A single squire and Helion awaited him there, and he could not help contrasting the modesty of his preparations with the evidences of pomp and splendor at the other end.

For the first time his composure showed signs of deserting him. He turned a disturbed face to his companion. "I expected to fight before a handful of people," he said. "I've never had to face a crowd like this before, Jacques. I confess to you that I find the prospect nothing short of appalling."

Coeur dropped a hand on his shoulder. "It will stir you up to your very best efforts."

A knight riding by shouted to an acquaintance, "Five of the biggest coins in my purse on the Burgundian!" The answer came back in a scornful tone: "I'll offer you the same wager. The Burgundian should win with a single thrust."

Coeur found himself sharing the nervousness of his companion. "What condition are you in?" he asked.

Some of D'Arlay's confidence returned. "I'm in better physical shape than ever before. I've been training faithfully for weeks. My sword arm is as hard as iron and I can step through a lively bout without feeling any fatigue. The Burgundian won't win with a single thrust, Jacques. That much I promise you."

2

Jacques Coeur scowled at the knot of admiring friends and respectful squires and heralds crowding the interior of the purple-and-rust pavilion. He scowled with even more feeling at Jacques de Lalain himself. The great champion, in a state of complete nakedness, was stalking up and down, glad of the chance to show off the power of his mighty shoulders and the bulging muscles of his legs. The expression on his arrogant face said as plain as any words, "Have you ever seen the like of me, you puny, ordinary mortals?"

"The point must be decided at once," said Coeur impatiently.

"The point has already been decided," declared the Burgundian. He stopped in front of Coeur and gestured regally. "I've nothing further to add to what I've already said. We will wear breastplates and helmets but with the condition I have named. There's no manner of sense in contesting the point longer, Sir Merchant."

"I'll inform the Sire d'Arlay that your overweening pride prevents you from listening to the voice of reason. I'll tell him you have closed your mind to all considerations of fair play."

Coeur brushed aside the silken flap and stalked out of the pavilion. The only hope left was that the storm, which had been threatening for days, would break and so make the meeting impossible. He glanced up at the sky and, to his dismay, saw that an aisle had opened in the clouds through which the sun was making a half-hearted effort to shine. There would be no help from the elements.

His appearance brought a roar of disapproval from the spectators. Twice already he had gone from one pavilion to the other in his efforts to convince the Burgundian that he must abide by the original agreement. Not knowing the real reason for the delay, the crowd made it clear that the blame was being laid at the door of D'Arlay. "Is this a meeting between two honorable knights in mortal combat," demanded a voice, "or is it a matching of wits, a contest in diplomacy?" The rabble in the front rows had reached the point where nothing but immediate action would suit. "Fight, fight, fight!" rose the cry from all around the enclosure. "Bring out your man, Jaquet—if he's not afraid to face the Burgundian!" The tension was increased by fear that officers of the Crown would arrive to stop the duel before the fighting began.

The Moneyman called as he walked down the enclosure, "The Burgundian wants to change the rules to his own advantage!" The spectators, however, had passed the stage where they were open to reason. The only response he got was further chanting of, "Fight, fight, fight!"

He found D'Arlay pacing nervously up and down inside his pavilion. The latter turned and asked in a strained voice, "Well, was an agreement reached?"

"I could do nothing with him," answered Coeur, his eyes full of smoldering anger. "He still contends that in yielding the choice of weapon he gave up his right and that he's entitled now to make these demands."

"He didn't yield the choice. I won it by the toss of a coin."

"I've dinned that into his ears a dozen times. All he says in reply is that he won't enter the lists unless you both wear breastplates. To that he has now added another condition. A hole over the heart must be cut from each plate. They must be heart-shaped and, of course, of equal size. He demands this as proof that his insistence on the use of armor is due to a sense of fitness and not to fear of your blade."

D'Arlay frowned. "A curious stipulation," he said.

"There's no doubt in my mind that he sees some advantage in it," declared Coeur. "My advice to you is to refuse his conditions."

D'Arlay was silent for several moments. "We're in no position to dispute with him any longer," he said then. "Listen to them out there! They're sure I'm the one who's holding back. Jacques, I must give in and fight him in the manner he demands. Accept his stipulations, in God's name, and let us have it over."

Coeur said, "It's for you to decide." To himself he added, "He's going to his death, but my hands are tied and there's nothing more I can do."

D'Arlay got to his feet. "What arrangements were suggested for the cutting of the plates?"

"An armorer will attend to that immediately. It will be done in the lists so all may see what is afoot." Coeur paused and then broke out with sudden vehemence: "Think well, Robin, before you agree. I tell you this man who is called the greatest fighter and most honorable knight in all Christendom is as sly as a fox and ready to take advantage of you in every way."

D'Arlay smiled without any hint of mirth and dropped a hand on the Moneyman' shoulder. "Don't lose heart, old friend. Come, take the word back to him that I have agreed." He turned to the servant. "I must wear all my best clothes today. Like a bridegroom, my Helion."

Coeur decided to make one more effort. "Robin," he said, "you and I have always agreed in our opinion of the Code of Chivalry."

D'Arlay, who had begun to disrobe, looked up and nodded in assent. "Yes, Jacques. My opinions haven't changed in any respect."

"And yet here you are," declared Coeur, in a bitter tone, "preparing to fight to the death with a knight much stronger and more skilled than you are. If you come out of this alive, it will be by the grace of Almighty God. And what is the reason? A dispute into which the pair of you fell over the wine cups. You're prepared to throw your life away in a futile quarrel."

A brazier of charcoal was burning behind them but there was still enough chill in the air inside the tent to make D'Arlay's teeth chatter. He began to dress with an urgency which rendered conversation difficult. "I can't deny," he said, "that the quarrel between us was a futile one."

"Then be wise enough now to refuse to go on with it. The conditions the Burgundian insists upon are a sufficient reason."

D'Arlay shook his head. "No, Jacques, my friend. The issue can now be settled only in the lists. And yet I assure you that I feel about such matters as I've always done."

"Is there nothing I can say or do to stop you from throwing your life away?"

Helion was slipping the gambeson over his master's shoulders. D'Arlay did not reply until the operation had been completed. "Do you think," he asked, "that I could live out my life with a charge of cowardice hanging over me?"

Coeur threw up his arms in a despairing gesture. "Chivalry," he declared, with intense bitterness, "flourishes on fear quite as much as on honest courage. Most knights abide by the Code because they're afraid of what others will think and say. Let me tell you this, Robin: This is a time when you should be above such fears. France needs every stout heart and strong arm today. Where does your real duty lie? Should you preserve your life to fight the English or risk it today against this Burgundian coxcomb who has no intention of taking any part in the war?"

"But don't you see," asked D'Arlay, with a resigned shake of his head, "that under the Code I would not be allowed to fight the English tomorrow if I didn't fight Jacques de Lalain today?"

3

The space on the slope, which had been reserved for the nobility, was rapidly filling up when Jacques Coeur stationed himself among the spectators there. He was in a mood of such preoccupation that he was barely conscious of the fact that close at hand a party of pikemen, who wore no insignia of any kind nor any distinguishing colors, were keeping clear a place capable of accommodating a score or more and from which a most favorable view of the enclosure was obtainable. He concluded that some great nobleman was taking this method of assuring an advantage to himself and his immediate retinue.

A herald entered the lists and stationed himself in front of the favored section to make an announcement of the conditions under which the duel was to be fought. Raising his voice, he laid special stress on the cutting of the heart-shaped holes in the breastplates of the contestants. As he spoke an armorer was at work in the lists, in full view of everyone, and the clang of his hammer and chisel on the steel provided a fitting punctuation to the words of the herald as he proclaimed, "This is done, brave gentlemen and fair ladies, to provide vulnerability, to place the two champions in constant jeopardy from the play of the blades." The crowds stirred and a hum of talk arose from all quarters. This was something new, something novel. It would make this gladiatorial encounter one long to be discussed and savored.

Jacques Coeur said to himself with deep inner disgust, "If they knew how much trickery goes on beneath the surface at all tournaments and all knightly meetings they would think less of this precious chivalry!"

If he had not been so bitterly concerned over the outcome, he might have found some relief in the beauty of the setting. No period in history has ever exceeded this one in its understanding and appreciation, and its use, of color. The spectators, massed solidly about the enclosure, presented a remarkable spread of contrasting hues. It was not only on the slope where the nobility clustered that this was to be found. There, the towering hennins of the ladies and their rich cloaks of so many delightful shades of red and green and blue (the wonderful blues of the Middle Ages!) and the costly plumes which bobbed on the heads of the men and the tufted magnificence of their enormously padded shoulders combined to create a man-made spectrum which was nothing short of breath-taking. The common people, who noisily filled the other side and swarmed about the pavilions so insistently that the bare points of pikes had to be offered to hold them back, were almost equally gay and diverse, with this exception, that the finery of the nobles was new and the colors on that side were sharp and untarnished and as spectacular as an aviary of tropical birds, while the clothes of the commonality, having been much worn and continuously exposed to wind and rain, had mellowed to shades of amethyst and topaz and rich blues and browns and warm greens and gray and common mulberry, the whole blending so miraculously that the rabble were even more rewarding to the eye than the aristocracy.

The voice of the herald sounded from the other side of the enclosure where he was making the same announcement for the benefit of the common people. Coeur heard the words repeated, "to provide vulnerability" and an admonition to the "good people, citizens and varlets of all degree," to remain orderly in "the face of whatever befall." A commotion to his right drew his attention and he saw that a party of men and women, all wearing masks, were filing into the space which had been kept free. The fact that they considered themselves under the necessity of concealing their identities, together with the richness of their attire, made it evident that they were from the court. The Moneyman studied them closely, thinking it should be easy for him to discover who they were. He was still engaged on this quest when he heard his name pronounced in a feminine voice behind him.

"My lord Coeur."

It was Valerie, accompanied by one of the De Burey pages, a somewhat gangling youth in a cloak which obviously had once belonged to a more mature member of the household, for it was lapped about him and the sleeves hung down over his fingers. Valerie herself was handsomely attired in a brocaded cloak with a collar of brown fur which framed her face effectively. On her head she wore a trim hennin of the same fur.

"I had to come!" There was a look of acute distress on her face. "My lord Coeur, is it true that—that he's in such great danger?"

"Yes, my child. He's in the very greatest danger. And there's nothing to be done to help him." The Moneyman regarded her with an air of sternness. "How is it that you are here? Did you have the consent of the Comtesse to coming?"

"No, my lord. They, my cousin and Monsieur the Comte, left many hours ago to come, and I—I persuaded Godefroy to bring me. I couldn't stay away while he was in such peril! He has been so kind to me, my lord Coeur, so considerate always!"

"I haven't seen the Comte and Comtesse de Burey here."

A brief smile lighted up her face. "It seems, my lord, that they had been told a different place. On the other bank. I very much fear they are there now. It was Froy who knew there had been a change of plan and that it was to be here." The smile had vanished as quickly as it came. "Is there nothing, nothing at all, to be done, my lord?"

"Nothing." Coeur shook his head with an air of depression which equaled hers. "All we can do, child, is stand here and watch—and pray that God and his patron saint will watch over him and bring him safely through."

While he talked, he had been keeping the newly arrived party within his vision, and he now saw something which made him gasp with surprise. A gust of wind had swept across the enclosure and, finding the mask of one of the ladies insecurely attached, had carried it away. Instinctively she clasped her face with both hands, crying, "Good St. Agnes!" And then, realizing that the mask could not be retrieved, laughed rather ruefully and said in a voice which reached Coeur's ears, "Sire, as the wind has played me this trick, I must either make myself absurd by hiding my face in my hands or withdraw from your presence."

Jacques Coeur addressed Valerie in an urgent tone. "My child! Move over here in front of me. Look to your right. At the lady who is unmasked. Look long and well, Valerie. It's important." He leaned down and whispered in her ear: "That is Agnes Sorel!"

She followed his instructions and remained for several minutes in a fixed and silent contemplation of the pale and beautiful lady who ruled the heart of the man who ruled the kingdom. She noted that the face of the King's favorite was not only pale but very thin and that her eyes, despite the smile with which she strove to make light of the mishap, had an unhappy look. She noticed also that the hand Agnes Sorel was holding near her face was thin almost to the point of transparency. More than anything else, however, she noticed how successfully the unfortunate lady strove to maintain a fiction of good spirits and how infinitely becoming to her fragile beauty was the dark blue-and-gray cloak which wrapped her about.

Valerie remained in silent regard so long that the Moneyman leaned over her and whispered, "Well, my child?"

"She has the loveliest and sweetest face I've ever seen," said Valerie, in a rapt tone. "I'm thinking, my lord, how mistaken you have been in seeing a resemblance in me. Truly, that is impossible! She's not only beautiful, my lord, she has an expression, a light in her eyes, which will never be found in any other face."

"I was not mistaken." Coeur was speaking in a tone just above a whisper. "You are her fleshly counterpart, my child. After you've lived as long as she has, and perhaps suffered as she has, you may acquire that expression, that light in the eyes, which comes from the sweet and stanch spirit within her."

"My cousin was right about her. I heard her tell the Comte that someday soon Agnes Sorel would reappear at court, pale and ill but as lovely as ever; and that, when she did, she would sweep all opposition away with the greatest ease."

Coeur did not reply at once. "My brave lady!" he said finally, blinking his eyes as though to conceal a suggestion of moisture. "Yes, my child, she's as lovely as ever. And she has swept all opposition before her! Ah, if I could only count on her support always! There would be no problem then. There would be no danger for France!"

One of the other ladies, whose face was not familiar to Jacques Coeur, had found a remedy for the situation by removing her own mask and covering Agnes Sorel's face with it. The favorite thanked her in a laughing voice and then said something to the King, who was wearing a domino which covered his face completely. He nodded his head and laughed in turn. By this time the rumor had spread that Charles of France was among the spectators and the masked party was usurping all attention.

Valerie had returned to her former position where she could no longer see the court group. "Did you spare a glance for the King?" asked Coeur, in a whisper.

She shook her head instantly and emphatically. "No, my lord. I thought the man nearest her must be the King, but I—I didn't dare look at him!"

A hand tugged at Coeur's sleeve and he faced about to find a youth beside him, dressed in the unrelieved black of the bombardiers. This was enough to capture his attention and interest at once. The newcomer was a pleasant-looking boy with dark blue eyes, and obviously he was in a much disturbed state of mind.

"I am Alain de Kersai," said the boy. "I respectfully request a word with you."

The name won all of the Moneyman's interest at once. "Alain de Kersai," he repeated. "You are cousin to Jacques de Lalain."

The boy nodded. "Yes, my lord Coeur."

"He objects to having you serve with the guns."

"Yes, my lord." Alain de Kersai looked about him apprehensively and then lowered his voice. "Jacques is a great knight-errant and I am proud of him. And yet I'm compelled to say that he's both blind and stubborn. It's because of his attitude to my serving with the guns that this duel is being fought."

"I understood so." Coeur was studying the boy's face with close interest, realizing that some conflict of mind had brought him. "You have something to tell me, I think."

"Yes, my lord. I've a confession to make." His voice sank still lower. "*I know something*. Something which would be of use to the Sire d'Arlay. I thought of telling him, but—but, my lord, I couldn't make up my mind. The Sire d'Arlay is championing my cause, and yet to tell might be a betrayal. I didn't know what I should do. And so—I did nothing."

Coeur placed an arm on the youth's shoulder. "Do you feel free to tell me what it is?"

Alain de Kersai hesitated. Then he began to speak in so low a tone that Coeur had difficulty hearing him. "Perhaps I should tell you so you can judge better. Jacques has a weakness of the eye which makes it hard for him to face the sun. Always he finds it necessary to maneuver so that he can be free of it. If his opponent knew that, he might contrive to keep Jacques in the sun as much as possible. It would perhaps balance the scales better—for we know, of course, that my cousin is stronger and more skilled than the Sire d'Arlay."

Coeur's eyes narrowed slightly as he considered the value of what he had been told. "I have small knowledge of such matters but it seems to me that this would be of service. It seems to me also that the Sire d'Arlay should be told."

"This also I should tell you. My cousin will carry a bitter enmity into the lists. Nothing will satisfy him short of the killing of his opponent. If his blade finds the vital spot, he will drive it home. And—and, my lord, he'll have no difficulty finding the heart! What I'm telling you now reflects on the honor of the family and yet I feel it must be told. My lord Coeur, he has been preparing himself for this duel with an eye solely to the final condition on which he insisted—the hole in the breastplate over the heart. He selected an arms master of the exact height and weight of the Sire d'Arlay and practiced with him every day. On the man's armor there was a red cross painted over the heart. For two months Jacques has been training himself to reach that mark."

"I knew there was something of the kind back of the condition!" exclaimed Coeur.

A flush of anger had taken possession of Alain de Kersai's face. "Day after day it has gone on! There has never been any deviation, always the same thing! He has become uncannily expert in that one respect."

"And in addition he has insisted they wear body armor and helmets so that D'Arlay's point may reach him a hundred times and do him no harm! And this is chivalry!" Coeur suddenly seized the youth by the arm. "Alain, I must go to my friend at once and tell him. Jacques de Lalain had enough advantage before, with his weight and great strength and skill. Now D'Arlay will have no more chance than a ewe led to the shambles! Are you willing to have me tell him?"

The boy nodded eagerly. "Yes, my lord!" he whispered. "I should have had the courage to go to him myself. If you can reach him in time, it may perhaps save him from the consequences of my—my weakness and indecision!"

But it was too late. Before the Moneyman could reach the foot of the slope the guards had spread their pikes out point to point to prevent any invasion of the enclosure. A fanfare of trumpets sounded, announcing that the contestestants were coming into the lists.

4

The wind was causing the Burgundian flag to twist and fold and unfold with a loud cracking sound as Jacques de Lalain emerged from his pavilion, preceded by two heralds sounding a note of defiance on their trumpets. He had reached his station in the center by the time the Moneyman had returned to his place on the slope, and was acknowledging the cheers of the spectators with a regal lift of his steel-clad hand.

The great champion was attired in white from the tossing plume in his helmet to the bleached leather leggings which he wore under the faude or iron petticoat suspended from his waist. Even the steel of his body armor had been burnished so diligently that it completed the effect. He looked enormous.

The sympathy of the spectators was with D'Arlay, but this did not prevent them from greeting the Burgundian with loud cheers. He was the living symbol of the principle of force which dominated the life of the day. He had never been beaten in the lists. The spectators, antagonistic to everything Burgundian, had nevertheless such respect for his prowess that they watched him with craning necks and loud whistles of awe. Rather than miss seeing him in action, they were content to have the insignificant Frenchman he was to face go down to defeat and perhaps death. The spectacle was the thing.

Trumpets sounded from the other end of the lists. The note produced by D'Arlay's heralds seemed thin and meek, as though to emphasize still further the all-too-obvious contrast between the two antagonists. It could not be denied that the comparatively unknown knight from Anjou looked unimpressive when he emerged. He walked down the slope to the lists with his usual hurried step, like a burgher making for his place of business rather than a champion stepping out to battle. There was no suggestion of the martial about him save that he was clothed in armor, and even in that respect there was something lacking. Armor was made to satisfy the vanity of the wearer as well as to protect his body, but D'Arlay's was as plain as the flapping robe of a hedge priest. Whereas the plumes of the Burgundian stood up above his helmet in snowy arrogance, his were gray and inclining to droop. His squire, carrying the sword, had forgotten to don his tabard with the De Burey arms and he was so embarrassed that he stumbled twice in following his master to the battle station.

The spectators, who were French almost to a man, watched the entrance of their champion in a dead silence.

Coeur looked down at Valerie whose face was pale. "God be merciful," he said, "and show him the way to prevail over this bloodthirsty Goliath as David did in the Valley of Elah!"

The same comparison had occurred to others. One of the royal party, after a glance at the figure of D'Arlay, said aloud in a resigned tone of voice, "All he needs is a slingshot in his hands."

It was D'Arlay, nevertheless, who opened the attack and he did so with such unexpected vigor that the Burgundian was put on the defensive at once. De Lalain abandoned the colossus-like pose he had struck and seemed in danger even of losing his balance as he struggled to pull himself together. A roar of approval went up from the closely packed ranks of spectators. The fight, it was clear, was going to be better than they had expected.

They were seeing something new, something completely novel in the bloody calendar of conflict. There was a frenzied jostling of shoulders and elbows as the spectators fought for better positions, a better chance to watch the streak of slender steel in the hands of D'Arlay as it wove about the seemingly inert blade of Jacques de Lalain, hissing and striking with the suddenness of an adder. They were accustomed only to the heavy two-edged sword and the cut and slash of cumbersome stroking like the swing of a blacksmith's hammer. This new weapon, about which there had been much skeptical talk in the town the last few days, had a magic quality. The Burgundian seemed almost as much at sea as the watchers. He was stumbling about like a bear in the first dazed and angry moments of a baiting.

A suddenly exultant Jacques Coeur held up a finger every time the leaping serpent's tongue ended with a grind of steel on armor. In a few minutes he had both hands in the air, fingers extended. "If it had not been for Burgundian guile and unknightly trickery," he cried, "the great Jacques de Lalain would be a dead man now!"

But in spite of the fact that long weeks of application had failed to supply him with skill to equal that of his opponent, the Burgundian had suffered no more than scratches on the surface of his breast armor. Alain de Kersai touched Coeur on the arm and said, "It's such a small mark, my lord, I fear it will take luck as well as skill to reach it."

The interest of the crowd, trained by much watching of gladiators in the lists to a technical expertness in all points concerning the use of weapons, was centering on this new method of swordplay. Someone in the group surrounding Charles of France said in an approving tone: "There's an undeniable gentility about the thing. It has the sharp bite of an epigram." Coeur heard the remark and nodded his head in agreement. D'Arlay, he recalled, had always contended that someday the sword would be the recognized weapon of gentlemen.

After several minutes had passed, Alain de Kersai glanced at Coeur and asked, "How do you think it goes, my lord?"

The Moneyman answered with a confident nod. "Robin has touched him nearly a dozen times. As far as I have been able to see, De Lalain has been inside his guard once only."

The young knight didn't seem happy in spite of this. He was silent for a moment and then he shook his head. "But, my lord Coeur," he said, "that single touch was no more than an inch from the unprotected heart."

"Robin also has been close."

"That's true. But I have been watching carefully and I've seen this: My cousin makes few thrusts but each time he seems to fail by very little. He's holding himself in reserve. I've a very great fear that soon he is certain to strike home."

Coeur did not answer immediately. Alarmed by what the young knight had said, he watched both contestants with an aroused intentness, noting that Alain had been right as far as the Burgundian was concerned. Jacques de Lalain gave no hint of anxiety over the dangerously facile attack that D'Arlay continued to press against him, depending clearly on the protection of his body armor. His return thrusts never varied: a straight drive down from the shoulder with all of his great strength back of it.

"Robin must end it soon."

"Yes, my lord Coeur. If he doesn't, it won't finish the way we hope."

Neither of them had made any mention of it but both had noticed that Jacques de Lalain's back was turned to the sun and that D'Arlay had been continuously under the necessity of fighting with the blaze of it in his eyes. The struggle continued under these conditions, the slender figure in somber mail still doing all the pressing. The Burgundian had set himself firmly on his massive legs and seldom moved except to retreat a step when the intensity of the attack put his defense at fault. There was still a suggestion of unruffled confidence in the figure under the tall white plumes, a hint that he was biding his time.

Coeur's early confidence began to wane. He realized that the weight of the armor must be exhausting D'Arlay's strength. How much longer could he remain on the offensive? "God and St. Martin direct his aim!" whispered the Moneyman under his breath with a sudden feeling of the most intense fear. "If he doesn't strike home soon, he's lost!"

He looked at Alain de Kersai and saw tears in the boy's eyes. "I like his chances very little," said the young knight. "Only a lucky thrust will save him now."

The chance for a lucky thrust clearly was small. The Burgundian, careless of all other attack, never failed to parry any stroke which came dangerously close to the exposed point.

A moment later the young knight cried out sharply, "Look!" D'Arlay had circled to his opponent's right and the Burgundian, forced to pivot about to face him, had shown unmistakable signs of discomfort at being thus exposed to the rays of the sun. Whether D'Arlay was aware of this or not, he continued to so maneuver that De Lalain had no opportunity of getting back to his firmer comfortable position. The result was at once apparent. The confidence of the great champion seemed to have been shaken. He was defending himself with a certain clumsiness and there was again a suggestion about him of a bear at the baiting post.

Alain de Kersai said in a tense voice, "The Sire D'Arlay has discovered the weakness for himself!"

"And he's making the most of it!"

"From now on"—there was a jubilant note in the boy's voice—"Jacques will know what it is to fight at a disadvantage!"

"God grant it's not too late!"

They had eyes only for D'Arlay's blade after that and so they saw each move which led to the finish. They saw D'Arlay pause and then circle swiftly around his opponent's right. They saw him feint and then drive his sword straight up in the direction of De Lalain's heart. The latter, for once, was not ready. There was no grinding of steel in contact. The thrust went home.

They saw the great champion stagger, and knew that the point of the sword had reached the unprotected portion of his breast.

Both were incapable of speech in this final moment of the long and doubtful battle. They stood in silence while a roar of almost incredulous delight rose from the closely packed rows of spectators. Coeur crossed himself reverently and thankfully when he saw that his friend's sword did not come away.

But they had reckoned without the reserves of strength in the great frame of the Burgundian. The latter's sword arm still had the power to strike. Seriously wounded, he managed to raise his weapon and thrust out at his opponent. Coeur and his companion had been praying for a lucky thrust. They saw it achieved now but not in the way they had hoped; they saw a blind stroke which sent the point of De Lalain's sword straight to the open space in D'Arlay's armor.

14

TUDDUAL arrived with a message from the Comte de Burey while D'Arlay was watching the fall of the snow from his windows in the Rue Grenier sur L'Eau, delighting in the way the whole world was turning white. The snow had been coming down heavily and soddenly for hours. It had piled up over the doorsteps, it covered the roofs, it filled the leads and gutters; and every window sill, every cornice, every turret and buttress was trimmed with ermine like the robe of a court lady.

The message took the form of a slip of paper on which the information had been painfully and almost illegibly scrawled that the Comte had something urgent to tell his brother and, being confined to his own fireside by a severe attack of some pestilential malady, was under the necessity of insisting that D'Arlay pay him a visit. The latter nodded to the herald and said he would accompany him back, although he knew that Robert de Poitevin, who had been attending him, would seethe with indignation when he heard.

As soon as D'Arlay reached the street there was a great commotion. People of all ages and conditions poured out of the other houses and stood knee-deep in the snow to watch him pass. A boy struggled through the drifts and with triumphant pride touched his sword as he went by.

The Hôtel de Burey was dark and cold when D'Arlay arrived. Servants scuttled through the drafty halls with blue faces and hands sunk deep in their sleeves. The wind could be heard in the upper reaches, battering at doors and causing pennons on the walls to rustle and flap and flutter. Candles guttered and a cross-grained fire in the entrance hall emitted clouds of smoke instead of heat.

D'Arlay found his brother ensconced in a small room at the head of a short flight of stone steps. He was wrapped voluminously in a hooded red robe. His bulbous nose, which was somewhere between brown and purple in color, suggested a worm coiled in a geranium bloom. Not content with the heat given off by the fire on the hearth, he had seen to it that some of the coals had been scraped out on to the stone floor and had both feet stretched over them in a sling. As the sling was looped over the top of a chair, there was an alarming lack of security about the arrangement. He blinked at his visitor and motioned to a chair.

"Ha, the hero of Paris!" grunted the Comte. "Nay, of all France. You are aware, no doubt, that your sword has become legendary and will be classed with the Cloak of Invisibility?" His voice dwindled away into a mumble. "You will go down in history, my stout brother. And I, Regnault de Burey, the head of the family, the head of one of the oldest and greatest families, moreover, am of no more moment in the minds of men than" —drawing on the argot of Paris—"the last echo of a fiddler's full dinner. I should be grateful to you, brother Robin. I've been smiled upon by people who have always disliked me. I've been singled out by Dunois to be tossed a greeting like a bone to a dog. I've been taken aside and congratulated. And all because I'm the brother of the Sire d'Arlay. Does it seem to you also that there is a tinge of irony about all this?"

D'Arlay sat down beside the muffled figure. "If this sling should break or slip," he said, "you might achieve a more lasting fame than mine as the accidental discoverer of a new cure for the gout."

The Comte paid no attention to this warning. He twirled one end of his mustache which was limp from lack of waxing. "Since you are a national hero," he said, "the question of your marriage assumes so much importance that our liege lord is taking it in hand. I've been informed that he has a wife for you and will summon you shortly to let you know the royal pleasure."

This accomplished the purpose of arousing D'Arlay's interest most thoroughly. The latter swung around and surveyed his brother with an air of intense alarm and dismay.

"It seems strange," he remarked, "that our liege lord, who has never before shown any signs of being aware of my existence, should suddenly decide to take such an interest in my affairs."

"It became certain that he would at the moment when the point of your sword wounded the Burgundian. If you had succeeded in killing him, your importance would have doubled. You are now in the nature of an asset. . . . It would be a good match for you, Robin. The girl is a royal ward and just turning thirteen. The marriage would take place at once but, naturally, it couldn't be consummated for a year or so. She has been a favorite of the King's—a nice little thing, with brown hair and eyes and a neat figure. You always get a modest answer from her, 'Yes, perhaps, thanks, maybe, please.' She'll make an obedient wife. It would be easy for you to become fond of her."

"Perhaps you'll condescend now to tell me her name."

"Her name is Amorette de L'Anguinais."

"I've never heard of her."

"She's a rich plum. Her father left her a sweet domain, on the eastern rim of Armagnac, and our liege lord has seen to it that no greedy fingers have been dipping into it. Your friend, the Moneyman, has looked after it with an even more jealous eye. I'm convinced her dowry would be ample for all our needs."

The Comte suddenly leaned forward and regarded his brother with an air of dramatic urgency. "In spite of all this," he said, wagging a forefinger at D'Arlay, "I've brought you here to warn you against this match. It would be a mistake. You must get away before any summons from the King can reach you. Do you understand? You must leave at once. Today."

D'Arlay was thoroughly mystified. "For years you've dinned into my ears the need to marry a rich wife. Here we have what seems to be a perfect arrangement, of the King's planning, moreover. And now you say I must avoid it by running away. Are you serious?"

"Robin! Attend closely to what I'm going to say. I'm the head of the family and I insist you obey me in this matter." The Comte's manner became even more urgent. "Don't you see that we have the chance now to make the family of De Burey the most powerful in all France?"

"On what do you base that sweeping assertion?"

"It's a matter of three months since you saw the little cousin. In a few minutes I shall take you up to renew your acquaintance with her." The Comte indulged himself in a smile with an edge of slyness to it. "You'll see a remarkable change in her. What doubts you may have had about the success of the scheme will vanish at once. . . . If she wins the degree of approval we expect, it may be deemed expedient to marry her off at once. A husband in the background is the best kind of cloak. . . . Well, why shouldn't you be the lucky man? If you married her, you could control the state through her influence with the King."

D'Arlay was so startled that for a moment he made no response. Then he began to laugh. "I suppose you are serious about this but I intend to treat it as a joke—as a joke in the very worst of taste. Understand this at once: I refuse to become the King's cuckold. And now, with your permission, I'll pay my respects to the ladies and return to the couch I should never have left."

The Comte did not seem disturbed. He nodded his head. "I didn't expect you to say yes at first. I expected you, in fact, to rear and snort and puff fire and fill the air with pious protestations. Your mind has always been like an uncured cheese with a fermentation of high-and-mighty notions going on inside it. All I ask, Robin, is that you think it over. The more you think about it, the more sensible it will seem. And in the meantime you must keep out of the royal clutches. My advice would be to get yourself to Arlay as fast as this pestilential weather will permit."

"All the thinking I could do in a hundred years wouldn't change my mind. The family will never become wealthy and powerful by the backstairs—not, at least, if it depends on me. As for the King, I can say no to him if I desire as easily here as at Arlay. I have no intention of running away."

"Isabeau is in attendance on the Queen and the little cousin is about to begin her dancing lesson with Old Ricciardo. I suggest," said the Comte, giving his brother a calculating side glance, "that we go up together and watch the lesson. Jacques Coeur is with her now, as it happens."

The Comte removed his feet from the sling and cautiously touched the ground with them. "The pain's gone!" he exclaimed, nodding his head with satisfaction. "There's been some kind of miracle here. I shall be able to walk or even cut a caper or two during the dancing lesson, if I feel like it."

2

The room to which he led his brother was being used for the drying of clothes. Two lines were stretched along the walls, from one end to the other, on which dangled garments, some of an intimate nature. It was a large room and quite obviously had been used once for less menial purposes although the nature of its former employment was hard to determine. There had been a chantry at one end but the enclosing screens had been removed, thus exposing to view the altar, or what was left of it. A family as poverty-stricken as the De Bureys could not afford to keep a chantry echoing with prayers for the souls of long-dead ancestors.

Valerie was standing in conversation with Jacques Coeur when they entered. She was facing the door and so she saw D'Arlay at once. She came forward to meet him, smiling in welcome and with hands outstretched. She did not say any of the things which might have been expected under the circumstances, no expression of her pleasure in seeing him again, no reference to the pride she had felt in his exploit in the lists, or her relief that he had recovered so quickly from his wound. In fact, she said nothing at all. But her eyes conveyed all this to him, and much more; they told him that his unexpected arrival was the greatest boon she could have asked on this stormy day, that his long absence had been for her an unhappy deprivation, that he remained her most highly prized friend.

He was finding it hard to speak himself, for the Comte had been well within the bounds of truth when he said there had been a remarkable change in her. She looked older and her manner had a suggestion of gravity about it. Also she was thinner, as though she had found the process of change in trying one; there was the hint of a hollow in her cheeks and the merest suggestion of a violet shadow about her eyes. In spite of this, perhaps in some degree because of it, she was lovelier than she had been when he first saw her. She had poise now and she walked with ease. There was grace in every move she made, in the carriage of her head, in the way she raised her arms, in the use she made of her hands. Her hair was dressed with restraint but it had lost none of its molten beauty, and it seemed to say, I am contributing to this portrait of a lady but at any time I could let myself go again most joyously in unruly curls.

As he watched her come toward him he knew that he could never marry the King's ward. He was saying to himself: "This is the second time I've fallen in love and once again the lady of my choice is placed by force of circumstances beyond my reach. This time I'm in love for all eternity and so I must reconcile myself to a lonely life."

It was D'Arlay who broke the silence. "It's a long time since I've seen you, Mademoiselle. A matter of many months."

"But I've been much luckier, my lord," she answered. "I saw you—just a month ago."

D'Arlay was so startled that he looked to Jacques Coeur for confirmation. The latter smiled and nodded his head. "It's true. She was at the duel. One of the pages knew where it was to be held and she talked him into accompanying her. In fact, she stood beside me and watched what was going on with an anxiety which at least equaled my own."

"I hope never again in all my life to feel so much anxiety, my lord," said Valerie.

"Old Ricciardo is waiting," said the Comte. He was shifting about from foot to foot and beating his hands together. "Perhaps we should all take a dancing lesson in order to keep warm."

The master was an Italian and he was so enormously fat that his stomach quivered like a bodge of oats as he came forward from the corner of the room where he had been waiting. In spite of his bulk he stepped lightly and with easy balance.

"What is it to be today, my lord and Mademoiselle?" he asked in a voice as high-pitched and thin as a bird's. "Will Mademoiselle go through the steps of the *pavane?* It is a dance of great dignity."

The Comte grunted in dissent. "The pavane? It's for giddy-gaddy dowagers of fifty or more and rheumatic old bucks who can't step to a faster air than a dirge. I suggest, Dancing Master, that you have her show us something of all measures. The pavane, if you must, but certainly the *Lège-de-moy* and the Calf's Feet and the *tricotet* and the *courante.* The courante above everything. I may tell you that I was the best dancer of the courante in all Anjou in my day. Ha, you should have seen when I swung my partner. Her skirts flew up so high——"

He broke off and began to hum the words of the course to which the courante was performed, *Sy vous ne savez dire, Yo!* His memories getting the better of him, he raised himself on his toes with both arms extended above his head. Giving his body a twirl, he brought his heels down and shouted with zest, "Yo, yo! Yo, yo!"

Coeur asked Old Ricciardo, "How is your pupil progressing?"

The huge round face lighted up with enthusiasm. "Ah, my lord, perhaps I shouldn't say so while she is here but, truly, Mademoiselle is in a way to become a very fine dancer. She has every quality. Such *diversità di cose!* Never have I had a better pupil!"

"Come, no more delay!" The Comte took Old Ricciardo by the arm and started him in the direction of the center of the room. "Get out your pipes and begin. Get the pavane over and done with first."

Coeur drew D'Arlay to a bench at one side of the room. As they watched the preparations for the lesson, finding it necessary to twist their heads about to see through the well-filled clothesline, the Moneyman began to speak in a low tone. "You were in an abstracted mood when you came in and from that I judged your brother had been telling you of the King's choice of a husband for his favorite ward."

"Yes, and I find myself in a serious predicament. I must run contrary to the royal will. I've no intention of marrying this girl who is, I understand, a mere child."

"She's the catch of the year, Robin. Make no mistake, there are a round score of eligible courtiers who would give anything to be in your shoes." Coeur was watching his friend closely. "Do you mind telling me your objections to the match?"

D'Arlay decided the real reason was a secret he could not share. Instead he said: "A disinclination to matrimony at the moment. Perhaps it's a disinclination also to having anyone, even our liege lord, select my wife for me."

"Don't you intend to marry in time?"

D'Arlay hesitated before answering. "There's nothing more certain than that I should marry. You know how deeply in debt my brother has managed to get himself. There seems no other way of saving the family lands. And yet—when it comes to the point I always find that I can't take a wife for no other reason than because she is rich enough to pay off the debts."

"Well." The Moneyman made no effort to urge him to a different decision. "It's your own life which is concerned and so you must make the decision yourself. Fortunately you are in a position at the moment to stand out against the King. You've become a national hero and our liege lord would hardly dare rouse public wrath by meting out any punishment."

As they talked, Valerie had been dancing as directed by Old Ricciardo. She had gone through the dignified steps of the pavane, holding her head high and swaying very little as she turned and curtseyed. Then he had sent her to the farthest extreme and she had danced the Lège-de-moy, with hands on her hips and her heels beating a furious rataplan on the floor in time to the fast tooting of the master's horn. After that she had gone to the tricotet, which happened to be her favorite. Holding her blue skirts no more than a modest inch off the floor, she had swayed and pirouetted, moving her feet all the time as fast as knitting needles in the hands of an industrious housewife. By the time she was through, her cheeks were flushed and her eyes were sparkling.

Jacques Coeur watched Valerie as she drew a fan from her sleeve and began to swing it back and forth.

"Well," he whispered, "what do you think of her now?"

"I've been sitting here in a state of wonder, not daring to believe my eyes," answered D'Arlay. "She has been most completely made over. It's nothing short of a miracle."

"Yes, it's a miracle. Even her voice has changed. Have you noticed that it's lower and more self-possessed? Your charming sister-in-law must be given the credit. She has brought about these improvements in our little Puss-from-the-provinces. We had many arguments but I always gave in and in the end I always acknowledged I had been wrong. She's a very clever woman." He gave D'Arlay a quick look out of the corner of one eye. "Could a better candidate be found?"

D'Arlay shook his head reluctantly. "I'm compelled to say that a better candidate could not have been found."

As Valerie danced, the Comte had hovered on the edge of things, humming loudly, skipping about and improvising dance steps of his own (the pain had left his feet apparently), and offering a great deal of advice. Now he clapped his hands together as a signal that he had something to say.

"We have come to the courante," he announced.

"But, my lord," protested Old Ricciardo, "one can't dance the courante alone."

"Didn't you hear me say 'we'? I shall dance with Mademoiselle. And I promise you, Master Ricciardo, you will say at the finish that never before has the courante been executed with more skill and zest. We will give to it as well just the right amount of"—he turned and winked at Valerie—"just the merest hint of naughtiness. Come, little cousin, take your position opposite me."

The courante can be danced by any number of couples. One participant sings a verse of the song while the gentlemen advance boldly toward the ladies who retreat before them with a simulation of coyness. All then join in the chorus and each man seizes his partner and gives her a vigorous twirl. Then they bow and separate, the gentlemen returning to their positions.

"It will be better with just the two of us," said the Comte. "I shall never have to change partners and, by'r Lady of Marmoutier, that suits me perfectly. Cousin, sing the first verse."

Valerie began in a gay voice:

> *"Penotte se vieult marier*
> *On ne scet à qui la donner."*

Then she clapped her hands and the Comte joined in with the chorus:

> *"Sy vous ne savez dire, Yo!*
> *Yo! Yo! Compère, commère.*
> *Sy vous ne savez dire, Yo!"*

He pranced forward with goatlike abandon as he sang, kicking his heels backward and tossing his arms about, his face wreathed in a toothy grin. Seizing Valerie in his arms, he swung her high in the air. Then he released her, bowed with an exaggerated sweep of his arm, and danced backward to his station.

"*Brava! Yo! Yo!*" he cried. "Now I'll give you a verse. A fanciful little thing I wrote myself. It's a trifle on the—the unconventional side, I'm afraid. It's a good thing Madame the Comtesse isn't here as I'm sure she would find fault with my sentiments."

The verse he proceeded to sing was rather more than unconventional. It was much better suited to a romp in a tavern, with greasy rufflers and blowsy women dancing to it. The Comte bawled it out at the top of his voice and then skipped forward with arms outstretched. This time he swung Valerie so far in the air that her skirts twirled about her ankles and threatened worse indiscretions. Releasing her, he raised himself on his toes and executed an elaborate pirouette, shouting for good measure, "Yo, yo! Yo, yo!—— Yo!—— Yo!"

"What's going on here?" demanded an angry voice from the doorway.

Silence fell on the room as Isabeau swept into it. The Comte's arms remained stretched above his head and he watched her with obvious uneasiness. Old Ricciardo stopped tooting on the horn and his mouth fell open with dismay.

Coeur leaned over to D'Arlay. "In public esteem you are the bravest man in all France. Have you the courage to stay and face this situation? Or would you rather withdraw before the fair Isabeau sees us?"

"I'm in favor of withdrawing," whispered D'Arlay.

Coeur motioned to Valerie to follow them. Then the two men got cautiously to their feet and tiptoed from the room.

BOOK TWO

1

A SENTRY called "Halt!" and swung a lantern over his head to inspect the party. When he recognized Jacques Coeur, he said: "I know *you*, my lord Moneyman. Many's the measure of wine I've had at the Grant Bande within seeing of your shop. Are these your people?"

"Yes. Direct us, if you please, to the headquarters of my lord Dunois."

The word that Jacques Coeur had arrived spread quickly through the camp. Men poured out of houses and tents to give him a welcoming cheer as he passed. They left bivouac fires in the fields and the shelter of hayricks. He found himself ringed about by faces which looked wild and dirty in the light of the torches. The soldiers were friendly, however, and he heard one phrase repeated over and over again, "The good Jaquet sees to it that we're well paid and fed." He had to acknowledge greetings so continuously that his right hand seemed to be rising and falling in perpetual motion.

The commander of the army occupied a large tent, through the open flap of which men passed in and out in a steady stream. Dunois sat on a stool with a stalk of wheat in his mouth and a tame pigeon on his shoulder. There were maps everywhere: on the ground, attached to the sides of the tent, on the backs of chairs.

"Well, Jaquet!" said the commander, nodding to the new arrival. "Have you come to witness the great victory my knights are gabbling about?"

Coeur took possession of a stool opposite him. His face had assumed an air of gravity. "I came, Bastard, because I heard things which disturbed me. I had reports of large bodies of our troops at Elbeuf, at Amfreville, even as far south as Beaumesnil. I heard of scattered operations north of the river, as far away as Pontoise and Gisors."

Dunois turned his head so carefully that the pigeon did not take alarm. He picked up a map and handed it to the Moneyman. "The crosses marked in red indicate where detachments of troops still linger." He smiled to himself and asked, "What conclusions have you drawn from these reports?"

"That the concentration you ordered before Rouen has not been carried out."

Dunois gave a nod. "Are you a master of military wisdom as well as everything else?"

"My servant Nicolas allows me no chance to feel any pride in myself;

I wear him, in fact, like a hair shirt. He says I believe myself to have the boldness of Alexander the Great, the military sagacity of Belisarius, the leadership of Caesar, the personal courage of Bertrand du Guesclin." Coeur had been speaking in a light tone but at this point his expression changed to one of complete gravity. "I make no such claims. I'm a merchant, a man of peace. But this much I have no hesitation in saying: I have some knowledge of strategy, enough to know when things are going wrong. . . . Do you expect to get the concentration completed in time?"

Dunois answered in a quiet voice. "They have affairs of their own to attend to, my fine knights. There are personal estates to be redeemed. Castles to be retaken. Ladyloves who beg not to be deserted. They are brave, but of what use is courage if no sense of discipline goes with it? They had their orders to join me here at once but they'll arrive in their own good time." He shook his head with sudden rancor. "We promised the King, you and I, that Rouen would be in his hands before the first snows fell. We have swept across Normandy without a single check. It has been one victory after another. But now I have little hope of making good our solemn assurance to our liege lord."

"Are the English in strength in the city?"

"Somerset and Talbot are both there. They're bitter hard fighters. Their forces are small but I can't risk defeat by attacking them with the strength now at my disposal."

Jacques Coeur did not put into words the angry thoughts which filled his mind. Was the triumphant march of the lilies of France to be interrupted by a nobility which held itself above obedience to orders? Riding through the camp a few minutes before he had seen the bodies of soldiers dangling from trees, some with willicoats wrapped around them as a sign that they had been hanged for rape, others with the entrails of sheep to show that their offence had been the pillage of the countryside. The thought ran through his mind. "If Dunois would hang a few nobles for disobedience, we would soon win this war."

Dunois asked a question. "And now, my master of strategy, what would you do if you were in my place?"

Coeur accepted the challenge promptly. "Many times I've stood at the Beauvoisine Gate in Rouen and looked at the walls of Le Petit-Appui against the skyline. If I were you I would treat Somerset and Talbot to a demonstration. I would concentrate the power of our cannon against the castle and blow it to pieces before their eyes. I would demolish it so thoroughly that the Englishmen would realize the fate awaiting Rouen if they were foolhardy enough to hold out."

The commander leaned over and gave him a pat on the shoulder. "Jean Bureau left me not more than an hour ago. I made that suggestion to him. We discussed it at some length and—we decided it would be impossible. You see, Moneyman, we lack cannon at the moment and we're short of bombardiers to handle them."

The Moneyman looked aghast at this information. "I was of the opinion that Jean Bureau was well equipped and organized for the whole campaign. What has gone wrong?"

"The smiths who cast the cannon have been at fault. The barrels show a tendency to crack and explode. Bureau has lost forty of them in the last month. Each time this happens half-a-dozen gunners are killed. The result? There is now a scarcity of trained handlers and the few who remain alive are becoming wary. They've no appetite left for serving in the pits. . . . I've little hope, Jacques Coeur, that Bureau could accomplish the reduction of Le Petit-Appui if I gave him orders to try."

The Moneyman gnawed his underlip in concentrated thought. Finally he asked a question. "Tell me, Bastard, is there no way of discovering when the bore of a gun is flawed?"

"Yes. When a gun has been fired and smoke is seen issuing from a crack in the barrel, it can be taken for granted that the next time it is discharged it will blow itself to pieces. But often when there is a crack all the smoke escapes through the muzzle and the touchhole and so no warning is given; and it is fired again, and it explodes, and the souls are freed from the bodies of many gunners."

"But," said Coeur, frowning thoughtfully, "if some way could be found to close the muzzle and the touchhole, then the smoke would find its way to any crack, and due warning would be given."

"Quite true. But how, Moneyman, would you go about closing them?"

"It would have to be done by hand. A man would be stationed at each end with cloths ready to wad into the hole as soon as the gun had been fired. There's no other way in which it could be done."

"And these unfortunate men would have to stay beside the cannon when it was fired instead of running for shelter. It would be sure death for them. Could you hope to find men who would volunteer for this suicidal part?"

After a moment's further consideration Coeur asked, "Are you content to have me see what I can arrange in this matter?"

"You have my full consent."

Coeur got to his feet. He had been in the saddle since sunrise and he was stiff and weary. In spite of his desperate need for rest, he delayed to ask another question. "When the King rides into Rouen in triumph, will the bombardiers have positions of special honor in the procession in recognition of the great part they've played?"

"I'm not sure," answered Dunois, "that the nobles will consent to the bombardiers riding in the procession. In the first place the good knights are still against the use of cannon. They refuse to see that all our victories have been won by blowing the walls down around the ears of Godon garrisons. In the second place, they abide by rules. There is no rule to say what position in a victory procession should be assigned to men who demean themselves by winning battles in new ways; hence the real victors will find themselves excluded."

The Moneyman began to speak in low and impassioned tones. "I'm the son of a merchant. You are the illegitimate son of a prince. Both of us have suffered from certain hardships and limitations because of this and I think we may open our hearts to each other in full confidence. Bastard, has it ever occurred to you that this is an absurd and topsy-turvy world? For a hundred years France has been beaten by a much weaker country. Have you thought that the Code of Chivalry is to blame? And consider how much trouble is caused because all honors and responsibilities are given to men without any consideration of their qualifications! They may be stupid and treacherous and corrupt but they are their fathers' sons. That is the only point to be considered, and so these oxheads, these vain peacocks, are given the power to govern and control justice and fight wars. These knights who are delaying you now wouldn't be in command of troops if it depended on their fitness to command."

When Dunois smiled at his vehemence but did not volunteer any comment, the Moneyman concluded, "We live in a wrong-headed world, Bastard, which worships blood and respects brawn but sees something vulgar in brains."

"You are uttering rank heresy, Moneyman," said the commander. "In fact, there's a smack of treason in what you've just said. I should refuse to listen to you. But," indulging himself in a smile, "as we are speaking in confidence, I may tell you that sometimes I think what a pleasure it would be to sell all my knights on the hoof. They should bring a good price in the market."

2

Jacques Coeur was given an old mill on the edge of the encampment for the use of himself and his party. In addition to Nicolas and two other servants, there was a scrivener and a neat little individual with a beard trimmed to a point who looked exactly what he was, a learned man from the University. It was to the latter that the Moneyman addressed himself as he glanced up through an opening in the ceiling into the black cavern of the mill above.

"My good Ferrand, this is a dusty hole and full of drafts. But it offers us shelter and we must make the best of it."

The room in which they found themselves was small and filled with spare querns. An opening in the floor led to a subterranean region through which water was rushing. Ferrand de Cordule said with a suggestion of a shudder: "I've a great fear of drowning and so it would be impossible for me to sleep down here. I will be almost equally uncomfortable above. There are, I think, bats. I've always had an aversion to bats and owls."

His suspicions were confirmed by a sound of rustling and a sudden trill from far up in the blackness. The scholar shuddered as he began to climb the ladder.

"If those who say you've made a compact with the Prince of Evil were to hear that," commented Coeur, with a laugh, "they would declare it was no earthly sound. Don't let it disturb your slumbers for tomorrow I expect much work from you."

Ferrand de Cordule stopped climbing and looked down over his shoulder. "I must confess, my lord Coeur," he said, "that I don't understand your desire to have these plans completed so rapidly." He had a packet of papers under one arm and he held them out as he spoke. "The war has just begun. It may be years before you can build the shops for which I'm drawing plans with such feverish haste."

"You're wrong, my friend. The war will soon be over. But even if it were to last for years, there would still be little enough time for all the things I want to do." He crossed the floor and looked up at the man of science. "War destroys old wealth and creates new. When peace finally comes to France, men will have gold in their purses and a desire in their minds to spend it on the blessings of peace and ease. We must be ready to take advantage of that when the time comes."

"But I fail to see——"

"You are a scholar. You know how to make steel. You know how to erect large buildings. But, my good Ferrand, you know nothing whatever about commerce and money. Less than nothing; because you have notions in your head which are wrong. Now I, I am a man of trade. When I look over those papers of yours, I know that a triangle means fire, a cross and arrow iron, a circle and dot gold—but otherwise they are a mystery to me. I can't make head or tail of your charts and plans. But—I know as much about money and its curious habits as you do of Vases and Philosophic Eggs and Athanors and Puffers. And I am telling you this out of the knowledge I have: For a year at least, after peace comes, France will be drunk with prosperity."

"It is true," said the scientist, "that I'm not familiar with the ways of commerce. But it would seem to me that the time to take advantage of prosperity is when prosperity is upon us."

"You will be startled at what I am going to say," declared Coeur. "I'm preparing to double the number of my shops. I must see that they are stocked with a wider assortment of goods. I must add at least two ships to my eastern fleet. I must build a new fleet to sail the northern seas and trade with the Hanseatic ports. In addition to that, Ferrand de Cordule, I must start to make goods myself, to have forges running and fires blazing and workmen by the thousands wearing the heart-and-shell device on their sleeves. And that is the part which concerns you. I look to you to build me the shops and forges I shall need."

"All this will take a great deal of gold," suggested Ferrand de Cordule.

"And I have little gold left at the moment. It's a strange position for me to find myself in—I, Jacques Coeur, whose coffers have always bulged with it. The war is proving more costly than I estimated. But—it matters not at all. My credit, with victory in sight, is so good that I can raise any amount I need."

The Moneyman had taken to pacing up and down the dusty room.

"Draw me the plans!" he exclaimed. "You still seem to doubt if it can be done. A *Vaillants Coeurs Rien Impossible!* Because men have labored singly over little forges to make bars of steel no thicker than the blade of a sword, must we always be content to work that way? I want workshops so long that from one end you won't be able to see the tilt hammers at the other. I want forges so large the fires in them will blaze like the pit itself. I have the mines and the ore now. Here in Normandy and in Bretagne and in Berri and Le Nivernais."

"Must I finish them tonight?" asked De Cordule mildly. "Or will you permit me to point out that we have been in the saddle all day and are sadly in need of rest?"

Coeur laughed. "I don't think I'm ever unreasonable in my demands. All I ask you to do is to finish the plans for me in half the time it would take anyone else."

"I can only say that I'll do my best." Ferrand de Cordule disappeared into the blackness above.

Dunois had ordered that sentries be placed about the mill. They could hear the one in front singing as he paced up and down. He had a deep voice which he was raising in a hunting song:

> "Of St. Hubert I sing, and the blaze and the brach hound,
> Red drips the blood from the tusks of the boar . . ."

He was interrupted at that point and they could hear him asking questions of a new arrival. A moment later the door swung open and Pregent Kennedy entered, dressed in the black uniform of the bombardiers. He remained in the doorway, blinking his eyes in the light of the torches.

"Welcome, Sir Scot," said Coeur, who had stretched himself out on the top stone of a quern for lack of a chair. "I've waited a long time for your report."

"You compel me to an admission, my lord Coeur," said Kennedy, in a tone which indicated reluctance on his part. "I've never mastered the art of writing. Is it a matter for shame? I will tell you that few men of high rank in my own Scotland can do anything with letters. They make their cross and that is all."

"It's equally true of France. No apologies are called for, Sir Scot."

"Not being able to write you, I was on the point of seeking you out when I heard that the bombardiers were being organized and trained. It was clear to me that it was more necessary to give my services there. I threw in with them at once and it was a good thing, my lord, that I did. They were a poor lot when I joined. I said to them, 'It's cannoneers I will make of you or may Master Clootie catch me on the prongs of his fork.' But I couldn't train bombardiers and seek out my lord Coeur at the same time; and so my report to you had to wait."

"Your decision was sound. Nothing has been lost through the delay." Coeur motioned to the servants to withdraw, which they did by climbing the ladder, and then he nodded his head at the Scot. "I'm all ears for what you have found in this matter."

"I went straight to the village you named. There was little to be learned there beyond what you already knew. When survivors began to creep back to the village, there was left only blackened walls and burned fields. They hid themselves in the ruins like rats and all they had to eat was the bark of trees and the frozen stalks of cabbages. Few of them lived through it. In the village today there are no more than five people who have any memory of the raid; and of these five none has any suspicion of the existence of our little mademoiselle."

"Up to this point," declared Coeur, "I find your report completely satisfactory."

The Scot nodded slowly. "Even had they an inkling of the truth," he said, "it is clear, my lord Coeur, they would never connect this mysterious survivor with—with a certain Mademoiselle de Voudrai."

Coeur frowned at him. "Have you seen fit," he demanded, "to carry your investigations beyond the instructions I gave you?"

"I have ears to hear."

"Is it in your mind to emulate the thirty young men of Timnath and plow with my heifer?"

The Scot did not seem in any sense disturbed by the harshness of the Moneyman's tone. He proceeded, as usual, to give an upward twirl to the ends of his mustache. "Scotland is a grand country in all respects save one," he said. "It is poor. A man may be born with a single shilling and die with the same shilling in his pouch—and not a second one to keep it company. If I'm to fatten my purse, I must do it before returning to my native heath."

"I intend to employ you in other matters and to pay you what you are worth."

The Scot indulged in a bleak smile. "If you do that, my lord, you will pay me a great deal of siller." He nodded his head slowly several times. "That's all I need to know. If you intend to continue the pleasant little gratuities, I shall serve you faithfully and—with the utmost discretion."

"Go on with your story, if you please."

Kennedy proceeded to tell in full detail of his search. It had been necessary for him to act with unusual caution but he had uncovered one fact which in his opinion pointed to the solution without any doubt. The oldest of the survivors, a baker whose oven had escaped the fire, recalled that a young wife in the village had been serving as foster mother to an infant from outside at the time of the raid. This young woman was described by the baker as "a roomy heifer who brought her own calves into the world once a year without fail and lost them all." The foster child, however, had displayed more vitality, surviving the perils of its first year and dying by violence (as the baker confidently asserted) with the woman when the Free Companies burned the village.

"Does the baker know who the real parents were?" asked Coeur.

Kennedy gave a negative shake of the head. "On the contrary, my lord, he's sure that no one in the village knew, not even the foster parents. The woman, who was a wanton glaverer about most things, never had a word to say about the child; which seems proof that she knew nothing herself. It was certain that the couple were being paid well. The husband bought a cider press and a brood sow and the woman wore a new tunic of fine green

Flemish cloth about the village. The real parents must have been people of substance, my lord."

"I've never had any doubts on that score. The girl herself is the proof." Coeur looked sharply at his companion. "You have more to tell me, I think."

Kennedy indulged in a slow wink. "Aye, that I have. What would you say if I told you that about the time the child was delivered to the foster mother, a young gentleman who lived in that district fought a duel with a nobleman from the south over the attentions of the latter to his sister?"

"My interest would be aroused but I would wait for more details."

"Quite properly, my lord Coeur. I never myself make the mistake of jumping to conclusions on scanty evidence. But listen to this! The sister had given birth to a child out of wedlock. As her lover was a married man, her shame could not be covered by marriage. The brother was killed in the duel and the lover was never seen in those parts afterward."

"It might be a coincidence," said Coeur thoughtfully. "But most certainly it's an interesting one."

"Aye, it is interesting." Kennedy gave his head a wag. "It's more than a coincidence, my lord. The duel was fought in a town less than a dozen miles from the village. It occurred a month after the birth of the child which in the meantime had vanished, though it was known in the town that a foster mother had been found for it. Everything fits together."

"What of the poor mother?"

"She felt her disgrace as much as might be expected. She died soon afterward. The circumstances of her death were—quite distressing, my lord Coeur."

"I am inclined to think," declared Coeur, after some moments of reflection, "that you have probed to the root of the matter. But there are important details still to be explained. You have mentioned no names."

"The mother's name was Céleste de Lansanne. The family was noble but poor. There were a dozen brothers and sisters at one time but only one has survived, a brother who has the estates, such as they are. I found him less communicative than a gravestone, my lord; for on a stone, after all, you find names and dates and sometimes indications of the character of the deceased. He told me nothing. He had mean little eyes, set close together, and his mouth jerked so much as he listened to me that I wondered at first if he had critters in his beard. He heard what I had to say and then motioned to the door."

"You got no confirmation from him?"

"Not a thing, my lord. I wasn't surprised. He had to consider that I might be seeking to make claims on the estate. He looked frightened when I demanded to know the name of the father. I'm disposed to think the father was a man of some consequence."

"Is it your opinion, then, that no one will ever make any move in the matter?"

"That is my opinion."

"And you've told me everything?"

"Everything, my lord."

Coeur seemed reluctant to accept this assurance. "I know you for a goundry rogue, Pregent Kennedy," he said. "How can I be sure you aren't holding something back?"

Kennedy drew himself up with an air of injured pride. "You have my word. Is that not enough? Then let me tell you that I am fond of the lass. I would do nothing to hurt her."

Coeur looked at him curiously. "I believe you mean it. I had to be sure because I also am fond of her and I want nothing to stand in the way of ascertaining the truth. When the war is over we'll go into the matter again. There will be ways of persuading this brother to tell us what he knows. In the meantime, Monsieur Kennedy, I depend on you to keep a still mouth."

3

The knights who had joined the bombards were making their headquarters in a small inn on the outskirts of the town around which the army was encamped. Escorted there by Pregent Kennedy, the Moneyman found the place filled with young men, some of them so very young that their cheeks had never known the scrape of a razor. They had discarded armor and were sitting around in the ease of loose tunics. As befitted men who fought in the stife of the guns, they were dressed in black from head to foot and, at first glance, seemed a somber company, an impression quickly dispelled by the eagerness of their eyes and the steady clack of their tongues.

"Look at them!" said the Scot pridefully. "Have you ever seen the equal of them, my lord?" He laid a hand on Coeur's arm. "Listen to them. Can you make head or tail of it?"

The words being bandied back and forth had no meaning at all for Jacques Coeur. He heard references to *tampions* and *fireballs* and *munions* and such expressions as *easing the orgues* and *sighting with the dispart*. The general discussion seemed to be concerned with the advantages of bronze over iron.

"My lords," said Kennedy, raising his voice until it could be heard over the din, "I bring you company tonight. This, my brave young men, is Jacques Coeur."

All conversation stopped and every head in the room came around on the instant. Alert eyes fixed themselves on the man who had made the resumption of hostilities possible. For a single second there was silence in the low-raftered room, and then an unexpected thing happened. With one accord the young knights got to their feet and cheered. They cheered so loudly that it sounded almost like a salute from one of their guns. They waved their goblets above their heads and shouted eager greetings to the Moneyman. The nearest thumped him heartily on the back, crying, "Here is our good Jacques!" A voice from the rear of the room shouted, "Buy us bronze barrels and plenty of good corned powder, and we'll blow the Godons back across the Channel."

Coeur waved to them. "When France is freed, we will have the bombardiers to thank for it!"

"The bombardiers and Jacques Coeur! The winning combination for France—the purse of Coeur and the guns of Bureau!"

Looking about him, Coeur saw that the common room of the inn had taken on the color of the company. Instead of lances and battle-axes on the walls, it had elevation bolts and missel rings and wooden fids. Hanging from a rafter was a copper hinge with a placard attached on which was lettered, "All that was left of the gates of Ourges after a direct hit." Another placard read, "Our pledges are not to fair ladies but to our country," and beside it, to lend significance, dangled one of the black patches which knights wore to denote vows.

Finding that the attention of the company had transferred itself elsewhere, the Moneyman took a seat with the Scot at a table near the end of the room. From there he watched what was happening with a lively interest. Plenty of drinking was being done but a certain ritual was invariably observed. The Knights of the Guns (as they called themselves) would stand up in line with arms linked in such a way that each man could drink from the goblet of his neighbor on the right. One would cry, "*Nous y voici!*" and the rest would say, "*En aval!*" as they emptied the goblets at one draught. Anyone who paused for breath was compelled to pay for the next round.

To add to the confusion in the crowded room, they had attached a hangman's noose above the main door of the inn and one of their number, keeping hold of the end, would let it drop around the shoulders of each new arrival. A quick pull on the rope would draw it tightly around the neck, and the shouts of laughter which greeted each successful operation were loud enough to drown out the scream of surprise and pain from the victim. When no victims presented themselves, two of the knights would sally out into the street, seize a passer-by, and propel him within by force.

D'Arlay came down the stairs soon after Coeur's arrival. He also was in black but he had succeeded in giving himself an air of elegance by a black plume in his cap and the use of onyx buttons on his doublet and in the tufts of his sleeves.

When he saw Coeur he waved a hand in greeting and walked over to the table where the latter was sitting.

"I was told a moment ago that you had arrived in camp," he said. "I'm more than happy to see you because you may know a way out of the difficulty in which we find ourselves."

"I know all about it," answered Coeur. "I've already seen Dunois. We hit upon a plan which may solve the matter."

He began to explain his belief that the loss of life could be prevented by packing the ends of the cannon after each discharge. D'Arlay listened intently and agreed at once that it was worth trying. He would see Jean Bureau in the morning, he said, and discuss the plan with him.

He added, however, that some very special inducement would have to be found to get the men into the mood to try anything so risky. Their courage had not been equal to the severe tests of the past few weeks.

After the matter had been thoroughly debated, D'Arlay looked at the Moneyman with an air of some reluctance and asked a question, "What word have you of Valerie?"

"Nothing for weeks. In the last letter from the Comtesse she said they were both well." Coeur studied D'Arlay with so much intentness that the latter began to wonder as to the reason. "Are you as much against me in this as ever?"

D'Arlay answered emphatically: "I am. My feeling, in fact, has increased."

"Then you'll understand my reluctance to answer your question. How do I know to what lengths you may permit this antagonism of yours to go, my dear Robin? You have a touch of the zealot in you, of the fanatic even. You might—— Well, it isn't necessary to speculate as to what you might do. Tell me this: when you saw the Comtesse last, did she give you any information?"

"She said nothing."

"There you are. She is a woman of discretion. Much as she likes you, she saw good reason for leaving you in the dark."

"She was right—and you also," said D'Arlay. "As I'm against you, I can't expect to be taken into your confidence."

Coeur asked suddenly, "You are very fond of the little cousin?"

After some hesitation D'Arlay nodded his head. "Yes. I am—I am very fond of her."

"Your fondness perhaps had something to do with your refusal of the King's ward?"

"I'm afraid so." A sigh accompanied the answer. "I saw the choice of our liege lord and she was—quite a nice child and rather pretty. I think she would have proven dull and prim; but that, after all, wouldn't have weighed much in the balance. I should have agreed to the match. But every time I tried to bring myself to the point of expressing my willingness, I would think of Valerie—and my resolution would weaken and disappear. I realize how foolish and wrong-headed I was about it. I've lost the best match in the proffer of the King. I've gained the royal dislike. And the great folly of it is that I know I must marry a fortune sooner or later."

"You've no idea that someday you may marry the little cousin?"

D'Arlay shook his head sadly. "No, Jacques, I've known from the start the impossibility of that."

Then, quite abruptly, Coeur began to laugh. He reached out and gave his companion's arm a vigorous shove. "My good friend, I've no fear of your attitude in the matter. I was—do you know how the Coquillards put it?—I was *tozing your ribs*. I would gladly tell you everything, knowing that you would never betray my confidence, if there was anything to tell. As a matter of fact, Robin, I may"—he leaned forward to add in a dramatic whisper—"*I may not go any further with it!*"

D'Arlay was too startled to make any comment immediately although the look on his face showed that he was delighted beyond measure. After a moment the Moneyman proceeded with an explanation.

"It's not that I've suffered a sentimental weakening. I have a streak of sentiment in me, as you've probably noticed, but I hold it sharply under control when it comes to matters of importance. The truth is that I may not need her. The war is being won and I seem to be getting my full share of the credit—in some quarters at least. The King has never been more cordial or more dependent on me. I always had a great reluctance to the idea, which was not mine as you will recall." He paused and then proceeded to sum up briskly: "It comes to this, then, that I'm not sure it will be necessary to proceed to the point of carrying out the plan. I may be content to—to consider that I have a weapon in reserve, for use if the need becomes great enough. I'll see to it, of course, that no one will suffer in the meantime. Our little Valerie can remain in the De Burey household and I will continue generous in my support."

"Have you told them of this?"

Coeur shook his head. "No, no! I haven't committed myself. I must always maintain a safe line of retreat. How can I tell what the future may bring?"

D'Arlay said in a fervent tone: "Jacques, my friend! I'm so happy I can't find words to tell you how deep my feelings go."

Alain de Kersai joined them when a supper of roasted boar's head and cold fish was served. "If my lord Coeur cares to listen to the talk one hears where Knights of the Guns assemble," he said, with an earnest air, "he may find cause for surprise."

"What is the nature of the talk?"

"It is new. In fact, my lord, we sometimes speak of ourselves as the New Men. It began when the Sire d'Arlay fought with my cousin, Jacques de Lalain, and got the better of him. Everyone started to speak then about the new weapon, the light sword. We didn't stop at that. We thought that times were changing and we were all in favor of the things we saw coming. We realized, my lord, that my cousin Jacques belonged to the past."

"That is true." Coeur nodded his head gravely.

"We're all rather amused over the follies of the past. Chivalry? It has been the absurdity of the ages."

The Moneyman, who had been finding it hard not to smile, became suddenly quite serious. "I'm very much interested, Alain," he said. "You see, I've felt that way about things for a long time. I've made no secret of it. You and the New Men will live perhaps to see great changes."

"To us, my lord Coeur, you are a symbol of the new age. You are a man of the people and yet you've risen to a place in the councils of the King. You don't believe the world so perfect now that any thought of altering it is wicked. That is what Jacques de Lalain and his sort think."

"No," affirmed Coeur seriously, "I don't believe the world to be perfect as it is. I'm doing what I can to change it."

"We've often said that," declared the boy excitedly. "In this very room we've talked about you and we've agreed that what you are doing is right. We are revolutionary in our ideas, my lord. Even you might be shocked at some of the things we believe."

"I doubt it, Alain de Kersai," said Coeur, with a smile. "You see, I am revolutionary in my ideas also."

2

THE WHITE ANTELOPE and red roses floated over the keep of Le Petit-Appui and so Coeur knew that the English were still holding out. He stood up in his stirrups and gazed down into the enclosure where the guns were voicing their demands for the capitulation of the garrison. Smoke belched up over the wattled wall.

There were half-a-dozen large bombards in action, raising their snouts from the great frames of oak, in which they were bedded, like the heads of serpents protruding from a pit. They were being fired in turn, and the work of reloading began almost as soon as the smoke ceased to erupt from the muzzles. That the unloading was slow was owing to the cumbersome nature of the machines and not to any lack of energy on the part of the men serving them. The latter moved with furious speed, darting about on the gravel floor like devil's attendants skipping on the edge of the Pit—an effect heightened by their close fitting black jerkins and hoods. They had to place powder in iron chambers separate from the bombards, carry these to the lower end of the tubes and clamp them tight with iron stirrups, and then set trains of the explosive to burning on the tops of the barrels. When the flames began to travel with a loud crackle like fire spreading across stubble, all work was suspended. The men in black, with the exception of two of their number, ran to places of safety behind a tall barrier. The pair who remained at their posts went into furious action as soon as the explosion was over, one rushing to the cannon's mouth, the other to the touchhole, to wrap the apertures with thick folds of felt.

The Moneyman smiled with pride. His plan had been put into practice and had solved the difficulty which a few days before had threatened to silence the guns. As a result, a large breach had already been opened in the outer wall of the castle and the bombards were now pouring their shot against the massive gray barbican. The English would have to give in soon.

He rode up to a young knight who sat his horse outside the entrance to the enclosure. "How long is the bombardment to last?"

"One more round, my lord," answered the knight. Then he stood up in his stirrups and waved his arms, cheering wildly. "A hit!" he cried. "A hit! A clean hit! Saw you ever a shot to equal it, my lord?"

A bombardier had raised his gun to the limit of its elevation (it had seemed, in fact, to be pointing at the sky), and the resulting shot had soared over the castle walls. By pure accident it had cut the pole which carried the flag of the defenders. The antelope and roses fell out of sight.

Other knights had been posted on horseback at intervals along the rise of ground. They now came riding up excitedly. The black flag with green lilies, which waved above the enclosure while the guns were being used, came sliding down; and men with blackened faces climbed over the top of the wattled wall and rushed up the grade to see the results of this miraculous shot. They jumped and danced and exchanged ecstatic slaps on the back. They began a song, "Poor Harry Sixt'" (for Henry of England was already showing signs of mental instability), which French soldiers liked to throw in the faces of the invaders.

Coeur took the first knight by the arm and drew him to one side. "Where is the Sire d'Arlay?" he asked.

"There," pointing down into the pit. "The one removing the wadding from the muzzle of the first gun. He'll be up in a few minutes. The guns will need half an hour to cool off."

When D'Arlay appeared, the Moneyman found it hard to recognize him. His friend's face was as black as a smith's, his hands were burned and covered with powder stains, his clothes were scorched and ragged. He raised his arms in front of him as though in self-defense. "No lecture, if you please," he said. "I weary of explaining my reasons for this."

"I've had the explanation already. None of the men were ready to risk their lives and so you thought it necessary to set an example. After which enough of them came forward to keep the guns well manned again. I heard all about it last night."

"Did you hear that the Scot, Pregent Kennedy, was the next man to offer himself? The pair of us still work together, a belted knight and a former captain of Free Companions doing the work of common men. A matter for much scandalized comment. I confess that my opinion of the Scot has climbed sky high."

"Do you know that at court your action is considered proof of madness rather than courage?"

"I'm aware that they laugh at me and say I'm a dangerous crackpot," said D'Arlay, his blackened face widening in a smile. "It doesn't matter. I don't care what they think."

"What brought me here today," Coeur said, "was to convince you that you needn't go on with this. You've shown the way and the guns are booming again. You've had more than your share of risks."

D'Arlay shook his head. "I'm not a bellwether. What would they say, the brave fellows who take as much risk as I do, if I left them now? No, I offered to tend one of the guns and I must go on. It may not be much longer. I predict that Le Petit-Appui will capitulate tomorrow and after that the English may decide it's useless to hold out any longer in Rouen. The war will be over if they do."

"It's true," said Coeur, "that the English leaders were showing a desire to discuss terms with us. But when some of the citizens of Rouen tried to let us in at a weak point in the walls, old Talbot came roaring up with a handful of men and gave our scaling party a warm welcome. We took a costly beating. Since then the English haven't talked about terms. Old Talbot is a seasoned fighter and he boasts that he has never laid down his arms. It's quite likely he may decide to fight it out here to the last man."

From where they stood they could see the French forces camping along an undulating ridge. Fires had been built at intervals for warmth as the wind was from the north and the air had turned raw. The sound of bugles reached them, thin in the distance but full, nevertheless, of the urgency of war. From the look of things a great army lay there, waiting the order to strike; but Coeur knew this was because of the craft Dunois had shown in his dispositions. Many needed companies were still missing.

Coeur laid a hand on his companion's arm. "Listen closely, Robin," he whispered. "The concentration isn't yet complete. If the English get an inkling of how weak we are, they'll decide to fight. . . . We aren't as close to the end as you think. You've done more than enough here. Wash that black off your face, have the surgeon attend to the burns on your hands, and be ready to ride on with me to see Dunois. I've talked to him and he wants to use you in more fitting ways than this."

D'Arlay shook his head. "You've convinced me I should stay here. We must reduce Le Petit-Appui quickly. That's the one way to make Talbot see reason, and the sooner we start the guns talking again, the better our chances will be. Until the castle falls, Jacques, I must remain at my post."

Pregent Kennedy joined them, walking with a limp, one hand going through the motions of curling a mustache end which had been burned away long before. He seemed blacker and more ragged even than D'Arlay. "You find us at our worst," he said. "In another hour or so—provided, of course, we—er, continued to survive—we would have succeeded in removing some of this filth. You have observed, no doubt, that none of the usual trappings of heroism go with serving the guns. Could you tell us from a pair of overworked chimney sweeps, my lord Coeur, or scarecrows left out for the winter in a cropped field?"

Coeur could not refrain from smiling as he inspected the grotesque figure of the Scot. "This is the first time I've seen you without a tartan somewhere on your person."

"Aye," agreed Kennedy in a gloomy tone. "I assure you that I feel undressed without my colors; but truly it would be a sorry thing to subject them to the devil's stife in which we spend our days. I lay this injunction on you, my lord: that if I'm killed, no matter where or when, and even if it's hard to find much that remains of the mortal guise of Pregent Kennedy, you will see to it that I'm buried in a proper and honorable grave—and that my tartan is draped about me."

"I will consider it a sacred obligation to do as you wish."

"Thank you, my lord. And also I thank you for the grateful and costly wine which you keep on our table. We toast your health in it every night."

As they talked, Coeur's eyes had been busy, darting along the French line and from there to the road which ran on to Rouen. It was clear that he was not pleased with what he saw.

"Does it seem to you," he asked his two companions, "that our line is thinly held hereabouts? Even more thin than at any other part?"

The Scot nodded his head. "Aye, my lord. It seems as thin to me as kilts in a wintry blast. And I'll tell you the reason. They still have it in their heads that it's devil's work we're doing here, sorcery or witchcraft or any evil name you care to put to it. They prefer to keep well to the wind of us."

"Do your neighbors ever visit you? Do they come over to watch the guns in action?"

"Not a mother's son of them has been near us. They jeer at us and call us imps of Satan and powderpolls. They cross themselves or hold their noses when we pass."

"Who are in command of the troops on each side of you?"

D'Arlay answered. "Jehan de Mottes on the right. Enguerrard de Tencon on the left."

Coeur received this information with a rueful look. "Two gallant knights," he said. "If it had been a matter of deliberate intent, we couldn't have picked two commanders more certain to fight in accordance with the dictates of chivalry—nor more certain to lose the day for France! Kind Father in Heaven, save me from the likes of Jehan de Mottes and Enguerrard de Tencon!" He shook his head back and forth in a mood of deep apprehension. "I'm not sure you could count on those two stiff-necked fools to lend a hand if the English attacked the guns!"

He continued to study the French position with growing discontent. "This isn't the planning of Dunois. He has to make the most of spare numbers but he would never leave his guns exposed so openly. Where is Jean Bureau?"

"At the headquarters of my lord Dunois," answered D'Arlay.

The Moneyman took a turn or two along the slope of the ridge. Then he pointed to the Rouen road. "Look!" he commanded. "Tell me what you see."

"Very little," said D'Arlay. "The air lacks clearness this afternoon. With a good light we can sometimes see the outline of the Beauvoisine Gate. But not today."

"We can see no more than half the distance today. Suppose that an English force suddenly appeared from the side road to the right? Suppose it headed at full speed in this direction? Would there be time for Jehan de Mottes and Enguerrard de Tencon to get their men to horse? Would there be time even to convince those two valiant blockheads of their duty? Or to get word to my lord Dunois of your plight?"

D'Arlay measured the distance with his eye. "No," he said, "there would be no time for anything except to rally to our own defense. It might prove a serious disaster for the arms of France."

"Go at once," urged Coeur, "to the man in command during the absence of Bureau. Point out the danger to him. Make him see we must take steps at once, that messengers must be sent to Jehan de Mottes and Enguerrard de Tencon. They must be told you have reason to expect an attack in force and that they will be needed—promptly and in full strength! Arrange a signal with them. You are higher here and would see the English first. A red flag flying on that knoll ahead of us will tell them the foe has been sighted." He kept his eye fixed on the Roman road as he talked. "Never have I been more sure of anything than about this. Talbot is too good a soldier to give in without making one effort to silence our guns. Conditions at the moment are perfect for an attack." His voice raised to a high note of urgency. "Make haste, D'Arlay! There's no time to be lost!"

2

Jehan de Mottes had answered the messenger sent to him earlier by saying in a gruff voice, "A knight doesn't carry pig's feathers!" which was a common saying at the moment and meant that he considered it beneath him to take any part in operations which involved common men, in this case the bombardiers. Enguerrard de Tencon had made no response at all.

When the guns started the *danse macabre* again—a term often applied to bombardments, referring to the strange rites once practiced in the cemeteries of Paris—and a first suggestion of crumbling began to show in the gray walls of the barbican, Coeur realized that for a matter of at least half an hour he had given no thought to the danger of attack which had seemed to him so imminent before. He forced his mind back to the realities of the situation, knowing that the danger was greater than ever. The responses of the two neighboring commanders made it unlikely that much help, if any, could be expected from them.

He walked to the edge of the mound and shaded his eyes with one hand, the better to see the Rouen road stretching on into the north. There was a haziness in the air which made it impossible to see far. He strained his eyes to study the shadows into which the highway dissolved, and at first he was sure it was imagination which made him fancy he detected movement and changing color. Gradually his conviction veered the other way. There *was* movement. He became certain of it. Imagination could not supply the flashes of light which he saw regularly and which might be made by the sun striking on armor or on the polished steel of weapons.

His worst fears had been confirmed. An armed party was moving down the road. He could see now the toss of horses' heads and a standard floating in the van. He knew that no French patrols would have ventured that far into enemy territory and so he was certain it was the English.

He began to shout: "To arms! Engloys! To arms!"

A squire sprang into action and planted the red flag as a signal that the enemy had been sighted. Two others started off to warn the neighboring companies, running as fast as their steel-encased legs would carry them. A fourth went forward to the slope where the New Men were waiting the word.

The young knights were already fully accoutered for action and were standing in rows along the top of the ridge, leaning on their upright lances. Their horses, held by squires, pawed the ground in front of them. Behind them were a half-dozen of the mounting platforms which knights used in getting to saddle when weighted down with armor. These consisted of wooden stands. For the heavier knights, however, there was an additional contrivance, a long wooden arm attached to the platform and curved like the ancient slings which had been called trebuckets. At the end of the arm was a steel torret and a hook. When the difficulty of mounting could be overcome in no other way, this hook would be attached to the belt of the weighty knight and the arm would swing him around into his saddle like a crane.

The mounting platforms would not be used. The New Men were light of frame and would need no more than the shoulder of a squire when the signal to mount came.

Jacques Coeur walked along the line until he came to Alain de Kersai. He looked into the face of the young Burgundian and was surprised to see the color in his cheeks and the sparkle of anticipation in his eyes.

"It will be sharp, Alain," he said. "I fear you can't count on any help. Your neighbors are so steeped in the gall of their sacred traditions that they may refuse to aid you."

"All the better," said the boy eagerly. "We want to do this by ourselves, my lord Coeur. If they come over to help, they will claim all the credit for beating the enemy off."

"But the odds will be heavy against you."

Alain de Kersai studied the approaching English for several moments. They were in clear sight now, a raiding force of considerable size. That they were lightly armed was apparent from the speed at which they rode. Coeur had already concluded from this that their purpose was to make a quick thrust and then get away; but there was no comfort in that, for they could wipe out the bombardiers in the short time they would allow themselves.

"They are no worse than five to one," said Alain. His manner was confident and cheerful.

The Moneyman looked along the line of young faces and saw everywhere the same exultant light, the same eagerness for the conflict. A sense of pity took possession of him. They were all so very young—some of them still looked like pages—so full of high spirits and the joy of living. It was an intolerable thought that they would soon be engaged in a fight to the death with the trained horsemen of the invading troop, that many of them would die under the blows of alien swords or be cut to pieces by the hoofs of maddened horses. He had always considered war a wasteful interruption to life, a cruel and senseless obsession of man. Now he began to realize in fuller measure the stupidity and cruelty of it. He felt a sense of responsibility for what would happen, knowing that but for his urging and his offer of finances the fighting would not have been resumed. "But it had to be!" he said to himself, in a mood which demanded justification. "France was bleeding to death. For each of these boys who die now, thousands of lives will be saved in the future."

"Alain," he said, "I would gladly give everything I possess to spare you this!"

"Would you rob us of our chance?" exclaimed the young knight. "My lord Coeur, this is the duty for which we've been trained—to guard the guns. So far we've had nothing to do, except to ride as escort when the batteries were on the move and stand to arms when a bombardment was on." He pointed excitedly at the English column which had come within a thousand yards or less. "They'll be on us in a few minutes, my lord! This is what we've longed for all these months." He raised his lance and gave it an exultant shake. "We'll show them now that the New Men can fight!"

Coeur glanced desperately to the right and then to the left. There was no sign of preparation on either side. It was certain that the brunt of the attack would be borne unassisted by a small company of green young men. In deep bitterness he realized that the commanders who thus refused to lend their aid would not be accounted cowardly or remiss, that no punishment would be meted out for the deaths of these gallant youths as there had been none for the slaughter of French archers in the lost battles of the war. "They will not carry pig's feathers!" he said aloud. "God grant a way to make them carry for all time the burden of the shame they have earned today!"

"Out of the way!" cried an urgent voice behind him.

The Moneyman hurried out through the ranks. His back was turned when the order was given for the charge. He did not look when the thunder of the action filled his ears, and he saw nothing until the impact of steel on steel drowned out the shouts of the contestants and even the wild screaming of wounded horses. Swinging about, he discovered with a sense of almost guilty relief that he could see from where he chanced to be only a small segment of the battleground. A clump of trees and an outward jutting of rocks closed off the rest. Within his vision, however, were rows of embattled figures on plunging horses. He saw the rise and fall of battle-axes at close range, the tossing of plumes in shiny helmets. He heard sounds which made him wish he could get far enough away to be out of hearing.

Someone ran by him shouting, "Out of the pit, everyone, they'll be here in a minute!" The Moneyman had no idea where he had left his own mount but it did not matter; he had no intention of riding off to safety while the frightful carnage went on below. He heard excited cries from close at hand but otherwise was not aware of company on the ridge until a hand touched his shoulder and a hoarse voice, which he thought was that of Nicolas, said in his ear, "Come, master, while there's yet time!" A horse, with blood streaming down one flank and nostrils flaring wide with fear and pain, came galloping up the slope. A loose piece of harness caught in the branches and the runaway animal was thrown to the ground, crushing someone (it did not seem to matter whom) under it. Through it all Coeur was aware that the guns went on firing steadily. "That is D'Arlay's doing," he said to himself. "He's determined to fire as many rounds as possible before the guns are lost."

The sound of battle lessened, then waxed and grew, and lessened again. Then the sound seemed to be coming from farther to the right. Coeur ran forward, tripping over a body and getting to his feet quickly without pausing to identify the victim. He found himself at the edge and looking over at the lower ground held by the troops of Jehan de Mottes. The English had changed their course and were riding hard and fast in that direction.

A few, a very few, of the New Men came riding back up the slope. More came on foot, climbing slowly and with obvious effort. The number returning seemed to Jacques Coeur pitifully small.

3

The talk in and around the large pavilion of Dunois that evening was all of the surrender of Le Petit-Appui, which had taken place at night-fall, and the death of Jehan de Mottes. Out of this rose speculation as to how long Rouen would hold out now that the English leaders knew the full power of the French cannon. It was whispered that already the English had authorized the burgesses of the city to open negotiations. There was a note of jubilation under all the talk and even Dunois was seen to smile.

The Moneyman had gathered the news by the time D'Arlay, well scrubbed and arrayed in his best black clothes, joined him there.

"The story that all these geese are telling and believing," said Coeur, a smoldering fire in his eyes, "is that Jehan de Mottes saved the guns and lost his life. That great ox, who allowed our fine boys to go to their deaths, is being made into a hero! I've tried to tell the real story but no one will listen to me. Here is the way they look at it: The English attacked and were repulsed. Jehan de Mottes was killed in the fighting. He was a knight. *Ergo*, he was responsible for the victory. I've had a dozen quarrels about it already!"

"What did happen?" asked D'Arlay. His hands were bound in black and they seemed to be causing him a great deal of discomfort. He was unable to keep them still.

"My belief is that the English leader didn't think it possible the rest would stand by while he attacked the guns. He suspected a trap and didn't want to drive any farther into our lines. When the young men checked his advance—he could have come on again, of course, after the first few minutes of fighting—he changed his plan. He swung around to his left and paid his respects to Jehan de Mottes in passing. Then, glad to have escaped the trap, he ordered his troop to return. And now we come to the part played by that gallant and honorable paladin, Jehan de Mottes. It seems he didn't have time to get all his armor on. He was fitting his *bavière* into place over his face when an English lance pierced above it. The point, by some queer trick of fate, found the tiny area where his brain was located. And now he will go down in the annals of this war as a hero!"

"Many others died today whose heroism will never be mentioned."

Coeur nodded his head soberly. Then he asked, in a hesitant tone as though he feared the answer, "What was the cost of our victory?"

"A heavy one. I find it hard to speak of it, Jacques. Alain de Kersai didn't come back. Nearly half of those fine lads were killed in three minutes of the most bloody fighting since the start of the Hundred Years' War!"

3

THE MEMBERS of the King's immediate train were eating a fine supper in a sour state of mind. In the center of the table was a roast swan with its body silvered and resting on green-colored pastry. Dunois sat in front of this elaborate but rather inedible dish and winked across its gilded beak at Jacques Coeur who sat on the other side.

Shortly before the company sat down, an English spy had been caught in the courtyard of the castle. His neck being committed to the rope in any event, the islander had boastingly asserted that his purpose had been to kill the three men who were most dangerous to England, whose removal, in fact, would make victory possible again for the invaders. He had named Dunois first, of course; but then he had amazed and chagrined the military leaders and the great knights by passing them over and asserting in a bold and confident voice that the other two were Jacques Coeur and Jean Bureau.

In spite of their mortified feelings, the knights were feasting mightily on three main dishes: roast beef, stewed kid, and chined salmon, and helping themselves to great handfuls of the roast train. All, that is, but Dunois himself. The commander was taking advantage of the fact that they were in Normandy to sup lightly on the rich angelot cheese for which that province was famous, contenting himself otherwise with a thin slab of white bread and a flagon of Malmsley wine diluted with water.

"The spy has been hanged," announced the commander, in a loud enough voice for everyone at table to hear. "It seemed a pity—a man of such rare and sound judgment."

This sally was received in glum silence. The general looked up and down the board with something of the expression of a cat which finds itself surrounded by mice, and reached a hand to the dish containing the feathered quills.

"Is it possible that the English," he began, picking his teeth fastidiously, "who are losing because of the guns are better aware of the importance of them than the French who are winning with them? And touching his thought of my good friend and gossip, the Moneyman——"

A hand touched the shoulder of Jacques Coeur and a respectful voice said in his ear, "His King's Grace desires the presence of my lord Coeur." He rose reluctantly and bowed first to Dunois and then to the rest of the company. He wanted very much to hear what the commander was going to say about his selection by the Englishman whose neck had been stretched. Well, he would hear about it later and so all he would lose was the opportunity to watch the glumly supercilious faces of the knights who were not going to find it to their liking.

The capture of the spy had created an atmosphere of unusual caution in the castle. The corridors, which ordinarily would have been dark and full of shadows, were now so well lighted by torches on the walls that no one could pass through them without being seen by many wary eyes. One captain of guards went to the length of halting the Moneyman and looking him over carefully, muttering in half-apology that one had to remember the uncanny skill spies had at disguise.

The chamber occupied by Charles of France was approached by a steep flight of stone steps at the head of which stood two guards with drawn swords. It was a small tower apartment and so brilliantly lighted that nothing could be concealed within it. On a table in front of the monarch were articles of clothing in a high but orderly pile. Coeur's quick survey told him that there were scarlet hoods and pointed hats of miniver and round beaver hats lined with velvet, not to mention a variety of rich cloaks and tunics. His master, he realized, had been immersed in the task of selecting a costume for his triumphal entry into Rouen.

"Ha, my good Jacques," said Charles, in a contented tone of voice, "I've made up my mind. By St. Martin of Tours, it wasn't easy! I had to be sure my decision was the right one. I shall wear"—the royal eyes lighted up as he reached into the pile and drew out a beaver hat—"this one. It is handsome and it will provide the best base for the crown. I shall change the lining to crimson and have the brim turned up all around."

"I'm sure you've made the right choice, sire."

"The King of Sicily will be on my right hand and my brother of Maine on the other. Behind us will ride"—the King sighed, for he had little liking for any of the trio he proceeded to name—"the three Comtes, St. Pol, De Clermont, and De Nevers. The order in which all my gentlemen ride has been settled to my satisfaction. The Comte de Dunois will head a party to greet me at the Beauvoisine Gate and I am naming you, my friend and counselor, to be at his right."

A sense of sardonic amusement took possession of the mind of the Moneyman. "Can it be that our liege lord doesn't want us in his train because my father was a merchant and the brave Dunois wears the bar sinister? Or does he consider in all honesty of mind that it will be an equal honor to welcome him into the captured city? I have a strong suspicion it's the first."

Charles was addicted to detail. His eyes beamed with satisfaction as he proceeded to enumerate some of the arrangements he had made. "You are to wear crimson. I suggest velvet although you can choose baudekin if you liking runs to that material strongly. Velvet is to be the note of the day—well, make your own selection. The hat, crimson. I advise a sugarbag shape and I must limit your ornamentation of the brim to seed pearls. Under no circumstances, diamonds; I consider them too ostentatious and, in fact, vulgar. I am trying to prevent the wearing of ostrich feathers but some of my gentlemen have an almost fanatical liking for them which I may find hard to control."

For a quarter of an hour longer he talked about the various arrangements for the great day. Coeur listened without making many comments. Whenever he did drop an amending suggestion his advice was so sound that Charles immediately adopted it. An old seneschal in a green-and-white tabard came in to stir up the fire on the hearth and to replenish the flagon of wine at the King's elbow. It was clear that he was a favored servant for he took in on himself to say, "Your King's Grace, the hour is growing late."

"There are two matters on which I desire your advice, good Jacques," said Charles, motioning impatiently to the seneschal to withdraw. "The first concerns the Lady Agnes. I may tell you, Moneyman, that she's to have another child and her health is not good. I don't accept the opinion of Robert de Poitevin who dins his gloomy predictions into my ears, but I'm forced to believe that she requires the most particular care. In spite of her condition, which makes travel hard for her, I'm ill content to have her far from my person. Now here is the difficulty. My duty will keep me in the field for the winter months. The child will be born in February and I am loth to see nothing of her in the meantime. What do you advise under the circumstances?"

Coeur gave the matter careful thought. He was delighted that the King desired Agnes Sorel near him, for it meant that he also would have the opportunity of seeing her and even of consulting her. He could tell her of the steps he had taken to meet her wishes in the matter of a successor and of the doubts he now entertained as to the need of doing anything more about it. So far he had told her nothing. In fact, he had not had a chance to speak to her for months. He had seen her, of course, on the few occasions when she had appeared at court, but all that had passed between them each time had been a bow from him and a smile from her, with a slight gesture of her thin hand to express her regret that anything more was impossible.

After several moments' thought he raised his head. "Sire," he said, "the terms of the capitulation will clear the English out of much of the province north and west of Rouen. I suggest, therefore, that the lady in question be directed to take up her residence at the Abbey of Jumièges and that she go at once before the winter sets in and—and before her condition will make travel impossible for her. There is a manor house a few miles away at Mesnil-sous-Jumièges which belongs to the abbey and which would provide her with ample room for her attendants. By giving her the manor house, the guest wing at the abbey would be available in case it became advisable for the court to pass any time at Jumièges. As you know, sire, the good fathers of Jumièges are well endowed and have added to their wealth by centuries of industry and thrift. They're in a position to entertain visitors well, even lavishly."

The King nodded his head with instant approval. "An excellent arrangement, my good Jacques. The idea of Jumièges had occurred to me but I wasn't aware of the existence of the manor house. I was afraid that the guest wing, which I have never seen, of course, would be restricted in size and hardly suitable for any—any duality of arrangements. You have removed my doubts and I shall act on the idea at once."

The royal attention then turned itself in another direction. It was apparent that the King was somewhat perturbed. He looked down at his lap and frowned. Finally he said in a hesitant voice: "I sent you, Moneyman, a list of appointments I proposed to make—governors and minor officials for the sections of Normandy which we have succeeded in winning back. You've returned it and I find, to my surprise, that you're suggesting an entirely different list. Is my judgment so faulty? I confess to being irked at your attitude and I'm demanding to know what reasons you can have had for this—this flouting of my wishes and my carefully considered judgments."

Coeur did not indulge in any of the protestations of loyalty and humility which constitute the usual approach to debates with royalty. His relationship with Charles had always been surprisingly direct. As a man of business he would lay the facts before his master and state his views with few reservations. When necessary he would dispute a point as man to man without any attempt to soften the effect of the facts. There had even been a camaraderie of sorts between them, dating back to the days when Charles lived in Bourges and depended on Jacques Coeur for the alleviation of his poverty. The King sometimes called his minister in affectionate tones "My old Jacques!" and the Moneyman would, on occasion, indulge in a facetious salutation which consisted of an oriental bow from the waist and an "Oh, King, live forever!" uttered in exaggerated tones.

The Moneyman lost no time, therefore, in voicing excuses for what he had done. He launched into a justification of his list. "Sire," he said, "I wish to point out first that it will take a great deal of energy and ability on the part of your new officers to set this country to rights. Think, liege lord: many sections have been harried and burned, they have been fought over several times, and the people who are flocking back to claim their lands and houses will be without food. Ways must be found at once to get food in for them, to bring it over roads that are almost impassable. Families have been broken up, and one of the first duties of your officers must be to assist parents in finding lost children and in getting homes for the poor little waifs who live like wild creatures in hedges and the slums of the towns. There will be bitter conflicts over the possession of lands and so there must be cool heads to settle disputes. I short, sire, the men into whose hands you give the reconquered provinces must be capable of restoring order out of chaos in the shortest possible time.

"And now, sire," went on the Moneyman, "look over this list of the men you have selected. I concede they would do certain things very well. They would bring dignity to their posts, they would preside at official banquets with a fine air, and they would see to it that their guests were properly seated. They would conduct tournaments and settle points of dispute between knightly contestants. Some of them might prove capable at collecting taxes and crown revenue. But, sire, none of them would turn a finger to bring in food for the starving people. They would think it of small concern to make fair settlement of disputes about the possession of houses and lands. Parents would never find their lost children." In his earnestness he placed both hands on the edge of the table and leaned forward toward the King. "The men I respectfully suggest as better fitted for these posts may not have the same prestige. But, liege lord, they are the kind of men who will labor day and night to get food into their towns and villages, to help the people in their misery and want, to let the humble and downtrodden sup at once on the sweet wine of restoration. I beg of you to consider these points well. It is important, as you have said so often yourself, sire, that the people who are being reclaimed from alien rule be helped to content and loyalty."

The feelings with which Charles followed this argument were reflected clearly on his face. At first he was resentful, then his rather gloomy countenance took on the aggrieved look of one who sees himself being thwarted of a pet desire, and finally he came around to an expression of reluctant agreement. He riffled through some papers in front of him until he found the documents in question. After glancing them over, he dropped them back on the table and called in a peremptory tone:

"Ulysse!"

The seneschal came in at a senile trot, his face showing a scandalized regret that his royal master should have an unanticipated want.

"Your King's Grace?"

"Ulysse!" The voice of Charles was sharp and reproachful. "*My bon morceau!* Has it been forgotten? Is the King of France of no consequence to his servants? Must his selection of officials be criticized, changed, torn to pieces, derided, laughed at? Are his few and simple wants always to be forgotten? Must he demand his bon morceau before it is produced for him?"

Leaving the room in a frenzy of self-reproach, the ancient seneschal gave Jacques Coeur a glance, nevertheless, which said he was convinced that the outburst was in some way the fault of the Moneyman. He returned in less than a minute with a silver platter on which reposed a glass bowl of a most beautiful garnet shade containing a mixture which defied quick classification. From long experience Coeur knew what the mixture was: a frothed-up bed of cream flavored with sugar, cinnamon, and a dash of verjuice. Beside the bowl was a small heap of cracked walnuts.

He proceeded to dip the nuts into the contents of the bowl and then to crunch them with relish—a reluctant relish because of his unhappiness in his servants.

After a half dozen or more had vanished down the royal throat, Charles progressed to a smile. "You are right!" he said to Jacques Coeur. "I had promised posts to many of these people and it seemed a convenient way of getting them settled in office. Why must the men about me be so lacking in the needed qualities? Yes, my good Jacques, you are right. I concede the wisdom of what you have said. We must have men capable of restoring order quickly."

The King got to his feet and dropped a hand on the shoulder of his Moneyman. "You are always right. What would I do without you, Jacques Coeur? I would be lost! I've always known it; and now, when there is so much talk and idle tattle, I acknowledge it to you openly. We must stand together, my old Jacques!"

The Moneyman was on his way out, glowing with the words of praise he had heard from his sovereign, when the King called him back.

"Jacques Coeur!"

"Yes, sire."

The mood of the monarch had changed. He had seated himself again and his attitude suggested deep gloom. His shoulders sagged, his arms rested limply on the table. Even a large emerald which he wore on a gold chain around his neck seemed to lack its rich glow.

"Jacques Coeur, Jacques Coeur! There are times when I feel I am losing everything worth while. Why, at this time when I am winning back all of France, must I lose those who mean the most to me? She is going to die! I speak sharply to Robert de Poitevin, I tell him he's a croaking beldame, I say he knows nothing. But down in my heart I'm sure he knows. Yes, Jacques Coeur, she's going to die!"

2

D'Arlay found the New Men squatting in groups on the earthen floor, engaged in a game called *honchet* which required the use of boards and men. One of them looked up and asked, "Will the procession be starting soon?"

D'Arlay peered through a crack in the oiled paper which covered the one window. "The sun is under and it's hard to tell the time," he said. "But I think it will start in a very few minutes now."

The players pushed aside the men and scrambled to their feet. There was a casual air about them as they strolled outside but D'Arlay knew that it was assumed. The yard of the inn was completely deserted. Everyone who could get away, even the stablehands, had gone to Rouen to see the King of France take possession of the city after all the years it had been in enemy hands. The young men grouped themselves about the entrance, their heads turning of one accord to the south.

A loud trumpet blast reached their ears, the work clearly of a whole company of heralds blowing lustily in chorus. It was possible, even at the distance, to detect the note of triumph in the concerted voice of the trumpets: the King of France had made his entrance into the ancient city through the Beauvoisine Gate.

"It will be a rare sight," said one of the New Men with a sigh. "They say the King will glitter with jewels from head to foot. My lord Dunois wears a sword set with diamonds which Jacques Coeur has given him."

"I've never seen the King," said another. His tone was wistful. "I suppose all the beautiful ladies of the court will be there."

After a pause the first speaker asked: "Do you suppose our comrades who died will be watching—and wondering why we're not in the procession?"

A third voice broke in, rough and scornful of such weakness, "The souls of our dead comrades will have better things to do than to watch a lot of elderly knights and fat dowagers dressed up in their finest clothes. I thought processions were great when I was a boy of five but now—I propose we choose sides and have a game of *La Soule*."

There was a long pause and then the first speaker nodded in agreement. "Maxime is right about it. If our comrades *are* watching, they won't want to see us mooning around. Why should we let anyone know our feelings have been hurt? Get out the ball!"

A large round globe, made of straw with a thin covering of leather, was produced and a game of La Soule begun. At first there was a listlessness to the struggle for possession of the ball. No signs of energy or enthusiasm were displayed. Gradually, however, the players became more interested, the action grew in warmth. In time the struggle was waging furiously and the loud shouts of the contestants made it clear that, for the time being at least, they had forgotten the slight which had cut them so deeply.

When D'Arlay returned to the inn he found that a letter had been delivered there for him. His name on the outside flap was inscribed in a hand he recognized at once, the hasty but well-formed writing of Jacques Coeur. It was a short note.

This is to tell you, my good friend, that I have reached a decision you will approve. I am now convinced it is not necessary to adopt *extreme means*. I am going to drop the plan and I propose to see the Comte at once and let him know. I send the word to you in this way because it seemed to me likely you would be low in mind today and it might serve to raise your spirits.

D'Arlay threw the sheet of paper into the fire and watched it burn. Then he turned and gave vent to his good spirits by a twirl of one foot as he started for the door.

"The highest of the bars has been taken away!" he said to himself.

3

The Comte de Burey had followed the campaign in the train of Charles of France. There had been little for him to do, beyond donning his armor (which chafed him painfully) in the mornings and keeping it on all day. After the entry into Rouen, however, things were changed in that respect. He became one of the busiest men about the King.

The duty assigned him had something to do with supplies of horses from the west (he was a little hazy about the matter himself), but it was not this which set him into such a lather of activity that the skirts of his short-ened houppelande flapped about his shanks and his bag sleeves were con-stantly in motion. Some days, in fact, he could transact his official business in fifteen minutes. Even when things were at a point of seemingly high tension, he was never engaged at it for more than an hour.

The demands on his time and attention came from participation in matters of a far from official nature. In the first place he was an active member of an exclusive court clique which indulged in orgies of com-petition in that fascinating new form of entertainment, cards. As the King was known to frown on all such pastimes, particularly now that he had girded himself to the duty of finishing the war and expected all his im-mediate attendants to take things as seriously as he did, the games had to be played as privately as possible. A tower room had been found for the purpose. It was so high and so difficult of access that it was unlikely the King would ever make his way to it; and here at all hours of the day and night the zealous players gathered. There were ladies (for the lure of cards was strong enough to induce bright-eyed young matrons as well as fat dowagers to essay the weary climb) as well as gentlemen competing for the possession of Tib and Tom and Tiddy, as the high cards were called. The stakes were steep, and so cardplaying proved profitable for the Comte de Burey. He was a good player, although none of his opponents realized it. Holding his cards tightly cupped in his unsteady hands and quite close to his eyes, he kept track of every piece of cardboard which fell on the table and noticed every expression on the faces of his opponents. As he mumbled to himself a great deal and had a tendency to fumble when playing his cards, they were disposed to laugh at him and treat him as of little account; but the fact stood that he almost always won.

But an even more profitable pursuit than cardplaying occupied a large part of his waking hours. As usual, when a victorious army has engulfed a large slice of territory, a busy traffic had developed in what was off-handedly called *lettres de marque*—that is, letters of safe-conduct, of identification, of leave of absence, of admission to military areas, of right to trade with the troops and the liberated inhabitants. Some were ob-tained properly and legally, after much running from one department to another, but the King's ministers were not prepared to issue such papers in unlimited quantities and so the demand had to be met by forged copies. Handsome prices were paid for both kinds and in short order an organization, working *sub rosa* and made up largely of crown officers, had sprung up to supply the ever-growing demand. The Comte's part in the transactions consisted in obtaining the signatures, real or forged. He spent hours each day waiting in anterooms for chances to get a minister's name down on the sheaf of documents he carried under his arm. The officers of the Crown were scattered throughout the huge rectangular palace the English had built on the river and which Charles had selected as his own headquarters while in Rouen (he had no option in the matter, for the city was a shambles of razed public buildings, of burned wooden houses, and of trade centers which the invaders had used as cannon foundries), some of them being located even in the oratories and the pantries and in temporary sheds erected on the mall and tennis grounds and in stuffy cubbyholes in stables and cattle sheds.

Frequently his pursuit of signatures took him to the office of the Moneyman which was located in the courtyard in what apparently had been a menagerie at one time, for there was a strong animal odor about it. Jacques Coeur invariably was busy but he would attend to the Comte's requests without making him wait. They were, needless to state perhaps, legal signatures the Comte sought when he went near the keeper of the King's purse. If Coeur knew that his visitor was engaged in the preparation of spurious documents as well, and it is inconceivable that he would not know, he said nothing about it.

One day, however, he looked at Regnault de Burey with a suggestion of annoyance in the pucker of his brow. "You must have a great number of friends, Naulty. And you must have a heart as big as a great spreading oak to go to so much trouble for them. I'm assuming, of course, that you wouldn't—shall we say, demean yourself?—by doing this for any kind of a reward."

The Comte did not relish the tone in which the words had been spoken. "You know quite well, Moneyman," he grumbled, "that I have need for every little round coin, silver as well as gold, which I can entice into the yawning maw that I call, somewhat inaccurately, a purse."

On two occasions Jacques Coeur said: "There's something we must talk about, Comte, as soon as I have half an hour to spare. As you know, they give me no peace here."

He did not find the needed half hour, however, until one day about a week after the French court moved into the palace vacated by the leaders of the English Army. He met the Comte outside the door leading into the crowded anteroom of the King and drew him down the corridor to his own quarters.

"Comte, I've come to a decision," said the Moneyman, digging his hands deep into the pockets of his cloak and frowning thoughtfully. "I may tell you in confidence that I no longer doubt the King will want me to remain in his service. He has given me the most positive assurances of his cordiality. For some time I have been skeptical as to the need for any special measure."

Sensing what was coming, the Comte frowned at his companion. "Do you mean," he demanded, "that the toads of doubt are hopping in your head as to the need of carrying out the plan?"

"That is what I mean. I mean much more than that, gossip Regnault. I have, in fact, made up my mind. I'm dropping the plan."

Seeing the end of all the good things he had been enjoying, the steady jingle of gold in his pockets, the secure future, the Comte protested energetically. Did he, Jacques Coeur, understand the risk he was taking? Was he not underestimating the amount of opposition which had developed at court? Could he be sure the cordial mood of the King would continue?

The Moneyman brushed such arguments aside. He contented himself with an assured nod and a final word. "My mind is made up, Comte. You understand, of course, that this will not mean a loss for you and the Comtesse. The payments will be continued to cover the cost of the girl's maintenance. There will be compensation for you also."

The Comte put little trust in promises, perhaps because he used the ones he made himself as a basis of valuation. He departed, therefore, in a thoroughly depressed mood, his mind occupied with schemes to repair this damaging blow to his prospects. Coeur called after him: "There's no need for repining, gossip Regnault. A great prosperity lies ahead of France in which all of us will share. You will pay off your debts and still have enough left to dine on golden plate. I promise it."

The Comte proceeded to the King's anteroom. Ordinarily his spirits lifted as soon as he breathed the atmosphere of the court, finding stimulation in the pervading sense of competition, the undercurrent of intrigue, the continuous battle of wits. Today, however, he remained sunk deep in gloom. He walked slowly into the long and drafty room, his eyes fixed on the floor, muttering indignantly to himself. He did not respond to greetings.

"This passes belief!" he thought, with an aggrieved shake of his head.

And then an idea occurred to him, a sure way out of this impending difficulty. It was such a brilliant idea that he stood still in the exact center of the room for several moments to consider it and to savor the gorgeous prospect it opened up. He slapped a hand against his thigh and said aloud, "Of course!"

"Of course what?" demanded a voice at his shoulder. "Is it new sap in your veins which is making you dream dreams? Or are you just sampling the visions of a withered old age?"

The Comte did not turn to identify the speaker. He walked triumphantly from the room, his head held high, his fingers itching for the pen which would put this dream or vision, whichever it was, into the process of consummation. "Does he think me some countinghouse varlet to jump at his beck and call?" he demanded of himself. "I have no need of the great Moneyman in this. I, Regnault de Burey, will take the reins into my own hands and there will be resolution and skill and craft in the driving!"

He made his way briskly to his own quarters. Two rooms had been assigned him in a tower on the river side, a small room for himself and an even smaller one for the three servants he had brought with him. "A pen, Hugan!" he shouted, when he reached the apartment. "Ink and paper, knave! And quickly."

It took some time to supply these most unusual needs, for the Comte was not a scholar and had little use for writing materials. Finally, however, his demands were filled and he set himself to the task of inditing a long letter to his wife in Paris. He labored over it a considerable time, his nose close to the paper, his lips repeating the words as he put them down. He deleted and rewrote and made an infinity of blots, saying to himself finally, "By'r Lady of Marmoutier, it is clear that neither my head nor my hands have a clerkly inclination!"

When the epistle was completed, he picked up the final sheet and read over the last paragraph with a sense of satisfaction in a task well done.

And so, my heart, I am sure you will agree with me that we must go on ourselves from where he has left off. This chance is too great to lose because some last-minute scruples fill the head of this puffed-up furrier. We must arrange it so our liege lord sees the little cousin before his liking for the De Maignelais vixen gets too strong a hold on him. If he likes the copy of his beloved original, the Moneyman will be in no position to call a halt.

Join me at once, sweet spouse, bringing our candidate with you. Need I point out she must be kept in the dark? Come in state. Bring all the best clothes the Moneyman provided for her—all her most charming gowns and hats and cloaks, the silkiest willicoats and all the laciest whimwhams. Our liege lord must see her at her best.

Set out immediately on receipt of this and spare not the horses in the coming!

4

ISABEAU read the letter from her husband with varying emotions. She was upset over this disruption of a program which had been proceeding so smoothly and profitably. She felt also some hesitation about going on with it. This was not because of scruples on her part but rather to an instinctive suspicion of any scheme hatched in the mind of her spouse. More than anything else, however, she experienced a deep anger with the Moneyman for the decision he had reached.

"It's always the way!" she said to herself bitterly. "When it comes to the point, men shy away and raise objections. They cannot do this, they must not do that! They prate of honor. Honor! It's no more than a mask they carry about, these self-appointed masters of ours, to hide themselves behind when they need an excuse for some weakness. . . . Men are made to be obeyed but not respected."

She reluctantly left the comfort of her own warm hearth and ventured out into the halls which the chill of winter had already claimed. Although she had thrown over her shoulders a cloak with a fur hood, she shivered and began to run, and it was with great unwillingness that she stopped on encountering the same physician who had been summoned to see Valerie on her first arrival.

"Messire," she asked, drawing the cloak about her more closely, "will Mademoiselle be well enough to undertake a long journey at once?"

The physician's eyes opened wide with surprise. "A long journey? Did I hear you aright, my lady? Did you mean a journey *now*, in this cold and bitter weather?"

"You heard me aright. Yes, Messire, a journey *now*."

"My lady! She's so ill she would die of shock if we were so ill-advised as to move her as much as from one room to another."

The Comtesse said to herself, "It's indeed aggravating that the little slut chose this time to become ill!" Aloud, she asked, "From what malady is it that she suffers?"

The physician lapsed at once into the vagueness in which medical advice was almost invariably cloaked. "A fever, my lady. There are many fevers but I haven't yet determined the exact nature of the one from which she suffers. The source of the disease? I do not know. If I did, I would become famous and rich. Of such matters, Aetius says—— But I must not distress you with opinions. This much I have done: I have bled her copiously, I have given her a clyster of herbs and scammony, I have had her bathed with hot water and distillations of oak leaf. I have even"— his eyes became filled with a zealous glow—"I have even tried something new. I am administering drinks to her of aniseed and polypody. To thin her, my lady, to remove the noxious matters from her body by reducing the flesh."

The Comtesse, who had shown a disposition to cut his explanations short by brushing past him, stopped suddenly. "To thin her!" she said indignantly. "Don't you realize, Messire, that she is already thin? Is it your idea to save her life by reducing her to such a paucity of flesh that her beauty will be lost? You will cease these new treatments at once, Messire! Polypody, indeed! Of what use is life to a woman without beauty?"

The physician was so discomfited that he stammered in replying. "But —but, my lady, I was acting in her best interests as I—as I conceived them."

The Comtesse completed the act of brushing by him, saying as she proceeded down the hall: "I will have no more of this stupidity, Messire. I order you to do nothing further until I have seen her myself."

She was disturbed, when she entered Valerie's bedroom, by the flushed condition of the patient's cheeks and brow. It was clear at once that her charge was quite ill, certainly more ill than she had supposed. The room was so warm that even Guillaumette, who was warming a sheet in front of the fire, had acquired a flushed look also.

Tossing feverishly from one side to the other, Valerie said in a weak voice, "I am so ill, Cousin, that I am like to burn up."

The Comtesse walked briskly into the room. Her first step was to whisk up the black-and-white cat which was ensconced on the foot of the bed and carry it to the door. Anatole-Raymonet arched his back and protested his ejection by a vain effort to rake the arms of his captor with his hind claws.

"Please!" protested Valerie. "When I am ill, my old cat always stays close beside me. He seems to know."

"This time," declared Isabeau, returning to the bedside, "he will be kept out of the room. I don't know why I tolerate the creature anyway. He's always in trouble. This morning he stole a fillet of fish in the kitchen. . . . Cousin, I have received word that we must proceed north at once. It's a matter of the greatest importance."

Valerie raised her head to look at her mentor but lacked the strength to sustain that position. She fell back on the pillow, saying in a tone of self-reproach: "How unfortunate that I should be ill! What are we to do, Cousin? Is it possible that I could be left behind?"

"It is *not!* You must get well as quickly as possible. You must exert your will to the utmost."

Valerie nodded her head feebly in agreement. "Yes, Cousin, I'll do my best."

"Is it necessary to tell you what is back of this summons?"

"No, I think not. I will—I will try hard to get well."

The Comtesse said in a bitter voice, "That physician is a fool! There's nothing to be done about it because all the others are just as bad." She turned to Guillaumette. "The air in here is very close. Light a vanilla stick at once."

She closed the door behind her emphatically but not quickly enough to prevent a black-and-white shape from bounding in and flying to its previous post on the foot of the bed.

Guillaumette walked over and patted Valerie's hand. "A lot of sympathy you had from her! Get well quickly, indeed! Does she think all you have to do is to say, I am better, and then step right out of bed?" The maid nodded her head and winked mysteriously. "I know what's wrong with her, Mademoiselle. She had a letter from *him.*"

Valerie remained still for several moments, a sign that her interest had been roused. "From the Comte?" she asked.

"One came from the master today but the one I meant arrived several days ago. It was from the other."

Valerie did not need to ask any questions. She knew that the letter had been from the Sire d'Arlay.

"She wasn't pleased with it, Mademoiselle," said Guillaumette, leaning over the bed and whispering. "She stayed in her room for hours. When she came out—— Ah, was she in a temper!" The maid nodded her head eagerly. "I wish I knew what was in it. Perhaps he has flipped his tail feathers at her and said good-by. Perhaps he was telling her——"

"You mustn't talk about such things to me, Guillaumette."

"I know, Mademoiselle. But, truly, she has been in a mood for such a long time!"

This was not an exaggeration as Valerie knew only too well. The Comtesse *had* been in a mood, almost from the time the Comte and D'Arlay had left to join the army. She had vented some of her ill temper on her charge. She had been extremely hard to please, never letting a day pass without pointing out faults. Valerie laughed too much ("A lady must not show much sense of humor, Cousin, the men don't like it and consider it vulgar"); she was impulsive, she said and did things as the mood seized her, which was wrong because ladies must always be cool and dignified; she was continually in a hurry, which was very wrong because haste must be left to servants. But the main fault, which she pointed out on innumerable occasions, was Valerie's failure to think like a lady.

"Inside yourself," the Comtesse had said on one occasion, "you are still a waif, the daughter of a wandering actor. Perhaps you *were* their child. If that is the case, nothing can be done to change you. But if it's in you to alter your way of thinking, I want you to understand that you must do so quickly. You'll never act like a lady until you're sure in your own mind that you are one."

Valerie had been honest enough to acknowledge that her mental attitude had not changed completely. "But more and more," she had added in her own defense, "I find myself doing the things you've taught me to do without conscious effort. I feel sure of myself most of the time."

"You must be sure of yourself all the time," Isabeau had said sharply. "I can't help you. It's something which must be felt and which can't be explained."

On every occasion thereafter, when Valerie did something which displeased her, she would say, "*There!* That is what I mean." Valerie would answer, "I'm not conscious of any fault, Cousin," and the Comtesse would raise her hands in a gesture of helplessness. "If you don't know by this time," she would cry, "how can I make you see?"

Valerie grew accustomed to hearing that accusatory, "*There!*" She could not understand why her mentor had changed in her attitude and become so critical. It seemed to her that the Comtesse took a pleasure in finding her at fault, or pretending to do so, that she was like a cat sitting at a mousehole ready to pounce.

On quite rare occasions Isabeau would revert back to a more helpful mood and even let drop a word of praise. It was as though she had said to herself, "After all, I stand to benefit if we succeed." Valerie welcomed these moments but she suspected the brief kindnesses of her mentor as much as her criticisms. She knew that the Comtesse was completely hostile to her and that everything the latter said and did must be weighed in the knowledge of this enmity. She had no way of judging the reason but she sometimes wondered if Isabeau knew that D'Arlay liked her and had become jealous.

All this ran through her mind now and added a malaise of spirit to the fever of her body. She said to the servant, "I feel very bad indeed, Guillaumette, and I mustn't talk any more." However, she added a few moments later, "I'm sure the Comtesse is going to be very angry with me because I won't be well enough to travel for a long time."

2

Valerie had been right. Christmas came and went, the cold days of January dragged slowly by. February, the least welcome of all months, was close at hand before she was well enough to travel. There was snow on the ground when they set out from Paris. All this time the pucker of impatience seldom left the heretofore smooth brow of Isabeau. There had been many days when she did not go near her charge and many more when she refused to address her.

The progress they made was slow. The roads were alive with travelers of all kinds: returning refugees with household goods on their backs; prosperous individuals who could be nothing else but army contractors; closemouthed fellows who were stamped as criminals of some sort; rouged, beribboned, noisy prostitutes; ladies of the court whose husbands were at the front and who wanted to be near them. Isabeau kept herself and her charge away from all contacts and saw to it that Valerie was well muffled about the face when they encountered other travelers.

They came at last to Rouen. The officer on the gate looked at their credentials and then called to someone in the rear: "Is that tug-mutton still about? If he is, send him in."

A few moments later Pregent Kennedy appeared. He smiled and winked at Valerie and then bowed to the Comtesse. "Welcome, my lady," he said. "And you also, Mademoiselle. The Comte de Burey has found it necessary to go on with the court to the Abbey of Jumièges and he instructed me to meet you on your arrival. I've been in and out of this place for five days, watching for you."

Isabeau answered sharply, as though she resented the suggestion that she had been placed under obligation to him, "I'm grateful for your kindness, Messire. Did the Comte leave any message for me?"

"Only that he considered it advisable for you to follow as soon as possible. Tonight, my lady, you will stay in a house where I have been quartered. It's a humble place but it's clean and comfortable. It stands close to the walls near the Cauchoise Gate and there's a view of the Church of St. Vigor from the window of the room you will have."

"Surely more suitable lodgings could be obtained for us!"

The Scot smiled acidly, making it clear that he had gained an unfavorable impression of the beautiful Comtesse de Burey and was not going to make any effort to hide the fact. He did not respond at once but busied himself adjusting a new tartan, with its rich dark green and blue background, about his neck. The war, quite apparently, had brought prosperity to Pregent Kennedy. He wore an English baldrick across one shoulder, a fresh one with gold embroidery on its velvet base, and his armor was new and highly shined.

"My lady," he said then, "there is nothing else. The English left the city in a sorry state, what with tearing down houses close to the walls to help in defense and burning over whole areas. The Comte had not succeeded in finding anything for you when I said that my companion and I, who share the only free bedroom in this house, would move to the attic and so make room for you. I assure you it's the best accommodation to be had at the moment."

The Comtesse was not at all happy about the arrangement. She said, "It must be a mean place to have one spare room only."

"On the contrary, my lady, it's quite large. But it belonged to a maker of shoes. There are five apprentices who live in the house. The ground floor is given over to the stock and the workrooms. The widow—he died a short time ago from a wound sustained in the siege—can't give up her room as she hasn't finished the period of mourning——"

"How much longer has it to go?"

"Until tomorrow, my lady."

Isabeau laughed. "One day? She has done so much better than most that no one will notice if she ends it now. That will give us two bedrooms, which is the very least we can get along with."

"The Widow Barbier," said the Scot, shaking his head, "won't stir from that room until the full time is up. She's most rigid, my lady. She stayed in bed for the first nine days as required, and now she has been sitting on the black sheet on the floor for a month and no one, saving her maid, has been inside the door in that time. My friend and I have been in the house for a month and we haven't laid eyes on her. Well, there was one occasion when the maid took us into the yard where we could see into the room. She"—the Scot's eyes began to beam—"is a buxom woman with a fine eye in her head and she won't remain a widow long."

"I'm not interested in the woman." Isabeau considered the situation and finally gave her head a reluctant nod. "If we can't have anything better, I suppose we must accept with good grace. Will you take us there at once, Messire?"

"It will be for one night only. I advise you to start for the abbey in the morning as the Comte will be waiting anxiously. And I assure you, my lady, we can't get back to the house too fast to suit me. You see, I don't trust this friend of mine."

Isabeau looked dismayed at this statement. "Are you afraid he will steal your things? Messire, what kind of place is this you are taking us to?"

"No, no, my lady. Lockie Bell is a fellow countryman of mine and I vouch for his honesty, even though he comes from Edinburgh. I meant in regard to the widow. I've been away from the house for three hours now, and how do I know what he has been doing in my absence? Has he forced the door and introduced himself to the notice of the lady?"

"I assure you," said the Comtesse, in a tone of angry reproof, "that I'm not interested in this rivalry for the favor of a shoemaker's widow. All I ask is that you take us to the house at once as we are sorely in need of food and rest and warm baths."

The Scot turned and winked for Valerie's sole benefit. "You should see the stock of shoes ready for sale and the great mounds of leather in the cellar! How he kept such a stock in wartime is a mystery. The yearly profits will be truly handsome—and the widow won't be able to manage it alone." He directed the rest of his remarks to the Comtesse. "It's my belief, my lady, that the time to catch a widow is when she emerges from her vigil on the black sheet. She's so hungry for companionship then that the first male face she sees seems to her to shine like that of an archangel—even if it's the lean visage of a middle-aged Scot."

Isabeau was amused in spite of herself. "I hope, for the poor lady's sake," she said, "that your companion has more to offer her than you have."

"Lockie Bell? My lady, he's a sour little fellow with bilious eyes and hair the color of a carrot which has been left too long in the ground. It's said of Lockie that the only prodigal thing about him is the number of yellow freckles on his face. He's small and thin and mean. But in spite of everything, my lady, I'm afraid of him. He has a way with women."

The house looked far from pleasing from the street and the first glimpse of the interior set the nostrils of the Comtesse into twitches of disapproval. The room to which they were shown, however, was large and had two beds which was, perhaps, better than they might have expected. Isabeau glanced about her, at the undraped walls and the ancient bench in a corner and the beds, one of which was large and the other quite small.

"Where will the servants go?" she demanded of the Scot who lingered in the doorway.

"The widow's maid has a room back of this. Your women can go in with her for one night. The men will have to do the best they can in the cellar. I've slept in my time on worse couches than a pile of leather."

The Comtesse dismissed him with a wave of the hand and then turned to Valerie. "I must have the large bed," she remarked. "The least discomfort makes it impossible for me to sleep. You will have to be very quiet, Cousin."

The maid who had been selected to accompany the Comtesse and whose name was Bona went below to make demands for fresh linen and hot water. It was some time before she returned, and she brought nothing but a very small wooden tub and a bucket half filled with steaming water. "They don't seem to know much about bathing here, my lady," she said.

The Comtesse looked at the meager supply. "There's barely enough for me. Fortunately, Bona, we will be having supper here and so Mademoiselle will not require a bath. I'm very tired. You must undress me and bathe me at once."

Valerie had been looking forward to the luxury of hot water but there was no appeal from this decision. She stretched herself out on her small and lumpy bed, keeping her eyes studiously away from the center of the room where Isabeau, not averse to showing that she was still slender and white of skin, was standing naked in the tub while Bona bathed her.

When this was finished, the Comtesse walked to the bed and lay down with a sigh of content. The maid began to pat and knead the flesh of her legs and stomach with quick and unsparing strokes of her strong hands. This was a matter of daily routine but Valerie had never been present when it occurred. A disinclination to watch so personal a ministration kept her eyes turned in another direction.

A second deep sigh of content and the rustling of a silk sheet gave notice that the rubbing had been finished. The maid left the room and in a few minutes the Comtesse stirred and called, "Cousin!"

The girl looked across the room. The Comtesse was lying under the sheet and her reddish hair was spread out artfully on the pillow.

"My child," said Isabeau, in a voice from which all trace of critical authority had vanished, "you must have thought me unfair and even cruel to you. I realize that I've been a hard taskmaster. But now that the time is drawing near for the test, I think you will say I was justified in being so severe. You see, Cousin, I had to be sure there were no flaws, no shortcomings in you. The risk in what we're trying is so great that we have to be very, very sure. . . . I've made life hard for you and there must have been times when you hated me. But as a result you're ready."

Valerie was completely disarmed by this speech. "There have been times," she said, after a moment, "when I thought you unreasonable. I was convinced you disliked me. After what you've just said, I can see how needful it was to be strict and exacting with me."

The brown eyes of the Comtesse, which could be so hard and unrelenting, smiled at her over the top of the sheet.

"I think you're going to succeed," she said. There was a pause and then she added, watching the girl intently as she did so, "We must all be on our guard from now on. A careless word might start talk and upset everything. You must suspect everyone, my child. Never discuss this matter and, if questions are asked, pretend you know nothing. This applies to my far-from-discreet husband, to the Scot, to the Sire d'Arlay. You must be careful even about what you say to Jacques Coeur." She laughed lightly. "You must be careful what you say to *me!*"

Valerie nodded her head gravely. "I'll be careful, Cousin."

"That's all I wanted to say. I hope now that there will be no more misunderstandings and no hard feelings between us." Isabeau closed her eyes. "I think I shall have a rest before supper. This continuous traveling has taken most of my strength."

Valerie brought herself to making a request which had filled her mind from the moment she saw the Scot. "Cousin," she said, "I ask your permission to go below and see Messire Kennedy. I'm sure you knew he was sent by my lord Coeur to find out what he could about my parentage. I'm burning to know what he has to tell. I—I'll be most careful, Cousin."

The eyes of the Comtesse opened and she studied her charge carefully for several moments. "Very well," she said. "He would think it strange if you didn't speak about it."

Valerie found Kennedy in the front storeroom below. He smiled when he saw her and said: "I've been expecting a visit from you. Here, sit down beside me. It's the best seat this place has to offer." He looked sharply at one of the apprentices who was busying himself in a corner of the room. "Out of here, Galbert!" he called. "Find some other task for yourself for the next half hour.

"And now, my little lady," he said, when the boy had left, "we may speak freely. It's plain to be seen that many things have been happening, and all of them for the best. The clothes on your back must have cost"—pausing a moment for a rapid calculation—"a round dozen nobles. I was not unprepared for the change as I have been hearing things. I've a well-trained ear for such matters, I assure you."

He got to his feet and began to pace about the room, flailing his arms to keep warm. He watched her out of one corner of his eye as he did so. "She's innocent of guile," he said to himself finally. "She holds up her head and there's a glow in her eye. She believes herself another Maid or —which she thinks the same thing—another Agnes Sorel. I must show care in what I say to her."

He said aloud, "There are questions you would like to ask?"

The girl responded to this invitation eagerly. "There are indeed, Monsieur. My mind is full of them. I want to know everything you learned when you—when you went to Berri at my lord Coeur's behest. I've heard so very little. Monsieur, I want to know about my mother and father, my real parents. I can't tell you how I've longed for this chance to see you alone and ask the questions which are never out of my mind."

"There are things I could tell you," admitted the Scot. "There are things I didn't tell the merchant, believing them to be for your ears alone."

"Can you tell me who I am?" she demanded, with a suggestion of breathlessness in her voice. "Can you tell me my rightful name?"

"Your mother's name was Céleste de Lansanne. Who your father was I don't know. To find out his name will require further inquiries, leading into a different part of the country. All that, my lady, must come later; perhaps when the war is over and Pregent Kennedy can undertake tasks in which there will be," he winked slowly, "a little profit for himself."

"Tell me everything you know," said Valerie eagerly.

"You will want to hear first what little I can tell you about your father. He was a grand handsome man, of goodly proportions and with hair as yellow as a Norseman."

Valerie's eyes were beginning to glow. "Was my father tall?"

"Aye, he was tall and as sturdy as a fine young oak. I heard stories of his skill with weapons."

The Scot proceeded to tell her the story of the duel which her father had fought with her mother's brother. The girl listened with absorbed interest and, when he came to an end, assailed him with an eager flood of questions. What part of the country had her father hailed from? Was he married at the time? Did he have a family? Did he see her mother after the duel was fought? She received little in the way of answers save negative shakes of the head. Finally she gave it up and turned instead to questions about her mother. On this score he proved much more communicative.

"She was of a good family, one of the best in those parts though not one of much wealth. For generations the heads of the family had shown a most deplorable tendency to let money slip through their fingers. On the other hand, they were, without exception, men of stout loins. Your mother, Mademoiselle, was the fourteenth to arrive, although, naturally, most of the earlier ones had died in infancy. All this had so reduced the family resources that there was no silver cup to present to the child at her christening."

"My poor mother!" Valerie sighed. "If I had thirteen uncles and aunts, some of them must still be alive."

"One only, an uncle. His name is Eduard and he lives on the family holdings today. A hard cullion, I found him, as grasping as a lowland lawyer. It was little I could get out of *him!*"

"Does he, my mother's brother, know that I'm alive?"

Kennedy shook his head emphatically. "On the contrary, he's sure you died before you were a year old and he's well content it should be so. It would do you no manner of good to ask him for help."

Valerie drew her head up proudly. "I would never ask him for help under any circumstances. From the little you tell me about him, I am sure he was not kind to my mother when—when she needed kindness so much." There was silence for several moments. "Monsieur Kennedy, tell me about my mother. That's what I long to know above everything else."

"She was a small person, small and dark of face. It seems that she had a liveliness of spirit for in the family she was called Flammèche. Even though she was the youngest and a little slip of a thing, she it was who ran the household. She would talk back fiercely to the lawyers when they said there was no more money and she made the servants do their work well. She sewed and she schemed and she saved." The Scot nodded his head in high approval. "A rare fine lady she must have been."

"How long did she live after I was born?"

"Not long. The tight-lipped brother would tell me nothing but I cuitered myself to an old harridan of a servant, with a face as sour as the last cucumber in the vat, and I had it from her that as soon as your mother was strong enough she left the house. Weeks later she was found with the family of a freeholder of land some distance away. She was earning her keep by working in the fields. But"—with a shake of the head—"there was more spirit than good sense in what she had done. The work was too hard for one of her gentle upbringing." He crossed himself. "Inside the month she was dead."

Valerie continued to ply him with questions. From the meager responses she received, she was able to piece together a picture of the mother she had never seen: proud, sensitive, brave, unwilling to face her shame in dependence but lacking the strength to break through the bars. Now that she knew this much, she realized there could be no happiness for her in the story. "But it's better to know the truth," she said to herself. "It's better to know something of my mother as she was, and to understand her and love her, even though there's pain in the knowing."

"There's one other thing I was told," said Kennedy after it seemed he had repeated everything he knew. "She was a good singer and she had a gift for mimicry. As a small girl she was often punished for imitating her parents and her brothers and sisters, as well as guests who came to the house."

Valerie smiled gravely. "That's the final proof," she said. "Now I'm quite sure this unfortunate lady was my mother."

A small man, easily recognizable as Lockie Bell from the description Kennedy had given of him, put his head in through a door at the rear. Behind him Valerie could see the face of Godefroy, the page who had accompanied them from Paris. Godefroy was a tall youth with the intense dark eyes of his native Provence and he had fallen in love with her as violently and hopelessly as is possible only with boys of his age.

"The widow," announced Lockie Bell, in a voice so resonant it seemed to be issuing from a vacuum, "has risen and dressed herself as she considers it only fitting for the Comtesse to have a room to herself. It's a very proper gesture on her part and adds to the high opinion I've conceived of her."

The maid of the household pushed in after him with supplementary information. "She's put on her new black dress. It's all silk, Messires, and has jet buttons as big as my ears. And she's going to prepare the supper herself. She's *such* a good cook!"

"Your mistress," declared Lockie Bell, "is an exceptionally fine woman in many ways and I'm prepared to have you give her that as my opinion."

Kennedy, who should have been pleased at the turn of events, was staring at his fellow Scot with an air which combined displeasure and suspicion. "How is it," he demanded, "that you seem to know so much about the lady of the house?"

The little man boomed out with laughter. "I've stolen a march on you, Pregent Kennedy," he said. "I've got the better of you. As usual. I've seen the widow and talked with her. I think I may claim, Pregent Kennedy, to be on a friendly footing with her already."

Kennedy scowled at him and avoided the necessity of making a rejoinder by drawing Valerie to one side and whispering to her, "You had better go now or that pretty Jezebel upstairs will think we're up to some mischief."

3

They arrived in due course at the Abbey of Jumièges which they found already filled to overflowing. Not only was Charles of France there with all his special train to occupy the guest dormitory, but the nobility of France had come flocking north over the snow-packed roads to bask in the light of the royal countenance. They were distributed over the country-side, in manor houses and castles and in taverns. The Comte de Burey greeted his wife on their arrival with the welcome intelligence that he had secured the exclusive use of a manor house about three miles east of the abbey.

"It isn't large," he said, eying her as though he feared her opinion of the place. "There's a sunny room for you, my spouse. I have to sleep in a dark, damp hole like a sepulcher." He had moles' feet attached to his garters but this remedy for the gout, which was believed to be infallible, did not seem to be doing him any good. He hobbled painfully. "The little cousin is looking well again, I'm *very* glad to see. Your letters frightened me about her. I expected to find her a lank-cheeked skeleton, wabbling along on broomstick legs." He took advantage of his wife's inattention to give Valerie's thigh a quick pinch. "And here I find her rosy and sparkling and well plumped out again with the sweet cushioning of youth."

They had not been in possession of their new quarters half an hour when Godefroy announced that the Sire d'Arlay had arrived and was dismounting in the courtyard. The Comte had already disposed of a flagon of wine in great gulping intakes and had retired to his dark, damp hole for a nap. The Comtesse flew from the room to make herself more presentable, leaving Valerie to greet the visitor alone.

When D'Arlay came into the room and saw her, he found himself swept away on a tide of emotion. He wanted to rush across to her and gather her up in his arms. He wanted to hold her tight, to bury his face in her hair, to feel her cheek against his own. A voice inside him was saying with a vehemence he had never felt before, *I love her, I love her, I love her!* Why, the same voice was demanding, should he continue to regard the obstacles which circumstances had erected between them? Why should he not forget everything else and declare his love in the tempestuous words which filled his mind?

Valerie was feeling something of the same emotion. She had been aware that a fondness for him was growing in her but certainly she was not prepared for the warmth of the feeling she experienced at the sight of his grave, dark face. She said to herself in alarm: "This is wrong. I must put him out of my mind. I—I must be sensible."

"I was surprised to hear at the abbey that you had arrived," he said. "My brother had told me Isabeau was coming to join him but it was most pleasant to hear that she was accompanied by a cousin who could be no one, of course, but you."

Valerie thought, "Why is he surprised?" Was it not to be expected, under the circumstances, that she would come? She looked up into his face but found no answer there. It was not capable of expressing anything else at the moment but the emotion which filled him.

"If you had arrived an hour later," he went on, "I would have missed you. Jean Bureau had sent me here to consult with my lord Dunois. I saw him last night and I had a foot in the stirrup to return to camp when

the word reached my ears that the Comtesse de Burey had arrived and—
and a cousin who has become of such importance to me——"

Isabeau swept into the room at this moment, crying, "Robin! How
happy I am to see you!" and holding out both hands to him in welcome.
Good use had been made of the few minutes she had allowed herself. All
trace of the fatigue of travel had vanished from her face under the hurried
ministration of Bona's expert fingers. Her hair was piled high on her head
and she had donned a gown which was striped green and yellow and blue
and had a train which twisted and shimmered behind her with the unmistakable susurrus of the richest oriental silk. Her ermine-trimmed sleeves
had fallen back, revealing to the elbow the whiteness of her arms.

D'Arlay said, "I'm happy to see you, Isabeau." He raised his hands to
take hers and then drew back, holding them out in front of him with an
apolegetic air. They were still heavily bandaged in black.

"What's wrong, Robin?" asked his sister-in-law. She looked at him reproachfully. "Have you been wounded? And I was not told!"

"It's just the usual thing. Powder burns. It's not serious, of course, but
I confess to finding the condition of my hands not only a great inconvenience but quite painful as well."

Valerie had retired to a chair at some distance, intending to take no
further part in the talk. At this, however, she rose and joined them.

"It may be more serious than you think," she said, in an anxious tone.
"Do they pain you continuously?"

D'Arlay nodded. "The master surgeon said the burns would heal
quickly but it's clear now he hadn't calculated correctly. The pain seems to
grow worse each day."

Valerie turned to the Comtesse. "Will you permit me, Cousin, to look
at them? I know something of the care of hands. Those who live on the
road, as we did, must understand how to cure them when they became
poisoned or burned."

The Comtesse made a gesture which meant that she would not stand
in the way if Valerie thought she could do any good. "But," she said, immediately after, "I think it would be wise if Robin went to his surgeon
again as soon as possible."

Valerie seated herself in front of D'Arlay. He held his bandaged hands
out for her inspection.

"How long is it, my lord, since you got these burns?"

"It was ten days ago."

She made a clucking noise to convey her sense of dismay. "Ten days!
That is bad, my lord D'Arlay. They shouldn't have taken so long to heal.
It's clear your surgeon didn't know much of burns." She glanced at Isabeau, who had seated herself close at hand and was watching what went
on attentively. "I shall need hot water, Cousin. May I ask Guillaumette to
get some? And I'll need linen for the fresh bandages."

"Of course."

While the water was being heated, Isabeau talked to D'Arlay in low
tones. Realizing that this was designed to exclude her from the conver-

sation, Valerie busied herself by clearing a table. As she did so, she cast an occasional glance at them, acutely aware of the proximity of the attractive brown hair of the Comtesse to D'Arlay's shoulder. The regularity with which they laughed or indulged in a mutual shake of head made her conscious of the close intertwining of their pasts.

When the water was ready, she had D'Arlay move to a chair at the table and seated herself beside him. Isabeau moved also, taking a position so close at hand that she could see everything.

Valerie found herself reluctant to begin. "I'll betray myself when I touch his hands," she thought. "She'll see how fond I am of him." D'Arlay was in the same dilemma. The first contact of her hand on his had sent a tremor through him. He watched the Comtesse apprehensively out of the corner of his eye. She was sitting close beside him and her gaily-striped skirt, which she had spread out like a fan, covered one of his feet with a deliberately proprietorial suggestion.

Valerie set to work finally. She soaked the bandages in the water and then peeled them from his hands with so much care and skill that he felt very little pain. As she went along, she gained more confidence and was no longer disturbed by the watchfulness of the Comtesse.

"What I know of medicines comes from the Egyptians [gypsies]," she said. "They use the very hottest applications for burns. But physicians have different ideas. They say the treatment should be cold and dry. Could anything be more wrong? See, my lord, he bound your hands so tightly that the blood can't reach the injured parts. Ah, the wicked, ignorant man, he has even covered them with potter's clay! At first the clay is well enough, for it relieves the pain. But to leave it on after is truly a most serious matter. In a few days, perhaps even sooner, your hands would have begun to mortify."

She worked swiftly. First she cut the blisters and separated the scars, removing the dead layers of skin and flesh with hot water, and with a sureness of touch which amazed him. Then she prepared a defensive to be applied to the inflamed parts and a hot emulsion in which the fresh bandage was to be soaked. It was clear that she put much reliance in the effect the emulsion would have. "I always carry the ingredients with me," she said. "It has seed of quince in it and fenegreeke and other things which I must not tell you because it's a very great secret. The Egyptians, with whom we traveled often, made me swear never to tell the whole recipe. But it's both soothing and healing in its effect, my lord. How much better your hands will feel!"

Then she applied an ointment. It was a basilicon unguent (she explained), made of white lilies and sweet almond and even with a little wax mixed in to give it body. As soon as it touched any part of his hands the pain stopped there at once; but D'Arlay could not be sure that this magic effect had anything to do with the ointment itself, for he was very certain that the touch of her fingers was enough to cure him of any ill.

When the bandaging had been completed, she nodded and got to her feet. "There!" she said. "I hope, my lord D'Arlay, you'll have less discomfort now."

D'Arlay smiled gratefully. "The pain has gone. You have wrought a miracle and I'm comfortable for the first time in a week. I'm deeply in your debt, Mademoiselle."

The Comtesse nodded to Valerie in dismissal and then engaged D'Arlay in conversation for some time. She found that he was uncertain as to Coeur's plans, having been actively in the field for months and out of touch with the Moneyman, but inclined to believe that the plan was to be abandoned. Isabeau, pretending to be in the same position, told him she had brought her charge to Jumièges to be in readiness for any decision Coeur might make. D'Arlay looked relieved and said, "I'm convinced, Isabeau, that you will have had your long journey for nothing."

When she complained of his neglect, he answered simply, "France is at war." To her plaintive suggestion that he might at least have written her, he held out his bandaged hands and said that he had been suffering from burns so continuously that the use of a pen was impossible.

"I think you've been mad!" she said. "There's no glory for a man of gentle blood in serving as you've done, even though people speak of your courage. Didn't you realize the mistake you had made when you weren't invited to ride in the victory procession?"

D'Arlay smiled and answered simply, "No."

It was, in fact, a very unsatisfactory talk for Isabeau. She dared not make any outward display of affection. Her husband, in spite of his afflictions, walked with a light foot and had a habit of entering rooms unexpectedly. D'Arlay was in a detached mood, uncommunicative and aloof. When he rose to go, saying that duty demanded his early return to camp, she felt that her efforts to win him back to the old footing had been without result.

The Comte popped into the room with the abruptness of a jack-in-the-box almost immediately thereafter. His eyes were still partly closed with sleep and his scant hair was standing up in ludicrous wisps.

"I feel," he grumbled, "as though I could spew up sick eels at the least provocation."

"Robin was here," said his wife. "He has just left."

The Comte gathered his scattering wits together at once. "You were properly discreet?" he asked.

"I told him nothing. The Moneyman gave him some hint of a change of heart but, luckily, they haven't seen each other for months."

The Comte stretched himself out in a chair and suppressed a yawn. "Everything seems to be working out to our advantage, my heart. Coeur is in Paris and isn't expected to return for some time. Agnes Sorel has given birth to her child, another girl. She had a difficult time and is now in such a state that no one is allowed to see her. She occupies a manor house close to the abbey."

Isabeau asked quickly, "Will she live?"

Her husband shook his head. "She's not expected to survive much longer. I asked the little medicine fellow about her and he gave me a gloomy shake of the head. The King still hangs on to a shred of hope, I'm told." He looked at his wife and smiled. "The portents are favorable. We have everything in our hands, my sweet spouse."

"Then," said Isabeau, with an air of satisfaction, "we must see that she's brought to the notice of the King at once. It must be done before Jacques Coeur returns."

"Of course." There was self-satisfaction even in the way he placed one knee over the other and swung his swollen foot back and forth. "I have a plan. It's not original, for I confess I took it, in its bare outline, from a book, but I think I shall improve on the original conception. The book, my lovely Isabeau, is one into which you have seldom dipped and from which you have derived less, perhaps, in the way of precept than you should. I refer to the Bible."

5

THE Comte and Comtesse de Burey were going to be late for the King's levee this cold morning of February seventh. Despite the fact that it was his own tardiness in getting out of bed which was responsible, the Comte proceeded to raise his voice in complaint as they jogged along the snow-packed road.

"We shall miss seeing him emerge with his face moist from sleep and his hair standing out like the bristles of a wild boar. It will be a great deprivation."

Snow had covered the vineyards which surrounded the abbey in all directions. More had fallen during the night and the branches of the trees drooped with the weight of it. The tall abbey towers had been turned into glistening columns of white against the dull gray of the winter sky. To anyone seeing them for the first time, these magnificent spires could have been nothing less than breath-taking; they were so high, so perfect, so symbolic of a faith which reached up from a rude and wretched earth for benediction from the skys. But the Comte and Comtesse de Burey had seen the twin towers on too many cold mornings to have any feeling about them at all. They did not even look up.

"It was along this road," said the Comte, "that the wicked wolf carried the weekly wash of the monks of Jumièges."

"What nonsense are you talking now?"

"Not nonsense at all, sweet spouse. I refer to the favorite legend of the abbey: How a wolf, which killed the faithful abbey mule, was cowed by the stern abbess of a nearby nunnery, where the wash was taken, into doing the work of the mule thereafter. A highly moral tale, my heart, even though I lack the piety to accept it literally." He gave his head a shake.

"And what a sad fate for the old wolf! No more light-hearted killings, no chases in the moonlight, no frolics with lively little she-wolves! Instead he spends his declining years carrying the soiled copes of fat priors and the befouled frocusses and the greasy drawers of monks." He glanced sideways at his wife who was staring straight ahead of her. "Can it be you are not interested in the moral of this tale?"

They turned in through the arched gateway of the Church of Notre Dame and proceeded on foot across the cloister garth. Their heels made a crunching sound on the packed snow. A young monk, crossing from the other side, dropped his eyes when he saw Isabeau and increased the speed of his footsteps. From the choir of St. Pierre came the sound of monkish voices raised in melodious plainsong.

They were the only ones late this morning. The anteroom in the palatially large guesthouse was empty and the royal seneschal, standing at the refectory door, raised a green-and-white striped arm with a gesture like St. Peter forbidding the Gate to eagerly flocking souls. "You know the rule, my lord Comte and my lady," he said smugly. "This door must remain closed until the levee is over."

They sat themselves down in outer space. The anteroom was dark and cold and the prospect of a long wait was not pleasant. Isabeau let her face sink into the folds of her fur gorget and said plaintively, "I think my feet may be frozen and I *know* I have taken a cold."

But waiting in all this discomfort was to have its reward. They had not been seated more than ten minutes when the outer door opened and an oddly assorted group came in with all the order and pomp of a procession. In the lead was a tall individual with a face as round and expressionless as a loaf of bread and a gait of exaggerated dignity. He was carrying a wand with a crook to which a white silk bow had been tied. This he tapped down sharply with each step he took. Behind him came a manservant carrying on outstretched arms a large velvet cushion on which reposed a wooden cradle. Third in line was a bulging female whose arms were filled with every conceivable object a baby might need, including a doll with painted cheeks and agates for eyes. Bringing up the rear was a young lady in a fur-lined cloak who stopped just inside the door and looked about her with the most complete self-possession.

"Jeanne de Vendôme!" exclaimed Isabeau. "I hadn't heard you were here."

The young woman shook back her hood, revealing a shock of reddish hair which frizzed out in all directions. There was an aggressive hook to her nose and an equally aggressive look in her gray-green eyes. She nodded to them and curtsied.

"It's a week since I came, Comtesse," she said. "But this is my first visit to the abbey."

Isabeau looked inquiringly at the file of servants and then at the cradle from which a thin and scarcely human wail was issuing. "You are married, my good Jeanne?" she asked.

Jeanne de Vendôme nodded her head and laughed. It was a strident laugh and without a trace of mirth. She had a habit, as was demonstrated later, of laughing at the most unexpected times, particularly when she was talking. "I have a husband," she said. "But the child is not mine. No, no *indeed*. I mustn't linger here, but if Madame the Comtesse cares to accompany me, I shall be happy to explain."

2

Isabeau followed the procession down a hall with high-barred windows to a room at the far end in which an adequate fire was blazing. Jeanne de Vendôme saw to it that the cradle was placed close to the hearth and then turned to the Comtesse.

"It's the child of the Lady Agnes Sorel," she whispered. "I've been engaged to take charge of it."

"You're fortunate to have such a good appointment."

The young woman tossed her head with a suggestion of protest. "It's not what I had hoped for. I desired a place in the household of the Queen. Still"—with one of her pointless laughs—"it's better than staying at home with my husband's mother and the three selfish pigs of brothers he keeps about the place."

"You're not likely to see the Queen now," said Isabeau. "But you're certain to see the King quite often."

Jeanne de Vendôme shook her head. "If the Lady Agnes lives, you mean, and I think very little of her chances. We're staying at the Manoir de Mesnil which belongs to the abbey, and so far His King's Grace hasn't deigned to visit us." The young woman handed her cloak to the maid and took up a position in front of the fire. She waved at the servants in dismissal. "Get along now, all of you. You'll attend to the tasks I set for you, if you please, and at once! Blanchette, the child will need another warm blanket."

When the servants had withdrawn, she nodded her head and laughed triumphantly. "At home my husband's mother has encouraged the servants to be insolent to me. I'm making sure that it's different *here!* They jump to obey when I speak to them." She dropped her voice to a confidential level. "The King is to see his child for the first time this morning. For him to visit *us* would have been an open acknowledgment of paternity, and *that* would not have done by any means. But he couldn't wait to see her any longer so out we had to come in all this cold. No one is supposed to know we're here so I must ask you to leave in a few minutes, dear Comtesse. We're to go back while dinner is being served." She indulged in a laugh, somewhat louder than any that had gone before. "I've been instructed in the need for the most complete secrecy. It's all very absurd!"

Isabeau looked down at the small white face in the cradle. "It doesn't seem a healthy child."

"What can you expect? The mother was very weak before the accouchement and it was a wonder either of them survived."

Jeanne de Vendôme joined Isabeau and looked down at her charge.

The child was bound up in rollers and bands and was so tightly strapped to the swaddling board that it seemed a miracle the poor little creature could breathe at all.

"I'm doing everything to keep it alive," said the young woman. "My appointment will end if it dies. But it's a puny thing, Comtesse."

"She would be a pretty child if she were not so very thin. How is the mother?"

"She hasn't long to live. Understand me, Comtesse; I speak from hearsay only. I've been a full week in the house and as yet I haven't laid an eye on my lovely and famed lady. It's given out that she's too ill to be seen and only her physician and her maid are allowed in her room. But I know the real reason for all the secrecy and the darkened rooms, Comtesse. It's her vanity. She can't bear to be seen."

"I can understand that," said Isabeau. "When I'm ill, I allow no one to enter my room except the physician."

The child's custodian tossed her head as though to say, "And you think I can't understand because I am not a beauty like you." She made no open response until the spell of resentment had passed. Then she said in a somewhat sulky voice: "Truly, my poor lady carries things to an extreme that's hard to believe. She allows no light in her room. None at all. Even the shutters are kept tightly closed. When her physician comes, he's received in darkness. She eats nothing and only occasionally does she take a sip of wine."

"She must be wasting away fast."

Jeanne de Vendôme nodded in avid agreement. "They say she's no larger now than a girl of eight or nine. I'm sure it would be a shock to see her. Even her head has become smaller. Her arms are no bigger around than my wrists." To demonstrate the last point, she drew back one sleeve and revealed a coarse wrist, covered with reddish hair. She nodded with assurance. "Make no mistake, Comtesse. She'll soon be a dead woman."

Isabeau looked at her companion attentively. The abnormal width between the eyes gave a suggestion of oddity to her face. There was, Isabeau saw now, an undoubted air of slyness about this Jeanne de Vendôme, and she made a mental note to the effect that the young woman could not be trusted far but might prove useful in spite of that.

Jeanne de Vendôme indulged in another of her pointless laughs. "Once, when a door opened to let someone in, I heard the Lady Agnes say, 'God forgive me for the life I have lived!' She pretends to be very pious now that the end is near. The chaplain has instructions to say whenever he has occasion to address any of us, 'Be good, be unselfish, be *virtuous*.' We're told not to discuss the child with anyone on the outside. It is not absurd?"

The baby whimpered faintly. Isabeau looked down at its small creased face with both awe and dread. Never having been brought to childbed herself, she knew nothing of motherhood and did not dare approach the cradle closely for fear of doing something wrong. It was perhaps because she had no knowledge of the care of children that she found herself wondering if it were necessary to keep the infant strapped down to the board and swathed in so many tight coverings.

The custodian broke in on her reflections with a question. "Have you heard that another note was found pinned to the King's pillow?"

The Comtesse looked at her with instantly aroused interest. "I didn't know. How strange that word of it could reach you and not get around at court. I've heard no whisper of it."

The girl nodded with self-satisfaction. "We hear things, even though we're this far away. It was three nights ago. One of the Grooms of the Chamber drew back the curtains—and there it was! It was in verse and *quite* amusing. It warned the King that Jaquet the Fox was gobbling up all France and that someday he would gobble up the King just like one of those turkeys he has brought in from the East."

"How did the King take it?"

"He was very angry at first and said nothing. Then he began to laugh and said, 'He's a generous fox, at any rate, for he has bought back Normandy for me.'"

The Comtesse plied her with questions about the incident in an effort to find out everything possible. She was particularly insistent in probing for information as to what the King had said and done.

Jeanne de Vendôme was willing to tell all she knew. "I heard it said," she whispered, "that later, when the King was in bed and sipping his nightly posset, he suddenly became thoughtful and said, 'A man must be very clever to become as rich as Jacques Coeur.' When someone answered, 'Or very unscrupulous, my liege lord,' the King made no comment. But he put the posset aside as though he found no further pleasure in it. It was strange, wouldn't you say, that he made no answer at all?"

Isabeau did not reply but to herself she said, "It was not strange. I know what was passing through the royal mind."

In the exhilaration of finding herself on such intimate terms with one of the great ladies of the court, Jeanne de Vendôme inclined her head closer and proceeded to tell of another incident. "Did you hear that a letter to my lord Coeur was addressed to our house? It carried the seal of the Dauphin and had come from his place of exile. I was told it was given to the King who had it opened. The Dauphin was proposing that the Moneyman help *him* to take his father's place on the throne. My lord Coeur laughed when the King handed him the letter and pointed out many reasons why it was a forgery. It was not only a forgery, he said, but a very clumsy one. The King listened to him with a face as white as chalk and said never a word. The enemies of my lord Coeur took much comfort out of the incident."

"My dear Jeanne," said the Comtesse, "let us make a compact between us. If you'll engage to tell me such information as you hear that may be worth passing on, I will, for my part, pay you a substantial reward."

"Dear Comtesse," answered the young woman, "I am very greatly in need of money."

3

On her return Isabeau found the anteroom in the sole possession of her husband. The Comte had taken advantage of her absence to acquire a tankard of wine and was in the act of imbibing from it when she entered. He stared at her over the rim with a fixed and expressionless eye.

The Comtesse hovered above him accusingly. "Are you too drunk," she demanded, "to understand something I must tell you? Something of the greatest importance?"

He lowered the tankard and wiped his lips fastidiously. "These are not ideal conditions, my spouse, to set a mind such as mine to skipping lightly down the path of understanding. I don't try to conceal from you that I'm slightly bosked. Nevertheless, I'm still capable of following a direct and intelligent statement of fact."

His wife frowned at him impatiently. "Listen to me carefully," she said. "Things have happened which I find most disturbing. The opposition to the Moneyman is growing stronger all the time. And bolder, much bolder. Regnault, we must act at once. Do you hear me, at once!"

The Comte placed the tankard on the floor beside him. He took the ends of his mustache between the thumbs and forefingers of both hands and strove, unsuccessfully, to give them a twist. "I shall arrange everything, my beautiful spouse," he declared.

6

LOOKING out over the top of the highest dunghill ever raised as a monument to French husbandry, Valerie had watched from her bedroom the round beaver hat of the Comte and the fluttering green hennin of the Comtesse disappear down the road. She shivered and thought how fortunate she was that she did not have to go out.

Guillaumette had placed a copper basin filled with water in front of the fire and now was engaged in warming the clothes her mistress would wear. "Hurry, Mademoiselle!" she called. "You'll freeze if you stay at that window any longer."

Valerie crossed the room at a run and, when she reached the fire, stepped forth with considerable reluctance from the bed blankets she had wrapped about her. The maid quickly dropped a woolen tunic over her head. "You had better wash before I put anything else on you," she said. "You shouldn't have gone to the window—you're blue with cold."

Valerie rolled her sleeves above the elbows, gave her hair a twist with one hand and attached it at the back of her head with a comb, then

proceeded to wash herself with the ice-cold water. She whistled as she did
so, happy in the knowledge that the Comtesse was not there to tell her
that whistling was unladylike.

A rap came on the door and Godefroy put his head in to announce,
"My lord Coeur has arrived."

Valerie looked up from the basin. "Are you sure? We were told he was
in Paris and wouldn't come back for a long time."

"He's here," said the page. "And asking for you, Mademoiselle."

The dressing was finished in quick order and it was no more than five
minutes later that Valerie made her way downstairs. The Moneyman was
pacing up and down the long room which occupied most of the ground
floor of the house. He was reading letters and, as he finished one, he stuffed
it into a pouch at the right of his belt and brought out another from a
pouch on the other side.

He stopped his pacing when he saw Valerie and gave her a warm, if
somewhat preoccupied, smile. "Ah, my little minikin," he said. "You look
completely recovered. That is good. I'm taking you with me on an important errand this morning."

Valerie said, "Yes, my lord?" in an interrogative tone which carried a
distinct note of alarm. She was thinking, "Am I to be shown to *him?*"

"To see the Lady Agnes Sorel. I was unexpectedly summoned back
from Paris by the King and found a note from her on my arrival, asking
me to see her and to bring you with me." The Moneyman looked down at
her with the undiminished amazement he always felt. "You grow more
like her all the time. My sweet lady will have a surprise when she sees you.
I'm afraid it's going to be a day of surprises for her, for I have something
to tell her which she won't like. I had intended to tell you also, my child,
but now I think it better to leave all discussion until after we've seen the
Lady Agnes."

"What does she know about me?"

"Nothing except that you are the one I selected in accordance with the
agreement between us. She doesn't know who you are nor what you look
like."

Valerie was apprehensive of the results of the meeting. "It's certain,
my lord," she said, "that she won't approve of me."

He smiled and gave her arm a reassuring pat. "Have no fears on that
score. It's not going to be as much of an ordeal as you seem to think. I
doubt if there will be any talk between you. She has been failing fast and
I question if her strength will allow of that. She wants to see you, and
that's all. I'm not sure of the wisdom of taking you; but her wish in the
matter was stated most unmistakably."

"Will I do as I am?"

After a moment's inspection the Moneyman nodded his head. "There's
no need to change but I suggest that you don your best cloak as well as
something attractive for your head." His hand had strayed in the direction
of the pouch containing the unread letters. He checked the motion half-

way, however, and stared down at her with renewed interest. "It's indeed strange," he remarked, "that none of my spies have picked up any hint of your existence, my child. They never miss anything."

Valerie frowned with surprise. "Spies! I don't understand, my lord."

Coeur laughed ruefully. "Did you think a man could become a minister of the King and wield as much power as I have had without taking steps to know what's going on? Unfortunately it's necessary to fall into the system that everyone uses who aspires to position and influence at court. Yes, I pay spies, many of them—the most expert listeners at keyholes, the most assiduous practitioners of the art of snooping and sneaking and tattling. During the time I've been Moneyman to the King I've employed no fewer than thirty-four of these admirable characters to keep me in touch with the spirit and the talk of the court. It makes my gorge rise to depend on such a scurvy lot—liars and cheats, all of them, and some with the best blood of France in their veins!"

Valerie left the room to dress for the journey. While waiting for her, Coeur paced up and down, thinking bitterly of the information these spies of his had poured into his ears immediately on his arrival. It had been made abundantly clear to him that the success of the French armies had not served to check the machinations of his enemies. The air of the court was filled with whispers. It was being said that Ferrand de Cordule was preparing poisons and spells for the elimination of all who opposed the Moneyman, even of the King himself! It was furthermore declared that De Cordule had succeeded in more concrete aims, such as the making of a copy of the King's seal with which Jacques Coeur would now be able to issue orders and proclamations without his liege lord's knowledge or consent. Most of the stories being circulated were trivial and absurd but they added up to a volume of calumny which might have the desired effect in the mind of the one man who counted, Charles of France.

He stopped his pacing and shook his head angrily as though to clear his mind of such unpleasant reflections. "What does it matter?" he asked himself. "Let them talk! I'm higher than ever in the favor of the King and the malicious tattle of these drones can have no effect at all!"

2

There were peasants standing knee-deep in snow about the Manoir de Mesnil where the Lady Agnes was reported to be dying. One of them gaped up at Jacques Coeur and asked, "Can you tell us how the great lady fares, lord?"

The Moneyman helped Valerie to alight. "She fares ill," he said.

The peasant crossed himself. "'Tis a bad thing, lord," he muttered. "A bad thing for the poor people of France. She has been our friend."

The manor house was a severe structure of dark gray stone with a single hint of graciousness in the carving of the pointed arches above the main door. It had a chapel which formed the base of a low rounded tower and a sloping roof from which small windows jutted unexpectedly.

As they approached the entrance, Valerie looked up at Jacques Coeur and said in an anxious whisper, "I'm so frightened that my knees are starting to tremble."

They were greeted inside by a manservant with a forefinger pressed ostentatiously to his lips. "Not a sound, my lord," whispered the man.

"Is your mistress worse, then?"

The servant was so close to the point of blubbering that the only answer he could give was a nod of the head. He clamped a hand over his mouth and glided away through a door in the rear.

Coeur became aware that a young woman was standing above them on the landing of the stone stairs. There was no light where she stood and all he could make out at first was the intentness of her eyes and the bold curve of her nose. He decided she must be the one who had been appointed to take care of the child. Jeanne de Vendôme was looking at Valerie, her eyes wide with surprise. "She sees the resemblance," thought Coeur.

The manservant returned with tears streaming down his face. "My lady will see you," he said, brushing an arm across his cheeks. "Her voice was so weak I could scarce make out a word. And, my lord, her old hound has started to bay again. It is a sign."

The man led the way through a door opening off the right of the hall. The room they entered was so dark that Coeur walked slowly and kept both arms extended in front of him. The fetid air gave him a strangling sensation in the throat. By the light of a single candle burning at the end of the room he made out a small grating in the far wall.

A voice from behind the grating said, "Ah, Jacques Coeur, to what a sorry state I have been brought!"

The Moneyman took a few steps nearer. His heart was pounding and he found it difficult to keep his voice steady.

"Dear Lady Agnes!" he said. "The thought of what you've been suffering has never left my mind."

"It won't be long now, Jacques Coeur. A few days, a few hours even. So little time to make my peace, and so much to repent!"

She had been propped up to a position where she could see him without being seen herself, for he could barely detect the outline of her head behind the grating.

"No one ever had less to repent, dear lady," he said. "It was my hope that today I would find you easier in body as well as mind. Is it possible your despondency is because of lying here in such unnecessary discomfort? You need fresh air and light. I would like to see all the shutters thrown wide open."

There was a pause and then she sighed deeply. "Allow me my final vanity. I want to be remembered as I was, not as I am. I shrink from the thought of any eyes resting on me. I have—I have changed so dreadfully! There is little more of me now than the skin on my bones—I, who was once so fairly endowed!" Her voice rose. "This hateful sick body in which I'm chained! It can't be mine! I was always well and people said I was fair to look at. My life was like a dream of loveliness. It was the touch of silk on the skin, the warmth of the sun in a garden. Eyes turned to me and they always smiled. Ah, Jacques Coeur, why must so sweet a dream end in this way—in suffering and ugliness?"

"You must believe, sweet lady," said Coeur earnestly, "that those who have admired and loved you can never think of you as anything but lovely still."

"If you saw me now, you would turn your eyes away quickly." He heard her move as she said this. It was evident from the slightness of the sound that her body had little substance left. Nothing more was said for several moments. "My good friend Jacques, have you brought the girl?"

"Yes. She's waiting in the hall."

"I find myself very curious about this lady who may inherit some of the dream in which I've lived. Is she lovely?"

"Yes, dear lady. Quite lovely. How could we have hoped to put her in your place if she were not?"

"I know of her, no doubt?"

"No, she doesn't belong to the court. She's young, no more than seventeen years."

A pause ensued. "So very young? Was that necessary?" There was the merest hint of dissent in Agnes Sorel's voice. "I'm glad your choice didn't fall on anyone I knew. It makes the thought of a successor a little less difficult."

Coeur waited for a moment and then began to speak in hurried tones. "I brought her here because you asked me to do so. But, my lady, I've made up my mind to go no further. I don't think it necessary; but, even if it were necessary, I would withdraw." He leaned closer to the grating in his desire to convince her. "I became the King's Moneyman at the invitation of our liege lord and not through any conniving and scheming of my own. I've filled the post honestly and loyally. If I must fight to hold my place now, I prefer to do so with my own weapons."

"What weapons, my lord Coeur?"

The Moneyman indulged in a sweeping gesture. "I possess a power all my own. It's something new and yet so potent that I feel disposed to put all my faith in it. The power of money, Lady Agnes. My finger is in every dish. There's scarce a man in the King's train who's not in my debt. As a last resort I could buy their support by the remission of obligations."

The voice behind the grating said wearily, "There are other ways of wiping out debts than by paying them. Dead men make poor collectors."

A door opened somewhere in the rear of the house and then closed again quickly, but not before a sound of unrestrained weeping had reached his ears. He thought, "It's a sign that the mistress has lived a good life when servants weep at her passing."

Agnes Sorel spoke now in a tone which showed how little strength she had left. "I didn't think it would be necessary this late to convince you of the need of proceeding. Don't put too much faith in this money power you speak of. The King is your largest debtor and you must know how he will feel. He hates to owe money but he has an equal aversion to paying off his debts." Her voice changed. She continued in low but excited tones: "I am dying, Jacques Coeur! Make no mistake about that. And when you stand on the brink of eternity, you see by a blinding white light. I can see everything so clearly! . . . Jacques Coeur, Jacques Coeur, you are in great danger! You must listen to me. You must do as I say. Don't let your pride stand in the way."

"It isn't pride, Lady Agnes."

She seemed almost out of breath when she spoke again. "Let me see the girl now. I won't have the strength to question her. Have more candles brought so I shall be able to see her well. My eyes grow poorer with each hour which brings me closer to the time when—when they will close forever."

"Are you certain you want to do this?"

"Quite certain. Perhaps I'll feel easier in my mind if I can approve your choice." She demanded with sudden impatience: "Is what I have done of such small importance that no effort need be made to carry on my work?"

The Moneyman returned to the hall where he found Valerie sitting on a bench against the wall. The candle had guttered so low by this time that she was little more than a shadow.

"You're to come now," he said. "Don't be disturbed. You won't have to see her or speak to her, and it won't take more than a few minutes."

She pressed close to him in the darkness and laid a hand nervously on his arm. "This place frightens me, my lord. It's like a house of the dead."

Coeur called an order to the manservant who answered it by bringing two candles. The Moneyman took them from him and led the way back. He seated Valerie close to the grating and placed both candles on a table beside her. Her nervousness was apparent in the tensity with which she twined the fingers of both hands in her lap. She kept her head up, however, and even ventured a look at the grating behind which her invisible judge sat.

Coeur drew up a chair beside her. "I've seen you so seldom of late," he said, "that I feel entirely in the dark about you. I assume that coming north has interrupted your studies."

"Not entirely, my lord." Her voice was steady enough. "I have a few books with me and I try to read in them each evening. It's hard because some of the books are not meant for—for beginners. I go very slowly, my lord Coeur." After a moment's pause she continued in a more animated tone: "Cousin Regnault has promised to get permission for me to see the books and manuscripts in the abbey library. He tells me there are wonderful things there. The Holy Word itself and many books with rich embellishments and even"—she looked doubtful of the propriety of going on—"even many of the old fabliaux, written out fairly and most easy to read. I'm looking forward to my visit."

"It's clear," said Coeur, nodding and smiling by way of encouragement, "that you're becoming quite a scholar."

No sound had come from behind the grating but there was a tension in the air which could be felt as surely as though the watcher herself could be seen. Coeur led Valerie on to talk of many things: her instructors, the advances she had made in other lessons, the people she had encountered during the long ride to Jumièges.

The girl soon lost all trace of self-consciousness and spoke with ease, even laughing when the things she spoke of roused her sense of humor.

A finger tapped on the grating. Coeur walked over and lowered his head to whisper, "Yes, my lady?"

"Send her away now, please. But we must have a talk, my lord Coeur, while I still have strength. I am—I am completely bemused! I can hardly believe what I've seen. I think this must be a—a fancy, a vision!"

Silence greeted him when he returned to his station at the grating after seeing Valerie back to the hall. It continued so long that he began to think Agnes Sorel had lapsed into unconsciousness. Then he heard a low sob, followed by others at irregular intervals.

"Jacques Coeur, Jacques Coeur!" she said, when the sobs had begun to subside. "What is this you've done? She's so much like me that—for a moment—I wondered if I had died and it was my own body that I saw." There was a long pause. "Who is this girl? Where did you find her?"

Coeur told the story as briefly as he could. Agnes Sorel made no comment until he began on the results of Pregent Kennedy's investigation of the girl's past. He could hear her stir then on her couch.

"But the names, the names!" she demanded, with a hint of excitement in her voice. "Who was her father?"

"That mystery has not yet been solved," said Coeur.

"Where was the village in which she was found?"

"In the south of Berri."

"I knew it!" The voice of the sick woman was pitched high and it was clear that she was much excited. "I was sure this close resemblance could not be accidental. Jacques Coeur, the father of this girl was my brother, my favorite brother who died three years ago. He told me of a romance he had had with a young woman of Berri and of her death after giving birth to a daughter. His wife was of a jealous turn and so he made no attempt to claim the child." She paused and he could hear her breathing. "There can be no doubt about it! None, Jacques Coeur! My brother and I were so much alike we were often mistaken for twins when we were young. It's not surprising the girl resembles me. I had a warning of the truth the instant she came into the room."

Jacques Coeur found himself willing to accept this conclusion without any question. After several moments of consideration he said: "You'll want me to investigate further, no doubt. It should be an easy matter to arrive at the facts now."

"Take whatever steps you think necessary. But for my part I need no further proof. I know, Jacques Coeur, that she's my brother's daughter; my mind is completely free of doubt."

The Moneyman seemed to have lost concern over what she was saying.

He leaned closer to the grating, so close, in fact, that he caught a glimpse of her on the other side of it.

"My lady," he said, "I've a little knowledge of many things. I'm not a physician but I know enough of medicine and the human body to be sure that you've talked overlong. I beg you to excuse me now, with the understanding that I am to return later, after you have rested. Perhaps you'll care to see me later in the day. If not, I must wait until tomorrow."

"No, I must finish what I have to say. If you go now, I may never see you again. Jacques Coeur, my best of friends, I confide my new-found niece to your care. She is sweet and intelligent and, I think, of fine and resolute character. I'm sure I can trust you to look after her well. It's my last earthly wish that she have a better life, a kinder one, than I have had." She was silent for several moments and then she began to speak again with an insistence which left her breathless after very few words. "You must find someone else. You must select a girl capable of accomplishing what we had in mind. As for my niece, see to it—see to it, Jacques Coeur, that she——"

The voice died away. Coeur did not wait for her to continue. Seizing one of the candles with urgent haste, he hurried in to her through a curtained arch in the wall beside the grating.

3

The room was so dark that at first he could make out nothing except that the small squares of light, which entered by way of the grating, cast a checkered pattern on the opposite wall. Then he saw that there was a window and made his way to it cautiously to open the shutters. This he accomplished with some difficulty, finding it necessary first to break the parchment which took the place of glass in the aperture. The shutters had not been opened in some time and it took all the strength he possessed to loosen the locks. When the wooden frames finally swung outward with a creaking of reluctant bolts, he filled his lungs with the fresh air which rushed in.

The room, he now saw, was so tiny that it was hard to determine the purpose it served in the household routine. It contained two pieces of furniture only, the couch under the grating, on which the dying woman lay, and a small table with medicines, a flask of wine, and a shallow glass.

Coeur turned his eyes toward the couch. He was so shocked by what he saw that with the utmost difficulty he compelled himself to draw closer. Agnes Sorel had lost consciousness. Her head was turned away from him on the soiled pillow but he could make out that her cheekbones protruded sharply and that the skin had sunk into deep blue hollows on each side of her brow. Of the beauty which had made a legend of Agnes Sorel not a vestige was left; she was a wraith, robbed of all semblance of her former self, no longer even a caricature of the famed Lady of Beauty.

He stood over her, the same thoughts running through his mind which she had given expression to a few minutes before—that it was doubly sad to see a life which had been lived in beauty and splendor come to such an ending. Then a more urgent consideration drove all other thought from his mind. He knew much more about medicine than he had taken credit for; and, looking down at the gaunt face of the patient, he realized that something must be done without any delay if she was to be summoned back to life.

He glanced at the medicines on the table and shook his head in instant and emphatic rejection. Then he poured a little wine into the glass and diluted it with water. Placing a hand under her head to raise it from the pillow, he held the glass to her lips and forced down her throat a few swallows of the liquid. "Come back, sweet lady," he said. "You must not leave us yet. Can you hear me?"

He was so intent on his efforts to revive her that he did not know he was being watched until an unfriendly voice broke the silence of the room.

"What has happened, my lord?"

He glanced up and saw that Jeanne de Vendôme was standing in the doorway, her eyes fixed on him intently. Still holding the glass to the lips of the dying woman, he studied the face in the doorway, and a conviction grew in him that something hostile and even malignant had entered the room with her. He was sure that this strange-looking young woman was to play an important part in his life.

"The Lady Agnes became unconscious as I talked with her," he explained. "She was scarce breathing when I reached her. Now she shows signs of coming around. See, she's breathing more naturally. I think she'll regain consciousness any moment."

"Am I to summon the physician, my lord?"

"Yes, at once." Coeur lowered the sick woman's head to the pillow and replaced the glass on the table before looking up. Jeanne de Vendôme had not moved. She was leaning against the frame of the door, her gray-green eyes watching him with a disturbing closeness.

"Your mistress needs immediate attention," he said sharply. "Go for the physician at once."

The young woman still did not obey. "How does it happen that the window is open?" she asked. "It's against all orders. My lady has most particularly instructed us that no light is to be allowed in."

"I opened the window. If I had not done so, it's quite possible your mistress would be dead now. That's a matter I intend to discuss with the physician. Is it Robert de Poitevin who is here today?"

"Yes, my lord. He has had instructions from the King to stay here and give my lady all his attention."

"That is good."

The girl still did not go. "You have broken so many rules," she said impudently, "that I'm not sure it's safe to leave you alone with her."

"You will go at once or I shall see to it that someone else is found for your post!"

Jeanne de Vendôme went then but with a swishing of skirts and a toss of the head which suggested both unwillingness and displeasure. In little more than a minute Robert de Poitevin came hurrying into the room, breathing indignation. Agnes Sorel had recovered some degree of consciousness by this time. Her eyes had opened and she was breathing easily. The little physician gave her one appraising glance and then shook his head protestingly in the direction of the open window.

"My lord Coeur, my lord Coeur!" he said in an outraged tone of voice. "This is a fault, a very grave fault indeed. My lady's orders are that no light or fresh air is to be allowed in any part of the house. What will she think of this?"

"The air in this house is more deadly than any disease," declared the Moneyman. "You would be well advised, good friend Robert, to use your own good judgment in such matters as this."

"My own judgment—and I think it good—is against the admission of the raw air from outside. It carries disease with it, my lord Coeur. It chills the body and lowers its powers of resistance. Air, my lord Coeur, is one of man's most deadly enemies."

The sick woman stirred slightly. The physician hurried over to the couch and regarded her with anxious solicitude. He touched a finger to her forehead and to her lips, frowned doubtfully, and then gave a quick nod of the head. "She has suffered no ill effects so far from this unseemly exposure to the—the elements," he declared. "But she must be removed at once to her bedroom. I say it to your face, my lord Coeur, I opposed her will to see you. I gave in to her most reluctantly. I know you too well. You're not a soothing person. You talk, you demand, you give orders. You're not made for sickrooms."

He broke off to clap his hands twice with an emphatic clack. When the manservant answered the summons, he instructed him to have the couch carried back to the bedroom at once.

Coeur looked down at the dying woman and was amazed to see that a change had come over her. The lines of her face had softened and some of her beauty had come back. It was clear that she had regained some measure of peace for there was the suggestion of a smile on her lips.

"My sweet Lady Agnes," he said in a low voice. "Have you anything else to say to me? Have you any further commands?"

If she heard him, she made no sign. Her eyes, perhaps resenting the light, remained closed. The physician took him by the arm and led him to a corner of the room.

"It will be a miracle," he whispered, "a veritable miracle, my lord Coeur, if our poor lady lives through the night."

One of the shutters had blown shut and the other was flapping back and forth. Coeur walked over and bolted it tight. He remained there in the dark for several minutes, his mind full of the past. He thought of Agnes Sorel as she had been when she came to the court, young and zestful for life, her beauty so startling in its flawlessness that men became speechless on first seeing her. "I pledged her my allegiance then," he said to himself. No one could say he had not kept his pledge. He had helped her, consulted her, considered her interests in all things. Between them they had kept Charles of France on the right path. It had been a perfect partnership, understanding, unselfish, complete in the confidence they gave each other. "No one has ever guessed how deep my allegiance has been," he said to himself. "And now this is the end."

The couch was being carried out. He waited until the sound of the servants' steps could no longer be heard. Then he said to the physician in a low tone, "It will be hard to reconcile myself to living in a world which Agnes Sorel has left."

4

When they emerged into the open air the noon sun had turned the countryside into a blaze of beauty. With the persistence of withwind, the snow had settled everywhere, leaving few traces of other color in tree or bush. The fields crisped and sparkled in this moment of supreme combination of winter sun and winter snow.

Nicolas stepped up and announced that a messenger had arrived from the abbey with word that Jacques Coeur was to return there at once. The Moneyman gave a nod of recognition to the horseman who had brought the word.

"The order is from the King?"

"Yes, my lord."

Coeur turned to Valerie. He was thinking, "How excited she will be when I tell her that the mystery of her birth has been solved at last!" He smiled affectionately as he raised her gloved hand to his lips. "I've something important to tell you, my child," he said. "But as I must leave you now, it will have to wait until I can find the time to see you again. By good St. Martin, it's the best of news! Your pretty eyes will sparkle with delight when I tell you what I've learned today—and what I have decided!"

"Then come soon, my lord."

As he struck off on the direct road to the abbey, with Nicolas in the rear protesting the headlong gait at which he rode, Jacques Coeur gave serious consideration to his future course. What Agnes had said about the attitude of the King had shaken his confidence to some extent but not entirely. "The life of the court is the only one she has ever known," he thought. "She judges everything by court standards. She hasn't any conception of the power I've acquired. She doesn't think it possible for anyone to fight his enemies with the weapons he has forged himself. I have influence and wide connections of which she knows nothing—and I have my sharp wits and the power of my great wealth."

He cried aloud, much to the alarm of Nicolas, "They'll find that Jaquet the Fox can fight, when pressed to it, like a wolf at bay or a lion on the prowl!"

7

THE ABBOT OF JUMIÈGES had decided on this particular day to partake of dinner in the refectory where the monks had their meals. Wearing his bishop's ring with the smallest trace of ostentation (for, after all, the right to wear it was the most prized privilege of the abbots of Jumièges), he sat in the center of the dais with a guest from the court on each side of him and watched the monks below in a silence which seemed almost to smolder. The guests dined sumptuously on gramose soup, a sided haddock, a roast of venison, and at the finish a *setewale*, which was the name given to an uncommonly rich pastry with ginger flavoring. They washed these fine dishes down with the very best of wines the cellars could provide and seemed to be enjoying themselves to the utmost. The good Abbot, however, contented himself with the three dishes being served to the members of the order: dried beans, cheese, and bread; and he ate of these with the sparse appetite of dissatisfaction.

"I'm deeply distressed, Messires," he said toward the close of the meal. "The honor paid us by the King in coming here is a great one, to be recorded in our annals and remembered with pride for all time. But it must be said that all this is upsetting to the discipline of my people."

One of the guests, sipping his wine with indolent enjoyment, remarked that "it should be refreshing for the members of the order to catch again a glimpse of the life of the outside world."

As though crushing an undesirable insect with a downward swoop of a sandaled foot, the Abbot gave this heresy the immediate dispatch it deserved. "It is to escape all contacts with earthly prides and pomps that these gentle fellows of mine have joined the order," he stated. His voice achieved an oratorical ardor. "They have put the temptations of life and the lusts of the flesh behind them. And yet they cannot fail, no matter how circumspectly they walk nor how resolutely they keep their eyes lowered, to see something of what is going on about them. And this must be said, Messires: You bring inside our doors the life of the outside world in its most beguiling and dangerous form." He shoved his wine cup away from him with an impatient gesture, as though it too belonged to the world which must be kept at a distance. "Observe, if you please, the monk at the end of the hall, the one who stands without movement and with his arms folded on his breast. It is Brother Pellion and he was discovered in laughing converse with a maid belonging to one of your ladies." The Abbot's voice grew deep with indignation. "She was a forward creature with a disrespectful tongue and a willingness to animal lust in her eye.

Brother Pellion has been standing on that spot for the better part of two days and he hasn't had a morsel of food in that time. There he will stand, in full sight of the food, until I grant him remission of his punishment or until he drops from exhaustion. It's more likely to be the latter, Messires."

One of the guests ventured a mild protest. "Is it not a severe sentence, considering the nature of the offense?"

The Abbot swallowed a crust of bread with a wry face as though he found it as bitter as chestnut husks. "The nature of the offense?" he exclaimed. He had intended to expatiate on the point but held himself in control and, after a moment of silence, went on with an explanation of the steps he had found it necessary to take. "I've imposed new rules to continue in force as long as we have courtly visitors. The brothers are not to be blamed, poor, bewildered fellows; but they must be saved the contamination of earthly contacts. Each must submit in turn to the *minuto* as fast as the infirmary can take them; an extra bloodletting will stifle bodily inclinations inside them. They are no longer to be allowed the freedom of the grounds. All their spare time must be spent in the carrells, improving their minds with the written word. They have always been allowed a half hour during dinner for conversation with their fellows. This privilege has been withdrawn. They must eat in silence."

The two guests had been wondering at the unwonted stillness throughout the hall. The members of the order had partaken of their frugal fare with no sound other than the clatter of spoons and cups on the table and the shuffle of the servants' feet. Their wants had been indicated in the sign language of the monastic world. The thumbs and first fingers of both hands bent in a circle meant, I desire bread. The tip of the first finger held to the first joint of the thumb was to be interpreted as, Pass the beans. Both hands joined obliquely together was a signal for an additional slice of cheese. Early in the meal a brother who sat just under the dais had in a forgetful moment raised his voice in speech. At the first syllable the bitter eye of the Abbot had fastened itself on him and the speech had broken off with the jarring suddenness of a note of music when a string snaps. For a full minute, while the long rows of cowled heads had remained bent over their platters, the accusing eye had transfixed the culprit, and not so much as the scrape of an imprudent heel had been heard in the hall.

"Brother Pellion was in charge of the bath," continued the Abbot. "I had foreseen difficulties when it became evident that the members of the King's train, who could not be received here, would look to us for bathing facilities. I had issued instructions that slips of paper were to be handed to applicants with the hour named at which each might come. But Brother Pellion, who is city bred and of weak fiber, fell into the habit of speaking with the servants who came to make arrangements for their masters and"—it was evident he had intended to add the word "mistresses" but it stuck in his throat—"I've replaced him with Brother Joseph who is old and has the use of one eye only."

The arrival of a pair of royal servants in green gilets, holding well-filled platters above their heads, created a diversion at this point. The Abbot called sharply, "Come, Brother Armand, what is this?" and the cellarer, in whose province such matters lay, hurried to the dais to make an explanation.

"It's a pittance, sent from the royal table for the delectation of the brothers, holy father."

"No pittance should be served without my permission," declared the head with a frown before which even Charles of France might have trembled. "What's the nature of the dish, if I may be allowed a belated word in the matter?"

The cellarer seemed reluctant to answer. "Cheese tarts," he said finally.

"Cheese tarts! Of what avail the minuto if my charges are to stuff their bodies with the richest of foods? I count it a grievous fault in you, Brother Armand, that you did not speak of this to me."

Animation had replaced the glum silence below. The rich pastries with their brown powdering of cinnamon on top were disappearing down monkish throats with a speed which threatened to exhaust the supply in no time at all. The smacking of heavy lips told of the satisfaction the creamy tarts had brought to starved palates.

The Abbot smiled bleakly at his guests. "I shall tender due thanks to our liege lord," he said. "But my conscience compels me to say it's well the responsibility for their spiritual welfare does not rest in his over-generous hands."

Brother Joseph, in spite of his years and the blindness in one of his eyes, had succeeded in getting an ample share of the unexpected pittance. He was still munching with a slow and circular motion of his jaws when the signal to rise was given. As he got to his feet he winked at the fat priest who had been sitting opposite him. The latter, interpreting the wink correctly, fell into step with him at the foot of the line.

The new custodian of the bath, employing a facility for speaking with no motion of the lips which years of practice had brought him, began to talk in the lowest of whispers.

"Brother Ossiprian, it will be this afternoon. *This* afternoon. Are you sure you understand what's expected of you?"

The other nodded by way of answer.

Brother Joseph was not content to let the matter rest there. He proceeded to coach Brother Ossiprian in what he was to do. The latter, who was head carpenter and spent most of his working hours in a dark workshop below the level of the ground, listened with frowning attention.

"You're not to leave your post for an instant. According to the understanding, the King and those with him will pass through the wine cellars and into your workshop an hour from now. Even though the King is of all men the most prompt, delays are possible, and so it may be they will not arrive until some time later. Now heed me well. You're to leave the door into the bathhouse ajar and you're to find tasks to busy yourself close beside it. When the King enters the other end, you are to give three quick taps with a hammer on whatever object engages your attention at the moment. Is that clear? Mind you, Brother Ossiprian, it's not to be two taps, nor is it to be four. They are to be quick, one after the other. *Three* taps, Brother Ossiprian. You will make no mistakes?"

"No, Brother Joseph," whispered the carpenter. "Three taps of the hammer. Quick taps. There will be no mistake."

As he spoke they passed the silent figure of the culprit, Brother Pellion. Without raising his eyes from the floor, the new custodian of the bath-house allowed one hand to brush the robe of his erring comrade and deposited in the side pocket a substantial wedge of cheese. With no motion of his lips Brother Pellion whispered, "A blessing on you, old friend."

The long double file broke up at the refectory door, the brethren going their various ways to the tasks awaiting them. The two ancient monks in the rear began to make their way across the cloister garth. Though free now of the danger of being overheard, they did not relax any of their precautions.

"You are to give the signal only if it's the King who enters," whispered Brother Joseph. "If others come first, pay them no heed. You understand, I trust?" After a moment he added as an encouragement to good performance, "The rewards are to be generous, Brother Ossiprian."

2

Regnault de Burey had known of the King's liking for detail when he made his plans. He had dropped a hint in the royal ear that the affairs of the abbey were in a state of sad confusion. This was not, strictly speaking, any concern of the King's; the responsibilities of the Abbot included the proper control of abbey affairs as well as watching over the spiritual well-being of his charges. "But it's well known, sire," the Comte had said during the brief audience allowed him to discuss the subject, "that the worthy Abbot has not scrupled to complain about the size of the party you've brought here. He implies quite openly that the presence of so many visitors has resulted in an upsetting of daily routine. I contend, sire, that if you would make a tour of inspection you would find that the confusion has always existed and is due to laxness in supervision."

Charles had decided at once that a tour of inspection was in order and had settled on that afternoon for the purpose. Starting out at the exact moment he had set, he led a small party of his ministers through the stables, the squillerie, the spicerie, the scalding pit, the pantries, and kitchens. Everywhere he found evidence that what the Comte had said was true.

"I must have a talk with the holy Abbot," he said cheerfully as he walked down the stone steps to the cellars. "He's not to be blamed for what has happened; at least we must be sparing in our view of him. His establishment is not equipped to take care of so many. But it's not to be gainsaid that things are sadly out of hand. Yes, I must have a talk with him at once." He glanced over his shoulder at the court official who followed closest on his heels. "Did you give an eye, my lord, to the confusion in the kitchen? And the stables! Truly the services of another Hercules are needed *there!*" A titter of approval greeted the royal jest. Charles, well pleased with himself, waited until his officers had enjoyed their laugh. Then he gave his head a sober shake. "It's said the accounts are ill kept. And did you notice that last summer's vines to catch flies are still hanging here and there?"

The party walked slowly through the cellars, casting appreciative eyes at the huge tuns of ale and the seemingly endless rows of bins where the fine wines were kept, the Saint-Emilion, the Malmsley, the Muscatel. Here was something to admire and commend without any reservations at all. The King, who liked his wine, nodded his head in approval several times and said to his attendants, "There's nothing amiss here and I must remember to speak a word for the cellarer when I have my talk with the worthy Abbot."

After the wine cellars came the workshop, where they had to step cautiously to avoid falling over saw benches and gantries and lathes. Here the aromatic scent of fresh shavings filled the nostrils instead of the acrid sweetness of the wines, but the King sniffed suspiciously and seemed intent on getting through as quickly as possible.

"What lies beyond?" he asked.

Guillaume Gouffier, who walked immediately behind, consulted a list and replied, "The bathhouse, my liege lord."

"Ha!" said the King, with deep satisfaction. "We now come to the source of the chief difficulty. I've had countless complaints of the long waits my good lords and ladies have had to endure for their turn to bathe. We must not overlook the fact that there are many of us and only one bath which might in all naturalness create an expectation of crowding. Still"—with a nod—"it's my understanding that none of the monks are due to bathe for many weeks. I think there has been bad management here."

The broad back of a solitary monk was to be seen at the far end of the workshop, bending over a lathe. He tapped briskly on an iron pipe and was so busy that he did not raise his head as the royal party passed.

The bathhouse beyond was a dark vault in which the light thrown by two forlorn cressets shone faintly. The one bath that it contained was sunk below the level of the flagged floor and it was large enough to accommodate three full-bodied monks at once. To meet the objections of the fair visitors, who preferred to bathe singly and not out in the open, the abbey carpenter had constructed screens about five feet high to be placed around the bath when desired. They were in use when the royal party appeared on the threshold and a sound of splashing came from behind them.

"It seems," said the King, pausing and frowning, "that our inspection is to be impeded by this insatiable demand for cleanliness which has suddenly taken hold of everyone."

And now it is possible to consider and perhaps admire the cunning and thoroughness which Regnault de Burey had shown in his planning. It had been necessary for him to estimate the progress of the King so accurately as to anticipate him at the bathhouse at almost this moment. He had helped Brother Joseph manipulate his list so that the steamy vault lacked all seekers after cleanliness other than the one now in the tub. Guillaumette, thoroughly flustered, even though she had been well coached, had to be standing inside the center screen when the door opened to admit the royal party.

Everything happened exactly as planned.

Guillaumette, berating herself mentally as a Judas but clutching avidly at the silver coins (but not as many as thirty) in the pocket of her skirt, brushed against the screen and caused it to fall outward. As a result Charles of France was treated to a tableau as unexpected and unconventional as any of the tales with which professional storytellers earned their fees.

Valerie had just stepped from the tub when the mishap occurred. The fall of the screen revealed her standing on tiptoe like Venus emerging from the waves, her arms outstretched for the towel which the maid held. The resemblance to the goddess did not end with the pose. There was a suggestion of eagerness about her as though she too was in process of entering a new life. Her hair had been piled high on her head to avoid wetting, where it was held by thin bands of blue velvet; and it was a mass of curls as richly golden as the popular conception of divine beauty. There was a hint of divinity also in the slender shapeliness of her figure.

"Guillaumette!" Valerie's voice rose to a sharp and very human tremble. "What have you done!"

"Mademoiselle!" wailed Guillaumette, scrambling frantically to raise the screen. "Oh, Mademoiselle! What have I done indeed!"

After the first moment of shocked inertia, Valerie moved swiftly. She did not, however, make the mistake that instinct urged on her of plunging back into the water, thus ending the episode with a loud splash, and on a note of farce. Nor did she rush with agitated leaps for the shelter of the side screen which was still standing. Instead she whisked the towel from the grasp of Guillaumette and wrapped it about her until nothing was to be seen but her head and the pleasantly sloped contour of her white shoulders. Then she moved so swiftly that the spectators, standing in frozen attention on the threshold, were hardly aware of motion on her part until the screen hid her from view.

"Oh, Guillaumette!" she gasped as she cowered in the dark corner, still holding the towel about her with a frantic insistence. "What a dreadful thing! I think I shall die of shame!"

"Can you ever forgive me?" sobbed the maid.

"How *could* you have been so careless! What will they think? Everyone will hear! Guillaumette, do you think we can get away before anyone finds who we are?"

The maid slipped the linen undergarment over the shoulders of her mistress with fingers which strove to make amends with haste for what she had done. "We'll get away as soon as we dare, Mademoiselle," she whispered. "I'll go first to make sure that no one is watching."

"Hurry, then, hurry!" said Valerie, with almost breathless urgency. She held up her arms so the warm winter tunic could be dropped over her head. "Guillaumette, you've had many chances to see the people here. Did you recognize any of those men?"

Candor forced Guillaumette to make an admission. "I'm very much afraid, Mademoiselle, that one was the King himself!"

Charles of France stumbled once or twice as he led the way back through the gloom of the carpenter shop. "Gouffier," he said, "it will be necessary to delay the inspection of the bathhouse until a more suitable time."

"Yes, sire," agreed Gouffier, with a smirk in his voice.

"I was informed," went on the ruler, "that we would find the place empty. It was so stated to me." He paused and, when he went on, a note of eagerness was permitted to show in his tone. "What an extraordinary thing! By'r Lady, I'm still unwilling to believe what I saw!"

The deep-set eyes of Guillaume Gouffier squinted up in surprise at his master. "If my liege lord will permit me to say so, I saw nothing extraordinary. We stumbled, most unexpectedly, on a very pretty girl in the act of stepping from her bath. It has happened before. I could quote several episodes in support of my statement, drawing them from history, both sacred and profane."

They passed from the carpenter shop into the long, cold crypt of the wine cellars where their footsteps echoed hollowly. The King sniffed the pungent winey odor and said: "On my honor, I feel the need for a stoup of the very strongest wine these bins can produce. It was like seeing——" The ruler paused and gave his head a bewildered shake. "Gouffier, I swear I saw a ghost back there."

"A ghost?" Gouffier presumed on the high standing he had in his master's regard to make light of the matter. "It was not a ghost I saw, sire. What I saw was a young woman fairly glowing with life and health. If there was anything ghostly about those warm, rounded limbs of hers, then, liege lord, I renounce forever the fear I have had of the supernatural."

"What I meant," amended the King testily, "was that she resembled someone so very much that she seemed like a ghost from the past."

The expression on his counselor's face showed such complete lack of understanding that Charles added, "Do you mean you failed to see the resemblance?"

"What resemblance, sire?"

Charles of France seemed reluctant to go any deeper into the matter. "Well, Gouffier, since you failed to see it, we'll let it rest there. But I must tell you that I was quite dazed by what I thought I saw in her."

Gouffier's face, which had a simian quality of slyness and malevolence about it, wrinkled up into a grin. "Sire, the young lady vouchsafed us no more than a fleeting glimpse of her charms. I am forced to an admission. My eyes were too busy elsewhere to reach any impression of her— her facial aspect."

The King offered no comment. He was making a mental note of the exact time when the episode had occurred so that it would be possible to discover from the monk in charge the name of the fair occupant whose turn in the sunken tub had been so rudely interrupted.

3

Valerie knew a journey was contemplated as soon as she returned to the manor house. Half-a-dozen saddles were warming on the hearth and there was a rope strung in front of the fire on which as many cloaks were suspended. She looked inquiringly at the Comtesse who was writing a letter in a corner of the room.

"Are we leaving, Cousin?" she asked.

The Comtesse frowned. She was such an indifferent scholar that the composing of a letter entailed the utmost effort and concentration. Valerie was convinced it was intended for the Sire d'Arlay and she said to herself, "She's sending him a message of farewell." Then she indulged in a second thought which left her with a guilty feeling of triumph. "It will do her small good." That D'Arlay had not been to see his sister-in-law since his visit on the first day of their arrival had been gleefully discussed and interpreted in the De Burey retinue, as Valerie had learned from Guillaumette. "He has given her up for good," was the way the maid summed up the situation. The reaction to this among the staff had been one of complete approval, as the popularity of the Comte's brother had grown with the fame he had won. "It's time he rode a new saddle," they said. Guillaumette's opinion, which she had expressed many times, was, "You ought to marry him, Mademoiselle, but if you do, watch out for Madame."

Valerie found it necessary to repeat the question, "Are we leaving today?"

"Yes." Isabeau sanded the letter and folded it with a frown. "We start for Paris as soon as the horses are ready."

"But, Cousin——"

"But, Cousin!" repeated Isabeau impatiently. Her eyes matched her hair in color and so it was clear that writing the letter had stirred her emotions. "Do you question the wisdom of leaving? I was sure you would be delighted. For my part, I can't get home soon enough."

"But——" Valerie felt a growing conviction that there was something back of this hurried exit she did not know about but which undoubtedly concerned her. "But, Cousin Isabeau, does my lord Coeur concur in this?"

The Comtesse drew her brows together. "Are we so beholden to my lord Coeur that we needs must consult him about all our plans and movements?"

Valerie was thinking: "Has it been decided I'm not suitable after all? Did that dreadful mistake this afternoon have anything to do with it?"

The Comtesse stood up, letter in hand. "Since you have had the bad grace to ask such a question, I'll tell you this: He knows of our leaving. It was settled between us."

"What has happened to change everything this way?"

"Nothing has happened. It's only that we think it better to return at once. Agnes Sorel will be dead before morning and the King will then depart without any delay."

"Am I to see my lord Coeur before we start?"

The Comtesse answered in a sharp voice: "No, Cousin, you will not see him. Didn't you hear me say we leave as soon as the horses are ready?"

The Comte entered the room at this point. He was cloaked and hatted for the journey and looked so much like a bear with a red nose that Valerie wanted to laugh. No fewer than three coats had been wrapped about him and his beaver hat had been pulled down over his ears where it was held in place by a woolen band wound many times around his head. He cut an absurd figure most certainly, and yet there was an air about him which suggested an expansion of his self-esteem.

He squinted at the girl and then asked his wife in an anxious whisper, "Has she any suspicions?"

Isabeau gave her head the merest shake and then said in a complaining voice: "My cousin has been questioning the wisdom of leaving this afternoon. She isn't sure yet we have the sanction of Jacques Coeur."

"Then your little cousin, Madame, shows less than her usual good sense. Does she think I would start at as late an hour as this on an impulse, a whim? I wouldn't stick my nose outside the door of this malodorous hole if I didn't have the best of reasons for it."

Godefroy entered and began to gather up the saddles. "We'll be ready to leave in another five minutes, my lord," he said.

The Comte groaned. "My bones will ache unbearably before we are through. I must have another glass of warm wine before I offer my protesting limbs to this torture."

"You've had enough wine already," declared his wife.

The Comte treated her to a steady look. "I'll have another drink, Madame, and you will order it for me without another word."

When Isabeau gave the order at once, Valerie said to herself in wonder: "This is indeed strange. What can have happened to bring this change between them?"

8

AT THE western boundary of the Hôtel Saint-Pol, where the King had taken up his residence on returning to Paris following the death of Agnes Sorel, there stood three houses. How they came to be there was a mystery. They backed against the meandering palace wall, which happened to be straight at this point, and so might well be a cause of worry to a nervous monarch who feared assassins. From the upper windows of these intruding houses it was possible to look down into the palace gardens, another disadvantage. Charles would have cleared them out long ago but for the fact that the indemnities to the owners were certain to be heavy; and so there they stayed like three burs in the tail of an otherwise sleek stallion.

The first of the three had once belonged to a family of some distinction and wealth but for the better part of a generation it had been used for commercial purposes. Men were seen to issue at all hours of the day from the ground floor which had been cut up into an infinity of tiny dark cubicles for the transaction of business, and bales of goods were constantly being craned in and out of the upper windows.

The third was equally large and had once been of corresponding importance; but the owners, less farsighted than the proprietors of the first, had given up when the roof began to disintegrate and the walls to crumble. It had been untenanted for many years, and people now took other routes to avoid passing it, because of their belief that it was haunted by evil spirits.

Between these two disreputable reminders of greatness long since departed was a house of a distinctly different type. It was much smaller, it was comparatively new, and it was as neat as a burgher's house in one of the suburbs which were stretching out far beyond the walls of the city. Its stone front had recently been scraped, the copper hinges on the door shone cheerfully, and over the entrance was a lantern enclosed in a new iron frame with the head of a griffon on top which must have come not long before from the forge of the smith. In spite of its immaculate appearance, there was something furtive about the little house. It seemed to shrink within the shelter of its gone-to-seed neighbors as though anxious to avoid notice. Its cleanliness did not succeed in achieving for it an air of virtue. It was like a strumpet who went about her ancient trade unobtrusively instead of romping and brawling in taverns and who preferred quiet attire to the vulgar finery of her competitors.

One afternoon in early March the Comte de Burey halted his retinue at the corner of the Logis de la Reine, which was still some distance from the neighborhood of the three houses, and instructed them to await his return there. He then proceeded on foot with Valerie, who had accompanied him. Guillaumette clumped along in the rear, her arms filled with bundles. It was a lovely day. Spring had put in an early appearance and a friendly sun shone on the dirty old city in an effort to coax out thin edgings of green along the banks of the river and in unexpected nooks here and there. The beauty, however, was lost on Valerie. She had been told nothing except that she was to make one of the party; but the purpose of this trip into the Marais, that part of the town where the great palaces clustered, was not hard to divine.

There was no one in sight when they stopped in front of the little house, but the Comte had no sooner raised the knocker on the front door than two men put in an appearance and ranged themselves beside him. They were armed with bills and short swords and they were prepared, quite obviously, to take things in hand if it developed that the newcomers had no right to be there. That contingency did not arise. The Comte said something in a low tone to the man who opened the door and they were admitted immediately.

Valerie looked about her with apprehensive eyes but was forced to the conclusion almost immediately that the interior was far from what she had expected. Nothing she had seen at the Hôtel de Burey or on her recent travels had prepared her for the richness and warmth of this unusual house. The walls were not bare and discolored with dampness but were covered with tapestries and hangings in cheerful colors. The floors were not wet and slippery but were hidden under carpets of the kind provided by the *tapissiers sarrasinois*, the latest Parisian guild, for the great and the wealthy of the city. Her feet sank into them as she walked diffidently behind Regnault de Burey. She had never seen anything like the furniture but she sensed that all of it was costly and rare.

A woman came from an inner room to greet them, saying in a stiff and precise voice, "And is this Mademoiselle de Voudrai, my lord Comte?"

The Comte stopped dead still and looked at the newcomer with unbelieving eyes. She was absurdly tall and thin with a neck which was swanlike in length if not in grace. A small head protruded forward from the end of it and a shovel nose, somewhat meaty in color, jutted out in turn from the head. It seemed almost inevitable that the weight of the nose would be too much, that it would bring about her collapse as the last small block will cause a child-built tower to fall. She would have been a completely comic figure had it not been for her eyes, which were sharp and hard.

"Can it be possible?" he whispered to Valerie. "What vision of beauty is this to banish the memories of all other fair women: Helen receiving the apple, Eleanor whose lusty charms won her two kings as husbands, Flora, Fredegonde, Héloïse?"

He knew who she was, however, even though he had not been prepared for her eccentricities of appearance. "Yes, Damoiselle Henriette," he said aloud, with a deep bow. "It's my understanding that she's to be left in your care."

The lean form of Damoiselle Henriette arched itself in a bow to Valerie. "I'm happy to welcome you, my lady," she said. "We have striven to anticipate every wish in the hope that you will be happy here. May I offer you refreshments before you leave, my lord?"

The Comte declined on the ground that he had left his escort some distance away and did not want to attract notice to them by too long a wait. He then kissed Valerie's hand. "It begins, my little pet," he said to her, in a cautious undertone. "You have nothing to fear. The staff has no other purpose but to see that you're comfortable. As for this drooping beanstalk, this disjointed old passionflower, I hardly know what advice to give. I would dub her harmless but for that eye of hers. Well, treat her almost as an equal—but never confide in her."

"I will try to be most careful in everything," the girl whispered back nervously.

The Comte drew himself up and bowed ceremoniously to each of them in turn. Then he said, "Farewell, Cousin," and departed through the front door.

"Would my lady like to go to her bedroom now?" asked Damoiselle Henriette, her head teetering on her grotesque neck as she turned in the direction of an inner door.

Valerie did not reply at once. She was wondering for the thousandth time if the sudden departure from Jumièges had been at the wish of Jacques Coeur. If he had known, and approved, why had she not heard from him since? Always before she had received notes at fairly regular intervals, and his long silence made her suspect that he did not know where she was. What disturbed her most was her uncertainty about the step just taken. Had she come to this house with the Moneyman's knowledge and consent? Isabeau had said that he knew, even going into details of the discussions there had been on the subject. And yet—the doubts she had felt at first still lingered in her mind. They had been augmented since arriving at this outwardly prim but aloof habitation situated so suspiciously on the edge of the King's greatest palace.

The tall woman repeated her question. Valerie collected her wits and replied in the affirmative. She then followed the Damoiselle up a flight of stairs to a large room on the floor above. She had no time to study the unusual pieces of furniture they passed on the way but her fears had not wholly vanquished her curiosity and so she marked each in her mind as worthy of examination later. Among them was a clock (she had seen clocks on the walls of great buildings and still thought of them as belonging in the realm of magic), surmounted with a gold globe and which ticked with an unbelievable regularity. She saw an esperver and did not know what it was (later generations would call it a hammock), even though it was suspended between stands as ornately carved as a chancel rail. It seemed to her suggestive that a chair at the end of the main room was built like a throne, with flying buttresses and napkin panels on the side decorated in quatrefoil. Through an archway leading into a room at the rear her eye picked out a monster buffet—an amazingly tall buffet even for an age which liked them tall and imposing—and she noticed it had castles elaborately carved on its top points and that gold and silver and enamel broke out all over it like a rash of adolescence.

She had passed all these marvels without pausing but she stopped when she came to the doorway of the bedroom. Inside was a bed which looked at first glance like a throne. It was unusual in having a full tester, the beds of the period being content, for the most part, with an overhang at the head. The posts were as big around as the barrel of a cannon and the curtains were of samite interwoven with gold, hanging in graceful folds like an emperor's robe. It was so high that the carvings above each corner of the tester touched the ceiling. The effect of this great height was to make the bed itself seem at first glance both short and narrow; but on stepping closer she found this to be a delusion, as it was capable of holding four tall men without any difficulty at all.

"It's called Pepin the Short," explained Damoiselle Henriette, in the tone of awe one might use on viewing the sacred relics in the Sainte-Chapelle.

Although she was familiar with the custom of giving names to pieces of furniture and decorations, particularly beds and standing cups, Valerie could not prevent herself from laughing. "Don't you think, Damoiselle Henriette," she suggested, "that it would have been more fitting to name this one after the giant Nemrod who was so tall his head touched the clouds?"

"Pepin was a great king," declared the other severely, "and the father of Charlemagne. It's the greatest of honors for one's bed to be named after a king."

Valerie's inner comment was that the bed should have been named Charles, for she had no doubts that he had slept in it. This conviction grew that night after Guillaumette had disrobed her and had tucked the covers up around her neck and had left her alone in the immense expanse of counterpane which, very clearly, had never been meant for one. She could not get to sleep, for the curtains had been drawn on all four sides and it seemed to her that she was looking up into a long tunnel of shimmering material with a quivering light in a lantern suspended from the top. The candle in the lantern was small and the only purpose it served was to distort the folds of the hangings and the floral designs into which the satin covering of the tester had been drawn; and, as she passed into the first stages of sleepiness, she fancied that she saw heads up there, some of them wearing crowns, and all of them staring down at her intently, as though wondering what a girl of the people was doing in a bed which had been built for a king. She would have sprung out of this closely muffled niche to seek a bed where darkness would close her away from these grinning, wicked faces but the languor which accompanies the near approach of slumber held her a prisoner, and in the end the faces faded away and the light of the candle seemed of no more significance than any star seen through a window at night. She fell off to sleep.

2

Valerie said little at dinner next day but Damoiselle Henriette, who sat at table with her, talked continuously as she pecked with the small appetite of ill-health at a salad of plums and Roman lettuce. Her conversation never deviated: the great but unacknowledged part women had played as nurses in all the great wars, the debt that France owed to Jeanne d'Arc, the ease with which a young woman known as Mademoiselle Margot had succeeded some twenty years before in beating all the men of France at tennis. "There's a lesson in this," she concluded. "Men haven't taken it to heart but to a few women the meaning is clear. Man's superiority is a sham, a self-fostered delusion!"

On rising to leave the table, she bowed to Valerie and said, "It's my earnest wish, my lady, that you'll always have a place for me in your household."

Left to herself, the girl strolled into a small room at the rear of the house where she had seen a few manuscripts and books. She picked up one of the books, a beautifully illuminated copy of an early part of the *Imitatio Christi*, but even the inspired text of that favorite book of the age failed to hold her. After a few minutes of laborious progress she let it fall into her lap.

She had been disturbed by Damoiselle Henriette's last remark. "That woman," she said to herself, "knows about everything. Or why should she think I'm to have a household of my own? Yes, she knows why I'm here and I am sure she regards me with contempt." Nothing but honeyed words had been spoken and yet she was certain she had seen in the sharp eyes of the tall woman an aloofness, a suggestion of sardonic acceptance of the situation. "If I am a success," so ran her thoughts, "all the ladies of the court will hate me, and plot against me, and, I suppose, envy me. I'll have no peace as long as I live. If I fail—everyone will consider it a great joke, I will be laughed at and my lord Coeur also." She was convinced, suddenly, that she would not succeed, that the idea had been doomed to failure from the start; that, in fact, the best thing she could do was to leave this house at once and run so far away that no one concerned would ever find her again.

But could she run away? Guillaumette had come to her that morning with a disturbed look on her face. "Mademoiselle!" she had whispered. "*We are prisoners!*"

"No, Guillaumette. You're imagining things."

"But, mistress, I'm not imagining things. Just a few minutes ago I was of a mind to step out for a breath of fresh air. But no sooner had I shown my face outside the door—there's only one door, for the house is built flat against the palace wall—than one of those two men we saw yesterday appeared from nowhere and grins at me. 'Where do you think you're going, my fair one?' he asks. I told him that was no concern of his and that it was clear to me he had been turned in at a pork-due.[1] He grins all the more and says to me, 'If you think you're going out, minikin, just think again. No one goes out, not even your mistress.' I said to him I would leave the marks of my fingers on his stupid face, but he said, 'It's orders, my old beauty.' And when I went to the Madame—— Do you know what the servants call her? Old Here-Comes-My-Nose-My-Ass-Is-Away-Behind. Well, it was the same. She jiggled that head of hers about and told me I must stay in the house and put my curiosity to bed."

Valerie had been warned that every possible precaution would be taken and so she was not particularly exercised over the fact that they were not to be allowed to show themselves on the streets at any time they desired. Now, however, she began to ponder seriously the position in which she found herself, and the knowledge that she was to all intents and purposes a prisoner added to her desire to be free of the chains they were forging for her.

She was deeply immersed in such thoughts when a sound behind her made her stiffen with alarm. She was alone in the room, and the noise, moreover, came from the part where no one could possibly be hidden, the rear wall which, if Guillaumette's information was correct, was against the high stone barricade of the Hôtel Saint-Pol. It was repeated. She sprang to her feet and turned about in time to see a section swing open in what she had assumed to be a wall paneled solidly in dark oak. A man stepped through the opening thus provided and closed the door after him. The panel sank back into place, and once more the wall presented an appearance of unbroken surface.

The intruder bowed to her and smiled, the smile having some trace of diffidence about it, as though he also was finding the situation a difficult one. He was of middle height and was wearing a handsome glaudkin of green velvet which covered him from head to foot. His face could not be called handsome but there was a rather amiable quality about his long nose and heavily lidded eyes. A gold chain was looped three times around his neck and his right hand toyed with it nervously as he took a few steps toward her.

"I must ask your indulgence for appearing so suddenly and so—so mysteriously, my child," he said. He smiled again and asked, "Do you know who I am?"

Valerie had dropped to her knees. Keeping her eyes on the floor, she answered, "Yes, sire."

"Come," said the King, reaching out a hand and helping her to her feet. "There is no need for further ceremony. I come today, not as the King of France but as a man who has seen you and who finds himself very much interested in you."

---

[1] On the Nativity of the Virgin the peasants of France were required to give one pig in eight to the nobleman on whose land they belonged. This was known as the pork-due.

Valerie found enough courage to raise her head and meet his eyes; but, after the first quick exchange of glances, she allowed her lids to drop again. That he had shown some embarrassment on entering was proof of his human qualities, but he was, after all, the greatest and richest king in the world and she found it impossible to summon immediately any of the assurance needed to meet the situation.

"It's extraordinary!" The King was staring at her fixedly, and it was clear that he was both puzzled and excited at what he saw. "A favor, Mademoiselle. Will you indulge me by looking me full in the face?" Valerie obeyed by raising her eyes. He studied her intently. "Extraordinary indeed! And now the profile, Mademoiselle." Valerie turned her head and kept it in that position for several moments. She heard him draw in his breath. "It's even more apparent that way. And now, sweet child, will you raise your head a little higher?" Before she could obey, he reached out and placed his hands on her shoulders. He drew her around until they were facing each other again. She could feel a slight tremor in his hands. "Would you close your eyes for a moment so that the lashes rest on the cheeks? And now, if you please, a smile. Thank you, that is the final proof! Truly it passes all belief! It is a miracle!"

He had thrown back the glaudkin, revealing under it a tunic of plum-colored velvet with bands of ermine about the neck and sleeves. Since her elevation to this new life, Valerie had seen much in the way of rich clothes, but she had never encountered anything to equal the costume Charles of France had donned for the occasion. Over the tunic, and extending from neck to waist, was a panel of silk as tawny as an orange skin and embroidered with gold thread in an intricate pattern designed around scarlet roses with diamonds in their hearts. There was a sapphire dangling from the gold chain and a spatter of precious stones in the front of his belt.

The King motioned her to sit down and then drew up a chair for himself, placing it directly in front of her. "I saw you a week ago," he said, leaning forward, and never taking his eyes from her face. "It was at the street fete to celebrate our victories. In the afternoon I went against the advice of all my officers—I put on a domino and sallied out to watch the merrymaking in the streets. I had a rich reward for my pains: I saw *you*, sweet child, sitting on horseback with the Comte de Burey watching the procession. I was not more than six feet from you but, of course, you didn't see me. I watched you for a long time, I saw everything that happened, I heard every word you said! I was concerned for a moment when one of the maskers stopped and tickled your cheeks with feathers at the end of a wand."

Valerie nodded and smiled. "He was a tall man and he was dressed like a clown."

"He said to you, 'I am the prince of fools, the monarch of hulverheads, the perfect product of the world of doddypolls.' And you said, 'That's a rash claim to make in a field where there's so much competition.' And then you laughed—a merry laugh, a charming laugh. I was entranced by it. As I stood there and watched and listened, I knew that I—I had become enamored of you."

Whatever composure Valerie had succeeded in gaining deserted her promptly. "Sire," she said, "I—I am overwhelmed! I don't know what to say."

The King took possession of one of her hands. "I have a confession to make to you. It wasn't an accident. It wasn't chance which led me to the spot where I saw you. It had all been arranged. I had seen you once before and I asked the Comte to contrive some way by which that very great pleasure could be repeated. It was planned with the utmost care, my sweet Valerie. And now I am happy—— Ah, how happy I am that I went to such efforts!"

The trace of embarrassment which had shown in his manner when he entered the room had vanished. He was completely in command of himself and of the situation. His eyes glowed with ardor as he captured her other hand and drew her forward toward him. "And now I have planned something else. I have planned *this*. This house is yours, with every comfort I could find for you, with servants to tend you and guards to give you security. I'm hoping to pay you many visits here. I desire you near my person."

Her confusion had increased as his had diminished. Lowering her eyes, she answered, "That will be as my liege lord wishes."

"No, no! That won't suffice me. I am seeking to ascertain your wishes. I shall come only as often as you desire to see me."

He broke off abruptly and began to ask her questions. Had she ever been in love? Was she prepared to cut herself away from her past life and all its relationships and act as though it had never been? Was she prepared to place herself unreservedly in his hands? Did she like children? Was she willing to bear them?

Her answers seemed to please him, particularly when she used a speech which Isabeau had prepared, "This is more honor than I can ever merit and greater happiness than I had ever dared to expect."

He kissed her hands impulsively. "Ah, my child, my pretty Valerie!" he exclaimed. "The resemblance, which still amazes me, goes deeper than the surface. How fortunate that this heritage of beauty and grace and sweet understanding has been given you! That it has come to you unimpaired!"

A moment later he released her hands and settled back in his chair. "And now let us talk," he said. "We must become acquainted with each other. You know nothing of me except that I'm the King of France. I know nothing of you save that you bear an amazing likeness to the loveliest of all ladies, and that everything about you pleases me. I've taken great care in the selection of the furniture, thinking to make this little nest a pleasant and beguiling habitation for you. Everything comes from one of the royal palaces or from estates which are in our hands. The buffet was used by the Englishman"—he was referring, quite apparently, to Henry V—"when he was in Paris. It's the only piece of its kind in France and that may balance the odium of its former ownership. The bed was in the Tournelles and I've slept in it many times." He paused over the last words as though to prevent any overlooking of the natural implication, that he expected to sleep in it many times more. "Do you like what I've done?"

"Everything is beautiful beyond belief, sire. I wish I could find the words to express how deeply honored I am."

The King brushed aside the need for further amenities with a wave of his hand. A thought had occurred to him which he hurried to put into words. "The Comte tells me you have a gift for mimicry. Show me what you can do. It will be an amusing step toward our—our better acquaintance."

"But, sire"—Valerie was reluctant to follow this suggestion, being convinced that what seemed to her a very modest gift would fail to amuse so great a personage as the King of France—"you would find it dull and—and trifling. I've imitated only the servants of my cousin and some low characters I had seen before. I'm certain, sire, they would interest you not at all."

The King smiled. "What of our good servant, the Comte de Burey himself?"

Valerie's brows puckered with uncertainty. Then, after a moment's thought, she smiled. "The Comte? Well—perhaps. He wouldn't be hard, as he has many odd traits, as you must have seen, sire. But—would it be proper to make light of him in this way?"

The King swung his chair around so that he could command a good view of the whole room. "From this moment on, my pretty one, the wishes of your king should weigh more with you than the feelings of Regnault de Burey. In any event, I swear myself to secrecy. He will never know that you have copied his ways for the amusement of Charles of France."

Valerie walked to the end of the room where she remained for several minutes with her back turned. When she swung around and faced him, the change in her appearance was so great that he gasped with surprise. "By good St. Martin," he cried, "you really look like him!"

She had drawn in her cheeks and thus given a suggestion of length and lankness to her face. One lock of hair had been pulled over her brows, and by some device, which had more to do with the spirit than the flesh, her expression had been changed to one of biliousness and misanthropy. She peered about her with shortsighted intentness as she came across the room with a shuffling gait. It was in the matter of the walk, however, that she proceeded to achieve her best effect. She moved as though her joints were stiff, placing her feet down cautiously and tenderly; with so much caution, in fact, that any stranger would have believed her to be suffering from a combination of gout and broken arches.

When she spoke, the King started in surprise, for the voice was so much like Regnault de Burey's that it was hard to believe it had been produced by anyone else. "The devil has his pincers on me today," she said, snuffling and grunting between words. "I think my flesh is being given a tweeze for every innocent little slip I've made in my whole life."

Charles of France threw back his head. "If all his misdeeds are remembered, our poor Comte will suffer torments through eternity," he said, laughing loudly.

Valerie proceeded with other imitations of the Comte, drawing on her memory of things she had heard him say. She gave a version of his meeting with Damoiselle Henriette which made the King laugh still more loudly. Finally she raised the small purse attached to her belt and gave it a shake. "That," she said, "is the sweetest sound ever to fill the ears of human beings. Don't tell me of the twittering of birds in bosky thickets or the chanting of heavenly choirs or the blast of a trumpet sounding the advance. No, by'r Lady of Marmoutier, nothing can compare with the clink, the jingle, the rasp, the sweet cuddling together of gold coins in a pocket which has been empty for years!"

Charles rose to his feet and walked over to where she was standing. He placed his hands on her shoulders and gave her an appreciative shake. "You are a clever little vixen!" he said. "And I love you for it. How much I shall enjoy seeing you imitate my ministers and the people closest about me! Of course that must needs wait on your opportunity to see them and know them. I intend, dear child, to make that chance come soon."

She allowed the lines of her face to resume their normal aspect and brushed the hair back from her forehead. The King nodded his approval without releasing her. "Even while I laughed, I was regretting the absence, if only for a few moments, of my lovely little charmer," he whispered. "Now you are again the perfect image of everything I most admire and love. Let me look at you closely before I go."

Suddenly he swept her into his arms and began to kiss her hungrily, on the mouth, the eyes, the ears, the cheeks, and brow. "I shall come back soon, my small one," he exclaimed. "I know that I am going to love you very much."

9

FRESH from the confusion in which they had existed at the Abbey of Jumièges, the members of the King's court were luxuriating in the magnificent accommodations of the Hôtel Saint-Pol. This great sprawling palace was capable of housing the whole train and with all the dependents they cared to bring. Even Jacques Coeur, who had always been allotted whatever space was left after the other ministers had been satisfied, had a large suite to himself in one of the most recent additions, a neighboring palace which had been acquired during the time of the King's grandfather and which was now incorporated within the rambling wall. True, it was a dark and granite-like structure in which even the rooms that the sun could reach were cold and dreary. The Moneyman found it necessary to keep candles burning beside him at all hours.

He had finished his day's work when the clomp of a spurred boot sounded in the anteroom and Nicolas put his head in to announce, "My lord Dunois to see you, master."

The commander of the French armies came into the room, nodding and smiling to the only one of the King's ministers for whom he had any respect. "Moneyman," he said, taking a chair, "I've come to give you a word of warning."

Coeur sighed. The air was full of rumors and hostile signs. Many friends had nervously taken advantage of favorable opportunities to whisper warnings in his ear. He had not needed these friendly words of advice, being capable of reading the portents himself. It had been clear to him for some time that the tide had turned and was running against him.

"What have you heard?" he asked.

"I've just come from the King." Dunois spoke in a tone which conveyed a suggestion of the dislike he felt for everything that had to do with courts and courtiers. "It's his intention to move quickly against the English in the west and south now that Normandy has been regained with such ease. Did you know of this?"

"No." Coeur almost choked over the word. It was inconceivable that Charles would make this decision without consulting him. It had been his arguments which had led to the breaking of the truce and the reconquest of Normandy. His money had made the campaign possible. He realized suddenly that the peril of his position was much greater than he had been prepared to believe. If Charles would go this far, he could be expected to go to still greater extremes.

"I knew the matter had to be decided soon," he said, after a short spell of bitter thought during which he had tried unsuccessfully to find some acceptable explanation for the affront. "After you, Bastard, I had more right than anyone to share my King's confidence, and to advise him in the making of war plans. I confess to a retching of the spirit at the injustice." His eyes had a strained look as he turned to face the army commander directly. "Is there no gratitude in kings?"

Dunois indulged in a gesture of resignation. "Kingship," he said, "is the hardest of all trades. There's little difference in being King of France and King of the Coquille. In each case you have selfish, cruel men around you, ready to go to any lengths for the favors and the preferment they demand —and prepared to sacrifice king and throne and country to that end. A successful king is tougher and more selfish and cruel than the men he employs. Look at poor Harry Sixt' of England—a gentle, unselfish, devout man. His country is drifting into civil war and he's losing all his dominions in France. He's a failure. I think we could have saved the Maid if we had thrown aside all dictates of strategy and expediency and marched to the rescue. We took what seemed the sensible course, the tough course, if you prefer: we left her to die." He sighed. "I'm a seasoned soldier and I've seen men perish by the thousands. But, Moneyman, the crew around the King are too tough for me."

After a moment's silence Coeur asked, "What did you hear?"

"The discussion was all of funds. The King is in a panic over what it would cost to drive the Godons out of Bordeaux and at the same time pay you for the cost of Normandy. The idea wasn't put into words exactly but the suggestion hung suspended in the air in full understanding of all that the expense of the western campaign could be blithely assumed if some way were found to escape settling with you."

"If I went to him and said, 'Sire, consider the debts paid,' what would he do?"

"I very much fear," answered Dunois, "that the pride of our liege lord is a complex thing. He might hesitate to put himself under an everlasting obligation to you. You would acquire thereby more stature than any subject should have. And I don't believe he would want the credit for Normandy to repose so exclusively and permanently in your hands. He would much prefer to accomplish the cancellation of the debts by other means."

Coeur had turned his head and was staring out of the window. There was nothing to see, for the room was high up and night was beginning to fall. He would have seen nothing in any event, his mind being too occupied with the unpalatable truths the old soldier was stating.

"The war," said the Moneyman finally, "has cost double what we figured at the outset. I've found it necessary to go back and back to the moneylenders. My estates have been put up one by one as security, even some of the goods in the shops as well. I could survive the loss of the original amount, but if it became known that none of the debt was to be paid, the Lombardy merchants would be about my ears in a moment. They would take everything away from me. They might even compel me to wear the green hat of bankruptcy."

"If I didn't know you to be as hard a fighter as any of them," commented the soldier, "I would feel very much concerned about you, Jacques Coeur."

The Moneyman achieved a mirthless smile. "Yes, I'm a fighter. I can be as tough as they can. But with this difference, Bastard, I am not selfish. My toughness has always been applied to different ends." He lapsed into silence and it was several moments before he resumed the discussion. "What you've told me caps the things I've been hearing for the past two weeks. A crisis has been reached. Need I say that I'm grateful, eternally grateful to you, old friend?"

The soldier got to his feet. His hand dropped to the jeweled hilt of his sword. "You made me a present of this, Jacques Coeur," he said, "and all Rouen was agog when I rode in with it at my side. You're too resourceful to reach such a stage, but if it should ever happen that you are in need of aid or of money, I shall be very unhappy if you don't come to me."

Silence prevailed in the room after Dunois had left. The pair of candles beside Coeur did little to combat the gloom which settled down with the passing of day. They had guttered to a low point when Nicolas came grumbling into the room.

"It's late, master," he said. "The Sire d'Antenne is out there but I'm going to tell him to take himself off."

Coeur straightened up in his chair. "Send him in!" he said sharply.

"But, master," protested the servant in sulky tones, "what he has to tell will keep until tomorrow surely."

The Moneyman half rose to his feet, his hands gripping the edge of the table. He was more angry with Nicolas than he had ever been before. "I told you to send him in!"

Nicolas knew when to submit. He vanished with alacrity and a few moments later the Sire d'Antenne appeared in the door.

Coeur was too disturbed over the situation in which he found himself to greet the informer in the usual facetious vein. He asked in a matter-of-fact voice, "Well, what is it this time?"

"As usual I've been fishing diligently in the sea of information and I've brought up a pearl," said D'Antenne. "You will be very much interested in my find, my lord Coeur. It has to do"—he was watching the Moneyman closely in spite of the lightness of his tone—"with the King's new mistress."

"The court is full of rumors about the wavering fancy of our liege lord," said Coeur indifferently. He turned away and resumed his staring out into the night. "You must bring me a better catch than that, splendid fellow, if you expect to rouse my interest."

"But this is a fact, not a rumor. The King has fallen in love. Madly, it's said. Who the lady is or where she comes from are mysteries to which no answers have been found. The King is so enamored of her that even the enemies of Jacques Coeur find it hard at times to reach his ear." He grinned maliciously. "That should be proof of the depth of his interest! Do you want to hear more?"

"Yes. At the usual rate."

The informer crossed one elegantly clad leg over the other. He was handsomely attired in sky-blue velvet with white trimmings and there was even the sparkle of a ring on one of his fingers. Coeur, noticing these signs of prosperity, said to himself, "This slimy purveyor of secrets has been taking his wares to profitable markets."

"The King has seen the lady in question three times and has spoken to her once only. Nevertheless, his surrender is so complete and overwhelming that she has already been established in a house with a train of servants to look after her. It's whispered he has ordered the letter S and the emblem of the surelle tree taken off all the silver he gave the Lady Agnes so that it can be presented a second time. The most curious thing about this is that the lucky lady is said to be as much like the Lady Agnes as though they were sisters——"

Coeur's features were too well schooled to give any inkling of the shock he had experienced. He sat quite still for several moments while the informer went on with other details. His mind was filled with alarmed speculations but, when he looked around at his visitor, his face gave no hint of this.

"Where did you hear this story?"

"From a close source. I prefer not to tell you the name of my informant. I wouldn't dare, in fact."

"Is the story likely to get into circulation?"

The Sire d'Antenne shook his head emphatically. "For the best of reasons the few who know about it are not telling. I question if more than three people have shared the secret."

"Why are you so certain of its truth?"

The informer raised one hand from his knee and gestured with it by way of answer.

"Where is the house?" asked Coeur.

"I could make myself a rich man if I knew."

"Can you prove the truth of this story by finding out about the house?"

D'Antenne gave some deep thought to this. "I'm not sure. Certainly it would be difficult, and it would be necessary to cross a few palms. With gold, not silver, and plenty of it."

Coeur named a sum. A covetous flush came into the cheeks of the informer and he answered without further hesitation: "I'll do your bidding even if I have to slit a throat or two and bestow the boon of my attentions on the fat wife of some court official."

"I must have it tonight."

D'Antenne indulged in further thought. Then he nodded his head. "If I get it at all, I shall have the information for you in a few hours."

2

Jacques Coeur started out to find his way to the apartments of the King. The route he followed took him through a gate leading into a tilting ground, at the far end of which he passed through another gate, high and ivy-clad, into a maze of formal gardens. After that it was a case of one gate after another, and then doors and staircases and dark passages without number. The Hôtel Saint-Pol was like a walled city.

In the course of his wanderings he had encountered people at every turn. Most of them he recognized, and all of them knew him, but for the first time since he had been summoned to court to become the King's Moneyman, he found himself ignored. Men and women turned away at his approach or acknowledged his greetings with a hasty word or reluctant nod. Even the servants and the guards (the palace swarmed with the latter), quick to sense a turn of sentiment or a dip in fortune, stared insolently through him as he passed. Nothing could be more indicative than this. Jacques Coeur read the signs aright but he was not prepared for what happened when he reached the double doors, with the lilies of France in gold leaf on the panels, behind which were the anterooms of the King.

A captain of guards was stationed there who looked at him and said in a voice which carried an undertone of regret, "I have orders not to admit you, Monseigneur."

Coeur was too stunned to speak at first. He had not expected a deliberate and public rebuff. It had never entered his mind, in fact, that he would be refused a chance to discuss the situation with his royal master. He studied the face of the captain for a moment, wondering if this was a ruse on the part of his enemies to prevent him from reaching the King.

"Are your orders from the King himself?"

"Yes, Monseigneur." The official looked about him hastily. Convinced that he could not be overheard, he added in a whisper, "The people of France will always remember that you brought them peace at last, my lord Coeur."

"It's unfortunate that the voice of the people doesn't penetrate within official cabinets." Coeur turned on his heel. "This is probably the last time we will see each other. Farewell, my good captain, and thanks for the kindliness with which you have carried out your orders."

He started slowly on the return trip, his head lowered in thought, thus saving those he passed the necessity of refusing to meet his eye or to acknowledge a greeting. There was no longer any doubt as to what the future held. Charles had closed his mind as well as his door. As Dunois had hinted, the King would now find some other means of avoiding the payment of the war bills than by accepting a voluntary cancellation.

He was passing through a passage even more lacking in illumination than the rest when he heard his name called in a feminine voice. He stopped and looked about him. The woman who had accosted him was standing in the shadow of a high-windowed alcove which in daylight would command a view of the tennis grounds. She placed a finger on her lips and beckoned him with her other hand to join her.

"My lord, I have something for you," she whispered. "It's from the Sire d'Antenne."

Coeur said, "He has lost no time if your message is what I think."

She was a young woman, small and dark and rather attractive. The Moneyman did not recognize her as one of the ladies of the court but it was clear she was above the station of a servant. He decided she must be the wife or daughter of some minor official. It was obvious that she was too nice to be concerned in any of the devious transactions of the Sire d'Antenne.

"I've a note," the girl whispered. "But I'm not to hand it to you until you give me the money."

"But, my dear lady," protested Coeur, "I don't carry that much gold on my person."

She looked troubled. "He said it was most important. That he had found what you wanted. I don't know what's in the note, my lord, but the importance of it was such that the Sire d'Antenne didn't dare take it to you himself."

Coeur's hand had been searching in a pouch he carried under his tunic. Having a fondness for unset precious jewels, he was in the habit of carrying some of his special favorites with him. When he extended his hand for her attention, an emerald of good size lay on the palm.

"This," he said, "is worth considerably more than the sum agreed upon. If you know anything of jewels, you will accept this without any question at all."

"I know very little." She was disturbed at the need to make a decision. She studied the emerald and then looked up into the face of the Moneyman. "I—I don't know what to do. It seems a very fine stone but I've no idea of its value. It has never been my luck to possess anything as costly as this."

"Please believe that I wouldn't deceive you. I assure you, my girl, that you may accept this with an easy mind."

She said in the tone of one who has decided to make a plunge, "Give it to me, my lord Coeur." She produced a small slip of paper which was doubled over and sealed tightly. The exchange was effected.

A kindly impulse caused him to ask a question, "How does it come that you are acting as go-between in this matter?"

She looked at him defiantly. "The Sire d'Antenne and I are friends."

"No, my dear." Coeur gave his head a shake. "No attractive woman can ever be a friend of the Sire d'Antenne."

She favored him with an angry look but then she threw her head back and laughed rather bitterly. "You are right, my lord. We began as friends but that didn't last long. I am his mistress. He has others, of course. I've always known it but I am so much in love with him that I—I try to forget." Her tone had become unfriendly. "Is there anything else you want to know?"

Coeur had been watching her compassionately, knowing that a liaison with the Sire d'Antenne could bring her nothing but grief and pain.

He broke the seal and convinced himself that the note contained the information he required. "I'm content," he said. "As content as your lover will be when he sees what you take him in payment." Then, in a kindly tone, he added, "I'm very sorry for you, my child."

The conversation had been carried on in guarded tones, but at this the girl began to laugh without any effort at restraint. "You are sorry for me? Then we are even. I, my lord Coeur, am sorry for you!"

This transaction with the emissary of D'Antenne, for the few minutes that it lasted, had succeeded in diverting the Moneyman's mind from the perils gathering about him. He was brought back to reality with a severe jolt when he reached the landing outside his suite of rooms. Nicolas was there, his arms filled with clothes which clearly had been hastily assembled. Behind the servant, a royal servitor with a pike in his hands leaned against the door.

Coeur knew what this meant and he asked one question only. "When did it happen, Nicolas?"

"A few minutes after you left, master. There are three of them in there now, going over your papers. They're strewing everything on the floor and quarreling among themselves. My lord Gouffier is one of them."

"That was to be expected." Coeur gave vent to a brief and mirthless laugh. "They must think me very careless if they hope to find anything of value within such easy reach of their fingers. They're wasting their time on household accounts."

"They've put seals on all the windows, master."

"But the enormity of what they do they can never seal up. It will go down in history as the greatest injustice of this age."

Now that the blow had fallen, Jacques Coeur felt a deep sadness but no anger. His mind went back to the past. He thought of his first shop at Bourges, of his first visits to the East, and of the series of inspirations which had led to his dominance. That he had become the richest man in the world and had paid for a war out of his own purse were no longer important. What he was thinking of, as he stood there outside his locked door, a discarded minister of the Crown, was his vision of a different and better world which he had hoped to see in his own lifetime.

"If they tear down what I have done," he said, aloud, "men will soon forget what I've taught them."

Coming back to the present he said to his man, "An abrupt and bitter ending, Nicolas, to twelve years of devoted service."

The critical tongue of his servant could find no other answer for once than, "Yes, master."

The Moneyman turned to the guard who had been watching them with open curiosity. "Where do you hail from, my friend?"

"From your own country, lord. From Berri."

"Will they believe in Berri that Jacques Coeur has deserved this? Will they think he has been a bad servant to the King?"

The man shook his head stoutly. "No, lord, no! They will never think ill of Jacques Coeur."

"Adversity is sometimes a friend. It shakes a man out of his complacency and sets him to the doing of better things." He drew a gold coin from his pouch and handed it to the guard. "Consider this, my good friend, a token that you saw the Moneyman of France at one of the supreme moments of his life."

Nicolas, who was scarcely able to see over the bundles he was carrying, did not seem to agree with this. "Adversity has never been a friend to me," he declared. "Where are we to go now, master?"

"We are going to the house of an acquaintance whose name had better not be mentioned here. Come, Nicolas. I have a disinclination to stay within these walls. Let's start at once, even though I lack a hat."

"They," said Nicolas, tilting his head back in the direction of the rooms, "think they are going to present you with a hat. A green hat."

3

The house in the Rue Grenier sur L'Eau was lighted up as though for a ball when they arrived. D'Arlay, however, was supping alone in the hall and showing a good appetite over a dish of mutton chops and a *salade* of the crests and livers of chicken. He raised a flagon of wine when he saw Coeur enter and called to him in a cheerful voice, "You're just in time to drink a pledge with me."

"You seem in a mood for celebration," said Coeur, advancing into the long room until he stood beside the chair of his friend.

"I am. I accomplished something today which made me very happy. I sold this house at a figure more than double what it cost me."

"Then you drove a good bargain."

"I had no idea of selling until a man who reeked of newly acquired wealth called two days ago and asked if I wanted a buyer. He told me there had been no building done in Paris since we took the city back from the English, or very little. The city is filled with homeless people and prices have gone to the skies."

"It always happens during a war. Money changes hands. Those who had it before sell their houses and estates to those who made fortunes during the fighting. Jacques Coeur was the richest man in the world a year ago but what do you think he's worth today? The man you sold to was an army contractor, no doubt?"

D'Arlay nodded. "He made the carriages for the cannon." Then he smiled. "The man has a marriageable daughter who will have a very large dowry. Perhaps I should have married her and kept the house."

Coeur looked at him with an increased interest. "Do you mean that the sale was for that purpose?"

"Naturally. I intend to apply the money I receive to the debts on the family estates. It will reduce them sufficiently to keep the creditors content. Having done that much, I shall consider myself no longer under obligation to marry a rich wife. I shall be free to—to marry the one I want."

Coeur seated himself at the table. He looked at his friend with an air which expressed both reluctance and self-reproach. "It seems," he said, "that I've been responsible for raising another obstacle in your path. Two things happened today which leave us, you and me, in unenviable positions."

He proceeded to tell of the steps the King had taken and of the information D'Antenne had given him about Valerie. D'Arlay's face, as he listened, displayed a wide range of emotion: incredulity, anger, dismay, and, at the finish, a gloom which seemed all the deeper because of his earlier exhilaration. The only comment he made was that Valerie's plight was the work of his brother and Isabeau. They had been very secretive and had refused to tell him anything, even keeping her whereabouts from him. He added that he was sure she did not know they were acting now on their own initiative.

Coeur was inclined to agree with him on the last point but he said that he wanted to be convinced. They must find some way of getting in touch with her and acquainting her with the facts. If self-interest had not prompted her to willing participation, they must then arrange her escape. It was to discuss these points that he had come.

"I've been in a glow of satisfaction for hours!" said D'Arlay, with a sudden display of bitterness. "Ever since the sale was completed, I've been making plans for the future. I was sure that things at last were shaping themselves in the right direction." A pause ensued and then he continued in a lower tone, "Has it occurred to you, Jacques, that my bad fortune may offset yours? That—that you have the game in your bandon?"[1]

"You mean that I can now rely on assistance from Valerie?"

"Yes." D'Arlay nodded his head somberly. After a moment he said, "Yes," again. He had placed his hands on the edge of the table and had, apparently, found something about them worth a prolonged study.

"That thought occurred to me as soon as I heard what they had done. I want you to know that I dismissed it without any hesitation or regret. I've no intention of profiting by it. I came here tonight to discuss plans with you for getting her out of their hands while there's still time."

D'Arlay looked up at that. "From what you've told me, it's quite clear that nothing else will restore you to the King's favor."

"I know that. You're thinking me inconsistent, no doubt. It's not inconsistency and it's not any sudden surrender to a chivalrous instinct. I wish I could honestly claim that my present attitude springs from the highest motives. But, now that the crisis has been reached which I foresaw, I realize that I would never have been capable of carrying through the plan I made to meet it. For a reason, my dear Robin, that I didn't know existed before; and not one in which I can take any satisfaction. My pride!"

"Your pride?" D'Arlay's tone made it clear that he did not understand.

"You will have to bear with me while I indulge in a long explanation." Coeur said this in a tone from which he could not exclude a suggestion of the readiness he always displayed to discussing himself. No subject interested him more. He was prepared to talk about his own motives and mental reactions as though they belonged to someone else. He had even developed a habit of referring to himself in the third person. "This Jacques Coeur," he would say, or, "This unusual figure who has risen from the ranks of the people," or even, "I sometimes find it hard to understand Jacques Coeur myself."

"I realize," he began, "that I'm unfortunate enough to have been born ahead of my time. The men of two hundred years hence will be doing the things I do today. They will be thinking then as I think now. My spirit is imprisoned in this strutting, bloody, foolish age. Pity me, Robin; I am a man of hard business sense and vision and here I am, living in the age of Chivalry!

"I know that I'm regarded as mad and dangerous," he went on. "What do I care what they think? Does an eagle listen to the jackdaws chittering among themselves about him? But I do care what the men of my own kind, the men of the future, will think—and what they will say about me. I would trade some of the years that are left me for a look into the future and a glimpse at what the history books will record about me."

He had risen and was pacing up and down the room. "Jacques Coeur

[1] In his own hands.

is always willing to say when he has been wrong. He now avows that you were right at the start and he was wrong. He doesn't want it recorded in history that he regained his post with the King through petticoat influence. He wants to be remembered as Jacques Coeur the pioneer and not Jacques Coeur the pander." He continued his pacing, gesturing freely. "I've led the world along new paths. I've changed the whole face of commerce. I've seen visions of the future and have tried to let the people of this mad age benefit by them. If an ungrateful King destroys all that I've done, I'll find a way to start over again. And I'll build a new empire of trade which will cover, if not France, the rest of the world!"

When he stopped at the table he had regained his composure. "I leave in the morning for Bourges, Robin. I must prepare to meet the storm. I'm going to see to it that no gold is left in any of my shops and that all my ships keep out of French ports. If they break me, I must be ready to make a new start.

"In the meantime," he added, "I've learned where the girl is. I shall leave it to you to take whatever steps seem necessary. But before you do anything, make sure she hasn't been carried away by visions of power and wealth and ease. She is human, Robin, and mustn't be blamed too harshly if she feels disposed to follow the path of opportunity."

"I'm sure she hasn't yielded to selfish motives."

Coeur smiled. "You're a man of stanch faith, Robinet de Burey, but you haven't been at court as much as I have! Still, I too have a great fondness for the child. And so I hope you are right."

D'Arlay had risen to his feet in a fever of impatience. "Where is she?" he demanded. "Tell me so I can start to work at once!"

Coeur drew out the paper and handed it to him. D'Arlay unfolded it with eager fingers. He read aloud:

"The middle house of the three which back on the western wall."

"Do you know the house?" asked Coeur.

D'Arlay nodded his head. "There are three houses built against the wall of the Hôtel Saint-Pol. They're so conspicuous that everyone has wondered why they haven't been torn down. This couldn't refer to anything else."

"Can you get into the middle house?"

It was D'Arlay's turn to surrender to a theatrical impulse. "I will not only get in," he declared, "but I will get her out of there, even if it has to be done over the prostrate body of Charles of France!"

"The less we have of heroics," said Coeur, in a dry tone, "the better it will be for all concerned. Get her out of the place by all means but not over the body of the King. Not over any bodies at all, in fact. We're in a sufficiently dangerous position as it is. I commend to you, Robin, the exercise of complete discretion."

10

AFTER three hours of the most exacting preparation, Valerie's toilet was completed. Isabeau, satisfied with her finally, had departed. Looking from the rear window of her bedroom, the girl could see the gardens of the palace over the high stone wall and the maze of turrets and spires and bell towers with their multiplicity of whirling girouettes and flying buttresses which gave a suggestion of a child's fairyland to the Hôtel Saint-Pol. This, then, she said to herself, was the beginning. This was the start of a life of ease and luxury, perhaps also of power and responsibility; certainly a life of trouble and worry and humiliation, and always of pain.

She left the window and began to pace slowly about the room. It was necessary to walk with deliberation for she had a very long train. To turn so that the train followed as easily and gracefully as the tail of a mermaid, and without any agitation or careening or doubling over of the material, called for the utmost skill. There had to be a discreet reaching back of one foot, not attaining quite the proportions of a kick (which would have been highly vulgar), to guide the stately and shimmering flow into its appointed course. She found herself perfect in this most difficult feat of ladyship and felt a natural glow of satisfaction. If one has a task to do, there is always a sense of pride in doing it well.

The three hours had wrought a miracle in her appearance. In the first place a new way had been evolved of doing her hair which had seemed excitingly successful. It was allowed to curl closely and naturally on her forehead and was then drawn back from her ears (which were permitted to show—a most daring innovation) in a series of loose waves. It was piled rather high on the back of her head where it was held in place by a comb with the letter V picked out in diamonds, which had arrived the day before without any note or identification of the giver—not that any was needed. She wore no hennin at all, and this was a deliberate and rather frightening innovation in an age when the outward hallmark of feminine gentility was extravagance of headgear. It was hard to decide whether the resulting effect was one of naïveté or sophistication. It had been the hope of Isabeau, in fact, that it would partake of both qualities. Seeing herself in the mirrors which servants had held up around her, Valerie's eyes had lighted and a tinge of natural pink had appeared in her cheeks; for neither inner mood nor outside circumstance counts at such a moment.

Words are poor instruments to convey an adequate conception of her gown. It was like a phenomenon of nature, such as a blending of colors in the sky at sunset. As words are the only available medium, it must be stated that the costume consisted of an undergown of the cherry-colored material Jacques Coeur had selected for her with such discrimination. Breath-taking in the bolt, it took on a new magic when seen close-fitted to the neck and shoulders and tapering to a tight V on the back of the hand, and falling to the floor in the voluptuous abundance which has already been noted. There was a strange quality to this sun-ripened red material; for although it shimmered with the impeccability of newness, it suggested age also, as though patient yellow hands had worked on it endlessly, their labor culminating in this brief beauty like the bloom of a century plant.

Above this was draped an overgown of deep ivory velvet which seemed to catch and reflect some of the warmth of her skin and hair. It was high-waisted almost to an effect of pertness, resting with daring insecurity on the extreme tips of her shoulders and coming to a very low V in front. It then cut away sharply below the waist to give full play to the beauty of the cherry skirt. The oversleeves were of the velvet. They fitted the roundness of her arm most snugly at the shoulder but then fanned out until they achieved a fullness to match that of her skirt. The relaxing of an arm allowed the hem of the sleeve to touch the floor!

This ivory overgown, with its gay and impertinent originality of design, was diapered in a pattern of gold thread which twined about tiny rosebuds of the cherry material. Sewn along the edges was narrow ivory lace, so old and fragile it seemed like cobwebs enjoying a last moment of beauty before crumbling into dust.

Her pacing took a three-sided course, for the giant bed, Pepin the Short, jutted out so far from the wall that it cut the room into that shape. She was still awed by this majestice piece of furniture. That morning she and Guillaumette had measured it, using a folded sheet for the purpose. Valerie herself had scrambled up one of the massive posts and had taken a tumble on getting down, so that the accuracy of the measurement was open to some question. It showed, and was probably not far wrong, that the bed from floor to top of tester was fourteen and a half feet high. The lantern suspended from its ceiling had been removed at Valerie's insistence, for it had gone on causing curious shadows which generally took the form of heads adorned with crowns.

Doubts multiplied in her mind as the light of day diminished. It was growing dark quickly and she seated herself at the rear window to look out at the palace which was dissolving into sharply etched masses of black. Lights began to show in windows, winking on in such numbers that it looked as though the stars had come down from their high station and were clustering close to earth. As she watched, her doubts rose to a peak and she found herself several times on the point of rising as the instinctive first stage of flight. "I can't! I can't!" she repeated over and over again.

To add to her uncertainty and bewilderment there was the continued silence of Jacques Coeur. She had received no message of any kind from him. Did he know of the turn things had taken? Was he in the confidence of the King? During the weeks which had followed their sudden departure from the neighborhood of the abbey she had been reassured on this point many times by the Comtesse. But doubts still persisted in her mind. Did the Moneyman know that Charles of France was coming to share supper with her this night?

She was beginning to feel a repugnance for the queenly magnificence in which she was attired. Looking down at the rich folds of the cherry gown, she had a desire to take it between her fingers and tear it to shreds. The perfume, which Isabeau had artfully sprayed on every layer of clothing, made itself so evident with each move that she felt cheapened. It was a very special perfume, a combination of Hungary Water, which was innocently concocted from tips of rosemary distilled with aqua vitae, and a distillation from much farther east which was not innocent at all—an exotic scent with a base of musk. The result of this blending was perfect for the purpose; and, because of that, Valerie hated it.

The room was becoming dark. Guillaumette was in the next room but her mistress made no move to summon her and have the candles lighted. Valerie was welcoming the gloom as a friend, because she had no desire to be seen in this suspicious finery. She continued to watch the lights in the windows of the palace, wondering what the people there, the disdainful ladies and the ambitious gentlemen, would think if they knew. They would hate her, of course, and fear her because of the power she might attain, and they would do everything to make her lot difficult. "What are they talking about now?" she asked herself. "About me, perhaps. Are they planning all the things they will do against me?"

For several minutes she had been conscious of sounds. First there had been a rustling in the vines which covered in dark green the wall outside her window, but she had paid no heed to this, believing it was caused by birds. Now she heard a hint of cautious footsteps, first on the roof above her and then on the landing outside her door. Suddenly she began to feel an acute alarm. She was on the point of calling out to Guillaumette when a familiar voice spoke to her.

"Don't be alarmed, Valerie. Make no sound, I beg of you. I'm in enough danger of being discovered as it is."

It was D'Arlay. He had opened the door just sufficiently to make sure that she was alone in the room. He came in now and closed it softly behind him. Pausing beside a table to deposit a bundle he had carried attached to his belt, he remained there in a listening attitude for several moments.

"It seems reasonable to believe now that no one observed my somewhat irregular method of getting in. I climbed a vine on the side of the wall from a low section of the roof of the next house. There was danger I might be seen from the street."

So much emotion had been stirred in Valerie that for a moment she said nothing at all. Then, in a low tone, she asked, "What brings you here?"

"I came because Jacques Coeur was able finally to trace you. Both of us had been striving to learn your whereabouts since you left Jumièges so unexpectedly; but without any success at all until yesterday."

Her emotions had narrowed down to one, a sense of indignation. "Do you mean," she asked in a tense voice, "that my lord Coeur doesn't know what has happened since we left?"

"He has known nothing. My brother and his wife refused to tell us about you. It has been a maddening situation."

"I thought it strange I never heard from him. Then—he doesn't know I have seen the King?"

"He heard it yesterday for the first time."

"But," she asked, "why have they done this? I don't understand at all."

D'Arlay suggested that they seat themselves. "You see," he said, "Jacques Coeur had changed his mind. He decided not to go on. My sister-in-law and my brother didn't agree with him. It's quite clear now that they made up their minds at once to proceed without him and that they arranged the sudden departure from Jumièges so he wouldn't be able to communicate with you."

"Did my lord Coeur think I was acting with them willingly?" she asked, after a pause during which they had looked into each other's eyes with the utmost gravity.

He shook his head. "No. But he wanted me to make sure on that point first of all."

"And you?"

"Valerie," said D'Arlay, finding it impossible to give expression to the intensity of his feeling, "I knew from the first that you had been deceived."

Indignation was now giving way in her mind to a faint stirring of hope. Perhaps it would not be necessary for her to go on. Perhaps it would not be incumbent on her to see again that constrained man with his possessive eyes and greedy long nose. Then, as she remembered how far the arrangements had been carried, she gave up in despair.

"The King," she said, in a whisper, "will be here in half an hour."

D'Arlay sprang to his feet at once. "Then we have no time to lose. Can we be sure of the half hour? If so, I think it can be managed." Then he paused and looked down at her earnestly. "It's only fair to tell you that— that your success is assured if you go on. It's quite clear that he, the King, has capitulated. Everything that Agnes Sorel had is within your reach."

Valerie answered with lowered head: "Never from the first have I had any desire for that kind of life."

"No one could blame you if you decided to accept this—this glittering opportunity."

She looked up at that. "Wouldn't you blame me?"

There was a long pause. "My feelings are too much engaged to take an impersonal view," he said finally.

What she thought of this was not apparent for another idea had occurred to her, causing her to ask in an anxious voice, "But what of my lord Coeur? Will his interests suffer?"

"He insisted you were not to give that any consideration. He has been dismissed from his post at court. He's now on his way to Bourges to raise his defenses against them. It's probably too late to do anything for him.

But—he would refuse, in any case, to benefit himself by sacrificing you. He wants me to take you to Bourges where plans can be made for the future."

She had been holding her feelings in close check but at this point she lost control of them. "Please, help me to get away!" she said, looking up at him beseechingly. "I can't stay here now. The thought of it sickens me!"

"I came prepared to help you."

"But how?" Now that it was possible for her to give up, she was frantic with anxiety to leave. "This house is closely guarded. Do you think I could climb down the vines?"

"I'm afraid not. They were so loosened by my weight in climbing up that I was sure near the end I wouldn't get the whole distance. But there's a chance to reach the roof of a low wing next door. If—if you're ready to take a certain risk."

"Yes, yes! I'm ready for any risk."

"Then," he said, nodding in the direction of the bundle on the table, "you will find clothes there. You must be dressed as a man to take this way of escaping."

"I don't care! I would do anything to get away now."

She took the bundle and retired to a small room adjoining the one they were in. Anxiety put speed in her fingers and she was back in a much shorter time than he had expected. It was so dark that he could barely see her. This was just as well, for she said in a constrained tone, "They are a very poor fit."

"They'll serve to get you out of here. Come. We've little time left."

Valerie's courage showed signs of deserting her when they climbed out of a window in the roof and found themselves on a slate surface which sloped sharply. In front of them the wall of the deserted house stood straight up, shutting off all view in that direction. To the left they could see the twinkling lights of the palace, to the right the city, with no lights showing at all. Peculiarly enough no sounds reached them from the palace, but out of the darkness that was Paris came the beat of horses' hoofs and the grind of carriage wheels and the voices of men raised in song and laughter and blasphemy.

She shivered and said, "I'm certain I shall never be able to climb down from here."

D'Arlay reached out a hand to her. "It always looks harder than it is. We must work our way along until we come to a flat projection near the back of the house. From there we can jump to a lower roof of the next house."

"Is it a long jump?" she asked in a sudden panic.

He did not answer at once. "It may seem long at first glance. But it's quite easy once you make up your mind to it. When I was a boy I used to play with the son of one of the servants who was about my own age. He was called Philbert the Climber and he wasn't afraid of anything. I often saw him climb the wall of a building and he would take jumps so long that I would be afraid to watch. He said it was easy. All he did was close his eyes and say, 'Here goes poor Philbert—O Lord, guide his feet!'—and then leap."

"And did the Lord guide his feet?" she asked nervously.

"Always. I never knew him to be hurt."

"If we—survive the jump, what do we do then?"

"Helion has horses at a tavern around the corner. We must leave Paris tonight, of course."

He could detect a note of dismay in her voice. "Must I go in these clothes?"

"Yes. There will be barely enough time for us to get out before the gates are closed for the night."

Valerie sighed and said, "Then we had better start before my resolution fails me."

The flat space, from which they would find it necessary to launch themselves, proved to be so small that there was barely room for both of them to occupy it at once. Another building, on the palace side of the wall, made it impossible for them to see anything beyond. "That," said D'Arlay, "was a foundry for the repair of armor. Lately it hasn't been used, and it's occupied only by a large family of rats. I went all through it while investigating the chances of getting in and out of this house and I found the entrance through the wall which the King uses. It has been most cleverly devised." He paused to calculate the time. "Being the most punctual of men, I judge that our liege lord is in the act of reaching at this very moment for the spring which releases it."

Valerie was not listening. Holding tightly to his arm, she peered down into the darkness.

"It seems a long way. Is it as much as—twenty-five feet?"

"No, it's fifteen at the most. The darkness makes it seem more."

They stood side by side for several moments and then D'Arlay said, "It would be wrong if I told you there was no danger in this."

"I know there is."

"But it's our only chance. If there had been any other way, I would have taken it instead of this." He stopped and looked down at her as though anxious to watch how she would receive what he was going to tell her. Her face was almost completely in shadow. "There's something I must say to you first. I love you very much."

Apparently she had been taken by surprise, for he could see her head turn up quickly toward him. They were standing so close together that he felt a tremor in her arm. When she spoke it was in a hesitant voice. "I—I thought you did, my lord Robin. But I wasn't sure."

"It began the first time I saw you. I kept it to myself and tried not to let you see how I felt because of the obstacles which stood in the way. They seemed insurmountable then. The main obstacle was removed when you told me back there that you would come with me."

She said nothing but he knew there was a question in her mind. "There was another which I'm sure you knew about. I was under the necessity of marrying a rich wife in order to save the family estates. I've provided for payment of the most pressing debts and I consider myself relieved of any further obligation. Even if I hadn't sold the Paris house, I doubt if I would have been in a position after tonight to help my brother. It may be necessary for both of us to leave the country. If that should prove to be the case, you and I will be starting life all over again. There will be no obstacles left. Unless—unless the state of your feeling for me should be one."

There was a long moment of silence and then she said in a whisper, "I know of no obstacle."

D'Arlay took her hand and raised it to his lips. "There is no time," he said rapturously, "to tell you how happy I am. Are you ready?"

"Yes. I'm ready."

"Then close your eyes for a moment and say, 'Here go poor Valerie Maret and Robinet de Burey. O Lord, guide their feet!'"

2

The quarterly wage payments were being distributed to the domestic staff at the Hôtel de Burey. The seneschal had arranged the money in tiny piles of silver with slips of paper under each on which the name of the recipient and the amount were written. This was for the convenience of the Comtesse, who insisted on presiding but had such scant facility with figures that everything had to be ready for her.

The servants stood in a long line (with expectations pathetically high in contrast with the smallness of the sums to be received), and the mistress called out each name in turn. The receipt was acknowledged in every case with a stock phrase, "God and Our Lady bless you, sweet mistress." Isabeau usually had something to say to each, a morsel of praise, a sharp demand for better service during the next quarter, an admonition of a personal nature. Today, however, she had nothing to say. Her mind was elsewhere, for her hands fumbled with the coins as she absentmindedly turned them over.

Her thoughts ran in one direction entirely. "He has been to see me three times only in the past year. Has he stopped loving me? Does he think the past can be dismissed so lightly? Does he consider me like the willing wife of a hatmaker or a woman of the streets that he treats me this way?" She moistened her lips and looked straight ahead of her with unseeing eyes. "I'll never let him go! I'll not permit anything or anyone to come between us! Has he any idea of the lengths I'm prepared to go to hold him?"

She had a few coins only to distribute when the Comte entered and crossed the room slowly, motioning to the seneschal to withdraw.

"Will Madame be kind enough to finish at another time?" he asked.

Isabeau needed no more than one glance at his face to realize that something was wrong. She said in a sharp voice, "You will all leave the room." When the last of them had gone, she looked up at him apprehensively.

"Well?"

"She has run away!"

"Do you mean——"

"I mean your so-called cousin who might be a real daughter to your rascally Uncle Gilles from the evidence we now have of her baseness and ingratitude! She ran away a few minutes before the King put in his appearance. Never in all history has a golden opportunity been lost on such a narrow margin of time." He hawked viciously. "I have just come from court. Need I inform you that our liege lord was in a silent mood, staring down the length of his nose and saying not a word? Once his gaze met mine and I read there such an intensity of dislike that I knew the fortunes of the house of De Burey were due to experience the greatest decline in its history."

The hand of the Comtesse was trembling with a fury she was unable to control. "How did the ungrateful creature get away?" she demanded.

The Comte threw back his head and neighed unmirthfully. "She had assistance," he said. "I had the whole story from the mouth of the Damoiselle Henriette herself. A most romantic tale, my spouse! A vine-covered wall was scaled by her rescuer as though for an elopement. There followed a change of attire and the girl went away with him, her chastely slender legs encased in masculine hose."

"And who," asked Isabeau, in a whisper so low he could barely catch the words, "assisted her in getting away?"

"Who? Must I humiliate myself by naming him? Madame, it was my brother. He was seen getting to horse with her a block away. It was your one-time admirer who seems to have transferred his vagrant affections to this yellow-haired wench."

His wife's hands were busying themselves with the silver coins which remained in front of her, spreading them with restless fingers, building them up into new piles and immediately leveling them again. He was shocked at the change which had come about in her appearance. There was a heavy flush on her cheeks. Leaning forward to observe her more closely, he perceived that the tip of her nose was covered with fine red lines.

"What will the King do?" she asked, after a long pause.

"I wish I knew what is in his mind," answered the Comte gloomily. "The story will be hushed up in order to spare his feelings and on that account he will be limited in the punishments he can administer. The girl will vanish from sight and never be heard of again. They—Robin and the Moneyman—will see to that. As for Robin, I doubt if our liege lord will be able to touch him. He's a popular hero since he poked his sword into the ribs of the Burgundian and he couldn't be shoved into the Bastille without stirring up talk all over the country. The facts would come out then and our liege lord would cut a ridiculous figure. I don't believe he would fancy the role of jilted lover." The Comte paused for a moment of gloomy thought. "If the whole story reaches his ears, the brunt of his displeasure will be kept for Jacques Coeur. The layer of the golden eggs will be killed and plucked—and not so much as a feather will come our way, sweet spouse."

"The whole story will reach the King's ears!" promised Isabeau.

The Comte was wearing a new cloak of plum-colored velvet, one of extreme cut with yellow and vermilion sleeves so huge that they increased his width twofold, and so richly embroidered and embellished and overlaid with buttons and links of chain that he resembled an eastern potentate. This magnificent garment he slipped off his shoulders and dropped on the edge of the table. "How will I be able to pay for this absurd vanity," he asked, "if no more golden eggs are found in the nest?"

His wife did not seem to have heard him. "The girl must be punished!" she said in a low tone, as though talking to herself. "She must be made to suffer in every possible way! I shall have to think of means of hurting her." She paused and then went on in a voice which contained a small shred of satisfaction: "She is fond of Godefroy. It would cut her deeply if we sent him home on the ground of cowardly conduct."

The Comte would not agree to this. "The boy has just reached the stage where he'll be useful to me," he said. "In any case it's Robin who deserves to be punished most. It will be to the point if you find ways of paying him back for the ill turn he has done us."

Isabeau answered quietly, "I had no thought of letting him escape easily!"

The Comte sank into a chair and scowled at the wall. "As he is my own brother, I'm forbidden to wish his death by hanging or to see him stripped of all his goods and turned out to beg. I can't curse those who begot him because they begot me also; though it's now my belief they were giving less attention to results when they brought him into the world. But it would suit me well if the King's torturer could acquaint him with the fine frenzy caused by hot eggs under the armpits or a leg bone crushed in the brodequins. Is it too much to ask that he itch eternally with the emerods and suffer all his days with a running of the reins?" His imagination continuing to work, he went on to name such other satisfactions as occurred to him. "I hope he will have to dine all his days on flyblown forcemeat and have nothing but viscous wine to sup. May St. Gatien, the patron saint of innocents, turn the other way when the good Robin walks in Paris of nights. May his slumbers be an endless nightmare. May——"

"I," said Isabeau, "am not content to indulge in idle words. I'm interested only in punishments we can inflict ourselves." Even her voice had changed and become deep, uneven, unnatural. "That much satisfaction at least is left to us. I'm going to see to it that they are all treated as they deserve!"

The Comte was too unhappy to continue the conversation. He got to his feet, snuffling loudly, and left the room. His wife remained at the table for several minutes, staring down at her hands which lay motionless among the broken mounds of silver. Then she rose also and procured ink and a quill pen. She began to write.

She wrote three letters, inditing them with painstaking effort in the uneducated round hand of a child. Each note was identical: an invitation to the recipient to wait upon her at once to discuss a matter of the utmost importance. She then addressed them to Guillaume Gouffier, Pregent Kennedy, and Jeanne de Vendôme. At the top of each she wrote the word *Urgent* and underlined it three times.

"I think I see the way," she said aloud. "I shall make them suffer as no one has ever suffered before!"

11

THERE was a time when it was believed, particularly in the preparation of pieces for the theater, that the most romantic of situations had been achieved when a pretty woman was compelled by circumstances to don male attire. This is a delusion which disappears rapidly whenever put to the test. As a matter of fact nothing is more certain to dispel romance than the troubles and vexations which immediately arise.

The first hint of difficulty on this occasion came when the trio, after a brisk canter through dark streets, came to the Porte Saint-Michel at the exact moment the lieutenant in charge signaled with an uplifted hand for the gates to be closed. D'Arlay called to him in an urgent voice, "One moment, if you please, Monsieur Lieutenant!" while he fumbled in his pocket for the necessary credentials.

The officer was a little fellow, wearing a cloak with enormously puffed-out sleeves which made him look like a monkey in a lion's skin. Most fortunately he recognized this late-comer. "Sire d'Arlay!" he said, bowing low. "You're just in time. One second more and"—gesturing eloquently—"it wouldn't have been in my power to help you." He bowed again so that the plumes in his hat touched the ground. "I saw you fight the Burgundian and it would have gone against the grain to do you a discourtesy. Is the sword at your belt the one you used on that glorious occasion?"

D'Arlay nodded affirmatively. "I own no other, Monsieur."

"These are your servants?" After a perfunctory glance at the papers, the officer let his eyes pass quickly over the two figures behind D'Arlay. Then, with what seemed almost a jerk, he brought them back to rest speculatively on Valerie. He raised his eyebrows and sidled over beside D'Arlay.

"When one stands guard at the gates of Paris," he whispered, "one sees things, my lord D'Arlay. How many times have I perceived bright eyes staring out from behind the closed curtains of carriages which were supposed to be empty! And the apple-cheeked little creatures who come in on the tail end of carts, looking for chances to better themselves! And the muffled-up ladies going out who prove to have beards when you take a look! But—*tcha, tcha,* Sire d'Arlay! Why do you think it necessary to put this one into leggings? No one can mistake her for what she is—at least no one as observant as I am of the—of the differences."

As they heard the gates clang to behind them, D'Arlay leaned back and spoke to Valerie. "He saw through your disguise at once. I'm afraid we're going to run into plenty of difficulty. Not even these ugly clothes Helion got for you—I left the selection to him as I was busy reconnoitering the ground, and I crave your pardon for the shoddiness of his choice—can conceal the fact that your face is lovely and that your legs, instead of being muscular, are undeniably pretty."

"My cloak comes to my ankles when I'm standing. I could wear a patch over one eye and put some stain on my face. But—will there be need for it? Surely I'm to wear proper clothes now that we're safely out of Paris!"

D'Arlay shook his head. "The King may decide to have you followed. It would be an absurd thing for him to do under the circumstances, but a wound to the pride is a great incitement to folly. We must ride hard and fast until we are well out of reach. Certainly it won't be safe for three or four days to stop long enough to find clothes for you. And can you think of any surer way of giving them a clue to our direction than a tailor who has supplied an outfit for a lady disguised as a man?"

It was clear that Valerie was unhappy over the situation but she said nothing more at the time. They rode until one o'clock through a light drizzle and then decided to spend what was left of the night at a roadside inn. She insisted on helping Helion with the horses and took the precaution of using a back door on entering. The late roisterers in the common room at the front thus had no chance to make the same discovery as the lieutenant of guards.

Fearing a hue and cry, D'Arlay had decided they must be up at dawn. As he and Helion were dressing hurriedly by the light of a very small candle, a tap came on the door between the two rooms. In response to his invitation to enter, Valerie opened the door a few inches.

"I am sorry to disturb but I—I find myself in a most distressing position."

D'Arlay buttoned his outer tunic at the neck, made sure that his servant was equally well along with his toilet, and then said, "Come in and tell us about it."

"I cannot, my lord. I am—only partly dressed. When I put on these clothes yesterday I found there were things I didn't understand about men's attire. There was no time then to ask questions and so I did the best I could. But I knew, as soon as I stepped out to join you, that there were things I had failed to do."

"I think I know what the difficulty is," said D'Arlay, in a completely serious voice. "The solution will be found in a belt of the strongest linen which you are supposed to wear next your skin or over the shirt if you prefer it that way. You have such a belt?"

"Yes, my lord. I have the belt in my hand."

"Have you noticed that there are a dozen or more holes along the bottom of the belt?"

"Yes, I noticed that."

"You will find a corresponding number of holes in the top of your leggings. Now, all you have to do is to take the short thongs of leather, which are usually kept in a small bag attached to the belt, and draw each one through a hole in the belt and then through the nearest hole in the leggings, and knot it. The leather thongs are called 'points,' as perhaps you know."

"But, my lord, there were no points in the bundle you gave me yesterday!"

"It's no wonder then," said D'Arlay gravely, "that you suffered from lack of that most necessary sense of security." He looked accusingly at Helion, whose expression was an acknowledgment of guilt. "It seems that Helion forgot to put any points with the bundle. I'm tempted to punish him by giving all his points to you and letting him spend the day in the expectation of disaster from which you suffered yesterday. Still, we must be sensible and so I'll divide my points and his into three equal shares and we'll all have to do the best we can until a more adequate supply can be secured. As you will be short on points, it will be advisable to draw them up as far as they'll go and then knot them tightly. Only in that way will your hose fit the legs snugly and without wrinkles."

"Thank you, my lord. I'm sorry to be so much trouble."

All the difficulties had not been solved, however. It developed a few minutes later that the belt could not be taken in enough to fit her waist comfortably. It was handed through the partly opened door and additional holes were punched in it. Then, in a most apologetic voice, she acknowledged that her shoes were too large and were threatening to drop off her feet with each step. The solution decided upon after some discussion was to sew bands of felt inside the heel and instep, and Helion was dispatched to the kitchen to obtain the necessary supplies.

When she finally emerged from her room, she looked so trim that D'Arlay's worries of the previous evening returned. "You're bound to attract too much attention," he said. "We must take other precautions before we risk showing ourselves again at an inn."

Valerie was in a subdued mood when they started out. She said very little and gave a strained smile when he rallied her on her lack of spirits. "I had a dream last night," she said. "It was a very cruel dream and I'm still depressed by it."

"Tell me what it was," he urged. "I'll expound it for you as Joseph did the dreams of Pharaoh."

She shook her head. "I don't want to talk about it yet. I'll tell you later."

The weather had cleared. They took to the road as the sun forced its way above the horizon. The gray of the sky turned to blue and there was a pleasant promise of warmth in the air. It was such a perfect morning, in fact, that her spirits began to lift. When they had been an hour on the road, she surprised herself by singing a few bars from a popular song.

For the sake of appearances D'Arlay was riding in the lead. Because in her improved mood she desired companionship, she set her horse to a gallop and came caracoling up beside him.

"This is the loveliest day I've ever known," she called.

D'Arlay had been thinking the same thing, although his sentiments were not inspired by the weather. He noted with approval the ease of her carriage and the lightness of her hand on the reins. The pressure of the air on her cheeks had brought color to them and her eyes were bright. She had gone abruptly to the other extreme in mood. She laughed and chattered and indulged in snatches of song and even gave him an imitation of Charles, rubbing a finger slowly down her nose and saying, "I come, not as King of France, but as a man——"

They were riding together now, their horses tossing manes in close accord. She looked across at him and smiled in sheer good spirits.

"You seem quite gay and happy this morning," he said.

"And haven't I the best of reasons?"

"Perhaps. I would be more disposed to feel as you do if I could read the future."

"I've forced myself to forget the future. I'm living in the present." She raised her free arm and gestured about her. "It's a lovely day. I can feel the breath of the south already. There are no signs of pursuit. Most of all I'm beginning to realize that it's true."

"What is true?"

"That—that I'm free of a shadow under which I've lived for more than a year."

He waited to see if she had anything to add and then asked her, "Have you no other reason for being happy today?"

Her eyes had become fixed on the road ahead. "Well—I ride in good company."

"That's better. But—it isn't the answer I had hoped for."

They were approaching a turn from which the road swung sharply downward and for a few minutes it was necessary for both to keep a careful watch ahead.

D'Arlay took up the conversation then. "It's only with the greatest difficulty," he said, "that I keep my arms to their regular tasks. Every moment since we started they've been demanding that I allow them to reach out and drag you over here into this saddle with me. There has been a madness of delight in me which has grown with each second. I'm filled with such a tumult that I—that I don't know how I control the impulse to shout aloud. Valerie, I'm so happy that if Charles of France were here with us I would slap his face with my glove in sheer exuberance!"

He sobered abruptly. "I'm weak at dissembling," he added. "If I allow myself to continue thinking like this, it will show in my eyes, in my manner. Everyone we meet will know you are a lady and that I love you. I must discipline myself, and I must begin now. We are three men riding together.

Helion is unmistakably my servant. Because of the clothes he chose for you, people will think you a servant also. I must treat you as one when people are around, and so I must avoid slips by maintaining the same fiction when we are alone. You see the good sense of this, I trust?"

Valerie watched him as he went through this difficult explanation. Smiling to herself and lowering her eyes, she answered in a respectful voice, "Yes, master."

"Of course," he said, "there's no one within miles of us at the moment and so it might be we could postpone the start of this—this most unpleasant pretense."

"Is it, then, no longer necessary for me to drop back at once and spend the rest of the day in the company of the sprightly Helion?"

"No," answered D'Arlay with a smile. "But it might be easier for me if you did."

Darkness caught them that night far from any roadside inn. They were lucky enough to sight almost at once a small farmhouse close to the road. To their dismay, however, D'Arlay's vigorous knock on the door was without results. No lights appeared and they could hear the loud clang resounding hollowly through empty rooms.

"The place seems to be deserted," said D'Arlay in a disgusted tone, after a last angry effort with the knocker.

"There's a barn behind it, master," said Helion, who had been investigating.

D'Arlay decided in favor of the barn. "It will be easier to break into," he said, "and it will have straw or hay for us to sleep on instead of bare floors."

The barn proved to be a ramshackle affair, with moonlight showing through gaps in the roof and the clay floor covered with a low mound of musty hay. Helion busied himself with the horses, tethering them in a corner and producing fodder for them from the feed-bags. Valerie and D'Arlay seated themselves together in the center. There had already been suspicious rustlings in the hay and, having no liking for rats, she wrapped her cloak carefully about her feet and ankles.

"And now," she said, "I can't postpone any longer the telling of my dream."

"Was it an unpleasant one?"

"It was about the Comtesse." Valerie was speaking in a repressed tone. "She came to me and told me something. I could read both hate and triumph in her face. What it was she told me I can't remember but of this I'm sure—it had to do with the future and it frightened me so much that I wakened up in terror and found that I was crying out, 'No, no!'"

"If you remember the rest so clearly, you must surely have some recollection of what she said."

Valerie shook her head. "My mind is blank on that point. It must be that she's planning some—some form of revenge for what we have done."

"That I can believe. But, Valerie, you mustn't worry about it. After all, what can she do? Neither of us, I most sincerely hope and trust, will ever see her again. But tell me more about the dream. Where did it take place?"

"In a very large room with a high ceiling and, it seemed, hundreds and hundreds of candles. There was a tapestry on one wall, representing the death of Absalom in the tree——"

"Was there," he asked, in an excited tone, "a drinking horn on a table under the tapestry?"

"Yes." Valerie nodded slowly. "I seem to remember that it had a silver eagle on top and that it stood on the feet of a bird."

D'Arlay was quite excited now. "That is the *Chambre de Charlemagne* at the Hôtel Saint-Pol. Have you ever seen it?"

She shook her head. "No. But it was very clear in my dream. There were many people about but they weren't close enough for me to see their faces."

"And Isabeau came to you in the *Chambre de Charlemagne* and gave you this message you can't remember?" He paused in thought. "It may be she's planning some sort of revenge which has to do with the King. Why otherwise would you see her in his chamber of which you have no waking knowledge at all?"

Valerie asked in a low voice, "Will she, Isabeau, be angry enough to go to such lengths?"

"I am sure"—nodding his head gravely—"that she'll be angry enough to do anything against us. She'll do anything that lies in her power."

They sat in an unhappy silence for several minutes. Then Valerie asked suddenly, "Did you love her very much?"

He nodded his head reluctantly. "I loved her so much when I was young that nothing else counted. Then she married my brother; and after that it was a sharp passion I felt, an angry passion, a determination to hold something of what I had lost. Gradually it cooled and then"—he smiled grimly—"then she had become a—an obligation from which I couldn't escape. I can tell you in all honesty, Valerie, that for many years my only desire was to break the bond." He paused and turned to face her anxiously. "I am ready to swear a solemn oath that at no time, not even when I was a boy and believed her the sun and the moon and the stars of my existence, did I feel for her the love that I have for you!"

2

There was still no sign of pursuit the next morning but, taking no chances, they rode long and hard. Valerie wore a patch over one eye and she never mounted or dismounted when there were spectators, for fear a lack of masculine ease would show or the feminine turn of a leg. She kept her cloak wrapped about her, which proved uncomfortable as the temperature rose with each league they rode southward.

This went on for two days more. The same discomforts had to be borne; but now a new one, and a harder to endure, made itself apparent—the lack of water. The inns at which they stayed were for the most part primitive, particularly in respect to bathing facilities. It was an accepted rule of the road, in fact, that travelers waited for baths and for the washing of their clothes until they reached their destinations. Argue and cajole as they might, they obtained no better than small basins of lukewarm water for the first nights of their southward flight.

On the fifth day Valerie could not resist the chance offered by a shaded bend in a stream close by the road. She reined in her horse.

"There are none about," she said. "Would it delay us too much if I took a bath there?"

D'Arlay looked doubtfully at the stream which flowed swiftly by. "I fear it's deep. Can you swim?"

Valerie smiled. "You seem to forget that nearly all my life has been spent on the road. I never bathed in a tub until I was sent to live with the Comtesse. In fact, my lord, I have some recollection of bathing at this very spot a few years ago when we were on our way to Tours. I—I swim with some skill."

D'Arlay stood guard on the road above the pool and Helion took up his station below. They knew when she plunged into the water by the loud gasp with which she proclaimed its unexpected coldness. It must have been very cold, in fact, for she returned fully dressed within a few minutes, looking refreshed but a little blue.

The bath had not been a complete success. "I found it very distasteful to dress again," she said, looking down at her muddy tunic and hose with a shudder. "I can't abide such dirtiness any longer. I must find a way to wash them tonight or my flesh will shrink from the need to get into them again tomorrow." She went on with some haste to explain herself. "You'll think this strange from one who lived so long on the road. It's because of what I had to endure then, my lord, that I have this feeling now. To be wet and unclean makes me think I am back once more in that kind of life, that the past has—has overtaken me. Something happens inside me. I have such distaste for these clothes that I feel I am imprisoned, body and soul." She looked up at him in an appeal for understanding. "I hope I don't sound ungrateful and hard to please."

"Tonight you shall have hot water to wash your clothes," vowed D'Arlay.

And water she had, a large and ancient tub filled to the top with it. It was steaming hot. Only the proffer of a heavy silver coin had reconciled the landlord to such an unheard-of luxury.

When D'Arlay made his way late in the evening to the one bedroom the inn boasted for the accommodation of guests, he found that Valerie had been making good use of the hot water. A line was strung across the space from corner to corner and on it her whole wardrobe was hanging limply like a file of scarecrows on a windless day. She had donned their common spare cloak in the meantime but, as the evening was unseasonably warm, had allowed it to drop about her waist. He caught the merest glimpse of a white shoulder as she hurriedly struggled into the cloak on the opening of the door.

"I regret profoundly that it has been necessary to turn the room into a washhouse," she said.

He sat down on one side of the bed and regarded her with a serious air. Valerie looked up at him and smiled, at the same time giving her head a shake.

"You are so very serious-minded, my lord Robin," she said.

He acknowledged that this was true.

"You allow yourself to worry about things when it isn't necessary."

"Yes. That also is true."

"And now tell me, what are you so concerned about at the moment that you haven't smiled since you came into the room?"

"I'm concerned about what we're to do tonight." He turned and indicated the bed, which was a truly enormous one. "Do you know that this is the only bed in the inn?"

"I hear the landlord say so." She did not seem disturbed. In fact, she was making no effort to hide the twinkle of amusement in her eyes.

"We must stay in this room, the three of us. Helion and I would gladly sleep outside the door but to do so would be to let everyone know you don't dress your sex."

"But I could sleep outside the door while you and Helion occupy the bed. As I'm the younger servant, it wouldn't seem amiss. Or unusual."

"Do you think I could sleep at ease, knowing you had the hard floor for your portion?"

"But what other course is open? Are you willing to agree that we all share the bed?"

D'Arlay shook his head emphatically. "No! No! Do you think I would ruin the reputation of the woman I love?"

"Who would know?"

"Stories of the kind get out somehow. No, Valerie, any other course but that."

Valerie indulged in a puzzled frown. "We must get through the night. If we don't do the one, we must do the other."

D'Arlay was sure he had the solution. "You shall occupy the bed while Helion and I sleep on the floor beside it."

Valerie gave her head another shake. "If it became known that we had spent the night together in one room, would anyone believe we had been so—so extremely conventional? Is honor satisfied when you sleep five feet from me instead of two? Is there innocence in bare boards and sin in a mattress?"

D'Arlay looked more worried than ever. "Then," he said, "I see no answer to this riddle at all."

What decision they would have reached if left to themselves can only be conjectured for at this moment a knock came on the door. D'Arlay opened it to find the landlord on the threshold with two dusty travelers beside him. The keeper of the inn bobbed his head in an excess of apology.

"There are more guests," he said. "It is a difficulty, lord. I must not turn them away; and this is the only bed I have. It is intended for five, lord." He lowered his voice for D'Arlay's ear alone. "They are worthy merchants who are going to the spring fairs in the south. They will be humble. They know their place and won't intrude on you more than is necessary."

"Can a man intrude further than to share your bed?" demanded D'Arlay.

He looked at the new arrivals without any effort to conceal his feelings. They were an oddly assorted pair. One was in his middle years and had succeeded in growing fat without achieving any of the benevolence of appearance or the jollity of manner which can mitigate avoirdupois. He looked vicious and grasping and inexpressibly vulgar. The other was small and thin and as active as a monkey. He had close-set eyes and black hair sprouting from ears and nostrils and on the back of his hands. There was a certain similarity about their clothes which had been gaudy and pretentious when new but now were soiled and sadly out of shape.

"I am a poor man, lord," insinuated the landlord. "I can't afford to turn away guests with money in their pockets."

D'Arlay darted a quick glance in Valerie's direction. She was keeping her back turned and he believed that he saw her shake as though with distress or inner laughter. After watching her for several moments he became convinced that it was the latter. "If that is how she feels," he thought with a sense of resentment, "why should I strive to find a way out of this dilemma?" It had not yet occurred to him that the arrival of these two unprepossessing guests had provided them with the solution of their problem, that the addition of two strange bedfellows would preserve her reputation.

He said to the landlord: "We rise at daylight. Otherwise I would insist that these new guests of yours leave before us. To save time, it's our intention to sleep in our clothes. They must be content to do the same."

The fat man said in a hearty voice: "That's entirely to my liking. I haven't been out of my clothes for ten days."

His point won, the landlord made a discreetly hasty exit. The smaller of the two stalked into the room with complete self-confidence. He grinned like a monkey and pointed a finger at the clothesline.

"You should feel at home here, Old Guts," he said to his companion. "Do you care to give a free exhibition of your skill? Or does it seem to you the rope is a trifle thin for a dancer of your weight?"

The fat man emitted a snort of dissent. "It's true enough, King Zoser, that I've taken on a pound or two. But when I step on a rope, I still have no more heft than a soul winging its way to paradise. I could take this rope, flimsy as a woman's virtue though it seems, and do a trick pavane or a back handspring or even a quarter-time mince. With or without music."

He laid a hand on one end of the line as though prepared to demonstrate the truth of what he had said. D'Arlay interposed hastily, "There will be no ropedancing here, if you please."

The fat man desisted at once with complete good nature but his companion was not so amenable. He scowled at D'Arlay and then turned his attention again to the articles of clothing strung on the line.

"You couldn't fit your long legs into these," he said. "They must belong to that small measure of ale over there in the corner. What's wrong with him that he has to be so particular about what he wears?"

"If we are to begin with questions," said D'Arlay shortly, "I have some to ask which you might find embarrassing to answer."

His realization that the newcomers were merchants, as the landlord had said, but that they purveyed entertainment and not goods, made D'Arlay think of demanding after all that they be sent away. When he whispered to Valerie what he proposed to do, however, she shook her head.

"No," she whispered, still finding it hard to control her amusement, "I think they may belong to the Coquille. They could do us a lot of harm."

"This is no laughing matter."

In the meantime the corpulent ropedancer had started to take off his shoes, sitting on the floor to do so. As he removed each he beat the mud from it on the side of the bed. Then he stretched himself out at full length on the mattress and gave vent to a contented snuffle.

The small one swung a bundle from his back to the floor and sat himself down beside it. It contained his stock in trade and he proceeded to take each article out in turn: a selection of wands, half-a-dozen balls, a leather cone marked with cabalistic signs, several knives, a cloth serpent with spring joints, a black silk cloak. After giving each the most careful examination he returned it to the bag, making sure it went back into its appointed place. By doing this he succeeded in putting himself into a complacent humor again.

"I'm young at my trade, Old Guts," he said, "but no one can say that I'm not good. Do you know a juggler as skilled as I am? Have you ever seen a saltimbanco with as many tricks?"

The ropedancer flexed his huge legs luxuriantly. "Can you keep six knives in the air at once?" he demanded.

There was a moment of silence. "I can keep four."

"I knew a man in the Low Countries who could do six, and never make a mistake."

The small man's temper flared up like a dry bulrush when thrust into coals. His beady black eyes snapped.

"So! You dribbling mooncalf, you great gobbet of *lard de carême!* You knew a man who could keep six in the air? It's a lie! You want to buy flutes, do you? I know a man who's going to feel my knife in his gizzards."

In an instant they were at it hammer and tongs. The little conjurer danced up and down in fury, screaming foul epithets. The fat man sat up in bed and bawled insults back at him.

D'Arlay took the juggler in hand and gave him a vigorous shake. "There's a limit to our patience," he said angrily. "Get to bed without more ado."

King Zoser subsided at once and gave D'Arlay an impudent grin. "Just as you say, Lord High-Sniffer. But I've got to do my flex first."

He walked to a spot in front of the one window (which was clamped down tight) and proceeded to contort his body in various ways. He held out each hand in turn and exercised the fingers for minutes at a time. He rolled his arms, twisted his neck, thrust his chest in and out with loud expulsions of breath, and cracked his joints with a sound like branches breaking in a storm.

The ropedancer shook his head at D'Arlay when the latter showed an intention of stopping this performance. "He has to go through it twice a day, lord. It keeps his muscles supple so he can do his tricks."

"It's true," whispered Valerie. "I know it because we often traveled in the company of such as these."

The juggler, his exercising finished, stretched himself out on the bed beside the ropedancer. Helion took his place on the other side of the fat man and seemed to fall asleep immediately. D'Arlay looked down at the small amount of space left and whispered to Valerie, "This will be like consorting with thieves or sleeping in a pig wallow. And yet it must be done. I'll sleep facing them and you take the outside."

After all five had settled into their places there were several minutes of silence, broken only by the loud breathing of Helion. Then the fat man began to snicker. "I'm reminded of a tale I heard once," he said. "It seems there were three people met at an inn, a hatter, a high toby, and a harlot. The hatter was on his way to a fair, just as we are. The high toby had slit the throat of a lagbelly merchant in Paris and was on a safety sweat. The harlot—— Well, I need not go into *her* reasons. The inn, as it happened, had one bed only, even as this one——"

"Spare our ears!" said D'Arlay. "I don't want to hear another word out of you, rogue, or I shall be compelled to wind this rope around your neck and teach you a new kind of dance."

The fat man said sulkily, "I thought only to speed your lapse into sleep with a merry tale, one to be repeated profitably to friends or whispered into the ear of a mistress like grace before meat." He twisted his bulk over on the other side, making the bed creak, and in a few minutes had forgotten his pique in slumber.

Realizing that it would be unwise on many counts to fall asleep himself, D'Arlay summoned up a train of reflection well calculated to keep him awake. He began for the hundredth time to speculate on what would happen as a result of Valerie's flight. He had no doubt that his own part in it would become known. He would have to leave the country. That would lose him his well-loved domain of Arlay but he would not be left destitute. There was plenty of gold to provide a start in some other part of the world. He went over in his mind the countries where sanctuary might be sought: Navarre, Spain, Portugal, Italy, Scotland, the Low Countries. When he reached the strip of Baltic country which housed the Hanseatic League he paused, for he had heard that fortunes were to be made there. In that far northern land he might still act in concert with Jacques Coeur.

An hour passed. The snoring of the three sleepers had merged into a steady antiphonal chorus. D'Arlay, who had not changed position, was inclined to believe that Valerie was still awake but he could not be sure until she said in a hesitant whisper, "My lord Robin?"

"Yes."

"Do you think he—King Zoser, the small, dark one—suspected?"

"He looked at you closely but I don't believe he saw anything wrong."

"I'm not sure. I could feel those eyes of his on me and it made me most uncomfortable. Do you think we should rouse Helion and get away while they're sleeping?"

"No, we would give ourselves away if we did."

There was a long pause. Then she whispered again, "My lord Robin?"

"Yes."

"Was ever a lady in such a position before?"

"I—I think it unlikely."

"Is it proof that I'm not a lady, after all, that I can feel amused over my plight? I'm so well accustomed to men like—like this King Zoser and the fat one that I don't seem to mind them very much."

He felt her shake as though she found it hard to keep from laughing. He was seized suddenly with the same desire and checked it with the greatest difficulty. "We must be careful," he whispered, "or we'll waken the others."

"Just imagine," she whispered back, "what the Comtesse would think and say if she knew!"

Her mood changed then with the unexpectedness he had already observed in her and which would always keep him, as she put it herself later, "trying to jump through hoops." He heard her give a deep and unhappy sigh.

"I've brought so much trouble to you and to my lord Coeur also."

"You must remember that it was he who began this." He stopped to make sure that all three of their bedfellows were still contributing to the chorus. "Try to get some sleep now as we shall have to get away earlier than we first planned."

"It will be much better if I stay awake."

In spite of her good intentions she fell asleep after all. His first intimation of it was when she ceased to toss and turn. Then he detected a broken rhythm to her breathing which turned gradually into an even volume of pleasant sound not unlike the purring of a kitten. He smiled to himself in the dark. "Now I must stay awake without fail."

A wave of happiness passed over him as he became conscious of the pressure of her shoulder against his. "It will soon be my right," he thought, "to hold her in my arms, to hear every night this sweet purring of content close to my ear!"

A more rosy note injected itself into his consideration of the future. The gold that he possessed, all of it safely stowed away, would be sufficient to assure them comfort wherever they went. His thoughts reached at last a land of everlasting enchantment where he and Valerie lived together, counting what they had lost as small. He pictured a white house on the side of a hill, from which perhaps the spires of the Eternal City could be seen, a road dead white in the sun winding down from it; the sound of children's voices in an olive grove back of the house. It might be, he said to himself drowsily, that adversity had been the prod needed to set his feet in the direction of happiness. . . .

The first light of dawn was showing through the window when he wakened. Valerie was lying in his arms, her head pressed against his cheek. The night had been warm and the cloak she wore had slipped off. He knew this because the shoulder resting on his right arm was bare and his other hand touched her elbow. He reached out cautiously with his left hand and found the cloak at the level of their knees. Drawing it up with the greatest care, he draped it over her. Then he sat up in bed and gave her shoulder a tug.

Valerie stirred at once. She drew a hand across her eyes and then looked quickly in the direction of the window. He heard her say in a horrified whisper, "I've been asleep!" It was not until she had raised herself to a sitting position that she discovered he was also awake.

They stared at each other, her eyes full of self-reproach. "I'm sorry, my lord Robin!" she whispered. "My only excuse is that we were long hours in the saddle yesterday. I was more tired than I realized."

"I hope you slept well."

She nodded. "I must have slept soundly and well, for I find myself completely rested."

"Then," thought D'Arlay exultantly, "her head did not find my arm an alien resting place! She came to me in her sleep as naturally as though she knew she belonged there!"

He was amazed to find how fresh she looked. Enough light came through the window for him to see that her eyes were wide open and that there was even a slight tinge of pink in her cheeks.

Valerie drew the cloak tightly about her and then put a foot to the floor. "If my lord Robin will be good enough to turn his head," she whispered, "I shall dress myself at once."

3

The morning of the seventh day found D'Arlay convinced that it would now be safe to change their traveling arrangements. They had spent the night at a large and pretentious inn where they had been allowed the use of three rooms. D'Arlay's was a large room with a hearth of its own and a towering armoire carved with the arms of a noble family (he could not be sure which family it was) and with ochre daubed on for background.

He was breakfasting there most substantially on a grilled fish and choice white bread, Helion acting as go-between with the kitchen, and Valerie standing behind his chair to anticipate his wants. The sun had climbed well above a ridge of hills in the east and was pouring cheerfully into the room. The fish was excellent, the wine cool. When Helion left the room, he took advantage of the chance to give her a more personal greeting.

"It's going to be a pleasant day for riding, my loved one."

She did not answer immediately. It was in a low tone that she finally said, "Yes, my lord Robin."

Laying down his knife but not turning in her direction at once, he allowed himself to say some of the things which he had been suppressing with great difficulty.

"You must have realized that I've been existing under an almost unbearable strain. To see you, to have you near me, and to be unable to tell you how much I love you!" To his own surprise he found himself giving voice to a rush of words which actually verged on the poetic. "I swear by God above me, and all the saints on the calendar, and all the shining angels with silver wings in heaven, that I love you more than any man has ever loved a woman since Adam's eviction! Even in those ill-fitting clothes that my dull, unfeeling clod of a servant selected for you, even with a patch over your eye and a deliberate dab of mud on your chin, you are the loveliest creature in the whole world."

"Aren't you breaking your own rule, my lord Robin?"

"I am!" He spoke with emphasis, even a trace of violence. "It was a foul rule, one that could be justified only by the peculiar circumstances in which we found ourselves. But now, by good St. Martin, it's no longer necessary! It's certain we're not being followed. I wanted to be sure in my mind, and now there can no longer be any doubts. And that means we have no further need for such rules. It means we can set about getting you proper clothes at once. It means——"

He turned in his chair then, expecting to find her as pleased as he was himself. Instead he found that she was wearing an artificial smile in the hope, obviously, of hiding her real feelings.

"Valerie!" He got to his feet and reached out to capture her hands. "You're not well? Has anything happened?"

"I had the same dream last night," she said, forcing herself to speak. "She came to me again, the Comtesse, and said the same things to me. She was wearing the same dress. I still can't remember what she told me but I know I was left with as much fear as before—fear for you and my lord Coeur as well."

"Could you see any of the others in the room this time?" he asked, after an uncomfortable pause.

She shook her head. "No. They were all as vague as the first time."

"You don't believe that it's Isabeau who wants to warn you of some danger?"

"No, no!" There was an almost fierce emphasis in her voice. "She comes to threaten me. She makes it clear how much she hates me. If the dream is a warning, it comes from—from another source."

"Is there anything more you can tell me about it?"

She wrinkled her brow in concentration. "One figure began to step forward. I was waiting anxiously to see who it was—and then the dream ended!" She said nothing more for a moment and then she began again in urgent tones: "We mustn't delay a moment! Much as I would like to get rid of these clothes, I can't stand the thought of waiting that long. We must get to Bourges and warn my lord Coeur. And then we must get away ourselves, far away—as far and as fast as we can!"

D'Arlay said, "It shall be as you wish, my heart." As Helion entered the room at that moment, he gave instructions that the horses were to be brought out at once and the landlord paid. Helion, looking surprised and not too pleased at this prospect of more hard riding, left the room. His master turned back to Valerie who had not succeeded in reaching a calmer state in the meantime.

"Where do you want to go after we leave Bourges?" he asked.

"To Spain, to the Indies, to Cathay! Anywhere, my lord Robin, if it's far enough away from *her* and the evil she's plotting against us!"

"And you're ready to go with me?"

She started to speak but changed her mind. Her eyes dropped and she frowned thoughtfully. Finally she looked up at him again. "If you want an answer to that, I think you should word the question differently."

It was his turn to frown. "I don't understand."

"I couldn't go with you except as your wife. So far I haven't heard you mention the word marriage."

"But"—he was both surprised and startled—"I've made it clear that I'm deeply in love with you."

"But isn't it true, my lord Robin, that the great gentleman who seduces a village maid lets her think that he loves her?"

D'Arlay looked seriously disturbed. "The point is well taken. I've been at fault. But it seemed to me that you couldn't fail to know what I meant."

"Robin," she said, addressing him thus for the first time, "you're a member of a very old family. You're a landowner in your own right and a great knight. As for me—no one knows who I am. I'm still no better in point of fact than the daughter of a strolling actor. When there is this difference in our stations, things can't be taken for granted as between equals. Not, at least, by me. I must always wait until you are ready to tell me what is in your mind."

"What is in my mind now," he declared, "is that I never want to be parted from you. I count all time lost until I can take you to a priest and have the marriage vows pronounced over us."

"We can't spare the time," said Valerie sadly. "Not even for that!"

Helion put his head in at the door to announce that the horses were ready.

No time thereafter was lost. Valerie would remain in the saddle so determinedly that she would have to be helped down at night. Even though they were now riding through the valley of the Loire, they did not linger to enjoy the beauties of that fabulous country. They paid no heed to the great winding river and the hills on the skyline; to the magic castles (which were even more beautiful in their reflection in the water); or the windmills turning as though ashamed of any form of hurry in a land of such enchanting peace; of the mule trains and the boats on the river in which men sang as they pulled at the oars; of the knights in armor who rode the river paths with cavalcades behind them.

To Valerie there was something about the valley of the Loire of much more importance than its serenity and charm. Another girl had ridden here in the garb of a man and had made an immortal name for herself. She knew the story of the Maid from beginning to end and was amazed to find that D'Arlay was almost completely ignorant of it. She would have liked to correct this serious flaw (which all members of the aristocracy shared at this time) by pointing out the places where Jeanne D'Arc had been and by recounting what happened in full detail. But the time could not be spared. Once she reined in her horse in front of an inn long enough to say: "She slept one night under that chestnut tree and when they asked in the morning if the rain had disturbed her she said, No, she had been listening to voices which drowned out the thunder." Another time, but without drawing rein: "When she crossed the river here the ends of a rainbow rested on each bank and heavenly music could be heard for miles hereabouts." It was then she asked, "Don't you feel, my lord Robin, that a benediction will always rest on this land because it was here the Maid led the armies of France?"

In spite of this determination to reach Bourges before the consequences she read in the dream could overtake them, she sometimes lapsed into a more normal mood. Once she asked him which country he would prefer if he were forced to go into exile. After some thought, he expressed himself in favor of Portugal. Her own choice was Italy. She explained it by saying that it was the home of great poets and painters and builders. "I know so little," she said. "It would be wonderful to live in a country where all the learning of the ages is being put into use."

D'Arlay fell into a mood of deep unhappiness at this point. "There's only one country where Frenchmen may live with any content," he said, "and that is France. And in all France there's no place to equal the domain of Arlay. Have I ever told you about it? Ah, my love, it passes all description! It stands on the slope of a green valley, and there's a stream below which is just like a beautiful woman because it's capricious and sometimes even quarrelsome and it winds about so much that it takes five miles to do one, and sometimes it's shallow and sometimes, most unexpectedly, it's very deep, and at all times it's the loveliest sight on which the eye can rest. The hills stretch away for many miles in all directions. The woods are dense and of the darkest green, and the trees about the house are like old friends. The winds which blow down the valley seem to sing rather than roar. In fact, the peasants have a song which they say comes from the sound of the March winds."

Valerie, listening to him attentively, caught some of his enthusiasm. "It seems perfect," she said.

D'Arlay sighed. "No, it has never been perfect. It has lacked a chatelaine. If you were there, it would be the most perfect place in the world. And now"—he gave an even deeper sigh—"that chance has been lost. You will never see Arlay."

4

D'Arlay was standing at the window of his room, looking down into the yard of the inn with some uneasiness. Steaming horses were being unharnessed there and rubbed down by a crew of vociferous servants.

When a knock sounded on the door, he answered in a preoccupied voice, "Come in!"

It was Valerie who obeyed the summons, and he needed no more than glance to know that she was the bearer of serious news. She remained in the doorway.

"We must get away! At once!" she said, in a tense whisper.

D'Arlay left the window and walked to the door. They faced each other for several moments in silence.

And then something happened which no one, lest of all the two participants, could have anticipated. He reached out, suddenly and with a touch of violence, and gathered her into his embrace, saying in a smoothered voice, "My poor Valerie, my sweet Valerie, you are frightened!" She responded with the same spontaneity. Her arms went up around his neck and she buried her face in the soft brown velvet of his shoulder. They stood thus for some time. Then, taking her face in his hands, he kissed her. It was a long kiss and it expressed everything he felt for her: love, devotion, passion, a tenderness beyond words. It was their first kiss and it had required the realization of imminent danger to bring it about.

He touched her hair and said, "My dear one, I must get you away from here at once." Then the flood engulfed him again and it was fully a minute before he was able to think of anything save the wonderful fact of her presence in his arms. When he finally stepped back, it was like awakening from a dream.

"What is it that has happened?" he asked.

Conscious of the time which had been lost, she began to explain in a hurried whisper. "When the new party arrived, I went into the hall and looked down the staircase, thinking it would be wise to see what manner of men they were. I recognized one of them at once. He was in charge and I knew he was of the court because I saw him when we were at the abbey. He has a face one doesn't easily forget."

"Do you know his name?"

"I heard the Comtesse speak of him at the time." She paused, her brow puckered in thought. "I seem to remember his name as Gouffier."

"Then I need to know nothing more! He may be following us, but it seems more likely he's bound for Bourges on some errand connected with Jacques Coeur." D'Arlay nodded his head emphatically. "In any event we must see that warning reaches Coeur at once. That means an all-night ride."

"You can't leave me here, so go with you I must." She gave him a confident smile. "I'm young and strong. There were many times when I had to drive or ride all through the night. I can do it again."

"I looked the place over before coming up. There's a gate behind the stables, so we can get away without being seen." He gave her grave face the most solicitous study. "We'll be eight hours in the saddle and riding hard the whole time. Are you sure you can stand it?"

"Quite sure." Then the gravity of her expression deepened. "Do you think my dreams were meant to warn us of this?"

"It's possible. I know this, that the presence of Gouffier with the party is an ill omen." Then his face took on a happy smile. "Tomorrow will be an eventful day in Bourges." His arms reached out for her again. "We will be married as soon as we arrive."

12

WHEN the clock struck one, Nicolas put his head in at the door of his master's room to ask, "Did you hear that?" At two he repeated the performance, speaking in a more urgent tone. Jacques Coeur paid no heed. He was seated at a long table, which quite apparently had been brought from the East for it was of fine red wood and built of a curious design. The top of the table was covered with papers on which he had written in his rapid flowing hand (quite different from the precise script of the period) and to which he was adding at a furious rate. He did not raise his head.

At three Nicolas decided to make himself heard. He began to speak in such a loud tone that his master looked up at once from the sheet on which he was engaged.

"Is it your wish to hasten the time," demanded the servant, "when you will take that post you think yourself so well fitted for, Moneyman in the Kingdom of Heaven?"

Coeur answered in an impatient tone, "I must finish what I'm doing while the matters are fresh in my mind." Then he looked up at his man and smiled. "You're thinking of your own need for rest as well as mine, Nicolas. Go to bed, then, in God's good name, so that I won't be interrupted any more by that ugly head of yours peering in at me. I weary of your solicitude, my dear Nicolas, and I weary of the complaining look you wear on your ill-natured face."

"Have I ever gone to bed before you, master?" Nicolas spoke in an aggrieved tone. "Never, as you know full well. Why should I start now after all these years of dancing attendance on you, and watching you, and waiting on you, and dandling round like a dog after the huntsman? No, master, I go to bed when you do and not a moment before."

He returned to the anteroom in which he spent nearly all his time.

"Three hours' sleep we've had in two days," he muttered. "What new devil is eating at his vitals that he can't stop work? Not that I care about myself——"

When he roused himself from the slumber into which he had fallen, the first rays of the sun were lighting the windows of the room. Sounds of industry reached him from below—the clang of hammers and the screech of saws (for the architects still had possession of the house and their workmen swarmed all over it), and, less evident but quite unmistakable, a hum of voices which indicated that the members of his organization summoned by Coeur to Bourges were also up and about. Nicolas stretched himself, after a guilty glance at the door leading into his master's room which fortunately was closed, and walked to a window. He could see all of one wing, on which a roof of high-slanting angles was being built. A man of some authority, carrying a roll of papers under one arm, was swinging himself up among the rafters and calling out orders as he did so. Nicolas had watched him climb on a score of mornings, expecting to see him fall and kill himself, but so far had not been rewarded by so much as a stumble.

In the courtyard, which the servant could see by leaning far out of the window, groups of men were standing about. He could hear one voice above the rest, a voice trained to make itself heard over the roaring of sea and wind.

"Ha!" said Nicolas with a smile. "It's clear Jean de Village wasn't drinking last night or he wouldn't be up so early." He leaned out still farther and called: "Jean! Jean de Village! Come up, the master will be asking for you in a minute."

In answer to this summons there appeared in the doorway a few moments later a man whose stature lent credence to the stories of giants which were used currently to frighten disobedient children. Coeur's great sea captain was not only inches taller than anyone else, he was even wider in proportion, with shoulders as massive as gun platforms and legs like the gnarled trunks of trees. Increasing the effect, he wore a grotesquely padded jacket of yellow cloth, tufted with black buttons and laced about with bands of sky-blue silk and so many chains that they clanked as he walked, and sleeves extravagantly puffed which made him lose all semblance to humanity. He seemed, in fact, like some gigantic animal straight out of the legends. His face was a leathery melon with a sickle mouth and eyes of bland and washed-out blue.

"Is the great man awake already?" Jean de Village demanded, stalking into the room.

"Awake already!" repeated Nicolas with a proper indignation. "The great man has been up all night, with his nose in his papers, while lesser men wallowed in slumber like swine. He hasn't slept a wink. Nor have I."

"You lie!" said the sea captain, with good-natured finality. "I can see by your eyes, you ugly old toad, that you've just roused yourself. And I'll tell you this: I'm no droil and I don't wallow in slumber like swine, I sleep with the thoroughness of a hibernating bear, but when I wake—I'll have you know, Master Nicolas, that I wake growling and that I'm likely to tear interfering servants like you to pieces."

Before Nicolas could make any move to prevent him, the sailor opened the inside door. He walked in, closing it after him with a resounding bang.

The Moneyman looked up and nodded. "Good morning, Jean."

"That rubber of salt in raw wounds," said Jean de Village, "that whining bergherst, that saw-toothed oracle of ill news—in other words, your servant Nicolas whose ungainliness of mood you suffer for some reason unknown to anyone else—tells me you have been standing every watch. This is not wise, good master and uncle-in-law. How can you keep a clear head for the problems which face you if you deny yourself the benefit of sleep?"

The Moneyman wrote the final words on a sheet and then, with a frown of abstraction, began to gather all the papers together. "My brave Jean," he said, "I have set down full instructions as to what must be done in all eventualities." He leaned back in his chair and passed a hand over his eyes with a gesture of the greatest weariness. He was pale and there were deep shadows under his eyes. "As soon as things are in order, I shall meet their charges and then, if necessary, leave the country. I am prepared"—he paused and sighed unhappily—"to abandon my shops and my factories in France, to see the work of a lifetime fall into ruins. But there's another side to the picture, my brave Jean, a brighter side. I'm going to start over again. I shall go to Rome—where His Holiness has a good opinion of me and will extend a welcome, of that I am assured—and from there I'll begin to build another empire."

He paused for several moments and then smiled at his companion with easy confidence. "Jacques Coeur," he said, "is greater than the business he has created in France. The business may die but if Jacques Coeur lives, he can build it all over again. That is what he will do now, either here or in Rome."

He began to gather the papers up and to seal them. "No other hand must touch them yet," he said, "not even that of my critical conscience, Nicolas the Unconvinced." As he sealed each note, he added it to a pile at his elbow which grew until it threatened to topple over. "I must save what I can before the blow falls. I've prepared notes to the number of twenty-two. Here, for instance"—holding up the last one of the lot—"are instructions to get your ships out of harbor as soon as the blow falls. If the time comes to open this one, you'll find I provide for a rendezvous off Marseilles and for one of the fastest in the line to patrol the coast and warn those coming in from the East not to put in at any French port. I have thought of every possibility and provided the answer for it.

"In the absence of D'Arlay, on whom I counted in this emergency," went on the Moneyman, "I'm confiding these to you. You must keep them with you always so that they can be produced as each need arises. Everything will depend on how quickly my plans are put into operation. All my factors will stand by me but every foot of the journey must be charted for them." He looked up at the sea captain and indulged in a somewhat uncertain smile. "A Vaillants Coeurs Rien Impossible! We shall have to demonstrate now the truth of the Coeur motto, Jean!"

The captain gathered up the notes and stowed them away in a capacious inside pocket. "Your desires will be obeyed," he said. "I assume from what you have said that I'm to turn everything over to D'Arlay if he arrives in time. That I'll do gladly."

Nicolas knocked at the door and, without waiting to be summoned, came into the room. "The Sire d'Arlay has just arrived."

"That takes a weight from my mind!" exclaimed Coeur, springing to his feet. "Bring him up at once. We'll breakfast here together, the three of us, Jean."

"He has a lady with him," announced Nicolas, with the same air of unconcern. "*The* lady, master. They both seem—in a state of mind. The Sire d'Arlay says he must see you at once."

A change had come over the Moneyman. The lines of fatigue seemed to have left his face, his color had improved, his eyes had lighted up. He gave the sailor's wide shoulder a reassuring tug.

"Truly, my Jean, this is good news. Go down and greet them for me. Bring them up in ten minutes. By that time I'll have finished all this."

2

D'Arlay had been waiting in the courtyard in a state of impatience which can readily be understood. As soon as he had helped Valerie out of the saddle, she had curled up on an outside bench and had fallen asleep at once. He looked down at her now and said to himself, "She rode like a veteran of the wars, my pretty bride-to-be." He was on the point of summoning a domestic and having her taken to a bed when he was joined by the man who had been seen earlier by Nicolas in the act of climbing the roof.

"Good morning, Sire d'Arlay."

D'Arlay recognized him as the architect from Paris who was building this amazing house for Jacques Coeur. "Good morning, Monsieur Pelle. You are at work early."

"I would hazard the opinion," said the architect, glancing at the recumbent form of the girl, "that you and Mademoiselle were in the saddle all night."

"We were. My companion rode with me stirrup to stirrup and it's no wonder she's now completely exhausted." D'Arlay glanced up at the unfinished walls hedging them in. "You seem to be making progress here."

The architect nodded morosely. "Is this your first view of it?" he asked.

"I was here when the walls were beginning to rise. I haven't been back since."

Monsieur Pelle burst suddenly into a flood of words. "This"—motioning about him—"could be the greatest monument in the world to the art of the builder. I, the most advanced thinker among architects, found at last a man who wanted a house along new lines, who had ideas of his own which were good. We worked together well at the start. We planned a house which was practical as well as beautiful. It doesn't consist of one huge Great Hall like a cathedral to reflect the glory of the owner—and grouped around it a huddle of rooms like ratholes in which he and his family and his dependents live and sleep in squalor. Instead, we have a well-balanced structure in which all rooms are of a comfortable size, with ample fireplaces and plenty of light. We built it as strong as any castle. This was to be a house at least a century ahead of its time, and yet a perfect one. Only for a man with the vision and genius of Jacques Coeur could such a house be raised."

The architect stopped and shook his head despondently. "And then what happens? The weak sides of the man begin to show themselves, his pride, his vainglory, his buffoonery. He needs must have the house original in matters where originality is out of place. Observe the designs in the stained glass of the windows! Nothing classical, nothing dignified! They must show ships, *his* ships, or the shops from which his wealth comes. Have you seen what he has carved over the door and windows? Mottoes! *Trade* mottoes, Sire d'Arlay! Have you observed the carved groups in bas-relief? Comic subjects instead of proper scenes from the Scripture, jokes at the expense of knights and the nobility. Over each door he must have a scene to designate the purpose of the room. A scullion with a ladle in his hand to show the kitchen, a head peering through sleeping curtains for a bedroom! Sire d'Arlay, the man has a touch of madness in him."

In spite of the impatience which possessed him, D'Arlay had already visited the ground floor and had observed some of the curious samples of Coeur's originality. He had counted a dozen mottoes, trite and threadbare for the most part, some of them repeated over and over in the carvings. He had smiled at a group in bas-relief showing two jesters on mules, tilting in imitation of brave knights in the lists, with broomsticks for lances and market baskets for shields, and had thought, "Jacques is paying his respects to chivalry." He had seen the figure of the Moneyman in various groups on the walls and had been puzzled as to the meaning behind the scenes. After taking it all in, he had realized that the house was a monument to the man himself; as, indeed, it was, a tribute to a daring spirit born centuries too soon, a man who sensed the ignorance of the dark age in which he was chained but who was not above flaunting his success openly before the fellow mortals he despised. It was, D'Arlay had concluded, a house to defy description or classification, a lovely, enduring, vainglorious, daring, amusing, sometimes vulgar house.

"Jacques Coeur has been an enigma to the world," he said to the architect. "Now he ceases to be that. Everything about him is revealed here. This house *is* Jacques Coeur."

"Yes," said the architect, in a grumbling tone. "It started to be Coeur *and* Pelle. Now it's all Coeur."

D'Arlay's mind went back to his urgent need for a talk with the master of this extraordinary structure. "Where is he?" he demanded. "I must see him at once! I have news of the gravest kind!"

"Where is he?" Monsieur Pelle made a despairing gesture, using both hands for the purpose. "That is what I ask myself a dozen times a day. He shuts himself up and no one is allowed to see him. I have had a hundred bitter arguments with that mule in human form who sits in his anteroom."

D'Arlay resumed his pacing, saying to himself: "I'll break in his door if he doesn't send for me soon! What possesses the man? Does he put no trust in me that he disregards my arrival in this way?"

It was with a sense of deep relief that he spied Jean de Village emerge from the main section of the house and come striding across the yard.

"Welcome, Jean!" he cried.

"Welcome, Robin!" boomed the giant, his face beaming like the ruddy sun of evening which it resembled in every respect. "My ears have been filled with the tales of your great deeds but my eyes have been empty of any sight of you. I would have given two years of my own life—and by St. Christophe whom I'm said to resemble, I value every minute of the life I am allowed!—to see you gobbon the ribs of the Burgundian with that lath of yours."

They shook hands with the warmth of old friendship but the smile which accompanied the act remained on D'Arlay's face no more than a moment. "Jean!" he cried. "There's danger ahead of us! Officers of the King are on their way here and will arrive soon. Jacques must know at once! Why does he hide himself away?"

Jean de Village smiled. "How long have you been waiting?"

"Half an hour. An hour. It has seemed longer than that—it has seemed an eternity!"

"You have waited," declared the sea captain, "exactly nine minutes. The great man was finishing some work on which he had been engaged all night when he heard of your arrival and he craved your indulgence for that much longer. I'm to take you in now."

The eyes of the huge man settled on the form of the sleeping girl. He stared at her for several moments with every evidence of interest and then he turned back to D'Arlay and winked.

"Is this the one?" he asked. "I've heard whispers about her. By St. Christophe, she's a pretty thing though I'm compelled to say she's a trifle on the small and meager side. I like my women large and lively and with something to swing when they walk."

D'Arlay resented the limited nature of this praise. "I am wedding her today," he announced stiffly.

Jean de Village swung around to face him, wearing a look of complete incredulity. "You are wedding her! Come, Robin, I've always known that someday you would marry the richest heiress in France. This girl, if the stories I hear are true, hasn't a name of her own or two whites to jingle in her purse."

"Do you think," demanded D'Arlay fiercely, "that any of us will be left with fortunes or lands in France? Have you no conception of the danger in which we stand? We'll all be driven into exile—if we have the good fortune to get away. I never expect to see Arlay again."

He reached down and gathered Valerie into his arms. When she stirred drowsily but did not waken, he looked at the giant sea captain and said, "She's been nearly twenty-four hours in the saddle, Jean. She may not be an heiress but I count myself the luckiest man in the world."

D'Arlay carried Valerie into the main hall. She wakened then and asked, "Where are we?" in a puzzled tone. She was so weary that, when her feet touched the floor, she could barely stand and found it advisable to cling to his arm for support. They ascended a marble stairway of most imposing proportions and entered the anteroom where Nicolas sat, clothed in gloomy authority.

The latter consulted a clock on the wall behind him. "You are early," he said accusingly. Then he motioned over his shoulder in the direction of an inner door. "But you may go in. He's expecting you."

D'Arlay stood no longer on ceremony but rushed headlong through the door. He called to Coeur, who was standing at a window: "Jacques, there's not a moment to lose! Gouffier is on his way here with a party of officers. It may mean he carries a warrant for your arrest."

Jacques Coeur did not seem disturbed at this announcement. He smiled at Valerie who had entered the room behind D'Arlay. "I have no words, Mademoiselle, to express the pleasure I take in seeing you," he said. "You've ridden all night, I judge, to bring a warning to Jacques Coeur. That was brave of you and I thank you with all my heart. But"—he spread out his arms in a gesture of resignation—"what is there for us to do?"

D'Arlay laid an urgent hand on his arm. "Get away at once, Jacques! We must all go. To Spain, to Italy, anywhere! We'll not get justice here."

Coeur's brows drew together in a frown. "Run away?" He shook his head. "I've been expecting this. It won't be hard to blow into thin air the shabbily trumped-up charges they may bring against me."

"It will do you no good to prove them false."

Coeur indulged in a laugh which had no trace of mirth in it. "This much good, Robin: My good name will be vindicated in the pages of history. This is not a situation, my friend, from which one may run away. It must be faced sooner or later. If I showed them my heels as you advise, it would be accepted as a confession of guilt; and Jacques Coeur would be remembered as a traitor and a thief."

The room in which they stood was large and handsomely appointed. There were tapestries on the walls and carpets on the floor. The chimney, heaped with six-foot logs ready for use, had columns and fluted pilasters of marble and panels patterned in gold overlay. The Moneyman walked to one wall which was covered by an oriental hanging. This he drew aside, revealing a high panel of overlapping steel plates confined in a thick metal frame. The purpose this served was apparent only when he ran one hand gropingly over the surface. A crack appeared at the edge of the frame and the panel began to turn inward.

Coeur said to Jean de Village, "Will you excuse me if I take my two friends inside for a talk? It will be for a few minutes only." He bowed to Valerie. "Will you be good enough to enter?"

The room into which they stepped was a small one, containing no furniture save two chairs and a plain table. There was a chimney with tiny windows on each side which admitted very little light. The Moneyman let the metal frame close after them. "No one else, not even Nicolas, has the secret of the spring," he said. "You'll see nothing here to excite you but someday it will be better worth a visit. Learned doctors and historians and scribes will strive to get their fingers on the papers I shall leave here. There will be plenty to make the search worth while then."

He ensconced his guests in the chairs and seated himself on a corner of the table. "So, our friend Robin found you and brought you away," he said to Valerie. "That's good. Before I hear how it all came about, I have this to say to you. You must both stay in France. Exile is a sad thing for a Frenchman. He knows that no other corner of earth will reward him for the effort of living. His thoughts turn backward to the sunny land he has left. He accepts exile as a last resort."

"But you——" began D'Arlay.

"Jacques Coeur is not to be measured by ordinary standards. He will be too busy with the tasks ahead of him to have time for repining or—or memories." The Moneyman nodded his head reassuringly. "The King is not in a position to bring charges against you. What have you done? No, you must stay and face it out." He paused and smiled first at one and then at the other. "You are to be wed?"

"As soon as we can find a priest."

"I knew it! It was written all over you, Robin. Although you are tired and dusty, your eyes shine with triumph, there is a hint of the conqueror in your stride." He reached out and shook D'Arlay's hand. Then he turned to Valerie and gave her cheek an affectionate apt. "I am glad, my children, and I wish you everlasting happiness."

"And now the story!" he exclaimed, after a moment. He nodded to Valerie. "You tell it. I count on your feminine sense of dramatic fitness to adorn the story properly. D'Arlay would recite it in a few precise words which would be good for nothing but a ledger."

She did his bidding, telling in full detail of the abrupt departure from the north, her translation to the little house against the palace wall, her meeting with the King (she skimmed over this part briefly), and her flight with D'Arlay. The Moneyman listened attentively and at the finish made one comment only. "I was right," he said. "I chose my candidate well. Men's preferences run in well-defined grooves."

Then he sat up straight and said, "And now I have something to tell you, my child. Your name."

Valerie straightened up in turn, all trace of drowsiness leaving her at once. She stared at him, her lips parted with eagerness.

"My name!" she repeated.

"Your father was Enguerrard Alphonse Charles Sorel. He was the favorite brother of the Lady Agnes. And so, my child, your name is Valerie Sorel."

The girl cried, "My lord Coeur!" She was so taken aback that for several moments she could say nothing more. She continued to watch him with eyes round with the excitement of this amazing announcement.

"The Lady Agnes recognized you as soon as she saw you that morning," he went on. "When I returned after taking you away, she told me her reasons for knowing that you were her brother's child, apart from the close resemblance you bore her. She had no doubts at all; as I had none when she was through."

Valerie had recovered enough of her composure to ask a question. "Did she know the circumstances of my birth?"

Coeur shook his head. "She was aware that her brother had an illegitimate child in Berri, a daughter, of whom all trace had been lost. Beyond that she knew nothing."

"Nothing of—of my mother?"

"I think not. We had little chance to talk about it, for the poor lady was drawing close to her end, as you know. She expressed one wish concerning you: that you would have a happier and fuller life than hers had been."

Valerie looked up quickly. "And that was the reason you changed your mind?"

"It was the final reason. Before that I had been aware of a great disinclination to proceed." He remained silent for a time, his head sunk in thought. When he resumed speaking, it was in a reflective mood. "Her word was always law with me. Even had I felt I must use every means in my power to hold the favor of the King, I would have bowed to her wish in this. Yes, she had only to speak and I—I did her bidding."

He walked across the floor and drew back a piece of tapestry which covered the upper part of one wall. This exposed a sculptured bas-relief, rather awkwardly executed but with fidelity to its main characters. These were three in number. The first was Coeur himself, for there was no mistaking the turban-shaped headdress, the furred cloak, and the chain at the neck. He stood before a lady who was reclining under a tree. On the head of the lady was a plain circlet and her hand was raised toward it in a gesture which suggested a doubt. Of the third figure only the head was seen, staring from the foliage of another tree. It was the King, for on his head was a crown; and on the regal countenance there was an expression of consternation.

D'Arlay walked over and studied the group with a puzzled frown. "What does it mean?" he asked finally.

Coeur laughed. "What does it mean? I provide the riddle but not the answer. When they find the way into this room, after I'm gone, they'll puzzle their wits just as you are doing now over the enigma I've left for their confounding. There's a hint in it of a certain truth—but no more."

They were interrupted by a sound of tapping on the wall which contained the secret door. A pause ensued and then Jacques Coeur said: "Nicolas, no doubt. He thinks it's time we stopped talking."

The tapping ended abruptly. "He shows less than his usual persistence," declared Coeur, with a frown. "Has something happened to stop him? I think we had better see what it's about." With his hand on the inner spring, however, he turned back and faced them. "There should be no talk yet of your parentage," he remarked to Valerie. "Let us keep the secret between us for the time being. There are certain legal aspects to be considered first."

"The situation we're in makes the secret safe," said D'Arlay. "We'll have no chance to talk, even if we wanted to."

The Moneyman had one more thing to say. "Never be afraid of life," he declared, in earnest tones. "The buffets of adversity are no more than tests of our spirit. I've never dreaded the future and I can look forward to what is ahead of me now with confidence that I shall always be the master of circumstances and never their servant. You are both young and I commend this philosophy to you."

He was speaking primarily for Valerie's benefit. She had become pale at the first sound, as though she sensed danger in it. Coeur had observed her reaction and he now touched her arm reassuringly. "If I have no fear of Gouffier and his errand, why should you?" he asked. "Come, we'll go out together and see what fate has in store for us."

The outer chamber proved to be empty but the hum of many voices came from the anteroom. The Moneyman opened the door and they were able to grasp at one glance what had happened while they were in seclusion. Gouffier and his party, who had traveled all night also, had arrived and taken possession. Jean de Village and Nicolas were standing together in a window embrasure and two men with drawn swords were stationed in front of them. Half-a-dozen other soldiers were in the room, lounging about insolently and talking in loud voices.

"Master!" cried Nicolas. He got no further with what he intended to say for one of the soldiers drove the handle of a sword into his side and growled an admonition to be silent if he desired to remain alive.

Valerie touched D'Arlay's arm. Looking down, he saw that her face was white and drawn. She began to whisper. "This is what the dream meant. There has been danger hanging over us ever since we ran away; and now, my Robin, it has overtaken us! I pray God for the strength to face it!"

D'Arlay lowered his head to speak in her ear. "Courage, my love! Whatever this is about, it can't touch us."

She caught her breath. "But it can, it can! I'm beginning to remember——"

Gouffier appeared in the doorway and all eyes turned in his direction. It was evident that he had been changing into more suitable garb after spending a night in the saddle. He was dressed from head to foot in green velvet and there were three tall white feathers in his hat. On his feet were low leather shoes with toes which curled up in the extreme of fashion.

He lingered in the doorway as though willing to prolong the suspense into which the others had been thrown by his arrival. There was triumph in the upward curl of his lips as he watched Jacques Coeur.

"Master Furrier," he said, rolling the phrase on his tongue with obvious satisfaction, "I come on instructions from our royal master. I am to inform you, first, that you have been dismissed from the post you held in the King's service——"

Coeur broke in bitterly: "The war is won and so I'm needed no longer."

Gouffier's nose twitched and his eyes became even more hostile. "Acting on further orders from my royal master," he declared, "I place you under arrest. You will surrender at once all weapons on your person and go with me and the royal guards assigned to take you to prison."

Coeur's face turned white and his hands began to tremble. It was clear he had not expected this. "I had no hope of a reward for what I've done for France and for my liege lord," he said, in a constrained tone. "But I didn't believe ingratitude could be carried to this extreme."

Gouffier, who was something of a dandy, produced a handkerchief from a receptacle under his belt and rubbed his nose with it. It had been well soaked in perfume. "Need I tell you," he asked, "that what you say will be made known to those who are to sit in judgment on you?"

Coeur turned to face the man who had been from the first his most active and unrelenting enemy. "All you need tell me, Guillaume Gouffier, is the nature of the charge which has been brought against me."

"The charge?" Gouffier indulged in a wry smile. "You know what it is full well, Jacques Coeur. Your guilty conscience has already told you that the facts of your heinous crime have been brought to light." He paused, savoring the pleasure he took in the announcement he was now to make. "You are charged with causing the death of the Lady Agnes Sorel by administering poison to her."

There was a moment of shocked and bewildered silence in the room and then Jacques Coeur said in a voice no one would have recognized as his: "I am charged with poisoning Agnes Sorel! It can't be true! It's so unheard of, so cruelly false, so—so bitterly absurd! No one could think of it in any seriousness."

"It is true, nevertheless, Master Furrier," declared Gouffier. There was the suggestion of a satisfied chirp in his voice. "I have the papers with me, duly signed and sealed with the royal seal. The charge is brought by the Baronne de Mortagne, more frequently called the Damoiselle Jeanne de Vendôme."

D'Arlay felt Valerie's fingers tighten spasmodically around his arm and heard her whisper tensely: "That was the name! She, the Comtesse, used it! I remember everything now!"

Gouffier suddenly transferred his attention to her. "I have a warrant also for a maiden known as Valerie Maret who has been indulging in the fiction of calling herself Valerie de Voudrai." A look of satisfaction grew in his eyes as he studied her. "I need not ask if this is the girl. The resemblance is even more marked than I had been led to suspect. I place you under arrest also, Valerie Maret, as an accomplice in the execution of this infamous crime."

3

As they made their way slowly down the marble stairs between walls of aquamarine and under a coved ceiling of beautiful design, Coeur turned his head backward. Valerie was following immediately behind him, a guard on each side holding her arms with what seemed unnecessary tightness. Her eyes were lowered and she stumbled as though she had fallen into a daze. Behind her stalked D'Arlay, his face a battleground of conflicting emotions—anger, despair, fear. Still farther back was Jean de Village. They were taking no chances with the gigantic sailor. One of the soldiers walked behind him with sword pointed at the small of his back.

Guillaume Gouffier, in the lead, began to talk in a voice silky with confidence. "You may be certain, my good ex-minister and one-time colleague, that this charge against you has not been loosely sworn. I've read the depositions and I may tell you that the evidence is conclusive. It was a pretty plot but—the truth is out now."

He paused before a sculptured group on the wall in which the figure of the planner and owner of all this magnificence stood out prominently. "This I will say for you, Jacques Coeur. Everything you did was on a grand scale. The little I have seen of this house has amazed me. Do you also find something ironic in the thought that you won't live to see it completed?"

Two of the soldiers were bringing up the rear of the doleful procession. One of them whispered to the other, "A pretty little fawn, Pierre, to be caught in a mess like this."

The other winked delightedly. "What a story, this, for us to tell! We were in luck to be chosen, Imbert." His thoughts turned to the future. "What crowds there will be to see them cut off Jacques Coeur's head! Or do you think they're more likely to break him on the wheel?"

"I've seen both done often. Breaking on the wheel takes longer. How they screech sometimes! But what I don't want to miss is the finish of this girl. You know what they'll do to her, don't you?"

The second soldier shook his head. "I don't know . . . but nothing's too bad for women poisoners."

"They burn them at the stake. There will be a fortune in it for the executioner when he rents out windows around the Place de la Grève to see this one dance on the faggots!"

BOOK THREE

1

THE CELL to which Old Philippe escorted Jacques Coeur was high up in the tower of Lusignan. It was a room of some size, much the largest and most comfortable of the many he had inhabited. It had a straw pallet, a chair, and a prisoner's bucket in one corner. There was a window which, he hoped, would yield him a view of the Vonne. The air had in full measure the dank jail smell and on the walls were the usual feeble drawings and the desperate messages of earlier occupants.

Old Philippe lit a second candle and placed it on the stone floor beside the pallet. He straightened up and stared at his new charge with his sunken eyes.

"The great Lord Coeur!" he said in a whisper. "That I have lived to see him here, a number in my charge! It's a strange world, a cruel world!" He shook his head at the inscrutability of fate and then added in a brisker tone, "You have one candle a week and no more, my lord, so use a care of the utmost."

Coeur asked in an indifferent tone, "Isn't it permitted to buy additional candles?"

"Yes, my lord, it's permitted," said Old Philippe. "It's customary in all cases where prisoners have the means at their disposal. Does my lord wish me to purchase more candles for him?"

"I was examined by the warden's men on arriving," said Coeur. "They took all the gold I had with me. To be returned, it was explained, if I leave here."

The turnkey nodded his head. "It's the custom. But it's possible that my lord was able to—to get the better of the guards and secrete about his person some part of his money? It is always done, it is winked at, my lord. How else could our fine gentlemen pay for better wines, for pittances with the meals, a white bread of Chailly even, a marrow bone for feast days, or a purée of eels? Or to have pets, a pair of white mice, a friendly toad, even in cases a cat? My lord did not fail, I trust, to keep a store of money hidden for his use?"

Coeur had been successful in this respect. Concealed in the leather of an inner belt about his waist were a score of gold coins—what was left of the secret supply he had been carrying when he was placed under arrest. It did not suit his purpose, however, to let this be known. Instead, he gave a doleful shake of his head.

"There will be money for everything," he asserted, "but only when I can get in touch with certain friends on the outside. If you, Master Turnkey, can assist me in getting word to them, there will be gold aplenty: gold for extra candles and the pittances, and gold for you too, more perhaps than you have ever had."

Old Philippe did not take up the suggestion. He waggled his ancient head and said: "It is too bad. It is too bad, my lord."

Coeur looked at him shrewdly, convinced it was going to be possible to reach an understanding. He did not pursue the point any further at the moment but asked a question, "Will Mademoiselle Maret be brought here?"

He had adopted a casual tone but he was burning with anxiety and impatience inside. Not since the day when they were arrested at the great new house at Bourges and taken away, under separate escorts, had he seen Valerie or heard directly from her. She had not been confined in any of the prisons where he had been held but beyond that he had not been able to learn anything. For all he knew she already had been placed on trial. It was certain that she had been questioned continuously and exhaustively and brutally as he had been, day after day, night after night. Perhaps, and he shuddered whenever this supposition crossed his mind, she had been put to the torture to force her into some kind of confession. If this had been done—and he had no doubts at all that sooner or later she would be stretched on the rack—it was possible that false evidence obtained in this way was already in the possession of his enemies and would be brought against him when he went on trial.

The turnkey's face had taken on the deliberately vacant look with which this query had been greeted at the other prisons. He shook his head.

"There is no one here of that name, my lord."

"But there has been word of her coming? It must be that she will be sent here soon."

"I've no knowledge of such matters, my lord."

Coeur reached out and grasped him by the turned-down collar of his soiled jerkin. "I promise you solemnly, my ancient one," he said, "and by any saint you care to name, or by the beard of the Eastern prophet, that a generous reward shall be yours if you become the bearer of tidings of her. If you will come to me the first time you hear anything of her, you'll be treated with a generosity such as you've never known before."

Old Philippe shook the ring in his hand and watched the keys swing back and forth. "This reward of such lordly proportions must wait on the time when you have word from those on the outside?" When Coeur nodded in agreement, the turnkey shook his head doubtfully. "An uncertain prospect, my lord. One does not wax fat on promises. The matter must be given thought. It must be turned over most carefully in the mind."

Coeur said to himself after the old man had left and the grating of the key in the lock had announced the closing of the cell for the night, "He'll do as I wish, for I could read his purpose in his villainous old eye." The satisfaction he would have felt ordinarily at having thus managed the first step toward the carrying out of a plan of defense was lacking, nevertheless. If Valerie was not brought to Lusignan, what did they propose to do with her? Perhaps her fate had already been settled. It was well within the bounds of probability that she had been tried, convicted, burned at the stake. He knew how strongly the weight of her punishment could be used against him in that event. Seating himself in his chair, he thought the situation over and became almost convinced that this was what had happened, that Valerie was dead.

When he awakened next morning, a faint light was showing through the window. He sat up on his straw pallet with a feeling almost of gratitude. This was the first time since his incarceration that he had occupied a cell which the light of dawn could reach.

Old Philippe arrived an hour later. He seemed, by way of contrast with his usual mood, quite cheerful. With an air of pride he demonstrated that he had been able to supplement the prison breakfast with an omelet, a loaf of white bread, and a bottle of wine.

"Saint-Emilion, my lord," he said, pointing to the wine. "The best in the cellars."

The prisoner looked at the iron tray containing these concessions without manifesting any great degree of satisfaction. "You have decided, then," he said, "to take me on faith."

The turnkey nodded briskly and emphatically. "We have talked it over, the others and I," he answered. "All of us feel that there is little risk in waiting."

"You've decided wisely." Coeur reached down into a corner of one pocket and drew out a coin. He tossed it to the old man whose ancient claws caught it neatly. "Something the Governor's men overlooked. I found it this morning."

The turnkey pocketed the coin and winked familiarly. "It's always so," he said. "It never fails that the clumsy fingers of the Governor's men overlook a few coins in the corners of pockets. Is it not odd, my lord, that prisoners always have such convenient pockets? They have corners into which coins creep, knowing they will be safe there. It is curious also, my lord, that the owner never discovers at first that he has been lucky. It is a day, two days, three, a full week, before the money is discovered."

Each day after that Coeur asked the turnkey, "Have my friends been located in the town yet?"

"No, my lord," was the invariable response.

"Are you sure," he demanded one morning, "that those you are depending on to find them are persons of diligence? Have they sufficient intelligence for the task?"

"It is my own brother-in-law and my good gossip the blacksmith I am using, my lord. I can assure you they would do anything short of strangling their wives or selling their immortal souls to the devil for the reward you offer. Also, my lord, they are acting with a man of the very best mind, a seller of books who came here from Paris."

"It's very strange. My friends must have traced me here by this time. There will be no mistaking them, Master Turnkey. Jean de Village will be the biggest man ever to show himself in the valley of the Vonne. When he puts his foot down, the very floors quiver. As for the Sire d'Arlay, he is prone to walk or ride with head bent forward and the sword he carries is longer than those of other men. They may be going under different names, Old Philippe. Have you cautioned your dawdling bloodhounds on that score?"

The turnkey bobbed his head. "A dozen times, my lord, I have said to them, Ask no names but watch for a sailor of mighty frame like the hull of his own ship. Be at ease, my lord; if your friends come, the word of it will run through the town like the pox."

Each day also the prisoner would ask, "Has there been any report of Mademoiselle Maret?" and each day the answer would be the same, "No, my lord, we've heard nothing concerning her."

2

The chill of fall was in the air and a damp wind blew along the ramparts overlooking the Vonne. D'Arlay looked up at the towers of the prison, beneath which the town seemed to cower and hide, and said to his companion, "They've caged the lion securely this time, Jean."

Jean de Village made no reply. He had been aware for several minutes that they were being followed. An owlish wisp of a man in gray cloak and bonnet was lingering at their heels and conducting himself with an elaborate pretense of unconcern. The sea captain stopped abruptly and bawled out a command.

"Come here!"

The little man advanced timorously, keeping his eyes on the huge sailor, and ready, quite obviously, to take to his heels at the first hint of violence.

"What do you mean by following us, you scum of the taverns, you foul breeze from the backstairs!"

The man gulped nervously and said in a thin voice, "I've been trying to get my courage up to ask if your name might be Jean de Village."

The sailor scowled down at the townsman for several moments and then said, "If you had asked me that question, I might have answered, yes."

"I thought so." The man sighed with relief. He drew closer to them and began to quote in a whisper, "A Vaillants Coeurs . . ."

"That's enough. Now, what business have you with me?"

"I am——" A cautious pause ensued. "My name is not important, my lord. Suffice it to say that I am come from Old Philippe who holds a post ——" Another pause to gesture back over his shoulder in the direction of the castle.

"What word have you for us?" demanded the sailor.

"This." The townsman dropped his voice still lower. "Go to the stationarius at the Sign of the Silver Missal. It is on a narrow street just off the Bail Gate. Tell the stationarius who you are."

He turned and began to slink away. Jean de Village called after him, "One minute: I have questions to ask, heart of a rabbit!"

"There's nothing more I can tell you." The little man walked cautiously along the rampart and, finding himself at a safe distance from them, increased his pace with greater confidence until he took advantage of an opening off the cobbled road to disappear from sight.

They located the Sign of the Silver Missal without any difficulty although they were surprised to find it swinging in front of a tiny booth wedged in between busy and prosperous shops, a mercer on one side, a butcher on the other. The booth had a counter and a row of shelves behind that, filled with books and manuscripts and supplies of paper and ink, and that was all.

The proprietor looked up when they stepped into the booth and his eyes took in the great bulk of Jean de Village. "Your wishes, Messires?" he asked.

"We're from the East," answered D'Arlay. "Having nothing much else to do we were drawn here by curiosity, to see what manner of books might be offered for sale so far away from the University of Paris."

"You are from the East," repeated the bookseller slowly.

"It surprises us," went on D'Arlay, "to find anything in the nature of a bookshop in a town where there is no seat of learning."

"You misjudge the West, my lord. There are rich abbeys hereabouts which are glad to add to their libraries from time to time. Also there are great seaports along the coast and men who have grown inordinately wealthy in the shipping trades. They ape culture and so they pay very good prices for books of romance and the chronicles of history. They buy from me all I can get my hands on."

"But," said D'Arlay, with a puzzled air, "how can you get books to sell?"

The bookseller hesitated. Then he raised both hands and smiled. "I might as well tell you, since I suspect it's no longer a secret. I had my booth in Paris, my lord, where, as you must know, the trade in books is controlled by the University with an iron hand. I starved on the meager profits. Most of the trade is in the lending of books to the students. Can you conceive of the difficulties? They are a careless, hell-bent lot, the students of Paris. Always they were leaving the books in taverns or getting drunk and damaging them, or handing them on to others who could not pay the fee, tiny as it was. Half my time was wasted in hunting my ill-used volumes, climbing up to evil-smelling garrets, and battling with innkeepers and pimps to get my property back.

"And when a volume was brought in," he continued, his voice acquiring heat as he dwelt on former wrongs, "which the owner or the poor écrivain, who had written it out, wanted to sell, was I permitted to make any profit for myself? No, Messires, I was not allowed to buy it and offer it for sale at my own price. First I must offer it to the public for a month. Always it was purchased within that time and"—his voice mounted to a still higher pitch—"I was permitted by law to retain two per cent of the price for my services in selling it! Could a man with a family of his own, a mistress, and a distaste for cheap wine, live on two per cent?"

"I concede it would be difficult," said D'Arlay.

"So, my lord, I came West. When my old friends in the trade in Paris are offered a book, they say, 'What a pity to sell it for the small price obtainable here.' They say that in the West the prices are much better and then they suggest the book be sent to me. It comes. I sell it. At double Paris prices, my lord. And"—dropping his voice to a whisper—"I allow myself twenty per cent instead of two! Half of that, naturally, goes to the stationarius in Paris who sent it to me."

The bookseller then drew a letter from under the counter. "You are the Sire d'Arlay?"

"Yes. And this is Jean de Village."

"I was sure in my mind about him. Messires, I have been expecting you for a long time. I am Pierre Dupain. I was beginning to fear I would not be of any aid to those who placed this letter in my hands." He shoved it across the counter. "I earnestly advise that you refrain from opening it until you are in your rooms and free of all watchful eyes."

D'Arlay secreted the letter inside his tunic. "We will exercise the greatest care," he promised.

"Permit me to advise also that you pass here at least once a day. If I have a message for you, I shall smile and nod you a good day. If there is none, I shall be too busy to see you as you pass."

In the double room they shared in a tavern on a dark side street D'Arlay opened the note. It was in Coeur's handwriting.

I am given better treatment here but I am completely in the dark as to what is happening. A means of communication has been set up which will enable us to write. *Be discreet* but send me word of anything you hear, particularly about Valerie. I have had no news of her since the day we were taken at Bourges.

Open Number Sixteen for instructions.

D'Arlay had sewn the notes of instruction, confided to him by Jean de Village, into the lining of his cloak. Number Sixteen contained information about the nearest supply of gold. They were to go to Father Etienne at the cathedral at Poitiers "who could be depended upon in all things." The gold in the possession of this friendly priest was to be held at his, Jacques Coeur's, disposal.

"It's ten leagues to Poitiers," said the sailor. "We can get there by nightfall if we set out at once."

3

Old Philippe wore a satisfied look and the tray he carried was loaded with fare other than that provided by the Governor of Lusignan. A well-tuned ear might have detected the faintest jingle of coins in his pocket.

"My lord," he said, depositing the tray on the floor beside the bed where Jacques Coeur was reclining, "I have news for you of the best."

Coeur looked up quickly. "It concerns Mademoiselle Maret?"

"It does indeed, my lord. She is here at last."

Coeur got to his feet and pumped the turnkey's arm up and down. "My friend!" he cried. "My ancient graybeard, my trusty one! The reward I promised shall be yours. When did she arrive?"

Old Philippe displayed some caution. "As to that, my lord, I am not fully informed. A few days back, I believe."

"And what of her health? What of her spirits? Her bearing?"

"I have not seen her, my lord. The reports I hear are that she has eaten very little since she arrived. A morsel of food, a sup of wine. Never more, my lord."

"Is she ill then? Is her lack of appetite due to the treatment she has received?"

"She is thin. Quite thin and pale."

"Has she"—Coeur forced himself to ask the question which had weighed so heavily on his mind—"has she been put to the torture?"

Old Philippe shook his head with a comforting positiveness. "I am told she hasn't, my lord. I am told her lack of appetite is due to lack of ease in her mind. She asks one question of everyone who has seen her. She asks it over and over again."

"What manner of question?"

"She seems concerned about being burned at the stake. It has been told her it is the law for women convicted of poisoning to be put to death in that way. She is right, my lord, it is customary. It seems to fill her mind. She talks of nothing else. She seems to have a great dread of the stake, my lord."

Coeur turned away. With lagging steps he walked to the window and stood there, staring out at the small square of sky which could be seen. "Yes," he said, in a repressed voice. "I'm not surprised. It's easy to understand that her mind would dwell on that. My poor child!"

When Valerie appeared in the door, Coeur's first impression was that she had become blind. She advanced slowly, giving no sign of seeing him.

She was dressed in clothes which had been supplied her in prison. The skirt dragged, the sleeves were badly soiled, there were rents in many places. Pieces of straw clung to all parts of her attire and to her hair. She was thin and there were deep shadows under her eyes. It was plain to be seen that long before she had abandoned all hope.

"How cruelly they have treated the poor child!" thought Coeur.

She remained standing just inside the door, her face turned toward the window, one hand held over her eyes to protect them from the unaccustomed light.

"Valerie!" he said.

She turned quickly at the sound of his voice. The look of wonder on her face changed at once to joy. She stumbled toward him with both arms outstretched.

"They didn't tell me I was to see you!" she cried. "I thought I was being taken to another cell. Oh, my lord Coeur, how I have longed to see you, to know how you fared!" Her eyes were becoming accustomed to the light and she peered up into his face intently. "Have they treated you well?" She paused and then burst out again: "Where is Robin, my lord? Have you any word of him?"

Coeur nodded slowly. "He's here in Lusignan. I've found a means of communicating with him."

"Will you send word to him, my lord, that I—that I love him so much he has seldom been out of my mind even—even when I've been gripped with the worst fears?"

"Yes, I'll send him your message at once."

He placed both hands on her shoulders and studied her with a troubled frown. "You mustn't let your confidence desert you," he said. "Everything is going to turn out well; be assured of that."

The girl allowed her head to droop. "I've given up all hope, my lord," she said. "At first I was certain you would find a way to save me. I waited, expecting each day the door would open and I would be told I was free. But nothing ever happened, and so I had to accustom myself to the truth, that you were a prisoner also and unable to do anything for me. I've been without hope for a very long time; how long I can't say, because I've lost all track of time. I've been in the dark so much that my only way of telling night from day is when meals are brought me."

"You mean they've been keeping you in a windowless cell!"

She nodded her head slowly. "Yes, my lord. It was hard to endure at first but now I'm reconciled to it. You can become accustomed to any hardship, even to hearing rats creeping on the floor and toads hopping in the dark." She raised her eyes and he saw that a look of fear had taken abrupt possession of them. "No, my lord, not to everything! Not to waiting, not to hearing nothing, not to the fear of death in such dreadful forms!" She lowered her eyes again. "I'm afraid that I'm a coward, my lord!"

As he listened to her, Coeur was thinking, "If it becomes necessary, I shall make a bargain with them, my life for hers. They're so anxious to proclaim my guilt to the world that they'll pardon her willingly enough to get a confession from me in exchange." This idea had been often in his mind but always before he had thrust it aside, knowing that he would sacrifice his honor as well as his life; for a confession would be an acknowledgment that he had killed Agnes Sorel, and history would so record it.

He brought forward the chair and seated her on it, turning it so that she faced the window. "Did you ever realize before how wonderful the sun is?" he asked. "Soon you will be able to leave this dark prison and go where you wish, to some place where you will bask in light and warmth."

"Soon?" There was a faint stirring of hope in the tone of her voice. "How I wish I could believe you! But—— No, I can't believe it. I know you are saying this to make me feel better."

"You must listen to me and accept every word I say. The trial is to be held here. The date has been set although I haven't yet been told what it is. It will be soon now for I have a feeling that they are coiled to strike. This much I have learned definitely. I am to go on trial alone. If I am freed of the charge—and I can't see how they can hope to convince even the most venal of judges on such an incredible accusation—then you will be set free without appearing in court. If I am convicted, you will be tried after me as an accomplice."

The girl could not repress a shudder as she heard the last words. He hastened to reassure her. "If everything else fails, my dear one, there is a way to save you—a way I am prepared to take. Ask no questions about it but allow yourself to believe this: that you will go free in the end. I swear by my belief in God and by my hope of divine forgiveness that this is the truth."

The expression on her face had changed as she listened. The despair which had possessed her when she entered was beginning to give way. "Do you mean it?" she asked in a whisper. "Can it be true?"

"Yes, my child." He was studying her with anxious eyes. "But to gain the freedom I promise you it will be necessary to help me. It's going to be hard for you. You must be prepared for"—he paused—"for the most diabolical and cruel pressure. They will try by every means to get a confession from you to be used against me."

"How can they hope for a confession from me?" Her eyes had opened wide with a conflict of emotion showing in them: surprise, incredulity, returning fear. "There's nothing I can tell them. Do they think I would invent lies to hurt you?"

"Have you been questioned?"

"Twice. The day after our arrest I was taken before Monsieur Gouffier, who questioned me for a long time. About a month later, when I was to be removed to a second prison, I was taken to him a second time. He kept me for an hour at least, asking me the same questions over and over again. Sometimes he asked them in different ways."

"Were you threatened? When you refused to say what he wanted, did Gouffier tell you they would adopt other methods?"

Valerie shook her head. "He was disappointed. I heard him say to one of the others, 'She's sly and she sticks to her story like a leech to the arm.' He looked very angry the second time, but he made no threats."

Coeur lowered his voice. "The only possibility they have of convicting us is to get a confession from one of us. They'll try to drag one from you first, I think." He leaned down toward her, his eyes fixed intently on hers. "Your ordeal will begin soon. They'll question you, hour after hour, day after day, trying to trap you, to force you into contradictions, threatening you. You'll become so weary you'll feel like telling them anything they want, anything to be free of them, and for a chance to rest. That's where the danger lies, my child. If you give in, you'll have peace—but for a few hours only. You will have signed your own death warrant as well as mine. They'll make you promises. They'll agree to let you go free if you appear as a witness against me. Put no trust in anything they say. Their promises are worth nothing. Once you've given in, they'll make what use of you they like and then they will hurry you to—to a cruel death."

"I know it," she whispered. "I've thought it over many times and I know the consequences if I am weak enough to give in to them."

The turnkey had left the door of the cell partly open and was standing in the hall. They could see him watching them and could hear the jingling of the keys as he twirled them about on one hand.

"Old Philippe won't allow us much more time," whispered Coeur. "There are so many things I wanted to tell you, but we must talk of those which count most." He dropped on one knee beside her and took her hand in his. "They're as cunning as serpents, these men who are supposed to stand for justice and the fair administration of the law. They may come to you and say I have confessed, and that your only hope of saving your life is to do the same. They may even tell you I've made statements incriminating *you*. That is the ruse they'll depend most upon—to divide us and set us against each other. Valerie! As you value your life, believe nothing they tell you about me. I have no more thought of acknowledging a crime I didn't commit than I have of denying my Maker. No matter what torture they may subject me to, I shall stand by the truth."

"Torture!" Valerie began to sob. "I can't stand pain," she said. "I've been healthy all my life and so I know little of sickness, but I can remember every injury I've had. I suffered so much from the sting of a bee that I was sure I couldn't bear it. An ache in the ear almost drove me mad." Her voice became choked with sobs and she had to stop until the flood of weeping subsided. "Kind Father in Heaven, what am I to do? I can't swear to lies; but can I withstand the pains of torture with this weak flesh of mine?"

"Come, child! You're in no danger. You mustn't yield to your imagination."

Now that her reserves of control had been exhausted, she began to talk of the most constant of her fears. "I've been told that when the executioner has a prisoner to be burned at the stake, he strangles her first. Is it true, my lord? Can I be sure of a merciful death before the flames reach me and consume me as they did the Maid?" She covered her face with her hands. "My lord Coeur, he's supposed to draw a knot around the neck and pull it so tight against the stake that one dies quickly. But is it not possible he will forget? Will he do it only if he's given a heavy bribe? How, how can the word be got to him? These thoughts run through my head all the time. Oh, merciful God, I think of nothing else! I shall go mad, my lord!"

Old Philippe put his head in at the door. "You've talked enough," he said. "I've been generous in letting you have so much time. Now, Mademoiselle, you must come with me."

Valerie buried her face in a handkerchief. In a few moments she stood up and replaced the damp linen in her belt. Her eyes were swollen and red but otherwise she had regained control of herself.

"I'm sorry I gave way," she said. "I'm not as weak as you will think now. I—I shall try very hard to be sensible and banish these—these weak fears."

"I know you will be brave," declared Coeur.

2

THE STONE STAIRS in the Tour de Mélusine, where both prisoners were lodged, seemed to curl endlessly upward. As the only light came from cressets at long intervals on the dark walls, the climbing of them was like going from one abyss of blackness into another. Two doors opened off each landing, one arched and high and with a peephole of the kind now known as a judas which could be opened only from the outside, and one low and with a small grating above it which indicated that the room beyond lacked all other means of obtaining light and air.

It was before one of the small doors that Old Philippe paused the next morning. He placed a bucket of steaming water on the floor while struggling to make the key turn in the lock. When the door creaked open, he was assailed by air of a particularly unpleasant heaviness, cold, damp, fetid.

"Mademoiselle!" he called, holding the lantern above his head and peering into the inky interior of the cell. "Mademoiselle! You are to dress and come with me. There is a hurry about it."

Receiving no response, he stepped into the room, carrying the lantern still higher and looking about him apprehensively. Was she dead that she did not answer? She had seemed the same as usual when he took her supper in the night before; but he knew from experience that strange and unexpected things happen in jails and that the most unlikely of inmates find ways of killing themselves. At first the room seemed empty. Then he caught a glimpse of her head protruding from the straw mattress on the floor.

The head moved, to his great relief; and, after a struggle, Valerie succeeded in extricating herself sufficiently to sit up. If Jacques Coeur had wondered about the straw clinging to her clothing the day before, he would have had the explanation now. To keep warm she had been compelled to slit the top of the mattress and wedge her body inside it.

"See!" said the turnkey. "I have brought you water. You are to make yourself neat and then come to the Council Room. The water," he added, "was promised to someone else who will now have to go without washing."

"This is the first hot water I've had since I came."

He had also brought a towel and, miracle of miracles, a tiny slab of hard soap. The ten minutes he allowed her, while he completed his round of cells on the same floor, proved sufficient: she was washed and dressed when he returned.

The Council Room was in the building known as the Queen's apartment. It was not large but it had many handsome Gothic windows and the furnishings were on a lavish scale. There was a massive table in the center and at the head of it sat Guillaume Gouffier, wearing the red cap and the red-and-white cloak of justice. He was flanked by two officials in similar attire.

"Valerie Maret," said Gouffier, "you have been before me twice already and you have been a very bad witness, as well you know. You have been stubborn and sly and"—he shot his head forward to look more closely at her—"and everything you have told me has been false! You've told me nothing but lies, clever lies to cover up your wicked deed and that of your partner. Today we must find nothing but truth in you." He seemed impatient to start on the task of involving her in the admissions which would cost her nothing less than her life. "If you are obdurate, it will be the worse for you!"

"I want to be a good witness, my lord," said Valerie in a supplicating voice, watching him with the frightened intentness of an animal caught in a trap. "I shall tell you the truth. I've tried always to tell you the truth, my lord, all of the truth."

"You've told me nothing but lies!" Gouffier glanced down the table at the clerk who was mending the point of a quill pen. "You must take down everything she says today, Master Herault. If she tries to evade us, we must see to it that she's trapped by her own falsehoods."

At the end of two hours the door opened and the Governor entered. He smiled and bowed to Gouffier and his associates and then looked at Valerie and raised his eyebrows in what seemingly was intended as a form of greeting. Auguste de Lenvers was an elderly man with a face like a comic mask. His eyebrows had an upward slant such as is seen in oriental idols, and his nose, not to be outdone, turned up even more abruptly. He looked, as a result, a veritable prince of good nature; an effect heightened by the fact that his stomach was round and full and his legs, as much of them as showed under his handsome velvet kirtle, were fat and grotesquely bowed.

"How have things progressed, my lord Gouffier?" he asked.

Gouffier scowled sulkily. "Badly," he muttered. "We can do nothing with her, hedge brat that she is. She stands by her story."

The Governor rubbed his hands gently and regarded Valerie with a smile which fairly oozed benevolence. "I'm disappointed," he chirped. "I expected, my lord Gouffier, that you would have the truth out of her as fast as a moneylender can coax the last coin out of a debtor's pocket."

"I give up," declared Gouffier. "She's yours now, my lord Governor. Take whatever steps you think necessary."

"I think," said the Governor, "we must now consider using—other methods."

2

Valerie spent a sleepless night. The Governor's words kept repeating themselves in her brain. "Other methods," he had said; and there could be no question as to what he had meant.

Most of the time she gave to prayer, kneeling on the edge of the rough mattress, her eyes turned fervently up to the darkness above her. "O God, Thou knowst I am innocent!" she repeated again and again. "Spare me the pain of torture. Find some way, O Lord, to soften their hearts before I'm dragged to the suffering of the rack. If this cannot be, O Lord, look down on me and lend me the strength and the stoutness of will to suffer this ordeal. Let me resist them to the end so that my tongue won't be guilty of uttering lies."

She was still praying when Old Philippe brought her breakfast in the morning. He nodded his head approvingly. "That is good," he said. Then he added: "I've brought you a fine breakfast. There are eggs as well as meat, and bread hot from the oven. And, see, a fine strong wine."

"Then I am to go below?" she asked, in a tense whisper. "Is it because of what—of what I must face that you think I need a good breakfast and the strong wine?"

Long experience had calloused Philippe's mind and it was with a sense of surprise that he now realized he was feeling sorry for her. This was due, of course, to the exceptional nature of the case. The old turnkey did not think her guilty. No one on the prison staff believed that Jacques Coeur, with her connivance and perhaps help, had poisoned Agnes Sorel.

"All I know, Mademoiselle," he said, "is that you're to go below with me. The Governor will be there, but not my lord Gouffier. It will be another questioning perhaps."

"And Gilles?" cried Valerie. "Gilles the executioner will be there! He will be ready with his hot fires and pincers!"

"Gilles will be there," conceded the old man. "But, Mademoiselle, you must not draw conclusions. There are other prisoners."

Valerie refused the food but took a drink of the wine. "No, Monsieur Philippe," she said in a voice which trembled, "it won't be for another questioning. The time for that is passed. He, the cruel fat man, said they would use 'other methods.' He meant the torture! Of course he did, Monsieur Philippe!" Her voice had lifted and it was apparent from the contorted expression of her face that she was on the verge of hysteria. "What else could he mean? What else?"

"If you aren't going to eat the fine, warm food, we might as well start."

"I can't eat anything. It would choke me. But I'm thankful to you for bringing it."

The keys began to jingle on the ring, a sign that the old man was growing impatient. "We must hurry," he said.

"Spare me a moment. I—I think I am going to my death. I must show a good front, good Monsieur Philippe, if this is to be my last day on earth."

She dipped her hands in what was left of the water he had brought the day before and laved her face, with particular care to remove all traces of weeping from about her eyes. She ran a quick hand over her hair and then adjusted her dress, brushing away the pieces of straw which adhered to it.

"Do I look better?" she asked. "I mustn't be a coward. I must seem brave and—and ready for anything they may do."

The turnkey led the way down the winding stairway. Valerie followed him with feet which had to be forced by sheer will power to do their duty. The calmness she had shown on leaving the cell was deserting her. Questions raced through her mind and she had to bite her lips to keep from crying out in panic. Would they stretch her on the rack and loosen her joints so that she would never be able to walk again? Would they suspend her on the estrapade over a blazing fire? Would they cut off the tip of her tongue as a final demand that she use what was left of it to tell the lies they required of her? Such things were done all the time, she knew, and there was no reason to hope that any leniency would be shown in her case.

They turned at the foot of the stairs into a long, dark vault with arched ceiling and no windows. Burning torches in tall iron stands supplied what light there was. Valerie was afraid to look about her for fear of what she might see. She was conscious of a heavy odor of burning.

The silence was broken by the voice of Auguste de Lenvers. "Valerie Maret, you are to come with me."

She followed him, her eyes lowered. She was able to see no more than the backs of his fat calves in parti-colored hose of red and yellow which looked ridiculously out of keeping with the occasion. He was wearing shoes of an extreme fashion, with tasseled points above the heels and toes which curled up a full foot so that he had to step with great care.

She was conscious now of others in the room, of a table at which several men were seated, of their red robes, and of the easy talk going forward among them. For one startled moment she caught a view of a huge and hairy man stripped to the waist who stood so far back that she could not make out any details of his face. She dropped her eyes again at once, knowing that this must be Gilles, Gilles the chief torturer whose cruelly expert hands would administer the instruments selected to break and tear and burn her body.

"You will sit here, Valerie Maret," said the Governor, coming to a stop and pointing to a wooden bench against the wall.

The bench was so high that only the tips of her toes touched the floor when she seated herself. She looked so small that one of the men at the table remarked on it to his companions.

"She seems a mere child," he whispered. "And, what's more, she has the appearance of being as innocent as one."

"I've never believed her anything but innocent," affirmed the man on his right. He drew his head to one side and gestured with his hands. "Innocent or guilty, it's no concern of ours, Messires. We do as we are told."

The Governor had seated himself beside Valerie with such an air of benevolence that one might have thought of him as her protector. He drew a scented handkerchief from a pocket inside his tunic and touched it daintily to his nose. If Valerie had been in a frame of mind which made observation of such detail possible, she would have seen that he was most meticulous about his dress and that his graying locks had been trimmed and curled so that they barely touched his collar, which happened to be the fashionable length at the moment.

"You must stay here," he began, "until they are through with another questioning. The prisoner has been found guilty of a most serious crime, the burning of a château in which two lives were lost, and it's believed he had accomplices. We are trying to get their names." Auguste de Lenvers gave his head a shake which indicated annoyance. "He's a stubborn fellow and we're having a great deal of trouble with him. For three days his head has been confined in the branks. It's a mask of iron, Mademoiselle, which is used for scolding women, but in this one the metal gag, which goes into the mouth and so prevents any talking, was provided with sharp spikes which cut into the tongue and the roof of the mouth with every move. We were sure he would be ready to talk. But there he is"—pointing beyond the table where the board of inquisitors sat—"and so far he hasn't uttered a word."

Valerie's eyes, much against her will, turned in the direction indicated. A man, naked save for a loincloth and with his head encased in an iron mask, was strapped in a low chair. At a command from the Governor an attendant emerged from the darkness behind Gilles and proceeded to remove the mask from the prisoner's head. Valerie shuddered. The man's face was inflamed and covered with clotted blood and the lips were so swollen that they stuck out like the jaw of an ape. His eyes were closed, his breathing labored.

"Are you ready to talk, Jean Milleteste?" called the Governor.

The unfortunate man saw the figure of Gilles, standing in readiness in the shadows. He uttered a despairing cry and sprang to his feet. The chair strapped to him hampered his movements and he had gone no more than halfway to the door when two prison attendants overtook him.

"Make ready with him," said Auguste de Lenvers.

The ropes which bound the prisoner to the chair were untied and he was then forced to a reclining position on a stone bench near the table of the questioners. With violent haste his arms and legs were strapped down securely.

"It's going to be necessary with this fellow to employ an ingenious device we have recently brought from the Low Countries." The Governor made this explanation for Valerie's benefit, speaking with a smack of the lips as though he relished the prospect. "We're informed it has never failed to bring results."

One of the red-robed men at the table leaned back to call over his shoulder, "Gilles, you black ape, what is the delay?"

A thin, piping voice answered from the other end of the vault. "The trap is ready, my lords. I am bringing it."

Valerie raised her head and saw the giant form of the torturer moving toward them. He seemed to become larger and more fearsome with each step. She saw also, with eyes which refused to linger on any one object, that the shadows from which he emerged contained the dreaded and much-whispered-about instruments used to produce unbearable pain. Not knowing what they were, but fearing them even more for that reason, Valerie's eyes passed hurriedly over the elevated frame of the rack, the innocent-appearing water dome, the coffin-like *chambre à crucer* which was a chest lined with sharp stones and spikes in which victims were kept for days and weeks at a time. A hearth at the far end was throwing a flickering light over these fantastic shapes.

Valerie saw that Gilles was carrying in his arms a round metal container more than a foot in diameter and with an open top. When he reached the bench where his victim lay, he reversed this object and placed it on the naked stomach of the recumbent man, pressing it down carefully to make sure no space was left around the edge. It could now be seen that the exposed surface had a circular indentation the size of a small frying pan.

Gilles proceeded to build a fire in the indented top of this instrument he had called a trap. Heaping it with charcoal, he achieved a small blaze which he pumped with a bellows until the fuel crackled. The man beneath began to twitch as the heat reached him through the iron. He struggled to get free of his bonds and his breathing turned to a frenzied pant.

Valerie forgot her own plight in the pity she felt for the suffering man. She watched with strained intentness, her hands clenched in her lap. "The iron is burning into his flesh!" she gasped. "Spare him this agony, my lord!"

The Governor had risen and was watching the proceedings with a fascination which manifested itself in a continual moistening of the lips and a tendency to jerk his hands about and to open and close his fingers. He turned to look down at her for the briefest moment and to say. "This is no more than the start."

Suddenly the victim gave a loud screech. It could be seen that his whole body was straining frantically to break the bonds holding him down to the bench. The scream was followed by others until they blended into a steady stream of unearthly sound. The vaulted chamber rang with the agonized clamor.

"This is what we learned from the Dutch," said the Governor, nodding down to her with excitement in his eyes. "There are rats in the trap, three of them, great fellows with strong, sharp claws. The heat has driven them crazy. Listen to them squeal! They're scratching and burrowing into his bowels in an effort to escape!"

Valerie emitted a cry as sharp as the screams of the victim and covered her face with her hands. Auguste de Lenvers turned quickly and leaned down over her while he dragged her hands away with angry haste.

"You were brought here to watch!" he exclaimed. "You must see what it's like. Come, we must have none of this!"

But her capacity for watching was over. She had fainted. With the impatient Governor still gripping both of her hands, her body slipped down on the bench and her head fell forward limply.

The screams of the victim had ceased. Gilles had removed the trap and the rats had leaped to the floor from the raw and bleeding mid-section of the bound figure. They were scampering wildly, seeking shelter and leaving red nail marks on the stones. The prisoner had given in. He was muttering now in a voice unnatural with pain. An officer at the table was taking down what he said with flying fingers.

The Governor watched two attendants carry the form of Valerie from the chamber. He seemed well satisfied.

"I shall give her two days to think it over," he said to himself. "Then she must make up her mind to tell us the things we want to hear—or be ready to have Gilles fit the trap over her own tender little girdlestead."

3

The seller of books raised his head and smiled. D'Arlay and his sailor companion shortened their strides, paused, then turned in at the booth under the Sign of the Silver Missal. There were no other customers.

"Do you realize," asked the man behind the counter, his intelligent eyes studying them both intently, "how strong the feeling in this town runs against the King and his officers in the matter of Jacques Coeur and the girl? No one believes them guilty. On the other hand, there is a general tendency to consider the Moneyman a hero. He made it possible for the King to free our country of the invaders. He finished the work the Maid began. I'm sure a similar feeling exists all over France."

D'Arlay answered in a tone of fervent agreement. "I am as sure of that as you are. How could anyone, except the court officers who will share the spoils and the King himself, who will be free of his loans, feel any other way?"

"It seems," said the custodian of the booth, in a low voice, "that the only reward for leaders, who come up from the masses to save France, is death. First there was Marcel and then the Maid and now our great and generous and farseeing Jacques Coeur." The bookseller paused and then added in a somewhat apologetic tone of voice: "You will know from this that I had other reasons for leaving Paris than my need for bigger profits. I held views which the authorities regarded with the deepest abhorrence."

"You should be careful who hears you."

"Life is a poor thing if you have to be careful in saying what you believe." The seller of books shook his head vigorously. "I thought I could see in the changes the Moneyman was making the start of better things in the world. And this will be the end of it. . . . It's the common belief in the town that you are here in Coeur's interest. You will find a readiness to help in almost any quarter where you may seek assistance."

He lifted his hand which had been lying flat on the counter. A note had been concealed under it. He pushed it across the board.

"I was told," said the seller of books, "that it's a matter of rather considerable urgency."

When the note was opened in the seclusion of their rooms, it was found to be of even greater urgency than Pierre Dupain had made them believe.

In two days [it read] V. will be subjected to the most barbarous and horrible of torture. Her spirit is stanch but she lacks the physical strength to withstand it. I pray you, I beseech you, to take the only means of saving her. Go to the King and ask him to forbid it. No one else has the authority or will to stop these beasts who hold our fate in their hands.

D'Arlay looked at his companion. "It's fortunate that the court is at Tours. How do you estimate the distance?"

"Nearly eighty miles, Robin."

"The king must be seen as early as possible tomorrow. We have two nights and one day in which to accomplish everything. This means I must ride to Tours alone. Don't shake your head, Jean, you would founder half-a-dozen horses on a ride such as this, and hold me back to boot."

4

D'Arlay betook himself to the lobby of the royal dining hall and paced up and down impatiently while the meal within progressed from one stately course to another. An hour later he was told that the King had withdrawn by a private door to his own apartments to read and write letters and that no one would be permitted to interrupt him. He began to suspect that word of his presence had reached Charles and that the King was avoiding him. Fuming inwardly, he sought out an official of the court who came from his own native Anjou and with whom he was on the best of terms. The latter informed him that the usual afternoon hunt was to be dispensed with as the King, after his period of rest and solitude, would have a consultation with a party of Spanish envoys. He would then almost certainly go for a solitary stroll in the gardens to improve his appetite for supper. It would be a case of catching him then or abandoning all hope of an audience that day.

"And there is nothing I can do in the meantime?"

"Nothing, my dear Robin. The only hope you have now is to get a hearing in the gardens. And, a word in your ear. Let none of the court officials know what you are about. They'll thwart you by some means if you do."

Late that afternoon, acting on the suggestion of his friend, D'Arlay gained entrance to the gardens by a side portal. No one was about but he thought it wise, in view of the warning he had received, to station himself in a clump of high shrubs where he could not be seen. Here he remained a long time. The shadows of evening began to fall and the conviction grew in him that he had been sent here on a wild-goose chase. He said to himself bitterly: "There's no honesty or decency in courtiers. Even my old friend Raoul has made himself part of this conspiracy to keep me from seeing the King."

He realized the next moment that he had done his friend an injustice. Wrapped in a long cloak which covered him from head to foot and with his habitual beaver hat pulled so low over his brow that it was not easy to distinguish the royal countenance, the King had entered the gardens alone and was strolling down a path which came close to the clump of shrubs. D'Arlay stepped out from his place of concealment and waited for Charles of France to draw closer.

"Sire," he said, with a low bow, "I am the Sire d'Arlay and I beseech a brief audience with you. It's a matter of life and death or I would not have intruded myself on you in this way."

The King halted some distance off. He peered at the intruder with the care acquired by all who live their days in constant danger of attack. When he had convinced himself of the identity of his petitioner, he gave an impatient grunt.

"So it's the Sire d'Arlay!" Charles of France regarded his visitor with a cold eye. "It's a long time since I have seen the Sire d'Arlay. It has seemed to me always that unpleasant things are connected with any mention of the Sire d'Arlay. He does not come to court. He does not marry, though suitable matches are suggested which have the sanction of his King. He holds beliefs which are not in accordance with his station in life and the obligations of knighthood." The King paused and seemed on the point of turning back. "You have not been a good subject, Sire d'Arlay."

"Sire, I accepted the gage of battle when Jacques de Lalain cast aspersions on the good name of the knights of France. I fought through the whole of the Normandy campaign in the most difficult service, and I performed daily the most dangerous of functions. There has never been a disloyal thought in my mind nor a seditious word on my lips. I've never asked a favor of my liege lord. I protest, sire, that I've been a good subject."

The King's eyes had been casting about, here and there and up and down, but never meeting those of D'Arlay. Suddenly he looked squarely at the latter for several moments. D'Arlay read such a degree of animosity there that he was sure his plea would be made in vain.

"There was an occasion——" began the King. Then he stopped. "Enough. This is the day of audience. I can't deny you the privilege I allow the humblest of my subjects. What is it you wish to say?"

"Tomorrow morning, unless you order it stopped, Valerie Maret will be subjected to torture at Lusignan. She will die under it, sire, or the unbearable pain inflicted on her will force her to confess a crime of which she is innocent."

There was a long pause. That the King was reluctant to discuss the case was clear, not only from his hesitation but also from the lack of ease he displayed in his manner. "It's my belief that the usual course is being followed," he said at last.

"Then, sire, justice demands that the usual course should not be followed."

Charles regarded his petitioner somberly. "It is clear, Sire d'Arlay, that you are at odds with what we have always deemed right and just, that you disapprove of torture as a means of reaching the truth."

"Yes, sire. I gave no thought to it before, accepting it in principle as something which had always been done and which must, on that account, be right and just. But now I see it close at hand, and with knowledge of the case. I realize now, sire, that it's both wrong and cruel." The arguments he had been preparing all afternoon began to roll forth. "Torture is a survival from the very darkest ages, a weapon of oppression which should no longer be used in these enlightened days. It's a system by which insensitive criminals can go free while innocent people, who lack the stamina to withstand it, must pay the penalty of guilt."

"It was talk of this kind which led the peasants to rise in the days of the Jacquerie," declared the King. He studied D'Arlay with bitter intentness. "Does your confidence in the innocence of the girl extend also to Jacques Coeur?"

"Yes, sire. Jacques Coeur is a great patriot and a faithful servant of the Crown. It's inconceivable that he could have poisoned the Lady Agnes."

"You are ill informed, Sire d'Arlay. It is conceivable to all who have studied the evidence. It is conceivable to me."

The King looked at D'Arlay and shook his head. "It comes to this," he said, "that there is a strong case against the prisoners. A prudent and fair king does not interfere with the working of his courts. I must tell you, therefore, that I have no intent to intervene on behalf of my guilty servant, Jacques Coeur, or his lowborn accomplice."

There was a determination in his voice and manner which left no doubt that his mind was made up. Realizing this, D'Arlay decided it would be necessary to use his final and, he hoped, most effective argument.

"It's easy to believe in the innocence of Valerie Maret," he said, "when one knows she was a niece—illegitimate, it is true, but a full blood relation nevertheless—of the Lady Agnes."

The King looked up at once with a startled expression. "A niece of the Lady Agnes!" he exclaimed. "Come, Sire d'Arlay, you carry your insistence too far! I was first led to believe she was a cousin of the Comtesse de Burey. Later I learned she was in reality the daughter of a common strolling player. Now you come to me with this unbelievable claim, hoping my sympathy will be stirred."

"The proofs can be obtained readily enough. But, sire, are proofs necessary to anyone who has seen her? Could such a close resemblance be explained in any other way than by blood relationship?"

The King's resolution was shaken. He frowned, he rubbed his chin, he gave D'Arlay a dozen quick and furtive glances as though to catch him off guard and glean further enlightenment in that way. Finally he said, "And if it were true—which I do not yet allow nor entertain as a possibility— what bearing could it have on the case?"

"It's difficult for me, a subject, to answer the question my liege lord has asked."

"If you have no answer, then we may consider this discussion at an end."

"I have an answer." D'Arlay spoke without hesitation or reserve although he knew that what he now proposed to say might be construed as treasonable. "After I have given it, you may say again that I am a bad subject and worthy of punishment. But, sire, innocent lives are at stake and I must not permit any considerations of prudence to control my tongue." He paused and then plunged headlong into what he had to say. "My liege lord, you must be aware of the feeling which exists in connection with the burning of the Maid. It's no secret that people ask why no effort was made to rescue her or to procure her release. There has never been any doubt in my mind that there were good reasons for the course followed. To attempt a rescue might have led to a military disaster. But, sire, many people don't know this and I am sure the question sometimes comes into your mind as to what the annals of the future will say about it. Sire! There can be no doubt at all that history will also record the part that Jacques Coeur has played in freeing France." He looked the King squarely in the eye as he continued: "Can you allow history to link these two events? Must it be recorded that you permitted your great servant to be convicted on evidence wrung by torture from the young and innocent niece of the Lady Agnes Sorel?"

The King was too startled to make any reply at once. He looked at D'Arlay as though he found it impossible to believe that any subject of his had dared to speak with such frankness. Finally he walked to one side and remained there for some time, his eyes fixed on the dark clouds with which the sky was overcast.

"Sire d'Arlay," he said when he returned, "you have spoken to me in words that no one has ever dared use before. That I resent them, and shall never forget nor forgive you for so speaking, must be clear to you. And yet, Sire d'Arlay, I'm compelled to admire your courage and to believe that nothing but a deep conviction could have induced you to say these things. And indeed you have probed cleverly!" he exclaimed with a sudden display of feeling. "No king can fail to think of what history will record of him and to wish his authority could run beyond his death to control the written word. I am so sensitive on this point that I have even considered you may be right. As I shall exact no punishment, I lay this command on you, Sire d'Arlay, that you never tell it that you dared to address me so, and that I listened. This must be a closed issue between us."

D'Arlay bowed. "You have my solemn promise, sire."

"The purpose of Jacques Coeur was clear," went on the King. "He intended to replace the Lady Agnes with this girl and to reap such benefit as he might through her influence. And now," he said, with sudden fury, "it becomes necessary, in order to establish his guilt, to tell the whole story in court! Things which I strove continuously to keep under cover will now be made known to the whole world!" He was breathing so hard that it was some moments before he continued. "The law must take its course. If Jacques Coeur and this girl plotted between them to remove the Lady Agnes from their path, they must pay the penalty. They will have a fair trial. One thing only must be held back. In deference to the memory of that lovely and sainted lady, the claim of this ungrateful girl to blood relationship must not be stated in court. I grant you one thing: the girl will not be put to the torture. I shall issue an order at once forbidding it." He scowled when he observed the relief which showed itself on his petitioner's face. "It's a proof of my fairness that I make this concession to a meddler who has offended me bitterly. You are a bad subject, Sire d'Arlay. It will be wise, Sire d'Arlay, if you never show your face again at court."

5

Guillaume Gouffier and Auguste de Lenvers sat in the Council Room and stared at each other bitterly. Two documents bearing the royal seal lay on the table between them.

"The King's messenger arrived half an hour after the time we had planned to begin the questioning," said Gouffier. "Thus we see, my lord Governor, that if the Sire d'Arlay had not taken it on himself to bring a copy of the order, we would now have the confession we need in our possession."

"That is true. The Sire d'Arlay is solely responsible for this upset in our plans."

Guillaume Gouffier glowered down at the two documents. He lifted one in a hand which seemed to loathe the touch of it. He allowed his eye to scan the words which had compelled them, most reluctantly, to close the torture chamber. "We must never forget," he said, in a low tone, "what the Sire d'Arlay has done for us. Never, Auguste, my friend."

A silence fell between them. The Governor had been summoned so summarily from his chambers to receive the King's commands that he had not had time for breakfast. He looked now at the tray of food which had been brought for him and which lay on the table beside the unwelcome documents. Starting to eat, he found that his appetite lacked the keen edge he usually brought to the first meal of the day. As he picked gingerly at the food, he kept an eye on the morose countenance of Guillaume Gouffier.

"I protest, my good Guillaume, that you are unduly downcast," he said finally. "Unless I'm at fault in my understanding of the King's order, it lays one prohibition on us only—we must not put her to the torture."

"And is that not enough to upset everything we had planned?"

"Not necessarily." The Governor devoted several moments to disposing of a mouthful of trousoned eel which, under ordinary circumstances, was his favorite breakfast dish. "The order enjoins us not to use torture which I take to mean the subjection of her tender limbs and fresh young body to the instruments in the torture chamber."

Gouffier commented impatiently, "Are you giving me a lesson, Auguste, in the interpretation of official language?"

The Governor smiled slyly. "Not at all, Guillaume. I am leading up to a suggestion which may enable us to achieve our purpose without going contrary in any way to the royal command. There's nothing in the order to prevent us from using other forms of persuasion which might prove just as effective."

"Be more explicit, if you please, my wise Auguste."

"There is," said the Governor, beginning to attack his food with some of his habitual zest, "the matter of cells. A cell can be so uncomfortable, so wearing on all the senses, that it has the same effect as torture. It is, naturally, a slower method but—— Ah, my still wiser Guillaume, it is very, very sure!"

Gouffier proceeded to give the problem some thought. "You have a cage?" he asked finally.

"Naturally. I was on the point of mentioning that possibility."

Valerie was led to a cell on the ground floor of the Tour de Mélusine. It was large and airy and light. More than that, it was furnished in a manner bordering on the elegant. There was a bed with a canopy and pillows with white linen covers and steps at one side with embroidered panels. There was a chair, large and padded and with rests for the feet as well as the arms, a cabinet for bedroom utensils, a crucifix on the wall, a row of pots containing flowers in one window. It was, clearly, destined for the occupancy of prisoners of the very highest order.

She came in with a white face and hands which trembled visibly (for, of course, they had not told her that the will of Charles of France now stood between her and the torture chamber), but the sight of all this luxury brought her some degree of reassurance. She looked about her and said, "It's a beautiful room."

The head turnkey, who was in charge of the arrangements, shook his head at her. "Wait, Mademoiselle, until I show you what is behind that curtain."

For the first time she became aware of the significance of a heavy brown tapestry which cut off one wall of the apartment. She grew pale again and asked in a frightened voice, "What is it, good master?"

The turnkey drew the curtain back and Valerie's hand went to her lips to suppress a cry of alarm. The space behind it was taken up by a cage with wide black iron bars. It was a grim-looking thing, with a huge lock on the door and panels of metal attached at each side. One panel carried the words, "Avow All or Suffer Herein," and the other, "The Eye of the Lord Is Turned Away from Ye." The proportions of the cage were of a sinister peculiarity. It was not high enough, clearly, to allow an occupant to stand upright nor long enough to permit of lying down. It was so designed that any unhappy individual compelled to remain inside it would perforce sit with knees drawn up or lie on the floor in the trying position known as the Jackknife.

The turnkey unlocked the door of the cage and said, "Mademoiselle is to go inside."

She looked about her at the comfort of the room and then at this grim receptacle, and shook her head. "I should have known," she whispered. "There is no kindness or justice in them."

Guillaume Gouffier and the Governor entered soon thereafter and found her ensconced behind the bars with her chin resting on her knees and a look of bewilderment and horror on her face. Dusting his nose with his handkerchief, Auguste de Lenvers approached the cage and looked down at her.

"Mademoiselle," he said, "it has been decided that the limits of your obduracy are to be tested in ways other than those used in the chamber you visited the other day."

"Yes, my lord," said Valerie, beginning to tremble afresh.

"But we haven't given up our intention of getting the truth out of you. You will stay where you are without being allowed out for any reason whatever, not even for illness or bodily disability, until you are prepared to talk. Do you understand that?"

"Yes, my lord."

"I would advise an early surrender to reason. Long tenancy of the cage has invariably an adverse effect on the health."

Guillaume Gouffier had been looking about him with a satisfied air. He now volunteered a suggestion.

"I think, my good Auguste, it would be wise not to draw the curtain. We must allow Mademoiselle, while she sits there in such obvious discomfort, to enjoy a view of the soft bed, the luxurious chair, the cool water in the basin and the other utensils needed for bodily uses, which will be hers as soon as she makes up her mind to be sensible."

3

JACQUES COEUR had completed his breakfast when the door of his cell opened with a scraping and squealing of hinges to admit the Governor.

Auguste de Lenvers was attired in festive garb, a white cloak over a blue tunic, a tall feather in his hat. With fingers tucked in his belt he looked about him, taking in the generous light pouring through the window and the neatness of the cell.

"You live in considerable comfort," he said, in a tone which implied that such had not been intended. "Well, it won't be for long. I've come to tell you, Jacques Coeur, that your trial begins today. The court will open in half an hour. It will be your wish, no doubt, to take some pains with your attire before going down."

The prisoner looked at him with disbelief. "The trial begins today!" he cried. "Surely you don't mean what you say, my lord Governor."

"I mean what I say, as you will discover immediately."

"Are you aware, are the judges aware, that I've had no notice?"

"I am giving you notice now, Jacques Coeur."

The prisoner indulged in an angry laugh. "You deign to jest at my expense. What can I do in half an hour? I haven't yet been told the nature of the evidence on which this infamous charge is based. How, then, can I be expected to meet it and offer my defense? Are the judges aware also that I've been given no opportunity to summon witnesses on my behalf?"

"You raise two points and I shall answer them in the order you have propounded them," said the Governor. He raised a finger. "First, the Bed of Justice, before which you are to appear, decided you were not to know the nature of the evidence. If you did, you would come before them with devious reasoning on your tongue and carefully contrived testimony to offer in defense. The course of justice would be delayed." Another finger went up. "Second, it's not intended to permit the calling of witnesses for the defense. It will be clear to you, therefore, that the decision to open proceedings today is in no sense a hardship. Further waiting would have been of no service to you."

Coeur had listened with growing consternation. "My lord Governor, this is contrary to all established rules!" he cried. "Have I heard you aright, that I'm not to be allowed to call my own witnesses? How can I be expected to prove my innocence if only the perjured evidence of this woman, and those who support her, is to be heard?"

Auguste de Lenvers smiled. "You should realize by this time, Jacques Coeur, that there is no expectation that you will prove your innocence. The case against you is strong and conclusive." He glanced about the cell a second time. "Is there anything you require before going below? Did they bring you hot water this morning? I gave orders you were to be well supplied. Has your razor a good edge? I like my prisoners to be presentable when they're led in for trial."

Coeur looked him steadily in the eye. "Truly I am being highly favored," he said. "I'm forbidden to defend myself. I'll go into court as completely silenced as though my mouth had been gagged. But at least I am allowed hot water and a sharp razor. Could I ask for more?" He gave vent to a short laugh. "You are most kind. I shall strive to repay your very great kindness by not bringing any discredit on you."

2

The Bed of Justice had been set up in the main hall. It took the form of a square surrounded by a frame partition not more than ten feet high over which black hangings had been draped. One corner of the square had been left open to serve as an entrance and opposite it was a dais with five chairs and a table. Here the judges sat in all the dignity and austerity of long robes trimmed with ermine and black hoods bearing the fleur-de-lys. A raised tier of seats ran along all four sides. Here were seated the distinguished guests (as he learned later, there had been a mad scramble to obtain places), ladies as well as men, and all in a high state of expectation. A second and lower row was occupied by officers of the court and lawyers. Out in the center, where every pair of eyes could rest on it, was a low-backed chair. This was for the prisoner.

All seats, including those of the five judges, were occupied when Jacques Coeur was led in. He had recovered his composure. There was even the suggestion of a cold smile in his eyes as he walked to the chair in the center. Here he paused and glanced around the line of closely packed seats, at the fine ladies and gentlemen rustling in silks and satins in the top row, and the lawyers below with paper on their knees and pens that were already scratching busily.

"This is indeed a great honor," he said. "For months I've dwelt in solitary confinement but at least I'm to be tried in the full light of day and even with much pomp and ceremony. I perceive that we have a goodly and distinguished company. All my acknowledged enemies are here, all who have reason to anticipate benefits from my downfall, all my debtors. But my most august judges, and you also, my ladies and gentlemen, I'm compelled to note one omission. None of my friends are here."

There was a moment's silence and then someone, probably one of the less favored who stood outside the wall of the Bed and could hear but not see, began to laugh. A titter ran along the tiers of seats in which even some of the lawyers, usually the most guarded and obsequious of men, joined.

"Strange as it may seem, I have friends," went on Coeur. "I didn't expect to find them here. I think, my lords and ladies, they could be found at this moment in the streets leading to this prison where Jacques Coeur goes on trial. I'm sure they fill the square in front of the cathedral and that they are taking a more sincere interest in the outcome than those who sit within these walls. I'm sure that all over France the eyes of millions who are my friends will be turned in this direction and that in their hearts will be prayers for the man of common birth who rose to be the King's Moneyman and who played a rather unusual part of freeing the land from the hated invaders."

Guillaume Gouffier, who sat at the center of the judges' table, said sharply, "The accused will take his seat so that the proceedings may start."

Coeur squared around to face his judges. He looked at each in turn and there was no longer any suggestion of a smile in his eyes. They had become hard, combative, doubly alert.

"In the performance of my duties as a minister of the King," he said, "I have always been fully conscious of the fact that I have enemies. I've been especially aware of the enmity of three men. Permit me to name them: Guillaume Gouffier, Antoine de Chabannes, Otto de Castellane. Is it a coincidence, or is it an indication of the nature of the justice which can be expected here, that these three men are seated among my judges? But even the presence of my most active ill-wishers among the five who are to judge me is not the greatest of the many shocks I have experienced today. Am I to believe my eyes when I see that the other two judges are—Jean Dauvet, the King's Attorney General, and Jean Barbin, King's Advocate! These two learned men will first try the case. Then, having completed their efforts to prove me guilty, they will take their seats with the three other judges—that most impartial and benevolent trio—and help to reach a verdict on their own efforts! Truly"—his voice rose until it resounded through the hall—"this is the most glaring mockery of justice! After this we may expect to see students at the universities mounting the platform to award themselves degrees and sinners deciding on their right to pass the gates of Paradise! After this we may accept it as truth that honesty has fled our courts of justice and innocent men are at the mercy of liars and cheats!"

The hall was in a tumult. From beyond the partitions, where the late arrivals stood, came the sound of much loud comment and even of scuffling, as proof that the words of the accused had aroused dispute. In the tier of seats where the favored ones sat ladies whispered behind fans and gentlemen in beaver hats expostulated over the effrontery of the prisoner. Guillaume Gouffier was pounding angrily on the table for order. "There will be no making of speeches!" he shouted repeatedly.

Coeur waited for several moments and then took advantage of a lull to continue with what he had to say.

"My words are not intended for the ears of the court," he declared. "I can't hope to win leniency from my judges nor need I fear that what I have said will deepen the enmity with which they approach their tasks. I'm hoping that a whisper of what I've said will reach those men and women who crowd the streets before my prison and fill the cathedral square and, in time, the people of France. I want my friends to know the odds I face. I want my countrymen to go on respecting Jacques Coeur and knowing him innocent, in spite of any verdict which may be rendered here. I want them to go on believing me innocent of this unthinkable and absurd and utterly revolting charge!"

He stopped speaking, glanced slowly about the room, and then sat down in the chair. Crossing one leg over the other, he raised a hand and then dropped it as a signal that the hearing should start.

3

The first witness was Agnes Sorel's maid, a small woman overcome with her grief. She was weeping when she came forward to testify and the fount had not dried up when she left. Sometimes it was no more than a gentle irrigation of the cheeks but, whenever the nature of the evidence warranted, she would puff and catch her breath and sometimes burst out into loud blubbering.

Guillaume Gouffier questioned her himself, establishing first her identity and the post she filled.

"Did you see the Lady Agnes constantly during her long illness?"

"Yes, my lord. I was always with her. I slept beside her bed—when I was able to sleep, my lord, which was seldom on account of the worrying. I took her to the *chaise percée*. I washed her in scented water twice a day——"

"I'm sure you were faithful, but——"

Nothing could stop the witness on this point. With swimming eyes she expatiated on the daily ritual of the sickroom. She was full of details about sponging and scrubbing and dosing. Gouffier gave up the effort to stem the tide and turned her over to Dauvet, the Attorney General, with a gesture of despair. The latter, skilled in the control of loquacity, brought her promptly to heel.

"You say your mistress allowed no eyes but yours to rest on her. Does that apply to her physician?"

There was a sternness in his voice which robbed her of the desire to wander.

"Yes, my lord. It was always dark in the room when he came."

"But there would be candles?"

"Not always."

Jacques Coeur heard this with satisfaction. "When I question this woman," he said to himself, "it won't be hard to make her admit how little there was to be done, that Agnes Sorel was dying and they all knew it. Later I shall get the same admissions from the physician himself." Now that the action had begun, he felt his interest quickening and even a small measure of optimism as to the outcome. He knew as much of law as though he had been a lawyer himself and he was sure it would prove easy to pick holes in the caset hey had built up against him.

Dauvet was proceeding with his questioning of the witness. "But you were not with your mistress the morning of February eight when she talked to Jacques Coeur?"

"No, my lord." The maid's manner and tone suggested that her absence on that occasion had been a calamity, a mistake of earth-shaking magnitude, and that all the dire things which had happened since could be traced back to it. "I didn't want her to see him. I told her she was not strong enough and that it would be better to send him away."

The Attorney began to lead the witness through a full recital of the

events of the morning when Coeur had seen Agnes Sorel. Her mistress
had spent a restless night and had shown symptoms of weakness during
the morning. Nevertheless, she had said at once that she would see the
Moneyman. The witness had assisted in moving her to her station in the
darkness back of the grating and had then returned to the bedroom. She
had proceeded to take advantage of the chance thus offered to introduce
some light into the room (by candle and not by opening the window) and
to do some necessary cleaning. She was engaged in this task when she discovered the Damoiselle de Vendôme looking at her from the doorway.
"He brought a lady with him," the latter said, meaning Jacques Coeur.
"A girl who looks so much like our mistress it would be hard to tell them
apart." The witness had answered, "That is impossible, for our mistress is
the most beautiful woman in the world and no one could look like her."
The custodian of the recently born child had given her head a toss and
said: "Then go and see for yourself. She's sitting in the hall, waiting for
him, and looking frightened." When the witness went on with her task,
Jeanne de Vendôme had said, "I'm going to see what this man is doing."
She had vanished, and in a few minutes the witness had gone out to the
hall to see the girl who resembled Agnes Sorel so much. The hall was
empty. She had said to herself, "This Jeanne de Vendôme may be of
gentle birth but she's a mischief-maker and a great flutterhead."

When Jeanne de Vendôme had come back to the kitchen in a state of
great excitement and had announced that Jacques Coeur had dared to
open the window of the room where her mistress lay and that she, Jeanne
de Vendôme, had seen him administering some liquid to her, the witness
had wanted to go at once to the assistance of her mistress. The physician
had forbidden this, saying he would go and would summon her when she
was needed. She had tried to tell him she was needed at once but he had
said sharply: "Get her room ready for her. It's filthy and the air is vile. Set
lemon sticks burning."

"How did you find your mistress when she was brought back?" asked
Dauvet.

"She was conscious, my lord, but so weak I was afraid she was dying.
I said, 'Oh, sweet lady, what has been done to you!' She opened her eyes
but didn't seem to recognize me. I said to the physician, 'Is she dying?'
and he said in an angry voice—but he wasn't angry, my lord, he's the
kindest of men—'Of course she's dying.'"

"Did he take measures to revive her?"

"Yes, my lord. He burnt some feathers under her nose. She opened her
eyes again and said in such a weak voice I could barely hear her, 'Am I
still alive, then?' She seemed disappointed, my lord, that it should be so."

"Did you remain in the bedroom after she had been taken back?"

"Of course, my lord. Did you think I would leave my poor sick lady? I
didn't leave, not for a single moment, until the next morning when Monsieur de Poitevin told me my mistress was dead."

"You hadn't realized she was dead until he discovered the fact and told
you?"

The grief of the witness led to a prolonged outburst. "No, my lord," she said finally, blowing her nose on a big handkerchief. "She had been lying still for so many hours! I thought a dozen times the end had come but when I asked him he said, No, she was still breathing. And then at last he said, 'She is gone, Bénédicte.' It seemed to me he was saying the end of the world had come."

Gouffier made a motion to his fellow judges and the five heads drew together. For several minutes they conferred in whispers.

The delay in the proceedings had lessened the tension in the court-room. People began to talk. Beyond the partition someone laughed.

The judges shifted apart and Dauvet resumed his questioning.

"Did you know what the prisoner gave to your mistress when he was alone with her?"

"No, my lord."

"Did Jeanne de Vendôme speak of it to you later?"

"No, my lord. As soon as my mistress died, the Damoiselle left and took the child with her. I didn't see her again."

"Did Monsieur de Poitevin speak of it?"

An incredulous look spread across the woman's face. "To me, my lord? Oh no, my lord. He never spoke of such matters to us. And none of us dared ask him questions. He would have flayed us if we had. "But"— hastily, as though fearing she had given a wrong impression—"he was always kind to us, my lord."

"From the moment it was known that Jacques Coeur had given your mistress a drink was there doubt in the minds of anyone in the house that the Lady Agnes was dying?"

There was so much malice and unfairness in the wording of this that Coeur controlled himself with difficulty from shouting a protest. The witness seemed puzzled at the form of the question and hesitated, frowned, and then said: "No, my lord. We knew there was no hope for her."

"That's all. The witness may retire."

Jacques Coeur got to his feet. "There are questions I desire to ask the witness, my lords," he said. He looked at the maid and smiled reassuringly. She resumed her seat and waited.

Gouffier turned in his chair and stared hard at the prisoner. The ex-pression on his face showed such a degree of malice that Coeur, who had become reconciled to anything in that quarter, was surprised and uneasy. The presiding judge said, "It's not the privilege of the accused to question the witnesses. The prisoner will resume his seat."

Coeur was unable to speak for a moment. That he was not to be allowed witnesses of his own had made it evident they were prepared to go to any lengths, but it had not entered his mind that he would be refused the right to question his accusers. He was so dumfounded that all he could do at first was to stare up at the satirically smiling countenance of his archenemy. Then he burst into a torrent of protest.

"It's always the privilege of the accused to ask questions of those who testify. How else can the truth be sifted from the evidence given? This is a right, my lords, that is accorded the lowest malefactor——"

"It's not a right accorded to you, Jacques Coeur."

"Does this mean I'm not to be allowed to make any defense?"

Gouffier's eye ran along the row of court officials seated on a bench beneath the dais. It came to rest on one who held a bundle of cloth on his knee. He made a motion and this officer rose to his feet.

"When the evidence has all been heard," said Gouffier, "the accused will be allowed time to make a statement. Until then he's to remain seated and he must be silent."

"Must I be silent while my fate is decided by judges who refuse me the ordinary rights granted without question to thieves and footpads?"

"The prisoner must be aware there are methods of compelling obedience. I hope it won't be necessary to resort to them. If, however, he persists——"

"I promise you, Guillaume Gouffier, that I have no intention of accepting this base injustice in silence."

"So be it," said Gouffier. He motioned again to the officer. "You will obey the instructions given you."

The officer walked across the court until he stood beside the prisoner. He was holding the cloth, which took the form of a hood in both hands.

"If the accused attempts to speak at any time without the permission of his judges, you will wrap that hood securely over his head. Keep a close eye on him, Usher, and nip in the bud any effort to utter as much as a single word aloud. We must have no scenes or interruptions; nor must we permit the utterance of seditious ideas in a court the King has set up for dispensing justice." Gouffier turned and spoke to the bench where a dozen lawyers sat, their hands full of documents. "Is the next witness ready?"

4

JEANNE DE VENDOME took the stand on the second day. There was a loud outburst of comment when she came into the main hall. The people who filled the space outside the frame partitions shouted and shoved and struggled furiously for a look at her and were with the greatest difficulty compelled to form a lane by which she could reach the Bed of Justice.

She had dressed herself for the occasion with an obvious desire to appear at her best but the result was not happy. Her dress was green, the shade of green which suggests poison, and there was too much of everything: too many loops of fur and embroidery; too much lace around the edges and too much of it standing up aggressively at the neck; too much padding about the hips. Her sleeves were so extravagantly long that only one hand could be seen (devoutly clutching a rosary with taut freckled knuckles) and the skirts were much too full and of such length that they swept the floor a full yard behind her with a swishing sound.

She walked with her head lowered and seemed subdued by the responsibility which rested on her. This was a pose; for, passing the chair where the accused sat, she raised her eyes for a single moment and stared straight at him.

Jacques Coeur said to himself, "She makes it very clear that she hopes to be the instrument of my ruin."

Jean Dauvet took the witness in hand. He left his seat at the table and escorted her to a chair just below it and a little to one side.

"Damoiselle de Vendôme," said Dauvet, taking up a position in front of her, "you have given us in preliminary hearings the information we needed about yourself and how you came to accept the post in the household of the Lady Agnes Sorel. In the interests of brevity, we don't propose to go over that again. The facts are duly noted down and we are content. Today we shall begin with your story of what happened on the occasion of the prisoner's visit to the Lady Agnes."

The witness bowed with an affected gravity, keeping her eyes determinedly lowered and drawing back her sleeves so that all could see the rosary clasped in one hand.

"What time on the morning of February eight did you first see Jacques Coeur?"

"It was between nine and ten. My charge—the child, I mean"—she indulged in her habit of speaking in a laughing tone, as though there was cause for amusement in the distinction—"had not been well. I had ordered a special posset and was on my way down the stairs to watch its preparation when the door in the front of the manor was opened. Jacques Coeur entered, accompanied by a lady."

"Did you recognize the lady?"

"No, my lord. I had never seen her before. But I was impressed instantly by the resemblance she bore to my—my mistress."

"You mean the Lady Agnes Sorel?"

"Yes, my lord. It was quite astonishing. I stood on the stairs and watched. I watched the girl and not Jacques Coeur because I was fascinated by her appearance. It was"—her voice raised in another outburst of meaningless laughter—"as though the Lady Agnes, fully restored to health and a little younger, had entered through the door."

"Did they see you?"

"Not at first. They stood in the hall for several moments without doing anything because it was in darkness like the rest of the house."

"But it was not too dark for you to catch the resemblance that the woman with the accused bore to your mistress."

"The house had been shuttered for weeks, my lord. My eyes had become accustomed to the gloom. And, of course, there was one candle in the hall. The resemblance"—the tendency to laugh was becoming more pronounced with each sentence she spoke—"was so very great, my lord, that it could not be missed, even in a dark hall and with a single candle."

"Did they make any move as they stood in the darkness of the hall?"

"Not at first."

"Did they speak to each other?"

"Yes, my lord. Jacques Coeur whispered something to the girl. I couldn't hear what it was he said."

"Did the girl answer him?"

"I don't remember that she did. I think she nodded only."

"But a little later they made a move? After their own eyes became accustomed to the gloom, perhaps?"

"Yes, my lord. Jacques Coeur spoke to her and she nodded again. Then she reached under her cloak—it was a long cloak with fur, for it was very cold that day—and brought out a small bottle. She handed this to him."

Jacques Coeur forgot everything else in the indignation inspired by this fabrication to connect Valerie directly with the alleged crime. He sprang to his feet.

"It's a lie!" he cried. "I declare——"

Blackness blotted out everything. Two powerful arms were clasped about him and were forcing him back into his chair. The hood had been wrapped around his head with such violent effectiveness that he could see nothing and found it almost impossible to breathe. He struggled to get free but had no success at all for the arms of the officer seemed like the folds of a python. He tried to cry out but the thickness of the cloth muffled his voice.

He could hear the officer swearing under his breath. "So, you didn't believe it, buzzard of Bourges! . . . You had to stand up and raise your voice to the noble judges, you maker of stinking furs! . . . One more such move and Antoine will smother you black in the face!"

When his head was released from the folds of the cloak he fell back in his chair and lay there limply while his lungs battled to resume their function. When his breathing became normal again, he sat up and wiped the perspiration from his face with an arm that trembled perceptibly.

"The accused now realizes," he heard Guillaume Gouffier saying, "that when he was forbidden to speak except in answer to direct questions, it was intended that the order should be obeyed. And now the questioning may continue."

Dauvet commenced at the point where he had left off. "Did they know you were on the stairs and so had seen the transfer?"

"No, my lord."

"Can you tell us anything about the bottle?"

"It was filled with poison."

"How did you know that?"

"Because, my lord, the physicians see to it that all bottles filled with poison have a special top. There is an arrow on it, painted red."

"Everyone knows that, of course. I wanted to bring out the fact that this particular bottle bore the distinguishing mark. It had the red arrow?"

"Yes, my lord. I was startled when I saw what it was the girl had handed to him and wondered what use they were going to make of it."

"It was natural for you to be surprised. Poisons are supposed to be carried only by physicians and, with the necessary permission, by medical students. As the accused and this mysterious lady were neither of them physicians nor students of medicine, it was to be expected that possession of a bottle of poison would be a matter of considerable surprise and even —alarm."

"Yes, my lord. I was frightened. It was like watching a Mystery."

Dauvet paused and looked meaningly at his fellow judges. "And what did the accused do with this lethal instrument that his accomplice had given him?"

"He nodded to her and hid it under his belt."

"He said nothing at all?"

"Nothing, my lord. It seemed to me they both understood and that no discussion was necessary."

"It's clear, at any rate, that there was none. You say you felt fear. Do you mean that you had a sense of impending tragedy?"

Jeanne de Vendôme paused. Then she allowed her voice to drop. "I was certain they were plotting some kind of mischief."

There was about this a suggestion of preparation in advance, even of rehearsal. At any rate an effect favorable to the prosecution had been achieved. The spectators within the enclosure were sitting forward on their seats watching the young woman in green. From outside the partitions there was a sound of much scuffling of feet and of unrestrained talk.

Coeur had recovered sufficiently to follow the evidence and at this point he felt a tug of real alarm. The story being told by the witness was not only completely false but clumsily conceived; but he would not be allowed to question her after she had finished and so it would stand unchallenged. Would it be accepted as truth? Looking with an almost feverish haste about the chamber, at the tense faces of the spectators, he realized that the story had produced the desired effect.

Jean Dauvet, satisfied with the impression that had been made, resumed his questioning.

"What happened after that?"

"He looked up and saw me on the stairs."

"What did he do then?"

"Nothing. But he looked startled, my lord. At that moment one of the menservants came into the hall and said that the Lady Agnes would see him. He followed the servant out."

"And the girl remained?"

"Yes, my lord. She seated herself on a bench in the hall and waited."

"How did she act while waiting?"

"It seemed to me, my lord, that she was nervous. She was listening closely and staring in the direction he had taken. At every sound she gave a start."

"How long did you watch her?"

"A few minutes only. Then I walked back up the stairs. The child was still restless and so I went to the kitchen by the backstairs to get what was needed for her myself. There I found Bénédicte, the personal maid of the mistress, and I told her that Jacques Coeur had brought a girl with him who resembled the mistress very much."

"How long did you talk to Bénédicte?"

"Not very long. I was busy getting the posset for the child."

"While you were attending to your duties, did you wonder what Jacques Coeur was doing?"

"Indeed, yes, my lord. I thought of nothing else. I was certain he had some ill purpose in mind. When the posset was ready, I gave it to a maid and told her to feed the baby. I would have attended to this myself except that I felt I should see what he was doing. I told Bénédicte so."

"The girl Bénédicte has already given us her story which confirms what you are telling us. What did you do next?"

"I went, my lord, to the small room with the grating where the Lady Agnes saw visitors."

"And what did you find?"

There was another long pause. Jeanne de Vendôme raised her eyes and stared hard at the prisoner before replying. The almost hysterical suggestion of laughter was no longer noticeable in her voice. It had become tight with feeling.

"I found—— My lord, I could scarce believe my eyes! He, Jacques Coeur, had opened a window. The room was so light I could see everything plainly. He was bending over my mistress with one hand under her head and with the other was administering a drink to her. I thought—— My lord, conceive of the situation! I had suspected his purpose on first seeing him and what was I to think when I found him thus?"

"What construction did you put on his actions?"

"I was afraid he was making her drink the contents of the bottle the girl had given him. I cried out to him to stop."

"What happened then?"

"He looked up. He seemed startled and, I think, afraid. He allowed the head of the Lady Agnes to fall on the pillow. He said my mistress had become unconscious while they talked and that he was trying to restore her."

"Did he say what he had given her?"

"I asked him and he said it was wine and water. He put the glass down on the table then."

Jean Dauvet paused with an air of deliberation. He looked along the tiers of seats with an air which said, "I know what you are thinking and that there is a doubt in the minds of all of you—a doubt which I shall now proceed to dispel." Then he turned back abruptly to the witness.

"You have told us you suspected the accused was in the house for the purpose of poisoning someone, your mistress almost certainly, as it was to see her that he had come. Then you saw him holding a potion to her lips. Why didn't you raise the alarm at once?"

Coeur, watching every move they made and striving to catch each intonation of voice, was convinced that this again had been carefully planned in advance. The raising of a doubt by the King's lawyer would be accepted as proof of the desire of the judges for a fair inquiry and it would make the answer of the witness more telling in its effects.

Jeanne de Vendôme hesitated most convincingly. "What could I have done, my lord?" she asked. "I had, after all, no more than a suspicion to act upon. If I had cried out for help and accused him of trying to poison my mistress, and it had been found that it was only wine and water he had given her, what situation would I have been in? He was powerful, the King's Moneyman, the friend and confidant of the Lady Agnes. I was the custodian of her child, an unimportant figure in the household. There are grievous penalties when one such as I brings false charges against one such as he. I was afraid, my lord. I didn't want to be put in prison."

Dauvet nodded encouragingly. "Mademoiselle, it's not hard to understand why you acted with some degree of caution. The penalties for false accusation are, as you have said, grievous. I think you've answered the doubt which had risen in my mind and, in all probability, in the minds of the other judges."

Dauvet proceeded with his examination. "The girl, Valerie Maret, was not in the room at the time?"

The witness shook her unruly shock of hair. "No, my lord. It has been told that she was in the room a short time before and saw the Lady Agnes. But she had gone when I came in."

"We have fixed the time that she left the room, after a few moments with the Lady Agnes, at ten minutes before you appeared. In the meantime"—he paused for effect—"things had happened."

He looked about the room as though appraising the effect this was having on the spectators. Satisfied, apparently, with what he saw, he turned back to the witness.

"And now go on with your story, if you please."

"I asked Jacques Coeur if I should summon the physician and he said yes. But instead of letting me go, he kept me in the room by asking questions."

"Did the thought occur to you that he was anxious to keep you longer so that the drink he had given the Lady Agnes would have its full effect?"

"Yes, my lord."

"But you did go for the physician?"

"Yes, my lord. I went to the kitchen and told Monsieur de Poitevin he should go in at once. He was very angry when I told him Jacques Coeur was in the room and had given her something to drink. He said, 'I shall have a quarrel with Jacques Coeur. He's a dangerous fellow.' Then he left."

"Did you go with him?"

The large green bows on the hennin worn by the witness shook negatively. She answered in a voice pitched small to suggest timidity and weakness. "No, my lord, I'm ashamed to tell you that I—I fainted."

Dauvet's voice took on a sympathetic tone. "To what do you attribute the fainting spell?"

"I think it was due to what I had seen and the strain of not knowing what I should do."

Only the presence beside him of the watchful officer with the cloak prevented Jacques Coeur from interrupting again. He wanted to say: "The maid did not speak of this fainting spell. There is a discrepancy here."

If Jean Dauvet was conscious of the discrepancy, he did not deem it necessary to clear the point up. He went on to another question.

"How long was it before you recovered?"

"They told me it was ten minutes before I became conscious again." She was still speaking in a small, hurt voice. "In falling my head had struck against the pail in which water was brought from the well. I felt quite sick and dizzy. I didn't have the strength to do anything until one of the menservants came in. Then I asked him what had happened to the Lady Agnes. He said she was so weak she might die at any moment. I asked him where the physician was and he told me that he had been summoned by the King."

"Was the serious condition of the Lady Agnes known to the rest of the household?"

"Yes, my lord. Everyone expected she would not last another day. They were sure nothing could be done to save her."

"Why did they think that?"

"Monsieur de Poitevin had said so before leaving for the abbey. He told Bénédicte that there was nothing to be done but—to wait."

"Where was your mistress?"

"She had been taken back to her bedroom. She was barely conscious."

"Did you see her?"

"No, my lord. It was Bénédicte who told me. I didn't see my mistress again."

"Did you tell Bénédicte what you had seen and what you suspected?"

Jeanne de Vendôme shook her head. "I did not. I knew that Bénédicte liked my lord Coeur and that she would make trouble for me if I told her. I spoke about it to the maid who helped me with the child. She became more frightened than I and said I mustn't speak of it again. She began to cry and say that the great Moneyman would have us put in prison if we said anything against him and that we would be whipped and even put to the torture. So, my lord, I said nothing more about it then."

"But after the Lady Agnes died, you decided you must speak, did you not?"

The mass of green ribbon which made up the hennin was agitated again by a vigorous nod of the head. She answered in a voice which had become suprisingly strident. "I couldn't keep silent any longer! It preyed on my mind, my lord, and I couldn't sleep. I used to dream about it and I would waken up crying. Finally I knew I would go mad if I didn't do something."

"And what did you do?"

"I went to my lord Gouffier and told him everything. I felt relief at once, my lord, even though I didn't know what might happen to me as a result of what I had done. I could sleep once more."

"And it was after you spoke to him that my lord Coeur was placed under arrest and charged with the poisoning of your mistress?"

"Yes, my lord."

Dauvet suspended comment for several moments. The sun was high by this time and was pouring through the windows near the top of the stone walls and lighting up the glum tapestries and the heavy black furnishings. For the first time since the trial began the chamber seemed warm and even cheerful. This, combined with the excitement of the evidence, had stirred the spectators to a high pitch. A hum of talk was rising from all quarters. Heads were nodding and hands waving in violent gesticulation as the story of the woman in green was discussed.

The Attorney looked at Gouffier and the latter responded by giving the table a sharp rap with a mallet.

"Silence!" he intoned. "If this talk doesn't stop at once, it will be necessary to clear the chamber and proceed without spectators."

This threat had the desired result. Silence settled down over the crowded court. Dauvet strode across the floor until he stood close by the chair where the prisoner sat. The balance of the examination was conducted from here.

"In my opinion," he said, in a louder voice than he had yet used, "it was most fortunate that you did as your conscience bade you. Since you brought to us these facts, which you have now stated openly before this Bed of Justice, other evidence has been found which bears you out. This new evidence, which vindicates you completely, will be introduced as soon as your testimony is complete." He glanced along the tiers of spectators with a triumphant smile before bringing his eyes back to the face of the prisoner. "There is one more point I must discuss with the witness. So much depends on the answer that I beg for complete silence in the chamber."

He raised a hand in the direction of the witness. "You have told us of seeing the girl hand to the prisoner a bottle which you recognized as a container of poison. Do you know what has happened to it?"

"Yes, my lord."

"Will you tell the judges what you know?"

The witness sat up straight at this, realizing that the crucial point of her evidence had been reached. Her eyes turned to the prisoner with the same satisfaction that could be read in those of the prosecutor.

"After I had recovered from the fainting spell," she began, "I went to the room behind the grating. The shutters had been closed again and it was so dark I could see nothing. There was a strange odor in the room. I had to light a candle. And then I—I found——"

"Speak louder, if you please. It's desirable that everyone should hear."

"I found the bottle on the table beside the couch. The stopper was out and was lying on the table beside the bottle."

"Did that account for the strange odor in the room?"

"Yes, my lord. I raised it to my nose and found that the strong smell came from it."

"Did you recognize the smell?"

"I can't tell you what it was, my lord. But I recognized it as an odor I've always associated with poison."

"Did you observe anything else?"

"I saw, my lord, that it was half empty."

"What did you do with the bottle?"

"I may have done something very wrong, my lord. I took the bottle with me and, when I told my story, I gave it to my lord Gouffier."

Dauvet motioned to a court official and the latter carried a bottle over to the witness.

"Is this the same one?"

"Yes, my lord."

"You are quite sure?"

"I am positive it's the same one. I recognize it by a scratch on the side of the glass."

"Smell what is in it and tell me if it is the same as what you noticed that day."

Jeanne de Vendôme took out the stopper and raised the bottle to her nose. Then she nodded her head. "It's the same, my lord."

Jacques Coeur had been following this evidence with an incredulous air. He now said to himself, "Is there no end to these shameless lies they have invented against me?"

The end had been reached for the time being. Dauvet smiled at the witness and said: "Thank you. That's all we need to hear. You are free to leave the court."

5

PREGENT KENNEDY had dressed himself for the occasion with the utmost care. The tartan around his neck had been mended, his cloak had been cleaned and pressed, his riding boots shone with the polish rubbed into them. This should have given him confidence, but there was, in spite of it, an air of wariness about him when he appeared in the open corner of the Bed of Justice. He glanced about him, bowed jerkily in the general direction of the judges' table, and said in an audible voice, "Here he is, Messires, Pregent Kennedy at your service."

One of the court officers urged him forward with a compelling forefinger on his elbow. Kennedy shook him off with a muttered, "Leave be, fellow, I beg to tell you that I'm a gentleman of Scotland and a soldier of France." He strode forward slowly and came to a stop beside the chair of the prisoner.

"My lord Moneyman," he said, in a low tone, "it's my intention to tell the truth touching such matters as may be brought up but I want you to know that I'm not here of my own free will."

"The witness," said Guillaume Gouffier, staring at him angrily, "will take his proper station at once. He will speak only in answer to questions from the judges."

The Scot obeyed to the extent of taking up his position in front of the table. "My tongue," he said, "may obey the order of the court but I'm making no promises for it. It's an unruly tongue and very likely to say what it pleases."

"Unruly tongues," declared Gouffier, "are often made obedient by the simple process of cutting them out. The witness will do well to bear this in mind."

Having thus, as he thought, reduced the Scot to the state of mental trepidation in which witnesses are supposed to exist, the King's minister said brusquely to the court official accompanying Kennedy, "Take this fellow to one side." Then he leaned forward in his chair and stared about the room.

It was clear that he had something of importance to say and was consciously trying to prepare the ground for it, to raise expectations. He looked first along the row of lawyers (who seemed to become more down-at-heel in appearance and more obsequious in attitude with each session), then his eyes lifted and traveled the crowded tiers where the nobility, male and female, sat in their satins and velvets and their arrogance. Finally he gazed out through the entrance of the walled Bed at the crowded areas where the common people scuffled and clamored among themselves.

"I think," he said, turning to his brother judges for their approval, "that the time has come."

It was not necessary, apparently, for him to explain further. The heads of the other four waggled in agreement. Raising a hand, he signaled to the officer standing guard on the door leading to the tower.

A few moments later this door swung open with an abrupt clang which had something of the effect of a blast of trumpets. All heads turned abruptly in that direction and, for the moment, all other sounds ceased.

First through the door came the Governor, Auguste de Lenvers. He had attired himself in peach-colored velvet (rather faded and napless, it must be stated, and not entirely above a suspicion of grease spots) and he walked with such a consciousness of drama on his puffy and perked-up features that he would have been a comic figure under any other circumstances. After him came the head turnkey, carrying a large iron ring on which the prison keys jingled. As there was nothing in prison procedure to make his presence essential, it must be assumed that the shambling figure with the keys was included in the procession to satisfy a desire on the part of the judges for a touch of symbolism. Behind the turnkey walked a slender figure in white with guards on each side holding her by the arms. To say that she walked is not strictly correct. She had been released from the cage (and hastily bathed and clothed and given strong stimulants) not more than an hour before and her legs were still too stiff and cramped to function normally. She progressed, in fact, with short and hesitant steps and was in constant need, obviously, of the support of the two guards.

Auguste de Lenvers stepped aside after entering the legal enclosure and waved a hand to the turnkey to do likewise. In a thin voice he instructed the guards to lead their charge to the center.

The entrance of Valerie Maret produced all the effect the judges may have hoped to achieve. She was extremely thin and pale but these results of her incarceration tended to increase rather than diminish her resemblance to the deceased Agnes Sorel. Those among the nobility present who had been often in court gasped with surprise. It was not hard for them to believe that the well-loved mistress of the King had risen from the grave to appear at this inquiry into the manner of her death.

A complete silence had fallen on the courtroom. Valerie, believing that her turn had come to stand trial (which meant to her that Jacques Coeur had already been convicted), was in a state of physical collapse and experiencing a degree of fear which can only be compared to the feelings of a rabbit in a snake pit. She had not raised her eyes as she was escorted across the room, and she continued to keep them down as she stood tremblingly in front of the judges.

Gouffier said in a sharp tone to the guards, "Turn her about so that all may have a chance to see her."

In obeying this order the pair had to hold her up by force as they pivoted on their heels, for she was no longer capable of any effort at locomotion. As the turning progressed, more gasps came from people who had not been able up to that time to get a good view of her face. If the judges had expected her appearance to be a sensation in court they were being amply justified.

"That will do," said Gouffier. He turned to his fellow judges. "I contend, my lords, that an important point in the case against the prisoner has been demonstrated."

At this moment Valerie fainted. The arms of the guards, linked through hers, kept her from falling, but her head slumped forward and her body went as limp as a doll's from which the sawdust has been lost. The puzzled faces which the guards turned to the judicial bench said as plainly as words, What do we do about this?

"Carry her out," instructed Gouffier in a tone of complete indifference.

The pair, uncertain of the method they should use, elected to walk out as they were, with the result that she dangled on their arms (and this was a grim piece of symbolism which had neither been planned nor expected) like a figure hanging at the end of a rope.

"And now," said Gouffier, "the Scot will step forward."

2

If he expected to find Pregent Kennedy in a chastened mood, the presiding judge was promptly disillusioned. That hardy exile from his native land had watched the scene just finished with a degree of emotion which manifested itself in a heightened color and a nervous twitching of the fingers as though they yearned for the cool feel of his sword handle. Whether or not this had hardened his resolution to oppose the desires of the court, it became at once apparent that he was not going to be an amenable witness.

Dauvet began on his interrogation, drawing from the witness, with some difficulty, the details of his meeting with Valerie Maret and of the trip to Paris where she had fallen under the eye of Jacques Coeur. Kennedy answered each question briefly, pausing to consider his reply with the greatest care and volunteering no information beyond what was asked.

"When did you learn that the prisoner had foisted the girl on a noble family under a name which implied a distant relationship to them?"

The Scot paused to consider. "I heard she was known as Valerie de Voudrai some time after she had been taken into the household of the noble family in question. And, my lord judge, if there was any foisting done, it was with the full knowledge and connivance of the family in question."

"We will tolerate no more comments of that kind. But, as you have made this statement, you will tell us what grounds you have for it."

"My grounds?" The Scot laughed. "Pure hearsay, my lord. Put it down that I repeated gossip, rumor, idle chatter, whatever you will. But put this down also. It was hearsay which I'm convinced is true."

Dauvet looked as though he would like to apply some disciplinary measures. Thinking better of it, however, he proceeded with his interrogation.

"Did the prisoner hire you to pay a visit to the southern part of Berri in the hope of getting more definite information about the parentage of the girl?"

"That is true."

"Was it as a result of this investigation you made that she assumed the name of Valerie de Voudrai?"

"No, my lord. Jacques Coeur had learned something of her parentage from other sources. I was sent to secure what information I could to clear up the point more definitely."

"And what did you learn?"

"Very little. I found proof of what was already known, that she was not the daughter of the deceased actor. Such facts as I was able to learn seemed to point to the accuracy of the information which had come previously to my lord Coeur."

Coeur had felt the same emotions as Kennedy when Valerie was led into court but in an intensified form. Back of the pity and anger he experienced had been a sense of guilt because it was through his scheming that she now stood in peril of her life. If anyone had dared to look at him while she was in the courtroom (it is doubtful if any did) it would have been seen that dejection had gained a stronger hold on him and that he slumped down in his chair with the air, for the first time, of a beaten man.

The examination was continuing:

"Did you discover positive proof that her real father was a member of the family of De Voudrai?"

"No, my lord. But I found evidence to convince me she was of illegitimate birth and that her father could have been of that name."

The King's Attorney frowned. He also sensed that this witness, from whom so much had been expected, was not disposed to give evidence unfavorable to the prisoner.

"Did the prisoner tell you," he demanded, "his reason for his anxiety about the parentage of the girl?"

"He did not."

"You knew he was spending large sums of money to educate the girl, to see that she acquired all the graces and niceties of deportment. You knew also, I'm certain, that a veritable fortune had been expended on her wardrobe. What did this suggest to you?"

"It suggested to me that he had gone"—the witness hesitated and then concluded with a word from his native tongue—"that he had gone *daft!* In Scotland, my lord, we would not spend as much money on the wardrobe of a queen."

"You must have guessed his reason for such liberality. Or did he take you into his confidence?"

The Scot shook his head. "He said nothing to me. It's true I indulged in a guess."

"And what did you guess?"

"I guessed," said Kennedy dryly, "that he was spending his good money on the girl because he wanted her for himself."

A ripple of laughter spread through the court. Gouffier frowned angrily and pounded on the table with the gavel of authority. Dauvet consulted with his fellow judges before resuming the examination. He left his seat and descended to the floor where he took up his station directly in front of the witness.

"It has been made clear to everyone in this court," he stated, "that the girl Valerie Maret bore a close resemblance to Agnes Sorel. That was the purpose in producing her at this stage. That the resemblance transcends anything in the probabilities of nature has been shown by the effect she produced when she entered this room."

The Attorney looked about him before proceeding. "This startling resemblance is the key to everything that has happened. It is my contention that it supplies the reason for the poisoning of the unfortunate lady." He swung around abruptly on the witness. "Did you realize the truth, Monsieur Scot? Did you know it was because of this resemblance that Coeur had picked her out, that he had spent a fortune to bedeck her like a princess of the blood, and that he had her taught to act and speak like a lady?"

Kennedy waited for a moment before replying. Then he contented himself with one word.

"No."

Dauvet was nonplused, not having expected such a flat lack of co-operation. "It's said you are the shrewdest member of a very shrewd race. How could you have failed to grasp the point of the masquerade being prepared under your eyes?"

"I failed to grasp the point for two reasons."

"State them."

"First," said Kennedy, "the masquerade, as you call it, was not being prepared under my eyes. I was with the Army. I may say that I was training men to handle the cannon and so playing an important part in preparing for the victory of France. Second, I didn't know the girl resembled the King's lady."

His questioner indulged in a scornful laugh. "You failed to see what everyone in this room grasped in one amazed second of time?"

"Aye," answered the Scot calmly. "I had never seen Agnes Sorel."

A tendency to titter on the part of the ladies in court was checked by an angry tap of the mallet. Dauvet studied the witness as though in doubt of the wisdom of continuing his examination. He decided to try once more.

"We're sure you are as anxious as the court that the full truth should be arrived at. Tell the judges if you can recall any time that the prisoner, Jacques Coeur, gave you any intimation, any hint, of his purpose in educating the girl Valerie Maret."

Kennedy snorted scornfully. "Does it seem to you likely, my lord, that if he plotted the murder of the Lady Agnes Sorel he would drop any hints of his purpose before a mercenary with the reputation, as you stated yourself, of being 'the shrewdest member of a very shrewd race'?"

Dauvet threw his arms in the air. "The witness," he said to his fellow judges, "is deliberately obstructive and hostile. There is no use wasting more time on him.

"The point is established in the minds of all who have studied this case," he went on, "that the accused saw some advantage to be gained out of the resemblance Valerie Maret bore to the Lady Agnes Sorel. What was it that he planned to do? The girl had beauty, vivacity, youth. It's not our function to inquire if he proposed to establish through her an influence at court. This Bed of Justice was not set up to probe into the political aspects of the case. Whatever the motive of the accused may have been, we are sure of one thing: that he could not hope to reap any advantage until the Lady Agnes had been removed from his path. That certainty raises many startling speculations. How can we tell how many other victims might have suffered the same fate if the facts in connection with the death of Agnes Sorel had not been brought to light so soon? His boundless ambition had created a feeling among all who shared the confidence of the King that he had become a menace to the state. He knew this full well. Was it in his mind to free himself of all opposition?" The speaker paused and gestured in the direction of the witness. "It was our hope that this man who had played some part in the beginning of the conspiracy would be in a position to throw light on the motives of the accused and the scope of his plans. It seems that he's not able to do so. Or"—frowning bitterly—"he has no intention of telling us what he knows. So be it! Fortunately we have enough evidence on the factual side to prove the prisoner's guilt. That will suffice. The ends of justice will be met even if we're not able to go further and draw aside the curtain which now screens the workings of a blood-guilty mind." He turned to Kennedy and said sharply, "You may retire."

The Scot drew himself up proudly and bowed to the judges. Then he tossed the tartan of the Kennedys across his shoulder and began to retrace his steps to the entrance. He gave no further sign of recognition as he passed the prisoner but their glances crossed for a brief moment. It was as though each had said to the other, "Greetings, friend."

3

On the morning of the third day the clerk found it necessary to repeat his summons for the first witness before any attention was paid. Then a florid little man entered the enclosure. He had a neatly trimmed beard and there was something about the hang of his tunic and the set of his hat which smacked of the scholastic. Dauvet greeted him with a cordial, "Good morning, Doctor," which not only confirmed the hint of his garb but established the fact at once that there would be no difficulty with this witness.

"Your name?"

"I am Olivier de Bousse, regent at the Bons Enfans St. Honoré."

"You are of the University. You have come a long way, my good doctor, to lend your testimony in a case you must find particularly distasteful. However, no one else could serve as well and we were under compunction to bring you all the way from Paris. I desire, my worthy doctor, to extend to you the thanks of the judges who make up this Bed of Justice. And now, were you ever in attendance on the Lady Agnes Sorel?"

"Yes, my lord." The witness spoke in rich, full tones as though addressing a classroom. "I was summoned to see her, with a number of other doctors from the University, at the request of Robert de Poitevin. This was at the time when it was first realized she was with child."

"It was in Paris?"

"Yes, my lord."

"What did you think of her condition then?"

Before committing himself to a reply, the witness ran his fingers through his beard—a favorite gesture. "She was in a condition of great physical weakness. That much must be allowed. She felt ill in the extreme and she talked as though she expected to die. In spite of that, my lord, I was convinced she was not in a dangerous condition. I studied her with the utmost care before reaching the conclusion that all the symptoms were the result of—of her expectations."

"You expressed this opinion at the time? To the other physicians in attendance?"

The witness nodded his head emphatically. "Assuredly, my lord. I am always outspoken in my opinions and I voiced my optimistic view to all of them. There were five of us, including Robert de Poitevin. Our opinions were not hastily reached, my lord. We gave long and prayerful consideration to her condition, realizing how great our responsibility was. We could not allow ourselves to err through a leaning to the bright side. We considered every possibility."

"Did any of the physicians disagree with you?"

"One. Robert de Poitevin. He felt her condition was somewhat dangerous. But permit me to say"—the witness smiled with a suggestion of unctuousness—"that our good Master Robert, having attended her for many years, had a deep personal interest which inclined him to alarms. Also permit me, my lord, to voice my own opinion which is that in temperament he rides a gloomy horse. He is prone to take the least favorable view of things. . . . However, after the last of our several consultations, he was more disposed to agree with the rest of us."

"Do you still consider you were right?"

"Yes, my lord. Her death has not changed my view of the case. Nor has it changed the opinions of the other doctors from the University who were with me then."

"Unfortunately we can't summon all to give their testimony here. I feel certain that the judges will agree with me that you, as the acknowledged authority on cases of this nature, are in a position to speak for the rest. Did you have occasion to see the Lady Agnes later?"

"Yes, my lord. It was when she was in Paris on her way to the Abbey of Jumièges. I was asked to see her and did so on two occasions. She was close to her time, my lord, and all her symptoms were aggravated, both in body and mind. She was more certain than ever that she would not survive the ordeal."

"And you?"

The great man from the University smiled knowingly. "My lord, it has been my experience that all ladies as they approach the period of accouchement are prone to have the same fear. It is an almost inevitable phase at some time during the long wait. Perhaps"—he raised his shoulders and hands in a gesture of acceptance—"it's a part of the punishment of Eve. It means nothing—nothing at all. I laugh at my poor little ladies when they tell me their fears. I will allow, however, that the Lady Agnes had this tendency in a somewhat exaggerated form. My opininon is that she could not be considered in actual danger. I left her with every hope and expectation that she would regain her health after bringing her child into the world."

"Were the other physicians in attendance at the same time?"

"Yes, my lord. All of them had been summoned. Again they were in agreement with me."

"What of Robert de Poitevin?"

"Well, my lord, he would be a very poor physician indeed if he had not entertained fears for the lovely lady who had confided herself to his care. I recall that he considered her too weak to be altogether certain of surviving the ordeal."

The feelings with which Jacques Coeur listened were influenced by his knowledge of the witness. When Olivier de Bousse had come into the enclosure, he had said to himself, "That great windbag!" The doctor, in his opinion, represented the least worthy element at the University. He was pedantic and opinionated and yet at the same time servile to all forms of authority; a coddler of the great ladies who came to him for medical attention, a theorist who covered up his lack of experience and judgment with a smother of learned words. The prisoner said to himself now, "It's very clear why this toady has been brought as a witness."

The reason became clearer with each question asked. The doctor seemed determined to convince the judges (if they needed to be convinced) that Agnes Sorel would have lived if nature had been permitted to take its course.

"Did you see her after the child was born?"

"Unfortunately, no. But I received reports from various sources which kept me advised of her condition. This was done"—proudly—"on orders from the King, who desired that I should know."

"Did you still hold to your view that she would regain her strength and, in time, her full health?"

"I did. Nothing that I heard had any effect on my opinion. Permit me to say this, my lord: I have known scores of cases where ladies lapsed into a condition as weak as that of the Lady Agnes and yet recovered in due course. My lord, it happens all the time."

"And do you then believe that she died of poisoning?"

"I am certain in my mind that she was poisoned."

"Can you define that further by telling us on what your opinion is based?"

"On the brief space that elapsed after the time when the poison is said to have been given her. Consider, my lord, she had been lingering for weeks without any visible, or actual, change for the worse. Suddenly she is dead! It happened within a few hours from the time the visit of the prisoner was paid to her."

It was now Dauvet's turn to hesitate and the reason again was a desire to phrase what he had to say with special care.

"There are some who have declared that no one could be guilty of administering poison to her because it was so apparent that she was on the point of death. You don't agree with that?"

The witness responded with indignant emphasis. "I do not, my lord."

"You think she would have overcome the weakness which kept her abed if someone hadn't wanted her out of the way?"

"It's not for me to say what God might have done. Death comes at strange times and in strange ways. But without Divine intervention to claim her soul, Agnes Sorel would have lived."

The royal questioner bowed and smiled as though putting a period at the end of a well-rounded and thoroughly satisfactory passage. "And now, my good doctor, I must ask you to enlighten us on certain matters which also have an important bearing on this case. Did you know at the University of Paris a man who went by the name of Ferrand de Cordule?"

"Yes, my lord. A doctor of science and, so I have been assured, a man of ability."

"Do you subscribe to that opinion?"

"I had respect for his knowledge. I had none for the man."

"Will you explain why you had no respect for the man?"

"If it's your wish. But I shall answer with some unwillingness, my lord. It's not fitting to criticize another scholar, even one whose field is science."

"It's important to have your opinion and I must ask you to overcome your scruples."

"So be it, my lord. I had no regard for Ferrand de Cordule because he dabbled in what we sometimes call the wicked sister of science. Black magic it is more often called, my lord. Let me explain what it is. The study of science leads men of weak fiber to experiments of a forbidden nature: the making of gold, my lord, the secret of perpetual life, the concocting of charms and spells and love potions."

"And the making of poisons?"

"The making of poisons above everything else. It's my opinion that this is the worst of all the evil practices which have grown out of these experiments in forbidden paths, in the shaking of fruit from the Tree of Knowledge. By so doing science becomes the servant of crime and violence."

"And did Ferrand de Cordule turn his hand to experiments in black magic?"

"It was well known at the University that he did."

"Was he known to have had success?"

The eyes of the witness widened. "A degree of success, my lord, that baffles the understanding. It was the general belief that he had succeeded in piercing the veil which God has drawn over what He has forbidden man to know. I had this from so many sources, and with so much convincing detail, that I never questioned its truth."

"And this dealer in black magic left the University some years ago?"

"Yes, my lord. He left to enter the service of Jacques Coeur."

"In what way could he be of service to Jacques Coeur?"

"This much I may state as a fact. He sailed to the East on one of Jacques Coeur's ships and spent much time in Egypt and the lands of the Turk and even farther east, in Arabia and Persia. He brought back many of the secrets of the East."

"What manner of secrets?"

"They were of many kinds. But most particularly they were concerned with the poisons of the East."

Dauvet held up a hand to the occupants of the dais, saying, "Let me have the confession, if you please." When a document was given to him he carried it to the witness.

"Do you recognize this handwriting?"

Olivier de Bousse took the paper and studied it carefully. Then he gave it back with an affirmative nod.

"Assuredly, my lord. It's the handwriting of Ferrand de Cordule."

The word "confession" had stirred up fresh apprehensions in the mind of the prisoner. Ferrand de Cordule had nothing to confess. The work he had done had been confined to the planning of workshops and the improvement of methods of forging and smelting. His journey to the East had been for the sole purpose of studying the making of steel in Damascus, and such secrets as he had brought back with him had dealt with that distinctly practical subject. If he had signed a paper containing accusations against his master he had done so undoubtedly under extreme pressure of some kind.

"Why are you sure it's his handwriting?" Dauvet was asking.

"I saw letters from him many times and also manuscripts he had prepared. There is no mistaking it. He had what you would call an individual style, my lord."

Dauvet walked to the dais and, when he returned to his station beside the witness, he carried the bottle of poison in his hand.

"Do you know what this is?"

"It's a poison."

"Can you identify it for us?"

The doctor took the bottle and examined it closely. He removed the stopper and smelled the contents. Finally he handed it back with a confident nod.

"It's an Eastern poison, my lord. It is rare and a most powerful one."

"It's the wish of the court that you read the description of the third page of the confession of Ferrand de Cordule and then tell us if the poison described there is the same as that contained in the bottle."

Olivier de Bousse read with great care the section of the letter pointed out to him. He then took up the bottle again and looked it over with even more attention than he had shown the first time. It was several minutes before he expressed an opinion.

"Undoubtedly, my lord, the reference in the confession is to this very poison."

Dauvet's voice had a triumphant ring as he dismissed the witness with a wave of the hand. "That will be sufficient, my worthy doctor. You have been instrumental in throwing much light on the problems before us. You have the thanks of the court."

When the man from the University had withdrawn from the enclosure, Dauvet picked up the document and said, "With the permission of the other judges, I shall now read the confession which Ferrand de Cordule has made. It is of the utmost importance and I must demand that the spectators remain absolutely quiet."

The first paragraph convinced Jacques Coeur that the letter was a forgery. Ferrand de Cordule's style had always been crisp and compact and straight to the point. This was written in a rambling, and in places almost incoherent, fashion. It was not only full of obscure allusions and references of a supposedly scientific nature (a practice that had been anathema to the precise scientist) but it contained gross errors which the prisoner detected at once and which, he knew, could not have been committed by the meticulous De Cordule.

That the officers of the King had gone to the extreme of forging a document to strengthen their case was the final proof that they would stop at nothing. Jacques Coeur felt an icy sensation at the heart. For the first time he saw his position as hopeless. "I am doomed," he thought. "Someday it will be known that this so-called confession is all lies, that every scrap of evidence brought against me is false. But there will be no satisfaction in that for me. I will be moldering headless in a criminal's grave when the truth is revealed."

His depression grew as another consideration crossed his mind. "If I am to save Valerie, it will mean that I shall be compelled to affirm all these lies that have been told—and then the truth will never be known!"

While these thoughts filled the back of his mind, he had been listening to the reading. It was an astounding document. The testator alleged that he had been lured from his post at the University by the promises of "much wealth and greatness in keeping" made by Jacques Coeur. There had been an understanding between them that he, Ferrand de Cordule, would devote himself to delving into the secrets of nature and that the Moneyman would provide him with everything he needed for the purpose. The tasks to which he had set himself had included the turning of other metals into gold (no claims of success were made on that score), the evolving of better mining methods, the concocting of perfumes and, above everything else, the making of poisons "of such rare subtlety that death follows soon on its use and no one can perceive the reason therefor." There had been an urgency in Jacques Coeur's instructions in the matter of poisons and the testator confessed that he had brought back from the East a poison which gave his master the power he craved.

Dauvet held up the bottle for all to see. "Here," he declared, "is the poison that Ferrand de Cordule brought back with him from the East. This is the poison that was given to Agnes Sorel and which caused her death. Had Jacques Coeur made any use of it before he gave it to her? A question, truly, for disturbing conjecture! Would it have claimed other victims later? That is a speculation God alone can answer now."

Dauvet folded the document and replaced it on the table. He then turned and faced the eager listeners.

"It was the purpose of the Bed of Justice," he declared, "to summon Ferrand de Cordule before it and, by process of examination, supplement his statement with the details which would have made the guilt of the accused still more clear. Unfortunately this is impossible."

He paused for effect and then continued in a low voice: "Ferrand de Cordule has gone to seek the leniency he needs. Two days after this confession was signed he was waylaid by thieves while returning by night to his house in Bourges. His body was found by the side of the road the next morning. And so this remarkable but guilty man was removed from the possibility of earthly punishments for the sins he had committed against nature and against his God."

Jacques Coeur gasped audibly. Then he glanced about the room, expecting to find traces on the faces there of the incredulity and horror he felt himself. He was disappointed in this. Everyone seemed to have accepted without reserve this announcement of the death of an important witness. There was some whispering and nodding of heads but not a suggestion of protest or of unwillingness to believe the explanation given.

"My old friend was foully murdered!" he said to himself, wishing passionately that he dared stand up and proclaim his belief for all the world to hear. "He was put out of the way so they could prepare this false confession without fear of complication or contradiction. And there's nothing I can do! I must sit here in silence, knowing that my friend's death brings my own closer."

4

The judges supped that night in the dining salon of what was known as the Queen's apartment. They were in high spirits. Confident that their task had been accomplished, that Jacques Coeur's guilt had been established, their talk ran largely on the division of spoils.

It was understood that the Crown would have to be satisfied before any other hands could be dipped into the dish. Charles would get the gold, the ships, the ex-Moneyman's share in the ransoms (there was a profitable traffic in captured English noblemen), and the buildings in which the shops were located. But the prisoner's many estates were a different matter, and the eyes about the board were filled with greed and contentiousness as they discussed what would be done with them. It was assumed that each would receive at least one of the estates and they fenced bitterly over the disposition of the richest plums.

Antoine de Chabannes, who like most old soldiers had a ravenous liking for sweets, kept reaching for the well-spiced gobbets royal and saying at intervals, "Saint-Fargeau must be mine." The château of Saint-Fargeau in Puisaye had been purchased by Jacques Coeur from the Marquis de Montferrat and it was the rarest prize of all.

Gouffier was taking no part in the discussion, from which it might have been inferred that he had already arranged for his own share of the spoils and had nothing to gain by bickering with his fellow judges. He was eating little.

Gouffier rose to his feet when Auguste de Lenvers appeared in the doorway and motioned in his direction.

"He wishes to see you," whispered the Governor, when Gouffier joined him.

"Jacques Coeur?"

"Yes. I was with him a few minutes ago and I can tell you that he's in a desperate mood. He looked at me as though he was already dead and was seeing me from the—the other side."

When Gouffier faced Coeur in his cell, after closing the door in the Governor's face, he realized that the description given by the latter had an aptness to it. The ex-Moneyman was sitting on the side of his bed. He looked up for a moment only, and in that brief crossing of eyes Gouffier was convinced of his resignation to the inevitable.

"I've selected you," said the prisoner, "in preference to any of the others to listen to a suggestion I am going to make. There's a forthrightness about your villainy which makes it possible to deal with you and avoid all preambles."

Gouffier smiled and nodded his head. "I'm gratified by your good opinion."

There was a pause and then Coeur spoke in a low and hopeless tone of voice. "I'll make a bargain with our royal master."

"What offer do you wish to make our liege lord?"

"A confession. Although I'm as innocent of the death of Agnes Sorel as the mother who bore her, I'm willing to sign a paper that I poisoned her as charged. In return Valerie Maret must be cleared of the charge of complicity and released at once."

Gouffier found it hard to keep the elation he felt from showing in his face. More than anyone he knew how much the King desired a confession from the servant he was treating with such treachery. Charles had been sensitive to the public clamor against the arrest of Jacques Coeur and he knew that no one was likely to believe any verdict the five judges might bring in. But a confession! That would ease the royal conscience and justify Charles to his subjects.

Gouffier prided himself on driving a hard bargain. He looked down at the prisoner and shook his head.

"We're proving our case right up to the hilt," he declared. "We don't need a confession from you."

Coeur roused himself sufficiently from his apathetic mood to say with a suggestion of impatience, "I know as well as you know yourself, Gouffier, that the King would give much to have me clear him in this way."

"But the price you ask is too high."

"It is my price."

The judge shuffled his feet in the intensity of his thought. "Are you aware," he asked finally, "that in certain high circles there is a desire to see the girl share your punishment?"

"I've told you my terms." Coeur's voice now displayed a note of resolution. "Do you think I would put my head in the noose and besmirch my own reputation for all time for any other reason than to save this girl I have involved in my ruin?"

"I tell you that you ask too much," repeated Gouffier. "It's possible the King would agree to dealing leniently with her but his goodness of heart would not go beyond a promise to save her life."

"Let me tell you, then, the least I will agree to. She's not to be brought to trial. She's to be publicly exonerated and released unconditionally before I put my signature to the paper in question."

"It couldn't be done that way!" cried Gouffier in emphatic dissent. "The girl could not be released until she had appeared to answer the charge. You would have our promise. Isn't that enough?" He paused and then demanded, "Don't you put any trust in our word?"

Coeur looked up and met his visitor's eye squarely for the first time. "None," he said. "I would refuse to believe any promise you made me. I would refuse to believe any promise the King made."

Gouffier frowned. "You've grossly insulted the King of France!" he cried. "You, a common furrier, have expressed a doubt of the honor of our liege lord."

"Yes," said Coeur calmly. "When you take my proposition to Charles of France, tell him that I refuse to accept his word. Tell him he must fulfill his part of the agreement before I carry out mine."

"That means we must be ready to believe your word!"

"You can do so without any hesitation or doubt. I'm not a king, Guillaume Gouffier, or a king's judge."

The visitor shrugged his shoulders. "Very well," he said. "I will take your message to the King. I may even advise him to accept." Then, abruptly, he began to laugh. "There's no one to hear me say this. Moneyman, I don't blame you. Where you are concerned, we're not to be trusted, any of us."

6

IT WAS LATE in the afternoon of the third day when Guillaume Gouffier, in his capacity of presiding judge, consulted a list lying in front of him and said: "We now come to the last witness. The ushers will summon Monsieur Robert de Poitevin."

The physician came in with a quick step and a frown. He did not look in the prisoner's direction and Jacques Coeur said to himself, "The good Robert is in a mood."

Without any explanation, Gouffier elected to conduct the examination himself. He stared down at the witness with a suggestion of wariness in his eyes and said, "You were in the manor on the morning Jacques Coeur came to see the Lady Agnes?"

"I was in the manor every morning for several weeks. I remained in constant attendance until her illness terminated in death."

"We are interested only in the morning when she saw him. Did you see him yourself when he arrived?"

"No, my lord. I heard of his arrival and went at once to my lady, urging her to refuse to see him. I was certain she lacked the strength to see visitors, even as close a friend as Jacques Coeur."

Gouffier assumed a smile which he endeavored to make ingratiating. "You tell us she lacked strength. That was natural, as she had been ill for a long time and she had just passed through the—the trying ordeal of motherhood. But after hearing the evidence of the learned doctor from the University, I'm sure you're not disposed to think that her condition at the time was serious."

The frown on the physician's brow seemed to deepen. "It was so serious," he declared, "that any strain could have brought about the end."

The presiding judge scowled. "We believed from what you said at the preliminary hearing that you thought she would recover."

The physician's breath exploded in an indignant snort. "Impossible, my lord judge! I made it clear that I entertained no hopes for her at all."

"Then you failed to express yourself properly."

"Or"—with growing heat—"you failed to grasp the meaning of what I said."

Gouffier leaned forward the better to glare at this witness who dared answer him back. "I shall tolerate no more of this insolence," he declared. "It's your opinion only and of no importance whatever. We will go on, if you please. . . . You told the Lady Agnes that it would be a mistake to see him?"

"I did indeed. My opinion had no effect on her. She said it was her last chance because her end was near——"

"Master de Bousse has explained about her fears on that score," interrupted the judge.

"She decided she must see him then or not at all. She insisted he was to be sent in."

"Have you any idea why she felt it incumbent on her to see him?"

"It was most natural," declared De Poitevin. "They had been close friends for many years. She had made him an executor of her estate, to act with me and one other. It's conceivable that they had many things to talk over before she died."

The insistence of the witness on the imminence of her death brought an angry flush to the cheeks of the judge. Gouffier paused and swallowed hard before continuing with the examination.

"Let us come, then, to the episode with which we are chiefly concerned. Do you recall that some time after the prisoner was admitted to his audience, the Damoiselle de Vendôme came to you?"

"Yes, my lord judge."

"Was she in an excited state?"

"She was very angry. I didn't pay much attention to that at first because she was always in a temper over something. She quarreled with the servants, she criticized her mistress, she told me I knew nothing of medicine, she spoke sharply of the King and all his ministers. She saw no merit in anyone. A very disagreeable person, in short."

"You say you paid no attention to her at first. Does that mean you saw reasons for doing so later?"

"Yes, my lord. When she told me Jacques Coeur had walked into the room beyond the grating. This made me very angry. I could hardly believe my ears when she said he had given the Lady Agnes something to drink."

"You went to the room at once?"

"I ran there! To my surprise the room was light. Coeur had dared to open the shutters."

"A suspicious circumstance in itself."

The witness had been ready to continue with his evidence. At this remark, however, he paused. He looked up at the judge.

"A suspicious circumstance, my lord? I don't understand you."

"It's clear," said Gouffier, "that the prisoner would not have gone so contrary to the wishes of the mistress of the house if he had not felt he needed light to accomplish his purpose quickly."

"On the other hand, my lord judge, would he not have desired darkness to cloak his misdoing if he had gone into the room with criminal purpose? Would he have made the room light so that anyone who happened to come near, as the Damoiselle did, could see what he was about?"

The flush deepened on the cheeks of the presiding judge. "Are you here as an advocate for the prisoner?" he demanded in a furious tone. "I wish you to understand that you're not permitted to express opinions before this Bed of Justice. You're here to answer questions and you must limit yourself in your responses to matters of fact and personal observation."

The witness drew himself up to his not-too-considerable height. "You invited discussion of the point, my lord judge. Perhaps it's to be regretted that I couldn't agree with your opinion as the significance of the opening of the shutters. But, at any rate, I gave you my honest view of it."

Jacques Coeur was following the evidence closely for the first time in three days. With a faint stirring of hope he said to himself: "My old friend Robert is testifying like the honest man I know him to be. They had better have a care or he'll tear such holes in their fabric of lies that all the perjury in the world won't serve to mend it!"

It was clear to him now that the judges had taken the witness for granted, to the extent, at any rate, of assuming he would not prove hostile. It was inconceivable to them that a man of humble station, dependent on the favor of those above him, could do other than support the ministers of his master, the King.

A light was beginning to grow in the eyes of the prisoner. "They're a stupid lot!" he said to himself. "They thought all they had to do was to silence me. The case has been prepared so carelessly that they have no control over their own witnesses."

Perhaps Gouffier had also reached the conclusion that greater care would have to be shown. He was beginning to phrase his questions so that the witness would have no further chances to express unwelcome opinions.

"What did you do on finding the prisoner beside the couch of the Lady Agnes?"

"I stated my disapproval most sharply."

"What explanation did he give?"

"He said she had fainted while talking to him and he had hurried to her side to give her a restorative."

"Was there any evidence that he had done so?"

"Yes, my lord. There was a cup on the table beside the couch. It was half filled."

"Did you assume that he had given her the rest?"

"I had already been told so."

"That's true. By the Damoiselle de Vendôme. What condition did you find her in?"

"She was not yet fully conscious. I saw at once that his visit had been harmful."

"Did you think her condition due to the dose he had given her?"

"I was certain it had done her no good. He had no knowledge of medicine. How could he tell what was needed?"

With each moment the prisoner was gaining a clearer insight into the situation which existed. The judges knew that the responses they would get from the witness on many points would not suit them. Nevertheless, it had been necessary to call him to testify. They were making the best of it by ignoring all the important aspects. There were a dozen questions he should be asked, vital questions. Did the witness see the bottle of poison on the table? Did he discover that the cup contained poison from the bottle? Did the Lady Agnes show symptoms of poisoning? Did he administer antidotes?

Jacques Coeur was certain that none of them would be asked.

It became apparent at once that he was right. Dauvet took up the burden and proceeded to examine the witness with minute care about the evidence he had already given. He refrained from asking anything on these important points. His questions were so cleverly phrased that the concurrence of the witness in the evidence given by others with reference to the poison could be assumed. After nearly an hour of this adroit maneuvering no one in the room, except the prisoner and the witness himself, could have believed otherwise.

Finally Dauvet looked up at his colleagues and received a nod from Guillaume Gouffier. He nodded in response and turned back to the witness.

"I have one more question to ask you, and one only. After Jacques Coeur had given the drink to Agnes Sorel and had left the manor house, were you certain she was dying?"

"It was clear she was sinking fast. But——"

"Thank you, Master Physician. That will do." A peremptory wave of the hand accompanied the verbal dismissal.

The hearing of evidence was completed.

2

Although Jacques Coeur had reconciled himself to the certainty that he would be declared guilty, it was with a sense of shock that he realized there was no longer any opportunity to combat the testimony offered against him. The small measure of renewed hope he had felt when Robert de Poitevin entered the court guttered down like a dying candle. His eyes had been fixed on the narrow window above the dais through which the last rays of the afternoon sun had made their way into the room and it seemed to him symbolic that the patch of sky turned dark as he watched. "It's all over," he said to himself. "There's no way of undoing what they have done with their lies."

Then he noticed that De Poitevin had not left his station in front of the judges' table. The expression on the face of the physician showed the amazement he felt that he had not been asked any of the questions he also knew to be vital. Gouffier said sharply, "The witness is not required any longer." The little man, with the greatest reluctance, turned to withdraw.

To the surprise of everyone Antoine de Chabannes elected to speak at this moment. An old soldier, who had grown stiff of movement and heavy in build and face with the passing of the years, he had seemed out of place among the more alert ministers of the Crown who made up the board of judges with him. He had said nothing at all. Sitting impassively beside the presiding officer, he had seemed to take little interest in the proceedings. Perhaps his mind had been occupied with visions of the fine round towers of Saint-Fargeau hidden away in the forests of Auxerrois and the rolling land he hoped someday soon to claim as his own. Perhaps also the desire to make these dreams come true influenced him. Raising himself in his chair, he said in a rumbling voice, "I desire to ask the witness a question."

The physician returned with willing briskness to his place. Guillaume Gouffier stared at his soldier colleague as though apprehensive of the nature of the question to be asked.

"It's late," said the presiding judge. "The hearing has been most thorough."

"It is a small matter, perhaps, but bear with me in this." The old soldier smiled and nodded his square shaggy head. "I've noticed a gap in the evidence. Did you," to the witness, "see the bottle of poison on the table as well as the cup?"

For the second time that day Jacques Coeur sat up straight in his chair. A glow came into his eyes that told of awakened interest, even that his mind had resumed its normal briskness. He sensed that of all the questions left unasked this had been the one the other judges feared the most. The angry flush, which came so easily to the cheeks of Guillaume Gouffier, spread up beyond the narrow line of his temples. He scowled at his inept neighbor as though he wished him many leagues away, even in a far country where the climate would be much warmer than the over-heated atmosphere of the Bed of Justice.

The spectators, sensitive to the currents of feeling among the chief actors in the drama, seemed aware already that matters had taken an unexpected turn. Silence suddenly fell on the room.

"No, my lord judge," said Robert de Poitevin in a loud voice, "I did not see the bottle of poison on the table. It was *not* on the table, my lord judge."

"But," said the old soldier, his dull eyes framed in a puzzled frown, and disregarding the impatient tug that Gouffier gave his elbow, "I'm sure the girl said it was there all the time and that she returned to the room later and go it."

"She was mistaken, my lord. It was not there."

Speaking in a voice he strove to keep composed but with very little success, Guillaume Gouffier addressed the witness. "It's clear that you were so disturbed over what had happened that you overlooked the bottle."

"No, my lord. That is not clear at all. You must know that the form of container in which all poisons are kept was designed so that it could never be overlooked. It's inconceivable that a man of medicine could fail to see a bottle of poison with its arrow beside a patient in whose welfare he took the absorbed interest I felt in the Lady Agnes Sorel!"

"It must be, then," said Gouffier, "that the accused made the grave error of returning to the room later and leaving the bottle on the table then."

"No, no, my lord! That could not be! The accused left the room before I did and he had no opportunity of returning to it."

Antoine de Chabannes did not seem aware even yet of the enormity of the blunder he had committed. He blinked his eyes and said to the witness: "I can't make head or tail of this. At any rate, Master Physician, you knew it was poison in the cup?"

Gouffier waved a peremptory hand at the witness to forbid an immediate reply. Glancing sideways at the old soldier, he said: "Since you raise the point, my lord, I must declare your question one to which the witness cannot give a proper reply. There's nothing on record to show that he tested the contents of the cup. I'm sure our colleagues agree with me that there's no object in pursuing your query further."

The witness was not to be shoved aside in that manner. In a loud voice he proclaimed, "I tested the contents of the cup!"

It must have been clear to Robert de Poitevin that he was daring the wrath of the King's ministers and, presumably, of the King himself. Nevertheless, he showed no hesitation, no disinclination to go on. He stood up straight, his round stomach stuck out in front of him, his eyes full of righteous zeal.

The court was in an uproar now. The spectators were chattering excitedly, the lawyers were scraping nervous heels and whispering. From beyond the partition came loud and unrestrained talk. Gouffier brought down his gavel and declared in an angry voice, "The hearing is over and the guards will clear the court at once!"

This evoked shouts of protest from the people on the other side of the partition. Cries of "Let him speak!" "The truth is coming out at last!" and "Brava, Robert de Poitevin!" filled the air. The pikes of the guards rang unavailingly on the stone floor.

The physician took advantage of a momentary lull to cry in a high-pitched voice which everyone could hear, "I tested what was in the cup! It was wine and water!"

Gouffier had the gavel raised but at this he lowered it silently and placed it beside him on the table. He motioned to the guards and ushers to restore quiet in the court. When this had been done, he began to speak in reluctant tones.

"In view of the statements of the physician who tended the Lady Agnes in her last illness," he declared, "it will be necessary to continue the hearing. Too much has been said—or perchance not enough. Either the Damoiselle de Vendôme has given false evidence before this court or Robert de Poitevin has been guilty of negligence in the care of an illustrious patient and of the further offense of endeavoring to obstruct justice." He glared down at the witness. "We must now ascertain which it is."

Jacques Coeur had been watching the scene with a deep sense of relief and deliverance. The break had come exactly as he had known it would —if it came at all. A single one of the forbidden questions had been asked and had received an honest answer; and doubts had been raised as to the validity of the whole case against him. Each additional question now would lead inevitably to others, until the effect perhaps would be like a landslide which begins with the dislodgment of a few stones. If the more astute of the judges did not succeed in getting matters under control (and this would be hard without giving the appearance of deliberately throttling the truth), the case which had been so maliciously constructed against him would be wafted out the windows of the Bed of Justice.

The prisoner looked up at the four bitter faces on the dais and the bewildered and uncomfortable countenance of the one who had started this upheaval. He had heard whispers of the designs Antoine de Chabannes entertained on his much-prized château and it seemed especially fitting that the bungling had been his. "What is your chance now to look over the vineyards and the woods of my fair domain and call them your own?" he said to himself.

Gouffier, whose face had not lost its suggestion of white fury, rapped for silence again. This time he was obeyed instantly.

"The remarks of this witness," he said, "have qualified the case against the accused to this extent: that we must now inquire more fully into the movements of our main witnesses at the time in question." He turned to Dauvet. "I'm out of patience with the turn things have taken. I leave the examination to you."

Dauvet rose to resume the role of questioner. He seemed wary of the witness and began with the greatest circumspection.

"Why do you say the accused had no opportunity to visit the room behind the grating after you both left?"

"I sent a servant at once to clear the room. Jacques Coeur left the house before this was completed."

"You are not speaking from direct observation of what happened. The servant in question will be recalled and then we shall see"—scowling at the witness—"if what you have stated is a mere assumption."

"You will find I'm right."

"We know this to be true: the Jacques Coeur and the girl smuggled the poison in. Agnes Sorel died quickly and unexpectedly thereafter and the bottle was found later by the Damoiselle de Vendôme in the room where the victim had been. Any discrepancy in detail will be cleared up later."

There was a pause and then the witness spoke in a voice which could be heard clearly in all parts of the court: "Agnes Sorel did not die quickly and unexpectedly. She had been on the point of death for many days."

"The court has heard the evidence of the learned doctor from the University who is quite certain she would have recovered. An opinion"— Dauvet glanced about the court and paused to lend additional emphasis —"in which all his colleagues share."

Coeur found it hard to restrain himself from shouting, "Olivier de Bousse is a quack and a liar!"

"This poison," said Dauvet, "was brought from the East and, as we have learned, it acts slowly and leaves no trace. You have"—with an ironic rise of voice—"no fault to find with that statement?"

"I have. I challenge the statement, my lord."

"Are you going to set yourself up against the combined wisdom of the practitioners of medicine at the University?"

De Poitevin did not give a direct answer. "I'm an authority on poisons, my lord judge," he said. "I've given a good part of my life to them. I've read of such magic potions but I've never seen them. Nor has any man of medicine of my acquaintance. In my opinion they are a myth like—like the fire-spitting dragon and the furnace which changes other metals into gold."

"Are you denying that De Cordule brought this poison back from the Orient? A poison which leaves no trace after death?"

The witness shook his head. "I doubt it but I'm in no position to deny it." Suddenly his voice gained in volume until it had an oratorical ring to it. "But I am denying, my lord judge, that this bottle contains such a poison!"

Dauvet was so completely taken aback that for several moments he said nothing. Then he asked, "Did you hear Olivier de Bousse identify it as the one described in the confession?"

"Olivier de Bousse knows nothing of poisons. If you'll bring him back and allow me to question him, I'll convince you of that in a very few minutes." Before he could be stopped, the witness reached up to the table and took the bottle in his hands. He gave it a vigorous shake. "Smell it, my lord judge. Is the odor a familiar one?"

Dauvet put the bottle to his nose briefly and then returned it to its place. "I fail to recognize it," he said.

"What did the odor remind you of?"

"I think it gave a suggestion of bitter almonds."

"Exactly!" cried the witness triumphantly. He sniffed loudly and then looked about him. "Everyone within a radius of ten feet," he declared, "must have recognized the odor given off. Twenty—nay, thirty, witnesses to it, my lord judge! . . . And now let me tell you what this poison is. It's not a rare poison from the East. It isn't even one of the rare varieties we use here, such as briony or turpeth or sea-hare or leopard's gall. It's one you hear of constantly because it's used a great deal." He turned to face the spectators on the seats nearest him. "I'm sure some of you who recognized the odor can tell the court what it is."

Gouffier's gavel hovered in the air but before it could descend a chorus of voices called, "Laurel!"

Robert de Poitevin cried, "You are right, it is laurel!" Then he swung back to Dauvet. "Yes, it's laurel, my lord judge. As many of you will know, it's made from the leaves of the laurel bush and it's potent enough to cause death quickly."

Jacques Coeur's heart was racing with new hope. He was thinking, "They were so confident they became careless. They didn't see to it that the poison put in the bottle was one from the East. They filled it with the first they laid hands on!"

Dauvet glowered. "The contents of the bottle will be examined again. You are very positive, Master Pill Maker. But let me tell you this: the point is of small moment. Olivier de Bousse says it came from the East. You say it didn't. It does not matter which of you is right. The poison in that bottle was given to Agnes Sorel and brought about her death. *That* is the point which counts."

"It was sixteen hours after Jacques Coeur left her that Agnes Sorel died," said the witness. "Laurel kills quickly. This is fortunate, for the victim suffers great agony. But it loses its power to kill after a certain time has elapsed. If it so happens that the victim survives an hour, he is almost certain to live. A longer period than an hour is a guarantee of survival. The fact that the Lady Agnes lived for sixteen hours is the most conclusive proof that her death was not due to a dose from this bottle."

The silence in the room was more dramatic than any tumult could have been. For the first time since the hearings began, not a single pair of eyes rested on the prisoner. The attention had been transferred to the pudgy figure of the physician.

"After Agnes Sorel died," the witness went on, in a reverent tone of voice, "we took out her heart to be embalmed. Three other physicians were present, all men of recognized worth. Call them and they will confirm what I am going to tell you. The blood of those who die from laurel poisoning is dark, their skin is livid. We found nothing of the kind. . . . My lords, when laurel kills, the face of the victim carries an indelible mark of the throes of death. The Lady Agnes Sorel died slowly and in peace. She drew her last breath with a smile on her lovely face, a smile as sweet and gentle as she herself had always been in life. The smile remained there after death. . . . My lords, she was not poisoned!"

The stillness which followed this speech was broken by a sound as though all the spectators had sighed in unison. It was a sigh of complete conviction, perhaps also of relief.

From the start of the proceedings Jacques Coeur had carried in his pocket an important letter. It was one of several which had not been taken from him at any of the prisons where he had been incarcerated because they dealt with business detail and had been deemed of no importance. This particular missive was one of the few weapons he possessed for his defense.

He looked cautiously at the upright figure of the usher standing as usual beside his chair. The man's mouth had fallen open and he was so absorbed in what he saw and heard that, clearly, everything else had been forgotten. The prisoner leaned out quickly and gave the motionless figure a vigorous shove. The usher gave a grunt of surprise and went over in a heap on the floor.

Coeur sprang to his feet and waved the letter in the direction of the judges' table. "Here," he cried, "is the final proof. A letter from Ferrand de Cordule. I can produce a dozen more like it. Compare the handwriting in this letter with that in the confession he's alleged to have written and you'll find that document nothing but a clumsy forgery. It's a pack of lies and absurdities!"

Coeur resumed his seat as the usher picked himself up from the floor. The spectators had listened to what he said with every evidence of excited interest, but the judges had paid him no attention at all. Four of them, all very solemn of face, had their heads close together in serious discussion. Antoine de Chabannes was taking no part in the talk. He sat apart and looked dismal and thoroughly penitent.

Suddenly Jacques Coeur began to laugh. It was a high-pitched burst of mirth to which he gave vent and it drowned out all other sounds in the court. He laughed so long and with such heartiness that his body shook. The usher made no move to stop him.

"Guillaume Gouffier!" Coeur called. "A certain agreement reached between us may now be regarded as null and void."

It was significant of the turn things had taken that the usher still made no move to control him.

One of the guards approached the prisoner and said in a tone of voice which carried a new note of respect, "You are to return to your cell, my lord Coeur."

3

Old Philippe had said that morning, as he took in Valerie's breakfast, "It will end today." He had then looked about the cell and added in a pessimistic voice, "Enjoy this comfort while you may, Mademoiselle."

Valerie spent the day in such a ferment of spirit that she could not remain still. She went at frequent intervals to prostrate herself before the crucifix and to pray fervently that the Lord would cause truth to prevail in the solemn room below where her fate as well as that of the Moneyman was being decided. She left her food untouched.

She had little real hope of the outcome. The reports Old Philippe had given her of the progress of the case had always been filled with gloom. The evening before he had said with many glum shakes of the head: "There's the confession, Mademoiselle. The Moneyman won't be able to answer *that!*" Her prayers, therefore, had a desperate note, as though she feared that nothing short of direct intervention from above would be of any avail.

When the light coming through the window began to fail, she knew that the hearing would soon be over if it had not ended already. From that moment on she kept listening for approaching footsteps. She was sure she would be able to tell what the verdict had been by the sound they made.

An hour passed, and then another. Valerie gave up listening. Her worst fears had been confirmed. The prison attendants had come to have a certain gruff affection for her. If the decision of the court had been in Jacques Coeur's favor, they would have come quickly to give her the glad tidings. They delayed their coming because the news was bad and they disliked the necessity of telling her.

The cell was in darkness when she finally heard footsteps approaching along the stone corridor. It was Old Philippe, for there was no mistaking the rheumatic hitch of his stride. He was walking slowly.

"My lord Coeur has been condemned!" she cried aloud. "God in heaven, what are we to do? It will be my turn next. And then—and then——"

Old Philippe came through the door holding a lantern in his hand. "You haven't lighted your candle," he said in a complaining tone.

"No," she answered, speaking from a far corner of the room. "It seemed —it seemed more fitting to wait in the dark."

Old Philippe lighted the candle with fingers that trembled from age. "It has been the same way often before," he said, grinning to himself. "They seem to think the dark hides them when it comes to the final word."

Valerie came forward out of the shadows and faced him. She was composed in manner, although her cheeks were pale and she kept her eyes averted. There was strain in her voice when she spoke.

"You have word for me. Is it—is it bad?" And then, without waiting for him to answer, she went on: "There's no need for you to tell me, Philippe. I know what the decision was. My lord Coeur was found guilty.

Oh, it was certain from the first! I knew it when I was taken into court that day. I didn't look up but I saw them. I saw my lord Gouffier. He was like a great, cruel cat, stretching his claws and ready to pounce on the poor mice trapped below!"

She had come close enough for him to see her face clearly. To his great amazement he discovered that she had in some way succeeded in changing her expression. Her lips were drawn back in an imitation of Guillaume Gouffier and there was the same deep indentation between her eyes. Although it was certain that she was near the point of a hysterical outburst, she began to speak with a perfect rendition of his voice.

"That will do!" She nodded and looked about her, one hand smoothing the other, a familiar habit of Gouffier's. "I contend, my lords, that an important point in the case against the prisoner has been demonstrated."

Then she drew herself up as though pronouncing the verdict. "You are declared guilty, Jacques Coeur, and sentence will now be passed upon you. Later we shall have before us this woman of low degree, this impostor, who acted as the accomplice——"

She began to laugh, a high-pitched outburst which changed quickly into a flood of tears. "You need not tell me, Philippe," she sobbed. "I know that he was found guilty and that now—that now—there is no hope for us!"

"But, Mademoiselle"—the old man spoke in a puzzled manner—"what is all this—this carrying-on? I didn't say the prisoner was found guilty. I didn't say the news was bad. I would say on the whole the news was good."

There was a moment of tense silence. The sobbing stopped. She repeated the word, "Good?" in a toneless voice. Then she reached out with a frantic urgency and seized his arm. "Good! Did you say good? Do you mean—do you mean he was acquitted?"

The turnkey slipped the ring back over one wrist and gestured with his free hand. "The charge of poisoning has been admitted to be false."

Valerie's knees gave way and she sank to the floor. She began to cry again, slowly at first and then with mounting volume and intensity.

"Is it true? You are not deceiving me? He has—he has really been acquitted? God, I thank Thee, humbly and earnestly, for saving him from them!"

"You will be free in a day or so, Mademoiselle. No charge is to be brought against you. But"—he gave vent to a sudden cackle—"the lady who told all the lies is in trouble now. It's said she'll have to do public penance for bringing false charges. I was glad to hear *that*, Mademoiselle. The lying, green-eyed vixen!"

"And what of my lord Coeur? Does he go free also?"

The turnkey shook his head. "No, Mademoiselle. The word is that he will be held and tried later on other charges. I saw the list—treason, robbing the royal purse, helping black heathen Turks. It's a fearsome list, Mademoiselle."

Valerie's sense of elation deserted her suddenly and completely. She asked in a stricken voice, "Does he know?"

"Yes, Mademoiselle. I've come from his cell just this minute. He was eating a good warm supper—some roast venison I begged from the kitchen for him—and talking with good cheer. He said to me that now you were free he could face them with a clear conscience and fight them claw and fang. He said he had beaten them once and would do it again. He was in a very good mood, Mademoiselle."

"But, Philippe, what does it mean? Why are they holding him and letting me go?"

The turnkey shook his head gloomily. "It's like a fork, Mademoiselle. If they don't catch him on one prong, they will on another. But you have no more worries. They won't put you back in the cage. Tomorrow perhaps the papers will be signed and then you will be free of them."

7

D'ARLAY had two horses saddled and ready at the entrance to the Lusignan prison when Valerie was released next morning. Unfortunately it had become known in the town at what hour she would be set free and the space in front of the grim stone pile was so crowded that he was compelled to remain on the edge of things. The clang of the gate swinging open brought cries of "Here she is!" as the eager townspeople fought to get closer to the foot of the paved ramp. D'Arlay caught no more than a glimpse of her face before she was engulfed. She was wearing a hood well down over her brow but he had seen enough to know that she was thoroughly frightened and bewildered.

By the time he reached her, the cloak she was wearing had been torn from her shoulders and was being divided into small pieces as souvenirs. One old woman, using a knife which she had carried in the palm of her hand, had succeeded in cutting off a lock of hair. Valerie gave a gasp of relief and joy when he reached her side after several minutes of battling.

"Robin! I'm nearly suffocated!" she cried, as she surrendered herself into the shelter of one arm. "Please, get me away from these people!"

He had to draw his sword finally and threaten to cut a path through the crowd in order to reach the horses. They mounted in haste and turned in the direction of a street which wound up to the higher reaches of the town. But they were not yet free. A gaunt figure, in a jerkin stained grotesquely with a jumble of colors, dashed out in front of them, raising one arm and shaking it excitedly.

"One moment!" cried this apparition. "You must hear what I have to say! If you refuse me your ears, you'll lose the chance to waken a blind world to the recognition of genius."

D'Arlay cried impatiently, "Out of the way, scarecrow!"

"Yes, I'm a scarecrow," said the man. "But also I'm an artist. I'm a great artist. So far the world has refused to see the genius which inspires my canvases. I am overlooked, brushed aside, sneered at. I starve in a cold garret. I can't afford to buy the colors I need. Monseigneur, if I were allowed the honor of painting Mademoiselle Maret, if I had the chance to capture the beauty she shared with the dead woman, it would be a different story. Everyone would want to see the picture. They would ask who this great artist is."

D'Arlay said, "We're leaving town as fast as our horses will carry us and so we can't help you to your deserved fame." He drew out a royal d'or and tossed it to the artist. "That, at least, will get you food and fuel and some of the colors you need."

The interruption had given Valerie a chance to look about her. She drew in her breath in surprise when she saw that all the windows in the tall and narrow houses fronting on the prison square were filled with heads. There were watchers even on the sharply sloping roofs. Children were being held up by chattering mothers so they would catch a glimpse of her and have something to remember when they grew up.

"It would have been just like this," she said to herself, "if I had been tried and found guilty and they had dragged me out to burn at the stake. I think people like this would enjoy it more to see me die in the flames!"

This train of reflection brought her close again to a state of panic and she cried beseechingly to her companion, "Please, we must get out of here quickly!"

By the time they had followed the course of the winding street to a wider thoroughfare above from which it was possible to catch a view of the river, she had recovered from her fear. She looked up at the sky where a September sun shone brightly, and cried out with pleasure.

"It seems a lifetime since I saw the sun last," she said. Then she began to feel a realization of what this meant. "Robin, I'm free! I'm not to go back to prison! They can't touch me now. I'm free!"

"Yes, you are free and they can't touch you again. Your patron saint must have pleaded your case well and so persuaded the Heavenly Father to reach down a protecting hand. Nothing else could have saved you."

"I'm so happy now." Abruptly her mood changed back. Her eyes had fallen on her skirt and had become conscious of a new disaster. "Robin! They've cut my skirt to tatters! There's hardly anything left of it."

D'Arlay laughed. "You're lucky, my sweet one, to have any clothes left at all."

In a moment she began to laugh with him. "What does it matter? I'm free and that's all I need care about." She looked down at the bright blue waters of the Vonne and exclaimed in wonder at the beauty of it. "How lovely the world is! And now I belong to it again, I'm a part of it and not a number in a dark cell."

For the next few minutes she rode beside him in a perfect transport of happiness. She kept turning her head from side to side for fear of missing something. She found beauty in the dirty streets and charm in the glum old houses. She looked at a tavern sign painted the green of bile and eagerly spelled out the name, *Le Dur-bec* (the hawfinch). She chattered with more abandon than was ever displayed by that shy species of bird, asking her companion an infinity of questions about himself. She hardly waited for his answers before going on to something else. The miracle of having someone to talk with seemed to have gone to her head.

Suddenly she stopped. She turned in the saddle and looked at him questioningly. "Robin, where are you taking me? I've been so full of the joy of finding myself alive again that I've not thought about it before."

D'Arlay leaned over and took possession of her nearest hand. "We go first to a sleepy little village about six miles south of here. Word has been sent ahead to the priest, Father Eligius, that we are coming and that we want him to marry us. Pierre Dupain says he's a right-thinking little man and so we may assume that he'll be ready with book and bell and candle to—to make the journey we are about to take together a much more proper proceeding than the last one we made in each other's company."

Valerie reined in her horse and gazed at D'Arlay with unbelieving eyes. "You are still willing to marry me?" She spoke in a tense whisper. "After all that's happened? Dearest Robin, I—I am a notorious woman! Only by a great miracle have I escaped the flames they light for women poisoners. You saw what happened back there. I'm afraid it will always be the same. People will go out of their way to see me, they'll whisper behind my back. My name will be coupled with Gilles de Retz who murdered all those babies. *Valerie Maret the poisoner!*"

"In Arlay," he said, still keeping possession of her hand, "we'll live in a world of our own. There are no close neighbors and no town within a dozen miles. Let the outside world talk about you if it has nothing better to do. The murmur of our own stream and the wind in the trees will keep us from hearing."

Her eyes had filled with tears. Keeping them lowered, she said in a whisper: "You would sacrifice everything for me, Robin? Is it through a sense of pity that you're ready to do it?"

"My reason for wanting to marry you is sheer selfishness," he answered. "I take the most intense pleasure in seeing you, in having you near me. I can conceive of no joy to equal the knowledge that you belong to me. I want you to sit beside me at meals, to lie beside me in bed, to ride with me, to share all my thoughts. I don't want to talk to anyone else as long as I live. If I can't have you, life will be a complete desolation. So you see," he added, after a pause during which he tried vainly to catch her eye, "there's nothing fine or self-sacrificing, nothing noble at all, about my attitude. I'm an intensely selfish fellow who insists on getting what he wants."

Valerie looked up then. Her eyes were still slightly misted but this did not obscure in any degree the happiness which showed in them. "I won't be able to resist such selfishness as that," she said.

They had been riding through streets which showed few signs of life. A man standing in front of a tavern had sprung into action suddenly as they passed and had run after them for a few yards, crying, "I know you, you're that woman!" but this had been the extent of the interest they had created since leaving the neighborhood of the prison. Now, however, they reached a small square sleeping in front of an old church of green stone. A smiling man with a basket under his arm confronted them.

It was Pierre Dupain. He waved a hand to them, saying, "You escaped the crowds more quickly than I thought possible. Nonetheless I came on time."

"This," said D'Arlay to his companion, "is a very brave man to whom you owe your life. If he hadn't shown the courage to establish a system of communication between us and Jacques Coeur in prison, we would never have been able to save you from the torture."

"Then you must be Pierre Dupain," said Valerie, extending her hand to him. "I heard about you from my lord Coeur. I shall be grateful to you, Monsieur Dupain, as long as I live."

The bookseller took her hand and kissed it. "A small risk to take in such a cause," he said. "As for saving your life, Mademoiselle, I think the credit for that goes to the one who made the midnight ride to Poitiers and convinced a certain great man that you should be spared."

Valerie turned quickly to D'Arlay. "What is this? I've heard nothing of a ride to Poitiers."

He brushed it aside. "It's a story I may tell you some time."

Pierre Dupain held up his basket, from which the neck of a bottle protruded. "A wedding breakfast," he explained. Then he added with a twinkle, "They say the efforts of a good cook are wasted on a bride and groom; but my wife is a *very* good cook, as you will perhaps discover."

"Was the word sent to the priest?" asked D'Arlay.

The bookseller nodded. "The messenger is back already and reports that the arrangements have been made."

"Au revoir, Pierre Dupain!" said D'Arlay, kicking his heel gently into the ribs of his horse. "Two people will always remember you with gratitude."

2

The priest in the nearby village was right-thinking, as had been reported, but he was much more: he was a gentle old man with a love for all mankind showing in his deep-sunken eyes and with an infinity of the wrinkles of kindly humor clustering at the wicks of his mouth. When the ceremony had been performed in his little church—it must have been one of the very smallest in all France and its tower was shaped absurdly like a salt shaker—he walked between them down the aisle with an arm over the shoulders of each.

"I count this an honor," he said. "You are brave young people. You, my daughter, have been through a terrible ordeal but you are very young and I don't believe you'll carry the scars of it long. You, my son, have assumed a responsibility which will not be easy. You will be much criticized and perhaps persecuted. The expression you wear tells me you'll count such difficulties a small price for the joy you'll know in this union. Keep the belief in your hearts that Our Lord will be lenient to you both and show you the way to real happiness."

His house was joined to the church by a covered walk over which vines clustered like a solid wall. They realized immediately how fortunate this was. A curious knot of people had already gathered in front of the edifice.

"Word has reached the village that you headed from Lusignan in this direction," whispered the old priest. "You must stay with me tonight and resume your journey at dawn. It will save you inconvenience; and I will be selfish enough to find much pleasure in your company."

Accordingly they had their wedding breakfast in a small walled garden back of the house. It was so small and the walls were so high that little sun reached it, no more actually than a splash of light on one side of the ivy-covered brick. However, it was pleasantly tangled with late flowers and there was a pear tree on which the fruit had turned a ruddy color.

They seated themselves together under the pear tree and Valerie spread a handkerchief on the ground to serve as cloth. Pierre Dupain had not overpraised his wife's cooking, for the breakfast she had prepared passed all commendation. There were hard-boiled eggs colored with saffron and flavored with cloves; a cheese of Montreuil, made from fresh cream and generously sprinkled with sugar; a bread of two colors, white and brown, the result of alternating layers of wheat and rye; and a pair of custards baked in flaky crust called darioles over which the hand of the good housewife had not been niggardly in shaking the cinnamon. The wine was light-bodied and it left the tongue and throat refreshed. Both of them were hungry and they finished the contents of the basket to the last crumb and drop.

"I had hoped," said Valerie, tidily clearing up all traces of the meal, "that there would be a chance today for me to get new clothes. The memory of the prison, and the taint of it as well, will always cling to what I'm wearing. These are things they found for me when they took me out of the cage. As you see, my lord Robin, they're very dull and also a very bad fit."

"I've lived this morning in such a glow of content that I've hardly noticed what you have on," he answered. He cast a belatedly appraising eye over her attire. "You're right, my heart. That dress doesn't sufficiently become you."

"Bice!" said Valerie bitterly, holding out her sleeve which was of the dull gray known by that term. "All my life I've had to wear it and all my life I've hated it! Once, when I was a very small girl, it was promised me I was to have a new dress for my birthday. I said to my mother—to Madame Maret—'Please, Maman, anything but bice!' She was a kind woman and she promised me it would be either pink or blue, the colors I craved most. I especially wanted pink. When I got the dress, which color do you think it was?"

"Pink, I hope."

She shook her head with the sadness of the memory she had brought back. "No, my Robin. It was bice. They hadn't been able to afford anything better. Now you will understand why I dislike this color so much."

After he had settled his wife comfortably in a corner of the wall with his cloak as a cushion, D'Arlay sought the old priest to see what could be done about the problem of clothes.

"I find it necessary to ride over to a somewhat larger place this afternoon," said the priest. "Perhaps I could get something for my lady there and bring it back in my bundle. What articles do you want, Monseigneur?"

D'Arlay began to indulge in expansive instructions. "Everything, Father Eligius. You may tell the tailor that I want the best he has. The materials must be rich. The fashioning must be becoming and with a degree of art."

The priest let fall a diffident hint. "It's a small town, my lord. You must not expect too much of it."

"As for color," went on D'Arlay, "I want pink, if you can get it. Otherwise blue."

"But—but, my lord! Have you a long ride ahead of you?"

"Yes. A continuous journey of perhaps two weeks."

"Then permit me to make a suggestion, my lord. The colors you name would not be practical for such a long journey. Nor would it be wise to select rich materials. I would most strongly advise a good wearing material. The color should be gray."

"Not gray!" cried D'Arlay. "Father Eligius, there are reasons, the very best of reasons, for this dress to be frivolous and gay and in no sense practical or sensible. It must be rewarding to the eye and the heart of my wife. I want a plume in the hat, an ostrich plume——"

"Monseigneur! We are not in Paris or Tours or Lyons!" protested the priest. "There will be no ostrich plumes in the town to which I ride. It will be a matter of very great luck if I'm able to get your lady as much as a colored ribbon for her hat."

Valerie was sleeping when D'Arlay returned to the garden but she wakened almost immediately and sat up against the wall. She had lost the happy mood of the morning.

"I'm realizing how selfish we've been!" she said, looking at him with guilty eyes. "My lord Coeur is still in prison and we haven't mentioned him all these hours. I confess, my Robin, that I've been selfish enough to want nothing but happiness today."

D'Arlay began to talk in optimistic terms. He was convinced that his friend had weathered the worst of the storm in escaping conviction on the poisoning charge and that he would be able to meet successfully any new charges they might bring against him. "He has been an honest and capable minister to the King," he pointed out. "They won't find a shred of real evidence against him. He has on many occasions made up deficits in the royal purse from his own funds and said nothing about it. The proof of this will be in the household books."

"But will they allow the books to be brought into court?"

"Perhaps not. But how can they expect to make a case against a man who has been as honest and disinterested as that? Any charges they make will be trivial and as false as the heart of Judas. The truth can't be kept from showing itself."

Valerie was far from ready to believe this. "It was a miracle which saved us!" she whispered tensely. "Can we be sure it will happen again? Can the truth prevail if they refuse to let him speak in his own defense or to call witnesses? Will they let him consult his own records?"

D'Arlay was not to be robbed of his optimism. "The odds against him can never be as great again as they were this time. Yet he won. If there isn't another miracle, there will always be the Coeur genius to find a way out—and the Coeur luck." He walked over and seated himself beside her. "Come, my love, this is not the day for doubts. We're entitled to happiness for a few hours and it isn't selfishness to want that much. I have many things to tell you and so I must begin at once. The good priest will be back before the afternoon is over and that is little enough time to tell you how much I love you."

3

They had supper with Father Eligius in a stone cubicle off the kitchen. It was so small that his housekeeper could not enter to serve them. Instead she handed the dishes in to them through a circular hole in the wall, having something to say each time. Once she remarked to Valerie, "Eat well of this, my lady, for truly you're as thin as a plucked crow." It was a simple meal, consisting of a late melon, a platter of stewed goat meat, and a steaming hot mixture of vegetables.

Valerie had regained her good spirits and she chatted about the future, assuring the old priest that she intended to have a large family and that she hoped they would all be girls with the exception of the much-needed heir. "There are too many knights in the world now and too much fighting," she said, in answer to his surprised query.

Father Eligius had shown discrimination in the matter of her new clothes. The dress was blue and a good match, moreover, for her eyes. No tailor was capable of such prodigies of labor as producing a lady's gown in a few hours and so she had asked no questions, assuming that they had belonged once to someone else. The hat had been made by the nimble fingers of the tailor's wife and it had a becoming blue ribbon in it. There had been no time to change but Valerie felt perfectly satisfied, and this added to her lightness of mood.

"And now," said Father Eligius, drinking the last drop of his one glass of wine which he had diluted liberally with water, "I mustn't indulge any longer my great liking for young company. You've had a hard day and tomorrow you must start out at dawn. Come with me and I'll show you to your room."

The good-natured face of the servant appeared in the aperture in the wall and she addressed a few words to D'Arlay, wishing them much happiness. He smiled and thanked her.

"Your servant is Angevin," he said as they followed the priest up a steep flight of stone steps. "I can tell from her voice. I think she must have been born not far from Arlay."

"Yes, Micheline is from Anjou. She's a widow and a faithful servant. But there are times when she holds her tongue on a loose rein."

There was a hall above and a bedroom opening off it. Pausing at the door, Father Eligius raised two fingers above them as he pronounced a blessing.

"You've been sorely tried," he said to Valerie, giving her a smile of real affection. Then he turned to D'Arlay. "In spite of it, she is very lovely, this very young wife of yours. You must always be kind to her."

When the door had closed behind them, the happy bridegroom placed a hand on each of her shoulders and smiled down at her. "Yes, you are lovely, my very young bride," he whispered. "My Valerie! My sweet minikin, with your hair curling so distractingly about your ears! I vow no candles are necessary when your eyes shine so brightly! I swear solemnly to treat you with more than kindness all the years of your life!"

She whispered back, "It makes me happy when you say such things to me." Then she added with a nod of the head, "I'm glad we know my parents were of gentle blood, because it makes me feel less—less unworthy."

Micheline had not shared his opinion in the matter of the lighting of the room and had resorted to the usual method. A candle was burning on the table. She had gone further than that, however. There was in addition a large cluster of unlighted ones. D'Arlay smiled when he saw what she had done. "Even if she hadn't spoken, I would have known she was Angevin from this," he said. Then, realizing the number of tapers the housekeeper had provided, he burst out involuntarily with, "Does she think me the Twenty Candle Bridegroom of Nantes?"

Valerie, it was clear, did not understand what he was talking about. She came over and stood beside him at the table. "Is this some custom of your part of the country?" she asked.

D'Arlay did not answer at once. He was regarding her with a somewhat guilty air. "I thought you knew or I wouldn't have said anything about it. Yes, it's a Western custom, one of those absurd jokes people think they must play at weddings. I'm sure this is the work of the servant and that the good old priest would be angry with her if he knew."

"But what is the custom?"

He took her by the shoulders again and frowned down at her sternly. "You are a married woman now and I suppose there would be no harm in telling you. If you are going to be shocked, you must blame your own curiosity. Well—when a bridegroom takes his wife in his arms on their bridal night, he must blow out the candle and light another one afterward. This—this keeps on. Thus there is evidence in the morning to satisfy the curiosity of relatives and guests. Now that I've satisfied *your* curiosity, are you very much shocked and angry with me?"

A blush had taken possession of her face but she answered with a shake of the head. "No. But in the morning I may speak my mind to that old woman downstairs." Probably with a desire to change the subject, she said that she was sure Father Eligius had surrendered his own room to them. Had he noticed that part of it was devoted to the priest's memories of his boyhood days? "There's a little cap he wore once," she said, "and a hoop and a toy horse with a wisp of real horsehair stuck to its neck. And there's a plate of colored pebbles from the seashore. Somehow it makes me feel very sorry for him."

D'Arlay dropped his hands from her shoulders. It was clear that he was ill at ease. "My sweet child," he said, "it would be much easier for us if we were following the usual ritual tonight. There should be a groom of the chamber to turn down the bedclothes and to make sure they've been properly aired and to perfume the place with rose leaves. Then there should be a bevy of friends and servants to bring you in and undress you and put you to bed. After that another lot should escort me in. That's only part of it but, as I have never been through it, I don't know all the rules. I find myself uncertain as to what to do. Do you have the same feeling?"

Valerie slowly nodded her head. "Yes," she whispered.

"When Naulty was married the whole household practiced what was to be done for weeks ahead. . . . Do you think I should return to the hall and come back a little later?"

She nodded quickly. "Yes, my Robin. It's most kind of you to think of it." She took her skirt in both hands (what the curious people of Lusignan had left of it) and drew it out. "This is quite ugly, as you see, and it's such a poor fit. I—I would rather be alone when I take it off."

Then she had a sudden thought. Going to the corner of the room where the childhood mementoes were kept, she took a handful of the colored pebbles. These she transferred to one of his hands.

"Take a walk in the hall," she suggested. "Walk very slowly. And each time you make a turn, transfer one of the pebbles to the other hand. By the time they're all in the other hand, you may come back."

"I will find it difficult to walk slowly, my heart," he said.

But when he reached the landing outside the door he remained there in deep thought for some time. Finally, nodding his head in decision, he began to descend the stairs. He put each foot down carefully so she would not hear.

Father Eligius was sitting in the small room at the front of the house, straining his eyes over a book which was so heavy in its board bindings that he held it on his knees. Clearly it was his most prized possession for he was turning the leaves with a reverent hand. He looked up when D'Arlay appeared in the door and all the wrinkles on his face gathered themselves together in a smile.

"I knew you would come, my son," he said. "I've been waiting for you.

Take this seat beside me. We'll talk and perhaps we'll drink a little wine. We'll talk so long that, when you go back upstairs, that gentle little wife, who has been treated so cruelly, will be soundly asleep."

They talked an hour or more. D'Arlay then returned to the bedroom with stealthy steps and was careful to make no sound in opening the door. But Valerie was not asleep, after all. She smiled at him from the bed and remarked, "How slowly you must have walked, my Robin."

A lighted candle on a table beside the bed was waiting to be blown out.

Envoy

THE story of the girl who was known as Valerie Maret until her sixteenth year, then for a brief and troubled period as Valerie de Voudrai, and after that for the balance of her days (which proved lengthy for those times and as happy as life could be in that or any age) as Valerie de Burey, has reached its climax. So far as she and the Sire d'Arlay are concerned, this long recital of events could now be considered as closed.

But the story of Jacques Coeur cannot be dismissed summarily at this point. His trial dragged on at Lusignan for nearly two years more, and on May 29, 1453 (the same day that Constantinople fell to the Turks, a very bad day for civilization), he was declared guilty on five of the twelve charges which had been brought against him. It would be waste of space to enumerate these charges, for never in all judicial history had a great political figure been arraigned on such trumpery, absurd, and baseless grounds. It had been *opéra bouffe* from the beginning, but the King of France had to be freed of his debts and the nobility could no longer abide the spectacle of great wealth and power in the hands of a furrier's son; and so Jacques Coeur was condemned to death (Charles, most magnanimous of monarchs, changed this to perpetual exile at such time as the judgments against him had been satisfied) and to the confiscation of all his property. He was compelled to make the *amende honorable* in the Palace of Justice at Poitiers, which meant appearing barefoot and carrying a ten-pound candle to confess his misdemeanors, on the same day Jeanne de Vendôme underwent the identical punishment for having sworn to false evidence against him. Anyone with the smallest grain of humor would have seen something absurd about this; but a sense of humor was the quality they lacked most of all in the brave days of chivalry, and this final phase of the judicial proceedings is recorded in history with full solemnity.

And then began a mad scramble for the spoils. First of all those gallant gentlemen, the five judges, were awarded for their fairness and skill in handling the case by a gift of estates. Even Antoine de Chabannes, that fumbling veteran, attained the goal on which he had fixed his greedy rheumy eyes, the fair domain of Saint-Fargeau. The goods in the great shops were put up at auctions, held in Paris, Tours, Bourges, Lyons, and Poitiers, and never before nor since have such bargains been known. The nobles and their eager wives bid in the jewelry and the gold and silver vessels and all the costly and curious objects from the East. The ladies competed bitterly for the silks and satins and velvets, and it is probable that the prices paid for these goods came closer to their real value. When the last fragment of candle had burned out (the auctions were conducted on the inch-of-candle method, by which the successful bidder is the last one to name a price before the light dies) the shops were closed, the shutters put up and bolted. The great enterprises of Jacques Coeur had come to an end.

To tell all this, as well as the unusual events which followed, would require more space than can be allowed. The balance of the story will be set down in the form of a few scenes; and these will be told as briefly as possible.

1

D'Arlay had been restless and unhappy since the conviction of Jacques Coeur. There was nothing he could do to help the unfortunate Moneyman (who was being kept in solitary confinement in one prison after another and was, according to rumor, being slowly poisoned) and this disturbed him so much that he could not keep still after his far-from-exacting daily duties as the master of Arlay had been finished. At such times Valerie could do nothing for him.

One day he took to horse to escape the Old Man on his shoulder and rode out to Tremblay Hill from which visitors caught their first glimpse of the manor house of Arlay. As he passed over the crest he was surprised to see a stranger coming from the other direction at a brisk trot. They had few visitors and so D'Arlay reined in his horse at once and watched this newcomer with an interest which grew almost to bursting point when he discovered it was Pregent Kennedy. He was sure the Scot would prove to be the bearer of important news.

"Greetings!" he shouted, waving a gauntleted hand. "Greetings, Sir Scot! I can tell by the light in your eyes that you have news for me which will pull me out of this fever in which I pass my days."

Kennedy answered while still some distance away: "Aye, that I have. The best of news." He raised his voice to a triumphant blast. "*We accomplished our purpose!*"

When he had reined in, the Scot proceeded with his explanation. His face, which seldom changed from its lean solemnity, was actually glowing with enthusiasm.

"Jacques Coeur is free!" he declared. "And never in the annals of Christendom has such a spectacle been seen. It was wonderfully done, my lord D'Arlay, most monstrously well done!"

"God has answered the prayers of the people of France!" said D'Arlay, crossing himself.

"Aye. There will be much rejoicing when the word is passed that the Fox is loose. But it will be a bitter day for the sour-faced King and his noble ministers!"

D'Arlay was too happy to say much at first. They had wheeled their horses, in the meantime, into the slow slope of the road which led through autumnal colored woods to the domain of Arlay.

"We had him out of there like that!" said Kennedy, snapping his fingers. "It was a"—he paused and then had recourse to his native tongue for the word he needed—"a *canny* trick we played on them. Every detail had been attended to. First, a fire broke out in the apartments of the Governor. Never have you heard such shouting, such clamor for everyone to help, and such running with buckets of water, and the Governor's lady coming out screaming in her shift. While this excitement held the attention of everyone, the Fox tied his turnkey up with ropes—there was a jingle of gold in the turnkey's pocket, you may be sure—and opened the door with the keys. The warder on the gate had been well anointed too and—he was out of the place before the Governor was through bellowing orders and his lady had borrowed a kirtle to cover her shapelessness. Ah, it was a fine bit of planning. I give the Fox due credit for it."

"The Moneyman arranged it himself?"

"Down to the last detail. All we had to do was to play our parts. The seagoing fellow was there, bellowing and ramping around and letting the weight of his hand descend on anyone who got in his way. There were other Coeur men, factors and sea captains, and all of them good fellows in a pinch. It was an inspiring sight to see how his men rallied around him in his need, my lord."

"All," said D'Arlay, with sudden bitterness, "but the one who should have been there most of all."

"You were kept in the dark by the Moneyman's orders." The Scot nodded his head sagely. "And a sensible thing it was. You had jeopardized your safety and your position as a landowner enough as it was. Your wise friend, who thinks of everything, had no intention of letting you play the scapegoat. I assure you, my lord, that none of us had any great part to play. There were half-a-dozen spry young fellows on hand to do all the little bits which might have fallen to your share." He added, after a moment's pause, "It was said also that your lady was expecting the arrival of a son and heir —another good reason for not sending you word of what was afoot."

D'Arlay was still far from satisfied. "There were good reasons for not letting me take part—that I grant you—and only one on the other side, the fact that I'll regret it as long as I live!"

They had reached a small wooden bridge spanning a stream swollen to a fair semblance of a roaring torrent by recent rains. D'Arlay led the way across. Then he turned back to his companion with an unhappy look on his face. "The hoped-for heir," he said, "proved to be a daughter. A pretty little thing who didn't manage to grasp one second of life. I think it should be possible to save more of the babies who come so hopefully into the world and depart so quickly! The physician and the midwife didn't succeed in making our poor little Anne breathe at all."

"And how is your lady now?"

"She's not strong yet. Perhaps this good news you bring will be the draught to set her on her feet again." D'Arlay's mind went back to the more pressing matter of the escape. "Do you feel free to tell me anything more of the plans? Is Jacques Coeur in a safe place?"

"The flight has been worked out as carefully as the escape. Aye, the Fox has found a safe lair for the time being." They were crossing a large glade and there was not even a vagrant bird within hearing distance; but the Scot from force of habit lowered his voice. "If it's your thought that you would like to see him before he gets out of the country, it could be arranged. I have the Moneyman's promise for you on that."

"I must see him," said D'Arlay eagerly. "I can leave at once if necessary."

The manor house boasted a long, flagged passage with an outside colonnade creating the effect of a cloister. It was here that the Scot was taken to see the chatelaine of Arlay. He found her rather wan and thin lying on a couch with covers tucked up around her neck.

After she had skillfully probed into all the important matters and had led him persistently into descriptions of everything which had occurred, Valerie raised her head slightly to get a better view of her visitor.

"And what of you, Monsieur Kennedy?" she asked. "The last time I saw you was in Paris—before all these dreadful things happened—and at the time you were contemplating matrimony. Did you marry the fair widow?"

Kennedy shook his head. "Not I!" he exclaimed. "It was the luckiest escape I've ever had in a lifetime salted and peppered and porreted with such escapes. But"—with a triumphant nod—"my friend, Lockie Bell, married her! Aye, he's a maker of shoes now, that gallant Lockie! You see, my lady, the Guild has a rule that a widow may carry on her deceased husband's trade if she remarries someone in the Guild. When the other makers of boots discovered she had taken into her bed an ugly little Scottish runt who didn't have a shilling to bless the union with and who, moreover, didn't know a last from a goloshing, there was such a storm that it looked as though the happy couple would have nothing left but the bed itself! But Lockie has a persuasive tongue and he convinced them he could become a maker of boots himself and so satisfy the requirements of the Guild.

"And now"—triumphantly—"Lockie Bell is serving his time in a basement which stinks most abominably of leather, learning to slash and clobber and cobble and sew. Every time I think of him, working away as though St. Crispin was there to jab him with an awl if he slackened in his efforts, I chuckle to myself with sardonic satisfaction."

After a long pause Valerie asked, "And so the fortune you came to France to make is still beyond your reach?"

"It's still to be made, Madame." The Scot crossed one leg over the other and gave his tartan the customary backward flick. "Now that this untimely and unmanly peace has been made and there's no profit in killing any more, I'm thinking of going on to Rome with the Moneyman. He says there will be fortunes to be picked up there now that he intends to make the city his headquarters. I hear the pious cardinals will pay well for men who can handle a sword and pink a churchly rival through the eye. I hear also that the gold and the rich goblets and the jeweled purses lie on the street for the mere stooping over. Aye, Rome is the place for one with the special talents of Pregent Kennedy."

2

It was a long ride that D'Arlay took to say farewell to his friend. After two weeks of steady journeying over the roads of the south, which were notoriously bad, he found himself one dark night on the bank of the Rhône. On the other side he could see a cluster of lights from Good King René's favorite city of Tarascon.

He waited here with Pregent Kennedy for the better part of two hours before they heard the beat of horses' hoofs. The voice of Jacques Coeur came to them out of the darkness.

"Are you there, Robin?"

D'Arlay answered eagerly, "Here I am," and ran forward. Someone slipped the hooding from a lantern and held it up cautiously so that a brief view could be had of the man who had escaped through the fingers of Charles of France. With a sinking of the heart D'Arlay saw that Jacques Coeur had become an old man. His cheeks had the prison flabbiness and they were so sunken that his nose jutted out from them like the beak of a bird of prey. His neck was scrawny and there was a stoop in his shoulders. He coughed continuously.

Only his eyes were the same. They were still alive, commanding, full of determination.

"I had hoped," said Jacques Coeur, leaning from his saddle to shake hands, "to have several days with you. But, as you know, we were detained. That leaves us a short time only until I launch myself on the last stage of my flight to freedom."

"But," demurred D'Arlay, still feeling the shock caused by his friend's appearance, "I expected to cross the river with you and share your journey through Provence."

Coeur shook his head emphatically. "King René is a kindly old dotard and he won't surrender me to his brother-in-law of France. But there will be eyes everywhere and all my movements will be reported in full. If you were with me, the fact would get to Charles quickly. You would then be in serious trouble, my good Robin. The King might think the grounds sufficient for a charge of treason. Certainly everything you possess would be confiscated." He gave his head another shake. "We mustn't allow him that satisfaction, our good friend Charles. There's a house down the road where we may rest for an hour and talk. Then I must—betake myself on the road to exile."

D'Arlay said, "It will be a hasty farewell, Jacques."

The Moneyman began to cough and it took him quite a time to control the spasm. "Don't let this habit of mine disturb you," he said breathlessly. "I didn't break out of prison to die of the lung trouble it has started in me. I'm a tough old bear, I'll have you know. If they think I'm done for, they'll get a shock when I come charging out of my lair at them! . . . I have many things to tell you and a list of instructions as long as that famous sword of yours. Come, we must get to work."

Two hours later D'Arlay watched Coeur and his party ride off on the road to the ferry. He thought, "I'll never see him again." There had been no more than a handshake between them and from the Moneyman a hearty, "Farewell, Robin. We have been good friends." D'Arlay himself had been unable to utter a word.

Now from the darkness he heard Jacques Coeur speak to Nicolas who rode beside him. He said in a tone which he did not think, clearly, could carry so far to the rear, "I'm an old man at last, Nicolas, for I find myself most uncomfortable in the saddle."

There was a sympathetic note in the voice of the servant when he answered, and this for the first time in the memory of all men, "Come, master, this won't do! You're far from being an old man."

"But I am, Nicolas. I can't be sure I shall ever set eyes on the ship that's waiting for us."

"I remember once you said you could outwork, outthink, and outwalk any man alive. I laughed at you then but I knew it was true. And you still can! I swear, master, you'll get your strength back in a day or so and outride all of us."

"You're trying to be kind; and God knows my need for sympathy must be great to make you change your tune, my old goad! But it's no use. Soft words can't patch up a weak body. I'm a broken man, Nicolas, doddering on my way to the grave!"

"Master, master! You can't mean what you're saying!"

The clatter of the hoofs on the hard road made it impossible for D'Arlay to hear anything more.

3

There had been no word from her husband for several weeks and Valerie was so worried that she was finding it hard to sleep of nights. She was wondering for the thousandth time whether the Moneyman had been recaptured and whether the Sire d'Arlay had been with him at the time. She was becoming certain as each day passed without any message that this was what had happened.

A servant appeared in the door to announce, "The Comte de Burey, mistress."

She had not seen her brother-in-law for some months and had heard nothing of him in that time. The thought leaped into her mind that he was the bearer of bad news.

"Show the Comte here, if you please."

She was startled when her brother-in-law entered the room. He had changed a great deal, being so much thinner that his face looked gaunt and long. This gave greater prominence to his eyes and nose.

In spite of everything that had happened, Valerie had kept a feeling of tolerance for Regnault de Burey and she was sorry to note how poorly he was dressed. From her first recollection of him he had been shabby, but the materials used for his clothes had been of the best and he had always looked what he was, an impoverished nobleman. Now he was attired in shoddy cloth which could not be made to fit him. His shoes were broken and patched and it was only too clear that the cracks in the leather had been painstakingly, but not successfully, clobbered.

"Ha, Little Cousin," he said, blinking his eyes at her in a manner which could be construed as affectionate. "You gain in beauty all the time, it seems; and the rest of us will soon be on the scrapheap with the broken wheels and discarded stewing pans, and the old clothes and the fish scales and the offal generally."

He grunted his disgust at the way life was treating him and it was several moments before he began to speak again. "The servants tell me that my brother is still away. What's the sly young dog up to? He must have lost his senses. If I had a wife like you, I wouldn't let her out of my sight for a minute. I said to myself when I started out, 'If she's going to yield to anyone while he's away, why shouldn't it be me?' "

Valerie was so delighted at finding that he had not come as the bearer of bad news that she smiled at him. She said, "If I ever decide to take a lover, Naulty, I promise to consult you first."

He was not taken in. "I may look forward to hearing from you, then, in a thousand years," he said. He ran a weary hand down the inflamed bridge of his nose. "I'm teetering on the brink of ruin."

"I'm sorry to hear you're in trouble." She did not add the word "again" as anyone else would have done.

"Job, sitting on his ulcers and boils and watching his wealth disappear in smoke and thunder, was rolling in content compared to the position I find myself in! Afflictions seek me out like flies to corruption. I am sick. I am poor. And Isabeau——" He paused and gave his head a lugubrious shake. "You've heard of the plight of my unfortunate spouse?"

Valerie said in an apprehensive tone, "No, we have few visitors and so we hear nothing of what goes on."

"That's strange. I thought everyone knew. Isabeau has the dead palsy."

Despite the state of her feelings toward the Comtesse, Valerie experienced a sense of shock. This grew into a closer approach to something like sympathy for the sufferer than she had thought possible when the husband of the sick woman went on into details.

"She had curious symptoms for a long time. She spoke with difficulty and sometimes used one word for another. She complained a great deal of hearing bells ringing when there was no sound at all, sometimes in the middle of the night. Then one day she fell over on the floor and lay there without moving. She hasn't moved since."

"When did this dreadful thing occur?"

"Over a month ago. The physician says she may stay like this for years. He even thinks it possible she may live out her allotted span without moving a single muscle. That's arrant nonsense, of course. He's full of nonsense, with his talk of what Paulus says and Galen thinks and his lack of ideas of what can be done for her." He went on in tones of the deepest scorn. "Jalop and scammony! Vapors of vinegar! He knows nothing, that chattering fool! He had her head shaved before I knew what he was about. My poor Isabeau! How she must have suffered as she felt him clipping off her lovely red curls—slightly sprinkled with gray if the truth must be told—and could do nothing to stop him."

"Do you mean that she can see and hear?"

The Comte nodded his head. "All her senses seem to be alive and active. She always had a great fear of being closed in. Sometimes she wouldn't sleep in a tester bed because she felt as though she would smother. She never wanted to ride in a carriage. Do you suppose"—he turned a pair of eyes on his companion which reflected a vicarious sense of horror—"that she feels that way now, being closed in and not able to move a finger to free herself? Would she scream to get out if she had the power? Truly, Little Cousin, it's a gruesome thought!"

He had succeeded in communicating some of the emotion he felt to Valerie. She wet her lips nervously and said: "This is truly awful! I—I hope some way can be found to help her—to release her!"

"The physician says that release will come only with death." The Comte sat in gloomy silence for several moments. "There's something even worse I must tell you. She can still move a part of her right cheek. I noticed it and so we began to communicate. When I ask her a question, she moves her cheek if the answer is yes. I can anticipate some of her wants. But, Valerie"—he paused again—"I've found there's something she wants to tell me. She has no way, of course, of letting me know what it is and I, so far, have been unable to guess. I haven't asked the right questions. It's truly a terrible situation!" He shuddered with so much feeling that his listener did the same. "There she sits, propped up in a chair with pillows, her eyes staring straight at me. I know that back of them is her burning desire to make me understand. I've asked a hundred questions but always her cheek remains still. But when I ask, as I do every day, if there's still something she wants me to know, the cheek quivers and shakes in eagerness."

"Do you suppose"—Valerie hesitated before putting her thought into words—"that it has to do with her wishes about her—her death? Does she desire to be released at once?"

Regnault de Burey considered the point in silence for several moments. "And if that is what she wants, what can be done to satisfy her?"

"Nothing," said Valerie hastily. "At least all you could do would be to tell the physician."

"I know what *he* would say, that brain of a cuckoo bird." The Comte snuffled with digust. "He would accuse me of an impiety in thinking of such a thing. No, Little Cousin, that is one question I dare not ask her. Suppose the answer was yes? Then I would be in a sorry dilemma. Ever after her eyes would be fixed on me and I would know what they were saying. They would be saying, You coward, you keep me here in a misery so great that death is the only release and you do nothing for me! . . . Well, enough of this! There are worms in my flesh when I think too much about it."

They sat and looked at each other in silence for a long time. Valerie asked finally, "May I offer you some refreshment?"

"Wine, if you please, Little Cousin. One sensation does not diminish with me as the years advance. My thirst."

The Comte watched her over the rim as he imbibed eagerly from the flagon which had been brought him. "It's indeed lucky," he said, after the edge had been taken from his thirst, "that I find you here alone. That brother of mine has no sympathy for me when it comes to the troubles in which I seem always to be involved. He would sit there with a face like a graven saint and say that I deserve all this. Perhaps I do, but, by'r Lady of Marmoutier, I refuse to let my younger brother tell me so! Now you, my Valerie, have a generous share of human kindliness. The fact that I am sorely in need of money will strike home to your friendly little heart at once."

Valerie looked at him doubtfully, remembering an admonition from her husband in this connection. "Don't let Naulty wheedle you into giving him money, no matter what tale of woe he may have."

"But, brother-in-law," she said, "I have so little—a few coins of my own only and some small bits of jewelry which could be sold perhaps. If your needs are great, it will be necessary to speak to Robin when he returns."

The Comte doubled up with a sudden pain. "I have the hip gout now," he said, groaning. "Every part of my body is clamoring for ointment. . . . I think, Little Cousin, I shall content myself with what you can gather together for me. It will be given with an ungrudging smile and no lecture will go with it." He gave a wheezing sigh. "I've been lectured so much that I weary of it."

Valerie had not expected to be taken up in this way. She stammered, "But, truly, it would require such a long time——"

"I can wait. To convince you that I haven't been prodigal with my resources, I may tell you that I haven't stirred a foot from these parts for the better part of a year. Look at me! Could you tell me from a dissipated apothecary or a nip-cheese lawyer? I've just sent my last mistress away. A man can't do more than that."

4

The stricken chatelaine of Montagne-Noire, the ancestral home of the De Bureys, sat in a mound of musty cushions, her eyes motionless in a face on which the palsy had stamped for all time an expression of extreme suffering. Her hair, which the physician had so ruthlessly sacrificed, was beginning to grow again in the form of a reddish fuzz, but there was not yet enough of it to hide the curious conformation of her skull. It was well for her peace of mind (if a mind could know any peace when caught in such a prison) that there was no mirror in the room.

It was a dark room with walls damp from the last rain and with the rank smell which comes from lack of airing. It was so dark, in fact, that even the most active eyes would not have been able at first to see the two women servants who leaned on the handles of brooms in one corner. They were watching their mistress.

"Look at her!" said one of them, in a whisper. "Sitting there like an ugly idol! What wicked thoughts has she got in her mind, do you suppose, Brigitte? Do you think she sees us?"

"Of course she sees us," answered her companion. "She never misses anything, that one. She's in a rage right now because she can't order us whipped."

"She's making up for everything now. How long is it since Bona went to the trouble of bathing her?"

"I can't remember."

The second servant was an emaciated creature with arms as thin as kindling wood and the slack face of the weak in mind. Clutching her broom in her hands, she ventured out to the center of the floor. After standing in front of the motionless figure for several moments, she began to dance about the Comtesse with awkward steps and grotesque motions of her arms. Every time her gyrations brought her in front of her mistress, she would pause and then lunge out viciously with the broom, aiming it at the face of the helpless woman and drawing it back only when it had come as close as an inch of its mark. Once, cackling insanely, she ran to the wall and scraped the end of the broom on the dampness. Then she returned to her triumphant caperings, permitting the soaked straws to brush closer with each thrust at the once-beautiful features of Isabeau de Burey.

The first domestic, who had been screeching with delight over the performance, said suddenly, "Someone is coming, Brigitte!"

The Comte entered the room a few moments after the two servants had vanished in giggling haste. He advanced slowly, for his eyesight was rapidly growing more deficient and his mind was busy elsewhere. He was wondering how far the few odd coins Valerie had been able to spare him would go in meeting his most pressing needs. They rattled about forlornly in his leather purse where, as he knew only too well, they had all the space to themselves.

Slowly and somewhat absent-mindedly he seated himself in a chair facing the rigid figure of the Comtesse. The atmosphere added to his sense of acute discomfort and he sniffed as he looked about him.

"This place is as sour as a cheese vat or a public jakes!" he said aloud. "Are they keeping pigs below that such a rank odor assails my nostrils everywhere I go? I tell you, my spouse"—looking directly at the Comtesse for the first time—"it's a sorry thing when the hand of a mistress is no longer felt in an establishment like this."

He paused as though, in his absent-mindedness, he expected her to reply. Something about the figure opposite him suggested that a response was in her mind and that she was striving desperately to make him understand. The Comte was not receptive to such influences. He stretched one leg out in front of him and groaned with the pain the effort had involved. "I swallow all the nauseous messes this dolt of a physician concocts for me and yet my gout gets worse every day." Then he drew himself up in his chair by employing both his elbows and stared intently at his wife.

"My poor Isabeau!" he said. "I hardly recognize you when I see you sitting there. How much longer must you endure this?"

It became apparent then, even to one as lacking in sensitivity as he, that the helpless woman was trying by sheer force of will to tell him something. He leaned forward with his elbows on his knees and studied her face, as though the answer might be found in surface indications. The rigidity of her expression had robbed her of almost all suggestion of humanity. The eyes were wide open and staring fixedly, the lips were parted and unpleasantly moist. The physician's insistence on shaving her head had completed the picture.

Was there something different about her? It seemed to him that there had been a change but he could not have told in what it consisted, except that he fancied her breathing had become more stertorous. After several moments of uncomfortable watching, he made up his mind to the duty from which he had been holding back.

"Is there still something you want to tell me?" he asked.

The place on her cheek which functioned normally moved several times, as though to lend emphasis to the reply.

"Has it to do with your condition?"

The cheek moved again, unmistakably.

"Do you want—do you want to go on living as long as we can keep you alive?"

He was staring at her intently as he spoke, realizing the necessity of interpreting her wishes accurately. There was not as much as a quiver.

"Are you then anxious to—to die?"

There was no mistaking the meaning of the muscular answer this time. The one active part of the palsied body had for a moment fairly pulsed with life and motion.

"But the physician says you may live for a long time. For years even." The Comte was speaking slowly and with obvious reluctance. "Is—is—is it your wish that something be done to release you?"

Again the cheek moved. The Comte slumped back in his chair. He had his answer now, the one he had more than half expected to hear, the one he had dreaded. She wanted to escape from this living death, and was asking him to accomplish it, to put an end to her suffering. This was what she had been trying to tell him for so long.

Finally he began to speak in a grumbling tone. "You always preferred that brother of mine, my sweet spouse. Oh, I knew it all along. You were not hiding anything from me. It was plain to be seen you regretted your bargain. Shall I send for the gallant Robin to render you this service?" He gave vent to a short and scornful laugh. "You needn't give me any answer to that, Isabeau. It would do no good to ask him. He's too honorable, too holy, to interfere with the workings of nature and the will of God! Or, if you prefer it in plain words, he's too squeamish. But I, the despised husband, the one you've always made the butt of your ill humors, I'm not too honorable. What's more to the point, I'm not squeamish. I have the courage, inside this unknightly body of mine, to face a situation like this squarely."

He paused and changed position slowly in his chair. "Tell me, sweet spouse, shall I send for Robin?"

There was no suggestion of motion in the cheek.

The Comte laughed again and in the same tone. "I thought not. You're looking to me in your final extremity." He remained sunk in uncomfortable thought for some minutes. Then he raised his head and began to speak in sharp tones. "There's one method only. Poison. If I can obtain some— and if my present resolution doesn't desert me—are you ready to have me use it?"

The Comtesse responded with an immediacy which left him with no doubt as to her feelings and wishes. She wanted to die and was prepared for the means he suggested. He cleared his throat protestingly and writhed about in his chair.

"Do you realize what they would do to me if they found out? They wouldn't believe it was by your wish. How could you have let me know, they would ask. When I told them you had conveyed your desire by moving a muscle in your cheek, they would laugh at me. Learned physicians from the University would go on the stand and say it was impossible. My high rank would not save me. They would send me to the executioner as they did Gilles de Retz."

He got to his feet and hobbled to the door. Over his shoulder he said, "I think I must have loved you very much once, Isabeau, or I wouldn't be ready to do this for you now."

He came back some minutes later. Locking the door after him, he walked to a table which lay within the restricted area of vision of his wife. On the top of it he laid a container with the telltale red arrow.

"Yes," he said, nodding. "It's the same, the very bottle of poison they tried to say was used by Jacques Coeur to kill Agnes Sorel. For all I know it was you and that sly wench, Jeanne de Vendôme, who gave it to them in the first place. It was Guillaume Gouffier who handed it to me. As a souvenir, he said, of a laudable but unsuccessful effort."

The Comte raised the container and gave it a shake. "There's something ironic about this," he said. "One might almost believe that fate had delivered it into my hands for this particular use." He looked across at the still figure of the Comtesse. "Well? Have you the stomach for it, my poor spouse? Are you still prepared to make an end of it when this must be the means?"

There was a long pause. Then the muscle in the cheek moved.

"So be it."

And then he became aware that there had been a change in her. The breathing became less stertorous until finally he could not hear it at all. The eyes of the unfortunate woman remained open but he knew that this meant nothing. He walked over to her and felt the part of her face in which the power of motion had been left. It seemed to his exploring fingers no different from the rest. It was cold and stiff to the touch.

He realized that he was holding the container of poison in his other hand. Hastily concealing it in his purse, he ran to the door and unlocked it. He raised his voice and began to shout.

"Hugon! Tuddual! At once! I think your mistress is dead!"

5

"The Pope's fleet may be pounding at the infidels in Constantinople this very moment," said D'Arlay.

Valerie made no response. She was looking ahead and thinking, "In an hour I shall have my little Alain in my arms."

"It was a slap in the face for the King of France when the Pope made Jacques Coeur one of his captains," went on D'Arlay. "And a great feather in the Moneyman's cap. If what we heard was true, that he has been given command of a squadron, he'll have a chance to prove that his genius knows no limits!" He paused and shook his head. "But what a sacrifice he has made! He'll never start in trade again. It's very doubtful if he'll have the strength after he returns from the East to do anything as ambitious as that."

Valerie asked in a musing tone, "Will he have grown much, do you think?"

Her husband looked at her in complete puzzlement for a moment. Then he sensed the direction in which her thoughts had been running, and he smiled and reached over to squeeze her hand in its fine glove of red stamped leather.

"Our son?" he exclaimed in mock indignation. "Of course he has grown. He will have grown out of all recollection!"

"I would know him," declared Valerie, "if he had become six feet tall in our absence! But will he know us—his wicked parents who have been away from him for three whole months? Robin, he may think us strangers! It will break my heart if he does."

D'Arlay exclaimed suddenly, "There's the girouette above the entrance tower! See, above that clump of three trees! We're home, my love, we're home again at last!"

With one accord they began to ride faster, rising in their stirrups and staring ahead of them.

"You mustn't be disappointed," said D'Arlay, "if he doesn't remember us at all. You must allow for the fact that our Alain is only a year and three months old. Children have no capacity for remembering at that age."

"I think you're wrong, my Robin. How can we tell what's going on inside those small heads of theirs? Besides, Alain is a special kind of child, a most intelligent child." She shook her head with a sudden shift of mood. "I hoped so much we would come back with full information about his— his family on his mother's side! Three months of traveling about, and searching, and talking to everyone! And what have we to show for it?"

"I'm sure, my love, we've learned everything there is to be found. You know beyond all question of doubt that your father was a brother of Agnes Sorel. I was surprised when that old curmudgeon of an uncle in Berri finally conceded us that much. I don't believe he would have done it if he hadn't been so concerned to convince us that you were illegitimate and in no position to make any claims on his property. That, alone, was worth all the trouble we took."

Valerie sighed. "I hoped so much to learn something more about my poor mother." She lapsed into silence as they began to jog down the incline into the arm of the valley which constituted the domain of Arlay. It was several minutes before she burst out with, "I'm sure it was a mistake to hire that wet nurse for Alain!"

"She seemed a capable young woman. Isn't it a rather late hour to be having misgivings?"

"I distrusted her. She has red hair. And you know, my Robin, that women with red hair never make good nurses."

"I didn't know it."

Valerie gave him the benefit of a serious frown. "They're too much interested in their own looks. And that isn't all. I caught her in one thing before we left and it should have been a warning. Alain needed a purgative and she actually gave it to the poor little child. It's a wonder he survived!"

"And what else, pray, was she to do?" asked her husband, with a blank look.

Valerie shook her head with an air of exasperation. "I thought everyone knew. Medicine must never be given to children. Their stomachs are not strong enough to stand it. But when one is needed, the nurse must drink it herself so the child gets the benefit of it through her milk. . . . I should have been firm and insisted on someone else before we left."

They rode by a thick copse of evergreens from which a flock of migratory birds rose suddenly and wheeled off to the south with more precision than any army of men ever achieved on the march. The road twisted and dipped again and they then found themselves riding across a broad meadow at the far end of which stood the manor house. High stone walls covered with ivy gave it seclusion and protection and its profusion of windows, even in the circular surface of the entrance tower, hinted at comfort within as well as an unusual degree of light.

D'Arlay looked at his wife. "Shall we race? You won the last time and I feel a deep urge to wipe out the disgrace."

Valrie nodded eagerly but the next instant reined in and shook her head. "I'm afraid it wouldn't be wise, Robin," she said.

"You will at any rate permit me to carry you in over the threshold. We've been away so long that it seems proper again."

"And for the same reason I must say another no. I—I am at the moment somewhat heavier, fair husband."

Helion, elevated to the important post of seneschal, came out on the *tête-de-pont* to welcome them. He was dressed in multi-colored magnificence, with one leg pink and one blue and his tabard a crisscross of many shades. "Master! And my lady!" he cried, fairly dancing with excitement. "It is wondrous to see you back from your long travelings. Most fortunately the nurse is here with Master Alain. And if you had only come an hour earlier, my lady, you would have been able to greet a young knight who came seeking you."

Valerie dismounted before asking further enlightenment. "And now, Helion," she said, gathering up her skirts which were long enough to drag a full yard behind her, and unwinding the green silk gorget about her neck, "who was this guest we arrived too late to see?"

"Mistress, I am ashamed to confess that his name has left my mind," said the new seneschal, after a moment's ineffectual effort. "But he came, my lady, at the behest of Godefroy de Monglat who had bested him in a contest of arms."

"Another of them!" Valerie stopped and looked up at her husband with her nose wrinkled to express exasperation. She seemed on the point of stamping her foot. "This is too much! Robin, something must be done."

"This is the third, is it not?"

"The fourth!"

D'Arlay smiled down at her. "It's a great compliment he pays you, my love."

Valerie sighed. "But they're so much trouble! They seem to think it incumbent on them to languish and to ogle me and even to pretend devotion. It has become very tiresome."

"If I don't object, why should you?"

"When I see Froy again, I shall beg him to find someone else as the object of his devotion. I'm a married woman now—and rather unusually devoted to my lord and husband—and so there's something unseemly about these visits of defeated knights." She sighed again. "He was such a clean and honorable boy! What a pity he has had to grow up into a chivalrous knight and make a spectacle of himself in this way!"

Helion said, as though it were an afterthought: "There's someone to see you, my lord. A messenger from Bourges."

"If you'll allow me, my love," said D'Arlay, turning in haste, "I shall see this messenger at once. It will be news about Jacques Coeur."

Valerie joined him in a very few minutes in the Great Hall where he had talked with the messenger. She was carrying her son in her arms and was fairly crowing with delight.

"Robin!" she cried. "He knew me at once, the little pet, and held out his arms to me. He's well and he's fond of his nurse. I'm ashamed now of the things I said about her. Ah, my husband, this son of ours is such a fine and manly little fellow——"

She stopped, becoming aware that something was wrong. D'Arlay's face was white.

"You must be ready for a shock," he said, in a low tone. "Reports have come from the East. Jacques Coeur is dead!"

Valerie cried, "Oh no!" and then subsided into silence as he proceeded with an explanation.

"It has been confirmed that he was put in command of a part of the fleet but it's not known yet whether he got into action with it. It may be that he met a Turkish fleet and was wounded in the fighting. This much only is known for certain, that he was taken ashore on the island of Chios and died there. The island belongs to Genoa and he has been buried in the church of the Cordeliers."

For a long time there was silence and then Valerie said: "This is the end of all his great dreams!"

D'Arlay nodded somberly. "He used to talk to me and explain the things he wanted to do. He was convinced that the world would never grow out of its interest in war and killing until life itself was made more comfortable and interesting and worth while. That was what he was striving to do. . . . I very much fear that in a few years everything he accomplished will be forgotten!"

For some time they sat and looked at each other, too unhappy to put their thoughts into words. Then D'Arlay began to speak again. "The poet Homer was born on the island of Chios—or he died and was buried there. It seems to me most fitting that an epic life like that of Jacques Coeur should end in the same place."

"The King's Moneyman and the saviour of France!" said Valerie, her eyes filling with tears.

A cry of protest rose at this point from the son of the house who had been deposited on the floor. He began to crawl in his father's direction. D'Arlay lifted him in his arms.

"How he has grown, this fellow, since we went away!" he said, with an air of pride. "At this rate he will grow into a taller and stronger man than his father. I suppose"—looking at his wife with a stealthy smile—"we must expect him to become a gallant knight someday. A fine fighting man like your champion, Godefroy. Or even Jacques de Lalain."

She looked up at him indignantly. "This is an ill time for joking, my Robin."

D'Arlay continued in a more serious vein: "Perhaps nature makes a mistake in letting any living creature grow to maturity where the killing instinct develops. Why must a nice, rosy-cheeked boy become a knight with no thoughts in his head but killing other knights or outdrinking them at their wine—and smelling of leather and horse sweat and the gambesons worn too long under their armor!"

"Don't you think," Valerie cried, "that men will come to their senses in time to spare us that?"

D'Arlay shook his head. "Jacques Coeur was the only one who saw the need for change and had the courage to work for it. And now he's dead." He turned to her and smiled. "Still—it will come before long. There will be a change. Men will begin to see the folly of all this. Everything Jacques Coeur wanted—and much more—will come to pass in time. I'm sure of that, my heart."